Stories and Tales

Available from the Simms Initiatives and the University of South Carolina Press

The Army Correspondence of Colonel John Laurens, ed.

As Good as a Comedy and Paddy McGann

Beauchampe

Border Beagles

Carl Werner, 2 vols.

The Cassique of Kiawah

Castle Dismal

Charlemont

The Charleston Book, ed.

Confession

Count Julian

The Damsel of Darien, 2 vols.

Dramas: Norman Maurice, Michael Bonham, and Benedict Arnold

Egeria

Eutaw

The Forayers

The Geography of South Carolina

The Golden Christmas

Guy Rivers

Helen Halsey

Historical and Political Poems (*which includes* Monody, The Vision of Cortes, The Tri-Color, Donna Florida, and Charleston and Her Satirists)

The History of South Carolina

Joscelyn

Katherine Walton

The Letters of William Gilmore Simms, Vol. 1

The Letters of William Gilmore Simms, Vol. 2

The Letters of William Gilmore Simms, Vol. 3

The Letters of William Gilmore Simms, Vol. 4

The Letters of William Gilmore Simms, Vol. 5

The Letters of William Gilmore Simms, Vol. 6 (exp. ed.)

The Life of Captain John Smith

The Life of the Chevalier Bayard

The Life of Francis Marion

The Lily and the Totem

Marie de Berniere

Martin Faber and Other Tales, 2 vols.

Mellichampe

The Partisan

Pelayo, 2 vols.

Poems, Descriptive, Dramatic, Legendary, and Contemplative, 2 vols.

The Remains of Maynard Davis Richardson

Richard Hurdis

Sack and Destruction of the City of Columbia

The Scout

Selections from the Letters and Speeches of the Hon. James H. Hammond, ed.

Simms's Poems Areytos

Social and Political Prose: Slavery in America/Father Abbot

South Carolina in the Revolutionary War

Southward Ho!

Stories and Tales

A Supplement to the Plays of William Shakespeare

Vasconselos

Views and Reviews in American Literature, History and Fiction, 2 vols.

Voltmeier

War Poetry of the South

The Wigwam and the Cabin

Woodcraft

The Yemassee

Stories and Tales

William Gilmore Simms

Introductions and Explanatory Notes and Texts established by John Caldwell Guilds

The University of South Carolina Press

Cloth original published by the University of South Carolina Press, 1974
Paperback published by the University of South Carolina Press
Columbia, South Carolina 29208

www.sc.edu/uscpress

Manufactured in the United States of America

24 23 22 21 20 19 18 17 16 15
10 9 8 7 6 5 4 3 2 1

ISBN 978-1-61117-481-6 (pbk)

Published in cooperation with the Simms Initiatives, a project of the University of South Carolina Libraries with the generous support of the Watson-Brown Foundation.

PREFACE

If it were not so cumbersome, *Uncollected and Unpublished Stories and Tales* would be an appropriate title for Volume V of *The Centennial Edition of the Writings of William Gilmore Simms.* None of the stories in this volume is included in *The Wigwam and the Cabin,* the one well-known group of his tales which Simms himself collected, and two of them have never before been published; hence in a sense (though five do appear in little-known collections made by Simms) these fifteen stories are either "uncollected" or "unpublished."

I owe debts of gratitude to many institutions and individuals for assistance in the preparation of *Stories and Tales.* I am grateful to Texas Tech University for the research grant under which I began and to the University of South Carolina for the research grant under which I completed work on the volume. Of many debts to librarians and libraries, none is so deep as to E. L. Inabinett and his staff at the South Caroliniana Library, where most of the work was done. Each member of the Editorial Board has contributed to Volume V, but my indebtedness to Mary C. Simms Oliphant, who generously granted me full access to her vast collection of Simmsiana, goes beyond an editor's debt to fellow editors. The following graduate students and research assistants at the University of South Carolina have in various ways contributed to the preparation of this volume: George Ellison, Kathleen Higgins, James E. Kibler, Mary Meats, Stephen Meats, Nell M. Nixon, Noel Polk, Laurie M. Price, Miriam J. Shillingsburg, Peter Shillingsburg, James West, and Margaret J. Yonce. Special recognition is owed George Ellison and Noel Polk for their assistance in planning and preparing the charts of emendations and textual variants. Finally, I should like to acknowledge my indebtedness to my colleagues, William S. Kable and Gordon Lindstrand, for their assistance in reading proof.

J. C. G.

CONTENTS

PART II

Apparatus

INTRODUCTION

In 1932 the writer of a dissertation on William Gilmore Simms quietly observed, "If Simms is ever reintroduced to a reading public, his short stories will probably be the medium."[1] Despite the gradual increase of interest in Simms since the publication of his letters, this volume is the first attempt to "reintroduce" a prolific and virile writer in what is perhaps his best genre—the short story or tale. Even critics contemporaneous with Simms recognized that his strongest abilities lay in the short story. Rufus W. Griswold, for instance, commented in his *Prose Writers of America:* "The shorter stories of Mr. Simms are his best works. They have unity, completeness, and strength, and though not written with elegance, are comparatively free from redundancies and weighty offences against taste."[2] A reviewer of *The Wigwam and the Cabin* (1845) wrote in *Godey's* that Simms's tales "have more nerve and not less beauty and grace than his larger works"[3]; and a critic in the *North American Review* noted: "Either from a lack of original power to sustain . . . a long flight . . ., or from a lack of sufficient culture to train his native energies up to such high-reaching aims, Guy Rivers seems equal only to the short and easy career of the magazine tale or story."[4] If these preferences perhaps seem inspired more by coolness toward Simms's novels than by warm acclaim for his stories, his shorter fiction, it should be remembered, did evoke praise from a recognized master of the craft, Poe, who, in his famous *Broadway Journal* review of *The Wigwam and the Cabin,* called Simms the "de Vega of American writers of fiction," and asserted: "His merits lie among the major and his defects among the minor morals of literature." Even though

[1] Hampton Jarrell, "William Gilmore Simms: Realistic Romancer" (Duke University Ph.D. thesis, 1932), p. 42.

[2] 4th ed.—reived (Philadelphia, 1856), p. 505.

[3] XXXI (Dec., 1845), 271.

[4] LXIII (Oct., 1846), 360.

Poe found Simms's "earlier works of length, such as 'The Partisan,'" marred by "many inaccuracies of style" and "the prevalence of the merely repulsive," he discovered much to admire in the "best fictions" and said of their author: "in invention, in vigor, in movement, in the power of exciting interest, and in the artistical management of his themes, he has surpassed, we think, any of his countrymen:—that is to say, he has surpassed any of them in the aggregate of these high qualities."[5]

This high estimate of Simms as a short-storyist by the contemporary who was the first American writer to give serious consideration to the short story as an art form makes the neglect of Simms by historians of the short story puzzling. Whereas the contributions of Poe, Irving, Hawthorne, and Melville to the development of the short story have been well noted, Simms's role has been almost completely overlooked. Certainly, Simms's accomplishments do not match those of these other forerunners; but his contribution to a genre that before the Civil War produced few real craftsmen was nevertheless far from negligible. In sheer bulk Simms probably produced more short fiction than any of his contemporaries, and although much of it is perhaps best forgotten, he did write enough stories of genuine excellence to rank, it would seem, among the four or five foremost figures in the history of the American short story before 1870. At the least, Simms the short story writer deserves as large a niche in our literary annals as Simms the novelist.

Why has Simms the short-storyist not received more recognition? The easiest and possibly best answer is that his stories, not readily accessible, have not been read. Those that he himself collected have long been out of print; many others have never been collected or reprinted since their original publication in out-of-the-way periodicals; and two of his best, in manuscript form at the time of his death, have remained unpublished until now. Simms's predilection for pseudonymity (or anonymity) almost precludes the possibility of all his writings being discovered, for he published widely and seemingly indiscriminately in journals, annuals, newspapers, and miscellanies. If it

[5] *Broadway Journal*, II (Oct. 4, 1845), 190. Poe's praise here, though primarily concerned with Simms as a writer of stories and tales, does not exclude Simms the novelist, whom Poe quotes himself as considering "'the best novelist which this country has, upon the whole, produced . . .'" (p. 190). In a recent article Claude Richard questions Poe's sincerity in this review; see "Poe and 'Young America,'" *Studies in Bibliography*, XXI (1968), 38.

can be fairly stated that William Gilmore Simms was never long with a story—he found it "much easier to invent a new story than to repair the defects of an old one"[6]—it should also be noted that he was never long between stories. During his forty-five years of literary productivity, it is known that he published at least eighty short stories or sketches, not including novelettes or stories of more than thirty-six thousand words. Simms began writing short fiction early and continued writing it intermittently throughout his career: his first known publication, "The Robber—an Eastern Tale," appeared in the *Album* in seven installments in 1825 (when he was only nineteen); and his last publication in 1870 (the year of his death) was likewise a story, the truly excellent "How Sharp Snaffles Got His Capital and Wife," published in *Harper's* for October, four months after his death. Furthermore, Simms's last literary energies appear to have been devoted to "Bald-Head Bill Bauldy" and "The Humours of the Manager," long manuscript stories "completed" in varying degrees shortly before his death and now published for the first time.[7]

Even in the period between 1842 and 1851, when, largely for economic reasons, Simms is said to have neglected fiction for other forms and pursuits, he did not abandon *short* fiction; when he had difficulty selling his novels, he relied more heavily than ever upon his short stories. In August, 1841, Simms had written J. H. Hammond: "You will perceive that Irving now writes almost wholly for magazines and Cooper & myself are almost the only persons whose novels are printed."[8] Himself a magazine editor during six years of the trying decade beginning in 1842, Simms nevertheless sold stories to other periodicals. Though he never prospered from the sale of stories, he apparently came to regret that he had expended time and energy on the writing of history, geography, and biography when with more profit and less toil he could have written fiction. *The History of South Carolina,* he remarked, "did not yield me as much

[6] Dedication, *The Wigwam and the Cabin* (New York, 1859), p. 4.

[7] Simms left, in varying stages of completion, at least eight other manuscripts of unpublished fiction, the longest of which are "The Brothers of the Coast. A Romance" (175 pp.), "Will O' Wisp; or The Irish Baronet" (187 pp.), "The Family Fortunes a Sketch" (69 pp.), and "Rawlins' Rookery; or The House of Eld and Glamour" (98 pp.). All are in the Charles Carroll Simms Collection, South Caroliniana Library.

[8] *The Letters of William Gilmore Simms*, ed. Mary C. Simms Oliphant, A. T. Odell, and T. C. Duncan Eaves, 5 vols. (Columbia, S. C., 1952-56), I, 271.

money as I have earned in three nights, penning legends for the Annuals."[9]

When, in the 1850's, Simms wisely diverted his main energies again toward the novel, he did not stop writing short stories and novelettes, though his production of shorter fiction did perceptibly slacken. This relatively steady output indicates that Simms's interest in the short story never waned. His own recognition that he wrote too much too hurriedly is revealed in his apology to readers of the *Southern Literary Gazette:* "As long as the Editor is compelled, as we have frequently been, to write one half of his book himself, one half of what he writes, must be trash."[10] Thus the bibliographer who uncovers stories to add to Simms's canon is not likely to add to the prolific Charlestonian's stature as an artist.

But in this collection and in *The Wigwam and the Cabin,* to be published intact as a later volume in the Centennial Edition, it is not the "one half . . . trash" of Simms that is our concern; rather it is the small core of stories that reveal both the representative and the best of William Gilmore Simms. Although these representative selections are necessarily uneven in quality, at his best Simms as a story-teller had few peers among his contemporaries, and he complemented his natural bent for story-telling with a fondness for theorizing about the art he practiced. Simms, in the words of Edd Winfield Parks, "was a good but not a great critic" whose "theories often seem better than his fictional and poetic practices."[11] Though never highly original, sometimes naïvely expressed, and frequently lacking in artistic sophistication, Simms's theories of short fiction represent generally sound thinking about a genre not fully recognized as a legitimate art form at the time they were written. An acquaintance with these theories seems a necessary preamble to a study of his stories.

Despite his lifelong concern with short fiction, Simms was not quick to formalize principles about the writing of "regularly planned . . . novels in little," as he once described his own stories to E. A. Duyckinck, "— not mere scenes or sketches."[12] As editor and critic Simms did not write about the short story nearly so much as he did about the novel; and when he did write about the short story, his

[9] *Letters,* V, 409.
[10] N.s., I (July 1, 1829), 80.
[11] *William Gilmore Simms As Literary Critic* (Athens, Ga., 1961), pp. 110, 111.
[12] Letter of December, 1854; *Letters,* III, 342.

main purpose seems to have been to distinguish between the short story (or novelette) and the novel (or romance). Simms's theories of the short story, one concludes, are the product of his stories, not his stories the product of theory. Nevertheless, through a close reading of his critical writings a fairly adequate idea of Simms's concept of the short story can be gained.

Two of the main distinctions Simms made between the short story and the novel have to do with plot and characterization: in plot or subject matter, the short story has more latitude than the novel because it may deal more freely with the supernatural, the improbable, or the unusual. In introducing his ghost story "Grayling; or, 'Murder Will Out,'" Simms lamented that our "story-tellers . . . venture on no subjects the details of which are not . . . susceptible of proof." "A love of the marvellous," he added, "belongs . . . to all those who love and cultivate . . . the fine arts"[13] ; this love of the marvellous was encouraged in Simms, certainly, by his great admiration for German romantic literature—a fondness he was never to outgrow, despite the battle waged against it by his innate sense of realism. As a practical solution Simms theorized that the short story, unlike the novel, may ignore probability—and even possibility—if it chooses to enter the province of fantasy; thus, in his stories and novelettes, Simms frequently made use of the supernatural, although he almost never employed it in his novels. If, however, the short-storyist does not clearly aim for the "wild and wonderful," he, like the novelist, must strive for verisimilitude. In the preface to *The Wigwam and the Cabin,* for instance, Simms stressed the value of "the general truthfulness of its treatment" of frontier life. "I have seen the life—have *lived* it—and much of my material is the result of a very early personal experience," he added.[14]

Though the short story allows greater latitude in the selection of plot than does the novel, this advantage, Simms believed, is counterbalanced by the necessary restriction upon character development in the short story. In fact, in 1866 he remarked that short stories are "the most difficult of all to write" because "no room is allowed you for the development of character" and "you have to rely chiefly on incident and this tasks invention to the uttermost." Yet Simms real-

[13] *The Wigwam and the Cabin,* pp. [1]–2.

[14] *The Wigwam and the Cabin,* Dedication, pp. 4–5.

ized that fully developed character is "the chief source & secret for the discovery & development of incidents"[15]; and it is possible that the very problem of interweaving character and incident in a brief space is responsible for the better disciplined form in his short stories than in his novels. Although Simms's stories, with a few exceptions, cannot be characterized as well-knit or closely constructed, they do possess a greater economy of style and a better sense of proportion than his longer works customarily do.

It may also be true, paradoxically, that Simms's short stories (despite his insistence that their scope automatically restricts character development) contain more realistic characterization than his novels. Simms's forte in characterization, it has commonly been recognized, is portrayal of people from the middle and lower classes of society. Though Simms once observed that "a character either wholly good or bad, never yet entered into the imagination of the dramatist or novelist,"[16] his own aristocratic heroes and heroines too often are wooden paragons of virtue. Apparently, loyalty to the Old South's concept of the perfect gentleman and lady was stronger in Simms than his penchant for realism; the epic must have its hero and heroine, and, since he looked upon the novel as a modern epic,[17] Simms created his leading characters in the epic mold. The short story, however, does not demand epic proportions, and thus the noble hero and genteel heroine need not appear. More frequently, then, than in his novels or romances, Simms peopled his short stories with understandable human beings, intermixtures of good and evil: " . . . the planter, the squatter, the Indian, and the negro—the bold and hardy pioneer, the vigorous yeoman—these are the subjects," he wrote of *The Wigwam and the Cabin.*[18] When Simms dropped his chivalrous inhibitions, he was capable of creating believable, flesh-and-blood characters; it must also be noted, however, that his villains are sometimes as stereotyped as his heroes and that perhaps the most memorable character in his novels, Porgy, is both chivalrous and gentlemanly.

[15] *Letters,* IV, 580, 589.

[16] *Magnolia,* n.s., I (July, 1842), 52.

[17] "The modern Romance is the substitute which the people of the present day offer for the ancient epic," Simms wrote in the preface to the revised edition of *The Yemassee* (New York, 1853), p. v.

[18] Dedication, p. 5.

Although, as we have seen, Simms made distinctions between the short story and the novel, to his mind all forms of fiction share many purposes, one of which is to give meaning and life to the history and traditions of the nation. Probably more than any other writer in the South, Simms was leader of the movement for a distinctive national literature in America. "The true and most valuable inspiration of the poet," Simms wrote in 1845, "will be found either in the illustration of the national history, or in the development of the national characteristics. His themes, if unallied to these, will be very likely to lack permanence and general interest."[19] In both his novels and his short stories Simms put this theory into frequent practice; the stories in *The Wigwam and the Cabin,* in Simms's own words, for instance, "represent, in large degree, the border history of the south." Though some critics accused him of a sectional rather than a national point of view, Simms had a ready answer: " . . . to be *national* in literature, one must needs be *sectional.* No one mind can fully or fairly illustrate the characteristics of any great country; and he who shall depict *one section* faithfully, has made his proper and sufficient contribution to the great work of *national* illustration."[20]

Closely associated with Simms's belief in the use of national themes in fiction is his view that all literature faithful to truth serves a moral purpose: "as truthfulness is never without its moral, and as the great end of the artist is the approximation of all his fiction to a seeming truth, so, unavoidably, he inculcates a moral whenever he tells a story," Simms once wrote.[21] Truthfulness, in Simms's sense, involves the treatment of vice as well as virtue, of low and vulgar characters as well as noble and generous ones. It was partly the inclusion of "brutal murders" and "lavish oaths" ("an unnecessary amount of the horrible and the revolting") that led William Peterfield Trent to declare that Simms's Border Romances "should never have been written, since they have nothing ennobling in them."[22] Trent's charge was not the first of its kind against Simms; against the much earlier charge of immorality in "The Loves of the Driver," Simms wrote a long

[19] "The Epochs and Events of American History, as Suited to the Purposes of Art in Fiction," *Southern and Western Monthly Magazine and Review,* I (Feb., 1845), 126.

[20] Dedication, *The Wigwam and the Cabin,* p. 4.

[21] "Modern Prose Fiction," *Southern Quarterly Review,* XV (April, 1849), 43.

[22] *William Gilmore Simms,* American Men of Letters Series (Boston and New York 1892), pp. 88–89, 328.

public letter in defense of the morality of realism in art. "Your Homers, your Shakspeares, your Chaucers, your Beaumonts, your Fletchers, your Shirleys, your Massingers, your Scotts, your Byrons—the whole tribe of great names," he expostulated, "employ the deadly sins of man, as so many foils to his living virtues and whether he falls or triumphs, the end of the moralist is attained, if he takes care to speak the truth, the whole truth and nothing but the truth! In this, in fact, lies the whole secret of his art. *A writer is moral only in proportion to his truthfulness.*" [23] Neither is truth to be considered synonymous with fact because the merely factual can belie truth[24]: the writer of fiction, unless indeed his province be the marvellous or supernatural, must adhere to the probable whether he ignores or follows the factual. Fiction, Simms once said, "is neither more nor less, than probable truth under intenser conditions than ordinary." [25]

To Simms truthfulness of treatment involves manner as well as matter. Although, for instance, the language spoken by his own aristocratic heroes and heroines seems stiff and stilted to modern readers, he objected to artificiality in the dialogue of other writers. His definition of realism includes realism in language, both in the sense of calling "things by their proper names" and in the sense of capturing regional peculiarities in speech. "We dare not speak of legs, or thighs, in the presence of many very nice ladies," Simms protested in a plea against society's "mock modesty," which, he added sarcastically, would condone the use of " 'female dog,' 'feminine dog,' or something equally inoffensive and equally stupid," but object to the "perfectly moral" use of " 'bitch.' " [26] Interest in Negro dialect and scrupulous efforts to produce its sounds accurately in print have made Simms, in the words of J. Allen Morris, "very nearly an authoritative writer in [the] particular field" of Gullah dialect. [27] By modern standards, Simms's language may seem Victorian (for instance,

[23] *Letters*, I, 259. For the attack (by a reader who termed himself "A Puritan") which prompted Simms's reply, see *Magnolia*, III (June, 1841), 285–286. "A Letter to the Editor [P. C. Pendleton] By the Author of 'The Loves of the Driver' " first appeared in *Magnolia*, III (Aug., 1841), 376–380.

[24] See, for example, Simms's review of *Uncle Tom's Cabin* in *Southern Quarterly Review*, n.s., VIII (July, 1853), 218.

[25] "Modern Prose Fiction," p. 52.

[26] *Letters*, I, 257, 265.

[27] "Gullah in the Stories and Novels of William Gilmore Simms," *American Speech*, XXII (Feb., 1947), 47.

"damn" in Simms is almost invariably "d——n"), but in theory, at least, he was a pioneer in realistic use of the spoken word.

Neither Simms's penchant for realistic portrayal of native scenes and characters nor his strong prejudice against English models should mislead one into considering him a literary isolationist. Though he decried American subservience to British culture, Simms at the same time encouraged Americans to read widely in the literatures of other European countries and to use them as guides for the establishment of their own. "When we shall have cultivated a more intimate acquaintance with the literature of France, Spain, Germany and Italy," Simms wrote in 1828, "we shall then at length have discovered that for the last quarter of a century, we have indeed been following blind guides."[28] And of all European literatures, to Simms's thinking, that of Germany served as the best model for America.[29] Certainly the strongest foreign influence on his own early fiction is that of the German romanticists. His earliest published tales, in the little-known Charleston journal, the *Album,* are all in the Gothic tradition: "The Robber—an Eastern Tale," "Moonshine," and a series of fictitious "Sketches." In addition, Thomas has claimed possible German sources for six Simms novels and sixteen other short stories (or novelettes), including "How Sharp Snaffles Got His Capital and Wife." Despite realistic tendencies, Simms's tales, much more so than his novels, are marked "by an accentuation of the bizarre and irrational"—elements which the author definitely associated with Germany.[30]

Partially as a result, perhaps, of his predilection for the bizarre and irrational and his conflicting love for realistic treatment of native

[28] "Introduction," *Southern Literary Gazette,* I (Sept., 1828), 6. See J. Wesley Thomas, "The German Sources of William Gilmore Simms," *Anglo-German and American German Crosscurrents* (Chapel Hill, N.C., 1957), I, 127–153; C. Hugh Holman, "European Influences on Southern Literature," *Comparative Literature* (Chapel Hill, N.C., 1959), II, 453–454. Although not so readily apparent as the German, the Spanish influence on Simms is also highly significant. See Stanley T. Williams, "Spanish Influences on the Fiction of William Gilmore Simms," *Hispanic Review,* XXI (July, 1953), 221–228; and *The Spanish Background of American Literature* (New Haven, 1955), I, *passim.* Among Simms's works reflecting his Spanish interest are *Pelayo, Count Julian, The Damsel of Darien, Donna Florida, The Vision of Cortes, The Lily and the Totem, Vasconselos, The Cassique of Kiawah,* and "The Maroon."

[29] See "German Literature," *Southern Literary Gazette,* n.s., I (Sept. 15, 1829), in which Simms states that "no portion of Literary history [is] of more importance to us, than that of Germany" (p. 197).

[30] Thomas, *op. cit.,* p. 129.

American themes, the short fiction of William Gilmore Simms covers a wide range in form, subject, setting, and purpose: it ranges from Gothic tale to tall tale, sketch to novelette; from English troubadour to Negro slave, European castle to Southern wigwam; from highly supernatural to starkly realistic, fanciful to historical, quasi-philosophical to quasi-scientific. This variety demonstrates Simms's versatility and wide interests, but it is nevertheless true that his chief accomplishments fall within a single category: the portrayal of the people, manners, and folkways of the South. If even his best stories mirror the prejudices and idiosyncracies of the Old South, this reflection also attests to the author's faithfulness in depicting his region, which to his mind was his "proper . . . contribution" to national letters. Simms's pictures of three important peoples in American history—the colonial Indian, the pre-Civil War Negro, and the Southern frontiersman or backwoodsman [31]—are the most complete in the American short story; in addition, his stories of the Indian, the Negro, and the backwoodsman generally possess a charm and picturesqueness lacking in much of his fiction.

III

The fifteen stories and tales selected for this volume range, in dates of original publication, from 1828 to 1870—excluding of course "Bald-Head Bill Bauldy" and "The Humours of the Manager," the manuscript stories now published for the first time. Only the Civil War decade is not represented: from the 1820's there are two stories; from the 1830's, two; from the 1840's, six; from the 1850's, two; and from 1870, one. Actually, since "Sharp Snaffles," "Bald-Head Bill Bauldy," and "The Humours of the Manager" were written mainly during the 1860's, that decade is well represented in dates of composition if not in dates of publication. In length the selections illustrate both Simms's "novels in little"—*Martin Faber,* "Carl Werner," "Maize in Milk," "The Maroon," "How Sharp Snaffles Got His Capital and Wife," and "Bald-Head Bill Bauldy"; and his "mere scenes or sketches"—"Indian Sketch," "Confessions of a Murderer," "The Unknown Masque," and "Ephraim Bartlett, the Edisto Raftsman." The other tales—"The Bride of Hate," "Mesmerides in a Stage-Coach," *The Prima Donna, Flirtation at the Moultrie*

[31] The term *backwoodsman* rather than the more familiar *frontiersman* is chosen as the more appropriate word.

House, and "The Humours of the Manager"—are medium-range stories seeming to fall within neither of these categories.

Though it has been pointed out that his short fiction is extremely versatile and wide ranging in subject matter and form, Simms himself preferred to divide it into only two large groups: "domestic tales," or "tales of the South," by which he meant all those tales in *The Wigwam and the Cabin,* for instance, and all others dealing with regional themes and settings; and "tales of the imagination," by which he meant those stories under the influence of German (and Spanish or other European) romanticism, usually with exotic settings and heavy philosophical or psychological undertones. There are instances, of course, in which these two divisions overlap, but it is surprising how many of Simms's stories fall neatly into one group or the other. Simms early visualized publishing "two separate miscellanies, one consisting of 'Tales of the South' purely—. . . and another of a more imaginative character." [32] Perhaps the success he experienced with *The Wigwam and the Cabin* only whetted his desire for his other "separate miscellany," for he waged a lifelong (albeit unsuccessful) campaign to interest a publisher in a collection of his "things purely imaginative." [33] On August 8, 1845, for instance, he wrote his old friend Duyckinck, editor of Wiley and Putnam's Library of American Literature (of which *The Wigwam and the Cabin* was a volume), a very strong plea: "A volume of Imaginative Stories—purely such, &, in my poor conceit, singularly original & successful as such,—such, indeed, as have no resemblance in American Literature, unless in the writings of Poe, and partially of Hawthorne—are to be collated out of my materials. I can give you some titles, the articles —some of which—are in your hands." [34]

Unable to persuade Duyckinck, and Wiley and Putnam, to issue a companion volume to *The Wigwam and the Cabin,* Simms then approached, in order, Burgess and Stringer [35] (who had published *Helen Halsey* and *Castle Dismal*), Paine and Burgess [36] (New York publishers with a declared exclusive interest in American books), and

[32] Letter of June 6, [1845], to E. A. Duyckinck; *Letters,* II, 66.

[33] Simms used this phrase both in a letter to James Lawson on June 7, [1845], and in a letter of June 25, 1845, to Duyckinck (see *Letters,* II, 71, 79).

[34] *Letters,* II, 99.

[35] See *Letters,* II, 109, 115–116, 119–120, 133.

[36] See *Letters,* II, 133, 154, 216. Actually Simms approached Burgess and Stringer, and Paine and Burgess, through his friend and agent Lawson.

Carey and Hart[37] (Edward L. Carey was one of Simms's favorite correspondents)—all to no avail. Finally, seemingly discouraged, he dropped the idea, however reluctantly, for more than twenty years, only to revive it again in 1868, when he wrote to his former publisher, J. S. Redfield, on September 4: "Now, it so happens, that I have a collection of *short* stories, suitable for periodical publication. . . . These are all in print, having been furnished to annuals & periodicals some 20 to 30 years ago. They were then considered highly successful. Many of them are of imaginative, psychological or spiritual character."[38]

Among the titles Simms suggested to Redfield were three of his long-time favorites that nearly always figured prominently in his proposed edition of "tales of the imagination"—*Martin Faber*, "Carl Werner," and "The Bride of Hate." An earlier choice, "The Maroon," was dropped by 1868 possibly because it had been collected in both *Marie de Berniere: A Tale of the Crescent City, etc. etc. etc.* (1853) and *The Maroon; A Legend of the Caribbees, and Other Tales* (1855), but more probably because of the author's hopes to publish it as a separate book.[39] It is perhaps significant that Simms made no mention to Redfield of "How Sharp Snaffles Got His Capital and Wife" (because it was already submitted to *Harper's?*) or "Bald-Head Bill Bauldy" (because it was not yet written?) or "The Humours of the Manager" (written but without a publisher). Why he did not recommend at least "The Humours of the Manager," which we know he had written (but not committed to a publisher) by September, 1868, is particularly curious. The answer, of course, could be that Simms had in mind for the Redfield collection only previously published "moral imaginative" stories. Yet the fact that he once had included *The Wigwam and the Cabin* (as well as *Castle Dismal*, *Confession*, and *Carl Werner*) among "several bretheren of the same order"[40] as *Martin Faber* reveals that he did not always clearly distinguish between his "domestic" and his "moral imagina-

[37] See *Letters*, II, 381–382.

[38] Later in the letter Simms stated of the stories here described as "all in print"—"all of them have been for 20 years out of print." *Letters*, V, 156–157.

[39] See Textual Introduction to "The Maroon," below, p. 709. Other titles variously suggested for the "tales of imagination" volume are, in Simms's own words, "Conrade Weickhoff," "The Star Brethren," "Annihilation" (later entitled "The Wages of Battle"), "The Lucumo of Etruria," "The Pilgrim of Love," "Ipsistos," and "Logoochie."

[40] Letter to Rufus W. Griswold, December 6, 1846; *Letters*, II, 224.

tive" tales. Simms must have had reasons unknown to us for not offering "The Humours" to Redfield; but the problem does point up the disadvantage, not to say folly, of unequivocally accepting Simms's generally helpful, but overly simplified partitioning of his tales into only two subject headings.

A more meaningful division—at least for the fifteen stories in this volume—might be a three-pronged classification: *moral imaginative, manners,* and *the backwoods,* as suggested below:

I. *Moral Imaginative*[41] (5)
   A. German: "Confessions of a Murderer," *Martin Faber,* "Carl Werner," and "The Bride of Hate"
   B. Spanish: "The Maroon"

II. *Manners* (5)
   A. Plantation: "Maize in Milk"
   B. Theatrical: *The Prima Donna* and "The Humours of the Manager"
   C. City: *Flirtation at the Moultrie House*
   D. Pseudo-scientific: "Mesmerides in a Stage-Coach"

III. *The Backwoods* (4)
   A. Dialect: "Ephraim Bartlett," "Sharp Snaffles," and "Bald-Head Bill Bauldy"
   B. Non-dialect: "Indian Sketch"

The only selection in the fifteen not fitting one of these headings more or less clearly is "The Unknown Masque. A Sketch of the Crescent City," which in fact fits two: moral imaginative (German) and manners (city). Other of the stories might also be classified variously, but, as a guideline used with discretion, this tripartite division may prove helpful. It should, for instance, be noted that all the stories might be divided, like the backwoods tales, into those that are primarily humorous and those that are not. All the stories of manners, for example, are humorous with the exception of "Maize in Milk" (not *primarily* humorous, at least) and *The Prima Donna.*

[41] The term "moral imaginative" is Simms's own (see, for example, the "Advertisement" *to Carl Werner, An Imaginative Story; with Other Tales of Imagination,* below, p. 89; and his December 6, 1846, letter to Griswold, *Letters,* II, 230), but, as indicated above, he used it and other terms variously.

Note, too, that none of the moral imaginative stories are humorous (although there are touches of grim humor in *Martin Faber* and "The Maroon"). Perhaps, too, it is worth observing that Simms uses dialect to relate only those backwoods stories which he intends to be humorous.

Although Simms himself seems to have held some of his "tales of imagination" in highest regard, the three stories in the present collection almost certain to have the biggest impact on the modern reader are "How Sharp Snaffles Got His Capital and Wife," "Bald-Head Bill Bauldy," and "The Humours of the Manager." These three tales alone put Simms front-and-center in the tradition of American humor, a tradition with which he has never adequately been linked because his humorous writings have not been known—just as Simms the short-storyist has been neglected because his short stories in general have not been known. Perhaps the chief contribution of this volume is to help correct this deficiency—and though not all of its contents will enhance Simms's reputation or please his readers, "Sharp Snaffles" and "Bald-Head Bill Bauldy," at the very least, in their somewhat different ways will inevitably do both.

Part I

STORIES AND TALES

[*One of Simms's earliest attempts at fiction, "Indian Sketch," was published in the November, 1828, number of the* Southern Literary Gazette, *a Charleston literary journal co-edited by Simms and James Wright Simmons. Explanatory and Textual Notes begin on page 557.*]

INDIAN SKETCH.

During a short excursion, some few years since in the Western country, I found, after a long and fatiguing ride over bad roads, on a hot and sultry day in June, that I was at length approaching something like a human settlement. The indication of the traces of human perseverance are to be met with in the wilderness some miles in advance of the habitations of the wanderers themselves. The long cross rail fence, the opening in the trees upon the sky, the clear whistle of the wind among the few remaining giants of the forest, and the distant hum of happy voices—together with the more clearly marked and intelligible lowing of cattle, neighing of horses, cackling of geese, and now and then the dark apparition of some bristly hog half wild and half tame, brushing suddenly by you, to your infinite alarm, particularly if night fall be at hand. Travelling, (as in all new countries, one must, if he wishes to travel without inconvenience from creeks running over their banks by frequent freshets, felled trees and often compelled to take a new road) on horseback, is calculated to render, after a long day's ride, the sight of a farm house one of those somethings in life, which, while we should blush to give it the character or appellation of a pleasure, is nevertheless an object of no little moment and concern. I found the one to which I was fast approaching a perfect cure to my fatigue and ill-humour of the day. Whether it was that I had already begun to calculate on the smoking and enticing supper of fried bacon, eggs, fresh water trout, fresh butter, and round and glowing biscuits made of new Ohio flour—or that the natural tendency of the frame to repose and quietude, induced the feeling of gratitude and pleasure that I enjoyed, I leave to bookmen, apt at enquiries of this nature, to determine. Certain it was that I was more than pleased. I had ridden the whole day through a seemingly interminable forest, that, when I had emerged from the density of one seemed to show forth a denser and darker in which I had to embowel myself—that I had at length arrived safe at my resting place for the night, and all that was left for me to do, was to see my horse fed, rubbed down, and watered (a duty which no traveller ought to neglect) and to provide for the content and appetite of his equally hungering and jaded master. It required no great effort to make the inmates of this well stocked but humble cottage understand the nature of my wants, and provide for them accordingly, practised as they were, by an almost daily recurrence of similar duties. The supper table of neat pine was quickly furnished forth—a white cotton cloth with fringe from its sides a foot deep, was soon spread over it, and the rude but well relished dainties of country life were before me, and I nothing loth, ready for the repast.

I ate my supper in silence. My host was a half breed, who had married an Indian woman of the Nation (Choctaw) and under the sanction of the tribe, had commenced the business of Innkeeper upon their principal road. It is never the character of the Indian to be communicative; and nature has in this simple particular provided him with an education, which makes him more polite than the civilized man. His native independence and secluded and wandering habits, by removing him from the necessity of society, throws him upon himself, and his mind becomes actively employed, while his tongue may be said to slumber. The half-breed has so much of the aborigine still about him, that he partakes of nearly the same ascetic and taciturn disposition. His words are always significant and full of meaning—his looks are taught to have a language of their own for the better filling out and illustrating the brief and pithy accents of his speech. The Indian women are of a degraded *caste* in the opinion of the men. They are considered and used as mere beasts of burthen. Seldom, if ever admitted to the confidence of equality or affection, they are kept at a humble distance from their superiors, who assume to themselves in practice, the full supremacy as Lords of the creation. Nothing can be more amusing to one who is at all intimate with the Indian character, than the various pictures which are given of them by the Poet and the novelist. Nothing more idle and extravagant. The glory of the Indians (as they were) is the hunt and the battle field; and in robbing them of the extent of country sufficient for the one pursuit, and exercising such a powerful restraint upon them, as a ready and well-armed frontier, in the other, we seem to have robbed them of all of that pride, love of adventure and warlike enthusiasm, which is the only romance, the North American Indian ever had in his character.

As I have said, my supper was discussed in silent solemnity. My host sat before me at the head of the table, eating only occasionally. His consort, a large, strapping Indian woman *stood up behind* his chair and waited upon us throughout the meal. The looks of both of them as well as of two young and tolerably well looking savages who sat in the corner of the room, seemed full of gravity and sadness. Although naturally gloomy and sullen, I could easily perceive that something unusual had taken place, and accordingly as soon as our repast was ended, after a preliminary compliment on my part of a twist of Tobacco, which seemed to have stirred up the spirit to an effort, I began my enquiries of the youngest of the group whom I soon ascertained to be the most communicative and intelligent. From him, I gathered the following interesting communication. There had been, it seems, (I use my own language, as his was broken and scarcely intelligible) a number of Indians, young men and women, employed by a neighbouring planter (a white man) to pick a quantity of cotton which he had on hand. For some days they pursued their labor, with a diligence and assiduity, which, accustomed as we are to hear of the indisposition of the Indians to all manner of employment, except that of hunting, was, at least to me, new and interesting.

At length on the last day of the time for which they had been employed, the Planter, after rewarding them for their labor, produced the all inviting jug of whiskey—and placed it before them. This there was no withstanding. Those who had tasted the "Fire water" before, now set the example for those as yet ignorant of its perniciously seductive influence, and they all, with the exception of Mewanto became immediately intoxicated. This young man, who amidst the general example thus placed before him and from a society, than which, he could have no other restraint, could thus stoically resist, it must be supposed was a man of no ordinary strength of mind. He was in fact the pride of his people, and amidst their general depravity they felt the moral superiority of the man, and were "ashamed of their nakedness." Mewanto, had among the many who had thus bartered the higher energies of their original character, for a sensual and momentary indulgence, one intimate, closely allied and dear friend, called Oolatibbe. He strove for a long while to prevent this young man from falling into the dangerous habits of his associates—but in vain. The prevalence of custom proved more effective than the advice and entreaties of friendship, and the youth, unaccustomed to the liquor, became in a short time deeply intoxicated. His friend, with some difficulty led him away from the small grove or thicket where the rest of the party were still carousing, and represented to him in the simple language of truth, the danger and the error of his present licentious and unhappy indulgence. He spoke with much warmth and a good deal of that native eloquence with which this people are said to be so admirably gifted—and I remember, my informant having used (for he adopted the figurative mode of speech so common, not only with them but every savage people) as the language of the young savage on this occasion, the following sentence. Alluding to the prostration of his people on the appearance of the whites, "that they had been as many as the leaves on the trees about them, but the white man had been the whirlwind that shook them down, and the remaining few were falling one by one, blighted and blasted by the cunning of their enemy, otherwise, wholly unable to remove them." The drunken man listened to him with a sort of stupid attention for some time, but at length suddenly starting back as if he had encountered some fearful object, he tore the knife from his belt, and before his friend could avoid the danger plunged it quickly into the bosom of Mewanto, who fell dead upon the spot.

He remained in a sort of stupor for a moment—but suddenly became sobered on the instant to behold with horror the dead body before him. A shriek or howl, which is indicative of some matter of death, and peculiar to the Indians, was the result of his first awakening to sensibility and reason. This, the rest of the Indians perfectly well understood, and it had the effect of bringing them all to their proper senses. A loud, wild and melancholy cry was sent up in general by the party—the murderer preceding them to the great council of the nation. They placed no restraint whatever upon him—and without any compunction he voluntarily delivered himself up to the council and demanded to be led to death. "To-morrow," said my informant in conclusion, "he will be shot."* And where is he now, said I, anxious to gather from the youth as

* We annex a poem by a native writer upon this subject, which (as we believe it has never been quoted before) may serve as an apt illustration of this article.

At midnight did the Chiefs convene,
With many a shriek of wild alarm,
'Till solemn silence hushed the scene,
As in prophetic charm;
When, wild the cry of horror broke,
As thus a dark brow'd warrior spoke:

"I come to die—no vain delay,
Nor trembling pulse unnerves my soul;
Ye fellow Chiefs, prepare the way—
Let death's dark clouds about me roll;
My bosom feels alone life's dread—
There is no feeling with the dead!

Our tribe has lost its bravest steel—
'Tis well the scabbard follow too,
Since life no longer can reveal
Aught that can glad my view:
From its own home, I madly tore
The jewel, that my bosom wore.

He cross'd me in my hour of wrath,
And still with cruel love pursued—
An evil spirit dimn'd my path,
A film o'erspread my gaze—I view'd
No more, the friend I lov'd so well,
But some insatiate foe from hell!

My hand had grasp'd its kindred knife,
A struggle, and I heard a cry—
It was the shriek of parting life,
For it is hard to die,
A friend or kindred soul to leave—
Now, there are none, for me will grieve!

Too late, too late I knew my friend,
Too late, had wish'd the deed undone!
'Twere vain, my bosom's grief to blend
With tears, that can restore me none,
(Tho' in unending streams they fell)
Of all the friend, I loved so well.

much more as possible, for his fit of talkativeness seemed to be nearly exhausted. "By your side," he returned. I started and beheld

---

Far, wand'ring on the distant hills,
  Yet, watching for the morning's dawn,
His spirit lingers near the rills,
  Now anxious to be gone:
And only waits my kindred shade,
To bear it to the grave I made.

His hatchet seen in gleaming light,
  When first the warhoop's cry is heard,
I've placed to meet his waking sight,
  When carols first the morning bird!
Nor did my bosom's care forget,
His rifle, knife and calumet!

Prepare the grave, I long to fly,
  To that far distant realm of bliss,
Where nought can dim the spirit's eye,
  Or, lead the heart like this;
Where, morning owns no clouded shade,
And life is light, and undecay'd.

Oh, brother, whom I madly slew,
  Then shall our kindred spirits join;
At morn the red-deer's path pursue—
  At eve the tented camp entwine;
Close at one time the mutual eye,
And on one blanket's bosom, lie."

No longer spoke the Warrior Chief,
  But sullen sternness clothed his brow,
Whilst fate and anguish, fix'd and brief,
  Proclaim'd him—ready now!
No counsel spoke—no pray'r was made—
No pomp—no mock'ry—no parade.

He walk'd erect, unaw'd, unbound;
  He stood upon the grave's dread brink,
And look'd with careless eye around;
  Nor did his spirit shrink,
The deadly rifle's aim to greet,
His bosom long'd its death to meet.

A moment's pause—no sound was heard;
  He gazed—then with unchanging look,
He spoke in pride, the signal word,
  With which the valley shook—
And when the smoke had cleared away,
The dark-eyed Chief before me lay.

the same young man, whose countenance had first struck me while at the supper table. The question involuntarily rose and I asked with some astonishment—"and is he not confined—and will he not escape." "He cannot fly, for did he not help to make the law himself." Thus was the powerfully moral rule of all christian denominations, "Do not unto others what you would not others should do unto you," faithfully and honestly obeyed on the most trying occasion in the annals of humanity, as if it had been one of the simplest duties of the domestic hearth.

I was curious to witness the final termination of this, to me, wonderful characteristic of a people, whom we have learned to despise, before we have been taught to understand. I turned round and fixed my gaze upon the condemned. What could a spectator, unacquainted with the circumstances, have met with there. Nothing of the precise and awful matter of fact, that connected itself with the fortunes and life of the object of observation. I addressed him—I brought him to the subject so deeply interesting to himself. He spoke of it, as of those common occurrences which we often speak of unconsciously. He took up the handle of a tomahawk and employed himself in carving upon it, a space for a bit of flattened silver which he labored to introduce into it. He spoke in detached sentences, during this little effort. In reply to a question which I put, touching the commission of the crime, and whether he was conscious that he was doing it or not, he replied—"Yes—he knew it all—he knew it was the one of himself, the best part—but he had put on a horrible shape and the evil one darkened his eye sight—that while he struck the blow, he knew perfectly well that it was his friend he struck, but that he was made to do it."

We conversed at intervals till a late hour—he seemed to sing at times or rather muttered a few broken catches of song, monotonous and highly solemn—at length, the rest having withdrawn, he threw himself upon a bear skin before the door, and I attended the little boy, who was with difficulty aroused from a deep sleep, to my chamber, which he pointed out.

It may be supposed, I slept little that night. I was filled with thoughts of the strange obedience which this ignorant savage manifested to his rude and barbarous, but really equitable laws. The highest moral obligation however instructing him, "that he must not expect others to do, what he would not do himself."

The next morning, a large crowd had assembled within and around the house in which I slept. I rose and went to the window. The open space in front of the house was covered with the Indians. A great deal of excitement seemed to run through them all. I dressed myself as quickly as possible and went down among them. They were crowded in the house as well as in the area before it. I looked about for the principal in this extraordinary spectacle—his were the only features unmoved in the assembly. He seemed busily employed in gathering up sundry little articles as well of ornament as necessity in the Indian's life. His dress seemed more studied—it consisted of a pair of pantaloons, seemingly much worn, and probably the cast off donation of some passing traveller. There was a buckskin hunting shirt on him, with several falling capes, all thickly covered with fringe, a belt of wampum, studded with beads of various colours, tolerably well arranged, encircled his waist—while his legs, which were well formed, were admirably fitted by a pair of leggings loaded with beads. Several other little ornaments were thrown about him, particularly over his neck and shoulders.

A difference of sentiment seemed to operate upon, and form a division among the assembled multitude, an air of anger, impatience and exultation, fully indicated the friends of the deceased thirsting for the blood of his murderer—while an appearance of sadness and concern, pointed out those who were more tenderly disposed toward him. At length, the victim himself made the first signal of preparation. He arose, and giving to a little boy who followed him, a bundle which he had been making up of beads, hatchets, arrow heads, knives, tobacco-pouch and some other little things, he led the way. I joined in the mournful procession. Our way lay through a long grove of stunted pines—at the end of which we were met, and accompanied by the three men appointed as his executioners, who were armed with rifles, which they wore under the left arm.

Never did I behold a man with a step so firm on any occasion, or head so unbent—a countenance so unmoved, and yet without any of the effort common to most men who endeavor to assume an aspect of heroism upon an event so trying. He walked as to a victory. The triumphal arch seemed above him, and instead of an ignominious death, a triumph over a thousand hearts seemed depicted before him.

The grave was in sight. I watched his brow attentively. I felt myself shudder and grow pale, but saw no change in him. He began a low song, apparently consisting of monosyllables only. He grew more impassioned—more deeply warm. I could not understand a single word he uttered—but, even though he stood as firm, proud and unbending as a Roman might be supposed to have stood, as if he disdained the addition of action to his words, the cadence, the fall, the melody and wild intonation of this high-souled savage's voice was to me an active eloquence, which I could not misunderstand. He paused at length. Then moving with an even pace, he took his place at the head of the grave prepared for him—beckoned the boy near, who had followed him, with the simple utensils of savage life, and when he had retired, motioned the executioners. I saw them prepare their rifles, and take their aim—I looked upon the features of the victim—they were steady and calm—I turned my head away with a strange sickness. I heard the single report of the three rifles, and when I turned my eye upon the spot so lately occupied by the unfortunate victim of an infatuation, which has slain more than the sword, they were slowly shovelling the earth into the grave of the murderer.

[*Like "Indian Sketch," the "Confessions of a Murderer" appeared in the* Southern Literary Gazette—*in the long missing November 1, 1829, number of the second or "new" series, with which number the journal died. Several years later "Confessions of a Murderer" provided Simms the germ for* Martin Faber, *his first piece of fiction published separately in book form. Explanatory and Textual Notes begin on page 563.*]

CONFESSIONS OF A MURDERER.

I was born in an obscure country village in D———; the place had not more than ten or twelve families, and that of my parents was one of the most intelligent and respectable. The village was one of that class which is never known to vary its position; it neither increased nor diminished, and my father was one of the principal, if not the only principal man in it. Would he had been less so. Had he thought more of his own and the business of his own family and less of those around, I should not this day recount the history of my own disgrace. But my father was the great man, the lion of the village, and I became no less so of my mama's fireside. I was a spoiled boy even before I could read—so early are the principles of the human mind subject to misdirection. I was perverse, unruly and puerile, and my father mended the matter very considerably by damning at me on all warrantable occasions. To him and to my mother I charge my crime and its punishment, and while they are wondering how so bad a scion should spring from so good a stock, they have been weaving the rope about my neck. I shall render amends to the laws of the land; they are accountable to God, and to his mercies I leave them.

I was a truant from school and exulted in it without punishment. I was brutal while a mere boy to all around me; was a boor in decent society; was insolent to my parents; rude and boisterous at table; savage and ferocious among my associates and received no punishment. Sometimes when I exceeded even the bounds of toleration, tacitly joined to my conduct by my father, I received some such rebuke as—'now my dear how can you do so,' or, 'I will be vexed with you, my son, if you do not behave.'

What was all this to an overgrown boy, nursed in full ideas of his own importance, licentious in his habits, and admitted to all and any irregularities, for which my father furnished an ample model. I bade defiance to threats, and scorned reproaches. I laughed at the soothings of my mother and took her gifts and favors, furnished in order to persuade me to do better, as things of course which she was obliged to give me. I was brought up a brute, and fulfilled to the letter the seeming objects of my education. Their lessons fitted me to be what I have been, and have reduced me to the miserable situation in which I now am. But let that rest.

I was sent to school, but learnt nothing, or what I learnt was entirely obliterated and counteracted by the nature of my education at home. I cared little to learn; my tutor dared not coerce me; he was a poor miserable hireling from the east, who cringed to all for his bread and who considered my father's influence as a matter which would not allow him to restrain or chastise his favorite son. Whatever I did, therefore, went by with impunity. However extravagant, violent or insolent my amusements, I was unpunished. Grown bold and confident, I even ventured to assume the burdens of my companions, announce myself as the offender and get them off free of punishment, while I escaped myself. One day, however, a circumstance occurred which could not pass so easily. It was under the master's own eye, and I was brought up to receive the award which his sense of justice or his lenity might think proper to bestow. He did not even flog me, he spoke to me like a father; as my father never spoke to me; his words were those of kindness, of friendship. I laughed in his face. He was indignant, as well he might be, and gave me a smart blow with his open hand on my face. I looked round upon my companions in order to ascertain if I should be supported, but they were kept in more subjection than myself and dreaded him accordingly. I submitted, though my heart rankled and my spirit burned within me for revenge. I had it—many years afterwards I had it. A deep and dreadful revenge. For the time, however, I contented myself with one more congenial with the little spirit of a bad and brutal boy. He kept me in, as a punishment, after the boys generally had been dismissed. He left me in the schoolroom and retired to his dinner. While in that room shut up, what were my emotions! The spirit of a demon was working in me, and the passion of my heart nearly exhausted my body; I threw myself on the floor and wept; hot, scalding tears. I rose—I strode for a long time to and fro; a sudden thought seized me; a mean and paltry revenge filled my bosom, as I stopt before a couple of large, new and beautiful globes that had just come to my teacher at a vast expense. I now perceived my revenge. Though small in proportion, to what it appeared to me that my wrongs required, I well knew that the injury of his globes would be almost the most severe revenge I could take upon their owner. A jug of ink lay beside them. I opened it carefully and poured its contents upon the beautifully varnished lines of the heavens and the earth. They were ruined, irrevocably ruined. These are trifles you will say, but you are mistaken. To people advanced in years the life of a boy is made up of trifles; but these incidents are developed with the growth of the child to maturity. The same feeling which prompted to the act just related, would prompt an incendiary to the firing of his enemy's dwelling; the same feeling grown mature with my years, prompted me to the commission of a murder—the crime which to-morrow I shall partially expiate upon the gallows.

Weakly could I describe his rage upon discovering what I had done. I was in the school-room, where he had left me, when he returned. For some time he did not perceive them, but walking up and down he spoke to me for a long time in a manner, which, had I not been acted on by something of the spirit of the arch-enemy of man, must have had the effect of compelling me to acknowledge and atone by the only mode in my power for my errors and misconduct. In vain—I was callous alike to reason and kindness. Suddenly, the globes caught his eye—he stopt short; he approached them; passed his hand over his face and actually shed tears. But human passion triumphed; he turned shortly upon me and smote me with his fist upon the face. The blow was a severe one and felled me to the earth. In the first movement of anger, he took me by the arm and with his school strap inflicted upon me a severe but richly deserved flogging. But I thought not so then. I did not for a moment consider the vast robbery I had made from that poor man's small stock of happiness and enjoyment. My feelings were all concentrated in my self—all my own and according with the manner of my education. The revenge of my boyhood did not rest here. A solemn convocation of the chief men of the village, at the head of which stood my father, highly incensed at the indignity, determined upon the offence. The man lost his school and another more indulgent and tractable took his place. What became of the unfortunate man thus turned out of employment by the babble of a boy, for some time I knew not. My revenge contemplated him reduced to necessity, and exulted at the picture which its own desires had presented. He was not the only sufferer. A wife and two infant children—girls—claimed his care. They departed from the village and took a road farther into the country. I did not care to follow them.

Years glided on, and brought something like an improvement to my physical appearance at least. I became manly, and rather graceful and active. My features underwent a considerable change for the better, and perhaps, my manners were less objectionable. My heart, however, remained the same. There was a spell upon it; it seemed seared and while it blighted the fortunes and the feelings of others, partook somewhat of the blight itself. My time, as before, was consumed in idleness. Such amusements as tended to the encouragement of this disposition were always an object of concern with me. Angling, hunting, and frolicking made the day and night of my existence; an existence that I now perceive has been all night. Talk not of the darkness of Greenland; the moral night is the worst of all darkness; the heart and the affections are there, prisoners in a dungeon of space and vacuity.

One morning, with my gun, I had wandered for some time through a part of the country into which I had never before penetrated. The game was plentiful and any thing but shy. I was easily seduced therefore into a long, but encouraging pursuit. I had gone some fourteen or fifteen miles from our village on the opposite river. My way led through a close and umbrageous forest. A grove of dwarf or scrub oaks, woven about with thick and sheltering vines gave a delightful air of quietness to the scene, which while I felt pleased with, my natural inquietude of disposition would not permit me to enjoy. Wheeling to return, I perceived for the first time a clear and sheltered creek, that stole in among the shrubbery and again made its way into the light at a considerable distance beyond. I followed its bendings. It was a sweet place and the hum of the wind among the tree tops alone broke the solemn and mysterious repose of silence. A small arbor arose upon a bank that jutted into the creek so far, that but for a small and narrow neck which united it to the main, might almost be considered an island. I approached it from the point where it was most sheltered, and saw not and was also unseen, by a tall and beautiful girl that reclined on a small hillock beyond it. We both started with surprise at the same moment. I cannot say that our emotions were those of love, but the surprise was productive of pleasure, to me at least, and I feel too much to her. I apologized for my intrusion, and how we grew familiar I cannot now say. My heart has been an Etna and preyed upon its own vitals. Suffice it—we parted, with a hope, though neither of us expressed it, to meet again. We did meet, and every successive day found me with my gun and on the same journey; I killed no birds, however, as before.

That girl was the most artless, the most innocent of all God's creatures! Strange that she should be condemned to a union with the worst and wildest!—need I say, that I, whose touch has contaminated all whose ill fortunes doomed them to any connection with me, blighted and blasted that innocence and changed the smile into the tear and the hope into the fear of that fond and confiding woman. We were both comparatively children; but I—I had lived many; many years of dissipation and crime. I had concentered a long life of wickedness into a few brief years and its concentrated venom fell upon her. But our commerce while it continued was productive of but few sorrows. She gave every thing up to her affection for me: she taught me to love, she loved me, as the young and morning flower has been seen to entwine itself about the deadly and poisonous nightshade.

I had grown to man's estate, my father was returning to a state of second childhood and his principal employment, at this time, was that of looking out a fitting and proper match for his son. Wealth, entered largely into the essentials required of the lady, and his labors were not entirely unavailing. He made a selection. His choice was concurred in by all parties, save myself, and I had, as yet, heard nothing of the matter. But that was no objection. It proved none. I had long been reduced to many straits for ready money. My pursuits rendered much of this necessary; for though my time was greatly given to my intercourse with Emily (such was her name) yet I had not so entirely divested myself of old employments and associates, as to do without this necessary. I saw no difficulty, at the same time, in marrying the heiress, and enjoying as before the society of the poor sweet girl I had dishonored. My resolution was taken, and a few days saw me in preparation for the bridal. For two days I went not to my place of rendesvous. I was too busily employed. On the third a smart but pensive faced boy, arrested me at the door of the mansion house of the lady to whom I was engaged. I recognized her with surprise and apprehension. I took her aside. Emily, said I, what brings you here. Can you ask, she replied; could I fail to see you for two whole days, nor fear every thing. Alas! you know not, I see, how long two days are to me. Where have you been, what has detained you, were you sick. I have been sick, Emily, I replied unhesitatingly, but am not now. To-morrow you will see me without fail. But where are you going now she continued. Is this the house you live in—'tis very handsome. But Walter, you will come, dear Walter? I will Emily, go now, and expect me. We parted. How like a child, a sweet confiding child, she spoke to me. Yet at the very moment that the accents of her voice were most tender and touching I had begun to hate her. She was in my way. I kept my appointment however. She was in waiting, and seemingly in very bad spirits. Had she heard any thing? She had. In a few words she gave me to understand that the rumour of my intended marriage had met her ear, and she now enquired of me if it was so. I denied it.

'Walter,' she exclaimed earnestly, 'I believe you, I cannot think for a moment you would wrong me so. But Walter, a something tells me that I shall not live very long, and I would be your wife before the time comes, when my sin will stand embodied before me. You have promised me frequently; say that you will marry me this week, I don't care what time, dear Walter, only let it be this week.'

Her eyes filled as she spoke and her heart palpitated violently as I pressed it against my own. It was the prayer of an apprehensive and almost subdued spirit. Disappointment, for I had long deceived her with promises, had worn and harassed her to a skeleton. But I had no notion of complying. I was inflexible; I was brutally stern, I repulsed and when in the tenderest and most endearing accents she repeated her request, I quickly and pettishly replied that it was impossible.

'It is all true then, as they have said,' she exclaimed passionately. 'Oh, God, now do I feel my infirmity. But think not,' she continued as her face assumed all the majesty and loveliness of inspiration, 'think not thus to injure me unpunished, unpursued. I will go to the village, I will see this lady for whose love mine and my spirit must be sacrificed. She shall know whether it be compatible with her honor or the dignity of the female character, to unite herself with one who has so grievously injured one of her own sex,' and she burst into a passion of tears.

I was alarmed—I had never seen her exhibit so much firmness of purpose on any occasion before. How could I expect it, there had been no occasion whatever for such an exhibition 'till now. I seized her hand. She withdrew it quickly and indignantly. 'Emily,' I exclaimed, while I again took hold of and retained it firmly. She struggled, her strength was opposed to mine and in the heat of the struggle I forgot that victory in such a case would be the greatest shame. I hurled her to the ground, she looked up to me imploringly, apparently strove to speak, but in vain, and she turned her face despairingly upon the still dewy grass and sobbed as if the strings of her heart kept breaking with every motion of her lips. I know not what demon possessed me at that moment. There seemed to be a more than customary silence around me. I knelt beside her, and the fury was in me. My eyes wandered wildly around the forest. I uttered no word, but my left hand grasped her throat, she partly turned her head and exclaimed, while the tones came rattling forth, 'Walter, spare me, do Walter; I am too young, too bad to perish in my sins, dear Walter, I will not reproach you, I will not accuse you, I ——— O ———God!' and she was dead—dead under my hands. I breathed not, I moved not for a minute. My eyes were in the air, on the water, in the woods, but I dared not turn them to the still imploring glance of that fixed and terrified look.

Need I say more, than that I am now about to suffer for that crime? Need I say that Emily Stephenson was the eldest daughter of the poor man, who had been driven from his occupation by the boy, whose manhood had now proved so fatal to him. She was his eldest, most beloved, and tenderly nursed child. I have seen him once since; he spoke not to me; but when he looked upon me, he passed his hands over his eyes as if they had been seared and scathed by a bar of blistering fire. He rushed from my presence but now, and I am alone.

* * * *

I look once more from the window of my dungeon; what a crowd are in waiting. There are parents in that crowd; Alas! is there one whose son's education has been like mine? let him beware!

[*After its initial publication in 1833 by J. and J. Harper,* Martin Faber *was published again four years later by Harper and Brothers in a two-volume collection entitled* Martin Faber, the Story of a Criminal; and other Tales. *The substantive revisions which Simms made for the 1837 edition have been incorporated in the Centennial edition text. Explanatory and Textual Notes begin on page 564.*]

MARTIN FABER;
The Story of a Criminal.

TO

MY DAUGHTER—

TO ONE, WHO, AS YET,

CAN UNDERSTAND LITTLE BUT HIS LOVE,

THESE PAGES ARE FONDLY DEDICATED,

WITH ALL THE AFFECTIONS OF

A FATHER.

ADVERTISEMENT TO THE SECOND EDITION.

The story of "MARTIN FABER" was published two years ago—it was published under some few disadvantages. It happened to be put forth shortly after the appearance of a book called "Miserrimus," and, unhappily, it was soon found that a monstrous family likeness existed between the two performances. The coincidences were numerous. "Miserrimus" told his own story—so did "Martin." The one was a tale of crime—so was the other. The one was published by Harper and Brothers—so was the other. The one filled about two hundred pages—so did the other. And, more unlucky yet, the same style of printing and binding was chosen for both publications. After this, the identity became too striking to escape the eyes of many, who dwelt learnedly upon the likeness. It was a burning shame to copy at all—so they said—and then for the American to copy after the Englishman! Patriots, too, had much to say on this latter subject.

As an offset to these coincidences, when we say, that, in no incident of "Martin Faber" could any resemblance be discovered to the supposed prototype—that the motives of action, and the influences governing the two, were entirely different—that the one was desultory and without a plan, and the other had both plan and purpose—that the one, perhaps, never, or scarcely ever, lived, and that the other, unhappily for our country, has, of late years, become a character too common to create surprise—when we say this, and, in addition, say, that the moral, under deliberate and just criticism, must be considered decidedly in favour of the American story, the reader will probably suspect that the likeness between the two works is not so very striking after all.

What is that moral? This question suggests another matter of complaint with some of the critics, who have done the work the honour to pronounce, if not a judgment, at least a sentence upon it. The moral has been objected to, and, strange to say, none of those, so objecting, have condescended to state what it is, or to designate their grounds of objection to it. They have generally sheltered themselves under the convenient *ipse dixit* of that venerable father of the art, whom they will do wisely never to forget, and who says—with a complaisance not restrained to his own time—

"I do not like you, Doctor Fell,
The reason why, &c.
But," &c.

In the first edition of "Martin Faber," the Advertisement which prefaced it ran thus:—

"The work which follows is submitted with great deference and some doubt to the reader. It is an experiment; and the style and spirit are, it is believed, somewhat out of the beaten track. The events are of real occurrence, and, to the judgment of the author, the peculiarities of character which he has here drawn—if they may be considered such, which are somewhat too common to human society—are genuine and unexaggerated. The design of the work is purely moral, and the lessons sought to be inculcated are of universal application and importance. They go to impress upon us the necessity of proper and early education—they show the ready facility with which the best natural powers may be perverted to the worst purposes—they stimulate to honorable deeds in the young,—teach firmness under defeat and vicissitude, and hold forth a promise of ultimate and complete success to well directed perseverance. By exhibiting, at the same time, the injurious consequences directly flowing from each and every aberration from the standard of a scrupulous morality, they enjoin the strictest and most jealous conscientiousness. The character of Martin Faber, not less than that of William Harding, may be found hourly in real life. The close observer may often meet with them. They are here put in direct opposition, not less with the view to contrast and comparison, than incident and interest. They will be found to develope, of themselves, and by their results, the nature of the education which had been severally given them. When the author speaks of education he does not so much refer to that received at the school and the academy. He would be understood to indicate that which the young acquire at home in the parental dwelling—under the parental eye—in the domestic circle—at the family fire-side, from those who, by nature, are best calculated to lay the guiding and the governing principles. It is not at the university that the affections and the moral faculties are to be tutored. The heart, and—*les petites morales*—the manner, have quite another school and other teachers, all of which are but too little considered by the guardians of the young. These are—the father and the mother and the friends—the play-mates and the play-places."

It will be seen from this, that the author somewhat earnestly insisted upon his moral. He thought it highly valuable, and, in his estimation, it was evidently meant to do great things. How it came, after this, that the book was immoral, has created as much surprise in his mind, as, doubtless, it must have created in many of those who subsequently read it. Two years have elapsed since its first publication, and many have been the criticisms, pro and con, which have been written upon the work; yet is he incorrigible enough to aver, that he does not yet perceive where the moral fails. This confession may shock some and astonish others—it is proof of inveteracy somewhere, certainly; but, as the modest adventurer, liable to suspicion, is apt to say in the newspapers, let us beg that, for a while at least, "public opinion may be suspended."

The story of "Martin Faber" is an exceedingly simple one, and one that occurs more frequently than the wellbred gentleman of city life is apt to imagine. He tells his own story, and appears, according to his own account, as, in great part, the victim of parental perversion. He is a selfish and wanton criminal, as persons, so situated in infancy and childhood, are very apt to become. Every now and then, in his narrative, the reason—the true cause—the parent germe of his error and his crime—is permitted to appear. His doings are atrocious;—that is to say, he is a winner of the love, and a violater of his faith with woman—he is a liar and a murderer. There is nothing, surely, uncommon, however unnatural, in these offences. This nature is, after all, a curious matter. We may define it, not to be paradoxical, as the very creature of art—remarkable for its imitation, for its ingenuity, for its facile susceptibility to all early impressions. We make what we call the nature, from the plastic material so put before us, and this is education. To commit murder is unnatural, strictly speaking; but, in the sense of the word, as adopted in common parlance, it is not unnatural. Martin Faber is not unnatural—you may see him daily. He walks London with audacity, where, we are told, there are five thousand persons well disposed to defy the laws, and cut your throat, for a shilling. We see him in New-York, in Massachusetts, at Mobile and New-Orleans—that is to say, if the newspapers do not lie, and if citizens are not hung frequently without a reason. The character, unhappily for humanity, is but too common to be considered altogether unnatural.

The only difference between the narrative of crime given in "Martin Faber," and that furnished by the newspapers daily, consists in this little particular. The author of the work has striven to trace it to its causes—to describe its sources—to probe the wound, and to declare its depth. He aimed to show the steps by which erroneous principle rises from indulgence, and becomes the parent of fierce will, unbending passion, and law-defying excess. All the offences which the criminal usually commits against society, are studiously thrown together—not to attract, but to discourage and deter. The mind of the reader is shocked with that man, in his true colours, as a monster, whom he not unfrequently shakes hands with, as a fellow-citizen, in the street. Nobody sympathizes with him in his progress—nobody deplores his fate, which is that of the detected felon. The virtuous triumph—the vicious are overthrown. It is shown that all his evils spring from his errors; it is shown that the good fortune which attends the good, results from their adherence to principle. What more is wanted for morality? There is no single scene in the whole narrative, calculated, by its voluptuousness, to offend a delicate sense, or to entice a weak one; on the contrary, the colouring of the volume—the moral colouring throughout, even where the grosser events are narrated—is that which precedes the thunder-storm—that wild, cloud-compelling aspect, which, to the well-regulated mind, would have all the effect of warning and discouragement. The author was careful, in all the work, that the crimes of the chief actor in it, should be without any of those enjoyments, to him, which might be supposed to have attracted him, and which might lead others to the same excesses. He labours up the steeps of sin—he plucks the fruit from the forbidden tree—and his reward is blight and ashes. He lives in fear and hate—distrusting and distrusted—and he dies with the fullest consciousness that there is nothing of hope for him in the future, and nothing of grateful recollection for him in the past. No smiles receive him—no tears lament him—none weep above his tomb.

It has been objected, in "Martin Faber," that his occasional references to the vague notion of fatality, have an injurious tendency—but I see not this. It is only another error of his education. It matters not much to the public what may be the opinions of the outlaw. He may think what he pleases, and do little harm, until that period shall arrive—which, from some aspects in the moral world, would seem not so very far off—when we shall take our models from the gallows, and sanctify to our children the fame of the cut-throat and the felon. On this subject we may remark, that it is the stale cant of the detected criminal, always to ascribe to an agency beyond his own, the crimes for which he is about to suffer. Nobody, who reads criminal confessions, but must have seen how frequent are such references; and nothing is more true to nature—the nature even of the outcast—than that he should thus, when hope has failed, seek this form of palliation before the public, for those offences which his conscience yet teaches him are beyond excuse. An instance occurs of this sort in the lying narrative of Vaux—James Hardy Vaux—in whose memoirs the reader may find it. In "Martin Faber" it makes no part of the story; and the unmeaning phrases—for they amount to nothing more—which he utters on this subject, were solely employed to preserve the truth of portraiture. It is melancholy to think, as we pause and listen to such confessions as have here been spoken of, how strangely the mind seems to delight, even when there is no apparent necessity for it, in its own self-deception; though we must feel that such deceit, when uttered by the criminal, conveys, of itself, no small compliment to that predominant virtue in the community, which he feels acting upon him all the time, and of which he is conscious, when too late, that he has been the unwise enemy.

In conclusion, and to refer again to the supposed resemblance of "Martin Faber" to "Miserrimus," we may add, that the chief incidents of the former work were first published in the Southern Literary Gazette, a periodical put forth in Charleston, South Carolina, about seven years ago. It filled some eight or ten pages in the second volume of that journal, where the reader, if curious, will find it. From the paper entitled, "Confessions of a Murderer," the work was subsequently elaborated—partly in 1829, partly in 1832, and finally revised for publication in 1833, when it appeared in its present form. In the process of elaboration, new persons and new events received their existence. Thus, the character of William Harding, which does not appear in the original production, was introduced, and all the softening and gentler features of the work were the fruit of an after labour. The sterner, darker features of the story—those in their nature most resembling "Miserrimus," were all conceived in the first instance, and nearly all of them appear in the story as it was first given to the public, in the shape of a contribution to a monthly magazine.

"And thus hath been my strife—unbroken, long,
My care of being. There can be no foe
Like that which follows, and is born of guilt."

CHAPTER I.

This is a fearful precipice, but I dare look upon it. What, indeed, may I not dare—what have I not dared! I look before me, and, but for that awful strife—that gross exposure—the hissing scorn—the deriding shout—but for these, the prospect of death, terrible to all men, would have few or no terrors for me. Without adopting too greatly the spirit of cant which makes it a familiar phrase in the mouths of the many, death to me will prove a release from numberless strifes and trials. I do not fear death. Why should I fear that which I may not avoid? I look behind me, and the survey of my crimes, and of the past, however I may regret many of them, and much of it, at least brings with it no fears of the future, and but few compunctious visitings. They were among the occurrences known to, and the necessary sequence in the progress of time and the world's circumstance. They might have been committed by another as well as by myself. They must have been committed! I was but an instrument in the hands of a power with which I could not contend.

Yet, what a prospect, does this backward glance afford! How full of colors and characters—How curiously dark and bright. I am dazzled and confounded at the various phases of my own life. I wonder at the prodigious strides which my own feet have taken—and as I live and must die, I am bold to declare,—in half the number of instances, without my own consciousness. Should I be considered the criminal, in deeds so committed? Had not my arm been impelled —had not my mood been prompted by powers and an agency apart from my own, I had not struck the blow—I had not scorned the supposed obligation—I had not rejected the terms upon which society tendered me its protection. The demon was not of me, though presiding over, and prevailing within, me. Let those who can think, when the blood is boiling in their temples, analyze its throbs and the source of its impulses—let the skin-dried ascetic, withered over the map and the crucible, undertake the examination as he may. I cannot—I dare not. The life which was given me had a different direction, and I had no right to defeat its purposes. I am a fatalist. Enough for me that it was written!

My name is Martin Faber. I am the only son of German parents—people of good family, and, so far as paying their debts, and not flying in the face of society could make them so, very good sort of people. I was born in the village of M——, a little settlement of some sixty or seventy families, of quiet habits, and not very brilliant minds. The Fabers were the first among them in fortune and respectability; and, possessed of a strong, shrewd, and somewhat improved sense, my father, Nicholas Faber, contrived, after no very long period, to make himself the first man in the village, which was one of those that, having attained a certain growth, always after remain stationary. It stagnated accordingly; and such being the case, the prospect was exceedingly remote of a diminution in the influence of our family. On the contrary, my father, each successive day, grew more and more supreme in the estimation of the people. He was the only active principle among them. He did their thinking, and they were very willing to depute to him a labour so excessively unpopular—not to say undemocratic. He was their oracle—their counsellor—his word was law, and there were no rival pretensions set up in opposition to his supremacy. Would this had been less the case! Had Nicholas Faber been more his own, than the creature of others, Martin, his son, had not now obliterated all the good impressions of his family, and been called upon, not only to recount his own disgrace and crime, but to pay its penalties. Had he bestowed more of his time upon the regulation of his household, and less upon public affairs, the numberless vicious propensities, strikingly marked in me from childhood up, had, most probably been sufficiently restrained. But it was fated that such should not have been the case. It was decreed that he should neglect or mislead, and that I should be misled. As I have already said—it was written!

The only child, I was necessarily the favorite. The pet of mama, the prodigy of papa, I was permitted to dogmatize and do as I pleased from my earliest infancy. I grew apace, but in compliance with maternal tenderness, which dreaded the premature exposure of the child's nerves, health and sensibilities, I was withheld from school for sometime after other children are put in charge of a tutor. In the mean time I had the freedom of the common, and, indeed, a common freedom in the indulgence of my own moods and passions. When sent to school, the matter was not greatly amended. I learned nothing, or what I learned was entirely obliterated by the nature of my education and treatment at home. I cared little to learn, and my tutor dared not coerce me. He was intelligent, and well taught—a man versed in the abstruser sciences; but wanting in decision and independence of character, the most necessary attributes of one in his vocation. This want was fatal to his usefulness; and Michael Andrews—for that was the name he bore—was, accordingly, but a tool—a poor, miserable hireling, who having a large and depending family, dared not offend by the chastisement of the favorite son of a person of so much consequence as my father. Whatever I said or did, therefore, went by without notice, and with the most perfect impunity. I was a truant, and exulted in my irregularities, without the fear or prospect of punishment. I was brutal and boorish—savage and licentious. To inferiors I was wantonly cruel. In my connexion with superiors, I was cunning and hypocritical. If, wanting in physical strength, I dared not break ground and go to blows with my opponent, I, nevertheless, yielded not, except in appearance. I waited for my time, and seldom permitted the opportunity to escape, in which I could revenge myself with tenfold interest, for provocation or injustice. Nor did I stop to inquire at any time whether it was injustice or not to which I had been subjected. I had no desire to discriminate nicely into the merits of my treatment. It was enough for me that my pride or my passion had been mortified—I sought equally for my atonement. To all alike, I carried the same countenance. It mattered not to me to whom these features were exhibited; and as for concealment, that was only my resort when cunning counselled, and as it became necessary to my purpose. To the servant, the schoolmaster, the citizen, and even to my parents, I was rude and insolent. My defiance was ready for them all, and when, as sometimes was the case, even at the most early stages of childhood, I passed beyond those bounds of toleration, assigned to my conduct, tacitly, as it were, by my father and mother, my only rebuke was in some such miserably unmeaning language as this—"Now, my dear—now Martin—how can you be so bad"—or, "I will be vexed with you, Martin, if you go on so."

What were such rebukes to an overgrown boy, to whom continued and most unvarying deference, on all hands, had given the most extravagant idea of his own importance. I bade defiance to threats—I laughed at and scorned reproaches. I ridiculed the soothings and entreaties of my mother; and her gifts and toys and favors, furnished in order to tempt me to the habits which she had not the courage to compel, were only received as things of course, which it was her duty to afford me. My father, whose naturally good mind sometimes made him turn an eye of misgiving upon my practices, wanted that stern sense of duty which would probably have brought about a different habit; and when, as was occasionally the case, his words were harsh and his look austere, I went, muttering curses, from his presence, and howling back my defiance to his threats. I was thus brought up without a sense of propriety—without a feeling of fear. I had no respect for authority—no regard for morals. I was a brute from education, and whether nature did or did not, contribute to the moral constitution of the creature which I now appear, certain, I am, that the course of tutorship which I received from all around me, would have made me so. You will argue from this against my notion of the destinies, since I admit, impliedly, that a different course of education, would have brought about different results. I think not. The case is still the same. I was fated to be so tutored.

CHAPTER II.

There was at the school to which I went, a boy about twelve years of age—the same age with myself. His name was William Harding—he was the only child of a widow—a lady, living a retired life—of blameless character, and a disposition the most amiable and shrinking. This disposition was inherited by her son, in the most extravagant and unhappy degree. He had been the child of affliction. His father had been murdered in a night affray in a neighbouring city, and his body had been brought home to the house and presence of his lady, when she was far advanced in pregnancy. The sudden and terrible character of the shock brought on the pains of labour. Her life was saved with difficulty, and, seemingly by miraculous interposition, the life of her infant was also preserved. He grew rapidly—tall and promising; but he was the creature of the deepest sensibility. His nervous organization was peculiarly susceptible. He was affected by circumstances the most trifling and casual—trembled and shrunk from every unwonted breeze—withered beneath reproach, and pined under neglect. A character so marked, presenting too, as it did, so striking a contrast to my own, attracted my attention, at an early period of our school association. His dependence, his weakness, his terrors—all made him an object of consideration to my mind which no other character in the school could have provoked. I loved him—strange to say—and with a feeling of singular power. I fought his battles—I never permitted him to be imposed upon:—and he—could he do less?—he assisted me in my lessons, he worked out my sums, he reproved my improprieties—and I—brutal and unforbearing with all beside—I bore with and submitted patiently on most occasions to his reproofs. William Harding was a genius, and one of the first order; but his nervous susceptibilities left him perfectly hopeless and helpless. Collision with the world of man would have destroyed him; and, as it was, the excess of the imaginative quality which seemed to keep even pace with his sensibilities, left him continually struggling—and as continually to the injury and overthrow of the latter—with the calm suggestions of his judgment. He was a creature to be loved and pitied; and without entertaining, at this period, a single sentiment savoring of either of these kindred emotions for any other existing being, I both loved and pitied him.

One day, to the surprize of all, William Harding appeared in his class, entirely ignorant of his lesson. The master did not punish him with stripes—that was not his usual course—but, as the school was about to be dismissed, commanding the trembling boy before him, he hung about his neck a badge made of a common card, on which was conspicuously printed, the word "idler."—With this badge he was required to return home, re-appearing at school with it the ensuing afternoon.

A more bitter disgrace could not, by any ingenuity, have been put upon the proud and delicate spirit of this ambitious boy. I never saw dismay more perfectly depicted upon any countenance. His spirit did not permit him to implore. But his eye—it spoke volumes of appeal—it was full of entreaty. The old man knew but little of the ambitious nature—he saw not the appeal—he knew nothing of the entreaty. The school was dismissed, and, in a paroxysm of grief which seemed to prostrate every faculty, my companion threw himself upon the long grass in the neighbourhood of the school-house, and refused to be comforted. I sought him out, and curious to know the cause of an omission which in him was remarkable, and which should therefore have been overlooked by our tutor, I enquired of him the reason. The cruelty of his punishment was now, upon receiving his answer, more than ever, apparent to my eyes. His mother had been ill during the whole of the previous night, and he had been keeping watch and attending upon her. I was indignant, and urged him to throw aside the card beneath the trees, and resume it upon his return to the schoolhouse. But, with a scrupulous conscientiousness, the due result of a circumspect mother's teachings, he refused to descend to the meanness and cowardice of such a procedure, and determined rather to bear his punishment. I was of a different temper. Grown bold and confident by the frequent indulgencies which had so often sanctioned my own aberrations, I had already, in many instances before, assumed the burdens of my comrades, escaping myself, while effecting their escape also. Should I now hesitate, when a sense of justice, and a feeling of friendly sympathy coalescing towards the same end, both called upon me for action. I did not. I seized upon the accursed tablet. I tore it from his bosom, and hacking it to pieces of the smallest dimensions, I hurled them to the winds, declaring his enfranchisement, at the same moment, with a shout. He would have resisted, and honestly and earnestly endeavored to prevent the commission of the act. But in vain, and with a feeling of the truest satisfaction, I beheld him return home to his suffering parent. But my turn was to come. I had no fears of the consequences, having been accustomed to violate the rules of school, with impunity. In the afternoon, Harding appearing without his badge, was questioned, and firmly refused to answer. But not so me. I had justified my act sufficiently, to myself, at least:—I was not now to forego my triumph; and, boldly advancing from my seat, in the face of the affrighted school, I announced my own handiwork, which, as I was feared by the schoolfellows generally, might never (though several of them had witnessed the whole affair) have been otherwise revealed. At the usual hour of dismissal, I was instructed to remain, and when all had departed, I was taken by the master, into a small adjoining apartment, in which he usually studied and kept his books, and which formed the passage way from the school-room to his dwelling-house. Here I was conducted, and wondering and curious, at these preliminaries, here I awaited his presence. I had been guilty of insubordination and insurrection, and was not altogether sure that he would not proceed to flog me. But not so. He spoke to me like a father—as my father had never spoken to me—his words were those of monitorial kindness and regard. He described the evil consequences to his authority if such conduct were longer tolerated; and contented himself with requiring from me a promise of apology before the assembled school on the following morning. I laughed in his face. He was indignant, as well he might be, and, under the momentary impulse, he gave me a smart blow with the open hand upon my cheek. I was but a boy then—some thirteen or fourteen years of age,—but, at that moment, I measured with my eye the entire man before me, and though swelling with fury, coolly calculated the chances of success in a physical struggle. Had there been a stick or weapon, of any description at hand, I might not have hesitated. As it was, however, prudence came to my counsel. I submitted, though my heart rankled, and my spirit burned within me for revenge;—and I had it—years afterwards I had it—a deep, a dreadful revenge. For the time, however, I contented myself with one more congenial with the little spirit of a bad and brutal boy. In school-boy phrase, he kept me in—he took from me my freedom, locking me up safely in the little study, into which I had been conducted.

CHAPTER III.

While in that room shut up, what were my emotions! The spirit of a demon was working within me, and the passions acting as they did, with an unwonted degree of violence upon my spirit nearly exhausted my body. I threw myself upon the floor, and wept—hot, scalding and bitter tears. But this weakness soon passed into one of a different character: and now I stamped, I raved, I swore. I heard the voice of Harding mournfully addressing me through the partition which separated the school room from my dungeon. He had come to sympathize with, and, if possible, to assist me. But I would not know—I would not hear him. The gloomy fiend was uppermost, and I suddenly became silent. I would not answer his inquiries—I was dumb to all his friendly appeals. In vain did the affectionate boy try every mode of winning me to hear and to reply. I was stubborn, and, at length, as the dusk came on, I could hear his departing footsteps, as he had slowly and sorrowfully given up his object in despair. He was gone, and I rose from the floor, upon which I had thrown myself. The first paroxysms of my anger had departed, and their subdued expression left me an opportunity more deeply to investigate my injuries, and to meditate my revenge. I strode up and down the apartment for sometime, when, all of a sudden, I beheld the two large, new and beautiful globes, which my teacher had but a little while before purchased at a heavy cost, and not without great difficulty, from his little savings. He was a philosopher, and this study was one of his greatest delights—ay, almost his only delight. My revenge stood embodied before me. I felt that I too could now administer pain and punishment—I felt that I, too, had power,—and there is no sweeter consciousness in life. Though small in proportion to what, it appeared to me, my wrongs required, I well knew that to injure his globes, would be almost the severest injury I could inflict upon their owner. I did not pause—the demon was impatient. I seized the jug of ink that stood upon the shelf below me, and carefully poured its contents upon the beautifully varnished and colored outlines of the celestial regions. They were ruined—irreparably ruined; and where the ink, in its course, had failed to obliterate the figures, I took care that the omission should be amended by employing a feather, still further to complete their destruction. This, you may say, is quite too trifling an incident for record. No such thing. "The child's the parent of the man." In one sense, the life of the child is made up of trifles; but by these trifles, chiefly, the standards of good judgment and just sensibilities are to be created and kept in exercise. The morals are formed most usually by our associates in play; and the tastes and exercises of the juvenile years will at all times indicate the character in age, of which they are the very seed and nucleus. The same passions which prompted the act just narrated, would move the grown-up incendiary to the firing of his neighbor's dwelling. The same passions prompted me in after years to exaggerated offences. How could it be otherwise? They were my education not less than my fate!

Vainly would I endeavor to describe the rage, the agony of wrath, which came over the face of my tutor upon discovering what I had done. It is fresh in my memory, as if the occurrence had taken place but yesterday. I was in the study, where he had left me, upon his return. Indeed, I could not effect my escape, or I had certainly done so. The room was dark, and for some time, walking to and fro, and exhorting me in the most parental manner as he walked, he failed to perceive his globes or the injury which they had sustained. In this style he went on, speaking to me, in a way, which, had not my spirit been acted upon by the arch enemy of man himself, must have had the effect of compelling me to acknowledge and to atone, by the only mode in my power, for my errors and misconduct. I had, indeed, begun to be touched. I felt a disposition to regret my act, and almost inclined to submission and apology. But on a sudden, he paused—the globes had caught his glance—he approached and inspected them narrowly. Passing his hands over his eyes, he seemed to doubt the correctness of his vision; but when he ascertained, for a truth, the extent of the evil, tears actually started from the decaying orbs, and rolled as freely as from the eyes of childhood, down his lean and wrinkled face. Then was my triumph. I gloated in his suffering, and, actually, under the most involuntary impulse, I approached, and keenly watched his countenance. He beheld my approach—he saw the demon look of exultation which my features put on; and human passion triumphed. He turned shortly upon me, and with a severe blow of his fist, he smote me to the ground. I was half stunned, but soon recovered, and with a degree of unconsciousness, perfectly brutish, I rushed upon him. But he was too much for me. He held me firmly with one hand, and in his anger now more fully provoked by my attack, he inflicted upon me a very severe flogging—almost the only one which I had ever received. It was certainly most richly deserved; but I thought not so then. I looked upon myself as the victim of a most unjustifiable—a most wanton persecution. I did not, for a moment, consider the vast robbery I had made from that poor old man's stock of happiness and enjoyment. My feelings were all concentrated in myself; and my ideas of justice, where my own interests or emotions were concerned, were in no degree abstract. I knew but one being in the world, whose claims were to be considered, and that individual, was, of course, myself.

I was now dismissed, and sore and smarting in body and mind, I returned to my home. I showed my bruises; I fabricated a story of greater wrongs and injuries. I dwelt upon the unprovoked aggression; taking care to suppress all particulars which might have modified the offence of my teacher. The flogging he had given me, had been a most severe one—and, the cause not being heard, would seem to have been most brutal. This was another part of my revenge, and it had its consequences. A solemn convocation of the chief men of the village, of whom my father was the dictator, incensed at the indignity, as it met their senses, and relying upon my *ex parte* representation, determined, without further hearing, upon the offence. Michael Andrews lost his school with every circumstance of ignominy; and in a most pitiable condition of poverty, in a few weeks after, was compelled to leave the place. I was yet unsatisfied—my revenge was not altogether complete—boy as I was—unless I could actually survey it. I went out to see him depart. I watched him, as in a miserable wagon, containing all his household gear, he drove into the adjacent country, attended by a wife and four young children. Silently, indeed, but not less certainly, did I exult in the prospect; as, from a little hillock which overlooked the road they were compelled to travel, I looked down upon their departure. They beheld me—they could not mistake the expression of my glance,—and the faces of all were immediately turned away. There is a dignified something in decent sorrow, and suffering borne in silence, which places it above the malice of the petty spirit, however reckless—while it forbids anything like the spoken taunt or triumph;—I had otherwise shouted my cry of victory in their ears. A sad train, they proceeded on their way into the country: a turn in the road in a few moments concealed them from my sight, and satisfied at length with my revenge, I did not care to follow them.

CHAPTER IV.

Under the direction of a more supple tutor than the first, I finished my education, if so we may call it. William Harding was still my associate. He was still the same nervous, susceptible, gentle youth; and though, as he grew older, the more yielding points of his character became modified in his association with society, he nevertheless did not vary in his mental and moral make very considerably from what I have already described him. Though disapproving of many of my habits and propensities, and continually exhorting me upon them, he yet could not but feel the compliment which my spirit, involuntarily, as it were, rendered to his; and he was not at any time averse to the association which I tendered him. Still he was like me in few respects, if any—no two people could have been more decidedly different; different in attributes of mind—different in purpose and pursuit—different in feelings and sentiments—different in all respects, whether in disposition, in character, or person. It is the somewhat popular notion that sympathy in pursuit, and opinions and sentiments in common, bring about the connexions of friendship and love. I think not—such connexions spring from a thousand causes which have no origin in mutual sympathies. The true source of the relationship is the consciousness of dependence and weakness on the one hand—of strength and capacity for protection on the other. This I know to have been the fact in our case; and I believe it to have its share in that of most of those associations which are styled friendly.

With little other society than that of William Harding, years glided away, and if they brought little improvement to my moral attributes, at least, as they brought with them no new provocations to the old nature, so they left in abeyance, and seemingly quite dormant, many of those, which, in my character, were decidedly immoral. Circumstance is the accoucheur in these cases; and virtue and vice, like cat and dog, would lie quietly together on the same hearth-rug for centuries, without the necessity of blow or broomstick, did not the inconsiderate hand sometimes throw them the bone, and unreasonably look to them justly and peacefully to make the division. My physical man decidedly improved in the progress of the years. My features underwent a considerable change for the better—my manners were far less objectionable—I had suppressed the more rude and brutal features, and, mingling more with society—that particularly of the other sex—I had seen and obeyed the necessity of a gentlemanly demeanor. But my heart occupied the same place and character—there was no change in that region. There, all was stubbornness and selfishness—a scorn for the possessions and claims of others—a resolute and persevering impulse which perpetually sought to exercise and to elevate its own. The spell of my fate was upon it—it seemed seared and soured—and while it blighted, and sought to blight the fortunes and the feelings of all others, without any sympathy, it seemed nevertheless, invariably, to partake of the blight. In the vexation of my spirit at this strange inconsistency of allotment, I used to curse myself, that I was not like the serpent—that I could not envenom my enemy, without infecting my own system, with the poison meant only for his. To this mood—this fatal mood—the creature of an original nature, made too active by an unhappy education, and most unfortunate indulgence—the want of employment gave activity if not exercise and exhibition. The secretions of my malignity, having no object of development, jaundiced my whole moral existence; and a general hostility to human nature and the things of society, at this stage of my being, vented itself in idle curses, and bitter but futile denunciations. I lived only in the night time. For that matter, my life itself has been a long and weary night, to which, if the starlight ever came, it brought bale only, and bitterness—a night, in which there has been little balm or beauty—a night of many tempests. Talk not of Greenland darkness, or Norwegian ice. The moral darkness is the most solid—and what cold is there like that, where, walled in a black dungeon of hates and fears and sleepless hostility, the heart broods in bitterness and solitude, over its own cankering, malignant, or misdirected purposes.

I had now grown up to manhood—to unemployed and objectless manhood. While all around were busy, and had duties to perform, the indulgence of my parents, and my own hopes of wealth, seemed to acquit me of any necessity or solicitude as to what labour I should engage in. This was another curse of my education. I was an idler, and learned the lessons of most idlers—those of dissipation—every species of irregularity, and a horribly consuming ennui. Harding was a student still—a close student—and it was only now and then, in the daytime, that I had his company. My time was in great part passed alone; for, festering in my own rankness of nature, I was too little disposed to seek society. One morning, pursuing a favorite amusement, I had wandered with my gun for some distance, into a part of the country, which was almost entirely unknown to me. The game, though plentiful, was rather shy, and in its pursuit, I was easily seduced to a greater distance from our village, and at length crossed a stream, which though not a river, was sufficiently large, particularly when swollen by freshets,—a not unfrequent event—to make something like a barrier and dividing line between two sections of the country. The day was fine, and without being at all conscious of the extent of my wanderings, I had proceeded some fourteen or fifteen miles. My way led through a close and umbrageous forest. A grove of dwarf or scrub oaks, woven about with thick vines and sheltering foliage, gave a delightful air of quietness to the scene, which could not fail altogether in its effect, even on a spirit so discontented and querulous as mine. Wandering from place to place in the silent and seemingly sacred haunt of the dreamy nature, I perceived, for the first time, a clear and beautifully winding creek, that stole in and out, half sheltered by the shrubbery growing thickly about it—now narrowing into a thin stream, and almost lost among the leaves, and now spreading itself out in all the rippling and glassy beauty of a sylvan and secluded lake. I was won by its charms, and pursued it in all its bendings. The whole scene was unique in loveliness. The hum of the unquiet breeze, now resting among, and now flying from the slowly waving branches above, alone broke, at intervals, the solemn and mysterious repose of that silence, which here seemed to have taken up its exclusive abode. Upon a bank that jutted so far into the lake by a winding approach, as almost to seem an island, the trees had been taught to form themselves into a bower; while the grass, neatly trimmed within the enclosure, indicated the exercise of that art, whose hand has given life to the rock, and beauty to the wilderness. I was naturally attracted by the prospect; and if I were not, a circumstance which occurred at the moment when I stood bewildered with the novelty of the prospect, would have determined me. A sweet but uncultivated voice suddenly broke through the copse, and the tones of a young girl saluted my ears with a song, in which education seemed somewhat to struggle and vie with simplicity. The words were these—I shall never forget them:—

I.

The bird had playful music,
  The heart was full of glee;
And life was rich in pleasantness,
  And sunny hours to me.
I knew not what it was to weep,
  I never had a care;
And all my days were happy ones,
  And all my friends were dear.

II.

Had anybody told me then,
  That future hours must come,
When mine would be an aching heart,
  For ever clad in gloom—
That I should hear no young bird's voice,
  Or, sadden'd by his lay,
Should seek to fly his gentle strain,
  Or banish him away:—

III.

I should have deem'd, in thoughtlessness,
  That, at my girlish pride,
The prophet speaker took offence,
  And only sought to chide—
I should have smiled at prophecy,
  So very idle then,
Nor feared, nor felt, as now I do,
  I shall not smile again.

The singer paused in the strain—a strain so simple, yet so thoughtful, that I paused also. It had really affected me; and after a few moments' hesitation, which vexed me as I felt it, I approached the spot whence the sounds had arisen, and reaching the point most sheltered, soon found myself in the presence of a tall and beautiful girl, about fifteen years of age, sitting within its shade. Her eyes cast down upon some needlework which she had in her hands, enabled me to survey, for sometime before she became conscious of my notice, the almost singular loveliness of feature and person which she possessed. She started, and trembled with a childish trepidation at my approach, which not a little enhanced the charm of her beauty in my sight. I apologized for my intrusion; made some commonplace inquiry and remark, and we soon grew familiar. The cottage in which her parents resided, was but a little way off; and after chatting with her for some time, and in a manner evidently not ungrateful to her, and certainly satisfactory to me, I was permitted to attend her home. What was my surprize to discover in the person of her father, my ancient schoolmaster, old Michael Andrews! Fortunately for me, however, I had been so completely changed in appearance by the forming hands of time, that he did not recognize me; and even had this not been the case, the condition of the old man himself was such, that I was secure from any fear of detection. His mind and memory were in great part gone. He still contrived, mechanically as it were, to teach the "accidence" to three white-headed urchins, belonging to the neighborhood, and in this way, with the industry of his daughters, the family procured a tolerable livelihood. I was treated kindly by the old people, and had certainly made some impression on Emily—the maiden I had accompanied. I lingered for some hours in her company—and, though timid, uneducated and girlish in a great degree, I was fascinated by her beauty, her gentleness, and the angelic smile upon her lips.

It was late in the day when I left the house of old Andrews. He had heard my name, and showed no emotion. He had evidently forgotten all the circumstances of my boyhood in connexion with himself. I could then venture to return—to repeat my visits—to see once more, and when I pleased, the sweet object, whose glance had aroused in my bosom an emotion of sense and sentiment entirely unknown to it before. We did meet, and each returning day found me on the same route. Our intimacy increased, until she became my own —and was my victim.

CHAPTER V.

That girl was the most artless—the most innocent of all God's creatures. Strange! that she should be condemned as a sacrifice to the wishes of the worst and wildest. But, it was her fate, not less than mine! Need I say that I—whose touch has cursed and contaminated all whose ill fortunes doomed them to any connexion with mine—I blighted and blasted that innocence, and changed the smile into the tear, and the hope into the sorrow, of that fond and foolishly confiding creature. We were both, comparatively, children.—She was, indeed, in all respects a child—but I—I had lived years—many years of concentrated wickedness and crime. To do wrong was to be myself—it was natural. That I should deceive and dishonor, is not therefore matter of surprize; but that there should be no guardian angel—no protecting shield for the unwary and the innocent, would seem to manifest an unwise improvidence in the dispenser of things. A few months of our intimacy only had elapsed. In the quiet and secluded bower where we had first met, she lay in my arms. I had wrought upon her imagination to the utmost. With a stern sense and consciousness, all the while, of what I was doing, I had industriously aroused all the natural passions of her bosom. Her lips were breathing and burning beneath my own. Her bosom was beating violently against mine. My arm encircled and clasped her closely. There was a warm languor in the atmosphere—the trees murmured not—the winds were at repose—no warning voice rose in the woods—no tempest blackened in the sky—the shrill scream of a solitary bird at that moment might have broken the spell—might have saved the victim. But the scream came not—the fates had decreed it—body and soul, the victim was mine. She was no longer the pure, the glad, the innocent and unstained angel I had first known her. Her eyes were now downcast and fearful—her frame trembled with all the consciousness of guilt. She gave up all to her affection for one so worthless—so undeserving as myself: yet, even then, she had won none of my affections, though loving me, even as the young and morning flower may be seen to link and entwine itself with and about the deadly and venomous nightshade. Mine were the professions of the momentary passion, which I had taught her to believe, and which, for the time, I had actually believed myself. But only for a time.

Our intercourse was continued in this way for several months. The consequences now began to threaten Emily with exposure, and she hourly besought me to provide against them by our marriage, as I had already frequently promised her to do. But I had no idea of making any such sacrifice. The passion which had prompted me at first, had no longer a place in my bosom. I did not any longer continue to deceive myself with the belief that she either was or could be any thing to me. She had few attractions now in my sight, and though still beautiful, more touchingly so, indeed, from a sadness which her features had been taught to wear, and which had now become habitual—I had learned to be disgusted and to sicken at the frequency of her complaints, and the urgency and extravagance, as I then considered them, of her requisitions. Still, I could not desert her entirely. I had not yet grown callous enough for that. I saw her frequently, and in various ways sought, not merely to evade her entreaties, but to soothe and alleviate her distresses.

To full manhood I had now attained, and it was advised by my father, that, as I had nothing else to do, I should employ myself in addressing a lady whom he had already chosen, as worthy to be the consort of so hopeful a son. Constance Claiborne was not merely young, beautiful and wealthy—she was amiable and accomplished. Our parents arranged the matter between them, before either of the parties most interested, knew or suspected any thing of what was going on. I had as yet heard nothing of the affair. But that was no objection. It proved none with me. I was not unwilling, for many reasons, that the marriage should take place. It will be sufficient to name one of these reasons. Though liberal, the allowance of money for my own expenditure, which I received from my father, had, for a long time past, been inadequate to the wants which my excesses necessarily occasioned. I had got largely into debt. I was harrassed by creditors; and had been compelled to resort to various improper expedients, to meet my exigencies. My more recent habits rendered a still further increase of stipend essential, for though, for some months, I had given my time chiefly to Emily, I had not yet so entirely divested myself of my old associates as to do with less money. My pride too, would not permit her to want for many things, and I had contributed, not a little towards the improvement of the condition of her family. It is well perhaps, that, in a chronicle of crimes, almost unvarying, I should not altogether overlook those instances of conduct, which, if not praiseworthy, were, at least, not criminal. The marriage was therefore determined upon. Constance was an obedient child, and, without any affection existing—without knowing, indeed, what her affections should be—she consented to become my wife. Still, though making up my determination, without scruple on the subject, I confess I was not altogether at ease when my thoughts reverted to the condition of the poor girl I had dishonored. But what was that condition. In pecuniary matters, I could make her better off than ever—and, so far as caste was concerned—she could suffer no loss, for she had known no society. I never thought of the intrinsic value and necessity of virtue. My considerations were all selfish, and tributary to conventional estimates. I saw no difficulty in marrying the heiress, and still enjoying, as before, the society of Emily. Matrimonial fidelity was still less a subject of concern; and, adjusting, in this way, the business and relations of the future, I hurried the arrangements and prepared assiduously for the enjoyments of the bridal.

CHAPTER VI.

A sense of caution—or it may be of shame—determined me to keep the proposed marriage, as long as I well could, from the knowledge of the one being whom it most injured. A few days before that which had been assigned for the event, I proceeded to the place of our usual rendezvous. I had not seen her for several days before; and her looks indicated sickness and suspicion. The latter appearance, I did not seem to observe, but her indisposition called forth my enquiries and regrets. I still strove to put on the guise of affection, but my words were cold, and my manner, I feel assured, wore all the expression of the most confirmed indifference. "You look unwell, Emily," I observed, putting my arms around her—"you have not been so, have you?"

"Can you ask," was her reply, as her eyes were mournfully riveted upon my own; "could I continue well, and not see you for three days? alas! Martin, you little know how long a period in time is three whole days to me in your absence. Where have you been—have you been sick—you look not as you are wont to look. You are troubled and something afflicts you."

Her manner was tender in the extreme—the suggestion even by herself of indisposition as the cause of my absence, seemed to awaken all her solicitude, and to make her regret her own implied reproaches.

"I have been slightly unwell, Emily," was my reply, in a tone gravely adapted to indicate something of continued indisposition; and the possibility that this was the case, brought out all her fondness. How like a child—a sweet confiding child she then spoke to me. With what deep and fervent devotion—and, yet, at the very moment when the accents of her voice were most touching and tender, I had begun to hate her. She was in my way—I saw how utterly impossible it was, that, feeling for me as she did, she could ever tolerate a connexion with me, shared at the same time with another.

"But—there is one thing, Martin—one thing of which I would speak—and, hear me patiently, and be not angry, if in what I say, I may do you injustice and may not have heard rightly. Say, now, that you will not be angry with your Emily—that you will forgive her speech if it seem to call in question your integrity, for, as I live, Martin, I think you intend me no wrong."

And as she spoke, her hand grasped my arm convulsively, while one of her own, as if with a spasmodic effort, wound itself about my neck. I saw that the time for stern collision was at hand—that busy tongues had been about her, and I steeled myself stubbornly for the struggle and the strife.

"And, what do they say, Emily—and who are they that say any thing which calls for such a note of preparation? Speak out—say on!"

"I will, Martin—but look not so upon me. I cannot bear your frown—any thing but that."

"Now then—what is said. What would you have, Emily?"

"There have been those to my mother, Martin—who have doubted your love for me, and, ignorant of how much importance it is to me now, who say, you are only seeking to beguile and to mislead me."

"They do me wrong, Emily—they speak falsely, believe me, as I live."

"I knew it, Martin—I knew that they did you wrong, and I told them so, but they sneered and laughed, and so they left me. But, Martin—they will speak to others, when I shall not be there to defend you, and we shall both suffer under their suspicions."

She paused here, and her eye sunk under the penetrating gaze of mine, but suddenly recovering, and hurrying herself, as if she feared the loss of that momentary impulse which then came to sustain her—she proceeded—

"I knew that I should suffer from you no injustice—I could not think it possible that you could wrong the poor girl, who had confided to you so far;—but Martin—do not smile at my folly—a something whispers me I have not long, not very long, to live, and I would be your wife—your married wife—before the time comes when my sin shall stand embodied before me. Let me have the *peace*—the *peace*, Martin, which our lawful union will bring with it; for now I have none. You have promised me frequently—say now that we shall be married this week—say on Thursday, Martin—on Thursday next that it shall take place."

I started when she concluded the sentence, as if I had been stung by an adder. Thursday was the day appointed for my marriage with

Constance. Had she heard of this. I fixed my eyes attentively and searchingly upon her own; but though filled with tears, they quailed not beneath my glance. On the contrary her gaze was full of intenseness and expression. They conveyed, in that dumb, but most expressive language, which is theirs only, the touching appeal of her subdued and apprehensive, though seemingly confident and assured, spirit. Disappointment, and the hope deferred that maketh the heart sick, had worn her into meagreness. Her cheeks were pale—her look was that of suppressed wretchedness, but these things touched me not. I had no notion of compliance, and my only thought was how to break off a connexion that promised to be so excessively troublesome. I had now become completely tired of her, and told her peremptorily that it was impossible, for a variety of reasons, to grant her request. She implored—she made a thousand appeals to every supposed impulse and emotion of manhood and affection; to my pride, to my honor, to my love. I was inflexible; and finally, when she continued to press the matter with a warmth and earnestness natural to one in her situation, particularly as I had given her no reason for my refusal, I grew brutally stern in my replies. I repulsed her tendernesses, and peevishly at length, uttered some threat, I know not what —something of absence, or indifference, or anger.

She retreated from me a pace, and drawing her hands over her eyes, seemed desirous of shutting out the presence of a character so entirely new and unexpected, as I now appeared to her. For a moment she preserved this attitude in silence—then suddenly again approaching, in subdued accents, she spoke as at first.

"Your words and look, Martin, just now were so strange and unnatural that I was almost afraid of you. Do not speak so again to your Emily, but oh, grant her prayer—her last prayer. I do not pray for myself, for though I could not live without your affections, I shall not need them long, but I pray you to give a name, an honorable name, to the little innocent of this most precious burthen. Let it not, if it lives, curse the mother for the boon of a life which its fellows must despise, and speak of with scorn and ignominy."

I withstood even this appeal. My heart was steeled within me, and, though I spoke to her less harshly, I spoke as hypocritically as ever. She saw through the thin veil which I had deemed it necessary to throw over my dishonesty, and a new expression took the place of tenderness in her features.

"It is all true then, as they have said," she exclaimed passionately. "Now, O God, do I feel my infirmity—now do I know my sin. And this is the creature I have loved—this is the thing—wanting in the heart to feel, and mean enough in soul to utter falsehood and prevaricate—this is the creature for whom I have sacrificed my heart—for whom I have given up, hopelessly and haplessly, my own soul. Oh, wretched fool—oh, miserable, most miserable folly. Yet think not," and as she turned upon me, she looked like the Priestess upon the tripod, maddened with the sacred inspiration—"Think not, mean traitor, as thou art—think not to triumph in thy farther seduction. Me thou hast destroyed,—I am thy victim, and I feel the doom already. But thou shalt go no farther in thy way. I will seek out this lady, for whose more attractive person, mine and my honor and affections, alike, are to be sacrificed. She shall hear from me all the truth. She shall know whether it be compatible with her honor and happiness, or the dignity of her character, to unite herself, in such bonds with a man who has proved so deadly, so dishonorable to her sex. And, oh, God"—she exclaimed, sinking fervently on her knee—"if it shall so happen that I save one such as I, from such a folly as mine, may it not expiate in thy sight, some portion of the sad offence of which I have been guilty."

She arose firmly and without a tear. Her eyes were red, her cheeks were burning with the fever of her whole frame, and she seemed, in all respects, the embodiment of a divine, a glorious inspiration. I was awed—I was alarmed. I had never before seen her exhibit any thing like daring or firmness of purpose. She was now the striking personification of both. She approached and sought to pass by me. I seized her hand. She withdrew it quickly and indignantly.

"Begone" she exclaimed—"I scorn, I despise you. Think not to keep me back. You have brought death and shame among my people in devoting me to both. You shall pollute me no more. Nay, speak not. No more falsehood, no more falsehood, for your own soul's sake. I would not that you should seem meaner in my sight, than you now really appear."

I seized her hand, and retained it by a fierce grasp.—

"Emily," I exclaimed, "what would you do—why is this? I ask but for delay, give me but a month, and all will be well—you shall then have what you ask—you shall then be satisfied."

"False—false! These assurances, sir, deceive me not now—they deceive me no longer. My hope is gone, forever gone, that you will do me justice. I see through your hypocrisy—I know all your villainy, and Constance Claiborne shall know it too. Ha! do you start when her name is but mentioned. Think you, I know it not all—know I not that you have been bought by money—that, vile and mercenary as you are, you have not only sold me, and this unborn pledge of your dishonesty and my dishonor, but you have sold yourself. Seek not to keep me back. She shall hear it all from these lips, that thenceafter shall forever more be silent."

She struggled to free herself from my grasp, and endeavored to pass by me, with a desperate effort—her strength was opposed to mine, and in the heat of the struggle I forgot that victory in such a contest would be the heaviest shame. Yet, I only sought, at first, to arrest her progress. As I live, I had then no other object beyond. I certainly did not intend violence, far less further crime. But the fate was upon me;—she persisted in her design, and in the effort to prevent her passage, I hurled her to the ground. I paused, in a deadly stupor, after this. I was no longer a reasoning—a conscious being. She looked up to me imploringly—the desperate feeling which heretofore had nerved and strengthened her, seemed utterly to have departed. The tears were in her eyes, and, at that moment, she would have obeyed as I commanded—she would have yielded to all my requisitions—she would have been my slave. She met no answering gentleness in my eyes, and with a choking and vain effort at speech, she turned her face despairingly upon the still dewy grass, and sobbed, as if the strings of her heart were breaking in unison with each convulsion of her breast. At that moment, I know not what demon possessed me. There was a dead—a more than customary silence in all things around me. I felt a fury within me—a clamorous anxiety about my heart—a gnawing something that would not sleep, and could not be quieted; and, without a thought of what I was to do, or what had been done, I knelt down beside her. My eyes wandered wildly around the forest, but invariably came back, and settled, in the end, upon her. There was an instinct in all this. She had the look of an enemy to the secret and impelling nature within me, and, without uttering a single word, my fingers with an infernal gripe, were fastened upon her throat. She could not now doubt the desperate character of my design, yet did she not struggle—but her eyes, they spoke, and such a language! A chain which I myself had thrown about her neck—that neck all symetry and whiteness—fell in my way. I sought, but vainly, to tear it apart with my hands, and could only do so—with my teeth. In stooping for this, she writhed her head about, and lifted her lips to mine. I shrunk back, as from the fang of a serpent. They had a worse sting, at that moment, in my eyes. Mournfully, as she saw this, she implored my mercy.—

"Spare me, forgive me, dearest Martin, I will never vex you again—spare me this time, and I will be silent. Kill me not—kill me not"—more wildly she exclaimed as my grasp became more painful—"I am too young to die—I am too bad to perish in my sins. Spare me—spare me. I will not accuse you—I—God! Oh, God!"—and she was dead—dead beneath my hands!

CHAPTER VII.

I breathed not—I lived not for a minute. My senses were gone—my eyes were in the air, in the water, in the woods, but I dared not turn them, even for an instant, to the still imploring glance of that now fixed and terrifying look of appeal. Still it pursued me, and I was forced to see—it was impossible that I could turn from the horrible expression—the dreadful glare, which shot from them through every muscle of my frame. The trees were hung with eyes that depended from them like leaves. Eyes looked at me from the water that gushed by us; and, as in a night of many stars, the heavens seemed clustering with gazing thousands, all bent down terrifically upon me. I started to my feet in desperation; and by a stern impulse I could not withstand, I pronounced audibly the name of my crime.

"Murder!"

Ten thousand echoes gave me back the sound. Tongues spoke it from every tree, and roused into something like demoniac defiance, I again shouted it back to them with the energies of a Stentor—then leaned eagerly forward to hear the replication which they made. But this mood lasted not long. I was a murderer! I whispered it, as if in terror, to myself. I seemed to doubt, and to desire some assurance of the truth.

"Am I not a murderer?" was my inquiry.

Spoken, however low, it still had its echo.

"Murderer!"—was the response of the trees, which had now tongues, as well as eyes. The agony grew intolerable, and a lethargic stupor came to my aid. I approached the corpse of my victim. Resolutely I approached it. How different was the aspect which her features now wore. She looked forth all her sweetness, and there was something—so I fancied—like forgiveness on her lips. Was it I that had defiled so pure an image—was it my hand, that, penetrating the sanctuary of life, had stolen the sacred fire from the altar? Oh, strange! that man should destroy the beauty which charms—the life that cheers and gladdens—the affection which has won and nourished him.

Deep in the centre of that forest stood an ancient rock. It was little known to the neighborhood, and its discouraging aspect and rude and difficult access had preserved it from frequent intrusion. I, however, whom no sterility could at any time deter, had explored its recesses, and it now suggested itself to my mind, as the place most calculated to keep the secret of my crime. A large natural cavity in one of its sides, difficult of approach, and inscrutable to research, seemed to present the idea of a natural tomb, and the suggestion was immediately acted upon. I took her body in my arms—I pressed her to my heart—but in that pressure I maddened. I had not yet destroyed, in her death, the distinct principle of life which she carried within her. I felt the slight but certain motion of her child—of my child—struggling as it were for freedom. I closed my eyes—I suppressed the horrible thoughts which were crowding upon my brain, and hurrying on my way, sought out the cavity assigned for her repose. But a single plunge, and she was gone from sight, from reach—she and her child—I was a double murderer. The rock was silent as the grave—it had no echoes—for, at that place and moment, I had no speech.

Will it be believed, the huge stride which I had taken in crime, contributed largely to the sense of my own importance. Such is our nature. We are proud of the power to destroy. I had never before doubted my capacity for evil—but I now felt—for I had now realized —I had exercised—this capacity. There is something elevating—something attractive to the human brute, even in being a destroyer. It was so with me. There was an increased vigor in my frame—there was new strength and elasticity in my tread—I feel assured that there was a loftier, a manlier expression in my look and manner. But, all was not so in my thought. There every thing was in an uproar. There was a strange incoherence, an insane recklessness about my heart, where, if I may so phrase it, the spirit seemed prone to wandering about precipices and places of dread and danger. I kept continually repeating to myself, the name of my crime. I caught myself muttering over and over the word "Murderer," and that, too, coupled with my own name. "Murderer," and "Martin Faber," seemed ever to my imagination the burden of a melody; and its music, laden with never ceasing echoes, heard by my own ears, was forever finding its way to my own lips.

CHAPTER VIII.

I left the rock, slowly and frequently looking behind me. Sometimes my fancies confirmed to my sight the phantom of the murdered girl, issuing from the gaping aperture, and with waving arms, threatening and denouncing me. But I sternly put down these weak intruders. Though this was the first crime, of so deep a dye, which I had ever committed, I felt that the thoughts and feelings which came with this act, had been long since familiar to my mind. The professional assassin could hardly look upon his last murder, with more composure, than I now surveyed the circumstances of my first. I was indeed a veteran, and in a past condition of society, I should have been a hero—the savior or the destroyer of a nation.

To be precipitate, was to be weak; so I thought even in that moment of fearful circumstances. I went back with all possible composure to the spot on which the crime had been committed. I examined the place carefully—took with my eye the bearing and distances of all the surrounding objects in their connexion with the immediate spot on which the deed had been done. In this examination, I found the pocket handkerchief of Emily, with her name written in Indian ink upon it. I carefully cut it into shreds, dividing each particular letter, with my pen-knife, and distributing the several pieces at slow intervals upon the winds. Where our feet together had pressed the sands, with a handful of brush, I obliterated the traces; and in the performance of this task, I drew off my own shoes, leaving, only, as I proceeded, the impression of a naked foot. While thus engaged, I perceived for the first time, that I had lost a rich, and large cameo, from my bosom. The loss gave me no little concern, for, apart from the fact of its being generally known for mine, the initials of my name were engraven upon the gold setting. How and where had it been lost. This was all important, and with indefatigable industry, I examined the grass and every spot of ground which I had gone over in the recent events. But in vain—it was not to be found, and with a feeling of uneasiness—not to describe my anxiety by a stronger epithet—I proceeded on my way home.

The poverty of Emily's family; the insulated position which they held in society; their inability to press an inquiry—were all so many safeguards and securities in my favor. There was some little stir, it is true—but I had so arranged matters that I passed unsuspected. The inquiry was confined to the particular part of the country in which she resided—a lonely and almost uninhabited region—and, but a distant rumor of her unaccountable disappearance reached our village—and there the connexion existing between us was almost entirely unknown. The family had but few claims upon society, and but little interest was excited by their loss. In a little while all inquiry ceased; and with a random and general conclusion that she had fallen into the river, the thought of Emily Andrews gradually passed away from the memories of those who had once known her.

CHAPTER IX.

The night came, appointed for my marriage with the beautiful and wealthy Constance Claiborne. Attended by William Harding, who, strange to say, in spite of the manifest and radical differences of character existing between us, was yet my principal companion, I was punctual to the hour of appointment. Every preparation had been made by which the ceremony should be attractive. A large company had been assembled. Lights in profusion—rich dresses—gayly crowded and decorated apartments, and the most various music, indicated the spirit of joy and perfect harmony with which our mutual families contemplated the union. I have already said, the bride was beautiful. Words cannot convey an idea of her beauty. She was emphatically a thing of light and love—

> "Which seen, becomes a part of sight."

In grace, one knew not with what, save herself, to institute a comparison. In expression, there were volumes of romantic, and interesting poetry, embodied in each feature of her face; and the steel of my affections, stern as it was, wherever she turned, even as the dutiful needle to the pole, turned intuitively along with her. Such was the maiden,—so much after the make and mould of heaven, whom a cruel destiny was about to link with one formed in spirit after the fashion of hell.

The ceremony was begun. We stood up with linked hands at the altar. The priest went on with his formula. The bride's hand trembled in mine, and her eyes were commercing only with the richly carpeted floor. I was about to answer the question which should have made us one, when a cold wind seemed to penetrate my body. My bones were numbed, and a freezing chill went through my whole system. My tongue refused its office, and, instinctively, as it were, bending to the opposite quarter of the apartment, my eyes fell upon a guest whom none had invited. There, palpable as when I had last seen her, stood the form of Emily Andrews. A pale and melancholy spectre, and full of a terrible reproach. I was dumb, and for a moment, had eyes only for her. She was motionless, as when I had borne her to the unhallowed grave in which she did not rest. My disquiet, so unaccountable to all around, seemed to indicate a reluctance to the ceremony. I felt that all eyes were upon me—the bride's hand was slowly withdrawn from mine, and that motion restored me. Mine were terrible energies. I seized her hand with a strong effort, and with a voice of the sternest emphasis, my eye still firmly fixed upon the obtrusive phantom, I gave the required affirmative. With the word, the figure was gone.—I had conquered. You will tell me, as philosophers have long since told us, that this was all the work of my imagination—a diseased and excited fancy, and in this you are probably right. But what of that? Is it less a matter of supernatural contrivance, that one's own spirit should be made to conjure up the spectres which haunt and harrow it, than that the dead should actually be made to embody themselves, as in life, for the same providence? The warning sound that chatters in my ear of approaching death may be, in fact, entirely unuttered; but if my senses, by an overruling fate, are calculated for the inception of such a sound, and compelled to recognise its presence, shall we hold it as less the work of a superior agency? Is it less an omen for that?

This was not all. At midnight, as I approached my chamber, the same ghastly spectre stood at the door as if to guard it against my entrance. For a moment I paused and faltered; but thought came to my relief. I knew that the energies of the soul, immortal and from the highest as they are, were paramount, and I advanced without fear. I stretched forth my hand to the key—in the face and in defiance of the spectre—and all was vacancy again before me. If my fancies had conceived the ghost, my own energies were adequate to its control. In this I had achieved a new conquest, and my pride was proportionately increased and strengthened. I was thus taught how much was in my own power, in controlling my own moods, compelling obedience from my own fears and fancies—in making even destiny subservient to my will!

CHAPTER X.

To the reflective mind, I need not say that no happiness awaited me on my marriage. Still less necessary to say that the amount of happiness which fell to the lot of my wife was equally, if not more limited. A temper like mine—so impatient, and so without resources—could not long suffer a dependant or an associate to remain at peace. She felt accordingly; and I am persuaded a greater curse could not well have fallen to her lot. I did not ill-treat her—to speak in common phrase—I employed no blows—no violence. But there are other penalties which virtue can be made to endure, not less frequently, and far more poignantly, than vice. I was a wretched, sleepless, discontent—always showing my teeth, and, when occasion offered, never withholding my venom. She suffered as a martyr—with a patience that was never to be disturbed; and I failed utterly, however much I strove, to drive her beyond the boundary of a yielding, an always conciliating humility. She loved me not from the first—how could she love me?—and only became my bride from the absence of a sufficient degree of firmness in her character, to resist the commands or the solicitations of her parents. Perhaps, too, as she knew little of me, and less still, at that time, of the nature of those feelings of which her heart could become susceptible, the constraint had been less upon her than, even then, I imagined it to have been. That she soon perceived her error and misfortune, I discovered not less quickly; and in due accordance with the discovery, my pride grew morbid and angry. I did not distrust—but I hated her; and with a fiend-like hatred, which can only be understood by a reference to the course of conduct which I thought proper to pursue in consequence. With a perversity of character, strange and contradictory—which, let philosophers account for as they may—when I found that she could love, that feelings were engendered in her bosom for another, hostile to her affection for me, though not at variance with her duty—I encouraged their growth. I nursed their developement. I stimulated their exercise; and strove, would you believe it, to make her the instrument of my own dishonor. But her sense of pride and propriety was greater than mine. Though soon conscious that her heart was another's, she unerringly held her faith to her husband, and my anger and dislike were exaggerated, when I discovered that my vice, even when allied to and assisted by her own legitimate feelings, could acquire no ascendancy over her virtue.

I soon found that she had been won, all unconsciously on his part, by the talents, the gentleness, and many attractions of mind and manner of my old associate and schoolfellow, William Harding. She listened to his language with unreluctant spirit, and a pleasure which she never thought to conceal. She was only happy in his presence and society; and with a feeling which she had never yet dared to name to herself, and from the analysis of which I feel she must always have shrunk, she gave him a preference over all others, in every thought, in every emotion of her being. Nor was he insensible to her regards. Sensitive, and easily wrought upon, whether by kindness or cruelty, her ceaseless consideration, exhibited in a thousand forms, of which she herself knew nothing, controlled him like an infant. He had always been very intimate with me—more so than any other of the village—and he was now almost an inmate of my house. With the free openness of heart which marked and made his character, he sought unreservedly for the society of Constance, and Constance only: and while I saw from this, that his intentions had no dishonourable object, I saw at the same time that he knew nothing of the precise feeling which prompted them. I had learned, with singular felicity, at an early period of my life, to study and to analyze the human heart. I exercised my habit with regard to these two, and was not long in discovering that their propensities were mutual. At first, while she was yet a charming creation in my sight, and before I had learned to disregard and be indifferent to the admiration which she excited in others, this predilection gave me not a little concern. I was for a season the victim of a jealous doubt—not so much the result of a fear, or of offended honor, as of a weak pride and vanity, that was vexed at the preference given to another in the bosom of one I would, at that time, have had exclusively my own. But this feeling went with the season. I grew indifferent at first to, then pleased with their association, and finally it became an object with me, so to encourage it, as, in time, to afford me sufficient opportunity and excuse for a dreadful and overwhelming revenge. To this object I addressed all the means in my power, but without the desired success. They were both honest—sweetly, nobly honest; as, from my own feeling and character, I had never expected man or woman to have been. Joining in thought—intermingling hourly in spirit, and in a communion which, if they had not been wonderfully immaculate, must have brought out their weaknesses, they were yet strong; and the most jealous scrutiny, the most bitter hate and hostility, could never have construed into impropriety a solitary feature in their conduct. Many were the modes which I adopted to stimulate their passions—to influence or to create desires—to put their passions into that fervour, which, once provoking discontent and the vague want which is the first symptom of the active appetite, will never rest again short of its surfeit. Thousands of opportunities did I throw before them in order to provide myself with victims. But they were children—weak enough for susceptibility, but not daring to do wrong.

They went through every ordeal like angels—without a speck of earth; and pining with strong affections, and suffering as they did in the noble struggle to restrain and keep them down, I was yet mortified to see that they could not be otherwise than successful. But the strife of their spirits in this labour had its influence, and, day by day, the cheek of Constance grew paler and paler, and there was a nameless anguish in her eye, as it sunk beneath my own, which spoke of that love—worst love of all—which has its birth untwinned by hope. Nor was she the only one with whose heart the contest promised to be vital. I beheld, at every succeeding visit, the increasing fever in the soul of my other victim. The worm was in the core, and kept up a ceaseless labour in the bosom of the gentle and too susceptible Harding.

CHAPTER XI.

Several months had now elapsed since our marriage; and in that time, as might have been expected, my young wife and domestic associations had lost most of their attractions—in my eyes at least. My resources were now always out of doors—carousing sometimes, but frequently solitary and savage. My favorite pursuit—one that had been a passion in boyhood, and which contributed not a little to the sternness of my mood—was to take long walks into the neighboring country, with my fowling-piece on my shoulder, and, with this apology for my wanderings, I had contrived to become familiar with the forests in that neighborhood for fifteen miles round. It was in a ramble of this sort that I had first encountered Emily, and this habit furnished a sufficient reason to others, for those long absentings from home in which my time had been chiefly given up to her. Sometimes, on these excursions, Harding would become my companion; not that he was a sportsman, but simply because of his contemplative character of mind, which luxuriated, and was enthusiastic, in its admiration of the gloomy beauty of the thick woods. His presence did not interfere with my mood; indeed, although the cause was essentially different, his silence was a fitting similitude of mine. We wandered thus from one wood to another, through path and cover, frequently without a word, and living only in our thoughts. It was on one of these occasions, while traversing a dense thicket, girded in by heavy trees, and almost impervious from the undergrowth, that we sat down together upon the trunk of a fallen pine, and fell into conversation. The sun was completely shut out from the spot, and the solemn hush of all things about us was such as to make the train of thought in our minds much gloomier than ever. Our dialogue was necessarily prompted by the circumstances of our situation, and, as if impelled throughout the whole scene by an irresistible monitor, I remarked to him thus, in spite of my own consciousness of the danger of such a topic—

"Harding, this is just the spot, it appears to me, that one would choose in which to commit a murder!"

"Horrible!" was his reply, "what could put such a thought into your head? This, is just the spot now which I should select for the inception of a divine poem. The awful stillness—the solemn gloom—the singular and sweet monotony of sound, coming from the breeze through the bending tree tops, all seem well calculated to beget fine thoughts,—daring fancies—bold and striking emotions."

"You talk of taking life, as if it were the crowning crime—it appears to me an error of society by which the existence of a being, limited to a duration of years, is invested with so much importance. A few years lopt from the life of an individual is certainly no such loss, shortening as it must, so many of his cares and troubles; and the true standard by which we should determine upon a deed, is the amount of good or evil which it may confer upon the person or persons immediately interested."

"That is not the standard," was his reply—"since that would be making a reference to varying and improper tribunals, to determine upon principles which should be even and immutable. To some men, from the operation of circumstances, or from their own improvidence, death would be welcome even by violence; and the feeling with which such a man would submit to the executioner, can surely afford no standard by which to determine upon the fate of others not so situated, and not having the same feeling or condition with himself. Life is a sacred something which we do not venerate enough. It is considered quite too lightly by society, and it appears to me, if we believe for a moment in the immortality of the soul and the doctrine of rewards and punishments, we have not the right, even in the case of the criminal, to doom him to a loss of it. The idea is horrible which conceives the murder of a human being, even according to the standard you suggest; for, leave the choice but a moment to the victim, and he will submit, in most cases, to the loss of all his possessions, and even of his liberty, to avoid that fearful rush of the soul into the dark and deep chaos which our ignorance depicts the future."

"Why, what would you say to a friend, William—to me, for example, if I told you I had been guilty of this crime?"

"Say!" he exclaimed, as his eyes shot forth an expression of the deepest horror—"say! God help me, I could say nothing—I could never look on you again."

I surveyed him with close attention for a few moments, then, with a deliberation that, under all the circumstances, was significant of a momentary madness, placing my hands upon his shoulders, I slowly exclaimed—

"Look—you shall look upon me again—you shall see and hear. I have been guilty of this same crime of taking life. I have been, and am, a murderer."

He sprung upon his feet with undisguised horror. His face was pale as death—his lips were parted in affright; and while I held one of his hands, the other involuntarily was passed over, entirely concealing his eyes. What prompted me to the narration I know not. I could not resist the impulse—I was compelled to speak. It was my fate. I described my crime—I dwelt upon all its particulars; but with a caution, strangely inconsistent with the open confidence I had manifested, I changed the name of the victim—I varied the period, and falsified, in my narrative, all the localities of the crime; concluding with describing her place of burial beneath a tree, in a certain ground which was immediately contiguous, and well known to us both.

He heard me out with wonder and astonishment. His terror shook his frame as with an ague, and at the conclusion he tried to laugh, and his teeth chattered in the effort.

"It is but a story," he said chokingly, "a horrible story, Martin, and why do you tell it me? I almost thought it true from the earnest manner in which you narrated it."

"It is true, William—true as you now stand before me. You doubt, I will swear—"

"Oh, swear not—I would rather not believe you—say no more, I pray you—tell me no more."

With a studied desperation—a malignant pleasure, increasing in due proportion with the degree of mental torture which he appeared to undergo, I went again over the whole story as I had before told it—taking care that my description of each particular should be made as vivid as the solemn and bold truth certainly made it.

"I am a murderer! William Harding!"

"May God forgive you, Martin—but why have you told me this—would you murder me, Martin? Have I done any thing to offend you?"

His excessive nervousness, at length, grew painful, even to myself. "Nay, fear not, I would not harm you, William, for the world. I would rather serve and save you. But keep my secret—I have told it you in confidence, and you will not betray me."

"Horrible confidence!" was his only reply, as we took our way out from the forest.

CHAPTER XII.

Several days had passed since this conference, and, contrary to his custom, Harding, in all this time, had kept out of my sight. His absence was felt by both Constance and myself. He had been, of late, almost the only companion known to either of us. Why I liked him I knew not. His virtues were many, and virtues were, at no time, a subject of my admiration. That he was loved by Constance, I had no question; that he loved her I felt equally certain—but it was the passion of an angel on the part of both; and it may be that knowing the torture which it brought with it to both of them, my malignant spirit found pleasure in bringing them together. It was not a charitable mood, I am satisfied, that made me solicitous that he should be as much as possible an inmate of my dwelling.

He came at last, and I was struck with his appearance. The change for the worse was dreadfully obvious. He looked like one, who had been for many nights without sleep. He was pale, nervous to the last degree, and awfully haggard.

"I am miserable," said he, "since you breathed that accursed story in my ears. Tell me, I conjure you, Martin, as you value my quiet, that you but jested with me—that the whole affair was but a fabrication—a fetch of the nightmare—a mere vision of the fancy."

Will it be believed, that having thus an opportunity, even then, of undoing the impression I had created, I took no advantage of it. I persisted in the story—I was impelled to do so, and could not forbear. There was an impulse that mastered the will—that defied the cooler judgment—that led me waywardly, as it thought proper. You have read that strange poem of Coleridge, in which the "Auncient Marinere" is made, whether he will or no, and in spite of every obstacle, to thrust his terrible narrative into the ears of the unwilling listener. It was so with me; but though I was thus compelled to denounce my crime, the will had still some exercise, and I made use of it for my security. I changed the particulars so materially from the facts, as they really were, that inquiry must only have resulted in my acquittal. The state of mind under which Harding labored, was of melancholy consequence, to him, at least, if not to me. Sad and disappointed, he left me without a word, and for some days more I saw him not. At length he came to me looking worse than ever.

"I shall go mad, Faber, with this infernal secret. It keeps me awake all night. It fills my chamber with spectres. I am haunted with the presence of the girl, you accuse yourself of having murdered."

"Go to—will you be a child all your life. Why should she haunt you?—it is not you who have murdered her—she does not trouble me."

"Nevertheless, she does haunt me. She calls upon me to bring you to justice. I awake and she is muttering in my ears. She implores—she threatens—she stands by my bed side in the darkness—she shakes the curtains—I hear the rustling of her garments—I hear her words; and when I seek to sleep, her cries of 'Murder,! Murder! Murder!' are shouted, and ring through all my senses, as the sound of a sullen, swinging bell in the wilderness. Save me, Martin—from this vision—save me from the consequence of your own imprudence in telling me this story. Assure me that it is untrue, or I feel that I shall be unable to keep the secret. It is like a millstone around my neck—it makes a hell within my heart."

"What! and would you betray me—would you bring me to punishment, for an offence which I have told you was involuntary, and which I unconsciously committed? Your sense of honor, apart from your feeling of friendship, alone, should be sufficient to restrain you. I cannot believe that you would violate your pledge—that you can betray the confidence reposed in you."

Silenced, but not satisfied, and far more miserable than ever, the poor youth, whose nerves were daily becoming more and more unsteady and sensitive under these exciting influences, went away;—but the next day, he came again—his look was fixed and resolute, and an air of desperate decision marked every feature.

"I am about to go to the Justice, Martin, to reveal all this story, precisely as you have told it to me—I cannot bear a continuance of life, haunted as I have been, by innumerable terrors, ever since I heard it. But last night, I heard the distinct denunciations of the murdered girl, couched in the strongest language, emphatically uttered in my ears. The whole scene was before me, and the horrors of the damned, could not exceed those which encompassed my spirit. I fled from the chamber—from the house. In the woods I have passed the whole night in the deepest prayer. My determination is the result of the soundest conviction of its necessity. I can keep your secret no longer."

I paused for a moment, and having prepared myself for all difficulties by a consideration of all the circumstances, I simply bade him—"Go then—if you are determined upon the betrayal of your friend and the forfeiture of your honor."

"Reproach me not thus, Martin"—was his reply. "Forgive me, but I must do so. I must either disclose all or commit self-murder. I cannot keep within my bosom that which makes it an Ætna—which keeps it forever in flame and explosion. Forgive—forgive me!" Thus speaking, he rushed from my presence.

CHAPTER XIII.

I was cited before the Justice, and the testimony of William Harding delivered with the most circumstantial minuteness, was taken down in my presence. Never did I see a more striking instance of conscience struggling with feeling—never had I conceived of so complete a conquest of one over the other. I denied all. I denied that

I had ever made him such a statement—that we had ever had any such conversation; and with the coolness and composure of veteran crime, wondered at the marvellous insanity of his representations. He was dumb, he looked absolutely terrified. Of course, however, in such an examination, my own statements were unavailing; and his were to be sustained by a reference to the localities and such of the details which he had made, as might ostensibly contribute to its sustenance or overthrow. Search was made under the tree where my victim was alleged to have been buried. The earth appeared never to have been disturbed from the creation—upon digging, nothing was found. So, with all other particulars. Harding's representations were confuted. He was regarded by all as a malignant wretch, who envied the felicity, and sought to sting the hand of him who had cherished and befriended him. The public regard fell away from him, and he was universally avoided. I affected to consider him the victim of momentary hallucination, and the christian charity thus manifested, became the admiration of all. I almost dreaded that I should be deified—made a deacon in life, and a saint after death.

Poor Harding sunk silently to his den. Sensitively alive to public opinion, as well as private regard, his mind reeled to and fro, like a storm troubled vessel, beneath a shock so terrible and unexpected. He had lived upon the breath of fame—he was jealous of high reputation—he was tremblingly alive to those very regards of the multitude, which were now succeeded by their scorn and hisses. What a blow had I given him—but he was not yet to escape me. I suffered a day or two to elapse, and then sought him out in his chamber. I entered, and looked upon him for several minutes unobserved. His head was between his hands, and his chin rested upon the table. His air was that of the most woful hopelessness. The nature of his feelings might be inferred, along with his personal appearance, from the nature of the companions beside, and the general condition of things around him. One boot was thrown off, and lay upon the floor—the other, as if he had grown incapable of further effort, was permitted to remain upon his foot. The mirror lay in the smallest pieces about the room; the contemplation of his own features, blasted as they had been with the shame of his situation, having prompted him, as he came from the place of trial, to dash his hand through it. On the table, and on each side of him, lay—strangely associated—his bible and his pistols. He had been about to refer, with an everyday philosophy to one or the other of them for consolation. It was in this situation, that I found him out. I brought with me increased tortures—while the people, who saw and wondered, gave me credit for christian benevolence. How many virtues would put on the most atrocious features, could their true motives be pursued through the hive of venomous purposes that so frequently swarm and occupy the secret cells and caverns of the human heart!

He saw me at length, and, as if the associations which my presence had called up, were too terrible for contemplation, he buried his head in his hands, and again thrust them on the table. As I approached, however, he started from this position—a mood entirely new, appeared to seize upon him, and snatching the pistol which lay before him upon the table, he rushed to meet me. He placed it upon my bosom, and deliberately cocked it, placing his finger at the same moment upon the trigger. A glare of hellish desperation, flowed out from his eyes, as with words that seemed rather shrieked than articulated, he exclaimed—

"And what is there that keeps me from destroying you? What should stay my hand—what should interpose to protect you from my just revenge—what should keep you from the retributive wrath, which you have roused into fury?"

I made no movement—precipitation, or any act or gesture, on my part, at that moment, would have been instant death. He would have felt his superiority. I maintained my position, and without raising a finger, I replied with the utmost deliberation:—

"What should keep you from taking my life! What a question! Would you be answered?—Your own fears.—You know that I would haunt you."

The pistol dropped from his hands, and he trembled all over. I proceeded.

"You should have no peace—no moment of repose secure from my intrusion—no single hour you could call your own. I should link myself to you, as Mezentius' dead, to his condemned and living victim. I would come between you and your dearest joys, nor depart for a solitary moment from a share in all the unavoidable duties and performances of life. We should sit, side by side, at the same table —sleep in the same couch,—dwell in the same dwelling. Would you rise to speak in the council, I should prompt your words—I should guide your action. Would you travel, I would mount the box and impel in the direction of my caprice. Would you love, I would figure in your courtship—go between yourself and mistress, and assist in your bridal. Your own wife should not have one half of the communion that I should enjoy with you!"

He was paralyzed with his agony.

"Terrible man!" he exclaimed, "What would you do with me; why am I made your victim—why do you persecute me? I have not wronged; I have not sought to wrong you. You, on the contrary, have destroyed me, and yet would pursue me further. You have been my evil genius."

"I know it—I deplore it!"

"You deplore it! Horrible mockery! How shall I believe your speech after what has happened. Why deny the story, yourself poured into my ears as the truth."

"It was the truth!"

"Yet you swore it was false!"

"Life is sweet—life is necessary, if not to human joys, at least, to the opportunities of human repentance. Would you have me give myself to an ignominious death upon the scaffold—disgracing my family, dishonoring myself, and dooming all who shared in my communion to a kindred dishonor with myself?"

"Why then did you tell me of this crime?"

"I could not help it. The impulse was native and involuntary, and I could not disobey it. It would not be resisted. It burned in my bosom as it has done in yours, and, until I had revealed it, I could hope for no relief."

"Dreadful alternative! Hear me, Martin Faber—hear me and pity me. You know my history—you know my hopes—my pretensions—my ambition. You know that for years, from my boyhood up, in despite of poverty, and the want of friends and relatives, I have been contending for glory—for a name. You know that the little world in which we live, had begun to be friendly to my aspirations—that they looked on my progress with sympathy and encouragement—that they pointed to me as one likely to do them honor—to confer a name upon my country as well as upon myself. You know that for years, in solitude, and throughout the long hours of the dark and wintery night, I have pursued my solitary toil for these objects.

You know that I have shrunk from the society that has been wooing me—that I have denied myself all the enjoyments which are the life of other men—that I have, in short, been sacrificing the present for the future existence—the undying memory of greatness, which it had been my hope, to leave behind me. This you knew—this you know. In one hour—without an object—to satisfy a wanton caprice—you have overthrown all these hopes—you have made all these labors valueless—you have destroyed me. Those who loved, hate me—those who admired, contemn me—those who praised, now curse and denounce me as a wanton and malicious enemy, seeking the destruction of his friend! I am not only an exile from my species—I am banished from that which has been the life-blood of my being—the possession of a goodly, of a mighty name! I have no further use in life."

"All is true—you have said but the truth. I am conscious of it all."

"Oh, speak not, I conjure you—I need not your assurances in my confirmation. I do not ask your voice. Hear me in what I shall say, and if you can, heal as far as you may heal, the wounds you have inflicted."

"Speak on!"

"I will seek to reconcile myself to the condition—to the exile to which you have driven me. I will struggle to give up the high hopes which have prompted and cheered me, through the unalleviated and unlighted labors of my life—I will struggle to be—nothing! All I ask is that you should give me peace—permit me to sleep once more. Say that you have not committed the crime, of which you have accused yourself. Give me this assurance, and free me from this gibbering and always present spectre, that, roused for ever by my fancies, refuses for ever to be gone!"

How easy to have granted his request! How impossible, indeed, would it appear, to have refused an appeal, urged under such circumstances. But I did refuse—I reiterated the story of my crime, as I had uttered it before, without any variation, and the nervously susceptible youth sunk down before me, in despair, upon the floor. In a moment, however, he arose, and—a smile was upon his lips. There was a fearful energy in his eye, which had never marked it before, and which it surprised me not a little to survey. With a strong effort, he approached me.

"I will be no longer a child—I will shake off this fever of feeling which is destroying me. I will conquer these fancies—I will not be their slave. Shall I possess a mind, so soaring and absolute, to bow down to the tyrant of my own imaginings? I will live for better things. I will make an effort!"

I applauded his determination, and persuaded him to go with me, as before, to my residence. This, though good policy with me, was the height of bad policy with him. The world looked upon me as the most forgiving and foolishly weak philanthropist—a benevolent creation of the very finest water. The readiness with which Harding again sought my hospitality, after his charges against me, was, of course, still further in evidence, against the honesty of his intentions. They looked upon his depravity as of the most heinous character, and numberless were the warnings which I hourly received, of the thousand stings which the—so-called—serpent was treasuring up for my bosom. But, I affected to think differently. I put all that was wrong in his conduct down to a momentary aberration of intellect, and urged the beauty and propriety of christian forgiveness. Was I not of a most saint-like temper? They thought so. How well did I know them—how little did they know me!

CHAPTER XIV.

It is strange, that, with my extended and perfect knowledge of human character, and my great love of mental and moral analysis, I should have suffered myself to be taken in by these external shows on the part of my victim. Strange, that so sudden—so unlooked for, an alteration from his wonted habit had not aroused my jealousy—my suspicion of some hidden motive. But, my blindness was a part of my fate, or, how should it have been that a creature so weak, so utterly dependent as Harding had ever been, should have deceived a spirit so lynx-eyed as mine. Led to consider him too greatly the victim of the nervous irritability, by which, indeed, his every action and impulse was distinguished, I had not looked for the exercise, in his mind, of any of that kind of energy, which would carry him undeviatingly and perseveringly to the attainment of any remote or difficult end, or to the accomplishment of a far and foreign purpose.

I had neglected entirely to allow for the stimulating properties of a defeat, upon a mind which had only lived for a single object. I had refused to count upon the decision of character, which, might, by probability, arise in a mind, however in all other respects, variable and vacillating, when concentrating itself upon the attainment of a single desire, and that, too, of a kind, so absorbing, so all impelling as the acquisition of fame. I did not recollect that Harding had himself acknowledged the existence of one only passion, in his bosom; or, I should have seen that his present change of manner, was but a thin veil disguising and concealing some ulterior project, subservient to the leading object of his spirit. I failed, therefore,—fool that I was—to perceive the occult design, which of a sudden had so completely altered all the obvious characteristics of my companion—his habits, his temper, and his hopes. Folly to suppose, that with the loss of public estimation, he would be content with life unless with a desperate effort to regain his position. And how could he regain that position? How, but by establishing my guilt, and his innocence of all malevolent intention. And such was his design. Assured, as he now was, that I was in truth a criminal—that I had committed the murder of which I had accused myself, and that I had only so varied the statement of its particulars as to mislead and defeat enquiry—and looking forward to the one single object,—that of restoring himself to the popular regards of which I had deprived him—he was determined, of himself, to establish my crime—to trace the story from the very imperfect data I had myself given him, and by perpetual associations with myself, and a close examination into my moral make, to find out the materials of evidence which should substantiate his now defeated accusations. How blind was I not to have perceived his object—not to see through his unaccustomed artifices! The genius—the gigantic genius of his mind, will be best comprehended from this curious and great undertaking, and from the ingenuity and indefatigable industry with which he pursued it to the end. Nor, from this fact, alone, but coupled, as under existing circumstances was the pursuit adopted, his strength of character and firmness of mind, are of the most wonderful description. The task was attended with an association, which, for a protracted period of time, still further exposed him to the scornful execrations and indignation of those, for whose good opinion, alone, he was voluntarily about to undergo all this additional load of obloquy. Under these aspects the effort was a high-souled and sublime one, and furnished one of the best proofs of the moral elevation of his genius. I regard it now, when too late to arrest its exercise and progress, with a sentiment little short of wonder and admiration.

All these occurrences, had, of course, been made known to my wife; and shocked and terrified as she had been—torn and distracted between a sense of duty to myself, and a feeling of deep, but unexpressed regard for my accuser—when, for the first time after the trial, I brought him to the house, with a highly proper spirit—seeing the affair as she had seen it—she declined making her appearance. I insisted upon it:—

"How can you require such a thing?" was her very natural inquiry. "Whatever may have been his motive, has he not sought your life. Has he not brought a foul and false accusation against you, making you a criminal of the darkest dye?"

"Look at me, Constance," I said in reply, as I took one of her hands in mine—"I am the criminal—I committed the crime he charged upon me, and which I myself had revealed to him. His accusation, so far as he was concerned, was neither foul nor false!"

And wherefore did I tell her this? Why should I have multiplied the evidence against me—why put myself at the mercy of another? It might be enough to say that I did not fear that Constance would betray me. As she was a pure and delicate woman, her love for him—treasured up in secret, and a source of trembling and self-reproach, as I knew it must be, to her heart—was my sufficient security. She would not have linked her testimony with his, however she might have hated me and loved him, fearing that her motives might be subject to the suspicion of others, as she herself would have suspected them. This consideration would have left me without fear, in that quarter, but this was not a consideration with me, in telling her the story. I could not refrain from telling it—in spite of myself I was compelled to do so—it was my fate.

I shall not attempt to describe her horror. She was dumb, and in silence descended with me to the apartment in which Harding had been left. To him this was a moment of fearful ordeal. The woman he loved, though hopelessly, he had struck, through her husband. He was not to know that I had most effectually acquitted him, to her, of the offence, for which he anticipated her scorn and hatred. His anxiety and wretchedness were again manifest until she relieved him, as with a boldness of spirit which I had never before seen her manifest, she walked forward, took his hand, and welcomed him as if nothing had happened. He looked first to me, then to her and silently, with a tearful eye, and frame violently agitated, he carried her hand to his lips. She retreated, and was deeply confused by this act. I saw her inmost soul, at that moment in her face. Why had she not loved me as she loved him? Why, oh, why?

That night, in my chamber, I said to her—"You love this youth—speak not—I would not have you deny it. I will tell you more—would you know it?—he loves you too, and there are few persons in the world more deserving the love of one another. Were I dead to-morrow you would most probably make the discovery, and—"

"Oh, Martin Faber, I see not why you should torment me in this manner. For heaven's sake, let me have peace. Make not all miserable about you; or, if you are bent on making me so, let not your malice exercise itself still further on this unhappy youth, whose life you have already embittered, whose prospects you have blighted—and to whom every hour of association with yourself, must work additional evil. Persuade him, for the repose of all, to leave the country."

"Would you fly with him! Beware, woman! Think not to deceive me—I see into your heart, and understand all its sinuosities. Look that your interest in this enthusiast gets not the better of your duty."

She turned her head upon the pillow, and sobbed bitterly:—yet, how wantonly had I uttered these reproaches. The angels were not more innocent in spirit than was she at that moment when I had inflicted upon her the tortures of the damned.

CHAPTER XV.

I am now rather to relate the labors of another than of myself, and to record the progress of Harding in the newly assumed duties of his life, of which, to their termination, I had little, if any suspicion.

In accordance with his design, and in this respect, my own habits and disposition favored him largely, he was with me at all hours—we were inseparable. He pretended a taste for gunning, and though a poor sportsman, provided with the usual accoutrements, he would sally forth with me, day after day, in the pursuit of the game, in which the neighboring country was plentifully supplied. Day by day, at all hours, in all places, we were still together, and seemingly in the same pursuit; yet, did we not always hunt. We chose fine rambles —pleasant and devious windings of country, secluded roads, hills and dales and deep forests, in which a moody and reflective spirit might well indulge in its favorite fancies. Of this make were we both. To-day we were in one direction—to-morrow in another, until the neighboring world and woods, for an extent in some quarters of twenty miles, became familiar to us in our excursions. I was struck with Harding's new habit of observation. In our rambles before he had seen, or appeared to see, nothing. Now nothing escaped his notice and attention. Tree and stump—hill and vale—wood and water—all grew familiar, and a subject of large and narrow examination. He seemed particularly solicitous of the true relations of things —of parallel distances—objects of comparative size, and the dependencies of a group, in the compass of his survey. As he had a great fondness for landscape drawing and some skill in the art, I put these peculiarities down to the account of this propensity, and gave myself no concern about it; but not unfrequently, turning suddenly, would I detect the fixed gaze of his eye, fastened inquiringly upon my own. On such occasions he would turn aside with a degree of confusion, which, did not, however, provoke my suspicions. There was no object in these wanderings that seemed too humble for his survey. He peered into every cup of the hills—into hollow trees—groped his way through the most thickly spread and seemingly impervious undergrowth, and suffered no fatigue, and shrunk back from no difficulty. Having hit upon a new spot, which looked romantic or dark, he would, before its examination, closely watch my progress —the direction which I took and the peculiar expression of my face. These practices were not unseen by me at the time, but I regarded them as having no object—I was certainly blind to their true one. It is only now that the mystery of his mind is unveiled—that his new-born daring is accounted for—that he now appears the rational and strong spirit I had never before considered him.

We had now, in these rambles, taken, with the exception of a single one, every possible route, leading into the neighboring country.

Bold and daring as I was, I had always avoided the path which led to the little islet and the scenes of my crime, though, certainly without exception, the most beautiful and attractive among them. This had not escaped his attention—though he had so contrived it, as not to appear to have a care or even to be conscious, of the route we were to pursue. It now happened, however, that we were called upon to retread spots which had grown familiar, and more than once my companion would exclaim—

"Have we not been here before—can we not take some new direction?"

Still I avoided the route too well known already to me, and still he had not ventured to propose taking it. He would not alarm my suspicions by a suggestion, though one which would have been so perfectly natural. He took another mode to effect his purpose, and one day, just as we were about to pass the little hollow in the woods, which led directly upon the path I so much wished to avoid, he saw, or pretended to see, some game which attracted him, and, without saying more, he darted into the avenue. I was compelled to follow, and, slowly, and with feelings I was ashamed to possess, but could not control, I prepared to call up to my mind the whole history of crime and terror, already sufficiently vivid to the eye of my memory. We pursued the devious route, and once more I found myself retracing a region, which though for months untrodden, was still as freshly in my recollection as when I made it the field of exercise for all the black and blasting passions running then riot in my soul. On we went from point to point, of all the places in my memory, each of which had its distinct association, and spoke audibly to my spirit of some endearment or reproach, some sorrow or delight. Here was the little lake,—here the islet where I first discovered her. Here the scene of her dishonor and of my triumph—here the place of our usual meeting, and here—the spot upon which she perished under my hands. I strove not to look. I felt all things too vividly in my soul, and though I closed my eyes, I could not shut out the images of terror which were momentarily conjured up by my imagination. I strove to gaze in all quarters but that which witnessed our struggle and my crime, but my eyes invariably turned at last and settled down on the one spot, where, at length, I beheld, under the influence of my imagination, the distinct outline of her figure, as it had, at the time, appeared before me. Slowly it seemed to rise from its recumbent posture, and, while I breathed not, I beheld it proceed along the road which I had taken, when bearing the inanimate burden from which that now guiding spirit had forever departed, to its place of final slumber in the body of the rock, which stood rigidly in the distance. I followed it, unconsciously, with my eyes. My respiration had utterly ceased—my hair was moist yet active—my lips were colorless and cold, and my cheeks were ashen pale. A palsying wind seemed to penetrate my bones, and though not a joint trembled, yet they were all powerless. I became conscious at last of my condition and appearance, from discovering the eyes of Harding anxiously bent upon mine and following in the direction of their gaze. There was something so expressive—so earnest in his look, that, though yet utterly unsuspicious of his design, I was nevertheless not a little struck, and somewhat offended by his seeming curiosity. I recovered myself the instant after making this discovery, and turned abruptly upon him. As if detected in an impropriety, his eyes fell, in evident confusion, from the look which I gave him; and tacitly, without a word, we prepared to proceed in our ramble. Not willing to suggest a solitary movement while in this region, which should prompt doubt or inquiry, I left the choice of road to himself, and saw with some concern that we were now taking the direct route to the cottage of old Andrews, the father of Emily. I had no fear of exposure from any such interview, for, I had so contrived it, that all suspicion had been diverted from myself in the minds of the family. I had busied myself in the little inquiries that had been made into her fate—had pretended not a small portion of sorrow and regret—had made sundry presents, which in the depressed condition in which they lived, had readily contributed still more to their blindness; and never having been recognized, in the dotage of the old man, as the boy who had contributed to his first great misfortune, I had escaped all imputations on the subject of the second. Besides, I had taken care to visit them frequently, though privately, for a short period of time after the event, and felt secure that I had no other position in their regard, than that of confiding and friendly consideration. But the subject had become irksome, and, in addition to this fact, I had, for the first time, revolved in my mind the possibility that my companion, coupling the conversation of the family, which would most probably turn upon the fate of their daughter, with my own story, might be enabled to gather from the particulars such information as would open the trail, and prepare the way for further evidence. But the cautious policy of Harding silenced my alarm, and indeed, my great error from the first, consisted in the humble estimate I had been taught to make of his character for firmness. There is no greater mistake, than in despising him to whom you have given any reason to become an enemy. Where there is mind, injury will engender malice, and where there is malice, there is a ceaseless prompter, which will one day couple the venom with the sting. Self-esteem in exaggerating my own strength to myself, had also taught me to undervalue that of others—in this way, I assisted his pursuit, and helped him on to his object.

We came soon upon the cottage. The old man sat glowering in idiotic abstraction in a corner chair, which he kept in a continual rocking motion. His mind seemed utterly gone, and though he spoke to both, he appeared to recognize neither of us. His wife was glad to see me, and thanked me repeatedly for some articles of dress which I had sent her a few months before, since which period, until then, I had not seen her. An unavoidable association called up the memory of Emily, and the tears of the old woman were again renewed. Harding with an air of common-place inquiry, and a manner of the most perfect indifference, almost amounting to unconsciousness, inquired into the story to which she had referred, and while she told it as far as it was known to herself, busied himself in plaiting into something like form, the remains of a handful of osiers which he had plucked on the way. He felt that, at such a moment and occasion, my jealousy, if I were really guilty, must be particularly active; and took care, therefore, to avoid the expression of much curiosity. Yet his very indifference, had not my fate otherwise ordained, should have alarmed my watchfulness, so utterly different did it appear from the emotion which he usually expressed when called upon to listen to a narrative so sorrowful and touching. But he heard it, as if in a dream. His mind seemed wandering, and I was lulled into the most complete security. Never was indifference so well enacted—never had mortal been more attentive to a history than Harding to this. All its details had been carefully treasured up, and where the old lady had associated me with the adventures of her daughter, his mind had taken deep note, and the record in his memory was ineradicably written. Over the chimney place stood a rude portrait of the murdered girl, to which, when the old lady called for his attention to her beautiful features, he scarcely gave a glance; and he, whom destiny had selected to bring the murderer of her child to punishment, provoked openly the anger of the mother, by his glaring inattention to the story of her supposed fate. We left the cottage after a somewhat protracted visit. I had no single concern—not the slightest apprehension, so completely had my companion played his part in the transaction—but he had not lost a word, not a look not an action, in all the events of that morning. His eye was forever upon me—his thoughts were dissecting mine, and the most distant association of cause and effect, drawn vividly together by his intellect, quickened into sleepless exercise and energy by the influences acting upon it, supplied him with the materials for commencing the true history of my crime.

We passed the rock on our return. I could not keep my eyes from it; and his eyes were on mine. He saw the same ashy paleness of my cheek and look, and he saw that this rock had something to do with my history. In the analysis of a story like mine—so terribly romantic as it was—his imagination became a prime auxiliar, and with its aid, where a dull man would have paused for facts, with the felicity of truth, it supplied them. He grew strong and confident in each hour of his progress in this labor.

CHAPTER XVI.

We had in our village, among its other wonders, a small building, which, by a stretch of liberal indulgence, had been denominated "the Academy of Fine Arts." It was almost our only lion, and we made the most of it. Its collection was poor enough and large enough, and always on the increase, from the habit prevailing among a few of our domestic artists of sending their pictures to the gallery, as frequently for sale as exhibition. This kept the collection always new; and consequently, to a certain extent, always interesting. It was a favourite lounge for this and for other reasons. In connexion with the establishment, an adjoining apartment had been given up to the village library, and there we got our books, and read the newspapers from all parts of the country. As we had our politicians, too, so we had our discussions; and thus, in a country like ours, where disputation is the mental small-beer of all classes, we had an additional attraction for the crowd, in the eloquence of our disputants. From the picture-gallery we adjourned to the library, from the library to the reading-room, and the transition was not great from the perusal of the journal to the forensic analysis of its contents. This apartment was a complete bear-garden—but our business is not there at this moment.

A week had not well elapsed after the ramble of Harding and myself, narrated in the previous chapter, when, lounging with my wife through the gallery aforesaid, I beheld one picture, crowded among the hundred upon its walls, from which I could not turn my eyes. It filled me with astonishment while awakening in my mind a thousand apprehensions—more painful, as they were vague and intangible. It depicted the scene of my crime—the crime itself—as truly done to nature (so my fancy assured me) as if the artist himself had surveyed its execution. There was the little copse upon the neck of land, the stream running alongside in faithful affinity—there lay the female form, pale and shadowy, and with, as I thought, a sufficient resemblance to Emily to have been held a portrait. She was painted as dead, and in the distance, moving off in the shadow of the wood, and with face averted, the figure of a man, which the active fear within me assured me was intended for myself. You may guess my emotion. My wife, who was with me, was struck with the picture, and annoyed me by her conjectures as to what could be its design. Her reference was to some pagan story—had she looked that moment in my face, she had not gone so far for the subject. Having recovered from the first shock, I inspected the piece more closely; and finding it for sale, from the label, I affected to be pleased with it, and paid its price to the keeper of the collection, who was its proprietor, having bought it (a great bargain, he said) from an old woman who was entirely unknown. Having secured it in my possession, and after examining it closely, I was more and more confirmed in the opinion that the whole of it had been copied from that dreadful event in my own history—such was my fear—my reason, indeed, suggesting innumerable parallel subjects for the exercise of the artist's fancy, having no connexion with me. The mysterious manner in which the piece had been sold to the academy contributed to my fears, and into this particular I had not the courage to inquire. I dreaded to increase my knowledge. After I had sufficiently indulged my curiosity, I took my wife into the apartment to which it had been carried.

"Constance!" I exclaimed, "look on this picture, and you see my story. This picture imbodies the tale I gave you and Harding some months ago. Do you remember it?"

She looked into my face with that uncertainty of glance which one might be supposed to wear when doubting the sanity of a companion. I went on—

"It is true, Constance. In that very wood so described, the girl, whose features you there see, became twice my victim. I took from her her honour, and finally her life. The artist who has described it, has done so narrowly."

"Heavens! and you speak so coolly—will you stay here, Faber?"

"Wherefore not? I tell you, Constance, you are not yet free."

And, apprehensive as I was, I could not yet restrain the malignant spirit which luxuriated always in the sensibilities and sorrows of others. She only wept, while, in her presence—for I knew she dared not tell the story—I cut up the telltale fabric with my knife, and saw the fragments, one by one, consuming in the flames. Fool that I was in all this—to suppose that the avenger of blood could be satisfied—to think that the artist had not other copies. So it was! Another and another, to the number of three, giving various aspects of the transaction, appeared in time upon the walls of the academy. I was too sagacious, however, to purchase any more. I had now begun to tremble! Still I had not the slightest suspicion of the author, and though my thoughts were restlessly employed upon the subject, they wandered to all persons and conjectured all things but the right. Still, daily, did Harding and myself pursue our rambles, and, each day, through his adroit ingenuity, yielded something more to the stock of that evidence with which he was to overwhelm me. By degrees, he had penetrated in all directions of that fatal wood; and, at length, our footsteps were bent, as in the most casual manner, up the steep sides of the rock, and over the very path, which, burdened with the dead body of Emily Andrews, I had once journeyed alone.

My eyes were again riveted upon that fearful chasm—I heard the dead fall of her delicate form, as it struck from side to side in its passage down—I heard the clattering of the loosened stones which had accompanied and followed her; and, at length, the same subtle imagination which had revived all the circumstances vividly before one sense, arrayed her reanimated form as vividly before another. I saw her arise from the chasm, pale and ghastly as when I had seen her descend. For a moment the spell of terror fixed every faculty, and in that moment, the searching glance of my companion, had gathered much towards the formation of his testimony. He had followed the direction of my glance, and the chasm, half concealed in the umbrage, and not very obvious to the gaze, grew distinctly before him. I recovered from the trance slowly, which had so stupified me, and we returned to the village.

In a few days more, and another scene, to me full of dreadful significance, stood up prominently in the collection of the academy. How well his imagination understood mine! How subtly, where all reason must have been at fault, had its nice and daring perceptions discovered the clue leading to the innermost soul and darkest secret of the criminal! There was the rock—there the chasm, and just above it, in a dim haze that made the outline and expression, but did not impair the felicity of the portrait, stood the phantom person of Emily, as my fancy had pictured it to my sight but a few days before. "God of heaven!" I exclaimed, in the bitterness of my fear, "what demon is it that can so imbody—so torture me with my own dreadful imaginings?" Through the means of an agent—vainly foolish as before—I secured this new accuser, and destroyed it in like manner with the first. But, horrible! another self made its appearance, and, in despair, I gave up the hope of arresting, in this manner, the progress of that mysterious inquiry, which, taking a form so equivocal and so silently industrious, was, in consequence, so doubly terrible. But Harding, for he was the artist, did not content himself with probing, in this stern but strange manner, the secrets of my soul, by an exercise of my fears and fancies. He privately took his way to the family of the murdered girl. He ascertained the day and date of her absence—took careful note of our association—of the expectations that had been formed in their minds, not less than in the mind of Emily herself, from the attentions I had paid her; and though the true nature and extent of our connexion had been totally unsuspected by her parents, our intimacy had been such as to warrant a belief, that, in the progress of events, something must necessarily grow out of it. He found that we had been almost in the daily habit of meeting, and in the very wood in which he had first perceived my terrors. He learned, that, in dragging the stream in its neighborhood, no traces had been found of the victim—that a search, made shortly after she had been missing, and on the same day, throughout the country, for many miles, had been ineffectual. He was conscious that few places of concealment offered themselves in the circuit so examined, except in the cavity of rock to which his mind had already adverted; and, associating the ill disguised apprehension and horror which I had exhibited while upon it, he came to the rapid conclusion that the mystery was to be developed there. Yet how was he now to proceed? There was still something wanting to unite together the several links in the chain of testimony which he had so assiduously and singularly woven. The circumstances, though strong, were not at all conclusive against me; and, having succeeded so poorly in the first instance, and with the public prejudice so strongly against him, he might well dread the overthrow of his design, in the event of any premature and partial development. Though perfectly satisfied that the chasm contained the remains of the murdered girl, he was yet well convinced how little the mere development of the body would avail, unless with some identifying circumstance, fixing the crime upon me. Accordingly, he devoted himself busily to the task of tracing in the details of the mother, all the particulars of my intimacy with the daughter. In this scrutiny he happened upon, read carefully, and copied a single note having my initials, merely, but without date, which I had sent her, enclosing some ornaments for her person and engaging to meet her on some day in the ensuing week. The style of expression was guarded in the extreme, and indicated the feelings of one who esteemed the individual he addressed, with a respectful consideration, which though not love itself, might in time, become so. The absence of a date, alone, presented a difficulty, which was only overcome, by a single passage which the note contained. It spoke of pressing engagements for a term of some days, which would so occupy the attention of the writer as to leave him no opportunity of seeing her for that period unless that which the note suggested was embraced. What engagements were there of so pressing a character upon me? Harding knew as well as myself the nature of my employments, and felt assured that the assertion was either false, or that the note had been written at the time, when my marriage arrangements had been made; the only circumstance he conceived likely to have been looked to in my mind, as calculated to interfere with the pursuit of any humbler object. This was conjectural, however, yet the conjecture furnished him with an additional clue which he suffered not to escape him. The old lady could say nothing as to the period when the note had been received—but the jewels were shown him, and carefully noting down their kinds and qualities, he proceeded to the several shops of our village in which such articles were sold. He inspected all of corresponding description, and submitting those in question, he at length found out to whom and when they had been sold. The dates were supplied, and were so far found to correspond with events, that it was indubitable that but four days after their purchase by myself, Emily Andrews had been lost to her family. The circumstances were now almost embodied in the estimation of the law; and assured, but still unprecipitate, Harding prepared calmly and quietly the whole narrative, and awaited impatiently the operation of looked for events, to unfold the entire history. And the time came!

CHAPTER XVII.

Fate had me in its power, and I was blind. If I were not weak enough, of myself, to reveal the secrets of my soul, and its crimes, I was not less the creature of a destiny, which, in the end, set at nought my profoundest cunning, and proved my wisdom to be the arrantest folly. I look back now with wonder at my own stupidity. A single survey into existing things, as in all other concerns I had certainly made it, and I should have laughed all inquisition to scorn. Now, I am its victim—the shallow victim of a most shallow design. Thus it is, however, that the wisest suffer defeat through a self-esteem which leads them into wrong, not merely in their estimate of themselves, but in their estimate of others. Thus was it with me;

and well, from my own experience, may I exclaim with the ancient, "*fata viam invenient.*"

Yet was I not unwarned—unthreatened. I had a presentiment that something was to happen—I was uneasy, discontented—wandering. My spirits were dreadfully depressed, and but half conscious, I took my way to the secluded cottage of Harding. Unannounced, I entered his study, and found him—on his knees, at prayer. A strange feeling possessed me, and I was almost tempted to kneel down beside him. But I dared not—I had never been taught to worship—I had never been taught to bend the knee, and tones of supplication were foreign to my sense and unfamiliar to my lips. Could I have knelt at that moment and fervently prayed for the grace I had not, I feel satisfied the heart of my companion would have relented of all its purposes. He would not, at that moment, have arrested the new-born exercises of a spirit so redeeming and atoning. The moment of indulgence was permitted to escape, and the fiat had gone forth. The doom was upon me!

We sallied forth, as had been, for so long a period, our morning custom. A grave solemnity marked the expression of Harding's countenance, mixed, at intervals, as we grew more and more communicative, with a faltering hesitation of manner, indicating, it is more than probable, a relaxing of his purpose. I can now comprehend all his feelings and emotions. His position was, indeed, a strange and sad one. Under a sense of duty the most sacred, not merely to the community, but to himself, he had undertaken the punishment of a criminal with whom he was in the daily habit of close communion—to whom, in worldly matters, he was somewhat indebted, and in whose welfare, he had at heart, and sincerely, a deep interest. The task of hypocrisy which he assumed, sufficiently painful to a mind like his, was doubly irksome under the operation of such circumstances; and, I am assured that could he, at that moment, have been persuaded of a change of heart in me—had I given him the slightest reason to believe that my crimes were regretted, and that it was my fixed purpose to become a better man,—he would, even then, just as the curtain was about to be drawn, which would unveil the whole catastrophe, have stayed his uplifted hand—he would rather have suffered the tortures of his imagination, and the rebukes of his ambition, than have cut off the penitent in his first approaches to pardon and atonement. But, at this very moment, I uttered some vile jest—discreditable to manhood and morality, alike—and the spell was broken. He was strengthened in his purpose, and solemnly he led the way, I following, unconsciously, to my own sacrifice.

A sudden turn brought us directly upon the scene of my crime, and there, to my surprise, a goodly company was assembled.

"What is this!" was my exclamation. "Why are so many of the villagers here. Know you, William, what is meant by this assemblage?"

"We shall see!" was his sudden and somewhat stern reply, as we continued to approach. My heart trembled, and leapt convulsively to my mouth—my knees faltered, but there was no retreat. We came up to the company before whom my appearance had scarcely been made, when, wildly from the group, rushed forth the mother of Emily—she seized me by my arm.

"Give me back my daughter" was her frenzied exclamation—"you will not keep her from me. My daughter—my poor sweet Emily."

They dragged her back to the spot, where, feebly and with an expression of subdued idiocy, old Andrews incessantly shook his stick in the direction where I stood, while his palsied head maintained a corresponding motion. I recovered myself, but my tones were husky and thick, and I am satisfied not so coherent as I could have wished them.

"What does all this mean, my friends; why this charge upon me—why this gathering—" was my inquiry.

"This gentleman will explain" said the Justice, pointing to Harding who had by this time taken a place midway between the company and myself, "you are charged," continued the officer, "with having first seduced, then spirited away the daughter of these old people, one Emily Andrews; and for your sake, Mr. Faber, I sincerely hope that you may be able to establish your innocence in spite of the strong circumstances which, it is said, will be brought against you."

I looked to Harding—I sought to crush him with that look—but he was untroubled, unappalled beneath it; and, though trembling with emotion, as seemingly determined in intention, as the martyr, fortifying if not establishing his faith, by the free offering of his blood. He proceeded, modestly, but confidently to his narration. He recounted the history of our intimacy—described once more the circumstances of the revelation which I had made to him of my crime. How it had burned in his brain like so many living coals. How he had come in his agony to me, and how finally, in order to escape from the suggestions of torture inflicted upon him by conscience and imagination, he had revealed it as it had before been heard, to the officers of justice. He showed how he had been overthrown by the search made in accordance with the story—how, writhing under the reproaches of the public and crushed in their opinion, he had been on the verge of madness and suicide—how I had sought him out in his closet—repeated my story, and how he had again believed it. A certain something, he said, assured him that I had told the truth, but not the whole truth—that I had suppressed and altered, so as to defeat inquiry; but that, though the causes which had led me to disclose so much unnecessarily, were unknown and unaccountable, he was taught, at length, really to believe in the commission of the crime. A desire to regain his station in society—to show that nothing of slander or malice had prompted him in the first instance, inspired him with the design, which, carried out perseveringly and properly, had resulted in his being able, he thought, most satisfactorily to prove the murder of Emily Andrews by Martin Faber, and accordingly, he proceeded to the developement of his particulars. How did I curse my own blindness as he proceeded in his narration. How did I wonder at the ingenuity with which, without any clue, he had unravelled, as it were with my own fingers, all my secret. He had watched all my motions—all my looks—all my words. He had suffered not a glance—not a whisper to escape him. With the assistance of his mother, who, herself, in disguise had sold them, he had carried on the affair of the pictures—he discovered who had bought them, and conjecturing for what purpose, he defied me to produce them. He described the involuntary terrors which my face had exhibited on approaching the spot upon which we stood—how the same emotion, so exhibited, had led him to suspect that the rock to which he pointed had also some connexion with the transaction. The facts gathered from the conversations with the family, leading to the final, and, as he thought, conclusive proof, in reference to the jewelry, he next dwelt upon; and, with a brief but compact summary, he so concentrated the evidence, that, though strictly speaking, still inconclusive, there was not an individual present but was persuaded of my guilt.

"And now," said he, "there is but one more witness for examination, and this is the rock of which I have spoken. I am persuaded that the body of Emily Andrews lies there. The expression of Faber's eye—the whole look with which he surveyed the chasm, could not have come from nothing. That rock, in some way or other, is associated with his crime. I have made arrangements for its examination and we shall soon judge."

Placing a little ivory whistle to his lips, a shrill sound went through the forest, and after the lapse of a moment, a sudden flash illuminated, and a loud explosion shook the earth around us. We proceeded to the spot, and when the smoke had cleared away, a shout from those who traversed the fragments, torn from the fissure which had been split by gunpowder, announced the discovery of the victim, and in her hands—conclusive evidence against me—torn from my bosom without my knowledge, while in the last convulsions of death,—lay the large brooch, the loss of which had given me so much concern at the time, and, on its back, chased finely in the gold setting, were the initials of my name. There was no longer any doubt —they seized upon and dragged me to prison.

CHAPTER XVIII.

He came to me in my dungeon—he, my accuser—my enemy—my friend. In the first emotions of my wrath, I would have strangled him if I could, and I shook my chains in his face, and I muttered savage curses and deep threats in his ears. He stood patiently and unmoved. His hands were clasped, and his eyes were dim, and for a while he had no language, no articulation.

"Think not," at last he spoke—"think not I have come to this work with a feeling of satisfaction. I have suffered more agony in its progress than I can well describe or you understand—I will not attempt it. If you cannot, from what you know of my character, conceive the grief and sickness of heart which must have come over me, during the long period and regular and frequent succession of hours, in which I was required to play the hypocrite—I cannot teach it you. I come not for this. I come to ask your forgiveness—to implore your better opinion—and that you may attribute to a necessity which gave me no other alternatives than death or shame, the whole of this painful episode in my life!"

He was a noble creature, and so I could not but think at that very moment; but, I was of the earth, earthy! I was a thing of comprehensive malignity, and my impulses were perpetually warring with the suggestions of my better reason. I may not wonder at my madness, though even then I knew it to be such.

"My blood be upon your head—my ignominy be yours—the curses of all of mine be on you—may all things curse you. Talk of my being a murderer, are you less so? Have you not hurried me to death—to a shameful death—dishonoring myself, dishonoring my family, when, probably, I might have atoned for the error of my youth, in the progress and better performances of my age? This is your religion, is it? this your love for me—for man! Hypocrite, that you are, begone! Come not falsely now to extenuate what you may not excuse—your priestly cant about forgiveness does not deceive me. Away—I curse you to the last!"—and his head sunk upon his breast, and his hands were clasped in agony, and I exulted in the writhings and gnawings of that heart, whose over-delicate structure, I well knew, could never sustain such reproaches.

"Spare me, spare me! As I live you do me wrong. Be not so merciless—so unforgiving. Fame, and the world's good opinion, were to me the breath of life. I could not have done other than I did and lived—I could not."

"Looked you then to me to do it? Was the world's good opinion nothing to me? Had I nothing to live for? Had I no aim in life? Oh—away! I sicken but to see you!"

Patiently, amidst all my reproaches, he persisted in the endeavour to conciliate my fiendish mood, suggesting a thousand excuses and reasons, for the obvious duty which I myself felt he had done to himself and to society—but I rejected them all, and, in despair, he was about to retire, when a sudden thought came over me.

"Stay, William—there is one thing—there is one way in which I can be assured that your motive was not malicious, and that you have been stimulated as you say, solely by a belief in the necessity of what you have done!"

"Speak—say, any thing, but grant me your forgiveness—give me your good opinion!"

"Ridiculous! the good opinion of a murderer—the hated, the despised of the community;—of what good is it to you or to any body?"

"True—true!—but even with the murderer I would be at peace—I would not have him die with an ill feeling towards me. But there is yet another thought which prompts the desire in this case. It is from my associate and companion that I would have forgiveness, for the violation of that confidence which grew out of that association. For this I would have your forgiveness!"

"The distinction is somewhat nice, but you shall have what you ask—cheerfully have it—upon one condition!"

"What is that, say on—I will gladly serve you."

"Justice demands a victim and I must die; but it is not necessary to justice that I should die in a particular manner. I would not die by the rope, in the presence of a gaping multitude—you must provide me with a dagger—a knife, any thing by which I may free myself from the ignominy of such a death."

"Impossible! that will be wrong—it will be criminal. Justice, it is true, may not care whether the rope or the steel shall serve her purposes, but she requires that her officer, at least, shall do it; otherwise it is not her act. It is your will, not hers, that would be performed—her claim would be defeated."

"Shallow sophistry!—this then is your friendship—but I knew it would be so—away, and may—"

He stopped me in my curse.—

"Stay!"—he exclaimed hurriedly, and with terror—"any thing but that. I will do as you require."

CHAPTER XIX.

The day of retribution—of a fearful trial, is come!—Horrible mockery!—the sunlight streams through the iron grating, and falls upon the straw of this accursed dungeon. How beautifully—how wooingly it looks—lovelier than ever, about to be forever lost! Do I tremble—would I yet live and linger out the hours in a life of curses, among those who howl their denunciations forever in my ears? Could I survive this exposure, this infamy, and cherish life on any terms and at all hazards! I would not die—not thus, not thus—

on that horrible scaffolding, I shudder but to think on it. Yet what hope would I rely upon? I have none to whom in this perilous hour, I could turn in expectation. No fond spirit now labors, unsleepingly, for my relief. I have not lived for such an interest—I have not sought to enlist such affections—none hope—none seek my escape—none would assist in its consummation! I am alone—I must die!—and what,—horrible thought!—if he should not bring the weapon?—if his shrinking and woman-like conscience should scruple still to interfere with the decree of justice, and I should be led out in the accursed cart, through the jeering multitude, and go through all the trials of that death of shame and muscular agony!—let me not think of it. Let me not think!—

And I closed my eyes as if to shut out thought, and rushed to the extremest corner of my cell, despairing of the appearance of Harding with the dagger he had promised. But a few hours were left, and the sharp and repeated strokes of the hammer, at a little distance, indicated the rapid progress of the executioner in his preparations for the terrible performance of his office. I groaned in my agony of thought, and buried my head still deeper in the meshes of my couch. But I lay not long in this hopelessness of soul. Thanks, thanks—the fates be praised—he comes—the bolts shoot back—the doors are unbarred—he is here! I shall not stand then on that fearful fabric! they shall not see the wretch writhe and dangle in his pain, for their amusement! He brings me that which shall enable me to give them my defiance, and disappoint the gaping multitude, already beginning to assemble. I shall defeat them still!

"Oh, Harding—I had almost given you up—I had begun to despond—to despair. I dreaded that the weakness of your spirit had yielded to your conscience, and that you had forgotten your pledge. God of terror! what a horrible agony the thought brought along with it. It is well you came; I had else cursed you with spectres that would have fastened on you like wolves. They would have drained the blood, at the same moment, from all the arteries in your system. Give me the knife."

"It is here, and, oh, Martin—I have had a terrible struggle with my own sense of what is right in the performance of this office. I have resisted the suggestions of conscience—I have overcome the rebukes of my own mind—I have done wrong, and do not seek to excuse myself—but I have brought you what you desired. Here, take it, take it at once and quickly before I repent me of having so weakly yielded in the struggle."

"I have it—I have it!" I shouted wildly, as I seized it, shaking the naked blade as if in defiance, in the direction of the scaffold. "I am secure from that shame—I shall not be the capped and culprit thing of ignominy which they would make me, in the eyes of that morbid rabble. I am free from the dishonor of such a death. Ah, Harding, thou hast almost redeemed thy fault—thou hast almost taught me to forgive thee for thy offending. Nay—I could almost forbear to howl my curses in thy ears, and avoid saying to thee, as I do—may the furies tug at thy vitals, like snakes, in all hours—"

"Forbear, forbear!" he shrieked—"oh, cruel; wantonly cruel as thou art—where is thy promise, Martin—where is thy honor—wilt thou deceive me?"

"Ha! ha! ha!—fool that thou art—didst thou not deceive and betray me? Where was thy honor, false hypocrite—where was thy forbearing mercy? Wert thou not cruel, wantonly cruel then? Hell's curses be upon thee—I would have thee live forever to enjoy them—thou shouldst have an eternity of torment—thou shouldst have an exaggerated sense of life for its better appreciation. Forbearance, indeed! No—I would invent a curse for thee that—and ha! thou art come in season, at the fit moment, to be my help in imprecation. Come forward—thou hast lips would make an oath tell—and tell to the quick. Come hither, come hither, my Constance!"

And I dragged forward the young and terrified wife, who had just then made her appearance in the dungeon, and forcing her upon her knees before me, I stood over her, like some fierce demon, waving the gleaming dagger in her eyes.

"Thou shalt kneel, Constance!—it is a solemn moment, and thou hast that to perform which requires that thy word and action should well suit its solemnity. Ay, fold thy hands upon thy breast—yet I ask thee not to pray—thou must curse and not pray. Speak then as I tell thee—speak and palter with me not, for, doomed as I am to death, and hopeless of escape, as I have nothing now to hope, I have nothing now to apprehend from man. Speak after me, then, as thou hast a love for life—as thou hast a leading and a lasting terror of a horrible death!"

Agonized with the situation of Constance, Harding advanced to interfere, but with a giant-like strength, I hurled him back with a single arm, and threatened, if he again approached, to bury the weapon in the bosom of the kneeling and terror-stricken woman. On a sudden, she recovered her energies, and in coherent but feeble tones, she called upon me to proceed.

"It is well thou art thus docile. Thou art wise, Constance—thou art obedient, as thou hast ever been. Keep thy hands folded, and speak after me—say, in thy wonted manner to thy God—bid him hearken to thy prayer—bid him, in tenderness and love for thee, to grant it as thou makest it. Promise him largely of thy increased love and obedience for this. Promise him thy exclusive devotion—say thou wilt live only for him; and strive to forget all the other attractions, whatever they may be, of life and society. I care not if thou keepest these pledges, it is enough for me that thou makest them."

She did as she was required. She implored the Father, fervently to sanction the prayer she was about to make—she vowed her whole love and duty, in return, so far as her poor capacities would permit, entirely to him. She spoke in the fullness of accumulated feelings, and with a devotion as deep and touching, as it was tearless and dignified.

"Well—that is enough. Thou hast been as liberal in promises, as I could well desire thee; and now for the prayer and petition thou hast to offer. Look on this man, Constance—the murderer of thy husband—the wretch, who, wouldst thou believe it, my Constance, has the audacity to have a love even for thee, in his cruel heart—the wretch, whom—thou wilt be slow to think so, my Constance, but it is nevertheless true—whom thou dost love—"

She looked up to me, as I proceeded, with a most imploring expression—but I had no touch of pity in my soul at that moment.

"It is true, and you dare not deny it, my Constance. You love the wretch who has murdered your husband, and, perhaps, when my bloody grave, which his hands have dug, has been well covered over, you will take shelter in his bosom—"

The wretched woman shrieked in agony, and fell at length upon the floor—but I allowed her no respite. It was now my triumph. After a few moments, making her resume her position upon her knees, I continued—

"Him, thou must curse! Say after me—God of heaven and earth, if thou be, as thou art said to be, just in thy provisions— Say on!"

She repeated: I went on.—

"If the power be in thee, as I believe, to do the will of thy creatures on earth—"

She repeated.

"If thou canst curse and bless—build up and destroy—yield pleasure or pain—make happy or miserable—"

She repeated.

"I call upon thee, with thy agents and ministering powers to curse with thy eternal wrath—to blister with thy unceasing severities—to torture with thy utmost varieties of pain—to make sore the body—to make bitter the life—to make wretched the spirit—to pursue at all seasons and in all lands, with thy unceasing and most aggravated asperities, this bloody man, the destroyer of my husband."

The youth, upon whom this imprecation was to fall, rushed forward—

"Speak it not! oh, speak it not, lady!—in charity speak it not. I can bear with the curse from his lips—from any lips—but thine. Sanction not, I pray you, this wantonness of cruelty—pardon rather, and forgive me that I have been the unwilling, and, at all times, the sad instrument of Providence in this proceeding."

"Back, back, William Harding—the curse must be uttered—it must be felt—it must be borne. Speak on, Constance Faber—speak on—as I have told it thee."

She looked up in my face with the calm resignation of a saint—and, as one entering upon the pilgrimage of martyrdom, she proceeded regularly in the formula, sentence after sentence, which I had prescribed; while, standing above, I muttered my gratification as every added word seemed to arouse new agonies in the bosom of the denounced. But, as she reached the part assigned to the application of the curse, she changed entirely the character of her prayer, and entreated these curses upon the head of Constance Faber, if she should ever teach her lips to invoke other than blessings upon any being of the human family, whatever, in the sight of heaven or of earth, his offence might be! The glare from my eyes must have been that of the hyena, robbed of his prey; could a look have blasted, she had been slain. A malignant shriek burst from my lips, as, with uplifted arm and furious stroke, I aimed the weapon at her bosom. Harding sprang forward, but the dagger, as she swooned away from the stroke, had penetrated her side. The youth, with unlooked for power, tore her from my grasp, before my blow could be repeated, and bore her out of my reach to the opposite part of the cell. The keeper and his assistants rushed in upon me. That was the moment of trial; and, as they approached, I shouted my defiance to all their power, and aimed the bloody dagger at my own heart; but, at that moment, the pale spectre of Emily came before me—I felt her breath, like a cold wind, blighting and chilling me to the soul, while her finger, resting upon my hand, scorched it as if with all the accumulated fires of damnation. The fates paralyzed me at that instant. I was a coward! I shrunk back from my own blow, and the dagger fell from my uplifted, but nerveless hands. They rushed upon me—they bound me down to the floor of my dungeon. I had no more strength—an infant might have fastened the shackles upon me, so completely had fate secured its victim. The dreadful spectre had departed, and, when too late, recollecting how ably my will heretofore had controlled its presence, I howled, in the silence of my cell, over the unperforming weakness of my hand. That hand had doubly failed me, for Constance yet lived—she was but slightly wounded. I, too, survived—still survived to all the horrors of death, and of such a doom as that before me.

CHAPTER XX.

The hour is come, and that mournful ghost is again before me. She points me to the scaffold, which rises dreadfully up before the barred window of my dungeon. They come—the stern guard, and the loathsome executioner. Oh, cursed weakness, that my own hand should fail me in that moment of release—of relief—that I should be unmanned at the very moment when I should most have been the man. But the fates had written it—I must fulfil my destiny. My eyes grow dim—I fail to see any longer the crowd—all is confused and terrible. What spectres are these that surround me? It is Emily,—and why does the old father shake his palsied hand in my face—will no one keep off the intruders?—they have no concern here. I have raved—but now all is before me. What a multitude—does this suffering of a fellow creature give them pleasure! Should I ask—I who have lived in that enjoyment! Would I had also been weak; I should have escaped this exposure—this pain. It is but for a moment, however—but a momentary thrill; and then—fate will have no secrets. I shall no longer be its blind victim—its slave. Will no one drive that old man from the foot of the scaffold? I would not see him there! It is old Andrews. Would he were gone—or that I could look elsewhere. But no matter—it will soon be over. I would I had a God at this moment—better to have believed—on earth there is nothing for me—such a faith, though folly, had been grateful. But now—now it is too late. The hour is come! The choking, cold hand is about my throat—dark—dark. The sunlight and the skies are gone—gone—gone—gone.

[*One of Simms's favorites among his "moral imaginative" tales, "Carl Werner. An Imaginative Story" was first published in 1838 in the two-volume collection entitled* Carl Werner, An Imaginative Story; with Other Tales of Imagination. *Explanatory and Textual Notes begin on page 655.*]

CARL WERNER.
An Imaginative Story.

ADVERTISEMENT.

The first story in this collection is founded upon a passage from an ancient monkish legend, which the lover of antiquarian lore will most probably remember. The treatment of the subject is, however, entirely my own; and the circumstance in the history of the two young men, upon which the catastrophe depends, is too frequent among the thoughtless of every nation to make it the peculiar property of any. The strifes between the rival moral principles of good and evil, have also been a subject of frequent celebration in the form of allegory; though, I believe, that, in this respect, my claim to originality will also be undisputed. In the character of the venerable guest of Matilda, it will be seen that I have ventured upon a faint delineation of one of the apostles, and that I have moreover presumed to suggest a notion of their continued toils on earth in the cause of heaven. Such a theory does not, it appears to me, seem altogether incompatible with the history of the strifes of good and evil, as afforded by the sacred volume; and, indeed, must somewhat help us in the hope which we entertain, according to the holy promise, of the final and complete triumph of the former. I trust, in what I have done, I will not be found to have trespassed beyond the limits of propriety. The other tales, with, perhaps, a single exception, belong to the same moral imaginative class with the first. They have been written at various periods in my brief career of authorship. Two of them, it may be well to state, were published with other titles than they bear in this collection. The change was made in consequence of my discovering subsequently that similar titles had been employed by other writers, which might, to the casual reader, suggest an idea of identity between them, which exists neither in the subject, nor the mode of treatment. They are only republished in this collection as they belong properly to the classification which distinguishes the work.

I.

"With what a sober and saintly sweetness do these evening lights stream around us. What a spiritual atmosphere is here! Do you not feel it?"

My friend did not immediately answer my question, and when he did, his reply was rather to the mood of mind in which I had spoken, than to the words which I had uttered. We were walking, towards the close of day, in one of the deepest parts of a German forest, through which the sunlight penetrated only with imperfect and broken rays. The vista, which was limited by the dusk, was covered with flitting shadows, and wild aspects, that won us farther at each succeeding moment in their pursuit. The cathedral picturesqueness of the scene warmed us both, and when my friend replied to me, I felt that our fancies were the same.

"You have no faith, I believe, in popular superstitions—you never yield yourself up to your dreams?"

Something of a feeling of self-esteem kept me from answering sincerely to this question. I felt, at that instant, a guilty consciousness of a growing respect for the legends of the wonder-loving land in which I wandered. My answer was evasive.

"What mean you—your question is a wide one?"

"Elsewhere it might be,—but here—here in Germany—it would seem specific enough. Briefly—you have no faith in ghosts—you do not believe in the thousand and one stories which imagination hourly weaves for the ear and the apprehensions of credulity."

"To speak truly, I have not often thought of this matter until now. The *genius loci* has somewhat provoked my fancy, and triumphed over my indifference—if indifference it be. Ghost stories, though frequent enough, are, as frequently, subjects of common ridicule; and the hearer, if he does believe, finds it prudent to keep his faith secret, if it be only to escape the laughter of his companions. This may have been the case with me, and from seeking to deceive my neighbors on this head, it is not improbable that I have fully succeeded in at last deceiving myself; and have come to doubt sincerely. But of this I will not be certain. I am not sure that I should not partake of the sensibilities of any timid urchin, at the sudden appearance of any suspicious object in any suspicious place."

"Ha! ha! I see you are no sceptic. You are for the ghosts—you certainly believe in them."

"Not so!" I replied, somewhat hastily; "I cannot be said to believe or disbelieve. I have no facts—no opinions—on the subject, and therefore cannot be supposed to have arrived at any conviction respecting it. I have scarcely given it a thought, and my impressions are rather those of the temperament and memory than the mind. Warm blood makes me jump frequently to conclusions upon which I never think; and the stories of boyhood, in this respect, will, long after the boy has become a man, stagger his strength with the images produced on his imagination by a granddame's narratives at that susceptible period. My notions of the marvellous arise almost entirely from my feelings—feelings kindled by such stories, and, it may be, rendered vivid by a natural tinct of superstition, which few of us seem to be free from, and which may, perhaps, be considered the best of arguments in defence of such a faith."

My friend made no immediate answer—a pause ensued in our speech, but not in our movement. We walked on, and the shadows became more thick around us. The scattered lights of evening grew fainter and fewer, and I perceived that the mood of my companion, like my own, had undergone a corresponding change. Sad thoughts mingled with strange thoughts in our minds, and when he again spoke, it was evident that he felt the night. He resumed the subject.

"I have not been willing to believe, but I feel, and feeling brings the faith. I have reason to suspect myself of a leaning to these superstitions, and discover myself inclining to conviction the more I indulge in solitude. Solitude is one of the parents of superstition. The constant wakefulness and warring strifes of selfish interests, which prevail in the city and among the crowd, drive away such thoughts, and, indeed, all thoughts which incline to reverence; and it is only when I get into the country—among these solemn shades and deep recesses—that I find my superstitions coming back to me with a thousand other sensibilities. It is then that my memory goes over the old grounds of my childhood; and that the fancies of an early romance become invigorated within me:—it is then that I give credence to the unaccountable story that we sometimes hear from the lips of more credulous or more experienced companions. Their earnestness and faith strengthen and awaken ours—the fancy grows into form, and the form, at length, from frequent contemplation, becomes almost sensible to the touch. We continue to contemplate until we believe; and there is not a faculty or sense that we have, which does not at last become satisfied, along with our fancies, of the rich reality which the latter have but dreamed."

"I am not so sure that they dream only," was my serious reply. "Why, if the doctrine of the soul's immortality be true—why should it not return to the spot which kindred affections have made holy—why may it not do a service to the living?—prevent a wrong?—reveal a secret, or by some ministry, which could not have been performed so well by any but itself, do that which may help the surviving to some withheld rights, to some suppressed truth—or to some unlooked for means of safety from tyranny and injustice?"

"True—that might have been an argument at one period in the history of the world; but the world has grown wiser, if not better, in later days!—a thousand modes are now in our possession for discovering the truth, to one at that time when spirits were allowed to return to earth. The days of miracle are gone by. The 'spirits from the vasty deep' do not come to us, however loudly we may call for them."

"Who shall say that?" was my reply. "Who shall answer for the necessity. It may occur now as it has occurred before, nor is it an argument against the belief, that man has grown wise enough to find out the truth for himself, after judicial forms, without the need of any such revisitings of the moon. If wisdom has grown mighty to find out the truth, crime has also grown proportionably cunning to conceal it; and virtue suffers the injustice, and vice escapes, even now, from a just punishment, quite too frequently, when it were to be desired that some honest ghost could be evoked from the grave, to set the erring judgment of man aright. Coleridge considers it a conclusive argument against the notion, that the ghost of a man's breeches should appear with him. This may be a good joke, but it is a poor argument. If it be once admitted, that for wise and beneficial purposes the just Providence shall permit the departed spirit to return to the earth, where it once abode, it will be necessary that it should put on that garb and appearance which shall make it more readily known by those whom it seeks; since its purpose, in its return to earth, might only be effected by its appearance in proper person. I can conceive of no difficulty in this; since it must be obvious that as the appearance of the spectre is the work of God, himself, with Him the toil is equally easy of giving the spirit its guise of flesh and fashion, and of preparing the mind of the spectator so that his eye shall behold the object, whether it appear in reality or not."

"The subject is one," said my friend, "which invariably forces itself upon me when I am in solitude. We are now in a place singularly accommodated to thoughts and things of this nature. There is a venerable gloom and gravity about these old trees. You see that none of them are young, yet the grounds have neither been cleared nor grubbed, to my recollection, for many years. The aged branches have stretched out innumerable arms, and bend, with their accumulated weight of years upon them, even to the ground. They have the air of a group of sainted Druids, such as the Romans annihilated. Black and frowning, yonder mountain overhangs the wood, protecting, yet threatening. It has the look of a blasted thing, and it must be a haunted one. The ruins which you behold at a little distance to the left, admirably consort with the rest of the picture. A gray mist seems to hang over and to hallow them, until even the beautiful knoll of green which rises in front of them seems offensively garish from the exceeding depth of its contrast. Those are the ruins of an ancient monastery, which the superstitious fancies of the neighborhood have long since peopled with a fraternity of immaterials, sufficiently numerous and wild to consecrate to their peculiar purposes a situation of the kind. They are not often intruded upon, except by myself; and as I have a story to tell which properly belongs to them, it will not be out of place if I tell it to you there. Some of the old monuments will give us a pleasant seat, and among the dead only, as we then shall be, we shall be in no danger of suffering interruption or disturbance from the idle footstep of the obtrusive living.

II.

"We are in Germany," continued my companion;—"of course I do not tell you this with any other object, than simply to remind you, that you are in a land, of all others, one of the most renowned for its superstitions, its wild fancies, its marvellous imaginations. The minds of its people have become spiritualized by the popular faith; and thought takes the shape of poetry at its birth, and fancy is busy every where. Their rivers and their rocks, their green knolls and sinking valleys, their dense forests, wild wastes, and deserted ruins, like these around us, are all haunted and venerable. The dell and dingle have their different spirits, the wood and rivulet theirs; and the gentle-hearted peasants who inhabit them are, in some instances, almost as rigidly tenacious of the privileges of the *genius loci*, as they are of their own rights and religion. A tale of *diablerie* will not, therefore, seem out of place, in a region so abundantly supplied with this material; and the story which I am about to relate to you, though differing materially from those which we are accustomed to hear, is yet as native to this neighborhood as any of the rest. The parties who figure in it, were born in the little hamlet of ——, not a mile distant, and you will hear the story from any of the villagers to whom you may refer for confirmation of it.

"It is now about fifty years since the events which I am about to relate to you are said to have occurred. The village of —— stood then pretty much as it does now, except that there were then two families in it, of which there are no descendants or surviving relics now. The family of Herman Ottfried was one of the most respectable in it; nor was that of Carl Werner less so. The former consisted only of Herman, and the fair Matilda, his sister; while that of Carl Werner existed in himself alone. He was an only child, whose mother had been long since dead, and whose father had died just before the time when my narrative begins. Herman was about twenty-five years of age, Carl Werner not more than twenty-one—yet they were inseparable friends. Matilda, the sister of Herman, was but seventeen; and it is more than probable, that the great intimacy between Carl and Herman, and the strong regard which the former professed for the latter, arose from the yet stronger feeling which he entertained for the sister. But of this anon. Herman was a good natured, laughing, and mischievous creature, ready always for fun and frolic, not easily apprehensive of danger, nor always scrupulous about proprieties in his pranks. He had good sense enough to keep him from any extravagant folly, or extreme rashness; and good feeling enough to restrain him from any excess which might inflict pain upon the deserving and the good. He was of graceful person, manly and strong, brave, generous, and well-principled. The favorite of the village, he was yet wanting in one of those traits of character in which all beside him were abundantly provided—he had no more faith in a ghost than he had in a sermon; and though not deficient in proper veneration, he had but slight regard for either.

"In this respect, as in several others, he differed greatly from his more youthful friend and companion, Carl Werner. Carl was superstitious to the last degree; his memory was perfectly crowded with legends the most extravagant, and he had a feverish and perpetual desire, continually, to increase his collection. He was, in very truth, a dreamer—one of those gifted men, who see strange sights and hear uncommon sounds, which are denied to the vulgar faculty; and his senses were accordingly employed always in scenting out and searching after the supernatural. But let me not be understood to say that Carl was a simpleton. Far from it. He was, in reality, as I have phrased it already, a highly gifted man. He was a poet—a man of quick and daring imagination—one whose verses were full of fire, and acknowledged to be of more than ordinary merit,—but he was rather too much of a mystic. Deeply impregnated with the traditionary lore of 'The Teuton,' and irritably alive to all its exciting influences, the fancy which was in him, the active and subtle spirit of his thoughts, gathered from all objects and associations food and stimulant for its own continued exercise. His very existence, so deeply had he drank of the witch beverage and been led away into the haunted forests of his fancy, had become rather metaphysical than real. His life was passed in dreams; and even his love for Matilda, so far from humanizing his mind and binding it to earth, seemed to have the effect of elevating it the more, and of making it hourly more and more spiritual; until, at length, he appeared to regard the maiden rather as a creation of his thought—a dream of heaven—than an object for the contemplation and the enjoyment of his senses. His life was thus diseased by his imagination, while yet in the green, in the blossom, and the bud.

III.

"Between Herman and his sister, the soul and person of Carl Werner were pretty evenly divided. When not with one, he was with the other; and when not separately with either, he was sure to be with both. Though the tastes and tempers of the two young men seemed greatly to differ to the common eye, their sympathies ran strangely together. Their sports and studies, though not alike, seemed nevertheless to bring them together always. Their habits were equally wandering, and while the poetry of Carl made him musing, meditative, and abstracted in his habits, it led him the more to delight in those practical tendencies in the mind of his companion, which suggested a character directly the reverse. Herman, too, was pleased with the fellowship of a thinking being, and one who could furnish names and definitions for all his own occasional and half-digested imaginings and thoughts. They had neither of them much system in their pursuits, and far less in their studies. Books they read, not by selection, but as they happened to fall into their hands; or, rather, Carl would read them, and describe their character and unfold their contents to his companion, who, in his own experience, could most generally remember adventures to correspond with and match those which Carl related to him. In this manner they became mutual dependants, and hence, some of the secret of their intimacy. They would follow—each—without much, or at best with a momentary opposition—the moods and promptings of the other—the momentary impulse being the sufficient governor,—and to that they most generally left the direction of studies and amusements alike. The feeling which prompted the one, if not exactly like that which filled the bosom of the other, was seldom offensive to it: and we need not wonder, thus situated and circumstanced, if they grew together, to the almost complete exclusion of all the village beside—the fair and gentle Matilda alone being excepted.

IV.

"Let not my preliminaries fatigue you. I cannot get on so well without them. My narrative has a comprehensive ground-work, and I must bring the several more striking features of the locality, in due order, and, not precipitately, before your eye. Having prepared you, I will now proceed:—

"Living, as they did, in the neighboring village, and possessed of tastes equally wandering, and, in the case of Carl, so mingled with romance, it will not be thought surprising if they spent a great deal of their leisure time among these old ruins. They were ruins then and no obtrusive utilitarian has presumed, as you may see, to take from their gray loveliness by making them more useful. The charm of the spot is the same now as then—if possible, indeed, the beauty of the ruins is even greater, for the walls have suffered from subsequent tempests, and desolation has made more complete her broken temple. Time is the ally of romance, and decay takes nothing from her honors! The source and secret of their beauty have been steadily increasing; and the domain, loved by the German youth of whom we speak, is, perhaps, scarcely less attractive now to us. Touched, as these dismembered and massive fragments at this moment are, by the mellow hues of the fleeting and flickering sunlight, they are, in my eyes, immeasurably beautiful; and seem to me as they did to Carl Werner, a fitting abode for the sleepless and sad spirit—doomed to its midnight vigil of a thousand years.

"The imagination of Carl Werner had peopled these ruins with a countless host of inmates, with wild traditions, with the most pitiable and strange narratives. It was the theatre where his invention became most active, and where he continually exercised it, as much for his own, as for the pleasure which it gave to Matilda and Herman. He had explored the many cells which abound among the ruins—he had groped through the ancient chambers, until he had, from conjectures frequently exercised, come to the belief that he could actually assign the various uses to which they were put:—and, in some cases, through the aid of local tradition and domestic history, he even ventured so far as to say who were their occupants. Though superstitious to the last degree, and most wilfully credulous, Carl Werner had no idle fears. The abbey was his favorite resort even at midnight, and with Herman, who was something of a daredevil, along with him, a ramble through the old chambers at night, when the rising moon began to peep through the cracks and fissures, was a favorite mode with Carl Werner of passing those pleasant hours. It is true, that, at such times, Matilda never ventured along with the two; but the warm and spirited fancy of Carl enabled him to embody for her ears, when they met, the sweet, strange thoughts of his mind, which, at such periods, formed the topic of conversation between him and his companion. These were themes upon which Carl never failed to be eloquent, and Matilda always loved to hear. At other times, the three would wander while the day lasted, in a sort of mental and dreamy unconsciousness, among the broken walls, turning thoughtlessly over the marble stones, laboring now and then to decipher the inscriptions, and toiling through the ancient grounds and over the green grave knolls about the edifice; until, as the sun began to wane, Matilda, with a growing and beautiful timidity—always becoming in a young and lovely woman—would hurry them homeward, leaving the unfinished story of Carl to find its conclusion at the evening fireside, which generally brought them all together like one family. They were soon to become one, it may as well be said, for, seizing a favorable moment, the gentle and fond Carl had whispered to the maiden that he loved her, and she did not hesitate long to promise that she would be his. The time was designated for the nuptials, and the two were quite as happy as mutual love, and so pleasant a hope, could possibly make them.

V.

"One afternoon, a few weeks prior to the time appointed for the marriage, Carl and Matilda went forth upon their usual rambles. Herman went not with them. He had gone away from the village on some alleged business, though, it is more than probable, that he had simply excused himself, with a delicate sense of propriety, from adding to a party which under existing circumstances could do very well without him. The fond Carl had more than once been indebted in this manner to the kind consideration of his friend. Thus, left to themselves, the lovers wandered off in the usual direction, and were soon embosomed in the haunted shades of the ancient abbey. They seated themselves among the monuments, and discoursed of the old time stories; and, with each remembered legend, the timid Matilda, with a most natural fear, would creep closer to her lover, and the fond Carl, with a most natural protection, at length encircled her waist with his arms; and the ghosts of ancient years were forgotten by the happy pair, in the delicious realities of their present situation.

"But a sudden step, as of one approaching, disturbed their dream of felicity. It was Herman. He came, with an air of impatient pleasure and slow regret, mingled up in his manner. As he drew nigh, he handed a letter to Carl, and bade him read it.

"'It is from my uncle, old Ulrich Ottfried of Amsterdam, and he writes for me to come to him immediately. The place he promised me is at length vacant, and I must lose no time to secure it—I must leave you.'

"'Leave us, dear brother!' exclaimed Matilda.

"'Leave us, Herman!' said Carl.

"'Ay, leave you!' replied the brother, 'leave you, to be sure. Would you have me sit here, purring like a tame cat all my life, when there I have a chance to be somebody, and see the great city.'

"'And will you leave us, Herman?' said the girl reproachfully, and the tears stood in her eyes.

"'Pshaw, 'Tilda! no tears now, I beg you. They're not true—they're not natural. You know you won't miss me, and there's no reason why you should. You have Carl there, and he'll be more to you than ever I can be. He suits you better; and I know him too well to be afraid to leave you to his hands.'

"'Dear Herman!' said Carl, 'but you will not go soon—you will stay to the wedding.'

"'I can't—the letter, you see, urges my instant departure; and I'm too anxious to get the place to risk the loss of it by any idle delay. It's true, I'm sorry to part with you; but, as I said, I leave you both in good hands. You love 'Tilda, and she loves you, and I believe you will be quite as happy with each other, as if I looked on myself, and saw all your happiness.'

"The hand of Carl pressed that of Matilda, and hers returned the pressure, at these words. Carl then demanded of Herman when he proposed to set forth. His prompt answer surprised and pained his hearers.

"'To-morrow,' said he, 'at early dawn, I travel.'

"'To-morrow!' exclaimed Matilda, 'dear brother, you cannot mean it!'

"'So soon, Herman!' said Carl.

"'Ay, to-morrow—so soon!' was the reply. 'It's hard. I find it harder than I thought, to leave you—you, dear 'Tilda—for you have been a dear, sweet sister to me always; and you Carl, who have been a brother after my heart's wish: I find it very hard to leave you, but I can't help it; nor, indeed, if I could, would I. The place is every thing to me, and I can make my fortune in it. My uncle, if I please him, promises to take me with him into business. Read the letter, Carl—see how fairly the good old fellow speaks. He *is* a good old fellow—he always loved me. I was his favorite, 'Tilda—he never thought much of you. But, never you mind—there's no good fortune that comes to Herman that you shall not share—both of you. So, it matters not much which of us the old man loved—it's the same thing; but go I must, and, as I've told you already, I go to-morrow.'

"This seemed a settled matter in the mind of Herman, and it produced a melancholy feeling in that of Carl. It seemed to impress Matilda even more gloomily, as well it might; for Herman was an only brother, and having neither mother nor father, the privation, she well knew, must be severely felt. She had no longer spirit to remain abroad, and closely attended by the young men, she returned, in sorrowful temper, to her cottage.

VI.

"You may be sure that was a gloomy evening in the house of Matilda; and not even the well-satisfied love of the betrothed, could make it otherwise to either of them. Herman was quite too dear to his sister and his friend, to suffer them, at such a moment, to feel their own felicity as perfect, just when they were about to be deprived of him, perhaps for ever. The maiden felt so unhappy, that she retired at an early hour, and the two young men wandered forth to talk over their several projects, and the various, and we may add, the sorrowful thoughts, with which their approaching separation had filled them both. They had been so long as one—so perfectly inseparable, hitherto—that it is not to be wondered at, if they were almost unmanned by it. Carl, indeed, suffered far more than Herman. The latter had the excitements of a new world in promise before him—the prospects of bettering his fortunes, and, besides this, he was of a more elastic and lively temper than his friend. He could very well bestow consolation, where other wanderers would have needed it. Carl had been always a dependant upon Herman, whose excellent spirits and generous mood had frequently neutralized the excessive morbidness of his imagination; and when the former thought of this, and of his weakness in many respects, he exaggerated to his own mind the greatness of the privation which he was about to undergo. Herman tried his best to console him, and in the earnestness of their mutual thoughts, they gave no heed to their wanderings. In the first moment of external consciousness, Carl looked up, and the ruins of the ancient abbey were before them. It was a fitting place for their last interview and private conference. The silence and the gloom of the spot accorded meetly with the sadness in their bosoms, and they at once entered the sanctuary. They seated themselves upon one of the broken monuments, and sat for some moments in a moody silence. At length, Carl spoke as follows:

"'I feel cold all over, Herman, as if a breath from that old vault had breathed upon me. Your contemplated journey affects me strangely. I know not how I shall bear it. I shall not often ramble among these ruins—I may have the disposition to do so—I know I will—but I shall not have the courage.'

"'Pshaw!' exclaimed the bolder Herman—'how you talk. I know you better than you do yourself, and venture to predict that when I am gone you will be here oftener than ever. You love these ruins.'

"'I do—I confess it!—they are to me sacred, if only for their recollections,' said Carl.

"'And ghosts!' continued Herman with a gentle laugh. 'You love their ghosts, I think, even more than their recollections.'

"'Ay, could I see them,' said the other. 'But they are shy ghosts, and—did you not hear a breathing?'

"Carl turned and looked in the direction of the old vault, as he spoke these words, but Herman only laughed at him. Carl laughed too, a moment after, when he perceived that his weakness had been observed by his friend.

"'You have nearly roused them, Carl,' said Herman, after his quiet chuckle had subsided. 'But for my laugh they would have been about you. You would have conjured the reverend abbot from that shattered vault, and a pretty story you would have of it.'

"'Perhaps'—said Carl; 'and you would have listened to the story, Herman, without a single interruption. Why is that? Why is it that you can enjoy a ghost story without believing in the ghost?'

"'Why do we enjoy a puzzle which we know can be undone?—a mystery—when a moment's reflection teaches us that it is no mystery? It is because the human mind finds a pleasure in that which is ingenious—in any thing which shows intellectual power. A fairy tale has a spell for all senses, not because we believe in its magic—in its subtlety—in its strange devices and wild conceits; but, that these subtleties, spells, and devices, appeal to natural desires and attributes of the mind of man. They are beautiful, and as the appreciation of that which is beautiful, forms the legitimate object in the exercise of taste, they commend themselves to every intellect or imagination that possesses even common activity. You, perhaps, are less fortunate than myself, since you believe in the ghost; and a natural sense of apprehension, which your faith necessarily excites in your mind, while the story is telling, subtracts from the perfect satisfaction with which—were you as incredulous as myself—you would hear or tell it. You tremble while you narrate, and your eyes are forever looking round to see the object which your fancy conjures up.'

" 'True, but I do not cease to tell the story. I go on—I would go on, though I beheld the ghost.'

" 'I doubt you!' boldly said the other. 'I believe you might try to do so, for I know the extent of your moral courage; but your imagination is too powerful for your control; and this I sometimes fear. I sometimes fear that you may suffer greatly, when I am gone, in the conflict between your imaginative faculty, and your good sense. While I was with you, I had no fear; for when you looked round for the ghost, I laid it with a laugh. It will rise and haunt you when I am gone.'

" 'How can you speak thus, or fear this, when, in the same breath, you deny its existence?' demanded Carl.

" 'Oh, I do not deny its existence *to you,*' said Herman—'we can always have the ghost we call for, for imagination is a god. It is the only creator under heaven. Yours is of this sort, and the worlds you people are sometimes too extensive for your sway. They will rebel against you.'

" 'I fear them not!' said Carl. 'It is my joy to create, and I sometimes pray that with my bodily eyes I may behold the dim but glorious visions of my mind. Yon old abbot, sleeping in the dust and sanctity of a thousand years,—could he rise before me now and answer a few questions, I should be most happy.'

" 'Do not trouble yourself to call upon him—he will not trouble himself to come.'

"'Yet, I am sure,' responded the reverent Carl, turning an anxious look upon the vault, as if soliciting the buried saint to give the lie to his comrade, 'yet, I am sure, that it is not because he cannot.'

"'What other reason!' said Herman. 'He cannot, my dear Carl, and if he could, he would not. He sees—if the dead may see aught—all around him that he hath ever known or loved in life; and for us, whom in life he never knew, he hath too little sympathy, to come at our bidding. There might be some motive for those lately dead to reappear at the requisition of those who still have human and earthly affections struggling with the cares and woes of earth; and I would that it were possible we could evoke them. I, too, should be a summoner, Carl—I, too, should pray that my bodily eyes might behold—not the objects of my mind, but the creatures of my heart! I would give worlds, if I had them, once more to behold my dear mother.'

"'Could she know your wish, Herman, would she not appear, think you?' demanded Carl.

"'The suggestion makes against your argument, Carl,' replied the other—'immortal as she is, she must know, she must hear my wish; yet she does not appear! wherefore does she not?—she cannot—it is written—she cannot; and it is, perhaps, wise and well that she cannot. It might alter my plans—it might affect my purposes—it might disturb the existing condition of things without making them better.'

"'Herman,—could I believe with you, I should be unhappy; but I cannot. I feel assured that the spirit may return, and make itself known. I do not say visibly to the eye, but in some way or other, to one or more of the senses. Do you remember the story of Dame Ulrica, and the silks that rustled in the tiring chamber?'

"'Ah, no more of that, Carl; and as you are now getting fairly on the track of the hobgoblins, we may as well stop our confabulation, else shall we not go to bed to-night. Of one thing be sure, if I can revisit you after death, I will———'

"'Will you promise me *that,* Herman?' demanded the other eagerly.

"'Ay, that will I, though I shall try to do it in such a manner as not to scare you. I shall sneak in like a gentle ghost, and shall speak to you in the softest language. Will you really be glad to see me?'

" 'Glad!—you will make me happy. It will be a prayer realized. Promise me, dear Herman!—we are about to separate, we know not with what destiny before us. The means of communication are few between us, and our anxiety to know of each other will sometimes shoot far ahead of our capacity to receive or yield intelligence. Promise me—though heaven grant that you may live long years after me—that should any thing befal you, and the power be with you, you will come to me—you will tell me of your own condition, and guide me aright in mine; for my sake, and for the sake of your dear sister, who will so soon be a part of my life. Will you do this—will you promise this, dear Herman.'

" 'I will—to be sure, I will, Carl,' was the reply.

" 'Seriously—solemnly?' demanded Carl.

" 'Seriously—solemnly!' said the other; 'but,' he continued—'if I am to take all this trouble, and expose myself to all risks of wind and weather merely to oblige you, you must do me a similar favor; for, though I do not believe in any such power on the part of the spirit once gone from earth, nor am I particularly curious on the subject; yet, while agreeing to satisfy you, Carl, I may just as well exact a similar promise from yourself. Dead or alive, Carl, it will always give me pleasure to see you. I have loved you as a brother, in life—I have no fear to behold you after death.'

" 'It is a pledge—a promise, Herman!' was the ready answer; and with the utterance of the pledge, a hollow laugh resounded from the dismembered vault of the aged abbot.

VII.

"They sprang at once to their feet. Herman laughed back in return, but he remained where he was. Carl trembled like a leaf, but he leapt over the stone on which he had been sitting, and made his way fearlessly towards the vault. Herman followed him. The marble of which the vault had been built was fractured in several places, so that the interior was clearly visible from without. Carl would have entered it, but Herman opposed his doing so.

" 'Why should you go in—we can see the venerable dust where we stand,' and the eyes of the two peered into the now silent chamber with a scrutinizing gaze that promised to suffer nothing to escape them.

"'Look!' said Carl; 'look, Herman! dost thou not see!' and he pointed to a corner of the vault while speaking.

"The eyes of Herman saw nothing, however, or he was not willing to acknowledge that they did; but Carl was more ready to believe, and consequently more able to see, for, even while he pointed out the object of his sight to Herman, he watched it as it glided away through an aperture of the vault—a pale bluish flame—a fragment, as it were, of light—that seemed first to crawl along the walls of the chamber, and then suddenly to disappear through one of its many fissures.

"'What is it that you see? I see nothing,' said Herman.

"'A light like that of a taper—a small, creeping light, that passed out of the corner to the east.'

"'Some slimy worm,' said Herman, 'though I did not see it at all.'

"'Strange!' exclaimed Carl; 'but you heard the laugh, Herman?'

"'Yes,' said the other, 'but whether it came from the vault, or from the opposite wall, I will not pretend to say. Some urchin may think to frighten us from the other side. We will look in that quarter.'

"Carl now followed his companion, but he followed him unwillingly. Like all true romancers, he had got just enough of the mystery. He was unwilling to press the matter farther, lest he should discover that which might jeopard his prize—which might enable him, indeed, to 'point the moral,' but which would spoil, rather than 'adorn, the tale.' This, however, was the desire of Herman. He would have given as much to discover that the source of the laugh was human, as Carl would have bestowed to prevent such a discovery. The hopes of the latter prevailed. They searched behind the suspected walls, but found nothing; and the benefit of the laugh was clearly with the superstitious Carl. After this they left the ruins. The hour was getting late, and as they had still a great deal to say of sublunary concerns, it did not need that they should take the haunted abbey for this purpose. The next morning Herman took his departure. Carl saw him a little way upon the road; and when they were about to separate, one of the last words of Carl was to remind him about his promise. Herman laughed, but freely renewed it. Was it a fancy of Carl, or did he hear the laugh faintly repeated among the rocks behind them, several seconds after his companion had disappeared. It might be an echo merely, but the circumstance troubled the mind of Carl, who could not avoid thinking of it for weeks after.

VIII.

"At length the dreams of the dreamer gave way to more urgent realities. He became a married man; and his bosom was too much filled with the thoughts of Matilda, and his eyes were too much occupied with gazing upon her, to permit of the intrusion of any busy ghost or wandering vision upon either thought or sight. Marriage has a wonderful tendency towards making men practical. The tendency, indeed, is sometimes too direct and rapid to be altogether pleasant. Not that this was the case with Carl. Far from it. He was improved in more respects than one in the change of his condition. His mind needed some qualifying and subduing influence to change its direction—to turn it from the too constant contemplation of those baseless fabrics which had heretofore but too much occupied its regards; and to bring it back to human necessities, and, through their medium, to the just appreciation of merely human joys. It is no less true than strange, that for the first three weeks after marriage, Carl did not dream at all, as had been, for as many years before, his nightly, and, to speak truth, his daily custom. For three whole weeks he lived a common man—had earthly notions of things—addressed himself to earthly labors—and did not once, in all that time, pay a single visit to the ancient abbey. But when the three weeks were over, he began again to dream, and to wander. The old abbey again received him as a constant visitor, and the presence of Matilda with him did not greatly lessen his devotion to the sanctity and superstitions of the spot.

"Perhaps, indeed, it was Matilda that somewhat contributed to the superstitions of her husband. She was a religious being—deeply impressed with the spirit of faith and worship, even if she lacked the divine intelligence which might have enabled her to discriminate between the holy things of the sanctuary, and those meretricious symbols, and mocking shadows, which the arts of one class, and the fears of another, have decreed for worship, and declared no less holy than the true. The *spirituelle* held a large place in her composition; and if her imagination lacked the activity of Carl's, her yielding weakness rendered her susceptible to the full influence of his. This weakness increased the activity of a faculty to which it was constantly appealing; and though the terrible forms and fancies to which the mind of Carl frequently gave birth and performance, only drove the timorous wife more earnestly to her prayerful devotions, she did not seek to discourage him in a practice which had so beneficial an effect. Unconsciously he practised upon her fears, moving her to devoutness through an unseemly influence; and with equal unconsciousness on her part, her fears stimulated his superstitious tendencies even to error, by giving continual employment to an imagination which daily became more and more morbidly active, and consequently dangerous.

"Herman had now been gone for some months. At first he wrote to them freely and frequently, but after a while his letters grew fewer and less satisfactory, and at length months went by without bringing them any intelligence of their neglectful brother. Matilda sometimes complained of this, and thought unkindly of Herman; but Carl, like a true friend, always found some excuse for his neglect, in the pressure of business, and the accumulation of other duties and friends.

" 'Besides, he need not write, Matilda, when he has nothing particular to say. No news is good news commonly; and when a letter comes, Matilda, you know you always dread to open it, for fear of hearing evil. Herman will not forget us, be sure.'

" 'But he may be sick, Carl.'

"That was always a suggestion which silenced her husband, and he felt doubly unhappy on such occasions, as, in addition to the fear with which such a suggestion seemed to inspire Matilda, there was an unpleasant consciousness in his own mind which dreadfully troubled him. At such times, strive as he might, he could not help thinking upon the promise which Herman had given him, and he felt that, however he might regret the death of his brother-in-law, such an event would be lessened of much of its evil, if that promise could be kept. Such thoughts he felt were criminal, and to do Carl all justice, we should add, that he strove manfully to resist them.

But he could not resist them, and they grew upon him. After a little while, he thought of nothing else. He did not need the gently-uttered fears of Matilda, who continually spoke of her absent brother, to remind him of his promise and of his mortality; and in his dreams the image of that well known friend, stretched out pale, and motionless, in the embrace of death, came but too frequently to his mind, not to lose, in time, many of its terrors.

IX.

"One pleasant afternoon, the two, Carl and Matilda, rambled forth, according to their usual custom, towards the ancient abbey. The sun was just about setting, and he made a glorious descent. His rays streamed through the broken walls by which they walked, and they paused to contemplate the picturesque effect of their scattered beams, gliding among tombs, in which the dust that once was life, and strength, and ambition, could no longer feel their warmth. While they looked, a cloud suddenly arose in the heavens, obscuring and shutting out the bright glories which had won their gaze, from the shattered walls which they had made golden but a moment before. The sudden clouding of the sky brought an instinctive gloom to their mutual minds, and without seeming to notice the absence of any connexion between the phenomenon upon which they looked, and the object in her thoughts, Matilda quickly remarked:

" 'I hope, Carl, that nothing is the matter with Herman.'

"Strange to say, the thought that something was the matter with her brother, was even then the busy thought in the mind of Carl. He replied after a moment's pause—

" 'Indeed, Matilda, I hope not.'

"A slight laugh rose from the ruins, and the conscious soul of Carl was smitten within him.

" 'Had he been sincere in the utterance of that hope?' was the question which he asked himself when he heard the laugh; but it was a question which he dared not answer. Matilda did not seem to have heard the sound which had touched him so deeply; and he was sufficiently collected to conceal his agitation from her. But while they spoke together, though but a few moments had elapsed, the cloud had veered round, and now hung in the sky directly before them. Somehow, this appearance affected Carl seriously. He coupled the cloud with his own thoughts, and his imagination grew busy in its contemplation. It did not seem a common cloud to his eyes; and its progress, from a speck in the pathway of the sun, to a mantle, in whose pitchy bosom the dying but glorious orb was to find his splendors utterly subdued, was a marvel to a mind so subtle as his. His fancies grew firm and strengthened when he saw that Matilda observed the wonder also.

" 'That is a strange looking cloud, Carl!' she exclaimed—'see how it rolls—over and over—onward and onward—and yet there is no wind. It is coming towards us.'

"The flight of the cloud seemed to have increased in velocity. It neared them rapidly, and was evidently descending. When above them, it seemed to open and to expand, and from its bosom Carl felt the warm drops upon his face.

" 'It rains!' he said, 'let us go into the abbey.'

" 'I feel none,' said Matilda.

" 'Indeed! it is full on my cheek!'

"The eyes of Matilda turned from the floating mass that had now passed over them, but when her glance met the face of her husband, she screamed in terror.

" 'Father of heaven!' she exclaimed, 'be with us! Carl, my husband, your face is covered with blood!'

" 'Say not so!' he cried, 'what can it mean?' He wiped his face with his handkerchief, and the stains were visible to his own eyes; and when he looked down upon his garments, they, too, were covered with the same sanguinary color. The wonder was greater still, when they looked in vain to find a drop upon the person of Matilda. Yet her arm had been fast locked within his, and the very hand which had sustained hers was sprinkled plentifully with the stains.

X.

"They hurried home in consternation. The thought of Matilda was upon her brother; and she regarded the events of the evening as ominous of his fate. But why did the blood stains fall only upon her husband? Why were her garments untouched? This was a mystery to her; but not to Carl. He thought he could explain it, but he forbore to speak. He dared not. His thoughts and feelings were not what they should have been. He was guilty, in his secret soul, of improper feelings, if not of improper wishes, and he knew it. Supper was soon served, and, like a good wife, regardful only of her husband, Matilda urged Carl to eat, for she beheld his abstractedness. He ate without knowing that he did so. She, however, could eat nothing, and as soon as the repast was over, she retired for the night. But Carl felt that there was no sleep for him; and a feverish mood, for which he could not account, prompted him to sally forth. He would have gone to his wife's chamber—he tried to do so—for he knew what were her apprehensions, and he wished to soothe them—but he could not. Something impelled his footsteps abroad—a spirit beyond his own drove him forward; and with a desperate mind he rapidly hastened to the abbey, as if there, and there only, he should find a solution of the marvel which had distressed him. His heart seemed to grow strong in proportion as his thoughts grew wilful; and without any of those tremors which had ever before possessed him when he rambled, with a purely mental and not a personal feeling, among the ruins, he boldly plunged into their recesses.

"The night was a clear, but not a bright one. The stars were not numerous, but they were unclouded. The air was still, and was only now and then apparent in a slight breathing, as it came through some little crevices in the wall. The silence of the place was complete—was its solitude complete also? Carl asked of himself the question, as he walked beneath the massive archway of the fabric—still solid and strong, though broken and impending; for, the masons of old, wrought, not less to make their works live than to live themselves. They live, like all good workmen, in their labors. The roof, broken in many places, let in the scattered starlight, and sufficiently, though imperfectly, revealed to him the place. He went forward, full of sad and truant thoughts. He took his seat upon one end of a dilapidated stone which had often sustained him before. His elbows rested upon his knees, and his hands supported his head. It was in this posture that he mused with feelings which sometimes brought him back to impulses and a course of reflection not unworthy of his better nature. They reproached him with the heartlessness of his curiosity, as if it were not the tendency of mind always—great mind, which overlooks the time, and lives for God, and for the species—to disregard nice affections, and the tender blossoms which decay.

" 'Herman, Herman!' he exclaimed, 'I have been unworthy of thee. Thou hast loved me with the love of a brother, while I have thought of thee even as the ancient augur of the victim, which he slaughtered for unholy wisdom! I have prayed in my secret soul—I have prayed for thy death—that I might have improper knowledge.'

"Again did a slight laugh come to his ears. He looked up with a shudder. A small blue light crawled along upon the opposite wall, like some slimy reptile, and while Carl watched its progress with solemn interest, the laugh was repeated almost beside him. He started, and almost at the same moment he felt one side of him grow chill. A breath of ice seemed to penetrate him from the east. He turned his eyes in that quarter, and the spectacle that then met his gaze paralyzed every faculty of his body. The form of Herman Ottfried was there, sitting beside him on the other end of the grave stone. He could not speak—he could not move. His eyes were riveted upon the spectre, and the glare which was sent back from those of the unearthly visitant, was that of hell. A scornful leer was in it—a giggling hate—a venomous but laughing malice.

" 'Ha, ha, ha!' The vaulted abbey rang with the echoes of that infernal laugh.

" 'Her—Her—Herman!' Carl tried to speak, but a monosyllable was all that he could utter.

" 'Mercy! mercy!' screamed the unhappy Carl, as he lifted his hands and strove to close his eyes against the dreadful presence. But the elbows refused to bend—he could not raise them. His knees in the mean time gave way, and he sank senselessly upon the damp ground of the abbey.

XI.

"When he unclosed his eyes, which he did in the fullest consciousness of his situation, and consequently in the extremest terror, he was rejoiced to find himself alone. The grave stone, at the foot of which he lay, was untenanted. The abbey was silent, and though he dreaded, at every step which he took while making his way out, to hear the dreadful laugh, and to behold the hellish visage, he yet suffered no farther interruption while in the abbey. When he had left it, however, and was about to enter the main street of the village, he was encountered by a drunken man.

"'Hallo, friend!' exclaimed the bacchanal, 'whither so fast? Stop and hear a song—stop and be merry.'

"And, in the voice of one satisfied with himself and all the world, the drinker carolled with tolerable skill, one of those famous dithyrambics in which the German muse has frequently excelled. The eye of the unhappy Carl was turned, half in hope, and half in despair, upon the man. He had heard of the soporific effects of wine—of its ability to drown care, and produce a sweet forgetfulness of his sorrow, and he felt inclined to the temptation; but a sudden thought of Matilda shot through his brain, at that lucky instant, like an arrow. He knew not the lateness of the hour, and was ignorant how long he had been from her. He knew that he had swooned away, and knew not how long he had remained in his stupor. It might be near daylight, and what,—if such were the case,—what must be her fears? Domestic love came to his succor, and he rejected the overtures of the bacchanalian, who nevertheless continued to pursue him. He followed the unhappy Carl to his very door, now persuading, and now striving to provoke him by every manner of taunt and sarcasm, to partake of the intoxicating cup which he proffered. But the sufferer was firm, though more than once it came to his thought that wine was good against sorrow. He was not yet so deficient, however, in other resources, as to fly to this doubtful succedaneum.

XII.

"It was not so late as Carl had fancied it, and his wife was still awake. He had not been away much longer than was his wont, when he went forth on his usual evening rambles; and though she had suffered from his absence, yet it was not through any apprehensions for his safety. Still she had no complaints, and the pleasure in her eyes when he did return, was, probably, one of the best arguments against his wandering forth again. She was still melancholy and apprehensive, and when she observed the anguish, not to say the agony, which was apparent in every feature of his face, her apprehensions underwent a corresponding increase.

"'What is the matter, Carl? What has troubled you?' she demanded of him in agitated accents.

"'Nothing, nothing!' with an effort, he made out to reply.

"'It is something—something terrible, dearest husband—your cheeks are haggard, your eyes are wild—you tremble all over. Tell me, tell me, my husband, what is it that troubles you.'

"'Nothing,' he again replied—'return to your bed,' (she had risen when she beheld his face,) 'return to your bed and heed me not. I will be better soon.'

"He quieted, if he did not satisfy her. She returned to the couch as he bade her; and he prepared to follow her. But there was one duty which he omitted that night, which, from his childhood, he had never neglected to perform before. He did not pray. He strove to do so, but his mind could not be brought to address itself in supplication. He forgot the words; and others, foreign to his object, took their places. He gave up the effort in despair. He could think of nothing but the terrible laugh, and the demoniac visage which had met him in the abbey. All the next day he was like one whose senses wandered. His wife strove to soothe his mood, which was fitful—and to attract his attention, which strayed continually; but he smiled upon her kindly, with a sickly smile, and gave no farther acknowledgment. As night approached he grew visibly agitated, and as he became conscious that his efforts at concealment were unavailing, he sought his chamber, to hide in its dimness what he might not otherwise conceal. But his agony seemed to increase with his solitude. Dreadful images were about him in his chamber, and a chuckle, like that he had heard in the abbey, was uttered, at intervals, even over his shoulder. He descended to the apartment in which he had left Matilda, preferring that she should see the agony that he could not endure alone. But her presence gave him no consolation, and her solicitude became an annoyance.

"'Trouble me no more!' he exclaimed, in tones which she had never heard from his lips before, replying to one of her fond appeals to know the cause of his sufferings. 'Trouble me no more—it is nothing—nothing which I may tell you.'

"She turned from him in sorrow not less deep, though less acute than his, and the tears filled her eyes. His heart reproached him as he beheld her action, and readily conceived her pain; but there was a wilful impulse in his bosom, which refused to permit of his making the usual atonement. Sullen and sad, he glowered about the apartment 'till night came on, and supper was announced, when Matilda saw that his agitation was visibly increasing. With the meek and blessing spirit of an angel, forgetting the harsh rebuff which he had given her, she approached him—threw her fond arms about his neck, and implored him to smile again upon her. He tried to do so, but the effort produced only a ghastly grin, no less shocking to her eyes than the effort had been irksome to his mind. He went to the supper table, and, unobserved by him, her glance watched him while he strove to eat. He left the table in horror, for the face of Herman stared at him from the plate. There was no hope of escape from the pursuing fiend, and the unhappy Carl rushed out of the house. Where should he go?

" 'To the abbey! to the abbey! I will speak—I will demand its meaning. I will know and hear all. If it be Herman, in truth—my brother and my friend—'

" 'Ha! ha! ha!'

"The infernal laugh was at his elbow. He turned in desperation to behold—not the gorgon stare which had so terrified him in the abbey, but a face rather good natured than otherwise—the face of the bacchanalian who had encountered him on the preceding night. A mischievous grin was upon the features of the stranger, whose broad mouth and little twinkling eyes, with the fat, hanging cheek, and the red and pimpled nose, seemed the very personification of fun and frolic. Not a feature in his face appeared of demoniac origin. The subtle malignity of the satanic attributes were entirely wanting, and in place of them, reckless mirth, indifferent to all matters but good cheer, was the prevailing expression. But the laugh! That, certainly, had been very like the laugh he had heard in the abbey. No two sounds could have seemed more alike to the ears of Carl. A new thought entered his mind with this conviction. This drunken fellow might have been the proprietor of the former laugh, as he certainly was of that which he had just heard. To him might be ascribed the design to frighten himself and Herman. When he looked into the cunning, merry, blubber-face of the reveller, conjecture became conviction. 'It must be so!' said Carl, half aloud.

"'To be sure it must,' exclaimed the other. 'We will have a glass together now, though you did refuse to be a good fellow last night. Come. Here's old Dietrich hard by. I can answer for his liquors, though I cannot for his conscience. I believe in the one, and—damn the other. Come, my friend, let's try him.'

"Carl was half disposed to be civil with the stranger. The notion which had suddenly possessed him that he and the ghost of the abbey were one and the same person, brought a singular relief to his mind; and he was half persuaded to forgive him the impertinence of the fright which he had received, in consideration of the solution of the mystery which the conjecture brought. The stranger pressed him, expatiating upon the sweets of wine, and the luxury of good company.

"'Wine,' says he—'wine, Carl——'

"'How the devil does he know my name!' thought Carl to himself, but he did not say it.

"'Damn my instinct,' said the other—'I find it the hardest thing in the world not to know, what, indeed, it is not necessary that I should know.'

"'What do you mean?' said Carl.

"'Oh, nothing—I was only regretting that my passion for wine—I had almost thought it an instinct—should sometimes make me indifferent to the sort of company I fall in with. Here, I've been on the eve of eulogizing the rich Hochheimer to you, who are a judge, doubtless, of the noble beverage, simply because, in my intercourse with mankind, I meet hourly with so many to whom the eulogy is a sort of key to their tastes, that it is now almost habitual with me to dwell upon it. To you, however, any idle talk upon the merits and effects of good wine would be only an impertinence.'

"'I am no judge—I drink little,' said Carl, to whom the seduction of appearing more than he was, or of knowing more than he did, had always been a very small one.

"'You belie yourself,' said the stranger—'I know that you are a judge—I see it in your face. Come with me—you shall give me your opinion of the wine of Dietrich.'

"'Nay, you must excuse me,' said Carl.

" 'Can't—never excuse a man from his wine,' said the other, bluntly. 'Excuse a milk-sop, of course—but never a man.' And as he finished a sarcasm which has led thousands of goodly young men to their ruin, he familiarly took the arm of Carl to lead him forward to the tavern. But Carl was not vain of being esteemed manly in this respect. His philosophy was that of an English poet, whom he never read:

'Who drinks more wine than others can,
I count a hogshead, not a man—'

and he gently, but firmly refused.

" 'Why, man,' said the other, 'Am I then mistaken in you. I thought you a good fellow, who loved good company, good wine, and a good story—'

" 'Good story!' exclaimed Carl, touched in the right place.

" 'Ay, a good story—a tale of the mountains—of the miners, and the red demons of the mines—the gnomes and the salamanders.'

" 'Have you, indeed, such stories?' inquired Carl, now rather curious.

" 'Ay, that have I, and, nearer home, of the old abbey here. I can tell you a ghost story of those ruins, that 'll make every hair of your head stand on end.'

"Carl hesitated and lingered, and his companion laughed at his hesitation. That laugh chilled him—it reminded him of what he had been willing to forget. It reminded him of the face of Herman—the ghastly grin upon his lips, and the dreadful laugh—so like to that of the stranger, which he had then heard. He broke away from the arm which held him.

" 'Not now,' said he, 'you must excuse me. I have business to attend to.' And with these words, amid the curses and the derision of his companion, he hurried forward to the abbey.

XIII.

"A spell, whose power seemed to be irresistible, prompted him in the direction which he took. A will, superior to his own, yet compassing and controlling it entirely, drove him onward to the abbey. What proper motive had he there? None. His duties were all elsewhere—with his wife—in his own home. What could he gain to see once more the dreadful spectre which had affrighted him? An unholy curiosity stimulated the answer to this question. Knowledge —Knowledge. To know that which is forbidden—to win the secrets of two worlds—was the hope of Carl, as it has been the unwise hope of thousands. He did not remember, while he indulged this vain desire, that the 'tree of knowledge, is not that of life;' still less can it be said to be that of happiness. Thought is not often happiness; and where thought takes the wings of the imagination, and strives ever after the ideal, it is too apt to be torture and strife, as it must finally be death. Death, indeed—death and time are the grand illuminators. To wait is to be wise. Alas! for Carl—he had not only to wait but to endure.

"'I must pluck up courage!' he mentally exclaimed. 'I demanded to see him; I must not shrink from the encounter. Let him speak to me—let him say he is happy—and I will ask no more.'

"What right had he to ask so much? Were it his right, would it not be revealed? Would the just God withhold from him a right? He did not ask himself these questions, for Carl, like all of his species, was but too apt to contemplate, through the medium of a shallow vanity, the deity in his own heart, as if the dwelling-place of fears and feebleness, of vain caprices and false-founded passions, could ever be the home of divinity.

"He entered the abbey walls—he trod among the crumbling ruins, but his heart shook within him. Again he sat upon the tomb-stone—again did the sudden and sinuous light crawl before him upon the walls. He felt the chill enter and curdle the blood within his bosom, and he knew that the spectre was sitting at his side. He dared not look round upon him. He almost sank upon the ground; but the resolve of his mind sustained him, and he tried to compose himself.

"'Why should I fear?' he said in his thoughts. 'If it be Herman, he will not harm me—if it be not Herman, what other has claim upon me!'

"As if the spectre had seen his heart, and in this manner commented upon its fears and weakness, the dreadful laugh which had so shocked him before, was again repeated. The blood ran cold in the bosom of the mortal, but his firmness had not departed. The resolve was still in his mind, and after a brief pause, in which he struggled successfully with his terrors, he turned his eye boldly to behold the spectre. The same dreadful presence met his glance as on the preceding night. But the novelty had passed away, and with it some of the terrors. He felt that he could now survey it, distinctly, resolutely, if not calmly. He did survey it—and what a spectacle! The face was that of his friend, that of Herman Ottfried, indeed; but, oh! how different. It was the face of his brother and his friend, but in place of the gentleness and good nature that made its prevailing expression heretofore, the features were all hell-stamped—the skin was all hell-dyed and darkened. Carl nearly fainted—his heart seemed to wither within him as he gazed. But he continued to gaze. His resolve, built upon high, but erring, moral purpose—was not now to be shaken. Nor, indeed, could he do otherwise than gaze. The eyes of the spectre, like those of the fabled basilisk, rivetted his own. The glare which shot from them, like a yellow vapor, seemed to exercise upon him the power of a spell. He gazed till he was infatuated; yet he writhed all the while beneath the scornful malignity of the spectre's glance.

" 'What would you with me?' he screamed, rather than spoke. He could easier scream than speak; and the words were scarcely intelligible to his own ears. He was once more answered by that infernal laugh. He shivered as he heard it, but it did not increase his terrors. It rather made him indignant.

" 'Who are you?' he cried, in tones more temperate, and with a spirit even more resolved than before. 'Who are you?—what are you? I know you not.'

" 'Herman—thy friend—he for whose death thou pray 'dst, that thou might 'st possess his secret. Would'st thou not hear it?'

"Such was the terrifying response of the spectre whom he had summoned.

" 'Thou liest!' cried Carl, boldly. 'I uttered no such prayer.'

" 'Thou did'st,' was the prompt reply, 'in thy heart thou did'st, and thy prayer is granted. Herman Ottfried is no more—he is beside thee.'

" 'I believe thee not!' was the courageous reply. 'My friend still lives; and if he did not, I would not believe that such as thou seemest, and art, should be his representative. He is good, and thou—'

" 'Art damned!—thou would'st say!' and the spectre concluded his sentence—'And thou say'st truly, Carl Werner. I am as thou say'st. Yet, look once more upon these features, and, blasted and blackened as they appear to thee, say if they are not those of him who was thy friend—of him who was Herman Ottfried.'

" 'I believe thee not!' cried Carl, trembling all over.

" 'Thou shalt—thou dost believe me, Carl Werner,' replied the spectre. 'Thou know'st that I am he. Did I not pledge myself to meet thee—to tell thee all—to give thee intelligence—to ease thy curiosity? I am come. I am ready. Art thou willing—art thou prepared to hear?'

" 'Not from thee—not from thee!' cried Carl, in agony. 'Away! leave me—trouble me not with thy falsehoods. My friend is living—Herman Ottfried, I know, still lives; and if he did not, thou never couldst have been the spirit which filled his frame, and gave impulse to his actions. He had no malice such as glares from thine eyes—he had no foul passions such as hang about thy lips.'

" 'Thou reasonest like a child, Carl Werner. Hear me and believe. The first truth is death—the second judgment. Mortality is a state of dreams and shows—presentiments which impose only on mortal senses. We throw off all disguises for the first time, when we arrive at the first truth, which we never know until death. We acquire all truth when we reach the higher form of judgment. In death, we know for the first time what we are and have been—in judgment, we know what we shall be.'

" 'Then thou canst tell me nothing,' said Carl, fearlessly—yet trembling all the while.

" 'Yes—I can tell thee what I am!' exclaimed the spectre in reply; but it needed no words to unfold that which was but too clearly discernible in the blasted and blasting expression of his countenance as he thus replied. Carl saw this expression, and the shudder that shook his frame sufficiently apprized the spectre that it was unnecessary for him to relate that which the quick imagination of Carl so readily conceived. He grinned fearfully as he witnessed the tremblings of his mortal companion, and the malicious and hateful expression re-aroused the courage of the youth.

" 'Yet, though I cannot but see that thou art one of the damned and blasted of heaven—one of the thrice blasted perchance———.'

" 'Thou art right!' exclaimed the spectre, while lurid fires of a hellish agony seemed to kindle in, and to dart forth from his eye—'thou art right; I am indeed, one of the thrice—ay, one of the seventy times seventy times damned of the Eternal; and I defy him amid all his fires.'

"He paused as he spoke these words, and his clenched hands were lifted in air, and thrust upwards, as if he would do battle even at that moment with the deity. Carl shuddered and shrunk from the fearful presence; but his soul grew strengthened within him in due proportion to the revoltings which he felt at such foul blasphemy.

" 'I believe thee!' he exclaimed, and his own clasped hands were raised in prayer while he continued—'I believe thee; but I believe not that thou art Herman Ottfried—it is impossible—I believe not that he is dead.'

" 'Thou shalt have confirmation to-morrow. His blood was upon thee yesterday—his shadow is before thee now. Dost thou not believe me—wilt not thou hear some of the secrets which thou didst once so desire to know. Where is thy curiosity—where is thy thirst, Carl, after knowledge? Has thy marriage changed thy nature, and art thou willing to be the mere cur of the household, and forego that noble ambition which made thee seek after wisdom, as if it were life—as if it were more than life to thee—as if it were happiness? Is it happiness to thee no longer? Is thy sense dulled for its enjoyment? Go to, Carl, I had not thought this of thee. Go to thy wife—get from her the needle and the net-work, and find in her example thy fitting employment. Thou hast not the soul for my secret—thou wouldst fear to hear it.'

" 'Fiend—foul fiend, and bitter devil!' cried the fierce Carl, provoked by the taunting of the spectre beside him—'I fear thee not, though I would not have thy secret. I hold thee to be a cheat, and thou but slanderest the noble spirit of my friend. Have at thy throat, monster, in the name of heaven and its blessed ministers. Have at thy throat! and let the great God of the heavens and the earth determine between us.'

" 'Ha, ha, ha!' was the only response of the spectre as Carl uttered these words. The replication of the crumbling walls to the infernal laugh was tremendous; but it did not shake the desperate courage of Carl Werner. He sprang upon his glowering and grinning enemy, with outstretched arms and fingers, and he aimed to clutch the fearful image—not a whit alarmed at the increasing fiendishness of its aspect—by the throat; but the object melted in his embrace, at the moment when it seemed most secure. His arms grasped his own body; and, stunned with confused thoughts and defeated passion, the unhappy Carl gazed around him in a stupor, which was not at all diminished as he found himself alone.

XIV.

"To a certain extent, this stupor brought with it a desirable insensibility. He trembled no longer. He was almost reckless. A reaction in his mind had taken place, and from having been one whom every thing before, however slight, could startle, he was now one whom nothing could affect or move. He rushed through the abbey. He thrust his fearless head into all its recesses—into tombs and niches, cells, and ruinous and long untrodden apartments, with most admirable indiscretion. He summoned his tormentor from the places in which he had hidden himself, and defied the presence which he invoked. But all was silent; and, exhausted with fatigue, and chafed with his disappointment, Carl at length departed from the abbey in hopeless despondency. The next day, even as the spectre had predicted, he received the fatal intelligence of the death of Herman. This news was but too confirmatory of what he had seen and felt. It gave life and body to his fears. The grief of Matilda was great, but it would be vain to undertake to describe that of her husband. To her, his agony—dearly, as she well knew, he loved her brother—seemed strange and unaccountable. She little dreamed of the nightly revelations which were made to his senses. With a praiseworthy sense of propriety and a manly tenderness, he had carefully withheld from her, though still longing to reveal, the fearful secret which he possessed. But how could he say to her that he had seen her brother, or seen him as he was—a thing upon whom the curse of God had fallen, and who had been delivered over by his judgment to the awful ministers of eternal wrath. He felt that he must keep his secret, and bear with its horrible burden as best he might. But, as evening drew nigh, the horrors of his heart grew less and less supportable. He felt that he must again perform his vigil. He must again repair to the place of his trial and his torture; and this, by a secret conviction of his mind, he felt must be done, until he had courage to hear, and was willing to believe, all the horrible intelligence which the spectre might think proper to convey. He had bound himself solemnly to the meeting, and he could not shrink from the terms of his pledge. Yet, where and when was it to end? This was the dreadful question which his soul answered in utter hopelessness.

" 'In my death. Yet it will end soon, for I cannot stand this strife much longer.'

"Such were his thoughts and words; and their truth would readily be believed by those who were conscious of the sudden and singular change which had taken place in his person. All the villagers remarked it. He was haggard and listless—he saw and heeded nobody—he moved through the streets like a ghost, and Matilda—the beloved wife of his affections—no longer filled his heart, and commanded the devotion of his eye. She strove to find out the secret of his sorrows, and to soothe them. But vainly would the physician seek to heal, while he remains ignorant of the cause of the distemper. We must lay bare the wound to extract the poison; and in the purity of her soul she did not even imagine the horrible nature of that secret which was preying upon his. Her efforts were in vain. Night came on, and though she strove to keep him at home, the spell was too powerful to permit her to succeed.

" 'Where is it you go, dearest Carl? Why, night after night, will you go forth in so much sorrow, and with features so wild, so full of apprehension; and when you return—so full of horror—so haggard—so dreadful? Tell me, dear husband, whither it is you go, and why it is you suffer in this manner.'

" 'Nay, do not heed me, dearest,' said the unhappy man, with a gentleness of manner which made his sorrows only the more touching—'do not trouble yourself about me. I have busy and vexing thoughts, and shall not look well until they are digested into form. When I resolve them, then will I remain with you, and be at peace.'

" 'What thoughts are they?' she demanded; but he smiled, and answered her evasively.

" 'Ask me not—not now,' he replied, and resisting her solicitations to be allowed to go forth with him, he rushed out of the house. She followed him to the door, and looked after him in the street; and her own apprehensions were greatly increased as she beheld the erratic impulse of his movement, and the feebleness of his step—the one betokening the disorder of his mind, the other the debility of his body. While she looked and trembled, with the big tear gathering slowly in her eye and stealing silently to her cheek, the accents of a mild but strange voice met her ears at a small distance, and, turning, she beheld an old man standing before her. He was a stranger to her, and evidently a stranger in the place, since his air and costume were very different from any that she had ever before seen. His beard was long and white like silver, and hung down neatly smooth and clean upon his bosom; his hair, equally long, and not less white, streamed with similar smoothness down his back and shoulders. It was evident that he was a person of very great age, yet his skin was clear, of a pure white and red, and unmarked by a single wrinkle. His mouth was small, and wore a sweet expression, and his eyes were full of benevolence. He carried a little staff, and a bundle which probably contained a single change of raiment—it certainly could not have held more; and he seemed like some venerable traveller, who had an unconquerable desire for travel, and had learned to narrow his wants to the smallest possible limits, consistent with the superior claims of an intellectual nature.

" 'Daughter,' he said, 'Peace be with you. Can you give me shelter and food for the night? I am a stranger, and would abide with you.'

"The heart of Matilda, like that of Carl, was open as day, and the stranger most probably had seen in her countenance that he would not be refused; for, even as he spoke, he prepared to enter. He was not deceived in the person he addressed. With a sweet voice, full of respect—for his venerable white hairs had impressed Matilda with a proper and gentle awe—she bade him welcome, and having closed the door—after giving a long lingering look to the form of her husband, who was rapidly passing from her sight—she led the way for her aged guest, into an inner apartment. There she spread before him the simple repast from which the unhappy Carl had fled. The old man blessed the bread ere he broke it, and blessed the giver. He then ate heartily, and at intervals conversed with Matilda, who sat with him at the table, though she ate nothing. Her heart was too full of doubt and sorrow to suffer her to eat, and while her guest spoke, the tears gathered unbidden, and without her consciousness, to her eyes. He saw them.

"'Daughter, you weep—you are unhappy. Why is it—what is your sorrow.'

"'Alas! father, are we not born to sorrows. Is there one who escapes?'

"'True, my child—sorrow is human, and to grieve is the attribute of man, and perhaps his blessing. They are blest who can weep. God loveth those whom he chasteneth; for it is through trial only that we gain virtue, and through virtue only that we gain heaven. The untried are the unblessed, for then is the work harder for them, and the prospect of virtue more remote. Such, my daughter, is not your case. The fire even now is purifying you, and if you grieve, you do not murmur. Sorrow, like a goodly medicine that is to work for our healing, must be submitted to without murmuring. Whence come your sorrows, my daughter—let me know them. I have travelled much among men, and I know many of the arts of healing. I have some skill which I may boast, in curing those hurts of the mind which come from our indiscretions, and are to be healed by our humility. Let me know what grieves you, and hear to my counsel.'

"'I grieve not for myself, my father, so much as for one that I love—my husband.'

"'You are married then?'

"'I am, and to one of the best of men; but he is thoughtful even to sadness, and I fear that his thoughts are sometimes too vexing for his mind, which they very much disorder. Something troubles him very greatly even now, and before you came he went forth in deep anxiety, which it was painful to me to behold. He will be away until near midnight, or even after; and when he returns, it will seem that some dreadful strife hath shaken him—his face will be pale as if with sudden fright—his eyes wild, staring, almost starting from their sockets, and his whole appearance that of a man almost distraught.'

"'And how long hath he been troubled in this wise, my daughter?' demanded the aged stranger.

"'But a few days,' Matilda readily replied; for there was something so encouraging in the appearance of the old man, that, although a woman rather disposed to reserve in her manners, she felt that she could have freely told him every secret of her bosom.

"'But a few days—and before this time, he hath shown none of these habits?'

"'None, father—none of this wildness and affliction. He hath been thoughtful ever, and fond of sad thoughts,—but he hath never been wild and stern as he is now, and never did he go abroad in this fashion after the night.'

"'You tell me of one,' said the stranger, after a brief pause given to thought—'You tell me of one who hath done a sudden wrong, and whom a just conscience is smiting sorely; or, one, perchance, who is fond of his error, or, from a false and unseemly pride, who persisteth in it.'

"'Oh, no, father—I cannot think it. Carl would never wrong human being. He is the most just and honorable of our village—that everybody says of him.'

"'That may be, my daughter, but is there no wronging of God and of one's self—which is also a wronging of God, as it perverts the service of the creature from the place and power to which it is due. Can you tell me that Carl Werner has not done this.'

"Matilda tried to think, before she answered, whether she had mentioned her husband's name. She did not recollect having done so, and yet the old man had pronounced it. Before she could resolve this thought or reply, the stranger continued:

"'It is always a bad sign to see one, on a sudden, depart from a good habit, my daughter. You say that your husband seldom or never went forth at night, but always preferred to remain at home, until now.'

"'Yes, father,—but it is with evident reluctance that he now leaves me. It is like tearing himself away that he rushes out of the house, soon after nightfall, and goes off I know not where.'

"'To return miserable,' said the old man. 'To bring him back to an old habit, my daughter, is probably to give him the peace of mind which you say he seems to lack. Have you striven to keep him at home, my daughter, since you have seen the evil of this habit?'

"'I have, my father, but without success,' was the reply.

"'You must do it,' said the old man with vehemence—'you must do it. A good wife, who loves her husband, and is beloved by him, has a thousand sweet arts of persuasion which will not fail to procure from him her wishes. Your husband loves you.'

" 'Of a truth, I think it.'

" 'Then, my daughter, if you love him, you shall not fail to persuade him, if you seek to do it. You must keep him at home. He must not go abroad. These nightly wanderings make his infirmity. They prove that he is subject to some evil influence, which thus exacts his obedience, and imposes upon him this form of service. You, and you alone, can save him; for, as the evil influence strives through the powers of hate, it can only be safely contended with by the powers of love. This is the war which is ever going on between the two great principles by which the world is divided. You must prove that the principle of love in your bosom is stronger than that of hate in the enemy of your husband. Can you prove this, my daughter; for, unless you can, Carl Werner is lost to you forever, as he certainly will soon be lost to himself.'

" 'I can—I will!' cried the devoted wife, with terror and love both equally mingled in her countenance; for the words of the venerable old man had deeply impressed her, and a something in his air and manner assured her that he was worthy of all confidence.

" 'I can—I will, my father—only tell me what I shall do—how work—what say.'

" 'Love needs no counsellor, my daughter, for it is God's nature, and is by instinct wise. True love, I speak of; and not the idle fancies which the profligate and vain have misnamed love. If you love Carl Werner with a true wife's love, you will seek that he should be always with you—you will seek to make him happy. These are your present tasks. You must begin by keeping him from this wandering habit. He must not go forth again at night—for he flies from the principle of love, to pay homage to the principle of hate. Withdraw him from that foul worship, and he is safe, and you are both happy.'

"It would be needless to dwell upon, or to detail, the farther dialogue which then took place between the young wife and her venerable guest. It is sufficient to say that the longer she listened to his counsel, the more she became impressed with its force, and with the necessity for its adoption. While she heard him she had no wish for sleep, and hours seemed to pass away like minutes until the clock struck the midnight hour, and she then grew more than ever alarmed at the absence of her husband. She was desirous of putting into use and exercise the advice which the old man had given her, and would have sallied forth, even then, to look after him, when the stranger dissuaded her from it.

"'Do you remain,' he said, 'while I go forth and seek him.'

"'You!'—she said—'no, father, you are too old and feeble, and your limbs are weary with the long day's travel.'

"He rose, as she spoke these words, and as he moved over the floor, she was answered. Where had those aged limbs acquired that strength and elasticity which they now exhibited?

"'But you know not where to seek him, my father.'

"He smiled; and she did not doubt, when she beheld that smile, that the aged man knew better where to find her husband than she did herself. He paused as he crossed the threshold, and bidding her be of good cheer, he blessed the house and departed.

XV.

"Meanwhile, what of Carl Werner? With a fearful instinct he proceeded, upon leaving his dwelling, to the place of meeting with the spectre. Vainly did he strive against the fascination which impelled him to seek the abbey. Why should he so wilfully seek that which was so full of torture? He had now no wish to hear the revelations of the dead—he had no thought, certainly, to profit by them, when brought by one whose very presence was so terrific; still less did he desire to owe his knowledge to a source so foul and fearful. These were his thoughts, nor his thoughts merely. These were his frequent resolves throughout the day. 'I will not go to-night,' his lips muttered at all hours; yet, with the coming of evening, his good resolutions failed him. A power which he strove vainly to resist, drove him onward; and like the criminal, reluctant yet compelled, he appeared regularly at the appointed hour at the summons of his tyrant. Carl felt that there was a judgment in all this. He felt that it was a decree of heaven against him for the unholy feelings and desires of his heart. Yet, where, and when, and how, was this to end? He dared not think! His knees trembled beneath him as he put this question to himself, and felt, with the increasing weakness and misery of every moment, that it could end only in his death.

"This conviction was despair. Despair has its strength, but it is the strength accorded by a demon at a fearful price. The price was hope and peace—the penalty was the loss of two lives—the life of the present, and the life to come. Carl felt that they were already gone, and all his thoughts were now given to the demon. The principle of hate grew active in his fears, and the principle of love grew feebler and feebler, in the continual decay of his hopes. The strife was not only against Carl Werner, but it was against the sweet young wife of his bosom. He felt it to be so, himself, as he found himself continually laboring not to think of her.

"We need not say, that in the abbey that night, the same hour of torture was passed by Carl, in company with the demon, as before. The belief that his friend was the victim and the slave of hell, sent forth by the infernal monarch to perform a duty which he dared not disobey, was the racking conviction to Carl. Vainly he demanded of the spectre to disavow the features he had assumed. His prayer was idle. Would the principle of hate yield up his chief vantage ground? As well might he implore indulgence from that power, whose only office is punishment. He raved to the demon—defied his malice, and vainly flattered himself that the passion which he showed to his tormentor, was, in reality, a re-assertion of his virtue. Thus do men hourly chain themselves with their own sophisms. The very tumult in his soul, and the violence of his lips, as they sprang from a feeling of hostility, were, in truth, only so many tributes to the principle of hate. The fearless calm, the gentle earnestness of love, were not in his heart. It was rather a place of fears and strife; and every moment of his paroxysm, increased the number of avenues through which sin might enter and perpetuate its sway. The conflict nearly destroyed the mortal. Almost exhausted, Carl rushed from the ruins; and, this time, he left the demon squat upon the tomb-stone, where he had sat all the time of their conference, glowing and grinning at the agony, and yelling forth his dreadful laughter, as he beheld the flight of the victim.

XVI.

"Carl was not permitted to reach his home in peace. A group of revellers stood in his path as he was about to enter the village. They danced and sang at his approach, and soon gathered around him with tumultuous cries. They sang in his ears the praises of revelry, and invited him to join them.

"'Be not churlish, brother,' was the cry—'why cherish care? why mate with sorrow? why deny thyself to live? The wine, the wine, boys, and here's health and a fresh heart to our new companion.'

"Carl envied them their felicity; and their language, for the first time in his life, seemed sweet in his ears. Hitherto, he had led the life of an abstemious and wholly studious youth, rejecting utterly those noisy and spendthrift pleasures which are so apt to lead astray the young. He began to think that he had erred in his practice, and had been guilty of injustice to a class of persons who were a great deal wiser than himself. The torments which he had just undergone, prepared him for this way of thinking. He hesitated, murmured, looked vacantly around him, and they took him gently by the arm, and renewed their solicitations. Among the foremost of these, he now recognized the bacchanalian who had before assailed him. But he was not intoxicated on this occasion; and while he spoke with the words and warmth of a boon companion, his language was carefully chosen and gently insinuating. Carl began to yield; his eyes were already turned in longing upon the tavern—his feet were at the guidance of the individual we have just spoken of—in his thought, the indulgence of wine began to assume the appearance of a leading and necessary object: and in another moment the powers of evil would have made large strides towards the possession of their victim, when another hand pressed the arm of Carl Werner, and a gentle, but strange voice, in his ears pronounced the name of his wife.

"'Matilda—she waits you, Carl—she suffers at your long absence. Will you not go to her?'

"The old man whom we have seen setting forth from the house of the wife in search of the husband, stood at his elbow. He had come in time. His words operated like magic, and Carl broke away from his conductors.

" 'Matilda—my wife—my poor wife!' he exclaimed—'Yes—let me go to her.'

"If the words of the aged man were so quick and powerful to move Carl Werner, his presence seemed to have no less an effect upon those who sought to lead the youth astray. They shrank away from the stranger with hisses, and though reviling him, they still fled. Carl was surprised at this, and the more surprised and horror stricken when he distinguished among the howls and hisses of the flying crew, the horrible laugh which had so much haunted him before. The old man took no heed of their clamor, but composedly conversed with Carl while they proceeded to the lodgings of the latter, with all the calmness and ease of one whom a confidence of superiority keeps from anger towards an inferior, as certainly as it protects from harm.

XVII.

"Carl felt better and happier in the embraces of his wife when he reached home, than he had felt for some days before. The principle of love was reviving within him. The conversation of their aged guest contributed largely to this improvement. They could not but acknowledge the influence which they could not but feel. Yet he could scarcely be said to converse. His words seemed so many laws settling doubts and silencing controversy. He spoke from authority—from an authority, seemingly, even beyond that of strong common sense and great experience. Carl was surprised and pleased to find himself able to listen to his words; and though the terrible strifes which he had recently undergone were still busy in his mind, he yet found pleasure in his new companion. Much of the old man's conversation seemed, indeed, to be intended for his particular case. He spoke of the 'various encounters' to which mortals were subject. The necessity of confidence in heaven's justice—the willingness to wait—the readiness to endure. He then spoke of the principle of love as he had spoken to Matilda. He insisted upon it as sufficiently strong to withstand the opposite principle of hate, and to trample over it in the end. The conflict, he said, would be long and perilous, and it would be continued through nations and individuals to the end of time;—patience, he said, and perseverance, prompted by the spirit of love, which is eternal, would be certain to achieve the victory. In the meantime, it would be necessary that the labors of love should be increased and strengthened. We should strive to love one another, as the best policy, and the noblest moral economy. Every falling off in our affections from each other, was a gain to the rebelling principle of hate, and kept back humanity from its hope of heaven. Every increase in the amount of human love, was a succor to the sovereign principle; as much so, as, in the warfare among men, would be the accession of new numbers. To love one another is to conquer evil, for as evil toils through the principle of hate, it can only be successful over us, by engendering in our bosoms hostility to our fellows, and a general faithlessness of each other, which must produce hostility. To confide, should be the first lesson, as it is always the first and noblest proof of love!

"This counsel strengthened Carl Werner and his wife, and made them both think. Carl felt calmer as he thought, and retired to his chamber with new and better resolutions. The old man prayed with the two before they retired; but though Carl knelt with the rest, he yet found it impossible to pray. He could only think, and his thoughts were confused, apprehensive, and not given, as he felt himself, to the sovereign principle of love. When he retired to his chamber, he resolved to pray alone; but he could not. He knelt by the bedside in vain. His tongue seemed to cleave to the roof of his mouth. His brain seemed to glow like fire, and he longed once more for the presence and the conversation of the aged man. He slept but little during the night, and when Matilda awakened at intervals, she heard nothing but his groans.

"The next day the old man sought an opportunity of conversation with Matilda in secret.

" 'My daughter,' he said, 'your husband must not go forth to-night. You must exert all your strength—all the strength of your love; spare no prayers, no solicitations, but you must keep him at home. He goes to pay homage to the principle of hate. He must break his bondage. He must withhold his homage; and he must prove that he renounces the hateful worship, ere the principle of love will come certainly to his aid. He will not find relief—he cannot be happy—till then; and he must do this himself. We can do nothing towards it, save by our prayers, and these will be of little avail, until, of his own resolve, he breaks to you the secret of his sorrow. When he freely and voluntarily declares to you the trouble of his mind, he will find relief. To confide our wo to a beloved one, is to find healing. He must acknowledge this truth, ere he can hope for healing; and it is a truth that he must teach himself. I warn you, therefore, unfold nothing that I have said to you, which shall move him to this determination, else it will be of no avail. We may tremble, but we must be silent; and if our fears become stronger than our hopes, we must then only resort to our prayers.'

"That day the old man gave Carl himself a lesson which had its effect in promoting the wishes of all, though, to the passing thought, it would seem to have no necessary connexion with the misfortunes of the latter. He saw him in a condition of stupor, sitting upon the threshold, and evidently unconscious of all things around him.

" 'My son,' he said, 'we do not all our duties when we have said our prayers. Indeed, we may be said to do none of them, if we do but this. Our prayers are offered that we may have strength and judgment to perform our duties rightly and thoroughly. The first of these is industry. The decree of God—one of the first—is one of the elements of religion. "Thou shalt earn thy bread in the sweat of thy face." He who prays merely, and toils none, is a hypocrite, and though he may deceive himself and his fellow men, he cannot deceive God by his professions.'

" 'Alas! my father—I would work,' said the unhappy Carl, 'but I cannot—I am sick—I am sad—too sad—too sick to work.'

" 'Hast thou tried, my son.'

" 'Of what use to try, my father. I feel that I should do nothing.'

" 'The will is the service, my son. God tasks not your service, but he receives the free tribute of your heart, and if the will is free to serve him, the amount of your body's service is of little regard. Try—let the will govern the limbs, and they will do much. Certainly, thy labor will lessen the troubles of thy mind, which, in most cases, spring from the tyrannous imbecility of the frame. Try, my son—thy labors will avail thee much more in thy sadness than all thy prayers.'

"Carl obeyed, and strove diligently to labor, and though he did but little, yet he felt better from what he did. The old man conversed with him while he toiled, and he gathered goodly counsel, and pleasant consolation, from his words. But as the day waned, the agonizing apprehensions of Carl were renewed. The fascinating spells of the demon began to work upon his mind, and his increasing disquiet became visible to his household. At supper he was unconscious of the meats before him, until the words of the aged guest aroused his consideration, while he prayed for a blessing upon the repast. Carl gradually grew fixed in mute attention as he listened to the terms of this prayer, which was, in some respects, peculiar. The old man prayed that 'the fond husband might ever be heedful of the affections with which he had been endowed by the confiding wife—that he might heed the meaning of her pale cheek, her tearful eye, and laboring bosom—that he might never estrange himself from one who looked so much, so entirely to him, for countenance and comfort—and that the ways of error into which frail mortality was ever but too prone to fall, might never seduce the regards of the comforter, from the weak but confiding heart to which they were entirely due.'

"Much more after this fashion was said by the old man, but these words had their effect. Carl looked upon his wife with eyes of closer inquiry than he had fixed upon her for many days. He saw, for the first time, that her cheek was pale—as if death had set his hand upon it—that her eye was full of tears—and that her bosom heaved with an anguish which her lips had never spoken. Her eye caught the glance of his own while he gazed, and she burst into a flood of tears—rose from the table—rushed to the spot where her husband sat, and threw herself at his feet. How dreadfully was he shocked by this movement! How bitterly did he reproach himself! He felt that he had been selfish—that, heedful of his own sufferings only, he had given neither eye nor thought to hers. He sank down upon the floor beside her; and he muttered broken words, imploring forgiveness. The venerable guest saw that the moment was come, when love was to obtain the mastery or forever fail; and without being seen by the two, he left the apartment. But his words had been deeply impressed upon the mind of Matilda, and she needed not his presence to prompt her in the performance of her task. She poured out her full heart to her husband, told him of her fears during his absence, of her sufferings as she beheld the sapping and overcoming character of his, and implored him, for the love which he had once vowed her, as earnestly as if she had lost it. Long and trying was their conference, and more than once the wife despaired of her object. But though she trembled, she yet implored, and the principle of love prevailed. The heart of Carl was touched—the seal removed from the fountain—and he poured forth, in her astounded but unshrinking senses, the whole strange and dreadful secret.

XVIII.

"He had scarcely done so, when he heard a tap on the window, as of one claiming admission. He started, he trembled—a guilty fear rose in his throat and choked him.

" 'It is he—the demon—the spectre!' he exclaimed, gaspingly.

" 'Bid him enter,' cried the old man, who had returned to the apartment without their perceiving either his departure or his entrance, and who seemed perfectly conversant with the whole narrative—

" 'Bid him enter, Carl.'

"But Carl hesitated and trembled. He moved not; and Matilda rose to her feet.

" 'I fear nothing!' she exclaimed—'I will throw open the window. If it be the spirit of Herman Ottfried, he will not harm me. If it be other than his, it cannot. God be with me—for I will do it!'

"The voice of the old man arrested her, as she was about to do what she had said.

" 'Daughter!'

"She turned, and saw that his eye rested anxiously upon Carl, and she then understood that the office belonged to her husband. She did not need to look upon him twice. He had been praying while she spoke, and he now rose.

" 'No, Matilda—the task should be mine. I have looked upon the fiend before—I do not fear to look upon him again. Still less do I fear—having your eyes upon, and your prayers for, me.'

"A horrible yell of laughter reached his ears from the outside, and half unmanned him. He shivered all over; but just then the aged guest repeated these words, as if for himself.

" 'The Lord is my strength, and my redeemer. He is with me, and I fear not the evil one. Be of good cheer, oh, my soul, for in this is thy strength. Thou shalt prevail in the strife with thy enemy, even as love prevaileth over hate, and the spirit of God over the spirit of the devil.'

"With a single blow of his fist, Carl threw wide the shutter, and though his voice trembled while he spoke, yet the words which he uttered were distinct—

"'Enter—if it be God's will—enter!'

XIX.

"The mocking spectre was once more before him—and the grin of malice and imagined victory was again visible upon his countenance, until he beheld the form of the venerable guest, still kneeling upon the floor, with eyes and hands uplifted to heaven, and seeming as if he beheld him not. Then his whole aspect was altered. His grin became a bitter scorn, and, though he still wore the exact features of Herman Ottfried, yet the whole expression was so changed to that of a hellish hate, that, even to the eyes of Carl, the likeness seemed almost gone.

"'Thou here!' exclaimed the spectre, addressing the aged man.

"'Thou seest!' was the reply.

"'I see—but thou art here in vain—thy prayers will avail him nothing—he hath bound himself to me. My power is upon his pledge. He cannot escape—he must meet me where I will; and when he forbears to come—when, urged by such as thee, he presumes to disobey, I will seek him with redoubled tortures, where he hides, and tear him from thy very altars. Carl Werner—I command thee. Come!'

"Carl trembled all over, and he felt an irresistible power dragging him forward. At this moment the old man spoke—

"'His pledge shall be fulfilled—but not to thee. Look, Satan!—God hath heard the prayers of love—and his messenger comes to release the thrall of hate. Look!—the pledge is redeemed?'

"As he spoke, he pointed to the opposite corner of the apartment, upon which his eyes had been earnestly fixed, even while the demon was addressing him. There, visible to all, stood another spectre, having the precise features of Herman Ottfried, and the very expression which he was wont to wear in life. The contrast between the one and the other spectre, both having the same features, was prodigious! They represented different principles. The one had borne the features of punishment—the other came with the mild attributes of mercy. Alike in every feature, they were yet as utterly unlike as night and day.

"The demon put on a look of agony, mingled with hate and disappointment, as, with a howl and hiss, he fled from the presence of the spectre whose features he had worn for the purposes of hate, but whose glance of benignity and love he could not withstand. Howling with hate, he fled; while the gentle spirit advanced into the apartment.

"'Oh, brother, dearest Herman!' cried the sister, with a joyful accent, as she rushed towards him. She sunk down upon the spot where she would have embraced him, and her eyes beheld his shadowy form melting away, even like the last gleam of a lovely sunset into the distant shadows.

"'Look to your wife, my son,' said the aged man—'she swoons—give her help.'

"Carl raised his wife, and in a little while she recovered—but the aged man had disappeared. They never saw him again."

[*First published in* Godey's Lady's Book *in 1841 under the title "The Passage of a Night; or, the Benefactress," the story was retitled by Simms for inclusion in* Southward Ho! A Spell of Sunshine *(1854). Explanatory and Textual Notes begin on page 681.*]

THE BRIDE OF HATE;
Or, the Passage of a Night.

"Thou and I long since are twain;
Nor think me so unwary or accursed,
To bring my feet again into the snare
Where once I have been caught; I know thy trains,
Though dearly to my cost; thy gins and toils;
Thy fair enchanted cup, and warbling charms,
No more on me have power; their force is nulled;
So much of adder's wisdom I have learned,
To fence my ear against thy sorceries."
Samson Agonistes.

I.

At length I was permitted to behold my benefactress. The messenger who brought my quarterly remittance was the bearer of a letter, the first which had ever been addressed by her to myself, in which this grateful permission was accorded. I read and re-read it a thousand times. My first emotions were those of pleasure;—a pleasure enhanced by the hope of satisfying a curiosity, which, awakened in my earliest boyhood, had never yet been gratified. Why had I been so kindly treated, so well provided for, so affectionately considered, in all the changes of my brief existence, my sickness and my health, by a lady of such high condition? Why, again, should she, whose care and consideration had been so unvarying and decided, have shown so little desire to behold the object of her bounty? Years had elapsed since I had become her charge. Years, to me, of continued satisfaction, if one small matter be excepted. There was one alloy to my enjoyment, which, in its most rapturous moments, my boyhood did not cease to feel. It was the mystery which overhung my origin. Who am I? was the question, not so natural to the boy, yet natural enough to the sensitive and thoughtful. I was both sensitive and thoughtful; and my boyish associates, on this very subject, contrived to keep me so. Their inquiries disordered me—their surprise at my ignorance alarmed me—their occasional doubts gave me pain, and the suspicions of their minds readily passed into my own. "Who am I?" was the perpetual inquiry which my mind was making of itself. I could address it no where else. My tutor, with whom I also lodged, declared his ignorance, and I believed him. He was too good a man, too kind, and himself betrayed too great an interest in the question, not to have spoken sincerely. He saw my disquiet and endeavoured to allay it; and the endeavour added to the burden, since it sufficiently declared his equal inability and desire. His anxiety, though unequal to, was not unlike my own. I know not if his conjectures led him to like conclusions with myself. I only know that mine were sufficiently painful to extort my tears and tremors.

Vainly, at each quarterly return of the agent of the Baroness, did I endeavour, by question and insinuation, to gather from him some clue to the facts of which I sought to be possessed. He had been the person who brought me to the school—who made the contract for my education and support with my tutor—and who, alone, through each successive period of my life afterwards, had been the medium for conveying the benefactions of my friend. To whom then could I so naturally apply? From whom could I hope to obtain better information? Besides, he always treated me with marked affection. I can remember, when a mere child, how frequently he took me upon his knee, how kindly he caressed me, what affectionate words he poured into my ear; the gentleness of his tones, the tenderness of his regards! Nor as I advanced in years did his attentions alter, though they assumed different aspects. He was more reserved, though not less considerate. If he no longer brought me toys, he brought me books; if he no longer took me on his knee, he lingered with me long, and seemed to regret the hour that commanded his departure. There was something, too, so I fancied, in what he said, did, and looked, that betrayed the fondness of one who had known me with a tender interest from the beginning. His arms, perhaps, had dandled me in infancy; he had been my follower, my attendant. But why linger on conjectures such as these? My speculations ran wild, as I thought, over the circumstances of my condition, and painfully resolved, hour after hour, the secret of my birth.

From Bruno, however, I could obtain nothing. When questioned, he affected a stolid simplicity which, even to my boyish understanding, seemed wholly inconsistent with his. I knew that he was no fool —still less was I willing to consider him a churl. My conclusion was natural. He knew something. He could tell me much. Could he not tell me all, and where could be the motive for concealment? The answer to this question inevitably overwhelmed me for a time, until the elasticity of the youthful heart could disencumber itself from the desponding tendency of a premature activity of thought. The only motive of concealment must be guilt. I was the child of sin—I was the foredoomed of suffering. My present anxieties gave a gravity and intensity of expression to my features which did not become one so youthful. I felt this—I felt the seeming unnaturalness of my looks and carriage, but how could I relieve myself? I felt the pain of thought—thought unsatisfied, and could already imagine how natural was the doom which visited the sins of the father to the third and fourth generation.

When I failed to extort from the cunning of Bruno the secret which I was persuaded he yet possessed, I turned naturally to the letter of my benefactress. I read and re-read it, each time with the hope of making some discoveries—of finding some slight clue to the truth, which might relieve my anxiety. An ambiguous sentence, the latent signification of a passage—and how many of these did my desire enable me to discover in a billet of twenty lines?—awakened my hopes and caused my heart to bound with double pulsation. But when I had gone through it again and again, until my head ached, and my senses seemed to swim, I was compelled to acknowledge to myself that there was nothing in the epistle that I had not readily comprehended at the first. It simply expressed the writer's gratification at the improvement and good conduct of the youth whom she had thought proper to educate and provide for, until manhood should bring around the period of independence; and expressed though without emphasis—and how earnestly did I look for this quality in every word, syllable and point!—a very natural desire to remark, with her own eyes, the personal deportment and carriage of her protegé—subjects which she seemed to regard as equally important with my intellectual improvement, and of which neither my letters nor my exercises—which were duly transmitted to her by my tutor—could give her much, if any, satisfaction. Failing to find any occult signification in the language, I next addressed my scrutiny to the style and manner of the letter—the hand-writing, the air, the roundings equally of letters and periods. How soon, where the hopes and anxieties are awakened, will the boy learn to think, examine and become analytical! To trace the mind of the writer in his penmanship is a frequent employment with the idly curious; but a deep interest led me to the same exercise. The style of the composition was clear and strong, but it struck me as quite too cold for the benevolent tenor which the note conveyed. Why should one speak the language of reserve whose deeds are the very perfection of generosity? Why should the tones be frigid where the sentiments are as soft as summer and sweet as its own bird-music? There was, to my mind, some singular contradictions in this. I could very well understand how one, doing, or about to do, a benevolent or generous action, should speak of it as slightly and indifferently as possible—nay, should avoid to speak of it at all, if to avoid it be within the nature of the occasion;—but this did not apply to the character of the epistle I examined. The writer spoke freely of her friendly purposes; but her language to the recipient was cold and freezing. If she had said nothing of what she had done and still meditated, and had spoken to me in more elaborate tones, I should have been better satisfied. But there was not an unnecessary word in the whole epistle—not one which I could fancy put in at the moment when the current of feeling being at its height forbade the reserve of prudence, or the cautious considerateness of deliberate and calculating purposes. There was evidently considerable pains taken—so my youthful judgment inferred—in the reserved language and manner of this letter; and why should my benefactress, moved only in what she had done by a high but ordinary sentiment of charity, strive to express herself in such language to a boy? This question led me into newer intricacies, from which, I need scarcely add, I did not readily extricate myself. The penmanship of the writer did not call for a less earnest examination than the language which she employed. It was evidently feminine in its character, but how masculine in its tone. The utter absence of ornament was a deficiency, which struck me as forming a surprising feature in the hand-writing of a lady. She used capitals constantly in beginning words as well as sentences; but these capitals exhibited the cold Gothic aspects of the Roman, rather than the lively ornamented outlines of the Italian letters. The T of her signature, for example, was a simple perpendicular stroke, carried much below the line, with a thick heavy cap upon it, having a dip at each end almost as great as that of an umbrella. The letters were remarkably clear, but how irregular. They seemed to have been written under a determination to write, even against desire and will—dashed spasmodically down upon the paper, not coherent, and leaving wide gaps between the several words, into which an ingenious hand might readily have introduced other words—such as I fondly conjectured might have given to the composition that friendly warmth and interest in my fate, which it seemed to me it needed more than any thing beside. My grand conclusion, on finishing my study, was this, that the writer had taken some pains to write indifferently; that the studied coldness of the letter was meant to conceal a very active warmth and feeling in the writer; and—though I may not be able to define the sources of this conjecture so well as the rest—that this feeling, whatever might be its character, was not such as could compel the admiration or secure the sympathy of mine. This conclusion may seem strange enough when it is recollected that Lady T. was my benefactress, who had always carefully anticipated my wishes; provided for my wants; afforded me the best education which the condition of the Palatinate afforded, and, in all respects had done, through charity, those kindly deeds which could not have been exacted by justice. The next moment I reproached myself for ingratitude—I prayed for better thoughts and more becoming feelings—but my prayer was not vouchsafed me. The conclusion which I have already declared, had taken a rooted possession in my mind, and I commenced my journey to the Castle of T—— with a mixed feeling of equal awe, anxiety, and expectation.

II.

I now remarked some alteration in the looks and bearing of my companion, Bruno, which also surprised me and awakened my curiosity. Hitherto, he had always seemed a person of little pretension, having few objects, and those of a humbler class; a mere yeoman, a good retainer—in which capacity he served at T—— Castle—modest in his deportment, without arrogance of any kind, and, in all respects, a very worthy personage. I do not mean to say that he now assumed the appearance of one who had become less so; but he certainly was no longer the quiet, subdued and somewhat melancholy man whom I had heretofore been wont to find him. A certain boyish lightness of manner and gaiety of speech distinguished him as we rode together;—and though these qualities might not be altogether inconsistent with what is becoming in a man of forty, yet were they, at the same time, very far from corresponding with the usual characteristics which he had borne in our previous intimacy. Until now I should have called him a dull person, possessed of good, benevolent feelings; rather grave and sombre in his discourse, and, altogether, having no qualities to recommend him to a higher destination than that which he filled in the Castle of the Baroness. Now, he suddenly became the man of spirit—his words were mirthful, his voice musical, his opinions playful and even witty, and not unfrequently he would burst into little catches of song, that sounded unpleasantly in my ears, since I could neither conjure up cause of merriment in my own mind, nor conjecture the sources for so much of it in his. Nor did this conduct seem the result of simple natural feelings—the play of health in an exercise which was agreeable, or of sensations which lie beneath the surface only, and obedient to the summons of any cheerful wayfarer, who, having no cares, is susceptible of the most ordinary pleasures. There was an air of positive exultation in his looks, a triumphant consciousness in his manner, which he vainly strove to hide, and in the business of which I quickly inferred from his frequent smile and searching gaze upon me, I, myself, had no little interest. When I commented on his gaiety and spirit, he would suddenly control himself; relapse, as it were by an effort, into his ancient gravity, and, possibly, mutter a few clumsy words of denial;—but his struggle to contain himself did not long continue, and before we reached the end of our journey, he had fully surrendered himself to the joyous mood which possessed him on our setting out.

Having no knowledge of Castle T——, I endeavoured by a series of direct questions to obtain from him as much information as possible in respect to it and the Lady thereof. He seemed to be surprised at the avowal of my ignorance on the subject of the Castle, and surprised me even more by expressing his wonder at the fact; concluding by assuring me that I was born in it—at least he had been told so. His mention of my place of birth necessarily provoked an eager renewal of my old inquiries, but to these I obtained no satisfactory answers. Enough, however, was shown me by what he said, and still more by what he looked, that he knew much more than he was willing, or permitted, to reveal. His reserve increased the mystery; for if any of my acquaintance had ever convinced me of their unequivocal regard, it was my old friend Bruno. That he should know, yet withhold, the secret, the desire for which was making my cheek paler every day, and filling my heart with the gloom that seldom afflicts the young, argued, to my understanding, a painful history, which, perhaps, when heard, I should wish for ever buried in oblivion. When I inquired after my benefactress, as I had frequently done before, his brow became clouded, and it was only at such moments that he seemed to part easily with that gaiety of manner which had striven to cheer our tedious journey. Stern glances shot from beneath his bushy grey eyebrows, and his lips became compressed, as closely as if some resolute purpose of hostility was gathering in his mind.

"It seems to me, Bruno, that you love me no longer. You will not answer my questions—questions which seriously affect my happiness—and yet it is clear to me that you can do so. Why is this? Why should there be any mystery in the case of one so poor, so humble, such a dependant as myself?"

"Love you, Herman! Do I not love you?" he exclaimed; and I could see a big tear gathering within his eye, as he replied in reproachful accents—"Ah, my son, you know not how much I love you; you know not now—perhaps you will shortly know, and when you do, you will see that what I have withheld from you, was wisely withheld. There is a season given for truth, Herman, and if Bruno forbears the truth in your ears, it is only that he may wait for the season."

"But why should you not tell me of Lady T——? I should like to form some idea of, and to love her, before I see her."

"Then you do *not* love her?" he demanded with some quickness; and I could perceive a smile gleam out upon his countenance, in which I fancied there was an expression of bitter satisfaction. His question confused me—it conveyed a reproach which he certainly never intended. Could it be possible that I did not love my benefactress—one to whom I owed so much—to whom, indeed, I owed every thing? I blushed, hesitated, stammered, and, before I could reply, he again spoke, and anticipated the feeble excuse which I was preparing.

"But how should you love her?" he exclaimed in tones rather of soliloquy than conversation. "How, indeed! It would have been wonderful, indeed, if you did."

Here he arrested himself in the manner of one who thinks he has said too much. The true feeling with which he spoke I gathered rather from the tone of his utterance than from what he said. The words, however, might have been made to apply much more innocently than the emphasis permitted me to apply them.

"How, what mean you, Bruno?" I demanded with an astonishment which was sufficiently obvious. He endeavoured to evade the effects of his error with the adroitness of a politician.

"How could you be expected to love a person whom you had never seen—whom you do not know—of whom, indeed, you know nothing?"

"Except by her bounties, Bruno."

"True, these demand gratitude, but seldom awaken love, unless by other associations. Mere charity, gifts and favours, have but little value unless the donor smiles while he is giving—speaks kind words, and looks affection and regard. The Baroness has erred, if your affection was an object in her sight, in not personally bestowing her bounty and showing to your own eyes, the concern which she felt in your success, and the benevolence she intended. Without these, her bounty could scarce secure your love; and the feeling which dictates it might have no such motive for its exercise—might be dictated by pride, vanity, the ostentation of a virtue; or, indeed, might be the consequence of a simple sense of duty."

"Duty! How should it be the duty of the Baroness to provide for my support and education."

"Nay, I say not that such is the case. I simply suggest one of the causes of that favour which men are very apt, when they name, to confound with benevolence."

"But why should you speak as if it were doubtful that the Baroness really desires to secure my affection. Do you know, Bruno, that she does not?"

"He or she who aspires to secure the affection of another will scarcely succeed by the mere act of giving in charity. The gift must be accompanied by other acts, other expressions, which shall exhibit the attachment which the giver desires to awaken. It must be shown that there is a pleasure felt in the benevolence, that the heart which bestows enjoys a kindred satisfaction with that which receives. As for any knowledge on the subject of the feelings of the Baroness, I pretend none. I but state a general truth when I say, that, if her object had been to make you love her, she should have carried her gifts in person, shown herself frequently to you, counselled you from her own lips, exhorted your industry and diligence, prompted your ambition, cheered your labours, and encouraged all your honourable desires."

"Ah, if she *had* done this, Bruno."

"Doubtless you would then have loved her, and then she would have been—"

He paused abruptly; the same stern expression of countenance denoted the suppression of a sentiment, such as more than once before during our dialogue had seemed to fill his mind with bitterness. I eagerly demanded of him the conclusion of the sentence, and with a smile which was half a sneer, he replied,

"Then she would have been—secure of your love."

I smiled also, and, perhaps, a like sarcastic sneer passed over my own lips, as he came to this lame and impotent conclusion.

"Bruno, you deceive me, and possibly wrong my benefactress. You know more than you will tell me. There is some strange mystery in this business—"

"Which I believe, Herman, but—"

"Which you know, Bruno."

"Perhaps so; but let me ask you, Herman, my dear Herman, do you believe me to be your friend?"

"I do."

"That I have ever shown you kindness, watched over you, counselled you, guided you, protected you, done all, in short, that a father could have done for the son he most loved?"

"Truly, good Bruno, I believe, I think, I know that you have been all this to me. You have supplied those performances, which, if your thinking be right, the benevolence of the Baroness imprudently omitted."

"Enough, Herman. Believe then a little more. Believe that he who has been friendly and faithful hitherto, without hesitation, without exception, without going back, and without sign of reluctance, will still be true, faithful and affectionate. There is something that I might say, but not wisely, not beneficially for you, and therefore I forbear to say it. But the time will come, I think it will come very soon, and all my knowledge shall then be yours. Meanwhile be patient and learn the first best lesson of youth—learn to wait! By learning to wait, you learn to endure, and in learning to endure, you learn one of the principal arts of conquest. I speak to you the lesson of experience, of my own experience. Never did a young man pass through a more trying term of endurance than myself. I have suppressed my nature, stifled the passions of my heart, kept down those struggles of my soul, which, as they would have vainly striven for any release, were premature; and, after twenty years of bondage I am at length free. Your visit to the Castle of T——, is the epoch of my emancipation."

III.

Having thus spoken, Bruno became suddenly silent, and no effort that I could make could induce him to resume the conversation. Yet, how had this conversation excited me!—what strange connexions did it occasion among the thoughts and fancies of my mind. Where had he obtained the power to speak with so much authority, words so full of animation, thoughts so far beyond his seeming condition. His words seemed to lift and to expand himself. His eye glittered with the fire of an eagle's as he spoke, his lip quivered with equal pride and enthusiasm, and his form, it seemed to rise and tower aloft in all the majesty of a tried and familiar superiority. The mystery which enwrapped my own fate, seemed of a sudden to envelope this man also. He had dropped words which indicated an alliance of our destinies, and what could he mean, when, at the close of this speech, he said, that my visit to the Castle of T—— was the epoch of his emancipation. The words rang in my ears with the imposing solemnity of an oracle, but though I felt, in vain did I strive to find something in them beyond their solitary import. They increased the solemnity and anxiety of those feelings which oppressed me on my nearer approach to the gloomy towers of T—— Castle. As we came in sight of them I could perceive that the countenance of my companion assumed an expression of anxiety also. A dark cloud, slowly gathering, hung about his brows, and at length spread over and seemed to settle permanently upon his face. He now seldom spoke, and only in answer to my inquiries and in monosyllables. Something of this, in the case of each of us, may have been derived from the sombre and gloomy tone of every thing in the immediate neighbourhood of this castle. The country was sterile in the last degree. We had travelled the whole day and had scarcely encountered a human being. But few cottages skirted the cheerless and little-trodden pathway over which we came, and a general stuntedness of vegetation and an equally general poverty of resource in all respects, fully accounted to us for, and justified the absence of inhabitants. Bruno, however, informed me that the country on the other side of the lake on which the castle stood, and from which it derived its resources, was as fertile and populous, as this was the reverse. A succession of little hills, rugged and precipitous, which were strewed thickly over our pathway, added to the difficulties of our approach, and the cheerlessness of the prospect. The castle was gray with years—one portion of it entirely dismantled and deserted—the residue in merely habitable condition—the whole presenting such a pile as would be esteemed as a ruin, among a people of romantic temperament, but carefully avoided by the superstitious as better calculated for the wanderings of discontented ghosts, than as a dwelling for the living. The wall which was meant to protect it from invasion on the side we came, was in a worse state of dilapidation than even the deserted portions of the castle, and we entered the enclosure through a fissure, and over the overthrown masses of lime and stone by which it had been originally filled. There were too many of these openings to render formal ports or gateways necessary. Within the enclosure I had an opportunity to see how much more desolate was the prospect the nearer I approached it. Its desolation increased the feelings of awe with which the mystery of my own fate, the ambiguous words and manner of Bruno, and the vague conjectures I had formed in reference to my benefactress, had necessarily filled my mind; and I was conscious, on first standing in the presence of the Baroness, of far more apprehension than gratitude—an apprehension not so creditable to my manhood, and only to be excused and accounted for, by the secluded and unworldly manner in which my education had been conducted.

The Baroness met me with a smile, and such a smile!—I could not comprehend its language. It was clearly not that of affection; it did not signify hatred—shall I say that it was the desperate effort of one who seeks to look benevolence while feeling scorn; that it was a smile of distrust and bitterness, the expression of a feeling which seemed to find the task of receiving me too offensive and unpleasant even to suffer the momentary disguise of hypocrisy and art. I was confused and stupified. I turned for explanation to Bruno, who had accompanied me into the presence; and the expression in his face did not less surprise me than that in the face of the Baroness. His eyes were fixed upon hers, and his looks wore an air of pride and exultation; not dissimilar to that which I have already described as distinguishing them while our dialogue was in progress. There was something also of defiance in his glance, while gazing on the Baroness, which puzzled me the more. Her eyes were now turned from me to him.

"And this then is the—the youth—the——" She paused. I could no longer misunderstand those accents. They were those of vexation and annoyance.

"The same!" exclaimed Bruno, "the same, my lady, and a noble youth you see he is; well worthy of your patronage, your love!"

There was a taunting asperity in his tones which struck me painfully, and at length stimulated me to utterance and action. I rushed forward, threw myself at her feet, and, while I poured forth my incoherent acknowledgments for benefactions, would have seized and carried her hand to my lips. But she shrunk back with an impulse if possible more rapid than my own, her hands uplifted, the palms turned upon me as if beckoning me away, her head averted, and her whole attitude and manner that of one suffering contact from the thing it loathes.

"No, no! None of this. Take him away. Take him away."

I rose upon my feet and turned to Bruno. His form was erect, his eye was full of a stern severity as he gazed upon the Baroness which seemed to me strangely misplaced when I considered his relative position with the noble lady to whom I owed so much, and, it would seem so unaccountably, so unnaturally. Bruno paused and did not regard me as I approached him. His eyes were only fixed upon his mistress. She repeated her injunction, with a wild and strange addition:

"Have you not had enough? Would you drive me mad? Away with him. Away!"

"Come!" he exclaimed, turning to me slowly, but with an eye still fixed upon the Baroness, whose face was averted from us. He muttered something further which I did not understand, and we were about to depart, he frowning as if with indignation, and I trembling with equal apprehension and surprise.

"Stay!" she exclaimed, "where would you take him, Bruno?"

"To the hall below, your ladyship."

"Right, see to his wants. His chamber is in the northern turret."

"There!" was the abrupt exclamation of Bruno.

"There! There!" was all the reply; a reply rather shrieked than spoken, and the manner of which, as well as the look of Bruno when he beheld it, convinced me that there was something occult and mysterious in the purport of her command. Nothing more, however, was spoken by either the Baroness or himself, and we left the presence in silence together.

IV.

We descended to the *salle à manger*, where we found a bountiful repast prepared. But neither of us seemed disposed to eat, though the long interval of abstinence since the morning meal, would, at another time, and under different circumstances, have justified a vigorous appetite and an enormous consumption of the various viands before us. I remarked one thing in the management of the feast which occasioned my astonishment. There was a regular taster of the several dishes, who went through his office before Bruno invited me to eat. I had heard and read of this officer and the objects of this precaution in the history of past and barbarous centuries, but that he should be thought necessary in a modern household and in a Christian country was a subject of very natural wonder; and I did not hesitate to say as much to my companion and friend. But my comment only met his smile; he did not answer me, but contented himself with assuring me that I might eat in safety. He even enlarged on the excellence of some of the dishes, most of which were new to me. I did little more in the progress of the repast than follow the example of the taster, who, his office over, had instantly retired, but not before casting a glance, as I fancied, of particular meaning towards Bruno, who returned it with one similarly significant! I observed that all the retainers exhibited a singular degree of deference to this man, that his wishes seemed anticipated, and his commands were instantly obeyed. Yet he spoke to them rather in the language of an intimate companion than a master. He was jocose and familiar, made inquiries into their exclusive concerns, and seemed to have secured their affections entirely. It was not long before I discovered that this was the case. From the *salle à manger*, as neither of us cared to eat, we retired after a brief delay, and leaving the castle, emerged by a low postern into an open court which had once been inclosed and covered, but of the inclosure of which only one section of the wall remained, connecting the main building with a sort of tower, which, as I afterwards found, contained the apartments assigned me by the Baroness. To this tower Bruno now conducted me. Crossing the court, we entered a small door at the foot of the tower, which my conductor carefully bolted behind him. We then ascended a narrow and decaying flight of steps, which, being circular, gradually conducted us to an upper chamber of greater height from the ground, than looking upward from below, I had at first esteemed it. This chamber was in very good repair, and, at one time, seemed indeed to have been very sumptuously furnished. There was, however, an air of coldness and damp about the apartment that impressed me with unpleasant sensations. But a single window, and that a small one, yielded the daylight from the eastern horizon, while two small, narrow doors that appeared to have been shut up for a century and more, occupied opposite sections of the northern and southern walls. The little aperture at the head of the stairs was closed by a falling trap, and fastened or not at the pleasure of the incumbent, by a bolt in the floor above. A massive bedstead of carved columns, and antique pattern, stood almost beside the trap, making flight easy by that means in the event of such a proceeding seeming desirable. A venerable table, of the same style and century as the bedstead, stood in the middle of the apartment, sumptuously covered with a rich damask cloth, the massive fringes of which swept the floor around it. The solitary window of the apartment was shaded by a curtain of similar hue, but of softer and finer material. But the upholstery and decorations of my chamber, or my prison, for such it seemed with all its decaying splendour, called for little of my notice then, and deserve not that of my reader. A casual glance sufficed to show me the things of which I have spoken, and I do not think I bestowed upon them more. There were matters far more serious in my mind and important to my interest. Two stools which the apartment contained, afforded seats to Bruno and myself; and I scarcely allowed myself to be seated, before I demanded an explanation of the strange scene through which we had gone with my benefactress.

"A little longer, dear Herman—be patient a little longer, and then you shall have no cause to complain of me. I shall strive soon to convince you of my wishes for your happiness and welfare, and, perhaps, of the continued labours which I have undergone, having your fortunes in view only. Yet, I do not promise you to unfold the mystery entirely, or even partially, which enwraps this castle, and its unhappy mistress. Perhaps, I cannot. I confess freely, there is something beyond my knowledge, though not, I trust, beyond my power. Should I succeed in what I purpose, and this very night may show, then may you expect such a revelation as will satisfy your curiosity and make you better content with your position. Of one thing I may assure you, your fortunes are better than you think them, the prospect is favourable before you, and the time is not far distant when you may realize my hopes in your behalf, and reap some of the fruits of my toils. But I must leave you now. Nay, do not stay me, and do not seek to question me further. I cannot now, I will not speak more on this subject. It is your interest that calls me from you."

I would have detained him for further questions, spite of his admonition, but he broke away from me, and was hurrying through the small southern door of the apartment, when he suddenly stopped.

"Herman, I had almost forgotten a most important matter. I must give you some cautions. This door, you perceive, has a bar, which drops within these fissures of the wall and secures it thoroughly. You will close it after me and keep it fast at all hours. Do not open it to any summons unless it be mine, and even my voice, or what may seem to be my voice, must not persuade you to violate this caution. When I desire entrance you will hear these sounds, but no words"—here he breathed, rather than whistled, a slight note, interrupted by a singular quaver, which seemed the very soul of mystery—"above all," he continued, "let no woman's voice persuade you to undo the bar."

"But suppose the Baroness should send?"

"Do not you hear? She may send, nay I am sure she will, she may come herself."

"But I must then open?"

"No, not then! Not for your life."

"Ha, Bruno! What may this mean?"

"Inquire not now, my son; but believe me that my precautions are not idle, not unnecessary. I live but to serve and save you."

"Save me! You confound me, Bruno."

"Yes, I have saved you until now, and require nothing but your obedience to be your preserver still. Do as I ask, as I command you! and all will be well, and we shall be triumphant."

His words were no less strange to me than had been those of the Baroness, and what was more strange than all, was that sudden air of authority, parental, indeed, which he now assumed for the first time. I did not, at the moment, feel the greater singularity of my own tacit obedience, without disputation, to the authority of this man. I acted, all the while, as if under the sway of an instinct. His eye, in the next moment, gave a hasty glance to the solitary window of my chamber, and to the door in the southern wall of the apartment.

"That door is almost unapproachable," he said, seeing that my eye followed the direction of his, "it leads to an abandoned terrace which overhangs the lake. The portion of wall which connected it with the castle is almost in ruins. Still it may be well that you should keep it bolted. The window, which is grated, and inaccessible, will yet afford you a pretty view of the neighbouring mountains, which, as there is a lovely moon to-night, you will be able to distinguish readily.

Should the hours seem tedious in my absence, you can amuse yourself by looking forth. But, let me warn you at parting, Herman, open to no summons but mine."

V.

He left me at these words, and left me more perplexed, if not more apprehensive than ever. My meditations were neither clear nor pleasant. Indeed, I knew not what to think, and, perhaps naturally enough, ended by distrusting my counsellor. The change in his deportment and language had been no less marvellous than was the reception which I had met with from the Baroness. The inference seems usually justified that where there is mystery there is guilt also; and Bruno had evidently been more mysterious and inscrutable than the Baroness. She, indeed, had spoken plainly enough. Looks, words and actions, had equally denounced and driven me from her presence; and ignorant and innocent of any wrong, performed or contemplated, I necessarily regarded my benefactress as the victim of sudden lunacy. Still, it was impossible to reconcile the conduct of Bruno, however strange and unaccountable it might seem, with the idea of his unfaithfulness. He certainly, so far as I knew, had ever been true to my interests. He had been something more. He had shown himself deeply attentive to all my feelings. Never had father bestowed more tender care on a beloved son, and shown more of parental favour in his attachments than had been displayed towards me from the first by this person. It was not easy now to distrust him; and racked by conflicting conjectures, I passed two weary hours, before any thing happened to divert my thoughts from speculations which brought me no nigher to the truth. In the mean while, I had made sundry attempts, by looking around me, to lessen the influence of my thoughts upon my feelings. I examined my chamber with the appearance, if not the feeling of curiosity. I mounted to the window, and, for a little while, was soothed by the soft, silvery light of the moon, as it seemed to trickle down the brown, discoloured sides of the rocks that rose in the distance, hill upon hill, until the last was swallowed up in the gloomy immensity beyond. The moon herself, in the zenith, was beyond my glance. But this prospect did not relieve the anxiety which it failed to divert. I turned from the pleasing picture, and resuming my seat beside the table in my gloomy apartment again surrendered myself up to those meditations which, however, were soon to be disturbed. My attention was called to the door through which Bruno had taken his departure, and which, though I did not then know the fact, led through a long dismal corridor, to a suite of rooms beyond. A distinct tap, twice or thrice repeated, was made upon the door. I was on the eve of forgetting the solemn injunctions of my companion, and had nearly risen from my seat for the purpose of opening it. I recollected myself, however, before doing so; and maintained an inflexible silence. But I could not stifle the beatings of my heart which, on a sudden, seemed to have acquired fourfold powers of pulsation. I almost tottered under my emotion; and nothing but a resolution of the most stern character, and the feeling of shame that came to my relief and reproached me with my weakness, enabled me to preserve a tolerable degree of composure. I kept silence and my seat—suppressed my breathings as well as I could, and with ears scarcely less keen than those of the watch dog, when the wolf-drove trots about the enclosure, did I listen to the mysterious summons from without. Again and again, though still in moderate force, as if some caution was necessary to prevent the sounds from reaching other senses than my own, were the taps repeated upon the door; and after a full quarter of an hour, passed in a condition of suspense the most trying and oppressive, I was at length relieved by hearing the tread of retiring footsteps preceded by the murmurs of a voice which I had never heard before, and none of the words of which could I distinguish. I breathed more freely for awhile, but for a while only. Perhaps an hour had elapsed; it might have been less, it certainly could not have been more; I had fallen into a sort of stupor, akin to sleep, for nature was not to be denied her rights, even though care had begun to insist on hers; when the summons was renewed upon the entrance, and, this time, with a considerable increase of earnestness. Still, I followed the counsel of Bruno, returned no answer, and strove to retain my position in the most perfect silence. The knocking was repeated after a little interval, but with the same want of success. Then I heard voices. A whispering dialogue was evidently carried on between two persons. How acute will the ears of anxiety become when sharpened by apprehension. I heard whispers, evidently meant to be suppressed, through a stone wall nearly three feet in thickness. The whispering was succeeded by a third summons, to which I paid as little attention as before, and then the whispers were exchanged for murmurs, sharp, quick murmurs, in the tones of that voice, which, once heard, could never have been forgotten. It was the voice of the Baroness. I could now distinguish her words; for, in her passion, she lost all her prudence. "Said you not that you saw them enter together?" The reply was inaudible, though the whisper which conveyed it was sufficiently so.

"And you saw Bruno go forth alone?"

Again the whisper, which must have been affirmative.

"And he took the way to the convent?"

The response was immediate, and I suppose affirmative, also, though still in a whisper too soft for me to hear.

"Then *he* must be here!"

The remark was followed by a louder knocking, in the intervals of which my name was called three several times in the voice of the Baroness; each time with increased emphasis, and evidently under the influence of a temper, roused from the first, and growing momently more and more angry, under disappointment. I began to reproach myself with my conduct. How could I justify this treatment of my benefactress? By what right did I exclude her, and what reason could I give to myself or others for such disrespectful treatment? The discussion of this question in my own mind led to various and conflicting resolves. My reflections all required that I should answer the summons and open the door to the mistress of the castle; but my feelings, swayed equally by the mystery of my situation, and the singular influence which Bruno had acquired over me, were opposed to any compliance. While I debated, however, with myself, I heard another voice without—the voice of Bruno—which seemed to produce as much annoyance and fluttering among my nocturnal visiters, as their summons had occasioned in my own excited heart. His tones were loud, and he seemed to be under as much excitement as the Baroness. The words of his first address were clearly audible.

"Ah, madam," he exclaimed, "it is as I apprehended; you have then violated your promise—you have dared!"—

"Dared—dared!" was the almost fierce exclamation in reply.

"Aye, madam, dared. You knew the penalty of faithlessness when you complied with the conditions; can it be that you would defy it. How is it then—"

"Stand from my way, insolent!" cried the Baroness, interrupting him in haughty accents, and evidently moving forward.

"Willingly," was the answer; "willingly, but I go with you for awhile. Dismiss the girl."

Strange to say, this command, for command it was, was instantly obeyed. I heard the Baroness clearly address a third person, of whom I knew nothing, but whom I conceived to be the person meant by Bruno, in terms which despatched her from the presence. The dialogue between the two was then resumed, but the sounds gradually died away from my ears, as it seemed, in consequence of the parties retiring to some more distant spot. My agitation may be fancied all the while. So long as the interlocutors were within hearing, I was more composed and quiet. When I ceased to hear them and to be conscious of their neighbourhood, my anxiety became utterly unrestrainable. I defied the fears which oppressed me, the warning which had been given me, the nice scruples of propriety and delicacy, which, at another time, I should have insisted upon as paramount to every other law. I lifted the bar from the door, which I opened, and emerged into the long and gloomy gallery of which I have already briefly spoken. I was resolved to pursue the parties, and satisfy that intense curiosity—a curiosity which was strictly justified by my own entire dependence upon the circumstances in progress—possibly, for life and death, weal and woe, bondage and freedom—which was preying upon me like a fever. With many misgivings, some momentary scruples, and a few fears, all of which I contrived to keep in subjection, I pursued this gallery with the most cautious footstep, resolved to hear the dreadful truth, for such I now esteemed it to be, upon which turned the mysterious history of my birth and fortunes. I groped my way almost in entire darkness, along a ruinous part of the castle. The gallery seemed to be winding, and there were openings in the wall, which I felt on each hand, at intervals, and which seemed to indicate other chambers and apartments. Through these, a chill wind passed, confirming me in the belief that they were ruinous and deserted, and satisfying me that the parties I pursued, were not to be found in either of them. At the end of the gallery, I was stopped by a door, and beyond it the voices were again heard, sometimes low, at other times in angry emphasis, but seemingly with little or no cessation, either of one or of the other. The words were seldom sufficiently audible to be syllabled clearly, and my curiosity would not suffer me to remain satisfied. I tried the door, which, to my great joy, was unfastened; and advanced with increased caution into a second, and small apartment which seemed a dressing room. A faint light gliding through a chink in the opposite wall, together with the distinct voices of the persons I sought, guided me to a spot, where I could see them with tolerable ease, and hear all their words distinctly. The chamber into which I looked was similarly furnished with my own. It seemed to have been equally unoccupied. An ancient ottoman received the form of the Baroness, who, as she spoke, alternately rose from, or sunk back upon its cushions. She scarcely uttered a sentence without accompanying it with great and corresponding action; now rising from her seat and advancing passionately upon her companion, with hand uplifted, as if to strike, eye flashing fury and resolution, while her lips poured forth a torrent of impetuous indignation and rage;—then suddenly receding at the close of her words, she would sink back as if exhausted upon the ottoman, burying her face within her hands, and sobbing with disappointed anger. Bruno, meanwhile looked the very embodiment of coolness and resolution.

"Ulrica," I heard him say, as I approached the aperture, "these are follies from which you should be now freed. They are frenzies which must only destroy you, while they do no good to your purpose, enfeeble you in my sight, and humble you in your own. Of what avail is all this violence—of what avail your further struggles to prevent that consummation which is, at length, at hand: let me implore you to be wise, ere it be too late. Welcome with a smile the necessity which you can baffle no longer."

"Welcome it with a curse, welcome it with death, rather. Well do you call it a necessity, it is a necessity like death, and as such, and such only, shall it have my welcome."

"And the wise welcome death with a smile, if only because it is a necessity," replied Bruno. "You cannot now escape me, you cannot longer evade compliance with my wishes. Long, long, and wearisome, indeed, have been my labours. I have, at length, triumphed! I have succeeded in my purpose, and am at length the master of your fate. I witness your struggles with sorrow, as they only drive you on the more certainly to humiliation—perhaps to madness. It is pity, Ulrica, genuine pity, and no other feeling which would move me to implore of you a willing concession of that which you can no longer avoid to make. The necessity is now inevitable, and I would spare you those further struggles which tend only to your exhaustion. You are so completely in my power, that your hatred and fury no longer awaken my indignation."

"Do you exult, wretch; do you then exult? Beware! You are not yet secure of your triumph."

"I am. Let this night pass only without harm to the boy, and all is well, and our triumph is complete. I am then your master."

"Master! Master! Away, insolent, and leave me. You are still my slave."

"No, Ulrica, you know better than this. The epithet is no longer applicable. I am your master and the master of your fate."

"Slave! Slave! Slave!" was the oft repeated and bitter exclamation, which came forth from her lips in foamed impotence.

"If to conquer is to acquire the rights of a master, then are these rights mine. Still I say not 'woe to the conquered.' No, Ulrica, again, and again, I conjure you to seek favour and to find it. It is still in your power—it is in your power while this night lasts—to receive indulgence. Be merciful to yourself as well as to him, the youth, who now, for the first time, from that awful hour of storm and meditated crime, the hour of his birth, enters the dwelling of——"

"Say it not, man—wretch, fiend! Hell's curses and consuming fire be upon that hour, and the vile thing of which you speak. Slave! Hence! Hence and leave me: and hear from my lips—lips which have seldom spoken the language of vengeance and of hate in vain, that the night is not yet over, and he who shouts at the close of one day may howl ere the beginning of another."

"I do not despise your threats, Ulrica—I fear them;—but I guard against them also. Did you fancy that you could penetrate to that chamber undiscovered by the watchful eyes that for the last seventeen years have been busy in penetrating every movement of your mind and soul."

"Accursed period! Fiend, wherefore will you torment me with the recollections of that time?"

"Curse not the time, Ulrica, but the deed which it witnessed, and the worse deeds to which it led—your deeds, Ulrica, not mine—your free and voluntary deeds, to which neither the counsels of wisdom, nor of others, but your appetites and evil passions impelled you. You have called me slave repeatedly to-night—it is your favourite epithet when you deign to speak of, and to me. It is now time that I should relieve myself from the epithet, as I am now able to prove myself your master, and the master of your fate. If, seventeen years ago, I was the bondman of your father, annexed to the soil, his serf—your slave—I have been emancipated from all such relationships by your crime. You asserted the power which was transmitted you, to command my obedience. You required of me a service, as a slave, which released me from all obligations of that condition; and though I wore the aspect, the demeanour, the burden of the slave, from that moment I resolved to be one no longer. When that boy——"

"Curse him!—Hell's curses be upon him and you!" was the fiendish exclamation, accompanied by looks equally fiendish.

"Those curses, Ulrica, will cling to your neck and strangle you for ever!" was the stern and indignant answer of Bruno to this interruption. "Of one thing be certain, they neither vex me nor baffle me in my purpose. They have never hitherto done so, nor shall they now, when my labours are on the eve of successful completion. But I resume: when that boy was born, I resolved to secure him from the fate of the others! Did it not prove my fitness for freedom when my mind was successful in the struggle with my master. How long has that struggle continued—what has been its history—what now is its termination? My triumph—my continued triumphs—my perfect mastery over you! I have baffled you in your purposes—prevented many—would I could have prevented all of your evil deeds and desires; protected the innocent from your hate—preserved the feeble from your malice, and secured, to this moment, the proofs equally of your crime and my superiority. Did these achievements seem like the performances of a slave? Did these betray the imbecility, the ignorance, or the pliability of the slave? No, Ulrica, no! He who can rank with his master has gained a sufficient, perhaps, the only sufficient title to his freedom! But that title was already gained when you descended to the level, and contented yourself with sharing the pleasures of the slave, when you were willing——"

A torrent of the most terrific imprecation, in a voice more like the bursting of a thunder bolt, drowned the narrative of the speaker, and prevented me from hearing the conclusion of a speech, the tenor of which equally surprised and confused me. What Bruno said was just enough to advance me to a mental eminence, from whence I could survey only a sea of fog, and haze, and mystery, much deeper than before. When his words again became intelligible, he had discontinued his reminiscences.

"Hear me, Ulrica. You know not yet the extent of my knowledge. You dream not that I am familiar with your secrets even beyond the time when I was called to share them. 'Till now I have kept the knowledge from you, but when I name to you the young but unhappy Siegfried! His fate—"

"Ha! Can it be! Speak, man, monster, devil!—How know you this? Hath that vile negress betrayed me?"

"It needs not that you should learn whence my knowledge comes. Enough that I know the fate of the unhappy Siegfried—unhappy because of your preference, and too vain of his elevation from the lowly condition of his birth, to anticipate the fearful doom which in the end awaited him; and to which, I, too, was destined. But the kind providence which has preserved me, did not suffer me to be blinded and deceived by the miserable lures which beguiled him to his ruin, and which you vainly fancied should mislead me. You would have released my limbs from fetters to lay them the more effectually upon my soul. You commanded my submission, you enforced it, but you never once deceived me. I saw through you from the first, and prayed for the strength to baffle and overcome you. I obtained it through prayer and diligence; and more than once it was my resolution, as it long has been in my power to destroy you, and deliver you without time for repentance, to the fearful agent of evil, which has long had possession of your heart. That boy has saved you more than once. The thought of him, the thought of what he was, and should be, to you, has come between me and my purpose.

You have been spared thus long, and it is with you to declare, in this place, and at this moment, whether you will be wise in season, whether you will forego the insane hatred which has filled your bosom from the hour of his birth, and accept the terms of peace and safety which I now offer you for the last time. Hear me through, Ulrica, and know that I do not heed your curses. I am too strong, too secure in my position, to be moved by the idle language of wrathful impotence. This night must determine equally for him and yourself. To-morrow, which witnesses his public triumph, will be too late for you unless to share it. I have already seen his Holiness who will be here at noon, armed with plenary powers to search and examine; and it needs only that I should point my finger, and your doom is written, here and eternally. You are not in the temper to die; and you may escape for repentance. Nor is the condition a hard one. The youth is noble, intelligent and handsome, he will do honour to any house. It is only to acknowledge——"

"Say no more, slave! Base, blackhearted, bitter slave! Say no more to me on this hateful subject. You have deceived me long; but you have not yet baffled me, as you insolently boast. Still less are you the master of my fate!—The master of my fate!—Ha! ha! ha! That were indeed, to be humbled to the dust. Away fool, and know that my foot shall yet be upon your neck, while your false tongue licks the ground in which you grovel. Away! I defy you now, and spit upon you with disgust and scorn. Give me way, that I may lose sight of your false and hateful aspect."

The words of the man were full of a calm, but bitter sorrow, as he stood before her.

"For your own sake and safety, Ulrica, I implore you. Be not rash; yield to the necessity which must go forward, yield to it with grace, and all may yet be well. There is still time for safety and for repentance. On my knees, Ulrica, I supplicate you to be more merciful to yourself, to me, to him!"

"Never, never!" she exclaimed, as, with violent hand and sudden blow, she struck the speaker, who had knelt before her, over the yet unclosed lips, and rapidly passed towards an opposite entrance. He did not rise, but continued to implore her.

"This, too, I forgive, Ulrica. Once more I pray you!"

"Slave! Slave! Slave! Do your foulest—base traitor, I defy you." She disappeared in the same instant, and Bruno rose slowly and sorrowfully to his feet; while, trembling with equal wonder and apprehension, I stole back with hurried but uncertain footsteps to my chamber, and hastily fastened the door behind me.

VI.

I naturally expected that Bruno, in a short time, would follow upon my footsteps, and deep, indeed, was the solicitude with which I waited for his coming. No words could convey to the understanding of another, the singular and oppressive feelings, doubts and anxieties which had been awakened in my mind by the strange and terrible scene which I had witnessed. The curious relation in which the parties stood to each other—the calm assurance and stubborn resolution which was shown by Bruno, in defiance of one whom I had regarded only in the light of a mistress equally without reproach or fear—her fury, which, as it awakened no respect in him, was the sufficient proof of her weakness and his power—his mysterious accusations, which I was too young to comprehend and too inexperienced to trace;—and not least, the fearful threats to which every sentence which he uttered, tended—subdued all my strength, and made me weaker in limb and in heart than the infant for the first time tottering on uncertain footsteps. There was something, also, in the brief space which he allowed the Baroness—but the single night on which she had already entered—for repentance before doom, which fearfully increased the terrors with which my imagination invested the whole fearful subject. And what could be the judgment—what the penalty—for those crimes, of which, as nothing was known to me, all seemed rash, dark and overwhelming? The more I strove to think, the more involved I became in the meshes of my own wild-weaving fancies; and, failing to fix upon any certain clue which might lead me to a reasonable conclusion, I strove, at length, in headache and vexation, to dismiss all thought from my mind, patiently awaiting the approach of Bruno and the morning for the solution of my doubts and conjectures. But Bruno and the morning promised to be equally slow in their approaches. The stillness of death now overspread the castle, and the buzzing of a solitary insect within my chamber, acquired, in the tomb-like silence of the hour, a strange and emphatic signification to my ear. Hopeless of Bruno's immediate return—as nothing could be more natural than the conclusion that his labours must be great that night in preparation for those morning results of which he had spoken so confidently, I determined to yield myself to slumber; and without undressing, I threw myself upon the massive and richly decorated couch of my chamber. But I might as well have striven for flight to the upper clouds, as to win the coy and mocking sleep which I desired. My imagination was wrought up to an almost feverish intensity. The breathing of the wind through a crevice startled and distressed me, and in the very silence of the scene and hour I felt a presence which stimulated my fancies and increased my anxiety and dread. I no longer strove to sleep. I rose and approached the little window, and looked down upon the court.—There, the moonlight lay, spread out like a garment, so soft, so spiritual, that thought naturally became mysticism as I surveyed it, and the vague uncertainties of the future crowded upon the arena of a present world. I could fancy shadows—which were images rather than shadows—which passed to and fro in the cold, thin, but hazy atmosphere, that tossed their wild arms above their marble brows, as, melting away in the distance, they gave place to wilder and pursuing aspects. Sounds seemed, at length, to accompany these movements, and that acute sense of the marvellous, which all men possess in proportion to their cultivated and moral nature, and which seems a quality of sight and hearing only—a thing all eyes and ears—conjured syllables from the imperfect sounds, and shrieks of pain from the vague murmurs which now really reached my ears from a distance, and which, probably, were only murmurs of the wind over the little lake that lay at the foot of the castle. As this conviction stirred my mind, I remembered the door to which the attention of Bruno had been drawn for a moment while he was discussing the securities of my chamber. I remembered that this door, as he described it, led to the terrace which immediately overlooked the lake. The remembrance, in my feverish state of mind, led me to desire to survey this scene, and I approached the door, and had already begun to undo the fastenings, which, by the way, I found far less firm and secure than my friend had imagined. The niches of the wall, into which the bar was dropped, were crumbling, and decayed to so great a degree, that the shoulder of a vigorous man, from without, might, without much effort, have driven it from the slight fragments which still held it in its place. Nor was even this degree of violence necessary to effect an entrance. From a further examination I discovered that the wall had been tampered with—a fragment of the stone dislodged, though not withdrawn, through the opening of which, a hand from without might readily lift the bar, and obtain access. The cement having been carefully scraped away, the stone was suffered to remain, so nicely adjusted to the place, that it was only in one point of view that I could discern a faint glimmer of the moonlight through the aperture. The suspicions of Bruno, not to speak of my own, received strong confirmation from this discovery; and my apprehensions being naturally aroused, I now strove for means to secure the door which I had been about to open. It was apparent to me that I was now threatened with danger from without. I looked about my chamber, and my eye rested upon the massive table standing in the midst. I immediately seized upon that, and piled it, though with some difficulty, against the door. While I meditated in what manner to increase my defences, my ear, which had acquired all the keen sensibilities of an Indian scout on the edge of an enemy's encampment, detected a light buzzing sound, which drew my attention to the terrace. But I had scarcely stooped to the aperture, when a scream—a torrent of screams—rang so suddenly on the late silent atmosphere, that I was staggered, almost stunned, as if a thunderbolt had on the instant fallen at my feet in the deep stillness of the unbroken forests. The sounds came from the terrace, and as soon as I could recover from the enfeebling effect of my first surprise, hearing the screams still repeated as wildly as ever, I obeyed the natural impulse of my feelings, and prepared to rush out to the scene of clamor. I dashed the table from the door, against which I had taken such pains to bear it, and tearing the slight fastenings away which otherwise secured the entrance, I threw it open and darted upon the scene. The object that met my eyes that instant, fastened my feet. There stood the Baroness, about twenty steps from me, and at nearly the same distance from a door in the opposite wall, which was open, and from which she had evidently emerged. Behind her stood a negress—a dwarf—the blackest, strangest, and most hideous looking animal I had ever in my life beheld. The Baroness had been approaching my apartment—her face was towards me, but her eyes were turned—nay, fixed and frozen, it would seem, as if in the contemplation of some object upon the parapet which overlooked the lake. Her attitude exhibited the intensest and strained action of insanity. One hand—the left—was uplifted, and averted, as if to hide her eyes from the object which they yet resolutely strained to see. In the other hand, glistening in the moonlight, was a poinard bared, and borne aloft, as if designed for immediate service. I shuddered with an uncontrollable emotion of sickness—heart-sickness—as I associated the dialogue to which I had listened, with this instrument of death. But, though her progress had evidently been towards my chamber, her eyes were not now given to me. Her thoughts—if thought she had—were all elsewhere. Her fancies were hurrying her to other worlds, and scenes, and objects, visible to no senses but her own. Wildly she pointed to the parapet overlooking the lake, and gazed and spoke—a speech whose every accent was a scream of agony—as if still in sight lay some object of hate and fear, which she vainly struggled not to see.

"There—there—will it never sink—will it never die—will those hideous eyes never turn away! Down, down!—Thrust it down when I command ye—the rock is heavy in its garments—the lake is deep, deep, and still, and silent—down with it slave—for ever from my sight! Or, if ye tremble, set me free and I will do it—I have no fears—none! none!"

Thus, fixed and terrible, ghastly and staring wild, with idiot frenzy, she stood gazing and intent upon the fancied object in her sight—immovable, seemingly, as a statue, and conscious of nothing beside. I lost my fears in the contemplation of hers, and approached her, though hardly with any distinct purpose. She seemed not to notice my approach—not even when the negress who followed in her train rushed to her at my appearance, and strove, with an excitement of manner only less than her own, to direct her attention upon me. But the wretched one turned not once aside at the interruption. Her eyes had but the one direction, and could not be averted; and her incoherent language was poured forth in rapid, though inconsecutive syllables, to the object of her mind's vision, which so effectually froze to darkness all her capacities of sight. Never did I behold—never could I have fancied or believed a spectacle so wild and fearful. Imagine for yourself a woman, once eminently beautiful—

of a dark and mysterious beauty—tall in form—majestic in carriage—in little more than the prime of life—wearing the dignity of age, yet, in every look, movement, feature, and gesture, exhibiting the impulsive force and passionate energy of youth;—her person bending forward—her eyes straining as if to burst from the burning sockets—her lips slightly parted, but with the teeth gnashing at occasional intervals with a spasmodic motion—her hair, once richly black and voluminously massive, touched with the grey that certainly ensues from the premature storms of a winter of the soul, escaping from all confinement, and streaming over her cheeks and neck—the veins of neck and forehead swelling into thick ridges and cording the features with a tension that amply denoted the difficulty of maintaining any such restraint upon them!—Imagine such a woman!—the ferocity of the demon glaring from her eye, in connection with the strangest expression of terror which that organ ever wore—the raised dagger in her hand—her hand uplifted—her foot advanced—and so frozen!—so fixed in the rigidity of marble!—the image above the sepulchre—no unfitting emblem of the dread and enduring marriage, which nothing can ever set asunder, between unrepented Guilt, and unforegoing Death!

I was nearly maddened even to behold this spectacle, and it was a relief to me, when with a no less terrible and terrifying energy she shook off the torpor which stifled life in all its wonted forms of expression, and renewed those fearful tones of memory and crime, which, though revealing nothing, amply testified to an equal and elaborate narrative of shame, and sin, and suffering.

"There! there!" she exclaimed, still addressing herself to some imaginary object which seemed to rest or to rise before her upon the parapet which overhung the lake—"There again!—its hands—its little hands—will nothing keep them down! They rise through the water—they implore—but no! no! It were a mistaken mercy now to save!—let me not look—let me not see—will you not fling it over—the lake is deep—the rock is heavy in its little garments—it will soon sink from sight for ever, and then—then I shall be safe. Ha! it goes—it goes at last!—Do you not hear the plunge!—the water gurgles in its nostrils—closes over it, and—God spare me, what a piercing shriek—Another! another!—Keep me not back—I will look if it be gone!—No! no! its little face smiles upon me through the white water!"

And this was followed by a shriek, piercing like that which she described, which penetrated to the very marrow of my bones. With the cry she bounded towards the parapet, looked wildly down into the lake at the foot of the castle, then recoiled with a scream to which every previous cry from her lips was feeble and inexpressive. The climax of her frenzy had been reached. I was just in time to save her. She fell backward and I received her in my arms. The shock seemed to bring her back to a more human consciousness. Her eyes were turned upon my own; and new intelligence seemed to rekindle them with their former expression of hate—her hand vainly strove to use the dagger against my person. In the effort it fell nerveless at her side, while a sudden discharge from the mouth and nostrils drenched my garments with her blood.

VII.

Bruno at that instant appeared and received her from my arms. The relief was necessary to me—I could not have sustained her much longer. I was sick almost to exhaustion. I felt unable to endure a sight to me so strange and terrible, yet I strove in vain to turn my eyes away. They were fixed as if by some fearful fascination. Hers, too, were now riveted upon me. At first, when I transferred her to the arms of Bruno, they were turned upon him; but, in the next moment, as suddenly averted with an expression of loathsomeness and hate, which suffering had not softened, nor the seeming approach of death diminished of any portion of intensity. On me they bestowed a more protracted, but scarcely a more kindly expression. Broken syllables, stifled and overcome by the discharge of blood, struggled feebly from her lips; and, fainting at last, she was borne to the chamber from which she had emerged at the beginning of that scene, the purposes of which seemed to me so inscrutable, and the progress of which was, in truth so terrible. Medical assistance was sent for, and every succour bestowed in the power of skill and humanity. Need I say, that a deep interest in her fate affected my bosom. A vague conjecture, dark and strange, which coupled the fate and history of this noble but wretched lady with my own, had naturally arisen in my mind, from the dialogue to which I had been a listener. What was she to me? I shuddered with an apprehension and painful terror whenever this question suggested itself to my thoughts. What was she not? What had she not been; and what had been her purposes—her baffled purposes? Let me not fancy them lest I madden.

"It is no subject of regret, Herman," were the first words of Bruno, when, yielding the Baroness up to her attendants, we retired to another apartment. "God has interposed to save us from a greater trial, and to save her from an exposure even more humbling than this. The dawn of another day, the sight of which she will now be spared, would have been worse than death to a spirit such as hers."

"But, will she die, Bruno? Can she not be saved? is it certain?"

"It is; and I am glad of it for your sake, as well as hers."

"For my sake?"

"Ay! the moment of her death puts you in possession of this castle and all her estates."

"Me!"

"You."

"And I am"——

"Her heir—yet not *her* heir. You are the heir to a power beyond hers, and which proved her destiny. Her death makes atonement at once to the living and to the dead. She now, involuntarily, compensates for a long career of injustice. But inquire no further; death, which will place you in possession of your rights, will, at the same time, deprive you for ever of a knowledge of certain secrets, which, had she lived till to-morrow's noon, must have been revealed in order to compel that justice which has been too long denied. It is fortunate that she will perish thus—fortunate for her—for you—for——"

He paused, and with an impulse which I could not withstand, I desperately concluded the sentence—

"And for yourself!"

"For me! Ha!—Can it be?—Herman, my son, what have you done?"

"Followed you through the corridor, when, this evening, you led the Baroness away from my apartment."

"And did you trace our footsteps—did you find us where we were—did you hear what was spoken?"

"All! All!"

He covered his face with his hands, and groaned aloud in the bitterness of an anguished and disappointed spirit.

"This pang," he exclaimed at length, "I had hoped to spare you. I have toiled for this at all seasons and hours, by night and day, in crowds and solitudes. Unhappy boy! your curiosity has won for you that partial knowledge of the truth which must only bring delusion, doubt and anxiety."

"But why should it be partial, Bruno. I know from what you have already said, that you know more, that you know all. You will complete my knowledge, you will terminate my doubts."

"Never! Never! If God has spared me, by his act, this night, that dire necessity from which, he well knows I would have shrunk, shall I now voluntarily seek it? No! No! The fearful chronicle of shame is sealed up for ever in her death. Blessed dispensation! Her lips can no longer declare her folly, and mine shall be silent, on her shame. You have heard all that you can ever hear of these dreadful mysteries."

"Nay, Bruno! Say not this, I implore you. Tell me, at least, tell me, that this most fearful woman is not——"

I shrunk from naming the word, the word signifying the relationship which I suspected to exist between us, which, indeed, seemed now to be infinitely more than a doubt, a suspicion. I looked to him to comprehend, to answer, without making necessary the expression of my fear. But he was silent, and I forced out the reluctant word.

"Tell me, Bruno, tell me at least, that this fearful woman is not—my mother."

"And of what avail if I should tell you this? Would that terminate your doubts—would that satisfy your curiosity?"

"It would—it would."

"No, Herman, I know your nature better—to know this would only lead to other and more annoying questions, questions which, if answered, would take peace from your mind for ever. You would know next—"

He now paused.

"Yes!" I exclaimed, "I would then seek to know—and I now do—what was he, Bruno—my father—and what is the secret of your power over her—and who are you?"

"Let it be a matter of thanks with you, Herman, in your nightly prayers, that you can never know these," was the hoarsely spoken reply. I threw myself at his feet, I clasped his knees, I implored him in tears and supplications, but he was immovable. He pressed me to his heart, he wept with me, but he told me nothing.

VIII.

At dawn we were summoned to the chamber of the Baroness. A crisis was at hand. His Reverence, the Cardinal ——, whose presence had been expected at a late hour in the day, and for another purpose, had been solicited to attend in haste, and had complied with Christian punctuality, with the demands of mortal suffering. But his presence effected nothing. The miserable woman clearly enough comprehended his words and exhortations. She listened without look of acknowledgment, or regret, or repentance. She heard his prayers for her safety, and a smile of scorn might be seen to mantle upon her lips. The Host was elevated in her sight, and the scorn deepened upon her countenance as she beheld it. Truly was she strong in her weakness. The sacred wafer was presented to her lips, but they were closed inflexibly against it. The death struggle came on; a terrible conflict between fate on the one hand and fearless passions on the other. The images of horror will never escape from memory. They are engraven there for ever. She raised herself to a sitting posture in the bed, without assistance. The effort was momentary only. But, in that moment, her glance, which was fixed on me, was the very life-picture of a grinning and fiendish malice. The expression horrified the spectators. His eminence once more lifted the sacred emblem of salvation in her sight, and the last effort of her struggling life, was to dash it from his hands. In that effort, she sank back upon the pillows, a fresh discharge of blood took place from her mouth, and strangulation followed. The sufferings of the mortal had given place to those of which there can be no mortal record.

* * * * * * * * *

And I was the master, undisputed, of all these domains. And Bruno had gone, none knew whither. Nothing more could I fathom of these mysteries, but there was one search that I instituted, one discovery that I made, which tended to deepen them yet more, in seeming to give them partial solution. That little lake, I had it drained, and just beneath the wall of the parapet, we found the tiny skeleton of an infant—bleached and broken into fragments, but sufficiently perfect to leave no doubt of its original humanity. A rude fragment of stone such as composed the outer wall inclosing the castle, lay upon its little ribs. Need I say that I gathered up, with the solicitude of a nameless love, every remnant of this little relic, that it was inurned with the tenderest care, and consigned to sacred keeping with the feelings of one, who knew not well that he might not even then possess, though he had never known, the love of an angel sister.

[The Prima Donna: A Passage from City Life *was published in pamphlet form in Philadelphia by Louis A. Godey in 1844. It has never been reprinted. Explanatory and Textual Notes begin on page 695.*]

THE PRIMA DONNA:
A Passage from City Life.

Mephistopheles.—Methinks, 'twere better far,
In place of these vain wanderings through the woods,
Didst thou requite the monkey for her love.
The hours to her are lamentably long,—
She stands beside the window, day by day,
To watch the shapeless clouds, and see them roll
Away, above the old walls of the town.
"Were I a bird!"—thus ever runs her song
Through the long day and the yet longer night:—
A moment cheerful,—but she lapses soon
To sadness, which is lasting: then she weeps
'Till tears refuse to come:—then quiet seems,
But lovesick, not the less.
Faust.—Oh, serpent, serpent!—GOETHE'S FAUST.

CHAPTER I.

I had changed my lodgings, seeking shelter in the suburbs, from the crowd and confusion of Broadway and the Park. The omnibus, at a shilling a ride, enabled me, while enjoying a seclusion akin to that of country life, to seek the city at any moment when pleasure or business called me thither. The second morning after my transition, I suffered myself to look round upon my new neighbourhood. I found myself in very good quarters for a single man. Our house was well arranged and spacious. It stood apart from all others, while, on either hand, the green of a well-stored vegetable garden gratified the eye, and the breezes from two quarters of the compass poured in at my windows. We were just in advance of the onward march of city improvements. Our pavements were incomplete, and the clang and clamour of cart, cab and carriage, were moderate accordingly, when compared with the stunning sounds with which they momently assailed me in Broadway. But, as if to qualify this advantage, there was just opposite, one of those annoyances which are to be found in the suburbs of every large city, in the shape of a cluster of low, crowded and filthy looking rookeries,—a nest of wooden structures, dingy, dark, narrow, and tumbling to decay, which still, however, gave shelter to a crowd of inmates. Every tenement of this nest, was filled from basement to attic;—the people were of the very poorest, and some of them, evidently, of the most dissolute, character. Rags and dirt were the conspicuous badges at every window, and no prospect could be more melancholy than that of the poor, puny, little children, who were despatched from rise of morn to set of sun, to glean, as beggars, from better furnished portions of the city, their daily supplies of pennies and "cold victuals."

I am not, however, one of those persons who sicken at the thousand aspects of human misery. Some experience of the world and its vicissitudes, acquired at a period when other men are usually about to begin their lessons, had fortified my senses, and prepared me to look with fortitude, if not indifference, upon those evils of life which are unhappily inevitable. I did not forego the prospect from the window, because it showed me suffering as well as sunshine; and, if I could not, in any great degree, alleviate the one, I saw not, in consequence, any good reason why I should reject or forego the other. My morning and afternoon contemplations included the 'rookeries.' I saw the outgoings and incomings of their motley population, and acquired, after a moderate period, a certain degree of interest, in some few of the several inhabitants. There was one old woman, a sturdy Meg Merrilies sort of body, who carried out, empty, a sack some five feet in length, which I am sure she always brought home full. What she brought, and what use she made of the commodity, I never troubled myself to inquire or even to conjecture. The simple appearance of the old dame at her departure and return, was enough for my curiosity. In going forth, her tongue sounded an alarum to the whole neighbourhood, which sufficiently apprised it of that important event. Very different was the manner of her return. She entered without beat of drum. Her tongue was most singularly silent, and the fierce, consequential air with which she sallied forth, was exchanged for that of the most quiet, meek and cautious of all humble adventurers. She was not my only acquaintance among the inhabitants of this motley settlement. There was a great, hulking, heavily built person most like a sailor in appearance, but one, evidently too well fed to relish a frequent journey to the cross-trees, who also secured some portion of my daily consideration. He, too, presented himself under different aspects, at his diurnal periods of egress and return. In the first case, he went forth, feeble, tottering, slightly lamed, and, I think, irrecoverably blind;—a decided improvement, however, always followed his morning visit to the city. He evidently met with Brandreth, the pill dealer, and Williams, the oculist, by the way. His eye-sight left him in no doubt about his "homeward bound" course; and his legs were then better able to pursue it. This was the more remarkable, as, at such periods, his arms were usually filled with stuffs, clothes, food and fragments of one description or another, in such quantity and weight as might have given a more vigorous person reason to stagger beneath the burden. He evidently pursued his craft with a success which convinced me that he might have arrived, in other days, at a post of high command even in Alsatia. There were other persons in this community, who, in their places and periods, also provoked, though in a far less degree, my observation and inquiry; and it would not, perhaps, be a very difficult matter, were I so minded, to awaken a similar interest in most of my readers in behalf of one or more individuals of its population, quite as mysterious as that of the "Stout Gentleman," of one of our most graceful writers, whom all are pleased to honour. Certainly, there were physical allotments among my friends of the 'rookery,' which, alone, were sufficient to impress the spectator with heedful deference. Brawny arms of Hibernian vigour brandished the broom, and flourished in the suds. Voices, of aristocratic authority, rose suddenly and stunningly upon the senses, and never did the damsels of Eleusinia declare themselves in a dialect of more unctuous emphasis and spirit in the hearing of assembled Greece. Of the mysterious character of those business operations which were pursued among them, I have already spoken. A very curious scandal-monger in literature might live for months in the periodicals by examining the domestic records of my suburban neighbourhood.

My tastes did not exactly lead me to institute any such examination. I was content to see the beauties of the scene afar off. Morning and evening glimpses satisfied my curiosity; and my old woman with her long sack, and my sturdy sailor with his imperfect eyesight, upon both of whom such radical changes took place in the progress of each diurnal sun, were studies which amply requited all my curious *cacoëthes*. The morning cries and clamour of the former aroused me from sluggish slumbers; and her usual period of return at evening, was equivalent to the tintinabulary summons to my evening repast—both of these important events happening to occur usually at the same hour of the day. A little pleasurable excitement, which was pleasurable, perhaps, only because of the excitement, served to reconcile me to a neighbourhood, the contemplation of which, while it failed to stimulate curiosity, did not contribute to the gratification of any of my usual tastes. I was just sufficiently remote from the scene I witnessed, to make it visible to me through that hallowing medium which turns the past into poetry, and elevates the foreign into dignity and grace. I must confess to a reluctance to any nearer approximation, which was so strong as to prompt me to make use of the back door of my lodging house, in the greater number of cases; and to seek, by a street in the rear, that outlet to the city, which, otherwise, could only have been marked by almost actual contact with the suds and sentiment of the 'rookery.'

CHAPTER II.

But a few days made a great difference in my mode of thinking and feeling in regard to some of the persons of my Alsatia. The cries and clamors of which I have spoken—as the familiar sounds from that neighbourhood, underwent a sweet and singular modification. A new and very different voice from the rest, aroused me one morning from my slumbers, and drew me to my window, with a sentiment of pleasurable anxiety, which was altogether new to my experience. Such a voice—of so much power—so much sweetness—so touching, so energetic, at once so expansive and insinuating, arch and tremulous—passionate, yet full of the most gentle fear.

I am not a musician myself. I am neither performer nor connoisseur, nor do I profess to have any great passion for that most pure and elevated of all the sensual luxuries:—but I should have been more or less than mortal to have withstood the

"Divine, enchanting ravishment,"

of that voice whose sudden song, penetrating the thick folds of sleep which enveloped me, commanded me to rise from my couch and compelled me to listen. The song was an English one—one of those simple old ballad ditties, the taste for which has undergone some revival in recent days;—but the air was decidedly foreign. The artifices of Italian music linked with the direct, natural and earnest language of English poetry, struck me on subsequent reflection, as suggesting a moral discord, which was unpleasant; but, while the performance lasted I was not sensible to this or any objection. I had no time to make it—no feeling for dissent or dissatisfaction, and it was only, long after the voice became silent, that, in seeking to be critical I found any thing to qualify its complete harmonies. I listened breathlessly while it proceeded. I was confounded to perceive that it came from a hovel, the very meanest of the group, which stood almost in the centre of the 'rookery.' If I wondered, however, at the first moment of the discovery, I had no time, just then, to yield myself up to mere astonishment. Delight occupied all the emotions of my soul; and it was not until the music had ceased for several moments, that I was able to shake myself free from that overpowering spell which its sovereign sweetness had imposed upon me. It was only when my ears ceased to find employment, that my eyes began to resume their accustomed exercise. It was only then, that, in examining the miserable dwelling from which such intoxicating sounds arose, I perceived the partial profile—at one of the low, unsashed windows—of a woman, seemingly very youthful, in whose style of face, I fancied I discerned the marked outlines of the English character, and yet, not entirely English. The black eyes—hair, long and glossy, of the same colour, which streamed upon a neck of unusual whiteness, seemed to distinguish one who had in her veins a warm, rich tincture of Milesian blood. I subsequently discovered, however, that she was of direct

English parentage. Still, her more remote ancestors might have come from the sister Isle.

I had now a new employment for my vacant hours, and a new motive for the survey of my 'rookery.' I watched and listened long enough, and often enough, to discover, in the next five days, sufficient cause for a greatly-increased wonderment. The girl—for she was young enough to be considered under this head,—was really beautiful. Her appearance, air, manner and behaviour, were such, also, as to justify the belief that she had come of good family, had been used to gentle nurture, and had been blessed with something more than an ordinary education. Yet how came she in such a place—so meanly habited—so poorly tended—so wretchedly provided for? The hovel which she occupied, was decidedly one of the meanest of the 'row.' The apartment in which I usually beheld her, and which I could easily overlook from mine, was almost entirely without furniture. A rude box beside the window formed the only seat which I perceived it to contain; and the bed, the foot of which was all that I could see, was spread out upon the floor. The wild and tender ballad which she sang—the style of her performance—the subdued and sweet resignation of her countenance the while,—how little did these correspond with the wretched state of every thing around her! What could have brought her to this condition? I mused over this question long, and approached it frequently. The answer which I found seldom satisfied me. I was unwilling to believe that mere misfortunes, the hazards of a capricious fate alone, could have so reduced worth, accomplishment and talent;—and yet, how difficult, —looking on her face of angelic purity of expression, and a placid resignation not less angelic,—to believe that she was the victim of guilt—the creature, self-impelled to sin, by her own bad passions, or pliant virtue.

CHAPTER III.

The more I thought, the more I was confused; and I became hourly more and more interested in the subject. My caution and my studies, and sometimes my landlady and supper, were equally forgotten. I became something of an amateur in music; though, after the few first days, my eyes were probably far more busy than my ears.

I almost lived at that window of my chamber which looked out upon the 'rookery.' My own movements, at length, came to be almost as much matter of observation and scrutiny to others, as were those of the fair singer to myself. Perhaps, I became somewhat indiscreet in the watch which I kept over her. Not content with the advantages of my position, I was tempted forth at evening by the sweet song of the syren, and without determining upon my movements, by the exercise of any previous thinking, I found myself, finally, under her very window.

This was a stretch of freedom rather large for one who had usually maintained, in his conduct, something like the regimen of a purist. It was an indulgence, the exercise of which soon brought me a rebuke, which, if it did not fully answer the intended purpose, of chiding me back to my own territory, at least served to remind me that I was an invader of that of another. The second time that I ventured to cross the street and place myself beneath the window of the musician, she was engaged in a touching little ditty, which I had never heard before, and the mournful sweetness of which brought to my soul as I listened a most luscious sentiment of grief. Perhaps I should have been amply satisfied to listen from my own chamber, had not the tones of her voice been unusually low. There was, that night, a faintness in her utterance which seemed to denote a full feeling in her heart of the sorrowful sentiment which other lips only sung. An undefinable curiosity made me throw by my books, extinguish my lamp, put on my cap, and steal forth to the 'rookery.' The evening was dark—a faint starlight through apertures in a dense mass of sullen clouds served only to confuse the aspects of general objects;—and secure, as I fancied myself, from all observation, I crossed the street, and placed myself against a lamp-post which stood in front of the miserable dwelling. Here I had not been many minutes before the music ceased. I could hear a brief conversation carried on in low but harsh tones in the apartment which had been so lately the prison of the sweetest song. The mean light of the chamber seemed extinguished, and while I waited for the strain to be resumed, the door below suddenly opened, and I was abruptly confronted by one, who, emerging from the dwelling, in almost rude accents, demanded my business.

CHAPTER IV.

There was surely something very impertinent in the demand. I had, by the common law, quite as much right to be where he found me as any body, so long as my presence did not conflict with the similar rights of any other citizen. The querist was a man, slight of frame, apparently decrepid in his limbs, and evidently an Italian. I could see by the lamplight, in the full glare of which he stood, that he was violently agitated. His thin, dark features were almost convulsed—his lips quivered, and his eyes emitted a fiery gleam, in which I fancied that I beheld the expression of a very malignant and personal hostility. This was all matter of very curious surprise to me, and it was only, I suppose, because of my exceeding surprise, that I did not, at the first moment, resent the impertinence of his demand. It may be that I felt also, that, however justly, according to law, I might maintain my position where I was, in spite of him or any body else, yet that, in my heart, and some of its desires, I was, in truth, a trespasser upon his rights. I certainly longed to get into his household—if it were his,—and to gaze my fill, at the sweet prisoner-bird thereof. That she was a caged songstress, I could not allow myself to doubt. I had caught, during the day, more than one glimpse of her sweet, sad countenance; and I fancied, more than once, that I read in her eyes as they encountered mine, the yearning to be free. Perhaps, in this reading of her eyes, my boyish vanity led me to fancy that I saw a great deal more. Perhaps—but there will always be time enough for the confessional. Enough to say that my conscience somewhat interfered in the desire which I certainly should have felt under other circumstances, of knocking my impertinent querist into the gutter, in answer to his demand.

As the matter was, I hesitated—actually stammered, and failed to reply in a satisfactory manner either to him or to myself, until provoked to a right feeling of resolution by the repetition, in broken English, of his inquiry:—

"What you do here? What you want?" The style of the question was unbearable—the manner in which his face was thrust forward into mine, was not to be endured, and I boldly blurted out the truth, or that which was truth, *per se*, with a look and accent of defiance.

"I stop here because it pleases me—because I wish to hear the music."

"Ah, ha!—it please you, dis music, eh? But you shall be go to you place—you shall nevare come stop here, no more,—nevare!"

And the shrivelled, angry, bilious, fiery-eyed little fellow, shook his finger almost in my face.

Human stomach could not stand this, and an involuntary emotion caused me to double my fist and raise my arm, with an action which left him in little doubt of my summary intentions. He receded at the sight, and, as I fancied, in order to effect a retreat as abrupt as had been his entrance upon the scene; but I was mistaken. It was only the better to prepare himself for defence. In another moment a stiletto glittered in his hand, and he assumed an attitude of the most determined preparation. This would not have discouraged me, —for I was conscious that a frame evidently so feeble as his, armed with any weapon, the use of which depended upon his muscle, could not oppose much obstacle to the blow of an arm like mine, endowed with no small share of masculine vigour, and under the direction, too, of some small science, the due result of an occasional exercise, in a very good school of the fancy. I felt confident that I could have "muffled his skylights" in a single instant, and long before his Italian weapon could be brought to bear upon the action. But a moment's reflection convinced me how seriously foolish would be any conduct which would bring me into a street-brawl with one like my opponent —so feeble in person—so superior in years—and so wretched in his condition. My arm was instantly lowered, and, murmuring something of a disinclination to chastise age, however impertinent, I was about to draw off from the ground and seek my own proper bulwarks. But he was not disposed to suffer this; availing himself of a change in my position, which half removed my face from him, he sprang towards me,—with what purpose I could only conjecture. I had just time to turn and grasp his uplifted arm, from which I wrenched the weapon. In another moment, such was my indignation, I might have used it upon him; but I was happily spared this folly, by the sudden appearance, from the house, of the young woman who had been the innocent occasion of all this difficulty. At her approach I withdrew the grasp which I had taken upon the fellow. He trembled like an aspen in the wind. His teeth chattered—with rage, not fear.

He shook his impertinent finger at me in hate and defiance; and when the hand of the woman was put upon his shoulder, as she threw herself between us, he flung her from him with a degree of violence, which almost renewed in my heart the desire to pummel him. The next moment he grasped her about the body and dragged her within the entrance. Her eyes were turned full upon me while she was passing from sight; and it was a small solace to my feelings at that instant, to fancy, as I did, that there was any thing but unkindness for me in their expression. I was but a youth at that period, and the vanity which seems natural enough to youth, must not be visited by the reader with too harsh an expression of opinion.

CHAPTER V.

However ruffled I might have been by this event, there was yet something in it which soothed and satisfied me. The heart of man is a very selfish substance, even in its impulses of greatest generosity. Perhaps, in a world, in which so superior and vast a proportion of the performance depends upon man, it is not unfitting that it should be so. He must be impelled by influences of self even to the execution of those social achievements which would seem to be most universal in their tendencies and aims. But this is no place to philosophize. It is enough for me to confess that I found pleasure in the conviction that the unknown songstress was unhappy, without finding it a cause of unhappiness to meet my glance—that she dwelt with one who was evidently not satisfied with her; and with whom—she being the creature of taste and sensibility which I readily assumed her to be—she could still less be satisfied. But in what relation did they stand to one another? This was a mystery to me which brought with it feelings of disquietude and pain. He was old enough to be her father. Was he so? I would have given something—though I knew not wherefore—could I have believed it. I prayed, unconsciously, that she was not his wife,—and shuddered, the next moment, with the apprehension that she might be something less, and something worse.

For two days after this I heard no music, and in all this time the windows remained closely fastened. I saw nothing of the songstress;—but the man, to whom I now addressed no moderate degree of my attention, but whom before, though I had seen, I had scarcely noted—he went forth as usual, just after my breakfast hour had been passed. I took the precaution now, to do my espionage through the blinds of my window, which I kept as carefully closed as my opposite neighbour. I could see that his eyes were cast upwards as he passed out and came in, and I readily conjectured, that, having noted my constant watchfulness from the window, the quick instinct of jealousy converted my appearance at night beneath his, into proofs, and

"Confirmation strong as holy writ,"

of evil purposes contemplated, and, possibly, evil deeds performed. Yet, truly, did I mean no evil. At the worst, that susceptible vanity of the youthful heart which makes it equally ready to exercise its own, and to believe that the affections of another are sympathetically awakened, was all my error. The strange surprise of hearing such music, and seeing such a face, in such a dwelling, was, perhaps, more than any thing beside, the source of that interest which the songstress awakened in my bosom. Had she come and gone, without bringing about the annoying little incident just mentioned, she would most probably have been nothing more in my eyes and thought, than any other among the "sweet singers of Israel."

CHAPTER VI.

It was impossible, now, that I should feel any such indifference. Curiosity was awakened, within me, and sharpened into activity all those other emotions which had been merely roused before. Every thing about her lowly household had now an interest in my sight which kept me feverishly alive to every sound which reached my ears from, and every movement of life which took place in, that quarter. Her ugly, little, bilious-faced and fiery-eyed protector, was, in particular, an object of excessive concern with me; and I followed his rickety movements, as he went abroad, and was careful to scrutinize them as he returned home, as if it were possible for me to derive from such a scrutiny a knowledge of those secrets which had become so annoyingly worth knowing. I was not long, however, permitted to maintain this watch upon his movements. On the third morning after the night on which we had encountered, I was impressed with the conviction, after resuming my usual post of survey at my window, that the dwelling of the suspicious pair was no longer occupied. An air of unusual stillness overspread the establishment. The windows and doors were all sealed up and silent. No smoke ascended from the chimney—no voice resounded from the enclosure—no old woman knocked at the gate for entrance—nobody went in and nobody came out. It presented a lamentable contrast to the busy hum of the thick clustering hive around it. I waited with some impatience for the breakfast hour. I hurried through the meal without asking whether I had satisfied appetite, and certainly without doing justice to my landlady's coffee biggin. I hastened back to my window, and waited for the customary departure of my male neighbour on his daily journey. He failed to appear as usual; and I was pained to think that I should hear no more music from the lips of the sweet, but melancholy stranger. My fears were well-grounded. My venerable landlady congratulated herself at dinner, that those noisy people, across the street, who sang so loud, had moved away under cover of the last night—the latter circumstance being one that awakened all the good old lady's apprehensions for the security of the rent due; in which an old lady of like dimensions with herself, had, it appears, considerable interest. But even this fear did not diminish her satisfaction at the removal when she recollected her escape from the music which annoyed her. The other sounds from the 'rookery,'—vile, various and discordant as they were—never offended a single sense in her whole system. They were natural and familiar, and, like certain other natural and familiar objects, they "signified love."

But to me this confirmation of my fears brought with it a degree of discomposure for which I was myself unprepared. I had sustained a loss, which pressed for the moment heavily upon me;—the loss of that object of secret sympathy which responds to our emotions, though in tears that we are not permitted to see, and in sighs that we cannot hear. I felt the privation so seriously, and my curiosity had been so highly stimulated, that I could no longer keep within the house, and actually sallied forth, on the wild-goose chase of looking-up the fugitives in such a city as New York.

A few hours ramble soon cured me of this folly, though it failed to bring me to my senses. I gave up the search after persons whose names I did not know, and who, if they had not left the city, could only have found shelter in some one of the thousand purlieus of destitution which cover its filthy spots. I returned home soured and dissatisfied, and went back, in sheer doggedness of purpose, to my solitude and studies.

CHAPTER VII.

It may have been three weeks, or more, after this, that there was a great stir in New York about a foreign Prima Donna—a singer whose excellence was equally indisputable and great. The newspapers which, in such matters, usually speak in the superlative style of *Euphrosine*, and in words as magnificent as those of Brobdingnag, now, in the excessive warmth of their enthusiasm, happened upon a newer set of phrases, which left the ancient forms of eulogy far behind them. The fountains of public admiration were opened. The praises of the new candidate for applause and sixpences, sounded from the high places of authority, were heard repeated at every corner. The singer was pronounced to be one who could sing louder, squeak longer, and prolong the note through a more numerous and symmetrical set of quavers than any vocalist of past or present celebrity. She was, in short, the last lion of the town, and absorbed in her own glory, for a season, its thousand phrases of hyperbole.

As a general rule I never suffer myself to do as all the town does; but on this occasion I fell into the current and went forward with the stream. I had my reasons, apart from any curiosity either to see the lion or to hear his roar, which induced me to depart from my wonted resolution. I fancied that the music of the new performer would impair my recollection of the old, and do away with the impression of that which I had lost so suddenly. Up to this time I still deceived myself with the fancy that all my interest in the unknown creature whom I so much missed, had been the pure result of her musical sweetness and superiority. I went—the house was full to overflowing—all hearts save my own were full of expectancy and impatience. The curtain rose—the crowd roared and clapped. With an indifference the most unfashionable, I looked up at the performer, and beheld in the famous Prima Donna, my own musical Unknown!

CHAPTER VIII.

It may be readily imagined that my indifference, from that instant, disappeared. I was now all eyes and ears and devoted attention. I drank in every sound, watched every expression, and was ready to believe any extravagance which the public enthusiasm might exhibit or express. She was triumphant in her performances that night. She was said, by the critics, even to have surpassed herself. Opinion had but one voice, and that was admiration; feeling but one emotion, and that was love. She was, indeed, a most lovely creature. Her form, which I now beheld entire, and in a perfect light, for the first time, was one, harmoniously rounded into grace, whose every movement seemed to swell into expression. She looked admirably the character she played—for the time she was—one of those sylphs of the moonlight and the sea, which breathed in poetic spirituality from the works of the ancient masters of English romance. Nor was the intellectual spirituality of her appearance, lessened by the unvarying sadness which prevailed upon her countenance,—a sadness not unfitly suited to the looks of a being otherwise pure and designing to be so,—born for heaven, and ultimately secure of it, but whom, a single, sad lapse, has banished into short but painful exile from its bright and blessing abodes.

I cannot say that I listened to, or even heard, the music. The seat which I occupied was in the pit, and so near to the footlights—the orchestra being between, that I could note every change in the expression of her face. I may have deceived myself, but I certainly fancied, that she at length saw mine. If she did, she read a volume in the quivering of my lip—in the tearful admiration of my eye. There was one period in her performance when I *know* that she beheld me. She had advanced to the outer edge of the proscenium in obedience to the action of the piece. My emotions had been gaining strength for a considerable time before. Heedless of the impropriety I had risen from my seat, and without a consciousness of my folly until forcibly drawn back to my place by some one behind me, my motion towards the stage had corresponded entirely with hers. The good people ascribed to a music frenzy the absurdity of my conduct. But she—she knew better; she saw the movement of my person—she beheld the outstretched action of my hand, and never could intelligence like hers, mistake the unequivocal language in my eye. Her countenance changed on the instant—I could see *that*, though I could see little else—her cheeks became flushed, her lips trembled and her voice for the first time faltered as she sung, while her eye was fixed upon me with a tearful but sweet intensity of gaze.

Let it be remembered that I was little more than a boy at this period—that I had seen very little of the witchery of dramatic representation—that I had no sort of suspicion of guile in the heart of one, who could personate innocence and grief quite as truly as her own form and features personated loveliness—that I looked upon the ideal in all things, and knew nothing of the real; and believed that truth was an undoubted presence, for ever manifested where it was professed. To those who have been once young, I need not undertake to account for this confidence in the humanities—to those who are still young, there will be no need for me to make any such attempt. Enough that I looked, listened and believed. I will not say that I loved. I am not sure that there is any passion in the heart of man worthy of the name of love, until the character is fixed by experience, and the heart subdued by some degree of suffering. Perhaps it will be quite enough to admit that my passions were active—my sensibilities—without referring to any more subtle influence.

CHAPTER IX.

I waited with indescribable impatience for the close of the performance, and was the first, when she retired from the stage, to leave the theatre. I went round and stationed myself at the place of private egress. My former adventure under her window had taught me to be cautious, and I took care to place myself as much in shadow as possible. Here I watched and waited, counting the moments as if they had been hours, and even reproaching the object of my admiration, as if she had known that I awaited her. In reality there was no great delay. It might have been a half hour after her share in the performance was ended when she came forth, conducted by her ancient protector. They passed close beside me, her garments brushed against me, and her eye, keen and quickened, as

I fancied by feelings like my own, rested full upon my face. Involuntarily, she seemed to pause, and I trembled with a secret joy which the restraints upon it seemed to heighten. Her attendant, however, hurried her forward, fortunately without beholding me, and I only lingered long enough behind to avoid awakening his suspicions.

I had not far to follow them. At the corner of the same street a carriage stood in waiting, into which she entered, closely followed by her protector. Vainly did I stretch my head forward to catch the words of direction which he uttered to the driver. My hope was about to be defeated, and all my labour taken in vain. There was but a single alternative. I bounded forward lightly, and, amidst the rattle of the carriage as it rolled away from the stand, placed myself upon the flat in the rear without detection.

Our course lay toward the suburbs, but on a side of the city as far as possible from that which they had left. My anxieties while we rode were prodigious. I heard the occasional words which were spoken by those within the vehicle—those of the man were most frequent,—hers were monosyllables only, and so faintly spoken that I could not divine their character. I would have given worlds to have risen upon the flat and looked in upon the ill-connected couple, but I dared not incur the risk of such a movement. At length we approached our stopping place. The speed of the horses was lessened —the carriage was about to stop, and I leapt to the ground in anticipation of this event. A tree, one of the few which city improvements had left in the neighbourhood, yielded me a covering from which I beheld without difficulty the new place of retreat which the fugitives had chosen. The edifice itself in which they lived was of that better sort, which amply testified to the successes and improved fortunes of the Prima Donna. It was now of brick, newly built, two stories in height, with green blinds, a small verandah on the southern side, and a little patch of green sward in front. You passed to the door of the dwelling through a low white paling gate, upon a neatly gravelled walk edged with box, trimmed grenadier fashion, in stiff, slender and unbroken lines. I made these observations that night after the departure of the carriage. I gave myself ample time for the survey, for it grew rapidly to the small hours of the morning before I left the spot and returned to my own lodging house.

Shall I confess my folly? The next night found me again at the theatre, and every night on which she did not perform, I was a ghostlike stalker through the lonely street—to me not lonely—in which she lived. She saw me not—she knew not of my proximity, though I sometimes fancied, with the vanity of a youthful spirit, that she suspected it. She had seen me at the theatre—she had seen me beneath the lamp on the night when I followed her home. She could not doubt the admiration which was expressed by my action and my eyes, and surely, she knew enough of the nature of man to know that where his heart is, there will his form be also. I drew conviction, on this head, from another fact. Nightly and constantly she sang while I traversed the *pavé* before her dwelling; and the strains were those of a sad tenderness, of a heart pouring forth the irrepressible moans of a defeated love. At the theatre, her eyes—so I persuaded myself—frequently sought out mine; and it seemed to me, at such moments, that her song trembled, and her voice became subdued, even though the burden of the music called for the greatest exertion of her powers. How small and shadowy are the tokens which persuade the youthful imagination into confidence and hope!

CHAPTER X.

The passion which this girl had awakened in my bosom was such as to lead me to a complete departure from many of my usual habits. I now remembered certain old acquaintance among the editorial fraternity—clever, good-humoured fellows—who, I well knew, possessed *carte blanche* at all the theatres. One of these, in particular,—a vivacious literary and political writer—a fellow who could write a comedy after supper and a review before breakfast, and who was sufficiently popular in the community to do as he pleased with every body—had been a frequent companion of my idle hours during my first acquaintance with New York. Him I had seen frequently at the theatre while my inamorata was playing, and his voice, through the medium of his papers, had been one of the loudest in her eulogy. I resolved on renewing my acquaintance with him, and availing myself, as far as I could, of the privileges which he possessed to procure some of those which I desired. I did accordingly. I called on him, and after listening to his good-humoured reproaches at what he was pleased to call my neglect of old friends, I plainly told him what I came for. I wished an introduction to the Prima Donna.

"Ah, ha!" said he—"so you too are among the thousand in the meshes of Mam'selle ———."

"She is then unmarried?" I exclaimed—"she is not the wife of ———"

"The little old Othello that has her in keeping! Well! of that the least said the better. We know nothing. Enough to tell you that she passes for his wife, and for aught that any body knows in New York, she may be."

"But you call her 'Mam'selle?'"

"True, but that means nothing. A miss is always more attractive in theatrical parlance than a mistress; and I have known, in Green Room history, a woman who had buried eleven husbands, more or less, who never once changed her maiden name in the bills! This is only a trick of trade, and the stage, as you should know, has, perhaps, a hundred and one tricks beyond any other craft or profession. Mam'selle ——— is assuredly married to the little old Italian; and if not married——"

A shrug of the shoulder finished the sentence of my editorial friend, very little to my satisfaction.

"The story goes," he continued, "that he happened upon the poor girl in London, while in a state of great destitution, just after she had lost a mother, or while the mother was in the last stages of decay. That he provided them with present means, and availing himself of their necessities, married the girl,——"

"Against her will?" I interrupted.

"No—not so—against her wish, perhaps, but not against her will. Destitution, and poverty, and hunger, have no will in such a place as London; and famine will reconcile a girl, however lovely, to a very strange connection. Mam'selle, who is English by birth, was thus persuaded to couple with this Italian, who makes himself very ridiculous here by his jealousies. He has already had a dozen quarrels where he had no cause for one; for, though the girl is a sort of rage at present—a distinction which she owes more to me than to herself—yet she is not deluded by applause, and takes it as humbly as if she knew its real value as well as the oldest veteran among us. If you really desire an introduction, after what you have heard, I don't see that there will be any difficulty. She will be at rehearsal to-day at 12, M., and the matter can be easily managed."

I readily embraced the proposition. He continued:

"A week more will finish her career in New York. The rage now, she will soon give place to another novelty, and in ten days more be among the things that were. We are to have, by the next packet, a celebrated Harlequin, who can jump twenty feet high, take the ceiling in his teeth, and hold on thereby sufficiently long, to enable him to poach a dozen eggs for his supper by a machine which he takes up with him for that purpose. His legs, meanwhile, not to be outdone, are to go through all the movements of the famous Tilsit Waltz, and at the close he professes to be able to shuffle them off, with his boots, and drop down, finally, with his stumps again falling into the dismembered sockets, as truly as if the position had undergone mathematical arrangement."

"Oh, nonsense!"

"Well, I doubt not that the report of his wonders is somewhat exaggerated, but the report is enough. It will kill Mam'selle most effectually for the season, so that, to know her in the day of her glory, you must know her at once. I shall look for you at 12."

CHAPTER XI.

I was punctual. The hour was fortunately chosen. Mam'selle was in the Green Room alone. Her ugly little protector was absent—where, it mattered not to me,—so long as he was absent; and I had at length the felicity of speaking to the fair creature, whom, hitherto, I had not been permitted to approach. My address, I had reason to believe, said little in my favour. I was flushed, confused, agitated. I feel that I stammered while speaking the most customary nonsense; and I was so little the master of my own faculties, that I could not tell whether her composure was less or more than mine. But, in either event, perhaps, I had no reason for annoyance. If the woman, in such a case, preserves her composure—if she be any thing of a veteran in the arts of life—it does not displease her to look on the bashfulness of the unsophisticated heart of youth. There is a compliment conveyed by his terrors which is grateful, because of its freshness, to the heart which is no longer so: and if she was not composed—if like myself she trembled and was confounded, then it followed that my emotion must have escaped her sight. My friend, the Editor, congratulated me on my leaving the apartment upon the obvious impression which I had made. Before we left her the company began to pour in—the various assemblage of a good stock-management. There were others too, not of the company,—who possessed the privileges of the interior—to whom the wires might be shown, and the mechanism of the magic, without danger. There were the Editors—a numerous tribe—the writers for the stage, some of the proprietors of the establishment, and a few of the dashing bloods of the town. To all of these the Prima Donna was the eye of attraction—the centre of the solar system in that little world. I felt myself very small and very awkward, when I witnessed the dashing freedom and consequential airs of most around me, as they approached to converse with one whose very glance had so completely unsettled my nervous system.—Finally, the little, old Italian, her protector, made his appearance, and with his *entrée* you would have fancied that we had suddenly fallen in with a mountain of ice. Every thing was frigid after his appearance. The dandies bowed at a more respectful distance, at the object of their previous devotion, while his little fiery eyes seemed to scrutinize every countenance with suspicion, and to find in every movement abundant cause to congratulate himself on having arrived in the very nick of time to prevent the worst of mischiefs.

To me, he gave less attention than I feared would have fallen to my lot. I had even begun to think that he failed to recognize me, and should certainly have believed so, but for a single sentence which he uttered with a sinister grin, as we underwent the usual forms of introduction to one another.

"You be love music, vera moch, sare, I remembair, eh?"

The remark was simple in the ears of all but the Prima Donna and myself. I took care to regard it as such in the reply I made at the moment; but I remembered it, and availed myself of the opening which it gave me—for purposes of explanation—to call upon the couple at their residence.

CHAPTER XII.

I did so, and found the Prima Donna alone. I was this time sufficiently calm myself, to see that she was terribly agitated. Her dress and whole appearance were disordered. Her hair had found partial freedom from restraint,—her eyes were red with weeping, —and the traces of recent tears were apparent upon her pallid cheeks. She met me with a look full of equal intelligence and alarm.

"Oh! why, why have you come hither? Leave me, leave me, I implore you, sir—it is not well—it is not right; and he will believe every thing that is wrong. Leave me, sir, leave me if you——"

How would she have finished that sentence had her tongue not failed in its office? I had barely time to form a pleasing conjecture on the subject—not to answer—when the little old Italian burst into the room, with the fiery, fearful, malignant aspect of a Sirocco. The poor woman sank upon a settee at his appearance, and covered her face with both her hands. The big tears oozed through her fingers, and her sobs were almost convulsions.

"Ha! ha! what for you come to my house. You lov' music, but I break up de music—look you, I break up de music—so! so!—"

And with the action of a madman, seizing upon a guitar which lay upon one of the tables, he dashed it into a thousand fragments by repeated blows against the elbow of the sofa. Then turning to me, he exclaimed—

"You is villain, sare. I is turn out, tree, five villain from my house dis day, and break up de music. You is great villain, and you is come to my house,—dere is no more music in my house,—what for you is come, eh?"

I had risen on his entrance. I could scarcely contain myself during his proceedings. The tears of the girl had awakened my indignation—his brutality scarcely left me prudence to forbear violence, which seemed to be almost the duty of a gentleman under existing circumstances. Nothing but a consideration of her claims, and the wretched relation in which she stood to this miserable tyrant, kept my hands from his throat. For her sake, I subdued my tiger,—for her sake, I strove to answer mildly. I contented myself with saying that I came to explain my conduct in the previous interview when he was so much offended. But the violent old wretch did not allow me to finish what I was saying. He gave me the lie direct.

"You come for make my wife lef' me, and go wid you. You tell lie—you is one villain, dat I shall make lef' my house for evare."

My blood was getting the better of my judgment, when the Prima Donna interposed. She rose from her seat with the manner of one who has conquered, but after a violent effort, and about whom still remain all the traces of the conflict.

"Oblige me, sir, if you please, by leaving the house; oblige me still more by avoiding it, and me, for ever. To acquire a friend is with me a misfortune—I need one, how much, Heaven only knows—but I wish for none. Leave me, sir; and, in going, believe me, that *I* at least suspect you of no evil, and am as grateful to you as if you meant nothing but good. If you fancy that you leave me unhappy, at least be satisfied that nothing which you could do or say would have the effect of making me otherwise."

"Ha! you speaks to him in dis manner. You will have me kill you to death, you ———"

I forbear to repeat the horrible epithet which the monster used on this occasion. His words provoked me to fury, but when he coupled them with a blow—a blow by his vile hands upon that pure, sweet, imploring and noble face,—my fury became violence. I grasped him in my arms. I lifted him as if he had been an infant, in spite of all his struggles. I hurried with him to the window, the sash of which was raised, and a moment longer would have sufficed me to pitch him into the street. But my better angel, in the aspect of the wretched woman, his victim, came to keep me from a deed which I might have repented in suffering and shame. She recovered from the blow which had staggered her against the wall, and grasped my arm in season. I put the reptile down unharmed upon the floor, and he seized the first moment of his liberty to hurry from the apartment, not without giving a glance at the woman, which spoke volumes of treasured bitterness and revenge.

CHAPTER XIII.

My situation was now one of considerable awkwardness, and it did not lessen my annoyance to reflect that it was one into which I had been hurried by my own unregulated passions and imprudent vanity. But this was no moment for reflections such as these. It was evident that I now had no business there, even if the business had been legitimate which had carried me there at first. To remain longer in the house of one who had ordered my departure in language of brutality, and whose conduct had provoked me to violence, was surely against all received rules of gentility. And yet, how to leave the poor woman to his rage? Would he not wreak upon her weak person and unoffending head, all the venom which would be idly shown against the bosom of superior manhood? This was my apprehension—the apprehension that made me linger,—it was evident that the Prima Donna, herself, was not entirely without it.

"Do not—do not leave me," she exclaimed passionately, as she beheld his departure, while with hands clasped in something like a mortal agony of fear, she approached me. "He will soon return—he is terrible in his anger—he will do some dreadful act."

"Fear nothing—I will protect—I will stand by you to the last."

I spoke with the look and language of a knight of the middle ages. Forgetful of the matter-of-fact and every-day character of the busy world around me—the age of money-changers and their greatest mart,—I was hurried away by my boyish feelings, and utterly lost in the seventh heaven of heroism. I would have taken her hand in mine as I addressed her; but the attempt brought about an instant change in her manner. The fear of doing, seemed suddenly greater than that of suffering, wrong; and in tears no less energetic if less passionate than before, she now entreated my departure.

"Go, for God's sake, and leave me, leave me for ever. I do not blame you—no, no! But you cannot know the mischief you have done. My husband will never forgive me for this folly; and every moment of your longer stay will increase the difficulties, perhaps the dangers, in my way."

I told her there should be no difficulties—no dangers—that I would stand by and shield her from all harm. At that moment I felt myself equal to every danger; and would have faced the giant Ascaparte himself in her battle. But she knew her own relation to her jealous liege, and resolutely insisted upon my departure. I lingered until longer delay would have been impertinence, and then prepared to comply with her demand. But before leaving I proffered my assistance in the event of any further difficulty. I put my card into her hand. She calmly tore it into fragments which she threw into the grate.

"No, sir, no: I thank you, but you can render me no help—I shall need no assistance. I only ask you not to see me—not to know me any more. Forget that you have ever seen me."

"Impossible!"

She silenced my raptures by an impatient movement of her hand, and the sad sorrow of her countenance was exchanged to an expression of dignified purity, as she thus rebuked my extravagance. My passion yielded to respect. Her beauty and talent aroused the one—her virtuous and becoming conduct commanded the other. I bowed and was turning away, when, as if moved by some fear that her sternness had given pain, her features softened—she advanced—gave me her hand for a moment, then left me hurriedly for an inner chamber.

CHAPTER XIV.

I find it difficult for me to close this narrative. The events startle myself as I recall them with an air of utter improbability;—and yet I know them to be true, and how many share my knowledge. The next week the famous Prima Donna—she who had been the orb of loveliest attraction, rising nightly in song and splendour before the eyes of the whole city—the next week she had not only survived her glory, but was a corpse! She went to rehearsal the morning after the scene which I have just described was over; and, though indisposed, she played successfully that night. I saw her, and saw that there was a serious sickness in her system; but I ascribed the sickness rather to her soul than to her body—to that poor heart—so fond, so young, so tender, so attractive,—sacrificed in the first hour of its maiden dawn to such a dreadful tyranny as that from which she suffered. For two nights after, being those of Saturday and Sunday, I saw nothing of her. Monday night she was announced to play, but her malady had increased—she did not appear, and her absence was accounted for by the manager. Tuesday produced a crisis in her professional fortunes. The great harlequin, who could jump twenty feet and take the ceiling in his teeth, made his appearance that night with wondrous éclat, and the Prima Donna, as my friend the editor had predicted, was almost as much forgotten as if she had never been. The next morning she was dead! The terrible annunciation came to me, while at the breakfast-table, in the morning papers:

"*Mysterious.* We are told, just as our paper was going to press, that Mam'selle ———, the lady who has been making such a sensation in the musical circles of our city for the last ten days, died suddenly last night, at the house of her protector, Mons. ———, in ———'s Place. There are some circumstances connected with this event which have awakened the suspicions of the police. An examination by the coroner takes place at an early hour this morning. The lady was young, very pretty, and singularly well constituted for the part of Prima Donna in the company to which she was attached. She was acknowledged by Mons. ———, to be his wife, and her virtue is stated to be beyond reproach, though, we understand, it has not been without suspicion. We trust for the credit of our city, that her death will be found to have taken place according to the ordinary events of nature."

What a shock did I feel when I read this paragraph. I felt as if sight had been suddenly deprived me; but I recovered instantly to the most acute excitement of feeling. I darted up from the table, hurried to my chamber, put myself in condition to go forth, and reached the dwelling of the lovely victim in time for the examination. I too had my suspicions of foul play, and in my heart I swore that the malignant wretch who claimed to be her husband, and who, I felt sure, must have been her murderer, should not escape from the talons of justice and a just punishment, if my vigilance could fix them upon him.

A crowd was already assembled, and the coroner busy in telling out jurors for the examination. The corpse of the victim was placed at length upon a table. The eyes were closed—the features composed—she had died seemingly without a struggle, and this appeared to prove that she had died without pain. The presumptions were, accordingly, in favour of the supposition that her death had been natural. Not a muscle seemed out of place, governed by extreme tension, or strained in the slightest particular. The blood-vessels of the neck and forehead were charged fully, and shone,—oh, how freshly with life and beauty,—through the clean transparent whiteness of her skin. I could have bent down, amidst all that crowd, and pressed my lips upon those rigid features which had teemed, but a few days before, with all that was pure, and sweet, and charming, in my sight.

The examination led to no discoveries, though it was conducted with considerable closeness and sagacity. The coroner was familiar with his duties, and not disposed to pretermit their exercise. He was acute in his inquiries and closely observant of the persons who were examined as witnesses. Among these was Mons. ———. His features, now passionless and cold, dark yet inexpressive, confirmed the impressions of my own bosom that he was guilty of her death. How was it that he, who, while she lived, had been jealous to madness of all her movements, should so soon, so suddenly, lose all interest in her fate, unless he himself knew the fitting solution of the mystery. This, though to me conclusive, of the one conviction, was quite as conclusive with all around me of his innocence. His composure was in his favour. Strange enough! as if a man who was innocent of her murder, could have looked with composure, upon the inanimate form of one who had lately slept upon his bosom, whose eyes had gleamed with fire, whose cheeks with youth—whose voice had sent forth such heavenward aspirations of tenderness and love.

A cautious verdict of the jury finished the investigation. She "died from the visitation of God." True: death from any cause, however strange,—however hurried—is still a visitation of God—God in that form of power which is most terrible to man. The glance of dire enmity and malignant hate which the Italian shot towards me from his half-shut eyes, as the verdict was declared, convinced me, not the less, however, that she died also from the "visitation of the devil." His black heart had decreed her doom—his viperous hands had compassed it—his Italian art had enabled him to do so with impunity. "After life's fitful fever she sleeps well!" —The murderer still lives, but is he, therefore, the less a token of God's eternal justice? Has he escaped punishment? Is he safe? No! no! The hangman is for ever present to his imagination—fear dogs his footsteps—he is haunted by the hounds of terror—he breathes the breath of sleepless apprehension—bitterness is in the bread he eats, and venom in the cup from which he drinks. He lives a prolonged form of death, only too happy if it could be that he might not live for ever.

THE END.

[*Simms first published "The Unknown Masque" in April, 1845, in the* Southern and Western Monthly Magazine and Review, *popularly known as "Simms's Magazine," which he edited in Charleston throughout 1845. Explanatory and Textual Notes begin on page 697.*]

THE UNKNOWN MASQUE.
A Sketch of the Crescent City.

"One unsummon'd came,
And placed his unknown feet upon the hearth,
And straight the room grew dark."

It was in the winter of 1825-6 that I paid my first visit to the "Crescent City." New-Orleans was not then the wondrous place that it has since become; but it was sufficiently so, even at that early day, to turn the head of a backwoodsman. Before that time, I had never been beyond the little country village in West Tennessee, which was the nearest market town to my father's plantation. I had never known the advantages of travel, nor seen any thing of the great world, 'till, at eighteen, I went down the Mississippi, to that Queen of Cities—so she is destined to become—sitting nearly at its mouth. All things were new to me, but I travelled with a friend, who, though not five years older than myself, had passed frequently over the same region, and was able to enlighten me on all the matters about which I was ignorant. He had relatives in New-Orleans—a sister married to a wealthy Creole, who spent a portion of every winter in that place. He made her frequent visits, and being of a lively imaginative turn, had contrived to discover all that was curious and attractive in and about the city. Its walks and theatres, its *cafés* and hells—for New-Orleans could then boast some eight or ten of these licensed and well named haunts of crime and dissipation—were all familiar to his experience. Not that he himself was dissipated. He was only curious. He could gaze without being fascinated, touch without being defiled, and was altogether a man of most extraordinary powers of caution and resistance, mixed up with eagerness and curiosity. To him I owe it, that I fell not into the snares, the secret and the danger of which he equally unveiled before my sight. As he had no doubts of himself, no apprehensions of his own weakness, he went every where without scruple, and I with him. I could tell some queer things about our wanderings—but these may serve hereafter. Suffice it now, that, in three weeks, I could myself have served as *cicerone* to the stranger in New-Orleans, with quite as much credit as one half the native citizens.

Through my friend's sister I obtained access to society. This is not so easy a matter where the French Creoles are concerned. They are a proud aristocratic people, and half detest and half despise, the new men of Anglo-Saxon blood, who seek their fortunes in the extreme south. The American trading population is their aversion. They think better of the same race when not engaged in commerce. This distinction favored me. But my friend's sister, Madame C——, provided me with a sufficient passport. I went under her wing. I had a little smattering of French which contributed to my progress, and being of lively but unobtrusive habits, I made my way with tolerable success, and soon had the *entree* of several noble houses. Invitations poured in upon me, and one delightful Wednesday in January, found R. F. and myself in the same chamber, eagerly and anxiously busy in adjusting our habits for the masque-ball of Madame Elinor de B——. This lady was a belle and a fortune. She was the young widow of the—at one time—celebrated Col. Eugene de B——, a famous swordsman and sugar planter. His death had been sudden; but he was twenty years the senior of his wife, and her grief was of no long duration. Eleven months before had she yielded his mortal remains to the earth, and we were now to enjoy, at her dwelling, the most splendid and picturesque masquerade that had ever taken place in New-Orleans. New-Orleans will long remember the event in the curious circumstances which it occasioned.

I was excited to the last degree with expectation. It was my first appearance in such a scene. I had heard of masqued balls in Europe —of their splendor—their intrigue—the humor which they brought forth, the wit and merriment which they stimulated—and, to confess a truth, I had some vague notions of personal adventure—of some romantic encounter with beauty, and wealth, and sensibility, combined under some quaint disguise which I was to penetrate, and find myself happy in a happy conquest. My friend R. F. had his expectations also. He did not withhold them from me. But he knew the object of his desires. That portion of the romance which arises from the mystery, was wanting to his case. His eye was fixed on no less a person than the widow herself, by whom the masquerade was given. He already knew her, and flattered himself that he had found favor in her sight. I can answer for it that she looked upon him graciously. He was not without his attractions. A more manly fellow never went from Tennessee—a more graceful never trode the apartments of splendor. Brave, frank, generous, R. F. was not wanting in other accomplishments. But he lacked wealth, and this deficiency most usually produces hesitation and doubt, in the sensitive mind, when approaching the woman who is endowed with it. Such is the result of our present modes of thinking in society.

I have said that Madame Elinor de B—— was a *belle*. She deserved to be so, and would have been so in spite of her fortune. She was but twenty-three at the time of which I speak, and never did more beautiful or princely creature glide through the measured majesty of dance. Her form was large and eminently symmetrical—her carriage was equally easy and dignified. Her features were not regular, but their united expression carried you away from any analysis of details which might have resulted in an unfavorable decision upon them. You saw not the deficiency of charms which dazzled the glance, and baffled the colder judgment, and the mind submitted with the eye, and the heart yielded, at the first summons, to a nameless influence which was always irresistible to enslave. Such was the effect of this lady's beauty upon others. In this way it won my companion. R. F. was her captive when he first visited New-Orleans. He had always been her worshipper. He had yielded to her beauty without resistance, and prudent and resolved in almost every other matter—in all affairs of dissipation for example—in his passion for Elinor de B——, he was quite as rash as the least prudent youngster that ever started from the leash at twenty-one.

Strange to say, the beauty of this lady had never satisfied myself. That she was a woman of many and imposing beauties, I could easily see and admit. It was the style and character of her beauty that did not please me. I felt that there was something strange in the very intensity of her glance. The eye was brilliant, but the effect upon myself was chilling. It was the brilliancy of the diamond, perhaps, but it seemed to possess its hardness also. The lady had a habit of looking on you fixedly—into your eye,—her own glittering the while with a thousand fires of which she seemed to be unconscious. Sometimes, while thus gazing upon you, your speech would utterly fail to command her attention. Her mind seemed to be wandering. These were peculiarities which I did not conceive to be pleasant ones. Her hair was of a light brown, her eye was hazel, her complexion dazzlingly fair, and distinguished by the most delicate but glowing red that ever kindled woman's cheek to loveliness. But there was something in the frequent quivering of her thin lips which produced an uncomfortable sensation; and she had a habit of drawing in her breath, at moments of abstraction, with a slight sobbing sound, such as an infant gives out, after having cried itself to sleep. I confess, these were matters, which, however slight they may seem to others, very much tended to qualify my admiration of her charms. R. F. did not perceive them himself, or regarded them as beauties.

—

The affair was one of the most splendid things that I had ever seen. Indeed, I could not well conceive of any thing in this country more magnificent. The huge double mansion of Madame de B——, in the *Rue des* ——— was illuminated from attic to cellar, and the long treble line of carriages which crowded the street at an early hour in the night, declared, as much as any thing else, for the sensation which the affair had produced throughout the city. The broad passage way through which you entered, was crowded as we made our appearance, and we had come soon in order to secure good places against the crowd. My eyes were dazzled with the glare of lights, and the glowing richness and grand varieties of costume. Knights and Princes, and Cardinals, Earls and Dukes, famous individual characters of all periods and both sexes, from the time of Solomon to that of Louis XVI., were encountered at every step, but mine is not a catalogue, and the reader must conceive them for himself. We struggled through the dense and shifting masses with great difficulty, till we reached the *dais* of reception. Madame de B—— shone like a star of the first magnitude, and as I presented Madame, the sister of R. F. whom I escorted, I felt very much like falling upon one knee in an obeisance to her beauty, which had never seemed to me so completely pure and unqualified as now. R. F. was almost convulsed with his rapturous and but half suppressed admiration. I could see, as I fancied, that she smiled particularly on him. She was aware of the habits in which we came. In this respect, she possessed an advantage over all the circle. It was one of the modes adopted for securing the company from the obtrusion of improper persons that each invited guest bore a card with her signature, and upon his acceptance of her invitation, apprized her of the costume in which he would appear. For a moment, I could see that her eye lingered upon the erect form of my friend, shrouded as it was, in the flowing garments of an Egyptian. Then we gave way to other visitors. At a signal, Madame de B—— disappeared from the hall of reception, and when she again re-appeared, it was only to be lost among the thousand masques, of whom nothing could be known but by conjecture. The music timed all our proceedings, whether we danced, or walked, or took refreshments. Now we grew together in groups, interested by the attractive and spirited dialogue of some two masks doing more than usual justice to their assumed characters,—and now we lingered over the prophecies of a saucy gypsy, or followed laughing upon the ludicrous footsteps of the Italian Harlequin. It was not long before the very monotonous and somewhat silly exordium on these occasions,—the "*Je te Connais!*" with which every thing in the shape of conversation begins, yielded to settled dialogue. The groups had subsided into pairs, each drawing aside the mask which promised most pleasure, or satisfied that vanity which did not relish being left alone. Of my own adventures and successes, I can say but little. My fortune was not a prominent or highly promising one. I had my companion, and changed her, often enough, and more frequently than was needful or prudent, if the truth were known; but I made no conquests—prevailed upon none to remove their masks, and was rather fatigued than delighted before the sports were well over. But such had not been the case with R. F. He came to me a little after midnight. The clock upon the mantle had been silenced, and, half tired, I was stealing a glance at my watch concealed in the folds of my vest, when he laid his hand upon my arm. I turned with a guilty consciousness.

"Fie!" said he, "looking at your watch! It would not do for Madame de B—— to see you."

"No! where is she—in what dress."

"Hush! she is not far off—there, as Zenobia. Is she not a glorious being."

"She is!—she approaches!"

At these words, R. F. turned and advanced towards her. She took his arm, and they disappeared among the crowd. It would seem that they understood each other. A group of masks, loud in merriment, drew nigh, and I shrunk back into the recess of a window half shaded by rich curtains of white and red, and there threw myself upon a pile of cushions. Here I could see much and remain, in great degree, unseen myself. Ten minutes had not passed before I again saw my Egyptian. He approached where I was sitting. I called him in subdued accents. But he gave me no heed. A moment after, he looked round upon me, without recognition and immediately turned away. I rose to follow him, but just then, a huge peasant woman of Savoy, with a long train following her, passed between us and arrested my progress. A second attempt and a third were not more successful, and at length I saw my Egyptian disappear in a distant circle. Hardly had I thus given him up, when he appeared again before me—but this time with a hurried step, and apparently coming from a different direction. I plucked him by the sleeve.

"This time I have you. Well—you have been with her? Does she smile?"

"Scarcely! There's something wrong—something mysterious. Do not be out of the way, W——. I may need your assistance."

"Indeed! What's the matter?"

I then gathered from him the following story. He had joined Madame de B——, as I had seen, and they had retired together into an alcove. There she had proceeded as if resuming a conversation which had been interrupted. The conversation was of a most interesting nature to my friend. Her remarks—her manner of uttering them—were of a kind to betray to him that she entertained a lively interest in himself and fortunes. There was only this difficulty about them, that he had not been privy to that first part which she seemed to assume had taken place between them before. He declared this difficulty. She recoiled from him.

"What mean you, Monsieur F——?"

"My dear Madame, no more than this, that, however grateful to me is what I now gather from your lips, this is the first moment when you have spoken to me on the subject."

"What! you forget!"

"On my honor"—

"Ah, Monsieur, how can this be so—when but a few moments ago, we were interrupted by that ever troublesome Parisian who would be a Count Poniatowski."

"You have been deceived. I was not with you at that moment. I was not present at such an interruption."

"Impossible."

"It is true! This is the first moment to-night, when I have been honored with your conversation."

"Ciel! and to whom have I spoken! There are two then."

"Two!"

"Yes! yes! Two Egyptians. Monsieur F—— if you love me, find out the other, and bring him to me. Remember—no strife, no quarrel—I must not be compromised."

—

This was the substance of what I got from F., and what took place between himself and the woman he pursued, and who certainly seemed to favor him. I told him what I had seen of the Egyptian whom I had approached, and who did not seem to know me.

"He, then, is the intruder, for I have not been near you since we parted, when you were looking at your watch. You must join me in the search for him. We will separate for this purpose. I will take one route, you the other. The word between us shall be—what?"

"Right! Ready!"

"Be it so! Spoken only by myself. You will need none!"

Turning to separate, we met the very person we were preparing to seek. His habit seemed the very *fac simile* of that of R. F. His person was the same in height and bulk. No wonder that Madame de B—— should be deceived. R. F. instantly approached him. His anxiety as to what had taken place between the stranger and the lady,—the doubt lest she might be compromised,—the vexation that the other had listened to words meant only for him, and words too, which, if they were of the kind to which he had been a brief listener, were of too precious a description to be lavished idly,—these considerations made the movements and the speech of R. F. equally prompt and decided. He tapped the stranger on the shoulder, and led him aside.

"A word with you, sir."

"A dozen, if you please," was the answer, in cold and measured accents.

"Who are you, sir, and by what right are you here?"

"Really, young gentleman, you challenge my rights as if your own were exclusive. Madame Elinor de B—— could better answer your question."

"It is by her that I am authorized to make the demand."

"Ah! it is by her then! Well,—go to her, and say that if she desires it, I will unmask for her satisfaction, in her presence;—but, mark me, only in her presence!"

"Enough! W——, you will remain with the stranger. See that he does not escape you."

This was said in a whisper, as R. F. disappeared. The simulacrum was no ways disquieted. Our proceedings had not been so quietly conducted, but that they had reached other ears, and curious eyes were peering around us. My friend soon found his princess. He communicated what had taken place with the stranger.

"Insolent!" was the exclamation of the haughty lady.

"Say but the word," was the whisper of R. F., "and I fling him from the window."

"No! no!" said she, with a pleased and flattering smile,—"no, monsieur,—that would only spoil the assembly; and besides, it may be some friend or acquaintance,—some stranger in the city,—who knows me well, and who should have been invited. There may be some mistake. I grant him the interview. Conduct him to the opposite apartment, to which I will lead the way. You will wait upon us at the door."

These instructions were not given unheard, and by the time that R. F. got back to where I was standing with the stranger, there was quite a smart little excitement in the assembly. Our Egyptian remained the while in a perfect state of composure. Nobody could have seemed more perfectly at his ease; and we all began to take for granted, as Madame de B—— had suggested, that, if not an invited guest, he should have been, and it would turn out, either that he was some distinguished friend of the family, or some one about whose invitation and costume there had been some mistake. When R. F. drew nigh and communicated the charge of Madame de B——, the stranger immediately took his way to the chamber. R. F. kept beside him, and I followed close behind, with some half dozen eyes, curious to see into the mystery, if any, and be the first to declare it to the crowd. When we reached the door of the room where Madame awaited him, the masque entered, and R. F. followed him. I closed the door and held it firmly. But, in a moment after, R. F. came out, the stranger positively refusing to unmask unless he did so. Then followed a few words from Madame. We could hear the dignified tones of her voice, sweet still, in spite of its majesty. A subdued murmur followed. Then silence, and then a shriek,—a shriek of horror and agony and terror, such as I never wish to hear again. This was succeeded by the noise of a falling body,—with the rattle of a chair, which seemed to have been crushed at the same instant. The whole thing was over in a moment, and in the next, R. F., not waiting for me to open it, drove the door with his foot. We rushed in, followed by a crowd, and there was Madame de B—— prostrate, senseless, with her face prone upon the floor. But the Egyptian was nowhere to be seen. How had he escaped? The windows were all closed. He had not passed by us. There was but one other door to the apartment, and that led into the ball-room and was locked.

We raised Madame de B—— from the floor. She was utterly unconscious. Her lips were livid,—her eyes open wide, and glaring upon us with a terrible vacancy, that declared more emphatically than any words, the degree of horror and affright to which she had been subjected. She recovered her consciousness after some hours, in which it was doubtful whether life remained in her heart or not.

—

Months after this event, R. F. had an interview with the woman whom he still loved most devotedly. She had corresponded with him meanwhile,—that is to say, she had answered his letters, but had given him no encouragement. His hopes depended upon a personal interview. That he had partially won her affections before, there is no reason to doubt. That he had extorted from her a confession of preference, I have every reason to believe. But all was changed after that fatal masquerade. When R. F. renewed his suit, she answered him only with tears. When he pleaded most earnestly, and fell upon his knee before her, she undid the fillet which bound her tresses, once of the most delicate and silk-like auburn, and showed him that they had become white, like those of the Queen of France, in the progress of a single night.

"Is it for such as I am now to think of love, Monsieur F——? How can I reward a heart so young as yours. Besides,—but no! Enough, my friend, that I can never marry."

She was inflexible. She did not live long after, but sunk away into premature old age and infirmity. Two acts of her life, almost immediately following the events of the masked ball, provoked much remark in New-Orleans. She bestowed one-half of her large fortune on a boy, supposed to have been the natural child of her husband, Col. Eugene de B——. The other half went to the convent in which she finally shrouded herself for the grave. Public conjecture took more than one form in regard to the circumstances of terror which had such an effect upon her. By some it was said that the strange Egyptian, when he uncovered his face, betrayed the decaying features of her late husband, and thence grew another suspicion that he had been unfairly dealt with;—others, somewhat less credulous, insisted that the affair was nothing more than the practice of a fraudulent confessor, who, knowing her superstitious tendencies, contrived this mode of alarming them; thus securing for his brotherhood a vast fortune, which otherwise might have fallen into the hands of a heretic from Tennessee,—my poor friend R. F. being understood by this unfriendly designation.

E——.

[*Simms's fascination with mesmerism provides the basis for "Mesmerides in a Stage-Coach," published in* Godey's Lady's Book *for September, 1845. Explanatory and Textual Notes begin on page 701.*]

MESMERIDES IN A STAGE-COACH;
Or, Passes en Passant.

"Here cease more questions.
Thou art inclined to sleep; 'tis a good dullness,
And give it way:—I know thou canst not choose."
* * * * * * * * *
"But release me from my bands
With the help of your good hands."—SHAKSPEARE. *Tempest.*

I.

I was in possession of a new power, a power strange and wonderful—not to be believed if not witnessed, and scarcely then. I had, at an earlier period, laughed, with the rest, at the wonders of Mesmerism, and congratulated myself, with the *soi disant* scientific, in the pharisaical dialect, that "I was not as one of those." But my opinions had undergone a change. I had seen the thing that I had pronounced nothing. It had been made apparent to my sight and understanding—nay, I had felt it with my hands. It was in my fingers, and I, too, was a professor. The silken bands of sleep—iron, if imposed by the Mesmerizer—it was in my power to impose at will. I had set to sleep my fairest enemy. A stubborn and capricious damsel, whom I had otherwise in vain striven to move, my superior will as a magnetizer had subdued to slumber. Her long white fingers rested in my own; I squeezed them—oh, how tenderly—and they were not withdrawn. Her large dark eyes, setting under the glance of mine, sunk from dewy softness into dark. My hands paddled in her long raven tresses, and her head drooped towards me as if it would have sought for rest within my bosom. Was not this a conquest? After this, could I dispute or doubt the rare powers of the magnetizer?

I did not, you may be sure. But circumstances seemed to deny me the privilege of their immediate exercise, now while the first fury of discovery was upon me. I was summoned to a distant part of our forest country, and in leaving my home and the fair friend—my first and only subject—I seemed to leave behind me all occasion for the repetition of my experiments. But the subject haunted me. Mesmerism was a truth, and every truth must have its use. Mesmerism was a power, and every power must have its value. What was the nature of this truth? What was the extent of this power? These were questions. So far, we see that it may be made subservient to the cause of humanity in lessening the amount of physical and mental suffering. It can subdue headache and fever; it produces insensibility to the minor influences of pain. The nerves of sensibility seem to be entirely under its control. Of its other attributes of *clairvoyance*, &c., I say nothing, as, in my own experience, I know nothing. But the rare sympathy which exists between the Mesmerizer and his patient, I was not permitted to doubt. Had I not, through its agency, subdued to tenderness one of my most stubborn enemies among the fair sex? Had she not, ay, even while laughing merrily at the absurdity of my manipulations, fallen beneath them, wept freely amidst her smiles, and, while the words of taunt were yet warm upon her lips, exchanged them for words of dependency, if not of love? Did I not, with uplifted hands, will her adhesion, and did she not follow me from room to room like a tame spaniel, anxious, even to suffering, when I left her sight, and satisfied, even to joy, when she again had me by the arm? Woman, was not that my triumph? Need I tell you that, though something mortified at the result, my once wilful beauty is no longer enemy of mine. I verily believe she was as sorry to see me depart for the great wildernesses of the west as my own wife and child—though she did not say so.

II.

In the stage-coach this new experience troubled me; I could think of nothing else. My mind ran upon long trains of experiments yet to be made. The truth gained was partial only; it was without its application, and till the uses of a truth are known, it must always be considered an imperfect truth. People will ask the why and the wherefore, and until you can give them an answer, they will suspect quackery. My head was full of vague speculations on this subject. My *causality,* which in my case is a rather large development, was interested to find an answer, to explain and solve this mystery, to be able to contend with, if not to satisfy scepticism. Perhaps neither tale nor drama is so absolutely interesting as, to a speculative mind, the analysis of a newly-discovered truth. The details of thought, by which, step by step, we reach a remote and unexpected consequence, sets the brain in as complete a whirl of excitement as the tragic action in romance. The only difference is, that he who *thinks* out his drama, does not show his emotions; and a man may seem to his neighbour excessively sleepy or abominably stupid, who is yet busy in the elaboration of an argument which shall set the North river in a blaze. I suppose I made some such appearance to my companions in the stage-coach. There were two of them. They were unknown to me and unknown to one another. They had taken their seats after me and at different stopping-places along the road. The first was a quiet, good-humoured country squire, who chuckled in an under-tone whenever he heard any thing particularly to please him, and, at the same time, with an adroit use of his tongue, made the huge quid of tobacco that distended his cheek revolve rapidly from one to the other—an action which was invariably followed by the wiping of his mouth with his coat sleeves. He was not a man to contribute much to the idle gossip of a stage-coach. The other was a person much younger and of much more pretension. He was probably not more than twenty-one, one of that order of clever ignorants who, as they acquire daily something new, leap to the rare conviction that it is a something that is yet to be taught to their neighbours—a conviction which kept him constantly busy in repeating aloud the lessons memorized the day before. He spoke of every thing, spoke constantly, and, accordingly, said nothing; but of this he had not the smallest idea. He naturally addressed himself to one or the other of us, but he might as well have spoken to the spokes of the carriage as to me, for, busy with my own psychological cogitations, I was conscious, when he condescended to address me, only of an unpleasant chattering murmur, which sometimes unhinged a very close-fitting speculation. I believe I made out to answer "Yes" or "No"—

responses which might or might not have corresponded correctly with his observations. He did not seem to succeed any better with our third person, who chuckled now and then, but did not often answer, or, if he did, it was in an equally negative manner with myself. But this lack of sympathy did not abridge the eloquence of the youth. Evening came on, night followed, and still his tongue was in exercise. A sudden thought struck me—"Why should I not silence this fellow—put him to sleep?" Upon this hint I proceeded. Circumstances favoured me. Our vehicle was a small one. I occupied one of the back seats, the elder of our party, the tobacco-chewing, chuckling farmer, the other, and our loquacious lad sat directly opposite me, our knees occasionally touching. I contrived that they should touch completely. The night was dark; the windows of the stage shut in. He could not see me at my manipulations. There were two incentives to the experiment. It *was* an experiment, and a very doubtful one. If successful, it was of some importance to my speculations. It was a *fair* experiment, as he had no sort of consciousness of my purpose, and his imagination could lay no claim to any of the results. His eyes had nothing to endure, and if he slept, it could not be chargeable to the strain upon them—to the intensity either of his gaze or mine. Though I fixed my glance strenuously towards the place which he occupied, I could not even distinguish the outline of his form. Enough, my will and my eyes went together. Occasionally I passed my hands before his face and brought them down in slow passes on each side, from his temples to his knees. I continued this for about twenty-five minutes. For the first five of these minutes, his loquacity seemed undiminished; but at the end of the next five, I flattered myself that there was a cessation of the fire. In two or three minutes more he was silent; a deep sigh escaped him at intervals, and we heard no more of him. He was asleep; whether in consequence of my proceedings or because of a natural stage-drowsiness, I did not then pretend to say. I had gained my object, the noisy mouth was sealed up, and I could resume my magnetic cogitations without any farther annoyance. But I was unsatisfied; I must know if he is asleep, and by my means. I lifted my hand and *willed* that his should follow it; they met against the window of the stage. But this might be accident. I again exercised my will, and the next moment he had risen and taken his seat with exquisite deliberation in the lap of my companion. "Hollo! stop! none of that!" was the exclamation from the lips of the chuckling farmer, now startled from a very pleasant condition of natural sleep. Then followed a struggle, in which, with no scrupulous hands, our farmer strove to push the invader of his premises back to his proper place. But this was no easy task. The young chatterbox, now silent enough, was tenacious of his new position, and seemed obstinately bent on retaining it at all hazards. Though a slender person, and his opponent a stout one, he seemed no easy customer, but exhibited a degree of nerve and strength which promised to lead to surprising and, perhaps, disquieting results, if I had not thought it advisable to interpose. I again exercised my will, and the patient sunk back into his seat at the very moment when his doggedness seemed most invincible. "Habet!" of that there was no longer question, and, satisfied with the result so far, I suffered the sleeper to enjoy his nap. Indeed, it would have been equally difficult and dangerous to try other experiments under existing circumstances, and I delivered myself once more up to the train of thinking which such experiments were well calculated to occasion.

III.

While thus engaged, the stage stopped before a cottage some fifty yards from the roadside. A light was burning in one of the windows by which it was made discernible. The driver hallooed to us within, a hoarse, sullen sentence of three words, seemingly of inquiry. I had noted this fellow before, and remarked his surly demeanour and violent carriage. Of course, I paid no attention to what he said, and after a few minutes delay, he thundered out what seemed to be a volley of oaths, of which he seemed always to have a sufficient supply coiled up in his jaws, and giving the lash to his team, we dashed ahead with a speed as reckless as if he had the finest macadamized road before him and a broad noonday sun burning over head.

I suppose we had driven half an hour, or even more—for I was deeply shrouded in the tangled depths of thought—when it suddenly struck me that I might be carrying my involuntary sleeper far beyond his place of destination. I now remembered that he had brought no baggage—nothing but an umbrella, cane and small valise

—when he had entered the stage. He was evidently bound for a short distance only. And with this recollection came another. What had been the rough inquiry propounded by the stage driver as we stopped before the cottage? At the moment, as it had not concerned me, I had given it no consideration; but it now struck me very forcibly that it was a demand to know if some one of us was not to stop there. I was not. The country squire was awake, and might answer for himself, and not thinking just then of the condition of young garrulous—imposed, as it had been, by myself—I took for granted that he should have been on the *qui vive* at such a moment, and with reference to such a matter, if he was at all interested in the result. The suggestion worried me. I had no design to do injury to the youth. My purpose could scarcely be considered mischievous; yet I might be doing him serious hurt. I might be carrying him from friends and family, from his sweetheart, from the bridal party, from the sick bed of some dear parent. Even now the maiden might be waiting for him at the altar, the priest wondering, with the marriage service open before him, the brother beginning to meditate upon pistols for two, and the poor girl preparing a rational fainting fit, natural enough as the catastrophe for a first jilting. Really, the consideration of these things troubled me. The consequences of my freak might be inconvenient, might be dangerous. God forbid that I should put asunder those whom he had joined together or was about to join together—rob the damsel of those sweet prospects of the future, the sweetest that social life is ever permitted to know, which makes all paradise before the eye of the betrothed—and probably incur for the youth the more dreadful but not more painful danger, of getting his brains blown out by a fierce brother or a savage cousin. With these conjectures troubling me, I proceeded somewhat hastily to undo what I had done. But my nervous system had become disordered. What if I should be unable to wake him? This was a subject of apprehension. Such cases were on record—nay, they were even numerous. A youth has been kept without eating for five days in consequence of the inability of the magnetizer to arouse him; and the story goes of a wife, mesmerized by her husband in 1839, who is asleep to this very day. Scandal, it is true, ascribes it to the will of the husband that she still sleeps, and not to the inadequacy of his powers. While I remembered these and other cases, I became apprehensive and fidgety, and my passes, made with a nervous rapidity, while they produced perspiration on me, seemed to have no sort of effect upon him. What was to be done? I stopped to meditate. It was necessary that I should compose myself or I should fail altogether. I reasoned with myself, brought back my wandering fancies, fixed my mood, and addressed all my resolution to the one object. This done and the results were apparent. The task was easy. A deep sigh escaped my patient, succeeded by a sort of hysterical gasping which lasted for a few seconds. He then leaned forward, put his hands affectionately on my knees and murmured something incoherently, but in tones equally soft and soliciting. Just at this moment our horses, which had been going at considerable speed, came to a dead halt, and looking through the glass, I saw a light from a cottage some twenty paces from the roadside. It was just such a comfortable box as we had passed a few hours before—a snug cabin of two stories, a piazza in front, and a neat white paling running before it along the road. These objects now caught the eye of my patient. He leaned forward, and I heard him mutter, slowly, and as if the subject were still matter of doubt—"Why, here I am; I must have slept." He rose as he said so, bundled up stick, umbrella and valise, and opening the door, prepared to leap out. He paused, only, it would seem, to take me by the hand and wish me well—a civility which was wholly unexpected, and due entirely, I suppose, to the rare sympathy which is supposed to exist between the mesmerized and his mesmerizer. I thanked him; he shook my hands fervently and leaped down to the ground.

IV.

I congratulated myself that the lad was now at home, that no evil consequences had followed my experiment; that no damsel had been jilted at the moment of highest expectation, no parson disappointed of his fee, no brains blown out by fierce brother or savage cousin. The house was astir, expectation was on tiptoe; a servant held a torch by the entrance; lights were to be seen in the corridor of the building, where a group was collected entirely of women. One portly dame could be seen in the centre, supported by a young girl on each side, whom, even at that distance, I could fancy pretty.

The scene reminded me of home. I envied my patient the felicity he must feel, thus leaving a miserable stage-coach and night-travel over villainous roads, in winter, for the quiet and dear enjoyments of the family circle. I watched him as he hurried up the walk to the house, saw him enter, and in the next moment throw his arms round the neck of the stately dame and imprint a kiss upon her cheeks. With the quickness of thought, he had bestowed a like salutation upon the damsels; but in the midst of it all what a hubbub followed. A chorus of feminine storm, the indignant roar of the maternal lungs, followed and admirably accompanied by the softer but more prolonged clamours of the daughters. The next moment I saw the young man descending the steps with a backward movement, his hands extended as if in protestation; his voice reached us in tones which seemed those of explanation and entreaty. But the storm was unappeased; the matron was raging, the young ladies weeping as if their hearts would break. What struck me as most singular, was that our driver should be evidently enjoying the scene as a matter of high regale. His laughter was unmeasured, unmitigated, and, mingled with the thunders of the dame and the plaintive notes of the damsels, made the sounds of strange difficulty for the imitative echoes of our Georgia forests.

"What can be the matter, driver?" I demanded.

"Matter! He's got into the wrong box, that's all, and bussed the wrong women."

"How? Isn't that his family—his mother and sisters?"

"No, indeed; he left them some fourteen miles back. I called out to him, but, d—n him, he didn't choose to hear, and I wasn't gwine to wait on him all night. He's been 'sleep, I reckon, and wasn't quite awake, that's cl'ar, when he got a kissing the old lady. If he don't move mighty quick, she'll get at him yet, tooth and toe-nail, for she's not too slow, if you once rouse her, with the broomstick."

I had congratulated myself rather prematurely that my experiment had been without bad consequences. You may be sure that I said nothing of my doings. The sight of the old lady's anger was a caution, particularly as I now beheld her, step by step, following the young man from the house to the coach, he facing her but retreating all the while, protesting, with extended arm, that it was all a mistake, that he had just wakened out of a sound sleep, and fancying himself at the door of his own mother, had allowed his affections to go before his eyes.

"A pretty tale, indeed," says the old lady; "but it won't go down. I know you very well, sir; you're Willis Dalton, of ——. I've heard tell of you before; you was always counted a most conceited, impudent person. I only wish I was a man for your sake; I'd lick the conceit out of you mighty quick, I tell you. But don't you think to get off. Wait till my son John comes home. If he don't settle off scores with you he's no son of mine."

The old lady did not absolutely lay hands on the youth, but she followed him so closely to the vehicle that we were all momentarily apprehensive that she would do so. Her action was considerable and her deportment excessively threatening. The unfortunate offender effected his return into the stage with a crab-like movement. He was evidently not a little afraid of an assault from behind. But she contented herself with the use of the one certainly feminine weapon, and forebore all others. But of this one she was unsparing. She remained at the stage door, thundering to the last, until the sharp crack of the driver's whip warned her that he was about to make a start. As she withdrew, the youth cried out, in no friendly tones—"Why didn't you call me, driver, when you reached my house?"

"I did!" was the short reply.

"Well, I suppose I was asleep. Why didn't you wake me?"

"None of my business. I stopped at your house and called you; if you didn't choose to hear, 'twas your own consarn. I wasn't gwine to wait on you all night and lose the mail; I'm behind time now."

They had an angry but a brief dispute, and getting satisfaction and consolation from no quarter, the youth sank back into his seat.

"At least," said I, by way of warming his vanity and so soothing his mood—"at least, you had a kiss of the young ladies, and I should say they were pretty girls enough."

"'Gad, yes, they are pretty; and the kiss, so far as they were concerned, was not out of the way. But to kiss that old hag and think she was my mother!"

"Do not blame her—her indignation was natural."

"So it was;—but how could I have made such a mistake?"

"You were half asleep."

"I suppose I was. But it was something strange that I should sleep. I never slept in a stage-coach before—never could sleep."

"And how will you do now? Where will you go?"

"I reckon I must go on till I meet the other stage. Perhaps I shall have to go to ——. Confound the old woman for taking it so much to heart; otherwise I might have staid there all night."

"Do you know her?"

"Only by hearsay. She's well off, and one of the girls is a belle."

"If so, the matter's easy."

"How?"

"Admit the kiss to have been *prepense*, a deliberately designed performance——"

"Ay, indeed, and get John Gilbert's bowie knife between my ribs," he said, interrupting me.

"No; make love to the belle and marry her."

"Well, that's not a bad idea."

"If you think so, why not act upon it?"

"More easy said than done. I should like very well to know the girls, and have often thought upon it before; but this cursed scrape."

And so we talked for an hour, until wearied, when we sank back to our separate musings. What was in his thoughts I could easily imagine—they were full of his novel adventures of the night. Mine had received their colour from the same circumstances, and I had just begun to persuade myself to make another mesmeric experiment upon the youth, when our mutual musings were cut short by an unexpected catastrophe—an event not unfrequent in the rugged roads and regions of the south—the upsetting of our stage. In a moment, we were rolling over the side of a hill, heels in air, and with such a strange proclivity to one another that, on rising, it was a matter of some uncertainty whether each man stood on his own or the legs of his neighbour. We scrambled out without any nice attention to the mire, and by the aid of one of the lamps of the stage, still left unshattered, we were enabled to obtain a partial view of the condition of the wreck.

V.

The little town of M—— was four miles off. It would take some two or three hours, according to our driver, before he could put the stage in fit traveling condition, and we resolved to walk this distance.

We lent a hand in righting the vehicle. It had sustained some small injuries; the sashes were broken and some bands of leather. The chief hurts were to the harness; and having seen our Jehu busy, over a rousing fire, at the work of repair, we set forth, with cautious footsteps, over an unknown road. We reached the —— at a late hour, but it was daylight before the stage arrived. Meanwhile, we entered the bar-room, and by the aid of segars, a warm fire, and an equally warm noggin, the components of which shall be nameless, we contrived to discuss the subject of our adventures with tolerable good humour and fortitude. Occasionally the bar-keeper looked in upon us and stirred the fire; now and then a stranger put in his head, but lingered not long, and at length we heard a vehicle drive up to the door. It proved to be not ours, but the returning stage from the west. It was, accordingly, the vehicle for my patient, Mr. Willis Dalton. There was but a single passenger, a tall, well-made person of thirty years or more, calm, sedate, somewhat stern of countenance, who entered the apartment, and with a lofty nod to the company, took his place at the opposite side of the hearth, wrapped up closely in a large masking cloak. We could see his face, but he sat with eyes almost shut and looking down upon the fire. His presence did not restrain us. Our conversation naturally ran upon the adventures of the night, and we contrived to make a merry discussion of it, in which our hitherto hum-drum squire, who did nothing but chuckle and chew tobacco before, took a very active part. The whole scene was renewed, and, by little and little, it assumed quite a dramatic and exciting cast. Even our youngster, whose propensity to chatter had been somewhat subdued since the occurrence, began to forget the offensive parts, and to dwell with some *goût* upon the kisses so unpremeditatedly acquired; and I am disposed to think, from the tone which he now assumed, that, in the ears of any other person not familiar as were ourselves with the whole history, he would have been at some pains to prove that the proceeding was not so entirely unpremeditated as it was known to us to be. Even as it was, a stranger would have gathered from his words and manner that he was a very audacious gallant, who knew how much a tender-hearted young damsel would endure from the lips of a very gallant and very handsome young gentleman.

I had noted more than once, while this conversation was in progress, that the stranger at the opposite corner of the fireplace betrayed some interest in it. He turned more than once at the voice of the several speakers, and, on several occasions, I noted that his brow was contracted and his lips compressed. At length, when our merriment had reached what seemed its climax, when we had rehearsed the old lady's rage and the daughters' screams with reiterated success, he turned suddenly round upon us.

"You are from ——, gentlemen?" he demanded.

"We are, sir."

"You came by the upper route—by ——'s and ——'s?"

"We did, sir."

"And passed by the house of Mrs. Gilbert. If I mistake not, that lady and her family is the subject of this very spirited conversation."

There was a pause. The features of the stranger lightened into a sort of fiendish grin. Young Dalton looked as blank as the full moon in a rainy night. The stranger rose to his feet, and approached him and laid his hand upon his shoulder.

"You, sir, seem to have been the source of all this merriment, the hero of this story. Your name, sir? I am John Gilbert, the son of that 'portly dame'—'twas so you called her—the brother of those damsels of whom your speech has been so free. It is fortunate, sir, that we have met."

VI.

Here was an explosion! We all rose to our feet; but just at this moment the surly stage-driver appeared at the entrance and warned us that the stage was ready. Dalton immediately turned, as well as myself, in obedience to the summons, but the fierce brother, the aforesaid John Gilbert, was not to be so bamboozled.

"Stop, sir; you cannot leave me yet. The stage must go or stay—but you remain. I must have this matter explained—atoned for. Here, landlord."

It was now Dalton's turn to show passion. He had been taken by surprise; besides, he felt that he had done wrong. But he was a lad of spirit; he was not to be bullied. He turned upon his assailant and confronted him like a man.

"Well, sir, be it so; I am ready."

"I'm glad of it. Landlord?"

The barkeeper made his appearance. Gilbert seemed to know him, for he called him by name.

"Freeman," said he, "is Colonel Alford in town?"

"He is, sir; I saw him yesterday."

"Do step to him; say that I want to see him here as soon as he can come. And, Freeman."

As the other was moving away he caught his arm and whispered in his ears. I caught but one word—"pistols." Freeman disappeared. I felt it necessary to interpose. I begged the gentlemen to be seated while I furnished an explanation, which, I confidently assured them, would set all things right.

"Impossible!" said the brother. Dalton himself looked doubtful; besides, his blood was up, and he seemed half indifferent whether the thing came to a fight or not. I begged them to be seated, and entered upon my narrative. I described the powers of Mesmerism, its strange effects, my own acquisition of it, and, in describing my experiment upon my young companion, I did not scruple to say whence the desire originated. The youth looked angry enough when I declared my purpose to have been to compel his silence, and the chuckling squire revolved rapidly his tobacco and laughed out merrily, with an approving nod of his head. But, at the close, I discovered that my labour had been taken in vain; nobody believed me; the marvellous properties of Mesmerism were too extravagantly stated to secure the faith of any of my hearers, and——

"Pshaw! what nonsense!" was the complimentary comment with which Mr. John Gilbert saluted my conclusion. Even Dalton, whom it so much concerned to prove my story true, regarded me as bent upon practising upon the party, and in a very simple manner, for reasons of my own. I was piqued.

"You are incredulous, gentlemen, but I can convince you."

"Do you mean to say that you or any man can put me to sleep at pleasure?"

"You may be a difficult subject, sir——"

"Ah, I see how it is," said he, interrupting me, while a smile of scorn and derision passed over his countenance, and was reflected from the faces of the rest. I became a little irritated.

"You do not hear me out. I say that you may be a difficult subject, and not easily impressible, but if you will suffer me to try, I fancy that I can produce such effects upon you as will lead to your conviction."

"Why, what will you do?"

"That remains to be seen."

"Agreed; you shall try. Will half an hour suffice for your experiment?"

"It will."

"I can spare that time. Meanwhile, this gentleman, *your friend*, will please remain in the apartment with us."

Dalton, the offender, was here referred to. An emphasis was laid upon the words italicized, which clearly betrayed the suspicions of the speaker. He regarded us as in collusion. Both of us answered in a breath, and to the same effect.

"We never saw each other before to-day."

"It matters not, gentlemen; I am willing that the experiment should be tried. *My* friend will be here in the meantime, and this affair will scarcely conflict with the other. Shall we go to a private chamber?"

To this we agreed; but private we were not allowed to be. This dialogue took place in the bar-room, and there were other parties. The surprising story which I had told had been noised abroad, and even at that early hour had attracted listeners. Among these was my stage-driver. He had made his appearance in order to give me the last imperative summons for departure; but the prospect of a fight which was then in progress, was too agreeable to be foregone. He was an amateur, loved nothing so well as the combat *à outrance*, and though under any other circumstances he would have been as solicitous about saving the mails as if life depended upon it, it was very evident now that his fine had no terrors when a fight was in prospect. He had heard the arrangement by which I proposed to prove the involuntary character of Dalton's conduct, and curiosity and doubt took the place of his ordinary appetite. The stubborn fellow made it a condition of my stay that he should be present at the manipulations from first to last; and in order to keep the stage for half an hour, I was compelled to keep him. Accordingly, our party in the chamber consisted of Dalton, Gilbert, the chuckling, tobacco-chewing squire, whose name was Moore, John Staggers, the stage driver, and myself. To this party was subsequently added Colonel Alford, and another gentleman whose name I forget.

VII.

Having secured the chamber, I prepared to put my experiment in execution; but I was stopped at the outset by Dalton.

"I claim," said he, "as a matter of right, that this gentleman should first try his experiment upon myself. He asserts that he has already succeeded with me and imposed his will upon me. It is a point of honour with me to prove that he cannot do so, and, accordingly, that he has never done so. It seems that I did sleep in the stage—that I do not deny;—but that he caused the sleep is out of the question."

A new ally came to my aid. Our chuckling fellow traveler, Moore, who had spoken before only in an occasional monosyllable, broke out —"But why did you get in my lap?"

"I get in your lap?"

"You did;" and the tobacco made a rapid evolution from one jaw to the other—"you did; and if you hadn't got out mighty quick, I'd ha' sent you through the windows. I was getting wolfish, I swow!"

I explained this mystery also. Some further chat ensued, but it was finally agreed that my first experiment should be tried on Dalton. I placed him accordingly, enjoined the utmost silence on the parties, and proceeded with the usual passes and manipulations. In twenty-one minutes by the watch my patient was pronounced asleep. This was a triumph almost against my expectations, for the young man had addressed all his firmness to the duty of resisting me.

"Now, gentlemen, try and waken him."

They approached, and several of the ordinary experiments were tried, but without success. By throwing water into his face they made him sneeze, but the effort was evidently merely muscular, for they produced no other sign of consciousness. His hands were punctured, a needle drawn through the skin; he was pinched, kicked, cuffed, lifted and dragged from the chair by John Staggers, the stage-driver, who, in every physical proceeding, was bent on having a finger in the pie, but all without disturbing the mesmeric sleep. When released, the patient sank down on the floor, with all that effortless insensibility which Dante describes in himself on hearing the piteous groans of Francesca's companion—

"Caddi come corpo morto cade."

Every body was satisfied but John Gilbert. He looked with undisguised contempt on the processes, and did not seek to conceal the opinion that there was some collusion between us. I felt disposed to be angry, but anger, generally unprofitable, would have been, at such a time, in such a place, and with a stranger who had evidently some reason for suspicion, an absolute folly. I accordingly subdued my irritable mood, and contented myself with inly resolving, if I could only reduce him to the condition of his opponent, to revenge myself in a manner equally effectual and inoffensive.

"It is now your turn, Mr. Gilbert."

"And you think to put me to sleep by this sort of mummery?"

"I do, sir. Are you willing?"

"Willing that you should try, sir? Yes; but the whole thing is very ridiculous."

"It may seem so to you, sir; and yet, you see the condition of my patient yonder."

"He? He's no more asleep than I am."

"You think so. Could any man practise so well, endure so much?"

"Ay," he retorted, "to escape worse."

"Enough, sir; let us begin."

At this moment, Colonel Alford entered. He did not need much explanation to understand the true situation of affairs. He had heard without what was in progress, and a few words sufficed to let him see where the several parties stood. A brief whispering conversation between Gilbert and himself informed him of the painful duty that the latter desired at his hands, a duty to be attended to as soon as the present subject could be dismissed. Alford accordingly disappeared, and his activity and absence only the more strenuously impressed me with the necessity of succeeding in my purpose if I wished to prevent bloodshed.

VIII.

I need scarcely say to my readers that, having undertaken such a performance, I must be a man of no small determination of my own. My will had been long acknowledged among my acquaintances as a remarkable feature in my character. I had good health and no small share of physical strength. I was goaded to my task by my pride, my desire to prevent mischief, and a lively curiosity to see what results might be produced in such a case and with such parties by the processes I had in view. Besides, I was exercising myself in a newly-acquired and highly stimulating attribute, and this alone, to the determined will and sanguine temperament, is provocative enough whatever may be the occasion. But with all my endowments as a Mesmerizer, I did not disguise from myself that I had a stubborn subject. Mr. John Gilbert was about my own age, size and general strength. That he had sufficient confidence in himself was evident. His health was good; his nervous system not easily excited. He was cool and composed, and having no faith in my ability to conquer, had no fears of my success. It was necessary that I should put my whole soul and all my resources into the experiment. I did so. I took certain precautions with him that I had not taken in the case of Dalton. I let down the curtains of the chamber, placed the mirror and every thing that might divert his glance out of sight, and requested the spectators to take their seats behind him. I seated myself with my back close to the bare wall, on a high chair, placing him upon a bench considerably below me. I then curiously examined his phrenological developments, and having located as well as I could the two newly-discovered organ's of mental and physical sleep, I subjected them to strong pressure and a gentle friction before I began the direct passes. I also touched more than once the region of physical weakness or infirmity, another organ the discovery of which we owe to that rare neurologist, Dr. Buchanan. But I need go no farther into such details, which are known to every practitioner of the school of Mesmer. I mention these to show that, being conscious of the difficulties in the case of my new subject, I took the proper pains to overcome them. The conflict between us was a protracted one. Thirty minutes had elapsed and he was still awake, and had it not been that I saw that some impression had been made, I should have given up the effort; but I was encouraged by some of the signs of progress. His pulse had sunk considerably; his skin, from being originally hard, dry and hot, was now soft and moist, and fast approximating to the exact temper of my own. There was a haziness about the pupils of his eyes which was unmistakeable, and his glance, instead of being a fixed, expressive gaze, was now an inane and unmeaning stare. With a strong effort, I concentrated my will more completely upon my object, and while keeping both of my eyes steadily upon the right one of his, I gave a slight waving motion to my head. His eyes closed; he opened them with an effort, and at that moment Colonel Alford with another gentleman entered the room;—he turned them to the entrance, while a feeble smile passed over his lips. It was the last effort at resistance, and I checked it instantly. "Look at me, sir!" I exclaimed, in the sternest accents; and his eyes closed beneath my glance. I renewed the passes, and the conflict was at an end. But the labour was an exhausting one. I had been forty-three minutes at work before I was able to assure myself of my conquest. I placed a chair behind him, threw a cloak over it, and leaned his head back upon it. Perfecting his sleep by some few farther manipulations, I delivered him to the company.

IX.

Col. Alford and his companion were doubters. They seemed to take for granted that Gilbert was amusing himself at my expense. I required them to test his capacity for endurance, which they did in a variety of ways. All the ordinary modes of disturbing sleep failed in the case of both Dalton and himself.

"Speak to him, Colonel Alford—speak to him of the business upon which he engaged you."

He did so, but without receiving any answer. After giving them ample time for trial, and after they had exhausted all their experiments, I proceeded to show them one of the wonders of this most wonderful mystery—the strange sympathy which exists between the Mesmerizer and his patient. I spoke to him.

"Mr. Gilbert, extend your hand to Mr. Dalton; you must be friends, good friends, henceforward."

I was obeyed; and commanding Dalton at the same moment, he rose and staggered to the spot where Gilbert was sitting and seized his hand, which was cordially shaken.

"That will do; resume your seat, Mr. Dalton."

This was done. I ordered a table and writing materials to be brought, and placing them before Dalton, commanded him to write as follows—

"On the honour of a gentleman, I never intended the slightest impertinence to the family of Mr. Gilbert. The whole thing was a mistake, the result of a condition in which I was scarcely conscious of what I was doing. I believed Mrs. Gilbert to be my mother and the young ladies my own sisters. I believed myself to have arrived that moment at my own dwelling.

"Signed WILLIS DALTON."

"What do you think of that, sir?" I said to Colonel Alford.

"Waking or sleeping, very good; but it will not be satisfactory to Gilbert," was his reply.

"We shall see, sir."

I had the table and writing materials transferred to the side of Gilbert. I placed the pen in his hand, and said to Alford—

"If, waking or sleeping, he writes that he is satisfied with this apology, and believes it a conscientious one, what then will you say?"

"That it will satisfy me."

I placed my finger on Gilbert's *benevolence* and *conscientiousness*, bade him read the apology of Dalton, and told him to write what he thought proper. He obeyed me, and wrote—

"Dalton is a good fellow. I am quite satisfied. He must go home with me."

"Sign it, Gilbert."

He did so, and I placed the paper in Alford's hands.

"Why, this is art, magic, witchcraft!" he exclaimed. "Do you know what you have done, Gilbert?"

But he spoke in vain to the sleeper, and turned to me with bewildered aspect. I placed his hand in that of Gilbert, then commanded the latter to speak to him. Alford renewed his question. He was answered, but very slowly.

"Yes, I know; it is all right."

"You are satisfied," I said to Alford, resuming my control over the patient.

"Perfectly—though it's monstrous strange."

"You shall see another proof of my power."

Thus saying, I prompted the veneration of both my patients, then commanded them to rise and embrace, which they did, and very lovingly too.

"Enough, gentlemen; we have made peace and prevented bloodshed, and I hear the wheels of the other stage at the door. We have nothing more to do than to put them into it."

"What, asleep?"

"Yes—why not? Take my right arm, Mr. Gilbert, my left arm, Mr. Dalton."

They did so, and I led them down stairs and was about to conduct them through the bar-room to the stage, and through a crowd of wondering spectators.

"Stop, sir," said the barkeeper. "Who's to pay the bill?"

"They will pay, each for himself;" and, at my command, they did so. I then conducted them to the coach and bade them get in.

"By the ——, I'll go with them and see the end of it," said Alford.

"If you will, I'll confer upon you the power of waking them."

He consented, and we entered the coach together, when I put him in communication with both the patients, gave him a few brief but sufficient instructions, and left the parties for my own stage—my Jehu, the aforementioned John Staggers, having again become importunate for the transmission of the mails. I had good reasons, for my own part, to promote and encourage his hurry. The village had gathered together; vague reports had gone abroad of what I had been doing. John Staggers himself had denounced me for witchcraft, and Doctor Vomit, the physician of the place, had begun to foment the hue and cry against me as an impostor, a quack, a swindler and magician. I had casually called the attention of Colonel Alford and the others in the room to the singular effect of my processes upon the pulse of the patient, showing how headache and fever might be relieved, and this decided invasion of Vomit's province had stirred up all his bile against me. Though he could not persuade John Staggers that I was a humbug, it was not hard to convince him that I was a wizard; and while Vomit was working the crowd, Staggers was not unwilling to leave me at their mercy. In telling me that the stage could wait no longer, he did only that which he could not well avoid doing; and had I not been almost as prompt in my movements as himself, I should certainly have been left to take my chance at a scamper through the village gauntlet, Doctor Vomit at the head.

X.

The ides of Mesmer, unlike those of March, had a pleasant termination. I returned through M—— a month after this event, taking such precautions as I fancied would leave me unrecognized. I still had some dread of Vomit and his myrmidons. I had suffered my whiskers to grow, had exchanged my hat for a cap, and muffling myself from ears to heels in my *fearnaught,* I stole to a private chamber in the inn, with as little noise as possible. I then sent for Alford. When he found out who I was, he shook my hand with unmeasured gratification, and gave me a lively description of the sequel to the affair, the further control of which I had entrusted to his hands—how he had made the parties kiss each other, kiss the driver, kiss the horses, leap and dance, sing and laugh, by his mere command; and how, even while they were engaged in the most affectionate embraces, how he had awakened them; how they had recoiled from each other in a sort of horror, and with what difficulty he had succeeded in persuading them of the facts to which he had been witness. The production of the written apology and its acceptance by Gilbert was conclusive; and subdued by the strangeness of the events, the exhortations of Alford, and somewhat by the natural tendency of the Mesmeric state to make gentle and placable the temper, he had consented to renew, at waking, the expressions of content and friendship which he had written while asleep.

"But the best is yet to come," said Alford. "Dalton has not only made peace with the old lady and the girls, but is desperately smitten with the youngest of them, who, it seems, as if she had some presentiment of what was to come, had apologized for his impertinence in the first instance, and, as Dalton has since assured me, was the least reluctant when the kissing was in progress, and the least complaining when it was over. The report goes that they are already engaged to be married, and I'm half inclined to think it true. As for myself, thanks to your instructions, I'm a glorious Mesmerizer. I put every body to sleep—my wife when she scolds me, my tailor when he duns me, the parson when he makes *me* sleepy, and even Vomit when he blackguards you. I challenged him to the trial, and as he had ridiculed the matter before hundreds, he could not get off. I had him sound in fifteen minutes, and made him swallow a half-dozen of his own pills, from the effects of which—Heaven help him —the poor devil has not recovered yet. He'll never trouble you again."

So much for Alford, whom I left the wonder of the village. When we reached Gilbert's, I persuaded the driver to let me out, and the first persons I encountered were Dalton and one of the young damsels walking in the shrubbery. He blushed when he saw me, and so did the young lady. I had little time to spare, but in the few moments which I staid, I saw enough to satisfy me how the land lay; and this morning I received through the mail a copy of the "——— Telegraph," with Alford's endorsement, and brackets around a small but significant paragraph, which runs thus—

"Married, on Thursday evening last, by the Rev. Mr. Humdrum, Willis Dalton, Esq., to Miss Lucilla Gilbert, youngest daughter of the late Hon. John Gilbert, all of this county."

So much for Mesmerism in a stage-coach.

[*"The Maroon. A Legend of the Caribbees" was first published as a serial, in six installments, in the* New York Illustrated Magazine *for 1847, though segments of it had appeared in earlier writings by Simms. It was later included in the collection first entitled* Marie de Berniere *(1853) and subsequently retitled* The Maroon; A Legend of the Caribbees, and Other Tales *(1855). The present subtitle is one of the revisions Simms made, probably in 1865, for a never realized separate edition. Explanatory and Textual Notes begin on page 704.*]

THE MAROON:
A Romance of the Carib.

"To hear no voices but from off the sea,
To see no aspects but of sun and cloud,
To live and be alone!—such is the doom!"

CHAPTER I.

The waters of the Caribbean sea, subject to some of the wildest vicissitudes that ever sweep the billows of the western hemisphere, were never more placid and lovely to the eye than on the morning of the 26th of August, in the year of grace one thousand five hundred and thirty-two. The exquisite calm of heaven—that delicious serenity and repose of atmosphere which seem never so lovely or so perfect as in those latitudes where the capricious winds may, at any moment, lash themselves and the ocean into immitigable fury, and where nothing is long secure against their violence—appeared to rest, with the bosom of the halcyon, upon the mighty deeps of sea. The sky was without a cloud—the breeze, soft and spicy as if borne fresh, on the very instant, from the aromatic islands of the east, was gentle without languor, and just sufficed to waft along, under easy sail, the high-pooped Spanish bark that might be seen to form, as it were, a natural and becoming portion of the vast and beguiling picture. She alone stood up, careering over the watery waste, relieving its monotonous levels, and looming out, beyond her natural size, in comparison with the uniform smoothness of the waters. A swift and well built vessel of the time, was the "Diana de

Burgos," named after a favorite beauty of old Spain. She had taxed all the genius of the architect of that day, in her modeling, to do honor to her namesake. And he had succeeded, so perfectly succeeded, that the emulous little bark had already acquired a peculiar reputation, such as that enjoyed by the Baltimore clipper of modern periods, for exquisite grace of air, and unparalleled fleetness of foot. She was the pride of the waters, and cleft them, or passed over them, as if endued with all the consciousness of the young and haughty beauty whose name had not been taken by her in vain.

Of her deeds, of her peculiar employment, in the western hemisphere, we shall say nothing. At that wild period, we know very well what was the usual history in the new world, as well upon the ocean as the land. "No peace beyond the line," was the common proverb of license among the rovers of all the European nations; and our "Diana de Burgos" carried within her graceful girdle all the requisite resources for deeds of strength and violence. Her loveliness of model did not conflict with her capacity for fight, and a single glance upon the swarthy groups that covered her deck, would satisfy any sceptic, without farther search, that she had already enjoyed no inconsiderable experience in the trade of war. Could her polished decks have spoken out, what revelations of blood and terror might they not have made! But her past history is nothing to us. It is enough that she still possesses sufficient materials of interest for a startling and a touching narrative.

At the moment when we ascend her sides—in that calm and lovely day—in that serene and delicious atmosphere—with that broad deep ocean, as smooth as it could well appear, to comport with the necessary degree of animation which, to form a picture, such a prospect seems to require, and, at the same time to disarm every sense of danger in the bosom of the most apprehensive—we shall find that no such calm and serenity prevails among her inmates. We discover them grouped about in small parties along her deck, here leaning against her masts, there crouched among bulk and cordage—variously placed in different attitudes—a hundred sturdy seamen and soldiers, speaking little, an occasional word or sentence only—but all looking as if thoroughly informed and anxious in relation to some matter of evidently increasing interest. The broken sentences to which we listen—the half-uttered inquiry, the faltering suggestion, have no meaning for our ears, though clearly of ready comprehension by all around.

Happily, a stir takes place among them; they rise to their feet—the groups separate; there is a sudden show of restraint, as from the approach of authority. A word has gone forth which leads to expectation, and the eagerness, but partially suppressed, which now, in every visage, follows prompt upon its former simple look of doubt and anxiety, may well encourage us to hope for the gratification of our own curiosity. Patience, the door of the cabin is thrown open!

The group which appears within is one to add somewhat to the interest of expectation. In the foreground appears a person seated in a chair, one of those ancient high-backed fabrics used, about that period, in all European countries which had reached any degree of civilization. This person is a man of countenance more striking than impressive. He is, we may be permitted to say at once, the captain of the Diana—Don Velasquez de Tornel—a personage, short and corpulent, with great hands and limbs, a neck thick and short, like that of a bull, and of a face plethoric and fiery red. His features are dark and fierce, and marked by the signs of an angry passion, the appearance of which he seems laboring to suppress. His eyes are small, intense, and catlike of expression, keen, vigilant, and cunning. His nose is short and sharp, his lips thick, and marked, at moments, by a slight quiver, which betrays the secret emotion. A thin, but grisly beard overspreads his chin and cheeks. He would seem to be a person about fifty years of age—a man of strifes and violence, of quick and irritable temper, and of restless, unforgiving moods. His feet are wrapped in bandages of flannel, and suggest the true reason why he remains seated at a time when his thoughts and passions would seem disposed to goad him into the most eager exercise. Thus seated, he is wheeled out upon the deck by his attendants; while, slowly following him, appears a female whose highly expressive features, and wild peculiar beauty, makes her less an object of interest than study. Her person is small, but highly formed; commanding, from its ease of carriage, its erectness, the bold defiance in her eye, and the imperious curling of her lip. The style of her beauty is not of the noblest order. It possesses but little of the spiritual, but is of a kind more likely to secure admiration during an age, and in a region, where the passions learn to triumph and command in the absence of the sentiments. She takes her place at a little distance in front of the spot occupied by Velasquez. Her arms folded across her breast, she preserves an erect posture, while her eyes, neither gazing upon, nor averted from him, seem to be filled with a twofold expression of wounded pride and lurking anxiety.

His glance surveys her keenly and unreservedly. There is a mixture of tenderness and suspicion in his gaze, while the sinister smile which now curls his lips gives to his whole countenance the air of a brooding and sleepless malignity. This silent watch is so prolonged as to be painful; but her features never swerve, nor does her expression alter. She looks as she did when she took her first position. There is evidently a motive for this inflexibility, which she maintains without faltering, so long as his eye is upon her. But when he turns away and summons the pilot to his side, then, it is seen, that her breast heaves as if to throw off the oppressive burden of self-constraint—then it is that her cheek pales and lip quivers, and all her countenance betrays a fear which it has hitherto been its business to suppress.

But a few words are spoken by the captain to his pilot; a question is asked—a command is given; and while the latter is retiring, he is reminded—to "see that all things are in readiness, and to keep a bright look out." The pilot withdrawn, the eyes of Velasquez once more, but slowly, address themselves to the lady. But she has recovered from the momentary emotion which oppressed her. Her features are once more inflexible; her look is steady; she has nerved herself to a resolute endurance of his gaze; and the muscles of her face, like the strings of her soul, are rendered tenacious by a will which his would vainly endeavor to overcome. Failing in this sort of examination, he addressed her—seemingly resuming a dialogue which the previous scene had interrupted.

"You have answered clearly, Maria! It is well for us both that you did so. It would have been a grief to me that I should visit your head with my wrath, even though it should be shown—Madre de Dios!—that you had merited it by such a crime as this. For, did I not pluck you from the accursed gipsy—have I not made you a lady, and bestowed my love upon you? It were a crime against god if you had been false to me!"

"I have answered you, Don Velasquez!"

"So you have, my beauty—so you have! But it is not enough to answer. Must one look angry because one is virtuous—eh?"

"But to be wrongfully accused—to be wrongfully threatened!——"

"Oh! oh! one gets used to such things, if all other things go right. Of course, I know that you are innocent. But how did I know it then? For you will admit, my life, that the affair looked very suspicious. There was I, groaning in my agony with this accursed pain, and where were you? Ah! well! you were not with this whelp of a musician. You did not sit looking up into his face while he was stretching his throat against the wind, and singing nonsense to his silly guitar? You did not prefer listening to him to tending on me, and, of course, Juan must have been mistaken in supposing that you suffered him—that you were willing that he should—ah! never mind! It is not easy to speak of such things without choking—but when this whelp of a musician did put his arms about you, it was only his impertinence, and you properly repulsed him—"

"Has not Antonio already assured you of this?" demanded the lady, coldly.

"True—true!——"

"And Perez?"

"Very true—and Juan, I say, must have been mistaken."

"He is a wretch!——"

"Nay, nay, do not abuse the child—my own sister's child—has good eyes, too; but, nevertheless, did not see—was mistaken—saw this Lopez presume—this guitar player—but did not see, as Antonio and Perez did, that you resented this presumption—that you frowned and threatened! But what an atrocious impertinence that such a poor, puny, beardless beast of a boy should thus behave himself. Is it not monstrous? But he shall sweat for it! should he not? Can such an outrage be excused? What think you, my life—should not this wretch of a musician suffer?—Say! answer me!"

The lady replied by a vacant stare.

"Ah! I see! You feel the enormity of his offence. You have not words sufficient to declare it. Well! you will be better able to acknowledge the propriety of the punishment I will inflict upon him."

These words were accompanied by a hideous grin. The tyrant readily conceived all the torture which he inflicted. He watched eagerly the features of the person he addressed, anxious to extort from them some acknowledgment of the heart's inward suffering; and seemed chagrined to perceive the steadiness of aspect with which the woman bore his scrutiny.

"Truly, my life," he continued, with less than usual of that cat-like play of feature which declared his peculiar malice, "truly, my life, it pleases me to perceive that you have no sympathies for this monster of a musician. I did fear, I confess, I did fear—that, though you might not have erred with him, you might have been foolish enough, through some misplaced sentiment of feminine tenderness, to have interposed and pleaded against his punishment. That would have been a weakness, my beautiful Gitana. We must punish such enormous guilt. We must punish it as it deserves! We must so punish such an offender as that he shall never so offend again!"

He paused—and gazed steadily upon the woman! But she too well knew the cool malignity of the tyrant—his peculiar and unrelenting nature—to suffer herself to be deceived by the obvious lure which he threw out that she should implore mercy for the criminal of whom he spoke. She also felt the importance of maintaining the same settled indifference and coldness of aspect as before. He allowed some lengthened moments to intervene, and resumed but with evident disappointment.

"And you have nothing to say, my life?"

"Nothing!"

"Madre de Dios! But it is so precious to me, that you so thoroughly acknowledge my justice. Ho! there—Juan!—bring forth this vile singer, this wretch of a guitar player—this audacious musician! He shall vex no longer with his midnight strummings, the sweet quiet of our Lady of Burgos—our chaste Diana—whom he makes unhappy by his presumption. See to it, Juan! bring him forth quickly!"

CHAPTER II.

There might have been seen, for a single moment, while the eye of Don Velasquez was averted, a convulsive quiver upon the lips of the woman. Her arms somewhat sunk in that moment, and were clasped together with a spasmodic intensity; yet the action was too gently performed—the movement quite too slight—to fix the regards of the person whose glance she chiefly feared. In that brief moment—

in those slightly expressed emotions—it could be seen that she felt her worst struggle was at hand. But it could be seen, also, that she was possessed of wondrous faculties for endurance. In what school she had acquired this capacity, it needs not that we should ask—it is enough that passion too, has its power of self-restraint, as well as virtue—and is never so intense, perhaps, as when it is subjected, by its own will, to the check of denial and delay. In the heart of the woman, this power of self-restraint, once acquired, is perhaps far more complete than in the heart of the man—if, for no other reason than that of her habitual subjection to the will of a superior, and the habitual exercise of a policy in society which is not necessary to him by whom society is controlled or commanded.

The individual named Juan now made his appearance. He was what is called, ordinarily, a handsome youth; with smooth features, long, oily and somewhat curling locks, which evidently demanded much of his attention—and a person which, though very slightly, was yet very symmetrically made. But the intelligence of his countenance was that of cunning rather than of thought; and in his small gray eyes, there might be seen a something of the malignant and cat-like expression which made so conspicuous a feature in those of his uncle. He was showily habited, with a gay cloak of silk, falling gracefully from his shoulders, in addition to the ordinary doublet, which he also wore, of a rich description of cloth, with slashed sleeves, and a great ruff at either wrist. A heavy gold chain about his neck, with a shining *agnus dei*, ostentatiously displayed, rather discovered his love of ornament than any very decided religious feeling in his breast. But without detailing the several parts of his costume, it will suffice to say that he was a sort of a sea-dandy, thought well of his person, and, for reasons of his own, was disposed to make the most of it. His manner was full of consequence and confidence, and, as he approached his uncle, it might be seen that he possessed no small share of influence in determining the character of the latter's counsels. He drew nigh to him and whispered a few moments in his ear.

"Be it so, my son! be it so!" said the other kindly, and with a sudden brightening of the features. Had the eye of Don Velasquez, at that moment, been directed suddenly to the features of the lady, he would have been somewhat gratified, as well as informed, by their frequent and excessive changes. On the appearance of the youth,

Juan, she had addressed to him a single glance of equal bitterness and scorn, and, while he stooped and whispered in the ears of his uncle, her look was that of a loathing such as one would naturally feel at contact, suddenly, with a reptile equally hideous and dangerous. But her features, under the control of a most watchful will, resumed their look of icy indifference before her tyrant could detect their changes.

The whispered dialogue with Juan over, the latter drew nigh to the lady, and proceeded to whisper in her ear also. She recoiled from him with unqualified disgust.

"Beware!" he exclaimed, but in subdued accents, "Beware, Maria, you are on the eve of the precipice, and a single word may incur for you the fate of your favorite."

"Assure me of that and I welcome it," she answered, with a sudden resumption of all the vivacity which could be made to gather in an eye of unexampled brilliancy and beauty.

The youth smiled spitefully, but said—"You are wild! That fate would realize no hopes for either of you. It would be death, and something worse than death—denial to the grave, and, of course, beyond it. But I am not now speaking of your death. It is through me, Maria, that you live. Nay, you live—need I tell you that—because I love!"

"What! if I proclaim you where you stand, the villain that you are," answered the lady in accents similarly subdued with his own.

"It would avail you nothing! He would regard it only as a mode of escape, which, in your desperation, you seek to adopt. Does it need still that I should prove to you how completely I control his ear and fashion his will."

"Alas! no!—But what is the purpose, as he understands it, of this whispered conference with me!"

"Ah! that is *my* secret," the other answered with a smile—"enough, that I speak of anything but that! My true purpose is with you, and for you, and myself! I will save this favorite of yours—save him unharmed aboard the vessel, with probably no greater penalty than close imprisonment, and"—he spoke this with a grin—"perhaps a denial of his guitar;—I will do this, Maria, if you will become wise as I would have you——if—"

"I understand you—but that is impossible! I tell you, Juan de Silva, I loathe you too much to keep terms with you. You have gone too far—you have shown me too vile an aspect—too serpentlike a tooth, for me to suffer your near approach, save as a most hateful and hated enemy. I will brave any fate before I suffer this!"

"Beware! your words but doom your favorite."

"Be it so!—Had he been the man I thought him, it had never come to this. It had been your fate not his, or mine! He deserves all that he finds, failing himself, and failing me, at the proper moment. Hark you, the dagger which his fingers clutched, when your felon hand rested upon his shoulder, was put into them by mine; and the name which my lips uttered when I gave it him, was that of Juan de Silva. And yet he struck not, but tamely submitted, sacrificing himself and me. Now, that you have heard all, judge for yourself what terms there can be between us!"

The lofty if not noble scorn which filled her features at this narrative, heightened wondrously the beauty of her countenance. Her companion, though evidently moved by her words, could not forbear betraying, with open admiration of his gaze, how much it stimulated his passion. He spoke, after a brief moment, lost in the absorbing pleasure of his gaze.

"I can forgive you, Maria, and adore you still. That this Lopez was thus base and insensible, should surely satisfy you that he was not meant to enjoy, or to deserve, a heart like yours. Be mine, and all is yours! I am here, the master. I can save this creature—will save him, for I fear him not, but—I must have your assurance."

"Never! Juan de Silva! Never!"

"Beware!"

"Never!"

"Once again, beware! You precipitate his fate!"

"I should precipitate myself upon a worse, if I sought to save him upon these conditions. I loathe and hate you, Juan de Silva; too much to endure your smiles, your favors, the snake-like and revolting coil of your venomous embrace."

"You have doomed him!" was the sullen answer from the scarcely parted lips of the youth. "His fate is sealed forever!"

He was about to turn away!

"Stay!" was the eager whisper of the woman.

"Well."

"What is that fate?" was the faintly spoken inquiry that reached his ears.

"You will know soon enough. His hour approaches."

"And I too am prepared for mine! I too can perish!" were the muttered accents which reached the retreating ears of the scowling Juan. He turned and fixed a simple glance upon her pallid but proud features. The glance was one of equal hate and mockery. It helped to strengthen her, and her high spirit prepared itself for the worst.

CHAPTER III.

"I was right, Sir," said Juan aloud, as he returned to the seat of his uncle who had been watching with some curiosity the progress of this conference, of which he heard not, of course, a single syllable. "She is prudent and sensible. She will not interpose with prayer, or argument, to balk the ends of justice. She will not meddle with his fate."

There was something like disappointment in the dark malignant features of Velasquez.

"Yet did she seem exceedingly slow in coming to her resolution!"

"By no means, Sir—she was prompt enough; but—" here the sentence was concluded in a whisper that reached only the ears of Velasquez—"but, it was my policy to persuade her, if possible, that her entreaties might avert his fate. Could I have succeeded, it might have served to confirm and strengthen our suspicions. But she is firm—she may be guiltless! But of the guilt of Lopez there can be no doubt. She denies not that."

Juan had his own motives for this statement. He did not despair yet, of finally overcoming the resolution of the woman. His passion, in this, somewhat baffled his judgment. But of this hereafter.

"Well, there is nothing left but to punish the one. Bring him forth."

Juan retired—the anxious soul of the lady followed his parting footsteps, but her eyes maintained a steady and unfaltering gaze, as before, neither resting upon, nor absolutely shrinking from the countenance of Velasquez. The pilot was again summoned to the side of the latter.

"Well?"—was the brief but intelligible inquiry. It was sufficiently understood.

"We approach, Señor."

"Good! see to your ship."

The pilot disappeared—a bustle announced new parties to the scene; and preceded by Juan, a youth came forward under the conduct of two soldiers. He was manacled, hand and foot, and moved with difficulty. The rattling of the chains was heard. It smote upon the soul of the woman, but she turned not once her head. The eyes of Velasquez were upon her. A savage grin lighted up his dark satanic countenance, and left no doubt in the minds of those who beheld, that he meditated a purpose of the deadliest malice. The youth in bonds was of graceful person, and handsome features, but they were not those of a man of character or courage. The cheeks were of a deadly paleness, the lips quivered with apprehension—the whole air and expression were those of one totally unequal to the trial that lay before him. His eye wandered restlessly and apprehensively to the countenances of one or the other of the three parties to whom the reader has been introduced, without daring to encounter the gaze of either. Velasquez watched his movements with the exultation of a cat in possession of her prey. The face of Juan bore a similar expression; while in the fine masculine spirit which made itself conspicuous, in the face of the woman, in spite of all her efforts to subdue it, there might be seen a strange conflict between tenderness and scorn.

"Unbind him!" said Velasquez.

"Oh, thanks! thanks!" muttered the victim, looking appealingly to his tyrant. The scorn deepened in its shadows upon the face of the woman.

"You know not yet for what you have to be thankful," was the sneer of Juan, as he busied himself in undoing the manacles.

"Speak to me, Juan. For what am I reserved; what may this mean, if it be not mercy?"

"It means freedom!" was the response, still in a whisper.

"Well—and that——"

"*May* be mercy!" was the ironical return of Juan, as he withdrew from between Velasquez and his prey. The latter now looked with features in which hope and doubt were still at a lively struggle, upon the face of his tyrant. He made a step toward him. The uplifted hand of Velasquez arrested his approach.

"Lopez de Levya, were I to have thee drawn up by the neck to yon spar, as the heretic English do those whom they would destroy, it were no more than thou deservest. But I am of a more merciful temper—I have taken the chains from thy limbs—"

A lively gratitude overspread the features of the person addressed —but he still trembled with a natural anxiety and doubt. He knew his tyrant.

"I mean to set thee free!"

"Thanks! thanks!"

"Nay, I will do more for thee than this. I will elevate thee to rare dignities. I will make thee a chief, a prince, a sovereign of land and sea. Thou shalt be able to stand up in thine empire, and none will say thee nay."

A pause! The culprit looked wildly at this language. It was something more than apprehension that shone in his face. There was no mistaking the hideous malice of the speaker; there was no doubting the ironical grin upon the lips of Juan; and the experience of the ship had seldom found mercy, or forgiveness, or generosity, in either. The eye of the woman was now fixed fully upon that of Velasquez; her intense interest in what she had to hear, making her somewhat relax in the stubborn vigilance of thought which had impressed itself upon all her features. Velasquez resumed:

"The quiet of this part of the Caribbean Sea, as thou well knowest, is seldom broken by the prows of Europeans. The savage steers his bark in other courses, dreading its wild currents and fearful whirlpools. Here, he who shall make his abode will be a sovereign beyond dispute. It may be ages before he will see upon his horizon, driven by hostile tempests, the white sails of a Christian vessel. No empire could be more secure from challenge—no state more certainly beyond the danger of overthrow."

Another pause, and a conviction of what was intended, at once passed into the soul of the woman. Her hands were griped convulsively together, and the paleness of her cheek increased. The culprit to whom Velasquez addressed himself simply appeared bewildered. Chains, confinement, terror, and probably want of food and sleep, had rendered his faculties obtuse. But Velasquez proceeded rapidly to his complete enlightenment.

"Look out upon the sea, good Lopez;" and his hand waved in the direction of the object to which the ship had been sensibly approaching. At a league's distance, a little island was distinctly perceptible, though seeming to be scarcely upheaved above the billows which encircled it. Trees in groups might be seen to wave upon it, the earth rose into moderate hills, and elevations as the eye penetrated the interior. Numerous wild fowl sailed in swift gyrations above it, and gigantic birds strode majestically along its white and sandy shores.

"That island, Lopez de Levya, I discovered, for the first time, when I last traversed this ocean. I made the discovery against my own will, being driven hither by stress of weather. I little dreamed at that time of its future usefulness; but when our weather-beaten pilot, old Gomez, in beholding its solitude, declared that it would be the spot, of all the world, in which Love would be most likely to find security, we called it in a merry jest, 'The Isle of Lovers,'—and when I remembered that it was farther said;—'One might be a sovereign here without paying his tenth to any crown,'—then did I conceive how fitly I might reward merit by bestowing this island upon the deserving—upon one who would desire security for his love, and a sovereignty beyond dispute."

The eyes of the culprit were gradually enlarging. He had slowly begun to guess the terrible destiny which was before him: and the first feeling of overwhelming apprehension, necessarily kept him dumb. He looked at his tyrant with eyes full of a vacant terror. The latter gave him but few moments for meditation, or doubt, as he thus proceeded:

"Thou hast done me great wrong, Lopez de Levya. Thou hast audaciously presumed upon the lady of my love. For this wrong will I reward thee! we are commanded, as thou knowest, my son, to forgive those who do us injury. I will go farther than the commandment. I will honor thee with wealth and territory, and the highest distinction. Henceforth, shalt thou be a prince, an absolute sovereign, Lopez de Levya; and as thy suitable empire, behold the 'Isle of Lovers' which I now bestow upon thee. There shalt thou make music to the night, with no constraint. None shalt say nay to thy strumming. If thou shalt please no damsel's ears with thy song, thou shalt at least offend in nothing the rights of others. Thou shalt sing thy areytos to the stars, and find them more gentle in thy sight, than such eyes as thou hast but too frequently offended with thy wilful fondness. Am I not right in this, lady mine?" and with a smirk quite as full of sarcasm as of tenderness, the persecutor of both parties, turned his gaze from the face of the wretched man to that of the scarcely less wretched woman. But he gained nothing by the scrutiny. Her glance was fixed, and obdurate, and conveyed no meaning in it, such as that which his jealous suspicions might have looked to see. He watched her features for a few moments with a dissatisfied expression, then resuming his former tones and aspect, he addressed himself to his nephew, Juan:

"Juan, my son,—we trust we have sufficiently said, to make this excellent prince understand what honors are designed him, in requital for his evil deeds. It is for thee to do the rest. Take the prince, therefore, conduct him to the boat, and do thou see him safely placed within the limits of his empire. Give him provision for a month, in which space of time, doubtless, he will be able to bring his subjects to proper subjection, and take his tithes of the produce of the land. Give him a crossbow and a spear, that he may coerce them should they rebel or fly;—and see that you forget not to hang his guitar about his neck, that he may regale his hours of recreation and repose with the precious ditties which he so much loves to sing in other ears. So shall he have pleasing recollections of one at least for whom he will scarcely ever touch guitar again."

CHAPTER IV.

The doom was pronounced—the hand of the executioner, the hand of his most bitter enemy, Juan de Silva,—was laid upon the shoulder of the victim, but he refused to yield his faith to his own fears. He still hoped against conviction—still shrunk from a belief in that punishment which, to the timid and dependent nature, such as his, seemed to involve terrors much more extreme than any threatened form of death. But when he at last yielded to the conviction which had long been entertained by all around,—unless, perhaps, by the woman, his supposed associate in crime,—then the whole strength of his soul,—feeble in its best moments—seemed to give way on the instant. Every show of manhood was forgotten. There was no pride to keep up appearances—no struggle to maintain a decent show of fortitude and firmness—but the miserable culprit sunk down into the most lamentable imbecility to the shame of all around him.

"Mercy! mercy! For the sake of the Blessed Virgin, have mercy upon me, Don Velasquez," he shrieked rather than pleaded, when the determined aspects of the men appointed to convey him to the boat, and the violent grasp of Juan, upon his shoulder, silenced all doubts as to the real intentions of his tyrant, to carry out his sentence, in full, as it had been delivered. The hard-souled sailors, as much in scorn as in pity, recoiled from the piercing feminine entreaty of the victim, and left him free for the moment, as if in doubt whether Velasquez might not yield to supplications, which were urged with such a humiliating disregard to manhood. Falling upon his knees, he crawled toward the spot where sat the arbiter of his fate, glowring in the enjoyment of that bitter-sweet morsel of revenge which is so grateful to the malignant nature. In his eyes,—had those of the victim not been blinded by his own tears—had he not been too base to venture to accompany his entreaties by a resolute look upon the face of him upon whose word his fate rested—he might have seen how hopeless were all his pleadings. But he saw nothing, as he crawled along the deck to the feet of the tyrant,—but the terrible danger which he was anxious to escape. Could he have seen the inexpressible scorn which dilated the nostrils and curled the lips of the woman,—could he have heard her bitter and only half suppressed accents of loathing—muttered between her gnashing teeth!—But they could not have changed his nature!

"Can he not die! Can he not die! Anything but this! And yet," she continued—herself unconscious that she spoke—"Yet how should it be that one who had not the soul to slay his enemy, in the moment when all that made life precious lay in the blow,—how should it be that he should aim the weapon at his own bloodless heart, though to escape this most loathsome tyranny!"

"Beware!"—was the single word, whispered close beside her ear, from the lips of Juan de Silva. "Beware! lest a worse fate befall thee even than his! Would'st thou peril life for such a reptile!"

She was silent at the suggestion. Not that she had any fears of death; but, just then, her quick thought and resolute spirit suddenly conceived its own method for escape and vengeance. Other emotions than those of scorn filled her bosom, as the whisper of Juan, like the hissing of a hateful serpent, filled her ears; and, in their sudden consciousness, she trembled lest her feeling should declare itself aloud, in spite of the resolute will which she invoked to curb and keep it in. The emotion, which her lips did not declare, was conspicuous, for the instant, on her countenance, and remained unseen, only in consequence of the absorbing nature of the event in progress at the feet of Velasquez. To this spot the abject culprit had continued to crawl, unrestrained by the stern commands of his tyrant not to approach him. To his knees he clung, though the latter strove to shake him off, and to spurn him away with the members which were too heavily swathed and bandaged to suffer him to use them with any efficiency for such a purpose.

His pleadings, which were of a sort to move loathing rather than pity, produced no feeling of either kind in the breast of Velasquez. They provoked his merriment rather. He grinned as he beheld the writhings of the wretched creature before him. He had a sorry jest for all his contortions. Verily, the Spanish adventurers of that day in America, were a terrible banditti! of these, Velasquez was a proper specimen. When his victim appealed to him for the sake of his widowed mother at Segovia, he answered—

"I shall tell her of thy possessions, Lopez;—she shall hear of thy elevation. She was always a woman of rare ambition. Did I not know her in her younger days? Know'st thou not that she once disposed her mantilla so that she might make a captive of me? Had she done so, verily, it might have been mine own son, for whom this Isle of Lovers hath been found. I shall tell her of thy fortune, Lopez. She shall rejoice in thy principality; and, it may be, will find her way out to thee, seeking to share in the wealth of thy dominions. Enough now,—take him hence, I tell thee;—Juan, son,—wilt thou not see the Prince bestowed upon his empire! I begin to weary of this gratitude."

Again the officers approached, and again they hesitated,—all but Juan—as the cries of the wretched imbecile rang through the vessel. The sailors would still have suffered him to urge his prayers for mercy, but Juan had no such yielding nature, and he knew, better than they, how profitless were all entreaties. *He* had resolved, for his own purposes, that there should be no relentings in the brutal spirit of Velasquez. He left the side of Maria de Pacheco, at the summons of his uncle, and, with his own hand, grappled the victim, while giving the word to the sailors chosen to assist him.

But, rising to his feet, Lopez dashed away from the grasp of his assailant, and once more rushed in supplication to Velasquez. His terrors gave him wonderful strength, and a faculty of speech scarcely less wonderful. He was positively eloquent. Never was prayer for mercy more passionate, or more pregnant with the best argument in behalf of mercy. They touched all hearts but the two, alone, whom it had been of any avail to move. These were immovable. Again were his entreaties answered by scurril jest, mocking suggestion and derisive laughter. The taste for the sports of the tauridor, who tortures the bull to madness before he bestows the *coup de grace*, could alone afford any likeness to the sort of pleasure which this sea despot enjoyed in the fruitless agonies of his victim. It was in a sort of defiance, produced by very shame and despair, that the culprit rose at length to his feet, and folding his arms upon his breast, submitted to his fate, from which, it was evident, that no degree of humiliation could possibly suffice to save him. A smile softened the features of Maria de Pacheco.

"It is well!" she murmured to herself. "A little sooner and the shame would have been spared to both!"

The victim seemed to hear her accents, though not to understand them. He turned a timid glance toward her, but her eye no longer sought his own. She was conscious that other eyes were then keenly fixed on both.

The boat was declared to be in readiness. The month's store of provisions, accorded by Velasquez, were thrown into her;—the spear and the crossbow followed; and the hands of the seamen, appointed to convey the Maroon, were fastened firmly on his shoulder. He was now subdued to submission, if not reconciled to his fate. He no longer opposed himself to their efforts, and though he still spoke the language of entreaty, it was no longer addressed to his tyrant.

"Oh! my countrymen,—Antonio, Pedro—is it you who do me thus—is it you, my countrymen, who help to give me up to such a dreadful doom."

Such was the touching appeal, made to ancient comrades, which the poor wretch uttered at the parting moment. They looked downward, in silence, but did not relax their hold upon him.

"And I am to perish on that desolate island;—and the people of my own land, leave me to this solitude! They hear the voice of my prayer, and shut their ears against it! I am never more to hear human speech—never more to look upon Christian face,—nor call any man brother or friend. Oh! Spaniards, brothers, friends, countrymen!—will you doom me thus—will you desert me thus to the solitude of the sea, which is worse than any death. Christians! help me—speak for me—save me!"

There was a moisture in the eyes of the weather-beaten seamen who stood around him. At this moment, the woman advanced suddenly, and stood before Velasquez. Juan beheld her purpose in her countenance, and whispered as she passed him—"Beware!" She heard, but did not heed the warning.

"Velasquez!"—she spoke with firmness—"Surely, you have carried this jest far enough. You cannot mean really to devote this wretched man to this place of desolation!"

"Jest!" exclaimed the other; "Jest, call you it? By my faith, but you have very merrily described a very serious ceremonial. Yet, if there be a jest designed at all, I see that it hath been omitted. Ho, Juan, bring forth the guitar of our Prince. See you that it be slung about the neck of Don Lopez. It hath a band of crimson—truly, the fitting color for a sovereign. It will help him to remember his old songs when in the enjoyment of his new seigniory. He shall have his ditty and jest together. It were cruel, Lady mine! to deprive him of that which hath been so much his nightly solace! Eh! what say'st thou?"

The person addressed, recoiled as if from the tongue of the viper. She was silent, unless the thought which moved her lips, but did not escape in words, might be construed into speech.

"At all events—it is *but* death,—*but* death, after all! He hath weapons, and the sea rolls at his feet. He hath but to will, and his exile ends in a moment!"

We shorten a scene which was only too painfully protracted. The victim was hurried to the boat. His feet pressed the lonely islet of which he was mockingly declared the Prince. He stood erect, but not in the consciousness of sway. His eyes were fixed upon the vessel from which he was torn, and in which he saw nothing but the country, the friends, the familiar faces, from which he was forever sundered. He was unconscious of the mocking performance, when Juan de Silva hung the guitar about his neck. The awkward appendage was no burden to him at such a moment. The faces of those who had placed him upon the sands were turned away. The sound of their parting voices had died away upon his ears. The boat was pushed from the shore;—yet he still stood, with a stare of vacant misery in his aspect, upon the spot where they had placed him. Long after the prow of the boat had been turned for the ship, he could be seen in the same place, with the ludicrous decoration upon his breast, while, with still uplifted hands, he seemed to implore the sympathy of his comrades and the mercy of his tyrant. But of neither was he vouchsafed any proofs. Mercy was none—sympathy was powerless to save. Even she!—But of her he dared not think! She had been his fate; and though, in his soul, he dared not blame her, yet when she rose to recollection, it was always to provoke a sentiment of bitterness which a nobler spirit never could have felt. He saw the boat rejoin the vessel. He saw once more her broad sails spread forth to catch the breeze. Gradually, they lessened beneath his gaze. The world which held his soul and his hope, grew smaller and smaller, contracting to a speck, which, at length, faded utterly away in the deepening haze which girdled the horizon. Then, when his eyes failed any longer to delude him with a hope,—did he fall prostrate upon the sands, in a swooning condition, which, for the time, wholly and happily obliterated the terrible sense of his desolation.

CHAPTER V.

It will not be difficult with many persons, to comprehend how a condition of utter solitude should not necessarily produce a sense of pain. To the man of great mental resources, and of a habit contemplative and thoughtful, such a condition would be apt rather to suggest ideas of complete security and repose, which would be friendly to the enjoyment of a favorite indulgence. To spirits whom the world has soured—whom the greedy strifes of men have offended,—men of nice sensibilities and jealous affections, whose friendships have proved false, and wounded, as so many deceitful reeds which have broken and pierced their sides;—to the heart of deep and earnest passions robbed of those upon whom all the heart's affections have been set;—these, all, might rejoice in an abode from which the trying services, and vexing necessities, and disquieting obtrusions, of social life, were shut out and excluded forever.

But Lopez de Levya was not one of these! He was young, and handsome, and hopeful, and this was his first trouble. The world still loomed out before his vision, the gay and songful paradise which youthful fancies describe it still. There were warm passions and eager sympathies in his soul still to be gratified; and though we may not regard him as a person to whom affections of any kind were very necessary, yet had he a bosom filled with those which grow from an intense appetite for praise—which could have their gratification only in a world of beings like himself. It would be impossible to describe the utter desolation which possessed the bosom of the unhappy wretch when he did finally awaken to realize the fact that he was left alone—utterly abandoned by his comrades,—upon an obscure islet of the Caribbean Sea!

It was a long time, indeed, before he could utterly conceive his own situation—a long time before he could persuade himself that the stubborn and unrelenting spirit of Velasquez had absolutely resolved that such should be his doom. For hours—until the midnight came with its sad and drooping stars, looking down mournfully upon the billows of the ever chiding ocean;—until the daylight dawned, and the red sun, rushing up from the Eastern waters, rose angry and fiery, and blazing down upon the little islet with the fierce glance of a destroying despot;—for the first dreary interval, from sun to sun, he still cherished the hope that this was but a trial of his strength—a cruel experiment upon his youth, and courage;—and, recovering from the first feelings of consternation, when at sunset the dusky white sails of the vessel finally disappeared from sight, the unhappy wretch still flattered himself that, with the morning, he should hail her outline once more upon his horizon, and catch the glitter of her foaming prow coming to his rescue.

And with this hope he clung to the beach all night. He slept not—how could he sleep? Even for one night how intense was the desolation of that scene. There was the eternal sighing and moaning of the sea, which, toward the morning, subsided into calm and slept on, as if still dreaming of future tempests. And there were voices all around him of strange animals and wild fowl,—sometimes a chirp, as of an insect, and sometimes the scream of some passionate bird;—and, anon, a great plunge in the waters as if of some mighty beast leaving its place of sleep upon the land.

It was among the misfortunes of Lopez de Levya that he was no hero, and all these sounds inspired him with terror. Not less terrible to him were those wild, deep mysterious eyes of the stars, slowly passing over him, and looking down, as if to see whether he slept, in their passage to the deep. Never was night and situation so full of charm, yet so full of the awful and the terrible. Beautiful, indeed, surpassingly beautiful and sweet, was the strange wild charm of that highly spiritual mingling of land and ocean;—that small and lovely islet, just rising above the deep, so thoroughly environed by its rocking billows, shone upon by that wilderness of stars; breathed over by that pure zephyr gliding in with perfume and blessing from the South; and haunted by unknown sounds, from strange creatures of the sea and sky, who, in a life of perpetual freedom, could never know the feeling of desolation or of exile.

But the wild romance and the wondrous beauty of the scene, were lost upon the man who had no higher idea of the possession of the intellectual nature than such as could be drawn from association with his fellow. The region, unoccupied by man, however beautiful in itself, could bring no joy, no peace to the bosom of the exile. Velasquez knew the real nature of his victim. He well knew that Lopez had no sympathy with the mute existences of sea and sky; of earth and air; and of those more exquisite essences, which, in such a situation, the imaginative nature would have joyed to conjure up from the spiritual world, he thought only with terror and reluctance. He did fancy that voices came to him upon the night air;—the voices of men and in a strange, unusual language;—and he instantly trembled with fears of the cannibal—the anthropophagi, who were supposed, at that period, to be the only inhabitants of these regions.

But the night passed over in security. He opened his eyes upon another day, in the solitude of that wild abode, ere yet the sun had warmed with his gay tints the gray mansions of the East. He opened his eyes upon the sea and sky as before. The billows were rolling slowly away at his feet, in long low courses, but slightly lifted by the breezes of the dawn. Vainly were his eyes stretched out over the watery waste, in the pathway of the departed vessel. The vast plain of ocean spread away before him unbroken by a speck; and when the sun rushed up visibly into the heavens, and laid bare the whole bright circumference of the deep, for many a league, undarkened by an object, then the conviction of his utter loneliness—his life of future loneliness—forced itself upon the heart of the wretched youth; and flinging himself once more upon the earth, he thrust his fingers into the sands, and cried aloud in the depth of his agony—

"Jesu! it is true!—it is true!—and I am left—left by my people,—to perish here alone!"

We spare his lamentations,—his entreaties,—as if there were still some human being at hand, who might afford him relief and consolation,—to whom he might appeal for succor and protection. Prayer he had none. The name of the Deity, of the Savior, and the Virgin, were sometimes upon his lips; but the utterance was habitual, as he had been accustomed to employ them in mere idleness and indifference. Three days passed in which despair had full possession of his faculties. In this time he lay crouching upon the beach during the days, and gazing vacantly in the direction in which the ship had gone. At night he retreated to higher ground, filled with apprehensions of great monsters of the sea,—of the seas themselves;—lest, rising suddenly, endued with a human or a fiendish will, they might gather round him while he slept, and hurry him off, beyond escape, to their gloomy abysses. A small clump of trees afforded him the semblance of a shelter. Here he lay from nightfall to dawn, only sleeping in the utter exhaustion of nature, and suffering, at all other times, from every sort of terror. The stars, looking down through the palm leaves overhead, with their mild, sad aspects, seemed to him so many mocking and malignant angels exulting in his condition. The moaning of the sea, and the murmurs of the nightwind, were all so many voices of terror appointed to deride him in his desolation, and impress his heart with a sense of unknown dangers. The rush of great wings occasionally along the shore, or the rustle of smaller ones in the boughs above him—perhaps of creatures as timid as himself,—kept him wakeful with constant apprehensions; and, at moments of the midnight, a terrible bellowing, as of some sea-beast rising to the shore, or leaving it with a plunge that echoed throughout the islet,—struck a very palsy to his heart, that, for the time, seemed to silence all its vibrations. Let us leave the miserable outcast, thus suffering and apprehensive, while we return to the inmates of the vessel by whom he was abandoned.

CHAPTER VI.

He was not wholly abandoned. Maria de Pacheco, the woman, who, like himself, was, in some degree, a victim also to the will, if not the tyranny, of Don Velasquez, was not the creature tamely to submit to injustice, however she might prudently seem to do so. We need not ask whether there was any real attachment between herself and the poor creature whom we have seen "marooned." It is probable that the degree of regard which she entertained for him was small. He was not the man to fix the affections, to a very large extent, of a woman of so proud and fearless a soul. The feebleness which he had shown, had probably lessened the attachment of a heart, which, in the possession of large natural courage of its own, might well despise that of one, who had displayed so little. But as little did she love the man of whom she had become the slave; we may add, almost without her own consciousness, and at the will of another, by whom she had been sold at a very early age. She was still comparatively young; but with advanced intellect, and an experience that left it no longer immature. Born under the burning sky of Andalusia, tutored in the camp of the Gitano, though not of Zingaro race, she had soon acquired an intensity of mood which was only surpassed by her capacity of subduing it to quiet, under a rigid and controlling will. Loathing the sway of her tyrant, revolting at his person, she was as little disposed to regard with favor the affections which had been proffered her, of his more subtle and malignant nephew.

The person of Juan de Silva, graceful and showy as it was, could not blind her to his heartless vanities, and that dangerous cunning of character, which so admirably coöperated with the mocking and fiendish coldness of his soul. If she loathed Velasquez, she feared, as well as loathed, De Silva; and feared him the more, as, in possession of the secret of his infidelity to his uncle, she was yet made fully conscious of the truth of his boast, that any revelation of it, which she might make to the latter, would avail but little against him.

But, though anxious, she was not the woman to despair! She revolted too greatly at her own condition of restraint, bondage and denial, to yield even temporarily to despondency. In the moment that saw her feeble and wretched lover consigned to the lonely islet of the Caribbees, she made a secret resolve to avenge his fate or to peril her own person upon her vengeance. She clearly had no absorbing passion for the victim. It was evident that she could still maintain a prudent restraint upon her feelings at the moment of their greatest trial;—but the highest and proudest heart needs something for affection—some other one upon which to lean for sympathy—and which, at least, makes a show of responsive interest in its affections. It was thus that she had turned a willing ear to the professed devotion of Lopez de Levya—to his tastes and his gentleness, contrasting as they did with the brutality of all around her, and making her somewhat indifferent to his feebleness of will and lack of courage.

But she had not fancied his imbecility to be so great as the hour of trial had shown it. Though scorning his weakness, she sympathized in his cruel destiny. The respite which had been given him from death, by the capricious tyranny of Velasquez, suggested to her mind, a hope of his future extrication. Food had been left with him sufficient for a month. What might not be done in that space of time, by a subtle thought, and a determined spirit?

In a moment, Maria de Pacheco had her plans conceived, and her soul nerved to the prosecution of a single purpose. But she had an opponent, not less subtle than herself, in the person of Juan de Silva; and the keen scrutinizing eye which he fixed upon her, as she turned from the spot upon which Lopez had been left, seemed to denote an indistinct conception of the purpose which had passed that very instant through her soul. But she was not discouraged by this fear.

"Well," said he, in a whisper—"you see how hopeless is the struggle! What is left for you, but—" and a smile of mixed fondness and significance closed the sentence. The ready expression of the woman's face was made to accord happily with the single word with which she furnished an equally expressive conclusion:

"Death!"

"No! no!" said he,—"You will not die—you shall not! You shall live to be far more truly the mistress of the Dian de Burgos, than she finds you now. Why should we be enemies, Maria?"

"Beware! your uncle's eye is upon us!"

He turned away, and this single sentence, as it seemed to denote a disposition to make a secret between them, brought a fresh hope to the soul of the young man. He smiled, and glided to his uncle. Maria smiled also, but it was with a sterner feeling—not a less hopeful one, perhaps, but one in which bitterness was a much more positive ingredient than delight.

"I must baffle *his* vigilance;"—she muttered to herself. "He only need be feared, and he must be met and vanquished! Ay! but how!—How! I must manage this;—and I will!"

Her eyes followed his retreating form as she spoke. They noted quickly the jaunty air of self conceit which marked his movements; they scorned the showy and quaintly cut garments which he wore, and the profuse decorations of his neck and breast—and the quick instincts of the woman at once suggested an answer to her doubts.

"How, but through his vanity! He would be loved, as he would be admired and watched. Well!—he shall be loved, loved as he desires! The task is a hard one enough truly—but it shall be done! Juan de Silva, you *shall* be loved! You, at least, shall believe it—you *will* believe it; and this will suffice!"

In this she expressed a portion of her policy. It will be all that we need to show at present. How she pursued this policy—by what constant, hourly practices—by what adroit feminine arts—and with what fixedness of purpose—need only be suggested. The details would be too numerous. But she was encouraged to perseverance by success. She had reason to believe that she had succeeded in disarming the jealousies, and in awakening the hopes, of her enemy. They both maintained a judicious regard for the exactions of Velasquez; but there were hours when he slept, or when he suffered, when they might throw aside their caution, and speak together without fear or interruption.

It is by no means strange that the most artful should be imposed upon by arts such as he himself employs. But what is so blind as vanity? What creature so easily baited as the self-worshipper, when the food tendered him is that which increases his love of self. To make such a one satisfied with himself, is most surely to gain his confidence in you;—to persuade him that he is as much an object of your idolatry as of his own, is to obtain access to the few open avenues which conduct to his affections.

Maria de Pacheco had not been vainly tutored in the arts of the *Gitana*. Beautiful in person, graceful in carriage, skilled equally in the song, the dance and the story, she put in exercise all her powers of attraction, to bind more securely the spells which she aimed to put upon the creature whom she yet loathed with most complete aversion. In three weeks after the "marooning" of her timid lover, she had succeeded in possessing Juan de Silva with the notion that the victim ceased to be remembered. So credulous do the most vigilant and suspicious become, when blinded by an absorbing passion.

The two were alone together on the vessel's deck, as she swept, one gloomy night, along the waste of sea in silence. Don Velasquez had but a little before been conveyed below. He slept! Maria had ministered to him in song and story as was her wont, with Juan beside her. The departure of Velasquez had left them free to resume a conversation which had been begun before. He had been emboldened by the tenor of a previous dialogue. His hand grasped that of the lady. She suffered him to retain it. He carried it to his lips. It was not withdrawn; but, could her features have been seen, through the dim veil of night which covered them, the infatuated youth beside her, blinded by her charms, and beguiled by her arts, would have shrunk with fear from the deep and vindictive loathing which they betrayed, even while she submitted so quietly to his caresses.

The secret thought of Juan de Silva was one of delighted vanity. Could that thought but have found its way into speech, it would have congratulated himself upon the admirable address which he himself had shown, in subduing a spirit which he had hitherto found invincible. He did suffer some words to escape him which conveyed to her mind this idea; and she compressed her lips more closely together, with difficulty maintaining the silence which, if broken at that moment, would have overwhelmed him with her loathing and her scorn.

"You have forgiven me all, Maria?" he whispered tenderly, fully assured of her answer.

"What was there to be forgiven?"

"The fate of Lopez!"

A slight convulsive shiver passed over the form of the woman, and it required a strong effort to keep from withdrawing herself from his embrace, with a show of horror such as one might express in detaching himself from the folds of a serpent. He continued:

"But it was in my devotion that I sought to destroy. It was because you were so loved, that he was so much hated. I was well assured that, for so mean a spirit, you could not long have suffered pain, and now"——

"You were right," she said, interrupting him; "right—but you;—what is your spirit, Juan?"

"My spirit!"

"Yes! your spirit! your courage, your pride, your character?—Your person is pleasing to the eye—your talents to the mind! You have grace, beauty and accomplishments, but"——

"But, what!"

The vanity of the youth had taken the alarm. He spoke eagerly and with anxiety. She hesitated to reply, the better to increase this anxiety; and he renewed his entreaties for explanation. She at length gave it.

"Shall I always be loved by the subordinate? Shall the person whom I love, be always the creature of another's will?"

"You mistake, my Maria. You should know by this time, that I can do what I please with my uncle."

"Why, so you may, but in what manner is it done? By treachery,—by falsehood,—by meanness,—by descending to low arts and petty falsehoods. Let the truth but reach the ears of Velasquez, and he will maroon you as quickly as he did Lopez de Levya."

"Perhaps so,—but there's no reason that the truth shall reach his ears?"

"That may be, but shall we live always in terror of the truth—always in the base security of a lie. I tell you, Juan de Silva, such is my spirit, that I demand in the object of my devotion, manliness of soul—the courage of speech without fear,—the spirit to act without subterfuge—the will to command for himself, and through himself, and not as the mere creature of another! And, why should you, with your talents for command,—why should you be the lackey of your uncle?—that feeble despot, who—but no! no!—what need? You will not, you cannot understand the nature which I feel,—the spirit which sways sovereign in my soul!"

"Ay, Maria, but I do feel, I do understand you."

"Impossible, Juan, or you would rather be with me the sole possessor of some desolate isle such as that given to Lopez de Levya, than—"

"But how, if we be sole here—here, with the lovely Dian de Burgos for our palace, and the seas of the west for our empire?"

She laid her finger upon his wrist—but a single finger,—and slowly murmured in his ears—

"This were, indeed, something, but I tell you, Juan de Silva,—you are not the man for this. Your uncle!——"

"And if I prove to you that I am, Maria;—if I show you that I can fling aside my scruples when it will serve my purpose to do so;—and that no ties which deny me the gratification of my passions, have the power to keep me in subjection—if, in short, I can say to you, Maria de Pacheco, the Dian de Burgos, henceforward, is mine solely,—wilt thou share with me the sovereignty?"

"Alas! Juan, I should dread lest old age seize me, ere I ascend my throne!"

"Demonios! but another week shall not pass ere thou hast it all!"

"Were it so!—but—" The pause was full of meaning.

"Wilt thou promise me, Maria!—"

"Will I not?"

"And thou wilt deny me no more, if I show thee that no voice speaks in authority here but mine?"

"Show me that, Juan;—make thyself supreme, and thou shalt be as a sovereign over Maria de Pacheco, as thou wilt then be over the Dian de Burgos. But thy uncle!"

"Speak not of him!—Enough! Think'st thou I love this servitude any more than thou dost? Think'st thou it better pleases me than thee that I should minister to one, brutal and bedridden, whose feebleness checks our adventure and lessens our spoils."

"But how wilt thou ——"

"Nay, sweet, let not the manner of the thing disturb thee. Better, indeed, that thou should'st not know. Thou shalt see if I lack manliness. Thou shalt see if I fail when the moment needs. I am no Lopez de Levya—no mere singer, my Maria. Ah! if I prove not myself worthy of thy spirit—if I show thee not! Thou didst not know me, Maria—thou doubtest still,—thou dost not know me yet. Yet, I tell thee, for a love such as thou can'st give me, thou shalt see me do such deeds as were terrible as death to other men!"

The unresisting hand of the woman was carried to his lips as he spoke, as if he would affirm thereon the resolution which he had expressed. Yet even as he kissed them, her fingers, moved by the feeling in her soul, could have grappled his throat in mortal struggle. They separated for the night, and the exulting spirit of Maria declared her conscious triumph in secret soliloquy.

"Ay! ay! methinks, I have thee. It is sure. I do not mistake the blindness which is in this passion. He will do! He will perform what he doth not yet promise. The son of the sister, shall do murder upon the life of the brother that has murdered him. He is mine! The Dian de Burgos shall be mine. Yet, it will need that it be done quickly. The month is nearly gone! Another week!—but one—one week! Well! I must be patient. I must subdue my soul, while I work with other weapons. Juan de Silva, I shall take thee in thy own snare, or I have never used the snare of woman!"

CHAPTER VII.

With her whole soul set upon a favorite project, Maria de Pacheco was not a person to slumber or prove afraid. She was not less sure of herself than of others. She knew the general character and temper of the Spaniard. She knew the spirit which prevailed among the crew of the Dian de Burgos. Though young, and a woman, she had been by no means an unobservant spectator of the various events which had taken place on board, since she had become an inmate of the vessel. Besides, she was a sagacious student of character, as are all women of any native intelligence. She possessed the faculty, which seems like an instinct, of seeing, as it were, at a single glance, into the moods of those around her. She knew that Velasquez, *her master*, was no longer the master in his own ship. She as well knew that Juan de Silva was not very popular as his successor. One event, which had taken place a few months before, now pressed upon her recollection, and suggested to her a new auxiliary in working out her scheme.

One of the lieutenants, or as he might be called in our time, a mate, was a Biscayan named Diego Linares. He was a stout and somewhat surly fellow, habitually;—and, in the exercise of his common character, had given a rude or insolent reply to Juan de Silva, who had rewarded him for it very promptly, with a blow upon the mouth. The dagger of the Biscayan would have answered the indignity, and was drawn for that purpose, when other parties interfered, and Juan, after the first feeling of excitement had passed over, sought, in various ways, and by various civilities,—which he never made unnecessarily cheap,—to atone for the rashness and folly of his act. The interposition of Velasquez, himself, was finally addressed to the conciliation of the parties;—since Diego was a man not easily to be dispensed with. His efforts were apparently successful. The anger of the Biscayan was seemingly subdued, but it was in seeming only. The wound still rankled, and might easily be re-opened. Maria de Pacheco saw more deeply into the secret feelings of the injured person than either Juan or Velasquez. She better knew the vindictive temper of Biscayan blood, which is perhaps much more tenacious of its resentments, than that of almost all other Spaniards, all of whom are vindictive.

With the first inception of her own resolution, she at once conceived that this resentment might serve her purpose hereafter, and had, accordingly, sometime before, addressed herself to the task of making a friend of the discontent. She sought him at periods when the eyes of Juan were withdrawn from her. She sought him with an art which none possesses in any degree to compare with her who has been tutored in the camp of the Zingali. She knew the habits of the Biscayan, could rejoice his ear with songs and ballads from the native province of Diego; and frequently, even when she sang before Velasquez, she adroitly chose for her themes such as were familiar to the ears of the former. These still drew him, loitering nigh, to listen, as he traversed the deck upon his midnight watch. Gradually, the parties came to speak together; and, by degrees just as insensible as those by which she had brought Juan de Silva to believe in her newly-born affections for himself, she found her way into the confidence of Linares for another purpose. She fomented his hate for Juan; and, at length, when sure of the future purpose of the latter, she kindled the other's fears for the safety of Velasquez. It would have been easy to arouse Linares to such a degree of fury, as to prompt him to rush upon and slay Juan, with the hope, subsequently of justifying himself before Velasquez, and such was the wish of Diego;—but the more vigilant woman saw how futile such a proceeding would be, knowing how completely Juan was in the possession of his uncle's confidence. Besides of what use to her, in her desire to rescue Lopez de Levya, that Velasquez should escape the design of his nephew?

"No! no! good Diego," she said to the excited Biscayan,—"this were only to destroy thyself. Would Velasquez believe either thy testimony, or mine, against Juan de Silva? Thou mightest slay the one, but thou would'st be sure to perish from the fury of the other."

"I know not,—the crew!——"

"Soft! I understand thee! It is well that the men love thee. They should!—Thou, in truth, dost all the business of the vessel—Velasquez incapable, and Juan de Silva no seaman, and, I trow, but little of a soldier. Let then the treachery advance which thou can'st not arrest, save at thy own peril. It may be that Juan will repent—that he will not do the bloody deed which he meditates. All then will be as before, and our secret suspicions may sleep. But, it will be enough that we should keep proper watch, and if thou hast friends in the vessel——"

She paused.

"They are all my friends—they care nothing for Velasquez, now that he can do nothing; and they hate the insolence of this Juan!"

"Good!—then there will only need, if thou hast friends, that thou choose from among them, so that two or three of them may be ready with thyself to avenge thy captain should he meet foul play. Be ready, and I will counsel thee should I see farther tokens of this conspiracy."

The Biscayan was not superior to the inducements which she had adroitly insinuated rather than expressed. He was made to behold at the same glance, his revenge obtained upon the man who had subjected him to indignity, and the promotion of his selfish fortunes.

CHAPTER VIII.

Maria had thus secured a second agent, and made a large step toward the attainment of her object. But the days passed, and the nights followed, and still, nothing decisive, on the part of Juan, tended to confirm the assurances which he had made to his wily confederate. She became anxious and apprehensive, particularly as the passion of the youth seemed to be cooling toward her. He was no longer communicative—no longer sought her as frequently as before. His manner was now hesitating, his brow clouded, and his whole appearance that of a man who was brooding over wild suspicions.

But Maria was too much an adept to suffer her own anxieties to be perceptible, while she watched his with apprehension. Her doubts put on the appearance of womanly reserve, of dignified pride, of feminine sensibility, solicitous to avoid exposure. But she was equally studious not to forego the exercise of any, the meanest of her attractions. Her dress was carefully studied, and with the happiest effect; and if her brow was clouded, it was with sadness the sweeter for the shade. She sang too,—never with more exquisite freedom, or with more voluptuous sensibility, than when she sat alone, in the darkness of night, upon the deck of the slowly moving vessel. This was the third night after the last interview, which we have described, with Linares. She was suddenly joined by Juan de Silva. She knew of his approach, but started with well feigned surprise, as his whisper reached her ears.

"Thou hast thought me a laggard, Maria."

"Nay, I have suffered no disappointment. I had no hopes of thee, Juan!"

He was piqued.

"That was because thou did'st not know me. But I have been busy in my task. It is not that I am irresolute, that I am slow. It is because I would be sure. It is not known to thee, perhaps, that Velasquez hath valuable possessions in Spain. These will serve us hereafter, my Maria, when we shall tire of the sea. I have secured the papers which conduct to these. The key of his coffers is at my girdle. And now—but, hark thee,—continue thy ballad. It has beguiled his fancies, and he is about to join us to be nearer thee. There! His bell sounds. I will bring him forth, and—dost thou heed me, Maria?"

His hand trembled with an icy chillness, as he laid it upon her wrist. Her own grew chilled with a sympathetic consciousness of what he designed.

"Thy song! Thy ballad!" he muttered convulsively as he left her, and, almost unconscious of what she did, she resumed, in accents that slightly faltered, the ballad of "Belerma,"—one of her favorite songs, which she had probably learned from a purer source than that of the Zingali camp.

"Quando vio aquel corazon
  Estando en èl contemplado,
De nuevas gotas de sangre
  Estaba todo banado."

Which may be thus freely rendered:

"When the precious heart before her
  Lay all open to her view,
As if conscious of her presence,
  It began to bleed anew."

The voice of Velasquez—a voice that had once been equally rich and powerful,—now feebly joined its accents with hers, as he tottered forth from the cabin, supported on the arm of his nephew, and sank into a seat which had been prepared beside her. Her tones subsided into silence as he approached.

"Nay, stop not," said he; "let me hear thee—I come out only to hear thee, for I feel not so well to-night—not well, not happy, Maria mine. Thy voice will persuade me to a better spirit, though it sounds more sadly than is thy wont to-night; and that ballad—methinks, beauty mine, thou would'st never grieve over my heart, as the lovely damsel, Belerma, mourned over that of Durandarte." And he sang feebly—

"Corazon de mi, señor,
  Durandarte muy preciado,
En los amores dichoso,
  Y en batallas desdichado."

She continued silent.

"Sing for me, Maria—deny me not;" he said entreatingly. "I know not that I shall ever ask it of thee again. I feel as if a sentence had gone forth upon me. I feel as if I had done thee wrong! My heart tells me that I have wronged thee. If thou wilt sing for me now, I know that thou forgivest me!"

"Thou should'st not give way to such fancies, uncle mine;" said the nephew; "methinks, thou art looking better to-day than thou hast done for months past; and know I not that thou hast always been fond of Donna Maria, even as the good knight, Durandarte, was fond of the true maiden, Belerma."

"Ah! Juan, but Velasquez is no Durandarte, to find his way to the heart of a fair maiden. These days bring forth no knighthood such as his. Who is it walks behind us? Methought I heard a footstep?"

"It is none but the page, Gomez;" said the nephew, in somewhat hurried accents.

A thrill ran through the veins of Maria, as she remembered that the page, Gomez, was the creature of Juan, and the person who, as a spy upon her actions, first discovered the strong intimacy between herself and Lopez de Levya. The tones of Juan betrayed to her something of his purpose, and she gathered from them the conclusion that he meditated the performance of his crime that very night. Her heart smote her. She felt her own criminality; but she loathed the tyranny of Velasquez, as much as she did the cold and cruel selfishness of Juan; and it was only in the death of both that she could possibly hope to extricate from his desolate condition, the unhappy Lopez, whom, if she did not actually love, she did not loathe, and for whom every sentiment of humanity required that she should suffer the bloody game of Juan to go on. But she looked round at the inquiry of Velasquez, and while she detected Gomez near them, she was also enabled to discover another and a taller form, among the shadows beyond him. In this person she fancied she saw Linares, and suddenly she commenced the Hymn to the Virgin, plaintive and touching, of the dying knight, Baldwin:

"O Santa Maria Señora,
No me quieras olvidar,
A ti encomiendo mi alma,
Plegate de la guardar,
En este trance muerte
Esfuerzo me querais dàr,
Pues a les tristes consuelas
Quieras à mi consolar.
Y à tu preciosa Hijo,
Por mi te plega rogar,
Que perdone mis pecados,
Mi alma quiera salvar."

Which in an English idiom we may render thus:

"Holy Mary, thee beseeching,
  Lo! my soul in anguish cries,
Take it to thy holy keeping,
  Grant thy mercy ere it dies.
In the death-trance quickly sinking,
  To thy throne for help I flee,
In my hour of terror drinking,
  Consolation still from thee:
From thy precious son entreating,
  Pardon for my past career;
And the soul, its doom awaiting,
  Rescue from its mortal fear."

CHAPTER IX.

She had two objects in choosing this Hymn. It was the appropriate chant of Velasquez,—equally for his lips and ears, at that moment of his impending peril; and she cherished the human hope that, as in the previous song, he would join his voice with hers, and thus utter the proper prayer to Heaven, just when it would most become his lips. Her quick instincts led her also to believe that Linares would receive it as an intimation that the time was approaching when it would be necessary for him also to act. But Velasquez took no part in the Hymn. His head sank upon his breast as she proceeded, and he seemed to drowse.

"Dost thou sleep, uncle?" demanded Juan.

He looked up when addressed, and, in the imperfect light, it could be seen that the eyes of the invalid were full of tears.

"Thy Hymn saddens though it soothes me, Maria. Why didst thou choose it? Yet I blame thee not. I would I could sing it with thee. I strove, but the voice failed me, and my heart felt strange as if with a sudden sinking. I remember me to have heard that Hymn, the last night that I slept in the dwelling of my poor mother, Juanita. I was innocent then! I was a lad! There was a woman who was blind,—they called her Dolores,—she sang it often beneath our windows, but I did not weep to hear it then as I do now. Yet I remember it well. I knew the ballad all by heart, and could have sang it with her; but I had wilder fancies, and I mocked the tenderness of her Hymn with a gay ballad of some bolder spirit. I could not mock her now. Thy voice hath soothed me, Maria, but sing to me no more to-night. I feel as I would sleep. Juan, give me thy arm."

The nephew started to his feet. Maria would have offered an arm also, but Juan repulsed her.

"Not thine!" he answered, in accents not so low but that Velasquez heard them.

"And why not hers, Juan?"

"She lacks the strength. Here is Gomez."

"Maria lack the strength? Is she not well, Juan! or am I so much feebler than before? It must be so! I feel it so! Well! Give me help. Gomez be it, then."

A cold sweat covered the face and forehead of Maria de Pacheco, as she beheld the officious Gomez start forward at the summons of Juan. She saw Velasquez grasped by them, as if for support, on either side. The words of the latter—

"It is very dark—go'st thou rightly Juan?"—rushed through her very brain with a dreadful import, the more terrible and startling, as, having herself receded toward the cabin, she did not see them approach. Then she was conscious that some one stood beside her. It was Linares, followed by another. She grasped his arm.

"Now! now! Linares!—It is doing! Hence! Quick!—God have mercy!"

A plunge, and a most piercing shriek, were heard while she was speaking. Linares started forward. There was a sudden uproar in the ship. The alarm was given, and the men were running to and fro, while a crowd gathered on the side where the deed had been done. Another scream from the waters—a scream of agony,—a cry for help, and then the stern accents of Linares prevailed over all others.

"Murderer of thy uncle,—bloody traitor, I have caught thee in the act!"

"Away!" cried Juan de Silva,—"and to thy duties. Behold in me thy captain."

"Never!" was the cry from the crew.—"Diego Linares!"

The heavy hand of Linares was upon the shoulder of the culprit. His confederate Gomez was in the grasp of an equally powerful assailant. The proceeding had been too well devised,—the action too prompt—to suffer the cunning Juan to escape by any subtleties, and he was already given to understand that the fate to which he was doomed was that to which his uncle had been already consigned. In the suddenly aroused sense of danger which he felt, his impulse was to call for Donna Maria.

"She is here!" cried Linares.

The proud woman had recovered all her strength of soul and courage, and in the conviction that the hateful and malignant spirit whom she had once feared, was now wholly in her power, she felt an exulting sense of pleasure in being able to discard the veil of hypocrisy which she had so successfully worn. She steadily advanced toward the clamorous group.

"Speak for me, Maria;" exclaimed the captive;—"tell these men, —say to Linares, that, in what I have done, I have but obeyed thy wishes!"

"As if my wishes should suffice to move the loving nephew to the murder of his first friend, and most loving uncle!"

"Demonios! do I hear thee, woman!"

He was grappled instantly and firmly by the vigorous Linares. A dozen willing hands were nigh to help him in the fearful deed which he designed.

"Must I perish! Has my toil of blood been taken for such as these! Maria dost thou indeed desert me! Speak!" cried the desperate man—"Speak! thou knewest my purpose—thou didst not disclaim my deed!"

"I know thee as a felon and a fiend—as one whom I loathe and scorn! Linares, trust him not! He who would keep no terms with one so confiding as his mother's brother, will keep no terms with thee. What said I to thee before? Do thy duty to thyself and me! Revenge Velasquez, thy captain, recover the wretched Lopez de Levya from the isle where he was put to perish, and be the master of thy ship and crew!"

"This then was thy scheme! Demonios! that I should have been blinded by this woman's subtleties."

"Thou wast the victim to thy own vanities—thy own quickness to crime—thy own coldness of heart!" said the proud Maria.

"Oh! tongue of the serpent! dost thou sting me thus! But thou exultest too soon. Think'st thou that I have lived for such fate as this! with this wealth at my girdle—with so much of life in my possession—shall I lose life? No! off there, ye base scum and offal—off!—Ye shall hang for this like dogs. I will live—I will!—"

His own terrible struggles arrested his words, by which they had been stimulated. He had much to live for, and the unwilling spirit of youth was not to be resigned so easily to the sacrifice of those delights, for which he had paid such heavy price. His strength which was not ordinarily great, was that of desperation at the moment. He fought with wonderful spirit and address, and it tasked three stout seamen so to recover the mastery over him, as to lift him to the side of the vessel to which the feeble uncle had been beguiled, and over which he had been suddenly thrown. Brought to the verge of the precipice, he succeeded in forcing himself back, so that his head only hung over the bulwarks. Suddenly however, the whole weight of the powerful Linares was thrown upon him; and the crack of the neck, as it was thrust down upon the sharp and narrow thwarts, could have been heard even above the spasmodic gurgle and hoarse scream of the victim, by which it was accompanied. The still quivering carcass which they committed to the deep, was no longer conscious of its fate. A second plunge declared the doom of the page Gomez,—whose cries had been silenced by the stroke of a dagger, while his master's death-struggles were most violent.

Deep and dreary was the silence which followed on board the vessel. The rage of all parties was satisfied, and a certain, but indescribable fear was upon every heart. But none of the fruits of the struggle had been lost. A single hour had in effect rendered Maria de Pacheco, as had been promised by Juan de Silva, the Mistress of the Dian de Burgos. A single sentence to Diego Linares, declared the present destination of the vessel.

"The Maroon—Lopez de Levya!"

She was obeyed—the ship was brought about, and her prow turned once more in the direction of the desolate Isle of Lovers.

CHAPTER X.

Let us now return to our "Maroon." Three days upon his desolate island, did not materially lessen its terrors, or increase its attractions, in the eyes of Lopez de Levya. He still shuddered, not less at its fanciful and unknown dangers, than at his isolation among them. But the necessity of looking about him—of looking upward, indeed, —of feeling himself in motion, and realizing, as thoroughly as he could, the sense of life, as well its consciousness of suffering,—led him, at the end of this period, to make an effort, which, in his previous feeling of despair, he had never thought it possible he should make again. The nature, even of the constitutionally timid man, does not easily succumb to fortune—does not usually,—except, perhaps, in the first moment of overthrow, yield itself submissively to fate. The first moment of weariness which succeeds the contest, is, perhaps, the one of greatest prostration; and after that, the recuperative energies arouse themselves, and the sufferer, together. The very sense of abandonment is usually one of awakening and new resolve. This is one of the marked characteristics of the human nature. Indeed, the natural impulse of every free moral agent is resistance. To oppose, to struggle farther,—to contend to the last, and even where consciousness of the conflict itself fails,—is one of the earliest, as it is one of the most necessary developments, of the moral instinct. Combativeness, indeed, is one of the most important of our moral qualities. It is one which,—arguing always the presence of a great and pressing necessity,—is, at the same time, continually counselling the means by which to contend against it.

Lopez de Levya, though feeble, was not entirely wanting in the natural instinct; and, armed with the Spanish crossbow, and the shafts which had been accorded him—a spear, a knife, and one or two other implements of use and necessity, which might, in the event of exigency, be converted into weapons, he now proceeded to explore his empire. A sense of his possessions was also rapidly beginning to make itself felt in his reasonings. That delightful human instinct which, in the consciousness of sway, reconciles us so readily to all its dangers, was about to contribute its assistance toward comforting our Maroon in his desolation. He was indeed a sovereign, though he commanded no subjects. Yet, the wild fowl which sped along the shore before his footsteps, or sprang aloft, wheeling in slow gyrations overhead, as he drew nigh their coverts, might be made to feel his authority as well as to minister to his wants. He could persecute, punish and destroy them, quite as certainly, and certainly with less danger to himself, than if they were of his own species; and a sense of fierce delight at this consciousness of his power to do mischief, was grateful to his heart, as it always is to that of the being who is himself peculiarly sensible to the influences of fear. He was beginning to regard with complacency a condition from which there was no escape. A thousand years might elapse, as Velasquez had malignantly assured him, without suffering the prows of any European vessel to approach so nearly to his islet as to discover the existence of its lone possessor. He must make the most of that existence. He must hoard, must economize his resources, as well of thought and enjoyment, as of covering and food. He must not destroy his subjects simply to exercise his authority. His power must be sparingly indulged for his own sake and safety. He laid aside his guitar with care and tenderness, protecting it from hurt and exposure, by hanging it beneath the friendly palm trees where he had passed the night. In the first paroxysm of his despair and madness, conscious that this dangerous but delightful instrument, was connected with his present sufferings, he was about to dash it upon the bleak sands and trample it under foot, or cast it from him into the engulphing and surrounding sea. He knew not, himself, why he forebore to do so. Some tender recollection in his thought procured its safety;—some conviction that it might minister to him in his wretched exile;—and the desperate passion which might have destroyed it,—was restrained. Yet bitter were the tears that he shed over it, as, arousing from the swoon that followed the departure of the vessel from his eyes, he found the cruel memorial still about his neck, where it had been hung by the mocking hands of his enemy. With the subdued temper that followed the first feeling of his despair, the instrument became doubly precious, as it not only spoke of future solace, but reminded him of former enjoyments. It constituted one of the few moral links which connected him still with the great family of man. He lacked the courage to part with any of his treasures, and the care with which he secreted his favorite instrument beneath the palm trees, was that of the tender mother, who leaves her infant for a while, solicitous of its comfort even while she has no fears for its safety; and sometimes looking back, not with any hope to see, but that her eyes involuntarily yield themselves to the course indicated by her heart.

This charge disposed of, Lopez de Levya grasped his spear with as much martial dignity as he could command. He felt for his knife at his girdle, he slung the crossbow over his shoulder, and, ready for any event, he sallied forth to explore his empire. But though his territory was a small one, such as an adventurous spirit would have traversed wholly, and surveyed thoroughly, in the course of a single day, our Maroon was quite too timid, too cautious in his footsteps, not to make it a work of longer time. Several days were necessary to his examination. He proceeded slowly, and winding heedfully about, and probing every copse before he penetrated it, he first assured himself against any possible danger from secret foes, before he made his search satisfactory. His domain was equally ample and compact; not wanting in variety, but having its elevations of rock, and its valley of verdure and its long wastes and stretches of sand, in a comparatively close compass.

The islet was not, as it had been thought by Velasquez, a mere series of sand hills, raised up by the sea, the creation of its own contending billows. It was a solid rock, whose gradual ascent, nowhere rising into more than a very gentle elevation, admitted of the easy accumulation of sand and soil, which, in process of time, had, in various places received a covering of very green and beautiful vegetation. The shrubbery was rather close than lofty. Among the trees were the plantain, the cocoanut, the breadfruit and the banana. The pine apple grew in gold and purple, unobserved by man; and slender vines, which shot out from the knotted and ancient bulbs, from crevices of the rock, ran wantonly over the sides of sudden hillocks, which they garnished with blue clusters of the grape.

Verily, our musician had an empire in truth. Velasquez little dreamed of the treasure he had given away in his malice. The sterile islet was a principality of fairy land, and Lopez de Levya grew more and more reconciled to life as he beheld the wealth which lay scattered around him. His possessions were beyond his wants. Nature had made ample provision, and millions might have been found, among the needy and oppressed children of Europe, to whom a life of exile and isolation in such an abode, would have been the most acceptable boon of heaven.

Nor were these vegetable possessions all that came to Lopez with his empire. Tribes of small wild animals wantoned before his footsteps scarcely seeming to fear his presence; and the nimble little marmozet of the tropics, with a petty, playful mischief, darting before him as he came, would fling the nuts from the tree tops, and chatter, in equal fun and defiance, at his sovereign authority.

Our "Maroon" began to grow interested in his possessions, and fate soon conducted him to other discoveries. His island, stretching away from north to south, was exceedingly long in proportion to its width. He had been landed at the northern extremity, at which point, it had been impossible to conceive its dimensions, except from its width, and this had led to conclusions which gave no reason to suppose its extent to be half so great as Lopez found it. At the close of the third day of his explorations, he had nearly reached its southern extremity. He had found the land gradually to rise as he advanced, until toward the close, taken in comparison with the uniform level of the sand and sea surrounding the spot to which he approached, and by which the island was terminated in this quarter, he discovered what might be considered a moderate mountain. It was certainly a large and imposing hill, seen from the low shores or the waters which surrounded them. Here, too, the groves thickened into something like a forest. Heated by his ramble, and somewhat fatigued, as the day was wearing to its close, he passed gladly for shelter into the shady recesses of its heights. He soon found himself in one of the coolest realms of shade which he had ever traversed. A natural pathway, as it seemed, conducted him forward. Gradually advancing, he at length emerged from the thicket only to stand upon the brow of a rugged eminence which rose, almost perpendicularly, overlooking the sea. A small flat of sandy beach, lay at his feet which was evidently subject to overflow at the rising of the tide. Not half a mile beyond could be seen a small cluster of little rocks, just peering above the sea, scarcely bigger it would seem than so many human heads, which the waves covered at high water. Between them he could distinguish the boiling and striving of the billows, which sent up a sheeted shower far above the rocks with which they strove. Long lines, stretching from several points and losing themselves among these rocks, betrayed the course of strong currents which were caused by the capricious whirlpools that lay within their embrace.

The eye of Lopez took in all these objects, but they did not bound his survey. Stretching far beyond,—did he only fancy, or did he really behold a slender dark speck which might be the outline of a shore corresponding with that on which he stood?—miles of ocean lay between them, but in that unclouded realm of sunshine and of calm, objects might be seen from an eminence, such as that on which he stood, at a surprising distance. It was only in glimpses now that he beheld, or fancied, the object in his gaze. Sometimes it would utterly disappear,—but this might be from the continued and eager tension of his vision;—again would it grow out boldly beneath his eyes;—but this might be in obedience only to the desires of his mind.

Long and feverishly did he watch, and many were his conjectures as to the distant empire which his hope or his sight had conjured up. He turned away, and his glances rested upon the smooth plane of yellow sand beneath his feet, which lay, inviting to his tread, glinting a thousand fires from bits of crystal, which reflected the now waning sunlight.

To this little esplanade, which looked so exceedingly inviting, our "Maroon" was persuaded to descend from his heights, by finding a convenient series of rude steps which wound below—little gaps in the hillside, or fractures in the naked rock, which one might almost be tempted to imagine,—so admirable was the assistance which they gave to the anxious footsteps,—had been the work of art. Following these, Lopez descended to the hard and sandy floor, and standing in the shadow of the rock, he once more looked forth eagerly upon the doubtful waste of sea.

There still lay the empire of his desire. It was along and over those billows that he was yet to see the glimmer of a saving hope. Such was still his dream, and seating himself upon the sand, he inscribed almost unconsciously the names of Spain, of the Dian de Burgos, and of the lowly hamlet in his own country, from which he had been persuaded regretfully to wander. Then followed rude outlines of the ship which had abandoned him, and then naturally enough, a portrait, something less rude, of the fair but passionate woman, for whose fatal love, he was suffering the dreadful doom of exile and isolation. His own name was written, but as quickly obliterated, and musing over the melancholy record, his heart failed him, and he sunk forward, prone, upon the faint memorials which the rising waters would soon wash away forever. Thus he lay, moaning, for many weary minutes, till, all at once, a coldness fell upon him, which chilled him to the heart, and aroused him to more immediate apprehensions. The shadow of the hill beneath which he lay was upon him. The sun was slowly receding from the heights.

Starting to his feet, he turned to reascend the hill, and recoiled with a feeling little short of horror, as he beheld the huge mouth of a cavern yawning directly upon him. This cavern was open to the sea. Its waters, at their rising, passing the little stretch of sand upon which he had lain, glided into the dim hollow, which now looked, grimly threatening, upon the easily alarmed spectator. The opening was not a very large one, but would easily admit of the passage of three or more persons at a time. Its lips were covered with a soft and beautiful clothing of green moss which made the darkness within seem yet more dismal. Long grasses, and thick shrubs and vines hanging over from above, contributed to increase the solemnity of its aspect, as showing the depth and certainty of its solitude; and the deep silence which prevailed within, added still more greatly to the impressive influence with which it possessed the soul of the "Maroon," while he timidly yet eagerly gazed upon the opening.

At the first discovery of this domain of solemnity and silence, he receded almost to the sea. He was not encouraged by the stillness. A voice from within, the cry of a beast, the rush of a bird's wing—had been more encouraging. His advance was very gradual,—but he did advance, his doubts being much less easy of endurance than the absolute presence of a real cause of apprehension. With trembling nerves he presented his spear, and got his knife in readiness. The spear was thrust deep into the throat of the cavern, but it provoked no disquiet within. Then, his hair erecting itself, and his heart rising in his throat as he advanced, he, at length, fairly made his way into the subterranean dwelling. There he shouted, and the sounds came rolling back upon him from so many hollow voices within, that he once more recoiled from the adventure, and hurried back in terror to the entrance.

CHAPTER XI.

But he gathered courage for a second trial. The answering echos were not followed by any evil, though they seemed to mock his ears with a laughter such as he had heard from the tyrant of the Dian de Burgos, when he devoted him to his melancholy exile. He passed again into the cavern, taking care, by his own silence, to provoke no such fearful responses as those which had driven him forth. A few feet brought him to a small dark pool which lay directly in his pathway, and which left but a narrow space between its own margin and the walls of the cavern. This he sounded with his spear, and found to be shallow. It was a lakelet left by the waves of ocean, by which, at its overflow, the cave was evidently penetrated.

Passing this pool, our "Maroon" found himself upon a dry floor, the foundation of which was the solid rock, but a slender coating of soil had formed upon it, which was, in turn, clothed with a nice smooth covering of green and velvet-like moss. Here he was gladdened by a glimpse of the sun, which, breaking through a chink in the rock, a slender crevice, glided along the rugged vaultside, affording to the timid adventurer, a more perfect idea of an angel presence, than he had ever before possessed. Another opening in the rock, almost immediately above, afforded sufficient light for his examination of the whole interior. The cave narrowed to a still slenderer gap, as he advanced, than was the one by which he had entered. This was the entrance to another apartment. It was sometime before he ventured to enter this and not until he had thrust his spear, its full length, into its recesses. He then clambered up, for the elevation of this inner chamber was greater than the first.

Here he was again refreshed with brief glimpses of the sunlight, which, peeping in through two openings of the rock, looked like two of the most natural and smiling eyes in the world. This apartment, though of less height, was of larger area than the other. It soon afforded him new subjects of curiosity if not alarm. In the centre of the chamber stood a rock, scarcely larger than a blacksmith's anvil, and having something of the appearance of one, on which lay the remains of a fire. Brands lay half consumed, the fires of which were now extinguished; but the ashes were there, still undisturbed, as if the flame had only recently gone out. Piles of an aromatic gum, lay upon a shelf of the rock, and other piles, in slender fragments, of wood of which our Maroon knew nothing, lay contiguous also. But what, more than anything beside, arrested and confounded our "Maroon" were certain numerous shreds of dark hair, soft, fine and very long, like the hair of women, which hung, neatly tied in separate volumes, from the tops of reeds, which were stuck about the vaulted roof of the cavern, and wherever a crevice could be found sufficiently large, in which to introduce their slender extremities. Examining several of these shreds of hair, the wonder of the explorer was increased to discover that the ends of them were shriveled as in the flame. There were other objects to excite his surprise, if not to occasion his alarm. Baskets of shells and pebbles, flowers which had decayed, a bow and many arrows,—all of the latter being broken—and a heavy string of large pearls which had been slightly injured in the fire, but which Spanish cupidity readily conceived would still possess considerable value in the Cuba market.

CHAPTER XII.

Here then was a curious discovery. The island was not inhabited. He had traversed it for three days and had found no footstep but his own. Had it ever been inhabited? Scarcely:—the impunity with which beast and bird enjoyed its securities, and of which he had sufficient proofs in his three days' experience, was conclusive of that question. But that it was visited by human beings, the witnesses in the cavern were numerous. Did they come frequently, for what purpose, and from whence? These were the next questions. That they came frequently might be inferred from various circumstances. The brands which had been swept from the altar, were in great heaps in one corner of the cavern. The shreds of hair were equally numerous and of different degrees of age. This difference was very perceptible upon the slightest examination. They came for a religious purpose. The shreds of hair, the altar, the aromatic woods and gum,—were all significant of sacred rites. From whence?

Surely, was the thought of the "Maroon," from that isle, or continent, the dim outlines of which had fixed his gaze but an hour before. A farther search led to farther discoveries, but all of the same character. Vast stores of these shreds of hair, seemingly the accumulation of centuries, were found in remote crannies and dark recesses of the vault. A thousand little baskets of shells, and white and blue fragments,—pebbles that seemed like glass,—and, more precious in the sight of Lopez, numerous strands of pearl, such as he had already discovered—which, dark and dingy with frequent smokes in the cavern, he found could be made clean by a little water. In a recess of the rock, the most obscure, he made the discovery of a niche which had evidently been used for a couch. It was softly lined with moss and leaves, and there were flowers in bunches at the head and feet which might have been grasped by the hands of youth and beauty. The impression of the head was perceptible upon a pillow of moss at one extremity, and suggested to our Maroon the idea of a far more comfortable couch for himself, than any which he had yet found upon his island. The sun had been rapidly sinking while he had been urging his researches, and the cheerless dusk of the horizon without, as he emerged from the cavern, determined him once more to return to its recesses. He did so, and, ascending the mysterious recess in the inner chamber, though with some hesitation, he soon sunk into a deep slumber, in which, though he dreamed of strange forms and aspects about him, he dreamed of nothing to impair the virtue of his sleep.

CHAPTER XIII.

But with his awakening thoughts, apprehension, rather than pride or exultation, followed the consciousness of his new discoveries. Had he not reason to fear the return of the strange people by whom the isle was visited, as it would seem, periodically? That they were a barbarous people he could not doubt—that they would resent his presence, and treat him as an enemy, he had every reason to dread. He should be a victim to some one of their cruel sacrifices. He should be immolated on the altars of one of the bloody deities of the Caribbean worship. The man, brave by nature, and in the situation of Lopez de Levya, might well entertain such apprehensions. How much more vividly would they occur to the imagination of one so timid and feeble of soul as our "Maroon." They kept him—assuming various forms of terror—in a cold sweat for several days; and though the impression was naturally weakened and dissipated the more familiar the images became, yet any immediately impelling thought brought them back upon his spirit with a ghastly and withering influence.

Three days elapsed after this discovery before he found himself able to recur to it without a vague and overpowering sense of terror. But the pearls shone in his eyes. He had grown wealthy on a sudden. He drew forth the numerous strings which he found suspended in the cavern. Every Spaniard of that day had an instinctive appreciation of treasure. Lopez had never seen so much riches at a glance before. He examined his pearls in the sunlight. He cleansed them of their impurities by the ocean's side. And he was the master of all this glitter. He had never dreamed of such vast possessions. In Spain—but when he thought of Spain, and felt the probability, in all its force, that he should never again behold its shores, he was almost moved in his desperation to fling his newly found treasure into the deep. But the latent hope, which dreamed of the possible approach of some future mariner, forbade the sacrifice, and restoring his possessions to the dark crevices from whence he had taken them, he stretched himself out upon the eminence which vaulted his possessions, and which had now become with him a favorite place of watch, to gaze upon the broad plane of ocean by which he was girded on every hand.

CHAPTER XIV.

No sign of hope for the "Maroon." The sun shines with a red and scorching influence. There is not a cloud in the sky to curtain the brazen terrors of his countenance. The ocean sleeps, smooth as glass, unbroken in its wilderness of range, spread out like an endless mirror of steel, that fired the very brain to gaze upon. And in the sky, on the return of night, might be seen the moon, bright but placid, nearly at her full, giving to the scene something of an aspect of melancholy, such as she habitually wears herself. Not a speck upon the waters,—not a speck,—and, while the lull continues, no possibility of a sail in sight. He looks toward the faint uncertain line of shore, which he has fancied to be beyond him on the south. It is no fancy now. It is certain. The subdued waves lessen the usual obstacles of vision. The line of land, if it be land and no mocking cloud, appears to rise. It undulates. There are inequalities which strike his eye, and which, seen at that distance, cannot be subject to doubt or disbelief. He trembles with mixed feelings of hope and terror as he comes to this conclusion. Once more to behold the human form—once more to look upon the friendly aspect of man, and to say Brother! But will the aspects be friendly that shall look upon him from that shore? Will they hearken to his cry of pleading? Will they understand him when he uses the endearing title of "brother" to the savage chief who leads the marauding party? These suggestions but fill our "Maroon" with dismay.

Crouching in the shade, his eye fixed on the opposite shores, as he believes them, he starts suddenly to his feet. He passes his hand across his brows—his fingers press his eyes, as if to remove some speck, some foreign atom, from his vision. Can he believe his eyes? Does he, indeed, behold an object upon the waters approaching him from that doubtful and hostile shore? He sees;—but now it disappears. It is gone! He looks in vain, his whole frame convulsed and quivering with the emotions of his soul! Again it rises into view. It disturbs the smooth surface of the deep. The brightness of the mirror is shaded by a speck, and that speck grows upon his sight. He can doubt no longer. It is a boat which he beholds—it brings with it a savage enemy—the fierce cannibal of the Caribbean Sea! He drops his spear, and his cross-bow—his hand grapples, not his knife, but his rosary. He falls upon his knees—he counts the beads with hurried hand and failing memory. He clutches the agnus Dei—he strains it to his lips, and with many a broken invocation to some favorite saint, he hurries away to put himself in shelter.

His search has fortunately enabled him to find many places of temporary hiding, such as would probably suffice for safety during the stay,—which was evidently brief always—of the savages by whom the islet was visited.

At first he thought of occupying a dense piece of copse which lay at a little distance in the rear of the elevation in which the cavern was found. But a doubt whether this would not be penetrated, in a desultory ramble of the intruders after fruit; and a curious desire to be in some situation which would enable him to watch their proceedings, led him to abandon this idea. The cave itself was obviously one of their places of greatest resort. It was here that their religious rites were performed. The islet itself was unemployed. It was a place set apart and sacred to some special and superior purpose. The vaulted chamber was the place of their mysteries. He determined that it should be the place of his concealment. He had sought out all its secret places. He had seen that certain of their remains—their shreds of hair,—their baskets of shell,—their broken arrows,—had been undisturbed for a long season; and behind these, in convenient fissures of the rock, which were wholly unlighted by the day, he prepared to bestow himself.

The suggestions of the naturally timid person, under a consciousness of approaching danger, are usually prompt enough. Lopez de

Levya hurried to execute the plan he had conceived. He entered the cave ere yet the strangers could behold any movement on the shore. His provisions—a supply for several days at least had been already transferred to the safe keeping of the vaulted apartment. These were all disposed of convenient to his reach, in the crevice of the rock in which his own person was to find security. And all prepared, he planted himself within the mouth of the cave, anxiously looking forth—yet not so as to be seen—for the unknown object of his apprehension.

CHAPTER XV.

The strange object is indeed a boat—a large canoe, with two banks of oars—one of those long and stately barges in which the Caribbean was wont to go forth for war or ceremonial. Its sides were gaudily and richly painted. Its poop was raised with a triumphal canopy of dyed cotton above it. Its prow was lofty and sharp, and bore for a figure head, the savage jaws of the Cayman, or American crocodile. The rowers of the boat were men, but all beside were women. These were eight in number—seven who sat forward, and near the prow, and one who sat in the stern, alone and under the canopy. The course of the boat was regulated by the oarsmen. The women at the prow were all richly clad in stained cotton garments. Their heads were tressed with strands of pearl, their necks, which were bare, were covered with similar decorations. Each in her hands bore a bunch of arrows and a basket. Beside them might be seen other baskets of aromatic gums, and bundles of a wood similarly aromatic. These females were all evidently matrons, none of them being less than thirty years of age, and all of them wearing the experience of look and bearing which is common to those who have been mothers. But she who sat alone at the stern, was evidently none of these. She could not have been more than fifteen years old, and looked wild and startled as a young fawn, for the first time venturing forth without its dam in company. She was quite as beautiful as she was young; her skin less dark than was usual among the Caribbean Indians—not much more dark, indeed, than was that of the Spaniard,—and the red blood coursing at moments, from her heart into her cheeks, suffusing it with the most exquisite teints of innocence and youth. She was well formed and tall. Her hair streamed down over her back and shoulders. Her bosom was quite bare, without pearl or any other ornament. Her dress was of white cotton, purely white, without any of those rich and gaudy dyes, which were so freely used by her people. Before her was a small earthen vessel half covered, from which a slight smoke continued to ascend, as if from a hidden fire below. Into this, at intervals, the maiden might be seen to fling a fine powder which she scooped out of a gourd that lay beside her. Numerous baskets of flowers and shells lay at her feet, and a bunch of arrows rested upon her lap.

The oarsmen were all habited as warriors. Their brows were grave. No words passed among them or among the women, until, as they drew nigh the shore, the latter suddenly broke out into a wild, and not unmusical chaunt, which made our "Maroon" recoil within his vaulted chamber, with an indefinite sense of terror. At this sound the rowers dropped their oars,—the boat lay upon her centre, and the women prepared to leave her, though they were still more than thirty paces from the shore. But the water was exceedingly shallow where the vessel lay;—the beach which formed the esplanade of the cave, stretching out boldly for some distance into the sea. Availing themselves of their knowledge of the bar, the women stepped forth upon a ridge where the ocean, disarmed of its billows, swept along gently to the level of their knees.

They brought forth their billets of fragrant wood—their baskets of shell—their sheaves of arrows—their vessels of odorous gums and incense. Then, taking the damsel from beneath the canopy at the stern, they bore her, with anxious solicitude, upon their shoulders from the vessel to the shore—her feet and drapery being kept sacred from the waves. One of their number seemed to counsel and direct the rest, and it was with feelings of new horror, that our "Maroon" beheld in her grasp, as she led the way to the cavern, a sharp broad instrument of stone, that greatly resembled a butcher's cleaver. His apprehensions were not now for himself. For what was the unhappy damsel destined? For the sacrifice? For what crime—what penance—what terrible superstition?—to appease the malice of what bloody god—was this poor child, so young, so beautiful—so evidently innocent—to be made the victim? Her sad and fearful looks—the tears which now gathered in her eyes—the wild chaunt of the women, and the stern grave aspects of the men—these all seemed to denote an occasion of wo and terror. The men did not leave the boat—they drew no nearer to the land. The shore seemed to be a consecrated one, which the masculine footstep was not allowed to pollute. The girl, still borne upon the arms of the women, and following her who seemed to be the officiating priestess, was carried into the cavern; the wild chorus of the women being resumed as they entered the gloomy portals, and reverberating from the walls within, with a sound at once sweet, awful and inspiring.

CHAPTER XVI.

Our "Maroon" was already crouched, close, in his place of hiding. He beheld in silence and safety, but with an awful beating at the heart, the whole of the strange procession. He saw the women circling the altar stone with wild contortions and a strange unearthly song. He saw them, from several branches of wood, draw forth the billets with which they kindled a flame upon the stone. The fire was drawn from the vessel which had been supplied with fuel on the voyage by the hands of the young damsel. She sat apart, on a low projection of the wall, to which she had been conducted, and but a few paces from the cavity in which Lopez found retreat. She took no part in the ceremony, though she seemed deeply interested in its progress. At certain pauses in the wild incantations, particularly when certain emphatic sounds or words closed the chaunt, she clasped her hands aloft, and her groan was audible, as if in supplication. The fire began to blaze suddenly above the stone, and its strange gleams played in lively tints upon the gloomy walls of the cavern. Then the circling dance and the chorus were renewed. Then, at certain sounds, the women paused, and, at such moments, the maiden rose, and, approaching the flame, threw into it fragments of wood or gum with which she had been supplied. At all such additions, the flame blazed up more brightly, and the chaunt was more wild and vigorous than ever. At length it ceased, and, in an instant, every woman crouched down around the stone where she stood, except the one who seemed to act as priestess.

She did not join in the chorus of the others, but in a low chaunt of her own performed some separate office. She now approached the maiden, and conducted her toward the altar. At her words the damsel bent over the heads of the kneeling women, separately, and her tears fell fast as she murmured in their several ears. She took from the neck of each her strands of pearl. They themselves unbound them from their own tresses, which now hung down mournfully, of great length, from every shoulder. The pearls were collected by the priestess and laid apart. Our "Maroon," from his place of watch, followed with keen eyes, and saw where she laid them. The women now receded. The girl embraced them each, with a deep sobbing, and they responded with mingling sighs and songs, while passing out of the chamber in which they left her with the officiating woman. When their voices were heard only faintly from the sea shore, where they had now assembled, the maiden was conducted to the altar place by her matron like companion.

Her mournful utterance announced some sadder ceremonial. The girl answered her by a cry and threw herself at her feet before the altar. The woman knelt upon one knee. The head of the maiden was supported upon the other from which the long black hair depended, half shrouding the drapery of the priestess. Very tender were the few words which then passed between the two. The girl clasped her hands together, and her tearful eyes were full of the sweetest but saddest resignation. The woman smoothed her tresses out with her fingers, stooped and kissed affectionately the lips of the child, and while everything betokened nothing less than the truest sympathy, and the most heartfelt and generous affection between them, what was the horror of our "Maroon," now deeply interested in the event, to see the woman possess herself of the broad knife of stone which lay on the foot of the altar. Timid and feeble as he was of soul, his fingers clutched his knife with a convulsive resolution, which, in the case of a braver spirit would have long before declared itself in action!

CHAPTER XVII.

The moment in which the Indian damsel lay thus prostrate and at the mercy of one who seemed about to complete the rites in which she had been engaged, by the sacrifice of the innocent creature in her grasp, was a moment of the most cruel humiliation to the imbecile Spaniard. His sensibilities were violently excited. Every sympathy of his heart was awakened. His better nature—his human training—his

Christian teaching—such as it was possible for him to acquire in that day of constant war and rapine—were all active in urging him to adventure his own life, in saving her who seemed about to perish before him. She too, so young, so resigned, and—not the least consideration—so really beautiful. But the necessary nerve was wanting to the "Maroon." He who dared not the single stroke, though prompted by the woman he professed to love, when it would have saved her from shame and himself from the bitter exile which he now endured, was not likely to exhibit any rashness—any ordinary courage, —though with such a threatening spectacle of death before him.

Happily for humanity, his apprehensions were all idle. The meditated sacrifice in which the priestess was about to officiate, contemplated not the life but the long and flowing locks of the damsel. These were severed at a stroke, and hung up in the chamber, from an arrow, the shaft of which was made to penetrate a crevice in the rock. Then the maiden rose, and taking the bunch of arrows which she had brought, she snapt them in twain before the altar which the matron still continued to supply, with aromatic gums and fuel. Some further ceremonies were performed—there was a solemn imposition of hands, while the virgin knelt before the priestess, and the lips of the latter were glued to the forehead of the girl. A brief dialogue, in subdued and murmuring tones, passed between them, and then the voices of both rose in a wild, sad chaunt, the burden of which was caught up by the voices of the females without. One embrace followed the subsidence of the strain, and the matron and the virgin parted—the former hurrying from the cavern, and the latter sinking down, in an agony of fear and grief, before the fitful blaze upon the altar.

Lopez de Levya drew a long breath. He began to grow courageous. The voices of the women without were dying away in the distance. Could they have retired to the boat, and could they be returning to the distant shore whence they came, leaving the maid alone as he himself had been left? Her evident sorrow and apprehension declared this to be the case. But it was evident that no such feeling moved her abandonment as had occasioned his. The proofs of a deep and tender interest had been shown her to the last. He had heard the sighs, the moans and murmurs, of the officiating matron. He had witnessed her fond caresses of the damsel. He had heard with quivering sensibilities the wild sad chaunt of the attending women, whose song still feebly fell upon his senses from without.

The scene which he had witnessed was a religious ceremony. But what did it contemplate? Was the maiden thus left to herself—and to him—destined for a sacrifice—to perish at last, before the altars of some strange and savage divinity? It might be so; but certainly no such purpose was designed at present, for he did not fail to perceive that an ample supply of food was left with her, sufficient for a month's consumption.

Or, was she destined herself to become a priestess officiating, like the matron, who had left her, in the same, and other mysterious rites, hereafter? This was the more probable conjecture. At least such was the thought to which after a rapid mental survey of probabilities, our "Maroon" arrived. Perhaps, a little more deliberation might have rendered it doubtful, whether the innumerable signs which the walls of the chamber presented, of repeated ceremonials like the present, were not proofs that the proceeding could not regard any such appropriation of the neophyte. It was a ceremonial evidently common to the tribe or nation. It was one through which, at a certain period, each virgin had to pass. It was indeed, a dedicatory, but it was an invocatory service also. We may, in this place, briefly declare the object of the ceremonial.

Among the Caribbeans, as among the Aborigines of the new world in most quarters, both sexes were dedicated, separately, and by different rites, to fortune. The period in life when they were to emerge from the salutary restraints of the parent, and to be left to the assertion of their own wits and the exercise of their own intelligence, was that chosen, in which to solicit for them the protection of the gods, who should confer upon them some especial spiritual guide and guardian. To propitiate the gods for this favor—to move them to an indulgent dispensation—to secure a friendly and favoring protector, and to inspire the young with wisdom, courage and faithfulness, were the objects of the ceremonial. In the case of males, they were thus consecrated when able to commence the labors of the chase. They were subjected to severer ordeals than the other sex since the leading desire, with them, was their proper endowment with hardihood and courage. Long abstinence from food, exposure to cold, and frequent stratagems by which to alarm them and try their courage, were resorted to by those having charge of their initiate. The maidens were more gently entreated.

Isolation rather than exposure, was the influence employed upon their courage. Food was provided them, but of a sort rather to enflame the fancies than the blood. This was to be chastened rather than exhilarated. Roots of rare efficacy, the virtues of which they knew,—herbs which assailed the brain and the nervous system were silently mingled with the food which was left for their sustenance; and the very fumes of the aromatic woods and gums with which they were appointed to feed their daily and nightly fires, possessed a partially intoxicating effect upon those who continued to inhale them. It was while under such influences that the visions of the youth were to be observed with heed. The images that were most frequent in their dreams—the scenes which they witnessed—the voices that they heard,—the laws which were declared—these were to be the oracles by which their whole succeeding lives were to be regulated. By these the young warrior was to be guided in the chase or the conflict, and the young woman, in the keeping of her household, the training of her young, and the exercise of her sympathies and tastes. The favorite, or leading aspect, or object, in their visions, was to become their guiding spirit forever after. It was customary in many tribes—perhaps in most—to adopt this object as their mark or sign;—and this was the *totem*, inscribed upon the arm or breast,—not dissimilar to those of knighthood in the middle ages, drawn from favorite objects of sight, or the events most conspicuous in their lives—with this difference, that, in Europe, the *totem* was inscribed upon the shield, the surcoat or the pennon,—among the savages of the new world, upon the naked person.

CHAPTER XVIII.

Night came on in the vaulted chamber of the lovely isle, occupied only by the Indian damsel and the "Maroon." Without, all was silent, except now and then, the bark of the marmozet as he bounded among the cocoanut trees above. Several hours had elapsed since the sounds of the wild chaunt of the women had failed upon his ears, yet our Spaniard maintained his place of hiding with religious quietude. Meanwhile, the girl fed the fires upon her altar. She sat upon a rude swelling of the rocky floor, her hands folded in her lap, and the ends of her shortened hair resting upon her shoulders. Her form was rather between the "Maroon" and the fire,—the blaze of which, as she heightened it by occasional supplies of fuel, made marvellously distinct in his eyes the exquisite outline of her delicate but well marked profile. And thus she sat, and such was her only office for several hours more.

It must have been full midnight, when our Spaniard, who had not slept an instant, discovered that sleep had seized upon the senses of the Indian damsel. Her form subsided into an attitude favorable to rest. She sunk upon one side, her head resting upon a sudden elevation of the floor, which conducted to the niche which seemed to have been employed as a couch on previous occasions, and where, for the last two nights Lopez himself had taken his rest. Her breathing was soft and regular. It denoted a calm and perfect sleep. He was encouraged and gradually withdrew from his place of concealment. His steps were cautiously taken. He drew nigh to the sleeper—surveyed her with a keen and pleasant interest;—then, farther to be sure, he stole forth into the antechamber of the vault, and gliding cautiously, maintaining a vigilant watch all the while, he emerged from the cavern, and stood upon the beach.

The waters of the sea had gone down. The gray sands were quite uncovered for a long stretch, the spot being wholly bare upon which the Indian bark had anchored during the afternoon. The moon was high in heaven, and at her full. No cloud obscured or sullied the blue serenity of the skies. The scene was eminently and wholly spiritual. There was nothing human visible in the surrounding aspects of ocean, sky and land.

Satisfied of this, our Maroon returned, with rather hurried footsteps, to the cavern. He stole back cautiously, however, so as not to disturb the damsel. She still slept, her position being totally unchanged. But the fire had grown faint upon her altars. He fed it with a handful of the fuel that lay contiguous. He knelt beside her, and in the reviving blaze, he examined closely the innocent features, which he had thought so very sweet and beautiful in the before imperfect light. The nearer survey did not lessen her loveliness in his sight. Her closed eyes, and her slightly parted lips, were studies for the sculptor, they were so delicate in their structure yet so admirably defined. The features might have been thought

Castilian. The forehead was high but narrow, the nose good, and the neck moderately large and smooth, rising into the gentle swell of a bosom which had not yet learned to heave with other than happy childish emotions. One of her hands, the fingers of which were long and taper, had stolen to her breast, the partial drapery of which it seemed to grasp. The other lay at her side, the fingers closing upon a handful of wood intended for the fire. Thus she slept.

The "Maroon" stooped and pressed his lips closely upon hers. She sighed deeply, but moved not. Again he repeated the kiss, and her eyes opened upon him. They closed involuntarily. Again they opened, and now with a wild, appealing expression. He had slightly retreated, as he found her about to waken. He had regained his feet. He stood somewhat apart, the altar being in some degree between them.

We have spoken of the personal appearance of Lopez de Levya, as being pleasing to the eye of woman. At this moment it looked manly as well as pleasing, and, in the doubtful light of the cavern, with his form erect, his features half shaded by the gloom, his knife at his girdle, and a rich red scarf about his waist, he might have served for the model of one of those brigands, a compound of Orson and Adonis, whom we see so commonly in Italian pictures.

The impression was not unfavorable upon the eyes of the Indian damsel. But her senses had evidently mingled the aspect before her with the object in her dream—the purpose of her watch and ordeal,—the beneficent creature vouchsafed by her savage gods, from whose guidance her future destiny was to be shaped and governed. The instincts of the Spaniard were sufficiently acute to see the impression that he had made, and to conjecture, in some measure its origin. He was well aware that the first impression of the European upon the Aborigines was that of a superior being. The devout appealing eyes of the damsel—her hands crossed upon her breast, satisfied our "Maroon" that she held him to be so. He advanced a single step, he smiled on her kindly, he raised one hand upward to heaven, while he placed the other on his heart. She followed all his movements with others like them. Her hand was lifted to heaven, and carried to her breast. She too smiled,—the smile of innocent hope, that might have brought with it warmer assurances. He spoke, sweetly and tenderly, but the words were lost upon incapable but not unheeding senses. She shook her head with a mournfulness of look that told him, plain as words could speak, how sorrowful she was that she knew not what he said. But he smiled encouragingly, and resorted once more to signs to assure her of his affection. These she understood.

The language of the heart is a very universal one. Charity and sympathy may speak, and be understood, though they have not a word in common with the hearer, from the centre to the pole. She answered his signs. She pointed to the fires before her. She threw a fresh supply of fuel upon the blaze, then rising to her knees, knelt before him, and crossed her hands upon her bosom. He stooped, and took her in his arms. She would have receded, but he held her tenderly in his grasp, and once more pressed his lips upon hers. She sunk submissive in his embrace. She spoke, but a single sentence, but one of its words smote his ear like a familiar accent. He had picked up a few of the Caribbean phrases from Spaniards who had been among this people. The girl had designated him as "the good White Spirit." The word "Spirit" had become a frequent one in the intercourse of the Jesuit missionaries with the heathen. God, and love, and heaven, good, bad, the sky, the sea, the boat, Castile, white and red man,—these, and several other words had, from the communion of the Spaniards with the tribes of the Caribbean Sea, grown to be a tolerably common property with the two races. Lopez rapidly ran over in the ears of the girl all of this description which he found it easy to remember on the instant. Some of these she repeated after him with ready acquiescence. Again she described him as the good white spirit—*her* good white spirit—and he now understood her.

He did not disabuse her. He feared to forfeit her reverence, in seeking to awake a humbler emotion; and as the master of her destiny, a celestial visitant, provided for her guidance, he proceeded to inforce her affections. He placed himself beside her—together they supplied the altar with fuel and incense, and when he kissed her lips, she crossed her arms upon her breast, and submitted with delighted reverence.

It was the benevolent spirit whose favor she implored, who then, in his most gracious aspect presented himself in compliance with her invocations. She had been taught to believe that he was difficult of approach,—slow to be won,—reluctant to appear;—

that it required earnest and long continued devotions, and a painful and protracted vigil. How fortunate was she among her sex, that, in her instance, he had departed from his wonted severity!—that, instead of presenting himself, as he was reported frequently to have done,—in harsh and ungenial aspects—in the shape of bird, or beast, or reptile,—he had assumed his noblest attributes of form, and put on features not only of the highest, but of the tenderest character. Verily, she was the favored among women! The tones of the Spaniard's voice were to her sounds of the sweetest music from the Caribbean heaven. His smile was that glance of the morning or of the evening, when the brightness is equally rare and benignant; and, when his hand rested upon her cheek or neck, she felt the thrill of an emotion through all her veins, such as she had been taught to believe was vouchsafed only to the favored few, the select of the Caribbean Elysium.

Their eyes took part in their constant intercourse, and never had Lopez looked or spoken with so successful eloquence. Though she comprehended but few of his words, yet nothing was thrown away of all that fell from his lips. As at the first, in the primal hour of creation, the speech which heaven bestowed upon its creatures was that of love, so love constitutes the basis of that ancient language which it is still so easy for the heart to comprehend. Assisted by this heart-manual, it was easy for Lopez to make his Spanish and her Indian words subservient to their gradual use; and ere they sunk exhausted into the mutual arms of sleep that night, they had commenced a course of study quite as rapid as the Robertsonian method, by which a modern or ancient dialect is to be mastered in six lessons.

The bridal hour of the two exiles thus strangely brought together, promised to be as happy in its progress, as the destiny in which it had its origin was solemn and peculiar. With the dawn, the two awakened to neither repining nor repentance. Life had suddenly put on her loveliest aspects to both. The Spaniard was no longer lonesome in his solitude, and the damsel was happy in the faith that she was favored among women, by the very Deity to whom her sex devotes the most dutiful and earnest solicitations.

CHAPTER XIX.

The passion thus begun, and sanctioned, as it would seem, by an especial Providence, was neither slow to ripen nor of modified character. The very isolation of their abode, separated from all the world beside, tended to compel their affections eagerly, and into the same channel. But it was not long before the Indian damsel learned to comprehend the purely human character of her companion. Her very love produced this discovery, since it could only exist in its natural intensity in the untutored mind, in the comparative loss of its veneration. The young Spaniard no longer repined at his desolate condition. The fate to which he resigned himself had received its consolations, and in the first few days of his happiness, if he thought at all of his late comrades, it was with something of fear and misgiving, lest they should come and tear him away from an abode, in which he was equally free and happy.

The morning after their first meeting, he stole from her side while she yet slept, and from the ante-chamber of the cavern awakened her with a soft sweet strain from his guitar. It was the first time he had touched the strings since the instrument had been hung about his neck in mockery. She started from the mossy niche where she lay, and lighting anew the fire upon her altars, sank before it in the attitude of prayer. A delirious delight was visible upon her countenance as the music reached her ears, and when Lopez looked in upon her, she bore the expression of one whose whole soul was lifted with a sense of the divine favor.

He made the guitar the instrument for her education. She had the sweetest voice, herself, and for his music, gave him wild ballads of her own people, of which he could appreciate the music only. But their words were rapidly interchanged. The lessons were constant, and conveyed through numerous media of which the teacher in civilized life, can have no notion. Life itself depended on their progress, and when this is the case, the tuition must be marvellously rapid—love as well as life,—their daily sports, their mutual progress,—the exercise of their tastes—their consultations upon sea, and sky, and grove,—the passage of the wild bird,—the bound of the marmozet—the gathering of fruit,—the song, the dance, the sigh, the smile,—all these provoked their lessons and exercised their industry in acquisition. It was not long before they declared themselves in syllables that took the place of simple sounds,—not long before the teacher could listen with delight to the childish prattler at his side, whose accents would have seemed uncouth in the ears of critics only. Day by day, teaching and taught, the horizon of their hopes and affections sensibly expanded before their minds, and the damsel did not cease to be less innocent because she had learned not only to understand her own emotions, but to comprehend the real nature of the companion from whom she had learned the first great lesson of the woman heart. She was not less happy that, in losing a God, she had found a lover and a Lord!

CHAPTER XX.

The world for a brief season seemed wholly surrendered to them. They lived for each other only; and as they saw no other forms, so they forgot for a time, that they were to be disturbed by other beings of a nature like their own. Lopez had no hopes—shall we call them fears?—that the Dian de Burgos would ever again appear to seek him out in his place of exile. He knew how serious and how terrible always were the jokes of his late tyrant, and never looked for his repentance. Nor did the poor Amaya—such was the name of the damsel—dream that her Caribbean kindred would ever sunder a union so marvellously wrought by heaven. Her barbarous rites were neglected in the prompt realization of her dreams. This was due in great measure to the teachings of the "Maroon." Already had he begun to bestow upon her some of his theology—crude and selfish as it was. The *Agnus Dei* which he put into her hands, was quite as frequently an object of her entreaty as it was of his. Their supplications at morning and at evening to the Virgin, were twined together; and it must be confessed, that, of the two, the poor pagan damsel was much more earnest in her prayers than the habitual Christian.

He taught her other lessons. Already had he began to conduct her fingers among the strings of his guitar, and she, rejoicing at the merry tinkle which she produced, soon promised to acquire its language. The instrument was constantly in her keeping, except when she summoned him to perform upon it. Then she sat beside him, on the edge of the great ocean, and while the waters rolled and tumbled toward their feet, she listened to his chaunt—his fierce ballads of Spanish chivalry—comprehending but little of the story, but feeling all the sweetness of the music, the more perhaps that the words were mysterious and vague.

But their sports were not always of this subdued order, though they were scarcely less romantic—such, at least, as she now taught and encouraged him to practice. The sea was scarcely an object of terror to the practised swimmers of the Caribbean Isles. Amaya, like all the damsels of her people, had been accustomed to embrace its billows from her infancy. She soon taught the more apprehensive Lopez to persue her in the waves. At the fall of the tide she led him off among the rocks, whose heads at such periods were distinctly visible. Here resting on their dark gray summits, he beheld her, with a terror in which she did not share, leap down into the boiling black abysses, and disappear wholly from his sight. Before he had yet recovered from his alarm, she reappeared, bringing up with her the peculiar oyster, whose immedicable wounds give birth to the beautiful pearl which is so much valued, though not in the same degree, by Indian and European. After this discovery, our "Maroon," encouraged the sport which had first alarmed his fears. He too acquired courage from cupidity, and, being no bad swimmer, he learned to follow her into the grim recesses of the rocks, when the seas were at repose. He reserved to himself the opening of the valves, so that he extricated the fruit from their embrace, without subjecting it to injury. Great was the wealth which he thus acquired, to say nothing of the ancient treasures of the cavern.

But these treasures, which he had not sought, were valueless where he was. His possessions, so unsuited to his present condition, first taught him to repine. When he looked upon his unprofitable stores, his thoughts immediately yearned for the native land, in which they had made him famous. With this recollection, his heart saddened within him. He looked earnestly along the ocean waste for some sign of his countrymen. He looked with a momentary indifference upon the sweet, wild and artless creature, who gambolled before his eyes, or crouched in confidence beside him.

Her keen glance beheld these changes. No change in his aspect ever escaped her vigilance. At such moments, she would incline herself timidly toward him—would draw his attention by little artifices,—

would appeal to him in awkward Castilian, which insensibly glided into her native Caribbee tongue;—the broken accents finally acquiring emphasis as they concluded in some sweet and foreign ditty—sometimes, with a playful fondness, she would assail his melancholy, by sudden plunges into the billows, striking out for the cluster of little rocks, hiding in whose hollows she would beguile him with a wild strain of her people, or in appealing fancies of her own, which might have found a fitting translation in such a ballad as the following:

THE LAY OF THE CARIB DAMSEL.

I

Come, seek the ocean's depths with me,
For there are joys beneath the sea,
Joys, that when all is dark above,
Make all below a home of love!

II

In hollow bright and fountain clear,
Lo! snow white pearl await us there;
And amber drops that sea-birds weep
In sparry caves along the deep.

III

A chrystal chamber there I know,
Where never yet did sunshaft go;
The soft moss from the rocks, I take,
Of this our nuptial couch to make.

IV

There, as thou yieldest on my breast,
My songs shall soothe thy happy rest,—
Such songs as still our prophets hear,
When winds and stars are singing near.

V

These tell of climes whose deep delight,
Knows never change from day to night,
Where, if we love, the blooms and flowers,
And fruits,—shall evermore be ours.

VI

Oh! yield thee to the hope I bring,
Believe the truth I feel and sing,
Nor teach thy spirit thus to weep,
Thy Christian home beyond the deep.

VII

'Tis little,—ah! too well I know,
Thy poor Amaya may bestow,—
But if a heart that's truly thine,
Be worthy thee, O! cherish mine!

VIII

My life is in thy look—for thee,
I bloom, as for the sun, the tree;
My hopes,—when thou forget'st thy woes,
Unfold, as flow'rs when winter goes.

IX

And though, as our traditions say,
There bloom the worlds of endless day,
I would not care to seek the sky,
If there thy spirit did not fly.

It was impossible even for a heart so selfish as that of our "Maroon," wholly to resist a confidence so sweet and touching. The wild grace of her action, the spiritual delicacy of her love, the delightful companionship with which she cheered his solitude—all succeeded, in the absence of any absolute temptations, to secure his continued devotion to her charms.

But a change was destined to cast its shadow over their otherwise happy dreams. Three weeks of delight, with little interval, and scarcely any respite, had passed since they first knew each other. No doubt of the security, as well as transport, of her condition, assailed the heart of the Indian damsel; and if the Spaniard ever thought of his home, it was only as one of those vexing fancies, which, as he could scarcely hope to realize it, it was but childish to encourage. He made the most of his present happiness, and resigned himself to the possession of Amaya, with the more satisfaction, indeed, since, in a choice among a thousand, she still would most probably have been the object of his preference. But he did not the less regard the dowry which she brought him. He subjected his treasure to daily examination, and when the weather served, to daily increase. His necessities made him a miser. He did not the less enjoy the treasure, which it seemed he could never spend.

CHAPTER XXI.

But a new prospect of freedom, in this respect, was about to open upon him. One morning, whilst our wealthy "Maroon" was still engaged in the cleansing and assorting of his treasure, close in his cavern,—he was surprised by the sudden and unexpected entrance of Amaya, with words of wonder on her tongue, and looks of terror in her face. He hastily put his pearls from sight and hurried with her to the entrance of the cavern. There, in the sea-monster which alarmed her with a nameless fear, he beheld an object of scarcely less terror to himself. This was an European vessel. It might—it must be a Spaniard—but it was still at too great a distance to enable him to solve his doubts, or to relieve or increase his apprehensions. It was evidently approaching his islet; and for what visitor other than Velasquez should he look?

In a secure cover, on the top of his cavern, our "Maroon," with the trembling Amaya beside him, watched the course of the stranger. The Indian girl beheld the anxiety of her companion, to describe the feeling at his heart, embodied in his looks and actions, by its gentlest name; and her own terrors increased accordingly. In the brief space of time between the first appearance of the vessel, and his discovery of her true character, Lopez de Levya, rapidly ran over in his mind the prospects of his condition—the probable object of the Dian de Burgos, and the effect of this return upon his fortunes. What had he to hope from Velasquez or the implacable Juan, his rival? What motive but that of mockery and a cruel curiosity would have brought either of them back to the spot where they had *marooned* him? And should they search for him what was his hope of concealment? He could hide from the Caribbeans, who had no suspicion of any presence but their own,—but from the people of the Dian de Burgos there was no concealment. They would search the island—they would discover the cavern, and not one of its crevices could be made safe against their penetrating eyes or their probing lances.

A cold sweat covered the limbs of the miserable creature as his rapid thoughts coursed over the whole ground of his condition. And yet, it will scarcely be believed that, thus doubtful of his own fate, he could yet think of concealing his newly gotten treasure. He hurried back into his cave, counselling Amaya still to maintain her watch upon the stranger. In secret he toiled to place his pearls in security. The crevice which let in the light on one side the vault, he busily crammed with the soft moss and leaves taken from the couch in which he had slept. The light being excluded, he placed his baskets of treasure along the ledge, and concealed them in like manner. Nothing but the closest search, under the stimulating influence of a suspicion that something was concealed, could have led to the discovery of his possessions. There was no way of hiding himself in the same manner, and full of the most horrible apprehensions, he joined Amaya upon the eminence.

It was now necessary to think of her. Should Velasquez suspect the treasure—should Juan obtain sight of her, or any of the Spaniards, she would be torn from his arms with unscrupulous violence. To conceal her, it was necessary that the cave should be kept from their knowledge. He conducted her into its recesses. He showed her where he himself had been hidden, and easily persuaded her to seek shelter in its dusky interior. She might hope to escape unnoticed, even if the cave were penetrated; but her safety, should the bark be the Dian de Burgos, lay only in showing himself. Upon this policy, trembling still to encounter the cruel Velasquez, and insidious and hateful Juan, the "Maroon" resolved. He continued his watch in secrecy, though passing from copse to copse; he left the neighborhood of his cavern, as the chewit flies always from the spot where her young are hidden.

The vessel approached that part of the island where he had been landed. This increased his fears that she was that of his tyrant. If he came to mock, it was the game of Lopez to implore and seem repentant. If to pardon, it was his policy rather to appear surly and provoke his enemy to continued hostility;—for, though anxious to reach Spain with his treasure, yet our "Maroon" well knew that, with Juan or Velasquez as a master, the very suspicion of his great possessions would be fatal to his life. Better, then, to delay the day of his restoration than peril everything on a hope so doubtful. But, in truth, Lopez de Levya was not in a condition of mind to resolve on any policy. He was now, as he had ever been before, the creature of events!

CHAPTER XXII.

These, for once at least, proved favorable to his fortunes. We have already detailed the fearful circumstances which had changed the dynasty on board the Dian de Burgos. Linares and Maria de Pacheco were now the masters, but the former had no control over the proud intelligent spirit by whom the whole proceeding had been counselled. He was a mere seaman—a bold, strong man, who, conscious of his own deficiencies, was not unwilling to supply them from the stores of one who had so much identified her fortunes with his own. She asked for little in return, and that he was disposed to accord. He was the captain of the ship, but she was the guiding spirit. He did not seek her affections. On this point, indulgent, perhaps, on all others, she had shown herself equally resentful and inflexible. But, it will suffice for us that they understood each other, and that Linares lent himself to her project of rescuing Lopez. The latter had but little esteem among the seamen, but he had been harmless, was really gentle in his nature in proportion as he was timid, and his cruel punishment had won their pity and their sympathies. The sailor of that day looked upon the "Maroon" as doomed to a much worse punishment than death!

Impatient, on the prow of the Dian de Burgos, stood the proud but anxious woman as the ship approached the shore. Concealed among a cluster of young palms, Lopez beheld her, and in the position which she held, her eager attitude and outstretched hand, he at once inferred some great change in her fortunes and his own. His heart was instantly strengthened. He came forth from his hiding place, and the ship, dropping her anchors, Maria de Pacheco was the first to descend into the boat which now hurried to the shore. We need not attempt to depict her raptures or his own. In her case they were those of a strong, impetuous nature—her very fondness being linked with an arrogance of will, which rather compelled and commanded, than solicited affection in return.

The submissive spirit of the "Maroon" did not dare to withhold the expression of a joy, and the declaration of an attachment, beyond any which he possibly could feel. Perhaps, of the two persons, there was much more in the gentle and dependent nature of Amaya, to persuade him into love, than in that of the imperious woman whom he had certainly learned to fear. But she brought with her something more than the poor Indian girl could offer. Her coming promised him a restoration to his country, and the privilege of growing famous in the use of his Caribbean treasures. The very dowry of Amaya was hostile to her claims. Of this dowry,—of Amaya herself,—he religiously forbore to whisper aught to the proud woman who stood beside him, and who naturally spoke and thought as if she were as much the mistress of his heart as she was of his fate.

She soon told him all her story, and he revealed such portions of his, as might satisfy her inquiries without provoking any doubts. He described the beauties of his islet. He showed her where he had often slept, beneath the palms. He gathered for her his fresh and luscious fruits, and in the delight and wonder with which she beheld this new paradise, and in the happy consciousness of the attainment of all for which she had striven, at such fearful sacrifice of pride and feminine feeling, she yielded herself up to the sweet and innocent attractions which gathered around her. It was with a vague feeling of terror that he heard her declare her purpose to explore his empire, and to see, for herself, the beautiful retreats and resources which had so singularly fallen to his possession.

CHAPTER XXIII.

The situation of our "Maroon" was one of considerable difficulty. There was no pretext by which he could avoid the contemplated exploration of his islet, by the woman who was the mistress of his fate, and, as she naturally enough assumed, of his affections also. What had she not periled for those affections? The conviction of her own sacrifices,—the belief that she had saved him from a cruel destiny, and that he felt the profoundest gratitude for her love,—had rendered her more subdued, and gentle of tone and carriage, than he had ever before seen her. She had no longer to contend with the brutal passions of Velasquez, or the subtle and insolent spirit of his nephew. There was no influence now to combat her imperious will, and to oppose itself to the exercise of her own passions. She had won the fearful game for which she had played, and she might well give herself a brief respite after the contest. The sweet and balmy climate of the islet, the picturesque beauty of its aspects,—

its delicious fruits,—the novelty of such an abode,—and, above all, that romantic passion for solitude—with a companion—which accompanies the fresher sensibilities of youth,—all tended to excite in Maria de Pacheco the desire which she expressed, at least to dream away a single night on the lonely domain of the "Maroon." Her early career in the haunts of the gipsy, was recalled to memory; and she longed to realize, anew, the wild sense of pleasure which her passionate childhood had felt, dreaming beneath the arch of Heaven, and gazing away long lapses of the night, in mute communion with the sadly bright, down-looking stars. Here, in a solitude which her lover had maintained for near a month, she might surely rest one night in safety. The boat might return to the ship—nay, *should* return, and she should share, for that night, with Lopez, the sovereignty of the island.

"They shall maroon me also, Lopez."

"They may!" was his suggestion.

"Nay, I fear not. Linares is faithful to me. He cannot well do without me."

"But he may be blown off with a tempest. They are fierce and sudden in these latitudes, and terrible in proportion to the beauty and serenity of the calmness now."

"Well, Linares will come back for us."

"But, should he founder?"

"*We* then are safe, Lopez!"

The answer silenced him for awhile. But he renewed the attempt—more cautiously, but with such suggestions as might have influenced his own nature. He described to her the unwonted terrors which had assailed him in his first acquaintance with the island. The lowing of strange beasts of the sea which sometimes came to sleep by night upon the shore. The screams of unknown birds of great expanse of wing, and power, glimpses of which he caught, rising and descending, as from the stars, at midnight. The awful plunges of wild monsters, from the shore into the sea, and the bellowing of whole tribes of strange animals, whose uproar seemed to shake the isle itself.

But these rather provoked the curiosity than the alarm of the fearless woman. The novelty of such sights and sounds precluded the images of terror which he sought to raise. She declared the very loneliness which still made him shudder, to be a consciousness highly desirable to her heart; and as for the great birds and beasts,—she had seen the elephant, and had heard the lion roar in his own desert of Sahara; and the very safety of her lover was a sufficient proof that she could be in no peril. Her will proved superior to his fears. The boat was filled with fruit and sent back to the ship, and Linares was entreated to lay his vessel at anchor for the night, when the two would come on board in the morning.

To keep Maria from the cave, was now the object of the "Maroon;"—to prolong his ramble till nightfall, among the groves, and along the seashore,—and, in the night, while she slept, to steal away from her side,—regain the cave, repossess himself of his treasure, and soothe the fears and the suspicions of Amaya, so that he might abandon her in safety, and without detection by the woman whom he most feared;—this was the notable scheme which he suddenly devised, when he found that Maria was fixed in her purpose of remaining on the islet.

To leave his treasure was out of the question. But for this treasure, he had not cared to leave the place. He was really very happy with the Indian damsel,—might have been completely happy but for the dowry which she brought, and which filled him with the proudest fancies of the figure that he should make in Spain. To say that he had no compunctious visitings of conscience at the thought of her abused devotion,—of his so soon and cruel abandonment of one who so thoroughly confided to his affections—would be to do him great injustice. But the sympathies of the heart, unless sustained and strengthened by a decisive will of the intellect, are never long to be relied on. They are at the mercy of every mind, who brings to its support a resolute and earnest character. Lopez was humbled when he thought of Amaya, but his remedy was to dismiss her from his thoughts with all possible rapidity. He was compelled to do so, for his companion required all his attentions.

We shall say nothing of her shows of fondness. Maria de Pacheco was not feeble or childish,—not wanton, indeed, in the display of her attachments. She was too proud, for the exhibition of love in its weakness and dependence. But she indulged the mood somewhat after the fashion of the Sultana of the East. She willed to love and to be loved, and she required obedience. It was necessary that Lopez should prove that he was not ungrateful for the risks which she had run, and the sacrifices which she had made, in his behalf. It was needful that his attachment should be as fond, and his behavior as dutiful, as it had been before the unfortunate discovery which had placed them both at the mercy of Juan. That he was reluctant, or forgetful in any respect, Maria was not suffered to perceive.

Excited as she was by her own emotions—the consciousness of a great battle fought, and a triumph gained,—the last trophies of which were now in her hands—she, perhaps, would have been slow to detect the wandering mood and the indifferent manner of her companion, even if he had betrayed either. But the timid nature is always solicitous how it alarms or offends the bold one; and on the score of his devotedness, Maria beheld nothing, as yet, to occasion her jealousy.

But his will, which kept him observant of her moods, was not sufficient to prescribe to her the course to be pursued, or to arrest her eager progress. Her impetuous spirit hurried her forward; and the ground which,—feeling his way at every step—it had taken Lopez several days to traverse, when he first undertook to explore his territory—was now overcome in a few hours. Vainly did he seek to detain her gaze—to arrest her progress, and inspire in her an admiration of objects which had never once fixed his own. His artifices, though never suspected, were always fruitless. She still made fearful progress. The seashore was abandoned, the cool groves received them—the plain rose beneath her footsteps,—they were already upon the slopes of that elevation, at the extremity of which lay the secret and the treasure of the "Maroon." He looked back in terror for the sun. His round red orb still shone high and proudly in the heavens; and it was with equal wonder and self-reproach that Lopez remembered how long it was before his timid spirit had suffered him to compass the same extent of territory. The paths naturally opened for her footsteps. They had often been traversed by his own; and it was with a mortal fear that Lopez momently caught glimpses of the small, naked footstep of Amaya, on the softer sands, as she had wandered beside him in their rambles.

But these were never seen by Maria de Pacheco. The earnest and intense nature seldom pauses for the small details in a progress. Her proud spirit was always upward as well as onward—always above the earth. She threw herself suddenly down beneath the thicket. There was a pause. Our "Maroon" enjoyed a brief respite from his terrors. He threw himself beside her, and her eyes closed in his embrace. To a fierce and intense nature such as hers, there is something delicious in the pauses of the strife, but it is only because they are momentary. The rest from conquest is perhaps the only real luxury of enthusiasm;—but the interval is brief, and is simply designed to afford a renewal of the vitality necessary for continued action.

"How sweet, how beautiful, is the repose of sky and shore and sea! What a delicious languor of atmosphere is this!"—and a moment after speaking thus, Maria de Pacheco shook off her own languor, and was once more upon her feet.

"Will she now return to the shore—to the palms where I told her I had slept?"

Such was the secret inquiry of his heart. She had no such purpose. Her curiosity was still unsatisfied. Besides, to walk simply upon the solid earth, after weeks on shipboard, is itself a luxury. The sun was still high, and bright, though sloping gradually to the sea. The step of Maria was taken forward, and Lopez followed, like a criminal, with reluctant footsteps, as if going to execution. They stood at length on the brow of the hill, which looked over to the Caribbean shore. The abrupt precipice arrested her farther progress, and she stood gazing with eager satisfaction upon the small, snug and lovely domain of the "Maroon."

CHAPTER XXIV.

The thoughts coursed rapidly through the brain of Lopez de Levya. He felt that she was on the brink of his secret. Another step, to the right or to the left, and the descending pathway would lead to the sandy esplanade at the mouth of the cave; and, with her restless glances, what could keep her from discovering its curious portal and penetrating to its inmost recesses. Were she to make this discovery without his assistance, her suspicions might well be awakened! He resolved with unaccustomed boldness. He made a merit of necessity. He put his hand upon her arm, and with a sweet significant smile looked upon her face as she gazed upward.

"I have reserved, for the last, my greatest curiosity. I have conducted you hither to surprise you. Follow me now and you will see how complete is my establishment!"

She did not reflect that he had been guided by her footsteps, and that his reluctance at her inspection of his territories had been declared from the beginning. She was sufficiently happy, and indulged in no recollections or reflections, which might occasion doubt or suspicion. He led the way and she descended to the beach. He conducted her to the cave, and with the eager delight of a curious child, she darted into its recesses. The antechamber was a wonder, but the interior aroused all that was romantic in her nature. It was just the sort of dwelling for one trained among the gypsies of the Alpuxarras. The chamber was so wild and snug! The stone, such a truly Egyptian fireplace! She did not dream of its uses as an altar, nor did he breathe a syllable on this subject. And the couch in which he had slept, in which there still remained a sufficient supply of moss and leaves, to render it suitable for the same purpose, was one to determine her instantly that it should be hers that very night.

We need not describe the consternation of Lopez as he listened to this resolve. It completed his disquiet and annoyance. He had trembled, at every step which she had taken—at every glance of her eye when the cave was entered. He feared her eager survey—her penetrating scrutiny; his eyes stole frequently and unconsciously to the remote corner of the cave in which he had concealed Amaya; and while he trembled at the possible discoveries of the Spanish woman, his companion, his heart smote him for those which the poor girl of Caribbee must have already made. For Maria de Pacheco, assuming the duty and devotion of her lover, had not spared her endearments. The silence and the secrecy of the cavern seemed to invite them. She had hung upon his neck with her caresses, and he had been compelled to requite them, though in fear and trembling. His conscience smote him when he thought of the unselfish and confiding passion of Amaya—her simple truth, her gentle nature, and the artless sweetness of her affections. But to withstand the imperious spirit of the woman at his side, was not within his strength and courage. His fears, and the newborn agonies of the Indian woman, may be more easily imagined than described.

CHAPTER XXV.

Again did the two emerge from the cavern. The sun had set! night was falling rapidly as is its wont in those regions, where the day makes, as it were but a single transition, from meridian brightness to the stillness and the dusk of midnight. An angry flush lay in the region where the sun went down, to the wary mariner denoting wind and tempest. But neither Lopez nor his companion thought of storm; nor did this fear impress the seamen on board the Dian de Burgos. The fruits from the shore—the momentary pause from the ordinary duties of the sea,—and a division of a portion of the treasures of Velasquez and Juan among the crew, by way of hush-money and bounty, called for something like indulgence. The Dian de Burgos was not without her luxuries. The stores of her late captain were fished up. Linares was disposed to be liberal to his former comrades; and wine and stronger beverages were not denied to their enjoyment. It was among the infirmities of Linares that he himself was not wholly insensible to the joys of the vine. As the heir to Velasquez he might certainly indulge his tastes. He did so; and while Maria de Pacheco luxuriated in the delights of love, he gratified his newly gotten liberty by sacrifices at the altars of a very different deity.

Ordinary precautions are soon forgotten in the acquisition of extraordinary pleasures. No one thought of tempest. The evening remained calm. There was little wind stirring, just enough to break into irregular but not threatening billows, the vast surface of the sea. The stars were out soon, large, bright and very numerous. A thin drift of clouds might be seen to scud slowly away among them from the west to the east. Lopez would have led his companion away from the cavern—would have persuaded her to a couch among the palms where, as he showed her, his own had first been made. But she had resolved upon the chamber in the cavern, and he was compelled to submit. They re-entered it with heedful footsteps. The interior was wholly dark, except where, in the inner apartment, the light of the stars made its way through the two small apertures which the Maroon had left unclosed. It was long before they slept. Much had Maria de Pacheco to relate. She gave him the details of the conspiracy against Velasquez. She suppressed nothing of her own share in the proceedings, and declared a very natural and feminine horror at the catastrophe, which she yet insisted on as necessary to her own safety and to his.

The "Maroon" listened to the narrative with conflicting feelings and in silence. The conduct of Maria established a new claim upon his gratitude; but it did not contribute to the strength of his former passion; and his thoughts, though fascinated by the terrible story to which he listened, were sometimes startled from their propriety, as he heard, more than once, what seemed to him a deep sigh from the hiding place of Amaya. It may have been in his fancy only that this intrusive monitor was heard, but it sufficed to keep him apprehensive. Fortunately, Maria de Pacheco heard nothing. She had no suspicions, and in the death of Juan and Velasquez her fears were all ended. In the recovery of the "Maroon" all her hopes seemed to be satisfied.

CHAPTER XXVI.

The night began to wane, the wind rose. It could be heard shrilly to whistle through the crevices of the rock, as if in threat and warning. But Maria slept, not deeply, and her head was on the arm of the "Maroon." When he sought to rise, which more than once he did, she started from her sleep with disquietude. If he but stirred she was conscious of it. Her sleep was troubled. Her dreams revenged upon her conscience the obtuseness which, by the force of her will, she imposed upon it in her waking moments. It enabled her to restrain, though unconsciously, the movements of her companion. He made repeated attempts to disengage himself from her grasp,—and rise. He wished to confer with Amaya. We may conjecture what he would have said. But he strove in vain. In watching for the moment when the sleep of Maria should become sufficiently deep to afford him the desired opportunity, he finally slept himself. Nature yielded at last, and his slumbers were soon quite as profound as those of his companion.

Without being well conscious that he slept at all, he was suddenly awakened, as if by a death-cold hand upon his wrist. He started, and was confounded when he unclosed his eyes, to behold the cavern brightly illuminated. The fire which had been suffered to go out by the Caribbean damsel, in the sweet experience of her first mortal passion, had been suddenly revived, and by her hands. She stood between him and the altar-place, her eyes wildly sad and staring upon him and his companion. A torch was still grasped in one of her uplifted hands. She had probably been inspecting closely the sleeping features of the woman who had first taught her to feel the agony which belongs to a consciousness of the infidelity of the beloved one. As at his awakening, the head of the "Maroon" was involuntarily uplifted, she cast the brand which she held upon the altar, flung one of her hands despairingly and reproachfully toward him, and darted headlong from the chamber.

CHAPTER XXVII.

Maria de Pacheco still slept. It was now doubly important to the "Maroon" that she should continue to do so. To rise softly—which he now succeeded in doing, without arousing her—to extinguish the brands and to steal forth, and see what was the course, and what the purpose of Amaya, was the next natural movement of Lopez. He soon smothered the flame and quenched the burning embers; but the night had grown dark,—the stars were shrouded, and, when he emerged from the cavern, he could see nothing. He stole back, trembling with doubt and apprehension, and wondering what next would follow. Maria had awakened.

"Where are you?"—was her salutation as he drew nigh—"Where have you been?"

"Hear you the wind, Maria? The night is very dark and gusty! We shall have a storm to-morrow."

"But we are safe, Lopez!" was the reply.

"I am not so sure of that," was the secret whisper of his guilty heart.

The night passed without farther interruptions. At dawn, the Maroon arose before his companion. He proceeded to his treasure which he now prepared to have in readiness to convey, without being suspected, on board the vessel. The richer pearls were hidden in his bosom, and in the folds of his garments. The rest were stored away carefully in the bottom of one of the largest baskets which he had found in his cavern, and which he pretended had been picked up on the shore. A few bananas were laid upon the top to prevent inquiry. His arrangements were all complete, before Maria awakened.

With the sunrise they had both emerged upon the beach. But the sun rose faintly and struggled on his course against numerous clouds. The wind came in sudden gusts sweeping the ocean into temporary anger. The lulls between were not less unpromising; and, to the old seaman, the signs were pregnant of one of those wild and capricious changes of the weather, which so frequently converted into a scene of wrath and horror, the otherwise sweet serene of those latitudes. But Maria did not heed these signs, in the consciousness of the attainment of her desires. Lopez was too anxious to leave the neighborhood of the poor Caribbean damsel, about whom his heart constantly reproached itself; and those whom we left on shipboard were quite too happy, in the enjoyment of their unfrequent saturnalia, to disturb themselves with anticipations of the future. It may have been a fancy only, but, looking back at the moment ere he stept into the boat which was to convey him from the islet, did he catch a glimpse of the slender form of Amaya among the palms, with her arm outstretched, and pointing to the cavern? A second and more earnest glance revealed him nothing.

Safely within the ship, his treasures made secure, and with the example of all around him persuading him to licentiousness, Lopez de Levya soon gave way to excesses which contributed to make him forgetful of the damsel he had deserted. He was received with half maudlin affection by Linares and the crew. The coarser pleasures in which these were indulging were transferred, with some qualifying refinements to the cabin of Velasquez. Here, from flagons of gold and silver, did our "Maroon" quaff the intoxicating beverage to the health of Maria de Pacheco, and the prosperous fortunes of the Dian de Burgos. The day passed in prolonged indulgence. The excesses which might have revolted Maria and her companion at another time, were now only the outpourings of a natural exultation which was due to a sense of newly-acquired freedom, and the acquisition of novel luxuries. The gradual progress of the hours brought on increase of wind which finally grew to storm. But this occasioned no disquiet and did not lessen the enjoyments of any of the parties. Linares, like a veteran seaman, full of wine as he was, first took care to see that his vessel was secure. He was in a good anchorage. His ship was stripped to the storm, and he had no reason to apprehend that she would drag her anchor under any pressure of the gale. A good watch was set, and, wishing for more freedom in his revels, he withdrew from the cabin to the more genial, if more rough association of the crew.

CHAPTER XXVIII.

Night came on—a night of storm and many terrors. Maria de Pacheco and our "Maroon" were not wholly insensible to its dangers. At moments, when the pressure of the wind was most severely felt, they would pause in the midst of their delights, and think of the solid security of the chamber in the rock. But the revel went on without reserve. The rich flagon stood before them in the cabin. They were alone with each other. They lived for each other, and there was no tyrannic power at hand to arrest them as they carried the intoxicating draught of rapture to their lips. No longer conscious of the proximity of other eyes, Lopez de Levya requited the caresses of his companion with an ardency quite equal to her own. They spoke of their mutual delights. They declared their mutual hopes of home, and in the increasing exultation which he felt in his security, and the increasing influence of the wine which he had quaffed, the "Maroon" revealed to Maria the wealth of pearl which were contained in his bosom and his baskets. He poured forth his milk-white, but transparent treasures, into her lap, and wound the lengthened strands about her neck. His form resting upon one knee before her, her head stooping to his embrace, neither of them perceived, for several moments, that, while they were most drunk with delight, they had a visitor.

The door of the cabin had opened silently upon them, and the deserted damsel of the Caribbees, standing erect, with hands drooping at her side, and eyes staring intently, but vacantly and wildly upon them, now stood beholding, herself for a while unseen, their almost infantile caresses. Stern and mournful did she stand, surveying this scene of tenderness, which every pulse of her passionate young heart taught her was indulged at her expense. She neither sighed, nor spoke, nor moved, after her first entrance. Was it an instinct of their own souls which taught them that another and a hostile spirit was at hand, and which made the proud Spanish woman start to her feet, with a sudden terror; while the "Maroon," sinking lower, upon both knees, looked round him in shame and trepidation at the unexpected presence?

To him the deserted woman gave but a single glance, but that declared every thing in their mutual histories. Advancing toward Maria de Pacheco, before her purpose could be divined, she suddenly tore the strands of pearl from the bared neck and bosom to which they seemed beautifully kindred, then, dashing them to the floor, trampled them under foot, and fled from the cabin with a shriek which sounded like that of doom in the ears of the "Maroon." He had apprehended a worse danger when he saw her so suddenly approach Maria. He had seen in the grasp of the Indian damsel, the same broad and heavy cleaver of stone, with which he had beheld the priestess, on the night of her first entrance to the cave, sever the long sable tresses from her neck, and devote them, in sacrifice, on behalf of her future destinies. That she would use this fearful instrument on the forehead of the Spanish woman, was the spontaneous fear in the heart of Lopez; but, at that moment, so suddenly had he been surprised by her presence, and so greatly was he confounded by his guilt and terror, she might have safely executed the deed of death, had murder been her purpose.

Inflamed with wine, stung by the indignity to which she had been subjected, Maria de Pacheco recovered from her astonishment much sooner than her paramour from his fears. Confronting him with a fierce and flashing glance from her dark imperial eye, she demanded, in choking accents, the explanation of the scene. But, filled with terror, partly intoxicated, and wholly confused and bewildered by the condition in which he found himself, the unmeaning mutterings from his lips gave no satisfaction to the eager and heated inquirer. With a speech full of equal scorn and suspicion, she flung away from his approach, and darted out upon the deck of the vessel in pursuit of the stranger.

There, all was storm and darkness. The black masses of night seemed to crowd and accumulate before her path, filling up the passages, and preventing her progress. The vessel pitched awfully. The woman could scarcely keep her feet, though quite as much accustomed to the motion of the ship as any of the seamen. She felt her way along the bulwarks. She saw nothing, heard nothing—nothing but the awful roaring of the winds as they fell upon the waves in the fury of a mortal conflict. She made her way to the prow. The excellent look-out of veteran seamen whom Linares had provided for the watch was nowhere to be seen. She called to them below, and a couple of drunken sailors scrambled up and tottered toward her. They had seen nothing. She could see nothing. Nothing was to be heard. Yet, more vigilant, more sober, and less passionate faculties might have detected, even while she made her inquiries, certain dull and heavy strokes, which, at pauses in the storm, seemed to arise from the deep, and to run along the cable. Little did Lopez de Levya divine the fatal purpose for which the Caribbean damsel carried with her that hatchet of stone.

Impatient, with a brain full of suspicions, and a heart severed by disappointment, Maria de Pacheco returned to the cabin, leaving the two half drunken sailors in possession of the watch. They might have been, and probably were, famous watchers at all other times. But the liquors of Velasquez had been equally potent and tempting, and they were still provided with a flask of the delicious beverage. They drank and sang together in defiance of the storm. What was the storm to them? The Dian de Burgos was as tight a creature as ever swam the seas, and hard and firm were the sands, in which their anchors found their rest. Besides, since they came on deck, the storm seemed somewhat to have subsided. The seas were not so high. The ship no longer plunged with that peevish and cumbersome motion, like a high mettled horse under the discipline of a cruel curb, but rose easily and gently with the play of the billows, as if she were smoothly posting, with a fair gale, along accustomed pathways of the sea. The observations of our watch were of this satisfactory complexion. It never occurred to them as possible that the ship really was in motion—that she no longer opposed the resistance of her mighty bulk to the winds and waters, but obeyed placidly the impulses which their united powers gave. They little dreamed how much of their consolation, was drawn from causes of their greatest danger.

CHAPTER XXIX.

Meanwhile, in the cabin of the Dian de Burgos, the tempest raged as fiercely as it did without, and entirely excluded the terrors of wind and sea. The ready instincts of Maria de Pacheco had conducted her to much of the secret of her paramour. She now recalled his reluctance to conduct her over the island,—the art, which, when on the eve of discovery, had made a merit of necessity, and led her into the recesses of the cavern—the uneasiness which seemed heedless of her endearments—the disquiet which they seemed to occasion—his disappearance at midnight—and the pearl, the treasure, of which he was so unaccountably possessed. The sudden appearance of the Indian damsel revealed the whole secret, and led to conjectures which made the course of the "Maroon" seem more odious to Maria than it possibly could have been under a frank and honest statement of the facts.

To have made this statement required nothing more than common courage. But this was the very faculty which Lopez wanted most. When his secret was extorted from him, as it finally was, and the whole of its details surrendered, the vexation of the Spanish woman was not so much because of the events, as because of his withholding them. It betrayed a want of confidence in her, and this was proof of deficient sympathy. Upon this sympathy she had staked her life—had periled all that was feminine in her nature—and the appalling terror, lest she should have periled all in vain—might well justify the fearful aspect, and the stern and keen reproaches, with which she encountered him.

She was at last pacified. It was her policy to be so. When the heart has made its last investment, it is slow to doubt its own securities. His declarations of attachment, when he had somewhat recovered his confidence, began to re-assure her. She yielded to his persuasions—to his blandishments and caresses, rather than to his reasons, or such as he urged in his justification.

It was in the midst of these endearments that a voice was heard, faintly singing at the cabin entrance—a voice which the "Maroon" but too painfully remembered. The tones, though faint were distinct. The song was in the dialect of the Caribbee, and it was one of which a feeble translation has been already given;—a ballad which the poor Amaya had been wont to sing to Lopez, when she would beguile him to join her in her sports of ocean. It rehearsed the delights and the treasures of the deep—its cool chrystalline chambers, always secure from the shafts of the sun—its couches of moss and sea weed—and of the sweet devotion of the sea maid who implored him to her embraces. The pathetic tenderness of her tone—the wild, but pleading earnestness of her plaint—the solemn sweetness and mysterious force of that invocation with which the separate verses were burdened,

"Come, seek the ocean's depths with me!"—

startled the guilty "Maroon" with a new and nameless terror.

He started to his feet, but remained stationary, incapable of motion. But the angry spirit of Maria de Pacheco, was aroused once more. She put him aside, and darted to the entrance of the cabin. As she threw it open, a white form flashed upon the darkness. It seemed as if a spirit had shot away from her grasp, and darting high in air, had disappeared in the black waste of sky and sea beyond. A shriek, rather in exultation than grief, was heard amid the roar of wind and water. It was followed by the human scream of Maria.

"*Madre de Dios!* the ship is moving. We are at the mercy of the seas! Ho! there, Lopez!—Linares! Awake! arouse ye—or we perish!"

Her cries were cut short by her terrors. The prow of the ship was lifted—fearfully lifted, as if by some unseen power from below. The water surged awfully beneath, and a terrible roar followed, as if from a herd of wild animals deep in the hollows of the sea.

"What is that Lopez! What is this?" whispered the woman to the faint-hearted paramour who had crept beside her. A terrible shock followed—another and another!—and the whole dreadful danger was apparent in an instant to both. They were among the rocks. The ship had struck,—and the ready memory of the "Maroon," well conceived the fearful condition in which they stood, borne by the irresistible and treacherous currents upon those silent and terrible masses of rock, where, in moments of the sea's serene, he had so frequently shared in the wild sports of his Caribbean beauty.

Well might he remember those rude and sullen masses. Often had he remarked, with a shudder the dark and fearful abysses which settled, still and gloomy, in their dark mysterious chambers. But he had now no time to recall the periods of their grim repose. Another moment, and the ship, awfully plunging under the constant impulsions of the sea, buried her sharp bow, with a deep groan, in the black and seething waters. The breakers rushed over them with a fall like that of a cataract. For a single instant, the Dian de Burgos hung suspended as it were, upon a pinnacle. Then, even as the still besotted, and only half awakened sailors, were rushing out on deck, she divided in the middle,—one part falling over into the reservoir among the rocks, the other tumbling back upon the seas, to be driven forward, by successive shocks, and in smaller fragments, to a like destiny.

In this fearful moment, Maria de Pacheco, was separated, by the numerous waves, from the side of the "Maroon." He heard her voice through the awful roar,—

"Where are you, Lopez—O! let me not lose you now!"

But he could make no answer. He heard no more. Her cries ceased with that single one. He had not strength to cry, for he was struggling himself with the seas, and with another peril. While the fierce currents bore him forward,—while the wild billows tore him away from the fragment of wreck which he had grasped spasmodically, in the moment when the ship went to pieces, he was conscious of a sudden plunge beside him,—of an arm fondly wrapped about his neck, and of a voice that sung in tones the most mournful and pathetic in his ears, even as he sank, and sinking with him, that fond ballad of the Caribbean damsel. It was a heart-broken chaunt, which had some exultation in it. The last human words of which the feeble and perfidious "Maroon" was conscious were those of the entreating sea nymph,

"Come, seek the ocean's depths with me!"

[Godey's Magazine and Lady's Book *for 1847 contained Simms's "Maize in Milk. A Christmas Story of the South" as a serial in four installments. "Maize in Milk" was also selected by Simms for inclusion in his* Marie de Berniere *and* The Maroon *collections. Explanatory and Textual Notes begin on page 761.*]

MAIZE IN MILK.

A Christmas Story of the South.

Kindle the Christmas brand, and then
  Till sunset let it burne;
Which quencht, then lay it up agen
  Till Christmas next returne:
Part must be kept wherewith to teend
  The Christmas log next yeare,
And where 'tis safely kept, the fiend
  Can do no mischiefe there.—Herrick.

CHAPTER I.

The Full Corn-Crib.

Tell me nothing of the crops! Suppose they don't grow—suppose there *is* a failure, and the corn falls short, and the cotton *sheds*, and the army worm appears and the catterpillar, and there is an early frost, and half the *bolls* never blow! These things will happen! We must look to lose our crops now and then, no matter what we plant. It can't be that we shall have things always as we wish them. We can't be always wise or always fortunate. But we can, if we please, be always good and good-natured, and loving, and cheerful, and thankful for what we do get, and for the things in which we are prosperous. There's no reason because of the drought that our hearts shall be dry also. There's no reason because we make short crops that we should be short to our friends, and because the winter comes on sooner than usual that we should be colder than usual to our neighbors—that our charities should freeze up with the weather, and our gratitude fail us because the sunshine fails us. We must only make the hearth-fire brighter; we must only make sunshine for ourselves, and gather our friends about the warming, and make merry within while all is melancholy without; and show to one another how cheerful everything may be, though the tempest blows never so angrily against the shutter. A man may soon learn to make his sunshine wherever and whenever he pleases, and to carry a happy heart under a thin jacket. He must be a man without regard to the seasons. His affections must not alter with the weather. He mustn't blow hot and cold because the wind does so. He must keep his soul firm and his sympathies steadfast, and his charities must be as quick to warm as his anger is quick to cool. His log must be kindled at Christmas though he may have never another left in his wood-yard. There must be a fire, you know, at Yule, and why shouldn't his hands kindle it as well as another's? The log was cut to burn!

But he is unfortunate, you say. Well, is that any good reason why he shouldn't warm his fingers in a cold season? But then he makes blaze enough to warm a dozen! Exactly so; and this only proves that even the unfortunate man is never so wholly unfortunate that he does not possess the happy privilege, under God, of making others happy. There's no waste if, when he sets his log ablaze, he calls in his neighbors to enjoy it. I tell you the log must burn for some one's comfort in the cold, bleak days of December, and it is something of a blessing in the poor man's cup that he is permitted to raise the blaze. But then, say you, it is his last log! Who shall say that? Who shall dare to say that God's charity must have a limit?—that this man, who knew so well how to warm his hearth for the blessing of his neighbors, shall be permitted to make no more pleasant fires? I tell you, short-sighted mortal, that even beside that last log you may yet see some celestial visitant in fustian habit. It is thus that an unquestioning hospitality is sometimes permitted to entertain an angel! With the smoke of that last log, around which the unlucky man, obedient to a custom which he learned in his better days, has gathered his humble neighbors, there goes up to heaven a rare incense which makes acceptable, and may make profitable also, that last sacrifice of wealth. Let the log burn, then! Wouldst thou throw water on the cheerful gleams which light up all these ruddy faces? Wouldst thou silence the merry crackling of that flaming pile? Wouldst thou put out those pleasant charities which thus, if only once a year, are kindled to make one's fellow warm? Out upon thee for a doubter of God's providence! Get thee to thy own home and put thy only stick upon the fire, and call in him who passes, that thou mayest not selfishly and sadly sit alone to see it burn! Then will the Father of those who gladden at the blaze, so gladden thee as that thou shalt never lack thy log at Yule.

Now, if thou wilt believe me, brother, there is a purpose in this long preamble. Just such was the tenor of that shrill but lively *crow* which issued from the capacious lungs of that famous old cock of St. Matthews, who held in fee the extensive domains of "Maize-in-milk." * The master of "Maize-in-milk" was a sovereign in his way, whose power was known only by its bounty. His was one of the finest plantations for peas, potatoes, Indian corn and short cottons, in Carolina—not a very great one, it is true; not so large nor so thickly settled as an hundred others in the same and other districts, but just such a snug, productive interest as enabled the proprietor to do the handsome thing by his neighbor and to entertain his guest like a gentleman. Colonel Openheart was one of those generous and frank planters whom men smiled to name, with pleasant recollections of the warmest welcome and the finest cheer. And even now, with his feathers somewhat ruffled by resistance and unexpected provocation, it was delightful to behold the bland visage and the good-humored smile which took all anger from his aspect. Anger, indeed! It was rare enough to see him angry. We tell you he was only ruffled, not roused, and just enough touched by opposition to show how animated he could become even in his benevolence. There he sits at the ample fireside, in which great logs of oak and hickory are yielding themselves up in flake and flash, and hiss and sparkle, his face glowing like the fire, warm, bright, capacious; cheeks smooth as a woman's, a beard carefully kept down by a persuasive razor, and his flowing locks just beginning to whiten at the ends, and slightly showing their snows against the warmer colors of his neck and cheek. And how his great blue eyes dilate under the high, broad forehead, as he looks around him with a mixed expression of amazement and satisfaction, taking in at the same glance the gentle and matron-like lady who presides at the evening board, from around which the chairs have already been withdrawn; and the tall and graceful damsel of fifteen, who, standing at her side, plies deftly the snow-white napkin over

* Indian corn not yet ripe, but ready in the *ear* for the table.

the dripping tea-cup. I am not sure that the comprehensive glance of Colonel Openheart fails to notice the nice little juvenile episode which escapes the eyes of the ladies, and which presents itself upon the great and antique sofa gracing the opposite end of the apartment. There, but scarcely enough in the foreground to constitute a portion of the picture, you may see Tom Openheart, a stout lad of nine or ten years, exhausted by a long day's squirrel hunt, with his own rifle and on his own pony, drowsing into gradual obliviousness of life and all its excitements, his arms thrown above his head, one of his legs secure on the sofa with his trunk, while the other wanders off, quietly conducted to a neighboring chair, to the leg of which Dick Openheart, a mischievous urchin of seven or eight, busily fastens it by the aid of his sister's handkerchief. The father's and mother's have already been disposed of in making secure the other equally pliant members of Tom Openheart; and anon, when the fastenings are all complete, you may look for some cunning explosion by which the Gulliver will be made to start from his slumbers in terror only to be taught the strangeness of his captivity.

I will not pretend to say that our excellent colonel sees this episode. The pleasant twinkle which lights the corner of his eye, and which is somewhat at variance with the words of his mouth, may be due to other influences; but it must be admitted, for the sake of history, that even were he to see the practice of Dick in this transaction, it is still not unlikely that he would suffer it to pass unchallenged. The good man would ascribe it to the season—to a natural levity—to any but a heinous and evil nature which called for rebuke and punishment. He had a queer notion that children were—only children, and that play was as necessary to their hearts, their growth, nay, their morals, as birch, logic and religion—doctrines which, in this era of juvenile progress, cannot be supposed likely to diffuse themselves greatly, and of which we venture therefore to speak without emotion. It is probable that Colonel Openheart's attention was wholly given to his good lady and his lovely daughter. They at least were his only listeners. There was an air of sadness upon the features of the excellent matron, which, however, were not wholly unlighted by a smile; while, on the other hand, the lips of the damsel were parted with an undisguised expression of merriment—positively on the verge of open laughter—the pearls of her mouth showing the white tips through their crimson setting, with a good humor and an arch delight that were clearly quite irresistible. Very sweet and very pretty was this expression of the face of Bessy Openheart, and the jade knew it. She was a blonde, and with features of wondrous regularity. Full of life and vivacity, there was yet a rich fountain of gushing waters at her heart, and her large blue eyes had learned how to fill with tears even before the happy smile could make its escape from her pretty little mouth. But we must not speak of her too soon. She is a mere child as yet—scarcely fifteen—just at that age when girlhood begins to falter with its own gaze, and when we begin to look upon it with as much trepidation as delight. But Colonel Openheart is about to resume.

"Not keep Christmas, Mrs. Openheart—not keep Christmas? Why, what in the world should I do with myself, my dear, or with you, or Bessy there, or Tom, Dick, Harry and the rest, from Christmas eve till New Year's? And what should we do with the neighbors—with Whitfield, and Jones, and Whipple, and Bond, and poor old Kinsale, and all their wives and little ones, all of whom have spent Christmas and New Years with us for the last hundred years or more. Some of them certainly did with my grandfather. Old Kinsale can tell you of the first dinner he ever took on this estate in the time of Grandfather Openheart, and that was a Christmas dinner. He can tell you every dish upon the table. There were ham and turkey just as now—there was roast and boiled—there was a round of beef—there were sausages and pillau—there were sundry pairs of ducks, cabbage and turnips, and potatoes; and for dessert, nuts, apples, mince-pies, plum-puddings, and more preserves than you could shake a stick at. More than thirty persons sat down to table, and to speak of the old man's Madeira brings tears of pleasure into the eyes of Daddy Kinsale to this moment. I tell you, old Billy Openheart is venerated to this day on account of his Christmas cheer. Not keep Christmas! Why, how would you avoid it, I'd like to know? They'd be here, all of them, fresh and fasting, I may say, before you could roll the Christmas log behind the dogs and dress up your windows with the holly and cacina. They'd be here to help you as they have been for the last fifty years. Bond and Whipple always came early for that purpose, and I think I have heard you say that little Susan Bond was the cleverest little creature in the world at dressing up the windows, and glasses, and flower-pots, with the green leaves and the scarlet berries. To think of the windows of "Maize-in-milk" looking bare at Christmas! Think of "Maize-in-milk" having no visitors at Christmas—no fun, no frolic, no dancing, no——! By the pipers, Mrs. Openheart, I don't know how to understand you. Talk of not keeping Christmas! Why, what in the name of blazes would you do with me, with yourself, with Bessy Clinton there, and dear little Rose, and Tom, and Dick, and Harry, and the rest, from Christmas eve till New Year's?"

"Well, to say the truth, dear husband, I did not think of spending Christmas at home at all, this season."

"Not spend Christmas at home!" cried the colonel, with renewed amazement. "And where, in Heaven's name, would you think to spend it?"

"Why, down in the parishes with Uncle Thomas. He's often asked us, you know——"

"With Uncle Thomas in the parishes! Go from home to spend Christmas! After that I should not be astonished at any of your notions. But, pray, Mrs. Openheart, when did you know your Uncle Thomas to spend *his* Christmas away from home?"

There was a pause, when the good dame, finding that her husband really waited her answer, meekly admitted that such an event had certainly never taken place within her remembrance.

"No—no! You may well say that. Well, only go to *him* and talk of spending Christmas away from home. Try *him*, Mrs. Openheart, by an affectionate invitation to come and stay with *us* Christmas week, and you'll get an answer will astonish you. You will certainly astonish him by the invitation. No—no; he's too much a gentleman of the old school—one of the good old Carolina stock, who knows what his duties are at Christmas—who knows what is due to his neighbors and to hospitality, and who knows——"

"But, my dear, considering what our expenses are, and how greatly they have been increased of late, Edward in Europe, and the sending of John and William to college—the purchase of the old Salem tract—the——"

"Poh! poh! poh! Positively, Emily, I am ashamed of you. This is only too ridiculous. You are for letting in at the spiggot and letting out at the bung. As for the Salem tract, it needs but one good crop, at good prices, and I pay for that; and that I should give up the acquaintance of my old neighbors, Tom Whipple, Elias Bond and Daddy Kinsale, because my eldest son is frolicking on the continent and two others have just had an introduction to those graybeards, Cicero and Homer——"

"Now, husband, you know I don't mean that you should give up the acquaintance of anybody——"

"You do, Emily, if you mean anything. It would amount to the same thing. Not to have my house full of my old friends, as usual, at Christmas, would be such a strangeness as would make them all feel strange. They'd look upon me as a broken man, or as a changed one, and in either case they'd become changed also; and then, in place of the cheerful household and pleasant neighborhood that we have had all along, there would be doubt, and coldness, and restraint —and all for what? Really, Emily, I can't see what you'd be driving at."

"But you could still see your neighbors."

"Not as before, Emily. A people so sparsely settled as our own, so very unsophisticated, and with that fierce sort of pride which distinguishes a life of comparative seclusion, are very easily made suspicious. They are, in particular, exceedingly jealous of any eccentricities on the part of the wealthy. Change your habit toward them in any respect—let your demeanor change in however slight degree, and they resent it as a something sinister, which is always personal to themselves. It wouldn't do to go out and see them at the fence; I must ask them in—and once in, the horse must be put up. And I can't say, 'Well, Bond'—or Whipple, or Jones, or Daddy Kinsale, as the case may be—'very glad to see you always, but sorry I can offer you nothing. Truth is, times are very hard, and that lark of mine in Europe and those two dogs, Jack and Will, they cost me a pretty penny now-a-days. Have to haul in my horns lest the sheriff pulls them off.'"

"Now, husband, you know I allude to nothing of this sort. It's only the usual waste that I'd have you avoid until you've got out of debt."

"Debt! Why, Mrs. Openheart, you speak as if I were over head and ears! What do I owe that I can't pay off with a single good crop?"

"You said the same thing last year."

The brave colonel seemed to wince at this suggestion.

"And as for waste—what waste? Do I waste anything at Christmas, or any other time? Is not all consumed that we cook? Is anything thrown away? Are there not mouths for all? What we and our guests do not consume, does it not go to the negroes? What they don't want, does it not go to the dogs and hogs, and ducks and chickens? I never see anything wasted. Really, Mrs. Openheart, I can't understand you. If you mean anything, it is that we are to kill no beef at Christmas, have no sausages, drink no egg-nog, and, I suppose, for the first time since we've been married, now going on fifty years——"

"Oh, husband—fifty years!"

"Yes, fifty years, more or less."

"Less by half—only twenty-six last November."

"Is it possible! And I said sixty! Well, it's certain I've counted the years by their pleasures."

A sweet, comical smile went round the circle. He continued—

"Well, as I was saying, here then, for the first time since our marriage, some forty-two years as you yourself admit, we are to have no mince-pies——"

"Nay, my dear; I didn't mean that we were to go without *them.* As you have bought the raisins, the citron and the currants, and as the hogs are already killed——"

"Oh! your only anxiety then is to keep these things from being wasted; but if that was your prudent intention, what do you propose to do with these nice things, after you have made them up, if we are to spend our Christmas with your Uncle Thomas?"

"Why, I thought of taking them down with us."

"Indeed! and precious little would Uncle Thomas, in his abundance, thank you for your pies. But, pray, in what respect should we be more wasteful in consuming them at home here, among our own poor neighbors, than down in the parishes, with the rich ones of Uncle Thomas? Really, Emily, I thought you were a better reasoner."

"Well, Edward, you do indeed make out a case against me, and if the mince-pies were the whole of our consumption in staying at home, as they will be in going down to the parishes, then your reproach would be conclusive; but you know, Edward, that these would form but a small part of our expense. They would not be alone: your Madeira, and Sherry, and Champagne—your beeves, your hogs, your turkies, and the horses of a dozen idle and worthless people eating at your corn-crib, and that not the fullest in the world——"

"It is full, Emily;—but I must stop you before you go too far. We can't always say who are the worthless in this world. I am sometimes disposed to think that the most worthless have their uses, and to suspect that the most worthy are not always of the value we put upon them. When I recollect how little I do myself in the way of work, and of how little real service I am to myself or to anybody else, in comparison with what I might be, I feel as if some malicious devil was jerking at my elbow in mockery, at those moments when I suffer myself to talk of the little worth or value of my neighbors. I tell you, Emily, I can't any longer bring myself to feel contempt for any human being, though I may sicken at the viciousness of some and sorrow over the idleness of others."

"Now, really, Edward, you shall not speak so slightingly of yourself. Are you not always busy? Do you not manage your own plantation?"

"After a fashion—but I'm not sure that my management is at all creditable to me or serviceable to my interests."

"*You* are never idle."

"I make chips enough, I grant you; but I am not sure that I am always profitably busy."

"Your negroes improve, increase, become more honest, sober, industrious, happy, more human every year."

"Thank God, I can conscientiously believe all that!"

"They love you, thank you, and go cheerfully to their tasks."

"Ay, ay; so they do, and so far.—But what is that fellow about? As usual, busy in tormenting his brother. Ho there, you dog—get you to bed, and wake up Tom that he may go along with you. What are you doing with the boy?"

"Only you call him up, papa," was the sly response of the dutiful urchin.

"Call him up yourself—push him—rout him up."

The boy stooped over the elder brother, and, with a closer eye, the worthy sire might have seen with what delicate consideration he introduced a feather of broom-straw into the ears and nostrils of the sleeper. A scream followed, then a roar and scuffle. The leg of Tom, as he started from his slumbers, was found to be inextricably involved with that of the chair, and both went over with a clatter that startled the good mother in her chair and shook the whole house from its propriety.

"Why, what have you done?"

The victim was not yet sufficiently awake to know well what was the matter with him, but struggled to throw out his fettered hands as in the act of swimming. The father saw his predicament, and as he and Bessy Clinton stooped to undo the ties with which the mischievous boy had fettered the lad, the urchin clapped his hands in exultation and flew away to the door.

"To bed, sirrah!" said Colonel Openheart, with a voice in which authority struggled hard with merriment; "to bed, before I give you the strap."

"No, no, papa! Don't I know it's Christmas time—and what's the use of Christmas if there's to be no fun, I want to know?"

"The boy has the right on't. What's the use of Christmas if there's to be no fun? There shall be fun, sirrah, but your share of it must cease for the night. To bed, both of you."

"But to-morrow, papa!" said both of the boys in a breath.

"You shall have the ponies, and we'll go to the river; and we'll take the dogs, and see if we can't put up a wild cat. There, enough for the night."

And the boys were kissed and disappeared.

"And these are to lose their Christmas—and the neighbors, and the negroes, and all, for no better reason than to save the waste, as if there could be any waste in making so many persons happy. And you, Bessy Clinton, that you should side with your mother for having Christmas away from home. You deserve a whipping for it, Bess."

"Ah, papa, you never whipped me yet."

"It's not too late to begin!" and he took the damsel about the waist, and she turned in his embrace and lifted her lips to his own, and he kissed her with delight as he said—"Well, well, we'll put it off till the New Year. I havn't the heart for whipping just now. But then——"

"But Bessy Clinton did not join with me, husband. She was quite opposed to it."

"Ah, that alters the case. You shall have Christmas at home. And Bessy Clinton, for your reward, hear farther——"

"What, papa?"

"You shall have your old friend, Mary Butler, to spend it with you."

"Oh! will she come, papa? Can you get her?"

"Ay will she. And more than that, mamma, I've bought in all the Butler negroes—bought them in for her benefit, to save them from that shark of a lawyer who manages the estate."

"Surely, Mr. Openheart, you haven't made such a purchase?" anxiously inquired the mother.

"Ay, but I have."

"What! bought in all the negroes?"

"All but a single family. Thirty-five workers, seventy-one negroes in all—and gave a pretty good price for them, too."

"How much?" asked the matron, with increasing concern.

"Two hundred and sixty dollars round."

"Good heavens! And how are you to pay for them?"

"I have three years to pay it in, Emily—first instalment next December of five thousand dollars, and the balance in equal parts the next two years. The terms are quite easy."

"But how are you to pay it, husband?"

"How? Why, surely, you don't suppose that I shan't make a sufficient crop next season to pay five thousand dollars!"

"Have you done so this?"

"No. Why do you ask when you know that this crop is a failure?"

"Ah—should the next be so?"

"'Pon my honor, Mrs. Openheart, you do contrive to suggest the prettiest prospects."

"But why did you buy these negroes, Mr. Openheart? You have more than you want already, and more than are profitable."

"True bill, Emily."

"You have scarcely any open land more than your present force can work."

"Go to clearing on the first of January. Plenty to clear, thank God."

"But that is fatal to your woodland; and really, Mr. Openheart, the question comes up again—why did you buy a property which you don't want, and which you know to be so unprofitable? Besides, the Butler negroes are particularly unserviceable. I don't know where you will find so many gray-headed people. Some of them haven't, to my knowledge, done a stitch of work for ten years; and there's at least a dozen old negroes who can barely totter along with the palsy."

"To tell you the truth, Emily, it was these very old negroes that caused me to buy—these and the dear child Mary Butler, who sat weeping in the house as the sale was going on, with these infirm old people hanging about her. They had dandled the child on their knee, and there wasn't one of them, from Daddy Enoch to Maum Betty, the one-eyed, whom she didn't regard as a personal relation. They wept and pleaded with her, and her weeping was so much pleading with me. Besides, I found that Skinflint, the man who acts as lawyer for Ingelhart and Cripps, the executors, was disposed to buy them at his own prices, and nobody would bid against him. Indeed, there was nobody willing to buy property just at this season—you will say they were wiser than your husband. Perhaps so. But they would have gone to Skinflint for nothing. His first bid was a hundred all round, and I at once doubled it. I was indignant at the fellow's bid, and wasn't to be deceived by the whisper that went about, intended to discourage others, that he was bidding in for the heiress. I knew better, and when he found I was in earnest he run upon me."

"But why did you let him do it? Why not stop at the two hundred?"

"Ask a man when his blood's up why he isn't cool. I was a fool—I know it, Emily, and you may reproach me as you will for it. I knew no more what I was about than if I had lost my wits. The sight of the dear, sweet little orphan in her sorrows, totally unmanned me. I had always seen her so happy and so bright before—and I could not help remembering what a pet she was of the dear angel mother. And poor Ben Butler was such a sterling fellow. Nobody wanted a dollar if he had it. I thought of all these things in a moment. I fancied I heard the father whispering in my ears, and that I saw the mother pleading with all her eyes, and my own grew to be quite blinded by my tears. And then old Enoch tottered to me in the piazza, staff in hand, and his gray beard hanging on his chest, and his old eyes, half shut up by age, were dripping too; and, taking my arm, he said to me, 'Mauss Openheart, you surely ain't gwine to let us go off to strange people?'—only these words, and they finished my struggles. Just then, Skinflint said one hundred round, and I mounted him with another. I knew his game the moment I heard his voice. And when he said to me, 'Really, Mr. Openheart, I had no idea that you wished to increase your force,' I swore in my own mind that he at least shouldn't have them. You've heard the whole story. The negroes are to be here to-morrow, and Mary Butler, and Skinflint himself, who is to bring the bonds and bill of sale."

"Well, Edward, I only hope that you may not suffer by your benevolence."

"Nay, never fear, Emily. I'm rash and headstrong, I know, and have done many foolish things, but I feel sure that I shan't suffer for this helping of the orphan, and keeping these poor dependent creatures from being scattered over the face of the earth. The probability is that my bonds will scarcely be presented for payment so long as the interest is regularly paid. The executors, Ingelhart and Cripps, can make no better investment of the money, and it will be a very nice sum for her when she is of age—or I am prepared to let her have the negroes back if she prefers it then. The plantation was not sold."

"And what will you do with these old negroes, Edward?"

The answer was somewhat impatiently spoken.

"Feed them first, Emily; clothe them, give them Christmas. We'll kill a beef for them to-morrow to begin with, and pray God to-night for good times, that we may be enabled to feed them always, from Christmas to Christmas, as well as now. So now to bed, and see that you rise before the sun, Bessy Clinton. You have to see to the pies and pastries. It's now one week to Christmas, and"—looking out from the windows—"a bright starlight night, in the language of the watchman. May we wake to a bright, dry, and honest winter morning!"

CHAPTER II.

So now is come our joyful'st feast,
  Let every man be jolly;
Each room with ivy leaves be drest,
  And every post with holly.
Though some churls at our mirth repine,
Round your foreheads garlands twine;
Drown sorrow in a cup of wine,
  And down with melancholy.
Slightly altered from George Wither, 1622.

The day of Christmas eve dawned propitiously upon the broad fields and groves of "Maize-in-milk." There never had been, in all the south, a brighter or sweeter December sunshine. Nature seemed to have yielded herself wholly to the moral of the season. She had put on her gayest habiliments; the earth sent up a perfume less penetrating and diffusive, perhaps, but not less sweet and persuasive than in the spring time, and the woods wore such robes as autumn had bestowed upon them—glorious, rich investitures of crimson and yellow, which made gum, oak and poplar look each like a sovereign prince begirt by his obsequious courtiers. Christmas in Carolina is very apt to be vexed with storm and rain, a fatal conjunction for thousands of schemes of juvenile delight and delinquency. But the present promises to be quite as favorable to the plans of happy-hearted creatures as the most amiable and philanthropic spirits could pray for; and, with the dawn, the three sons of Colonel Openheart, Tom, the good-fellow, Dick, the mischievous, and Harry, the little, starting from a sleep which teemed with the most happy dreams of turbulent enjoyment, had darted into the chamber of their excellent sire, and were hauling him out of sleep and bed at the same moment. He, too, had been in the enjoyment of the happiest heart fancies, such as are natural to the fond and hopeful parent. In his sleeping visions, he had beheld the return of his son Edward, now traveling in Europe, a tall and handsome youth, refined by foreign observation, and with a mind generously expanded to the appreciation of all that was excellent and noble in foreign standards. William and John were also returned from college, availing themselves of the brief respite of a single week accorded them during the great religious holiday of the year. And other forms, almost equally dear, and other images quite as sweet and persuasive, had passed beneath his waking fancy, while his real and earthly nature slept. Sweet glimpses of dear Mary Butler, and his own fair daughter, Bessy Clinton, and vague and indistinct forms and aspects, in innocent relationship with these, all of which aroused the fondest hopes and the most grateful imaginings in the fond father's bosom. It was the season when all sights and sounds are sweet and wholesome to the heart which desires and exercises itself in wholesome influences—when, as the great bard expresses it—

"*The* bird of dawning singeth all night long:
And then, they say, no spirit dares stir abroad;
The nights are wholesome; then no planets strike,
No fairy takes, nor witch hath power to charm,
So hallow'd and so gracious is the time."

And merrily, indeed, and with most vigorous throat, did the hundred voices of Mrs. Openheart's poultry yard respond to each other through the watches of that calm December night. Nor were these the only voices whose music somehow melted in with and formed a part of the dreams of the excellent colonel. All around the fine old mansion house of "Maize-in-Milk," the mock-birds had made homes for their young among the ancestral oaks and cedars. Of these, the bold choristers had maintained immemorial possession; and, as some of the trees spread their great limbs even up to the windows of the dwelling, against the panes of which their leaves rattled in the gusty night, it was easy for the Puck of the southern groves to send his capricious music through every chamber. These had Colonel Openheart been long accustomed to hear, but it seemed as if, at the approach of the season when

"a chyld was i-born,
Us for to savyn that al was forlorn,"

the voices of the birds grew more full and numerous, and a generous and glad spirit, a soul of exultation, gave new impulse to their merriment and music. Their fitful and capricious strains formed fitting echoes to the fancies that swarmed in the good man's visions; and his own heart caught up their echoes, and even while his boys were breaking into his chamber with their clamorous exhortations, he might have been heard to murmur in his sleep broken fragments of one of the ancient English carols—

> "Now thrice welcome Christmas
>   Which brings us good cheer,
> Minced-pies and plum-porridge,
>   Good ale and strong beer," &c.

And this was the boys' welcome as they bounced into the chamber, and dispelled, with a single shout, all the visions of his sleep.

"Why, what a mischief, boys, is the matter, that you rout me up at midnight?"

"Midnight, father—why, the sun's a-rising!"

"Well, what then? Is that any good reason that the father shouldn't sleep? You don't know what fine dreams you have driven away by your uproar."

"Oh, this is no time for dreaming, father. Come, up with you, and let's go to the river, and shoot off the big cannon."

"Well, I suppose there's no resisting you," said the indulgent sire, as he prepared to obey the requisition.

"You will ruin those boys, Colonel Openheart," murmured his excellent help-meet, with some querulousness of accent, occasioned by the rude disturbance of a slumber which had been as precious full of dreams in her case as in that of her husband.

"Nay, never fear," was the reply; "the boys are not so easily spoiled. The danger is with the girls. Boys are naturally good—a little more boisterous than their sisters, but better on the whole. You women are always apt to confound honest impulse with misdoing. We must let them play. Childhood is the season for play, and play is necessary for the heart; and so, boys, let's go to play heartily, as others go to work. Now that you have roused me, get you gone till I get up and dress myself. I shan't stay long."

In a moment, their merry voices might have been heard upon the lawn in front, ringing clearly out in the dry sweet atmosphere. A gentler song suddenly took wing in an adjoining chamber, and the eyes of father and mother both twinkled with a lustre that came directly from the heart, as they heard the soft but melodious accents of Bessy Clinton, singing, as if in preparation for the coming day, a familiar old Christmas ballad.

"When in Bethl'em, fair citie,
Chryst was born to die for me,
Then the angels sang with glee,
In Excelsis gloria.

"Ah! with what a lovely bright,
To the herdsmen shone the light,
Where he lay in lowly plight,
In Excelsis gloria.

"Heavenly king, to save his kind,
Bear we still his birth in mind,
Singing ever as we find,
In Excelsis gloria.

"Praying, as we sing, for grace,
To behold, in bliss, his face,
Whose dear coming saved his race,
In Excelsis gloria."

"And you think boys better than girls—naturally good, husband—not so easily spoiled?" was the quiet but ironical inquiry of the wife, as the last murmurs of the girl's song subsided away, and were followed by a triumphant shout from below and a tremendous explosion from a huge blunderbuss, to discharge which they had not waited for the father.

"The rogues!" exclaimed Colonel Openheart. "But I did the very same thing myself when I was a lad—the very same thing—nay, something worse. I made a mine of a whole canister of powder, and nearly shook down the old house on Briar Hill with a single blast. That's the nature of the animal. Don't let it worry you, my dear Emily; they shoot and shout while Bessy Clinton smiles and sings, and I am content that they should both enjoy themselves in their different ways. But the rogues are impatient; hear how they clamor!

Emily, dear wife, a kiss! God has blessed us in our children—eight living out of thirteen, five already blessed, and the others blessing us! We have not lived in vain, dear wife! And, hark you, is that Bessy Clinton again? No; it's dear little Rose. She has awakened at last, and sounds her little pipes in song also. How like her voice to Bessy Clinton's, and how like both to your own! But the horses are at the door, and those rogues are ten times as noisy as ever. And you don't like their singing, Emily, so much as Bessy Clinton's, eh?"

"Surely not. How can you ask?"

"Nor I—nor I," said the good-natured father, as he hurried below, leaving the now thoroughly awakened mother to the embraces of the two girls, who entered from an inner chamber, bearing in their hands great bunches of holly, prankt gayly with their own and the red berries of the cassina.

"You are late this morning, dear mother," said Bessy Clinton with a kiss; and little Rose echoed the opinion and followed the example.

"Late? You are as impatient as Dick and Harry," said the mother. "I am sure it's an hour sooner than you rise usually."

"Ah! but it's Christmas eve, mother, and we have to do a great deal. We shall have them here, pretty soon, and must get an early breakfast. Good old Mr. Bond will be here betimes to help us, and Squire Whipple won't be long after him."

"And Susan Bond's a-coming too, mamma, and Sally," was the eager assurance of little Rose, anxious to put in.

"You are all too like your father, too impatient, children. But now that you are here, Bessy Clinton, make yourself useful. Put the pin in this tippet, and—ah! child, how you're sticking me!"

"I'm so sorry, mother!"

"You're always so impatient! There, that will do. Pick up your holly branches and your berries: such a litter as you make. And come, we will hurry down and see about breakfast, so that it be in readiness when your father comes back. By this time he's half way to the river."

And they descended the stairs, Bessy Clinton singing pleasantly, while her fingers wove the green bushes and the red berries artfully together, from another of the ancient carols with which the English tastes of an affectionate grandsire had long since made her familiar.

"I am here, the Lord Chrystmasse,
Give me welcome, youth and lasse,
For I come to heal trespasse,
    Hurtes of soule to heale;
Dieu gardez—this I bring,
And ye need, with welcoming,
To rejoyce the man I sing,
    Come for sinners' weale.

" 'Tis Chryste's coming that ye see,
He who died upon the tree,
That your souls, from sin set free,
    Might be his once more;
In this blessing, make your cheere,
Yet of evyl joys beware;
Satan spreads his fatal snare,
    Though his sway be o'er:

"Welcome me, the Lord Chrystmasse—"

Etcetera! The song was hushed in the sound of carriage wheels. The neighbors had already begun to make their appearance. Sure enough, there was good old Mr. Bond in his homely "Jersey," and Susan Bond in her nice white dimity and old-fashioned tippet, and little Sally, to the delight of Rose, in her faded calico, that sat upon her rounded limbs like the sack upon her great-grandmother; and they brought along with them bouncing Joe Dillon, a great chubby-cheeked lad of one of the farther neighbors, of whom the family at "Maize-in-Milk" as yet knew nothing. And such a tumbling out of the frail vehicle as followed, and such a tumbling out of the house to receive them as took place, is quite beyond description. Mrs. Openheart met old Mr. Bond on the threshold, and Bessy Clinton took charge of Susan, while little Rose led off Sally—the little also—followed by the chubby boy at halting paces. And between Bessy Clinton and Susan Bond, the work of the day began almost instantly. The myrtle and the holly, the cassina and the bamboo, were instantly in requisition, and over the great heavy windows and doors, and all about the huge mirrors and antique family pictures, you could see the arches, and the wreaths and festoons beginning to grow up in green and crimson, giving to the spacious walls and rooms a charming aspect of the English Gothic. How sweet is work when our tastes go with the toil, and when beauty compensates industry. Our happy maidens were conscious of this pleasure in the progress of the labors of their hands; and now they put up and pulled down, re-arranged and altered, their tastes becoming more and more critical the more they were exercised. And "there now, Susan, that will so please father," declared at length that Bessy Clinton was herself quite satisfied.

Leaving the girls thus happily engaged, let us follow the boys in their excursion to the river. You should have seen the lads mount each on his own pony, not excepting Harry the little, who did not seem a bit too little for the marshtacky, brought all the way from Pocotaligo, which he straddled like an infant centaur. Colonel Openheart, mounted on a strong, black parade horse, upon which he had more than once marshaled his regiment, led the way, Tom trying hard to keep beside him in the narrow road, and Dick more ambitiously darting half the time ahead. They were followed by Swift, Sure and Slow, three famous dogs, which were the admiration of all the hunters of St. Matthews. Then came Bedford, the Superlative, a stout, gray-headed negro, who officiated as high sheriff over the plantation, carried out the wishes of his master, and reported progress nightly—a shrewd, sensible negro, cool and steady, confident in his opinions, yet perfectly respectful, who served God and his master as well as he knew how, and, murdering the king's English, seldom committed any more heinous offences. The way of the cavalcade lay over hill and dale, gentle eminences and pleasant slopes, and chiefly through woods which were as old as the hills themselves. Colonel Openheart was fond of trees and foliage, and had so contrived his fields as to maintain a fine body of wood between each. Through these his several roads meandered, and he could pass to the survey of one field after another without once leaving the shelter of the original forests. These were of pine, or oak and hickory, interspersed with a pleasant variety of gum and poplar, and shrub trees of every sort. Long reaches of swamp occasionally relieved the uniform aspects of the hill foliage, by the gigantic forms of cypress, ash and other trees of deciduous character. The brightness of that sunshiny December morning had its effect upon all parties. A cheery smile sat upon the face of the father, and brightened benevolently in his large blue eye; the white teeth of Bedford, the Superlative, never displayed their massive outlines more conspicuously than while riding along with the boys, responding to their eager inquiries; and they, the lads, their young souls spoke out only in shout and caracole, in impatient question that stayed for no reply, and in the expression of an exulting confidence in the joys of the day, which nature herself seemed to counsel and encourage. The autumn still lingered among the tree tops in robes of saffron and purple; and the life which animated them beside, showed itself momently in groups of squirrels, white, black and gray, which, darting from tree to tree, seemed really only to sport themselves for the amusement of the cavalcade and the annoyance of the dogs. Sometimes a covey of partridges flushed up from the brown and half-withered foliage along the track, and a couple of great turkey-hawks might be seen to rise sweeping the air over the open fields in wide circles, with keen eye bent upon the long grasses in which the rabbit might be supposed to have slept the previous night. The track pursued by the party, though a narrow, was a sufficiently open one. Made studiously circuitous, it was a good two miles to the river, and every fifty or hundred yards afforded some pleasant or picturesque changes to the eye. Now they skirted a hill upon whose brow sits a crown of the noblest pines, green, towering and magnificent; and now they wind along a copse of bays, a thicket, whose leaves suffer only enough from the winter's frost as to give forth those sweets of which none of the persuasions of the summer could beguile a single breath. A uniform dark green overspreads this region, save here and there where a great gum-tree, rising in the midst, shakes a head of glorious yellow aloft in lonely majesty. And now they pass into the levels of the swamp, through some choice cotton fields, in which, however, Colonel Openheart sees but little promise, during the present season, of realizing the usual bountiful returns. They are already nearly stripped of fruit—the white pods which commonly sprinkled these fields, as if strewn with blossoms of the dogwood, until the last of January, being quite beyond his power to pick until that period, show now but a scattered whiteness here and there, which rather mocks than satisfies the sight.

"Bad business here, Bedford, this season."

"Monstrous bad!" says Bedford, with a closing of the lips and a lugubrious shaking of the head. "Monstrous bad, sir; but such a *portentious* drought as devoured us, and such a *tempestious* tornado as beat us down after it, *jest* as the field was agoing to blow in September, was a ravaging of us that no cotton could stand under."

"We must do better next year, Bedford."

"Ef it's the will of Providence, there shall be another guess *desemblance* in our swamp next year."

"It must be, Bedford," was the rather emphatic reply of the colonel.

The negro was silent. The master proceeded—"The old Salem tract must be put in order with the beginning of the New Year. You know that I have bought the force of our old friend, Ben Butler. They will be here to-day. We must work them on that tract, and must contrive to pay for them, in part, out of next year's crop. They are not the best negroes in the world, as you know, but we must manage them with prudence. I look to you, Bedford, to do your best"—the negro touched his beaver—"and I do not doubt that you can meet all my calculations. The seasons can scarcely be so bad again as they have been for the last two years."

But these details are sufficient. Crossing a pretty but shallow stream, which was skirted by a growth of gum and traversed by occasional cypresses, of immense size, that strode clear away, six or eight feet deep, in the water, the party emerged upon a hammock beyond which lay the river, and the impatient boys cantered away in front while the colonel and Bedford continued at a more moderate pace. When the two latter reached the banks of the river, the urchins were already dismounted, and each had his pony fastened to the swinging limb of a tree; and here the object which had brought them to this point was at once presented conspicuously to the sight. Here, commanding the river, which was a broad and turbid stream, with a vast stretch of drowned swamp spreading away on the opposite side, was a tiny fortress, a redoubt of earth, with its bastions and its merlons, and a neat little two-pounder, looking out with impudent aspect upon the raftsmen going down the stream. In a moment, the colonel unrolled a nice silken banner upon which the fair hands of Bessy Clinton had wrought a palmetto, and it was soon run up the staff and floating gayly above the juvenile ramparts. And it was to hear the thunder of this piece, and to see the smoke and fire issue from its jaws, that our boys, Tom, Dick and Harry, would at any time abandon the more staid and regular amusements of the household. The smaller piece at home, manufactured from an old ship's blunderbuss, and set on a rude block before the house, though in itself a delight, and which they could venture to discharge themselves, was not to be spoken of in the same breath with the more formidable engine by which the river was commanded. Strange passion which the boy has for guns and uproar! Colonel Openheart encouraged this passion among his sons, and the fantastic notion of a fort at his *landing* on the river was a sort of tribute to the memory of his father, who had been one of the defenders of Fort Moultrie against the British. The fact—then proved for the first time—that a rifleman of the American forests made a first-rate artillerist, was one to be remembered by the son of one who had been conspicuous among those by whom the fact was so well proven; and the possession of a small British piece, which was one of the trophies awarded to his father's valor, had prompted the little battery that crowned the water approaches to "Maize-in-Milk."

But the signal is given! The eager hearts of the boys are bounding violently against their ribs; their eyes are dilating; their heads stretched forward, and their whole souls filled with delicious expectation. The torch is applied, and the roar follows. Then they rush forward into the smoke, Dick leading the way, and even little Harry, convulsed with frenzy, rolling and tumbling about in the sulphurous fog. Twice, thrice the discharge is made, and then the signal is given to resume the march. Each lad unfastens his horse, Bedford performing the office for little Harry, who is too proud, however, to admit of any help in clambering up his pony's sides. The adventure of the morning is over, and now back to the domicil for breakfast, with what appetite they may.

There they found old Mr. Bond and pretty Susan Bond, and other guests, already arrived—for their excursion to the river had somewhat encroached, in spite of all their efforts at early rising, upon the breakfast hour. The breakfast consisted of all the varieties known to a Carolina plantation of ante-revolutionary establishment. I don't know that it would be worth while to enumerate the various "creature comforts" under which the table groaned; and yet there may be some young persons among my readers to whom a *catalogue raisonée* may not be altogether without its uses. And first, then, for the inevitable dish of Indian corn, in its capacity of vegetable rather than breadstuff—hominy! Now, your yellow corn won't do for hominy—the color and the flavor are alike against it. It must be the genuine semi-transparent flint, ground at a water-mill, white as snow, and swelling out in two huge platters at convenient places upon the table. A moderate portion of each plate is provided with this vegetable, boiled to a due consistency, neither too soft like mush, nor too stiff, hard and dry for easy adjustment with a spoon. It requires long experience on the part of the cook to prepare this dish for the just appreciation of an adept. There must be no rising lump in the mass; there must be no dark speck upon the surface. The spoon should lie upon it without sinking below the rims, and hominy should always be eaten with a spoon or fork of silver. I name all these little particulars, as I assume the time to be approaching fast when Great Britain and Ireland, and one-half the continent of Europe will be fed out of the American granaries, and when *hominy* will arrive at its position of true dignity and distinction in the *cuisine* of the Old World. The Carolina breakfast-table would be a blank without hominy.

That of "Maize-in-milk" had its usual bountiful supply on the present occasion, and was not without its variety of breadstuffs. There were loaves and cakes of wheat, corn and rye, all the growth of the plantation—Colonel Openheart not being one of those conceited wiseacres who rely only upon the cotton market and neglect every other interest. It may be that he relied still too much upon the profits and prospects of the cotton market so as to indulge in a too ready habit of expenditure, but he never was that purblind proprietor who forgets the farm in the staple—a class of people still quite too large in Carolina for their own and the good of the country. His table rejoiced in its rice cakes and waffles also, among his breadstuffs—rice being also one of the grains of his own production. But of these, enough is said already. Among the meats on table, to say nothing of cold corn beef and boiled venison, we must spare a passing sentence to the sausages and black-puddings. Christmas on the southern plantation is emphatically the sausage season. Then it is, as old Mr. Bond was wont to say, that every negro is heard to whistle, and every mouth looks oily. But perhaps it is not every reader who knows what black puddings are. Well, we shall not pretend to enlighten those who are unhappily ignorant. It is enough to say that a black-pudding is something in the nature of the Scotch *haggis,* so sublimely sung by Burns, without the deficiencies and infirmities of that venerable compound. It is less unsightly to the eye and less unfriendly to the taste, more delicate in its flavor, and perhaps even more various in its ingredients. You shall find it a goodly commodity, taken along with its kindred, sausage and hominy, at a southern breakfast, when the Yule Log is blazing. Colonel Openheart had just killed his usual hundred head of hogs, and this was one of the great events to bring happiness to the negro quarter. The great beef had also been slaughtered, and plenty and pleasure were conspicuous in every visage. No wonder the breakfast went off swimmingly. The boys were the happiest creatures in the world, and the achievements of the great gun were thrust into all ears. Not that they were either obtrusive or uproarious in the house with the guests or at the table. On these points, our colonel, though very indulgent generally, was something of a martinet, and breakfast was discussed and dispatched with a degree of order and quietude which only was not solemnity and stiffness. After breakfast the girls continued the work of decoration, and the boys went out to play. The lady of the house had her preparations still in some degree to make, and the worthy colonel took charge of good Mr. Bond, and they went together to the farm-yard, comparing notes, and discussing peas, ploughs and potatoes as they went. Soon, however, their attention was drawn to farther arrivals. First came poor old Kinsale, a worthy old Irishman—a farmer of small degree, who had been so long in America as to insist that yams and Spanish were the real potatoes of green Erin, and that the Irish potato had never been otherwise than sweet from the days of Sir Walter Raleigh. He was a good old man, seventy-six years or more, for whom Colonel Openheart sent his own horses and carriage every Christmas. Unlike Irishmen, who are not generally tenacious of early customs, he still wore small clothes and long stockings, having no better reason for his adherence to ancient fashions than the possession of a pair of legs which were formed after the best of ancient models. The youngsters of the day, however much they might smile at the tottering gait and rheumy eyes of old Kinsale, were not without a sufficient degree of taste to prompt envy of his calves. The red bandana about his neck, and the great hanging cape and flaps of his Marseilles vest were in odd contrast with the modern *sack*, of newest pattern, which had lately beguiled him by its cheapness, its bright colors and glittering buttons, at a Charleston slop-shop. The old fellow was now all agog for the war with Mexico, and his first demand was for the last newspapers which spoke of that event. But that the approaches of age were quite too unequivocal to suffer such an absurdity, it might have been that we should have heard him talk of volunteering in the Palmetto Regiment. But he was still strong to totter about field and stable; he disliked the house, and placing his chair under the shade of a group of great oaks that circled the centre of the lawn before the mansion of "Maize-in-Milk," he indicated to the other gentlemen the propriety of choosing that as the place for the reception of the arriving company. So here they all took seats together, with the newspapers in the grasp of old Kinsale, and a variety of potatoes of the largest dimensions, yam, Spanish and brimstone at his feet. These, with a laudable brag of Colonel Openheart, he had displayed as the largest which had been made anywhere that season. A few superior cotton-stalks were also beside them, with some mammoth turnips and great ears of corn. While they sat together, in rolled the barouche of Captain Whitfield with his family, five or seven in number, soon followed by Squire Whipple and a Mr. Bateman, who had just bought a snug farm in the neighborhood, and had been invited to share the Christmas hospitalities of "Maize-in-Milk." All of these were farmers of moderate resources, well to do in the world without being wealthy, a comfortable and improving people. Colonel Openheart's pleasure was to feel himself in a neighborhood with which he could sympathize, and with this object he had been for a long period engaged in the politic task of endeavoring to secure the affections of those around him. He made but little difference between his neighbors, except such as was called for by moral differences among themselves; and if he thought of the poverty of any among them, it was only that he might remember the needy with more seasonable assistance.

But now other guests began to make their appearance, and as a stately carriage came whirling down the road, dear Bessy Clinton ran out to the trees where her father was seated, exclaiming—"It's Mary Butler, papa—that's the carriage;" and the eager eyes of the damsel sparkled as dewily bright as if the sunshine which they showed was about to issue from a tear. Sure enough, it was Mary Butler,—but who is it with her? Bessy Clinton had never been so fortunate as to know Elijah Skinflint, Esq., the lawyer of Messrs. Ingelhart and Cripps, to whom the temporary charge of Mary Butler had been confided. Mr. Skinflint, though he owned a plantation a few miles above that of Col. Openheart, was a practicing lawyer at a distant court-house, which he seldom left, except hurriedly, to cast an eye upon the doings of his overseer. His lean and angular person, red, searching, ferret-like eyes, and gaunt, erect frame, were quite new to our Bessy Clinton, who, though anxious to embrace Mary Butler, somewhat shrunk from the idea of approaching the grim guardian who came along with her. But, Skinflint and all his terrors were forgotten, when her father lifted Mary from the carriage; and the fond damsel bounded to her friend, and took her about the neck with as much fervency as if all the blood from her heart had gone into her arms. She was about to lead the lovely orphan away, when the voice of her father called her back; and she suffered a formal introduction to the redoubted lawyer, who had himself suggested the proceeding. Skinflint was evidently struck with the appearance of Bessy Clinton; who, for her age, was a tall and womanly-looking creature. I need not say she was a very lovely one. Skinflint appeared to think her so, and threw as much gentleness and animation into his glance, when he spoke with her, as a long practice in a very different school permitted him to do. He would have given her his arm in moving towards the house, but the damsel, too anxious to have Mary Butler to herself, contrived not to appear to see the awkward half-tender of civility which the learned barrister had made. In this way she got off, and the two girls were out of sight in an instant. The gentlemen again went towards their trees, where they soon forgot the other sex in a discussion which was equally shared between politics and potatoes.

Skinflint was something of a politician, but he met his match in old Kinsale. If the one was expert at weaving the knot of Gordius, the other had a prompt Alexandrine method of unloosing it. His sturdy, practical mind, and clear, direct judgment, made him more than a match for the lawyer, who soon contrived to get as far from him as possible. In a little while the attention of all parties was drawn to new objects which appeared upon the highway. These were the negroes of the Butler estate, whom Col. Openheart had so rashly purchased, and at such high prices. He had sent all his carts and wagons to bring them to their new abodes, with all their prog and furniture. And a quaint and merry-looking cavalcade they made. The carts, four in number, the wagons, too, and a great ox-cart, were all laden heavily with baggage and bedding. Grinning little urchins lay on the top, and the able-bodied walked beside the vehicles. Each carried something in his hands, or a wallet upon his shoulders. More than one old fiddle was to be seen among them, and the song with which they accompanied the crazy music of its strings, only ceased when they came in sight of the group beneath the trees. Col. Openheart, followed by his guests, went out to the roadside to speak to them as they passed. He had a pleasant word for each, and shook hands with old Enoch, the patriarch of the plantation, where the latter sat in the wagon which brought up the rear. Bedford appropriately made his appearance at this moment, and took charge of the cavalcade, which he conducted to the quarters prepared for them. Affectionate memories of his friend, Ben Butler, caused the eyes of Col. Openheart to grow dim as he shook hands with the aged negroes; but a very different sentiment was in those of Lawyer Skinflint. Be sure, that excellent citizen had thoughts in his mind, as he beheld the scene, which he would never have ventured to declare in any of his pleadings. But the worthy colonel neither saw nor suspected anything, and his deportment to Skinflint, whom he did not love, was quite as courteous and kind as to any other of his guests. For that matter, as the day advanced, Skinflint began to grow in favor. He evidently took some pains to make himself agreeable. He was a man of considerable experience and information; had traveled; was well read, and not entirely wanting in those finer tastes which so happily garnish even the conversation of the merely sensible. He could be sportive when he would; and a vein of dry humor, which at the bar was causticity, seasoned his most ordinary conversation. He was habitually a hard man,—cold, ascetic; sarcastic, selfish; with but little sympathy for humanity in its susceptibilities, and in those pliant movements of the heart and fancy, which the worldling is apt to regard as weaknesses. But he knew how to humor the moods of others; and, with an object in view, he could play the pleasant companion for an hour, or a day—nay, quite as long as he had anything to gain by it. And he had something to gain at "Maize-in-Milk;" at least, we already half suspect the grim bachelor of being more than pleased with the graces and charms of dear Bessy Clinton. We don't know that any eye but ours beheld him, as, frequently, in the progress of the day, his glance was fixed on the fair face and beautifully rounded form of the maiden, with a positive show of interest and pleasure. The insolent! He to presume on the affections of that sweet creature —that incarnation of all that is delicate and dear in humanity and woman!

But the day passes,—O! most pleasantly to all; and the young increase in numbers as the hours melt into the past; and the brightness grows in every eye as, sporting on the lawn, they seem to hurry the footsteps of the sun. And he sets at last! Then emerging from an ancient closet, our host brings forth the rude charred fragments of a half-burned log. It is the Yule Log of the last year. The hall chimney is carefully denuded of all its fires—the sticks are taken out, the hearth is swept. The great back-log, chosen for the fire of the new year, is brought in, and the fragments of last year's log are employed to kindle it. Our colonel delighted to continue, as nearly as he could, with propriety, the customs of his English ancestors; and his own shoulders bore the log from the wood-pile, and his own hands lighted the brands of the new year's fire as the sun went down. Doubtless, there is some superstition in all this; but such superstitions are not without their charm, and have their advantages. The superstitions which tend, in some degree, to make us forgetful of self, are equally serviceable to humanity and religion.

The tea-things are removed; the night advances, the sable fiddler has made his appearance; and, seated in the piazza, attended by an urchin with a rude tamborine, he brings forth sounds which have a strange effect upon youthful feet and fancies. The dance begins, and, for two hours, the girls and boys foot it merrily in the great hall. Then a few steal away to another apartment, and there the eggs are broken. One seizes upon the bowl, another upon the dish, and they proceed to manufacture a noggin of eggs—that luscious draught not to be foregone, styled, in homely parlance, *eggnog!* not an inebriating beverage in that temperate household. The dance ceases; the draught is enjoyed; the more youthful disappear, and the sweet voice of Bessy Clinton, as she sings another of her ancient Christmas carols, is the signal for the separation of the company that night at the mansion of "Maize-in-Milk." Verily, Lawyer Skinflint never, in his life before, appeared so devotedly fond of music. He hung upon the tones of the sweet songstress as if she were especially the sweet singer in Israel, while she poured forth, at her father's summons, the old "Carol for Christmas Eve."

Where, among the pasturing rocks,
The glad shepherds kept their flocks,
Came an angel to the fold,
And, with voice of rapture, told,
    That the Saviour, Christ, was born!

Born in Bethlehem, sacred place,
Of a virgin full of grace,
In a manger, lowly spot,
Symbol of his mortal lot,
    Lo! the Saviour, Christ, is born!

Dread and glorious was the bright
Of that sudden, shining light,
Which, around the angel then,
Token'd to the simple men,
    That the Saviour, Christ, was born!

But the voice that fill'd the blaze,
Cheer'd them in their deep amaze;—
"Tidings of great joy I bring,"
In the coming of your King:
    The true Shepherd, Christ is born!

CHAPTER III.

And never did a Christmas morning dawn more cheerily on human eyes than did this, so much looked for at "Maize-in-Milk," in St. Matthews. The harmony of heart within, seemed to lend its aspect to the outer world; and though at sunrise a heavy white frost lay upon the fields and woods, yet the day was sweetly mild and the atmosphere vigorous and bracing. The song birds are seldom forest birds. They fly to the shelter and countenance of man, from the deep thickets where the hostile vermin keep shelter. Perhaps there is an intellectual consciousness which they feel that the human is the most justly appreciative audience. So, the smaller birds of game harbor only in the neighborhood of fields which are cultivated by man, not for the reason assigned by M. Chateaubriand, but simply because these furnish most readily the food which they desire; and because, here, also, in the neighborhood of human habitations, they are less likely to fall victims to the prowling owl and fox or the vigilant hawk. Now the proprietors of "Maize-in-Milk" had, from time immemorial, been disposed to acknowledge the confidence which the feathered tribes thus tacitly seemed to repose in their forbearance; and, in the immediate proximity of the homestead, no hostile gun was permitted to ruffle a bird's feathers. The song-birds laughed merrily at noon-tide and morning in the roof-tree, and had no apprehension, and the partridge led her young along the roadside, skirting the hedge of box and myrtle, having no fear of being thought a trespasser. Our Christmas morning, on the present occasion, was particularly distinguished by these free forest visitors, who came about the habitation, to the great delight of the guests, as if they not only were disposed to assert their privileges, but as if they knew that the season was one for Sunday clothes and merry-making. When poor old Kinsale rose, therefore, some time before the sun, and before any other of the household—for old age requires fewer hours for sleep than youth—very sweet and pleasant was the sight that greeted his aged eyes. Sitting in the great massive porch of the building, which faced the south, a wide lawn spread out before him covered with green trees. These were of the various sorts of oak and orange, with a sprinkling of laurel and other trees, most of which were aged like himself, but showing far greater proofs of vigor. Their heavy tops were populous cities of song birds. Here the red-bird flourished, with his crimson tufts, satisfied with his glorious plumage and his brief but complacent note. Here was the imperial mock-bird, one of which, well known to the household, and fed with crumbs by the children—old Puck—very soon discerned a stranger in the portico, and was sending forth a short, sharp and querulous inquiry, which might be translated, "and who are you, my good fellow? and what do you want?" But, though pleased with the familiarity of the bird—for if there be anything which age most loves, it is society—old Kinsale was not the person to invite them by his presence. The summer of childhood is always most effectual, and, failing to conciliate the suspicions of old Puck, who hopped off at his call to one of his remotest twigs,—the old man turned his attention upon the great trees of the park, and finally, beyond them, to the open fields. It was the policy of the proprietor of "Maize-in-Milk" to maintain about his household, as much of the aspect of spring and freshness as he could. His fields on the right were accordingly covered with a vigorous growth of wheat, which, in his hands, was a crop of respectable production for Carolina. While his less considerate neighbors were satisfied to get but eight bushels of this luxuriant grain from the average acre, he, by skilful dressing, and the free use of lime, contrived to extract nearly thrice that quantity. On the opposite side was to be seen a broad tract of rye, green and growing, while beyond, on every hand, spread a wall of thickly wooded copse and forest, by which each of his fields was girdled, and through which lay pleasant walks and openings to the corn and cotton fields still farther distant. The settlements at "Maize-in-Milk," standing upon a hill, gave a very extensive view on every side. Looking from the rear of the dwelling, the eye might discern, a few miles off, the great gray tops of the cypress that looked forth from the dark recesses of the swamp. For these objects old Kinsale had an eye. They had harbored the aged man in the revolution from some of his tory neighbors.

But he was not suffered long to indulge in his solitary survey. Soon the children came skipping forth, Tom, Dick and Harry, each clamoring with new discoveries. Santa Claus visits us in the south, too, but under no such Dutch appellation. We do not confound the day of St. Nicholas with that of Christmas, though we distinguish them, in the old houses, by similar customs borrowed, however, from our English ancestry. With us, the good genius of the nativity, in a merely social point of view, is good old Father Christmas himself. The benevolent old graybeard makes his presents to the children, under this more seemly appellation. And the urchins are very well accustomed to look for his coming. They hang their stockings in the chimney-place, each with a sprig of ivy, or cassina, or holly, or sumach, either or all, in tribute to the venerable visitor. These he withdraws, and leaves in place of them such gifts as he deems best suited to the character and the deserts of his protegé. To some of these a bunch of hickories conveys a rebuke and threat, which by no means makes the coming of Father Christmas a merry one.

Our lads and lasses at "Maize-in-Milk" had done their best to merit, or, at all events, to receive the bounties of the ancient patron. Tom had hung his new boots, the first pair that had ever embraced his ankles, upon sticks pendant over the fender. Dick more ambitious of favor, had occupied a chair fronting the fire-place, with one or more suits of clothes, hat and shoes included, from each of which, capable of holding them, might be seen the protruding green and red of the sumach and the holly. Harry, without pockets to his breeches, had put his cap, shoes and stockings. The girls had also made provision for their guest. The tiny stockings of dear little Rose were placed conspicuously not to escape attention, while Mary Butler, Susan Bond and Bessy Clinton, had set their nice white baskets, beautifully dressed with flowers mingled with holly, on different sides of the fire-place in their chamber.

And now came forth the boys, each bounding tumultuously with his treasure, which had come with the dawn of Christmas. They had all slept with an eye open, eager to see what sort of visage the old man would put on. Dick swears he saw him, a big man, in a sort of white over-all or shirt, with a great basket on his arm, a great pair of horns on his head, and a long beard, like moss, hanging to his knees. Tom thinks he saw him, but is of opinion that he had on petticoats, and looked something like his mamma; while little Harry slept through it all. As for the girls we can only say that when asked what they saw, Bessy Clinton and Mary Butler smiled knowingly, but said nothing; while dear little Rose insists that Father Christmas was a big lady like her own mamma.

But for their gifts!—Old Kinsale had the first sight of these. The treasures of each were spread before him, and he was called upon to decide on their value. Tom emptied his boots to display a pair of spurs, a buck-handled knife and very pretty flagelet; with all of which he seemed very well contented. Dick held himself quite as lucky with one small qualification. His trophies were, a knife also, but smaller than that of Tom's, a bag of marbles, an India-rubber ball, a *bilboketch,* or cup and ball, a joint-snake, and *a bunch of hickory switches.* There was something in every pocket or receptacle among his clothes, from which the holly sprig had been taken. Little Harry was quite satisfied with certain toys that leapt like frogs, barked like dogs, or rolled and grunted like hogs. He was also indulged in a tipsy Turk, with his *chibouque,* manufactured in *papier maché.* The gifts of Father Christmas to the girls were in less doubtful taste. Dear little Rose had her toys, it is true; but Bessy Clinton found in her basket a beautifully bound copy of the common-prayer and a fine ladies' gold watch. A single sentence written in antique characters, evidently by King Christmasse himself, warned her to use the first gift properly that she might not lose the value of the second. Mary Butler had a ring with the initials of Bessy Clinton. Susan Bond was not forgotten. Her tribute of holly disappeared, and a very pretty musical-box, with a handsome set of chess-men, and a beautiful copy of Pilgrim's Progress, remained in place of it. The ancient sire had chosen judiciously. He knew the tastes of all parties and their deserts too. They were all satisfied equally with his liberality and justice; and, in their satisfaction with their treasures, the great gun was almost forgotten. Its sharp and loud report routed the rest of the sleeping household, and each urchin, lying in wait, made the house ring again as the several members came forth, with "Merry Christmas, papa! Merry Christmas, mamma!" "I've caught you,—I've caught you!" And this led to a new distribution of gifts. Father Christmas had done his duty, but the ordinary sire of the household must do his—and the mother and the sister and all;—and the custom did not confine these claims to the children, but extended to the house-servants, none of whom forgot that the advent of Father Christmasse, gave them claims upon *massa* and *missis,* which were to be urged early in the morning with vociferous cries, as soon as they should show their faces.

Before this rout had well subsided, the girls, Bessy Clinton, Mary Butler and Susan Bond, were busy at another and equally essential part of the ceremonies of the season. Each had a pile of eggs before her, and there were huge bowls and dishes spread out, and great vessels of sugar and a decanter of wine; and the eggs were broken, the whites emptied into the dish, the yolks into the bowl, and Susan Bond, seizing upon the bowl, began to beat away with a spoon like mad, stirring in every now and then a modicum of sugar with the yolks, till they lost their golden hue, and put on one more silvery and less rich. At the same time, our Bessy Clinton, even more busy, and at the more laborious process, was beating the white and mucilaginous portions of the egg into a thick foam of such final consistency that she could turn the vessel upside down without losing a drop of the commodity. This was the standard point, which, once attained, the yolk and white were again to be united, the wine was to embrace the two in its ardent grasp, and the whole was then fit for the palate of Father Christmasse himself, the King of the Feast. This is egg-nogg —a noggin of which is the necessary preface to a Christmas breakfast, after the old fashion in Carolina. This discussed, and breakfast followed, ample and various as the preceding day; and then all parties sallied forth, in several groups, to ride, to ramble and to hunt. Two or three of the young men, taking Tom Openheart along with them, and calling up the hounds, set off to chase the deer. Numerous *drives* on the ample estate of "Maize-in-Milk" promised abundant sport. We shall not follow the hunters, but content ourselves with saying that their efforts were rewarded with a fine fat doe and a monstrous wild cat, four feet from snout to tail, inclusive, that made famous play with hounds and hunters, and was only caught after three hours' running and doubling, and a most terrific fight.

Meanwhile, breakfast scarcely over at Maize-in-Milk, a new collection of shining faces appeared about the porch of the dwelling, in waiting for the appearance of "old maussa" without. These were the *field* negroes, under the lead of ancient Enoch, including those not only of the plantation proper, but those also who had just been bought of the Butler estate. The household servants, as we have already hinted, had made sure of their "Christmas" as soon as the family budged out of their several chambers. And such a chorus of cries and salutations! Such a happy variety of voices in the same monotonous chaunt of "Merrie Chrystmasse." There were voices of lame, halt and blind; beginning with old Dolly, a white-headed matron of ninety-three, whose memory was a complete chronicle of the revolutionary warfare. Blind and deaf, she sat between her great, great grand-children, on the steps of the porch, and shook her palsied head, with a feeble chirrup, which was drowned in the more vigorous burden of a hundred more, whose lungs deferred but little to her weight of years. And there was Binah, the mute, and Tony, the one-armed, and Polly the half-witted, and Diana, the rheumatic, and a dozen more of both sexes, whom the master only knew as dependents for whom he had to provide, and who were of more trouble and expense to him than thrice their number of the rest. But of this, our excellent proprietor did not complain. Indeed, these poor creatures were particular objects of his attention. He was content to take the evil with the good, and he regarded these old heir-looms as so many subjects of his father, who, having served their time faithfully, deserved to be protected and provided for during the future, in consideration of the past. There was no discharging the operative the moment he ceased to be useful.

And such a clamor as was raised, as our Col. Openheart came forth at the head of his guests, as if his benelovence was now to be assailed by storm. The jaws of eighty or more were instantly unclosed upon him; and "God bless you, maussa,"—"Merry Christmas, old maussa," —"How all is, dis merrie Christmas?"—"Hoping you live tousand merry Christmas more,"—"And all de chillans." These were some few of the burdens of their common song. Some had it in rhyme, borrowed probably from the school-boys:

"Christmas come but once de year,
Da's wha' mak' we come up yer *(here)*."

Or,

"Enty dis da Christmas come?
Yer's de nigger look for some!"

Or,

"Merrie Christmas, maussa, for true,
You' ole niggers pray for you;"

And, from another voice, as if by way of chorus,

"Gee 'um only you good cheer,
An' you'll hab de happy New Year."

For this scene our excellent proprietor had been accustomed to prepare. In this respect he followed the example of his ancestor, and, indeed, of most of the very old native proprietors. A sort of pedlar's variety was produced from a huge case, which had been brought up from the city a few days before. To some were given knives and scissors; caps, shawls and handkerchiefs. Others had hatchets, razors, tobacco, and cases of pins and needles. Some chose cotton or wool cards,—for most of the negro women of *character* on a plantation, carry on some little domestic manufactures of their own; and others were quite content with queer clumsy toys, and great grinning masques, with which they could amuse or frighten the more simple of their own or of neighboring plantations. Money is seldom given, never by a judicious proprietor, as it is sure to be spent perniciously at some neighboring groggery.

This distribution of Christmas presents occupied an hour or more. In some instances, but not often, and only when Col. Openheart could trust the good sense of the recipient, he was permitted to choose his article for himself. They all withdrew, more or less satisfied—their greasy, grinning faces doing ample justice, by their expression, to the bounty of the master, and the fullness of the hogmeat upon which they had been feasting for a week past.

Lawyer Skinflint was not satisfied with the spectacle he witnessed. He thought it a mode of spoiling them. They would always expect such favors. It invited familiarity. It would provoke jealousy among themselves. It would be productive of many other mischiefs which we shall not mention. To all these Col. Openheart opposed evasive answers only. It was not the season for discussion, nor was he, in his old age, to discuss or doubt the propriety of a practice which his grandfather and father had pursued before him without being thought worse persons than their neighbors. The excellent lawyer only ceased his pleadings with the appearance of the ladies in the portico, when he addressed himself with a benignant smile to Mrs. Openheart, and, after a few studied phrases about the day, turned to play the gallant with lovely Bessy Clinton; a new *rôle* which seemed by no means native.

The horses were now in readiness, the carriage and barouche. All parties were preparing to go forth. Col. Whitfield, with his wonted promptness, offered his services to Mrs. Openheart and Mrs. Whipple for a drive; while Misses Whipple and Jones, failing to persuade Bessy Clinton, Mary Butler and Susan Bond from the saddle to the barouche, very civilly offered to take up good old father Kinsale. Having ascertained how Bessy Clinton went, the lawyer determined to engage also in equestrianship, though really inclining, by reason of his peculiar physique, to the cushions; and he, Col. Openheart,

Mr. Bond and the two boys, became the companions of the three girls, and were soon mounted upon the liveliest and pleasantest pacers in the whole parish. It was a day for horseback, and the "righte merrie" cavalcade dashed at once up the highway for a mile; then, turning aside, proceeded to pay an annual visit, in especial, to the old fort, overlooking the river, remarkable for its local traditions; where you may yet see the proofs of the devil's presence, in one of his ancient frolics, in the tracks of his tail and carriage wheels—a legend which, at some future and convenient season, we shall have to put in print. The description of the scenery along the route taken by our party we must reserve for the same occasion. Enough to say of it that it harmonized admirably with the bracing air, the calm, generous sunshine, and the rapid but easy motion of the horses. All parties were delighted—eyes were in a glow, cheeks were brightly flushed, and even our lawyer, who kept his horse neck-and-neck, like a young gallant, with that of Bessy Clinton, talked of nothing but purling brooks, green leaves and love in a cottage the whole way. The sweet, gentle-hearted girl heard him with respectful kindness, and answered without hesitation or reserve. She had no suspicions of his gallantry, to put her on her reserves; and all things might have gone, with him, "as merry as a marriage bell," but for a slight incident which happened on the route.

Dashing suddenly into the main road, on their way back to "Maize-in-Milk," they came unexpectedly upon another party, the sight of which kindled the eyes equally of Col. Openheart and Bessy Clinton. "Why, Bessy," said the Colonel, "that is Mrs. Berkshire's carriage, surely. What brings her from the city?" The words were scarcely spoken, when the head of a young man was thrust forth from the carriage, which was in front, and suggested a new conclusion to our worthy proprietor of "Maize-in-milk." "It is she, and that is her son, Fergus, just from college," and, with the words, giving his horse the spur, our colonel dashed ahead, and was soon alongside of the vehicle and the persons in question. In another moment the carriage was stopped, Colonel Openheart alighted, and changing places with young Berkshire, the latter soon joined the young ladies by whom the rear was brought up. A handsome, tall, high-spirited young fellow was Fergus Berkshire. He spoke to Bessy Clinton as to an old acquaintance, and our lawyer watched, with some uneasiness, the sudden flush upon the cheek of the damsel as she hailed the youth's approach. He soon explained the motive of the sudden appearance of himself and mother.

"The old mansion-house and estate were in bad condition, and something was to be done with it before he went to Europe. Of course," he added, "it is our purpose, now, to spend our Christmas at 'Maize-in-Milk.'"

Bessy heard and answered him with undisguised pleasure.

"You know, Fergus," she answered, "you are always at home with us."

"We took that for granted," said the youth, "though I almost feared that a three years' absence had caused you to forget us all."

"And you go so soon again?" she inquired.

"Yes; mother is anxious to comply with the earnest wishes of my poor father, whose instructions were, that, after leaving college, I was to pass two years in foreign travel. We shall spend a couple of weeks here, with your permission, get our new overseer fairly under weigh, then proceed to the city and to New York, so that our preparations may be complete for sailing in the May packet."

He was silent and so was Bessy Clinton. A certain gravity which was unusual overspread her face. We will not trouble ourselves just now to ask wherefore this was so. Let it suffice, that from whatever source her emotion may have sprung, it did not make her forgetful of the courtesies; and the introduction of the new comer to the rest of the company, took place *selon les règles*. Our lawyer's share in this proceeding was conducted with sufficient stiffness; but it escaped the notice of all parties, except possibly young Berkshire himself; who, by the way, did not seem greatly to consider the presence of our excellent Skinflint. He soon contrived to get himself close beside our heroine, and on her bridle-hand, and they jogged along together rather too slowly, it would seem, for the attorney, whose steed had suddenly become possessed of the idea of going forward with all possible rapidity. An hour brought all parties home safely to "Maize-in-Milk," and after the interchange of the usual courtesies with the newly arrived, the company was left to dispose of itself as the several members pleased, until dinner time. We will but remark that Berkshire was the first person to emerge, after making his toilet, and sweet Bessy Clinton was the first to find him in the parlor.

The person who next entered to them was Skinflint, who listened demurely to the conversation of the young people, without taking part in it, wondering to himself all the while, what, in the name of common sense, people could find to please their minds in the prattle about their days of childhood. Fergus Berkshire and Bessy Clinton made much more of the theme than sour old Skinflint had ever made of his childhood. He, unhappily for himself, had never known the period. He was born a man,—hard, wiry, inflexible, calculating, selfish,—with his coat buttoned up to his chin, and his hard intellect busy from the first in stifling all his natural affections.

Old Colonel Openheart was one of those to whom the every-day world would give the title sneeringly of a man of affectations. He was certainly no humdrum personage. His Christmas dinner, for example, was not a good dinner merely. It was a *Christmas* dinner. He did not summon his guests to eat, simply, and to drink. The mere swill was not his object. The intellectual tastes were to be consulted, the fancies, the very superstitions, which, in the progress of the ages would naturally accumulate about the practices of a people on peculiar occasions. His Christmas was a season of equal thanksgiving and enjoyment. There was to be a natural ebullition of the feelings at such a time. There should be exultation. High and humble should equally show gratitude; and the natural expression of gratitude is good humour and cheerfulness. The high was to be high only in the exercise of an ability to make the lowly glad and happy; the humble was to exult in gratifications which showed them consciously in possession of bounties bestowed, in the first instance by the Lord of all, and intermediately by those whose only boast was in being able in some degree to follow his example in its bounties and its sympathies. Colonel Openheart strove for these objects. We have glimpsed at some of his household modes of doing this. His Christmas dinner, as it appealed somewhat to the superstitions and the fancies, was designed for this end also. And when the great hall was thrown open to his guests, dressed in a deep Gothic garment of green boughs and branches, sprinkled with red berries and blue, with candles distributed between, and a great oak wood fire blazing at the extremity —with a stately arch of green at each end of the table, and one of triumphal aspect and colossal size spanning its centre—the entering company felt themselves transported to the old baronial domains of our Anglo-Norman ancestry, and their minds were naturally elevated with the moral sentiments which grew out of their recollections of history. The quaint masking was not without its influence. The device was a homily; and when the head waiter made his appearance bringing in, as the first dish, the "boar's head," done after the ancient Saxon method, dressed in rosemary and with a huge lemon in its open mouth, they were all in the mood to join in chorus with the host, who, knife in hand, began chanting merrily the ancient carol:—

> "*Caput api defero*
> *Reddens laudes Domino.*
> "The bore's head in hand bring we
> With garlands gay and rosemarie,
> I pray you all sing merrily,
> *Qui estes in convivio.*
>
> "This head you must understand,
> Is chief service in this land,
> Looke wherever it be scanned,
> *Servite cum cantico.*
>
> "Be glad, gentles, lord and lasse,
> That to cheer you this Chrystmasse,
> We do bid the bore's head passe,
> Clad in rue and rosemarie."

Set in the centre of the table, this "armed head" was soon surrounded by the several solid meats for which John Bull has always been renowned, and the taste for which has been amply inherited in the south, with certain "graffings" of our own. Ham and turkey, for example, are certain as the day at our Christmas, and when venison is procurable it is never omitted from the board. But ours is no mere catalogue. The reader must imagine the variety. He must suppose the presence of roast and boiled—the beef and the venison pastry,—the duck as well as the turkey, and much of these to have been stricken wild in the woods and waters, with all the provoking freshness of the game flavor upon them. Wines of ancient denomination,—Madeira that had been walled up for thirty years, and sherry that had grown pale, indeed, from weight of years, was at hand;

but our host confined himself, on this day, chiefly to his new supply of natty English ale,—a potation which did honor to the British breweries. The dessert was composed of the fruits of Cuba and the north, nuts and figs, not forgetting pindars, groundnuts, or peanuts as they call them north of the Delaware. Nor had the damsels of the household neglected the usual preparation of mincepies and plum-puddings. In the latter article, in particular, our worthy colonel was resolute to do honor to his ancient English origin, and the plum-pudding was as certainly upon his Christmas table as was the soused head of the boar.

Day slipped away unconsciously while the parties were still at table. It seemed as if the quaintness of the feast, and the admirable humor of "Mine Hoste" had penetrated all hearts, and made each wholly forgetful of his cares. Even the excellent attorney was subdued to a temporary oblivion of the acridity which belonged to the profession, and the peculiar rigidity with which he practised it, and at the close of a certain number of glasses of old south side Madeira, to which he did (like Desdemona—eh?) "seriously incline," he might have been seen pelting our Bessy Clinton with almonds across the table, with a studied slyness of intention which his skill did not enable him to realize, and the familiarity of which made young Fergus Berkshire look rather graver than his wont. Suddenly the great gun in the park in front was heard to explode, and then followed a huzza from Tom, Dick and Harry, and a cloud of urchins whom they had gathered to the event. This uproar was succeeded by one of more gentle influence. The violin was heard in an adjoining apartment, the tamborin responded with its lively jingle, while the heavy foot of old Jake Priester, the white-headed Butler of the establishment, gave notice to the young people of stirring preparation, which would task all the lightness of their heels and hearts. But these were preparatory notes only, for old Jake always took some time to get his foot and fiddle in tune, and to put little Christier, his grandson, in training with his tamborin. Of the dance which followed we shall say nothing, except that "*will-he, nill-he,*" Skinflint was resolute to dance with sweet Bessy Clinton. This was a bold resolution of the attorney. He had certainly taken lessons in his youth; but that day had gone by many years, and his practice had been much more constant and devoted in the courts of law than in those of beauty. Still he had not forgotten the figures, and the wine of Colonel Openheart had enlivened his head, if it had not strengthened the virtue in his heels. He was not to be outdone by any young fellow, however fresh from college. But how, in the Virginia reel which followed, he contrived to get entangled between Bessy Clinton and Fergus Berkshire, and to take his length on the floor in consequence, is not easily understood. He himself ascribed it entirely to the awkwardness, or the malice of young Berkshire, whom he did not remember accordingly with any especial affection. While the young people were dancing in the mansion of "Maize-in-Milk," the blacks were busy in the "Negro Quarter." Thither Colonel Openheart soon withdrew, accompanied by Whitfield, Whipple, Bond and the older portion of the company. The negroes had their fiddle also—nay they had three of them, such as they were—one belonging to "Maize-in-Milk," one from the Butler estate, and one who volunteered from a neighboring plantation. Such wholesale *abandon* as they showed—so much recklessness of care, and toil, and vexation of spirit—would delight a philanthropist from Utopia. Every house had its circle, with open doors—and the grounds between their several cabins were filled with jigging groups—tossing heads, kicking shins, rompings and rollicking—with the rare impulse of so many happy urchins just let loose from school. They had their supper too, and devoured a good-sized barbacued steer, and several hogs, to say nothing of sundry possums made captive the night before. Of bread the consumption was intolerably vast; and some fifty gallons of *persimmon* beer—an innocent domestic beverage of their own manufacture—somewhat resembling cider,—were finished before the fiddlers and dancers showed signs of weariness. It grew to the shortest possible hours before "Maize-in-Milk" was everywhere fairly wrapt in slumber.

CHAPTER IV.

We trust that our readers have not forgotten our last Christmas at "Maize-in-Milk." Since that period, two anniversaries of this happy season have elapsed—we will not say how happily—at that ancient manor. But times have somewhat changed since then. The weather now has grown less favorable to field sports. The sun is far less cheering. The fields look gloomy. The woods, stripped of their foliage, have a ghostly aspect that chills and discourages. It lacks some three weeks to Christmas, yet the cotton fields, which at good seasons were wont to look white until the middle of January, are now absolutely bare. The naked stems, shorn of *boll* and fruit, stunted, slender, and with few and feeble branches, declare that the season has been unfriendly and that the crop is short. The spring rains were unfavorable to a *stand;* the rich swamp bottoms were inundated when the plant should have been up; the growing season continued wet and cold; and when the partial crop, which did promise to mature, was about to do so, a new enemy appeared in the caterpillar and the army worm. These filthy insects, worse than the locusts of the East, swept the fields in a single night. The leaves of the plant first disappeared beneath their devouring ravages; the unopened bolls then perished; and they fastened finally upon the stems and fruit, though with an appetite somewhat diminished. The worthy proprietor of "Maize-in-Milk" was the first to suffer. His fields were chiefly of that class which felt the evil consequences of excessive moisture. The heavy rains of spring, the continued inundations throughout the summer, and the numerous pest which a burning sun drew forth from the rank moisture of the fen and forest, were peculiarly injurious to the low but rich swamp tracts which constituted his most productive acres. His best lands, his chief reliance, failed him, and he might be seen, towards the close of a cheerless day, the second week in December, alone, and riding gloomily and slow from his river fields toward his dwelling. He felt all the sadness of the prospect. There were considerations working in his mind which rendered this failure particularly distressing, if not absolutely fearful. The two previous seasons, though not so absolutely lost as the present, were yet not productive. They had not enabled him to diminish the debt which he had incurred by the purchase of the Butler negroes. Not a cent of this money had been paid beyond the interest, and that, for the year about to finish, was not to be realized from the products of the present crop. Economy is not, unhappily, a frequent virtue in the household of a southern planter of the old school. His income lessens, but that does not imply any lessening of his expenses. He does not like to approach or to consider this necessity. His training, in fact, has been such as not to suffer him to do it. He knows not well how to put down his horses; to forbear the dinner parties and pleasure parties to which his neighbors have become accustomed as well as himself; to put his family and negroes upon short commons, and to sell unnecessary property in time to save himself. Colonel Openheart was no simpleton. He did not lack courage. He was not blind to his danger. He was not insensible to the claims of his creditors. But the habit of living like a prince, and training his children to do the same, and feasting his poorer neighbors like a feudal lord—these made the necessity of contracting equally difficult and irksome. He felt how childish was the pride which made him unwilling to confess his inability, but the habit of thinking and acting in one way only was incorrigible. He did not lack the courage to say to himself, there must be no more of this fine living; but how say it to his wife, whom he had married an heiress, who had always been accustomed to the luxuries he was required to suppress, and whose mature years might render it peculiarly difficult to submit to any change—and how say it to dear Bessy Clinton, whom the world looked upon as an heiress; and to the boys at college, how cut off their allowance; and Ned, in Europe, who had been no small spendthrift, how declare to him that his drafts could no longer be honored? These were all duties which thrust themselves for serious consideration upon our excellent proprietor, and darkened his brow to a corresponding shadow with that which rested on the natural landscape. Some of these duties had already been attended to. Ned had been long since summoned home from Europe; the boys at College had been warned that with the close of the present year they must be satisfied with but a pittance of the money which had hitherto supplied their wants; and to his wife and Bessy Clinton the amiable husband and father had dealt in hints of his approaching difficulties, which neither of them understood. A secret instinct warned our proprietor that his great trouble was with Skinflint, the attorney of Ingelhart and Cripps, executors of the estate of Butler. There had already been some negotiations between them which had given Colonel Openheart a taste of the quality of this person. He was, it is true, exceedingly polite and specious, but very searching, very scrupulous and very expensive. One thing more than all had impressed our planter with disquiet in relation to the attorney; it was a gradual approach to forwardness, consequence, and the show of an imperious will on the part of the other, in due proportion to the evidently increasing necessity for indulgence on the side of

Openheart. The latter was made to anticipate the sting of being at the mercy of one with whom he could have no sympathy; and it was very clear that the attorney was impatient for the moment when he could compel that recognition of his importance which as a man Openheart had apparently shown no disposition to entertain. Our proprietor paced his cheerless fields with a momently increasing cheerlessness of mood. He was joined by old Enoch, to whom for several minutes he said nothing. At length, shaking his head, he exclaimed—"Old man, this might have been better!"

"How better, maussa, enty de rain and de caterpillar?"

"I know all about the rain and the caterpillar; I know the mischief they have done, and wish to hear nothing on that subject;—but had you minded what I said, had you taken in the upper fields instead of the lower, they would not have been drowned, and we should have saved sixty acres there at least; but no, you must have your own way—you must know better than anybody else."

"Well, maussa, you nebber been say plant dem and leff de lower field; you say '*I tink* you better plant dem upper,' and *I* been tink diffren, so I tells you, and you say '*Well!*'"

The answer was conclusive. Colonel Openheart, instead of issuing his orders, had left it to Enoch's discretion, contenting himself with giving a suggestion instead of a command. This is a frequent error of the old planter of Carolina.

"Well, it is too late now to complain. How are your cattle?"

"De winter is mighty hard 'pon *dem*, maussa."

"How many hogs have you got in pen for slaughter?"

"Sebenty-tree."

"Instead of a hundred and fifty. How do you account for that, Enoch, when we turned out more than two hundred and fifty into the swamp last spring, and your hog-minder has been carrying out his three bushels of corn daily for six months to keep them up?"

"Well, maussa, dere's no telling; but de varmints in de swamp is mighty hard 'pon de pigs dis season—de wild cat, de niggers, and dem poor buckrah, Moses Daborne, 'Lishe Webter, Zeke Tapan, and dat half Ingin, Sam Johnson. Ef you could only clear de swamp of dem white niggers, you could raise hog tell you couldn't count dem."

"The old story! Enough. Ride up to the post-office and bring me the papers and letters."

Our proprietor was once more alone. "The world goes wrong with me on every side. I am either destined or I am imbecile. I have certainly been weak and erring, profligate, thoughtless; as wildly confident of the future as ever was poor boy with a pocket full of shillings and a long holiday before him. I must amend promptly or all is lost. If Ingelhart and Cripps, or rather, if Skinflint will indulge, one good crop will gain me time—two good crops at good prices, and all would be safe. But there's the rub! This swamp cultivation is so uncertain, and these good prices are so doubtful, and—the d——l take these lawyers and merchants; they get everything at last!" And then he mused in silence, looking neither to the right nor left as he went forward. Passing out of the open fields, he penetrated a dark avenue which ran through a dense and umbrageous swamp-forest, which formed, as it were, a boundary between the river-lands and uplands, and was crowded with an immense growth of cypress, ash, poplar and pine—so densely arrayed that, though in midwinter, when all but the evergreens were stripped of foliage, the beams of the sun were seldom suffered to find entrance. The day being clouded, the darkness of this region was still more oppressive, and a slight shiver shook the frame of our already desponding proprietor as he entered the narrow and dismal passage. At this moment an owl shrieked above him, a huge fowl, bald but horned, whose great human eyes and horrid screech might well disquiet with unpleasant forebodings the mood of one so circumstanced as our worthy planter. "How like," he exclaimed, "to the voice of Skinflint. I almost fancied at first that it was he crying out to me." He looked up as he spoke, and beheld the bird sitting upon a great limb almost overhead, and looking directly down upon him. He rode on, the little incident oppressing him unpleasantly, and much more than his pride was willing to admit. "Why does that fellow cross my fancy thus? What is he to me? What can he do? He can have no purpose but for his clients, and these may be satisfied—let the worst come to the worst—by a timely surrender of the property." But a second thought taught him not to lay this flattering unction to his soul. He had bought the Butler negroes at high, and the same sort of property was now selling at low prices. The loss must be large, and must be made up out of his own estates. Then the interest, then his own debts, which, to meet this interest, already had been suffered to grow to a heavy item! Altogether, the prospect was such that our proprietor of "Maize-in-milk" was only too happy to exclude the subject altogether from his thoughts. But this was not so easy, and his gloomy mood continued till he reached his dwelling, where, soon after, the contents of his mail gave it an increase of sting and bitterness. "A letter from Mr. Skinflint," he remarked quietly to his wife, "in which he speaks of being here in three days. That must bring him here to-morrow. Let us see—the letter is dated the 12th. Yes, indeed, to-morrow we may look for him."

"What does *he* come for?" said the simple-hearted but shrewd mother, looking up at Bessy Clinton. The latter did not see the glance, and did not appear to hear the inquiry.

"You forget," said the colonel, "that he has the management of all the business of the Butler estate."

"Did you say that Mary Butler was coming, papa?"

"Not unless this letter says so, which I see comes from Bloomsdale, and is addressed to you."

Bessy Clinton received and read the epistle with eagerness. "There, mamma, it is from Mary, and she and her aunt both are coming, and will be here on Saturday."

"We shall have a full house, then, for Fergus Berkshire rode in this morning to say that his mother would be up from the city in three days and would spend the Christmas with us."

The communication was received in grave silence—Colonel Openheart, his letters still in his hand, steadily watching the fire as flake by flake crumbled away into the mass below.

"We shall have a full house, Mr. Openheart," repeated the lady.

"Yes."

A pause.

"Why, husband, you seem to be in a dream!"

"Yes—yes, I hear."

"I am glad you do, for it is necessary that you should write at once for supplies for Christmas. The sugar is almost out; we must have several pounds of green tea, and perhaps a little black, for

Mrs. Berkshire asked for it when she was here before. She has learned the use of it at the north, where I am told they drink no other kind. And raisins, and currants, and almonds, apples and——"

We need not follow the good housekeeper through the catalogue. Our worthy proprietor was almost in despair, yet he subdued his feelings with great firmness and strength of will. Bessy Clinton alone perceived that something was wrong. Her eye perused the countenance of her father with a modest interest that did not suffer him to see that he was watched. She saw that his face had grown somewhat paler than its wont. She had already remarked that he had grown thinner during the past few months, and she now fancied that his hair had put on a more snowy complexion. She saw and mused, but was properly silent. Colonel Openheart reopened one of the letters which he had just received. It was the polite request of his grocer that his account should be attended to. The sum total was set down that there should be no mistake—$718.44; and here were wants which must increase it considerably, and no crop, and no means of payment but by a great sacrifice of property.

"I wish that there were no such season as Christmas."

"Oh, papa!" exclaimed Bessy Clinton, in reproachful accents, "how *can* you wish so?"

Mrs. Openheart looked up in surprise.

"At least," said the proprietor, "I may be permitted to wish that this Christmas were fairly over."

"What, papa, just when I am calculating upon this as the most merry Christmas of any that we have ever had!" and the sweet girl, as she spoke, had glided to the chair where her father sat, and with arm that circled his neck was bending round and looking up affectionately in his face. A slight moisture gathered in his eyes, which it was just possible for him to subdue.

"May you ever find it happy with you at Christmas, Bessy, and at all other seasons. God bless you, my dear child; you are of more comfort to me than all the others. But I can scarcely share with you in your delights this Christmas."

"And why not, papa?"

"You know that I have made no crop this year; there was a failure last year also, and another partial failure the year before, and my expenses have been very heavy. Bills must be paid, and——"

"Didn't I warn you of it, husband, when you would buy those Butler negroes?" said the good wife, with an exulting shake of the head and finger.

"Yes, Mrs. Openheart, you did," answered the husband, mildly, "but that was only after they were bought; and the question now is, not exactly as to your credit as a prophet, but to mine as a paymaster."

The sagacious lady felt the gentle rebuke and was silent.

"There are debts to be paid, Bessy Clinton," continued the father, affectionately, though sadly; "and this it is which makes me tremble even at the additional charges which this Christmas is to bring upon me."

"But our friends must be received with proper welcome, Colonel Openheart," said the lady.

"Oh, true," was the answer, as if it were a matter of course that certain appearances should be maintained even though at the sacrifice of everything—"true, true, your groceries shall be ordered, and we shall be prepared, I trust, to welcome with proper warmth every guest who may honor us with his presence—not forgetting that bird of evil aspect and voice, Richard Skinflint, Esq., himself. But I am afraid it will cost us greatly, and we must look to contract our expenses among ourselves, and make up in this way what our hospitality may dissipate. I will order what you desire. This year there shall be no changes. Merrie old Christmasse must visit the children too, as usual, and as we continue our own luxuries, the negroes must have theirs. The New Year must not be clouded to our inferiors because we are gloomy."

"But we shall not be gloomy, papa," said Bessy Clinton, twining herself about him and kissing his cheeks fondly. "This dark weather will disappear; hereafter you will have good seasons and good luck. Let me prophesy—me, Bessy Clinton, among the prophets—that next year will be a famous crop year, prices high——"

"And grocers low," was the somewhat sober conclusion of the father. "You are a good girl, Bessy, and I will probably remind you of your prophecy next Christmas, as your mother takes care to remind me of hers—that is, when they happen to be true. But what is here? Looking at Skinflint's letter and the grocer's, I have omitted one that would seem to be from Ned."

"From Ned?" exclaimed mother and daughter in the same breath.

"It looks like his hand, and is from New York. Sure enough, it is he. He reached New York on Friday last, in the Sylvie de Grasse, from Havre, and will be in Charleston by the Wilmington boat."

"When, papa, when?"

"To-morrow."

"To-morrow! Dear, dear Ned, how I long to see his face again."

The ejaculations of Bessy Clinton were sufficient for the rest. The mother's eyes were full of bright tears, and in the grateful thoughts of a favorite son arrived at home and manhood, the cares which troubled the father were temporarily forgotten.

The next day brought Skinflint. He was received with respect and kindness, if not cordiality, though neither our proprietor nor the worthy matron, his wife, beheld his coming with any satisfaction. The former could not forget that it was in the power of this man, with whom he could have no sympathies, materially to impair his fortunes; and the latter had suspicions which never crossed her companion's mind, that Skinflint's eye was fixed upon her daughter with an expression which already denotes the foregone conclusion of the hawk, who sees, from his swing in air, where the partridge is about to nestle. Any notion that such was the passion of the attorney, never once troubled the thought of Colonel Openheart, whose pride of character could not for an instant tolerate the idea of any sympathies between a creature of such avid and selfish character and his purely-minded and generous child. But Mrs. Openheart said nothing of her conjectures, and the fears of her husband with regard to Skinflint were wholly of a different character. They rode out together a little while after the arrival of the latter, and crossed the cotton and cornfields in their route to the river. There was an unpleasant grin upon the lips of Skinflint as the mean appearance of the cotton stems denoted the complete failure of the crop. He had heard something of this before, enough to satisfy him that things were going on as he wished them. A southern planter is apt to be suspicious of your comments when he is conscious that his crop is obviously inferior, and the eye of Colonel Openheart was soon sensible of the expression on the countenance of Skinflint.

"Not much cotton here this year, colonel," said he, switching his boot as they rode.

"*None,* sir, none, as you may see," was the sudden, almost sharp reply.

"Hum!" A pause. "How is your corn crop, colonel?"

"Turn your horse's head with mine, and you shall answer your own question."

They rode aside to other fields. The corn-stalks, low and slender, told their own story of a blight quite as great as that in the cotton field.

"Why, colonel, you will hardly make enough to do you, at this rate."

"Shall have to buy a thousand bushels at least, sir," responded the other, almost fiercely.

Skinflint knew the fact a month before, but it was the nature of the creature to extort the acknowledgment of the sufferer by making him lay bare his sore as frequently as possible, though at each effort he tore away some portion of the skin.

"And corn already seventy cents," was the muttered commentary of the executioner.

"Seventy-*five* here," was the stern correction which the proprietor interposed.

"Indeed!" exclaimed Skinflint; "then in three weeks more it will be a dollar."

"Possibly *two*, sir," was the second moody amendment.

"Scarcely, colonel," was the speculative suggestion of the attorney. "Prices here, whenever they pass beyond a certain point, bring in competition from other quarters. Here, sellers must be governed by some regard to the Charleston market, which in turn takes its color from the extent of the crops in Maryland and North Carolina. Now, as the crops this year in these two states have been of average character, it follows that the article will scarcely exceed eighty cents in Charleston. Allow for the cost of each transition and freight by railroad or wagon, and you must see that it can by no possibility exceed one dollar here, unless with reference to some very great scarcity. I don't think, all things considered, that you will have to give more than a dollar, though it may possibly, in two months more, go two-eighths above it, particularly as I suppose that none of your neighbors have done better than yourself."

"You mistake, sir—few of them but have done better."

"Indeed! But that is very unfortunate! But you have past seasons to rely upon, colonel. You have made good crops heretofore, and can very well afford to contend with the evils of the present."

"Unfortunately, sir, I have no such source of consolation. This is the third, though the worst by far, of three successive failures."

"Indeed! But suffer me to ask, Colonel Openheart, to what do you ascribe these failures?"

"Why, sir, I do not see what good can possibly arise to either of us from the inquiry. Perhaps the shortest way would be to adopt the suggestion of my neighbors, and to assume that all the mischief lay in the incapacity of the proprietor."

An audible "Hem!" answered this cold conclusion, which shut the door upon any farther annoyance from this score at least, and a somewhat protracted silence followed, broken at length by Colonel Openheart, whose mind had been gradually steeled by the tone, manner and comments of his companion, to a resolute approach to the very subject which, over all he most dreaded and could have wished to avoid. It was with something of desperation, therefore, that he himself opened the business of his debt to the estate of Butler.

"I take for granted, Mr. Skinflint, that there can be no reason why, in the present condition of my affairs, I should not have every indulgence from Messrs. Ingelhart and Cripps. Miss Butler is still a minor, and the investment is notoriously safe. I am aware that the entire payment is now due, but it must be evident to you that in the failure of my crops and the low prices of cotton for the last three years, so large a payment was impossible except at great sacrifice of property. Besides, as you are aware, the negroes were bought at very high prices."

"Quite too high," said Skinflint, with some gravity, well remembering that but for the generous impulse of Openheart he would have had them at his own prices. The recollection did not make him more accessible to the suggestions of the proprietor. "There may be some difficulty about the matter; and I am free to confess, Colonel Openheart, that your own statement holds forth nothing encouraging to a creditor, particularly in such a case as ours, where we represent the interests of a minor. The investment may be safe at present, but when you speak of a failure of three crops in succession, upon the successful making of which your only chance of payment depends, we are a little disquieted. Another failure diminishes our securities and necessarily increases your responsibility to other creditors, and the game may finally depend upon the degree of speed which the creditor may make in securing the stakes."

Openheart winced at this cool suggestion, but he had to control his emotions. The matter was one simply of business, and he felt that he had nothing to do but to put aside all the sensibilities—quite unnecessary in such a case and with such a companion—of the gentleman. He answered quietly, though it tasked some effort to do so—"But the property is always there, secured by mortgage, which you may foreclose at any moment."

"But the property may not be always there."

"How, sir?"

"It is a perishable property, and your real estates, which are the collateral securities, may be subject to the more perfect liens of other creditors. Besides, sir, negroes are falling in value, and the foreclosure of mortgage at this moment may be of vast importance even to your own safety, since the probabilities are that they will bring much better prices now—though still far less than when you bought—than they would in twelve months hence."

"Am I to understand from this, Mr. Skinflint, that your instructions are to foreclose if payment be not now made?"

"By no means, sir. What I say, is simply to suggest some of the difficulties in the way of a decision at this moment. I must reflect on the condition of affairs, and will communicate with my clients."

"It is understood, Mr. Skinflint, that you have the entire confidence of Messrs. Ingelhart and Cripps, and that your opinion will be almost certain to determine their conduct."

"I flatter myself," replied the attorney, with a mixed expression of meekness and complacency, "that I am not wholly without my influence over the minds of those gentlemen. But you will permit me to ask, Colonel Openheart, with what purpose your remark is made?"

"Surely, sir, my purpose was a very simple one—it was only that I might express the hope that your dealings with me and your knowledge of my affairs were such as would enable you to assure your clients of the undoubted security which they possess, collaterally, for the bonds which they hold of mine in behalf of the estate of Butler."

The lawyer looked grave for a moment, then smiling and turning round to his companion with an air of great amenity and frankness—"Colonel Openheart, it may be that I shall find it equally my pleasure and my interest to serve you in this manner. I think it likely, sir, that I shall have to seek a favor at your hands before I leave you. Now, sir, one good turn deserves another, and——"

"A favor at my hands, Mr. Skinflint? And, pray, what is it?"

"Excuse me, sir—not just now. Sufficient for the day, &c. Excuse me—not yet—not yet! Meanwhile, sir, if you please, we will suspend the conversation on this subject."

The manner of Skinflint struck our proprietor unpleasantly. Without question, Colonel Openheart was an aristocrat, and the familiar, very frank and friendly tones of his companion, were decidedly more grating upon his ears than the keen, avid utterance of the calculating and selfish man of business. They made him uneasy for a moment, as he could not possibly divine in what way he was expected to requite the service of the attorney. He was relieved when he recollected that Skinflint had lately bought a plantation in his neighborhood, and being a lawyer, naturally looked to fill some seat either in congress or the legislature. The large influence of Colonel Openheart was unquestionable, and he now worried himself with asking if he could conscientiously support such a person. But the adage of which Skinflint had reminded him, and which is always a favorite one with those who recoil from trouble, determined him to dismiss the evil to the day when it must come up; and thus satisfied, our colonel readily complied with the evident desires of his companion to canter off in the direction of the dwelling.

They left the fields accordingly, after a ten minutes' ride, and took their way out into one of the main roads of the country. They were scarcely entered upon this, when they encountered Bessy Clinton and Fergus Berkshire, on horseback, emerging from one of the long and lonely avenues leading out into the pine lands. Could Colonel Openheart have seen the scowl that showed itself upon Skinflint's brow at this unexpected meeting! The two young people rode slowly and seemed totally absorbed in their own affairs. There was an evident flush upon the face of Bessy Clinton, while the cheeks of Fergus seemed rather pale than otherwise. The parties exchanged greetings, and while the colonel and his companion walked their horses, the youth and damsel gave their steeds a free rein and were soon out of sight in the direction of the dwelling.

"A good-looking young fellow, that," said Skinflint, "with some natural cleverness. But ours is not an age of industry and exertion—

and once give a fellow a chance with plenty of money on foreign travel, and you may be sure that all's over with him. I have good reason to believe that young Berkshire made a monstrous hole in his own and mother's capital when he was abroad. His dissipation while in Paris was said to be notorious."

"Said by whom, Mr. Skinflint?"

"Oh, by everybody. The thing was all over town when he first came home from Europe."

"Town is a famous place for scandal, Mr. Skinflint, and 'they say' is a proverbial liar. I know nothing of Berkshire's doings while abroad *except while he was in Paris*, and there my son Edward happened to be with him during his whole stay. Edward speaks of him *there* as a close and eager student of the language, the country and the fine arts. I very much doubt if the charge of dissipation was ever less properly made than against Fergus. He shows no traces of it now; and, indeed, by his general intelligence, equal readiness and modesty, and large acquisition of facts, he shows that he could have employed but little time in excesses, or his intellectual gains must have come by instinct. As for his expenditures—but it may be that your profession has brought you to a knowledge of straits in the family with which I am unfamiliar, and I must not oppose my conjectures to your facts. Still I cannot persuade myself that either he or his mother is in any difficulty."

"Nor do I say it. I have no knowledge of their affairs myself, but it was said that they would probably have to put down the city establishment and have to retire wholly upon the country."

"Said probably by those who speak rather from their wishes than their wit. Mrs. Berkshire, while a very liberal and lofty-minded woman, is yet a very prudent one. She has, I think, trained her son very admirably, and——"

"All that may be, Colonel Openheart, but the best of training will not always or often secure our children against the temptations of a new sphere and an intoxicating novelty in society."

"*Always*, sir—good training will always secure the young against any temptation. But the question is as to the quality of training. What is *good* and what is *bad* training is hardly settled yet among philosophers. It certainly is not among parents and schoolmasters, who seem to me to pride themselves most upon their system where the regimen is the very worst."

"You may be right, sir, and I am not prepared to discuss a mere abstraction; but though this young man's education may have been as you think it, still the exception is possible, you know; and while such are the reports in the city, *if I were a father* I should be very jealous of the familiarity of any such person with a daughter of mine."

Colonel Openheart half wheeled his horse, about to survey the speaker. "Really, Mr. Skinflint, I have reason to thank you for your counsel and so has my family; but, believe me, we have none of us any apprehensions either from the vices of Fergus Berkshire or the weaknesses of my daughter. *Her training*, at least, has been such that we can confide everything to her delicacy, which, in the case of women, is the best security for their discretion. Still, sir, I thank you—I thank you."

There was something in the tone and manner of Colonel Openheart that warned Mr. Skinflint he had ventured a little too far.

"Pardon me, Colonel Openheart," he said, quickly, "but I meant not to advise. My remark was purely general, and did not specially relate to your case. This young man may be a very good young man. *Of my own knowledge*, I can say nothing against him."

"Can you upon the knowledge of any other person? If you can, Mr. Skinflint, you shall see that I am as vigilant in the protection of my fireside as any man in the country."

"Why, no, sir, not upon the *knowledge* of any one in particular—but what is said by many, sir, places the matter said in that category which, among legal men, constitutes a proverbial notoriety, and such is not supposed to need proving."

"Good law, no doubt, but most awful morality! Can you mention, among those who deal in this *notoriety*, one person who professes to speak from his own knowledge?"

"No; I am not sure that I can."

"Then I think that we may safely venture to dismiss the story, since the truth that no man will father is very apt to prove a falsehood. Your law rule, which rejects all hearsay testimony, will justify our irreverence."

We need not pursue the dialogue which Skinflint, confident as he usually was, could not but see had terminated to his disadvantage.

His tone was judiciously lowered, though without lessening any of the unfavorable impressions which his companion had contrived to form of his character and heart. Our proprietor treated him, however, with a peculiar civility, the stateliness of which, as it kept him at a distance without affording him definite cause of resentment, was sufficiently irksome, and he longed in his heart to have an opportunity to punish the patrician for the privilege which he exercised, being an honest man, of behaving fearlessly like one. It was the error of Skinflint to suppose that, having shown Colonel Openheart that he was somewhat in his power, he had acquired the right to prescribe to him in moral and social respects. He was soon made to see that there were some personal barriers which not even his legal and moneyed strength would enable him to break down. The character which is well grounded upon principle and well trained by habit, never yields in any misfortune, never succumbs to any condition, though these may menace every social and domestic security that we possess.

At dinner, Colonel Openheart was the hospitable landholder—that noble, old English character which we do not sufficiently value, but which is the source of England's best securities. He seemed to forget that he had cause of apprehension or annoyance, and the ease, the dignity, the grace with which he presided, the perpetual watchfulness that saw that no one remained unsupplied, these all served to extort from the secret thought of Skinflint a wholesome wonder as to the source of so much equilibrium. Dinner was late, and with night came the mail, bringing a hurried letter from Edward, which our proprietor, for reasons of his own, and with (for him) unwonted circumspection, forbore to read aloud. This letter told him of the young man's safe arrival in Charleston, and of his intention to be *en route* for the plantation in another day. Was it the postscript which informed the father that it was the writer's purpose to take Bloomdale in his way, and if possible bring Mary Butler and her aunt along with him, that kept him from reading it aloud?

The two gentlemen sat up late. We did not mention that Fergus Berkshire did not stay to supper, but left the company as soon as dinner was over, with an apology, in which he pleaded necessary business. He ceased to be the subject of Skinflint's comment, but the occasional glance of the latter, as the youth engaged the attention of Bessy Clinton, did not escape the eyes of the vigilant mother.

The intimacy between the young man and the maiden seemed to disturb the equilibrium of the attorney, and probably rendered him much more precipitate than he would have been in a matter which, as he sat with Colonel Openheart that night—the family having retired—he proceeded to bring up. We will not adopt his language, the substance of which was a formal proposal from him, Richard Skinflint, attorney at law, for the hand in wedlock of the fair maiden, Bessy Clinton Openheart. Many long speeches, circuitously conceived and cumbrously worded, prefaced this offer. Colonel Openheart looked upon the speaker with unmitigated astonishment, but he was prudent, kept his temper and his secret, and calmly answered the lawyer that he, Skinflint, should be permitted an interview in the morning with his daughter and hear his answer from her own lips. Skinflint said something in reply to this in approbation of the excellent custom prevailing in certain countries, where the parents adjusted among themselves the contracts of marriage, and the young people were sufficiently dutiful to submit. But Colonel Openheart's reply was brief and to the purpose. His daughter must determine for herself in a matter so vital to her own happiness. The night passed over with due rapidity. The morning brought breakfast and the promised interview. Conducting his daughter to the library, he instructed her to await the coming of Mr. Skinflint, and to give becoming ear to his communications. The latter was apprised that the damsel was in waiting, and with something more of flurry and agitation than ever troubled him in his ordinary practice, he stole half on tiptoe into the designated apartment. How he purred and prabbled, with what studied and formal phrase he proceeded to a declaration in which, if the heart be only warm and faithful, the lips may bungle and the tongue falter without dread of censure or ridicule, we will not say. Enough that his proposals, when Bessy Clinton fully understood them, were quite as confounding to that damsel as they were to her father. We need scarcely say that they met with ready rejection. What a blind thing is selfishness! Here, now, was a person of great worldly shrewdness, singularly sagacious in common business transactions, yet blundering with the inconceivable notion that he could possibly prevail with youth, beauty, tenderness, and the most generous and confiding faith. Taught by selfishness to regard wealth as the only power, he had forgotten that such subjects as affection, duty, taste, sweetness and grace, must always acknowledge far different authorities. It was impossible for sweet Bessy Clinton to be unkind or harsh, and though greatly surprised, if not indignant, at the proposal, she replied with gentleness. She was sorry that Mr. Skinflint had set his heart—his heart!—on his handmaid, but really the thing was out of the question. She was very grateful, but begged respectfully to be excused. Do not suppose that there was any mocking in her response. The irony is wholly ours. His pill was quite as much sweetened as it well could be, but was still such as he found it difficult to swallow. He would have argued the case, as he recovered his courage, precisely as he would have done before a jury in the matter of cow and calf, in trespass or replevin—and did argue it. The damsel heard him quietly to the end, and affirmed the previous verdict. He hurried to Colonel Openheart as to a court of appeal, but the colonel disclaimed jurisdiction; and ordering his horses, with fury but ill-concealed, Skinflint prepared to take his departure before dinner. With genuine politeness, regarding the circumstances, our proprietor did not urge him to delay. With nice and delicate consideration, he complied with his wishes, conversed with him without reserve and with studied kindness, but studiously forebore any absurd, apologetic or sympathetic discourses. The parties separated on good terms, Skinflint shaking his host's hand warmly and smiling in his face affectionately as he took his departure; but ere he was well out of sight, he shook his hand menacingly back upon the habitation, and swore, in muttered accents, through his closed teeth, a bitter oath of vengeance. Our proprietor knew enough of the person to apprehend that he had made a fast enemy, but he remembered the proverb, and put off his regrets and sorrows as well as he might to the day of evil that should compel them.

We pass over three days, and still Edward had not arrived. "He is sick in Charleston," said the anxious mother. "He is at Bloomdale," said the more knowing daughter. "He is spending time and money wherever he is," said the dissatisfied father, "instead of being at his law." The fourth day brought the truant as an escort to Mrs. St. Clair and Mary Butler. He had been delayed at Bloomdale at the requisition of the ladies, and the excuse was readily received by the parents, particularly as it was urged by a tall, handsome and wellbred youth, more than six feet high, admirably proportioned, and carrying himself like a prince of the blood royal. The father forgot his troubles as he saw his own youth restored and reflected in his son. He was not suffered to forget them long. That very evening brought him a letter from Skinflint, as the attorney for Ingelhart and Cripps. "Sense of duty, &c. Foreclosure of mortgage, &c. Unavoidable, &c. Very sorry, &c. With sentiments of profound respect, &c. *(Signed)*

"RICHARD SKINFLINT."

The proprietor crumpled the graceless epistle in his palm and hurled it into the fire. The wife alone saw the act. The young people were busy around the evening table, examining a world of curiosities which Edward had brought home from Europe. They little knew of the bitterness that dashed the cup of joy even while it was at the old father's lips. He uttered no sigh, no word. He would not cloud the happiness of that youthful circle. He resolved upon the exercise of all his manhood. Taking his hat, he went forth into the night. It was a lovely starlight. The skies were never more thickly studded with the saintly watchers, and all were bright and beautiful as if they had never felt a cloud. He walked down the noble avenue of oaks and cedars towards the high road. Ere he reached the gateway, a vehicle dashed by in considerable haste, which he recognized as that of Skinflint. This person was also a proprietor, and planted only a few miles distant. Though not a resident at his place, for his professional duties in the city would not suffer this, he yet contrived occasionally to visit his plantation, where, when not the guest of his neighbors, he was of his overseer. The angry feeling in Col. Openheart's breast was strongly excited as he detected the carriage of his enemy. He himself remained unseen in the shadow of the ancestral trees, but he clearly discerned the head of Skinflint as he thrust it forth for examination while passing the avenue of the man whom he now fondly thought to victimize. Colonel Openheart conjectured his thoughts, and the fierce idea rose in his mind of a deadly grapple with the scoundrel. Had they met on foot or on horseback in the high road, it had been scarcely possible, in the present mood of our proprietor, to have foreborne inflicting some indignity upon the base and malignant creature. But he passed, never dreaming that Openheart was so near. Had he fancied it, his head had never shown itself from the carriage window.

We must hurry over a week in order to realize the more important events in our narrative. We are again on the threshold of Father Chrystmasse. Our lady proprietor at "Maize-in-milk" has received the necessary supplies from the grocer. The hogs are killed, the mince-pies are made, and the usual guests, invited and uninvited, are already pouring in. The songs of Bessy Clinton and Mary Butler are ringing through the dwelling, and every customary chorus, gathered from the early poets in tribute to the season, has been employed to guide the merry damsels in the decoration of mantel and mirror, and window, and to cheer them in the prosecution of their pretty tasks. For a week beforehand the dance was continued nightly in the great hall. There were now Fergus Berkshire and Edward Openheart, and one or more of the latter's old acquaintances, to say nothing of neighboring maidens just rising into womanhood, whom the hospitalities of "Maize-in-milk" had brought together. Two days before Christmas, John and William made their appearance from college; and Tom Openheart, now a lad of twelve, and very tall for his age, was permitted to add to the strength of the company, in regard to the interests of certain of the damsels who were about his own age. Altogether, the auspices were particularly favorable to the sports of the young. Our ancient friends, Jones, Whipple, Whitfield, Bond and daughter, and good old father Kinsale—who in growing older did not seem to have grown a jot more feeble than he was twenty years before—also came with the day preceding Christmas, and wore their pleasantest aspects. But the weather had a cold, forbidding complexion still, and our proprietor found it difficult to keep from his own visage the doubts and apprehensions which were working in his mind. At this moment a stranger rode into the enclosure, who proved to be the sheriff of the district. He declared his purpose very civilly, regretted the necessity under which he was placed, showed his credentials, and would receive either the money on the bond, or the negroes. There was no remedy; Colonel Openheart submitted with simple fortitude. The negroes were at the sheriff's service. He excused himself to his guests and accompanied the officer to the negro-quarter.

"But why not wait till sale day, sir?" was the inquiry of Colonel Openheart. "They shall then be forthcoming."

The officer hesitated, but at length remarked—"I should do so cheerfully, sir, having myself every confidence in your honor; but I have been counseled that I shall be held rigidly responsible unless the levy is at once made, as some reason exists for suspecting that your son will be employed to *run* the negroes to Texas."

"By whom, sir, has this intimation been given?"

"By Mr. Skinflint, acting for Ingelhart and Cripps."

"The scoundrel! But I have no more to say. Make your levy."

The negroes were by this time assembled and listening with eager anxiety.

"You must go, my people," said the proprietor, addressing them with a voice which his emotions hardly suffered to be articulate—"you must go, I cannot help it. I would have saved you, but cannot. I have done for you all I could; I can do no more!"

He turned away to conceal his emotion, and hurried into the neighboring woods. The strong man wept like a child as the loud outcries and lamentations of the slaves still pursued him. He had been to them a father and a benefactor, had watched them in sickness and indulged them with moderate tasks when well. As he thought upon the parting, he recovered all his strength. He came forth, and said to the sheriff—"You will bring them up to the house?"

"Why, sir," said the officer, with considerate sensibility, "I had proposed taking them through the woods. It would mortify you before your guests."

"I thank you, sir," was the respectful but proud answer—"I thank you; but I must request that you will bring them to the dwelling before you depart. I have something to bestow upon them. My guests will know all before long, and may as well hear it at once."

The negroes were brought accordingly.

"You see, my friends, I have some troubles for my Christmas. They are rather new to me in my old age, but it is probable that I shall become familiar with them before I die."

Something more was said—enough to show that our proprietor, in his unaffected grief, had lost nothing of his manliness. He proceeded to open the cases in which the Christmas presents were kept. These were not to have been given till the ensuing day, but this delay would have deprived the Butler negroes of their share of gifts. With hasty hand our proprietor bestowed his wares.

"Now take them, Mr. Sheriff, as quickly as you please, so that our young people may not see them. They are down the road, and if you pursue *that* path, you will escape them. Good morning, sir, good morning," and the speaker retired among his guests. He maintained his courage manfully, was once more the courtly and considerate host, still solicitous of the wants and wishes of the meanest, until, some two hours having elapsed, an uproar without drew attention to the windows. What was the surprise of Col. Openheart to see all the negroes returned, and to find them quite clamorous in the publication of their delight that they were not to lose their present master. One of their number presented himself with a letter, which our proprietor opened with no little curiosity, for as yet nothing had been got from the negroes by reason of the multitude of voices which threw any or much light upon the mystery. The letter was from young Berkshire. We give it without curtailment.

"Dear sir:—Meeting with the sheriff, and being in want of a sufficient force for my Cedar Island plantation, I have ventured to assume your bond, with interest, being perfectly satisfied to pay the same price for the negroes at which you bought them. As I hold them to be amply worth the amount, I leave it entirely with yourself to retain them, if you please, paying me at your leisure—though I should prefer to have them, on my assumption of your several responsibilities in regard to this property. Whatever may be your decision, which you can make at your leisure, it will at least be proper that they should remain in your keeping until after the holidays. Very faithfully, and with great respect, I am, my dear sir,

"Your obliged friend and servant,

"Fergus M. Berkshire."

Colonel Openheart had not a word to say. The act was so handsome that he at once gave the letter into the hands of old Kinsale, who read it twice aloud to the company. The proprietor went out to the negroes and sent them back happy to their habitations. The young people soon after made their appearance. They had heard something of the matter, and Edward Openheart, as soon as all the facts were made known to him, at once rode over to Berkshire's to give him his own and the thanks of the family.

"Tell him, Ned, that he shall have the negroes, and tell him what you please besides, from your own heart."

Such was all the message of the father. Berkshire looked somewhat anxious when the young man paused.

"Do you bring any letter, Ned?"

"No."

"No message from anybody?"

"None but that from my father. What do you expect?"

"Nay, never mind; you will hear soon enough."

The young man seemed dull and disappointed, and was not easily persuaded to give a detailed account of his fortunate interposition to arrest the departure of the sheriff with the property. His narrative was briefly to the effect that, having occasion to ride a few miles up the road, he had suddenly, on his return, encountered the troop, with the sheriff and Skinflint at their head. The former had been summoned to the house of the latter, where he had stayed the last night, and they had gone out together the next day on their official mission immediately after breakfast, Skinflint waiting some four miles off for the return of the officer. He had timed his proceedings with the basest cunning and malevolence. He knew that "Maize-in-milk" was crowded with guests and neighbors, and that the pride of the proprietor would be touched to the quick by such a humiliating exposure as that which he meditated. He had not anticipated the issue. Fergus Berkshire met the party even while Skinflint was receiving from the sheriff a description of what had taken place. The exulting grin had not passed from his features as Fergus drew nigh. A few words sufficed to put him in possession of all the facts.

"I will assume this obligation," he said to the officer, by whom he was well known.

"Costs, interest, &c.?" said Skinflint.

"I will assume them all."

"It must be in writing," muttered Skinflint.

"Very good, sir."

The sheriff produced the papers with which the providence of the lawyer had furnished him, and a pocket inkstand and pen enabled Berkshire to prepare and sign an adequate obligation under the instructions of Skinflint himself, with which he had to confess himself satisfied. No unnecessary words passed between the parties.

"Go home to your master, good people," said Berkshire to the negroes. The sheriff he asked to dine with him, to Skinflint he bowed and bade good morning.

"The rascal!" exclaimed Ned Openheart; "if I had him under my horsewhip! But, dear Fergus, you will go back with me to 'Maize-in-milk?'"

"Not to-day, Ned," said the other, somewhat sadly.

"To-night, then?"

"No; you must excuse me, but I have good reasons for not visiting your house to-day."

"Pshaw! you fear that we shall be thanking you and all that sort of thing, but I promise you on my honor we shall say nothing about it."

Berkshire was firm, and Ned rode away somewhat wondering what had so suddenly come over the fellow. The mystery was explained as soon as he got home. Sweet Bessy Clinton had seized the first moment, when she could divert her father from his guests, to place before his eyes a written proposal from Fergus Berkshire for her hand, and to throw herself in tearful silence upon the old man's neck.

"And when did you get this, Bessy Clinton?"

"Last night, sir."

"And what do *you* say, Bessy?"

"Oh, father, I *do* think Mr. Berkshire is an honorable gentleman."

"I agree with you, Bessy; and were I you, I would certainly accept his offer."

"Thanks, dear father, thanks."

"Well, my child, go and write to him yourself. He deserves it."

Fergus Berkshire *did* come to "Maize-in-milk" that night.

If Richard Skinflint found himself discomfited so unexpectedly that day, the next, which was Christmas, brought him new sources of disquiet and new mortifications in a communication from Mrs. St. Clair, advising him that her niece had accepted the hand of Mr. Edward Openheart, and that the marriage was arranged to take place the ensuing May. "As this event," said the letter, "is the contingency upon which her minority determines, and as I have yielded my consent to the contract, which was the sole condition coupled with this contingency, it will be necessary that Messrs. Ingelhart and

Cripps should be prepared for the settlement with the future protector of the heiress in anticipation of the expected event."

Skinflint did not sleep that night—nor, for that matter, did several of our parties; but the provocation to wakefulness among them was the result of very different feelings. At "Maize-in-milk" there was now no check to the happiness of all the circle. The revolution was complete. The horizon was no longer overcast. The moon and stars were all out. Instead of the shrieks of the owl, a mockbird sang at the window, and the cheek of our proprietor grew warm and his face lightened as the several couples wheeled gayly in the great hall in the mazes of the dance—the tear of joy gathered brightly in his eye, and he murmured to his placid spouse, half unconsciously—"Thank God, it is a happy Christmas after all!"

[Flirtation at the Moultrie House, *under the full title given below, was issued by printer Edward C. Councell in Charleston in 1850. Although Simms's name does not appear on the title-page, the present editor follows William Peterfield Trent and others in assigning the epistolary tale to Simms. It is the one selection in the present volume whose authorship cannot be proved; but internal evidence is strong enough to support the conclusion that it was written by Simms. Explanatory and Textual Notes begin on page 779.*]

FLIRTATION AT THE MOULTRIE HOUSE:

In a Series of Letters, from Miss Georgiana Appleby, To Her Friends in Georgia, Showing the Doings At the Moultrie House, and the Events Which Took Place at the Grand Costume Ball, On the 29th August, 1850; With Other Letters.

ADVERTISEMENT

The publisher happened upon these curious epistles in a strange manner. They were found, in a small reticule, near the Steam Boat Ferry Wharf, on last Saturday night, by one of the imps of the printing office. It may be as easy for the reader, as the printer, to guess at the circumstances which brought them all together in the same budget. They may have been recovered by Miss Appleby from Miss Sophronia Kirkland: or they may have been dropt by that treacherous friend herself, on her way to or from the island; or they may have got into third hands by a concurrence of circumstances which we cannot explain. Of one thing, however, the curious may be assured,—that we print from the originals;—they are all to bè seen at the office of the publisher.

LETTER FIRST.

Miss Georgiana Appleby, Moultrie House, to Miss Sophronia Kirkland, near Clarkesville, Ga.

Oh! my Sophronia, my other self, you should be here. But for your absence, I should be the happiest creature in the world. I should want for nothing. Wanting you, however, I am still human, and still feel that none of my blessings are perfect. Yet, heaven knows, I ought to be content,—nay, more,—I ought to be happy. The place, itself, far exceeds my expectations. We reached Charleston on Tuesday, and the very next day came to the Island. And O! the sea, my Sophronia, the blue, the bright, the ever boundless sea! You know that my eyes had never before beheld the ocean. I was overwhelmed by the sight. It is beyond description. It is a power to be felt and feared, and loved, and worshipped, but hardly to be spoken of. The Moultrie House opens its great doors directly upon it. The big billows roll directly up to its portals, and subside in the sweetest murmurs and chidings at its feet. At high tide, the water spreads up and away to within a hundred yards of the entrance, and if you wish to enjoy the embraces of the Atlantic, in vulgar speech, take a sea bath, you can do so with a "hop, skip and jump," such as we learned to take when little ignorant school girls, at dear old Athens. I have already been in several times, with twenty others; and O! such rolling and rocking, such tumblings and tryings to swim in the shallowest places. There is no sort of danger. The shore slopes gradually down, and all you do is to run out and meet the breakers, which come in curling and falling over, one upon the back of the other, turning you over on your back also, and making you scramble and sprawl about, in the most comical manner, to get on your feet again. It is delicious frolicking, I tell you. But, cousin Tom says, I must hurry, for the boat will soon go to the city, and he is to carry my letter to the post office. Come to me, my Sophronia, heart of my heart, and soul of my spirit, and make me altogether happy by sharing with me my happiness.

Your own only,

GEORGIANA APPLEBY.

LETTER SECOND.

FROM THE SAME TO THE SAME.

I am more than ever delighted, best sister of my affections. The more I see of this place, the more I am charmed. It is at once so strange and so attractive. Think of being surrounded by the sea like Robinson Crusoe, only not alone. The Island is about four miles long. It has a great hard beach, almost like rock, after the seas go down, over which we ride on horseback, or in carriages, and hoof and wheel make no impression on the sand. We sit in the long piazza, which goes clean round the house, both stories, and look out upon the ships going in and out the harbor, with their broad white sails swelling out in the wind, like the wings of mighty sea-birds. Then you see the beautiful little pilot boats, like swallows darting along the waves. Then suddenly, some great sea-steamer, rushes up, foaming and fretting, puffing and panting, full of people staring at us, with much hunger in their faces. The truth is, there are charming enough people at this place, whom they would like very much to devour. Then come the big black porpoises,—a sort of sea-hog, and very good eating they say,—plunging one after the other, clean out of the sea, and playing about as happily, as if they did not care to come ashore again,—and I suppose they don't. Oh! my Sophronia, could you see these things with me. Could I know that you, too, were gazing on them at the same moment with myself. But you don't look at the sea all the time. It is one of the beauties of this place, that, by looking out straight in a certain direction, you could see three thousand miles, directly into Limerick, in Ireland,—if, indeed, your eyes did'nt fail you, as is the case with mine. Augustus Colleton, said to me yesterday:

"There you see Europe."

"Where?" said I.

"In that direction," said he. "It certainly lies out there. It depends entirely upon the extent of vision. It is hardly three thousand miles."

I strained my eyes a great deal, but could see nothing but the ocean. I suppose when I become used to it, I shall see Ireland as well as other people. But, looking out in one direction, as I tell you, I could see nothing but the ocean. I had only to turn a foot, and on the right, there was the loveliest headland, and the greenest shrubbery, and the great ghostly light-house, that every night robs the sky of one of its brightest stars, and stands up there smiling at me. By looking a little farther, the shores extend, and form around the harbor. Then you see a great fortress, full of open jaws, grinning with cannon. This they call fort Sumter. On the Island itself is fort Moultrie, filled with cannon also. But cannon is not their only possession. Oh! Sophronia, my heart, there are several of the handsomest officers in the world, and they are so gay, and so gallant, and so generous. They give parties every now and then, and have the band to play for us; and they all dance, and their balls are the most delightful in the world. Then, by looking a little farther, there is the beautiful city of Charleston, where I can tell you, there is enough to be seen to keep your eyes and heart busy for a twelvemonth. Oh! the shopping I have done, I have almost broken grandmama! But I must not talk of these now. I have a world of things to show you already, and I have some things chosen on purpose, for my own heart of hearts, my Sophronia. There is to be a grand costume ball, and we are all preparing for it. What part shall I play? I have altered my mind, a thousand times,—would that you were here, my Sophronia, to give me counsel. But I am at the bottom of my sheet. Love of my soul, thine through eternity.

GEORGIANA.

LETTER THIRD.

FROM THE SAME TO THE SAME.

Oh! I have not told you half, my sweet Sophronia. Whatever the attractions of the breeze, the sea, and the prospects without may be,—and they are admitted to be quite equal to any of the watering places in this country, and superior to most,—they must still be spoken of as secondary to the attractions of society within. These Charleston people are really very pleasant companions. A little stiff and apparently haughty at first, but the ice once broken, as frank, and courteous, as kind and conciliating, as any people in the world. We Georgians, in particular, have had no reason to complain. They seem to have singled us out for their special attentions. They have made quite a pet of poor little me, and I am gladly welcomed to all their circles.

Such fun as we have, and O! Sophronia, so much flirtation as goes on here. I never saw the like. There's Mrs. ——, but no! I wont be scandalous. Only you should see the airs and graces, of that fright, that odious face and figure,—that Emily ——, whom we met at Marietta. She is here, and cutting all sort of capers, and making as much fuss about herself as if she had beauty, grace, taste, wealth, and all the acomplishments at command. Such a flirting as she carries on, but between us, the labor is altogether on her side. She forces herself upon the young fellows, and is quite bold about it. The other day, Augustus Colleton, made up a fishing party entirely on my account, and, would you believe it, she followed us out into the piazza, and brought up the subject of fishing, and said,—the odious creature!—"And you are going a fishing to-morrow, Mr. Colleton. Oh! what a happy time you will have. Fishing is one of the sweetest sports in the world! I know nothing I love so well!" What could he do but ask her to become one of the party. Yet her anxiety arose only from the fact, that she has set her cap for a Mr. S——, a widower here,—a merchant, and a man of fortune, whom she has been following up and down, without any prospect of success. You may think so, when I tell you, that though he was one of the fishing party, he never thought to ask her. Oh! but we had a nice time of it. I caught more than twenty *whiting*, a favorite fish here; and Augustus was so good as to watch my line for me, and always to take them off of my hook. Soph, my heart, I do begin to think I have got *him, himself*, upon it. Oh! Lord, should it be so, my Soph, what in the world am I to do with him?

GEORGIANA.

LETTER FOURTH.

You ask me, soul of my soul, "who is Augustus Colleton?" Did'nt I tell you all about him already? Oh, he is the handsomest, modestest, the sweetest gentleman in the whole world; and could I halve my heart,—could I rob my precious Sophronia of any, the most chee-chee portion of it, I feel as if I could give that portion to Augustus. He is tall and slender, and graceful, with the brightest black eyes, and the glossiest black hair, and the bushiest black whiskers, and such a love of a moustache, that it seems to be a very nesting-place for cupid. He is all devotion to me, Soph;—follows me everywhere, makes up the prettiest parties, and contrives the nicest schemes, for getting us together, and he talks in such sweet, low accents, and he says such poetical things always, so different from every body else,—so full of moonlight, and midnight, and zephyrs, and ambrosia, that you see in an instant, that he was born to be a poet, as was the case with Mr. Horace, of whom cousin Tom talks so constantly. I have told Augustus all about you,—that you are my other self,—more than my sister,—more than a lover possibly could be,—myself in fact,—the soul part of my own life and being. You may be sure, Soph, I did justice, as well as I could to your charms and graces. I told him what a mind you had,—how brilliant, how deep,—what an unselfish and noble soul,—how full of self-sacrifice and devotion. I told him that, though you had ten times the wealth and beauty of poor little me, you were all meekness and humility, and were the last person that ever thought of your own possessions. He longs to see you, for my sake, and, oh, Soph! my precious, I long that you should see him for my sake also; for, of a truth, my heart, he grows more precious in my sight than all other of the sons of men. Can't you come to me, Soph?—What is to keep you? Run down, my heart, next week, when you will be in season for the Costume Ball;—bring all your pearls, and diamonds,—all your jewels, and put on all your charms. You shall go as Cleopatra, and I trust you will find your Cæsar,—not to die for him, and lose your crown, but to live for him and be crowned with happiness. You with him, and I with my Augustus, and

"Oh! if there be an Elysium on earth,
'T will be this, 't will be this?"

Your own

GEORGIANA.

LETTER FIFTH.

You will come, my Sophronia? Oh! bless you for the promise. Augustus heard it with delight. He sympathizes with me in all things. He asked a great deal about you, and I gave him a particular description of your person. I told him that you were born to be a queen, you carried yourself so nobly. That you were a Juno, a Cleopatra, a Zenobia,—with such a carriage, so graceful, so dignified, so beautiful, so grand. And he said,—"Oh! your friend is a Goddess,—better be a Goddess than a Queen,—for a Goddess needs no help from fortune; now, a Queen does, and your friend, you tell me, is poor."—"Poor indeed!" said I. I was quite indignant, and told him all. I let him understand that you had the means to queen it with any body in the land. I told him of your Georgia plantation on the Chattahoochie, and your Alabama plantation on the Tombecbe, and your stocks, and houses, and negroes, and soon figured it up so as to silence all his doubts as to your right to play Cleopatra, and drink pearls in vinegar every morning, if you pleased.—"You seem very fond of your friend," said he; and then, with a sigh, he went on,—"and I am half sorry for it." "Why," said I. "Ah!" he answered, "I am afraid, your friendship leaves no room in your heart for other friendships or affections." Oh! how poor little me trembled, my Sophronia. I knew not what to say, and half guessed what he might next say, for he was sitting quite close to me on the settee, in one corner of the great piazza, and his hand just then accidently rested on my own; when who should come, poking in among us, but that odious Emily ——, who is always getting in the way of people who get on very well without her; and when she appeared, Augustus, who heartily despises her, started up abruptly and hurried away. But I have succeeded, my Sophronia, in making him feel the value of my friend; and if any thing should happen, my precious,—if,—if, he should really prevail over my remaining affections,—he shall first be taught to know how to love and cherish you, as devotedly as he does myself. Come, and come quickly. I shall not sleep till I see you.

GEORGIANA.

LETTER SIXTH.

Miss Georgiana Appleby, to her sister, Miss Eudocia Appleby, Georgia.

Wish me joy, dear little sis, for, my heart of hearts, the friend of my soul,—my soul itself,—my Sophronia, has come to me, and completed all my happiness. I knew when she was to arrive, and sent Augustus up to the city to meet her at the rail-road, and bring her at once to the Island. Oh! she was so good to come to me. She never looked more beautiful before. Augustus is greatly charmed with her, I see that, and it contents me; it would have made me so miserable to be the wife of a man who could not love my friend. I have now no doubt of Augustus' feelings. They are every where remarked; and I confess to you, dear little sis, that, next to Sophronia, he has all my heart. Heigho! when next you hear from me, it may be all over, and I shall be betrothed. Grandmama is willing. She likes him; and cousin Tom says he is a famous fine fellow; though Tom don't think him quite so great a genius as I do. Tom is stupid enough to say, indeed, that he is no genius at all, but a sensible fellow enough. This he only does to vex me; for he knows how I hate all the tribe of merely sensible fellows. But, I can't say much more. I hear Sophronia's voice in the piazza, and she calls me. I must go to her. Who can she be talking with? Bless me! It is Augustus, and I thought he had gone up to the city in the one o'clock boat. I must join them. One word more only, dear little sis, and that must be about the costume ball. It takes place now in a few days, and will be a famous affair. I am to go as Amy Robsart, in Scott's novel of Kennilworth. They say I look the character so well: and Augustus is to go as Sir Philip Sidney. Soph has not decided what character to take.

Your

GEORGIANA.

P. S. Don't be foolish now about coming here 'Docia. You're too young and inexperienced yet, and the flirtation here is awful! If you were to see even the elderly gentlemen here who engage in it, it would completely shock you. There's a Mr. H—— here, a married gentleman, who always takes advantage of his wife's absence to flirt with us girls from Georgia. I saw some of his tricks summer before last, at Clarkesville, and I could tell you of others. 'Twont do for you at all. In a year or two, when you can go under the care and protection of Augustus and myself, the case will be otherwise. But just yet, never think of it.

Your loving sister,

G. A.

LETTER SEVENTH.

Mr. Tom Appleby, at the Moultrie House, to his friend Mr. Richard Meriwether, of Coweta, Ga.

DEAR DICK:

That cock won't fight. I have had enough of the mountains. This sea-shore is new to me, and so long as it keeps comfortable at this place, so long I stay; at all events while hot weather lasts. Here, I have as good cock-tails as heart could desire, and as pleasant a game of whist as would please old Billy Harris. There are other things. Sea-bathing I relish monstrously. It is perfectly glorious to rollick among the great breakers, and dash through seas of foam. You know that I pride myself upon my swimming; but, if I could do the thing famously in fresh-water, I do it ten times as well in salt. I am, here, sword-fish, shark, and porpoise, at the same moment; and execute such plunges in the Atlantic as would astonish a Hoosier with the idea of such a fish as never swam in the Mississippi. I don't go to any mountains, I tell you. There are good fellows here, and I have no time unoccupied. I have buried a button at ten paces, with my pistols here, seven shots in ten, and clipped it the other three. There is a fine grove here behind the sand hills, which makes the greatest pistol gallery in the world. Shrimps, you never ate, I reckon, and hardly oysters. I now include them in my articles of faith. I believe in shrimps. I have a perfect faith in oysters. They open the soul; they warm the sensibilities. They make the heart susceptible and tender. I feel their influence. I have half fallen in love with one of the Charleston girls, as fair as a lily and gentle as a zephyr. But, no more of this. It may be, after all, nothing but a flirtation, and the jade is an adept at that sort of thing. This is a famous place for flirtation, I find, and the practice, which might worry a too earnest fellow, has nevertheless, something very graceful and pleasant in it. Talking of flirtation, by the way, let me say to you, that if you are really serious in the affair with cousin Georgy, the sooner you are here the better. There is a handsome fellow, one Augustus Colleton, of some one of the parishes in South-Carolina, who is making locomotive progress in the heart of Georgy. He is no mean rival, I assure you; something of a dandy, a clever fellow enough, though I suspect, at bottom, a fortune hunter. He contrived, in the most natural way in the world, to sift me as to Georgy's fortune, which, of course, I did not exaggerate. If you are serious, I repeat, the sooner you are here the better. By the way, push down in season for a great Costume Ball which takes place on the 29th. Bring with you your dress of the Texan hunter. It shows your person off to the best advantage, and I know how well you can play the part. It will be the very thing for the occasion. I shall go as a Cumanche chief.

Yours truly,

Tom Appleby.

LETTER EIGHTH.

Tom Appleby, at the Moultrie House, to his uncle, Edward S. Appleby, Esq., of Georgia.

Dear Uncle:

I enclose you a printed report, from one of the newspapers of Charleston, describing the great blow-out at the Moultrie House the other night. You will see among those who figured on the occasion, your humble servant, as a Cumanche. Dick Meriwether went as a Texan Hunter, and did it famously, as usual. Georgiana went as "Amy Robsart," and was very pretty; while her "dear friend,"—Soph. Kirkland,—who is likely to prove a *dear* friend, indeed,—was very magnificent as Cleopatra. The whole affair was a very splendid one, though there was less of a crowd than would have been there, (and was anticipated) had it not been for this cursed *broken bone fever*, as they call it; an attack of it, which has prevented me from writing you before, I am just rising from. It seized me very suddenly, the day after the ball, coming on with headache; which, at first, I ascribed to my too frequent potations of champaigne and madeira, the night before. It stuck to me, in the shape of ache, soreness and fever for three days, and leaves me mighty weak about the legs and back. But I feed well, and have never lost my appetite. The ball, let me tell you, was a huckleberry much above my percimmon. I never saw any thing like it before. The newspaper notice will give you some notion of it. The supper tables were glorious, feeding eye and appetite at the same time, and to the great satisfaction of both.

Think of the oysters alone costing more than forty dollars, and you will have some notion of all the rest. It is estimated that the supper cost about a thousand dollars. I have no doubt it comes very near that mark. The wines were in great profusion, and the popping of champagne was as frequent as that of musketry at the battle of San Jacinto. We did not break up till three o'clock in the morning, and then a dozen of us took to the beach, and stripping for the sea, had a glorious buffeting for twenty minutes with the breakers. I got to bed at day light, slept like a top till dinner time, and then awakened with a stitch in my side, which turned out to be this abominable epidemic,—which makes you sore, but gets no sympathy. It is quite a gratification here, to see one's neighbor hobbling along as if he had a sudden twinge of the gout. But I am so weak, that I must shorten my letter. To-morrow, I must write you something about Georgiana, and her proceedings.

Your faithful nephew,

TOM APPLEBY.

LETTER NINTH.

Tom Appleby, at the Moultrie House, to his uncle, Edward S. Appleby, Esq., Georgia.

DEAR UNCLE NED:

I promised to tell you all about poor Georgiana. You must know there has been the devil to pay and no pitch hot,—such a flare up among bosom friends and kindred souls,—such sighs and sorrows,—complaints and tribulation,—it would be impossible for me to describe. I told you before, that Georgiana, had made a conquest, seemingly, of one Augustus Colleton, of Savannah river. He was completely smitten,—so every body thought,—and became the very shadow of Georgy wherever she went. They were to be found constantly together; walked the piazza and the beach by moonlight; listened to soft whisperings in the shade, waltzed together nightly in the ball-room, and played frequently together in the *tableaux vivants*. All seemed to go on as musically as the marriage bells, and all of us thought it would lead to that. I confess, I was'nt pleased to see it, because I knew Dick Meriwether's liking for Georgy, and I thought him by far the best fellow for her. But this chap, Colleton, was quite a gentleman, easy, courteous, graceful, very handsome, and of good family enough. He was something of a fop, and a little too sentimental for my taste; but he could swallow a cock-tail like a man, and played billiards like a beauty. I could'nt object to his attentions to Georgy,—and all I could do was to write to Dick, and give him a hint of the way in which the grey cat was like to jump. He came in season to see enough to sicken him. For the first day after he arrived, he could scarcely get to talk at all with Georgy; she was so much taken up with Colleton. But the very next day, who should come also, but Soph Kirkland. Poor Georgy was not satisfied unless her friend could congratulate her on her sweetheart. Colleton was sent up to the rail-road depôt to bring Soph down; my poor little cousin, being on the sly, and never telling me a word about it. The consequence has been awful. Colleton, almost in a moment, became the adorer of Soph, and she was not unwilling. The truth is, he is a good looking fellow, and very agreeable. You know that Soph is a beauty, and Colleton saw it. It appears too, that simple little Georgy, was foolish enough to tell him all about Soph's fortune. The game was soon up with *her;* and for two days before the ball, I could see that Georgy was quite neglected for Soph. For a while, Georgy refused to see it; but, at last, the thing was forced upon her in a way not to be mistaken, or misunderstood.

The night of the ball, Soph waltzed several times with Colleton. He did ask Georgy out with him, on one occasion; but his indifference was evident to all. Well, about midnight, Georgy happened to look round and ask for Soph. She had disappeared. The poor girl thought she might be taken sick, and ran out to look after her. She found her, a moment too soon, in one of the ladies' parlors, seated on a sofa, and with Mr. Augustus Colleton at her feet! Poor Georgy just clasped her hands together, and staggered back. The guilty couple started up in confusion, and began a sort of explanation; but Georgy would not stop to listen. She wheeled about, made off, came once more to the ball-room, and, though greatly stung, yet the poison was not mortal. She called up all her strength, and resumed her dancing with more eagerness than ever. It is wonderful how she bore up; and, fortunately, Dick Meriwether put in at the right time, and was very attentive. She looks on him with a sweet smile now, and he is full of hope. But she suffers! I see that. As for Soph, she has tried to make some explanations, but Georgy shakes her head. She feels that "her other self," her "better half," her "soul of souls," and most "precious of hearts jewels," is very mortal, like all the rest; and that she has stolen from her the only hope which she had nursed so fondly. Soph's conduct would be unpardonable, if love were not such an irresponsible power. As for friendship among women, let a handsome fellow get between the parties, and it is wonderful how soon it cools off! Thus matters stand at present. I must break off here. I am going on a fishing party with some gentlemen who are now in waiting. More to-morrow.

Your affectionate nephew,

TOM APPLEBY.

LETTER TENTH.

Tom Appleby, at the Moultrie House, to Edward S. Appleby, Esq., of Georgia.

DEAR NUNCLE:

We had glorious sport yesterday. Five of us, in the space of three hours, caught *seven* hundred fish,—trout, whiting, cavalli, black-fish, and other species. A great fishing region this: the very place for one like you, who enjoy it so well. The danger is, that you might be caught yourself; a bachelor is always in danger, I am told, till fairly laid up in lavender; and here the tempters are as numerous as those who assail Robert le Diable, in the old abbey. Still, I recommend you to venture. Come here and spend the month of October at all events. This is the most delightful month, they tell me, at this place. I shall try it, and so, perhaps, will Dick Meriwether; but Georgiana has resolved to be off next week. I do not oppose her. She is sadly discomfited. The loss of her friend is, perhaps, not so serious a matter, and I confess I do not greatly deplore the loss of the one lover, as I know the value of him that is left. Dick's hopes, by the way, are rising. He is frequently with Georgy, and she seems to find pleasure in his company. Soph and herself do not often meet; they sit at opposite extremes of the table. They occupy separate quarters of the parlor; and seldom exchange a word, except when passing. Soph has written Georgy, trying to excuse her offences. Georgy showed me her answer to this; but not the letter itself. She was calm, and uttered no reproaches. "I have made some mistakes," she says quietly,—"equally in love and friendship, but I have only myself to complain of. It must be my care now to commit no more of either sort." Soph evidently feels ashamed of herself. She does not look any of us in the face; but in all probability the consolations of Mr. Colleton re-assure and satisfy her. He is certainly sufficiently devoted. The report this evening is, that the question was popt just before dinner, at the extreme east corner of the upper or ladies' piazza. Mrs. G——e, of Charleston, happened suddenly to emerge from one of the neighboring chambers, and caught a fervent word or two, which seems to convey no other meaning. Since then, Mr. C. seems to be more excruciating than ever, and Miss K. more happy. They are even now about to sally out for a drive. Mr. C's. buggy is at the door, and he keeps a splendid trotter. There they go, with a hundred eyes following them. But Georgy calls to me, and I must go too. We are also for a drive. Dick Meriwether joins us, and I am in hopes that the sight of Soph's happiness, will not prejudice Georgy's.

Your affectionate nephew,

THOS. APPLEBY.

LETTER ELEVENTH.

Miss Sophronia Kirkland, to Miss Georgiana Appleby.

Can you forgive me, my own Georgy! Ah! indeed you must. How could I help it. Alas! I little knew how terrible a passion was love! What friendship can withstand it? We were ignorant children, my precious, when we believed ours to be so strong. Mine has failed in the encounter. Oh! Georgiana,—the deed is done. I am affianced. How could I resist the pleadings of Augustus? Ask your own heart, how impossible. Not that I suppose that your heart will so fully respond to such a question, in his case, as mine. It was a fancy only, my precious, that you loved him, or he you. Hearts are united in heaven. Would heaven unite one to many, or to more than one? That would be to destroy all the harmonies of earth. No! where we think we love, when we can expect nothing in return, we really do not love. It is a delusion. I know that you do not love Augustus; you cannot, for he is wholly devoted to me. Ours is a genuine passion, such as no one need mistake. Do not accuse me,—do not reproach me,—love me as ever, my Georgiana. I could not help what has been done. The heart of Augustus was linked to mine in heaven, and I but obey the decree of heaven which draws me irresistibly to him on earth. Once more, Georgy, forgive me, and let us once more embrace as before.

Ever your

SOPH.

LETTER TWELFTH.

Miss Georgiana Appleby, to Miss Sophronia Kirkland.

Never, Sophronia! We can never be as we have been before to each other,—we had better never meet. Be happy if you can. I am very willing to think that your loves are sanctioned by heaven. I have made some mistakes with mine, perhaps. I have mistaken both love and friendship. It must be my future care to commit no more such mistakes. I do not reproach you. I have only to complain of myself. I trust that *you* will make no mistakes in the matter of your happiness.

GEORGIANA APPLEBY.

LETTER THIRTEENTH.

Miss Georgiana Appleby, Moultrie House, to her sister, Miss Eudocia Appleby, Georgia.

Oh! sis, my child! I have seen the wreck of all my hopes and all my happiness. Soph Kirkland is a traitor to friendship. She has sacrificed her faith to me, at the pleadings of another. She has done worse. Oh! sis, she is a most treacherous creature. I had made a conquest. You heard. Augustus Colleton. He was so handsome,—so graceful,—so attentive to me. She has inveigled him from me, and me so confiding. He never would have abandoned me but for her arts, her cunning, her most unwomanlike tricks. I caught him at her feet, with one of her hands in his, and his arm about her waist. I could only exclaim, "Oh! Soph!" Could you have seen the blushes of the guilty thing, and his confusion. The truth is, my sis,—and that makes me feel it so,—he had been on his knees to me before!—oh! the perfidious! I would not have him *now*, if he came with wings, like an angel, and promised to carry me straight to paradise. I am so vexed, and so sad; but they shall never see it. You would be surprised how I stand it. But I must hurry. I am going to ride with Mr. Meriwether, who is here. I begin to think he is one of the handsomest men in the country, and he is so gentle, and truth and fidelity look out in all his features. Good bye, sis, I think of coming home next week.

Your affectionate sister.

GEORGIANA.

LETTER FOURTEENTH.

Tom Appleby, Moultrie House, to his uncle, Edw'd S. Appleby, Esq., Georgia.

DEAR UNCLE:

I shan't come now till October. Georgy lets me off from seeing her home. Dick Meriwether will take that office on himself. It's all fixed between them. He proposed to her last night and was accepted, and if I might judge of Georgy's looks this morning, she has found consolation in full for the loss of her former friend and lover. They will stay a week longer. But Soph's conscience could'nt stand it. She went off for Clarkesville this morning, with her old aunt, who really sees nothing of what goes on, and hears as badly; and with Mr. Colleton in attendance. I have no doubt they are shortly to be married; but not a word do we hear on that subject. We are now all getting on as smoothly as may be. The company here increases and improves, and we are in the best of spirits, busy preparing for a series of tableaux for to-night, in which Dick and myself play conspicuous parts. So, no more for a week at least, from

Your affectionate nephew,

THO'S APPLEBY.

NOTE.—Here the correspondence ends abruptly. We include the report of the grand costume ball, at the Moultrie House, as comprised in one of the letters of Mr. Thos. Appleby, to his uncle. The details, by the editor, may throw some light upon the previous history.

PUBLISHER.

APPENDIX.

GRAND COSTUME BALL AT THE MOULTRIE HOUSE.

This splendid entertainment took place at the time appointed, on the 29th of August. We have been seeking for some days to present our readers with a fair, if not a full report of the proceedings; but domestic and national politics have, to this moment, defeated our desires, and wholly occupied all that portion of our columns not devoted to business; and we are still compelled to limit the space which we should otherwise accord to this *fête,* which we are pleased to regard as one of the most favorable of the symptoms in our local policy—as significant, indeed, of the determination of our people, hereafter, to seek their amusements, where they will always prove most grateful when found,—at home! Our readers, in the interior as well as on the seaboard, are already in possession of the fact that the Moultrie House, on Sullivan's Island,—a splendid mansion for summer resort, and of very recent erection,—has, at once, attained the highest reputation, and has been thronged, the whole season, with the most fashionable and attractive society. The guests of the house itself were sufficiently numerous for a most magnificent turn-out; and, but for the peevish little epidemic which has been making sore the ribs and joints of our citizens for the last two or three weeks, the crowd from the city and the interior would have swelled the number beyond the accommodation of the Island. Hundreds were cut off from the entertainment by ugly twitches in knee and ancle, which forbade the idea of doing justice to any but a rheumatic or gouty character; and the fear of the aforesaid twitches, kept crowds from the country, who were otherwise prepared to come. As the day approached, accordingly, fears were entertained that the affair was destined to be a failure. The result was an agreeable disappointment to all who felt such an apprehension. The managers, senior and junior, maintained their hopes and labors together, and they have every reason to congratulate themselves on having done so. So far from proving a failure, there has been no such successful display, in these precincts, for many years. The Junior Managers, in particular, deserve the highest commendation for their generous exertions and their admirable tastes. We must put their names on record in connection with this compliment:

JUNIOR MANAGERS.

E. M. Beach, Esq.	A. Herbemont, Jr. Esq.
W. G. Desaussure, Esq.	Lt. J. B. J. Weld, U.S.A.
F. J. Porcher, Esq.	Theo. Stoney, Esq.
R. D. Spann, Esq.	C. K. Prioleau, Esq.
H. C. King, Esq.	E. C. Jones, Esq.
J. J. Edwards, Esq.	M. A. Pringle, Esq.

They were admirably seconded by the courteous keeper of the Hotel, Mr. Young, by his vigorous, energetic and excellent assistant, Mr. Pine, and by the *artiste* employed on the occasion, Mr. Eugene Bell. The Senior Managers, who, like the Juniors, were distinguished by a beautiful *rosette* upon the left breast, were as follows:

SENIOR MANAGERS.

Hon. J. Bond I'On.	A. Herbemont, Sr. Esq.
J. L. Petigru, Esq.	H. W. Conner, Esq.
W. G. Simms, Esq.	Otis Mills, Esq.
W. A. Carson, Esq.	Robert Hume, Esq.
C. T. Lowndes, Esq.	P. J. Porcher, Esq.
Hon. W. J. Grayson.	W. B. Pringle, Esq.
James Gadsden, Esq.	Edwd. Gamage, Esq.

At an early hour on the appointed evening, a goodly show of costumes began to be seen, in the grand passages of the buildings; and curious eyes began to peer in at the doors and windows of the several rooms assigned as the theatre of performances, long before the committee was prepared to throw them open. When, at length, the doors were unclosed, a most magnificent and faery-like prospect was unfolded to the view. The decorations, which were confided to Mr. Bell, were such as to do him great credit, and to satisfy all the anticipations of the assembly. Five of the largest rooms in the house, opening by folding doors into each other, were draped in the richest and most beautiful style, with festoons of blue, white and crimson, ornamented with *rosettes* and bouquets, and stars of gold and silver. In the centre, a raised *dais* allotted to the orchestra, was magnificently clothed in a drapery which fell in heavy but graceful folds, the chief loop in the midst, forming a wave of white, bearing, in crimson letters, the name of "Moultrie." The drapery of doors and windows was fashioned after the same model, with the same materials; and the extended area of five apartments was equally various and unique in its attractions. The chandeliers consisted of variegated lanterns, the lights gleaming in stars from above; while, along the walls, similarly disposed they added to the golden richness of the drapery, in the intervals of which they were displayed. In front, the central section of the immense piazza, more than a hundred feet in length, and sixteen in breadth, was enclosed with canvass and well-lighted for the promenaders. The supper room, one hundred by thirty-eight feet, with its three immense tables, the whole length of the room, was brilliant in its display; being decorated in a style no less superb than that of the ball rooms; every window wreathed in flowing and falling robes, and the great blue, white and crimson festoons embracing the columns and binding them together in the most graceful manner. By a judicious arrangement, the committee succeeded in separating the appartments assigned to the ball entirely from the rest of the house. There was no clamour, no confusion, except such as the uninitiated might suppose to exist in the fanciful evolutions of the foreign dances.

These were numerous, we may say in this place, and were continued, with little intermission, from 9 o'clock, P. M., to 2, A. M.; allowing only the proper intervals for the supper. They alternated agreeably from the cotillion to the waltz, and from the waltz to the polka. Many of the dancers were not simply prepared to *walk* through the figures, but to enter with great enthusiasm into the full spirit of the movement, with equal grace, taste, and propriety. But let us not anticipate. We have described the scene; it is time that we bestow our regards upon the actors. The orchestra pours forth its most triumphant music; and the gentlemen guests begin to appear; the gay gallants, the bachelors tired of their desolation, and non-descripts of many sorts, all habited according to the most capricious fancy. Grouped about the rooms, or promenading, they waited with eager expectation for the coming of the ladies; nor had they long to wait. A regal trumpet sounded from without, and a score of gentlemen ushers, of the epoch of Philip of France, and of John of England, suddenly entered, dividing on each hand, as they appeared, and making way between their ranks, for one in whose presence they were immediately forgotten. This was no less than Queen Constance, personated by Mrs. G—m—ge, of Charleston. She was accompanied by her son, Prince Arthur; the fair boy whose fate was so fearful and so mysterious; the part, equally well dressed and sustained, by Master J. McPh–s–n. Her confessor,—rather a juvenile keeper of a Queen's conscience, by the way, was represented by Mr. F. W—; whom, we were rather shocked to see, after a while, forgetting his *cloth* and professional duties, carrying on a series of bold flirtations, with a dozen different damsels, and fully completing the circle of his offences, by engaging in the merits and mysteries of the Polka. The whole group formed a very striking dramatic spectacle. The Queen's dress was a rich embroidered muslin train over white satin and point lace. Her crown and girdle were composed of the most magnificent jewels, in which she literally blazed; a veil of lace completed the costume.

Hardly had she entered, when she was closely followed by Mr. H—r—t, as Richard the Third; and so closely did he seem to follow in her train, that one might suppose he fancied her the very Lady Anne on whom his heart was set. We remarked, however, nothing sinister in his countenance; certainly, nothing of that murderous occult purpose which Kean, in Richard, does not entirely conceal from the audience, even when playing the lover to the princess whom he had widowed. We were disposed to find fault with Mr. H—r—t, for the exceedingly small development of *hump* between the shoulders. No doubt the Richard of history was a much more *personable* man than Shakspeare has made him; but Mr. H—r—t, should have dressed according to the dramatist.

Other characters began rapidly to appear. A bright little creature, recognized as Miss Gr–y–on, of Charleston, suddenly appeared as "Spring." Her costume was very felicitous, consisting of a pink silk skirt and green silk bodice, with an *illusion* over-skirt. The trimming consisted of wreaths and bouquets; the hair being dressed with flowers also. We perceived that she was closely pursued by a venerable monk, the veritable Peter the Hermit, who preached the crusades; and who seemed very desirous of realizing the line of the poet,—"Winter lingering in the lap of Spring!" It was a fine group of January and May. This latter character was understood to be personated by Mr. Fl—m—g, of Philadelphia; but Peter the Hermit soon cast his wintry garments, and suddenly re-appeared as a handsome French chasseur. His dress was rich and elegant, and he played both parts with equal ease and spirit.

Our eyes were next caught by a Greek girl, whom we understood to be Miss S. F—rd, of Georgetown. Her dress was a rich brocade, the skirts embroidered with crimson and gold; bodice of black velvet, with rich lace sleeves; her cap was elegantly embroidered. A couple of Turks hung about this lady, and neither party seemed for the time to acknowledge the national antipathy. Who these Turks were, we have not been able to ascertain, but have heard that one of them came from Marlborough district.

From the Greek damsel, we turned away only to behold a new candidate for admiration, in the person of Miss Fanny P–k–r, of Columbia, who appeared as Rebecca, the Jewess, in Scott's Ivanhoe. She looked the part admirably. Her dress was a very beautiful one, of satin and velvet. Her jewels were in profusion. The turban which she wore was of satin and velvet also, ornamented with an elegant veil, with large jewels and lofty floating plumes. The followers of the Jewess were numerous. There were several sailors, French, English and American; several postilions, one or two knights, and a German philosopher, each of whom seemed desirous of converting her to a faith,—in himself; but, we believe, with very little success. Rebecca seemed to be looking out only for "Wilfrid of Ivanhoe," and he failed to make his appearance. In his absence, however, we perceived that the close devotions of Mr. B—d—g, representing "The Southern Traitor," were by no means stinted; and we did not see that the fair Jewess was at all scrupulous in bestowing her smiles upon the ultra-Carolinian.

Here followed, in odd contrasts of costume, a score of gentlemen. There is Dr. Ben. T–p–r, as a sailor in the merchant service, so well delineated, that the door keeper refused him admittance, as a regular Jack Tar. Col. C——h——m, with admirable spirit, personated the same character. Mr. B–d–g appeared as "The Southern Traitor," or rather as a personification of the Palmetto State;—the decorations of his costume, fancifully arranged, consisting of cotton, rice, and spears of the palmetto. Then there was Mr. Dan'l L–n–e, as a French boatman, constantly seeking service, but only among the ladies. Mr. DeS–s–re, as an English postilion, was no less assiduous in the same way. Mr. T–v–u, as a pirate, seemed bent on making his way, and his *prey* also. His dress was picturesque,—a pink striped shirt, blue striped inexpressibles, and a cap of striped purple. Mr. M–ni–d, as an English Jockey, looked the character to the life. Mr. O'H——a's costume was a very rich one, which attracted much attention, but we failed to find a fit name for it. We labored under the same difficulty in respect to the habit of Mr. Thos. Fr—st, but have since been told that it was that of an Italian boatman. His dress was of white pantaloons ornamented, a jacket of blue, edged with black, and a hat similarly decorated. Mr. Julius Bl—ke's dress was neat and fanciful, but we did not ascertain the character.

This groupe passes, and here we have a bevy of beauties, closely attended by sundry cavaliers. Of these hereafter. The ladies deserve all our eyes, and fix them. Here comes Mrs. Be—ch, of Charleston, personifying the flag of the United States, in other words, the States themselves. This was quite a fanciful idea. The dress consisted of a blue skirt, studded with silver stars, a white cashmere tunic, with scarlet stripes and edged with silver fringe; the sleeves of blue, looped with a star; a cap decorated with stars, a perfect galaxy, soaring through which rose the American eagle. The whole habit was fanciful in a high degree.

Next came Miss C. Sm–th, of Charleston, as "Edith Plantagenet," in Scott's novel of "The Talisman." Her dress was a handsome white one with a rich veil, and she bore a beautiful chaplet on her arm. The costume was probably derived from that scene, in the rocky hermitage of the Priest or Santon,—the mad Saint,—where the Prince of Scotland first beholds the beautiful Princess of England,—the sister of the fierce Richard Cœur de Leon.

Miss Julia Ma–g–lt appeared as a Mexican *poblana*, and looked the character she assumed. She wore the *rebosa*, over her head and shoulders, with the natural grace which distinguishes the simplest peasant girl of Mexico. Her dress was of white and red, bordered with blue. The blue and red portions were covered with hieroglyphics. The costume was equally striking and perfect.

Mrs. St–n–y, of Charleston, wore a tri-colored dress, her hair dressed with cockades.

Miss C–t–r, of Savannah, was very happy in the personation of a sea nymph. Her dress was of white muslin, trimmed with sea weeds; she wore a wreath and necklace of shells. In her hand she carried a wreathed horn, such as might, with its music, evoked by such a nereid, have won old Triton himself to worship our island nymph.

These were attended by groups of delighted worshippers of the sterner sex. Among them, we noticed Mr. Y–t–s, in the habit of a French postilion,—a scarlet dress, pants ornamented with blue stripes and minute bells; jacket of black ornamented, and cap with corresponding ornaments.

Mr. A–h–by was a peasant of France of the reign of Louis XIV. Mr. Wil–ie appeared in the costume of a French marshal. Mr. M–ot as a Greek sailor. Mr. El–ott as an American sailor. Mr. C–n–y as a corsair, in a particularly rich costume. Mr. H. W. C–n–r, Jr., as a Tyrolese peasant, and Mr. D. P–i–u as a Spanish Matador, in a robe of deep scarlet, of velvet and satin, and looking as tender and benignant, as if he had never entered the ring with any beings fiercer than those which then surrounded him.

Here come another splendid procession of fair women. Here is Miss C–rt–r, of Charleston, as a Novice, with sundry gentlemen interposing to prevent her from consummating their destruction by taking the veil. She wore a double skirt of white muslin, a muslin veil and chaplet of white roses upon her head, and, at her side, a rosary and cross.

She was succeeded by Miss M–l–s, of Charleston, as a Flower Girl, with white dress and apron, decorated with wreaths and bouquets, and carried in her hands a handsome basket of flowers. With her came

Miss G. A–l–by, of Georgia, as "Amy Robsart," in Scott's novel of "Kennilworth," a sweet and graceful creature, who looked well the sad and gentle heroine whose habit she assumed. She was closely followed by a noble looking Texian Hunter, who was understood to be Mr. Richard M–iw–r, of Georgia. Also,

Miss C. C–nn–r, of Charleston represented happily a German Peasant Girl, in a dress of white, trimmed with blue and pink ribbons, and wore a straw bonnet trimmed with wild flowers. These ladies were followed, or attended, by groups of gentlemen, in and out of character. We observed that sundry grave seniors were as busy as possible mingling in the business of flirtation. Messrs. Pinckney, Rutledge, Williams, Mills, Porcher, Carson, Petigru, Simms, Heyward, Bryan, Hume, Connor, Screven, Jones, Whitaker, Lindsay, Gamage, Cheesborough, Jervey, Dukes, and others, appeared in citizens dress; distinguished, when managers, with a rosette upon the left breast; while numerous ladies, undistinguished by particular costumes, were yet distinguished by the art and elegance which had disposed the ordinary dresses of society.

Mrs. Hu—e, Mrs. M–l–r and Mrs. M–ls, of Charleston, were in full dress; so were Mrs. H—be—t, Mrs. T–y–r and Mrs. E–m–e, of Columbia; Mrs. P–ch–r, Mrs. B–y–n, Mrs. P–k–y, Mrs. F–m–n, of Charleston; Mrs. and the Misses C–lc–h, of Sumterville; Mrs. E–ns, Miss H–ry, Miss V–dy–e, Mrs. W–l–ms, Miss E. S–th, Miss B–ks, of Charleston; Mrs. G–l–son, of Beaufort; Miss L–a–s, of Charleston; Miss McN–ty, of Savannah; and Mrs. D–ve, Mrs. W–lt–r, Mrs. W–ng–n, Mrs. S–th, Mrs. C–t–r, Miss T–m–r, all of Charleston. Several of these were in magnificent ball dresses. Miss N–th wore a beautiful fancy dress.

Mrs. M–nk appeared as Lady Abbess; a noble figure, looking the sweetness and benevolence, with the dignity that belongs to the character. She was followed by a lovely train of Nuns and Novices, not one of whom however, but looked the sentiment of the old song, which says, "I won't be a nun!" Among these, one of the few whose names we procured, was Mrs. G—d—n, of —. She wore, with special grace, the costume of the Nun,—a dress of virgin white, with the veil and chaplet.

The Misses B——ke, of Charleston, appeared as "Soubriettes," in white dresses, pink aprons and caps.

Miss Ga–l–d, of Georgetown, came as a Flower Girl. She was followed by a splendid creature, Miss S. K–kl–d of Georgia, shining in jewels, as "Cleopatra,"—triumphant, as in the moment when she first makes captive of Mark Antony. She was closely followed by Mr. A. C—ll—n, of Savannah river, as Sir Philip Sidney; and certainly, he wore the garb and name of that preux chevalier with the happiest propriety and spirit.

Miss Ellen Fl—n, of Darlington, prettily personated the "French Fisherman," in blue jacket and white pants. A blue cap, ornamented with silver, completed the costume. Miss H—a—d of Charleston, was a "Greek Girl." Her dress was a rose-colored crape over white satin, with bodice of rose-colored velvet, and a corresponding cap. Miss A. G–lm–n, of the Island, wore a pretty fancy dress. Her bright eyes, and smiling face, looking still more sweet and fanciful. Miss Hu—d, of Charleston, was a "Cracovienne," in that costume; pink crape, over white satin; a pink satin tunic and pink hat, trimmed with black lace and looped up with pink flowers. Miss Hu—d, her sister, was in the same group, as a Swiss Peasant, and was closely followed by two Cossacks of the Don, whose fierce whiskers and moustaches, and wild eyes, seemed quite subdued by a hitherto unknown emotion. One of these Cossacks was Mr. A. M–l–r, of Charleston. The name of the other we did not learn.

Miss P–kn–y, of Charleston, came as "Twilight," a very happy personation. The dress was of white and pink tulle, with a turban of the same material, studded with stars. The dress was a very becoming one.

Mrs. P–ti–u, of the Island, wore a very rich fancy ball dress, with turban and feathers.

Mrs. R–g–r, as "Night," was a fine contrast to the more light and morning dresses of those about her. Her dress was of glowing black, rich and rare. Her veil, of raven black, was gleaming with stars, and she wore a tiara of the same burning jewels about her head. The costume was a very striking one, as if intended to realize the poetic atmosphere with which Byron seeks to clothe his oriental damsel:—

"She walks in beauty, like *the night,*
Of cloudless climes and starry skies,"

Miss R–g–r, of Charleston, was a "Soubriette," for the occasion. She wore a crimson figured skirt and black bodice, with a bewitching little cap.

Miss S–h–k–r, of Charleston, appeared as Flora, in an appropriate white dress, with straw hat and flowers; Miss W—ner, of Alabama, was very winning in the habit of a "sylph of the season," seeming to walk upon the air and in a cloud of amber; while Mrs. Sw—in, of Florida, as an Indian princess, did full justice to the forest beauties of the Apalachian.

These ladies all had hosts of attendants; a singular variety indeed of costumes, characters, nations and periods. We distinguished among them, Mr. R. P–kn–y, of Charleston, as a citizen of Herculaneum, in a rich dress; Mr. C. M—ig—t, as a member of the French Provisional Government; Mr. R. M—w—r, of Georgia, as a Texian Hunter, with hunting shirt, jaunty cap of fur, buck skin leggins, bowie knife and pistols; Mr. Geo. Re—d, of Charleston, as a Hunter also; Mr. S–on–y, as an officer of the French Republic; Mr. Sm—th, of Charleston, as an Austrian General.

Mr. J. W—k—r, in fancy dress.

Messrs. M—ns, B—e, O'H—a and Sch—ffer as members of the French Provisional Government.

Lt. W—ld, as an American Army Officer.

Mr. Sm—th, as a French Postilion, in a very attractive dress.

Mr. Sc—n and Mr. W–ld–n, as Firemen, of different companies, in full dress.

Mr. B—e, as a Marshal of France.

Mr. H–w–t, as an Italian Count.

Mr. W—, as a Field Marshal of Napoleon.

Mr. E—w—ds, as a Spanish Cavalier, and again as a Greek.

Mr. W–k–r, as a Russian Peasant.

Mr. S–m–ns, as a Castilian Cavalier; and last but not least, of those of whom we have succeeded in making a record,—

Mr. R—g—r, as a Chinese Juggler, or John Chinaman; a part which he looked and sustained equally well. His dress was quite an attractive one, and the character was performed with great vivacity.

We had thus far made our notes, when the signal for supper was given, and our work was arrested. In this way several characters escaped us. We have tried, but vainly, by the help of the recollections of others, to supply our own lack of memory. That we have omitted many we do not doubt. The omission is unintentional. The company consisted of a fraction above three hundred only; and a supper was provided which would have sufficed a thousand. Never has a supper table been set forth with better taste, more judiciously, more aptly or excellently, than on this occasion. This was due chiefly to the skill and taste of Mr. Pine, of the Moultrie House, to whom this duty was confided. He has made himself famous by its performance. Beauty, grace, variety, excellence, abundance, viands and vines, fruits, and flowers, meats and sweets, all that could delight the eye and provoke and satisfy the appetite, was spread before the brilliant assembly, from which arose one spontaneous voice of applause and congratulation. Mr. Pine and Mr. Young both deserve the highest praise for their performances on this occasion. They went to their tasks with a hearty good will, which is almost always apt to ensure success, and they infused this feeling into all their subordinates, their officers and servants. The dances were continued until a late hour, and the check to pleasure was due rather to the exhaustion of the frame than to the fatigue of the fancy, or any dulling of the edge of delight and enjoyment. No ball has ever been more succesful in making a whole company happy.

["Ephraim Bartlett, the Edisto Raftsman" was published in 1852 as an installment of "Home Sketches, or Life Along the Highways and Byways of the South," a series which Simms wrote for the Literary World, *edited by his friends, the Duyckinck brothers. Explanatory and Textual Notes begin on page 792.]*

EPHRAIM BARTLETT,
The Edisto Raftsman.

I resume my narrative. In my last, we had just hurried across the common road, once greatly travelled, leading along the Ashley, to the ancient village of Dorchester. Something was said of the fine old plantations along this river. It was the aristocratic region during the Revolution; and when the Virginians and Marylanders, at the close of the war, who had come to the succor of Carolina against the British, drew nigh to Charleston, their hearts were won and their eyes ravished, by the hospitalities and sweets of this neighborhood. Many brave fellows found their wives along this river, which was bordered by flourishing farms and plantations, and crowned by equal luxury and refinement. Here, too, dwelt many of those high-spirited and noble dames whose courage and patriotism contributed so largely to furnish that glorious chapter in Revolutionary history, which has been given to the women of that period. The scene is sadly changed at this season. The plantations along the Ashley are no longer flourishing as then. The land has fallen in value, not exhausted, but no longer fertile and populous. The health of the country is alleged to be no longer what it was. This I regard as all absurdity. The truth is that the cultivation was always inferior; and the first fertile freshness of the soil being exhausted, the opening of new lands in other regions naturally diverted a restless people from their old abodes. The river is still a broad and beautiful one, navigable for steamers and schooners up to Dorchester, which, by land, is twenty-one miles from Charleston. There is abundant means for restoring its fertility. Vast beds of marl, of the best quality, skirt the river all along the route, and there is still a forest growth sufficiently dense to afford the vegetable material necessary to the preparation of compost. As for the health of the neighborhood, I have no sort of question, that, with a dense population, addressed to farming, and adequate to a proper drainage, it would prove quite as salubrious as any portion of the country. Staple culture has been always the curse of Carolina. It has prevented thorough tillage, without which no country can ever ascertain its own resources, or be sure of its health at any time.

Cooper river, on the right, is at a greater distance from us. This, too, was a prosperous and well cultivated region in the Revolution. In a considerable degree it still remains so, and is distinguished by flourishing country seats, which their owners only occupy during spring and winter. The cultivation is chiefly rice, and the rice plantation is notoriously and fatally sickly, except among the negroes. They flourish in a climate which is death to the European. But of this river hereafter. I may persuade you, in future pages, to a special journey in this quarter, when our details and descriptions may be more specific. Between the two rivers the country is full of interest and full of game, to those who can delay to hunt for it. He who runs over the railroad only, sees nothing and can form no conception of it. A few miles further, on the right, there is a stately relic of the old British parochial establishment, a church edifice dedicated to St. James, which modern veneration has lately restored with becoming art, and re-awakened with proper rituals. Built of brick, with a richly painted interior and tesselated aisles, surrounded by patriarchal oaks, and a numerous tenantry of dead in solemn tomb and ivy-mantled monument, you almost fancy yourself in the midst of an antiquity which mocks the finger of the historian. In this neighborhood flourished a goodly population. Large estates and great wealth were associated with equally large refinement and a liberal hospitality, and the land was marked by peculiar fertility. The fertility is not wanting now, but the population is gone—influenced by similar considerations with those which stripped the sister river of its thousands.

Until late years, the game was abundant in this region. The swamps which girdled the rivers afforded a sure refuge, and the deer stole forth to the ridges between, to browse at midnight, seeking refuge in the swamps by day. We have just darted through an extensive tract named Izard's camp, which used to be famous hunting-ground for the city sportsmen. Twenty years ago I have cracked away at a group of deer, myself, in these forest pastures, and even now you may rouse the hunt profitably in the ancient ranges. There are a few sportsmen who still know where to seek with certainty for the buck at the proper season. The woods, though mostly pine, have large tracts of oak and hickory. The scrubby oak denotes a light sandy soil, of small tenacity, and, most usually, old fields which have been abandoned. Along the smaller water-courses, the creeks and branches, long strips of fertile territory may be had; and the higher swamp lands only need drainage to afford tracts of inexhaustible fertility, equal to any Mississippi bottom. The introduction of farming culture will find these and reclaim them, and restore the poorer regions.

A thousand stories of the Revolution, peculiar to this country, would reward the seeker. Nor is it wanting in other sources of interest. Traditions are abundant which belong more to the spiritual nature of the people than their national history. The poorer classes in the low country of the South were full of superstition. Poverty, for that matter, usually is so, but more particularly when it dwells in a region which is distinguished by any natural peculiarities. Thus the highlands of Scotland cherish a faith in spectral forms that rise in the mist and vapor of the mountain; and the Brownie is but the grim accompaniment of a life, that, lacking somewhat in human association, must seek its companions among the spiritual; and these must derive their aspects from the gloomy fortunes of the seeker. The Banshee of Ireland is but the finally speaking monitor of a fate that has always more or less threatened the fortunes of the declining family; and the Norwegian hunting demons are such as are equally evoked by the sports which he pursues and the necessities by which he is pursued himself. In the wild, deep, dark, and tangled masses of a Carolina swamp region, where, even by daylight, mystic shadows harbor and walk capriciously with every change of the always doubtful sunlight, the mind sees and seeks a spiritual presence, which, though it may sometimes oppress, always affords company. Here, solitude, which is the source of the spiritual and contemplative, is always to be found; and forces herself—certainly at one season of the year—upon the scattered forester and farmer. The man who lives by pursuit of the game, the deer or turkey, will be apt to conjure up, in the silent, dim avenues through which he wanders, some companion for his thought, which will, in time, become a presence to his eye; and, in the secluded toils of the farmer, on the borders of swamp and forest, he will occasionally find himself disturbed by a visitor or spectator which his own loneliness of life has extorted from his imagination, which has shaped it to a becoming aspect with the scene and climate under which he dwells. Many of these wild walkers of the wood are supposed to have been gods and spirits of the Indian tribes, who have also left startling memories behind them; and though reluctant to confess his superstitions—for the white hunter and forester dread ridicule more than anything beside —yet a proper investigation might find treasures of superstition and grim tradition among our people of this region, such as would not discredit any of the inventions of imagination.

One of these traditions occurs to me at this moment, the scene of which is at hand but a short distance from us, but not visible from the railroad. Here is not only a haunted house, but a haunted tract of forest. The tale was told me many years ago, as derived from the narrative of a raftsman of the Edisto. The Edisto, of which we may speak hereafter, is the great *lumber* river of South Carolina. Its extent is considerable, penetrating several district divisions of the State, and upon its two great arms or arteries, and its tributary creeks or branches, it owns perhaps no less than one hundred and fifty mills for sawing lumber. It supplies Charleston, by a sinuous route, almost wholly; and large shipments of its timber are made to the island of Cuba, to Virginia, and recently to New York, and other places. Its navigation is difficult, and, as it approaches the sea, somewhat perilous. Many of its rafts have been driven out to sea and lost, with all on board. It requires, accordingly, an experienced pilot to thread its intricacies, and such an one was Ephraim Bartlett, a worthy fellow, who has passed pretty much out of the memories of the present generation.

Ephraim was a good pilot of the Edisto, one of the best; but he had an unfortunate faith in whiskey, which greatly impaired his standing in society. It did not injure his reputation, however, as a pilot; since it was well known that Ephraim never drank on the voyage, but only on the return; and as this was invariably by land, no evil could accrue from his bad habit to anybody but himself. He rewarded himself for his abstinence on the river, by free indulgence when on shore. His intervals of leisure were given up wholly to his potations; and between the sale of one fleet of rafts, and the preparation for the market of another, Ephraim, I am sorry to say, was a case which would have staggered the temperance societies. But the signal once given by his employers, he would shake himself free from the evil spirit, by a plunge into the river. Purification followed —his head was soon as clear for business as ever; and, wound about with a bandanna handkerchief of flaming spot in place of a hat, it would be seen conspicuous on the raft, making for the city. With cheerful song and cry he made his way down, pole in hand, to ward off the overhanging branches of the trees, or to force aside the obstructions. Accompanied by a single negro, still remembered by many as old 'Bram Geiger, his course was usually prosperous. His lumber usually found the best market, and Ephraim and Bram, laying in their little supplies in Charleston, with a sack over their shoulders, and staff or gun in hand, would set out from the city on their return to Lexington, the district of country from which they descended. On these occasions, Ephraim never forgot his jug. This was taken with him empty on the raft, but returned filled, upon his or Bram's shoulders. They took turns in carrying it, concealing it from too officious observers by securing it in one end of the sack. In the other might be found a few clothes, and a fair supply of tobacco.

On the particular occasion when Ephraim discovered for himself that the ancient house and tract were haunted, it happened that he left the city about mid-day. It was Saturday, at twelve or one o'clock, according to his account, when they set out, laden as usual. They reached the house, which was probably twelve or thirteen miles from town, long before sundown; and might have stretched away a few miles farther, but for a cramp in the stomach, which seized upon Old 'Bram. Ephraim at once had resort to his jug, and a strong noggin was prepared for the relief of the suffering negro. At the same time, as Bram swore that he must die, that nothing could possibly save him under such sufferings as he experienced, Ephraim concluded to take lodgings temporarily in the old house, which happened to be within a few hundred yards of the spot, and to lie by for the rest of the day. The building was of brick, two stories in height, but utterly out of repair—doors and windows gone, floors destroyed, and the entire fabric within quite dismantled. It was a long time before Bram was relieved from his suffering and fright. Repeated doses of the potent beverage were necessary to a cure; and, by the time this was effected, the old fellow was asleep. In the meantime, Ephraim had built a rousing fire in the old chimney: had gathered *lightwood* (resinous pine) sufficient to keep up the fire all night; had covered the old negro with his own blanket, which he bore strapped beneath the sack upon his shoulders; and had opened his wallet of dried meat and city bread for his supper. Meanwhile, the fumes of the whiskey had ascended gratefully to his own nostrils; and it seemed only reasonable that he should indulge himself with a dram, having bestowed no less than three upon his companion. He drank accordingly, and as he had no coffee to his supper, he employed the whiskey, which he thought by no means a bad substitute. He may have swallowed three several doses in emulation of Bram, and in anticipation of a similar attack, before he had quite finished supper. He admits that he certainly drank again when his meal was ended, by way of washing down the fragments. Bram, meanwhile, with the blazing fire at his feet, continued to sleep on very comfortably. When Ephraim got to sleep is not so certain. He admits that he was kept awake till a late hour by the fumes of the whiskey, and by strange noises that reached him from the forest. He recalled to memory the bad character of the dwelling and neighborhood as haunted; and is not so sure, but thinks it possible that this recollection prompted him to take another draught, a stirrup cup, as it were, before yielding himself to sleep. But he denies that he was in any way affected by the whiskey. To use his own language, he had none of the "how-come-you-so" sensation upon him, but insists that he said his prayers, rationally, like any other Christian, put several fresh brands upon the fire, and sank into the most sober of all mortal slumbers.

I am the more particular in stating these details, since a question has been made in regard to them. Bram had his story also. He admits that he was sick, and physicked as described—that Ephraim had gathered the fuel, made the fire, and covered him with his blanket, while he slept—but he alleges that he awoke at midnight, when Ephraim himself was asleep, and being still a little distressed in the abdominal region, he proceeded to help himself out of the jug, without disturbing the repose of his comrade; and he affirms, on his honesty, that he then found the jug fully half emptied, which had been quite full when he left the city; and he insisted that, in giving him his several doses, Ephraim had always been very careful not to make them over strong. Bram admits that, when he had occasion to help himself, as the attack was still threatening, he preferred to take an over dose rather than peril his safety by mincing the matter. It is very certain, from the united testimonies of the two, the whiskey had, one half of it, most unaccountably disappeared before the night was half over. I must suffer Ephraim to tell the rest of the story for himself, and assert his own argument.

"Well, now, you see, my friends," telling his story to a group, "as I said afore, it was mighty late that night afore I shut my eyes. I reckon twarn't far from day-peep when I slipped off into a hearty sleep, and then I slept like a cat after a supper. Don't you be thinking now 'twas owing to the whiskey that I was wakeful, or that I slept so sound at last. 'Bram's troubles in the stomach made me oneasy, and them strange noises in the woods helped the matter."

"But what were the noises like, Ephraim?"

"Oh! like a'most anything and every thing. Horns a-blowing, horses a-snorting, cats a-crying, and then sich a rushing and a trampling of four-footed beasts, that I could 'a-swore it was a fox hunt for all the world. But it warn't that! No! 'Twas a hunt agin natur'. The hounds, and horses, and horns that made that racket, warn't belonging to this world. I felt suspicions about it then, and I reckon I knows it now, if such a matter ever is to be made known. Well, as I was a-saying, I got to sleep at last near upon day-light. How long I did sleep there's no telling. 'Twas mighty late when I waked, and then the noise was in my ears again. I raised myself on end, and sat up in my blanket. The fire was gone out clean, and I was a little coldish. 'Bram, the nigger, had scruged himself into the very ashes, and had quite kivered up his head in the blanket. How he drawed his breath there's no telling, since the tip of his nose warn't to be seen nowhere. Says I, ''Bram, do you hear them noises?' But never a word did he answer. Says I, to myself, 'the nigger's smothered.' So I onwrapt him mighty quick, and heard him grunt. Then I know'd there was no harm done. The nigger was only drunk."

"Nebber been drunk dat time," was the usual interruption of 'Bram, whenever he was present at the narration.

" 'Bram, you was most certainly drunk, sense I tried my best to waken you, and couldn't get you up."

"Ha! da's 'cause I bin want for sleep, so I nebber consent for ye'r (hear). I bin ye'r berry well all de time; but a man wha's bin trouble wid 'fliction in the stomach all night, mus' hab he sleep out in de morning. I bin ye'r well enough, I tell you."

"You old rascal, if I had thought so, I'd ha' chunk'd you with a lightwood knot!—but the nigger *was* asleep, my friends, in a regular drunk sleep, if ever he was; for when I hearn the noises coming nigh—the hounds and the horses—I drawed him away from the ashes by the legs, and laid him close up agin' the wall t'other side of the fire-place, and pretty much out of sight. I kivered him snug with the blanket, and let him take his sleep out, though I was beginning to be more and more jub'ous about them noises. You see, 'twas the regular noises of a deer-hunt. I could hear the drivers beating about in the thick; then the shout; then the dogs, yelping out whenever they struck upon the trail; I know'd when they nosed the cold trail, and when the scent got warm; and then I heerd the regular rush, when the deer was started, all the dogs in full blast, and making the merriest music. Then I heerd the crack of the gun—first one gun, then another, then another, and another, a matter of four shots—and I felt sure they must ha' got the meat. The horns sounded; the dogs were stopped, and, for a little while, nothing but silence. Oh! I felt awful all over, and monstrous jub'ous of something strange!"

"But why should you feel awful, and what should there be so strange about a deer-hunt near Izard's Camp—a place where you may start deer even at this day?"

"Why, 'twas Sunday, you see, and nobody now, in our times, hunts deer, or anything, a-Sundays; and it 'twan't till after midnight on Saturday that I heer'd the noises. That was enough to make me jub'ous. But when I remember'd how they used to tell me of the rich English gentleman, named Lumley, that once lived in the neighborhood, long afore the old Revolution; what a wicked man he was, and how he used to hunt a-Sundays; and how a judgment come upon him; and how he was lost, in one of his huntings, for a matter of six months or more; and when he was found, 'twas only his skeleton. Well I reckon, to think of all that, was enough to give me a bad scare—and it did. People reckoned he must have been snake-bit, for there were the bones of the snake beside him, with the rattles on, eleven and the button; he must have killed the snake after he was struck. But it didn't help him. He never got away from the spot till they found his skileton, and they know'd him by the ring upon his finger, and his knife, and horn, and gun; but all the iron was ruined, eaten up by the rust. Well, when I heer'd the horns a-Sunday, I recollected all about Squire Lumley, and his wickedness; and, before I seed anything, I was all over in a shiver. Well, presently I heerd the horns blowing merrily again, and the sounds come fresher than ever to my ears. I was oneasy enough, and I made another trial to wake up 'Bram, but 'twas of no use. He was sounder than ever."

"I 'speck I bin sleep den, for true," was the modest interruption of 'Bram, at this stage of the narrative. With a grave shake of the head, Ephraim continued—

"I went out then in front of the house, and the horns were coming nigher from behind it. I was a-thinking to run and hide in the bushes, but I was so beflustered that I was afeer'd I should run right into the jaws of the danger. Though, when I thought of the matter agin', I got a little bolder, and I said to myself, 'what's the danger, I wonder. I'm in a free country. I'm troubling no man's property. I've let down no man's fence. I've left no man's gate open to let in the cattle. This old house nobody lives in, and I wouldn't ha' troubled it, ef so be Bram hadn't been taken sick in his bowels. What's the danger?' When I thought, in this way, to myself, I went in and took a sup of whiskey—a small sup—only a taste—by way of keeping my courage up. I tried to waken Bram again, for I said, 'two's always better than one, though one's a nigger,' but 'twas no use; Bram's sleep was sounder than ever. It was pretty cl'ar that he had soak'd the whiskey mighty deep that night!"

"Ki! Mass Ephraim! How you talk! Ef you nebber been drink more than me, dat night, you nebber been scare wid de hunters dat blessed Sunday morning."

"The nigger will talk!" said Ephraim, contemptuously, as he continued his narrative.

"Well, I felt stronger after I had taken that little sup, and went out again. Just then there came a blast of the horns almost in my very ears, and in the next minute I hear'd the trampling of horses.

Soon a matter of twenty dogs burst out of the woods, and pushed directly for the house as if they knowed it; and then came the riders —five in all—four white men and one nigger. Ef I was scared at the sounds afore, the sight of these people didn't make me feel any easier. They were well enough to look at in the face, but, lord bless you, they were dressed in sich an outlandish fashion! Why, even the nigger had on short breeches, reaching only to his knees, and then stockings blue and red streaked, fitting close to his legs;—and sich a leg, all the calf turned in front, and the long part of his foot pretty much where the heel ought to be. Then he had buckles at his knees, and buckles on his shoes, jest for all the world like his master. And he wore a cap like his master, though not quite so handsome, and a great coat of bright indigo blue, with the cuffs and collar trimmed with yellow. His breeches were of a coarse buff, the same color with the gentlemen, only theirs were made with a finer article—the raal buff, I reckon. They had on red coats that were mighty pretty, and all their horns were silver mounted. Our Governor and his officers, nowadays, never had on prettier regimentals. Well, up they rode, never taking any more notice of me than ef I was a dog; and I saw the nigger throw down a fine buck from his saddle. There was only one, but he had a most powerful head of horns. While they were all getting off their horses, and the nigger was taking 'em, I turned quietly into the house ag'in to try if a kick or two could get Bram out of his blankets. But, lord have mercy, when I look in, what should I see but another nigger there spreading a table with a cloth as white as the driven snow, and a-setting plates, and knives, and forks, and spoons, and bottles, and salt, and pepper, and mustard, and horse-radish, all as ef he had a cupboard somewhere at his hand. I was amazed, and worse than amazed, when I seed my own jug among the other things. But I hadn't the heart to touch it. For that matter, the nigger that was setting out the things kept as sharp an eye upon me as ef I was a thief. But soon the dishes began to show upon the table. There were the pots upon the fire, the gridiron, the Dutch oven, and everything, and the most rousing fire, and Bram still asleep in the corner, and knowing nothing about it. I was all over in a sweat. Soon, the gentlemen began to come in, but they took no sort of notice of me; and I slipped out and looked at their horses; but as the nigger was standing by 'em, and looking so strange, I didn't go too nigh. But the deer was still a-lying where he first threw it, and I thought I'd turn the head over and see the critter fairly, when, as I'm a living man, the antlers slipped through my fingers jest as fast as I tried to take 'em,—like so much water or smoke. There was a feel to me as ef I had touched something, but I couldn't take hold no how, and while I was a-trying, the nigger holla'd, in a gruff voice, from the horses—'Don't you touch Maussa's meat!' I was getting desp'rate mighty fast, and I thought I'd push back, and try what good another sup of whiskey would do. Well, when I went into the house, the gentlemen were all a-setting round the table, and busy with knife and fork, jest as ef they were the commonest people. There was a mighty smart chance for feeding at the table. Ham and turkey, a pair of as fine wild ducks, English, as you ever seed; a beef tongue, potetters (potatoes), cabbage, eggs, and other matters, and all for jest five men and their servants. Jest then, one of the gentlemen set his eyes on me, and p'inted to one of the bottles—says he, jest as if I had been his own servant—

"'Hand the bottle.'

"And somehow, I felt as ef I couldn't help myself, but must hand it, sure enough. When he had poured out the liquor, which was a mighty deep red, yet clear as the sunshine, he gin me back the bottle, and I thought I'd take a taste of the stuff, jest to see what it was. I got a chance, and poured out a tolerable dram—supposing it was a sort of red bald face (whiskey)—into a cup and tossed it off in a twinkle. But it warn't bald face, nor brandy, nor wine, nor any liquor that I ever know'd before. It hadn't a strong taste, but was something like a cordial, with a flavor like fruit and essence. 'Twarn't strong, I say; so I tried it ag'in an' ag'in, whenever I could git a chance; for I rather liked the flavor; and I warn't mealy-mouthed at helping myself, as they had enough of the critter, and, by this time, they had begun upon my own old bald-face. They seemed to like it well enough. They tried it several times, as if 'twas something new to them, and they didn't find it hard to make the acquaintance. I didn't quarrel with them, you may be sure, for I never was begrudgeful of my liquor; and, besides, wasn't I trying their'n? Well, I can't tell you how long this lasted. 'Twas a good while; and they kept me busy; one after the other on 'em calling out to me to hand 'em this, and hand 'em that, and even the nigger motioning me to help him with this thing and the other. He didn't say much, and always spoke in a whisper. But, it so happened, that, when I was stretching out for one of the bottles, to try another taste of the cordial, one of the cursed dogs would come always in my way. At last, I gin the beast a kick; and, would you believe it, my foot went clean through him—through skin, and ribs, and body, jest the same as if I had kicked the wind or the water. I did not feel him with my foot. I was all over in a trimble; and the dog yelped, jest as if I had hurt him. Sure enough, at this, the great dark-favored man that sot at the head of the table, he fastened his eye upon me and said in a big threatening voice:

"'Who kick'd my dog?'

"By this time, my blood was up a little. What with the scare I had, and the stuff I'd been a-drinking, I felt a little desperate; and my eye was sot upon the man pretty bold as I said:

"'I was just reaching for my own liquor,'—(now, that warn't exactly true, I confess, for I was reaching for one of their own bottles) —'when the dog came in my way, and I just brushed him with my foot.'

"'Nobody shall kick my dog but myself,' said he, more fierce than ever; and looking as if he meant kicking! That made me a sort o' wolfish, and, just then, something put the old story of Lumley and the rattlesnake fresh into my head; and, I couldn't help myself—but I gin him for answer as nice an imitation of a snake's rattle—you know how well I kin do it, my friends—as ever he heerd in his born days.

"Lord! you should have seen the stir and heard the racket. Every fellow was on his feet in a minnit, and before I could dodge, the great dark-featured man, he rose up, and seized my jug by the handle, and whirled it furious about his head, and then he sent it at me, with such a curse, and such a cry, that I thought all the house a-tumbling to pieces. Like a great wind, they all rushed by me, men and dogs, and nigger, throwing me down in the door-way, and going over me as ef I was nothing in the way. Whether it was the jug that hit me, or them rushing over, and trampling me down, I can't say; but there I lay, pretty much stunned and stupified; not knowing anything for a long time;—and when I opened my eyes, and could look around me, there I was with Bram stooping over me and trying to raise me from the ground."

"*Dat's* true!" said Bram, laying special emphasis on *dat's* (that's) and shaking his head significantly. Ephraim continued:

"The strangers were all gone in the twinkling of an eye,—they had swept the platters,—carried off every thing clean,—carried off tables and chairs, bottles and cups, plates and dishes, dinner and drink, pots and ovens, and had even put out the fire; sence, when Bram waked up, there was not a sign of it to be seen. My jug was broke all to pieces, and lying beside me at the door, and not a drop of liquor to be had. What they didn't drink, they wasted, the spiteful divels, when they broke the jug over my head."

Such was Ephraim's story, grown into a faith with many, of the Haunted Forest and House near Izard's Camp. In Ephraim's presence, Bram does not venture to deny a syllable of the story. He only professes to have seen nothing of it, except the full jug when they arrived at the house, and the broken and empty vessel when he awoke from his sleep. In Ephraim's absence, however, he does not scruple to express his doubts wholly of the ghostly visitors and the strange liquor. His notion is, that Ephraim got drunk upon the "*bald-face*" (whiskey) and dreamed the rest. His only subject of difficulty is that the jug should have been broken. He denies, for himself, that he took a drop too much—considering the state of his stomach.—We must resume our journey hereafter.

[*"How Sharp Snaffles Got His Capital and Wife" was published posthumously in* Harper's Magazine *for October, 1870. Explanatory and Textual Notes begin on page 794.*]

HOW SHARP SNAFFLES GOT HIS CAPITAL AND WIFE.

I.

The day's work was done, and a good day's work it was. We had bagged a couple of fine bucks and a fat doe; and now we lay camped at the foot of the "Balsam Range" of mountains in North Carolina, preparing for our supper. We were a right merry group of seven; four professional hunters, and three amateurs—myself among the latter. There was Jim Fisher, Aleck Wood, Sam or Sharp Snaffles, *alias* "Yaou," and Nathan Langford, *alias* the "Pious."

These were our *professional* hunters. Our *amateurs* may well continue nameless, as their achievements do not call for any present record. Enough that we had gotten up the "camp hunt," and provided all the creature comforts except the fresh meat. For this we were to look to the mountain ranges and the skill of our hunters.

These were all famous fellows with the rifle—moving at a trot along the hill-sides, and with noses quite as keen of scent as those of their hounds in rousing deer and bear from their deep recesses among the mountain laurels.

A week had passed with us among these mountain ranges, some sixty miles beyond what the conceited world calls "civilization."

Saturday night had come; and, this Saturday night closing a week of exciting labors, we were to carouse.

We were prepared for it. There stood our tent pitched at the foot of the mountains, with a beautiful cascade leaping headlong toward us, and subsiding into a mountain runnel, and finally into a little lakelet, the waters of which, edged with perpetual foam, were as clear as crystal.

Our baggage wagon, which had been sent round to meet us by trail routes through the gorges, stood near the tent, which was of stout army canvas.

That baggage wagon held a variety of luxuries. There was a barrel of the best bolted wheat flour. There were a dozen choice hams, a sack of coffee, a keg of sugar, a few thousand of cigars, and last, not least, a corpulent barrel of Western uisquebaugh,* vulgarly, "whisky;" to say nothing of a pair of demijohns of equal dimensions, one containing peach brandy of mountain manufacture, the other the luscious honey from the mountain hives.

Well, we had reached Saturday night. We had hunted day by day from the preceding Monday with considerable success—bagging some game daily, and camping nightly at the foot of the mountains. The season was a fine one. It was early winter, October, and the long ascent to the top of the mountains was through vast fields of green, the bushes still hanging heavy with their huckleberries.

From the summits we had looked over into Tennessee, Virginia, Georgia, North and South Carolina. In brief, to use the language of Natty Bumppo, we beheld "Creation." We had crossed the "Blue Ridge;" and the descending water-courses, no longer seeking the Atlantic, were now gushing headlong down the western slopes, and hurrying to lose themselves in the Gulf Stream and the Mississippi.

From the eyes of fountains within a few feet of each other we had blended our *eau de vie* with limpid waters which were about to part company forever—the one leaping to the rising, the other to the setting of the sun.

And buoyant, full of fun, with hearts of ease, limbs of health and strength, plenty of venison, and a wagon full of good things, we welcomed the coming of Saturday night as a season not simply of rest, but of a royal carouse. We were decreed to make a night of it.

But first let us see after our venison.

The deer, once slain, is, as soon after as possible, clapped upon the fire. All the professional hunters are good butchers and admirable cooks—of bear and deer meat at least. I doubt if they could spread a table to satisfy Delmonico; but even Delmonico might take some lessons from them in the preparation for the table of the peculiar game which they pursue, and the meats on which they feed. We,

* "Uisquebaugh," or the "water of life," is Irish. From the word we have dropped the last syllable. Hence we have "uisque," or, as it is commonly written, "whisky"—a very able-bodied man-servant, but terrible as a mistress or housekeeper.

at least, rejoice at the supper prospect before us. Great collops hiss in the frying-pan, and finely cut steaks redden beautifully upon the flaming coals. Other portions of the meat are subdued to the stew, and make a very delightful dish. The head of the deer, including the brains, is put upon a flat rock in place of gridiron, and thus baked before the fire—being carefully watched and turned until every portion has duly imbibed the necessary heat, and assumed the essential hue which it should take to satisfy the eye of appetite. This portion of the deer is greatly esteemed by the hunters themselves; and the epicure of genuine stomach for the *haut gout* takes to it as an eagle to a fat mutton, and a hawk to a young turkey.

The rest of the deer—such portions of it as are not presently consumed or needed for immediate use—is cured for future sale or consumption; being smoked upon a scaffolding raised about four feet above the ground, under which, for ten or twelve hours, a moderate fire will be kept up.

Meanwhile the hounds are sniffing and snuffing around, or crouched in groups, with noses pointed at the roast and broil and bake; while their great liquid eyes dilate momently while watching for the huge gobbets which they expect to be thrown to them from time to time from the hands of the hunters.

Supper over, and it is Saturday night. It is the night dedicated among the professional hunters to what is called "The Lying Camp!"

"The Lying Camp!" quoth Columbus Mills, one of our party, a wealthy mountaineer, of large estates, of whom I have been for some time the guest.

"What do you mean by the 'Lying Camp,' Columbus?"

The explanation soon followed.

Saturday night is devoted by the mountaineers engaged in a camp hunt, which sometimes contemplates a course of several weeks, to stories of their adventures—"long yarns"—chiefly relating to the objects of their chase, and the wild experiences of their professional life. The hunter who actually inclines to exaggeration is, at such a period, privileged to deal in all the extravagances of invention; nay, he is *required* to do so! To be literal, or confine himself to the bald and naked truth, is not only discreditable, but a *finable* offense! He is, in such a case, made to swallow a long, strong, and difficult potation! He can not be too extravagant in his incidents; but he is also required to exhibit a certain degree of *art,* in their use; and he thus frequently rises into a certain realm of fiction, the ingenuities of which are made to compensate for the exaggerations, as they do in the "Arabian Nights," and other Oriental romances.

This will suffice for explanation.

Nearly all our professional hunters assembled on the present occasion were tolerable *raconteurs.* They complimented Jim Fisher, by throwing the raw deer-skin over his shoulders; tying the antlers of the buck with a red handkerchief over his forehead; seating him on the biggest boulder which lay at hand; and, sprinkling him with a stoup of whisky, they christened him "The Big Lie," for the occasion. And in this character he complacently presided during the rest of the evening, till the company prepared for sleep, which was not till midnight. He was king of the feast.

It was the duty of the "Big Lie" to regulate proceedings, keep order, appoint the *raconteurs* severally, and admonish them when he found them foregoing their privileges, and narrating bald, naked, and uninteresting truth. They must deal in fiction.

Jim Fisher was seventy years old, and a veteran hunter, the most famous in all the country. He *looked* authority, and promptly began to assert it, which he did in a single word:

"Yaou!"

II.

"Yaou" was the *nom de nique* of one of the hunters, whose proper name was Sam Snaffles, but who, from his special smartness, had obtained the farther sobriquet of "*Sharp* Snaffles."

Columbus Mills whispered me that he was called "Yaou" from his frequent use of that word, which, in the Choctaw dialect, simply means "Yes." Snaffles had rambled considerably among the Choctaws, and picked up a variety of their words, which he was fond of using in preference to the vulgar English; and his common use of "*Yaou,*" for the affirmative, had prompted the substitution of it for his own name. He answered to the name.

"Ay—yee, Yaou," was the response of Sam. "I was *afeard,* 'Big Lie,' that you'd be hitching me up the very first in your team."

"And what was you afeard of? You knows as well how to take up a crooked trail as the very best man among us; so you go ahead and spin your thread a'ter the best fashion."

"What shill it be?" asked Snaffles, as he mixed a calabash full of peach and honey, preparing evidently for a long yarn.

"Give 's the history of how you got your capital, Yaou!" was the cry from two or more.

"O Lawd! I've tell'd that so often, fellows, that I'm afeard you'll sleep on it; and then agin, I've tell'd it so often I've clean forgot how it goes. Somehow it changes a leetle every time I tells it."

"Never you mind! The Jedge never haird it, I reckon, for one; and I'm not sure that Columbus Mills ever did."

So the "Big Lie."

The "Jedge" was the *nom de guerre* which the hunters had conferred upon me; looking, no doubt, to my venerable aspect--for I had traveled considerably beyond my teens—and the general dignity of my bearing.

"Yaou," like other bashful beauties in oratory and singing, was disposed to hem and haw, and affect modesty and indifference, when he was brought up suddenly by the stern command of the "Big Lie," who cried out:

"Don't make yourself an etarnal fool, Sam Snaffles, by twisting your mouth out of shape, making all sorts of redickilous ixcuses. Open upon the trail at onst and give tongue, or, dern your digestion, but I'll fine you to hafe a gallon at a single swallow!"

Nearly equivalent to what Hamlet says to the conceited player:

> "Leave off your damnable faces and begin."

Thus adjured with a threat, Sam Snaffles swallowed his peach and honey at a gulp, hemmed thrice lustily, put himself into an attitude, and began as follows. I shall adopt his language as closely as possible; but it is not possible, in any degree, to convey any adequate idea of his *manner,* which was admirably appropriate to the subject matter. Indeed, the fellow was a born actor.

III.

"You see, Jedge," addressing me especially as the distinguished stranger, "I'm a telling this hyar history of mine jest to please *you,* and I'll try to please you ef I kin. These fellows hyar have hearn it so often that they knows all about it jest as well as I do my own self, and they knows the truth of it all, and would swear to it afore any hunters' court in all the county, ef so be the affidavy was to be tooken in camp and on a Saturday night.

"You see then, Jedge, it's about a dozen or fourteen years ago, when I was a young fellow without much beard on my chin, though I was full grown as I am now—strong as a horse, ef not quite so big as a buffalo. I was then jest a-beginning my 'prenticeship to the hunting business, and looking to sich persons as the 'Big Lie' thar to show me how to take the track of b'ar, buck, and painther.

"But I confess I weren't a-doing much. I hed a great deal to l'arn, and I reckon I miss'd many more bucks than I ever hit—that is, jest up to that time—"

"Look you, Yaou," said "Big Lie," interrupting him, "you're gitting too close upon the etarnal stupid truth! All you've been a-saying is jest nothing but the naked truth as I knows it. Jest crook your trail!"

"And how's a man to lie decently onless you lets him hev a bit of truth to go upon? The truth's nothing but a peg in the wall that I hangs the lie upon. A'ter a while I promise that you sha'n't see the peg."

"Worm along, Yaou!"

"Well, Jedge, I warn't a-doing much among the *bucks* yit—jest for the reason that I was quite too eager in the scent a'ter a sartin *doe!* Now, Jedge, you never seed my wife—my Merry Ann, as I calls her; and ef you was to see her *now*—though she's prime grit yit—you would never believe that, of all the womankind in all these mountains, she was the very yaller flower of the forest; with the reddest rose cheeks you ever did see, and sich a mouth, and sich bright curly hair, and so tall, and so slender, and so all over beautiful! O Lawd! when I thinks of it and them times, I don't see how 'twas possible to think of buck-hunting when thar was sich a doe, with sich eyes shining me on!

"Well, Jedge, Merry Ann was the only da'ter of Jeff Hopson and Keziah Hopson, his wife, who was the da'ter of Squire Claypole, whose wife was Margery Clough, that lived down upon Pacolet River—"

"Look you, Yaou, ain't you gitting into them derned facts agin, eh?"

"I reckon I em, 'Big Lie!' Scuse me: I'll kiver the pegs *direct-lie,* one a'ter t'other. Whar was I? Ah! Oh! Well, Jedge, poor hunter and poor man—jest, you see, a squatter on the side of a leetle bit of a mountain close on to Columbus Mills, at Mount Tryon, I was all the time on a hot trail a'ter Merry Ann Hopson. I went thar to see her a'most every night; and sometimes I carried a buck for the old people, and sometimes a doe-skin for the gal, and I do think, bad hunter as I then was, I pretty much kept the fambly in deer meat through the whole winter."

"Good for you, Yaou! You're a-coming to it! That's the only fair trail of a lie that you've struck yit!"

So the "Big Lie," from the chair.

"Glad to hyar you say so," was the answer. "I'll git on in time! Well, Jedge, though Jeff Hopson was glad enough to git my meat always, he didn't affection me, as I did his da'ter. He was a sharp, close, money-loving old fellow, who was always considerate of the main chaince; and the old lady, his wife, who hairdly dare say her soul was her own, she jest looked both ways, as I may say, for Sunday, never giving a fair look to me or my chainces, when his eyes were sot on *her.* But 'twa'n't so with my Merry Ann. She hed the eyes for me from the beginning, and soon she hed the feelings; and, you see, Jedge, we sometimes did git a chaince, when old Jeff was gone from home, to come to a sort of onderstanding about our feelings; and the long and the short of it was that Merry Ann confessed to me that she'd like nothing better than to be my wife. She liked no other man but me. Now, Jedge, a'ter that, what was a young fellow to do? That, I say, was the proper kind of incouragement. So I said, 'I'll ax your daddy.' Then she got scary, and said, 'Oh, don't; for somehow, Sam, I'm a-thinking daddy don't like you enough *yit.* Jest hold on a bit, and come often, and bring him venison, and try to make him laugh, which you kin do, you know, and a'ter a time you kin try him.' And so I did—or rether I didn't. I put off the axing. I come constant. I brought venison all the time, and b'ar meat a plenty, a'most three days in every week."

"That's it, Yaou. You're on trail. That's as derned a lie as you've tell'd yit; for all your hunting, in them days, didn't git more meat than you could eat your one self."

"Thank you, 'Big Lie.' I hopes I'll come up in time to the right measure of the camp.

"Well, Jedge, this went on for a long time, a'most the whole winter, and spring, and summer, till the winter begun to come in agin. I carried 'em the venison, and Merry Ann meets me in the woods, and we hes sich a pleasant time when we meets on them little odd chainces that I gits hot as thunder to bring the business to a sweet honey finish.

"But Merry Ann keeps on scary, and she puts me off; ontil, one day, one a'ternoon, about sundown, she meets me in the woods, and she's all in a flusteration. And she ups and tells me how old John Grimstead, the old bachelor (a fellow about forty years old, and the dear gal not yet twenty), how he's a'ter her, and bekaise he's got a good fairm, and mules and horses, how her daddy's giving him the open mouth incouragement.

"Then I says to Merry Ann:

"'You sees, I kain't put off no longer. I must out with it, and ax your daddy at onst.' And then her scary fit come on again, and she begs me not to—not *jist yit.* But I swears by all the Hokies that I won't put off another day; and so, as I haird the old man was in the house that very hour, I left Merry Ann in the woods, all in a trimbling, and I jist went ahead, detarmined to have the figure made straight, whether odd or even.

"And Merry Ann, poor gal, she wrings her hainds, and cries a smart bit, and she wouldn't go to the house, but said she'd wait for me out thar. So I gin her a kiss into her very mouth—and did it over more than onst—and I left her, and pushed headlong for the house.

"I was jubous; I was mighty oncertain, and a leetle bit scary myself; for, you see, old Jeff was a fellow of tough grit, and with big grinders; but I was so oneasy, and so tired out waiting, and so desperate, and so fearsome that old bachelor Grimstead would get the start on me, that nothing could stop me now, and I jist bolted into the house, as free and easy and bold as ef I was the very best customer that the old man wanted to see."

Here Yaou paused to renew his draught of peach and honey.

IV.

"Well, Jedge, as I tell you, I put a bold face on the business, though my hairt was gitting up into my throat, and I was almost a-gasping for my breath, when I was fairly in the big room, and standing up before the old Squaire. He was a-setting in his big squar hide-bottom'd arm-chair, looking like a jedge upon the bench, jist about to send a poor fellow to the gallows. As he seed me come in, looking queer enough, I reckon, his mouth put on a sort of grin, which showed all his grinders, and he looked for all the world as ef he guessed the business I come about. But he said, good-natured enough:

"'Well, Sam Snaffles, how goes it?'

"Says I:

"'Pretty squar, considerin'. The winter's coming on fast, and I reckon the mountains will be full of meat before long.'

"Then says he, with another ugly grin, 'Ef 'twas your smoke-house that had it all, Sam Snaffles, 'stead of the mountains, 'twould be better for you, I reckon.'

"'I 'grees with you,' says I. 'But I rether reckon I'll git my full shar' of it afore the spring of the leaf agin.'

"'Well, Sam,' says he, 'I hopes, for your sake, 'twill be a big shar'. I'm afeard you're not the pusson to go for a big shar', Sam Snaffles. Seems to me you're too easy satisfied with a small shar'; sich as the fence-squarrel carries onder his two airms, calkilating only on a small corn-crib in the chestnut-tree.'

"'Don't you be afeard, Squaire. I'll come out right. My cabin sha'n't want for nothing that a strong man with a stout hairt kin git, with good working—enough and more for himself, and perhaps another pusson.'

"'What other pusson?' says he, with another of his great grins, and showing of his grinders.

"'Well,' says I, 'Squaire Hopson, that's jest what I come to talk to you about this blessed Friday night.'

"You see *'twas* Friday!

"'Well,' says he, 'go ahead, Sam Snaffles, and empty your brain-basket as soon as you kin, and I'll light my pipe while I'm a-hearing you.'

"So he lighted his pipe, and laid himself back in his chair, shet his eyes, and begin to puff like blazes.

"By this time my blood was beginning to bile in all my veins, for I seed that he was jest in the humor to tread on all my toes, and then ax a'ter my feelings. I said to myself:

"'It's jest as well to git the worst at onst, and then thar'll be an eend of the oneasiness.' So I up and told him, in pretty soft, smooth sort of speechifying, as how I was mighty fond of Merry Ann, and she, I was a-thinking, of me; and that I jest come to ax ef I might hev Merry Ann for my wife.

"Then he opened his eyes wide, as ef he never ixpected to hear sich a proposal from me.

"'What!' says he. 'You?'

"'Jest so, Squaire,' says I. 'Ef it pleases you to believe me, and to consider it reasonable, the axing.'

"He sot quiet for a minit or more, then he gits up, knocks all the fire out of his pipe on the chimney, fills it, and lights it agin, and then comes straight up to me, whar I was a-setting on the chair in front of him, and without a word he takes the collar of my coat betwixt the thumb and forefinger of his left hand, and he says:

"'Git up, Sam Snaffles. Git up, ef you please.'

"Well, I gits up, and he says:

"'Hyar! Come! Hyar!'

"And with that he leads me right across the room to a big looking-glass that hung agin the partition wall, and thar he stops before the glass, facing it and holding me by the collar all the time.

"Now that looking-glass, Jedge, was about the biggest I ever did see! It was a'most three feet high, and a'most two feet wide, and it had a bright, broad frame, shiny like gold, with a heap of leetle figgers worked all round it. I reckon thar's no sich glass now in all the mountain country. I 'member when first that glass come home. It was a great thing, and the old Squaire was mighty proud of it. He bought it at the sale of some rich man's furniter, down at Greenville, and he was jest as fond of looking into it as a young gal, and whenever he lighted his pipe, he'd walk up and down the room, seeing himself in the glass.

"Well, thar he hed me up, both on us standing in front of this glass, whar we could a'most see the whole of our full figgers, from head to foot.

"And when we hed stood thar for a minit or so, he says, quite solemn like:

"'Look in the glass, Sam Snaffles.'

"So I looked.

"'Well,' says I. 'I sees you, Squaire Hopson, and myself, Sam Snaffles.'

"'Look good,' says he, '*obzarve* well.'

"'Well,' says I, 'I'm a-looking with all my eyes. I only sees what I tells you.'

"'But you don't *obzarve*,' says he. 'Looking and seeing's one thing,' says he, 'but obzarving's another. Now *obzarve*.'

"By this time, Jedge, I was getting sort o' riled, for I could see that somehow he was jest a-trying to make me feel redickilous. So I says:

"'Look you, Squaire Hopson, ef you thinks I never seed myself in a glass afore this, you're mighty mistaken. I've got my own glass at home, and though it's but a leetle sort of a small, mean consarn, it shows me as much of my own face and figger as I cares to see at any time. I never cares to look in it 'cept when I'm brushing, and combing, and clipping off the straggling beard when it's too long for my eating.'

"'Very well,' says he; 'now obzarve! You sees your own figger, and your face, and you air obzarving as well as you know how. Now, Mr. Sam Snaffles—now that you've hed a fair look at yourself—jest now answer me, from your honest conscience, a'ter all you've seed, ef you honestly thinks you're the sort of pusson to hev *my* da'ter!'

"And with that he gin me a twist, and when I wheeled round he hed wheeled round too, and thar we stood, full facing one another.

"Lawd! how I was riled! But I answered, quick:

"'And why not, I'd like to know, Squaire Hopson? I ain't the handsomest man in the world, but I'm not the ugliest; and folks don't generally consider me at all among the uglies. I'm as tall a man as you, and as stout and strong, and as good a man o' my inches as ever stepped in shoe-leather. And it's enough to tell you, Squaire, whatever *you* may think, that Merry Ann believes in me, and she's a way of thinking that I'm jest about the very pusson that ought to hev her.'

"'Merry Ann's thinking,' says he, 'don't run all fours with her fayther's thinking. I axed you, Sam Snaffles, to *obzarve* yourself in the glass. I telled you that seeing warn't edzactly obzarving. You seed only the inches; you seed that you hed eyes and mouth and nose and the airms and legs of the man. But eyes and mouth and legs and airms don't make a man!'

"'Oh, they don't!' says I.

"'No, indeed,' says he. 'I seed that you hed all them; but then I seed thar was one thing that you hedn't got.'

"'Jimini!' says I, mighty conflustered. 'What thing's a-wanting to me to make me a man?'

"'*Capital!*' says he, and he lifted himself up and looked mighty grand.

"'Capital!' says I; 'and what's that?'

"'Thar air many kinds of capital,' says he. 'Money's capital, for it kin buy every thing. House and lands is capital; cattle and horses and sheep—when thar's enough on 'em—is capital. And as I obzarved you in the glass, Sam Snaffles, I seed that *capital* was the very thing that you wanted to make a man of you! Now I don't mean that any da'ter of mine shall marry a pusson that's not a *parfect* man. I obzarved you long ago, and seed whar you was wanting. I axed about you. I axed your horse.'

"'Axed my horse!' says I, pretty nigh dumfoundered.

"'Yes; I axed your horse, and he said to me: "Look at me! I hain't got an ounce of spar' flesh on my bones. You kin count all my ribs. You kin lay the whole length of your airm betwixt any two on 'em, and it 'll lie thar as snug as a black snake betwixt two poles of a log-house." Says he, "Sam's got *no capital!* He ain't got, any time, five bushels of corn in his crib; and he's such a monstrous feeder himself that he'll eat out four bushels, and think it mighty hard upon him to give *me* the other one." Thar, now, was your horse's testimony, Sam, agin you. Then I axed about your cabin, and your way of living. I was curious, and went to see you one day when I knowed you waur at home. You hed but one chair, which you gin me to set on, and you sot on the eend of a barrel for yourself. You gin me a rasher of bacon what hedn't a streak of fat in it. You hed a poor quarter of a poor doe hanging from the rafters—a poor beast that somebody hed disabled—'

"'I shot it myself,' says I.

"'Well, it was a-dying when you shot it; and all the hunters say you was a poor shooter at any thing. You cooked our dinner yourself, and the hoe-cake was all dough, not hafe done, and the meat was all done as tough as ef you had dried it for a month of Sundays in a Flurriday sun! Your cabin had but one room, and that you slept in and ate in; and the floor was six inches deep in dirt! Then, when I looked into your garden, I found seven stalks of long collards only, every one seven foot high, with all the leaves stript off it, as ef you wanted 'em for broth; till thar waur only three top leaves left on every stalk. You hedn't a stalk of corn growing, and when I scratched at your turnip-bed I found nothing bigger than a chestnut. Then, Sam, I begun to ask about your fairm, and I found that you was nothing but a squatter on land of Columbus Mills, who let you have an old nigger pole-house, and an acre or two of land. Says I to myself, says I, "This poor fellow's got *no capital;* and he hasn't the head to git *capital;*" and from that moment, Sam Snaffles, the more I obzarved you, the more sartin 'twas that you never could be a man, ef you waur to live a thousand years. You may think, in your vanity, that you air a man; but you ain't, and never will be, onless you kin find a way to git *capital;* and I loves my gal child too much to let her marry any pusson whom I don't altogether consider a man!'

"A'ter that long speechifying, Jedge, you might ha' ground me up in a mill, biled me down in a pot, and scattered me over a manure heap, and I wouldn't ha' been able to say a word!

"I cotched up my hat, and was a-gwine, when he said to me, with his derned infernal big grin:

"'Take another look in the glass, Sam Snaffles, and obzarve well, and you'll see jest whar it is I thinks that you're wanting.'

"I didn't stop for any more. I jest bolted, like a hot shot out of a shovel, and didn't know my own self, or whatever steps I tuk, tell I got into the thick and met Merry Ann coming towards me.

"I must liquor now!"

V.

"Well, Jedge, it was a hard meeting betwixt me and Merry Ann. The poor gal come to me in a sort of run, and hairdly drawing her breath, she cried out:

"'Oh, Sam! What does he say?'

"What could I say? How tell her? I jest wrapped her up in my airms, and I cries out, making some violent remarks about the old Squaire.

"Then she screamed, and I hed to squeeze her up, more close than ever, and kiss her, I reckon, more than a dozen times, jest to keep her from gwine into historical fits. I telled her all, from beginning to eend.

"I telled her that thar waur some truth in what the old man said: that I hedn't been keerful to do the thing as I ought; that the house *was* mean and dirty; that the horse was mean and poor; that I hed been thinking too much about her own self to think about other things; but that I would do better, would see to things, put things right, git corn in the crib, git 'capital,' ef I could, and make a good, comfortable home for *her*.

"'Look at me,' says I, 'Merry Ann. Does I look like a man?'

"'You're are all the man I wants,' says she.

"'That's enough,' says I. 'You shall see what I kin do, and what I *will* do! That's ef you air true to me.'

"'I'll be true to you, Sam,' says she.

"'And you won't think of nobody else?'

"'Never,' says she.

"'Well, you'll see what I kin do, and what I *will* do. You'll see that I *em* a man; and ef thar's capital to be got in all the country, by working and hunting, and fighting, ef that's needful, we shill hev it. Only you be true to me, Merry Ann.'

"And she throwed herself upon my buzzom, and cried out:

"'I'll be true to you, Sam. I loves nobody in all the world so much as I loves you.'

"'And you won't marry any other man, Merry Ann, no matter what your daddy says?'

"'Never,' she says.

"'And you won't listen to this old bachelor fellow, Grimstead, that's got the "capital" already, no matter how they spurs you?'

"'Never!' she says.

"'Sw'ar it!' says I—'sw'ar it, Merry Ann—that you will be my wife, and never marry Grimstead!'

"'I sw'ars it,' she says, kissing *me*, bekaize we had no book.

"'Now,' says I, 'Merry Ann, that's not enough. Cuss him for my sake, and to make it sartin. Cuss that fellow Grimstead.'

"'Oh, Sam, I kain't cuss,' says she; 'that's wicked.'

"'Cuss him on my account,' says I—'to my credit.'

"'Oh,' says she, 'don't ax me. I kain't do that.'

"Says I, 'Merry Ann, if you don't cuss that fellow, some way, I do believe you'll go over to him a'ter all. Jest you cuss him, now. Any small cuss will do, ef you're in airnest.'

"'Well,' says she, 'ef that's your idee, then I says, *"Drot his skin,"** and drot *my* skin, too, ef ever I marries any body but Sam Snaffles."'

"'That 'll do, Merry Ann,' says I. 'And now I'm easy in my soul and conscience. And now, Merry Ann, I'm gwine off to try my best, and git the "capital." Ef it's the "capital" that's needful to make a man of me, I'll git it, by all the Holy Hokies, if I kin.'

"And so, after a million of squeezes and kisses, we parted; and she slipt along through the woods, the back way to the house, and I mounted my horse to go to my cabin. But, afore I mounted the beast, I gin him a dozen kicks in his ribs, jest for bearing his testimony agin me, and telling the old Squaire that I hedn't 'capital' enough for a corn crib."

VI.

"I was mightily let down, as you may think, by old Squaire Hopson; but I was mightily lifted up by Merry Ann.

"But when I got to my cabin, and seed how mean every thing was there, and thought how true it was, all that old Squaire Hopson had said, I felt overkim, and I said to myself, 'It's all true! How kin I bring that beautiful yaller flower of the forest to live in sich a mean cabin, and with sich poor accommydations? She that had every thing comforting and nice about her.'

* "Drot," or "Drat," has been called an American vulgarism, but it is genuine old English, as ancient as the days of Ben Jonson. Originally the oath was, "God rot it;" but Puritanism, which was unwilling to take the name of God in vain, was yet not prepared to abandon the oath, so the pious preserved it in an abridged form, omitting the G from God, and using, "Od rot it." It reached its final contraction, "Drot," before it came to America. "Drot it," "Drat it," "Drot your eyes," or "Drot his skin," are so many modes of using it among the uneducated classes.

"Then I considered all about 'capital;' and it growed on me, ontil I begin to see that a man might hev good legs and arms and thighs, and a good face of his own, and yit not be a parfect and proper man a'ter all! I hed lived, you see, Jedge, to be twenty-three years of age, and was living no better than a three-old-year b'ar, in a sort of cave, sleeping on shuck and straw, and never looking after to-morrow.

"I couldn't sleep all that night for the thinking, and obzarvations. That impudent talking of old Hopson put me on a new track. I couldn't give up hunting. I knowed no other business, and I didn't hafe know that.

"I thought to myself, 'I must l'arn my business so as to work like a master.'

"But then, when I considered how hard it was, how slow I was to git the deers and the b'ar, and what a small chaince of money it brought me, I said to myself:

"'Whar's the "capital" to come from?'

"Lawd save us! I ate up the meat pretty much as fast as I got it!

"Well, Jedge, as I said, I had a most miserable night of consideration and obzarvation and concatenation accordingly. I felt all over mean, 'cept now and then, when I thought of dear Merry Ann, and her felicities and cordialities and fidelities; and then, the cuss which she gin, onder the kiver of 'Drot,' to that dried up old bachelor Grimstead. But I got to sleep at last. And I hed a dream. And I thought I seed the prettiest woman critter in the world, next to Merry Ann, standing close by my bedside; and, at first, I thought 'twas Merry Ann, and I was gwine to kiss her agin; but she drawed back and said:

"'Scuse me! I'm not Merry Ann; but I'm her friend and your friend; so don't you be down in the mouth, but keep a good hairt, and you'll hev help, and git the "capital" whar you don't look for it now. It's only needful that you be detarmined on good works and making a man of yourself.'

"A'ter that dream I slept like a top, woke at day-peep, took my rifle, called up my dog, mounted my horse, and put out for the laurel hollows.

"Well, I hunted all day, made several *starts*, but got nothing; my dog ran off, the rascally pup, and, I reckon, ef Squaire Hopson had met him he'd ha' said 'twas bekaise I starved him! Fact is, we hedn't any on us much to eat that day, and the old mar's ribs stood out bigger than ever.

"All day I rode and followed the track and got nothing.

"Well, jest about sunset I come to a hollow of the hills that I hed never seed before; and in the middle of it was a great pond of water, what you call a lake; and it showed like so much purple glass in the sunset, and 'twas jest as smooth as the big looking-glass of Squaire Hopson's. Thar wa'n't a breath of wind stirring.

"I was mighty tired, so I eased down from the mar', tied up the bridle and check, and let her pick about, and laid myself down onder a tree, jest about twenty yards from the lake, and thought to rest myself ontil the moon riz, which I knowed would be about seven o'clock.

"I didn't mean to fall asleep, but I did it; and I reckon I must ha' slept a good hour, for when I woke the dark hed set in, and I could only see one or two bright stars hyar and thar, shooting out from the dark of the heavens. But, ef I seed nothing, I haird; and jest sich a sound and noise as I hed never haird before.

"Thar was a rushing and a roaring and a screaming and a plashing, in the air and in the water, as made you think the univarsal world was coming to an eend!

"All that set me up. I was waked up out of sleep and dream, and my eyes opened to every thing that eye could see; and sich another sight I never seed before! I tell you, Jedge, ef there was one wild-goose settling down in that lake, thar was one hundred thousand of 'em! I couldn't see the eend of 'em. They come every minit, swarm a'ter swarm, in tens and twenties and fifties and hundreds; and sich a fuss as they did make! sich a gabbling, sich a splashing, sich a confusion, that I was fairly conflusterated; and I jest lay whar I was, a-watching 'em.

"You never seed beasts so happy! How they flapped their wings; how they gabbled to one another; how they swam hyar and thar, to the very middle of the lake and to the very edge of it, jest a fifty yards from whar I lay squat, never moving leg or arm! It was wonderful to see! I wondered how they could find room, for I reckon thar waur forty thousand on 'em, all scuffling in that leetle lake together!

"Well, as I watched 'em, I said to myself:

"'Now, if a fellow could only captivate all them wild-geese—fresh from Canniday, I reckon—what would they bring in the market at Spartanburg and Greenville? Walker, I knowed, would buy 'em up quick at fifty cents a head. Forty thousand geese at fifty cents a head. Thar was "capital!"'

"I could ha' fired in among 'em with my rifle, never taking aim, and killed a dozen or more, at a single shot; but what was a poor dozen geese, when thar waur forty thousand to captivate?

"What a haul 'twould be, ef a man could only get 'em all in one net! Kiver 'em all at a fling!

"The idee worked like so much fire in my brain.

"How kin it be done?

"That was the question!

"'Kin it be done?' I axed myself.

"'It kin,' I said to myself; 'and I'm the very man to do it!' Then I begun to work away in the thinking. I thought over all the traps and nets and snares that I hed ever seen or haird of; and the leetle eends of the idee begun to come together in my head; and, watching all the time how the geese flopped and splashed and played and swum, I said to myself:

"'Oh! most beautiful critters! ef I don't make some "capital" out of you, then I'm not dezarving sich a beautiful yaller flower of the forest as my Merry Ann!'

"Well, I watched a long time, ontil dark night, and the stars begun to peep down upon me over the high hill-tops. Then I got up and tuk to my horse and rode home.

"And thar, when I hed swallowed my bit of hoe-cake and bacon and a good strong cup of coffee, and got into bed, I couldn't sleep for a long time, thinking how I was to git them geese.

"But I kept nearing the right idee every minit, and when I was fast asleep it come to me in my dream.

"I seed the same beautifulest young woman agin that hed given me the incouragement before to go ahead, and she helped me out with the idee.

"So, in the morning, I went to work. I rode off to Spartanburg, and bought all the twine and cord and hafe the plow-lines in town; and I got a lot of great fishhooks, all to help make the tanglement parfect; and I got lead for sinkers, and I got cork-wood for floaters; and I pushed for home jist as fast as my poor mar' could streak it.

"I was at work day and night, for nigh on to a week, making my net; and when 'twas done I borrowed a mule and cart from Columbus Mills, thar;—he'll tell you all about it—he kin make his affidavy to the truth of it.

"Well, off I driv with my great net, and got to the lake about noonday. I knowed 'twould take me some hours to make my fixings parfect, and git the net fairly stretched across the lake, and jest deep enough to do the tangling of every leg of the birds in the very midst of their swimming and snorting and splashing and cavorting! When I hed fixed it all fine, and jest as I wanted it, I brought the eends of my plow-lines up to where I was gwine to hide myself. This was onder a strong sapling, and my calkilation was when I hed got the beasts all hooked, forty thousand, more or less—and I could tell how that was from feeling on the line—why, then, I'd whip the line round the sapling, hitch it fast, and draw in my birds at my own ease, without axing much about their comfort.

"'Twas a most beautiful and parfect plan, and all would ha' worked beautiful well but for one leetle oversight of mine. But I won't tell you about that part of the business yit, the more pretickilarly as it all turned out for the very best, as you'll see in the eend.

"I hedn't long finished my fixings when the sun suddenly tumbled down the heights, and the dark begun to creep in upon me, and a pretty cold dark it waur! I remember it well! My teeth begun to chatter in my head, though I was boiling over with inward heat, all jest coming out of my hot eagerness to be captivating the birds.

"Well, Jedge, I hedn't to wait overlong. Soon I haird them coming, screaming fur away, and then I seed them pouring, jest like so many white clouds, straight down, I reckon, from the snow mountains off in Canniday.

"Down they come, millions upon millions, till I was sartin thar waur already pretty nigh on to forty thousand in the lake. It waur always a nice calkilation of mine that the lake could hold fully forty thousand, though onst, when I went round to measure it, stepping it off, I was jubous whether it could hold over thirty-nine thousand; but, as I tuk the measure in hot weather and in a dry spell, I concluded that some of the water along the edges hed dried up, and 'twa'n't so full as when I made my first calkilation. So I hev stuck to that first calkilation ever since.

"Well, thar they waur, forty thousand, we'll say, with, it mout be, a few millions and hundreds over. And Lawd! how they played and splashed and screamed and dived! I calkilated on hooking a good many of them divers, in pretickilar, and so I watched and waited, ontil I thought I'd feel of my lines; and I begun, leetle by leetle, to haul in, when, Lawd love you, Jedge, sich a ripping and raging, and bouncing and flouncing, and flopping and splashing, and kicking and screaming, you never did hear in all your born days!

"By this I knowed that I hed captivated the captains of the host, and a pretty smart chaince, I reckoned, of the rigilar army, ef 'twa'n't edzactly forty thousand; for I calkilated that some few would git away—run off, jest as the cowards always does in the army, jest when the shooting and confusion begins; still, I reasonably calkilated on the main body of the rigiments; and so, gitting more and more hot and eager, and pulling and hauling, I made one big mistake, and, instid of wrapping the eends of my lines around the sapling that was standing jest behind me, what does I do but wraps 'em round my own thigh—the right thigh, you see—and some of the loops waur hitched round my left arm at the same time!

"All this come of my hurry and ixcitement, for it was burning like a hot fever in my brain, and I didn't know when or how I hed tied myself up, ontil suddently, with an all-fired scream, all together, them forty thousand geese rose like a great black cloud in the air, all tied up, tangled up—hooked about the legs, hooked about the gills, hooked and fast in some way in the beautiful leetle twistings of my net!

"Yes, Jedge, as I'm a living hunter to-night, hyar a-talking to you, they riz up all together, as ef they hed consulted upon it, like a mighty thunder-cloud, and off they went, screaming and flouncing, meaning, I reckon, to take the back track to Canniday, in spite of the freezing weather.

"Before I knowed whar I was, Jedge, I was twenty feet in the air, my right thigh up and my left arm, and the other thigh and arm a-dangling useless, and feeling every minit as ef they was gwine to drop off.

"You may be sure I pulled with all my might, but that waur mighty leetle in the fix I was in, and I jest hed to hold on, and see whar the infernal beasts would carry me. I couldn't loose myself, and ef I could I was by this time quite too fur up in the air, and darsn't do so, onless I was willing to hev my brains dashed out, and my whole body mashed to a mammock!

"Oh, Jedge, jest consider my sitivation! It's sich a ricollection, Jedge, that I must rest and liquor, in order to rekiver the necessary strength to tell you what happened next."

VII.

"Yes, Jedge," said Yaou, resuming his narrative, "jest stop whar you air, and consider my sitivation!

"Thar I was dangling, like a dead weight, at the tail of that all-fired cloud of wild-geese, head downward, and gwine, the Lawd knows whar!—to Canniday, or Jericho, or some other heathen territory beyond the Massissipp, and it mout be, over the great etarnal ocean!

"When I thought of *that,* and thought of the plow-lines giving way, and that on a suddent I should come down plump into the big sea, jest in the middle of a great gathering of shirks and whales, to be dewoured and tore to bits by their bloody grinders, I was ready to die of skeer outright. I thought over all my sinnings in a moment, and I thought of my poor dear Merry Ann, and I called out her name, loud as I could, jest as ef the poor gal could hyar me or help me.

"And jest then I could see we waur a drawing nigh a great thunder-cloud. I could see the red tongues running out of its black jaws; and 'Lawd!' says I, 'ef these all-fired infarnal wild beasts of birds should carry me into that cloud to be burned to a coal, fried, and roasted, and biled alive by them tongues of red fire!'

"But the geese fought shy of the cloud, though we passed mighty nigh on to it, and I could see one red streak of lightning run out of the cloud and give us chase for a full hafe a mile; but we waur too fast for it, and, in a tearing passion bekaise it couldn't ketch us, the red streak struck its horns into a great tree jest behind us, that we hed passed over, and tore it into flinders, in the twink of a musquito.

"But by this time I was beginning to feel quite stupid. I knowed that I waur fast gitting onsensible, and it did seem to me as ef my hour waur come, and I was gwine to die—and die by rope, and dangling in the air, a thousand miles from the airth!

"But jest then I was roused up. I felt something brush agin me; then my face was scratched; and, on a suddent, thar was a stop put to my travels by that conveyance. The geese had stopped flying, and waur in a mighty great conflusteration, flopping their wings, as well as they could, and screaming with all the tongues in their jaws. It was clar to me now that we hed run agin something that brought us all up with a short hitch.

"I was shook roughly agin the obstruction, and I put out my right arm and cotched a hold of a long arm of an almighty big tree; then my legs waur cotched betwixt two other branches, and I rekivered myself, so as to set up a leetle and rest. The geese was a tumbling and flopping among the branches. The net was hooked hyar and thar; and the birds waur all about me, swinging and splurging, but onable to break loose and git away.

"By leetle and leetle I come to my clar senses, and begun to feel my sitivation. The stiffness was passing out of my limbs. I could draw up my legs, and, after some hard work, I managed to onwrap the plow-lines from my right thigh and my left arm, and I hed the sense this time to tie the eends pretty tight to a great branch of the tree which stretched clar across and about a foot over my head.

"Then I begun to consider my sitivation. I hed hed a hard riding, that was sartin; and I felt sore enough. And I hed hed a horrid bad skear, enough to make a man's wool turn white afore the night was over. But now I felt easy, bekaise I considered myself safe. With day-peep I calkilated to let myself down from the tree by my plow-lines, and thar, below, tied fast, warn't thar my forty thousand captivated geese?

"'Hurrah!' I sings out. 'Hurrah, Merry Ann; we'll hev the "capital" now, I reckon!'

"And singing out, I drawed up my legs and shifted my body so as to find an easier seat in the crutch of the tree, which was an almighty big chestnut oak, when, O Lawd! on a suddent the stump I hed been a-setting on give way onder me. 'Twas a rotten jint of the tree. It give way, Jedge, as I tell you, and down I went, my legs first and then my whole body—slipping down not on the outside, but into a great hollow of the tree, all the hairt of it being eat out by the rot; and afore I knowed whar I waur, I waur some twenty foot down, I reckon; and by the time I touched bottom, I was up to my neck in honey!

"It was an almighty big honey-tree, full of the sweet treacle; and the bees all gone and left it, I reckon, for a hundred years. And I in it up to my neck.

"I could smell it strong. I could taste it sweet. But I could see nothing.

"Lawd! Lawd! From bad to worse; buried alive in a hollow tree with never a chaince to git out! I would then ha' given all the world ef I was only sailing away with them bloody wild-geese to Canniday, and Jericho, even across the sea, with all its shirks and whales dewouring me.

"Buried alive! O Lawd! O Lawd! 'Lawd save me and help me!' I cried out from the depths. And 'Oh, my Merry Ann,' I cried, 'shill we never meet agin no more!' Scuse my weeping, Jedge, but I feels all over the sinsation, fresh as ever, of being buried alive in a beehive tree and presarved in honey. I must liquor, Jedge."

VIII.

Yaou, after a great swallow of peach and honey, and a formidable groan after it, resumed his narrative as follows:

"Only think of me, Jedge, in my sitivation! Buried alive in the hollow of a mountain chestnut oak! Up to my neck in honey, with never no more an appetite to eat than ef it waur the very gall of bitterness that we reads of in the Holy Scripters!

"All dark, all silent as the grave; 'cept for the gabbling and the cackling of the wild-geese outside, that every now and then would make a great splurging and cavorting, trying to break away from their hitch, which was jist as fast fixed as my own.

"Who would git them geese that hed cost me so much to captivate? Who would inherit my 'capital?' and who would hev Merry Ann? and what will become of the mule and cart of Mills fastened in the woods by the leetle lake?

"I cussed the leetle lake, and the geese, and all the 'capital.'

"I cussed. I couldn't help it. I cussed from the bottom of my hairt, when I ought to ha' bin saying my prayers. And thar was my poor mar' in the stable with never a morsel of feed. She had told tales upon me to Squaire Hopson, it's true, but I forgin her, and thought of her feed, and nobody to give her none. Thar waur corn in the crib and fodder, but it warn't in the stable; and onless Columbus Mills should come looking a'ter me at the cabin, thar waur no hope for me or the mar'.

"Oh, Jedge, you couldn't jedge of my sitivation in that deep hollow, that cave, I may say, of mountain oak! My head waur jest above the honey, and ef I backed it to look up, my long ha'r at the back of the neck a'most stuck fast, so thick was the honey.

"But I couldn't help looking up. The hollow was a wide one at the top, and I could see when a star was passing over. Thar they shined, bright and beautiful, as ef they waur the very eyes of the angels; and, as I seed them come and go, looking smiling in upon me as they come, I cried out to 'em, one by one:

"'Oh, sweet sperrits, blessed angels! ef so be thar's an angel sperrit, as they say, living in all them stars, come down and extricate me from this fix; for, so fur as I kin see, I've got no chaince of help from mortal man or woman. Hairdly onst a year does a human come this way; and ef they did come, how would they know I'm hyar? How could I make them hyar me? O Lawd! O blessed, beautiful angels in them stars! O give me help! Help me out!' I knowed I prayed like a heathen sinner, but I prayed as well as I knowed how; and thar warn't a star passing over me that I didn't pray to, soon as I seed them shining over the opening of the hollow; and I prayed fast and faster as I seed them passing away and gitting out of sight.

"Well, Jedge, suddently, in the midst of my praying, and jest after one bright, big star hed gone over me without seeing my sitivation, I hed a frésh skeer.

"Suddent I haird a monstrous fluttering among my geese—my 'capital.' Then I haird a great scraping and scratching on the outside of the tree, and, suddent, as I looked up, the mouth of the hollow was shet up.

"All was dark. The stars and sky waur all gone. Something black kivered the hollow, and, in a minit a'ter, I haird something slipping down into the hollow right upon me.

"I could hairdly draw my breath. I begun to fear that I was to be siffocated alive; and as I haird the strange critter slipping down, I shoved out my hands and felt ha'r—coarse wool—and with one hand I cotched hold of the ha'ry leg of a beast, and with t'other hand I cotched hold of his tail.

"'Twas a great b'ar, one of the biggest, come to git his honey. He knowed the tree, Jedge, you see, and ef any beast in the world loves honey, 'tis a b'ar beast. He'll go his death on honey, though the hounds are tearing at his very haunches.

"You may be sure, when I onst knowed what he was, and onst got a good gripe on his hindquarters, I warn't gwine to let go in a hurry. I knowed that was my only chaince for gitting out of the hollow, and I do believe them blessed angels in the stars sent the beast, jest at the right time, to give me human help and assistance.

"Now, yer see, Jedge, thar was no chaince for him turning round upon me. He pretty much filled up the hollow. He knowed his way, and slipped down, eend foremost—the latter eend, you know. He could stand up on his hind-legs and eat all he wanted. Then, with his great sharp claws and his mighty muscle, he could work up, holding on to the sides of the tree, and git out a'most as easy as when he come down.

"Now, you see, ef he weighed five hundred pounds, and could climb like a cat, he could easy carry up a young fellow that hed no flesh to spar', and only weighed a hundred and twenty-five. So I laid my weight on him, eased him off as well as I could, but held on to tail and leg as ef all life and etarnity depended upon it.

"Now I reckon, Jedge, that b'ar was pretty much more skeered than I was. He couldn't turn in his shoes, and with something fastened to his ankles, and, as he thought, I reckon, some strange beast fastened to his tail, you never seed beast more eager to git away, and git upwards. He knowed the way, and stuck his claws in the rough sides of the hollow, hand over hand, jest as a sailor pulls a rope, and up we went. We hed, howsomdever, more than one slip back; but, Lawd bless you! I never let go. Up we went, I say, at last, and I stuck jest as close to his haunches as death sticks to a dead nigger. Up we went. I felt myself moving. My neck was out of the honey. My airms were free. I could feel the sticky thing slipping off from me, and a'ter a good quarter of an hour the b'ar was on the great mouth of the hollow; and as I felt that I let go his tail, still keeping fast hold of his leg, and with one hand I cotched hold of the outside rim of the hollow; I found it fast, held on to it; and jest then the b'ar sat squat on the very edge of the hollow, taking a sort of rest a'ter his labor.

"I don't know what 'twas, Jedge, that made me do it. I warn't a-thinking at all. I was only feeling and drawing a long breath. Jest then the b'ar sort o' looked round, as ef to see what varmint it was a-troubling him, when I gin him a mighty push, strong as I could, and he lost his balance and went over outside down cl'ar to the airth, and I could hyar his neck crack, almost as loud as a pistol.

"I drawed a long breath a'ter that, and prayed a short prayer; and feeling my way all the time, so as to be sure agin rotten branches, I got a safe seat among the limbs of the tree, and sot myself down, detarmined to wait tell broad daylight before I tuk another step in the business."

IX.

"And thar I sot. So fur as I could see, Jedge, I was safe. I hed got out of the tie of the flying geese, and thar they all waur, spread before me, flopping now and then and trying to ixtricate themselves; but they couldn't come it! Thar they waur, captivated, and so much 'capital' for Sam Snaffles.

"And I hed got out of the lion's den; that is, I hed got out of the honey-tree, and warn't in no present danger of being buried alive agin. Thanks to the b'ar, and to the blessed, beautiful angel sperrits in the stars, that hed sent him thar seeking honey, to be my deliverance from my captivation!

"And thar he lay, jest as quiet as ef he waur a-sleeping, though I knowed his neck was broke. And that b'ar, too, was so much 'capital.'

"And I sot in the tree making my calkilations. I could see now the meaning of that beautiful young critter that come to me in my dreams. I was to hev the 'capital,' but I was to git it through troubles and tribulations, and a mighty bad skeer for life. I never knowed the valley of 'capital' till now, and I seed the sense in all that Squaire Hopson told me, though he did tell it in a mighty spiteful sperrit.

"Well, I calkilated.

"It was cold weather, freezing, and though I had good warm clothes on, I felt monstrous like sleeping, from the cold only, though perhaps the tire and the skeer together hed something to do with it. But I was afeard to sleep. I didn't know what would happen, and a man has never his right courage ontil daylight. I fou't agin sleep by keeping on my calkilation.

"Forty thousand wild-geese!

"Thar wa'n't forty thousand, edzactly—very far from it—but thar they waur, pretty thick; and for every goose I could git from forty to sixty cents in all the villages in South Carolina.

"Thar was 'capital!'

"Then thar waur the b'ar.

"Jedging from his strength in pulling me up, and from his size and fat in filling up that great hollow in the tree, I calkilated that he couldn't weigh less than five hundred pounds. His hide, I knowed, was worth twenty dollars. Then thar was the fat and tallow, and the biled marrow out of his bones, what they makes b'ars grease out of, to make chicken whiskers grow big enough for game-cocks. Then thar waur the meat, skinned, cleaned, and all; thar couldn't be much onder four hundred and fifty pounds, and whether I sold him as fresh meat or cured, he'd bring me ten cents a pound at the least.

"Says I, 'Thar's capital!'

"'Then,' says I, 'thar's my honey-tree! I reckon thar's a matter of ten thousand gallons in this hyar same honey-tree; and if I kint git fifty to seventy cents a gallon for it thar's no alligators in Flurriday!'

"And so I calkilated through the night, fighting agin sleep, and thinking of my 'capital' and Merry Ann together.

"By morning I had calkilated all I hed to do and all I hed to make.

"Soon as I got a peep of day I was bright on the look-out.

"Thar all around me were the captivated geese critters. The b'ar laid down parfectly easy and waiting for the knife; and the geese, I reckon they waur much more tired than me, for they didn't seem to hev the hairt for a single flutter, even when they seed me swing down from the tree among 'em, holding on to my plow-lines and letting myself down easy.

"But first I must tell you, Jedge, when I seed the first signs of daylight and looked around me, Lawd bless me, what should I see but old Tryon Mountain, with his great head lifting itself up in the east! And beyant I could see the house and fairm of Columbus Mills; and as I turned to look a leetle south of that, thar was my own poor leetle log-cabin standing quiet, but with never a smoke streaming out from the chimbley.

"'God bless them good angel sperrits,' I said, 'I ain't two miles from home!' Before I come down from the tree I knowed edzactly whar I waur. 'Twas only four miles off from the lake and whar I hitched the mule of Columbus Mills close by the cart. Thar, too, I hed left my rifle. Yit in my miserable fix, carried through the air by them wild-geese, I did think I hed gone a'most a thousand miles towards Canniday.

"Soon as I got down from the tree I pushed off at a trot to git the mule and cart. I was pretty sure of my b'ar and geese when I come back. The cart stood quiet enough. But the mule, having nothing to eat, was sharping her teeth upon a boulder, thinking she'd hev a bite or so before long.

"I hitched her up, brought her to my bee-tree, tumbled the b'ar into the cart, wrung the necks of all the geese that waur thar—many hed got away—and counted some twenty-seven hundred that I piled away atop of the b'ar."

"Twenty-seven hundred!" cried the "Big Lie" and all the hunters at a breath. "Twenty-seven hundred! Why, Yaou, whenever you telled of this thing before you always counted them at 3150!"

"Well, ef I did, I reckon I was right. I was sartinly right then, it being all fresh in my 'membrance; and I'm not the man to go back agin his own words. No, fellows, I sticks to first words and first principles. I scorns to eat my own words. Ef I said 3150, then 3150 it waur, never a goose less. But you'll see how to 'count for all. I reckon 'twas only 2700 I fotched to market. Thar was 200 I gin to Columbus Mills. Then thar was 200 more I carried to Merry Ann; and then thar waur 50 at least, I reckon, I kep for myself. Jest you count up, Jedge, and you'll see how to squar' it on all sides. When I said 2700 I only counted what I sold in the villages, every head of 'em at fifty cents a head; and a'ter putting the money in my pocket I felt all over that I hed the 'capital.'

"Well, Jedge, next about the b'ar. Sold the hide and tallow for a fine market-price; sold the meat, got ten cents a pound for it fresh

—'twas most beautiful meat; biled down the bones for the marrow; melted down the grease; sold fourteen pounds of it to the barbers and apothecaries; got a dollar a pound for that; sold the hide for twenty dollars; and got the cash for every thing.

"Thar warn't a fambly in all Greenville and Spartanburg and Asheville that didn't git fresh, green wild-geese from me that season, at fifty cents a head, and glad to git, too; the cheapest fresh meat they could buy; and, I reckon, the finest. And all the people of them villages, ef they hed gone to heaven that week, in the flesh, would have carried nothing better than goose-flesh for the risurrection! Every body ate goose for a month, I reckon, as the weather was freezing cold all the time, and the beasts kept week after week, ontil they waur eaten. From the b'ar only I made a matter of full one hundred dollars. First, thar waur the hide, $20; then 450 pounds of meat, at 10 cents, was $45; then the grease, 14 pounds, $14; and the tallow, some $6 more; and the biled marrow, $11.

"Well, count up, Jedge; 2700 wild-geese, at 50 cents, you sees, must be more than $1350. I kin only say, that a'ter all the selling—and I driv at it day and night, with Columbus Mills's mule and cart, and went to every house in every street in all them villages. I hed a'most fifteen hundred dollars, safe stowed away onder the pillows of my bed, all in solid gould and silver.

"But I warn't done! Thar was my bee-tree. Don't you think I waur gwine to lose that honey! no, my darlint! I didn't beat the drum about nothing. I didn't let on to a soul what I was a-doing. They axed me about the wild-geese, but I sent 'em on a wild-goose chase; and 'twa'n't till I hed sold off all the b'ar meat and all the geese that I made ready to git at that honey. I reckon them bees must ha' been making that honey for a hundred years, and was then driv out by the b'ars.

"Columbus Mills will tell you; he axed me all about it; but, though he was always my good friend, I never even telled it to him. But he lent me his mule and cart, good fellow as he is, and never said nothing more; and, quiet enough, without beat of drum, I bought up all the tight-bound barrels that ever brought whisky to Spartanburg and Greenville, whar they hes the taste for that article strong; and day by day I went off carrying as many barrels as the cart could hold and the mule could draw. I tapped the old tree—

which was one of the oldest and biggest chestnut oaks I ever did see—close to the bottom, and drawed off the beautiful treacle. I was more than sixteen days about it, and got something over two thousand gallons of the purest, sweetest, yellowest honey you ever did see. I could hairdly git barrels and jimmyjohns enough to hold it; and I sold it out at seventy cents a gallon, which was mighty cheap. So I got from the honey a matter of fourteen hundred dollars.

"Now, Jedge, all this time, though it went very much agin the grain, I kept away from Merry Ann and the old Squaire, her daddy. I sent him two hundred head of geese—some fresh, say one hundred, and another hundred that I hed cleaned and put in salt—and I sent him three jimmyjohns of honey, five gallons each. But I kept away and said nothing, beat no drum, and hed never a thinking but how to git in the 'capital.' And I did git it in!

"When I carried the mule and cart home to Columbus Mills I axed him about a sartin farm of one hundred and sixty acres that he hed to sell. It hed a good house on it. He selled it to me cheap. I paid him down, and put the titles in my pocket. 'Thar's capital!' says I.

"*That* waur a fixed thing for ever and ever. And when I hed moved every thing from the old cabin to the new farm, Columbus let me hev a fine milch cow that gin eleven quarts a day, with a beautiful young caif. Jest about that time thar was a great sale of the furniter of the Ashmore family down at Spartanburg, and I remembered I hed no decent bedstead, or any thing rightly sarving for a young woman's chamber; so I went to the sale, and bought a fine strong mahogany bedstead, a dozen chairs, a chist of drawers, and some other things that ain't quite mentionable, Jedge, but all proper for a lady's chamber; and I soon hed the house fixed up ready for any thing. And up to this time I never let on to any body what I was a-thinking about or what I was a-doing, ontil I could stand up in my own doorway and look about me, and say to myself—this is my 'capital,' I reckon; and when I hed got all that I thought a needcessity to git, I took 'count of every thing.

"I spread the title-deeds of my fairm out on the table. I read 'em over three times to see ef 'twaur all right. Thar was my name several times in big letters, 'to hev and to hold.'

"Then I fixed the furniter. Then I brought out into the stable-yard the old mar'—you couldn't count her ribs *now*, and she was spry as ef she hed got a new conceit of herself.

"Then thar was my beautiful cow and caif, sealing fat, both on 'em, and sleek as a doe in autumn.

"Then thar waur a fine young mule that I bought in Spartanburg; my cart, and a strong second-hand buggy, that could carry two pussons convenient of two different sexes. And I felt big, like a man of consekence and capital.

"That warn't all.

"I had the shiners, Jedge, besides—all in gould and silver—none of your dirty rags and blotty spotty paper. That was the time of Old Hickory—General Jackson, you know—when he kicked over Nick Biddle's consarn, and gin us the beautiful Benton Mint Drops, in place of rotten paper. You could git the gould and silver jest for the axing, in them days, you know.

"I hed a grand count of my money, Jedge. I hed it in a dozen or twenty little bags of leather—the gould—and the silver I hed in shot-bags. It took me a whole morning to count it up and git the figgers right. Then I stuffed it in my pockets, hyar and thar, every whar, wharever I could stow a bag; and the silver I stuffed away in my saddle-bags, and clapped it on the mar'.

"Then I mounted myself, and sot the mar's nose straight in a bee-line for the fairm of Squaire Hopson.

"I was a-gwine, you see, to supprise him with my 'capital;' but, fust, I meant to give him a mighty grand skeer.

"You see, when I was a-trading with Columbus Mills about the fairm and cattle and other things, I ups and tells him about my courting of Merry Ann; and when I telled him about Squaire Hopson's talk about 'capital,' he says:

"'The old skunk! What right hes he to be talking big so, when he kain't pay his own debts. He's been owing me three hundred and fifty dollars now gwine on three years, and I kain't git even the *intrust* out of him. I've got a mortgage on his fairm for the whole, and ef he won't let you hev his da'ter, jest you come to me, and I'll clap the screws to him in short order.'

"Says I, 'Columbus, won't you sell me that mortgage?'

"'You shill hev it for the face of the debt,' says he, 'not considerin' the intrust.'

"'It's a bargin,' says I; and I paid him down the money, and he signed the mortgage over to me for a vallyable consideration.

"I hed that beautiful paper in my breast pocket, and felt strong to face the Squaire in his own house, knowing how I could turn him out of it! And I mustn't forget to tell you how I got myself a new rig of clothing, with a mighty fine over-coat, and a new fur cap; and as I looked in the glass I felt my consekence all over at every for'a'd step I tuk; and I felt my inches growing with every pace of the mar' on the high-road to Merry Ann and her beautiful daddy!"

X.

"Well, Jedge, before I quite got to the Squaire's farm, who should come out to meet me in the road but Merry Ann, her own self! She hed spied me, I reckon, as I crossed the bald ridge a quarter of a mile away. I do reckon the dear gal hed been looking out for me every day the whole eleven days in the week, counting in all the Sundays. In the mountains, you know, Jedge, that the weeks sometimes run to twelve, and even fourteen days, specially when we're on a long camp-hunt!

"Well, Merry Ann cried and laughed together, she was so tarnation glad to see me agin. Says she:

"'Oh, Sam! I'm so glad to see you! I was afeard you had clean gin me up. And thar's that fusty old bachelor Grimstead, he's a-coming here a'most every day; and daddy, he sw'ars that I shill marry him, and nobody else; and mammy, she's at me too, all the time, telling me how fine a fairm he's got, and what a nice carriage, and all that; and mammy says as how daddy'll be sure to beat me ef I don't hev him. But I kain't bear to look at him, the old griesly!'

"'Cuss him!' says I. 'Cuss him, Merry Ann!'

"And she did, but onder her breath—the old cuss.

"'Drot him!' says she; and she said louder, 'and drot me, too, Sam, ef I ever marries any body but you.'

"By this time I hed got down and gin her a long strong hug, and a'most twenty or a dozen kisses, and I says:

"'You sha'n't marry nobody but me, Merry Ann; and we'll hev the marriage this very night, ef you says so!'

"'Oh! psho, Sam! How you does talk!'

"'Ef I don't marry you to-night, Merry Ann, I'm a holy mortar, and a sinner not to be saved by any salting, though you puts the petre with the salt. I'm come for that very thing. Don't you see my new clothes?'

"'Well, you hev got a beautiful coat, Sam; all so blue, and with sich shiny buttons.'

"'Look at my waistcoat, Merry Ann! What do you think of that?'

"'Why, it's a most beautiful blue welvet!'

"'That's the very article,' says I. 'And see the breeches, Merry Ann; and the boots!'

"'Well,' says she, 'I'm fair astonished, Sam! Why whar, Sam, did you find all the money for these fine things?'

"'A beautiful young woman, a'most as beautiful as you, Merry Ann, come to me the very night of that day when your daddy driv me off with a flea in my ear. She come to me to my bed at midnight—'

"'Oh, Sam! *ain't* you ashamed!'

"''Twas in a dream, Merry Ann; and she tells me something to incourage me to go for'a'd, and I went for'a'd, bright and airly next morning, and I picked up three sarvants that hev been working for me ever sence.'

"'What sarvants?' says she.

"'One was a goose, one was a b'ar, and t'other was a bee!'

"'Now you're a-fooling me, Sam.'

"'You'll see! Only you git yourself ready, for, by the eternal Hokies, I marries you this very night, and takes you home to *my* fairm bright and airly to-morrow morning.'

"'I do think, Sam, you must be downright crazy.'

"'You'll see and believe! Do you go home and git yourself fixed up for the wedding. Old Parson Stovall lives only two miles from your daddy, and I'll hev him hyar by sundown. You'll see!'

"'But ef I waur to b'lieve you, Sam—'

"'I've got on my wedding-clothes o' purpose, Merry Ann.'

"'But *I* hain't got no clothes fit for a gal to be married in,' says she.

"'I'll marry you this very night, Merry Ann,' says I, 'though you hedn't a stitch of clothing at all!'

"'Git out, you sassy Sam,' says she, slapping my face. Then I kissed her in her very mouth, and a'ter that we walked on together, I leading the mar'.

"Says she, as we neared the house, 'Sam, let me go before, or stay hyar in the thick, and you go in by yourself. Daddy's in the hall, smoking his pipe and reading the newspapers.'

"'We'll walk in together,' says I, quite consekential.

"Says she, 'I'm so afeard.'

"'Don't you be afeard, Merry Ann,' says I; 'you'll see that all will come out jest as I tells you. We'll be hitched to-night, ef Parson Stovall, or any other parson, kin be got to tie us up!'

"Says she, suddently, 'Sam, you're a-walking lame, I'm a-thinking. What's the matter? Hev you hurt yourself any way?'

"Says I, 'It's only owing to my not balancing my accounts even in my pockets. You see I feel so much like flying in the air with the idee of marrying you to-night that I filled my pockets with rocks, jest to keep me down.'

"'I do think, Sam, you're a leetle cracked in the upper story.'

"'Well,' says I, 'ef so, the crack has let in a blessed chaince of the beautifulest sunlight! You'll see! Cracked, indeed! Ha, ha, ha! Wait till I've done with your daddy! I'm gwine to square accounts with *him*, and, I reckon, when I'm done with him, you'll guess that the crack's in *his* skull, and not in mine.'

"'What! you wouldn't knock my father, Sam!' says she, drawing off from me and looking skeary.

"'Don't you be afeard; but it's very sartin, ef our heads don't come together, Merry Ann, you won't hev me for your husband to-night. And that's what I've swore upon. Hyar we air!'

"When we got to the yard I led in the mar', and Merry Ann she ran away from me and dodged round the house. I hitched the mar' to the post, took off the saddle-bags, which was mighty heavy, and walked into the house stiff enough I tell you, though the gould in my pockets pretty much weighed me down as I walked.

"Well, in I walked, and thar sat the old Squaire smoking his pipe and reading the newspaper. He looked at me through his specs over the newspaper, and when he seed who 'twas his mouth put on that same conceited sort of grin and smile that he ginerally hed when he spoke to me.

"'Well,' says he, gruffly enough, 'it's you, Sam Snaffles, is it?' Then he seems to diskiver my new clothes and boots, and he sings out, 'Heigh! you're tip-toe fine to-day! What fool of a shop-keeper in Spartanbûrg have you tuk in this time, Sam?'

"Says I, cool enough, 'I'll answer all them iligant questions a'ter a while, Squaire; but would prefar to see to business fust.'

"'Business!' says he; 'and what business kin you hev with me, I wants to know?'

"'You shill know, Squaire, soon enough; and I only hopes it will be to your liking a'ter you l'arn it.'

"So I laid my saddle-bags down at my feet and tuk a chair quite at my ease; and I could see that he was all astare in wonderment at what he thought my sassiness. As I felt I had my hook in his gills, though he didn't know it yit, I felt in the humor to tickle him and play him as we does a trout.

"Says I, 'Squaire Hopson, you owes a sartin amount of money, say $350, with intrust on it for now three years, to Dr. Columbus Mills.'

"At this he squares round, looks me full in the face, and says:

"'What the old Harry's that to you?'

"Says I, gwine on cool and straight, 'You gin him a mortgage on this fairm for security.'

"'What's that to you?' says he.

"'The mortgage is over-due by two years, Squaire,' says I.

"'What the old Harry's all that to you, I say?' he fairly roared out.

"'Well, nothing much, I reckon. The $350, with three years' intrust at seven per cent., making it now—I've calkelated it all without compounding—something over $425—well, Squaire, that's not much to *you,* I reckon, with your large capital. But it's something to me.'

"'But I ask you again, Sir,' he says, 'what is all this to you?'

"'Jist about what I tells you—say $425; and I've come hyar this morning, bright and airly, in hope you'll be able to square up and satisfy the mortgage. Hyar's the dockyment.'

"And I drawed the paper from my breast pocket.

"'And you tell me that Dr. Mills sent you hyar,' says he, 'to collect this money?'

"'No; I come myself on my own hook.'

"'Well,' says he, 'you shill hev your answer at onst. Take that paper back to Dr. Mills and tell him that I'll take an airly opportunity to call and arrange the business with him. You hev your answer, Sir,' he says, quite grand, 'and the sooner you makes yourself scarce the better.'

"'Much obleeged to you, Squaire, for your ceveelity,' says I; 'but I ain't quite satisfied with that answer. I've come for the money due on this paper, and must hev it, Squaire, or thar will be what the lawyers call *four closures* upon it!'

"'Enough! Tell Dr. Mills I will answer his demand in person.'

"'You needn't trouble yourself, Squaire; for ef you'll jest look at the back of that paper, and read the 'signmeant, you'll see that you've got to settle with Sam Snaffles, and not with Columbus Mills!'

"Then he snatches up the dockyment, turns it over, and reads the rigilar 'signmeant, writ in Columbus Mills's own handwrite.

"Then the Squaire looks at me with a great stare, and he says, to himself like:

"'It's a *bonny fodder* 'signmeant.'

"'Yes,' says I, 'it's *bonny fodder*—rigilar in law—and the titles all made out complete to me, Sam Snaffles; signed, sealed, and delivered, as the lawyers says it.'

"'And how the old Harry come you by this paper?' says he.

"I was gitting riled, and I was detarmined, this time, to gin my hook a pretty sharp jerk in his gills; so I says:

"'What the old Harry's that to *you*, Squaire? Thar's but one question 'twixt us two—air you ready to pay that money down on the hub, at onst, to me, Sam Snaffles?'

"'No, Sir, I am not.'

"'How long a time will you ax from me, by way of marciful indulgence?'

"'It must be some time yit,' says he, quite sulky; and then he goes on agin:

"'I'd like to know how you come by that 'signmeant, Mr. Snaffles.'

"Mr. Snaffles! Ah! ha!

"'I don't see any neecessity,' says I, 'for answering any questions. Thar's the dockyment to speak for itself. You see that Columbus Mills 'signs to me for full *con*sideration. That means I paid him!'

"'And why did you buy this mortgage?'

"'You might as well ax me how I come by the money to buy any thing,' says I.

"'Well, I do ax you,' says he.

"'And I answers you,' says I, 'in the very words from your own mouth, What the old Harry's that to you?'

"'This is hardly 'spectful, Mr. Snaffles,' says he.

"Says I, ''Spectful gits only what 'spectful gives! Ef any man but you, Squaire, hed been so onrespectful in his talk to me as you hev been I'd ha' mashed his muzzle! But I don't wish to be onrespectful. All I axes is the civil answer. I wants to know when you kin pay this money?'

"'I kain't say, Sir.'

"'Well, you see, I thought as how you couldn't pay, spite of all your "capital," as you hedn't paid even the *intrust* on it for three years; and, to tell you the truth, I was in hopes you couldn't pay, as I hed a liking for this fairm always; and as I am jest about to git married, you see—'

"'Who the old Harry air you gwine to marry?' says he.

"'What the old Harry's that to you?' says I, giving him as good as he sent. But I went on:

"'You may be sure it's one of the woman kind. I don't hanker a'ter a wife with a beard; and I expects—God willing, weather pre-mitting, and the parson being sober—to be married this very night!'

"'To-night!' says he, not knowing well what to say.

"'Yes; you see I've got my wedding-breeches on. I'm to be married to-night, and I wants to take my wife to her own fairm as soon as I kin. Now, you see, Squaire, I all along set my hairt on this fairm of yourn, and I detarmined, ef ever I could git the "capital," to git hold of it; and that was the idee I hed when I bought the 'signmeant of the mortgage from Columbus Mills. So, you see, ef you kain't pay a'ter three years, you never kin pay, I reckon; and ef I don't git my money this day, why—I kain't help it—the lawyers will hev to see to the *four closures* to-morrow!'

"'Great God, Sir!' says he, rising out of his chair, and crossing the room up and down, 'do you coolly propose to turn me and my family headlong out of my house?'

"'Well now,' says I, 'Squaire, that's not edzactly the way to put it. As I reads this dockyment'—and I tuk up and put the mortgage in my pocket—'the house and fairm are *mine* by law. They onst was yourn; but it wants nothing now but the *four closures* to make 'em mine.'

"'And would you force the sale of property worth $2000 and more for a miserable $400?'

"'It must sell for what it'll bring, Squaire; and I stands ready to buy it for my wife, you see, ef it costs me twice as much as the mortgage.'

"'Your wife!' says he; 'who the old Harry is she? You once pertended to have an affection for my da'ter.'

"'So I hed; but you hedn't the proper affection for your da'ter that I hed. You prefar'd money to her affections, and you driv me off to git "capital!" Well, I tuk your advice, and I've got the capital.'

"'And whar the old Harry,' said he, 'did you git it?'

"'Well, I made good tairms with the old devil for a hundred years, and he found me in the money.'

"'It must hev been so,' said he. 'You waur not the man to git capital in any other way.'

"Then he goes on: 'But what becomes of your pertended affection for my da'ter?'

"''Twa'n't pertended; but you throwed yourself betwixt us with all your force, and broke the gal's hairt, and broke mine, so far as you could; and as I couldn't live without company, I hed to look out for myself and find a wife as I could. I tell you, as I'm to be married to-night, and as I've swore a most etarnal oath to hev this fairm, you'll hev to raise the wind to-day, and square off with me, or the lawyers will be at you with the *four closures* to-morrow, bright and airly.'

"'Dod dern you!' he cries out. 'Does you want to drive me mad!'

"'By no manner of means,' says I, jest about as cool and quiet as a cowcumber.

"But he was at biling heat. He was all over in a stew and a fever. He filled his pipe and lighted it, and then smashed it over the chimbly. Then he crammed the newspaper in the fire, and crushed it into the blaze with his boot. Then he turned to me, suddent, and said:

"'Yes, you pertended to love my da'ter, and now you are pushing her father to desperation. Now ef you ever did love Merry Ann, honestly, raally, truly, and *bonny fodder*, you couldn't help loving her yit. And yit, hyar you're gwine to marry another woman, that, prehaps, you don't affection at all.'

"'It's quite a sensible view you takes of the subject,' says I; 'the only pity is that you didn't take the same squint at it long ago, when

I axed you to let me hev Merry Ann. *Then* you didn't valley her affections or mine. You hed no thought of nothing but the "capital" then, and the affections might all go to Jericho, for what you keered! I'd ha' married Merry Ann, and she me, and we'd ha' got on for a spell in a log-cabin, for, though I was poor, I hed the genwine grit of a man, and would come to something, and we'd ha' got on; and yit, without any "capital" your own self, and kivered up with debt as with a winter over-coat, hyar, you waur positive that I shouldn't hev your da'ter, and you waur a-preparing to sell her hyar to an old sour-tempered bachelor, more than double her age. Dern the capital! A man's the best capital for any woman, ef so be he *is* a man. Bekaise, ef he be a man, he'll work out cl'ar, though he may hev a long straining for it through the sieve. Dern the capital! You've as good as sold that gal child to old Grimstead, jest from your love of money!'

"'But she won't hev him,' says he.

"'The wiser gal child,' says I. 'Ef you only hed onderstood me and that poor child, I hed it in me to make the "capital"—dern the capital!—and now you've ruined her, and yourself, and me, and all; and dern my buttons but I must be married to-night, and jest as soon a'ter as the lawyers kin fix it I must hev this fairm for my wife. My hairt's set on it, and I've swore it a dozen o' times on the Holy Hokies!'

"The poor old Squaire fairly sweated; but he couldn't say much. He'd come up to me and say:

"'Ef you only did love Merry Ann!'

"'Oh,' says I, 'what's the use of your talking that? Ef you only hed ha' loved your own da'ter!'

"Then the old chap begun to cry, and as I seed that I jest kicked over my saddle-bags lying at my feet, and the silver Mexicans rolled out—a bushel on 'em, I reckon—and, O Lawd! how the old fellow jumped, staring with all his eyes at me and the dollars!

"'It's money!' says he.

"'Yes,' says I, 'jest a few hundreds of thousands of *my* "capital."' I didn't stop at the figgers, you see.

"Then he turns to me and says, 'Sam Snaffles, you're a most wonderful man. You're a mystery to me. Whar, in the name of God, hev you been? and what hev you been doing? and whar did you git all this power of capital?'

"I jest laughed, and went to the door and called Merry Ann. She come mighty quick. I reckon she was watching and waiting.

"Says I, 'Merry Ann, that's money. Pick it up and put it back in the saddle-bags, ef you please.'

"Then says I, turning to the old man, 'Thar's that whole bushel of Mexicans, I reckon. Thar monstrous heavy. My old mar'—ax her about her ribs now!—she fairly squelched onder the weight of me and that money. And I'm pretty heavy loaded myself. I must lighten; with your leave, Squaire.'

"And I pulled out a leetle doeskin bag of gould half eagles from my right-hand pocket and poured them out upon the table; then I emptied my left-hand pocket, then the side pockets of the coat, then the skairt pockets, and jist spread the shiners out upon the table.

"Merry Ann was fairly frightened, and run out of the room; then the old woman she come in, and as the old Squaire seed her, he tuk her by the shoulder and said:

"'Jest you look at that thar.'

"And when she looked and seed, the poor old hypercritical scamp sinner turned round to me and flung her airms round my neck, and said:

"'I always said you waur the only right man for Merry Ann.'

"The old spooney!

"Well, when I hed let 'em look enough, and wonder enough, I jest turned Merry Ann and her mother out of the room.

"The old Squaire, he waur a-setting down agin in his airm-chair, not edzactly knowing what to say or what to do, but watching all my motions, jest as sharp as a cat watches a mouse when she is hafe hungry.

"Thar was all the Mexicans put back in the saddle-bags, but he hed seen 'em, and thar was all the leetle bags of gould spread upon the table; the gould—hafe and quarter eagles—jest lying out of the mouths of the leetle bags as ef wanting to creep back agin.

"And thar sot the old Squaire, looking at 'em all as greedy as a fish-hawk down upon a pairch in the river. And, betwixt a whine and a cry and a talk, he says:

"'Ah, Sam Snaffles, ef you ever did love my leetle Merry Ann, you would never marry any other woman.'

"Then you ought to ha' seed me. I felt myself sixteen feet high, and jest as solid as a chestnut oak. I walked up to the old man, and I tuk him quiet by the collar of his coat, with my thumb and fore-finger, and I said:

"'Git up, Squaire, for a bit.'

"And up he got.

"Then I marched him to the big glass agin the wall, and I said to him: 'Look, ef you please.'

"And he said, 'I'm looking.'

"And I said, 'What does you see?'

"He answered, 'I sees you and me.'

"I says, 'Look agin, and tell me what you *obzarves.*'

"'Well,' says he, 'I obzarves.'

"And says I, 'What does your *obzarving* amount to? That's the how.'

"And says he, 'I sees a man alongside of me, as good-looking and handsome a young man as ever I seed in all my life.'

"'Well,' says I, 'that's a correct obzarvation. But,' says I, 'what does you see of *your own self?*'

"'Well, I kain't edzackly say.'

"'Look good!' says I. 'Obzarve.'

"Says he, 'Don't ax me.'

"'Now,' says I, 'that won't edzactly do. I tell you now, look good, and ax yourself ef you're the sawt of looking man that hes any right to be a feyther-in-law to a fine, young, handsome-looking fellow like me, what's got the "capital?"'

"Then he laughed out at the humor of the sitivation; and he says, 'Well, Sam Snaffles, you've got me dead this time. You're a different man from what I thought you. But, Sam, you'll confess, I reckon, that ef I hedn't sent you off with a flea in your ear when I hed you up afore the looking-glass, you'd never ha' gone to work to git in the "capital."'

"'I don't know *that,* Squaire,' says I. 'Sarcumstances sarve to make a man take one road when he mout take another; but when you meets a man what has the hairt to love a woman strong as a lion, and to fight an inimy big as a buffalo, he's got the raal grit in him. You knowed I was young, and I was poor, and you knowed the business of a hunter is a mighty poor business ef the man ain't born to it. Well, I didn't do much at it jest bekaise my hairt was so full of Merry Ann; and you should ha' made a calkilation and allowed for *that*. But you poked your fun at me and riled me consumedly; but I was detarmined that you shouldn't break *my* hairt or the hairt of Merry Ann. Well, you hed your humors, and I've tried to take the change out of you. And now, ef you raally thinks, a'ter that obzarvation in the glass, that you kin make a respectable feyther-in-law to sich a fine-looking fellow as me, what's got the "capital," jest say the word, and we'll call Merry Ann in to bind the bargin. And you must talk out quick, for the wedding's to take place this very night. I've swore it by the etarnal Hokies.'

"'To-night!' says he.

"'Look at the "capital"' says I; and I pinted to the gould on the table and the silver in the saddle-bags.

"'But, Lawd love you, Sam,' says he, 'it's so suddent, and we kain't make the preparations in time.'

"Says I, 'Look at the "capital," Squaire, and dern the preparations!'

"'But,' says he, 'we hain't time to ax the company.'

"'Dern the company!' says I; 'I don't b'lieve in company the very night a man gits married. His new wife's company enough for him ef he's sensible.'

"'But, Sam,' says he, 'it's not possible to git up a supper by to-night.'

"Says I, 'Look you, Squaire, the very last thing a man wants on his wedding night is supper.'

"Then he said something about the old woman, his wife.

"Says I, 'Jest you call her in and show her the "capital."'

"So he called in the old woman, and then in come Merry Ann, and thar was great hemmings and hawings; and the old woman she said:

"'I've only got the one da'ter, Sam, and we *must* hev a big wedding! We must spread ourselves. We've got a smart chaince of friends and acquaintances, you see, and 'twon't be decent onless we axes them, and they won't like it! We *must* make a big show for the honor and 'spectability of the family.'

"Says I, 'Look you, old lady! I've swore a most tremendous oath, by the Holy Hokies, that Merry Ann and me air to be married this very night, and I kain't break sich an oath as that! Merry Ann,' says I, 'you wouldn't hev me break sich a tremendous oath as that?'

"And, all in a trimble, she says, 'Never, Sam! No!'

"'You hyar that, old lady!' says I. 'We marries to-night, by the Holy Hokies! and we'll hev no company but old Parson Stovall, to make the hitch; and Merry Ann and me go off by sunrise to-morrow morning—you hyar?—to my own fairm, whar thar's a great deal of furniter fixing for her to do. A'ter that you kin advartise the whole county to come in, ef you please, and eat all the supper you kin spread! Now hurry up,' says I, 'and git as ready as you kin, for I'm gwine to ride over to Parson Stovall's this minit. I'll be back to dinner in hafe an hour. Merry Ann, you gether up that gould and silver, and lock it up. It's *our* "capital!" As for you, Squaire, thar's the mortgage on your fairm, which Merry Ann shill give you, to do as you please with it, as soon as the parson has done the hitch, and I kin call Merry Ann, Mrs. Snaffles—Madam Merry Ann Snaffles, and so forth, and aforesaid.'

"I laid down the law that time for all parties, and showed the old Squaire sich a picter of himself, and me standing aside him, looking seven foot high, at the least, that I jest worked the business 'cording to my own pleasure. When neither the daddy nor the mammy hed any thing more to say, I jumped on my mar' and rode over to old Parson Stovall.

"Says I, 'Parson, thar's to be a hitch to-night, and you're to see a'ter the right knot. You knows what I means. I wants you over at Squaire Hopson's. Me and Merry Ann, his da'ter, mean to hop the twig to-night, and you're to see that we hop squar', and that all's even, 'cording to the law, Moses, and the profits! I stand treat, Parson, and you won't be the worse for your riding. I pays in gould!'

"So he promised to come by dusk; and come he did. The old lady hed got some supper, and tried her best to do what she could at sich short notice. The venison ham was mighty fine, I reckon, for Parson Stovall played a great stick at it; and ef they hedn't cooked up four of my wild-geese, then the devil's an angel of light, and Sam Snaffles no better than a sinner! And thar was any quantity of jimmyjohns, peach and honey considered. Parson Stovall was a great feeder, and I begun to think he never would be done. But at last he wiped his mouth, swallowed his fifth cup of coffee, washed it down with a stiff dram of peach and honey, wiped his mouth agin, and pulled out his prayer-book, psalmody, and Holy Scrip—three volumes in all—

and he hemmed three times, and begun to look out for the marriage text, but begun with giving out the 100th Psalm.

"'With one consent, let's all unite—'

"'No,' says I, 'Parson; not all! It's only Merry Ann and me what's to unite to-night!'

"Jest then, afore he could answer, who should pop in but old bachelor Grimstead! and he looked round 'bout him, specially upon me and the parson, as ef to say:

"'What the old Harry's they doing hyar!'

"And I could see that the old Squaire was oneasy. But the blessed old Parson Stovall, he gin 'em no time for ixplanation or palaver; but he gits up, stands up squar', looks solemn as a meat-axe, and he says:

"'Let the parties which I'm to bind together in the holy bonds of wedlock stand up before me!'

"And, Lawd bless you, as he says the words, what should that old skunk of a bachelor do, but he gits up, stately as an old buck in spring time, and he marches over to my Merry Ann! But I was too much and too spry for him. I puts in betwixt 'em, and I takes the old bachelor by his coat-collar, 'twixt my thumb and forefinger, and afore he knows whar he is, I marches him up to the big looking-glass, and I says:

"'Look!'

"'Well,' says he, 'what?'

"'Look good,' says I.

"'I'm looking,' says he. 'But what do you mean, Sir?'

"Says I, 'Obzarve! Do you see yourself? Obzarve!'

"'I reckon I do,' says he.

"'Then,' says I, 'ax yourself the question, ef you're the sawt of looking man to marry my Merry Ann.'

"Then the old Squaire burst out a-laughing. He couldn't help it.

"'Capital!' says he.

"'It's capital,' says I. 'But hyar we air, Parson. Put on the hitch, jest as quick as you kin clinch it; for thar's no telling how many slips thar may be 'twixt the cup and the lips when these hungry old bachelors air about.'

"'Who gives away this young woman?' axes the parson; and the Squaire stands up and does the thing needful. I hed the ring ready, and before the parson had quite got through, old Grimstead vamoosed.

"He waur a leetle slow in onderstanding that he warn't wanted, and warn't, nohow, any party to the business. But he and the Squaire hed a mighty quarrel a'terwards, and ef 't hedn't been for me, he'd ha' licked the Squaire. He was able to do it; but I jest cocked my cap at him one day, and, says I, in the Injin language:

"'Yaou!' And he didn't know what I meant; but I looked tomahawks at him, so he gin ground; and he's getting old so fast that you kin see him growing downwards all the time.

"All that, Jedge, is jest thirteen years ago; and me and Merry Ann git on famously, and thar's no eend to the capital! Gould breeds like the cows, and it's only needful to squeeze the bags now and then to make Merry Ann happy as a tomtit. Thirteen years of married life, and look at me! You see for yourself, Jedge, that I'm not much the worse for wear; and I kin answer for Merry Ann, too, though, Jedge, we hev hed thirty-six children."

"What!" says I, "thirty-six children in thirteen years!"

The "Big Lie" roared aloud.

"Hurrah, Sharp! Go it! You're making it spread! That last shot will make the Jedge know that you're a right truthful sinner, of a Saturday night, and in the 'Lying Camp.'"

"To be sure! You see, Merry Ann keeps on. But you've only got to do the ciphering for yourself. Here, now, Jedge, look at it. Count for yourself. First we had *three* gal children, you see. Very well! Put down three. Then we had *six* boys, one every year for four years; and then, the fifth year, Merry Ann throwed deuce. Now put down the six boys a'ter the three gals, and ef that don't make thirty-six, thar's no snakes in all Flurriday!

"Now, men," says Sam, "let's liquor all round, and drink the health of Mrs. Merry Ann Snaffles and the thirty-six children, all alive and kicking; and glad to see you, Jedge, and the rest of the company. We're doing right well; but I hes, every now and then, to put my thumb and forefinger on the Squaire's collar, and show him his face in the big glass, and call on him for an *obzarvation*—for he's mighty fond *of going shar's* in my 'capital.'"

[The manuscript of this previously unpublished companion piece to "How Sharp Snaffles Got His Capital and Wife" is in the Charles Carroll Simms Collection of the South Caroliniana Library. Explanatory and Textual Notes begin on page 803.]

"BALD-HEAD BILL BAULDY," And How He Went Through the Flurriday Campaign!—

A Legend of the Hunter's Camp—

I.

Second Saturday Night.

The second week was at an end. Saturday had come! We had toiled, successfully, all the week; but Saturday, had been our crowning glory. We had achieved two bucks, fat as shoats in a fine mast season, a huge she bear, a doe, and two wild turkey gobblers; and had come out, triumphantly, in a hand to hand fight with a saucy panther who gave us battle from the jump; and the sun was yet an hour from his setting!

Our *amateurs* sang cock-a-lory! They, too, had achieved some goodly work, having done most execution in the struggle with the panther.

The Colonel, who was the dandy, the Beau, *par excellence* of our group, and who was supposed to be somewhat effeminate, had shown genuine pluck; and, after giving the panther two mortal shots, had the honour to be knocked over by the dying beast, and of bearing off, as trophies of his valour, three deep scratches on face, arm and bosom. He will swear by these to the day of his death!

All parties were duly exultant! But how to get our "birds" down the mountain to the camp? Our amateurs were puzzled.

Not so the hunters professional. Their ready wit, and long experience, made them equal to all emergencies. The great she bear was slung with leathern straps between two of the mounted men, while panther, bucks and doe, each tasked a single rider; and we made our way down in safety to our lonely hollow, between the gigantic masses, on every hand, of the Balsam Mountains, while our little cataract, sent up to our ears a lively chaunt of welcome and rejoicing, long before we came in sight!

All parties now went to work with a *vim!* It was cold weather, be it remembered, and our amateurs, in spite of furs and flannels, were made to shiver. Rousing fires were soon kindled, and, without taking off our own, we very soon had stripped the jackets from the carcasses of all our victims; and the work of dissection went forward, under the dexterous butchery of the professional hunters, who are all first rate butchers, as well as excellent tanners.

Of course, the peach and honey drams were not forgotten, and these were freely imbibed, at moderate intervals, while the anatomists went on with their work.

It was now a slash in the meat, and now a swallow from the drink, and in the increasing rigours of the evening, no harm followed from the frequency of our potations!

The preparations for supper went on also. Our cook knew his task. The one employed, at present, enjoyed quite a reputation for the excellence of his *cuisine*. He had joined our party during the week; and, as the hunters very soon learn to know in what each person is most an expert, "Bald Head Bill Bauldy"—otherwise "William Bauldy"—at once received his appointment, as Chief Cook and Bottle Washer during the encampment!

Bald Head Bill—so called because of a head as clean of hair as the palm of a damsel's hand; the scull polished as marble, and shining bright in the sun, as a sudden moonlight—had distinguished himself in the army; but much more as a cook than a soldier! Of this hereafter.

He wore a wig of monstrous dimensions; a great shaggy mass of reddish brown hair, by which his natural deficiencies of cranium, were concealed. It was only as a favour to the amateurs of the party that he showed his naked skull, to illustrate the truth of the story which he subsequently told us of his experiences and adventures in the "FLURRIDAY WAR." But of all these matters, anon!

Well, you will please suppose supper at an end, and our hunters all happy and at ease, around a roaring fire; that our tent, pitched behind us, is amply supplied with convenient mattresses and any quantity of blankets, shawls and wrappers; that we can lie with our feet to the fire, or sit grouped around it, and spin our yarns to the common merriment; while our baggage wagon, at hand, held its full stores of the creature comforts; the coffee, sugar, bread stuffs, bacon, and the demijohns of peach, honey, and mountain dew; all of which, like the famous cruse of the widow, seemed inexhaustible. At all events, there was no lugubrious party, to look into the faces of the group, and mournfully announce the total evaporation of the spirits!

The hour for the "Lying Camp" had come, and "Big Lie" was duly installed, as before, on the broad stone of patriarchal authority, which he filled with a dignity becoming his *fauteuil.*

Brave old Jim Fisher still held this eminent position, and he was fully equal to any that he undertook. He ordered a stoup of *the* beverage, all round, by way of inauguration, and the ceremonials soon gave way to the tale-tellers.

II.

How to Cross an African River.

"Big Lie," after a little *"hemming and hawing,"* apologetic, for the liberty he was about to take, now called upon Major Henry, the oldest of our amateurs, for "a lie that should run like the truth!"

Now, Major Henry was quite a wit and humourist, and almost as famous, as a *raconteur,* as he was, in his professional capacity, as a Lawyer. But the good things of the wit and humourist, of a high civilization, and of the purely conventional life of the city, are very apt to be thrown away upon the rude hunters of the mountains, who require the greatly salient in their narrations, and need striking incident to command attention. The quiet humours, the latent fun, and irony, are not so easily perceptible to them;—and the exaggerations of the "Lying Camp," especially, called for the startling, the wild, extravagant; for the droll rather than the wit!

Major Henry was conscious of all this, and was disposed to dodge his responsibility to the circle; but the more he *shied* the duty, the more authoritatively did "Big Lie" insist upon it;—and the Major was forced finally to respond; which he did, by telling an anecdote of a famous African negro, well known as an ancient boatman on the Congaree, who, in process of time, had devolved upon him the task of navigating the flat boat at McCord's Ferry, on that river.

This old African, who claimed to have been a Prince in his own country,—as was the boast of nearly every old African I ever knew,—had grown saucy from age and infirmity. His very impudence finally became so amusing, as to disarm the anger of those who provoked it; and, day by day, Cudjo grew more and more audacious; showing but little reverence for white or black, old or young, man or woman; wagging his tongue with wondrous familiarity in all directions, with a license as free as that of the wind which blows on all it listeth.

That he was a good flat-boatman and did his duty at the ferry, reconciled all parties, in *some* degree, to his impertinences, even where his humour might have failed to do so!— —Cudjo, by the way, was not his princely African name, but as he died finally, in the very odour of sanctity with that name, in the bosom of the Fetisch Church of Mumbo Jumbo, we respect his memory too much to declare his regal title or royal claim, as a Prince among the Gullahs!

"We were crossing McCord's Ferry, on the Congaree, on one occasion," said Major Henry, "Col. McCord and myself, when there was a heavy freshet, the waters being very high; so high that polling was difficult; the river was roughened by a heavy blow, and the winds swept our poor little flat about, making it very difficult, and indeed, somewhat doubtful, if we should be able to make the opposite shore, or even regain that which we had left. The boat was old and rotten, and one of the poles had broken. Two only remained, and these were managed by Cudjo, and a young assistant negro named Tony, which name was sometimes abridged to 'Scrub.' Cudjo had but little of the strength of youth remaining, and the vigour of his arms bore no sort of proportion to that of his tongue.

"Cudjo was in a strait on the present occasion. All his labours seemed to be fruitless in impelling the flat, which simply whirled about, as it were, in a circle, making no headway; and, after the work of a goodly hour, we found ourselves within a few yards of the point of land from which we had taken our departure.

"Cudjo, suddenly threw down his pole, put his arms akimbo, and confronting McCord, said as abruptly as gruffly,—

" 'Misser McCode, de white people ob dis country, is jis' so many bloody big fool! Dey hab no sense!'

" 'What moves you to think so *now*, Cudjo?'

"'Wha' moob me, you axes? Enty you kin see for you'saff? Whay de sense, I wants for know, ob trying to cross ribber like dis yer Cong'ree in flat boat, wid long pole wha' can't reach de bottom when de fresh come down. Yer we is now, jis a'turning and a twisting all about; we can't git across and we can't git back; de water takes us one way; de win' takes us anoder way; you can't hole on to de bottom wid de pole, and when you does, de strain ob de water and de win togedder, brecks de pole in you' han'; and dar you air; wid not'ing else for do but set down in de bottom ob de flat, and sing de Hallelujah, when you can't see Jarusalem! Lawd ha' massy! I tell you, Misser McCord, you buckrah people all so many d——d fool! In my country, we nebber hab flat to cross river! Nebber hab boat! Nebber hab de worry to work de pole, tell your berry eyes is a swimming in de sweat!'

"'How then, Cudjo, do you cross the river in your country?'

"'Misser McCode,—you hab no sense? You can't 'tink for you'saff? Hab for tell you ebbry'ting?—Look-a-dar;—out-a-yonder;—on de bank?—Wha' dat you see?'

"'I see nothing but an alligator.'

"'Das him! Well, you sees alligator! Das's alligator, I 'speck, 'bout twelve foot long! He's baby to da alligator in my country; but, he kin *do*, ef you *mek* 'em do! Da' same alligator, you sees dar, kin carry you 'cross de ribber,—dis berry ribber, Congaree!'

"'Well, I've no doubt, if he's willing; he's strong enough!'

"'I don't ax ef he's willing, Misser McCode! I only axes ef he's strong! I *meks* 'em willing! In my country, when I comes to de ribber and wants to git across, I looks 'bout me! I sees de alligators a-sleeping all along de bank ob de ribber! I picks out de biggest ob 'em all, wha's strong enough for carry me! Well, I creeps up to 'em sly as fox at de hen roos'. When I gits close enough, I jumps on he back! Dat wakes 'em up; and de moment he wakes, and feels someting heabby on he back, he push for de ribber! I hole on, buckle my leg roun' em so, and 'pur (spur) 'em fast as I kin! Well, wha' den? He push for de ribber, and carry me 'cross! Das's no d—— fool ob a flat, wid long pole, or long rope, and no bodders wid de fresh or de win'. We jis goes ahead, you see, jis as ef he was hoss, or mule, all de same! Ah! Masser McCode, ef de people ob dis country, dis buckrah people, only bin hab sense!'

"'But Cudjo, how do you *guide* your alligator horse, or boat?' quoth McCord.

"The saucy negro interrupted him with an air of scorn, as he replied,—

"'Misser McCode, you hab no sense! I hab for tell you ebbry ting! Wha' da dat?'—

"Holding up his right hand thumb.—

"'That's your thumb!'

"'Ah! *you* hab t'umb enty! Well, you guide 'em wid dat! You 'tick (stick) your t'umb in he eye! Dat will guide em 'cross de ribber.'

"'But, suppose Cudjo, I want him to carry me *down* the river?'

"'Well, wha' den? Ef you wants em to go down de ribber, 'tick you t'umb in he *right* eye! Den he go down.'

"'But,' says McCord, 'suppose I wish him to go *up* the river, Cudjo?'

"'My God, Misser McCord, you hab no sense? I hab for tell you ebbry t'ing? Enty you got 'noder t'umb? Well, you want 'em for go *up* de river? 'Tick you udder t'umb in he leff eye; dat shall mek 'em go *up* de ribber!'

"'But suppose, Cudjo, I want him to go neither up nor down, the river, but to go, just as we wish to go now, straight across;—how then shall I manage him?'

"'My God! Misser McCode, you hab no sense? You can'nt tink for you seff? I hab for tell you ebbry 'ting? Enty you got *two* t'umb? 'Tick bote t'umb in he eye; dat will mek him carry you 'traight cross de ribber!'

"'But, Cudjo, suppose he should,—just when we are in the middle of the river,—take it into his head, to go straight down to the bottom?'

"Here the African was at his wits end; his resources were exhausted; he fidgetted; looked dubiously at McCord and then at me, and, having no other alternative, seizing his pole, and working fiercely at the flat, he replied—

"'Ah! Misser McCord, ef de alligator go *down* to *de bottom,* and hab you on he back;—da berry bad! You hab for swim out de bes' way you kin!'

III.

Here Henry's story, or anecdote, reached its final conclusion. While he was telling it, we noted that "Bald Head Bill" was restless and fidgetting, showing himself somewhat impatient, and evidently, with difficulty, restraining himself from interrupting the narrator. But, as soon as the Major had finished,—he cried out,—

"I'll be dod-derned, Major, but you've got hold of a leetle piece of my history of the campaign I had in Goodwyn's Rigimint in the Flurriday War! You've hearn me tell it, fellows, more'n a dozen times!"

"Yes, to be sure; that's true, Bauldy;" was the cry from several.

"I'm very sorry," said Henry, "to have used up any of your thunder, Bauldy; but, I certainly never heard of your Florida Campaign; and I reckon there's several others here that never heard it. I move you, 'Big Lie!' that 'Bald Head Bill' shall tell us his adventures in that same campaign, and we shall then see how much like *his* alligator is to that of my African Prince, Cudjo."

The motion was seconded, and "Big Lie" gave the order.

Bauldy, so eager before, was now disposed to play the bashful; but, after some petty affectations, he consented, and proceeded after the following fashion.

IV.

How Bauldy Volunteers to Fight the Seminoles.
First Fight with a Bear.

"Well, fellows and you Gentlemen, you all ricollects, I reckon, about the great Flurriday War, with the Siminole Injins, not quite a hundred years ago. You remember thar was all sorts of great fighting, and skrimaraging in that country, and no great deal of killing on any side, 'cepting the massacr*ee* of Dade's Regiment of 'riglars, that let themselves be cotched in a dern'd ambuscado, when the Ingins chawed 'em up to a man.

"The poor fellows *fit* well, though, but had no chaince; and the Siminoles jist popped 'em down and sculped 'em, as ef they had been so many rabbits in a ring! I dont reckon, with all their cannon and shooting, they killed a single red skin.—

"That warn't all, ef you remember. The Siminoles come mighty nigh to captivating St. Augustine, and sculping all the people, women and children; and so thar was a call for volunteers from Georgy and Sout' Carlina, to go down and save St. Augustine, and whip off the red skins.

"Thar was a grand to do, specially, you see, as that sassy savage, Osceola, had corked up Giniral Gaines in a sort of hollow; and thar was some other generals, in pretty nigh the same fix; and, I reckon, of all on 'em, Giniral Clinch, who knowed the country, and the nater of the beasts that waur in it, he did about the best fighting of 'em all! As for the big Giniral Scott, he made a big fuss, and marched his grand army in three columns, and beat his drums, whenever he come nigh to the swamps and thicks, as ef to give fair notis to the Seminoles to lie low and keep dark;—and so they did! They squatted close in the bush and thick, and on the edge of the swamp, and grinned like Chesse-cats, as they seed the big armies marching by, with the big gineral, seven foot in his boots, making the drums beat, and the horns blow, whenever he rode ahead! 'Twas fine marching, I reckon; but marching warn't the thing, and there was no fighting. The grand army did not pick up a single red sculp.

"But I ain't to tell you of the whole war, but only the part that I, Bill Bauldy, had in it.

"Well you must know that I happened to be in Lexington Destrict, South Carolina, when Col. Goodwyn, of Columbia, called for

[*one page of MS missing*]

ways they hev in rigilar armies. We waur over six hundred men; all young fellows like myself, and a stout set of chaps they waur; and, once fairly in a skrimmage, they went at it, with tooth and toenail; and sich a hollering as made the woods shiver agin! I confess, I wan't much of a sodger, and hed no more idee of fighting than I had of flying to Heaven on the wings of the wind, as is writ in Holy Scripters. I was always a peaceable man, that only wanted to be let alone; and ef so be I hed pleased, I could have passed myself off for a man past his time of sarvice, seeing that my head was jest as bald of hair as a yellow tarrapin's belly. Besides, I was mighty apt to ketch cold, ef I didn't wear my wig all the time, sleeping and waking. Knowing that, I bought two new wigs from Bedell in

Columbia, and stowed 'em, convenient away in my skairt-pockets. Then I was ready for Flurriday, and all blazes!

"And twas mighty soon that the Colonel hed us in marching order; and, almost afore I know'd whar I was, I was down in Flurriday, and hunting up the Ingins. And in the s'arch, which was mighty like hunting for a needle in a haystack, we was in the saddle from morning to night, and sometimes from night to morning; now pushing over the hot sand hills, and now hafe wading, hafe swimming over the lakes, and lagoons; and then agin in great thicks, whar you couldn't see twenty feet before you! Well, we got into some skrimmages on the Withlachooche and other swampy rivers; but all I seed of the Siminoles was in the hearing of their bullets out of the swamp. Then we'd charge the swamp, and Lawd! they waur no whar!

"Twas in the second skrimmage on the Withlacoochie that my mar', on a suddent, went dead, sprawling right onder me, with a Siminole bullet through her head! I was pitched off, thinking, all the time, twas in my own head that the bullet lodged! I own up; I waur mighty skear'd that time! But that tuk me out of the troop! I hed no money to git another horse, and thar waur none to spar' in the rigiment. I had to go into the infant-*ry*. But I got an adssessment of the vally of my mar', and a sartipcate from the Quarter Master, for a hundred and fifty dollars, that government was to pay me; but, though I sent in my bill and the order to government, by our ripresentative, I never got a copper of money, and haint got it to this day. Our rip (representative) said thar was no use to try, onless I was willing to give a hundred out of the hundred and fifty to sartin high ossifers of government, who always expected two thirds of all the money of the sodgers, to get the rest for 'em. I told him, I'd see all the d——d rogues of Congress in Hell's blazes before I'd give 'em a copper!—And he then tells me a long story of a poor widow woman, one Amy Dardan, who had been trying to get the money from government, for her mar', ever sence the old war of the Revolution; and he said that the very *intrust* on that mar's money, 'cording to the adssessment, would be enough to buy up the whole state of Delawar', or Rhode Island; so, as government would hev to pay so much, they detarmined to pay nothing at all; and so the poor woman never got the hide of her mar' or a copper of her money! A'ter hearing that, I gin it up, and hed no more use for Congress or Washington government!

"Well, a'ter the loss of my mar', I had to go into the infan*try*, as I tell'd you; and then we hed a few more skrimmages. I own up, I warn't fond of fighting any how; and this gitting shot at, when you couldn't see your inimy, always brought on me an attack of the 'misery,' in my innards!

"So, you see, one of the ossifers said, seeing as how I couldn't keep up with the rigiment when we was on double quick, guine into a skrimmage,—

"'This fellow Bill Bauldy is not good on a march, and he's no 'count in a fight. What shill we do with him?'

"Another one, that hed a quicker sense of a fellow's vartues, he said,

"'He looks as ef he mout be a first rate cook! Hev' you ever done any cooking, Bauldy?'

"Well, felows, you all knows my vartues as a cook by this time, so I spoke up bold, and said,

"'I'm fust rate at that business. I kin cook any thing from a frog to an alligator terrapin; from a pairch to a blue cat; from a chicken to a turkey gobbler; from a pea to a cabbage! I'm fust rate as a cook!'

"'We'll try you, my good fellow,' said the Kurnel; 'and ef you only does hafe so well as Rafe Parkinson, you'll do!'

"Now, you see, Rafe Parkinson *was* a good cook enough—nothing to name in the same day with me—but he never could git his belly full of fighting; and soon as he haird an alarum, any thing of a skrimmage guine on, the dern'd fool would drop his gridiron, ketch up his musket, and run, fast as he could drive, whar he haird the firing; and one day he got a bullet through his body, thet stopt his cooking and fighting the same day together. Twas jest a'ter that, that the oss'fers put me in his place; so I gin up my musket, mighty glad to git shet of it, and took to the gridiron, the sasspan and the spiggot.

"Twant easy work, I tell you, for all the ossfer's mess waur powerful hairty feeders, and thar waur nothing that they could lay hands on that warnt grist to their mill. They ate plentiful: and thar was a mighty fine supply of all things in the pervision wagons! We hed the finest hams, and the best haird-tack; and beef a plenty, and cured fish; and leetle fish in boxes, called 'sartins' and a hundred nice things besides, to say nothing of any quantity of good Monongahely! Them chaps fed well off the government, though I could'nt git a dollar for my mar'! They kept me busy cooking from morning to night, and sometimes, when we waur in camp for rest, pretty much all night. Some on 'em would want something to eat all hours of the night! Then I hed to carry in dinner and breakfast, and supper, and wait upon table; and all I hed to help me was a poor little mangy drummer boy, that couldnt beat, and so they gin him to me for a '*scullion*' as they called it.

"Twas mighty hard work, I tell you; but then I got plenty of fine feed myself; and thar waur sartin 'parquizites,' as they called 'em, in their leavings on table, sich as hafe bottles of wine, and fine Spanish cigars, that I tuk to jist as naterale, as a duck takes to water. Lawd bless you, when they warn't fighting, them fellows lived like fighting cocks! Thar was hairdly nothing that they hedn't got! Some of the kurnels carried their crockery with them, and I've hairn tell of one gineral that carried sartin crockery wessels with him, wharever he marched, sich as no gentleman ever puts on his side board! Fact, as I'm a living sinner!

"Well, a'ter dinner always, when the off'sers left the table, I'd begin to pick up, eating as I went. I never missed any of the good things, and I was death on the liquor when I could git it, and never let a hafe bottle, or a cigar pass me, right or left, when they left 'em on the table.

"They had a smart chaince of them big long cigars, they call '*Plantation*,'—a-most a foot long I reckon; jist what them Cuba planters makes for their own smoking. They're the finest as well as the biggest cigars that I ever put betwixt *my* teeth. They waur all smuggled in, when we waur at St. Augustine, and the off'sers shet one eye on the smuggling, and the other they sot on the shares. Twas jist the way to sarve a government that won't pay a man for his gray mar', killed in the sarvice.

"The Cappin' of the schooner had only to count out his hundred boxes, and flip ten on 'em to one side, and then ninety to t'other side, and so we shar'd. Ten in the hundred's mighty good sharing, I tell you, only for shetting your right peeper, and seeing nothing but with the left! And the Cappin got his market mighty quick for all the rest. Any ten of them boxes, that I hed to stow away in our wagon, would ha' paid for my gray mar'.

"Well, I larne'd, in that school of the kitchen, to smoke cigars instid of Powhatan pipes! And I larned to love 'em mightily! But I durstn't let the offsers see me at it; and so, of an a'ternoon, when they waur all dressing and drilling, and filing and marching, on the parade, I used to slip off to the 'thick,' a-most down to the river, and git under some big tree, hiding away snug, and thar smoke my 'plantation' to my own satisfaction. I never stopt short of three of an a'ternoon, and I swallowed smoke sometimes pretty free at night time, whenever I got a chaince.

"Meantime, I made my little drummer boy, 'Scullion' we called him,—la'rn his business! Ef the little rascal didn't wash up all the plates and dishes, and hev the pots and pans all clean, when I come back from my smoking, I 'gin him Jesse! I thrashed him, ontell I made him larn his lessons!

"Well, 'twas jest in one of these a'ternoons, when the rigiment was a drilling, I slipt off to the 'thick' along the river, and laid myself down and lighted my 'long nine', and gin myself up for a grand smoke! But fust, afore that, I hed drunk up a full hafe bottle of as good liquor, as ever was left to take care of itself on a dinner table. So, when I come to lie down, onder the tree, and got the cigar in my mouth, I felt a leetle overkim,—drowsy like,—though I didn't get quite to sleep! And thar' I puffed, and I watched the beautiful blue and white smoke clouds curling upwards all about my head, jest as ef they knowd I was a-watching em, and loved to see 'em curling up, beautiful in the sun; and I had sweet thoughts, of a thousand things that waur all pleasurable; and I thought to myself, how happy I waur; and ef this sort of life could only last forever, with hairdly nothing to do, 'cept to lick the scullion boy drummer, and make him larn his business; and with jist a plenty always to eat of fine things; and to drink of fine liquors; and to smoke of fine cigars, I would'nt kear to be a King or even a President!

"Well, jist as my head was chock full of this pleasant thinking, a-most like a dream, what should I hear, but pit-a-pat, pit-a-pat, right behind me, as ef a soft foot was sot down upon the dry leaves, making a sort of crinkle. And, says I to myself, ef it should be a beautiful young woman now! Lawd-a-marcy! ef it should only be Susannah Sykes, the prettiest gal in all Lexington Destrict!

"Pit-a-pat! Pit-a-pat!—It come closer and closer; and, at last, I felt a sort of breathing jist over my shoulder. Twas my right shoulder. Then, suddent, I haird a sort of snort, and, turning my head a leetle, for I was too lazy to git up, Lawd love you, what should I see but a great big brown b'ar, a-most as big as an elephant, with his great snout jist over my shoulder!

"My hairt jumpd into my very mouth. I had no we-pon, and didn't know what to do! The b'ar hed the whip hand of me, I knowd, for he was on his legs, and I hafe stretchd out on my back. But Natur tell'd me what to do. 'Twas all Natur, for I never thought about it, ontell the thing was done; but, suddent, without trying to git up, I tuk the 'long nine' out of my mouth, and clapt the fire eend to his nose!

"Lawd love you! Ef iver you seed a b'ar back out from a skrimmage, you'd ha' seen it then! Soon as he felt the fire at his nose, he snorted deep; then stept backward, about three steps, going tail foremost; then he stopt to rub his nose, with one paw a'ter the other!—

"Soon as I seed that, I sees that I had got the whip-hand of *him!* So I puts the 'long nine' back in my mouth; draws a couple of good whiffs; takes another cigar out of my pocket; lights thet, and puts it in my mouth besides. Then I drawed quick on both cigars, and I gits up, and faces the b'ar, and makes at him; puffing, as haird as I could, all the time!

"Soon as he sees me coming at him with two blazing stars in my mouth, he begins to back agin; snorting free, as ef he was still feeling the fire! He went on, waddling backward, tail foremost, clumsy enough and cur'ous to see; and I a'ter him, puffing my cigars hairder than ever! When he sees that, he fairly turns tail and runs; mighty awkward, but mighty fast, as you know a b'ar kin run; and, in three minutes, by the sun, he was out of sight—and kivered up in the 'thick'! I should'nt be afear'd to say that he was rubbing his nose to this very hour! It's mighty sartin, to my thinking, that ef he's living now, he's never forgot that transaction!

"That was my first fight with a b'ar; and I licked him fair, though he did git the whip hand of me at the beginning! And now,—'Big Lie,'—don't you think twould be good to liquor all round, jist to keep the cold wind off a man's stomach?"

V.

How Bauld Head Bill Lost His "Sculp."

We liquored all round, every hunter acknowledging the propriety of protecting that delicate region, the stomach, from the atrocious invasion of the east wind, which, even in the days of Abraham, was proverbial for its bad character!— —After wiping his mouth, which he did expertly, with the sleeve of his coat, "Bald Head Bill" proceeded with the narrative of his experiences in the "Flurriday War," after the following fashion.

"That fight with the B'ar, in which I licked him so fairly, gin me courage for any thing! A'ter that, I begin to see how easy twaur, for a man, ef he'd only set right about it, to lick the whole creation of beasts. I seed that every thing warnt to be done by main force, and strength, but by skill and slight of hand, and knowing a thing or two,—knowing which eend of the cigar to put to your own mouth, and which eend to clap to the muzzle of your B'ar! And let me tell you that leetle as that idee may seem to you, fellows, there's ten pussons in every twenty thet kaint come to a right onderstanding about it!

"You may reckon, I spose, thet, a'ter thet transaction, I believed more in them Spanish cigars than ever; and I only wished our offsers had got the ninety boxes, instid of the ten out of every hundred! I went rigilarly at them every day, and never passed by any hafe bottle of liquor that stood next to 'em convenient for the handling. And every a'ternoon of parade, I jist set my scullion drummer boy at l'arning his business, and went off sly to take my smoke. I was more in love with that one tree in the thick whar I licked the b'ar than ever; and them hours I puff'd away in smoke, jist a hafe sleeping onder that tree, waur about the most heavenly hours I ever hed in all my born days, day or night.

"But, somehow, thar's an eend to every good thing some day, and I've found out, a'ter the tryings of forty years, that a man's pleasures don't last any longer than any thing else; and sartinly they never do outlast his liquor! My smoking onder that tree was to come to an eending mighty short and suddent, and more suddent than sweet!

"One hot a'ternoon, when I hed jest swigged pretty nigh on to a pint of good Jamaica, which we got by smuggling as well as the cigars, I gin my 'Scullion' a thundering lickin' to make him l'arn his lessons the quicker.

"And the darn'd dirty little rascal, he runned off, soon as my back was turned, and when I was off for my smoke in the 'thick.' He runned off, and without stopping to clean up a single dish, or plate, or knife, or fork, or nothing thet was needcessary for the supper table thet night! Lawd bless you, and keep you from being sich a fool as to ixpect gratitude from man or beast. A'ter all my lickin's and kickin's of that scullion, to show him how to l'arn the business, he runned away, leaving me to git on eeny how I could!

"But I didn't know nothing 'bout it jest at that time. I went for my smoke. I hed five of them 'long nines' in my pocket, and my skin was jest as full of liquor as it could well hold, without leaking out; and I was jist about as happy that day, as King Nebuchadozzor, jest afore they turned him out to eat grass! I laid down at full length, cigar in mouth, and drawed easy upon it, and I looked up and watched how the creamy and blue clouds of smoke, twirled up and twisted round, and floated among the tree tops and kept going up and up, till I seed them where they stopt to rest, cla'r away up in Heavin! And I hed the sweetest thinkin' at thet time, 'specially about Susannah Sykes, the purtiest white gal in all Lexington Destrict! And it did seem to me as ef I seed her own beautiful self or a beautiful picter of her, coming down to me, through the tree tops, as ef she had jist come down from the blessed skies!

"I own up, I was a-feeling of my liquor, boys. The Jamaica was a working in my brain; and what with the Jamaica, and three of them 'long nines,' I felt a leetle onsartin about the motion of the airth, and more then onst, it did seem to me, as ef twarnt the skies a-coming down to me, but the airth gitting upwards, and swelling onder me, and carrying me up towards the skies; and twas then I seed Susannah, coming through the trees. A'ter thet, come more of them happy thinkin's, and I felt all overish with happiness, when, all on a suddent, I haird an alarum!

"There waur a shouting and a shooting! Thar waur rifle shots and musket shots; and now I haird a yelling; and now a shouting, and then the drums a beating and the bugles a blowing, and I know'd thar waur a sharp scrimmage guine on!

"But, somehow I didn't feel like gitting up to go into it; for, you see, I waur only a cook; and not a sodger; and then, agin, I hed no we'pon! Besides, twouldnt do for the only good cook in the Gineral's mess to be shot down like that chuckleheaded fellow, Rafe Parkinson! You kin git any number of sodgers, thet's jest fit to be killed, and not good for nothing else;—but it's not one sodger in a thousand that you kin convart into a decent cook! I know'd all that, and feelin' what a loss twould be to the offsers, ef I was to be shot, I laid low, and kept dark; jest lying whar I was, snug in the 'thick', and drawing my long nine easy with easy breeth!

"And so I let the shooting and the shouting go on, without so much as letting the woods know that I haird any thing about it. And sometimes the noise would come closer and closer; and then I'd feel mighty oncomfortable; but then agin twould go far off; and I could jest make out to hyar the drums; so I begin to think that the darn'd red skins hed got the whip hand of our sodgers, and was a driving them ahead! And that, agin, made me think of the orful massacr*ee* of poor Major Dade's Rigiment, all cut to mammocks, with never a hair left on any man's head for a woman's fingers to play in!—

"Them thinkin's made me mighty oneasy; for, ef our sodgers waur all driv' off, what would bekim of me? Whar would be the 'parquizites'; the cigars, the Jamaica, and the easy time I hed of it, after licking the scullion boy, every a'ternoon? And how was I to git to the Rigiment, with the dern'd red skins all between me and them?

"And then, the next, and worst consideration, in that thinking!—'Sposing the red skins should captivate me; wouldn't they massacr*ee* me, jest as ef I waur a part of Dade's Rigiment?

"I begun to be orful skear'd, and to look about me; when, Lawd love you, as I lifted my head, what should I see, but a dern'd infarnal red skin, a'most ten foot high, with his tomhog in one hand and his rifle in t'other, sneaking along through the bushes like a catamount. And the dern'd sharp-eyed fellow seed me jist as I lifted my head, and I seed him, quick as blazes, ketch up his rifle, and p'int!

"When I seed that, I squatted low as I could lie; flat to the ground; and the bullet tore the bush jist right over my head, and I haird the report of the rifle, loud as a seventy six pounder, the minit a'ter!

"I do believe that the dern'd savage tried his best to murder me that very time! I'm sure he did his best to hit me with that bullet.

"Well, he jist missed me, you see; but the thing warn't to eend thar. I know'd he'd be looking a'ter me yet, and what was I to do; without no we'pon to fight; and mighty leetle stomach for it, a'ter eating so hairty a dinner and smoking them long nines!

"I don't know as how I did any much thinking jist then! It was all feelin' and skear! My hairt was in my mouth! But I laid close, flat as a terrapin to the ground, with my head drawed into my shoulders, jist making as leetle show as possible.

"I waited and listened! I haird nothing! But I felt sure the cussed red skin was a-working all round me, like a painther, and feeling his way, leetle by leetle, along my tracks.

"Soon I haird a stick crack, and the dry leaves rattle, but I didn't dar' to look up. But all on a suddent, I felt him plump upon my back! He had jist jumped like a painther upon me, and I know'd my time was up, and I caved in for dead, with all the 'misery' in my innards.

"In another minit, his fingers waur in my wool—that is, in my wig, and I reckon in a minit more I'd ha' felt his knife working round my head; but the wig come off, in his hands, and I haird him cry out

" 'Hegh!—A-poo-coola chee!'

"And with that he jumped off my back, jist as suddent as he hed jumped on, and I haird him a running.

"Then I looked up, and seed him guine at full speed, with the wig in his hand, and he run a'most fifty yards afore I seed him stop and git behind a tree!

"I was a-thinking to git up and driv at him, jist as I was, without any we'pon, thinking, you see, how I had driv off the b'ar, by a fair skear!

"But I hedn't the hairt for it, and my cigars had gin out! I jist had to lie close and watch for him, with my head jist lifted high enough to see over the bushes. Meantime, as my head begin to feel a leetle bit coolish, I tuk my t'other wig out of my pocket, and clapt it on!

"And so I laid, and waited and watched; and soon I sighted the red rascal sneaking round agin, jist as he did before. But I seed him only for a minit, as he worked his way round the tree, and was kivered by the bushes.

"Well, I reckon, a full quarter of an hour must hev slipt by—I thought it an hour,—when suddently, I felt the savage beast on top of me agin, coming down at a jump. Then I haird him cry out agin—

" 'Hegh!—A-coola-la! Coola-la: Etchee-ma-la-la!'

"In his own sarpent-like way of speaking, twas bekaise he seed I hed as good a head of hair on as ever, in spite of the sculp he tuk before! He jerked agin at my wig, and off it come in his hands, and then he bolted agin, and took fairly to his heels, for another hundred yards.

"By this time, I begin to think how twas. You see, the red rascal thought I was a white witch or wizard, may be, and they're mons'ous afeard of witches.

"Dern his buttons! he hed now got both of my wigs and I hed no more. I could guess that he waur a studying them wigs behind the tree. What his studies come to, I kaint say: but I warn't to git off. He come at me agin, but didn't jump upon me this time. He squatted on me, right across my back, astraddling me, as ef I was a horse, and he poked me in the side with his knife, sticking me a leetle only, but meking me feel mighty oncomfortable.

"Well, I twisted about onder him, and then he laughed like a great frog, and got up and turned me over with his feet, till his face looked fairly into my face!

"Then he made a motion for me to stand up, and when I did so, he tuk one wig a'ter the other, and clapt one on his own head and tother on mine. And oh! Lawd! how the conseeted rascal laughed at the i*deee!*

"But twan't for long! He soon shook his tomhog over my head, and p'inted me to march.

"And so I knowd I was captivated by the Siminoles and I was all over in a trimble, thinking of the captivation of poor Gineral Dade, and all his rigiment, and how they waur all massacr*ee*d.

"But I must licker now! I feel all over, when I think of that time, as ef the cussed knife of that red skin waur about to wipe its way clean round my forehead, sculp or no sculp! I must licker to ease off my feelings! Hyar's to you, fellows, and may you never hev sich a feeling as I hed about that time when I was captivated!"

VI.

Bauldy a Captive. How Rescued from the Torture!

Bald Head Bill, swallowed his liquor, wiped his mouth, groaned bitterly with his memories and resumed.

"We walked on, the cussed red skin pushing me before him, every now and then, when he seed me falling behind, with the sharp eend of his knife. I could hairdly keep my legs, or hold up my head, and thar was a something gathering all the time in my eyes, that a'most blinded me from seeing. And somehow, I tried to think of Polly Hopkins, my mar', and thin agin of Susannah Sykes of Lexington Destrict, jist for a sort of divarsion, and to keep from thinking of Dade's Rigiment; but Lawd love you, I could think of nothing else; for jist as I tried to think of Susannah, I was minded that I, prehaps, would never see her agin! And jist then, I'd feel the sharp p'int of the red skin's knife, poking me for'ard from astarn!

"We marched, as I reckon, about three miles in this way, going down and keeping close to the river-swamp all the time. Then we come to a lagoon, and thar was a dug out. The cussed red skin made me git in and take up the paddles; and he sot a-watching me, with rifle and tomhog and knife ready, ef I didn't work the dug out as he wanted. So he'd p'int to this side and that side, and I paddled him through the lagoon, ontill we got out into the river, and then he p'inted me to cross to t'other side. Thar we got into another lagoon, and run up a bit ontell we got to a sawt of hammocky island. It looked so; as I could see nothing but water all about me.

"And sich a place as twas! The snuggest hiding place in the whole world; a rigilar swamp thick all round about it, so thick, thet you had to pass into the darkness of night before you got to the camp of the rid skins; and thar they all was, more than fifty warriors, with twice as many squaws, and a great swarm of boys and papooses, of all sizes and ages, and most of them jist as stark-naked as ef they waur jist then mother born.

"And only three miles off from our campment, whar we had been a-watching, and scouting, marching and counter-marching, for a month and more, in sarch of the red skins, and could never find 'em!

"It was cl'ar to me that thar had been a scrimmage! Thar was a great hubbub among 'em; the warriors having a grand dispute about something, and the old men putting in their palaver to keep 'em quiet.

"But the women made the cussedest racket of all.

"When they seed me, they made a rush at me; but my captivator kept 'em off at arm's length, ontill he hed shown 'em all how he could pull off my sculp, at a jerk, without drawing a drop of blood. That made 'em all mighty cur'ous; walking all round me, and trying to feel me.

"But when he showed 'em that I hed two sculps, and clapt one a'ter the other on his own head, the hubbub got to be quite an uproar. And the warriors passed the wigs from one to t'other: then they come up to me and felt my head all over, and rubbed it; and oh! how they laughed!

"Them fools thet tell you a red skin never laughs, knows nothing about the matter. I tell you, I've haird more laughing and joking in that Siminole camp, while I was in captivation thar', than I ever haird in any of our camps, the whole time I was on sarvice.

"But, while they waur all busy, looking at my head and feeling of it, and the wigs; on a suddent, a young woman, a bright sassy looking squaw, snatched away one of the wigs, clapt it on her own head and took to her heels.

"She hadnt too much clothing on to keep her from running fast and she show'd as pretty a pair of legs, as ever a trotting horse showed on 'Hampton's Race Course' at Columbya.

"The Ingin that had captivated me tuk a'ter her in double quick time, and a dozen more, men and women, tuk after him. Fast as the gal was, they run her down, and my captivator got back the wig, and 'gin her a sound box on the jaws for her pains.

"Then she and an old woman jumped at him, like two she-tigers; but the old men, they come between and parted them;—the warriors looking on and laughing at the sport without trying to lift a finger. 'Twas a fine race for two hundred yards, I reckon; and I laughed too;—I couldn't help it, though I ixpected every minit to be massacr*ee*d!

"And though you sees me hyar this minnit, and hears me talking, I warn't then so fur off from the tomhog as you may think. I sometimes wake up in a dream, and don't feel quite so sartin, remembering that time, that I'm edzackly a living man! The skear was sich, that I feels it now crawling through all my flesh and curdling to my bones.

For, you see, them red skins are mighty quick about the business when thar's massacr*ee*ing to be done. They makes mighty short work of it, and don't give a fellow much time, ef its only to say his prayers!

"And so twas with me. A'ter they had tired themselves down with studying my head and wigs, and I reckon that every man, woman and child, had a feel of my head; they went into a sawt of consult, or counsel, and, a'ter some long and tall talking, they come to me, and they looked into my face and eyes, and walked round me several times; then a sawt of Priest, or Prophet, come along, and he went round me, throwing up his hands and making a great howling.

"Says I to myself, says I—'It's my funeral ceremonies they're a'ter now!'

"Sure enough! Three strong young fellows seized upon me from behind, and in less than three minnits, they had tied me up to a young sapling. The dern'd red skins hed found out that I warn't no wizard, and not much of a sodger; and I'll be dern'd ef one of 'em didn't absolute spit in my face! Oh! how I wanted to knock him down!

"But my airms were tied, you see, and my body was tied, and I was stropped agin the tree, not so tight but I could twist about a leetle.

"Then who should come up but a dozen leetle brats of boys, not one of 'em more than ten years old. And they had their leetle bows and arrows, and they crack'd away at me, twelve steps off; and some of the arrows hit me in the breast, and some in the face, and one of 'em a'most brushed my eye; and some of the arrows hed leetle spikes in 'em, and when these touched me, and I'd twist about, and wriggle like, how the leetle red divils would laugh and yell as ef they had done great things!

"They was at me, in this way, for a good half hour, the old warriors looking on and setting 'em on, jist as you'd set a fice-puppy on a rooting pig!

"But, on a suddent, thar was a divarsion in my favour. Before any body could say Jack Robinson, an old squaw, that looked as ef she was a thousand years old,—the ugliest old hag you ever did see,—she comes up, and stands betwixt the boys and me; and behind her comes a young woman, that I reckon was her da'ter, and she carried a papoose on her back, and the old woman, she hits me with her fist three good polks right in my face. Then there was a great grunt from the men, the warriors. And they all cried out

"'Hegh!'

"But nobody did nothing. Then the old woman whipt out a knife, and she cut the grape vines that tied me. Then she gin me, I reckon, a dozen sound blows, one a'ter another, all in the face, and she motions me to the young woman and the child. And, without more ado, they strops the leetle red brat on my back, and I knows from that, thet I'm to be a child minder. Oh! I felt so mean!

"But when I considered that I warn't to be burnt alive, or tom-hogged, or shot to misery, by them cussed leetle red skins, I felt easier in my hairt and conscience; and I tuk the child, and thinking to please the old woman and the young one, I made much of the brat, tho' it was about the ugliest, dirtiest little mawmouth that I ever did see; and it smelled, for all the world, like an old pole cat in September!"

VII.

How the Alligator Relieves Bauldy of the Papoose.

"Now, my friends, jist you consider, for one minnit, the change in my fortin! Thar was I, only a few months ago, a sprigh young fellow, dashing away among the gals, and pretickilarly cavorting about Susannah Sykes, the purttiest critter, of the woman kind, in all Lexington District!—

"Then you sees me next, mounted on my mar', Polly Hopkins, with a bran new coatee and breeches, boots and spurs, cap on my head, and sabre at my side, pushing down with six hundred more handsome fellows, under Col. Goodwyn, to fight the red skins in Flurriday!

"A'ter that, and when the cussed red rascals, shot my mar', you sees me marching on my own two legs, among the infan*try!* Then, bekaise I was a bad hand for foot-walking, when the order was 'double quick,' I was permoted to be Chief Cook, of the Gineral and his staff!—

"And thar', in that honorable cumpassity, you sees me injoying the good things of the grand table, a'ter the ossfers had done;—thar' I had, day by day, the old Jamaica and other lickers, and a good handful of fine Spanish cigars, smuggled all the way from Cuba, to smoke off the misquitars!—

"Warn't I the happiest man!—

"And jist when I was the very happiest man, you sees what a change; with hairdly nothing to eat, fit for a Christian sinner, and a white riprobate, with a cuff on one cheek, and a clip on t'other;—with a red skin to poke me with his knife, when I went too slow; and to shake his tomhog at me, ef I went too fast; and an old woman, ugly as Satan, and I reckon jist as bad, to lay a stick over my shoulders when she was in a bad humour;—thar I had to tote the cussed leetle dirty wretch of a red skin papoose, from daylight to dark; and ef the brat cried, I got a whack over my back; and ef I got in any one's way, I got another, with a kick to balance!

"Jist consider, and ax yourselves, if I was n't about the most unfortunit pusson that ever walked on his naked feet among the snakes, with the tigers driving him from behind, all in full cry! And jist consider, as I did, ef twarn't a thousand times better to have swallowed the bullet of the red skin, and let him take the nateral sculp from my head, instid of the whig!

"Oh! I was the most desprit man!—all day with that brat of a papoose; all day kicked and cuffed about by every body, and never let to have any peace at night! Ef I warnt carrying the brat, I was fetching wood and water for the Fillystines; and they'd rout me up, with a kick, at any hour of the night, to do any dirty sawt of work, that they didn't want to do for themselves!

"I waur desprit, I tell you; and the thought come into my head more than onst, to make a short eending of the misery, by running upon some sharp knife, or jumping plump into the river; or taking some red skin by the throat, jist when he hed his tomhog ready, and gitting myself knocked in the head at onst, and git rid of all the misery.

"But then, you see, when I come to consider, I couldn't bring myself squar' up to any of them *idees!* For, you see, a stick from a sharp knife, even ef it don't kill you, will make you mighty oncomfortable; and gitting drowned is apt to choke a pusson from taking in so much water, without the leetlest drop of licker in it; and as for being tomhogged,—that, you see, would give a pusson gitting the knock, a very great pain in the head; and I 'membered that a pain in the head was always mighty hard upon me to bear.

"But, still them idees come up to me, day a'ter day, though I hed my argyments always ready to put them down. And one day, with the brat of a red skin in my arms, walking by the side of the river, I got the leetle wretch to sleep, and laid it down on the dry leaves at the foot of one tree, and laid down myself in the shadow of another big tree; and thar I sot, thinking of my dreadful, horrid, miserable, owdacious situation, ontill I was all over in a sawt of bloody sweat of agony and rejection! And I looked upon the river;—so smooth and sweet, so cool and comfortable, it flowed along;—I thought to myself—

"Drowning would be better! That's sartin!

"But drowning's very onpleasant, with swallowing and choking with so much water! And then, says I,—I should never see Susannah Sykes any more; and some other man will git her;—prehaps, some of my own rigiment, when he gits back! He'll tell her how I hed to carry a cussed red skin papoose, smelling like a pole cat, and that I drowned myself in my misery, and was eat up whole by the Flurriday fishes, that air as big, some of them as a yearling calf!

"And the poor gal would marry him, as she had no more chaince of me!

"Lawd! Lawd!

"The *idee* was enough to shake the very snakes out of the soul of a sinner!

"And I groaned in the sperrit and the flesh together; and I felt like guine home right away, and thrashing the dern'd lying trooper out of his breeches.—

"And jist then, when I felt all over wolfish, with the hair growing innards, I haird the cussed leetle red skin, pole cat papoose give a great screech, as ef the devil had it on an eend!

"And so he hed!—

"When I looked thar was the leetle wretch snatched up by an alligator, more than two hundred feet long!"

"Two hundred feet!" was the exclamation of one of the group of listeners—

Bauldy answered impatiently:

"I don't mean edzackly! I never measured the beast! He mout have been only fifty five feet and a few inches. Don't you stop me *now!*

"Yes!" he continued—"Two hundred or fifty five, or it mout be only twenty five or sixty, I kin tell you he was big enough for any pusson hyar, no matter what his gairth might be!

"And thar he was, with the brat in his jaws, moving off for the river, at a double quick. I could see the heels of the leetle red skin, hanging out of one side of his jaws, and the head out of the other; the mouth wide open, and screeching at every squeeze the beast gin it!"

VIII.

How the Alligator Runs Away with Bauldy.

Bauldy, here, professing to be quite overcome by his feelings, solicited our sympathies, and we all liquored together.

After a long, deep groan, he resumed as follows:

"You may jedge, men, of my feelin's and sitivation! You sees the dangers of my sitivation! Ef that brat of a papoose was carried off by the alligator, what was to become of me?—What was my chaince, for keeping in the flesh, or holding my soul safe in my body? Jist none at all! I'd be beat, and kicked, and knifed, and sculped, and tom-hogged, and shot to death with arrows, and burnt into the airms of etarnity, with pitch pine knots!

"I know'd all this, and, quick as a jerk, I jumped up, and made a'ter the alligator! I screeched too, with the hope to skear him, but that only made him run the faster, holding on to the red papoose, as ef he loved it.

"Fortenittly, I was closer to the river than him, and as I was fast as a runner, though slow at 'double quick,' I double quicked my running, and got up to him, jist as he slipped into the river.

"Right away, I jumped upon his back and straddled him!

"Now, as God's my Jedge, I never haird before that ere story of Major Henry, about Col. McCord, and the Congaree nigger boat-man, Cudjo.

"But Natur tell'd me what to do!

"I straddled the beast in the small of his back, doubled my legs onder his belly, and gin him my heels, with all my might. Onluckily, I hed no spurs! I mout ha' done better ef I had! But I did the best!—

"But my seat was a mighty oneasy one, for I hed no purchase of arms or hands, 'cept by hugging him round the neck, and this I tried fust; but, jist then, it flashed across me, as I seed his sharp leetle eyes, looking out from his pine-knotty head, that I could manage him by *gouging*, much better than by spurring. Gouging is a nateral art, you see, wharever a pusson hes got strong fingers and thick nails! I l'arned to use both of 'em at school, but not in writing nor 'rithmetic; and so one a'ter the other, I stuck my fingers into his eyes!

"Now, that made the beast see straight! He bellowed out like a great buffalo bull and made right for the shore agin. By the time he got thar, I could see he was mons'ous sick at the stomach, and jist as he touched the land, he womited the leetle red skinned brat of a papoose, cl'ar out among the bushes;—it bellowing all the time, as ef twaur murdered! and I reckon the sharp teeth of the alligator hed hurt its dilikit feelin's, hyar and thar! I could see the blood a trickling from side and shoulder.

"Well, I was jist making ready to let go and jump off my water-stallion, when Lawd love you, he gives a bellow, wipes his long tail right round me, so as to tie me down to his back, and then pushes off into deep water as fast as he could go!"—

IX.

Alligator Bull Fight.

"Here was a fix! You'll all say—'That was a fix!' I could git *on*, but I couldn't git *off!* But, my gitting on was down-stream, and jist as rapid as a steam boat. It was jist one long plunge for'ard! But I kept my fingers in the sockets of his eyes, and I worked 'em thar, so as to make him bellow as we went.

"But he went on!—

"Soon, I seed the river a-widening; and I thought ef the dern'd beast, would have twisted his tail off of me, I'd hev tried a swim,—though not much of a swimmer,—before the land got too fur off! But, for all my fingers working in his sockets, he held me fast! I was captivated by him! His tail curled, like a snake, over one of my thighs, fixing it fast, and lapped the other. Ef I only hed a knife now, I could have made him let loose, for I seed jist whar to cut through his leather, betwixt the j'ints, but the cussed red skins, when they captivated me, hed tuk my knife, three dollars in gould, my tobacco box and pipe, and I reckon three good long nines! And thar' was a fortygraph of Susannah, and she a gal of only twenty seven. It didn't look a bit like her, hows'ever; so I didn't kear so much for the loss of that!

"But, without no knife, and tied up as I waur, I could do nothing but work my fingers in the cussed brute's sockets. All the time, the land was gitting further and further off, on both sides. But the beast went on, guine down stream all the time, and giving out a great bellow, whenever I'd work my thumbs about his peepers.

"But, all on a suddent, he stopt short, and made a motion to wheel about. I soon l'arned what was at the bottom of his change of thinking.

"A terrible great bellow, from another beast, sounded in my ears, close on my left, and then I haird a rush through the waters, jist like fifty wild horses waur a-rushing through the woods!

"Twas another alligator, full speed a'ter my stallion.

"Now, at first, twant easy to say, ef he was a'ter me, or at my alligator! You know that the great king alligators, has, every one of 'em, a sawt of territory of his own. Thar he rules, and no one dar say—'Who is you?' He's king, I tell you, all thar, in that country!

"Now, from all I could l'arn in the country, the case was this. My water-stallion, not seeing well whar he was guine, had gone down into the enemy's country; and the king of that country was a'ter him with horse, foot artillery, dragoons and the rest.

"The strange King-'Gator, come along rushing,—and bellowing like thunder! At first my stallion tried to turn about and run back, as I tell you; but, I reckon, I was a-hurting his peepers jist then, and keeping him on his track. Finding he couldn't git off, he faced about for a fight. I reckon he was a brave beast, though I rode on his back!

"And the two great bull alligators drove at each other, with a wicked will! Sich a bellowing! Sich a churning of the water! It was all foam, and it splashed up into my eyes and over my face and head and shoulders, jist like a sudden souse coming down from one of our mountain falls, a hundred feet or more!

"And now they rushed agin each other, and I was terribly jostled between 'em when their hard sides come together. The great beast that was attacking us, made a mighty plunge at me, I'm a-thinking, with his jaws stretched wide as the great Cave of Kentucky, and his great white grinders showing like double saws ready to take off a fellow's leg at a single snap! I was dreadful skear'd, thinking he'd hev one of mine. But jist then, my stallion made a wheel, and the other shot past him like a flash, not able to stop himself easy, a'ter he hed made thet desperate start.

"But soon he wheeled about, and was for taking us on 'tother flank, but my nag was too quick for him, and shot round sprigh as a sparrow, and got a leetle headway on the back track, up the river.

"But the other was at him agin, savage as a meat axe; and whether it was me he was a'ter, thinking of his supper all the time, or whether it was only bekaise he had a love for fighting, kaint be said; I only knowed that I was in the misery all the time, thinking of my legs, and I kept 'em doubled-up, close as wax, round the belly of my stallion, and spurring him with my heels, and working his eyes in the sockets, to keep him up on the long stretch!

"But soon to'ther Bull, as they say in the army, changed his tick-tacks, and now fou't with his tail, making a flank movement to do so, and threshing at the starn of my stallion, ontell in self defence, he hed to ontwist, and loose my thigh, that he might put his own tail in fighting order, and to the same usage. And so they jist gin each other the flail, shot a'ter shot, the long tails coming down upon the river jist like thunder!

"At this sort of skrimmaging, I soon seed thet my stallion was a gitting the worst of it, and he felt it too; for, a'ter trying it for five minutes, he fairly begun to run, and now that he hed his tail free, he made pretty good time of it; but the spiteful inimy warn't willing to let him or me off; and he had the heels of my nag, and come up with him mighty soon, steering up close beside him, jist like a ship of war that wants to board at close quarters.

"Well, that gin me a new chaince. I could feel that my stallion was gitting badly whipt, and, as they say in the army, dam moralized! So I watched my chaince, and when the inimy bull was scraping his scaly sides agin my leg, I jist throwed myself over upon him and straddled him instid of my old stallion!

"Twas mighty well done, I tell you. I couldn't jump it, you see; having my feet upon nothing; but jist throw'd myself over him, hugging him round the neck fast, 'tell I could fling my legs over. Soon as I had ixicuted that grand army manoover; taking him in both flanks, and buckling close to his body; I stuck my thumbs into his peepers, without onst axing him, 'by you leave, old Gentleman!'

"With that he squirmed all over, as ef he hed a spasm in his bowels; and then he broke out in sich a bellow as shook the river to its very bottom; and it was c'lar to me that he hed lost all his stomach for the fight, as he let my old stallion make off at the rate, I reckon of fifty miles an hour—more or less!"

X.

The Great Bull Alligator Goes Down with Bauldy into the Bottomless Depths.

"Now, my friends, jest consider me in my new sitivation! I do think that was the greatest horse swap that ever I made in all my born and living days! My first stallion was pretty much broke down; and I reckon his eye sight warn't the best! What with the ride he hed taken onder me; and the spurring and gouging; and the fight with the other fellow; who did give him some heavy blows; he was in no fix for much more travel thet night.

"My other stallion, that I got in the swap, was, as I tell you, good for five hundred miles, more or less from day peep to sundown!

"Lawd! It would hev blessed your innards to hev seen how we went down the river under my whip and spur;—thet is under my gouging and kicking! The other stallion warnt a sarcumstance to the new one, and, as we went, shooting away, like a rocket, I begun to feel mighty proud, and to think over my swap, jist as happy, as ef I hed traded off a bloody, sore backed, lazy mule, fourteen years old, for the finest blooded racer that ever old Johnson brought out from old Virginny!

"But whar was I guine, at this grand speed of my stallion? The Lawd only knows; and, heving nothing and nobody else to trust to, why, you see I was forced to lean upon him! I knowd I was guine down stream, not up; and that I was leaving my red skin captivators fur behind me; the cussed old woman, and the etarnal leetle brat of a papoose that smelled so like a polecat! Thar was a satisfaction in them thinkin's!

"But, as I driv on and on, and my alligator stallion didn't onst offer to slack his speed, I begun to be skeary, and to think he was guine to carry me too fur out of my beat, and out of his own! And so I thought of some plan to stop him, jist only that we might take an osservation.

"So, it come to me from Natur, that ef I was to gouge one eye and let to'ther alone, it would make him wheel about, right or left—no matter which,—and run me up on dry land onst more.

"I noticed that the river was spreading out mighty wide, into what peoples calls a Lake, and I noted agin, that the water was so cl'ar that I could see down to the very bottom, and a'most count the shells that was a lying thar. I'm sure, ef you hed dropt a silver picayune thar, I could ha' seed it, lying upon the bottom, all was so beautiful cl'ar in that water, though I reckon it was a thousand foot deep!

"Well, as I considered all things, and seen a beautiful green rising of the shore kivered with almighty big oaks, I gin my stallion a desprit screw in his *right* eye, and it would have done your hairt good to hev haird him.

"How he did bellow!

"How he did turn about and twist about, even ef he didn't jump Jim Crow! But he a'most jumped himself out of the water; then he come down with a thundering squelch; run ahead about twenty feet, and then, O! Lawd,—he went right down, down, down, and carried me onder,—for, in the same minnit, he quiled his tail about my thighs, jist as my t'other stallion, and fastened me close as wax, to his saddle.

"Down! Down! Down! we went, till thar was no more airth, and no more sky, and I begun to feel, all over, what people onderstands by drowning, and hanging, and all sawts of a massacr*ee*."

XI.

Out of the Depths.

"How long I lived in thet sitivation, who can tell! I kaint calkilate. I thought it was a month of Sundays; a whole year of holidays, and thar was no fun in Sundays or Holidays! My breath was fair stopt short; I know'd thet I couldn't stand it long! I felt death in my head and in my innards! I was a gonner! I know'd I was guine down all the time, on that cussed Bull alligator's back, and he holding on to me, never onst letting go, with his rascally scaly tail tying my knee and thigh fast to the saddle.

"I kicked; I twisted; I tried all ways; but nothing would do! I'd ha' givin all in the world jest to get one breath of air: but no! and I jest give in! I could do no more. Says I,—'I'm a gonner at last!' Who'd ha' thought it! And I so young a man! A man what had hairdly seen the world, and had no wife! and Susannah Sykes a widow woman left behind me to git what husband she could—prehaps to marry some dern'd impudent trooper of my old rigiment! Oh! Lawd! O! Lawd! to deliver myself to death, without making any fight of it! Without any chaince to fight! 'Twas mighty haird.

"And then the thinking! Lawd a massy! It did seem to me, as ef every thing wicked I ever did, in all my life, come up to my ricollection; from the time of stealing apples and peaches out of old Geiger's orchard, to the time when Sarah Grimes and me, was caught in the thunder storm, and—

"But thar's no need to be telling about that! She's married off now, and hes three children!—

"Well! But—

"As I was telling you, down I went, on that cussed critter's back, 'tell I thought I was in the very bowels of the airth! and then I stopt short! I couldn't think, nor see, nor breathe, nor do nothing but die! I felt a thousand fingers squeezing my throat. I felt a thousand hands a squeezing in towels down my throat! I felt Death all over! I was dead! dead! dead! and I hed no more feelin' of the sitivation!

"But, all on a suddent, I waked up, and felt my feet a scraping on hard ground! The bull alligator was still onder me; but, he seemed to shuffle me off, and then I haird him bellow out, like the King of all the Buffaloes, onder a misery of the innards.

"And then I haird no more!—

"And then I seemed to be sleeping! and I reckon I did sleep; for I waked up at last;—I warn't dead;—I aint dead yit;—I waked up at last, and found myself on the beautifulest sandy beach of a sawt of island, you ivir did see.

"Whar was I?

"I seed nothing! I haird no alligator! I looked round and listened. Thar warnt a sound. Not a leaf twinkled! Not a breath stirred! Not a bird sang! Not a beast bellowed; and all I could hyar was jest a leetle sawt of onderground singing, like some body that sings softly, and is a crying all the time. This, I soon knowed, was the sound of the leetle billows that broke over the sands and whistled in the great conchs that waur scattered all over the beach about me.

"But soon, I haird nothing, not even the waters, for I felt myself suddenly overkim with sleep; and I went off into a doze; into a drowse; and then into a big sleep, thet wrapt me up in its arms, jest as ef I was a baby, jest done suck at its mammy's buzzom!"—

XII.

Bauldy, After a Series of Serious Experiences, Is Made Captive by the Calypso of Flurriday; a Type Unknown to Ulysses.

"I waked up a'ter a long stretch of sleep, to feel the river jist playing about my feet.

"I felt stronger! But at first, I only crawled away, higher up the sands, to git out of the reach of the water. I hed enough of water a'ready, for one day.

"A'ter awhile, a'ter crawling a hundred yards or so, I sot up, and looked about me. 'Twas jest before sun setting.

"I could see I was on a sawt of island. The sands waur bright and shiny; and they jist sloped up gradywally ontill they come to a grand forest of the biggest trees I ever did see. Thar was oak and laurel among 'em; the tops so high, that you could see the skies fair resting on 'em, jist as ef they hed been so many pillars.

"Soon I felt strong enough to git up and walk, and I pushed for them big trees. Twas beautiful shady, and when I got fairly into the woods, I begin to hyar all sawts of noises, of birds and beasts too, I reckon.

"Thar was all sawts of singing; and soon I seed the beautifulest birds a-flying all around me; birds of all colours; some they called pair-o-kites, and other kinds, I never seed or haird tell of before! Then thar was a continyall barking and bouncing about of the squari'ls; but I seed no harmful beasts, and not even a snake!

"Well, a'ter a pretty tall walk, I gits out of the thick woods, and comes upon palmeto trees, and orange trees, that growd like in the fields, as ef rigilar laid out. Them palmetoes waur standing on leetle sand-hills.

"Walking on, I comes to another beach of sand spread out sloping to a big water, what they called a lake; and, keeping on along the edge of the lake, I gits to the most 'strowdinary place of all.

"First I passed into a hollow, all of white sand, the airth gradywally rising into hills; thet was a'most chalky white; and, as I gits on, I finds the chalk hills meeting a top of me, and kivering me as ef I was in a house. But the pathway was wide and spread with white sand; and now I begins to see conchs and shells, the biggest and beautifullest I ever did see; that growed all along the path; and thar waur leetle breaks, hyar and thar in the hills, and I could see the smooth waters of the lake, shining between them, onder the slanting sunset.

"And in every one of these openings, I seed a most mighty big alligator, that jest stood and looked at me, and never moved, and seemed to stand thar as a sentinel! I gin him the left always, and stood on, between the hills and onder them arches.

"I now seed the hills widen; and the sides of them was stuck full of shiny shells, and great chrystals that gin light; and 'fore I know'd whar I was, I found myself in a most tremendous big hall, all kivered over with shells and chrystals and they gin the light; but, all round, thar was openings to the lake, and they gin light besides.

"And Lawd! to see the alligators, going and coming through them openings, jist as ef they waur on business, carrying messages from one to t'other. Some was big, and some leetle enough, and all of 'em seemed to be busy. They'd look at me, and pass on; and when they'd meet one another, they'd give a grunt or a bellow, jist according to their size and disposition.

"Well, I went on, for this one hall, as I may call it, soon narrowed down to a sawt of gallery or passage, and when I got through thet, thar was another hall, not so big as t'other, but a heap purtier.

"By this time, I was mons'ous cur'ous, and pushed on; and the alligators were guine in and out, through the openings to the lake; but they didn't seem to mind me at all, and I hed nothing to say to them.

"And I was jist on another sawt of chamber opening, when, right ahead of me, stood a most powerful alligator right in the way! I thought I know'd him; and he was one of my stallions, the last I rode on! I knowed him by his sore eyes; and he knowed me too, for jist as soon as he seed me, he bellowed like thunder, and turned tail, and made for the other room beyont!

"That encouraged me. I felt, you see, as ef I had licked him, in a fa'r fight, jist as I did the b'ar. And so I followed him, through a dusky passage, and, Lawd ha' massy, what I then seed, was a wonder to hyar and tell on!

"Now, fellows, it dont much matter whether you does or doesn't believe what I'm guine to tell you. It's so strange and wonderful that I never quarrels with a pusson who says to me,—'I kaint believe that!' I could'nt believe it myself, you see, ef I hedn't seen it with my own mortal sight; and I'll 'scuse any of you, ef you shakes your head, heving no faith, for you know, seeing's believing as they say, and feelin's the naked truth; and as none of you has ever seen these things like me, or been made to feel them like me, so, I shaint quarrel with any of you, even ef you should say,—

"'Bauldy, you know thet's a lie!'

"But 'taint no lie, I'm telling you, though its mighty strange and onpossible to be believed! Ef you could only onderstand, and hev the right faith;—for its the faith only, you know, that kin iver see the truth;—then you'd find every bit as true as ef twas writ in the Holy Hokies of Nebuchedsneezar; and the 'Columbian orator' to boot!

"You kin believe, as you please, and be the worse off for your onbelieving; but whether you b'lieve or don't, all the same to me. I'll push on with the history.

"Well, as I tell'd you, I followed my big stallion alligator, seeing as how he looked skear'd, and had sore eyes; and I thought, all the time, I hed lick'd him fair, as I did the big b'ar on the Withlacoochie, only with the fire eend of my cigar!

"I followed him, through the dark passage, and on a suddent, came into a great hall, beautiful as ef twas all made of shiny chrystals and beautiful shells. And they gin out sich a light as fair dazzled my eyes. But thar was light coming in from the openings on the lake, besides, and, through one of these, like through a great arched window, the sun shined in, and jist over the head of a grand looking woman, that sate a-rocking on a great shell, that I reckon was a living beast out of the sea, for it jist kept heaving her up and down, soft and easy, like a boat rocking on the little billows along the shore!

"When I fixed my eyes on this woman, I was fair dazzled of the peepers; and mighty skeared besides; though, at a distance—for I was at one eend of the hall and she at the other—she looked mighty sweet and beautiful.

"She was built a-most like other women, but she was of a bright reddishy complexion like the Ingins, and she had long black hair that kept floating and playing all round her naked shoulders, as ef she kept up a breeze thar all the time, with nothing else to do! She had'nt much other clothing, I kin tell you, 'cept some thing that spread round her like a wail, made of the finest silk hair; and her figger was sich as to make a fellow's blood churn up to his brain, setting him fairly a fire!

"And I could see, even at that distance that she hed coal black eyes; and when she sot them upon you, it looked as ef they were a shooting little lightning bullets at you, that went through you at every pop!

"Well! I stopt short and did'nt know well what to do; preticklarly as I seed that great bull alligator march up to her very feet, and put out his great tongue as ef to lick her toes. Her feet were bare enough—had neither shoes nor stockings, and they rested on a purty little pavement of shells close fitting together, and mixed together of all colours.

"Well, thar, at the feet of that beautiful strange critter of a woman, thar, that stallion alligator of mine, gin a great bellow; then he wheeled about, wagged his tail like a dog that ixpects his feed, and looked haird at me!

"I seed then that the woman looked at me too; and says I—

"'What's the to do, now? I wonder ef that great beast and the woman kin onderstand one another.'

"But I reckon they did; for, a minnit a'ter, what does the great beast do, but he twirls his tail about, and actyally carried it up to his eyes, as ef to show that he hed got the infatenzy in 'em! Then he bellowed agin and looked haird at me!

"Now, it's most wonderful to say, but its all true, fellows! I seed that beautiful woman stoop down to the beast and look at his eyes; and she seemed to feel em; shè sartainly touched 'em! Then she said something that I couldn't hear, and on a sudden, more than twenty leetle bits of alligators, that I hed'nt seen,—all lying about her, and waiting, jist like little sarvants, they jumped up, and come towards me.

"Lawd love you, how skear'd I was! I was fair fastened to the ground! My feet stuck thar;—my tongue seemed to dry up in my throat! I couldn't talk, and I couldn't walk! I couldn't fight, and I couldn't run; and yit thar was twenty on them leetle devils, big enough, but nothing like my two stallions; they jist come towards me, in three columns, 'minding me of Gineral Scott's grand marching through the Ingin country;— so I reckon the ticktacks of the West P'inters and the stallion alligators must be purty much the same,— that is a'ter a dicklyration of war!

"I ixpected them to dewour me at onst, in a single mouthful. They was enough to do it; but to my wonderment, when they got up to me, they made a sawt of military movement, by files, right and left oblique, spread out like riflemen for a skrimmage, and made a parfect ring around me.

"Says I, to myself, says I—

"'I'm captivated agin!'

"But I couldn't move nor speak; but jist kept my eyes rolling from side to side to see what was guine to happen next. And I thought agin of Gineral Scott, when the offsers and the troops made a ring about him, and he made a speech, giving 'em thanks for their sarvices, and telling 'em how beautiful they *could* ha' fout ef only the red skinned innimy hed only gin 'em the chaince!

"But as for my making a speech, Lawd 'a' massy, I warnt then quite sartin that I hed a tongue at all.

"Suddent then, all them little army of leetle alligators begun to bob their heads at me, open their jaws, give a leetle bit of a bellow, and wag their etarnal long tails. This they did three times, as rigilar as ef they hed the word of command and had been under West P'int drill for a hundred years. Twas beautiful to see how they did it!

"Then, without any word of command, they made another army involution, and, half of them in front and half in the rear, they wheeled about and tuk up the line of march to whar the woman sot, watching them all the time, and talking, I reckon, to the great bull alligator. He kept thar close to her feet, and I seed her an'inting his eyes with something that they brought her in a shell.

"Now, one body of them leetle alligators, leading the way before me, and another body, following close behind, was jest the same as saying,

" 'March!'

"And they made me feel it so, when the bloody beasts in the rear, come close up and kept pressing me for'ards, with their horny snouts.

"They did'nt hurt me, that's true—and not one of 'em tried to bite; but, jist as sartin as ef they did, they pressed me on for'ard, showing me what they wanted, ontill, they got me alongside of my big stallion alligator, and at the feet of the strange, queer, astonishing reddish woman, that was, I reckon, a sawt of Queen among the alligators!

"My big stallion wheeled about and looked me full in the face, with his cussed little sharp eyes, bulging out from onder the lightwood knot of horny scales above them.

"But he did'nt offer me any provvication; and, in a minnit, the strange woman, gin out a kind of sound, like a frog's chuckle, and jist as they haird it, all the alligators, big and leetle, my old stallion among 'em, they wheeled about and made off, going through the openings, and all making for the lake, as happy as boys jist let out from school!

"And thar' I stood, by my own solitary self, not knowing what was to come next. I seed that I was captivated;—a prisoner, and heving no wepons, and no chaince for escape!

"But all was so wonderful and cur'ous, that I hafe lost the feeling of skear. Says I to myself, says I,—

" 'What's to come next?'

"I didn't hev to wait very long for the answer. The woman she eyed me close, with her bright sharp lightning-like eyes, big and black, and she shook her head till the long hair floated about her as ef the wind was a-rising in it; and I could then see that it was long enough to wrap her body round and round about, close to her feet!

"And she stared at me; and she laughed;—no—not laughed—she made no sound; but she smiled,—and sich a smile! Lawd, love you! She showed through them thick pulpy lips of her'n, sich a double row of the whitest teeth, every one sharp as a dog's grinder, that I begun to think, she would dewour me without turning me over to the cook, or using any salt to the dressing!

"But when I next looked, the smile was sweeter. The mouth was shet. Thar was only the leetlest show of teeth when she smiled agin! And I could see that she had a sawt of loving twinkle in her eye, all the time; and she leaned her head o' one side; and she tossed it; shaking the long hair out, from side to side; then she shot the fire from her eyes, straight into mine; and suddenly when I least ixpicted any sich thing, she flung out from her body, some twenty foot of tail, caught me round the waist, and before I could cry out, or kick, she pulled me into her lap, and gin me sich a hug as a she painther might give to the male one who had brought her home a young calf to feed upon."

XIII.

Bauldy Discovers the Places of Skulls and Skeletons. Great Excitement. Bauldy Escapes from Captivity in the Midst of War.

"In sich a sitivation as this, I think men, its reasonable that a man should licker."

We all agreed with him and liquored accordingly.

"Well, now," said he, resuming, "Jist you consider my fix! Thar I was, setting in that strange critter's lap, with her tail quiled all about my body, and not able to move, while she hugged me to her buzzom, and kissed me, jist as ef I was her newly married husband!

"Up to that minnit, I hed not seen that she had a tail at all! She looked, for all the world, like a nateral Injin woman, only she was a heap purtier, and a thousand times cleaner than the best on 'em.

"She hed kept the tail quiled onder her, jist as a snake quiles himself; and when she throwed it out, it was by a quick jerk, and it worked round me, tight as a thunder snake, when he's got a rattler in his gripe! As I tell you, her body, all on it, was jist as smooth as any Ingin woman's; but the tail was raal alligator; it was a scaly tail, scales all over,—only working twenty times more easy than any alligator's.

"And, setting in her lap, tied to it, I may say, she kissed me on my cheeks and mouth, and bit me, every time till the blood come! She had raal genovine dogteeth, or shirk's, I reckon!

"But, she didn't mean to bite or hurt me, that's sartin. She did nothing but squeeze and fondle! And O! Lawd, how I thought upon

Susannah Sykes of Lexington Destrict. And, O! Lawd! says I to myself, says I, how dreadful a thing to be married to sich a critter aginst ones will and liking! And O! Lawd! to think that I should be the husband of a Mar'maid!

"I hed hearn tell of Mar'maids before, but I never altogether believed in sich critters; but seeing is believing, and feeling's the naked truth! I knowd now that thar waur sich critters, and that I was captivated by a rigilar Mar'maid!

"Now, fellows, you must'nt ixpect me to tell you all. Thar's some things, you know, not to be mentioned among civil, decent white people! Only onderstand, I was at the marcy of a Mar'maid, the Queen of the alligators, who had a parfect army, a rigiment, I may say, of the most powerful bull alligators always in her sarvice! I jist hed to submit, and say no more about it!

"Now, how long I staid in this sawt of captivation, heving nothing to eat but fish and eystars, and shrimps, and whatever they could catch out of the river and the sea, I kaint tell you. It might have been thirty days or sixty months. I did'nt keep any count of time. The Queen fed me upon shrimps and clams and eystars and all kinds of fish; but every thing had to be eat raw. She tried her best, I confess, to make me relish cat and trout, and rock, and sheephead, and cavalli, and other things out of the sea; but twas hard work for me to come it, considerin' that I was a born cook by Nater!

"She picked out the best, biggest and fattest eystars for me, and showed me the nicest fish and the nicest parts of the fish.

"I did l'arn something onder her!

"But twas no go; and when she seed me, picking up sticks and building up a fire, she seemed to onderstand what I was about, and she jist grinned, after her fashion, and said nothing about it! The alligator sarvants brought in the fish.

"When I hed cooked some, a'ter my way, but without no salt, I offered her some, and she tried to eat; but she flung 'em away, and took to the raw baits.

"But I went on cooking for myself; and ef you kin onderstand how a white man kin git on, with fish and eyestars, without never a morsel of bread, why, you may believe me when I tell you, I made out to make a pretty hairty meal every day, and sometimes three times a day!

"Now, how long I lived in them quarters, onder them sarcumstances, I kaint raally tell you! It may have been twenty one days. I don't think rally twaur more than sixty nine or thirty one. But the days and nights passed away without my counting 'em.

"I hed too much to think about and to worry me. I hed to think about my captivation; and how long I was to be kept away from my people; living in the city of alligators, and with that strange Queen of Mar'maids; jist doing as she pleased, and not able to turn from one side to the other without being watched.

"When she hed'nt got me in her own sight, why she hed a dozen of them dern'd leetle sarvant alligators, that followed me all about, and seed a'ter me; and, go whar I would, they was always hyar and thar, ahead or astarn, or on the flanks of me, and I reckon, ef they hed seen me moving off, they'd ha' mounted me, every mother's son on 'em!

"But how to git off! Thet was the question thet worried me. I didn't know well whar I was. I guessed I was on some island, for, turn which way I would thar was the water. 'Twas wide, too, and spread out jist like a lake; though I could see the trees on the t'other side. Twas a mighty beautiful place, and ef I could only hev had Susannah Sykes thar, with jist hafe a dozen of the fambly and neighbours, from old Lexington, I could have spent the rest of my days thar, and never would hev got vexed with the Lawd, if they hed never come to an eending!

"There was some fine hammock land on the island that would hev brought any thing, from corn to cotton, from pindars (ground nuts or ground peas) to potatoes; and one piece of bottomy land, where I'm sure I could make five hundred bushels of rice to the acre! Ef I only hed that island now, in any raal white man's country, I'd live like a fighting cock!

"But 'twant living now that I was. In truth, I felt it was a sawt of dying out from all the world; and the Queen of the Mar'maids pretended to be mighty fond of me, yet she kept me in a contenuyall skear!

"Them teeth of her'n, 'specully when she laughed or tried to laugh,—for twan't nothing better than a grin—they waur all so white and shiny and sharp, that I never seed 'em but I thought of the white double saws in a shirks (shark's) jaws, and the white sharp grinders in the mouth of the great alligator stallion that carried off the Ingin baby. Why, fellows, she never kissed me onst, and she was always awrapping her tail round me, drawing me up to her buzzom, and kissing me as ef for dear life, without drawing the blood.

"Well, onst, soon a'ter I was captivated, she made me go with her to the river or lake to swim. She could walk like a human, had legs and feet like ourn, but, all between her toes was webbed, and the toes tied together by the flesh, same as a duck or goose, or any of them water birds. Onst in the water, fellows, Lawd, it was wonderful to see how she could swim; and dive and cavort; throw herself fair out of the water, lash it with her tail into foam; then plunge down, head foremost, into the very deeps of the sea and airth, and come up again, and swim off, while her long black hair was spread out over her back, from head to heels, like a great black wail over a woman in mourning!

"It was a most wonderful sight! And when she'd come up from diving, she'd bring up handsfull, of shells from the bottom, and pelt at me, jest as you see boys pelt one another with nuts or apples. And the alligator nation, they'd swim about a'ter her, ten thousand I reckon, but they always keept at a 'spectful distance off, and she never let 'em take any liberties with her; and, in fact, I never seed any of 'em try! It did seem as ef they sawt of worshipt her, as ef she waur their God as well their Queen!

"Well, when she got me into the water onst, I hed a time of it; and I took good kear never to let her catch me in it again! Why, she'd catch me round the neck and round the middle, and roll over with me, and buckle me to her with her long tail, and then dive down to the bottomless pit of the deep, ontill my breath was a'most gone; and I thought all was over with me!

"I never did like the water, and warn't no great swimmer at the best. I reckon I would ha' been drowned a hundred times over, in her alligator play with me, but that the water of that lake was different from any other. It didn't seem, when you was onst in it, that 'twas much thicker than the air in damp or foggy weather. You could breathe in it, in a sawt of way, and when you was deep down, it didn't lie heavy on your back.

"But I never let her git me in to it but onst, and when she found I didn't like it, she let me alone! She appeared to want to be good natured and coaxing, and she was mighty loving, a'ter her fashion; but it was a coaxing and a loving that somehow kept me in a continuyall skear, and I fought shy of her whenever I could; and when she'd let me, I'd jist wander away, ixploring the island, and finding out all I could; for I seed that twould be a mighty fine place for a leetle settlement, and I calkilated that, ef I could onst git off, and git among my people, I could git up a good force of twenty stout fellows, and git boats, and cross the river, and captivate the island, and kill off the whole alligator nation in short order!

"Well, one day, when I was a navigating and explorating the island, and when thet Queen of the Mar'maids was taking her a'ternoon swim, I got off about hafe a mile, and when I got to a sartin line, all them leetle spy alligators stopt following a'ter me.

"I couldn't tell what to make of thet, but I warn't sorry to git shet of 'em; so I pushed ahead, and went on, 'tell I got into a thick wood.

"Twas mighty dark and thick, so thick that the sun's blazes couldn't git in, only hyar and thar, with a faint leetle light that jist sarved to show what a dark and dismal place it was.

"I could hear the squarrls jumping and barking among the trees, and evey now and then an owl, would sweep out, singing his great 'Whoo-Whoo-Whoo! Whoo-Whoo!'

"And then I'd hyar the rush of some big birds with great rattling wings,—I reckon they waur eagles;—and by a leetle pond, I seed more than a hundred great white cranes that walked about the pond and never seemed to mind me; and onst, I seed a beautiful flash of flying birds that looked most like leetle rainbows, and by their cries, I knowed them to be parroquitos.

"But in the midst of my looking, I stumbled over something, and when I picked myself up and looked, what should it be but the skillyton of a man, with the flesh picked off clean to the bone.

"How my flesh did creep at the sight! But how much worser did I feel, when as I could see better, I seed a whole pile of skillytons, more than a hundred, I reckon, all stretched out, and all picked clean to the bones.

"Oh! twas dreadful! Thar, without eyes to see, they seemed to look out from the sockets at me, and I thought I haird them all say at onst,—

" 'You see what you're to come to yit, by that Mar'maid woman!'

"Lawd! Lawd! I could onderstand now, mighty well what them sharp white teeth of my Mar'maid was good for; and my flesh crawled to think how, when she kissed me, she always gin me a bite that drawed the blood. The infarnal critter was a-tasting me all the time, and calculating the meal she was to make of me!—

"I tuk hairt;—some thing told me;—and I squatted down and sarched and examinated the skillytones, and I felt sure that they was all of 'em the skillytones of *white* men like myself; for you see, the skulls were all the skulls of white men, not niggers or Ingins. They waur all broad and high, with big fronts, the eyes setting low onder the foreheads. Now, the nigger you know, hes his eyes high up, and most of his head is on the back of it; and the Ingin's skull is sharp and narrow, and runs back too; not so wide as the nigger's, but longer backward and more like a woman's!—and Ingin and nigger skulls are all mighty thick! Now, all these skulls were thin, and in the front part pretickilarly, some a'most as thin as paper!—

"I got out of that cussed place as soon as I could, and made my way out of that infarnal thick wood; but I fair staggered as I went, with my flesh crawling over me, jest as ef I was gitting on a coating of snakes!

"Now, when I got back to the skairt of wood, whar all the leetle spies of alligators drapt off from me, Lawd! what should I see, but the whole rigiment of 'em, lying squat about and waiting for me.

"And soon as they seed me, they tuk up the line of march, some in front, some in rear, and some on the flanks of me, jist as ef they were a rigilar troop, edicated at West P'int!

"And so we marched on, not heving a word to say to one another, tell jist as we got in sight of the beautiful place where the Queen of the Mar'maids kept me in captivation; they all set up to bellow, with their small v'ices, a sort of howling and singing together, jest as you hyar in a frog pond, in a cloudy night when rain is ixpected!

"By the time we reached the grand hall, the Queen had done her bathing, swimming, playing and cavorting in the river, and thar she sate, shining bright, and with that cussed snake smiling, so like a grin, upon her beautiful wisage. When I stood before, she jist shook her head good humouredly, and one of the leetle alligators, he set up a small bellow, as ef to tell her every thing.

"Then she motioned to me to come to her, and when I did so, suddent she whisked her tail around me, and drawed me into her lap! And then she bussed me, mighty affectionate; drawing the blood from my mouth, for with every buss, she always gin a leetle bite! The infarnal critter was jist a trying to see ef my blood and flesh, feeding as I was, on fish and eysters, was ready for her dewouring! I onderstood it all!

"And, though she hugged me close, and bussed me so keen, I could see that thar was a sawt of twinkle of suspicion in her eyes, as ef she begun to think that I was suspicioning her!

"I was dreadful oneasy, but I did my best to make b'lieve, I was as fond of her as she waur of me! But I hardly sleept a wink that night, thinking of the skillytones, in that dark wood, and what chainces thar waur before *me,* to git out of my perdicament!

"But the Lawd was marciful! The very next a'ternoon, when she went out to bathe, and swim, and cavort, and I hed to go out to see her, though she couldn't git me to come in the water, thar was a mighty change. Some thing happened,—what twas I never could guess,—that put an eend to my captivation and skear.

"When she went down to the river, heving a hundred bull alligators following close a'ter her, and jist as many running before, I followed slow behind, the leetle sentinel alligators sticking close to me one.

"I jist went down to a leetle sandy flat, kivered by the shade of three big palmeto's, and laid myself down, it may be about a hundred yards from the water.

"Then the cussed leetle spy alligators, they laid themselves down all about me. I could see the river, all in front, and I could see the Queen of the Mar'maids, every now and then, as she flashed through the water and cavorted! But I hairdly cared to look; and I was fair blind with thinking of my captivated sitivation, and them thousand skillytons; when, all on a suddent, I haird the greatest uproar in the river.

"Twas the roaring of ten thousand bull alligators; and the whole river was churned into white foam, and the noise was awful!

"And I could see the Queen of the Mar'maids, tossing her long arms in the air; and I could see her tail fairly curling, like a bow over her head; and off she went like a shot from a rifle, pushing down the stream, and followed by a thousand alligator bulls, she was out of sight in a minnit.

"And, jist at the greatest of the outcry, all the leetle sentinel spy alligators, that was a watching me, picked themselves up, and began to bellow; and they too rushed off for the river; and soon I saw their hundred le'ttle pine-knot heads bobbing one a'ter t'other, and going down the river, following, fast as they could, the hundred thousand bull alligators and the Queen.

"Then I ran down to the water side; and, far as I could see, thar they waur, all pushing for dear life, and the whole face of the river was kivered with foam!

"What could be the matter? When they all got out of sight—the Queen of the Mar'maids, and the bull alligators, and the leetle spy alligators,—I could still hear the mighty bellowing below, as ef a thousand battles was a guine on, all at the same time, and prehaps fully five miles off.

"I was mightily conflusterated; but, while I was a looking about me, and wondering what could be the 'casion for the great fuss and uproar and ixcitement—for it was cl'ar to me that thar was some tall fighting guine on below,—what should I see, but a nice new little dug-out, a cypress canoe—come floating across the river, right towards me!

"Oh! how I watched that dug out! As it come nigher and nigher, I could'nt hold myself in!

"I jumped into the river, when it was about thirty yards off, and waded out, 'till I hed to swim; but I got to the dug out, and cotch'd fast hold of it! And thar, inside, was a pair of as good new paddles of ash, as you would wish to handle; and thar was a sack and a bundle; by which I knowed that it had been fresh used by somebody thet didn't know, or kear how to make a boat fast to a sapling.

"I didn't wait to say 'good bye' to anybody! I jumped in. There was nobody and nothing to see me. You couldn't see, any whar, a single knot of an alligator's head above water. They waur sartinly all below, and fighting for dear life; for I could hyar the great bellowing; and every now and then a mighty big roar, as ef from the throat of some mighty stallion alligator, some big fellow, sich as I had straddled in my last ixtrimity.

"And as I pushed off, and struck across for t'other side of the river,—I hed seen enough of this side—I thought of the Queen of the Mar'maids, and how she would miss me, ef ever she got back!

"And then I wondered what sawt of fighting she could do ef thar waur a fight sartinly guine on! And then I axed myself, ef evey nation of alligators hed its own Queen; and I begun to consider, what sort of Queen the other was; and ef the two would hitch together in the skrimmage! I could see, in my thinking, what work *my* Queen would do with that tail of her'n, and how she would make them dog teeth meet in the flesh, at every grin!—

"But, when I thought of them teeth, and ricollected how clean all them skillitones had been picked to the bones, I bent and buckled to my paddles, and worked my way, till I sweated like a bull in fly time, pushing up stream.

"Twaur mighty haird work, I tell you;—but, whenever I'd begin to feel faintish, I'd think of them skillitons and them dog teeth of my Mar'maid, and I'd pull the harder!

"When, at last, I struck the shore, and made a landing, I jest had strength enough to make the boat fast to a sapling; to walk into the woods, a leetle way; jist to kiver myself out of sight, and then to throw myself at the bottom of a big tree, say a short prayer, and give myself up to the blessed sleep! I reckon t'want three minnits before it wrapt me up, jist as ef I was in a blanket! But, in them three minnits, Lawd! how I did long for a drink! I'd ha' given a hundred dollars, ef I hed it, jist thin, for a good swallow of peach and honey! And what say you fellows, for a kiss of the sarpent now?—"

A pause while we liquored.

XIV.

The Catastrophe. Bauldy's Greatest Miracle of All; and His Escape From Susannah Sykes.

"And now, fellows, the most extonishing part of the history of my campaign in Flurriday, is yet to come; for, I reckon, you'll all say, a'ter you've hairn me out, that nothing could be more strange and surprising, in what's gone before, than what I've got to tell you now!

"How long I slept onder that tree, it's not easy to say. The haird work of paddling up stream, me one and alone,—a matter, I may say, of sixty or twenty miles, more or less, tharabouts, or some whar,—pretty much knock'd me up and knock'd me down too!

"Then the skears I hed; the dangers I went through; the troubles; captivated by the Ingins; sculped; shot at and knifed; and then made to nurse the cussed dirty little red skin papoose; then the ride, first upon one alligator-stallion, then, swapping, and shifting to another; and then the captivation to that Queen of the Mar'maids; then the dreadful sight of the skillitons of our people, chawed up and gnawed to the bone, by that same Queen of the Mar'maids, I reckon, with her cussed sharp white dog-teeth;—well, all them dreadsome and fearsome ixperences, they waur enough to knock me down, and make sleep easy to me for a month of Sundays; so, thar's no knowing how long I had been sleeping onder that big tree, on the edge of a mighty great thick of swamp forest.

"But I was suddently waked up by mighty rough usage! First, I felt a kick in my side, and ribs; then I felt myself pulled and jarked about, by the arms and shoulders; and, when I opened my eyes and straightened myself out, to see what alligator hed got hold of me now, what should I see but a squad of four or five of our own Rigiment, all pulling at me at onst!

"And I cried out loud:

"'Oh! Lawd be praised, I'm safe at last!'

"So I said, though it did seem mighty strange that our own people should handle me so roughly. So I says—

"'Hello! fellows! Hev' you no sawt of feelin' for a man's ribs, that you kick so haird!'

"With that one kicks me ag'in, and says,—

"'It's the ribs we're feelin' for you d——d bloody desarter!'

"'Desarter!' says I.

"'Yes,' says he, 'a dern'd bloody desarter! We always know'd you was a d——d coward; but nobody ever suspected you of the courage to desart! Git up, you d——d blasted sneak, and git yourself hung as soon as possible! You aint decent enough to be shot!'

"And not a word of ixplanation would they hear to; but jist kept on, kicking and hauling at me, 'tell they made me git up, and soon as I did so, they roped my hands behind my back, and the Sargeant, he punched me in the rear, with his sword, 'tell I went ahead. I tried my best to tell 'em every thing, but they gin me no answer 'cept in cusses, and no sawt of satisfaction 'cept in kicks! All they'd say was,

" 'Keep your jabber 'tell you gits before the drum head court martial.'

"And twan't long before they got to camp; and twas a mighty great supprise to me to diskiver that the camp was jist whar I had left it months ago; and, when I calkilated, and looked about me, I was more supprised to find that I had landed jist at a p'int, that took me back to my old tree, whar I used to smoke my long nines on the sly!

"I could now onderstand that, in the scrimmage with the Ingins, they had licked the red devils off, gin 'em chase, and then come back whar the tents were all left standing, onder a rear guard.

"Well, they soon hed me in camp and up before the Gineral and all the off'sers; and thar, right in front of me, stood the cussed leetle dirty scamp of a scullion boy, that I used to lick so, every day, to l'arn him his edication as a cook. The moment I seed him, I smell'd a snake! The ongrateful varmint,—a'ter all I hed done for him to ratify agin me!—

"But I hedn't much time to look at him, or to think of him either; for thar' was the Gineral looking at me, with a great black thunder-storm over his eyes, and them sot upon me, as ef he meant to blast me black with the lightning! He did look bigger than ever; and blacker than ever; and his nose was redder than ever; and as much like a great firecoal, hot as blazes; and as he tuk off his great parade hat, with its bunch of feathers, and dashed it down upon the table, he fair snorted at me, like an angry bull at a yaller handkerchief!

"And I fell all over in a heap, wilting up, and running together, and quaking, like a great platter of seablubber, jist brought ashore by the rollers.

"Says he, with a v'ice of thunder—

" 'What hev you got to say for yourself, you scoundrel?'

"That tuk me all aback agin! I hed'nt the strength to say nothing; and I shook all over! My tongue was dried up fair, and stuck fast to the roof of my mouth! Then says the Gineral:

" 'He feels his guilt! Read the charges and pacifications, Mr. Adwokit!'

"Then the adwokit, who was no other than Captain Firebrand, he read, and as I haird them charges, I felt the rope growing round my neck, and the bullets going through my bowels!

"What do you think they charged upon me?

"Well, twas a mighty long catlog!

"First, they charged me with desartion from the company. Then they charged me with cowardice; skulking onder an alarum of the inimy; hanging back in an advance; stealing cigars and liquor;—beating the scullion boy cruelly, that he mightn't tell on me; and, Lawd knows how many things besides; among 'em,—would you b'lieve it, —they charged that I did the smuggling at St. Augustine, and kivered up the transactions of Capt. Chubb, of the schooner Sukey Gunja, gitting the ten boxes out of the hundred for *my* pay;—smuggling the boxes, onder hides, in the baggage wagons, and selling cigars and Jamaica, all smuggled, out to the onder offs'ers and soldiers; besides, drinking 'em and smoking 'em myself; and, last of all, they charged me with stealing my own cigars and liquor, and gitting drunk upon the liquor every a'ternoon and night! The very things the d——d raskals had done themselves!—

"I seed what some of it meant. The government hed smelt the rat, and got wind of that smuggling business; and they wanted to put the porkypine saddle upon *my* back! The d——d cunning wipers!

"Then they called up the rascal scullion boy to prove the pacifications, and he swore to a thousand lies! He swore that, when he cotched me drinking the liquor, and carrying off the cigars, I licked him to make him keep a shet mouth; and he told how he followed me, time a'ter time, every a'ternoon, to the edge of the 'thick', where I drunk and smoked by my one self. That I always carried a full bottle; that I never brought it back full or empty; that, if I come in at night, I never come in quite sober; but sometimes, when I was overdrunk, that I slept in the 'thick' all night! But thar was no eend to it!

"They had other witnesses that swore about the smuggling, a most etarnal pack of lies! And then they brought up the file of soldiers that hed found me sleeping onder the tree; and they said they hed found me, deep, dead drunk asleep; that they hed to kick and punch, and pull, and haul me about, to make me open my eyes; and that, when they got me up, I could hairdly walk, and staggered about like a blind man;—that I hed'nt quite slept off the drunk!

"Did you ever hyar sich a cussed story, and jist a'ter I hed gone through all that ixperience of captivation by the Ingins; by the alligators; by the Queen of the Mar'maids; and the hard row of two hundred miles, I reckon—more or less—paddling off from the Mar'maid's island, in a poor dug-out, and without a morsel to eat, or a mouthful to drink!

"Them fellows that brought me up, then showed more than a dozen chunk bottles that they said they found in the 'thick' whar I was sleeping;—and they showed five 'long nine' cigars that they swore they tuk out of my pockets;—when, as you all know, I was robbed of them vary last cigars by the cussed red skins when they captivated me!

"I now begin to see that thar was a sawt of conspi*ra*cy agin me to hev me hung, shot, and butcher'd!

"And Lawd love you, I hed no witnesses at all; and I could see, from the looks of all the offsers, that I hedn't no one friend among 'em, to stand up for me, and take my part, and argyfy my defences.

"'And now, scoundrel!' says the Gineral,—'What hev you got to say for yourself?'

"Well, seeing as how twaur pretty much over with me, with every body swearing agin me, and nobody to back me; I was desprit! and, a'ter a leetle time, of trying to settle my thoughts and feelin's, I got the strength, and made bold to tell them the whole of my ixperences and idventures, first about my captivation by the red skin, at the time of the skrimmage—

"With that the Gineral says—

"'We've hed no scrimmage, in the last seven days.'

"'Oh!' says I, 'but this was more than a month ago!'

"Then says he, 'What the devil is the fellow talking about? But go on,' says he—'go on!'

"And he squared a one side, looking at me with his left eye, which he could cock wonderful! So I went on to tell about my captivation by the red skin, and how he carried me off, and how he tried to sculp me, and carried off my wigs, and was skear'd at first—

"'Why, man, what do you talk about,' said the Gineral. 'The wig's on your head now!'

"With that, I felt my head, and, sure enough, thar was the wig.

"'But,' says I, 'whar's to'ther one?'

" 'Why, to'ther one's in your pocket!' says the sargeant,—'I felt it thar when I sarched you, while you was asleep. Them five cigars was in it!'

"I felt in my pocket, and sure enough, t'other wig was thar! For a minnit, I was dumbfoundered; but, in the next minnit, I seed through it all! They *hed* been scrimmaging with the Ingins; hed killed or captivated the red rascal that captivated me; and found my wigs upon him; and, to fool me, they had clapt one upon my head agin, while I was asleep, and rammed the t'other one in my pocket.

"It was all a cussed trick to make a fool of me, and hev' their fun; and, thinking so, I begun to feel easier, and reckon'd twa'nt so ser'ous a matter a'ter all! I begin to feel that twas no hanging or shooting matter; and, from the laughing of the off'sers, I rether thought the whole thing was a plan to skear me, and hev their fun out of my skear! Them fellows was up to all sawts of tricks, and thar was no eend to their skylarking when they was off duty.

" 'But,' says the Gineral, 'let him go on with his own redickilous story in his own way. It is a leetle amusing!'

"So I went on, and tell'd the whole; all my idventures; day a'ter day; the captivation among the Ingins; the nussing the d——d leetle dirty papoose; and how he was tuk off by the alligator; and how I jumped on the alligator's back, and rode him, and gouged him, and made him womit up the leetle red skin; and, how he carried me off; and then, how he fought with t'other alligator stallion; and how I swapt hosses, gitting astraddle of the bigger and stronger one; and how he carried me off, through the lake, to the island of the Queen of the Mar'maids; and how she hugged me up and kissed, and bit me; and then how I got off in the dug-out, and got safe back to the old 'thick,' a'ter a captivation of, I reckon, three months, more or less!

"Lawd! how the fellows laughed!

" 'And to think!' says the Gineral, 'that all that stuff should come out of one bottle of Jamaica! Why, Bauldy,' says he, quite good humoured, 'How long do you say you were absent from camp?'

" 'Well,' says I, 'Gineral, thar's no keeping right time among the Ingins, or among the Mar'maids either; but I rether reckon, if twarnt two or three months, twaur something over sixty days or thar abouts!'

" 'Now,' says the Gineral, turning to the offsers of the mess;—

" 'Now, Gentlemen, can you remember when Bauldy cooked our last dinner?'

"And, with one v'ice they all answered—

" 'Yisterday, Gineral!'

"Yisterday! was iver hair'd the like of sich bold lying! I was dumbfoundered! They went on:

" 'We missed him only last night, at ten, when we called for supper! Neether he, nor Blox (the scullion boy) was to be found; and thar was nobody to cook breakfast this morning, till Blox come in. He cooked the breakfast.'

"Blox, you see, was the scullion boy; and all the cooking he know'd, he larned from me. And see the thanks, I got!—

"Then the off'sers went on, and said, 'Blox put us on the trail, a'ter breakfast, and told how he had followed him, and found out all his tricks. So we diskivered how the liquor and cigars went!'

" 'So, you see, Bauldy, all the stuff you have been telling us, was nothing but a drunken dream! Instead of being absent sixty days, you were not gone sixty hours, and were dead drunk all that time! Now, what ought to be done with a cook that is not forthcoming when we want our supper?—That has no breakfast ready for us in the morning?—This is a dreadful crime, and dezarves ixemplairous punishment! Have you any thing to say in your defence: any thing that may be pleaded, in behalf of marcy!'

"I confess I was in sich a fix of bewilderment, and ixtonishment, that I couldn't say nothing! I hed told the truth, and the whole truth; and, by the Hokies, as you knows, fellows, nothing but the truth; for, you see, I've tell'd you every thing jist as it happened, and as I tell'd the off'cers. You'll b'lieve me, though they wouldn't! But they wouldn't b'lieve nothing, though twas the very angels thet come down to tell 'em. They was the ongodliest set of onbelievers I ever sot eyes upon! Says I to 'em—says I—'twas all I could say—says I, 'I've tell'd you every thing:—

" 'I sartinly was sculped and captivated by the Ingin; and had to mind child more than a month of forty days. I reckon.

" 'I sartinly did ride them alligators:

" 'I sartinly was captivated by the Queen of the Mar'maids, and she tuk me to wife, and sartinly hugged and kissed and bit me;—I've got the marks of the bites now on my mouth;—it's all sore yit—'

"And I showed em my sore mouth.

"They laughed, wild fairly, and said twas bekaise I smoked up all their long nine cigars, and then burnt my chops with the Jamaica.

"The onbelieving sinners! They would hyar to nothing and jist laughed at my sufferin's. And so I cried like a baby, and then they laughed the more.

"But, suddent, the Gineral, put on his grand looks, like a thunder-storm, and he clapt on his great parade hat, with all its white feathers; and he said—

" 'Now, Gentlemen, let us dispose of this case. It is cl'ar to you that William Bauldy, otherwise Bald Head Bill Bauldy, has been found guilty of all the charges, and the pacifications onder them. He as good as pleads guilty; for, you see, all the stuff that he's been telling us is either meant to lead us off his track, or it's nothing but a drunken dream, all born of a bottle of Jamaica. Is he guilty or not guilty!'

" 'Guilty!' was the magnamimous v'ice.

" 'What shall be his punishment?'

" 'Death!' was the answer, all magnamimous together!

" 'How shall he die!'

" 'Shot to death!' says one.

" 'Hung!' says another. 'Shooting's for a brave man.'

"And some went for whipping and branding; and driving out of camp!—

"A'ter they had all done, the Gineral he said—

" 'Gentlemen, I confess to a great onwillingness to put Bauldy to death. I am always onwilling to hang, or shoot any man, ef he's got but a single vartue left in him; for, you see, the vilest sinner may be saved, only give him time; that is,—ef he's got a single vartue to brag upon! Now, we know that Bauldy don't love fighting. We knew *that*, when we tuk him out of the ranks and made a cook of him! Twas for that very reason, that we tuk him out of the ranks and made him cook! Now, as for his desartion, I don't think he meant to desart. But the Jamaica got the better of him and he overstayed his time. Now, I grant you that to overstay his time, and not git our supper, or breakfast, when we put our faith intirely in him, was a great crime, desarving of death; but Jamaica is a great temptationer, and, as he shows you, begits bad dreams. And, I'm afear'd, Bauldy loves to sin with liquor, ef he doesn't love Mar'maids. He's kivered all over with vices, and crimes and temptations; but he's got *one* vartue which you'll all admit; and I'm for letting him off easy, considerin' that one vartue! He's a fust rate cook! He was born to be a cook! It was cl'ar he was never born to be a sodger! Now, we've never had sich good cooking, and sich good health, as we've all hed, ontill Bauldy was promoted to be our cook! He's good at a'most every sawt of cookery. Who kin fry a trout, a pairch, or a bream, with Bill Bauldy? Who kin bile a bluecat, to make it eat hafe so sweet? and, I never swallows a bowl of his tarrapin soup, but I feels more vartuous and happy a'ter it! Then thar's his tarrapin pies! Now, I'm bold to say, however them Beaufort people may brag about their tarrapin pies, Bauldy's beats them all hollow! A'ter eating one of his pies, I always lies down and sleeps with a good conscience, and rises up with an idee of dinner.

" 'It's a great vartue!' says he, 'to be a great cook, and redeems many vices! A great sodger, Gentlemens, is *one* thing, and a great thing; but a great cook is a greater;—he's a sort of life-presarver, and comforter, and saviour of the body, which, you know, is next to being the saviour of the soul! I puts great prophets and great cooks in the same rank, and wants to be marciful to their faults, bekaise of their vartues! And, considerin' *our* case, more than his'n, I'm for taking him to marcy! Ef we don't, who'll be the greatest sufferer—We or Him! Ef he's hung, 'twill be only death at last; but ef we kin git no good cooking done, for the rest of this campaign, it's death and darnation both to *us!* I tell you, last night's supper, and this morning's breakfast, both cooked by Blox, waur enough to kill any man's appetite, and distroy his stomach! And I'm cl'ar to let Bauldy off, 'till the eend of the campaign, when you kin do with him what you please! As for Blox, the rascal, who has showed himself so quick to watch his master's vices, without l'arning his vartues, I sentence him to a Baker's dozen, with a hickory on his bare back, well laid on, and order that Bauldy idminsters the punishment at onst!'

"Didn't I make them Baker's dozen tell at every crack on the leetle rascal's shoulders!

"That day, we hed caught in camp about two hundred tarrapins more or less! And didn't I do my best. I waited on table, and watched the Gineral, and the mess, as they ate; and ef *they* warn't happy, who was? As the Gineral ate the soup, and swallowed the pie, he took a long breath, wiped his chops with the towel, and said—

" 'Gentlemen, did'nt I tell you so! With all his vices, Bauldy's soul is worth saving. His one vartue is a very great one!'

"And we got on well, to the eend of the campaign, 'cept for one skrimmage, when the Siminoles made a hambush for us, and nearly captivated my baggage wagon, with all the mess kettles, and pots, and pans, and me in the bargin!—But I knocked down one impudent redskin with the frying pan, and driv' the hosses over him. We got *his* sculp; and the Gineral said,

" 'Bauldy's always at home with a frying pan! Ef I was to take him into a battle, he should hev a frying pan or a gridiron, or something of the sawt, instead of a musket!'

"At the eend of the campaign, and when we was disbanded, we had *seven* sculps to show; and one was sculped by me;—and they did say thet them *seven* sculps cost the government some twenty four millions of dollars!—Some did go so fur as to say two hundred millions; but I reckon that was an overcount!

"All the time I was with the Brigade, I tried my best to make the off'sers see the truth of my ixperience in captivation to the Ingins; the alligators, and the Mar'maid Queen; but, to the last, they purtended not to believe it! When we was a-parting, for good and all, and the Gineral and the mess was taking the goodbye drink together, the Gineral called me up, and says he—

" 'Bauldy, we won't hang you this time! You're a good fellow, ef you only know'd it, and you've got a great vartue! But Bauldy, you must leave off lying. 'Twont pay! Hyar now, take a pull of this Jamaica! Ef I waur to give you the whole bottle now, you'd see the Queen of the Mar'maids at the bottom!'

" 'Ah, Gineral!' says I, getting bold, a'ter I swallowed, 'that want of faith in you, and the whole mess, will keep you out of Heaven yit! Ef ever I spoke the truth at all, Gineral, it's about that woman; that Queen of the Mar'maids.'

" 'Well,' says he, good natured—'I suppose that story is jist as near the truth as any thing you do say, Bauldy! All your truth, my dear fellow, lies in the kitchen! After eating your tarrapin soup and tarrapin pie, I kin believe equally in you, and the sixty nine particles!'

"What he meant by the sixty nine particles, I never know'd, and I could only think of them things we use in dressing soups and pies, and sich dishes—sich as pepper and spice, and allspice, and nutmeg, and inyons, and, Lawd love you, a hundred more things instid of sixty nine!

"I went out of the sarvice poorer than when I went into it. I hed hairdly no clothes left. The sutler's account eat up all my pay before I got it. Government never paid me for my mar' Polly Hopkins; and the worst was last! When I got home to Lexington, I pushed right to see Susannah Sykes; and thar' I found one of our Brigade, playing Cock Horse, with a Doodle Doo, all about her, and she wouldn't look at me! When I popt the question to her,—which I did desprit,—she turned up her nose and said—

" 'I've hairn all about you, Mr. Bauldy! You may go back to your Queen of the Mar'maids, with her alligator tail! I ain't the pusson you thinks me!'

"The story, you see, had got before me. Jim Crowder hed told her every thing. He was the sergeant that captivated and brought me into camp as a desarter. He got ahead of me. Well, in three weeks a'ter that, she married Jim; and ef I've got any satisfaction in the world, it's the knowing that the two on 'em lives like cat and dog together; and some do say that he threshes her; others say she threshes him! I hopes both stories is true! I'm only glad I'm not the husband! Last time, I seed Susannah, 'twas at church, and she turned up her eyes, like a dying duck in a thunderstorm, and had the impudence to ax me to walk home with her. But she couldn't come it. And, the Lawd be praised, I'm a free white man to this very day! —Amen!"

[Two manuscripts of "The Humours of the Manager" exist in the Charles Carroll Simms Collection of the South Caroliniana Library, one complete rough draft and one incomplete revised version. The text published here is based upon both these manuscripts. Explanatory and Textual Notes begin on page 828.]

THE HUMOURS OF THE MANAGER.

I.

It is now several years since I passed a pleasant evening at the residence of the late Dr. Francis of New York. Nobody needs be told that the Doctor was a famous original in his way, was one of the most remarkable of the reminiscents of the city, and was never more happy than when he had about him a circle of good listeners. Not that he was at all unwilling, himself to listen, when other parties had any thing to say.

I need hardly mention, to those who knew him that the wonderful memory of the Doctor, his capacity for seizing upon the salient in his subject, and his buoyant and piquant manner, made him a most agreeable talker, while his anecdotes of persons and events perpetually opened new avenues for conversation.

Our excellent humourist, Cozzens, the Litterateur, has somewhat caricatured the venerable reminiscent in the character of Dr. Bushwhacker, in a recent volume; but the exaggeration is good natured and quite too slight to occasion offense to any, the best friends of the worthy original. His manner, we may say to those who did not personally know him, was bold, free, burly, in brief, genuinely Irish. His voice was loud, of Boreas tenor, cheery, fresh, and as full of stimulating geniality, as a stiff breeze in November. He loved society, lived in it whenever he could, always enjoyed it, and possessed most of those essential elements of experience, thought, observation and knowledge of men and manners, which endow the social circle with vitality. His long professional as well as private association with men, in the growth of a great city like New York, and his intimacy, especially, for more than half a century, with so many remarkable persons of that and other American cities, shown in lively delineations, brought them before you with a lifelike freshness, which showed equally the personal and the intellectual man. The style of Dr. Francis was the very best for a reminiscent. He was none of those demure "damnable faces," preliminary to his speech, which Hamlet denounces in the actors. He had something to tell and told it,—dashing into his subject, as the Poet counsels, *in medias res,* like a gallant Colonel of Cavalry leading his troopers in a charge. His manner, frank and full of bonhommie, was that of a liberal and portly Virginia host at his dinner table: and so, with a spirit and humour all his own, he recalled for his guests, as the subjects severally came up, his memories of the past, in men and things, which it is usually grateful to the curious, to study and remember.

With these tastes and these resources, Dr. Francis made welcome at his house, all the celebrities, of whatever class or profession who happened to find their way to New York. He especially welcomed the young in art and letters. It was his theory that the association of age with youth was equally beneficial to both parties. Nor did he wait for this untill the parties had become famous through other auspices than his own. It was quite enough for him to conceive the possibility of future distinction for the young beginner, or incipient genius, in any province. He could quietly guide them with counsel, and pleasantly encourage them with hope. The consequence of this hospitality was, that you rarely spent an evening with the Doctor without finding yourself in very grateful and sometimes very remarkable company; the more grateful, indeed, as the rëunion was most commonly unpremeditated. You dropt in—as it happened—and there you met—to use the style and manner of the host:—

"My friend, the eminent Dr. Swedenborg, who has just got back from a late tour of exploration in the spiritual world. He has had some adventures and experiences there which he will report to us in due season. He has enjoyed some most interesting conversations with Sir Isaac Newton, Lord Bacon, Dr. Franklin, George Washington, Edmund Burke, and George the Third, the last of whom he describes as having quite recovered his wits, though the measure of development is still appropriately small for a crowned head. Of these conversations we shall no doubt have a full report as soon as the publishers are ready. But for these we shall need to wait awhile. His adventures have fatigued him as you may see, since they seem to have made no such material progress in the spiritual world, such as we now boast in the utilitarian. They know nothing of steamboats and railways, to say nothing of telegraphing; though they are beginning, under Franklin's auspices, to turn their attention in this direction, with the view to a direct intercourse with the mundane world....

"Dr. Swedenborg,—my friend Dr. Mucklewhabber, the great German peripatetic Philosopher, who has made his ten miles an hour, on foot, along with Hugh Miller, and botanized, mineralogized and moralized at every step in the progress. He too has his book in preparation, five volumes quarto, with thirty thousand illustrations. It is my great felicity, my dear friends, that I can bring two such eminent philosophers together."—

Couple such speaking with a hearty jovial manner, a sonorous voice, lively action, great round rubicund face, with white hair blown about the head in wild confusion, and you can conceive the portrait of our venerable reminiscent. His local recollections have been published in a pleasant and portly volume, which is yet very incomplete. There are hundreds of topics, illustrative of his experiences among men; full of interest, of which Dr. F. discoursed knowingly, enough to furnish the materials of another volume, which might be made one of singular interest. Such a volume might be commended safely to Mr. Tuckerman or Mr. Duyckinck.

One of the evenings passed at the house of Dr. Francis, has been recalled to me by happening, in a late publication, a chronicle of the New York stage, upon certain passages relating to the once well known Charles Gilfert, famous for his music, and manager, at different periods, of the Bowery and Charleston Theatres. Francis was intimate with Gilfert, was his physician, as he was frequently employed by the leading actors, and the subject of Gilfert's humours being adverted to by one of the company, they became the subject of the evening's conversation, mixed up with incidental references to famous performers. Several gentlemen were present who had also known Gilfert as well in Charleston as in New York, as well in the full flush of his fame as a musician, and late in life, when, hopelessly insane, the strings of the fine instrument were all jangled, and out of tune. Each of these persons had something to contribute to the topic. It may be grateful to many of the present generation, to hear of one who has passed from it forever—himself an original, a fellow of infinite jest, of gay capricious humours, a man of very decided talent,—thought, indeed, in his day, to be a musical genius of high order—a person of equal tact and improvidence, shrewdness and recklessness,—cleverness in sundry respects, but of most unprofitable life; loose of morals, capricious of mood; a *bon vivant*, a gamester, selfish, but distinguished by noble charities; in brief one of those anomalies in endowment and character, the very caprices of whom have been too often supposed the certain indicatives of genius.

By birth a German, the mental man of Charles Gilfert was decidedly of the national type; though, living, as he did, at different periods in all the great cities of Christendom, mingling much with distinguished persons in all places, having the freedom of various circles as of all the theatres, he became cosmopolitan in mind and manner. At his ease in all situations—having a cool self possessed and quiet humour which gave vivacity to his conversation, and a quick power of conception, the fruit of a lively fancy,—he had the art to seize upon the latent humours of the company and bring them into active play—sometimes in the character of the wit, and not unfrequently in that of the Humourist and Droll.

The several reminiscents at the reunion of which we write, had each his contribution of anecdote illustrative of these characteristics. The Charleston gentleman told the following:

"Gilfert was of medium height, of heavy build, somewhat loose of limb, careless in his gait, and remarkable by his green spectacles, under or over which he was accustomed to look, when he was disposed to indulge in a sly mood and when his humours were quizzical, or when he wished to probe you, without in any way discovering himself. His green spectacles, could upon occasion, as we shall see, be exchanged for blue. Careless in business, especially in the payment of debt, to which he was quite as reluctant as Sheridan, he also possessed that happy art of Sheridan by which he could not only baffle his creditor for the time, but even procure additional loans. With all his cleverness, however, his credit grew finally so bad in Charleston that nobody would trust him, and even when he had become *quasi* manager of the Theatre in that city, the Lease could only be obtained on his wife's credit, and in her name. She was the Proprietor, he the Manager, and just as careless in the management of the Theatre, as he was in his private affairs.

"Mrs. Gilfert was greatly honored and respected in Charleston, not only as a noble actress, but as a woman of elevated tone and character. She preserved her purity from all reproach, in spite of the familiarities, the freedoms and levity of the stage; while her bearing was as dignified and lofty, as her character was above question.

"Nor was Gilfert, himself, however loose his own moral, the person to permit any blot upon her fair name or any indignity to her person whether on or off the stage. He shot one of the actors—Young, I think, in a duel because of some liberties taken with her person, which were not warranted by the situation or the character represented. He was concerned in several duels, as principal or second, and was tenacious of what, in that day, was called 'the Point of Honour.' I remember his training young Cogdale of Charleston, for the fight with rifles, when he killed Wigfall, of Edgefield District, a kinsman of Wigfall, distinguished as a former Senator in Congress, from Texas, and more recently as a Brigadier in the Confederate armies.

"Mrs. Gilfert was unquestionably one of the most finished of actresses in her day in America. She was a Miss Holman, one of a highly gifted family especially in Dramatic Art. She had been highly educated, and few women have ever shown themselves more capable of appreciating and nicely discriminating the characters which they sought to personate. She was equally eminent in Tragedy, and in High Comedy. Her Lady Townly was a conquest over art and nature; and, by all contemporaries was admitted to be superior in finish and general excellence to any previous or contemporary performance of the part. Her Lady Macbeth was one of those grand representations which fasten upon the imagination forever. It was never surpassed in this country, and was held by good judges at the time to be second only to the personation of that character, by the great Siddons, to whose school she belonged. She survived her reputation, lingered too long upon the stage, became *passée,* and her temper grew visibly soured by the decline of public favour, which, as is usual in such cases, she could not be persuaded argued a decline of power in herself. I remember perfectly the feeling of the community of Charleston growing cold, if not hostile towards her, in consequence of her assumption of a carriage, which she perhaps considered only dignified, but which her audiences held to be arrogant and scornful.

This was while she held the Theatre as its lessee. The enterprise failed. Gilfert's reputation as a musician, was still greatly esteemed, and during the declining periods of the engagement, involving also a decline in the dramatic tastes of the community, his talents as a pianist and violinist, were frequently taxed on the stage as an added attraction to the dramatic performance. He was chary of these appearances, and the announcement of them was always welcomed by a good audience.

"But, with all the popular admiration of his music, as a performer, it was a long time before the Charleston public knew him also as a fine composer. He kept his secret, though composing much, and published his compositions abroad under a foreign nom de plume—that of a German nobleman—the Baron Von Something—I forget now what. When asked why he should forego the advantage he possessed, by reason of his local reputation, he answered shrewdly, in his half broken English—

" 'Ah! my friends, you mistake. This reputation is not for Charles Gilfert, as composer, but for Charles Gilfert, the mere violinist and pianist. People are apt to be jealous of authors who set up to be more than one person, or to do more than one thing, and the very persons who praise my touch on the piano, or my bow on the violin, will be apt to say—"Ah! yes! he play well—but composition!—that is quite another thing." That is the way with the world. They will be willing to admit that you are something, and somebody, but you must not be too much thing or body. That makes them jealous. Besides, there is another good reason. The people of this country have too little self esteem, to venture to judge for themselves, in matters of the fine arts, without the sanction of foreign opinion. The arts must cross the water, like old Madeira, to be recognized as legitimate. Your people are provincial now. They will outgrow it; but now, and for a good many years they receive and will continue to receive their opinion from abroad. They do not make their own opinion in matters of art. They are afraid to be laughed at, and find it safer to sneer at the home production, than risk their reputation as critics by daring to approve in advance of the foreign verdict. Now, you see, my friends that where a people do not *make* opinion, they cannot confer reputation. The wit as the wine must cross the water. What says the Poet, "Tis Distance lends enchantment to the view." The local associations take all the charm from the object. "Familiarity breeds contempt." How should these people, that meets me every day in the market place, buying my little basket of beef and turnips, mutton and onions and other things—who sees me looking through my green specks, and walking the streets like any Hob the Miller,—nay, perhaps—who knows—who meets me sometimes coming home from a midnight lark with you young fellows, and not always able to keep a right line as I go,—perhaps, embracing the wall, or a lamp post, to preserve my equilibrium—how should they believe that I am one of the Grand Masters of Musical Composition —one of those great geniuses that expects to go down to posterity—famous, I say, as any of the grand old composers. They will believe it of the Baron Von, &c. whom they have never seen, but not of Charles Gilfert, who is but five feet seven inches in their eyes.'

"And he would close his rambling harangue, by thrusting his fist jocularly into the sides of his companion, and staring at him, through his green glasses, with the most comical expression. He had seriously spoken, however, when he affirmed his own convictions of his rank as a musical genius. Here, his self esteem was indomitable, and he continued firm in this conviction of his future fame to the last." One of the anecdotes of the evening will sufficiently illustrate the soaring hope and grand aspirations of his imagination on this subject. But of this hereafter. Our Charleston friend continued his reminiscences.

"While Gilfert, or rather his wife, was Proprietor of the Charleston Theatre, an original tragic Drama was submitted to him called 'The Female Assassin.' It belonged, as its title implied, to that superlatively sensational school, of which 'Abollin, the Bandit,' 'Schinderhannes' &c. were the redoubtable specimens in that day. We hear, in our times, a good deal of critical talk, in regard to the sensational in literature. But when was the sensational *not* an element, whether in prose fiction or the Drama, and briefly in every province of the fine arts. Athens, in the days of her greatest glory, under Pericles, was quite as sensational as New York, but without the myriad agencies of the latter city, in diversifying and accumulation of those sensational objects which appeal to the sensuous nature—to human passion, curiosity and the love of change.—

"Enough, that 'The Female Assassin'—the new drama, anticipated some of the monstrosities of the modern stage. Gilfert received the manuscript very graciously. It was commended to him as it came from one of the fashionable gentlemen of the city—one of the genuine *sang azul*—who could number thirty quarterings on his escutcheon. Such a man was to be conciliated. Besides, he was a passionate lover of the Drama, a constant visitor of the theatre—a man of fancy, who kept a famous stud, a member of the jockey club, who entered his blooded horses annually for the turf. He was also fond of cards, and—bled freely. These qualifications commended him especially to Gilfert's favour, and he was admitted to all the privileges of the Theatre. He joined with Gilfert and his coterie in most of those sacred circles in which the parties were silent, and the play was deep. The amateur Dramatist had a taste for beauty, was admitted to the green room, and at the rehearsals, and made the acquaintance of all the most pretty and sprightly actresses. Though on the shady side of forty, the heroines of the stage gave him such welcome as would better comport with one more youthful of age and aspect. They too had reasons for conciliating his favour. He was rich, liberal, gave fine dinners, delicious suppers, and occasionally very handsome presents. The gracious smiles of a favorite young actress were apt to be rewarded with some rich jewel, ruby or diamond, which it sufficiently delighted the Donor's heart, to see displayed the next night, upon the damsel's head or bosom.

"But, with all his sporting proclivities and all his admiration for the tender gender, the passion of the gentleman for dramatic authorship was paramount, and quite as earnest and exacting as that of Richelieu. His play was his ideal triumph. It was to glorify him. He was impatient for the hour when the plaudits of the theatre, were to lift him to the seventh heaven of self satisfaction. The seeming delight with which Gilfert had received the MS. was a hopeful augury. He had delivered it with modest misgivings. He went home assured. In a week, he sought the manager. Gilfert received him with open arms. He was surrounded by a group of good fellows. He broke through the circle, embraced the amateur, and cried out—

"'Ah! my dear friend, I am so happy to see you. That is a glorious play of yours. It will make a ——— of a sensation. It is full of strong points and magnificent sensations. Fred Brown shall do the hero—Mrs. Hughes the heroine. I have conceive all the cast already. It is a grand thing. It will make a most ——— grand glorious sensation.'

"The delighted Dramatist took his seat, amid the circle. The Madeira was put in circulation. The company toasted the promised play, and cheered the author, who made a modest speech in reply. Gilfert echoed it, and slapping the amateur upon his shoulders dubbed him with all of his anticipated fame. All went merrily as marriage bells. The Madeira continued to circulate. The circle squared into a whist party; and the dramatist, somewhat lighter of pocket, went off, with head in the skies, and feet treading the etherial plains.

"So week after week elapsed, and at every visit of the author to the manager, he met with the same enthusiastic reception; was assured of his successes, and dismissed with the passionate phrase, 'Your play will make a most ——— grand sensation!'

" 'The fact is,' quoth the manager, 'I build, my dear Colonel, upon that grand drama to put us all right with the public and the Treasurer. The theatre has not been doing handsomely this season. There is a most ——— falling off in the popular taste for theatricals. It is for your tragedy to bring us up—to bring up the theatre—to revive the failing tastes of the ——— people, and begin the new era of prosperity—what the pious people calls "a revival." Your play shall save us, my friend. It will make a most ——— grand and glorious sensation.'

"Fancy these assurances repeated week after week, throughout a tedious term of three months. Meanwhile, our Dramatist bled freely. He was hailed with equal welcome by actors and actresses. He declaimed with the one class and flirted with the other; made sweet faces, gave fine presents; gamed with the manager's circle and lost his money like a gentleman. Gilfert still enthusiastic in his assurances, in behalf of the new tragedy, had yet shown no signs of putting it upon the boards.

"But, we are told that the hope deferred is a sickening of the heart. Our dramatist was no longer satisfied with the fine speeches of the manager. The theatrical season was passing rapidly away; warm weather was coming on; the month of May was approaching, and in the hot climate of Charleston, theatres are not apt to find much patronage after the month of May, rarely after April. Our Dramatist felt all these things, and began to doubt the good faith of the manager. He was in this mood when he was suddenly startled one morning at seeing the announcement of a Benefit for one of the actors. The next day, a stock actress took her benefit. And so through the week. The endurance of our amateur was at an end. He felt that he had been bamboozled. He had heard something of the tricks of managers—of their heartless treatment of Dramatic authors—of their ignorance, selfishness and stupidity in regard to new pieces—and the pride of the author, as well as of the fashionable gentleman was at once in arms.

"He hurried to the theatre where he found Gilfert surrounded by the well known circle. There was the round table; there the corpulent decanter of old Madeira; with convenient goblets; and there too, ready for use, were sundry new packs of cards. And Gilfert met him with the well known welcome—an embrace this time and a fervent German kiss.

"'Ah! my dear friend; happy to see you. Take a seat. Here, Gentlemen—a glass for Col. ———. My friend, we will drink to the success of that grand tragedy and the restoration of the Theatre.'

"But our Dramatist was upon his dignity. He declined to be seated and declined to drink. Gilfert, with the tenderest consideration, taking his hands fervently within his own, exclaimed:

"'My dear friend, what is the matter with you. You will not sit. You will not drink! Ah! I see. I look into your eyes and see that you are bilious. Your skin is sluggish. Your digestion is not good. It is your liver! That ——d liver, in this climate, is always getting out of order. You must take some blue pill tonight and a bottle of Congress water in the morning.'

"'Thank you, Mr. Gilfert, but I have no complaint to make of my liver. My digestion is good, and my liver, I have every reason to believe, is working properly. My object here, Mr. Gilfert, is to——'

"'Don't you trust that liver, my friend. It is very deceptive. Your skin is most certainly inactive; and there is that unmistakable blueness about the eyes, just under them, making a sort of half circle, that tells me certainly that there is something wrong about the liver. The blue pill, my friend, and then——'

"'I thank you, Mr. Gilfert. But I have not come hither in search of medical advice. I have come, Sir, to request that you will return me my Drama.'

"'W-h-a-t! return you your Drama, my dear friend. Mein Gott! Give you my own soul! What! give you back that play which is to make the fortune of the theatre! That play, which, as I'm a living sinner, is to make the grandest ——dest sensation ever yet made in the dramatic world! It is impossible! Ask me rather to commit suicide. Blow my brains out with a pistol. Swallow laudanum and arsenic: or go down there, only two hundred yards off and drown myself in Ashley river, well knowing what the sharks, crabs and eels will be doing with the poor carcass of Charles Gilfert, in half an hour after. No! No! my friend! That tragedy is to come off on these boards before long, and you shall witness the grandest——'

" 'Thank you, Mr. Gilfert, but with my consent, my play shall not be presented on these boards. These fine words, Mr. Gilfert can delude me no longer.'

" 'Delude you, my dear friend.'

" 'Ay Sir, delude me. I am now satisfied, Mr. Gilfert that you do not mean to play my piece.'

" 'Not mean to play that grand Drama! Mein Gott! and how you knows that.'

" 'The theatrical season is nearly over. Your actors are taking their benefits.'

" 'And what that mean? Nothing! That, my friend, is a mere *ruse de theatre*. We shares with the actors all these benefits. We only uses their personal popularities, to fill the house. That is all. Come! Come, my friend; don't be unreasonable. Sit down, and take a bumper of this fine old Madeira, with all these gentlemen, your friends and mine. They will turn out strong as thunder when your piece is played.'

" 'Thank you, Mr. Gilfert; but no more of this. I beg to repeat my request that you return my M.S.'

"There was much parlaying after this, in spite of the dogged resolution displayed by the amateur. Gilfert went over all the old grounds, protesting, adjuring, entreating, and winding up with the frequently repeated assurance not only that the piece should be played; but that it would prove the 'd——est, grandest of all Dramatic sensations.'

"All in vain. The blood of the amateur was not to be allayed by the old sedatives, and, in very despair at last, Gilfert proceeded to look up the precious M.S. Throwing open his escritoir, he soliloquized in the following fashion for the benefit of the author.

" 'It is terrible unfortunate! I have made such great calculations upon this drama. I know what a most grand monstrous sensation it would make. The theatre have had such losses this season. That play would build it up! Would make all right in the Treasury. Mein Gott! Mein Gott!—But, if you are in earnest, my friend,—resolute I say—if you will not have the piece played, as I could put it on the boards—with entire new scenery—with Fred Brown as the hero,—Mrs. Hughes as the heroine,—and the beautiful Miss Tilden as the foil, and Mrs. Gray as the chambermaid——'

"'There is no chambermaid in my tragedy, Mr. Gilfert.'—indignantly.

"'To be sure there is no chambermaid. How I should make that blunder.—But, what say you now, my friend. You are really not in earnest?'

"'I am in earnest, Mr. Gilfert; and repeat my demand for my MS.'

"'Mein Gott!—Demand! Eh bien!'

"And taking down a huge pile of MSS. from a shelf, he proceeded to turn over, and canvas their titles. Here, a new dilemma beset him, and turning to the author, some what awkwardly, he said—

"'Ah! one thing, my dear friend—what is the name of that famous grand drama of yours?'

"'What, Sir! you do not even remember the name of that drama which was to produce so great a sensation?'

"'And—what's in a name! That is the very question that Shakspeare asks. I know the play well enough, but I never remember names. I have not the faculty.'

"'My play, Sir, is called "The Female Assassin"!'—Impatiently and striding the floor.

"Gilfert, turning over the pile of MS.S. play by play, kept muttering, '"Female Assassin"! "Female Assassin"!' till he had gone through the whole collection.

"'Tis not there!' he said, putting away the one collection and taking down another of similar dimensions, with which he went through the same process, with a like result.

"'Tis not there! Where the d——l is that d——d "Female Assassin."'

"A third pile resulted in no discovery. The manager was evidently gravelled. The author grew frightened.

"'You do not mean to tell me that my play is lost!'

"'Lost! Oh! No! nothing is ever lost in this house but money; and that is so lost that somebody is sure to find it!—Ah! Stop! Here is more of them.' And, from a fourth receptacle, he drew another pile of MSS. But the 'Female Assassin' still eluded his search.

"'Where, the d——, is that "Female Assassin"!'

"'You can not find my play, Sir!' cried the author, who now proceeded, with trembling fingers, to turn over the several piles of MS.S. for himself.

"'It is not here,' replied Gilfert utterly at his wit's ends. He proceeded from shelf to shelf, from drawer to drawer, untill he had explored every possible hole and corner which could possibly hide the 'Female Assassin,' but without result.

"'Some of them d—— woman actors have carried it off. There's that woman, Mrs. Gray, she is always poking every where, among the play books and she's curious as ——— after all new pieces. When she happens upon a good thing,—a grand thing, like your play, she carries it off; and there's Mrs. Hughes, and Miss Tilden,—all the same—whenever they gets hold of a piece with grand situations, like your Female Assassin—they seizes upon it, to study it in private, and see what parts is to suit them. There will be a regular fight among them about that heroine. I know it, just as sure as if I see them at it now. They've got it somewhere among them, my dear friend, and I'll see after it; and then, my dear friend, if you are so unjust, so unreasonable, as to deny us the privilege of playing it,—why, then,—Mein Gott!—you shall have the play; though it will cut us out of the very grandest d——t sensational that ever filled a treasury.'

"'My piece gone—missing—lost no doubt!' cried the author in a fit of despair for which Gilfert had no consolation. 'My only copy!'

"Savage were the eyes which he fastened upon the manager, who could only repeat, helplessly,

"'Lost! Nothing, I tell you, my dear friend, is ever lost in this house but the money!'

"'My play, Mr. Gilfert! My play!'

"'Mein Gott! What shall I do! What shall I say. It is not here, you see. But I will look with all my specks. I will go to these women.'

"'D——n the women!' was the ungallant response. 'I say, Sir; my piece, my tragedy!'

"'Oh! don't you be angry, my friend. There is no wisdom in that. I will try recover your piece. That is all I can say. D——n the Female Assassin!' *(sotto voce.)* Then as the wretched author bestrode the apartment, almost speechless with rage, Gilfert, in utter desperation, becoming impatient himself, exclaimed—

"'I would do any thing, my dear Colonel—I am willing to do any thing. I will try recover your play. But, in the mean time, take any of them pieces,'—pointing to the enormous piles of MS.S. 'Take a dozen of them, if you please! There's none of them that's worth a d——n!'

"This was the *coup de grace,* designedly administered. Here the scene ended. The author's rage, now at white heat, rendered him utterly speechless, and glaring at the manager, with eyes of a hyena, he darted headlong from the theatre, leaving Gilfert breathless; but in a mood to share in the laughter of the circle, which had beheld with rare but suppressed merriment the whole affair—a scene quite as dramatic, perhaps, as any in the lost performance!"

II.

How Gilfert Made a Trip to Saratoga. How He Bled the Cashier, and Completed His Professional Education.

The Carolina Reminiscent continued his narrative, illustrating the "Humours of the Manager" in a new province.

"It was probably at the close of this very dramatic season, which did *not* bring forth the grand sensational Drama of the 'Female Assassin,' that Gilfert, in company with two of his Charleston associates, prepared to visit Saratoga. One of these gentlemen was a well known and highly talented amateur actor. He had played on several public occasions, for the Benefit of the Greek Cause, and other objects of popular concern, and had always so acquitted himself, as to make it a subject of regret, as well as surprise among his friends, that he had not made the stage his profession. Where the endowment of nature was so evident, and where the acquisitions of art, had so admirably seconded the natural gift, it seemed almost criminal to forego the exercise of the faculty. It is very certain that Dan G—— could do nothing half so well as tread the stage and face the footlights.

A wit and a wag, full of fun and humour, prompt at retort, and good at an extempore speech, he was yet, above all things, a born actor. Handsome of face, fine of figure, graceful of action, with a keen quick perception of what the part required, and prompt to seize upon all its susceptibilities, I have rarely met with any man who seemed so completely made for the profession. In society, he was the life of every circle; humourous, droll, animated, imitative, with a fine flow of speech, and a lively and perpetual play of fancy, which, like summer lightning, illuminated with incessant flashes, the ordinary topics of discourse; Daniel G—— was one of those men who seem to take no account of their own resources, whether for profit or ambition. He was content, simply, to shine for the occasion, in society, and occasionally to burst forth upon an audience, as the hero of the stage, in some amateur performance, in which he found few foils, and rarely an equal.

"The other party to this proposed excursion of Gilfert, was an amiable and intellectual young Lawyer, of some literary proclivities,—a man of considerable cleverness and popular in society. I will slightly cover the true name under that of Colonel Bondy,—for he was a Colonel—in the militia—as well as a Lawyer.—Bondy was young, a great frequenter of the Theatre—fond of its excitements—happy in its pleasantries and freedoms, and admitted, because of his fellowship with Gilfert, to all the privileges of the green room. He was at that time of life, and of that temperament, to make these theatrical privileges very grateful to him. He conciliated Gilfert accordingly, and was eager to accompany the two associates to Saratoga, looking forward to the beyond, of Montreal and Quebec. It was to be an excursion for the summer.

"But, scarcely had they arrived in New York, safely housed at the most fashionable hotel of that day, when Gilfert made a most startling discovery. With well acted consternation in face and manner, he exclaimed:

" 'Mein Gott! What a misfortune! What shall I do?—I have left the money draft for all my expenses, in Charleston! Mein Gott! Mein Gott! Two thousand Dollars! What shall I do?'

" 'Oh! never mind it, Gilfert,' said Bondy—'You can write for it, and get it in the course of a couple of weeks. Meanwhile, I have enough money for both of us.'

"Gilfert embraced him.

" 'Bondy, my dear friend, you are a fellow after mine own heart. You are my guardian and preserving angel! Daniel my boy, what a glorious thing it is to have a friend who has money enough for both! When that is the case, nobody wants money for himself. Bondy, my dear fellow, I thank you. I accepts your offer with the same frankness with which you make it; and to show my feeling for you, my dear boy, let me have a couple of cool hundreds to begin.'

"What Col. Bondy thought of his friend's moderation, just at their entrance into New York, and when they had barely reached the hotel, he did not say. He showed no misgivings, however, even if he felt them, but gracefully enough delivered the two cool hundreds into the hands of his friend.

"From that moment, Gilfert disappeared from the party and from the hotel. He was absent all day and all night, and the next day, when they roused him from a late slumber, to make himself ready for the North river steamer for Albany, according to previous arrangement, they found him looking wearied, haggard and seemingly quite exhausted.

"But he rose, dressed himself; had his trunks sent down; and, soon after, showed himself below in the bar-room, where the three friends joined together in the enjoyment of a Julep. Almost ready to depart, Gilfert turned to Bondy, very cavalierly, and to his great surprise, said coolly,

" 'Pay my Bill, Bondy, my dear fellow, when you pay your own, and get the tickets for the steamer.'

"Bondy could only whisper to Dan—

" 'What the d——l has he done with the $200, I let him have yesterday?'

"Dan laughed, shrugged his shoulders, and only said—

" 'Patience, Tom, and shuffle the cards.'

" 'Yes! but d——n the fellow, *he* must n't be shuffling the cards at my expense!'

"Without mishap, they reached Saratoga in very good mood, but, scarcely had they arrived at the hotel, and tried its *strong* waters, when Gilfert, in his most quiet manner, said—

" 'Bondy, my dear fellow, let me have a couple of cool hundreds if you please.'

"The request was complied with.

" 'The theatre is good,' said Bondy, *sotto voce,* to Dan.

" 'Nothing better—*in its way;*' was the equivocal reply.

"As before, the moment Gilfert had obtained the money, he disappeared from the sight of his two friends. They saw no more of him till the next morning, at a late breakfast, when, without any preliminaries he said to Bondy,

" 'My dear fellow, you must let me have a couple of cool hundred this morning.'

"By this time, the mystery began to be somewhat oppressive to the imagination of Bondy.

" 'Where the d——l can he go, Dan? We must find out. How the d——l can he hide himself in such a place as this,—and what the deuse can he do with all that money? Six hundred dollars in a week! He will drain me dry! When I said I had money enough for both, I contemplated only our *necessary* current expenses. I can't stand this drain much longer!'

"Dan could give him no consolation—laughed merrily, as usual, and said—

" 'Patience, Tom! Patience! And have faith! It is a Christian virtue. Have faith!'

" 'Faith, indeed! How the devil shall faith pay our way? How much money have *you* brought, Dan? And why don't he try *your* purse?'

" 'He knows too well that it won't stand any trial, much less a strain. "Who steals *my* purse, steals trash!" That is the true reading, Tom! The fact is, Tom, I had somewhat calculated on you, myself. You are the proper cashier of the party. You are really the only monied man, just now, of the three. So Patience, and bleed freely! It is so much bread cast upon the waters. It will come home to you after certain days.'

" 'And, at this rate, I shall have to *go* home before many days! It is, in truth, a serious matter, Dan! And he calls upon me for the money, as cooly as if twere his own, and walks off without even a poor "thank'ee, Tom." '

"There was but little consolation in Dan's reply.

" 'To be sure! It is the way among friends! You proffer me your purse as a friend, and I help myself. Do you expect me, every time

I do so, to respond with the schoolboy, who has had a ginger cake given him—"Thank'ee Grandy"?—Nonsense!—Let him have the money, and see how it will end.'

"As before, the next day another cool two hundred was asked for and given; but Bondy, by this time, was desperate. Gilfert had again disappeared. Bondy raved.

" 'I started with fifteen hundred dollars. He has already had eight hundred. I have barely six hundred left, and here is this d——d expensive hotel bill to pay, *his*, as well as my own; and he spares himself nothing! I can't stand it, Dan! I must go home! I shall have seen nothing! No going to Niagara, now; no Canada; no Montreal; no Quebec! It's a d——ble disappointment—all my plans defeated. And you tell me to be patient when I am desperate! When I am literally bleeding to death!'

"It was with great difficulty that Dan kept him quiet for a day or two longer—'just to see how it will end!'

" 'Gilfert,' said he, 'is a queer genius, Tom. Full of eccentricity, full of talents, and, what music! How he charmed the whole saloon in that half hour at the piano the other night!'

" 'Oh! d——n the piano! D——n his genius, and the devil d——n his eccentricities! You forget, Dan, that I have to foot his Bills.'

"He was however, persuaded to remain a little longer; but, as he said, he was miserable.

" 'I take no pleasure in the d——d place. The waters do me no good.'

" 'You do not take enough brandy with them. Come, let's try a julep now.'

"The julep had a sedative influence. Dan beguiled Bondy into a convivial party that night, and made him laugh a little, and involved him in a nice little flirtation with a Salem belle, who blended fashion, love and piety, into a prettily incongruous medley, and Col. Tom Bondy survived the night.

"The next day he was destined to a surprise. Dan and himself slept in the same chamber, though, of course, on different beds. Strange to say, Gilfert, whom, hitherto, they had had to awaken every morning, now awakened them; and sate down, cigar in mouth, while they made their toilets. When they had done, Gilfert, who had been humming all the while—puffing his cigar at intervals—some new musical notes; rose up, flung his cigar stump into the chimney, and passed over to Col. Tom Bondy, who was arranging his collar at the glass.

"He put his hand affectionately on his cashier's shoulder. Bondy shrunk at the touch, and his immediate reflection was—

"'Another d——d cool $200.'

"Gilfert said—

"'Bondy, my dear Boy, I'm beginning to be concerned about you. You are looking very badly, Bondy. You are horribly bilious! Your very eyes are jaundiced! You don't *look* happy, and you *must* be sick. You ought to be happy here, Tom, flirting with the young women every night! I hear of you, Bondy! The flirtation is very good. I don't quarrel with that! But, my dear Bondy, you must n't get sick. These waters don't agree with you. Don't drink 'em. People of good sense never do. Drink brandy. *Eau de vie! Uisquebaugh!* Schnapps!—any thing that has got the soul of the Gascon in it! But for these medicinal waters! What says the play, Dan?—"Throw physic to the dogs!" That's my doctrine. But, in your case, Bondy, a little physic now—a very little—will do you good! A bit of blue-pill tonight, and a quart or two of this d——d water tomorrow, before breakfast, will help you now! 'Twould hurt *me!* I'm for something better! Dan, my boy, give that bell-rope a jerk.'

"The waiter promptly came.

"'John,'—said Gilfert—'Do you see that?'—

"Holding up a bank note of five Dollars. John saw it.

"'Now, John, do you see me, and these gentlemen.'

"John admitted that he saw them all.

"'You see, John, that we are all able-bodied white men,—with one exception. Our friend here,—you see for yourself, John,—is an invalid! He has filled his stomach with the infernal water of this place; and he is swollen! He is bilious! He is wretched,—and—Mein Gott, what will happen unless he gets instant relief.'

"John recognized the exigent fact.

"'Now, John, go below, and bring us up three of your biggest brandy smashes; cool as Nova Zemble; hot as Vesuvius; strong as Behemoth, and delicate as the Dove that went out of the Ark, keeping allways *above the waters!* Take that Bank note, John. Liquidate for the liquids; and put the residuum of change into your own pockets. Away, John! The sooner thou disappearest, the sooner shalt thou reappear!'

" 'Great God, Gilfert—and you give that fellow all the change out of five dollars only for bringing you three drinks?'

"Bondy could not contain himself. He was aghast.

" 'To be sure, Bondy. I give John the proper mode of knowing a gentleman when he sees him. I love to encourage infant merit, Bondy.'

"Bondy could only groan.

"Gilfert resumed his seat, and continued to speak in the same vein as when he began.

" 'Dan,' he said, 'you have noticed Bondy's condition. Why have you not told me of it before? Don't you see that his bile is terribly disordered? Look at the yellow in his eyes! The very *colour of gold!* Look!'

"Here he took from his pocket a handful of gold pieces, English guineas all, the Benton 'Mint Drops' not yet having shown themselves to American eyes.

"The eyes of Bondy opened wide. He stared at Dan and at Gilfert alternately, not knowing what to say, and quite bewildered as to what to expect. Meanwhile, the waiter reappeared, bringing three huge goblets of the desired beverage.

" 'Drink, Bondy, my boy, and drink in faith; for, if this beverage does not cure you—and the dose must be repeated every two hours throughout the day,—I must see that you swallow the blue pill to-night! If Bacchus cannot relieve you, we must call upon Mercury! We shall keep you in the hands of one or other of these Gods, untill that gold-yellow gets out of your eyes! But, that I know you, Bondy, to be one of the least selfish and most liberal fellows in the world—liberal to lavishness, and lavish to waste, I should suspect you, from the colour of your eyes, to be a worshipper of Mammon—a lover of lucre—a mere miserable miser,—decidedly the meanest of all mortal creatures! But, I know better, Bondy! I have tried you and you have not failed me. I owe you a debt, Bondy—'

"Here a long pause. What was coming next? Bondy's ears tingled with expectation.

" 'A debt, Bondy—which I can never—repay!'

"Bondy's saffron cheeks grew to a deeper saffron; then paled into a sort of dingy snow, and, in a moment after grew red as scarlet.

" 'A debt of—*gratitude,* Bondy.'

"Bondy, *sotto voce*—'Eight hundred dollars!—Gratitude be d——d!'

" 'Bondy, my dear fellow, your liberality has enabled me to complete my education.'

" 'Education!' exclaimed Bondy. 'Education!'

" 'Yes, education!—You see that there are some branches in science, in which my education had been greatly neglected. I felt my weakness. I knew that there were masters in my own arts, whose arts I could not fathom. But I was ambitious; and I was humble, Bondy! I knew that I had to *feel my way,* and pay for my education. In Charleston, I got on very well. There were a good many pigeons in Charleston, who thought themselves eagles. But the sciences had made greater progress, here, in New York. One night, in that city, opened my eyes,—to my own depth of ignorance. I resolved to study the profession thoroughly, and you afforded me the means to do so. I shall never forget you, Bondy, in my debt,—of gratitude! I shall never be able to repay you!'

"Bondy was again aghast.

" 'But it will be a satisfaction to you to know that Charles Gilfert is now one of the masters, and that your bounty has enabled him to become so!'

"Bondy was terribly bewildered. Dan was keeping his countenance as well as he could, readily conceiving the tortures of the 'only monied man' among them.

" 'Yes, Bondy, yes! I do not know, my dear friend, that you observed a certain group of *gentlemen*—so called—who came up with us in the boat. They were "swells." I did not mingle with them, *there,* though I knew them all. Thanks to my *spectacles!* They might have known a gentleman in *blue* glasses, whom they did not recognize in *green.* You will have noted, perhaps, that whenever I have left you boys, I put on my *blue* specks. I had a philosophical reason for it. Well, I visited these gentlemen,—so called—nightly. They are all scientific men. I got from you $200 nightly. That paid for each night's lessons! I had to take several lessons. It's damned expensive education, Bondy, this science. There are a thousand points of difficulty,—as difficult to round as the Cape of Horn, or Hope; but I had "*good hope*" to round them, being rather quick at catching sight of the invisible, and rather clever at doing the impossible! Enough, now, my dear Bondy, that, thanks to you, my education is complete. I graduated last night with all the honours,—and something more substantial!—I-BROKE-THE-BANK-LAST-NIGHT!—Look there, Bondy, my boy—your $800 or thereabouts, I set as so many nest eggs, and there are the chickens! Help yourself!'

"With these words, he drew from his pockets, coat and pantaloons,—from his hat,—from half a dozen different receptacles about his person,—roll after roll of bank notes, and hands-full of gold and silver, all of which he cast down upon the table before the amazed eyes of his two companions.

" 'Help yourself, Bondy! Don't be particular! Help yourself, Dan, my boy—don't spare it! There are other banks to be broken; and my scientific education is complete—for the present. There are new points of nicety, every now and then coming up, for, "*Ars est longa*"! you know; and I may have to pay for a little more schooling occasionally. For the present, boys, we'll do! We shall now be able to see the Canadians. I have not counted these chickens, but I have a shrewd notion that you will find five or six thousand in that pile. Count boys, and help yourselves to the prettiest figures.'

"Whether Dan had been in the secret or not, remained a secret from Bondy to the day of his death. But he recovered his health and temper from that moment; and the bilious aspect of his visage became thoroughly cleared. Still, though satisfied, and in fact delighted, at getting back his 'cool hundreds,' Bondy frequently referred to Gilfert's processes for acquiring his education, at the expense of his friend, as scarcely legitimate in morals."

III.

Our Carolina companion now gave way to other narrators; a brief anecdote was given by a Philadelphia *litterateur* to the following effect.

"One of our very best artists, a gentleman of the old school, and the most exquisite of the idealists of female heads, happened to visit Gilfert when he was manager of the Bowery. As an old acquaintance, of many years standing, who, by the way, acknowledged gratefully the help of Gilfert at a time when such help was of great importance to the painter,—he was admitted to the sanctum of the manager, the green room, and wherever else he pleased to go,—surveying all that is curious in the mechanism and management of a great Theatre. While in the green room, the eye of the painter was caught by the exquisite imitation of *flesh colour* in an article of dress hanging from the wall.

" 'How very beautiful, Gilfert,' said he,—'I have never before seen such an exquisite imitation, of the flesh. What is this garment?'

" 'Ah! my dear S——, you don't know? Dat is Madame Hutin's breeches!'

"The painter, who was as delicate as a girl, and one of the purest and best of men, turning over the pantalettes, exclaimed,—discovering a rent in them,—the opening of a seam—

" 'Heavens, Gilfert, you must contrive to have the attention of Madame Hutin drawn to this rent! It occurs very awkwardly!'

" 'Ah! Mein Gott, my dear S——, you will always be a child! You do not understand! My friend, you have never seen Madame Hutin! Well! She is a grand artiste! She knows, almost as well as you painters do, how to produce delightful surprises and beautiful effects! She study the public. She knows well the charming susceptibilities of the masculine gender; and—she leave that seam in her breeches open on purpose! Ah! She knows the secret for making beautiful effects! She is a most interesting woman,—before the footlights, and in them tights!' "

Dr. Francis here followed up the subject, in a degree, by an account of the first exhibitions of the foreign danseuses and especially of Madame Hutin, among the then sober and startled citizens of Gotham. He showed how rapidly they advanced,—the progress once begun,—in the acquisition of new tastes, and the appreciation of fine effects—delicate situations, aerial costumes, and piquant attitudes.*

* "Feb. 7. 1827. After the performance of 'Much Ado about Nothing,' a grand Pas Seul, 'La Barage Coquette,' was enacted by Madame Francisguy Hutin—her first appearance in America, and the first introduction of the modern French school of dancing on the American stage. The House was crowded and an anxious look of expectation dwelt on every face; but when the graceful Danseuse came bounding like a startled

IV.

He was followed by one of the veteran editors of New York, at whose office Gilfert was a frequent, almost daily visitor, especially when he desired a fresh puff for some new rarity in tragedy or ballet. At this period Gilfert already began to give proof of that growing eccentricity of mind and mood which gradually became insanity. The progress of the disease, however, was so slow that, for a long time, no apprehensions were felt, and no anticipations had of the final and full development of the malady. He was simply queer, eccentrical, full of strange caprices, fanciful and fantastic conversations. Of the origin of the infirmity, *quien sabe?* Irregular habits, disappointed hopes, a mortified self esteem, the failure of the Theatre in his charge, the Bowery, these, no doubt, all combined with determination of the blood to the brain, to establish the disease at last. His fancy was always exuberant, and was continually cropping out, in his talk, at this period, when his malady was yet only incipient. Some idea of his talk is derived from the recollections of the New York editor of forty years ago.

"Ah! my dear editor,"—he would say—"how wags it to day? Are you exuberant? Do your spirits mount. Are you etherial, on the wing—capable, in a word, of giving to the Bowery a most glorious puff for tomorrow. Sit down while I tell you. Ah! my

---

fawn, upon the stage, her light and scanty drapery floating in air, the cheeks of the greatest portion of the audience were crimsoned with shame, and every lady in the lower tier of boxes, immediately left the house. But Time works wondrous changes, and though, for awhile, Turkish trowsers were adopted by the lady, they were finally discarded, and the common ballet-dresses were gradually endured and are now looked upon as a matter of course. Madame Hutin was a skilful, graceful and daring dancer, and was greatly admired by the admirers of her peculiar school of art." *Records of New York Stage, Vol. I. pp. 528.*

"*March 1.* Mons. and Mde. Achille made their first appearance in America and Mde. by some was considered fully equal to Hutin. She was, perhaps, as graceful but not so dextrous and daring."—*Records N. Y. Stage Vol. I. pp. 529.*

To Gilfert we are indebted, whatever the merit or mischief, for the introduction of all the first French dancers; Charles Rinzi, Vestris and wife, as well as Achille, Celeste, and Hutin.

friend, it is a melancholy truth that these wretched people need to be told that the Bowery is the very temple of Art, of Fashion, of Terpsichore, and Melpomenene, and all the goddesses in tights—tripping so gaily on the light fantastic toe! You must give them a telling lesson in tomorrow's paper. You can't lay it on too thick. None of these milk and water things you do for Tom Hilson, and be d——d to him. Tom Hilson, the Pious! Oh! he's d——d pious in his pretences, and particularly appeals to virtuous sinners like himself—a d——d numerous class, who clothe the sinner's nakedness in white garments cut out by a saintly tailor. Tom Hilson and his piety, be d——d! I've found him out. I'll tell you how. You must know I went to Heaven the other night, having a little leisure time on my hands. We had closed the Bowery for a few days to repair and put in new scenery. Well, when I got to the gates of Heaven, I saw sitting there, looking rather drowsy, as if very tired of the situation of door keeper—not a paying situation as I know by the Bowery—the worthy old Saint, Peter of the Fishes and the Keys. He hardly looked up as I spoke to him.

" 'Do you know me?' says I.

" 'Know you,' says he, 'haven't that honour.'

"He spoke civilly and like a well bred gentleman—'Well' says I, 'you must know that I am Charles Gilfert, manager of the Bowery.'

" 'Bowery' says he, 'what's that?'

" 'What, old gentleman' says I—'you don't know the Bowery Theatre?'

" 'I do not,' said he.

" 'Not know the Bowery Theatre? Why what can you have to interest you in your studies here that you don't know the Bowery. Perhaps, you'll have some knowledge of the Park. It is just possible.'

" 'No! I have not. What's the Park?'

"I was confounded at his ignorance. But I tried him farther. 'Of course you know Tom Hilson?'

" 'Have n't the honour,' said he.

" 'What! don't know the pious Tom. He's of your church. He's d——d pious, is Tom Hilson, and yet you dont know him.'

" 'Have n't that honour.'

" 'Honour indeed! mighty small honour you'd have in the acquaintance of such a scamp. But I knew how twould be. I knew his church-going, and sanctimonious phiz was only so much lying and pretence. Of course the man who pretends to be pious, without being known to you, Saint Peter, must be a swindler and living on false pretences.'

"So you see how I found Tom Hilson out! * But, I wondered at the good saint's ignorance. I thought he ought to know every thing, and I told him so. He answered me shortly—

"'I mind my own business.'

"'Well,' said I, curious to see how much or how little he did know. 'Well' said I,—'if you don't know the Bowery Theatre, of course you are intimate with New York generally?'

"'New York:' said he—'what's that?'

"'What! dont know New York?'

"'No!'

"Mein Gott! Will Wall Street believe it, and Broadway, and the Bowery! Utterly unknown to the very saint that keeps the keys of Heaven! 'Well,' said I, 'my good fellow, if you dont know New York, it must be very well known to the sharp old gentleman down stairs;—he who keeps the Pit, you know!'

"To this he made no answer.

"'Then,' said I—for I wanted to see in how much his education had been neglected—'of course, my dear Saint, you know all about the world—that is, the Earth.'

"'Yes, I have some vague recollection of being there once, long ago. It is a poor little planet lying off yonder, filled with all manner of strange animals; but we take little count of such places up here.'

"'Indeed!'—said I, a good deal puzzled, and a little tired too,—'Well,' said I, 'Saint Peter, I think I'll walk in and take a seat and rest myself awhile, when we can talk more at our leisure.'

"'No, you won't,' said he, doggedly.

"'What!' said I, 'you won't let me in?'

* Gilfert was strongly prejudiced against Hilson—the reason is not known; but was probably due to some dramatic rivalry or collisions. Those who knew Hilson well describe him as a gentleman and scholar, and do not believe that he either was pious, or that he simulated piety. But, it was a part of Gilfert's humour to ascribe characteristics to individuals without much regard to propriety. Indeed, it is quite possible that he had no hostile feeling to Hilson, and that his portrait of him was drawn by his insane humours; for which we need not attempt to account, rather than by any unfriendly attrition between them.

" 'Can't!' he said.—'Impossible!'

" 'Look you, old fellow,' said I, 'you can't be serious! Why, man! I'm on the Free List every where!' "

V.

Such is a sample of his frequent discourse, while still in that harmless condition of his disease which occasioned no apprehensions, and amused from the fantastic character of his conceits, and the frequent humour of his talk. And this phase of his malady continued for some time. The disease grew slowly, but it grew steadily, untill it became necessary to put him under *surveillance,* if not absolute constraint. At length, however, confinement followed, but the restraint was still slight; only watchful, and sometimes so relaxed, that he was enabled on several occasions to make his escape from his keepers. On one of these occasions of escape, he made his way to the police office, or "Watch House" in the neighborhood of the Bowery Theatre. He laboured under a violent paroxysm of terror. His eyes were dilated, his face ghastly pale, his hair stood on end, and with arms stretched out he rushed into the police office, shrieking out to the officers as he came—

"I yield me! I surrender! Take me! Bind me! I confess the deed! I am a murderer! I have committed a horrid murder. Seize me and bind me! I surrender. I do not resist!"

The officers endeavoured to pacify him. They all knew him, knew his condition, and conjectured his escape from his keepers; and having some experience with such persons, they chimed somewhat in with his humours, in order to soothe them.

"Why who have you murdered, Mr. Gilfert?"

"It was not meant for him! I did not see him when I smote. It was the accursed Lobster upon whom I drew my sword."

"A Lobster, Mr. Gilfert?"

"Yes! a horrid Lobster—red, fiery, and climbing up my bedposts! Up he came, shining in crimson armour, with two great eyes glaring upon me with desperate purpose. I loathe—I dread the whole race! The lobster hath ever been my dread, my terror, my aversion!—and to see one, the most terrible of his kind, climbing up the bedpost, drove me desperate! I rose—I seized my sword from the wall—I smote the monster through the body; and oh! mein Gott! when he fell asunder, there was a little negro inside of him! With the same blow I slew them both! I confess! I confess! I surrender!"

VI.

Here our excellent host, Dr. Francis, took up the word.

"I attended Gilfert," said he, "in his last illness. I was with him when he died, and a sublimer death-scene was never beheld. Nothing like it on the stage! During his illness, and the continued advance of his malady, I was frequently impressed by the wonderful exhibitions of that imagination which he possessed, and which, even when disordered, was illustrative of the presence of genius. As a general rule, most insane persons exhibit the morbid activity and perpetual unrest of the idealizing organs. The marvellous, the fanciful, the imaginative, the humourous, all intensified, and are conspicuous in all they say and do. The wildest exaggerations of fancy, showing itself savagely in some cases, humourously and playfully in others, according to the differences of temperament, will always find a corresponding vehemency of expression. The language will be that of elevation always, except in cases of a dull fatuity, where the intellect was from the beginning feeble. In such cases, I have found the utterance, coarse, vulgar, even obscene, *especially in women*, even where, as in the case of Ophelia, they have been of the best families and have lived in circles of high life, and of unquestionable purity and refinement. That this should be so, is due, I apprehend, only to the originally feeble and inferior character of the intellectual endowment. But, in the case of men like Gilfert, where the gift of imagination, or of fancy, is large—and Gilfert, by the way, though a fine musician, was not merely a musician but an artist—a composer of very large merit—then the ideas—incongruous as they are—incoherent, distorted and exaggerated, in all respects, will be of strange brilliancy, grandeur, and audacity, and will always be clothed in a language, elevated, swelling, and ambitious;—though, in all cases, it will be found effortless and unpremeditated. There will be a Cyclopean vastness in the conceptions, and this vastness of form and proportion, will be fitly habited in a corresponding magnitude or grandiloquence of speech. This was so with Gilfert; and I have frequently been startled, with a delighted wonder, at the occasional outbursts of his thought; the conception of grand audacity, and the style of speech worthy of Nat Lee, under a similar affliction. It will be sometimes euphuestic, no doubt, like the fantastic writings of Lyly; stiltish as those of the Spaniard, Gongora; and strangely distorted at all times, sometimes hideously so, like the monster man created from the shambles,—'The Frankenstein' of Mrs. Shelley. You would be pleased to hear but pained also; surprised by beauty in the embrace of deformity; the blending of the fine Caucasian, Ferdinand in the Tempest, with Ariel at one moment, and the beast Caliban at another. But there were moments when the outburst would be one of singular and pure beauty, as if the music in his natural endowment, had clothed itself, for the moment, in language, simply from having no other instrument at hand. These however, were brief, spasmodic efforts—soon succeeded by incoherency and the most errant wanderings of the thought. The death-scene—the actual moment of the last agony—not, in his case, an agony—the actual transition from consciousness to death—afforded me one of the most remarkable of those instances of symmetry and propriety amidst all the sublime of his insanity; and, as I have already said, was one of the most beautiful, as it was certainly the most happy passage, that ever mortal made from Earth to Immortality. After a long silence, like sleep, a last effort, as it seemed, equally of the intellectual as the animal nature, seemed suddenly to inspire him. His face appeared absolutely illuminated. His eyes were rapt, as in the contemplation of a beautiful vision—looking upward with the most intense sentiment of devotion, mingled with delight; and, rising from his bed, with hands clasped and arms outstretched to Heaven, he stood upright upon the floor, while he ejaculated:—

"'Ah! Mein Gott! I thank thee! The prayer is granted at last! I live! I triumph! Charles Gilfert is immortal! Hark! You Hear? How they chaunt! The divine chorus—the grand effort!—It is Raphael, Gabriel, Michael, and they are all singing together the music of Charles Gilfert! Charles Gilfert is acknowledged! He is lifted up, he will sit with all the grand masters! His music is selected for the grand chorus of Heaven! It was too good—too grand for Earth;—and the archangels claim it for their own! Sing on! Sing on! ye Gods of Glory! Oh, the beautiful, and the beloved! Sing on my

Raphael, my Gabriel, my Michael!—Ah! it is so grand—so beautiful!—It has the wings—it is bathed in the sunlight—in all the beautiful hues of the rainbow,—and it goes up, and upward, upward till it buries itself in its face, at the feet of God! Ah! the divine triumph! And it is the music of Charles Gilfert! Oh! Mein Gott! I thank thee!—for the grand blessing,—Mein Gott! Mein Gott, I thank thee! I will sing for thee forever.'

"And thus, in a trance of rapt enthusiasm, a vision of supremest happiness, he fell backward, still murmuring in the same strain, and dying sweetly, with these last words upon his lips, and this last beautiful *hallucination* animating all his soul!"

Part II

APPARATUS

GENERAL INTRODUCTION TO THE TEXT

The editorial policy established for Volume I of *The Centennial Edition of the Writings of William Gilmore Simms* (see I, 437-440) has been continued in Volume V, with the exception of some streamlining to preserve space in this volume's sometimes lengthy and complex tables of emendations and textual variants. Whereas no symbols were employed in the textual apparatus of *Voltmeier*, two symbols have been used in *Stories and Tales:*

> A wavy dash ~ indicates a reading identical to the one that appears before the bracket. The wavy dash is used only to identify changes in accidentals and changes in paragraphing. Where changes in accidental readings have been combined with changes in substantive readings, the wavy dash has not been used.
>
> A caret ‸ indicates the absence of a mark of punctuation. The caret has been used only in conjunction with the wavy dash.

In addition, pointed brackets < > are used to enclose inserted editorial matter (such as ellipses) in the tables of emendations and textual variants.

Other principles not called into question by Volume I, but adhered to in this volume are the following:

(1) Throughout Volume V all titles have been regularized. The textual introduction to each story gives an exact transcription of the story title as it appears in copy-text. Emendations in chapter titles are recorded in Table I when they occur.

(2) In the two manuscript stories, all emendations that occur within one line of Centennial edition text have been listed under a single reference to the applicable line. (Thus, for example, the three

emendations in 477.17 of "Bald-Head Bill Bauldy" are listed in a single citation to 477.17 rather than in separate citations requiring three lines.) In addition, when the emendations consist of the addition, alteration, or deletion of quote marks involved in a single quotation (or closely related quoted passages), all emendations are listed in a single citation even if the quotation should run over to an additional line. (For example, the quotation beginning at 546.21 in "The Humours of the Manager" and ending at 546.22 requires five emendations which are listed under a single citation to 546.21-22.) If, however, the quotation calling for emendation extends three or more lines, the necessary emendations are listed in separate citations to the individual lines. This practice, it is believed, not only preserves space but helps the reader to see relationships among emendations.

(3) In establishing the texts of the manuscript stories—"Bald-Head Bill Bauldy" and "The Humours of the Manager"—the editor has made only those emendations necessary to produce the best reader's text that Simms himself could have expected. Since dialect provides much of the artistic flavor in both stories, in the dialect portions no attempt has been made to regularize spelling or punctuation—no matter how inconsistent—except where misreadings might occur. (All such emendations are listed in Table I to the applicable story.)

One of the chief problems in deciphering Simms's handwriting is establishing his intent in the use of capital letters. The following principles—almost identical to those established independently by Miriam J. Shillingsburg, "An Edition of William Gilmore Simms's *The Cub of the Panther*" (University of South Carolina dissertation, 1969), pp. 53-54—have been followed in this volume:

(a) The letters B, D, F, I, J, K, L, O, Q, R, T, X, Y, and Z are, almost without exception, distinguishable in their capital forms.

(b) All other letters pose problems. A, C, G, M, N, P, S, U, V, and W are seemingly used indiscriminantly with reference to lower and upper cases. Because neither size nor shape can consistently be relied upon in determining capitalization among this group of letters, the editor has depended almost exclusively upon contextual meaning. Even more puzzlingly ambiguous in Simms's handwriting are the letters E and H. Simms's lower case "e" is always recognizable as such—that is, he never wrote a lower case "e" where he intended a capital; but, on the other hand, he frequently used his equally recognizable capital "E" where obviously he intended the lower form. In such cases, context can be the only reliable guide. Similarly, Simms's lower case "h" never appears where he intended upper case; but, conversely, he frequently wrote the capital form where he obviously intended lower case. Again, contextual meaning has been the determining factor in establishing the reading. Consequently, Simms's manuscript "e's" and "h's" have been read as lower case unless the context clearly calls for capitalization.

INDIAN SKETCH.

In "Indian Sketch," his earliest fictional portrayal of the Indian, young William Gilmore Simms mocks the romantically conceived "savage" of "the Poet and the novelist" and insists upon more realism in the treatment of the Indian. Although this unpretentious sketch is marred by some almost incredibly clumsy phrasing, it is noteworthy not only for its unsentimentalized understanding of Indian character, but also for its narrative skill and power in the highly effective final three paragraphs. "Indian Sketch" is Simms's earliest successful use of the Southern backwoods as the subject for fiction. Though he was to stray from it for too long and frequent intervals in his literary career, Simms had at twenty-two discovered his forte.

Albert Keiser has called Simms's treatment of the Indian "probably the most balanced" in American literature (*The Indian in American Literature*, 1933, p. 296), though he apparently knew nothing of Simms's short fiction and based his judgment upon his reading of the novels. For Simms's own best exposition of the subject, see "Literature and Art Among the American Aborigines," *Views and Reviews in American Literature, History and Fiction*, First Series (New York: Wiley and Putnam, 1845), pp. 102-117; first published as "Literature and Art Among the Indians," *Southern and Western Monthly Magazine and Review*, I (March, 1845), 153-164.

Textual Introduction

"Indian Sketch" was first published, anonymously, in the *Southern Literary Gazette*, I (Nov., 1828), 142-149. A revised and somewhat expanded version, entitled "The Choctaw Criminal," was included in *The Book of My Lady. A Melange.* (Philadelphia: Key & Biddle, and Boston: Allen and Ticknor, 1833), pp. 277-290. Simms later used "Indian Sketch" as the germ for "Oakatibbe, or the Choctaw Sampson," published serially in the *Family Companion and Ladies Mirror* (Nov. and Dec., 1841) and in the *Southern and Western Monthly Magazine and Review* (April and May, 1845) before being included in *The Wigwam and the Cabin*, First Series (New York: Wiley and Putnam, 1845). The differences between "Indian Sketch" and "Oakatibbe" are great enough that they must be considered separate stories; "Oakatibbe" will be included in *The Wigwam and the Cabin* volume of the Centennial edition.

Since no manuscript exists, the first periodical printing, the *Southern Literary Gazette* publication of "Indian Sketch," serves as copy-text. The copy-text has not been emended to include Simms's revisions in "The Choctaw Criminal," including the new title. In the judgment of the editor "Indian Sketch" is more effectively introduced and ended than "The Choctaw Criminal," and the historical collation (see Table II below) reveals that Simms's revisions in "The Choctaw Criminal" pad the narrative and clutter the style.

Table I: Emendations and Textual Notes

Listed here are all changes in the copy-text of "Indian Sketch." The original reading appears to the left of the bracket, the emended Centennial edition reading to the right. Where no bracket appears the reading is the same in both texts and the refusal to emend is explained in parentheses.

4.8 of] or
5.1 shot,] ~.
5.38 res ore] restore
6.13 bosoms] bosom's
6.26 blankets] blanket's
6.29 brief.] ~,
6.39 moments] moment's

8.23 multitude, (Though the sense here seems to call for a semicolon, like other nineteenth century writers Simms frequently used commas where today semicolons would be preferred.)

Table II: Textual Variants

Below is a list of the variants between "Indian Sketch" in the *Southern Literary Gazette* (1828) and "The Choctaw Criminal" in *The Book of My Lady* (1833).

From left to right the chart of variants has the following text sequence:

LEFT MARGIN: Centennial edition key
FIRST READING: 1828
SECOND READING: 1833

7.14 147.8 unacquainted] 282.25 one unacquainted
7.14 147.8-9 there. Nothing] 282.26-27 ~? ¶ ~
7.18 147.12 it,] 282.31 ~∧
7.21 147.15 labored] 283.2-3 laboured
7.24 147.18 not,] 283.7 ~∧
7.30 147.24 times] 283.14 ~,
7.30 147.24 muttered] 283.14 ~,
7.32 147.26 bear skin] 283.17 bearskin
7.34 147.28 chamber,] 283.19 ~∧
7.34 147.28-29 out. ¶ It] 283.19 ~ ~
7.35 147.29 supposed,] 283.20 ~∧
7.36 147.30-35 thoughts of the strange obedience which this ignorant savage manifested to his rude and barbarous, but really equitable laws. The highest moral obligation however instructing him, "that he must not expect others to do, what he would not do himself." ¶ The next morning, a large crowd had assembled within and around the house in which I slept. I rose and went to the window
] 283.21-284.2 a thousand discordant fancies on the subject; and could not help the doubt which perpetually beset me, that before day he would be off, and out of all danger. I could not believe in the strange degree of obedience which this rude savage was about to manifest to his stern and primitive, but really equitable laws. Every movement in the household below, led me to the window, in the full expectation that it

could indicate nothing less than the flight of the criminal. But I was mistaken. The moral sublime had too unfrequently been the subject of my own experience, to enable me, in this instance, to appreciate it at a glance. ¶ A large crowd the next morning had assembled in the neighbourhood

8.5 147.36-39 covered with the Indians. A great deal of excitement seemed to run through them all. I dressed myself as quickly as possible and went down among them. They were crowded in the house as well as in the area before it.
] 284.3-8 thickly covered with Indians, all labouring under the natural excitements of the occasion. I hurried on my clothes with as much despatch as possible, and went down among them. The house was crowded as well as the arena before it. After surveying the mass,

8.16 148.8 fringe,] 284.17 ~;

8.18 148.10 while] 284.19 whilst

8.18 148.10 admirably] 284.20 closely

8.19 148.11 loaded
] 284.21 fantastically worked and literally loaded

8.20 148.11-12 ornaments were thrown
] 284.22-23 ornaments, medals, and trinkets hung

8.22 148.14 A difference of sentiment
] 284.25 Some difference of sentiment no less than of feeling

8.22 148.14 and] 284.26 and to

8.23 148.15 multitude, an] 284.27 multitude. An

8.23 148.15-16 impatience] 284.27 ~,

8.24 148.16 deceased] 284.28-29 ~,

8.25 148.17-19 an appearance of sadness and concern, pointed out those who were more tenderly disposed toward him.
] 284.30-32 on the other hand, sadness and concern were the leading traits of expression in the countenances of those interested in the criminal.

8.27 148.19 length,] 284.32 ~‸

8.28 148.20 signal] 285.1 open sign

8.28 148.20-24 arose, and giving to a little boy who followed him, a bundle which he had been making up of beads, hatchets, arrow heads, knives, tobacco-pouch and some other little things, he led the way. I joined in the mournful procession. Our way

] 285.1-9 arose from the ground where he had been reclining rather than sitting; and giving to a little boy, who stood in attendance, a bundle of beads, arrow-heads, &c. which he had been making up as a part necessary in the burial ceremonial—with the majesty of a chief, he drew the huge bear skin partially over his shoulders, and led the mournful procession. I took the way with the party. The path

8.32 148.24 pines—] 285.10 ~;

8.33 148.25-28 accompanied by the three men appointed as his executioners, who were armed with rifles, which they wore under the left arm. ¶ Never

] 285.10-18 from thence accompanied to the place of death, by the three executioners, each carrying his rifle unostentatiously beneath his arm. The criminal walked beside them, and in his own language gave them due directions for the performance of their duty. From one, he took the weapon with a smile, and looked hastily at the flint, while uttering a sentence which would seem to have been a jest at the expense of the owner. Never

8.36 148.28 with a] 285.19 with

8:36 148.28 occasion, or] 285.19-20 occasion—

8.38 148.30 endeavor] 285.22 endeavour

9.4 148.34 before him] 285.26 in his sight

9.5 148.35-36 was in sight. I watched his brow attentively. I felt myself shudder and grow pale, but saw no change in him. He

] 285.27-286.1 was now before us. The place of death, the scene, the trial and all its terrors, were at hand. I watched his brow attentively as he looked down upon the fearful paraphernalia; but while I felt the shuddering run like a cold wind through my own frame, I could behold no sign of change in him. After a momentary pause, he

9.10 148.40 proud] 286.4 ~,

9.21 148.51 eye] 286.19 eye again

9.22 149.1 spot] 286.19 ~,

9.22 149.1 unfortunate] 286.19-20 unhappy

9.22 149.2 infatuation,] 286.20 ~∧

9.24 149.3 the] 286.21 the fresh

Confessions of a Murderer.

I was born in an obscure country village in D———; the place had not more than ten or twelve families, and that of my parents was one of the most intelligent and respectable. The village was one of that class which is never known to vary its position; it neither increased nor diminished, and my father was one of the principal, if not the only principal man in it. Would he had been less so. Had he thought more of his own and the business of his own family and less of those around, I should not this day recount the history of my own disgrace. But my father was the great man, the lion of the village, and I became no less so of my mama's fireside. I was a spoiled boy even before I could read—so early are the principles of the human mind subject to misdirection. I was perverse, unruly and puerile, and my father mended the matter very considerably by damning at me on all warrantable occasions. To him and to my mother I charge my crime and its punishment, and while they are wondering how so bad a scion should spring from so good a stock, they have been weaving the rope about my neck. I shall render amends to the laws of the land; they are accountable to God, and to his mercies I leave them.

I was a truant from school and exulted in it without punishment. I was brutal while a mere boy to all around me; was a boor in decent society; was insolent to my parents; rude and boisterous at table; savage and ferocious among my associates and received no punishment. Sometimes when I exceeded even the bounds of toleration, tacitly joined to my conduct by my father, I received some such rebuke as—'now my dear, how can you do so,' or, 'I will be vexed with you, my son, if you do not behave.'

What was all this to an overgrown boy, nursed in full ideas of his own importance, licentious in his habits, and admitted to all and any irregularities, for which my father furnished an ample model. I bade defiance to threats, and scorned reproaches. I laughed at the soothings of my mother and took her gifts and favors, furnished in order to persuade me to do better, as things of course which she was obliged to give me. I was brought up a brute, and fulfilled to the letter the seeming objects of my education. Their lessons fitted me to be what I have been, and have reduced me to the miserable situation in which I now am. But let that rest.

I was sent to school, but learnt nothing, or what I learnt was entirely obliterated and counteracted by the nature of my education at home. I cared little to learn; my tutor dared not coerce me; he was a poor miserable hireling from the east, who cringed to all for his bread and who considered my father's influence as a matter which would not allow him to restrain or chastise his favorite son. Whatever I did, therefore, went by with impunity. However extravagant, violent or insolent my amusements, I was unpunished. Grown bold and confident, I even ventured to assume the burdens of my companions, announce myself as the offender and get them off free of punishment, while I escaped myself. One day, however, a circumstance occurred which could not pass so easily. It was under the master's own eye, and I was brought up to receive the award which his sense of justice or his lenity might think proper to bestow. He did not even flog me, he spoke to me like a father; as my father never spoke to me; his words were those of kindness, of friendship. I laughed in his face. He was indignant, as well he might be, and gave me a smart blow with his open hand on my face. I looked round upon my companions in order to ascertain if I should be supported, but they were kept in more subjection than myself and dreaded him accordingly. I submitted, though my heart rankled and my spirit burned within me for revenge. I had it—many years afterwards I had it. A deep and dreadful revenge. For the time, however, I contented myself with one more congenial with the little spirit of a bad and brutal boy. He kept me in, as a punishment, after the boys generally had been dismissed. He left me in the school-room and retired to his dinner. While in that room shut up, what were my emotions! The spirit of a demon was working in me, and the passion of my heart nearly exhausted my body; I threw myself on the floor and wept; hot, scalding tears. I rose—I strode for a long time to and fro; a sudden thought seized me; a mean and paltry revenge filled my bosom, as I stopt before a couple of large, new and beautiful globes that had just come to my teacher at a vast expense. I now perceived my re-

First page of "Confessions of a Murderer," *Southern Literary Gazette*, n.s., I (Nov. 1, 1829). From the only known copy, in the Kendall Collection, South Caroliniana Library, University of South Carolina.

9.24 149.3 murderer.
] 286.22-23 murderer. The following poem is devoted to the same subject.

CONFESSIONS OF A MURDERER.

Although Simms used the "Confessions of a Murderer" as the germ for *Martin Faber*, differences between the two are so great that they are best considered separate stories. The "Confessions," it might be noted, bears approximately the same relationship to *Martin Faber* as "Indian Sketch" does to "Oakatibbe," or "The Unknown Masque" to *Marie de Berniere*. In each case the early periodical publication is "elaborated" upon for book publication, and a new, much longer story emerges which, unfortunately, is not necessarily artistically superior. At the time of the publication of the "Confessions of a Murderer" in 1829, perhaps no better example of the confessional horror tale had appeared in American literature.

Despite the fact that the "Confessions of a Murderer" was published, anonymously, in the *Southern Literary Gazette* in November, 1829, it was not until almost a century and a half later that a copy of it was discovered among materials in the Kendall collection of the South Caroliniana Library. The discovery of the long-missing number of *SLG* made possible, for the first time, the unequivocal validation of the claim by Simms (in indignantly denying having plagiarized F. M. Reynolds's "*Miserrimus*") that the origin of *Martin Faber* lay in one of his own early published writings, the "Confessions of a Murderer" (see Textual Introduction to *Martin Faber*, below, pp. 572-573). In turn it is possible that Simms's inspiration for the "Confessions" can be found in still earlier issues of *SLG*. Nine months before the publication of the "Confessions of a Murderer," "The Criminal, from the German of Schiller" appeared in the *Gazette* for February, 1829 (I, 287-297), and was concluded in a second installment in March (I, 366-376). There are striking enough resemblances in the "Confessions of a Murderer" and the *SLG* version of Schiller's "The Criminal" (i.e., *Der Verbrecher aus verlorener Ehre*) to suggest, very strongly, that Simms had Schiller's story in mind and perhaps in hand when he sat down to write the "Confessions." For a fuller account see John C. Guilds, "The 'Lost' Number of the *Southern Literary Gazette*," *Studies in Bibliography*,

XXII (1969), 266-273; J. Wesley Thomas, "The German Sources of William Gilmore Simms," *Anglo-German and American-German Crosscurrents* (1957), I, 139-140, had earlier listed similarities between *Martin Faber* and *Der Verbrecher* without of course having seen the "Confessions of a Murderer."

Textual Introduction

Copy-text for the "Confessions of a Murderer" is the *Southern Literary Gazette,* n.s., I (Nov. 1, 1829), 266-269.

Table I: Emendations and Textual Notes

Listed here are all changes made in the copy-text of the "Confessions of a Murderer." The original reading appears to the left of the bracket, the emended Centennial edition reading to the right. Where no bracket appears the reading is the same in both texts and the refusal to emend is explained in parentheses.

14.19 many; (Possibly Simms intended a comma here, but the semicolon parallels the semicolon after "children" in the same line and adds emphasis.)

MARTIN FABER; THE STORY OF A CRIMINAL.

The publication of *Martin Faber* cast young Simms into the public eye of literary America for the first time. Charles Fenno Hoffman, reviewing the book at length in the *New York American* for September 28, 1833, wrote in part—"we do not hesitate to say, that since Godwin carried that singular and impressive style, first introduced in modern fiction by our countryman Charles Brockden Brown, to such perfection in Caleb Williams, no work of that school has come under our notice which shows more power than the little tale before us." Hoffman concluded his generally favorable review, containing several passages quoted directly from the book, as follows: "We may seem to have already bestowed too much space upon a book that purports to be meant only 'for the use of children;' but a writer of such approved discernment . . . must well know the ill effects of letting one's own powers lie idle; and will therefore enter into our views, when we express our unfeigned wish to hear soon again from the author of Martin Faber."

William P. Trent has the following to say about the strange sequence of events set off by Hoffman's review:

> On the Monday after "Martin Faber" was published, he [Simms] called on the Harpers, who referred to the criticism in the "American," and asked if he knew Hoffman. Receiving a prompt negative, they showed some surprise, which they explained by stating that a Doctor Langtree had said that Simms and Hoffman were bosom friends, which accounted for the favorable nature of the latter's criticism. On this slight provocation our warm-blooded author grew angry, and, after getting further proofs, proceeded, in company with his friend Randell Hunt, to call upon the talkative physician. Langtree (Samuel Daly Langtree, afterwards editor of the "Knickerbocker") rather evaded Simms's questions by answering that he had not read "Martin Faber." Whereupon Simms demanded a statement in writing of what had really been said. Langtree declining, the fiery author would have proceeded to violent measures, had not his friend Hunt interposed and induced Langtree to write his denial. When Langtree begged that the paper should be shown to the Harpers only, Simms declared that he would show it to anybody. He forthwith took it to Mr. Peabody, publisher of the "Knickerbocker," who had heard Langtree's remarks. Peabody, with an eye to business, advised him to publish the statement, as it would sell his book, to which Simms replied that he was a gentleman before he was an author. [*William Gilmore Simms* (1892), pp. 79-80]

Whatever the merits of this episode and the record of it handed down by Trent (no record of it exists elsewhere, either in print or in Simms's private memorabilia) it does capture the great, perhaps excessive, concern of the hitherto unknown author for his personal and literary reputation. That at least two leading New York magazines also reviewed *Martin Faber* shows that the young Charlestonian's talents were beginning to be recognized outside his native region. The *Knickerbocker* (then edited by Timothy Flint) noticed "obvious defects in the style" of *Martin Faber*, but called them "defects incident to youthful genius and talent" and concluded—"this story will excite and sustain interest, though we cannot but doubt the tendency of tales of such unmitigated horror" (II [Oct., 1833], 317). The *American Monthly Magazine*, opening its review with the surmise that *Martin Faber* "is an attempt to beat *Miserrimus* on its own ground," also claimed to see much merit among many faults: "It is not without a moral although it is not a very obvious one,—that children should have their dispositions educated as well as have their heads stored. The book is faulty, but is is [*sic*] within an ace of being a very clever thing notwithstanding.—We suspect it to have been done in a hurry, and never to have undergone a cool revisal" (II [Oct. 1, 1833], 141).

In the "Advertisement to the Second Edition" in 1837, Simms successfully rebuked the charge that F. M. Reynolds's "*Miserrimus*" (London: Thomas Hookham, 1833) was the model for *Martin Faber* by pointing to the 1829 publication of the "Confessions of a Murderer" as its origin (see above, pp. 18-22). One is struck by the accuracy of Simms's memory concerning the emergence of *Martin Faber* from the earlier and shorter "Confessions": (1) if Simms wrote the preface for the second edition of *Martin Faber* in 1836, as seems probable, "about seven years ago" pinpoints the 1829 publication of the "Confessions of a Murderer"; (2) the statement that the "Confessions" filled "some eight or ten pages" in the *Southern Literary Gazette* is erroneous in its estimate of pages, but Simms may have confused columns with pages (the "Confessions" occupies eight columns on four two-column pages in *SLG*); (3) the dates given for the "elaboration" of the "Confessions" into a full-length *Martin Faber* are essentially correct (see Textual Introduction, below); and (4) Simms is right in saying that the "sterner, darker features . . . nearly all . . . appear in the story as it was first given to the public"—that is, the character of William Harding and "the softening and gentler features" were added as "the fruit of an after labour." In brief, there can be no doubt that Simms used the early *SLG* sketch as the germ for his first book of fiction. This genesis is apparent in language as well as in plot, as, for instance, a comparison of the opening paragraph in the "Confessions" with the paragraph beginning, "My name is Martin Faber," in the 1833 *Martin Faber* (pp. 7-9) reveals. See Guilds, " 'Lost' Number," pp. 269-270.

Trent gives a very full account of the "*Miserrimus*"-*Martin Faber*-"Confessions of a Murderer" controversy and quotes at length a statement by Simms said to be included among "certain 'Personal and Literary Memorials,' scribbled off by the young author on the fourth day of June, 1834, while he was smarting under the stupidity and malignity of some of his early critics" (*Simms*, p. 77). Although the notebook Simms labeled "Personal and Literary Memorials" now in the South Caroliniana Library does not contain the passage Trent quotes, it is easily possible that Trent had material available to him that has since been lost, and the authenticity of the following passage, said to be Simms's "own words," can most probably be accepted at face value:

> But, as I have said, the period of its publication was a period to me of bitter excitement. I had set out to produce an original book, and flattered myself to have succeeded; what, then, was my surprise to perceive, in several of the newspapers, notices, which, though in all respects highly favorable, yet charged the work with a glaring resemblance to 'Misserrimus,' a work then only recently put forth in England, which, until after this period, I had never read, and a few of the leaves only of which I had glanced over in the bookstore of Mr. Maltby at New Haven. The misfortune of 'Martin Faber' consisted in being about the same length with 'Misserrimus,' in being printed in similar form, with similar binding, and in comprising, like the work to which it bore so unhappy a resemblance, the adventures of a bad man. There was not a solitary incident, not a paragraph, alike in the two productions; and a vital difference between the two was notorious enough in the fact that the criminal in 'Misserrimus' was such, without any obvious or reasonable cause, while 'Martin Faber' from the first sets out with an endeavor to show how and why he became a criminal, and has a reason for his offenses. 'Miserrimus,' on the other hand, does his evil deeds wantonly, and simply because of a morbid perversity of mind, which could only have its sanction in insanity. They all praised, however, to a certain extent, some of them evidently without reading it. [pp. 77-78]

Poe, the greatest of Simms's Southern literary contemporaries, did not review *Martin Faber, per se,* apparently in either the 1833 or 1837 editions, but in later reviews of works by Simms he singled out the tale for special praise. For example, in his review of *The Damsel of Darien,* Poe mentioned parenthetically that *Martin Faber,* by then in its second edition, "well deserved a permanent success" (*Burton's Gentleman's Magazine,* V [Nov., 1839], 283); in his *Broadway Journal* review of *The Wigwam and the Cabin,* Poe called *Martin Faber* one of Simms's "best fictions" and said of its supposed resemblance to "*Miserrimus*"—"we perceive that the individual minds which originated the two stories have much in them of similarity—but as regards the narratives themselves, or even their tone, there is no resemblance whatever. 'Martin Faber' is the better work of the two" (II [Oct. 4, 1845], 190). In a longer review of *The Wigwam and the Cabin* in *Godey's Lady's Book* (XXXII [Jan., 1846], 41-42) Poe devoted even more space to *Martin Faber,* and its comparison with "*Miserrimus*":

> Mr. Simms, we believe, made his first, or nearly his first, appearance before an American audience with a small volume entitled "Martin Faber," an amplifica-

tion of a much shorter fiction. He had some difficulty in getting it published, but the Harpers finally undertook it, and it did credit to their judgment. It was well received both by the public and the more discriminative few, although some of the critics objected that the story was an imitation of "Miserrimus," a very powerful fiction by the author of "Pickwick Abroad." The original tale, however—the germ of "Martin Faber"—was written long before the publication of "Miserrimus." But independently of this fact, there is not the slightest ground for the charge of imitation. The thesis and incidents of the two works are totally dissimilar;—the idea of resemblance arises only from the absolute identity of *effect* wrought by both . . . .

. . . whatever may have been his [Simms's] early defects, or whatever are his present errors, there can be no doubt that from the very beginning he gave evidence of genius, and that of no common order. His "Martin Faber," in our opinion, is a more forcible story than its supposed prototype "Miserrimus." The difference in the American reception of the two is to be referred to the fact (we blush while recording it), that "Miserrimus" was understood to be the work of an Englishman, and "Martin Faber" was known to be the composition of an American as yet unaccredited in our Republic of Letters. The fiction of Mr. Simms gave indication, we repeat, of genius, and that of no common order. Had he been a Yankee, this genius would have been rendered *immediately* manifest to his countrymen, but unhappily (*perhaps*) he was a southerner, and united the southern pride—the southern dislike to the making of bargains—with the southern supineness and general want of tact in all matters relating to the making of money. His books, therefore, depended entirely upon its own intrinsic value and resources, but with these it made its way in the end. The "intrinsic value" consisted first of a very vigorous imagination in the conception of the story; secondly, in artistic skill manifested in its conduct; thirdly, in general vigour, life, movement—the whole resulting in deep interest on the part of the reader. These high qualities Mr. Simms has carried with him in his subsequent books; and they are qualities which, above all others, the fresh and vigorous intellect of America should and does esteem. It may be said, upon the whole, that while there are several of our native writers who excel the author of "Martin Faber" at particular *points*, there is, nevertheless, not one who surpasses him in the aggregate of the higher excellences of fiction. We confidently expect him to do much for the lighter literature of his country. [pp. 41-42]

By and large, the second edition of *Martin Faber*, issued in two volumes in 1837, did not attract the wide critical notice of the first (but see the *Knickerbocker*, IX [May, 1837], 528); nor did its reception have the same impact upon the author, who by 1837 had published four major novels, *Guy Rivers*, *The Yemassee*, *The Partisan*, and *Mellichampe*. But throughout his career Simms was fond of reciting the circumstances of the storm caused by the initial publication of *Martin Faber*, recitations which almost inevitably led to assessments of the book's merits. His long biographical letter to R. W. Griswold dated December 6, 1846, reads in part—

> the work which, in my literary career succeeded to the publication of "Atalantis," was "Martin Faber," a gloomy & passionate tale, which, assumed by certain *European* critics as well as American to have been provoked by the British tale "Miserrimus" was in fact expanded from a tale which I published ten years before in a Magazine in Charleston . . . . "Martin Faber" belongs to the family of which Godwin's Caleb Williams is the best known model. But those who read the two works will fail to see any imitation on the part of the American author. [*The Letters of William Gilmore Simms*, 5 vols. (1952-1956), II, 223]

At this point Simms mentioned that he was enclosing a copy of Hoffman's review in the *New York American* "as a sample of the criticism which followed the publication of M. F." "All admitted the power & interest of the work," he added, "but some cavilled at the moral. The hero charges his crimes upon fate—an ordinary habit with such persons, & this is charged upon the author. He uses crime for his material, & in his case, as a young American beginner, the practice, unavoidable for any writer of fiction that ever lived, was supposed to be criminal." Later in the same letter Simms included *Martin Faber* (as well as "Carl Werner") among his several publications "marked chiefly by the characteristics of passion & imagination—by the free use in some cases of diablerie and all the machinery of superstition & by a prevailing presence of vehement individuality of tone & temper. They constitute, in all probability, the best specimens of my powers of creating & combining, to say nothing of a certain intensifying egotism, which marks all my writings written in the first person" (*Letters*, II, 224).

It is also significant that, when in 1868 Simms wrote to J. S. Redfield attempting to elicit his help in finding a publisher for a collection of "imaginative" short stories (see Introduction, above, pp. xxii-xxiii), the now veteran author recommended *Martin Faber* and "Carl Werner" as examples of his stories "of larger dimensions approximating the usual Dime-sized novellette . . ." (*Letters*, V, 157). Forty years after outlining its essential plot in the "Confessions of a Murderer," Simms, then—in desperate financial straits, to be sure—was still hoping to re-sell *Martin Faber* in slightly refurbished format.

W. P. Trent made short shrift of *Martin Faber*—"most readers of the present day would turn with loathing from the book; and few would read far enough to note the early appearance of a fault which was to mar all of Simms's future work,—careless inattention to details, consequent upon hurried writing" (*Simms*, p. 82); and scholars that have followed Trent have likewise given the book scant attention, harsh attention, or no attention at all. J. V. Ridgely, *William Gilmore Simms* (1962), devoting some three paragraphs to *Martin Faber*, finds it a "foolish story" with "no intrinsic merit," and excludes it from serious consideration (pp. 43-44). Two earlier notes, Floyd H. Deen, "The Genesis of *Martin Faber* in *Caleb Williams*," *Modern Language Notes*, LIX (May, 1944), 315-317, and Edward Stone, "*Caleb Williams* and *Martin Faber*: A Contrast," *MLN*, LXII (Nov., 1947), 480-483, debate the merits of Godwin as the source for Simms's book, with Stone defending Simms's "originality" and concluding that "it may seriously be doubted that Godwin's novel had any noticeable influence on the shaping of *Martin Faber*" (p. 483). Eugene Current-Garcia, "Simms's Short Stories: Art or Commercialism?" *Mississippi Quarterly*, XV (Spring, 1962), 56-67, quickly dismisses *Martin Faber* as "a fantastically implausible, self-confessed tale of murder and seduction, told by a typically Byronic figure . . ." (p. 58). Worthy of note, however, is J. Wesley Thomas's excellent if brief discussion of the possible German influence on *Martin Faber*, correctly concluding that Schiller's *Der Verbrecher aus verlorener Ehre* was the probable inspiration ("German Sources," pp. 139-140).

Although *Martin Faber* contains many errors in style, structure, plot, and language, it nevertheless is a work of sufficient power and imagination to account for Poe's claim that it possesses "evidence of genius, and that of no common order." Its place as one of America's first fictional studies of the psychology of crime—its causes and effects—earns it a secure position in the history of our early literature. Crude and cumbersome as it is, *Martin Faber* has a narrative sweep, a sustained power of interest, unusual in American literature in the 1830's.

In many instances, unfortunately, the revisions which Simms made for the 1837 edition cannot be considered improvements, for they too frequently lengthen rather than compress, hardly an advantage to a work already verbose. But he did make at least two major revisions which, in the judgment of the editor, constitute important improvements: (1) the seemingly unaccountable shift in point of view—from first person to third person—which marred the final chapter of the 1833 version was corrected in the 1837 edition, giving the book a consistent first person narrator throughout; and (2) the site for William Harding's picture-hanging, psychological testing of Faber was changed from the village barbershop, in the 1833 edition, to the village art gallery in 1837. Although Trent scoffs at an author who gives a "stagnated" village "an art gallery, where exhibitions are held yearly with a hundred pictures lining the wall" (p. 82), the idea of an art gallery in a small village (capable also, it is to be remembered, of a fashionable wedding) is not so difficult to accept, perhaps, as the idea of the village's barbershop serving as the exhibition place for paintings. The important point, of course, is that Simms recognized the incongruity of having the paintings hung in the barbershop, and attempted to correct the error. It is quite possible, also, to defend the sharp shift in point of view in Chapter XVIII in the 1833 text, by choosing to look upon it as an artistic method of indicating the narrator's sudden, traumatic shift in identity, brought on by a rejection of self. And the modern reader should not overlook the fact that, in its psychology of sex, *Martin Faber* seems well advanced for its time; in the seduction scene, for instance, Simms explicitly makes the point that Faber succeeds with Emily Andrews by skillfully and industriously arousing "all the natural passions of her bosom" (Chapter V). In brief, there is life and vivacity in the work that augurs well for an author yet in his twenties. These ideas serve simply to suggest that an imperfect *Martin Faber*, like many other Simms stories and tales, warrants closer consideration than American literary scholarship has thus far given it.

Explanatory Notes

18.dedication The daughter is Anna Augusta Singleton Simms, six years old in 1833.

30.29 The quotation is a paraphrase of Wordsworth's "My Heart Leaps Up When I Behold," line 7, which reads: "The Child is the father of the Man."

35.31-36.16 This unidentified poem is probably by Simms.

43.10-11 Priestess upon the tripod: Pythia, the priestess of Delphi, who sat upon a sacred tripod and exhaled an intoxicating vapor before giving prophetic utterances.

49.8 Quotation unidentified.
60.34 Mezentius' dead: Mezentius was a legendary king of the ancient city of Caere in Etruria, who was expelled by his subjects for cruelty. He was killed by Aeneas. See *Aeneid*, VII, X.

Textual Introduction

First published, anonymously, in 1833 as *Martin Faber; the Story of a Criminal* (New York: J. & J. Harper), the story was revised and expanded by Simms for inclusion as the title-piece of *Martin Faber, the Story of a Criminal: and other Tales*, 2 vols. (New York: Harper & Brothers, 1837). The story was also republished, with only accidental changes from the first edition, as "Martin Faber, The Story of a Criminal. By the author of the Yemassee, Pelayo the Goth, &c &c &c.," in *The Romancist, and Novelist's Library* (London: J. Clements, n.d. [1838 or 1839?]), No. 26, pp. 401-409. Since Simms never mentions *The Romancist*, it is quite possible that the London publication of his story occurred without his knowledge.

Simms says in the preface to the second edition that *Martin Faber* "was subsequently elaborated" from the "Confessions of a Murderer" in three stages—"partly in 1829, party in 1832, and finally revised for publication in 1833." The only existing details of publication come from W. P. Trent, who gives as his source the "certain 'Personal and Literary Memorials'" of Simms (already referred to in the Explanatory Introduction; see above), which apparently have been lost since Trent's use of them. According to Trent,

> When "Martin Faber" was finished, Simms contracted with Babcock, a New Haven publisher, to have a thousand copies printed at his own risk. When six or eight sheets had been printed, he inclosed them to the Harpers, saying that they might have the book "on their terms, they assuming the cost of printing and all the risk and trouble of publication." This modest proposal was accepted, and the story was published at once, probably in September [1833]. It had a fine run. In four days, only one copy was left, which was reserved for the author, who likewise received one hundred dollars, greatly to his delight. [p. 77]

Trent (p. 81) also records an 1834 reissue of *Martin Faber* ("... when 'Martin Faber' was reissued in 1834, he [Simms] wrote a preface . . ."), but no substantiation for this statement can be found; if *Martin Faber* was reissued in 1834, with a new preface by Simms with "lengthy animadversions upon his reviewers," it has escaped all bibliographers and librarians. Perhaps Trent, or his copy editor, has confused 1834 and 1837.

As early as July 19, 1834, Simms mentioned in a letter to Lawson his plans "to prepare a revised edition of Martin Faber & other things, making two volumes, 8mo. which, it appears to me might sell" (*Letters*, I, 61; see also I, 63). Less than a year later, on June 10, 1835, Simms wrote Lawson that Harper and Brothers "are about to publish a new edition of Martin Faber, with other Tales, making two volumes,—the contents of which I have just revised & sent on by the boat" (*Letters*, I, 70-71). Although in listing his publications for an unknown correspondent in a letter dated January 16 [1849], Simms gave 1836 as the publication date for a "New Edition" of "Martin Faber & other Tales," no copy with that date has been located. Perhaps Simms's memory of having completed the "new" *Martin Faber* volume in the summer of 1835 accounts for this apparent error in an otherwise surprisingly accurate list of his writings (*Letters*, II, 471).

It should be noted that Simms at times included *Martin Faber* among his "novels," at other times among his "tales"; the Centennial edition includes it in the volume of *Stories and Tales* because its length (approximately 35,000 words by Simms's estimate) makes its inclusion appropriate.

The 1833 edition has been selected as copy-text, and the substantive revisions Simms made for the 1837 edition have been incorporated in the Centennial edition text.

Table I: Emendations and Textual Notes

Listed here are all changes made in the copy-text of *Martin Faber*. The original 1833 reading appears to the left of the bracket, the emended Centennial edition reading to the right. Where no bracket appears the reading is the same in both texts and the refusal to emend is explained in parentheses. Where an explanation of the change is necessary it follows in parentheses.

18. <no prefatory sonnet> (Preceding the "Advertisement to the Second Edition" in the 1837 collection is a "PREFATORY SONNET" that is omitted from the Centennial text of *Martin Faber* because it appears to apply to the volume as a whole rather than specifically to the title story:

PREFATORY SONNET.

Divided from my child a thousand miles,
  A thousand trials keep us still apart,
And, ere again her eye upon me smiles,
  Cold, in a foreign grave, may sleep my heart.
Such is the fate which now my fortune dares—
  And should she lose me—young and desolate one—
Number her fondly, Father! with thy cares,
  Spare her the many trials I have known.
And, stranger! thou wilt sacred hold her name,—
  Thou'lt watch above her childhood with a word
Of kindness, that may soften even thy blame,
  Such as she ever from her sire hath heard.
Be thy reprovings gentle—wrong her not
  With dark entreaty; but, as some young flower
The very winds should worship, guard her lot,
  Give her thy love, and shield her with thy power.)

19.14-42 <quotation from 1833 Advertisement>] <1833 Advertisement> (Copy-text for the "Advertisement" to the first edition is the 1833 text itself.)

23.1 "This] ‸~ (The 1833 text opens with double quotes and ends with double quotes, following the nineteenth century tradition. The use of quotation marks between the opening and closing paragraphs in the 1833 text is inconsistent.)

23.2-5 and the prospect, to most men full of terrors, has few or none] and, but for that awful strife—that gross exposure—the hissing scorn—the deriding shout—but for these, the prospect of death, terrible to all men, would have few or no terrors

23.7-8 many] numberless

23.8 terrors] trials

23.8-9 death.] death. Why should I fear that which I may not avoid?

23.9-12 though I may regret my crimes, they give me no compunctious apprehensions] the survey of my crimes, and of the past, however I may regret many of them, and much of it, at least brings with it no fears of the future, and but few compunctious visitings

23.13 a] the

23.19 variously] curiously

23.26-28 blow.] blow—I had not scorned the supposed obligation—I had not rejected the terms upon which society tendered me its protection.

23.29 may] can

23.31-24.2 impulses. I cannot.] impulses—let the skin-dried ascetic, withered over the map and the crucible, undertake the examination as he may. I cannot—I dare not. The life which was given me had a different direction, and I had no right to defeat its purposes.

24.3-4 <no rule> (In the 1837 text there is a rule which separates the paragraphs, and this may possibly be authorial—perhaps to indicate a break in the continuity of the narrative.)

24.4-20 of good family—of German extraction—the only son. I was born in M—— village, and my parents were recognized as among the first in respectability and fortune of the place. The village was small—numbering some sixty families; and with a naturally strong and shrewd, and a somewhat improved mind, my father, Nicholas Faber, became the first man in it. The village of M——, was one of those that always keep stationary. The prospect was slight, therefore, of our family declining in influence. My father, on the contrary, grew every day stronger in the estimation of the people.
] the only son of German parents—people of good family, and, so far as paying their debts, and not flying in the face of society could make them so, very good sort of people. I was born in the village of M——, a little settlement of some sixty or seventy families, of quiet habits, and not very brilliant minds. The Fabers were the first among them in fortune and respectability; and, possessed of a strong, shrewd, and somewhat improved sense, my father, Nicholas Faber, contrived, after no very long period, to make himself the first man in the village, which was one of those that, having attained a certain growth, always after remain stationary. It stagnated accordingly; and such being the case, the prospect was exceedingly remote of a diminution in the influence of our family. On the contrary, my father, each successive day, grew more and more supreme in the estimation of the people. He was the only active principle among them. He did their thinking, and they were very willing to depute to him a labour so excessively unpopular—not to say undemocratic.

24.25-26 his] his own

24.27 in] upon

24.30-32 why speak of this?] it was fated that such should not have been the case. It was decreed that he should neglect or mislead, and that I should be misled.

24.33 a] the

24.34 schooled] permitted

24.35 earlier] earliest

24.36 too soon] premature

24.37 her] the

24.38 are usually] are

25.1-3 When sent, the case was not very greatly amended.] In the mean time I had the freedom of the common, and, indeed, a common freedom in the indulgence of my own moods and passions. When sent to school, the matter was not greatly amended. (1837 reading of "mended" for "amended" is just as likely a compositorial error as an authorial revision. Simms's dictionary defines "amend" and "mend" identically.)

25.6-11 His name was Michael Andrews. He was] He was intelligent, and well taught—a man versed in the abstruser sciences; but wanting in decision and independence of character, the most necessary attributes of one in his vocation. This want was fatal to his usefulness; and Michael Andrews—for that was the name he bore—was, accordingly, but a tool—

25.23-27 discriminate between those to whom this conduct was exhibited.] stop to inquire at any time whether it was injustice or not to which I had been subjected. I had no desire to discriminate nicely into the merits of my treatment. It was enough for me that my pride or my passion had been mortified—I sought equally for my atonement.

25.27-30 countenance.] countenance. It mattered not to me to whom these features were exhibited; and as for concealment, that was only my resort when cunning counselled, and as it became necessary to my purpose.

25.33 sometimes] sometimes was the case

25.37 'Now] "~

25.37 bad'] ~"

25.37 'I] "~

25.38 so.'] ~"

26.1 was such a rebuke] were such rebukes to

26.4 and the] and
26.8 give] afford
26.8 natural good sense,] naturally good mind
26.9 the] that
26.13 for] to
26.16 or] or did
26.23-24 twelve,] twelve years of age—
26.25 widow] widow—a
26.28 degree] and unhappy degree
26.34-27.1 But] He grew rapidly—tall and promising; but
27.5 So marked a character] A character so marked
27.5-6 a contrast, so strikingly with] so striking a contrast to
27.8 a consideration] consideration to my mind
27.9 would] in the school could
27.12 worked] worked out
27.13 he helped my understanding in its deficiencies, he] he
27.13-14 I—] I—brutal and unforbearing with all beside—
27.23 these,] these kindred emotions
27.26 perfectly] entirely
27.27 stripes,] stripes—that was not his usual course—
27.29 of] of a common
27.30 'idler.'] "~"
27.37-28.1 saw it not.] knew but little of the ambitious nature—he saw not the appeal—he knew nothing of the entreaty.
28.5 and] and which
28.7-8 now] now, upon receiving his answer,
28.9 whole] whole of the
28.12 school] schoolhouse
28.12-15 But he would not descend to the meanness of such an act, and resolutely determined] But, with a scrupulous conscientiousness, the due result of a circumspect mother's teachings, he refused to descend to the meanness and cowardice of such a procedure, and determined rather
28.17-18 already] already, in many instances before,
28.19 escape] escape also
28.20 coalesced] coalescing
28.21 calling] called
28.24 declaring, at the same time, his freedom,] declaring his enfranchisement, at the same moment,

28.29 for the consequence] of the consequences

28.30 Harding] In the afternoon, Harding

28.31-37 I boldly pronounced my handiwork, no one else venturing to speak, fearing my vengeance, though several in the school, had been cognizant of the whole affair.
] But not so me. I had justified my act sufficiently, to myself, at least:—I was not now to forego my triumph; and, boldly advancing from my seat, in the face of the affrighted school, I announced my own handiwork, which, as I was feared by the schoolfellows generally, might never (though several of them had witnessed the whole affair) have been otherwise revealed.

29.3 his] the

29.10 tolerated] longer tolerated

29.11 ensuing] following

29.14 his] the

29.14 boy] boy then

29.26-27 conducted. ¶ While] conducted. ¶ *CHAPTER III.* ¶ WHILE (In the 1837 text the long second chapter of the 1833 text was divided into two chapters. From this point on the chapter numbers in the 1837 and Centennial texts are one more than the 1833 up to the eighteenth or final chapter of the 1833.)

29.28-29 acting] acting as they did, with an unwonted degree of violence

29.31-32 I] But this weakness soon passed into one of a different character: and now I

29.33 On a sudden I] I

29.35 sympathize] sympathize with

30.9 gone off] departed

30.9 gave] left

30.10 and] and to

30.13 large price] heavy cost

30.15-16 delights] delights—ay, almost his only delight

30.16 embodied (The "imbodied" reading in the 1837 seems more likely to have been a compositorial error than a substantive authorial revision.)

30.17-18 punishment] punishment—I felt that I, too, had power,—and there is no sweeter consciousness in life

30.23 them] me

30.30-35 the exercises of his juvenile years will at all times indicate what they will be when he becomes old] by these trifles, chiefly, the standards of good judgment and just sensibilities are to be created and kept in exercise. The morals are formed most usually by our associates in play; and the tastes and exercises of the juvenile years will at all times indicate the character in age, of which they are the very seed and nucleus (Commas which appear in the second sentence of the 1837 passage after "will" and "times" are rejected; the 1833 copy-text is followed in these instances.)

30.36 grown] grown-up

31.2 my] my education not less than my

31.10 injury] injury which

31.11 way,] style

31.12 on] upon

31.12 man] man himself

31.17 caught] had caught

31.17 eye] glance

31.24 suffering] countenance

31.25 I wore] my features put on

31.30 and,] and in

31.36 man's small] man's

31.37 self] myself

32.15 weeks] weeks after

32.18 went] went out

32.21 I exulted] Silently, indeed, but not less certainly, did I exult

32.24 me,] me—they could not mistake the expression of my glance,—

32.27 above,] above the malice of the petty spirit, however reckless—

32.29-32 As it was, they proceeded on their way into the country. I was, at length, satisfied with my revenge, and] A sad train, they proceeded on their way into the country: a turn in the road in a few moments concealed them from my sight, and satisfied at length with my revenge, I

33.1 associations] association

33.2 make,] make very considerably

33.5 felt] could not but feel

33.8-11 any] any—no two people could have been more decidedly different; different in attributes of mind—different in purpose and pursuit—different in feelings and sentiments—different in all respects, whether in disposition, in character, or person

33.14 differently. Such] not—such

33.16 the] the consciousness of

33.17 the strength and] of strength and capacity for

33.17-19 This, I verily believe, was the fact in our case] This I know to have been the fact in our case; and I believe it to have its share in that of most of those associations which are styled friendly

33.22-24 attributes—they, at least, bringing no provocation, left in abeyance and dormancy, many of those which] attributes, at least, as they brought with them no new provocations to the old nature, so they left in abeyance, and seemingly quite dormant, many of those, which, in my character,

33.24-29 immoral.] immoral. Circumstance is the accoucheur in these cases; and virtue and vice, like cat and dog, would lie quietly together on the same hearth-rug for centuries, without the necessity of blow or broomstick, did not the inconsiderate hand sometimes throw them the bone, and unreasonably look to them justly and peacefully to make the division.

33.30 man was] man

33.30-31 their progress] the progress of the years

33.31 underwent] underwent a

33.39 and] and to

34.2 of] of all

34.4 In this respect, in] In

34.5 character] allotment

34.6 infecting (The 1837 "affecting" is rejected as being a likely compositorial error; also, the copy-text reading seems to be more appropriate in regard to context.)

34.7-9 mood,] mood—this fatal mood—the creature of an original nature, made too active by an unhappy education, and most unfortunate indulgence—

34.15-18 night time—my life has been a long night, in which there has been no starlight—in which there have been] night-time. For that matter, my life itself has been a long and weary night, to which, if the starlight ever came, it brought bale only, and bitterness—a night, in which there has been little balm or beauty—a night of (The copy-text spelling of "night time" is followed instead of the hyphenated 1837 form.)

34.22-33 cankering and malignant purposes. ¶ Many years had now elapsed since my adventure with Michael Andrews, my old schoolmaster. I had grown up to manhood, and my personal appearance, had been so completely changed by the forming hand of time, that I had not the same looks which distinguished me at that period
] cankering, malignant, or misdirected purposes. ¶ I had now grown up to manhood—to unemployed and objectless manhood. While all around were busy, and had duties to perform, the indulgence of my parents, and my own hopes of wealth, seemed to acquit me of any necessity or solicitude as to what labour I should engage in. This was another curse of my education. I was an idler, and learned the lessons of most idlers—those of dissipation—every species of irregularity, and a horribly consuming ennui. Harding was a student still—a close student—and it was only now and then, in the daytime, that I had his company. My time was in great part passed alone; for, festering in my own rankness of nature, I was too little disposed to seek society

34.37 on the opposite side of] at length crossed

34.38 was yet] was

35.1 divisions] sections

35.3 I] I had

35.7 effect] effect, even

35.7 as] so

35.8 even as] as

35.14 with] by

35.24-36.21 prospect, and approaching it from the point most sheltered, came suddenly into] prospect; and if I were not, a circumstance which occurred at the moment when I stood bewildered with the novelty of the prospect, would have determined me. A sweet but uncultivated voice suddenly broke through the copse, and the tones of a young girl saluted my ears with a song, in which education seemed somewhat to struggle and vie with simplicity. The words were these—I shall never forget them:—

I.

The bird had playful music,
  The heart was full of glee;
And life was rich in pleasantness,
  And sunny hours to me.
I knew not what it was to weep,
  I never had a care;
And all my days were happy ones,
  And all my friends were dear.

II.

Had anybody told me then,
  That future hours must come,
When mine would be an aching heart,
  For ever clad in gloom—
That I should hear no young bird's voice,
  Or, sadden'd by his lay,
Should seek to fly his gentle strain,
  Or banish him away:—

III.

I should have deem'd, in thoughtlessness,
  That, at my girlish pride,
The prophet speaker took offence,
  And only sought to chide—
I should have smiled at prophecy,
  So very idle then,
Nor feared, nor felt, as now I do,
  I shall not smile again.

The singer paused in the strain—a strain so simple, yet so thoughtful, that I paused also. It had really affected me; and after a few moments' hesitation, which vexed me as I felt it, I approached the spot whence the sounds had arisen, and reaching the point most sheltered, soon found myself in

36.22 shade, whose] shade. Her

36.24 presence] notice

36.26 timidity] trepidation

36.27 eyes] sight

36.30-32 off, and] off; and after chatting with her for some time, and in a manner evidently not ungrateful to her, and certainly satisfactory to me,

36.33-37.3 father, my old tutor. But, fortunately for me, he was not in a condition to recognize me] father, my ancient schoolmaster, old Michael Andrews! Fortunately for me, however, I had been so completely changed in appearance by the forming hands of time, that he did not recognize me; and even had this not been the case, the condition of the old man himself was such, that I was secure from any fear of detection. (Copy-text spelling of "recognize" is retained instead of 1837 "recognise.")

37.5 'accidence'] "~"

37.8-9 slight impression] impression

37.20 and] until

37.21 she] and

37.26 me] mine

38.2 wrought] wrought upon

38.4 worked industriously upon] industriously aroused all

38.17 yet had she not] yet, even then, she had won none of

38.20-22 nightshade?] nightshade. Mine were the professions of the momentary passion, which I had taught her to believe, and which, for the time, I had actually believed myself. But only for a time.

38.31 an habitual] a

38.32-33 than ever,—] and which had now become habitual—

38.34-35 extravagance] extravagance, as I then considered them,

38.35 not yet] not

38.36 entirely.] entirely. I had not yet grown callous enough for that.

39.1 thought advisable] advised

39.4 son. And she was so.] son.
39.22 crime] crimes
39.26-27 an affection existing,] any affection existing—without knowing, indeed, what her affections should be—
39.35 With regard to our connexion, I] I
40.4 the] the proposed
40.6 that] that which had been
40.7 of] of our
40.10 wear] put on
40.12 features] expression
40.22 a] the
40.28 fervid] fervent
40.29 that] when
41.9-10 say, that] say any thing
41.17 false] falsely
41.37 as] when
41.38 with] by
42.4-5 dumb language] that dumb, but most expressive language, which is theirs only,
42.18 given] given her
42.19-20 tendernesses (The 1837 "tenderness"—though substantive—seems unlikely to be authorial.)
42.21 of] something of
42.35 stood] withstood
43.11 influenced with] maddened with the sacred
43.24 rose] arose
43.35-36 already are] now really appear
44.5 more] longer
44.9 with] by
44.35 silent] quieted
44.37 at length, invariably] invariably came back, and
45.3 were] were fastened
45.6 was] fell
45.9 round] about,
45.9 shrunk] shrunk back
45.12 Spare] Spare me
45.12 forgive] forgive me
45.20 for] even for
45.33 in] from

46.1 forth] forward
46.1 replication] replication which they made
46.3 desired] seemed to doubt, and to desire
46.5 "I am a murderer!"] "Am I not a murderer?" was my inquiry.
46.11 bore] wore
46.16 won] has won
46.17 nourishes] nourished
46.25 present] present the idea of
46.26 seized] acted
46.26 her] her body
46.33-34 reach.] reach—she and her child—I was a double murderer.
46.37 stride] huge stride which
46.38-47.1 importance.] importance. Such is our nature. We are proud of the power to destroy.
47.2 had] had now
47.4 in] even in
47.8 in] in an
47.13 Murder] Murderer
47.17 on] finding its way to
47.22 Though] Though this was
47.24 the] this
47.24 long] long since
47.29 thought I] I thought
47.31 in] on
47.32 spot] place
48.11 intials] initials
48.11 on] upon
48.21 of] of the
48.23 the crime] her unaccountable disappearance
48.24 in which,] and there
48.29 passed] passed away
48.29 had] had once
49.3 dressed] crowded
49.5 our] the
49.21 encircle] penetrate
49.27 picture] spectre

49.29-31 rest.] rest. My disquiet, so unaccountable to all around, seemed to indicate a reluctance to the ceremony.

49.34 eye] eye still

50.2 of] of my

50.8 unuttered] entirely unuttered

50.9 spirit] senses

50.9 is] are

50.10 shall] and compelled to recognise its presence, shall

50.15 of] of the

50.16-17 advanced] advanced without fear

50.17-18 key,] key—in the face and in defiance of spectre—

50.19 fancies] fancies had

50.22-23 power,] power, in controlling my own moods, compelling obedience from my own fears and fancies—

50.25 I] To the reflective mind, I

50.26 in] on

50.26 is it necessary that I should tell you of the small] necessary to say that the

50.27 that] which

50.27-31 wife] wife was equally, if not more limited. A temper like mine—so impatient, and so without resources—could not long suffer a dependant or an associate to remain at peace. She felt accordingly; and I am persuaded a greater curse could not well have fallen to her lot

50.31-34 that is to say, I employed neither blows nor violence; but] to speak in common phrase—I employed no blows—no violence. But there are other penalties which virtue can be made to endure, not less frequently, and far more poignantly, than vice.

50.34-51.5 wretched discontent, and when I say this I have said all. She suffered with patience, however, and I sometimes found it impossible, and always difficult, to drive her beyond the boundary of yielding and forgiving
] wretched, sleepless, discontent—always showing my teeth, and, when occasion offered, never withholding my venom. She suffered as a martyr—with a patience that was never to be disturbed; and I failed utterly, however much I strove, to drive her beyond the boundary of a yielding, an always conciliating

51.6 first, and] first—how could she love me?—and

51.7 sufficient firmness of] a sufficient degree of firmness in

51.8-17 command. The discovery of this fact, which I soon made, offended my pride. I did not distrust, however—I hated her; and, with a strange perversity of character,
] commands or the solicitations of her parents. Perhaps, too, as she knew little of me, and less still, at that time, of the nature of those feelings of which her heart could become susceptible, the constraint had been less upon her than, even then, I imagined it to have been. That she soon perceived her error and misfortune, I discovered not less quickly; and in due accordance with the discovery, my pride grew morbid and angry. I did not distrust—but I hated her; and with a fiend-like hatred, which can only be understood by a reference to the course of conduct which I thought proper to pursue in consequence. With a perversity of character, strange and contradictory—

51.19 love, and] love,

51.21 duties] duty

51.24 Though] Though soon

51.27-28 feelings, could gain] legitimate feelings, could acquire

51.29-31 She was won by the gentleness, the talent, the high character of my old friend,
] I soon found that she had been won, all unconsciously on his part, by the talents, the gentleness, and many attractions of mind and manner of my old associate and schoolfellow,

51.32-37 and unconcealed pleasure. She delighted in his society; and with a feeling which she had never dared to name to herself, she gave him a preference, in
] spirit, and a pleasure which she never thought to conceal. She was only happy in his presence and society; and with a feeling which she had never yet dared to name to herself, and from the analysis of which I feel she must always have shrunk, she gave him a preference over all others, in

51.37-52.12 Nor—boy as he was—sensitive and easily wrought upon by respect and kindness—was he at all insensible to her regards. He became, as an acquaintance, almost an inmate of our house. He was always with us—and with the openness of heart common to such a character, he unreservedly sought for the society of Constance. I soon discovered their mutual propensities, for, at an early period, I had learned, with singular felicity, to analyze character.
] Nor was he insensible to her regards. Sensitive, and easily wrought upon, whether by kindness or cruelty, her ceaseless consideration,

exhibited in a thousand forms, of which she herself knew nothing, controlled him like an infant. He had always been very intimate with me—more so than any other of the village—and he was now almost an inmate of my house. With the free openness of heart which marked and made his character, he sought unreservedly for the society of Constance, and Constance only: and while I saw from this, that his intentions had no dishonourable object, I saw at the same time that he knew nothing of the precise feeling which prompted them. I had learned, with singular felicity, at an early period of my life, to study and to analyze the human heart. I exercised my habit with regard to these two, and was not long in discovering that their propensities were mutual.

52.12 and while] while

52.17 fear] fear, or

52.18-19 him over myself, in the bosom of one, I strove to have] another in the bosom of one I would, at that time, have had

52.20 first] first to

52.22 as to give] as, in time, to afford

52.22 excuse and opportunity] opportunity and excuse

52.23-31 But they were both honest—honest as I had never been—as I never expected man or woman to have been! Twining and intermingling, hourly in spirit, the most jealous scrutiny, the most bitter hate and hostility, could never detect the slightest feature of impropriety
] To this object I addressed all the means in my power, but without the desired success. They were both honest—sweetly, nobly honest; as, from my own feeling and character, I had never expected man or woman to have been. Joining in thought—intermingling hourly in spirit, and in a communion which, if they had not been wonderfully immaculate, must have brought out their weaknesses, they were yet strong; and the most jealous scrutiny, the most bitter hate and hostility, could never have construed into impropriety a solitary feature

52.32-38 chose to stimulate their passions—to influence their desires—to put their spirits into flame; and many were the opportunities with which I sought, in hurrying them to crime, to provide myself with victims.
] adopted to stimulate their passions—to influence or to create desires—to put their passions into that fervor, which, once provoking

discontent and the vague want which is the first symptom of the active appetite, will never rest again short of its surfeit. Thousands of opportunities did I throw before them in order to provide myself with victims. But they were children—weak enough for susceptibility, but not daring to do wrong.

53.1 the] every

53.1 one] a

53.2-12 suppressed and strong affections, I beheld the cheek of Constance grow paler, day by day, and saw, at every visit—the increased wildness of look—the still exaggerated emotions struggling for utterance and life, in the bosom of the young and
] strong affections, and suffering as they did in the noble struggle to restrain and keep them down, I was yet mortified to see that they could not be otherwise than successful. But the strife of their spirits in this labour had its influence, and, day by day, the cheek of Constance grew paler and paler, and there was a nameless anguish in her eye, as it sunk beneath my own, which spoke of that love—worst love of all—which has its birth untwinned by hope. Nor was she the only one with whose heart the contest promised to be vital. I beheld, at every succeeding visit, the increasing fever in the soul of my other victim. The worm was in the core, and kept up a ceaseless labour in the bosom of the gentle and too

53.14 Some] Several

53.14-19 this time, my house and young wife had lost most of their attractions. My favorite habit,
] that time, as might have been expected, my young wife and domestic associations had lost most of their attractions—in my eyes at least. My resources were now always out of doors—carousing sometimes, but frequently solitary and savage. My favorite pursuit—one that had been a passion in boyhood,

53.19 and one] and

53.20 my mood of sternness] the sternness of my mood—

53.21 and with] with

53.21-35 shoulder as apologetic for my idle wanderings, the neighboring forests for ten or fifteen miles round, soon became familiar to my survey. Sometimes, on these occasions, Harding would become my companion; and as he was highly contemplative in character, his presence did not at all interfere with the gloominess of my mood.

] shoulder, and, with this apology for my wanderings, I had contrived to become familiar with the forests in that neighborhood for fifteen miles round. It was in a ramble of this sort that I had first encountered Emily, and this habit furnished a sufficient reason to others, for those long absentings from home in which my time had been chiefly given up to her. Sometimes, on these excursions, Harding would become my companion; not that he was a sportsman, but simply because of his contemplative character of mind, which luxuriated, and was enthusiastic, in its admiration of the gloomy beauty of the thick woods. His presence did not interfere with my mood; indeed, although the cause was essentially different, his silence was a fitting similitude of mine. We wandered thus from one wood to another, through path and cover, frequently without a word, and living only in our thoughts.

54.1-2 wood, thickly sown with undergrowth, and penetrable with difficulty, that] dense thicket, girded in by heavy trees, and almost impervious from the undergrowth, that

54.3 tree] pine

54.3-6 Our] The sun was completely shut out from the spot, and the solemn hush of all things about us was such as to make the train of thought in our minds much gloomier than ever. Our

54.6 was] was necessarily

54.7-9 and unconsciously I remarked] and, as if impelled throughout the whole scene by an irresistible monitor, I remarked to him thus, in spite of my own consciousness of the danger of such a topic

54.10 such a spot, which] spot, it appears to me, that

54.13 choose] select

54.28-55.8 But, even by such a standard, Martin, it would be a crime of the most horrible complexion, for, leave the choice to the one you seek to murder, and he will submit, in most cases, to the loss of all his worldly possessions, and even of his liberty, in preference to the loss of life." ¶ "What would you say, William if you knew
] To some men, from the operation of circumstances, or from their own improvidence, death would be welcome even by violence; and the feeling with which such a man would submit to the executioner, can surely afford no standard by which to determine upon the fate of others not so situated, and not having the same feeling or con-

dition with himself. Life is a sacred something which we do not venerate enough. It is considered quite too lightly by society, and it appears to me, if we believe for a moment in the immortality of the soul and the doctrine of rewards and punishments, we have not the right, even in the case of the criminal, to doom him to a loss of it. The idea is horrible which conceives the murder of a human being, even according to the standard you suggest; for, leave the choice but a moment to the victim, and he will submit, in most cases, to the loss of all his possessions, and even of his liberty, to avoid that fearful rush of the soul into the dark and deep chaos which our ignorance depicts the future." ¶ "Why, what would you say to a friend, William—to me, for example, if I told you

55.5 depicts (It is possible that Simms intended "depicts as" here rather than "depicts.")

55.10 say!—] say! God help me,

55.11 upon] on (Note "look upon" at 55.16; the change to "look on" here, though probably authorial, eliminates the echoic effect of 1833 copy-text.)

55.12 looked] surveyed

55.12-15 moment, then, placing my hands upon his shoulder with a deliberation which was significant of the deepest madness, I spoke:
] few moments, then, with a deliberation that, under all the circumstances, was significant of a momentary madness, placing my hands upon his shoulders, I slowly exclaimed—

55.16 again] again—you shall see and hear

55.20 ashen pale] pale as death

56.16-17 way] way out

56.32 in] to

57.22 murdered.] ~"

57.25 me.] ~"

57.26 does] does haunt me

57.30 "Murder,!] 'Murder,! (Although omitted in 1837, the comma in this reading is retained.)

57.30 Murder!"] Murder!'

58.6 become] becoming

58.23 he was] you are

58.23 his] your

58.24 his] your

59.9 alledged] alleged
59.29 *abandon*] hopelessness
60.1 refer] refer, with an everyday philosophy,
60.2 or to the] or
60.3 brought] brought with me
60.18-19 exclaimed—"And] exclaimed— ¶ "And
60.33 should] could
61.5 I] that I
62.1 That] You know that
62.6 hour, you] hour
62.9 contemn] contemn me
62.11 my] his
62.28 to] refuses for ever to
63.16-17 all] all that was wrong
63.19-20 so.] so. How well did I know them—how little did they know me!
63.34 object] end
64.2 to] upon
64.5 vascillating] vacillating
64.6 end] desire
64.7 attainment] acquisition
64.11 passion] leading object
64.32 it] it to the end
66.18 itself] itself still further
66.29 narrate] relate
67.17-18 dependencies (The 1837 reading—"dependances"—is likely compositorial.)
67.18 Having] As he had a
67.29 impervious] romantic
67.32 then] at the time
67.36 not then regarded] never before considered
68.5 what] of the
68.11 known] known already
68.12-13 me] my suspicions
68.17 upon which to exercise his skill] which attracted him
68.20 the] to my mind the
68.21 of] of my
68.24 recollections,] recollection
68.35 look] gaze

68.35 but in] but

68.37-38 I beheld, at length,] at length, I beheld, under the influence of my imagination,

69.7 and] yet

69.8 ashen] ashen pale

69.12 the] in the

69.15 offended at] struck, and somewhat offended by

69.16 on the instant of] the instant after

69.16 turned round] turned

69.17 some] an

69.17-18 fell from the look which I gave him in evident confusion; and,] fell, in evident confusion, from the look which I gave him; and tacitly,

69.25 was] had been

69.37 perceived] revolved

70.8 a] any

70.9 contempt] injury

70.10 one day will] will one day

70.13 him] him on

70.17 recognize (The 1837 "recognise" is not accepted.)

70.19 some] a few

70.22 common-place] commonplace

70.27-30 His] He felt that, at such a moment and occasion, my jealousy, if I were really guilty, must be particularly active; and took care, therefore, to avoid the expression of much curiosity. Yet his

70.33 to] upon to

71.5 destiny] destiny had

71.8 no] no single

71.21 auxiliar (The 1837 reading "auxiliary"—though a possible authorial revision—is more likely to be compositorial.)

71.22 fact] facts (The sense of the sentence requires "facts.")

71.23 them, and he] them. He

71.23 confident and strong] strong and confident

71.24 progression in his labor] his progress in this labor

71.25-73.27 A week from this had not gone by, when, while under the hands of our village hair-dresser, I beheld a picture crowded among the hundred upon his walls, which filled me with astonishment, and awakened in my mind some moving apprehensions. I beheld the scene of my crime truly done to nature, and just by the little copse upon which the deed had been committed, stood a female form, pale and shadowy, and with a sufficient resemblance to Emily, to have been considered a portrait. You may guess my emotion. Having recovered from the first shock, I inquired, as if without the desire for an answer, where he got and who had painted it, and was told in reply that an old lady had brought it there for sale—the lady was unknown. Finding the price low—merely nominal, indeed, he had readily bought it; relying on the merits of the piece to insure it a ready sale. I affected to be pleased with it and paid him his price. Having secured it in possession, I examined it closely, and was confirmed in the opinion that the whole was copied from events in my own history. Beyond this I could perceive nothing farther. The preparation of the piece was a mystery, and I had not the courage to seek its developement. I cut up the tell-tale fabric with my knife, and witnessed its destruction, fragment by fragment, in the flames. Fool that I was, I did not dream that the artist had yet other copies. And so it was—another and another, to the number of three, appeared in the crowded shop of the hair-dresser.

] We had in our village, among its other wonders, a small building, which, by a stretch of liberal indulgence, had been denominated "the Academy of Fine Arts." It was almost our only lion, and we made the most of it. Its collection was poor enough and large enough, and always on the increase, from the habit prevailing among a few of our domestic artists of sending their pictures to the gallery, as frequently for sale as exhibition. This kept the collection always new; and consequently, to a certain extent, always interesting. It was a favourite lounge for this and for other reasons. In connexion with the establishment, an adjoining apartment had been given up to the village library, and there we got our books, and read the newspapers from all parts of the country. As we had our politicians, too, so we had our discussions; and thus, in a country like ours, where disputation is the mental small-beer of all classes, we had an additional attraction for the crowd, in the eloquence of our disputants. From the picture-gallery we adjourned to the library, from the library to the reading-room, and the transition was not great from the perusal of the journal to the forensic analysis of its contents. This apartment was a complete bear-garden—but our business is not there at this moment. ¶ A week had not well elapsed after the ramble of Harding and myself, narrated in the previous chapter, when, lounging with my wife through the gallery aforesaid, I beheld one picture, crowded among the hundred upon its walls, from which I could not turn my eyes. It filled me with astonishment while awakening in my mind a thousand apprehensions—more painful, as they were vague and intangible. It depicted the scene of my crime—the crime itself—as truly done to nature (so my fancy assured me) as if the artist himself had surveyed its execution. There was the little copse upon the neck of land, the stream running alongside in faithful affinity—there lay the female form, pale and shadowy, and with, as I thought, a sufficient resemblance to Emily to have been held a portrait. She was painted as dead, and in the distance, moving off in the shadow of the wood, and with face averted, the figure of a man, which the active fear within me assured me was intended for myself. You may guess my emotion. My wife, who was with me, was struck with the picture, and annoyed me by her conjectures as to what could be its design. Her reference was to some pagan story—had she looked that moment in my face, she had not gone so far for the subject. Having recovered from the first shock, I inspected the piece more closely; and finding it for sale, from the label, I affected to be pleased with it, and paid its price to the keeper of the collection, who was its proprietor, having bought it (a great bargain, he said) from an old woman who was entirely unknown. Having secured it in my possession, and after examining it closely, I was more and more confirmed in the opinion that the whole of it had been copied from that dreadful event in my own history—such was my fear—my reason, indeed, suggesting innumerable parallel subjects for the exercise of the artist's fancy, having no connexion with me. The mysterious manner in which the piece had been sold to the academy contributed to my fears, and into this particular I had not the courage to inquire. I dreaded to increase my knowledge. After I had sufficiently indulged my curiosity, I took my wife into the apartment to which it had been carried. ¶ "Constance!" I exclaimed, "look on this picture, and you see my story. This picture imbodies the tale I gave you and Harding some months ago. Do you remember it?" ¶ She looked into my face with that uncertainty of glance which one might be supposed to wear when doubting the sanity of a companion. I went on— ¶ "It is true, Constance. In that very wood so described, the girl, whose features you there see, became twice my victim. I took from her her honour, and finally her life. The artist who has described it, has done so narrowly." ¶ "Heavens! and you speak so coolly—will you stay here, Faber?" ¶ "Wherefore not? I tell you, Constance, you are not yet free." ¶ And, apprehensive as I was, I could not yet restrain the malignant spirit which luxuriated always in the sensibilities and sorrows of others. She only wept, while, in her presence—for I knew she dared not tell the story—I cut up the telltale fabric with my knife, and saw the fragments, one by one, consuming in the flames. Fool that I was in all this—to suppose that the avenger of blood could be satisfied—to think that the artist had not other copies. So it was! Another and another, to the number of three, giving various aspects of the transaction, appeared in time upon the walls of the academy.

73.28 had] had now

73.34 evidence which] evidence with which he

74.13 which had for a time] slowly, which had so

74.14-15 village. In] ~¶~

74.15-20 fearful meaning was in the shop of my hair-dresser.] dreadful significance, stood up prominently in the collection of the academy. How well his imagination understood mine! How subtly, where all reason must have been at fault, had its nice and daring perceptions discovered the clue leading to the innermost soul and darkest secret of the criminal!

74.21-23 above, in a dim haze that made vague the expression and outline, but did not impair the features,] above it, in a dim haze that made the outline and expression, but did not impair the felicity of the portrait,

74.23 imagination] fancy

74.24 borne] pictured

74.24-32 Who was it, that, with so much felicity, could embody my imaginings. I was thunderstruck, and, through the means of an agent, I secured this new accuser, and destroyed it in like manner with the former. But another self made its appearance, and, in despair, I gave up the hope of arresting, in this way, the progress of that inquiry, which, taking so equivocal a form, and pursuing a course so mysterious, was
] "God of heaven!" I exclaimed, in the bitterness of my fear, "what demon is it that can so imbody—so torture me with my own dreadful imaginings?" Through the means of an agent—vainly foolish as

before—I secured this new accuser, and destroyed in like manner with the first. But, horrible! another self made its appearance, and, in despair, I gave up the hope of arresting, in this manner, the progress of that mysterious inquiry, which, taking a form so equivocal and so silently industrious, was, in consequence, so

74.33 not alone] not

74.33-34 probing the secrets of my soul, by exercising] probing, in this stern but strange manner, the secrets of my soul, by an exercise of

74.36 he took] took

75.1-2 of] and extent of

75.2 the] her

75.37 weeks] some days,

76.15 were] had been

77.2 *invenient.'] ~"*

77.21-22 indicating] indicating, it is more than probable,

77.22 of] of his

77.36 have rather] rather have

78.1 this] this very

78.6 were] was

78.8 you] you, William,

78.9 somewhat sudden and] sudden and somewhat

78.15 frenzied (The 1837 reading "phrensied" is not accepted.)

78.27 charged,"] ~" (Except for this emendation, copy-text is followed in 78.25-29 despite the fact that the punctuation in the 1837 more closely conforms to modern usage.)

78.31 which] which, it is said,

78.38 made, in his ears,] made to him

79.1 heart] brain

79.3 inflicted] inflicted upon him

79.14 taught] taught, at length, really to

79.16 malice] slander or malice

79.21 wonder at] curse

79.23 as] as it were

79.26 them to the barber] them

80.15 convulsion] convulsions

80.18-19 name.] name. There was no longer any doubt—they seized upon and dragged me to prison.

80.22 him] him if I could

81.2 life!] ~" (The 1837 text adds the quotes, but also replaces the exclamation point with a period; the Centennial edition follows copy-text and retains the original punctuation.)

81.6-7 sense.] better reason. I may not wonder at my madness, though even then I knew it to be such.

81.8 death] blood

81.11 a] to a

81.12 when] when, probably,

81.13-14 age?] age? This is your religion, is it? this your love for me—for man!

81.19 writhing] writhings

81.19 gnawing] gnawings

81.28 amidst (Copy-text reading is retained over 1837 "amid.")

81.33 Harding] William

82.31 years] hours

83.1 on] on it

83.3 would] could

83.8 scruple, thus,] scruple still

83.19-20 couch.—Thanks, thanks—] couch. But I lay not long in this hopelessness of soul. Thanks, thanks!

83.22 I live again—I] I

83.22-24 fabric.] fabric! they shall not see the wretch writhe and dangle in his pain, for their amusement!

83.24 it] them

84.4 wildly—] wildly, as I seized it,

84.13 oh] "~

84.26 he] I

84.28 him] me (Simms apparently overlooked making this revision in altering the point of view from third person to first for the 1837 text.)

84.28 he] I

84.28-29 waving] like some fierce demon, waving

84.31 that] that thy

85.2 the criminal] I

85.3 while he] and

85.6 her husband] me

85.24 man] man, Constance

85.28 is] is nevertheless

85.29 him, as he] me, as I

85.30 he] I

85.30 his soul. He proceeded—] my soul at that moment.

85.36 he] I

85.36 respite.] respite. It was now my triumph.

85.38 he] I

86.3 repeated: He] repeated. I

86.21 in] at

86.25-26 thee. She] ~"¶~

86.26 his] my

86.29 he] I

86.29 while he, standing above, muttered his] while, standing above, I muttered my

86.32-33 entreated] changed entirely the character of her prayer, and entreated

86.36-38 the eyes of the disappointed criminal was that of a hyena, robbed of his prey.] my eyes must have been that of the hyena, robbed of his prey; could a look have blasted, she had been slain.

86.38 his] my

87.1 he] I

87.2 weapon] dagger

87.3 blow] stroke

87.4 his grasp, before his] my grasp, before my (There is no comma after "grasp" in 1837; copy-text is followed.)

87.5 his] my

87.6-22 the prisoner. As they approached, he aimed the bloody dagger at his own bosom, but, at that instant, fear came over his heart—the fates had paralyzed him—he was a coward! he shrunk back from the stroke and the dagger fell from his hands. Without difficulty he was in a moment secured. Constance was but slightly wounded, yet happily, enough so, to be entirely ignorant of the horrors of the scene so malignantly forced upon her. In his cell, the wretch howled over the unperforming weakness of his hand, which had not only failed to secure him his victim, but had left him without the ability to defeat his doom.
] me. That was the moment of trial; and, as they approached, I shouted my defiance to all their power, and aimed the bloody dagger

at my own heart; but, at that moment, the pale spectre of Emily came before me—I felt her breath, like a cold wind, blighting and chilling me to the soul, while her finger, resting upon my hand, scorched it as if with all the accumulated fires of damnation. The fates paralyzed me at that instant. I was a coward! I shrunk back from my own blow, and the dagger fell from my uplifted, but nerveless hands. They rushed upon me—they bound me down to the floor of my dungeon. I had no more strength—an infant might have fastened the shackles upon me, so completely had fate secured its victim. The dreadful spectre had departed, and, when too late, recollecting how ably my will heretofore had controlled its presence, I howled, in the silence of my cell, over the unperforming weakness of my hand. That hand had doubly failed me, for Constance yet lived—she was but slightly wounded. I, too, survived—still survived to all the horrors of death, and of such a doom as that before me.

87. * * * * * * * *] *CHAPTER XX.* (Asterisks divide the eighteenth chapter in 1833; 1837 and Centennial editions begin their twentieth chapters at this point.)

87.23-26 come! O] come, and that mournful ghost is again before me. She points me to the scaffold, which rises dreadfully up before the barred window of my dungeon. They come—the stern guard, and the loathsome executioner. Oh,

87.26-28 I should fail at that moment of escape—] my own hand should fail me in that moment of release—of relief—that I should be unmanned at the very moment when I should most have been the man.

88.5-6 There is an old man at the foot of the scaffold, that I would not see] Will no one drive that old man from the foot of the scaffold? I would not see him

88.11-12 —The] The choking, cold hand is about my throat—dark—dark. The

88.13 gone."] ~‸

Table II: Textual Variants

Below is a list of the variants between the original 1833 text of *Martin Faber* and the revised 1837 text.

From left to right the chart of variants has the following text sequence:

LEFT MARGIN: Centennial edition key
FIRST READING: 1833
SECOND READING: 1837

19.14 1.2 deference] vi.28 ~,
19.14 1.2 doubt] vi.28 ~,
19.16 1.4 something] vi.30 somewhat
19.23 2.1 honorable] vii.9 honourable
19.24 2.1 young,—] vii.9 ~‸
19.32 2.15 develope] vii.22 develop
19.32 2.17 education] vii.24 ~,
19.36 3.1 fireside,] vii.29 ~‸—
19.39 3.5-6 heart, and—*les petites morales*] vii.33 heart, and the smaller morals
19.39 3.6 manners,] vii.33 ~‸—
19.41 3.9 are—] viii.3~‸
19.41 3.9 father] viii.3 ~,
19.41 3.9 mother] viii.3 ~,
19.42 3.10 play-mates] viii.4 playmates,
23.epigraph 5. <no epigraph>] 13. <epigraph>
23.1 5.1 "This] 13.1 THIS
23.2 5.4-5 and the prospect, to most men full of terrors, has few or none
] 13.3-6 and, but for that awful strife—that gross exposure—the hissing scorn—the deriding shout—but for these, the prospect of death, terrible to all men, would have few or no terrors
23.7 5.9 many] 13.10 numberless
23.8 5.9 terrors] 13.10 trials
23.8 5.10 death.] 13.11-12 death. Why should I fear that which I may not avoid?
23.9 5.10-6.1 though I may regret my crimes, they give me no compunctious apprehensions

] 13.12-14.2 the survey of my crimes, and of the past, however I may regret many of them, and much of it, at least brings with it no fears of the future, and but few compunctious visitings

23.13 6.2 a] 14.3 the

23.13 6.3 of] 14.3 ~,

23.18 6.9 prospect,] 14.9 ~‸

23.19 6.10 colors] 14.10 colours

23.19 6.11 How] 14.11 how

23.19 6.11 variously] 14.11 curiously

23.19 6.11 bright.] 14.11 ~!

23.21 6.14-15 taken—and] 14.14 ~; ~—

23.22 6.15-16 declare,—] 14.15 ~—

23.23 6.16 instances,] 14.16 ~‸

23.24 6.18 criminal,] 14.17-18 ~‸

23.25 7.2 prompted] 14.19 ~—

23.26 7.4 blow.
] 14.21-23 blow—I had not scorned the supposed obligation—I had not rejected the terms upon which society tendered me its protection.

23.29 7.5 within,] 14.25 ~‸

23.29 7.6 may] 14.25 can

23.31 7.8 impulses. I cannot.
] 15.1-6 impulses—let the skin-dried ascetic, withered over the map and the crucible, undertake the examination as he may. I cannot—I dare not. The life which was given me had a different direction, and I had no right to defeat its purposes.

24.3-4 7.9-10 <no rule>] 15.7-8 <rule>

24.4 7.10 Martin Faber] 15.8 MARTIN FABER

24.4 7.10-8.6 of good family—of German extraction—the only son. I was born in M—— village, and my parents were recognized as among the first in respectability and fortune of the place. The village was small—numbering some sixty families; and with a naturally strong and shrewd, and a somewhat improved mind, my father, Nicholas Faber, became the first man in it. The village of M——, was one of those that always keep stationary. The prospect was slight, therefore, of our family declining in influence.

My father, on the contrary, grew every day stronger in the estimation of the people.

] 15.8-16.6 the only son of German parents—people of good family, and, so far as paying their debts, and not flying in the face of society could make them so, very good sort of people. I was born in the village of M——, a little settlement of some sixty or seventy families, of quiet habits, and not very brilliant minds. The Fabers were the first among them in fortune and respectability; and, possessed of a strong, shrewd, and somewhat improved sense, my father, Nicholas Faber, contrived, after no very long period, to make himself the first man in the village, which was one of those that, having attained a certain growth, always after remain stationary. It stagnated accordingly; and such being the case, the prospect was exceedingly remote of a diminution in the influence of our family. On the contrary, my father, each successive day, grew more and more supreme in the estimation of the people. He was the only active principle among them. He did their thinking, and they were very willing to depute to him a labour so excessively unpopular—not to say undemocratic.

24.20 8.6-7 counsellor—] 16.7 ~:

24.23 8.10 own,] 16.10 ~‸

24.25 8.14 his] 16.13 his own

24.27 8.16 in] 16.15 upon

24.29 9.1 had,] 16.18 ~‸

24.30 9.2-3 why speak of this?] 16.19-22 it was fated that such should not have been the case. It was decreed that he should neglect or mislead, and that I should be misled.

24.33 9.4 a] 16.24 the

24.33 9.4-5 favorite] 16.24 favourite

24.33 9.5 mama] 16.25 mamma

24.34 9.6 schooled] 16.26 permitted

24.35 9.7 earlier] 17.1 earliest

24.36 9.9 too soon] 17.2-3 premature

24.37 9.10 her] 17.3 the

24.37 9.10 health] 17.3 ~,

24.38 9.11 sometime] 17.4-5 some time
24.38 9.12 are usually] 17.5 are
25.1 9.13-14 When sent, the case was not very greatly amended.
] 17.6-9 In the mean time I had the freedom of the common, and, indeed, a common freedom in the indulgence of my own moods and passions. When sent to school, the matter was not greatly mended.
25.6 9.18-10.1 His name was Michael Andrews. He was
] 17.13-19 He was intelligent, and well taught—a man versed in the abstruser sciences; but wanting in decision and independence of character, the most necessary attributes of one in his vocation. This want was fatal to his usefulness; and Michael Andrews—for that was the name he bore—was, accordingly, but a tool—
25.11 10.1 who] 17.20 ~,
25.12 10.3 favorite] 17.22 favourite
25.18 10.11 connexion] 18.3 connection
25.20 10.14 I,] 18.6 ~‸
25.20 10.14-15 nevertheless,] 18.6 ~‸
25.22 10.18 myself] 18.9 ~,
25.23 11.1-2 discriminate between those to whom this conduct was exhibited.
] 18.11-16 stop to inquire at any time whether it was injustice or not to which I had been subjected. I had no desire to discriminate nicely into the merits of my treatment. It was enough for me that my pride or my passion had been mortified—I sought equally for my atonement.
25.27 11.3 all] 18.16 ~,
25.27 11.3 countenance.
] 18.17-21 countenance. It mattered not to me to whom these features were exhibited; and as for concealment, that was only my resort when cunning counselled, and as it became necessary to my purpose.
25.31 11.4 and] 18.22 ~,
25.32 11.6 all,] 18.23 ~;
25.33 11.7 sometimes] 18.24 sometimes was the case
25.34 11.9 toleration,] 18.26 ~‸
25.37 11.12 'Now] 19.3 "~

25.37 11.12 now Martin—] 19.3 ~, ~,
25.37 11.13 bad'] 19.4 ~?"
25.37 11.13 'I] 19.4 "~
25.38 11.14 so.'] 19.5 ~."
26.1 11.15 was such a rebuke] 19.6 were such rebukes to
26.3 11.18 importance.] 19.9 ~?
26.4 12.1 at] 19.10 ~,
26.4 12.2 scorned] 19.10 ~,
26.4 12.3 and the] 19.11 and
26.5 12.3 gifts] 19.12 ~,
26.5 12.4 toys] 19.12 ~,
26.5 12.4 favors] 19.12 favours
26.8 12.7 give] 19.15 afford
26.8 12.8 natural good sense,] 19.16 naturally good mind
26.9 12.10 the] 19.18 that
26.13 12.16 for] 19.23 to
26.16 13.1-2 education,] 19.26 ~;
26.16 13.2 did] 20.1 ~,
26.16 13.2 or] 20.1 or did
26.17 13.4 certain,] 20.3 ~‸
26.19 13.6 me,] 20.4 ~‸
26.21 13.9 education,] 20.7 ~‸
26.23 14.1 was] 21.1 was,
26.23 14.2 twelve,] 21.2 twelve years of age—
26.24 14.3 Harding—] 21.3 ~;
26.25 14.4 widow] 21.4 widow—
26.25 14.5 life—] 21.5 ~,
26.27 14.7 son,] 21.7 ~‸
26.28 14.8 degree] 21.8 and unhappy degree
26.33 15.1-2 difficulty,] 21.15 ~;
26.33 15.2 seemingly] 21.15 ~,
26.34 15.4 But] 21.17-18 He grew rapidly—tall and promising; but
27.3 15.8 shrunk] 21.21 shrank
27.5 15.10 So marked a character] 22.2 A character so marked
27.5 15.11 a contrast, so strikingly with] 22.3 so striking a contrast to

27.6 15.12 attention,] 22.4 ~‸

27.8 15.15 a consideration] 22.7 consideration to my mind

27.9 15.16 would] 22.8 in the school could

27.11 16.1 upon:—] 22.11 ~:‸

27.12 16.2 worked] 22.12 worked out

27.13 16.3-4 he helped my understanding in its deficiencies, he] 22.13 he

27.13 16.4 improprieties—] 23.13 ~;

27.13 16.5 I—] 22.13-14 I—brutal and unforbearing with all beside—

27.18 16.11 quality] 22.21 ~,

27.23 16.18 savoring] 23.1 savouring

27.23 16.18 these,] 23.1-2 these kindred emotions

27.25 17.3 surprize] 23.4 surprise

27.26 17.4 perfectly] 23.5 entirely

27.27 17.6 stripes,] 23.6-7 stripes—that was not his usual course—

27.29 17.9 of] 23.10 of a common

27.30 17.10 printed,] 23.11 ~‸

27.30 17.10 'idler.'—With] 23.11 "~"‸~

27.37 18.2 saw it not
] 23.20-22 knew but little of the ambitious nature—he saw not the appeal—he knew nothing of the entreaty

28.3 18.5-6 neighbourhood] 23.25 neighourhood

28.3 18.6 school-house] 23.26 schoolhouse

28.4 18.7 and] 24.1 ~,

28.5 18.8 omission which in him] 24.2 ~, ~, ~ ~,

28.5 18.9 and] 24.2 and which

28.6 18.10 enquired] 24.4 inquired

28.7 18.12 now] 24.5 now, upon receiving his answer,

28.8 18.12 ever,] 24.6 ~‸

28.9 18.14 whole] 24.7 whole of the

28.12 18.18 school] 24.11 schoolhouse

28.12 18.18-19.2 But he would not descend to the meanness of such an act, and resolutely determined
] 24.11-15 But, with a scrupulous conscientiousness, the due result of a circumspect mother's teachings, he refused to descend to the meanness and cowardice of such a procedure, and determined rather

28.16 19.4 indulgencies] 24.17 indulgences
28.17 19.5-6 already] 24.19 already, in many instances before,
28.19 19.7 escape] 24.21 escape also
28.20 19.9-10 coalesced] 24.23 coalescing
28.21 19.10 calling] 24.24 called
28.21 19.11 action.] 24.24 ~?
28.22 19.12 and] 24.26 ~,
28.24 19.14-15 declaring, at the same time, his freedom,] 25.1-2 declaring his enfranchisement, at the same moment,
28.25 19.16 and] 25.3 ~,
28.25 19.16-17 earnestly] 25.4 ~,
28.25 19.17 endeavored] 25.4 endeavoured
28.26 19.18 vain, and] 25.5 ~; ~,
28.29 20.3 for the consequence] 25.8 of the consequences
28.30 20.5 school,] 25.9 ~‸
28.30 20.5 Harding] 25.10 In the afternoon, Harding
28.31 20.7-10 I boldly pronounced my handiwork, no one else venturing to speak, fearing my vengeance, though several in the school, had been cognizant of the whole affair.] 25.12-19 But not so me. I had justified my act sufficiently, to myself, at least:—I was not now to forego my triumph; and, boldly advancing from my seat, in the face of the affrighted school, I announced my own handiwork, which, as I was feared by the schoolfellows generally, might never (though several of them had witnessed the whole affair) have been otherwise revealed.
28.38 20.12 remain,] 25.20 ~;
29.1 20.13 master,] 25.21 ~‸
29.2 20.15-16 passage way] 25.24 passage-way
29.3 20.16 his school-room] 25.24 the schoolroom
29.3 20.17 and] 25.25 ~,
29.4 20.18 curious,] 26.1 ~‸
29.10 21.9 tolerated] 26.9 longer tolerated
29.11 21.11 ensuing] 26.11 following
29.13 21.13 be,] 26.13 ~;
29.14 21.14 his] 26.14 the
29.14 21.15 boy] 26.15 boy then
29.16 21.18 and] 26.18 ~,

29.18 22.3 weapon,] 26.20 ~‸

29.21 22.7 revenge;—] 26.24 ~;‸

29.21 22.8 afterwards] 26.25 afterward

29.24 22.12 school-boy] 27.3 schoolboy

29.25 22.14 study,] 27.5 ~‸

29. 22.14-16 conducted. ¶ While] 27.6-28.1 conducted. CHAPTER III. ¶ WHILE

29.27 22.16 room] 28.1 ~,

29.28 22.18 passions acting] 28.3-4 passions, acting as they did, with an unwonted degree of violence

29.29 23.1 spirit] 28.4 ~,

29.31 23.2 scalding] 28.6 ~,

29.31 23.3 I] 28.7-8 But this weakness soon passed into one of a different character: and now I

29.33 23.4 On a sudden I] 28.9 I

29.34 23.6 school room] 28.11 schoolroom

29.35 23.7 sympathize] 28.12 sympathize with

30.7 24.1 floor,] 29.2 ~‸

30.9 24.2 gone off] 29.4 departed

30.9 24.3 gave] 29.5 left

30.10 24.5 and] 29.6 and to

30.11 24.6 sometime] 29.8 some time

30.12 24.7 new] 29.9 ~,

30.13 24.9 large price] 29.10-11 heavy cost

30.15 24.12 delights] 29.13-14 delights—ay, almost his only delight

30.16 24.13 embodied] 29.14 imbodied

30.17 24.14 I too] 29.15 ~, ~,

30.17 24.14-15 punishment] 29.16-17 punishment—I felt that I, too, had power,—and there is no sweeter consciousness in life

30.20 24.17 globes,] 29.20 ~‸

30.23 25.3 them] 29.23 me

30.24 25.5 colored] 29.25 coloured

30.30 25.15-17 the exercises of his juvenile years will at all times indicate what they will be when he becomes old] 30.8-14 by these trifles, chiefly, the standards of good judgment and just sensibilities are to be created and kept in exercise. The morals are formed most usually by our associates in play; and the tastes and exercises of the juvenile years will, at all times, indicate the character in age, of which they are the very seed and nucleus

30.36 26.1 grown] 30.16 grown-up
30.37 26.2 neighbor] 30.17 neighbour
30.37 26.3 after years] 30.18 after-years
31.2 26.5 my] 30.20 my education not less than my
31.3 26.6 endeavor] 30.21 endeavour
31.8 26.14 and] 31.2 ~,
31.9 26.15 me] 31.3 ~,
31.9 26.16 manner] 31.4 ~,
31.10 26.17 globes] 31.5 ~,
31.10 26.17 injury] 31.5 injury which
31.11 26.18 way,] 31.6 style
31.11 26.18 me,] 31.6 ~‸
31.11 27.1 way,] 31.6 ~‸
31.12 27.1 on] 31.7 upon
31.12 27.2 man] 31.8 man himself
31.16 27.8 But] 31.13 ~,
31.17 27.9 caught] 31.14 had caught
31.17 27.9 eye] 31.14 glance
31.21 27.15 rolled] 31.19 ~,
31.24 28.1-2 suffering] 31.24 countenance
31.25 28.3 I wore] 31.26 my features put on
31.26 28.5 and] 32.1 ~,
31.28 28.7 recovered,] 32.3 ~;
31.30 28.10 and,] 32.6 and in
31.30 28.10 anger] 32.7 ~,
31.36 29.1 man's small] 32.14 man's
31.37 29.3 self] 32.16 myself
32.1 29.6 world,] 32.19 ~‸
32.2 29.7 individual,] 32.20 ~‸
32.3 29.9 and sore] 32.22 ~,
32.4 29.11 bruises;] 32.24 ~—
32.7 29.16 me,] 33.2 ~‸
32.14 30.9 and] 33.12 ~,
32.15 30.10 weeks] 33.13 weeks after
32.18 30.13 went] 33.17 went out

32.18 30.14 as] 33.17 ~,
32.21 30.17-18 I exulted in the prospect;] 33.20-22 Silently, indeed, but not less certainly, did I exult in the prospect,
32.24 31.3 me,] 33.24-25 me—they could not mistake the expression of my glance,—
32.27 31.6 above,] 34.2-3 above the malice of the petty spirit, however reckless—
32.28 31.7 anything] 34.4 any thing
32.28 31.8 triumph;—] 34.5 ~;^
32.29 31.9-11 As it was, they proceeded on their way into the country. I was, at length, satisfied with my revenge, and] 34.6-9 A sad train, they proceeded on their way into the country: a turn in the road in a few moments concealed them from my sight, and satisfied at length with my revenge, I
32. 32. CHAPTER III.] 35. CHAPTER IV.
33.1 32.7 associations] 35.7 association
33.1 32.8 he] 35.7 ~,
33.1 32.8 nevertheless] 35.7 ~,
33.2 32.9 make,] 35.8-9 make very considerably
33.5 32.13 felt] 35.12 could not but feel
33.7 33.2 Still] 35.15 ~,
33.8 33.3 any] 35.16-36.1 any—no two people could have been more decidedly different; different in attributes of mind—different in purpose and pursuit—different in feelings and sentiments—different in all respects, whether in disposition, in character, or person
33.13 33.6 connexions] 36.3 connections
33.14 33.7 differently. Such] 36.4 not—such
33.14 33.7 connexions] 36.4-5 connections
33.16 33.10 the] 36.7 the consciousness of
33.17 33.11 the strength and] 36.8-9 of strength and capacity for
33.17 33.12-13 This, I verily believe, was the fact in our case] 36.9-12 This I know to have been the fact in our case; and I believe it to have its share in that of most of those associations which are styled friendly

33.21 33.15 away,] 36.14 ~;

33.21 33.15 and] 36.14 ~,

33.22 33.16-34.1 attributes—they, at least, bringing no provocation, left in abeyance and dormancy, many of those which
] 36.15-19 attributes, at least, as they brought with them no new provocations to the old nature, so they left in abeyance, and seemingly quite dormant, many of those, which, in my character,

33.24 34.1 immoral.] 36.19-26 immoral. Circumstance is the accoucheur in these cases; and virtue and vice, like cat and dog, would lie quietly together on the same hearth-rug for centuries, without the necessity of blow or broomstick, did not the inconsiderate hand sometimes throw them the bone, and unreasonably look to them justly and peacefully to make the division.

33.30 34.2 man was] 36.26 man

33.30 34.2-3 their progress] 37.1 the progress of the years

33.31 34.3 underwent] 37.2 underwent a

33.32 34.5 objectionable—] 37.3 ~.

33.35 34.9 demeanor] 37.7 demeanour

33.39 34.15 and] 37.13 and to

34.2 34.18 of] 37.16 of all

34.3 35.1 seemed] 37.17 ~,

34.3 35.2 invariably,] 37.17 ~‸

34.4 35.2-3 In this respect, in] 37.18 In

34.5 35.4 character] 37.19 allotment

34.6 35.7 infecting] 37.21 affecting

34.7 35.7 system,] 37.22 ~‸

34.7 35.8 mood,
] 37.23-25 mood—this fatal mood—the creature of an original nature, made too active by an unhappy education, and most unfortunate indulgence—

34.10 35.9 activity] 37.26 ~,

34.15 35.16-18 night time—my life has been a long night, in which there has been no starlight—in which there have been
] 38.7-11 night-time. For that matter, my life itself has been a long and weary night, to which, if the starlight

ever came, it brought bale only, and bitterness—a night, in which there has been little balm or beauty—a night of

34.20 36.4 hates] 38.15 ~,

34.20 36.5 fears] 38.15 ~,

34.21 36.6 solitude,] 38.16 ~‸

34.22 36.6-14 cankering and malignant purposes. ¶ Many years had now elapsed since my adventure with Michael Andrews, my old schoolmaster. I had grown up to manhood, and my personal appearance, had been so completely changed by the forming hand of time, that I had not the same looks which distinguished me at that period] 38.17-39.6 cankering, malignant, or misdirected purposes. ¶ I had now grown up to manhood—to unemployed and objectless manhood. While all around were busy, and had duties to perform, the indulgence of my parents, and my own hopes of wealth, seemed to acquit me of any necessity or solicitude as to what labour I should engage in. This was another curse of my education. I was an idler, and learned the lessons of most idlers—those of dissipation—every species of irregularity, and a horribly consuming ennui. Harding was a student still—a close student—and it was only now and then, in the daytime, that I had his company. My time was in great part passed alone; for, festering in my own rankness of nature, I was too little disposed to seek society

34.33 36.15 favorite] 39.7 favourite

34.34 36.16 gun] 39.8 ~,

34.35 36.16-17 country,] 39.8 ~‸

34.36 37.1 shy,] 39.10 ~;

34.37 37.2-3 on the opposite side of] 39.12 at length crossed

34.38 37.3 which] 39.13 ~,

34.38 37.4 was yet] 39.13 was

34.39 37.5 freshets,] 39.14 ~‸

35.1 37.7 divisions] 39.16 sections

35.3 37.10 I] 39.18-19 I had

35.7 37.16 effect] 39.24 effect, even

35.7 37.16 as] 39.24 so

35.8 37.17 even as] 39.25 as

35.14 38.9 with] 40.8 by

35.16 38.11 breeze,] 40.10 ~—
35.17 38.12 from] 40.11 ~,
35.17 38.13 above, alone] 40.12 ~—~,
35.18 38.15 silence,] 40.13 ~‸
35.20 38.17 lake] 40.16 ~,
35.23 39.3 art,] 40.20 ~‸
35.24 39.6-7 prospect, and approaching it from the point most sheltered, came suddenly into
] 40.22-42.6 prospect; and if I were not, a circumstance which occured at the moment when I stood bewildered with the novelty of the prospect, would have determined me. A sweet but uncultivated voice suddenly broke through the copse, and the tones of a young girl saluted my ears with a song, in which education seemed somewhat to struggle and vie with simplicity. The words were these—I shall never forget them:—

I.

The bird had playful music,
  The heart was full of glee;
And life was rich in pleasantness,
  And sunny hours to me.
I knew not what it was to weep,
  I never had a care;
And all my days were happy ones,
  And all my friends were dear.

II.

Had anybody told me then,
  That future hours must come,
When mine would be an aching heart,
  For ever clad in gloom—
That I should hear no young bird's voice,
  Or, sadden'd by his lay,
Should seek to fly his gentle strain,
  Or banish him away:—

III.

I should have deem'd, in thoughtlessness,
  That, at my girlish pride,
The prophet speaker took offence,
  And only sought to chide—
I should have smiled at prophecy,
  So very idle then,
Nor feared, nor felt, as now I do,
  I shall not smile again.

The singer paused in the strain—a strain so simple, yet so thoughtful, that I paused also. It had really affected me; and after a few moments' hesitation, which vexed me as I felt it, I approached the spot whence the sounds had arisen, and reaching the point most sheltered, soon found myself in

36.22 39.9-10 shade, whose] 42.8 shade. Her

36.24 39.12 sometime] 42.10 some time

36.24 39.13 presence] 42.11 notice

36.26 39.16 timidity] 42.14 trepidation

36.27 39.18 eyes] 42.16 sight

36.30 40.3 resided,] 42.19 ~^

36.30 40.3-4 off, and
] 42.19-22 off; and after chatting with her for some time, and in a manner evidently not ungrateful to her, and certainly satisfactory to me,

36.33 40.5 suprize] 42.43 suprise,

36.33 40.6-8 father, my old tutor. But, fortunately for me, he was not in a condition to recognize me
] 42.24-43.5 father my ancient schoolmaster, old Michael Andrews! Fortunately for me, however, I had been so completely changed in appearance by the forming hands of time, that he did not recognise me; and even had this not been the case, the condition of the old man himself was such, that I was secure from any fear of detection

37.5 40.10 'accidence'] 43.7-8 "~"

37.6 40.12 neighborhood, and] 43.9 neighbourhood; ~,

37.8 40.16 slight impression] 43.12 impression

37.10 40.18-41.1 uneducated] 43.15 ~,

37.15 41.8 connexion] 43.21 connection

37.17 41.10-11 object,] 43.24 ~∧

37.20 41.15 and] 44.3 until

37.21 41.16 she] 44.3 and

37. 42. CHAPTER IV.] 45. CHAPTER V.

37.25 42.5 say] 45.5 ~,

37.26 42.8 connexion with me] 45.7 connection with mine

37.29 42.12 children.—] 45.11 ~.∧

37.32 43.2 dishonor] 45.16 dishonour

37.32 43.2 not therefore] 45.16 ~, ~,

37.33 43.3 surprize] 45.16 surprise

38.2 43.10 wrought] 46.3 wrought upon

38.4 43.12-13 worked industriously upon] 46.5-6 industriously aroused all

38.10 44.3 sky—] 46.13 ~;

38.17 44.14 yet had she not] 46.23-24 yet, even then, she had won none of

38.19 44.16 with] 47.1 ~,

38.19 44.17 about] 47.1 ~,

38.20 44.17-18 nightshade?] 47.2-5 nightshade. Mine were the professions of the momentary passion, which I had taught her to believe, and which, for the time, I had actually believed myself. But only for a time.

38.29 45.11 was] 47.15 ~,

38.30 45.11 be] 47.15 ~,

38.31 45.13 beautiful,] 47.17 ~—

38.31 45.14 an habitual] 47.18 a

38.32 45.16 than ever,—] 47.19 and which had now become habitual—

38.34 45.18 extravagance] 47.22 extravagance, as I then considered them,

38.35 46.1 not yet] 47.23 not

38.36 46.2 entirely.] 47.23-24 entirely. I had not yet grown callous enough for that.

38.8 46.4 soothe] 48.1 sooth

39.1 46.7 thought advisable] 48.4 advised

39.4 46.11 son. And she was so.] 48.7 son.

39.5 46.12 beautiful] 48.8 ~,
39.7 46.15-16 interested,] 48.11 ~‸
39.16 47.11 expedients,] 48.23-24 ~‸
39.17 47.13 essential,] 48.26 ~;
39.20 47.17 pride] 49.3 ~,
39.21 48.1 little] 49.5 ~,
39.22 48.3 well] 49.6 ~,
39.22 48.4 crime] 49.7 crimes
39.25 48.7 was therefore] 49.10 ~, ~,
39.26 48.9 an affection existing,
] 49.11-13 any affection existing—without knowing, indeed, what her affections should be—
39.28 48.11 scruple] 49.15 ~,
39.30 48.14 dishonored] 49.17-18 dishonoured
39.31 48.15 condition.] 49.18 ~?
39.32 48.17 concerned—] 49.20 ~,
39.35 49.4-5 With regard to our connexion, I] 49.24 I
40.1 49.10 arrangements] 50.3 ~,
40. 50. CHAPTER V.] 51. CHAPTER VI.
40.4 50.2 the] 51.2 the proposed
40.6 50.5 that] 51.5 that which had been
40.7 50.6 of] 51.6 of our
40.8 50.9 appearance,] 51.9 ~‸
40.10 50.10 enquiries] 51.10 inquiries
40.10 50.11 wear] 51.11 put on
40.12 50.13 features] 51.13 expression
40.12 50.14 indifference. "You] 51.13-15 ~. ¶ "~
40.15 51.4 ask,] 51.18 ~?
40.17 51.7 alas] 52.1 Alas
40.18 51.9-10 been—] 52.3 ~?
40.19 51.10 sick—] 52.3 ~?
40.20 51.11 troubled] 52.4-5 ~,
40.21 51.14 suggestion] 52.7 ~,
40.22 51.14 herself] 52.7 ~,
40.22 51.15 a] 52.7 the
40.26 52.4 case,] 52.14 ~‸
40.27 52.6 child she] 52.15-16 ~, ~
40.28 52.7 fervid devotion—and,] 52.16-17 fervent devotion!—and

40.29 52.8 that] 52.17 when
40.32 52.13 connexion] 52.22 connection
40.34 52.17 if] 52.26 ~,
40.35 52.18 injustice] 53.1 ~,
41.2 53.3-4 integrity,] 53.4 ~;
41.7 53.11 her,] 53.10 ~—
41.9 53.13 And,] 53.12~‸
41.9 53.13 Emily—] 53.12 ~?
41.9 53.14 say, that] 53.13 say any thing
41.13 54.1 Now] 53.17 ~,
41.13 54.1 said.] 53.17 ~?
41.14 54.4 Martin—] 53.19 ~,
41.15 54.4 me,] 53.20 ~;
41.17 54.9 false] 53.24-25 falsely
41.20 54.11 so, but] 54.1 ~; ~
41.24 54.17 mine,] 54.7 ~;
41.25 55.2 her—] 54.10 ~,
41.29 55.7 but] 54.14~,
41.30 55.9 live,] 54.16 ~;
41.32 55.11-12 embodied] 54.18 imbodied
41.33 55.13 Martin,] 54.19 ~‸—
41.36 55.17 next] 55.23 ~,
41.37 56.1 as] 54.24 when
41.38 56.2 with] 54.25 by
42.1 56.4 this.] 55.1 ~?
42.2 56.6 but] 55.2 ~,
42.3 56.7 contrary] 55.4 ~,
42.4 56.9 dumb language] 55.5-7 that dumb, but most expressive language, which is theirs only,
42.8 56.14 meagreness] 55.11 meagerness
42.9 56.15-16 wretchedness,] 55.12 ~;
42.11 56.18 connexion] 55.15 connection
42.16 57.7 honor] 55.21 honour
42.18 57.11 given] 55.25 given her
42.19 57.13 tendernesses] 56.1 tenderness
42.20 57.13 peevishly] 56.1 ~,
42.20 57.14 threat,] 56.2 ~—
42.21 57.15 of] 56.2 something of
42.25 58.3 then] 56.9 ~,

42.27 58.6 now] 56.11 ~,
42.31 58.12 long,] 56.16 ~;
42.32 58.13 honorable] 56.17 honourable
42.32 58.14 burthen] 56.19 burden
42.35 59.1 stood] 56.22 withstood
42.35 59.2 me,] 56.23 ~;
43.3 59.8 true] 57.3 ~,
43.3 59.9 exclaimed] 57.3-4 ~,
43.4 59.9 God,] 57.4 ~!
43.4 59.10 sin.] 57.5 ~!
43.5 59.11 loved—] 57.6 ~!
43.7 59.14 prevaricate—] 57.8 ~!
43.9 59.17 Oh,] 57.11 ~!
43.9 59.17 fool—] 57.11 ~!
43.9 59.18 folly.] 57.12 ~!
43.10 60.1 me,] 57.13 ~∧
43.10 60.1 Priestess] 57.13 priestess
43.11 60.2 influenced with inspiration—] 57.14 maddened with the sacred inspiration;
43.11 60.3 Think] 57.15 think
43.11 60.3 traitor,] 57.15 ~∧
43.12 60.4 farther] 57.16 further
43.13 60.5 destroyed,] 57.17 ~∧
43.15 60.8 mine] 57.20 ~,
43.15 60.9 honor] 57.20 honour
43.17 60.12 honor] 57.23 honour
43.18 60.13 herself,] 57.24 ~∧
43.19 60.15 dishonorable] 57.25-26 dishonourable
43.19 60.15 oh, God"—] 57.26 O God!"
43.21 60.18 I, from] 58.2 ~∧ ~
43.22 61.1 sight,] 58.3 ~∧
43.23 61.2 guilty.] 58.5 ~?
43.24 61.3 rose] 58.6 arose
43.26 61.6 embodiment] 58.9 imbodiment
43.29 61.11 approached] 58.13 ~,
43.31 61.14 Begone] 58.16 ~!
43.35 62.3 sight,] 58.22 ~∧
43.35 62.3-4 already are] 58.23 now really appear
43.37 62.6 grasp.—] 58.25 ~.∧

44.1 62.7 Emily,] 58.26 ~!
44.2 62.8 delay,] 59.1 ~;
44.2 62.9 well—] 59.2 ~:
44.5 62.13 more] 59.5 longer
44.5 62.14 forever] 59.6 for ever
44.6 62.16 villainy] 59.8 villany
44.8 62.18 mentioned.] 59.10 ~?
44.9 63.2 with] 59.11 by
44.9 63.2 money—] 59.11 ~?—
44.11 63.5 dishonor] 59.14 dishonour
44.11 63.5 yourself.] 59.14 ~?
44.12 63.7 that thenceafter] 59.16 ~, ~,
44.13 63.7-8 forever more] 59.16 for evermore
44.14 63.10 endeavored] 59.19 endeavoured
44.16 63.12 and] 59. 20 ~,
44.16 63.12 struggle] 59.21 ~,
44.20 63.18 me;—] 59.26 ~;∧
44.20 64.1 and] 60.1 ~,
44.21 64.2 paused,] 60.2 ~∧
44.22 64.3 stupor,] 60.3 ~∧
44.24 64.7 her,] 60.6 ~∧
44.28 64.12 eyes,] 60.11 ~;
44.28 64.12 and] 60.11 ~,
44.33 65.1 silence] 60.18 ~,
44.35 65.5 silent] 60.21 quieted
44.37 65.8 at length, invariably] 60.24 invariably came back, and
45.1 65.12 me,] 61.1 ~;
45.2 65.13 fingers] 61.2 ~,
45.3 65.13 were] 61.3 were fastened
45.4 65.15 design,] 61.4-5 ~;
45.5 65.16 spoke,] 61.6 ~—
45.6 65.18 neck all] 61.7 ~, ~
45.6 65.18-66.1 symetry] 61.8 symmetry
45.6 66.1 was] 61.8 fell
45.9 66.4 round] 61.11 about,
45.9 66.5 shrunk] 61.12 shrunk back
45.11 66.8 mercy.—] 61.15 ~∧

45.12 66.9 Spare] 61.16 Spare me
45.12 66.9 forgive] 61.16 forgive me
45.12 66.9 Martin,] 61.16 ~!—
45.13 66.11 silent.] 61.18 ~!
45.14 66.12 exclaimed] 61.19 ~,
45.16 66.15 me.] 61.21 ~!
45.16 66.15 Oh,] 61.22 ~—
45. 67. CHAPTER VI.] 62. CHAPTER VII.
45.18 67.1 not] 62.1 ~,
45.19 67.3 woods,] 62.3 ~;
45.20 67.4 for] 62.4 even for
45.33 68.8 in] 62.20 from
45.33 68.8 tree,] 62.20 ~;
45.33 68.8 and] 62.20 ~,
46.1 68.12 forth] 63.3 forward
46.1 68.12 replication] 63.3-4 replication which they made
46.3 68.14-15 desired] 63.6 seemed to doubt, and to desire
46.5 68.16 "I am a murderer!"
] 63.8 "Am I not a murderer?" was my inquiry.
46.7 69.1 Murderer!"—] 63.10 ~!" ^
46.11 69.7 bore] 63.15 wore
46.13 69.10 image—] 63.18 ~?
46.15 69.13 strange!] 63.21 ~^
46.16 69.15 won] 63.23 has won
46.17 69.16 nourishes him.] 63.23 nourished him!
46.19 70.1 neighborhood] 63.25 neighbourhood
46.19 70.1 aspect] 63.26 ~,
46.20 70.2 access] 64.1 ~,
46.22 70.6 mind,] 64.4 ~^
46.23 70.7 large] 64.5 ~,
46.25 70.10 present] 64.7-8 present the idea of
46.26 70.11 seized] 64.9 acted
46.26 70.12 her] 64.9 her body
46.31 71.2 and] 64.17 ~,
46.33 71.5 reach.] 64.19-20 reach—she and her child—I was a double murderer.
46.37 71.8 stride] 63.23 huge stride which
46.37 71.9 crime,] 64.24 ~^

46.38 71.10 importance.
] 64.25-26 importance. Such is our nature. We are proud of the power to destroy.
47.2 71.12 had] 65.2 had now
47.4 71.14 in] 65.4 even in
47.5 71.16 vigor] 65.5 vigour
47.7 72.1 But,] 65.8 ~∧
47.8 72.2 There] 65.9 ~,
47.8 72.3 in] 65.10 in an
47.10 72.4 heart,] 65.11 ~;
47.12 72.8 myself,] 65.14-15 ~∧
47.13 72.9 muttering] 65.15-16 ~,
47.13 72.9 over the] 65.16 ~, ~
47.13 72.10 Murder] 65.16 Murderer
47.14 72.11 Murderer,] 65.17-18 ~∧
47.14 72.12 Faber,] 65.18 ~∧
47.17 72.15 forever on] 65.21 for ever finding its way to
47. 73. CHAPTER VII.] 66. CHAPTER VIII.
47.20 73.5 arms,] 66.5 ~∧
47.22 73.7 Though] 66.6-7 Though this was
47.22 73.7 crime,] 66.7 ~∧
47.22 73.8 dye,] 66.7 die
47.24 73.10 the act,] 66.9 this act
47.24 73.10 long] 66.9-10 long since
47.25 73.12 murder,] 66.11 ~∧
47.26 73.12 composure,] 66.12 ~∧
47.27 74.1 society,] 66.14 ~∧
47.28 74.2 savior] 66.15 saviour
47.29 74.4 thought I] 66.16 I thought,
47.31 74.6 in] 66.19 on
47.32 74.7 spot] 66.20 place
47.32 74.8 took] 66.20 ~,
47.32 74.8 eye] 66.20 ~,
47.33 74.10 connexion] 67.2 connection
48.1 74.12 pocket handkerchief] 67.4 ~-~
48.2 74.13 Indian] 67.5 India
48.3 74.15 letter,] 67.7 ~∧
48.3 74.15 pen-knife] 67.7 penknife

48.5 75.1 brush,] 67.10 ~∧
48.6 75.1 and] 67.11 ~,
48.6 75.3 leaving,] 67.12 ~∧
48.8 75.5 perceived] 67.14 ~,
48.8 75.6 rich,] 67.14 ~∧
48.9 75.6 cameo,] 67.15 ~∧
48.9 75.7 concern,] 67.16 ~;
48.11 75.9 intials] 67.17 initials
48.11 75.9-10 engraven on] 67.18 engraved upon
48.11 75.10 How] 67.19 ~,
48.12 75.11 lost.] 67.19 ~?
48.12 75.11 all important] 67.19-20 ~-~
48.13 75.12 industry,] 67.20 ~∧
48.14 75.15 found,] 67.23 ~;
48.19 76.3 favor] 68.3 favour
48.21 76.7 of] 68.6 of the
48.22 76.8 and,] 68.8 ~∧
48.23 76.9 rumor of the crime] 68.8-9 rumour of her unaccountable disappearance
48.23 76.9-10 village—in which,] 68.9-10 village; and there
48.24 76.10 connexion] 68.10 connection
48.26 76.14 while] 68.13 ~,
48.27 76.14 and] 68.14 ~,
48.29 76.17 passed] 68.16 passed away
48.29 76.18 had] 68.17 had once
48. 77. CHAPTER VIII.] 69. CHAPTER IX.
49.3 77.11 dressed] 69.10 crowded
49.5 78.1 our] 69.13 the
49.5 78.1 said,] 69.14 ~∧
49.10 78.8 romantic,] 70.1 ~∧
49.11 78.9 poetry,] 70.1 ~∧
49.11 78.9 embodied] 70.1-2 imbodied
49.14 78.13 maiden,] 70.5 ~∧
49.21 79.8 encircle] 70.15 penetrate
49.23 79.11 instinctively,] 70.18 ~∧
49.26 79.15-16 Andrews. A] 70.22 Andrews—a
49.27 79.16 picture] 70.22-23 spectre
49.27 79.18 moment,] 70.24 ~∧

49.29 80.3 rest.
] 70.26-71.2 rest. My disquiet, so unaccountable to all around, seemed to indicate a reluctance to the ceremony.
49.34 80.8 eye] 71.7 eye still
49.36 80.10 gone.—] 71.9 ~.‸
50.2 80.13 of] 71.12 of my
50.2 80.14 fancy,] 71.13 ~;
50.6 81.1 embody] 71.18 imbody
50.8 81.4 death] 71.20 ~,
50.8 81.4-5 unuttered] 71.20-21 entirely unuttered
50.9 81.5 spirit] 71.21 senses
50.9 81.5 is] 71.22 are
50.10 81.7 shall] 71.22-23 and compelled to recognise its presence, shall
50.13 81.11 door] 72.2 ~,
50.15 81.14 of] 72.4 of the
50.16 81.15 highest] 72.5 Highest
50.16 81.16 paramount,] 72.6 ~;
50.16 81.16 advanced] 72.6 advanced without fear
50.17 81.17 key,
] 72.7-8 key—in the face and in defiance of the spectre—
50.19 81.18 fancies] 72.9 fancies had
50.22 82.5 in
] 72.14-15 in controlling my own moods, compelling obedience from my own fears and fancies—in
50. 83. CHAPTER IX.] 73. CHAPTER X.
50.25 83.1 I] 73.1 To the reflective mind, I
50.26 83.2 in] 73.2 on
50.26 83.2-3 is it necessary that I should tell you of the small
] 73.3 necessary to say that the
50.27 83.4 that] 73.4 which
50.27 83.4 wife.
] 73.4-10 wife was equally, if not more limited. A temper like mine—so impatient, and so without resources—could not long suffer a dependant or an associate to remain at peace. She felt accordingly; and I am persuaded a greater curse could not well have fallen to her lot.

50.31 83.5-6 that is to say, I employed neither blows nor violence; but
] 73.10-14 to speak in common phrase—I employed no blows—no violence. But there are other penalties which virtue can be made to endure, not less frequently, and far more poignantly, than vice.

50.34 83.7-11 wretched discontent, and when I say this I have said all. She suffered with patience, however, and I sometimes found it impossible, and always difficult, to drive her beyond the boundary of yielding and forgiving
] 73.14-20 wretched, sleepless, discontent—always showing my teeth, and, when occasion offered, never withholding my venom. She suffered as a martyr—with a patience that was never to be disturbed; and I failed utterly, however much I strove, to drive her beyond the boundary of a yielding, an always conciliating

51.5 83.12 not] 74.1 ~,

51.6 83.12 first,] 74.1-2 first—how could she love me?—

51.6 83.13 bride] 74.2 ~,

51.7 83.14 sufficient firmness of] 74.3 a sufficient degree of firmness in her

51.7 83.14 character,] 74.4 ~^

51.8 84.1-4 command. The discovery of this fact, which I soon made, offended my pride. I did not distrust, however—I hated her; and, with a strange perversity of character,
] 74.4-18 commands or the solicitations of her parents. Perhaps, too, as she knew little of me, and less still, at that time, of the nature of those feelings of which her heart could become susceptible, the constraint had been less upon her than, even then, I imagined it to have been. That she soon perceived her error and misfortune, I discovered not less quickly; and in due accordance with the discovery, my pride grew morbid and angry. I did not distrust—but I hated her; and with a fiend-like hatred, which can only be understood by a reference to the course of conduct which I thought proper to pursue in conse-

quence. With a perversity of character, strange and contradictory—

51.18 84.4 which,] 74.18 ~‸

51.19 84.6 love, and that] 74.19 love—that

51.21 84.9 duties] 74.22 duty

51.21 84.10 growth.] 74.22 ~—

51.21 84.10 developement.] 74.23 development—

51.22 84.11 strove,] 74.24 ~—

51.22 84.12 it,] 74.24 ~?—

51.23 84.13 dishonor] 74.25 dishonour

51.24 84.14 Though] 75.1 Though soon

51.25 84.16 husband,] 75.2 ~;

51.27 84.18 to] 75.4 ~,

51.27 84.18 by] 75.5 ~,

51.27 85.1 feelings, could gain] 75.5-6 legitimate feelings, could acquire

51.28 85.1 ascendancy] 75.6 ascendency

51.29 85.3-4 She was won by the gentleness, the talent, the high character of my old friend
] 75.7-10 I soon found that she had been won, all unconsciously on his part, by the talents, the gentleness, and many attractions of mind and manner of my old associate and schoolfellow

51.32 85.6-9 and unconcealed pleasure. She delighted in his society; and with a feeling which she had never dared to name to herself, she gave him a preference, in
] 75.11-17 spirit, and a pleasure which she never thought to conceal. She was only happy in his presence and society; and with a feeling which she had never yet dared to name to herself, and from the analysis of which I feel she must always have shrunk, she gave him a preference over all others, in

51.37 85.10-86.3 Nor—boy as he was—sensitive and easily wrought upon by respect and kindness—was he at all insensible to her regards. He became, as an acquaintance, almost an inmate of our house. He was always with us—and with the openness of heart common to such a character, he unreservedly sought for the society of Constance.

I soon discovered their mutual propensities, for, at an early period, I had learned, with singular felicity, to analyze character

] 75.18-76.10 Nor was he insensible to her regards. Sensitive, and easily wrought upon, whether by kindness or cruelty, her ceaseless consideration, exhibited in a thousand forms, of which she herself knew nothing, controlled him like an infant. He had always been very intimate with me—more so than any other of the village—and he was now almost an inmate of my house. With the free openness of heart which marked and made his character, he sought unreservedly for the society of Constance, and Constance only: and while I saw from this, that his intentions had no dishonourable object, I saw at the same time that he knew nothing of the precise feeling which prompted them. I had learned, with singular felicity, at an early period of my life, to study and to analyze the human heart. I exercised my habit with regard to these two, and was not long in discovering that their propensities were mutual

52.12 86.4 and while] 76.10 while

52.17 86.10 fear] 76.16 fear, or

52.17 86.10 honor] 76.16 honour

52.18 86.12-13 him over myself, in the bosom of one, I strove to have

] 76.18-19 another in the bosom of one I would, at that time, have had

52.20 86.15 first,] 76.21 first to,

52.20 86.16 with] 76.21 ~,

52.21 86.16 association,] 76.22 ~;

52.21 86.16 finally] 76.22 ~,

52.21 86.17 me,] 76.23 ~‸

52.22 86.17-87.1 as to give] 76.23 as, in time, to afford

52.22 87.1 excuse and opportunity] 76.24 opportunity and excuse

52.23 87.3-9 But they were both honest—honest as I had never been—as I never expected man or woman to have been! Twining and intermingling, hourly in spirit, the most

jealous scrutiny, the most bitter hate and hostility, could never detect the slightest feature of impropriety
] 76.25-77.10 To this object I addressed all the means in my power, but without the desired success. They were both honest—sweetly, nobly honest; as, from my own feeling and character, I had never expected man or woman to have been. Joining in thought—intermingling hourly in spirit, and in a communion which, if they had not been wonderfully immaculate, must have brought out their weaknesses, they were yet strong; and the most jealous scrutiny, the most bitter hate and hostility, could never have construed into impropriety a solitary feature

52.32 87.10-14 chose to stimulate their passions—to influence their desires—to put their spirits into flame; and many were the opportunities with which I sought, in hurrying them to crime, to provide myself with victims.
] 77.11-20 adopted to stimulate their passions—to influence or to create desires—to put their passions into that fervour, which, once provoking discontent and the vague want which is the first symptom of the active appetite, will never rest again short of its surfeit. Thousands of opportunities did I throw before them in order to provide myself with victims. But they were children—weak enough for susceptibility, but not daring to do wrong.

53.1 87.15 the] 77.20 every

53.1 87.16 one] 77.21 a

53.2 87.16 and] 77.21 ~,

53.2 87.16-88.5 suppressed and strong affections, I beheld the cheek of Constance grow paler, day by day, and saw, at every visit—the increased wildness of look—the still exaggerated emotions struggling for utterance and life, in the bosom of the young and
] 77.22-78.10 strong affections, and suffering as they did in the noble struggle to restrain and keep them down, I was yet mortified to see that they could not be otherwise than successful. But the strife of their spirits in this labour had its influence, and, day by day, the cheek of Constance grew paler and paler, and there was a nameless anguish

in her eye, as it sunk beneath my own, which spoke of that love—worst love of all—which has its birth untwinned by hope. Nor was she the only one with whose heart the contest promised to be vital. I beheld, at every succeeding visit, the increasing fever in the soul of my other victim. The worm was in the core, and kept up a ceaseless labour in the bosom of the gentle and too

53. 89. CHAPTER X.] 79. CHAPTER XI.

53.14 89.1 Some] 79.1 SEVERAL

53.14 89.2 marriage;] 79.2 ~,

53.14 89.2-4 this time, my house and young wife had lost most of their attractions. My favorite habit,] 79.2-8 that time, as might have been expected, my young wife and domestic associations had lost most of their attractions—in my eyes at least. My resources were now always out of doors—carousing sometimes, but frequently solitary and savage. My favourite pursuit—one that had been a passion in boyhood,

53.19 89.4 and one] 79.8 and

53.20 89.5 my mood of sternness,] 79.9 the sternness of my mood—

53.21 89.6 neighboring country;] 79.10 neighbouring country,

53.21 89.7 and with] 79.11 with

53.21 89.7-90.1 shoulder as apologetic for my idle wanderings, the neighboring forests for ten or fifteen miles round, soon became familiar to my survey. Sometimes, on these occasions, Harding would become my companion; and as he was highly contemplative in character, his presence did not at all interfere with the gloominess of my mood] 79.11-80.6 shoulder, and, with this apology for my wanderings, I had contrived to become familiar with the forests in that neighbourhood for fifteen miles round. It was in a ramble of this sort that I had first encountered Emily, and this habit furnished a sufficient reason to others, for those long absentings from home in which my time had been chiefly given up to her. Sometimes, on these excursions, Harding would become my companion; not that he was a sportsman, but simply because of his contemplative character of mind, which luxuriated, and was enthusiastic, in its admiration of the gloomy beauty of the thick woods. His presence did not interfere with my mood; indeed, although the cause was essentially different, his silence was a fitting similitude of mine. We wandered thus from one wood to another, through path and cover, frequently without a word, and living only in our thoughts

54.1 90.2-4 wood, thickly sown with undergrowth, and penetrable with difficulty, that
] 80.7-9 thicket, girded in by heavy trees, and almost impervious from the undergrowth, that

54.3 90.5 tree] 80.10 pine

54.3 90.6 Our
] 80.11-14 The sun was completely shut out from the spot, and the solemn hush of all things about us was such as to make the train of thought in our minds much gloomier than ever. Our

54.6 90.6 was] 80.14-15 was necessarily

54.7 90.7-8 situation, and unconsciously I remarked—
] 80.16-19 situation; and, as if impelled throughout the whole scene by an irresistible monitor, I remarked to him thus, in spite of my own consciousness of the danger of such a topic—

54.10 90.9 such a spot, which] 80.20-21 the spot, it appears to me, that

54.12 90.12 reply,] 80.23 ~;

54.13 90.13 This,] 80.24 ~∧

54.13 90.14 spot] 80.25 ~,

54.13 90.14 now] 80.25 ~,

54.13 90.14 choose] 80.25 select

54.15 90.17 sound,] 81.1 ~∧

54.16 90.18 tree tops] 81.2 tree-tops

54.17 91.1 thoughts,] 81.3 ~∧

54.18 91.3 life,] 81.5 ~∧

54.18 91.4 crime—it] 81.6 ~. It

54.19 91.5 society] 81.6 ~,

54.21 91.7 lopt] 81.9 lopped

54.22 91.9 shortening] 81.10 ~,

54.26 91.14 reply—] 81.16 ~,

54.27 91.16 tribunals,] 81.18 ~^

54.28 91.18-92.8 But, even by such a standard, Martin, it would be a crime of the most horrible complexion, for, leave the choice to the one you seek to murder, and he will submit, in most cases, to the loss of all his worldly possessions, and even of his liberty, in preference to the loss of life." ¶ "What would you say, William if you knew] 81.19-82.15 To some men, from the operation of circumstances, or from their own improvidence, death would be welcome even by violence; and the feeling with which such a man would submit to the executioner, can surely afford no standard by which to determine upon the fate of others not so situated, and not having the same feeling or condition with himself. Life is a sacred something which we do not venerate enough. It is considered quite too lightly by society, and it appears to me, if we believe for a moment in the immortality of the soul and the doctrine of rewards and punishments, we have not the right, even in the case of the criminal, to doom him to a loss of it. The idea is horrible which conceives the murder of a human being, even according to the standard you suggest; for, leave the choice but a moment to the victim, and he will submit, in most cases, to the loss of all his possessions, and even of his liberty, to avoid that fearful rush of the soul into the dark and deep chaos which our ignorance depicts the future." ¶ "Why, what would you say to a friend, William—to me, for example, if I told you

55.10 92.11 say!—] 82.18-19 Say! God help me,

55.11 92.12 upon] 82.19 on

55.12 92.13 looked] 82.21 surveyed

55.12 92.14-16 moment, then, placing my hands upon his shoulder with a deliberation which was significant of the deepest madness, I spoke:
] 82.21-25 few moments, then, with a deliberation that, under all the circumstances, was significant of a momen-

tary madness, placing my hands upon his shoulders, I slowly exclaimed—

55.16 92.17 Look—] 82.26 ~!
55.16 92.17 again.] 82.26-27 again—you shall see and hear.
55.19 93.3 sprung] 83.3 sprang
55.20 93.4 ashen pale] 83.4 pale as death
55.20 93.5 and] 83.5 ~,
55.21 93.6 other involuntarily] 83.6 ~, ~,
55.22 93.7 concealing] 83.7 ~,
55.24 93.11 but] 83.11 ~,
55.25 93.12 caution,] 83.11 ~∧
55.26 93.14 victim—] 83.13 ~;
55.28 93.17 tree,] 83.16 ~∧
55.34 94.7 said] 83.23 ~,
55.35 94.9 true] 83.25 ~,
56.1 94.13 not—] 84.3 ~;
56.1 94.14 you—] 84.3 ~;
56.1 94.14 more,] 84.4 ~;
56.2 94.14 you—] 84.4 ~,
56.6 95.2 it—] 84.9 ~,
56.8 95.6 murderer!] 84.12 ~,
56.9 95.7 Martin—] 84.13 ~;
56.14 95.15 secret—] 84.19 ~.
56.16 95.18 way] 84.23 way out
56. 96. CHAPTER XI.] 85. CHAPTER XII.
56.21 96.7 him] 85.6 ~,
56.23 96.10 Constance,] 85.8-9 ~∧
56.24 96.11 her] 85.9 ~,
56.25 96.13 that] 85.11 ~,
56.31 97.8 one,] 85.19 ~∧
56.32 97.9 sleep. He] 85.20 sleep; he
56.32 97.10 in] 85.21 to
57.3 98.1 that] 86.6 ~,
57.4 98.3 it.] 86.8 ~?
57.7 98.7 waywardly,] 86.12 ~∧
57.11 98.13 me; but] 86.17 ~. But
57.14 98.17 facts,] 86.20 ~∧
57.16 99.2 labored,] 86.23 laboured

57.16 99.2 consequence,] 86.23-24 ~‸

57.18 99.6 me] 86.27 ~,

57.22 99.10 girl,] 87.4 ~‸

57.22 99.11 murdered.] 87.4-5 ~."

57.23 99.12 life.] 87.6 ~?

57.24 99.13 you?—it] 87.7 ~?‸ It

57.25 99.15 me.] 87.8 ~."

57.26 99.16 does] 87.9 does haunt me

57.27 99.17 awake] 87.10 ~,

57.28 100.1 bed side] 87.12 bedside

57.30 100.4 and] 87.14 ~,

57.30 100.5 "Murder,! <. . .> Murder!"] 87.15-16 '~! <. . .>~!'

57.32 100.8 Martin—] 87.18 ~,

57.33 100.8 vision—] 87.18 ~;

57.36 100.13 neck—] 87.22 ~;

57.37 100.14 me—] 87.24 ~?

57.37 100.15 punishment,] 87.25 ~‸

58.1 100.18 honor] 87.27 honour

58.6 101.7 become] 88.7 becoming

58.7 101.9 away;—] 88.8 ~‸

58.8 101.9 day,] 88.9 ~‸

58.8 101.10 again—] 88.9 ~;

58.10 101.13 Justice] 88.12 justice

58.11 101.15 me—] 88.14 ~.

58.12 101.16 haunted] 88.14-15 ~,

58.12 101.17 terrors,] 88.15 ~‸

58.16 102.4 damned,] 88.20 ~‸

58.23 102.14 Go then—if he was] 89.2-3 Go, then, if you are

58.23 102.15 his] 89.3 your

58.24 102.16 his] 89.4 your

58.24 102.16 honor] 89.4 honour

58.25 102.17 Martin"—] 89.5 ~,"‸

58.26 103.1 all,] 89.7 ~‸

58.28 103.3-4 forever] 89.9 for ever

58. 104. CHAPTER XII.] 90. CHAPTER XIII.

58.30 104.1 Justice] 90.1 justice

58.31 104.2 Harding] 90.2 Harding,

59.2 104.10 and] 90.9 ~,
59.4 104.13 dumb,] 90.12 ~—
59.5 105.2 unavailing;] 90.14 ~,
59.6 105.3 localities] 90.15 ~,
59.9 105.7 alledged] 90.19 alleged
59.11 105.10 So,] 90.21 ~∧
59.16 105.18 christian] 91.7 Christian
59.16 106.1 manifested,] 91.7-8 ~∧
59.21 106.7 storm troubled] 91.13-14 ~-~
59.23 106.11 multitude,] 91.17-18 ~∧
59.25 106.13 him] 91.19 ~!—
59.29 107.2 *abandon*] 91.25 hopelessness
59.30 107.3-4 appearance,] 91.27 ~∧
59.31 107.6 around] 92.2 ~,
59.32 107.6 off,] 92.2 ~∧
59.32 107.7 floor—] 92.3 ~;
59.34 107.10 room;] 92.6 ~—
59.38 107.16 bible] 92.11 Bible
60.1 107.17 refer] 92.12-13 refer, with an everyday philosophy,
60.2 107.17 or to] 92.13 or
60.2 108.1 situation,] 92.14 ~∧
60.3 108.1 brought] 92.15 brought with me
60.3 108.2 tortures—] 92.15 ~,
60.4 108.3-4 christian] 92.17 Christian
60.10 108.11 up,] 92.24 ~∧
60.13 108.16 new,] 93.1 ~∧
60.13 108.16 and] 93.1 ~,
60.15 109.1 bosom,] 93.4 ~∧
60.16 109.3 desperation,] 93.6 ~∧
60.17 109.4 as] 93.7 ~,
60.18 109.5-6 exclaimed—"And] 93.8-9 ~— ¶ "~
60.21 109.10 wrath,] 93.12 ~∧
60.23 109.13 gesture,] 93.15 ~∧
60.25 109.16 and] 109.17 ~,
60.26 109.16-17 replied] 93.18 ~,
60.26 109.17 deliberation:—] 93.18-19 ~∧—
60.28 110.2-3 answered?—] 93.21 ~?∧

60.28 110.3 fears.—] 93.22 ~∧—
60.28 110.3 You] 93.22 you
60.31 110.6 proceeded.] 93.24 ~—
60.33 110.9 should] 93.27 could
60.34 110.11 living] 94.2 ~,
60.35 110.12 depart] 94.3 ~,
60.36 110.13 moment] 94.3 ~,
60.38 110.16 couch,—] 94.6 ~∧—
61.5 111.7 I] 94.14 that I
61.7 111.9 What] 94.17 what
61.7 111.10 me;] 94.18 ~?
61.8 111.11 victim—] 94.18 ~?
61.9 111.12 wronged;] 94.19-20 ~—
61.12 111.16 it!] 94.23 ~.
61.14 112.1 happened.] 94.25-26 ~?
61.14 112.1 story,] 94.26 ~∧
61.15 112.2 truth.] 94.27 ~?
61.16 112.3 truth!] 95.1 ~.
61.18 112.6 least,] 95.4 ~∧
61.21 112.9 dishonoring] 95.7 dishonouring
61.22 112.11 dishonor] 95.8-9 dishonour
61.23 112.12 Why then] 95.10 ~, ~,
61.25 112.15 burned] 95.13 burnt
61.28 113.2 Faber—] 95.16 ~,
61.29 113.3 history—] 95.17 ~,
61.33 113.9 live,] 95.23 ~∧
61.33 113.9-10 aspirations—] 95.23 ~;
61.34 113.11 encouragement—] 95.25 ~;
61.35 113.12 honor] 95.26 honour
61.38 113.16 wintery] 96.2 wintry
62.1 113.17 That] 96.3-4 You know that
62.2 114.1 me—] 96.5 ~;
62.3 114.2 men—] 96.6 ~;
62.4 114.5 greatness,] 96.8 ~∧
62.5 114.5 hope,] 96.9 ~∧
62.6 114.7 hour, you] 96.10 hour
62.7 114.9 labors] 96.13 labours
62.9 114.11-12 contemn—] 96.15 contemn me—

62.11 114.14 my] 96.17 his

62.11 114.15 species—] 96.18 ~;

62.13 114.18 further] 96.21 farther

62.15 115.3 you—] 96.24 ~!

62.17 115.6 and] 96.26 ~,

62.17 115.6 heal] 97.1 ~,

62.20 115.10 exile] 97.5 ~—

62.22 115.12 me,] 97.7 ~‸

62.23 115.13 labors] 97.8 labours

62.25 115.17 crime,] 97.11 ~‸

62.28 116.3 to] 97.15 refuses for ever to

62.30 116.5 appear,] 97.17 ~‸

62.30 116.6 appeal,] 97.18 ~‸

62.31 116.7 refuse—] 97.19 ~.

62.31 116.8 crime,] 97.19 ~‸

62.33 116.10 sunk] 97.21 sank

62.35 116.13 eye,] 97.24 ~‸

63.3 117.2 mind,] 98.4 ~‸

63.12 117.15 evidence,] 98.15 ~‸

63.15 118.2 so-called] 98.19 ~‸~

63.15 118.2 serpent] 98.20 ~,

63.16 118.3 But,] 98.20 ~‸

63.16 118.4 all] 98.21-22 all that was wrong

63.18 118.6 christian] 98.24 Christian

63.19 118.8 so.] 98.25-26 so. How well did I know them—how little did they know me!

63. 119. CHAPTER XIII.] 99. CHAPTER XIV.

63.21 119.1 strange,] 99.1 ~‸

63.24 119.6-7 unlooked for,] 99.6 ~-~‸

63.25 119.7 habit] 99.7 ~,

63.26 119.9 But,] 99.8 ~‸

63.27 119.10 or,] 99.9 ~‸

63.28 119.11 dependent] 99.10 dependant

63.30 120.1 irritability,] 99.13 ~‸

63.32 120.4 energy,] 99.16 ~‸

63.34 120.6 object] 99.18 end

64.2 120.9 to] 99.21 upon

64.3 120.11 character, which,] 100.1 ~‸ ~‸

64.4 120.12 however] 100.2 ~,

64.5 120.13 vascillating] 100.3 vacillating

64.6 120.15 end] 100.4 desire

64.6 120.15 kind,] 100.5 ~∧

64.6 120.16 all impelling] 100.5-6 ~-~

64.7 120.16 attainment] 100.6 acquisition

64.8 121.1 passion,] 100.8 ~∧

64.8 121.1 bosom; or,] 100.8 ~, ~∧

64.9 121.2 manner,] 100.9 ~∧

64.10 121.4 project,] 100.11 ~∧

64.11 121.4-5 passion] 100.11 object

64.11 121.5 therefore,—] 100.12 ~∧—

64.12 121.6 design, which] 100.13 ~∧ ~,

64.12 121.7 sudden] 100.13 ~,

64.14 121.10 suppose, that] 100.16 ~∧ ~,

64.18 121.15 intention.] 100.21 ~?

64.19 121.17 was] 100.22 ~,

64.19 121.17 truth] 100.23 ~,

64.21 122.2 enquiry] 100.26 inquiry

64.22 122.3-4 object,—] 100.27 ~∧—

64.32 123.1 it] 101.14 it to the end

64.33 123.1 fact,] 101.14 ~∧

64.34 123.4 mind,] 101.17 ~∧

64.36 123.5-6 association,] 101.18 ~∧

64.37 123.8 those,] 101.21 ~∧

65.6 123.17 occurrences,] 102.3 ~∧

65.8 124.2 myself,] 102.6 ~∧

65.10 124.6 spirit—] 102.9 ~,

65.11 124.7 it—] 102.10 ~,

65.12 124.8 it:—] 102.11 ~.∧

65.14 124.12 life.] 102.14 ~?

65.16 124.14 dye] 102.16 die

65.17 124.15 said] 102.17 ~,

65.18 124.16 mine—] 102.18 ~;

65.18 124.17 criminal—] 102.18 ~.

65.22 125.5 me—] 102.24 ~?

65.30 125.17 fear,] 103.9 ~∧

65.31 126.1 me,] 103.9 ~∧

65.32 126.2 it—] 103.11 ~;
65.34 126.5 and] 103.15 ~,
65.35 126.5 silence] 103.15 ~,
65.37 126.9 struck,] 103.18 ~‸
66.1 126.11 offence,] 103.21 ~‸
66.3 126.14 as] 103.23 ~,
66.5 126.18 her] 103.27 ~,
66.8 127.4-5 moment] 104.4 ~,
66.9 127.6 why?] 104.5 ~!
66.10 127.7 her—] 104.6 ~,
66.14 127.13 to-morrow] 104.11 ~,
66.18 128.1 itself] 104.17 itself still further
66.19 128.3 embittered] 104.18-19 imbittered
66.19 128.4 blighted—] 104.19 ~,
66.20 128.5 yourself,] 104.20 ~‸
66.22 128.8 him!] 104.23 ~?
66.25 128.14 bitterly:—yet,] 105.2 ~‸—~‸
66.26 128.15 reproaches.] 105.2-3 ~!
66.27 128.16 moment] 105.4 ~,
66. 129. CHAPTER XIV.] 106. CHAPTER XV.
66.29 129.1 narrate] 106.1 relate
66.29 129.1 labors] 106.1 labours
66.30 129.3 Harding] 106.2-3 ~,
66.30 129.3 newly assumed] 106.3 ~-~
66.32 129.7 respect,] 106.6-7 ~‸
66.33 129.7 favored] 106.7 favoured
67.2 129.13 game,] 106.12 ~‸
67.3 129.13 neighboring] 106.13 neighbouring
67.5 130.3 yet,] 106.16 ~‸
67.7 130.5 dales] 106.18 ~,
67.8 130.7 favorite] 106.20 favourite
67.9 130.9 direction—] 106.21 ~,
67.10 130.10 neighboring] 106.22 neighbouring
67.10 130.11 extent] 107.1 ~,
67.10 130.11 quarters] 107.1 ~,
67.12 130.14 before] 107.4 ~,
67.13 130.15 Now] 107.5 ~,
67.17 131.4 dependencies] 107.11 dependances

67.18 131.5 Having] 107.12 As he had a
67.19 131.6 drawing] 107.13 ~,
67.22 131.11 eye,] 107.17 ~‸
67.24 131.13 which,] 107.19 ~‸
67.29 132.3 spot,] 107.26 ~‸
67.29 132.4 impervious] 107.27 romantic
67.30 132.5 progress—] 108.1 ~,
67.31 132.6 took] 108.2 ~,
67.32 132.8 then] 108.4 at the time
67.35 132.11-12 new-born] 108.7 newborn
67.36 132.13-14 not then regarded] 108.9 never before considered
67.38 132.17 route,] 108.11 ~‸
67.38 132.17 neighboring] 108.12 neighbouring
68.2 133.2 though,] 108.15 ~‸
68.2 133.2 certainly] 108.15 ~,
68.4 133.5 attention—] 108.17 ~,
68.4 133.5 it,] 108.18 ~‸
68.5 133.6 care] 108.18 ~,
68.5 133.7 what] 108.19 of the
68.11 133.14 known] 108.25 known already
68.12 133.16 me] 108.27 my suspicions
68.14 134.1 purpose,] 109.3 ~;
68.15 134.3 woods,] 109.4 ~‸
68.17 134.5-6 upon which to exercise his skill,] 109.7 which attracted him,
68.18 134.7 follow, and,] 109.9 ~; ~‸
68.20 134.10 the] 109.11 to my mind the
68.21 134.11 of] 109.13 of my
68.23 134.13 region,] 109.14 ~‸
68.23 134.13 which] 109.15 ~,
68.24 134.15 recollections,] 109.16 recollection
68.26 134.18 went] 109.18 ~,
68.29 135.4 lake,—] 109.23 ~‸—
68.30 135.6 dishonor] 109.24 dishonour
68.33 135.10 soul,] 110.1 ~;
68.35 135.13 look] 110.4 gaze
68.35 135.14 but in] 110.4 but

68.37 135.17 I beheld, at length,] 110.7-8 at length, I beheld, under the influence of my imagination,
69.3 136.4 taken,] 110.12 ~∧
69.3 136.5 burden] 110.13 ~—
69.4 136.6 forever] 110.14 for ever
69.4 136.6 departed,] 110.14 ~—
69.7 136.11 and] 110.18 yet
69.7 136.11 colorless] 110.19 colourless
69.8 136.12 ashen] 110.19-20 ashen pale
69.9 136.13 and] 110.21 ~,
69.12 136.17 mine] 110.24 ~,
69.12 136.18 the] 110.25 in the
69.13 137.1 expressive—] 110.26 ~,
69.13 137.1-2 earnest] 110.26 ~,
69.14 137.3 was nevertheless] 111.1 ~, ~,
69.15 137.4 offended at] 111.1-2 struck, and somewhat offended by
69.16 137.5 on the instant of] 111.3 the instant after
69.16 137.6 turned round] 111.4 turned
69.17 137.7 some] 111.5 an
69.17 137.8-9 fell from the look which I gave him in evident confusion; and,
] 111.5-6 fell, in evident confusion, from the look which I gave him; and tacitly,
69.20 137.11 movement] 111.8 ~,
69.22 137.14 saw] 111.10 ~,
69.22 137.14 concern] 111.11 ~,
69.24 137.18 for,] 111.14 ~∧
69.25 138.1 was] 111.15 had been
69.28 138.6 which] 111.19 ~,
69.30 138.8-9 recognized] 111.22 recognised
69.35 138.16 regard,] 112.1 ~∧
69.36 138.17-18 irksome,] 112.3 ~;
69.37 139.1 perceived] 112.4 revolved
69.38 139.1-2 possibility] 111.5 ~,
70.5 139.9 alarm, and] 112.12 alarm; and,
70.5 139.9 error] 112.12 ~,
70.7 139.12 mistake,] 112.15 ~∧

70.8 139.13 a] 112.16 any
70.9 139.15 contempt] 112.17 injury
70.9 139.15 malice,] 112.18 ~;
70.10 139.17 prompter, which one day will] 112.19 prompter which will one day
70.11 139.18 Self-esteem] 112.20 ~,
70.12 140.2 others—] 112.22 ~:—
70.12 140.2 way,] 112.22 ~^
70.13 140.3 him] 112.23 him on
70.16 140.8 and] 113.1 ~,
70.17 140.9 recognize] 113.2 recognise
70.19 140.12 some] 113.5 a few
70.22 140.16 Harding] 113.8 ~,
70.22 140.16 common-place] 113.9 commonplace
70.24 141.2 and] 113.12 ~,
70.26 141.4 form,] 113.14 ~^
70.27 141.5 His
] 113.16-19 He felt that, at such a moment and occasion, my jealousy, if I were really guilty, must be particularly active; and took care, therefore, to avoid the expression of much curiosity. Yet his
70.33 141.10 to] 113.23 upon to
70.34 141.11 it,] 113.24 ~^
71.2 142.3 chimney place] 114.6 ~-~
71.5 142.6 destiny] 114.10 destiny had
71.6 142.9 mother,] 114.12 ~^
71.8 142.11 no] 114.14 no single
71.9 142.12 apprehension,] 114.15 ~—
71.10 142.13-14 transaction—] 114.16-17 ~;
71.11 142.14 look] 114.17 ~,
71.12 142.16 forever] 114.19 for ever
71.18 143.6 it;] 114.27 ~,
71.20 143.10 mine—] 115.4 ~,
71.21 143.11 was—] 115.4 ~,
71.21 143.12 auxiliar] 115.5 auxiliary
71.21 143.12 and] 115.5 ~,
71.22 143.13 fact] 115.6 facts
71.23 143.14 truth,] 115.7 ~^

71.23 143.14 them, and he] 115.7 them. He

71.23 143.15 confident and strong] 115.8 strong and confident

71.24 143.15-16 progression in his labor] 115.8-9 his progress in this labour

71. 144. CHAPTER XV.] 116. CHAPTER XVI.

71.25 144.1-146.2 A week from this had not gone by, when, while under the hands of our village hair-dresser, I beheld a picture crowded among the hundred upon his walls, which filled me with astonishment, and awakened in my mind some moving apprehensions. I beheld the scene of my crime truly done to nature, and just by the little copse upon which the deed had been committed, stood a female form, pale and shadowy, and with a sufficient resemblance to Emily, to have been considered a portrait. You may guess my emotion. Having recovered from the first shock, I inquired, as if without the desire for an answer, where he got and who had painted it, and was told in reply that an old lady had brought it there for sale—the lady was unknown. Finding the price low—merely nominal, indeed, he had readily bought it; relying on the merits of the piece to insure it a ready sale. I affected to be pleased with it and paid him his price. Having secured it in possession, I examined it closely, and was confirmed in the opinion that the whole was copied from events in my own history. Beyond this I could perceive nothing farther. The preparation of the piece was a mystery, and I had not the courage to seek its developement. I cut up the tell-tale fabric with my knife, and witnessed its destruction, fragment by fragment, in the flames. Fool that I was, I did not dream that the artist had yet other copies. And so it was—another and another, to the number of three, appeared in the crowded shop of the hair-dresser.
] 116.1-120.1 We had in our village, among its other wonders, a small building, which, by a stretch of liberal indulgence, had been denominated "the Academy of Fine Arts." It was almost our only lion, and we made the most of it. Its collection was poor enough and large enough, and always on the increase, from the habit prevailing

among a few of our domestic artists of sending their pictures to the gallery, as frequently for sale as exhibition. This kept the collection always new; and consequently, to a certain extent, always interesting. It was a favourite lounge for this and for other reasons. In connexion with the establishment, an adjoining apartment had been given up to the village library, and there we got our books, and read the newspapers from all parts of the country. As we had our politicians, too, so we had our discussions; and thus, in a country like ours, where disputation is the mental small-beer of all classes, we had an additional attraction for the crowd, in the eloquence of our disputants. From the picture-gallery we adjourned to the library, from the library to the reading-room, and the transition was not great from the perusal of the journal to the forensic analysis of its contents. This apartment was a complete bear-garden—but our business is not there at this moment. ¶ A week had not well elapsed after the ramble of Harding and myself, narrated in the previous chapter, when, lounging with my wife through the gallery aforesaid, I beheld one picture, crowded among the hundred upon its walls, from which I could not turn my eyes. It filled me with astonishment while awakening in my mind a thousand apprehensions—more painful, as they were vague and intangible. It depicted the scene of my crime—the crime itself—as truly done to nature (so my fancy assured me) as if the artist himself had surveyed its execution. There was the little copse upon the neck of land, the stream running alongside in faithful affinity—there lay the female form, pale and shadowy, and with, as I thought, a sufficient resemblance to Emily to have been held a portrait. She was painted as dead, and in the distance, moving off in the shadow of the wood, and with face averted, the figure of a man, which the active fear within me assured me was intended for myself. You may guess my emotion. My wife, who was with me, was struck with the picture, and annoyed me by her conjectures as to what could be its design. Her reference was to some pagan story—had she looked that moment in my face, she had not gone so far for the subject. Having recovered from the first shock, I inspected the piece more closely; and finding it for sale, from the label, I affected to be pleased with it, and paid its price to the keeper of the collection, who was its proprietor, having bought it (a great bargain, he said) from an old woman who was entirely unknown. Having secured it in my possession, and after examining it closely, I was more and more confirmed in the opinion that the whole of it had been copied from that dreadful event in my own history—such was my fear—my reason, indeed, suggesting innumerable parallel subjects for the exercise of the artist's fancy, having no connexion with me. The mysterious manner in which the piece had been sold to the academy contributed to my fears, and into this particular I had not the courage to inquire. I dreaded to increase my knowledge. After I had sufficiently indulged my curiosity, I took my wife into the apartment to which it had been carried. ¶ "Constance!" I exclaimed, "look on this picture, and you see my story. This picture imbodies the tale I gave you and Harding some months ago. Do you remember it?" ¶ She looked into my face with that uncertainty of glance which one might be supposed to wear when doubting the sanity of a companion. I went on— ¶ "It is true, Constance. In that very wood so described, the girl, whose features you there see, became twice my victim. I took from her her honour, and finally her life. The artist who has described it, has done so narrowly." ¶ "Heavens! and you speak so coolly—will you stay here, Faber?" ¶ "Wherefore not? I tell you, Constance, you are not yet free." ¶ And, apprehensive as I was, I could not yet restrain the malignant spirit which luxuriated always in the sensibilities and sorrows of others. She only wept, while, in her presence—for I knew she dared not tell the story—I cut up the telltale fabric with my knife, and saw the fragments, one by one, consuming in the flames. Fool that I was in all this—to suppose that the avenger of blood could be satisfied—to think that the artist had not other copies. So it was! Another and another, to the number of three, giving various aspects of the transaction, appeared in time upon the walls of the academy.

73.28 146.3 had] 120.2 had now

73.29 146.5 author,] 120.3 ~;

73.31 146.7 persons] 120.5 ~,

73.31 146.8 things] 120.6 ~,

73.32 146.9 and,] 120.7 ~‸

73.34 146.11 evidence which] 120.9-10 evidence with which he

73.35 146.12 degrees,] 120.10 ~‸

73.37 146.16 path,] 120.14 ~‸

74.7 147.10 ghastly] 120.25 ~,

74.9 147.12 and] 120.26 ~,

74.9 147.13-14 companion,] 120.27-121.1 ~‸

74.13 148.1 which had for a time] 121.6 slowly, which had so

74.14-15 148.2-3 village. In] 121.7-8 ~¶~

74.15 148.3 more,] 121.8 ~‸

74.15 148.4-5 fearful meaning was in the shop of my hairdresser.
] 121.9-15 dreadful significance, stood up prominently in the collection of the academy. How well his imagination understood mine! How subtly, where all reason must have been at fault, had its nice and daring perceptions discovered the clue leading to the innermost soul and darkest secret of the criminal!

74.21 148.6 chasm,] 121.15 ~—

74.21 148.6-8 above, in a dim haze that made vague the expression and outline, but did not impair the features,
] 121.16-18 above it, in a dim haze that made the outline and expression, but did not impair the felicity of the portrait,

74.23 148.9 imagination] 121.19 fancy

74.24 148.9 borne] 121.19 pictured

74.24 148.10-149.1 Who was it, that, with so much felicity, could embody my imaginings. I was thunderstruck, and, through the means of an agent, I secured this new accuser, and destroyed it in like manner with the former. But

another self made its appearance, and, in despair, I gave up the hope of arresting, in this way, the progress of that inquiry, which, taking so equivocal a form, and pursuing a course so mysterious, was
] 121.20-122.3 "God of heaven!" I exclaimed, in the bitterness of my fear, "what demon is it that can so imbody—so torture me with my own dreadful imaginings?" Through the means of an agent—vainly foolish as before—I secured this new accuser, and destroyed it in like manner with the first. But, horrible! another self made its appearance, and, in despair, I gave up the hope of arresting, in this manner, the progress of that mysterious inquiry, which, taking a form so equivocal and so silently industrious, was, in consequence, so

74.33 149.3 not alone] 122.5 not

74.33 149.3-4 probing the secrets of my soul, by exercising] 122.5-7 probing, in this stern but strange manner, the secrets of my soul, by an exercise of

74.36 149.7 he took] 122.9 took

75.1 149.11 and] 122.13 ~,

75.1 149.12 of] 122.13-14 and extent of

75.2 149.13 the] 122.15 her

75.3 149.14 belief,] 122.16 ~‸

75.6 150.1-2 learned,] 122.20 ~‸

75.7 150.2-3 neighborhood] 122.21 neighbourhood

75.13 150.11 ill disguised] 123.2 ~-~

75.15 150.14 Yet] 123.5 ~,

75.26 151.14 tracing] 123.20 ~,

75.28 151.17 copied] 23.23 ~,

75.29 151.18 note] 123.24 ~,

75.29 151.18 initials,] 123.24 ~‸

75.30 152.2 person] 123.26 ~,

75.33 152.6-7 addressed,] 124.3 ~‸

75.34 152.7 which] 124.3 ~,

75.34 152.8 might] 124.4 ~,

75.35 152.10 difficulty,] 124.5 ~‸

75.35 152.10 overcome,] 124.6 ~‸

75.37 152.13 weeks] 124.8 days,

76.1 152.15 period] 124.10 ~,

76.5 153.3 time,] 124.16 ~^

76.6 153.5 made;] 124.17 ~—

76.7 153.6 to] 124.19 ~,

76.8 153.8-9 however,] 124.21 ~;

76.9 153.10 clue] 124.22 ~,

76.11 153.12-13 received—] 124.24 ~;

76.11 153.13 and] 124.25 ~,

76.14 153.17 and] 125.2 ~,

76.15 154.1 whom] 125.3 ~,

76.15 154.1 when] 125.3 ~,

76.15 154.1 were] 125.4 had been

76.17 154.4 that] 125.6 ~,

76.19 154.6-7 embodied] 125.8-9 imbodied

76.20 154.7 and] 125.9 ~,

76.20 154.8-9 prepared] 125.10 ~,

76.21 154.9 quietly] 125.11 ~,

76.22 154.10-11 looked for] 125.12 ~-~

76.22 154.11 events,] 125.12 ~^

76. 155. CHAPTER XVI.] 126. CHAPTER XVII.

76.25 155.3 soul,] 126.3 ~^

76.31 155.11 Now,] 126.10 ~^

77.2 156.4-5 *invenient.'*] 126.17 ~."

77.4 156.8 discontented—] 126.20 ~,

77.5 156.9 and] 126.21 ~,

77.12 157.1 moment] 127.8 ~,

77.21 157.15 indicating] 127.21 indicating, it is more than probable,

77.22 157.15 of] 127.22 of his

77.27 158.6 welfare,] 128.2 ~^

77.30 158.10 and,] 128.7 ~^

77.34 158.16 mán,—] 128.11 ~^—

77.35 158.17 drawn,] 128.12 ~^

77.36 159.1 have rather] 128.14 rather have

78.1 159.5 this] 128.18 this very

78.2 159.6-7 morality,] 128.19 ~^

78.3 159.8-9 and solemnly] 128.21 ~, ~,

78.6 159.13 were] 128.26 was

78.7 159.14 this!] 128.27 ~?
78.8 159.15 here.] 129.1 ~?
78.8 159.15 you] 129.1-2 you, William,
78.9 159.17-18 somewhat sudden and] 129.3 sudden and somewhat
78.10 160.1 leapt] 129.5 leaped
78.12 160.3 company] 129.7 ~,
78.15 160.7 daughter] 129.11 ~,
78.15 160.7-8 frenzied] 129.11-12 phrensied
78.15 160.8 exclamation—] 129.12 ~;
78.16 160.9 poor] 129.13 ~,
78.17 160.11 spot,] 129.14 ~^
78.17 160.12 feebly] 129.14-15 ~,
78.21 160.17 and] 129.19 ~,
78.21 160.17 satisfied] 129.20 ~,
78.23 161.1 friends;] 129.22 ~?
78.24 161.2 gathering—] 129.23 ~?
78.25 161.4 explain] 129.25 ~,
78.25 161.4-5 Justice] 129.25 justice
78.25 161.5 Harding] 129.26 ~,
78.27 161.7 myself, "you] 129.27-130.1 myself; "You
78.27 161.7 charged, "] 130.1 ~,"
78.28 161.9 away] 130.2 ~,
78.28 161.9 people,] 130.3 ~—
78.29 161.10 and] 130.3 ~,
78.31 161.13 which] 130.6 which, it is said,
78.34 161.18 intention,] 130.11 ~^
78.35 162.1 fortifying] 130.12 fortifying,
78.36 162.3 modestly,] 130.13 ~^
78.36 162.3 confidently] 130.14 ~,
78.38 162.6-7 made, in his ears,] 130.17 made to him
79.1 162.7 crime. How] 130.17 crime—how
79.1 162.7 burned] 130.17 burnt
79.1 162.8 heart] 130.18 brain
79.1 162.8 coals. How] 130.18 coals—how
79.2 162.9 me,] 130.19 ~;
79.2 162.9 how] 130.19 ~,
79.3 162.11 inflicted] 130.20-21 inflicted upon him

79.4 162.12 it] 130.22 ~,
79.7 162.17 public] 130.26 ~,
79.9 163.1 closet—] 131.1 ~,
79.11 163.5-6 altered,] 131.5 ~^
79.13 163.8 unnecessarily,] 131.6-7 ~^
79.14 163.9 taught] 131.8 taught, at length, really to
79.16 163.12 malice] 131.10-11 slander or malice
79.19 163.17 Faber, and] 131.15-16 ~; ~,
79.20 163.18 developement] 131.16 development
79.21 164.1 wonder at] 131.17 curse
79.21 164.2 narration.] 131.18 ~!
79.23 164.4 as] 131.20 as it were
79.23 164.5 secret.] 131.21 ~!
79.26 164.9 herself,] 131.25 ~^
79.26 164.9 disguise] 131.25 ~,
79.26 164.9-10 them to the barber,] 131.25 them,
79.28 164.12 and] 131.27 ~,
79.34 165.3 proof,] 132.9 ~^
79.36 165.6 speaking,] 132.12 ~^
80.4 165.14 chasm,] 132.20 ~—
80.6 165.18 examination] 132.23 ~,
80.9 166.2 and] 132.25 ~,
80.10 166.4 shook] 132.27 ~,
80.11 166.5 and] 133.1 ~,
80.12 166.7 fragments,] 133.3 ~^
80.12 166.8 fissure] 133.3 ~,
80.14 166.9-10 victim, and] 133.5 ~; ~,
80.15 166.12 convulsion] 133.7 convulsions
80.16 166.13 death,—] 133.7 ~^—
80.17 166.14-15 time, and,] 133.9 ~; ~^
80.18 166.16 name.
] 133.11-12 name. There was no longer any doubt—they seized upon and dragged me to prison.
80. 167. CHAPTER XVII.] 134. CHAPTER XVIII.
80.22 167.4 him,] 134.3 him if I could,
80.25 167.8 language,] 134.8 ~—
80.28 167.13 describe] 134.12 ~,
80.32 168.5 hours,] 134.17 ~^

81.2 168.11 life!] 135.2 ~."
81.4 168.13 but,] 135.4 ~^
81.4 168.14 earth,] 135.4-5 ~—
81.6 168.17 sense.
] 135.7-9 better reason. I may not wonder at my madness, though even then I knew it to be such.
81.8 169.1 death] 135.10 blood
81.10 169.4 murderer,] 135.13 ~—
81.11 169.5 a] 135.14 to a
81.11 169.6-7 dishonoring myself, dishonoring my family, when
] 135.14-16 dishonouring myself—dishonouring my family—when, probably,
81.13 169.9 age?
] 135.17-19 age? This is your religion, is it? this your love for me—for man!
81.14 169.9 Hypocrite,] 135.19 ~^
81.17 169.13-14 last!"—and] 135.22-23 ~!"^ And
81.17 169.14 sunk] 135.23 sank
81.19 169.16 writhing] 135.24-25 writhings
81.19 169.16 gnawing] 135.25 gnawings
81.19 169.16 heart,] 135.25 ~^
81.21 170.1 me,] 136.1 ~!
81.21 170.1 live] 136.1 ~,
81.23 170.5 did] 136.5 ~,
81.25 170.6 you then] 136.6 ~, ~,
81.27 170.9 you!] 136.9 ~.
81.28 170.10 amidst] 136.10 amid
81.30 170.13 reasons,] 136.12 ~^
81.31 170.15 all,] 136.14 ~;
81.33 171.1 Harding] 136.17 William
81.35 171.4 stimulated] 136.19-20 ~,
81.36 171.5 done!] 136.21 ~.
81.37 171.6 Speak—say,] 136.22 ~, ~^
82.1 171.9 hated,] 136.25 ~—
82.2 171.9-10 community;—] 136.25 ~^—
82.2 171.10 any body] 136.26 anybody
82.3 171.11 True—true!—] 136.27 ~! ~!^
82.10 172.5 condition!] 137.10 ~.

82.11 172.6 that,] 137.11 ~?—

82.12 172.8 victim] 137.13 ~,

82.14 172.11-12 multitude—] 137.16 ~;

82.15 172.13 knife,] 137.17 ~—

82.22 173.4 sophistry!—this then] 137.27 ~!^ ~, ~,

82.24 173.7 curse.—] 138.3 ~.^

82. 174. CHAPTER XVIII.] 139. CHAPTER XIX.

82.27 174.1 trial,] 139.1 ~—

82.27 174.2 come!—] 139.2 ~!^

82.28 174.2 mockery?—the] 139.2 ~?^ The

82.30 174.5 looks—] 139.5 ~,

82.30 174.6 forever] 139.6 for ever

82.31 174.7 years] 139.7 hours

82.32 174.9 forever] 139.8 for ever

82.33 174.10 exposure,] 139.9 ~—

83.1 174.13 scaffolding,] 139.12 ~—

83.1 174.13 on] 139.12 on it

83.2 175.1 whom] 139.14 ~,

83.3 175.1 would] 139.14 could

83.3 175.2-3 labors] 139.15 labours

83.6 175.7 die!—] 139.20 ~!^

83.7 175.8 what,] 139.20 ~^

83.8 175.10 scruple, thus,] 140.1 scruple still

83.11 175.15 agony!—let] 140.5 ~!^ Let

83.12 175.15 it. Let] 140.5 ~— let

83.12 175.16 think!—] 140.6 ~!^

83.19 176.9-10 couch.—Thanks, thanks—] 140.16-17 couch. But I lay not long in this hopelessness of soul. Thanks, thanks!

83.22 176.12 I live again—I] 140.19 I

83.22 176.12 stand then] 140.20 ~, ~,

83.22 176.13 fabric.] 140.20-22 fabric! they shall not see the wretch writhe and dangle in his pain, for their amusement!

83.24 176.14 it] 140.23 them

83.27 177.1 Harding—] 140.26 ~,

83.31 177.7 it.] 141.4 ~!

83.31 177.7 came;] 141.4 ~.

83.35 177.12 oh, Martin—] 141.9 ~! ~,
84.2 178.1 it,] 141.15 ~—
84.2 178.1-2 once and quickly] 141.16 ~, ~ ~,
84.4 178.4 wildly—] 141.18-19 wildly, as I seized it,
84.5 178.5 blade] 141.19 ~,
84.8 178.10 dishonor] 141.24 dishonour
84.10 178.13 Nay—] 141.26 ~,
84.12 178.15 do—] 142.1 ~,
84.12 178.16 vitals,] 142.2 ~‸
84.13 179.1 shrieked—oh, cruel;] 142.3 ~. "Oh, ~—
84.14 179.3 honor] 142.5 honour
84.16 179.5 ha!—] 142.7 ~!‸
84.17 179.7 honor] 142.8 honour
84.18 179.8 cruel,] 142.10 ~—
84.19 179.10 forever] 142.11-12 for ever
84.22 179.15 and] 142.16 ~,
84.26 180.3 he] 142.21 I
84.27 180.5 and] 142.23 ~,
84.28 180.6 he] 142.24 I
84.28 180.6-7 waving] 142.24-25 like some fierce demon, waving
84.30 180.8 Constance!—] 142.26 ~!‸
84.31 180.10 that] 143.1 that thy
84.33 180.13 curse] 143.3 ~,
84.33 180.13 Speak then] 143.4 ~, ~,
84.34 180.14 speak] 143.4 ~,
84.35 180.15 death,] 143.5 ~‸
85.2 181.4 but] 143.12 ~,
85.2 181.5 the criminal] 143.13 I
85.3 181.6 while he] 143.13 and
85.5 181.9 sudden,] 143.16 ~‸
85.5 181.10 and in coherent] 143.17 ~, ~ ~,
85.6 181.11 her husband] 143.18 me
85.13 182.3 him;] 143.27 ~,
85.15 182.6 pledges,] 144.3 ~—
85.16 182.9 Father,] 144.6 ~‸
85.18 182.11 duty,] 144.8 ~‸
85.22 182.17 promises,] 144.14 ~‸
85.24 183.1 man—] 144.16 man, Constance—

85.25 183.2 wretch,] 144.17 ~‸
85.27 183.5 wretch,] 144.19 ~‸
85.28 183.6 is] 144.21 is nevertheless
85.29 183.8 him, as he] 144.22 me, as I
85.30 183.9 expression—] 144.23 ~,‸
85.30 183.9 he] 144.23 I
85.30 183.10 his soul. He proceeded—] 144.24 my soul at that moment.
85.32 183.13 husband,] 144.27 ~;
85.36 183.18 he] 145.4 I
85.36 184.1 respite.] 145.5 respite. It was now my triumph.
85.38 184.3 he] 145.7 I
86.1 184.4 Him,] 145.8 ~‸
86.1 184.5 earth,] 145.9 ~—
86.2 184.6 — Say] 145.10 —Say
86.3 184.8 repeated: He went on.—] 145.11 repeated. I went on—
86.10 184.17 powers] 145.20 ~,
86.13 185.3-4 pursue] 145.24 ~,
86.15 185.6 man,] 145.26 ~—
86.16 185.7 youth,] 146.1 ~‸
86.18 185.9 lady!—] 146.3 ~!‸
86.18 185.10 not.] 146.4 ~!
86.20 185.12 wantoness] 146.6 wantonness
86.20 185.13 cruelty—] 146.6 ~;
86.21 185.13 me] 146.7 ~,
86.21 185.14 in] 146.8 at
86.23 185.17 Harding—] 146.10 ~!
86.24 186.1 Faber—] 146.12 ~,
86.25 186.2 thee. She] 146.13-14 ~" ¶ ~
86.26 186.3 his] 146.14 my
86.27 186.3 saint—] 146.15 ~,
86.29 186.6 he] 146.17 I
86.29 186.7-8 while he, standing above, muttered his] 146.18 while, standing above, I muttered my
86.32 186.12 entreated] 146.22-23 changed entirely the character of her prayer, and entreated

86.36 186.17-187.1 the eyes of the disappointed criminal was that of a hyena, robbed of his prey.
] 147.1-3 my eyes must have been that of the hyena robbed of his prey; could a look have blasted, she had been slain.

86.38 187.2 his] 147.4 my

87.1 187.3 he] 147.5 I

87.2 187.4 weapon] 147.6 dagger

87.3 187.5 blow] 147.7 stroke

87.3 187.6 unlooked for] 147.8 ~-~

87.4 187.7 his grasp, before his] 147.9 my grasp before my

87.5 187.8 his] 147.10 my

87.6 187.10-188.6 the prisoner. As they approached, he aimed the bloody dagger at his own bosom, but, at that instant, fear came over his heart—the fates had paralyzed him—he was a coward! he shrunk back from the stroke and the dagger fell from his hands. Without difficulty he was in a moment secured. Constance was but slightly wounded, yet happily, enough so, to be entirely ignorant of the horrors of the scene so malignantly forced upon her. In his cell, the wretch howled over the unperforming weakness of his hand, which had not only failed to secure him his victim, but had left him without the ability to defeat his doom.
] 147.12-148.8 me. That was the moment of trial; and, as they approached, I shouted my defiance to all their power, and aimed the bloody dagger at my own heart; but, at that moment, the pale spectre of Emily came before me—I felt her breath, like a cold wind, blighting and chilling me to the soul, while her finger, resting upon my hand, scorched it as if with all the accumulated fires of damnation. The fates paralyzed me at that instant. I was a coward! I shrank back from my own blow, and the dagger fell from my uplifted, but nerveless hands. They rushed upon me—they bound me down to the floor of my dungeon. I had no more strength—an infant might have fastened the shackles upon me, so completely had fate secured its victim. The dreadful spectre had de-

parted, and, when too late, recollecting how ably my will heretofore had controlled its presence, I howled, in the silence of my cell, over the unperforming weakness of my hand. That hand had doubly failed me, for Constance yet lived—she was but slightly wounded. I, too, survived—still survived to all the horrors of death, and of such a doom as that before me.

87. 188. * * * * * * * *] 149. CHAPTER XX.

87.23 188.7 come! O
] 149.1-5 come, and that mournful ghost is again before me. She points me to the scaffold, which rises dreadfully up before the barred window of my dungeon. They come—the stern guard, and the loathsome executioner. Oh,

87.26 188.8 I should fail at that moment of escape—
] 149.6-9 my own hand should fail me in that moment of release—of relief—that I should be unmanned at the very moment when I should most have been the man.

87.31 188.13 Emily,] 149.13 ~‸

87.33 188.15 intruders?—] 149.15 ~?‸

88.1 188.17-189.1 fellow creature] 149.17-18 ~-~

88.1 189.1 pleasure!] 149. 18 ~?

88.2 189.2 enjoyment!] 149.19 ~?

88.2 189.3 weak;] 149.20 ~,

88.5 189.7-8 There is an old man at the foot of the scaffold, that I would not see
] 150.2-3 Will no one drive that old man from the foot of the scaffold? I would not see him

88.7 189.10 gone—] 150.4 ~,

88.10 189.15 now] 150.9 ~,

88.11 189.15-16 come!—The
] 150.10-11 come! The choking, cold hand is about my throat—dark—dark. The

88.13 189.17 gone."] 150.12 ~.‸

CARL WERNER. AN IMAGINATIVE STORY.

After the publication of *Carl Werner . . . with Other Tales of Imagination* (probably in the late winter of 1838), Simms complained to his New York friend James Lawson in a letter of January 3, 1839: "Touching Carl Werner and the Poems [*Southern Passages and Pictures*] I lack all information. Whether they have been sold or not, been praised or blamed, is equally a thing unknown to me. The books have not yet reached our market" (*Letters*, I, 139). Although Simms continued to query Lawson about the critical reception (and possible sales) of *Carl Werner* in letters of March 30, June 18, and July 7, 1839 (see *Letters*, I, 141, 147, and 149), the book actually received rather prompt and favorable attention. The *New York Mirror* of December 22, 1838, for instance, called *Carl Werner* "by far the most attractive [work] that has been given the publick by Mr. Simms. There is more power and brilliancy, both of imagination and of language, in these brief romances, than we often find expended in a novel . . ." (XVI, 207). The *New York Review* of January, 1839, commented on *Carl Werner:* "We consider this work as among the most noticeable of the appearances of the current quarter. It is a production of no common order in the class of works to which it belongs" (VII, 267); and the *Boston Quarterly Review* of April, 1839, though registering disapproval of the author's "free use of the supernatural" and his introduction of "a little more German *diablerie* than comports with our taste," nevertheless stated that the "Tales are written with considerable power, and contain many passages of great beauty" (II, 261). But the review that apparently irked Simms (when he finally saw it) is the one in the *Knickerbocker* of January, 1839, which reads in part:

> These volumes, by Mr. SIMMS, contain several tales, after the German school, and are well worth perusal. 'Carl Werner' and 'Conrade Weickhoff' please us better than the rest, though we doubt not that with some, the tales founded on Indian traditions may be greater favorites. In this collection, the author seems to us to have had in his eye, as respects style and subject, BULWER's 'Pilgrims of the Rhine,' though he falls far below his model, in finish and effect. There is a peculiar manner, and a very careful elaboration, requisite to transfuse the German spirit into the English, and it is not a German castle nor a German heroine, that can insure a German tale. A thorough study of the language, an appreciation of the beauties of the German poets and novelists, a knowledge of the superstitions of the people, and of the traditions to which they have given rise, through

the medium of their native tongue; these are essential pre-requisites to the proper understanding of the character and peculiarities of the Germans. [XIII, 80]

In a letter of December 27, 1839, to Lawson, Simms claimed that the *Knickerbocker* had given "the performances of the most miserable pretenders" longer reviews and "larger commendation" than it had *Carl Werner* and other of his recent publications: "This, I do not complain of as a lack of friendship but as an act of injustice" (*Letters*, I, 156). Even years later Simms continued to feel that *Carl Werner* never received its due, either in criticism or in sales; in writing to E. A. Duyckinck on June 6, 1845, about the possibility of a volume "of a more imaginative character" to serve as a companion piece to *The Wigwam and the Cabin*, Simms complained about the untoward circumstances surrounding the publication of the *Carl Werner . . . with Other Tales of Imagination.* "These were put forth at a most unfortunate season," he wrote, "during the money pressure, and just as the public mind had been made eager & selfish in consequence of the Cheap Literature passion. I made nothing by the venture. Adlard [the publisher] had no facilities, and books of Tales at $2. when similar collections were selling at 12 or 25/100 were not to be thought of. A selection from these tales, with others not yet collected, would form a neat vol. for 37 or 50 and would, I think, sell. I am willing that you should propose these two volumes to W & P. [Wiley and Putnam] on terms the most favorable to them" (*Letters*, II, 66-67). As revealed in the Introduction (see above, pp. xi-xxiv), of course, Wiley and Putnam accepted *The Wigwam and the Cabin* but, like all other publishers, rejected the idea of a collection of "Carl Werner" and other "moral imaginative" tales. Never quickly or easily discouraged, Simms reminded Duyckinck on August 8, 1845, that *Carl Werner* "failed of circulation from the simple fact that it was an expensive book . . . just . . . when the great revolution in cheap literature had begun. I could wish that you would read these two volumes, which, it strikes me, contain as adequate proofs as I have ever shown, of the imaginative & inventive power" (*Letters*, II, 98). See also Simms's letter of December 6, 1846, to R. W. Griswold, in which the indefatigable Charlestonian classified "Carl Werner" among the "best specimens of my powers of creating & combining" (*Letters*, II, 224, quoted in part in the introduction to *Martin*

Faber, above, p. 569). Even as late as September 4, 1868, Simms was seeking a new publisher for "Carl Werner," perhaps as a separate book (letter to J. S. Redfield, *Letters*, V, 157).

If Simms was displeased with contemporary notices of *Carl Werner*, he would have discovered even less to please him in the book's subsequent reception. Devoting less than a paragraph to the "worthless" collection, Trent found it "hard to conceive" the object Simms "had in view, except to show that he had been reading translations from the German . . ." (p. 115). The only twentieth century scholar to give "Carl Werner" more than passing notice is J. Wesley Thomas, who includes it in his study of Simms's German sources, as a story in which "the German influence . . . is largely confined to mood and style":

> "Carl Werner" is a Faustian story dealing with the strife between the principles of hate and love for a man' soul. . . . Although the story obviously imitates the "German manner," it does not closely resemble any particular German tale. A possible source is suggested in the "Advertisement" to the collection in which "Carl Werner" appears: "The first story in this collection is founded upon a passage from an ancient monkish legend, which the lover of antiquarian lore will most probably remember." Simms's source may have been Hoffmann's *Die Elixiere des Teufels*, which had appeared in English translation as early as 1824. . . . The essentials of Simms's story—the struggle between good and evil forces for a man's soul, the two *Doppelgänger*, and the kindly priest—are all present in Hoffmann's story. The same elements, however, appear in Fouque's *Sintram*, a work which was also available to Simms in translation. The pact, which nearly causes the destruction of the hero, is, of course, reminiscent of the Faust legend. ["German Sources," pp. 132-133]

As the title-piece in a volume of tales which, according to Simms, "with, perhaps a single exception belong to the same moral imaginative class with the first," "Carl Werner, An Imaginative Story" in a sense stands at the head of this class of Simms's stories. Certainly it is not his best moral imaginative tale; but perhaps it illustrates best what Simms had in mind in using the term. To Simms a moral imaginative tale is not simply, or even necessarily, a story exploiting the supernatural; it may well be, as in "Carl Werner," a "form of allegory" celebrating the "strifes between the rival moral principles of good and evil." (Apparently to make his allegory clearer, Simms once considered changing the subtitle of "Carl Werner" to "the Good & Evil Genii"; see Textual Introduction, p. 658.)

Explanatory Notes

89.1-2 ancient monkish legend: Perhaps Hoffman's *Die Elixiere des Teufels* or Fouque's *Sintram.* For J. Wesley Thomas's theory, see immediately above.
92.18-19 'spirits from the vasty deep': *I Henry IV*, III, 1, 52.
116.8-9 This quotation has not been identified.
117.7 'tree of Knowledge, is not that of life;': *Paradise Lost*, IV, 221; IX, 751-752; IX, 848-849.
120.4 seventy times seventy times damned: Matt. 18:21-22. Could this be a compositorial error (for "seventy times seven") or is the misquotation intentional?
132.20-21 "Thou shalt earn thy bread in the sweat of thy face": Paraphrase of Gen. 3:19.

Textual Introduction

First published "Carl Werner. An Imaginative Story." in *Carl Werner, An Imaginative Story; with Other Tales of Imagination*, 2 vols. (New York: George Adlard, 1838), I, 1-89, "Carl Werner" has been republished only once, under the new title, *Matilda: or, The Spectre of the Castle. An Imaginative Story* (Boston: F. Gleason, 1846). Since Simms's name does not appear on the title page, and since he never mentions *Matilda*, there is a strong possibility that he did not know of its existence and that this separate edition was pirated.

The 1838 book version of "Carl Werner" is used as copy-text. Although there are a few substantive additions to the text (see especially those for the last two pages in the Table of Textual Variants) of *Matilda*, the editor has rejected them as unlikely, under the circumstances, to be authorial.

If Simms had been successful in finding a publisher for "Carl Werner" in 1868, the story apparently would have been re-titled "Carl Werner, or the Good and Evil Genii," as suggested in his letter of September 4 to Redfield (*Letters*, V, 157). In the same letter, Simms estimates the length of "Carl Werner" at "about 22000 words."

Table I: Emendations and Textual Notes

Listed here are all changes in the copy-text of "Carl Werner." The original reading appears to the left of the bracket, the emended Centennial edition reading to the right. Where no bracket appears the reading is the same in both texts and the refusal to emend is explained in parentheses. Where an explanation of the change is necessary it follows in parentheses.

93.29 living."] ~‸ (Double quotes are not used at the ends of other chapters.)
96.27 you. .] you.
99.25 her's] hers
100.30 con solation] consolation
102.4 of which] of that which (The omission of "that" from copy-text seems an inadvertent error by Simms or the compositor.)
104.7 befal] befall
104.26 They] "~
109.30 her's] hers
114.11 so] ~, (Although a space is left after "so" in copy-text, there is no punctuation. The space is not enough for a dash; the punctuation must be a comma or semicolon. A comma is selected as the more probable.)
119.20 presentments] presentiments
124.21 counsel."] ~'
128.11 Warner] Werner
130.3 If] "~
130.28 encounters] ~' (There is no punctuation after "encounters" in copy-text, though a single quote appears to have been pencilled or inked in. Cf. 131.14.)
131.14 love!'] ~‸ (There is a remote possibility that the single quote at the end of the paragraph was intended to go with the opening single quote at 130.28 to enclose a long indirect quotation.)
135.30 redeemed? (Simms possibly intended an exclamation point after "redeemed," but the question mark is almost equally appropriate.)

Table II: Textual Variants

Below is a list of the variants between "Carl Werner" (1838) and *Matilda* (1846).

From left to right the chart of variants has the following sequence:

LEFT MARGIN: Centennial edition key
FIRST READING: 1838
SECOND READING: 1846

89. [ix] ADVERTISEMENT] PREFACE
89.1 [ix].1 first story in this collection] [iii].1 following story
89.3 [ix].3-7 treatment of the subject is, however, entirely my own; and the circumstance in the history of the two young men, upon which the catastrophe depends, is too frequent among the thoughtless of every nation to make it the peculiar property of any.].3 management of the plot, however, belongs to me.
89.7 [ix].8 have also] [iii].4 have
89.8 [ix].9 though,] [iii].5 ~‸
89.15 [ix].18 entertain,] [iii].12-13 ~‸
89.15 [ix].18 promise,] [iii].13 ~‸
89.16 [ix].19-31 former. I trust, in what I have done, I will not be found to have trespassed beyond the limits of propriety. The other tales, with, perhaps, a single exception, belong to the same moral imaginative class with the first. They have been written at various periods in my brief career of authorship. Two of them, it may be well to state, were published with other titles than they bear in this collection. The change was made in consequence of my discovering subsequently that similar titles had been employed by other writers, which might, to the casual reader, suggest an idea of identity between them, which exists neither in the subject, nor the mode of treatment. They are only republished in this collection as they belong properly to the classification which distinguishes the work.] [iii].14 former.
90.1 1.1 "WITH] 7.1 '~

90.3 1.4 it?"] 7.2 ~'

90.6 1.8 uttered. We] 7.5-6 ~ ¶ ~

90.9 1.12 vista,] 7.8 ~‸

90.9 1.12 by the] 7.8 by

90.11 1.14-15 pursuit. The] 7.10-11 pursuit. ¶ The

90.14 2.3 "You <. . .> faith,] 7.13 '~‸

90.15 2.5 dreams?"] 7.14 ~'

90.17 2.7 felt,] 7.16 ~‸

90.20 2.12-13 "What <. . .> one?"] 7.19 '~'

90.21 2.14 "Elsewhere] 7.20 '~

90.24 2.19 credulity."] 8.2 ~'

90.25 2.20 "To] 8.3 '~

90.28 2.24 frequently,] 8.6 ~‸

90.36 3.9 place."] 8.13 ~'

91.1 3.10-11 "Ha <. . .> them."] 8.14-15 '~'

91.3 3.12 "Not so!"] 8.16 '~'

91.3 3.12 I replied, somewhat hastily; "I] 8.16 replied I somewhat hastily. 'I

91.7 3.18 memory] 8.20 the memory

91.8 3.20 think;] 8.21 ~,

91.9 3.21 boyhood] 8.22 my boyhood

91.9 3.21 will,] 8.22 ~‸

91.11 3.23 on his] 8.23 upon his

91.11 3.24 narratives] 8.24 narrative

91.12 3.25 marvellous] 8.24-25 marvelous

91.13 3.27 and,] 8.26 ~‸

91.14 4.1 tinct] 8.26 tint

91.15 4.2 which may, perhaps, be] 8.27 which may be, perhaps,

91.16 4.3 defence] 8.28 defiance

91.16 4.3 faith."] 8.28 ~'

91.19 4.7 us. The] 8.31-32 us. ¶ The

91.19 4.7 of evening] 8.32 of the evening

91.24 4.14 "I] 8.37 '~

91.30 4.22 indeed,] 8.42 ~‸

91.30 4.23 reverence;] 8.43 ~,

91.31 4.24 into] 8.43 in

91.34 5.1 childhood;] 9.2 ~,

92.3 5.10-11 believe;] 9.8 ~,

92.5 5.14 dreamed."] 9.10 ~'

92.6 5.15-16 "I <. . .> only," <. . .> "Why] 9.11 '~' ~ '~

92.13 5.25 injustice?"] 9.18 ~.'

92.14 5.26 "True] 9.19 '~

92.15 5.27 world;] 9.20 ~,

92.15 6.1 better,] 9.20 ~‸

92.16 6.1 later] 9.20 latter

92.19 6.7 them."] 9.24 ~'

92.20 6.8 "Who <. . .> that?" <. . .> "Who] 9.25 '~' ~ '~

92.21 6.10 occurred] 9.26 occured

92.27 6.17 now,] 9.31 ~‸

92.38 7.6 this;] 9.42 ~,

93.4 7.12 not."] 10.2 ~'

93.5 7.13 "The <. . .> one," <. . .> "which] 10.3 '~' ~ '~

93.10 7.20 recollection,] 10.7 ~‸

93.11 7.22 bend,] 10.9 ~‸

93.11 7.22 accumulated] 10.9 accumalated

93.17 8.2 left,] 10.13 ~‸

93.17 8.3 consort] 10.14 consert

93.18 8.4 over] 10.15 ~,

93.25 8.13 myself;] 10.21 ~,

93.26 8.16 the old] 10.22-23 the

93.29 8.20 living."] 10.25 ~'

93. 8. II.] 11. CHAPTER II.

93.30 8.21-22 "We are in Germany," <. . .> "of] 11.1 'We are now in Germany,' ~ '~

93.33 9.3 marvellous] 11.4 marvelous

93.34 9.4 faith;] 11.5 ~,

94.4 9.11 theirs;] 11.9 ~,

94.5 9.11 gentle-hearted] 11.10 gentle hearted

94.9 9.17 material;] 11.13 ~,

94.15 9.25 "It] 11.19 '~

94.23 10.9 been long since] 11.26 long since been

94.25 10.11 twenty-five] 11.28 ~‸~

94.25 10.12-13 twenty-one] 11.28 ~‸~

94.26 10.13 Matilda,] 11.29 ~‸

94.27 10.14 seventeen;] 11.30 ~,

94.30 10.19 anon. Herman] 12.2-3 ~ ¶ '~

94.31 10.20 good natured, laughing,] 12.3 ~-~, ~∧
94.34 10.25 rashness;] 12.6 ~,
95.4 11.9 "In] 12.14 '~
95.8 11.14 continually,] 12.17 ~∧
95.13 11.22 was,] 12.22 ~∧
95.17 11.27 too] 12.26 to
95.24 12.10 dreams;] 12.32 ~,
95.26 12.12 the effect] 12.34 effect
95.27 12.14 until,] 12.35 ~∧
95. 12. III.] 13. CHAPTER III.
95.32 12.20 "Between] 13.1 '~
95.35 13.1 both. Though] 13.3-4 ~ ¶ ~
96.7 13.11 reverse. Herman] 13.10-11 ~ ¶ ~
96.10 13.14-15 imaginings] 13.13 imaginations
96.13 13.18 or,] 13.15 ~∧
96.16 13.23 him. In] 13.19-20 ~ ¶ ~
96.18 13.25-26 follow—each—] 13.21 ~, ~,
96.19 13.27 opposition—] 13.22 ~;
96.19 14.1 other—] 13.22-23 ~;
96.20 14.2 governor,—] 13.23 ~,∧
96.21 14.4 alike. The] 13.24-25 ~ ¶ ~
96.25 14.9 beside—] 13.28 ~,
96. 14. IV.] 14. CHAPTER IV.
96.27 14.11 "Let] 14.1 Let
96.30 14.15 and,] 14.3 ~∧
96.31 14.16-17 proceed:—] 14.4 ~:∧
96.32 14.18 "Living, as they did,] 14.5 ∧~∧ ~∧
96.33 14.19 and,] 14.6 ~∧
97.2 15.2 gray] 14.9 grey
97.3 15.3 then—] 14.10 ~∧
97.5 15.6 more] 14.12 ~,
97.7 15.9 secret] 14.14 the secret
97.9 15.11 is,] 14.16 ~∧
97.11 15.15 are,] 14.18 ~∧
97.13 15.18 spirit—] 14.20 ~,
97.15 15.20 "The] 14.22 ∧~
97.15 15.20 peopled] 14.22 peopl ed
97.20 16.1 ruins—] 14.27 ~;

97.21 16.2 conjectures] 14.28 conjectnres

97.23 16.5 —and,] 14.30 ‸~‸

97.31 16.16 that,] 15.5 ~‸

97.34 16.20 which,] 15.8 ~‸

97.35 16.20 periods,] 15.8 ~‸

98.5 17.5 timidity—] 15.16 ~,

98.6 17.6 woman—] 15.17 ~,

98.9 17.11 for,] 15.19 ~‸

98.10 17.12 favorable] 15.20 favorite

98. 17. V.] 15. CHAPTER V.

98.15 17.18 "One] 15.25 ONE

98.16 17.19 marriage,] 15.25 ~‸

98.22 18.5 Thus,] 15.32 ~‸

98.25 18.10 the old] 15.35 he old

98.26 18.10 and,] 15.35 ~‸

98.31 18.17 "But] 16.5 ‸~

99.1 18.23 " 'It] 16.9 '~

99.3 18.26 no] 16.11 ne

99.3 18.27 it—] 16.11 ~,

99.5 19.1 " 'Leave] 16.12 '~

99.6 19.2 " 'Leave] 16.13 '~

99.7 19.3 " 'Ay] 16.14 '~

99.10 19.8 " 'And] 16.17 '~

99.11 19.9 eyes.] 16.18 ~'

99.12 19.10 " 'Pshaw] 16.19 '~

99.16 19.15-16 afraid to leave you to his] 16.22-23 afraid to his

99.17 19.17 " 'Dear] 16.24 '~

99.19 19.19 " 'I] 16.26 '~

99.25 19.27 "The] 16.31 '~

99.29 20.5 " 'To-morrow] 16.34 '~

99.30 20.7 " 'To-morrow] 16.35 '~

99.32 20.9 " 'So] 16.36 '~

99.33 20.10 " 'Ay] 16.37 '~

99.37 20.16 if I] 16.41 I

100.3 20.21 fellow—] 16.44 ~,

100.3 20.22 'Tilda—] 17.1 ~,

100.4 20.23 But, <. . .> mind—] 17.1 ~‸ ~,

100.5 20.25 share—] 17.2 ~,

100.5 20.25 So,] 17.3 ~∧
100.6 20.26 loved—] 17.3 ~,
100.8 21.3 "This] 17.5 ∧~
100.12 21.8-9 severely] 17.8-9 seversly
100.13 21.11 returned] 17.10 retured
100. 21. VI.] 17. CHAPTER VI.
100.15 21.12 "You] 17.11 '~
100.16 21.13 Matilda;] 17.11 ~,
100.20 21.19 maiden] 17.16 maid
100.24 22.2 one—] 17.19 ~,
100.25 22.2-3 hitherto—] 17.20 ~,
100.26 22.4 it. Carl] 17.21-22 ~ ¶ ~
100.28 22.6 him—] 17.23 ~,
101.9 23.2 a moody] 18.4 moody
101.10 23.4 "'I] 18.6 '~
101.13 23.9 so— <. . .> will—] 18.9 ~, ~,
101.15 23.11 "'Pshaw] 18.11 '~
101.15 23.11 Herman—] 18.11 ~,
101.18 23.16 "'I do—I confess it!—they] 18.14 'I do, I freely confess it. They
101.20 23.18 "'And] 18.16 '~
101.21 23.20 recollections.'] 18.17 ~.'
101.22 23.21 "'Ay] 18.18 '~
101.24 23.24-25 "Carl <. . .> vault,] 18.20 '~∧
101.28 24.3 "'You] 18.24 '~
101.32 24.9 "'Perhaps'—] 18.28 '~,'∧
101.35 24.14 "'Why] 18.31 '~
101.35 24.15 —a] 18.31 A
101.37 24.17 mind] 18.33 miud
101.37 24.18 ingenious—] 18.33 ~;
102.1 24.20 magic—] 18.35 ~,
102.1 24.21 subtlety—] 18.35 ~,
102.3 24.22 spells,] 18.36 ~∧
102.11 25.7 myself—] 18.44 ~,
102.14 25.11-12 "'True <. . .> on—] 19.1 '~;
102.15 25.12 though] 19.1 tho'
102.16 25.13 "'I] 19.3 '~
102.24 25.24 "'How] 19.10 '~

102.24 25.24 when,] 19.10 ~∧
102.24 25.25 breath,] 19.10 ~∧
102.26 26.1 "'Oh <. . .> *to you*] 19.12 '~ to you
102.26 26.2 Herman—] 19.12 ~;
102.31 26.8 "'I] 19.16 '~
102.34 26.12 years,—] 19.19 ~;
102.36 26.15 "'Do] 19.21 '~
102.36 26.15 him—] 19.21 ~;
103.1 26.17 "'Yet,] 19.23 '~∧
103.3 26.20 yet,] 19.25 ~∧
103.4 26.22 "'What] 19.26 '~
103.4 26.22 reason!] 19.26 ~,
103.5 26.24 sees—] 19.27 ~,
103.7 26.27 sympathy,] 19.29 ~∧
103.16 27.11 "'Could] 19.37 '~
103.18 27.13 "'The] 19.39 '~
103.20 27.16 not?] 19.41 ~'
103.21 27.17 is,] 19.42 ~∧
103.21 27.18 cannot.] 19.42 ~,
103.24 27.22 "'Herman] 20.1 '~
103.25 27.23 cannot.] 20.1 ~∧
103.29 28.3 "'Ah] 20.6 '~
103.29 28.3 that, Carl;] 20.6 ~∧ ~,
103.31 28.5-6 shall we] 20.7 we shall
103.31 28.6 to-night] 20.8 to night
103.32 28.7 death,] 20.9 ~∧
103.33 28.8 "'Will] 20.10 '~
103.35 28.10 "'Ay] 20.12 '~
103.35 28.10 will I] 20.12 I will
104.1 28.15 "'Glad] 20.15 '~
104.7 28.23 any thing] 20.20 anything
104.12 29.3 "'I] 20.25 '~
104.13 29.5 "'Seriously] 20.26 '~
104.14 29.6 "'Seriously] 20.27 '~
104.14 29.6 other;] 20.27 ~,
104.17 29.10 for,] 20.29 ~∧
104.18 29.11-12 from earth] 20.30-31 from the earth
104.19 29.13 you,] 20.32 ~∧

104.21 29.16 brother,] 20.34 ~‸

104.22 29.17 after death] 20.34-35 ~. ~

104.23 29.18 "'It] 20.36 '~

104.23 29.19 answer;] 20.36 ~,

104.24 29.20 laugh] 20.37 langh

104. 29. VII.] 21. CHAPTER VII.

104.28 30.1 leapt] 21.2 leaped

104.28 30.2 had been] 21.3 was

104.33 30.9 "'Why] 21.8 '~

105.3 30.14 "'Look] 21.11 '~

105.5 30.17 "The] 21.13 ‸~

105.13 31.1 "'What] 21.20 '~

105.13 31.1 it that] 21.20 that

105.13 31.1 nothing,] 21.20 ~.

105.14 31.3 "'A <. . .> small,] 21.21 '~‸

105.16 31.6 "'Some] 21.23 '~

105.16 31.6 Herman, 'though] 21.23 ~. 'Though

105.17 31.8 "'Strange] 21. 25 '~

105.17 31.9 Herman?'] 21.25 ~.‸

105.18 31.10 "'Yes] 21.26 '~

105.20 31.13 look in] 21.28 look to

105.22 31.15 "Carl] 21.29 ‸~

105.26 31.20-21 'point the moral,'] 22.3-4 " ~ "

105.27 31.21-22 'adorn, the tale.'] 22.4 "~‸~~"

105.31 31.27 found] 22.8 they found

105.32 32.2 Carl. After] 22.9-10 ~ ¶ ~

105.35 32.6 purpose. The] 22.12-13 ~ ¶ ~

105.36 32.8 road;] 22.14 ~,

106. 32. VIII.] 22. CHAPTER VIII.

106.6 32.17 "At] 22.21 ‸~

106.7 32.19 man;] 22.22 ~,

106.14 33.6 condition.] 22.29 ~‸

106.17 33.9 fabrics] 22.31 ~,

106.20 33.13 less true than strange] 22.33-23.1 less strange than true

106.21 33.15 for as many years before, <. . .> and,] 23.2 for many years before‸~‸

106.22 33.16 truth,] 23.3 ~‸

106.22 33.16 custom. For] 23.3-4 ~ ¶ ~
106.25 33.19 time,] 23.6 ~‸
106.25 33.20 single visit] 23.6 visit
106.26 33.21 over,] 23.7 ~‸
106.30 33.26 "Perhaps, indeed,] 23.10 ‸~, ~‸
106.35 34.6 class,] 23.15 ~‸
107.2 34.8 the true] 23.16 true
107.2 34.9 composition] 23.17 compisition
107.6 34.13-14 appealing;] 23.20 ~,
107.10 34.20 practised] 23.24 practiced
107.11 34.21 influence;] 23.25 ~,
107.13 34.24 giving continual] 23.26-27 giving a continual
107.16 35.1 "Herman] 23.29 ‸~
107.20 35.7 Herman;] 23.33 ~,
107.24 35.11 " 'Besides,] 23.36 '~‸
107.25 35.13 commonly; <. . .> comes,] 23.37 ~, ~‸
107.28 35.17 " 'But] 23.40 '~
107.29 35.18 "That] 23.41 ‸~
108.2 36.5 while,] 24.6 ~‸
108.5 36.11 pale,] 24.10 ~‸
108.6 36.12 death,] 24.10 ~‸
108.6 36.12 but too] 24.11 too
108. 36. IX.] 24. CHAPTER IX.
108.8 36.14 "One] 25.1 ‸~
108.13 36.21 among tombs] 25.5 among the tombs
108.22 37.10 " 'I] 25.14 '~
108.23 37.12 "Strange] 25.15 ‸~
108.25 37.15 moment's] 25.17 moments
108.25 37.15 pause—] 25.17 pause——
108.26 37.16 " 'Indeed] 25.18 '~
108.27 37.17 "A] 25.19 '~
108.28 37.18 Carl] 25.19 ~,
108.29 37.19 " 'Had] 25.21 '~
108.32 37.24 deeply;] 25.24 ~,
109.3 38.5 seem] 26.2 seem to be
109.4 38.6 progress,] 26.3 ~‸
109.4 38.7 mantle,] 26.4 ~‸
109.9 38.12 " 'That] 26.8 '~

109.12 38.16 "The] 26.11 '~

109.14 38.18 them,] 26.12 ~‸

109.14 38.19 to expand] 26.13 expand

109.16 38.21 "'It] 26.15 '~

109.17 38.22 "'I] 26.16 '~

109.18 38.23 "'Indeed] 26.17 '~

109.18 38.23 on my cheek!] 26.17 upon my cheek.

109.19 38.24 "The] 26.18 ‸~

109.21 38.27 screamed in] 26.19 screamed

109.22 39.1 "'Father] 26.21 '~

109.24 39.4 "'Say] 26.23 '~

109.26 39.7 they,] 26.25 ~‸

109. 39. X.] 27. CHAPTER X.

109.31 39.14 "They] 27.1 ‸~

109.32 39.15 was upon] 27.1 was on

110.4 40.1-2 it. Supper] 27.8-9 ~ ¶ ~

110.4 40.2 and,] 27.9 ~‸

110.10 40.11 chamber— <. . .> so—] 27.15 ~, ~,

110.11 40.12-13 and he wished to soothe them—but he could] 27.15-16 and he could

110.12 40.14 abroad—] 27.16 ~,

110.21 40.25 "The] 27.24 '~

110.24 41.3 complete—] 27.27 camplete;

110.26 41.6 fabric—] 27.29 ~,

110.28 41.7 wrought,] 28.1 ~‸

110.38 41.22 always—] 28.11 ~,

111.1 41.24 species—] 28.12 ~,

111.3 41.26 "'Herman] 28.14 '~

111.6 42.3 soul—] 28.17 ~,

111.7 42.4 death—] 28.17 ~;

111.8 42.5 "Again] 28.19 ‸~

111.17 42.17 speak—] 28.27 ~,

111.19 42.20 unearthly] 28.29 earthly

111.20 42.21 it—] 28.29 ~,

111.20 42.21-22 hate—] 28.29 ~,

111.21 42.23 "'Her] 28.31 '~

111.23 42.25-26 "'Ha, ha, ha!' The vaulted abbey rang with the echoes of that infernal laugh.] 28.32-33 <omitted>

111.25 42.27 "'Mercy] 28.33 '~
111. 43. XI.] 29. CHAPTER XI.
111.30 43.6 "When] 29.1 ‸~
112.1 43.15 abbey] 29.7 Abbey
112.4 43.18 "'Hallo] 29.9 '~
112.5 43.19 song—] 29.10 ~,
112.6 43.21 "And] 29.11 '~
112.17 44.12 what,—] 29.21 ~,‸
112.17 44.13 case,—] 29.21 ~,‸
112.19 44.16 pursue] 29.23 pursne
112. 45. XII.] 30. CHAPTER XII.
112.27 45.1 "It] 30.4 ‸~
112.32 45.8 was,] 30.8 ~‸
113.3 45.15 "'What] 30.13 '~
113.5 45.18 "'Nothing] 30.15 '~
113.6 45.20 "'It] 30.16 '~
113.7 45.22 wild—] 30.17 ~,
113.8 45.22-23 me, tell me] 30.17 me,
113.8 45.23 you.] 30.18 ~?
113.9 46.1 "'Nothing <. . .> replied—] 30.19 '~,
113.12 46.5 "He] 30.22 ‸~
113.14 46.8 which,] 30.24 ~‸
113.16 46.11 brought] 30.26 bought
113.18 46.13-14 places. He gave up the effort in despair.] 30.27 places.
113.22 46.18 fitful—] 30.30 ~,
113.29 47.2 even] 31.3 ever
113.34 47.8 "'Trouble] 31.8 '~
114.1 47.13 "She] 31.12 '~
114.9 47.24 him—] 31.18 ~,
114.18 48.9-12 "'To the abbey! to the abbey! I will speak—I will demand its meaning. I will know and hear all. If it be Herman, in truth—my brother and my friend—'] 31.25-26 <omitted>
114.21 48.13 "'Ha] 31.26 '~
114.22 48.14 "The] 31.27 ‸~
114.22 48.15 desperation] 31.27 desparation
114.23 48.15 behold—] 31.27-28 ~,

114.24 48.17 otherwise—] 31.29 ~,
114.27 48.21 fat,] 31.32 ~∧
114.32 49.1 prevailing] 31.36 prevaling
114.32 49.1-2 That, certainly,] 31.36-37 ~∧ ~∧
114.35 49.5-6 conviction. This] 31.39-40 ~ ¶ ~
114.37 49.8 that which] 31.41 that
115.1 49.10 cunning,] 31.42-32.1 ~∧
115.2 49.12 conviction. 'It] 32.1-2 ~ ¶ ~
115.3 49.13 "'To] 32.3 '~
115.5 49.17 his] 32.5 hs
115.6 49.18 in the one] 32.6 in one
115.6 49.18 and—] 32.6 ~∧
115.8 49.20 "Carl] 32.8 ∧~
115.10 49.23 and] 32.10 had
115.16 50.3 "'Wine <. . . > he—] 32.15 '~,
115.17 50.4 "'How] 32.16 '~
115.19 50.6 "'Damn <. . .> other—] 32.18 '~.
115.22 50.10 "'What] 32.20 '~
115.23 50.11 "'Oh] 32.21 '~
115.23 50.11 regretting] 32.21 regreting
115.24 50.13 indifferent] 32.22 innifferent
115.29 50.20 that it] 32.26 that
115.31 50.22 would be only] 32.28 would only be
115.32 50.24 "'I] 32.30 '~
115.33 50.26 of knowing] 32.31 knowing
115.35 51.1 "'You] 32.33 '~
115.38 51.5 "'Nay] 32.36 '~
116.1 51.6 "'Can't] 32.37 '~
116.1 51.7 other,] 32.37 ~∧
116.2 51.7 Excuse] 32.37-38 Excnse
116.2 51.8 man.'] 32.38 ~∧
116.2 51.8 And as] 32.38 As
116.6 51.14 he never] 33.2 he had never
116.9 51.16 man—] 33.4 ~.
116.10 51.17 and he] 33.5 and be
116.11 51.18 "'Why <. . .> other,] 33.6 '~.
116.12 51.20 wine,] 33.7 ~∧
116.13 51.21 story—] 33.7 ~.

116.14 51.22 "'Good] 33.8 '~

116.15 51.24 "'Ay] 33.9 '~

116.17 52.1 "'Have you,] 33.11 '~‸

116.19 52.3 "'Ay <. . .> and,] 33.12 '~‸

116.22 52.7 "Carl] 33.15 ‸~

116.28 52.15 "'Not] 33.20 '~

116.30 52.17-18 companion,] 33.21 ~‸

116. 52. XIII.] 34. CHAPTER XIII.

116.31 52.19 "A] 34.1 ‸~

116.31 52.19 seemed to be] 34.1 seemed

116.32 52.21-22 compassing and controlling] 34.2 compassed and controlled

117.4 53.5 Knowledge] 34.7 Konwledge

117.5 53.8 has] 34.8 had

117.7 53.10 the 'tree of knowledge, is not that of life;'] 34.10 "the tree of knowledge is not that of life,"

117.8 53.12 happiness;] 34.11 ~,

117.9 53.13 the imagination] 34.12 of imagination

117.14 53.19 "'I] 34.16 ‸~

117.17 53.23 "What] 34.19 '~

117.18 53.25 from him] 34.20 him from

117.19 53.26 Carl,] 34.21 ~‸

117.21 54.2 dwelling-place] 34.23 ~‸~

117.24 54.5 "He] 34.25 ‸~

117.27 54.9 curdle] 34.28 cnrdle

117.29 54.12 round] 34.29 rouud

117.31 54.15 "'Why] 37.3 '~

117.33 54.17 me!'] 37.4~.‸

117.34 54.18 "As] 37.5 ‸~

118.1 54.24-25 successfully] 37.9 successively

118.3 54.27 preceding] 37.11 preceeding

118.4 55.2 it,] 37.12 ~‸

118.6 55.5 indeed;] 37.14 ~,

118.7 55.5 but,] 37.15 ~‸

118.9 55.9 heretofore,] 37.17 ~‸

118.10 55.10 darkened.] 37.18 ~,

118.12 55.12 resolve,] 37.19 ~‸

118.12 55.13 built] 37.19 bullt

118.14 55.16 basilisk,] 37.22 ~.
118.17 55.20 while] 37.24 whlle
118.19 55.22 " 'What <. . .> screamed,] 37.26 '~∧
118.22 55.26 shivered] 37.28-29 shiver- | ered
118.24 56.1 " 'Who] 37.31 '~
118.27 56.5 " 'Herman] 37.34 '~
118.27 56.6 pray'dst] 37.34 prayd'st
118.28 56.7 not] 37.35 now
118.29 56.8 "Such] 37.36 ∧~
118.30 56.9 summoned.] 37.36-37 ~.'
118.31 56.10 " 'Thou <. . .> Carl, boldly. 'I] 37.38 '~ boldly. I
118.32 56.12 " 'Thou] 37.39 '~
118.33 56.13 prayer] 37.40 prayers
118.33 56.13 granted.] 37.40 granted thee.
118.33 56.14 no] 37.40 now
118.35 56.15 " 'I] 37.42 '~
118.37 56.18 should] 37.44 sholud
118.38 56.19 thou—] 37.44 thou——
119.1 56.20 " 'Art] 38.1 '~
119.6 56.27 " 'I] 38.6 '~
119.7 57.1 " 'Thou] 38.7 '~
119.12 57.7 " 'Not] 38.11 '~
119.15 57.11 couldst] 38.13 could'st
119.15 57.11 have been] 38.13-14 have
119.18 57.15 " 'Thou <. . .> child,] 38.17 '~∧
119.26 57.26 " 'Then] 38.24 '~
119.26 57.26 canst] 38.24 can'st
119.28 58.1 " 'Yes] 38.26 '~
119.31 58.5 replied. Carl] 38.28-30 ~ ¶ ~
119.34 58.9 conceived. He] 38.32-33 ~ ¶ ~
119.37 58.13 " 'Yet] 38.36 '~
120.1 58.16 " 'Thou] 38.38 '~
120.1 58.17 a hellish] 38.38 of hellish
120.2 58.18 and to] 38.39 and
120.4 58.20 seventy times] 38.40 seventy
120.6 58.22 "He] 38.42 ∧~
120.8 58.25 diety. Carl] 38.44-39.1 ~ ¶ ~
120.11 59.3 "I] 39.4 '~

120.12 59.4-5 while he continued] 39.5 which
120.14 59.7 is dead] 39.6 dead
120.15 59.8 "'Thou] 39.7 '~
120.17 59.11 not thou] 39.9 thou not
120.18 59.12 so desire] 39.9 desire
120.21 59.16 which made] 39.12 which has made
120.23 59.19 Is it happiness to thee no longer?] 39.14 <omitted>
120.23 59.20 its] 39.14 thy
120.24 59.20 Carl,] 39.14 ~‸
120.25 59.22 net-work] 39.16 net work
120.28 59.26 "'Fiend] 39.18 '~
120.32 60.4 monster,] 39.21 ~‸
120.33 60.6 throat!] 39.22 ~,
120.35 60.8 "'Ha] 39.24 '~
120.36 60.9 words. The] 39.25-26 ~ ¶ ~
120.38 60.12 upon] 39.28 upou
121.5 60.19 body;] 39.32 ~,
121.7 60.22 at all] 39.33 all
121. 60. XIV.] 40. CHAPTER XIV.
121.8 60.23 "To] 40.1 ‸~
121.10 61.1 in] 40.2 of
121.20 61.15 predicted,] 40.11 ~‸
121.23 61.19 would be] 40.14 would
121.28 62.1 reveal,] 40.19 ~‸
122.1 62.12 torture;] 41.4 ~,
122.9 62.21 "'In] 41.11 '~
122.11 62.23 "Such] 41.13 ‸~
122.18 63.6 vainly] 41.19 vain
122.22 63.11 which was] 41.23 that was
122.22 63.12 were in] 41.23 were
122.25 63.15 "'Where] 41.26 '~
122.26 63.17 and] 41.27 aud
122.30 63.22 "'Nay] 41.31 '~
122.35 64.3 "'What] 41.36 '~
122.35 64.4 but] 41.36 bnt
122.37 64.5 "'Ask] 41.38 '~
123.1 64.8 door,] 41.40 ~‸

123.5 64.13 body. While] 41.43-44 ~ ¶ ~

123.8 64.17 and, turning,] 42.2 ~∧ ~∧

123.11 64.21 seen. His] 42.5-6 ~ ¶ ~

123.11 64.21 long] 42.6 very long

123.12 64.23 hair,] 42.7 ~∧

123.14 64.25 shoulders. It] 42.9-10 ~ ¶ ~

123.14 64.26 very great] 42.10 great

123.18 65.4 probably contained] 42.13 contained

123.19 65.4-5 raiment—] 42.14 ~,

123.23 65.11 "'Daughter] 42.18 '~

123.25 65.14 "The] 42.20 ∧~

123.29 65.19 respect—] 42.23 ~,

123.30 65.21 awe—] 42.24 ~,

123.31 65.22 door—] 42.25 ~,

123.32 65.24 sight—] 42.27 ~,

124.3 66.9 "'Daughter <. . .> weep—] 42.34 '~,

124.3 66.10 it—] 42.34 ~,

124.4 66.10 sorrow.] 42.34-35 ~?

124.5 66.11 "'Alas] 42.36 '~

124.7 66.13 "'True <. . .> child—] 42.37 '~,

124.11 66.18 untried] 42.40 united

124.16 66.26 daughter—] 43.4 ~,

124.21 67.5 counsel."] 43.8 ~.'

124.21 65.5-6 <no chapter division>] 43.8-44.1 CHAPTER XV.

124.22 67.6 "'I] 44.1 '~

124.24 67.8 "'You] 44.3 '~

124.25 67.9 "'I] 44.4 '~

124.27 67.11 mind,] 44.5 ~∧

124.31 67.18 him—] 44.10 ~;

124.32 67.18 if with] 44.10 if

124.32 67.19 fright—] 44.10 ~;

124.35 67.22 "'And] 44.13 'Add

124.37 67.24 "'But] 44.15 '~

125.3 68.3 "'But] 44.19 '~

125.5 68.5 "'None, father—] 44.21 '~,

125.6 68.7 thoughts,—] 44.22 ~;

125.9 68.10 "'You] 44.25 '~

125.10 68.11 thought—] 44.26 ~.

125.12 68.14 or,] 44.28 ~∧

125.14 68.16 "'Oh <. . .> father—] 45.1 '~,

125.15 68.17 being] 45.1-2 beings

125.15 68.18 village—] 45.2 ~,

125.17 68.20 "'That] 45.4 '~

125.18 68.21 self—] 45.5 ~,

125.21 68.26 "Matilda] 45.8 ∧~

125.25 69.4 "'It] 45.12 '~

125.25 69.4-5 sudden,] 45.12 ~∧

125.29 69.9 "'Yes, father,—] 45.15 '~;

125.32 69.13 "'To] 45.18 '~

125.36 69.19 "'I have,] 45.22 '~∧

125.37 69.21 "'You] 45.23 '~

126.3 69.27 "'Of] 45.27 '~

126.4 70.1 "'Then] 45.28 '~

126.13 70.14 than that] 45.37 than

126.15 70.16 daughter;] 45.38 ~?

126.16 70.18 himself.'] 45.39 ~∧

126.17 70.19 "'I] 45.40 '~

126.21 70.25 "'I <. . .> father—] 46.1 '~,

126.21 70.26 do—how work—] 46.1 ~, ~,

126.22 70.26 say.] 46.2 ~?

126.23 70.27 "'Love] 46.3 '~

126.29 71.8 forth] 46.9 forth from home

126.33 71.13 "It] 46.12 ∧~

127.7 72.1 "'Do] 46.22 '~

127.7 72.1 'while] 46.22 ∧~

127.8 72.3 "'You!'—she said—] 46.23 '~∧ she said,

127.10 72.6 "He rose,] 46.25 ∧~∧

127.13 72.10 "'But] 46.28 '~

127.14 72.12 "He] 46.29 ∧~

127. 72. XV.] 47. CHAPTER XVI.

127.18 72.18 "Meanwhile] 47.1 ∧~

127.19 72.19 upon] 47.2 after

127.21 72.22 abbey.] 47.3 ~∧

128.4 73.23 "This] 47.20 ∧~

128.6 73.26 peace—] 47.22 ~,

128.11 74.6 Warner] 48.1 Werner
128.14 74.10 "We] 48.4 ‸~
129. 75. XVI.] 49. CHAPTER XVII.
129.1 75.14 "Carl] 49.1 ‸~
129.4 75.18 him with] 49.3 him
129.6 75.21 "'Be <. . .> cry—] 49.5 '~;
129.8 76.2 companion.'] 49.7 ~‸
129.9 76.3 "Carl] 49.8 ‸~
129.17 76.14 looked] 49.15 look
129.18 76.16 these,] 49.16 ~‸
129.21 76.20 and] 49.19 aud
129.23 76.23 tavern—] 49.21 ~;
129.24 76.25 of—] 49.22 ~;
129.31 77.6 "'Matilda <. . .> Carl—] 50.1 '~,
129.33 77.8 "The] 50.3 ‸~
129.33 77.8 setting] 50.3 sitting
130.1 77.13 "'Matilda—my wife—] 50.7 '~, ~,
130.1 77.13-14 exclaimed—'Yes—] 50.7 ~. ~,
130.7 77.20 fled. Carl] 50.12-13 ~ ¶ ~
130. 78. XVII.] 51. CHAPTER XVII.
130.15 78.4 "Carl] 51.1 '~
130.20 78.12 seemed so] 51.6 seemed to be so
130.20 78.12 laws] 51.6 ~,
130.23 78.15 experience.] 51.8 ~.—
130.28 78.22 'various] 51.13 "~
130.32 79.5 principle] 51.17 principles
131.3 79.13 increased] 51.22 incressed
131.10 79.22 for] 52.1 ~,
131.11 79.24 us,] 52.2 ~‸
131.12 79.26 faithlessness of] 52.3 faithlessnesss to
131.14 80.2 love!'] 52.5 ~."
131.15 80.3 "This] 52.6 ‸~
131.16 80.5 calmer] 52.7 ~,
131.18 80.7 retired;] 52.9 ~:
131.22 80.13 alone;] 52.12 ~,
131.28 80.21 "The] 52.18 ‸~
131.30 80.23 "'My <. . .> he said] 52.20 '~ said he
131.36 81.5 relief— <. . .> happy—] 52.26 ~, ~,

132.3 81.12 healing.] 52.30 ~.—

132.5 81.14 that he] 52.32 he

132.10 81.21 "That] 52.36 ‸~

132.11 81.22 effect] 52.36 effects

132.15 82.1 " 'My son,' he said] 52.41 '~ said he

132.20 82.7-8 elements] 53.1 elemeuts

132.20 82.8-9 "Thou <. . .> face."] 53.1-2'~'

132.24 82.13 " 'Alas <. . .> father—] 53.5 '~,

132.26 82.16 " 'Hast <. . .> son.] 53.7 '~?

132.27 82.17 " 'Of] 53.8 '~

132.28 82.19 " 'The] 53.9 '~

132.33 83.1 son—] 53.14 ~;

132.36 83.3 "Carl] 53.16 '~

132.36 83.4 though] 53.16 thongh

133.13 83.24 him,] 53.30 ~‸

133.18 84.3 "Much] 53.34 '~

133.21 84.7 pale—] 53.37 ~‸

133.22 84.8 it—] 53.37 ~,

133.22 84.9 tears—] 53.38 ~,

133.24 84.12 a flood of tears—] 53.40 tears,

133.25 84.13 table—] 53.40 ~,

133.27 84.16 himself! He] 53.42-54.1 ~!—he

133.28 84.18 sufferings only,] 54.1 sufferings

133.29 84.18 had given neither] 54.1 had no

133.30 84.20 muttered] 54.3 mnttered

133.31 84.22 come,] 54.4 ~‸

133.35 84.27 task.] 54.7 ~.—

134.5 85.11 fountain—] 54.14 ~,

134. 85. XVIII.] 55. CHAPTER XVIII

134.7 85.14 "He] 55.1 '~

134.7 85.14 tap] 55.1 gentle tap

134.8 85.16 trembled—] 55.2 ~;

134.10 85.18 " 'It is he—the demon—] 55.4 '~! ~!

134.10 85.18 spectre!'] 55.4 ~‸

134.10 85.18-19 he exclaimed,] 55.4 exclaimed the frightened Carl,

134.11 85.20 " 'Bid] 55.6 '~

134.12 85.21 apartment] 55.6 ~,

134.13 86.1-3 narrative— ¶ " 'Bid] 55.8 ~. '~

134.16 86.4 "But] 55.10 '~

134.18 86.6 " 'I <. . .> exclaimed—] 55.12 '~;

134.19 86.7 If] 55.12 '~

134.19 86.8-9 be other than his, it] 55.13-14 be the spirit of another, he surely

134.20 86.9 me—] 55.14 me and protect me;

134.21 86.11 "The] 55.16 '~

134.23 86.13 " 'Daughter] 55.18 '~

134.24 86.14 "She] 55.19 '~

134.27 86.18 rose] 55.22 arose

134.28 86.19 " 'No, Matilda—] 55.23 '~;

134.29 86.20 before—] 55.24 ~;

134.30 86.21 fear—] 55.24 ~,

134.30 86.22 upon, <. . .> for,] 55.25 ~‸ ~‸

134.31 86.23 "A] 55.26 '~

134.32 86.24 him. He] 56.1 ~; he

134.34 86.27-87.1 " 'The <. . .> redeemer. He] 56.3 '~; he

135.4 87.6 "With] 56.7 '~

135.5 87.7 and though] 56.7 and although

135.6 87.9 distinct—] 56.9 ~.

135.7 87.10 " 'Enter— <. . .> will—] 56.10 '~! ~,

135. 87. XIX.] 57. CHAPTER XIX.

135.8 87.11 "The] 57.1 ‸~

135.8 87.12 him—] 57.1 ~;

135.14 87.19 whole] 57.7 whols

135.16 87.22 gone.] 57.8-9 gone. It was, indeed, a diabolical countenance.

135.17 88.1 " 'Thou here!'] 57.10 'Art thou here! Thou canst not save him!'

135.18 88.3 " 'Thou] 57.12 '~

135.19 88.4 " 'I <. . .> vain—] 57.13 '~;

135.20 88.5 nothing—] 57.13 ~;

135.20 88.6 to] 57.14 t

135.21 88.7 escape—] 57.15 ~;

135.21 88.7-8 where I will;] 57.15 when and where it be my pleasure;

135.22 88.8 forbears to come—when,] 57.16 dares forbears to come; when

135.22 88.9 presumes] 57.16-17 presumes for a moment
135.24 88.11 thy] 57.18 the
135.26 88.13 "Carl] 57.20 '~
135.27 88.14 forward. At] 57.21-22 ~ ¶ ~
135.27 88.15 spoke—] 57.22 ~:
135.28 88.16 " 'His <. . .> fulfilled—] 57.23 '~!
135.28 88.17 thee.] 57.23 thee, fiend!
135.29 88.18 messenger comes] 57.24 divine messenger comes now
135.30 88.19 thrall of hate.] 57.25 terrible thrall of hate!
135.30 88.19 Look!—the] 57.25 Behold our triumph! the
135.31 88.21 "As he spoke,] 58.1 ^~^
135.33 88.24 him. There] 58.3-4 ~ ¶ ~
135.35 88.27 wear in life.] 58.5-6 wear when among the living.
135.35 88.27 life. The] 58.6-7 living. ¶ ~
136.1 89.2 features] 58.8 form and features
136.3 89.4 punishment—] 58.9 ~;
136.6 89.7 "The] 58.12 ^~
136.6 89.7 of agony] 58.12 of extreme agony
136.7 89.8 as,] 58.13 ~^
136.7 89.8 howl and] 58.13 terrific howl and a
136.8 89.9 spectre] 58.14 ~,
136.9 89.11 could not] 58.15 had not the power to
136.9 89.12 withstand. Howling with hate,] 58.15-16 withstand; howling with rage,
136.10 89.12 hate, he fled;] 58.16-17 hate and disappointment, the spirit from pandemonium vanished from their sight;
136.10 39.13 gentle spirit] 58.17 heavenly spectre
136.12 89.14 " 'Oh] 58.19 '~
136.12 89.14 Herman!' cried] 58.19 brother!' exclaimed
136.14 89.17 embraced] 58.21 embrac ed
135.15 89.18 last] 58.22 last faint
136.17 89.20 " 'Look <. . .> son,] 58.24 '~!
136.17 89.21 man—'she swoons—] 58.24 ~. 'She swoons!
136.19 89.22 "Carl] 58.26 ^~
136.19 89.23 recovered—] 58.26 ~;
136.20 89.24 saw him] 58.27-28 looked upon his venerable countenance

THE BRIDE OF HATE; OR, THE PASSAGE OF A NIGHT.

"The Bride of Hate" has been particularly pointed out by J. Wesley Thomas as one of the stories in *Southward Ho!* (1854) for which "specific German sources can be detected." Thomas enumerates striking parallels between Simms's tale and E. T. A. Hoffman's "Das Majorat": (1) almost identical settings, (2) over-all plots with only minor variations, and (3) closely similar climactic scenes; but Thomas's theory seems to be that Simms "found inspiration" in Hoffman, not that Simms exploited him (see "German Sources," pp. 137-138). For whatever reason, "The Bride of Hate" is one of Simms's better constructed tales, with a consistent point of view, almost no digressions, an artistic beginning, a perfectly anticipated and logically motivated ending—all written in a cold and lifeless prose that leaves the story flat and colorless despite its mechanical correctness. This observation does indeed suggest an artificial "borrowed" story rather than an example of true creativity. Perhaps Simms's chief contribution in this story, however, lies in technique. Despite its Gothic trappings, Simms employs in "The Bride of Hate" a technique somewhat anticipatory of the realistic method of Henry James: the point of view is limited to that of a single vessel of consciousness who discovers bit by bit the truth about himself.

In most respects the title Simms originally gave to the story, "The Passage of a Night; or, the Benefactress"—soon modified in his thinking to "The Benefactress, or the Passage of a Night" or simply "The Benefactress" (see *Letters,* I, 375; II, 79, 99, 124, 381)—is more appropriate than "The Bride of Hate." The highly effective opening sentence, "At length I was permitted to behold my benefactress," sets a tone of irony and mystery which, as a title, "The Benefactress" reiterates and supports whereas "The Bride of Hate" does not. Unfortunately, perhaps, then, Simms decided to change the title when he selected it for inclusion in *Southward Ho!,* as the paragraph establishing the framework for "The Bride of Hate" reveals.

This paragraph, introducing the German traveller who supposedly relates the tale to fellow passengers en route by ship from New York to Charleston (the voyage to Charleston, like the ancient pilgrimage to Canterbury, serving as the link for the various stories), reads as follows:

> When this little narration had ended, an intelligent German of the party, from whose grave features and silent tongue we had expected nothing, now pleasantly surprised us by volunteering a legend of his own country—a domestic legend of dark and gloomy character. We expressed our gratification at the offer, drew our chairs into the circle, lighted fresh cigars, and listened to the following tale, which, as if parodying the title of a previous story ["The Bride of Fate," pp. 138-165 in *Southward Ho!*], he called—[here follows, on the next page, "The Bride of Hate; or, the Passage of a Night"].
>
> [*Southward Ho!*, p. 181]

Explanatory Notes

137.1-9 The epigraph is from lines 929-937, *Samson Agonistes.*

Textual Introduction

On February 24, 1841, Simms wrote to James Lawson: "Godey has just sent me an impression of a story called 'The Passage of a Night' which I sold him when I was in New York, and which he is about to publish. It reads well, to my thinking" (*Letters*, I, 233). "The Passage of a Night; or, the Benefactress. A Tale" was published shortly thereafter, in *Godey's Lady's Book*, XXII (March, 1841), 115-127. Although the story was not published again until 1854 when Simms re-titled it "The Bride of Hate; or, the Passage of a Night" and included it in *Southward Ho! A Spell of Sunshine* (New York: Redfield, 1854), pp. 182-217, Simms had proposed it to Harper and Brothers in 1843 for publication in a collection of his short stories which never materialized (see *Letters*, I, 375), and throughout the rest of his life contemplated including it in the collection of "moral imaginative" short stories for which he never found a publisher. See *Letters*, II, 55, 79, 99, 124, 381-382; and V, 156-157.

The original periodical publication serves as copy-text for the Centennial edition. Although its new title in *Southward Ho!*, "The Bride of Hate," obviously is Simms's and is therefore adopted here, none of the variants between the periodical and book texts of the story itself appear to have authority.

Table 1: Emendations and Textual Notes

Listed here are all changes in the copy-text of the story originally entitled "The Passage of a Night; or, the Benefactress." The original reading appears to the left of the bracket, the emended Centennial edition reading to the right. Where no bracket appears the reading is the same in both texts and the refusal to emend is explained in parentheses. When an explanation of the change is necessary it follows in parentheses.

137. The Passage of a Night; or, the Benefactress. A Tale.] The Bride of Hate; or, the Passage of a Night.

137.1 "AT] At

138.6 'Who am I?'] "~"

138.17 "Vainly] ∧~

139.3 "From] ∧~

139.20 "When] ∧~

140.13 generosity *?*] ~ ?

140.15-16 There was <. . .> contradictions (Subject-verb agreement error in copy-text has not been emended if the sentence begins with an expletive.)

140.28-29 There was <. . .> pains taken (Cf. 140.15-16.)

141.33 "I] ∧~

142.37 "Having] ∧~

143.23 "It (This is the first paragraph in copy-text in which the beginning double quotes are appropriate to the context.)

144.21 nothing?] ~"

147.35 parts] ports (The passage calls for emendation; "parts" for "ports" is an entirely possible misreading of Simms's hand. "Ports" appears in *Southward Ho!*)

149.27 *salle a mangér*] *salle à manger*

150.18 *salle a mangér*] *salle à manager*

151.25 thought] though

154.2 surrenderd] surrendered

154.27 awhile <. . .> a while] a while <. . .> a while

156.7 awhile (Although the parallel uses of "a while" at 154.27 suggest that "awhile" here may be a printer's error, or a misreading of Simms's hand, either form is possible and there is not sufficient justification for emendation.)

158.26 of ——] of—— (A closed dash after "of," indicating an interruption, fits the sense of the passage.)
163.31 momeint] moment
168.12 hers.] ~"
168.14 hers.] ~"

Table II: Textual Variants

Below is a list of the variants between "The Passage of a Night; or, the Benefactress" in *Godey's Lady's Book* (1841) and "The Bride of Hate; or, the Passage of a Night" in *Southward Ho!* (1854).

From left to right the chart of variants has the following text sequence:

LEFT MARGIN: Centènnial edition key
FIRST READING: 1841
SECOND READING: 1854

137.epigraph 115. epigraph *Samson*] 182. epigraph—*Samson*
137.1 115.a.1 "AT] 182.1 ‸~
137.4 115.a.6 re-read] 182.5 reread
137.5 115.a.7 pleasure;] 182.6 ~‸
137.13 115.a.17 charge. Years] 182.14 ~;—years
137.13 115.a.18 satisfaction,] 182.15 ~‸—
137.14 115.a.19 enjoyment] 182.16 enjoyments
138.3 115.a.25 on this very subject, contrived] 182.21 contrived on this very subject,
138.4 115.a.26 me—] 182.22 ~;‸
138.5 115.a.27 me—] 182.23 ~;‸
138.8 115.a.31 no where] 182.26 nowhere
138.9 115.a.33 ignorance,] 182.27 ~;
138.11 115.a.36 disquiet] 183.3 ~,
138.11 115.a.36 endeavoured] 183.3 endeavored
138.12 115.a.37 endeavour] 183.3 endeavor
138.14 115.a.39 unlike] 183.6 ~,
138.17 115.a.43 "Vainly] 183.9 ‸~
138.17 115.a.44 Baroness] 183.9-10 baroness
138.18 115.a.44 endeavour] 183.10 endeavor
138.21 115.b.1 who,] 183.14 ~‸

138.22 115.b.2 afterwards] 183.15 afterward
138.23 115.b.3-4 whom then] 183.16 ~, ~,
138.24 115.b.4 From whom] 183.17 whence
138.29 115.b.11 Nor] 183.22 ~,
138.29 115.b.11 years] 183.22~,
138.34 115.b.17-18 something, too, so I fancied,] 183.27-28 something too—so I fancied—
139.1 115.b.24 thought,] 183.32~∧
139.3 115.b.27 "From] 183.35 ∧~
139.15 115.b.43 this—] 184.9 ~:∧
139.16 115.b.44 carriage,] 184.10 ~;
139.17 115.b.46 unsatisfied,] 184.11 ~∧—
139.20 116.a.1 "When] 184.14 ∧~
139.22 116.a.4 re-read] 184.16 reread
139.24 116.a.6 truth,] 184.18 ~∧—
139.25 116.a.8 —and] 184.19 (∧~
139.26 116.a.9 lines?—] 184.21 ~∧)
139.34 116.a.20 expressed] 184.30 ~—
139.35 116.a.21 —and] 184.30 (∧~
139.36 116.a.22 point!—] 184.31 ~)—
139.38 116.a.24 protege] 184.33 protégé
140.5 116.a.31 hand-writing] 184.39 handwriting
140.7 116.a.34 examine] 185.2-3 ~,
140.16 116.a.45 contradictions] 185.12 contradiction
140.26 116.a.59 feeling] 185.23 ~,
140.27 116.a.59 height] 185.24 ~,
141.1 116.b.6 hand-writing] 185.37 handwriting
141.8 116.b.16 irregular.] 186.5 ~!
141.12 116.b.21 words—such] 186.10 ~, ~,
141.13 116.b.22 conjectured] 186.10 ~,
141.15 116.b.24-25 any thing beside] 186.12-13 anything besides
141.18 116.b.29 —though] 186.16 (∧~
141.20 116.b.31 rest—] 186.18 ~∧)
141.22 116.b.34 enough] 186.20 ~,
141.23 116.b.35 Lady T.] 186.21 the baroness
141.25 116.b.38 Palatinate afforded,] 186.24 palatinate ~;
141.26 116.b.38-39 respects] 186.24 ~,
141.30 116.b.44 declared,] 186.29 ~∧

141.31 116.b.45 in] 186.29 of
141.31 116.b.46 Castle] 186.30 castle
141.33 116.b.48 "I] 186.32 ∧~
142.1 116.b.52 a humbler] 186.35 an humble
142.2 116.b.53 yeoman,] 186.36 ~;
142.2 116.b.53 retainer—] 186.36 ~,∧
142.3 116.b.54 Castle—] 187.1 castle; ∧
142.3 116.b.55 kind,] 187.2 ~;
142.4 116.b.56 I do] 187.2-3 I I do
142.8 116.b.61 gaiety] 187.7 gayety
142.9 116.b.62 and] 187.8 ~,
142.15 117.a.2 discourse,] 187.14 ~;
142.17 117.a.5 Castle of the Baroness] 187.16 castle of the baroness
142.17 117.a.6 spirit—] 187.17 ~;∧
142.19 117.a.7 witty,] 187.18 ~;
142.19 117.a.8 and] 187.18 ~,
142.19 117.a.8 unfrequently] 187.18 ~,
142.29 117.a.21 inferred] 187.29 ~,
142.30 117.a.22 I, myself,] 187.30 ~∧ ~∧
142.31 117.a.23 on] 187.31 upon
142.31 117.a.23 gaiety] 187.31 gayety
142.31 117.a.24 himself;] 187.32 ~,
142.32 117.a.25 and, possibly,] 187.33 ~∧ ~∧
142.33 117.a.26 denial;—but] 187.34 ~.∧ But
142.37 117.a.31 "Having] 187.38 ∧~
142.37 117.a.31-32 endeavoured] 187.38 endeavored
143.1 117.a.34 Lady] 188.1 lady
143.2 117.a.36 Castle] 188.3 castle
143.18 117.a.57 gaiety] 188.20 gayety
143.20 117.a.59 grey] 188.21 gray
143.28 117.a.68 you?] 188.29 ~!
143.31 117.b.3 know,] 188.33 ~∧—
143.32 117.b.5 you,] 188.34 ~∧
143.32 117.b.5 withheld,] 188.34 ~.
143.34 117.b.8 the] 188.36 a
143.35 117.b.9 Lady T——] 188.37 the baroness
144.1 117.b.15 was] 189.2 was even

144.5 117.b.19 every thing] 189.6 everything
144.8 117.b.23 exclaimed] 189.9 ~,
144.16 117.b.34 How,] 189.18 ~!
144.16 117.b.34 demanded] 189.18 ~,
144.17 117.b.36 endeavoured] 189.19 endeavored
144.21 117.b.40 nothing?] 189.23 ~"
144.24 117.b.44 favours] 189.26 favors
144.26 117.b.46 Baroness] 189.28-29 baroness
144.28 117.b.48 showing] 189.30 ~,
144.34 117.b.56-57 Baroness] 189.37 baroness
144.35 117.b.57 education.] 189.38 ~?
144.37 117.b.59 favour] 190.1 favor
145.1 117.b.63 Baroness] 190.4 baroness
145.2 117.b.64 affection.] 190.4 ~?
145.10 118.a.5 Baroness] 190.13 baroness
145.15 118.a.10 labours] 190.18 labors
145.15 118.a.11 honourable] 190.19 honorable
145.17 118.a.12 Bruno.] 190.20 ~?
145.18 118.a.13 Doubtless] 190.21 ~,
145.22 118.a.17 before] 190.25 ~,
145.22 118.a.17 dialogue] 190.25 ~,
145.23 118.a.19 and] 190.27 ~,
145.24 118.a.20 replied,] 190.27 ~:—
146.1 118.a.38 know] 191.3 ~,
146.3 118.a.41 Baroness] 191.6 baroness
146.8 118.a.47 faithful] 191.10 ~,
146.11 118.a.51-52 Meanwhile] 191.14~,
146.18 118.a.60 soul,] 191.21~^
146.20 118.a.63 Castle] 191.23 castle
146.24 118.b.1 connexions] 191.28 commotion
146.27 118.b.5 condition.] 191.31 ~?
146.28 118.b.6 and to expand] 191.32 and expand
146.33 118.b.12 envelope] 191.36 envelop
146.35 118.b.15 Castle] 192.3 castle
147.2 118.b.17-18 oracle, but] 192.5 ~; ~,
147.5 118.b.22 Castle] 192.9 castle
147.12 118.b.31 every thing] 192.16 everything
147.13 118.b.31-32 neighbourhood] 192.16-17 neighborhood

147.18 118.b.39 of] 192.23 ~,

147.21 118.b.42 populous,] 192.26 ~‸

147.27 118.b.50 esteemed as a] 192.32 esteemed a

147.27 118.b.50 ruin,] 192.32 ~‸

147.35 118.b.60 parts] 193.2 ports

148.4 118.b.69 Baroness] 193.8-9 baroness

148.8 119.a.5 Baroness] 193.13 baroness

148.18 119.a.18 Baroness] 193.23 baroness

148.22 119.a.24 Baroness] 193.28 baroness

148.32 119.a.36 for benefactions] 193.39 for her benefactions

148.37 119.a.42 from] 194.5 with

149.3 119.a.47 Baroness] 194.9 baroness,

149.5 119.a.50-51 and, it would seem so unaccountably, so unnaturally] 194.11-12 and, in respect to whom it would seem so unaccountable, so unnatural

149.9 119.a.54 addition:] 194.14 ~—

149.13 119.a.58 Baroness] 194.18 baroness

149.22 119.b.2 Bruno] 194.29 ~,

149.25 119.b.5 Baroness] 194.31 baroness

150.11 119.b.32 towards] 195.17 toward

150.18 119.b.42 *salle a mangér*] 195.25 *salle à mangér*

150.19 119.b.43 and] 195.26 ~,

150.21 119.b.45 inclosed] 195.28 enclosed

150.21 119.b.46 inclosure] 195.28 enclosure

150.23 119.b.48 afterwards] 195.30 afterward

150.24 119.b.49 Baroness] 195.31 baroness

150.29 119.b.56 ground, than] 195.36 ~‸ ~,

150.30 119.b.58 and, at one time,] 195.38 ~‸ ~‸

150.30 119.b.58 seemed indeed] 195.38 ~, ~,

150.34 119.b.63 horizon] 196.3 sky

150.34 119.b.63 small,] 196.4 ~‸

150.35 119.b.64 doors] 196.4 ~,

151.1 120.a.2-3 bedstead of carved columns,] 196.9 bedstead, ~‸

151.9 120.a.13 prison,] 196.17 ~‸—

151.10 120.a.14 splendour,] 196.18 splendor ‸—

151.11 120.a.15 deserve] 196.19 deserves

151.16 120.a.21 seated,] 196.24 ~‸

151.18 120.a.26 longer,] 196.27 ~‸—

151.21 120.a.29 labours] 196.30 labors

151.23 120.a.32 castle,] 196.33 ~∧

151.24 120.a.33 Perhaps,] 196.33 ~∧

151.24 120.a.33 cannot] 196.33 can not

151.24 120.a.33 freely,] 196.34 ~∧

151.25 120.a.34 thought] 196.34 though

151.29 120.a.39 you,] 196.38 ~;

151.30 120.a.41 favourable] 197.1 favorable

151.33 120.a.45 cannot] 197.4 can not

151.34 120.a.46 not] 197.5 ~,

151.38 120.a.51 apartment,] 197.9 ~∧

152.4 120.a.56 me] 197.14 ~,

152.7 120.a.60 entrance] 197.17 ~,

152.12 120.a.66 Baroness] 197.22 baroness

152.13 120.a.67 hear?] 197.23 ~.

152.13 120.a.67-68 send, nay <...> will,] 197.23-24 ~∧— nay, ~∧—

152.14 120.a.68 herself."] 197.24 ~'

152.25 120.b.12 Baroness] 197.37 baroness

152.25 120.b.13 all,] 197.37 ~∧

152.26 120.b.14 parental,] 197.38 ~∧

152.31 120.b.20 chamber,] 198.4 ~∧

152.33 120.b.23 his,] 198.7 ~;

152.36 120.b.28 grated,] 198.11 ~∧

152.37 120.b.29 neighbouring] 198.12 neighboring

152.37 120.b.29 mountains, which,] 198.12 ~; these,

153.5 120.b.36 apprehensive] 198.18 ~,

153.9 120.b.42 Baroness] 198.23 baroness

153.10 120.b.43 mystery] 198.24 ~,

153.12 120.b.45 Baroness] 198.25 baroness

153.12 120.b.46 words] 198.26 ~,

153.14 120.b.48 and] 198.27 ~,

153.21 120.b.58 favour] 198.36 favor

153.22 120.b.59 attachments] 198.36 ~,

153.22 120.b.59 towards] 198.37 toward

153.23 120.b.61 and] 199.1 ~,

153.24 120.b.62 hours,] 199.2 ~∧

153.24 120.b.62 any thing] 199.2 anything

153.26 120.b.64 mean while] 199.4 meanwhile
153.29 121.a.1 feeling] 199.7 ~,
153.29 121.a.2 and,] 199.8 ~∧
153.30 121.a.2 while,] 199.8 ~∧
153.31 121.a.4 discoloured] 199.10 discolored
154.1 121.a.10 and] 199.14 ~,
154.2 121.a.11 apartment] 199.15 ~,
154.2 121.a.11 surrenderd] 199.16 surrendered
154.4 121.a.14-15 which, <. . .> fact,] 199.19 ~∧— ~∧—
154.5 121.a.15 long] 199.20 ~,
154.10 121.a.21 so;] 199.24 ~,
154.11 121.a.23 heart] 199.26 ~,
154.16 121.a.29 seat—] 199.31 ~;∧
154.17 121.a.30 could,] 199.32 ~;
154.17 121.a.30 and] 199.32 ~,
154.18 121.a.31 watch dog,] 199.33 ~-~∧
154.22 121.a.37 and] 199.37 ~,
154.24 121.a.40 footsteps] 200.1 ~,
154.26 121.a.42-43 distinguish. I] 200.3-4 ~¶~
154.27 121.a.43 awhile] 200.4 a while
154.27 121.a.44 hour had] 200.5 hour
154.27 121.a.44 elapsed; <. . .> less,] 200.5 ~∧— ~∧—
155.3 121.a.62-63 murmurs, <. . .> murmurs] 200.20 ~∧—~—
155.5 121.a.65 Baroness] 200.22 baroness
155.8 121.a.68 inaudible] 200.25 not audible
155.13 121.b.5 and I suppose] 200.30 ~, ~~,
155.13 121.b.6 affirmative,] 200.30 ~∧
155.18 121.b.11 Baroness] 200.35 baroness
155.26 121.b.22 summons] 201.5 ~,
155.34 121.b.32 Baroness] 201.13 baroness
156.1 121.b.39 Aye] 201.19 Ay
156.4 121.b.42-43 Baroness] 201.22 baroness
156.9 121.b.48 Baroness] 201.27 baroness
156.13 121.b.54 seemed,] 201.31 ~∧
156.17 121.b.59 neighbourhood] 201.35-36 neighborhood
156.22 121.b.66 gallery] 202.2 ~,
156.26 122.a.2 woe] 202.6 wo

156.32 122.a.9 way] 202.13 ~,
156.34 122.a.12 each] 202.15 either
156.34 122.a.12 hand,] 202.15 ~∧
156.36 122.a.14 these,] 202.17 ~∧
156.38 122.a.16 pursued,] 202.19 ~∧
157.1 122.a.18 gallery,] 202.20 ~∧
157.3 122.a.21 cessation,] 202.22-23 ~∧
157.6 122.a.25 unfastened;] 202.26 ~,
157.7 122.a.26 second,] 202.27 ~∧
157.8 122.a.27 dressing room] 202.27-28 ~-~
157.10 122.a.30 spot,] 202.30 ~∧
157.13 122.a.34-35 Baroness] 202.34 baroness
157.17 122.a.39 companion,] 202.38 ~∧
157.17 122.a.40 uplifted,] 202.38 ~∧
157.18 122.a.40 eye] 202.38 her eye
157.18 122.a.40 resolution,] 202.39 ~∧
157.21 122.a.44 hands,] 203.3 ~∧
157.22 122.a.45-46 meanwhile] 203.4 ~,
157.27 122.a.52 sight,] 203.9 ~∧
157.30 122.a.56 wise,] 203.12 ~∧
157.32 122.a.58 curse,] 203.15 ~∧—
157.33 122.a.59 necessity,] 203.16 ~;
157.36 122.a.64 cannot now escape me, you cannot] 203.19-20 can not ~ can not
157.37 122.a.65-66 wearisome,] 203.21 ~∧
157.38 122.a.66 labours] 203.21 labors
157.38 122.a.66-67 have, at length,] 203.21-22 ~∧ ~~∧
158.1 122.a.68 am] 203.22 ~,
158.1 122.a.68 fate.] 203.23 ~!
158.4 122.b.3 feeling] 203.26 ~,
158.10 122.b.10 wretch;] 203.32 ~∧—
158.14 122.b.15 Master!] 203.37 master!
158.17 122.b.18 master] 204.1 ~,
158.18 122.b.20 Slave! Slave! Slave!] 204.3 Slave! slave! slave!
158.18 122.b.20 oft repeated] 204.3 ~-~
158.21 122.b.24 woe] 204.6 Wo
158.21 122.b.25 again,] 204.7 ~∧
158.22 122.b.26 favour] 204.7 favor

158.29 122.b.35 Hence! Hence] 204.15 ~ hence
158.29 122.b.36 me:] 204.15 ~!
158.37 122.b.46 soul.] 204.24 ~?
159.7 122.b.55 favourite] 204.32 favorite
159.16 122.b.66 demeanour] 205.2 demeanor
159.24 123.a.8 labours] 205.11 labors
159.25 123.a.9 when] 205.12 When
159.28 123.a.13 master.] 205.15 ~?
159.31 123.a.18 all] 205.19 *all—*
160.1 123.a.26 perhaps,] 205.26 ~‸
160.3 123.a.29 slave,] 205.29 ~;
160.6 123.a.31 thunder bolt] 205.31 thunderbolt
160.9 123.a.36 eminence, from whence] 205.35 ~‸ whence
160.15 123.a.43 'Till] 206.2 ‸~
160.18 123.a.46 devil!—] 206.4 ~‸
160.24 123.a.54 which,] 206.10 ~‸
160.25 123.a.55 providence] 206.11 Providence
160.33 123.a.66 power] 206.20 ~,
160.35 123.a.68 evil,] 206.22 ~‸
160.35 123.a.68 long] 206.22 so long
160.36 123.b.1 him, the] 206.23 him, and the
160.37 123.b.2 you] 206.24 *you*
161.10 123.b.15 Holiness] 206.35-36 holiness,
161.15 123.b.21 intelligent] 207.1 ~,
161.15 123.b.21-22 handsome,] 207.2 ~;
161.16 123.b.22 honour] 207.2 honor
161.20 123.b.28 my <second occurrence>] 207.7 *my*
161.20 123.b.28 fate!—] 207.8 ~‸
161.21 123.b.29 were] 207.8 ~,
161.21 123.b.30 Away] 207.9 ~,
161.29 123.b.40 forward,] 207.17 ~;
161.35 123.b.47 towards] 207.23 toward
162.1 123.b.52 you.] 207.27 ~!
162.7 123.b.59 deep, indeed,] 207.33 ~‸ ~‸
162.9 123.b.61-62 another,] 207.35 ~‸
162.16 124.a.5 her weakness] 208.6-7 the weakness
162.18 124.a.7 and] 208.8 ~,
162.19 124.a.9 uttered,] 208.10 ~‸

162.22 124.a.13 Baroness] 208.13 baroness
162.27 124.a.19 rash] 208.18 vast
162.27 124.a.19 dark] 208.18 ~,
163.2 124.a.33 to] 208.29 in
163.3 124.a.35 labours] 208.31 labors
163.5 124.a.37 confidently,] 208.32-33 ~^—
163.6 124.a.38 and] 208.33 ~,
163.13 124.a.48 to] 209.3 for
163.14 124.a.49 court.—] 209.4 ~^
163.15 124.a.50 There,] 209.4 ~^
163.18 124.a.53 a] 209.7 the
163.20 124.a.56 atmosphere,] 209.9-10 ~^
163.31 124.b.2 momeint] 209.22 moment
164.6 124.b.20 which,] 209.36 ~^
164.7 124.b.21 bar,] 209.37 ~^
164.9 124.b.24 in] 209.39 from
164.17 124.b.34 piled] 210.9 placed
164.26 124.b.46 terrace,] 210.19 ~;
164.32 124.b.54 darted upon] 210.25-26 darted out upon
164.33 124.b.55 eyes] 210.26 ~,
164.33 124.b.56 Baroness] 210.27 baroness
164.37 124.b.60 strangest,] 210.31 ~^
164.37 124.b.61 hideous looking] 210.31 ~-~
164.38 124.b.62 Baroness] 210.32 baroness
165.1 124.b.63 towards] 210.33 toward
165.4 124.b.67 intensest] 210.36 intense
165.7 125.a.2 poinard bared,] 211.1 ~, ~^
165.11 125.a.7 towards] 211.5 toward
165.21 125.a.21 still,] 211.16 ~^
165.21 125.a.21 it] 211.16 ~,
165.30 125.a.32 appearance,] 211.25 ~^
165.33 125.a.36 had] 211.28 took
166.8 125.a.53 grey] 212.4 gray
166.10 125.a.56 of neck] 212.6 of her neck
166.17 125.a.65 sepulchre] 212.14 ~!
166.19 125.a.68 unforegoing] 212.16 unforgiving
166.22 125.b.1 when] 212.18 ~,

166.25 125.b.6 an equal and elaborate narrative] 212.22 a long narrative equal
167.5 125.b.27 towards] 212.39 toward
167.11 125.b.35 and new] 213.7 a new
167.13 125.b.38 effort] 213.9 ~,
167.23 125.b.50 averted] 213.20 ~,
167.31 125.b.60 was,] 213.29 ~∧
167.32 125.b.62 succour] 213.30 succor
167.33 125.b.63 say,] 213.31 ~∧
168.4 126.a.4 been;] 214.2 ~?
168.8 126.a.8 Baroness] 214.5 baroness
168.12 126.a.14 hers.] 214.10 ~"
168.14 126.a.18 hers.] 214.13 ~"
168.24 126.a.29 But] 214.23 ~,
168.37 126.a.43 Baroness] 214.36 baroness
169.8 126.a.56 doubt] 215.7 ~,
169.12 126.a.62 act,] 215.11 ~∧
169.13 126.a.62 which,] 215.12 ~∧
169.16 126.a.67 silent,] 215.16 ~∧
169.25 126.b.10 word.] 215.25 ~:—
170.2 126.b.29 these] 216.1 these things
170.6 126.b.35 Baroness] 216.6 baroness
170.7 126.b.35-36 Reverence, the Cardinal] 216.7 reverence, the cardinal
170.19 126.b.52 fearless] 216.20 fearful
170.20 126.b.53 memory] 216.21 my memory
170.22 126.b.55 bed,] 216.23 ~∧
170.26 126.b.61 life,] 216.28 ~∧
170.27 126.b.62 effort,] 216.29 ~∧
171.2 127.a.7 and] 217.3 ~,
171.5 127.b.3 inclosing] 217.7 enclosing
171.8 127.b.7 keeping] 217.10 ~,
171.9 127.b.7 one,] 217.11 ~∧

THE PRIMA DONNA: A PASSAGE FROM CITY LIFE.

The Prima Donna and "The Humours of the Manager" are the two stories by Simms which best reflect his interest in theatrical life and manners. Though Simms's characteristic sententiousness greatly reduces its effectiveness, *The Prima Donna* presents a knowledgeable picture of life in the Bowery and the theatrical environs of New York in the early nineteenth century, seen through the eyes of a curious and sensitive (if self-centered) observer of the arts. The narrative begins as a well-ordered story of manners, then bows to Gothic influence and deteriorates. Looked upon as a story of manners, which it primarily is, *The Prima Donna* has merit; looked upon as the dramatic portrayal of the inner struggle of a protagonist (like, for instance, James's John Marcher) selfishly unwilling to commit himself fully to anything until it is too late, the story fails.

Explanatory Notes

172. Epigraph The quotation from *Faust* is taken *from the* "Forest and Cavern" section. The translation is probably Simms's own.

173.28 Meg Merrilies: Coarse gypsy woman in Scott's *Guy Mannering*.

174.25 "Stout Gentleman": Presumably the unnamed principal in the story of that name by Washington Irving, first printed in 1822.

174.31 damsels of Eleusinia: Eleusinian women danced and sang in honor of the goddess Demeter in the annual festival of the Eleusinia in Athens. See *Pausanius* I, 38, 6.

176.5 "Divine, enchanting ravishment,": Milton, *Comus*, l. 245.

180.21 "muffled his skylights": "skylight" is (or was) nautical slang for "eye"; in the slang of pugilism, "muffled his skylights" may mean delivering a stunning blow. See John S. Farmer and W. E. Henley, compilers, *Slang and Its Analogues* (New York, 1965), IV, 379.

182.8 "Confirmation strong as holy writ,": Paraphrase of *Othello*, III, iii.

182.19 "sweet singers of Israel": The line from Coleridge's "Faith, Hope, and Charity" reads, "Songster sweet of Israel" (*The Complete Poetical Works* [Oxford, 1912], p. 428, l. 14).

183.27 "signified love": *Merry Wives of Windsor*, I, i.

190.14 Tilsit Waltz: Tilsit is a small city in East Prussia; meaning otherwise unknown.
194.35 Ascaparte: Elizabethan writers frequently alluded to Ascaparte, thirty-foot giant in the romance of Sir Bevis of Hampton.
197.29 The quotation is from *Macbeth,* III, ii.

Textual Introduction

Simms's first mention of the composition of *The Prima Donna* occurs in his letter of August 15, 1840, to James Lawson: "I wrote a Tale entitled 'The Prima Donna' intending it as the first of the five for Snowden [William W. Snowden, publisher of *Ladies' Companion*], but it grew so greatly under my hands that I could not afford it at the price he offers and accordingly sent it to Godey. Should Godey not wish it, Mr. Beile [John P. Beile, Charleston bookseller] will bring it on to you" (*Letters,* I, 183-184). The following January Simms wrote Lawson that "I have . . . a story in the hands of Godey called 'The Cantatrice' or 'The Muse of the Ballet'. He chooses between the two names" (January 8, 1841; *Letters,* I, 212). In a letter of February 24, 1841, Simms informed Lawson: "I have . . . sold him [Godey] a story called 'The Prima Donna.' This name will be changed, & it may be called 'The Muse of the Ballêt' " (*Letters,* I, 233). For some reason, however, Godey delayed publication until early 1844, when the story was issued under separate cover as *The/ Prima Donna:/A/Passage from City Life* (Philadelphia: Louis A. Godey, 1844). Simms marked the event in his letter of April 4, 1844, to Lawson: "I see that Godey has published as the first of a select Library, a story called 'The Prima Donna' which I furnished him for his Ladies Book" (*Letters,* I, 413). In the middle 1850's Simms may have toyed with the idea of revising *The Prima Donna* and republishing it as "The Muse of the Ballet," the title that he perhaps preferred. In the Charles Carroll Simms Collection in the South Caroliniana Library is a manuscript title-page, written in Simms's hand, reading as follows: "The Muse of the Ballet/Chapter 1./The Brooding Bachelor." There is no manuscript accompanying this title-page, which is actually the other side of another manuscript title-page which reads: "Rawlins' Rookery;/or/The House of Eld and Glamour./ a Biography,/ a Budget and a 'What Not.'/ Edited by/W. Gilmore Simms, Esq./ Author of 'The Forayers'

Eutaw,' 'The/Partisan, The Yemassee &c./ [quotation from John Lyly]/ Redfield: New York/1857." A possible theory is that Simms first wrote the title-page for "The Muse of the Ballet" with the probable intention of reworking *The Prima Donna,* but that, for whatever reason, he soon discarded this idea and, turning the expensive sheet of paper over, wrote out the title-page for "Rawlins' Rookery" and the eighty-five manuscript leaves of it still intact.

The 1844 edition of *The Prima Donna*—its only publication—is copy-text.

Table I: Emendations and Textual Notes

Listed here are all changes made in the copy-text of *The Prima Donna.* The original reading appears to the left of the bracket, the emended Centennial edition reading to the right. Where no bracket appears the reading is the same in both texts and the refusal to emend is explained in parentheses. Where an explanation of the change is necessary it follows in parentheses.

179.33 thurst] thrust
179.34 blunted] blurted
184.10 Brodignag] Brobdingnag
185.28 procenium] proscenium
189.21 married ——] ~—— (Throughout *The Prima Donna* a spaced long rule has signified an unstated name or word; a closed dash has signified an interruption. The context clearly calls for emendation.)
189.28 girl, ——] ~—— (Cf. 189.21.)
192.9 you ——] ~—— (Cf. 189.21 and 189.28.)

THE UNKNOWN MASQUE. A SKETCH OF THE CRESCENT CITY.

"The Unknown Masque" is the one story in the present volume that warrants inclusion under two of the three classifications suggested in the Introduction: it is a "moral imaginative" tale with a demonstrable German source, and it is equally clearly a story of New Orleans "manners," as its subtitle indicates. This combination produces an interesting, attractive sketch, containing the best elements of the much expanded "Marie de Berniere" which grew from it, yet lacking the sentimentality and sensationalism of that novelette.

Trent (p. 14) records that Simms visited New Orleans in 1824-25—at which time Simms would have been eighteen or nineteen, very much like the young narrator in "The Unknown Masque," who "at eighteen" paid his "first visit to the 'Crescent City' " in the "winter of 1825-6." The peripatetic Charlestonian registered the impressions of his 1831 visit to New Orleans in "Notes of a Small Tourist—No. 10," published on May 17, 1831, in the Charleston *City Gazette*, of which he was editor (see *Letters*, I, 34-38). Simms's statement, "New-Orleans has grown prodigiously . . . since 1825" (*Letters*, I, 35), seems to confirm the earlier, 1825 visit on his part; at any rate, it is abundantly evident that, before writing "The Unknown Masque," Simms had tasted the pleasures of New Orleans at first hand, and had had opportunity to observe its customs and manners.

Although J. Wesley Thomas concentrates on "Marie de Berniere" as one of the outstanding examples of German influences in Simms's work, he does not mention "The Unknown Masque"—and indeed the ideas and details he lists ("German Sources," p. 136) as borrowed from Schiller's *Der Geisterseher* apply almost exclusively to portions of the novelette not included in the original sketch. And it is significant that what Thomas calls the "most striking scene in 'Marie de Berniere' " is in fact the essence of "The Unknown Masque"—that is, the masked ball scene featuring the strange appearance and even stranger disappearance of the "second" Egyptian and culminating in the shocking, unaccountable effect of the experience upon the beautiful young widow heroine. According to Thomas, this scene "was probably derived from an uncanny occurrence in the eleventh chapter of Eichendorff's *Ahnung und Gegenwart*, which novel, having not been translated, was one of the German works Simms apparently read in the original" (p. 136). It is clear, however, that in expanding "The Unknown Masque" into "Marie de Berniere," Simms depended more and more upon literary sources, largely German, and less and less upon personal experiences. In brief, "The Unknown Masque" is much more a domestic story of manners and much less a literary import from Germany than "Marie de Berniere."

It is possible that Poe as well as Eichendorff influenced Simms's composition of "The Unknown Masque." Not only is "The Unknown Masque" reminiscent of Poe's "The Masque of the Red

Death" (1842) in title, but also, in a general but important sense, in setting, plot, and theme. That is, Simms, like Poe, uses a gay masked ball as the scene for the unexpected and frightening appearance of an uninvited ghostly visitor who strikes terror in the heart of at least one beholder. One also wonders if Simms did not have Poe's Ligeia at least partially in mind in describing the strange beauty of Madame Elinor de B——: "Her features were not regular, but their united expression carried you away from any analysis of details which might have resulted in an unfavorable decision upon them. You saw not the deficiency of charms which dazzled the glance . . . ." In "Ligeia" (1838) Poe had written: "Yet her features were not of that regular mould which we have been falsely taught to worship . . . although I saw that the features of Ligeia were not of a classic regularity—although I perceived that her loveliness was indeed 'exquisite,' and felt that there was much of 'strangeness' pervading it, yet I have tried in vain to detect the irregularity and to trace home my own perception of 'the strange' " (*The Complete Works of Edgar Allan Poe*, ed. James A. Harrison [New York, 1902], II, 250). And any reader recalling Poe's emphasis upon the "strangeness" and "intensity" of Ligeia's "brilliant" black eyes that "so delighted and appalled" the narrator (*Works*, II, 251, 253) would be struck by Simms's description of Elinor beginning, "I felt that there was something strange in the very intensity of her glance. The eye was brilliant, but the effect upon myself was chilling." Simms probably was not conscious of similarities between what he had read in Poe and what he wrote in "The Unknown Masque," but there is no reason to question that, in 1845, he was steeped in Poe and had assimilated some of his ideas and techniques. One of the most discriminating reviews Simms ever wrote, a justly appreciative appraisal of Poe's *Tales*, appeared in the *Southern and Western Monthly Magazine and Review* in the same year as "The Unknown Masque" (see *SWMMR*, II [Dec., 1845], 426-427).

Explanatory Notes

198. Epigraph These lines have not been identified.

204.8 Count Poniatowski: Possibly Jozef Anton Poniatowski (1763-1813), Polish prince and marshal of France.

207.2-5 Marie Antoinette's hair is reputed to have turned white overnight, or over a short period of time. Simms may have gotten this from Byron's note to the first lines of "The Prisoner of Chillon." See *The Complete Poetical Works of Byron* (Boston, 1935), p. 402 and p. 1026n.

Textual Introduction

Simms published "The Unknown Masque./ A Sketch of the Crescent City" in the *Southern and Western Monthly Magazine and Review*, I (April, 1845), 262-269, the Charleston literary journal of which he was sole editor. Like most of his contributions to the magazines he edited, "The Unknown Masque" is not signed by name, but by the pseudonym "E——," which Simms had previously used in the *Album* and the *Southern Literary Gazette*, other Charleston periodicals he had edited.

Though "The Unknown Masque" was never again published as a complete and separate short story, Simms used it as the germ for the novelette, "Marie de Berniere; A Tale of the Crescent City," much as he had used the "Confessions of a Murderer" as the germ for *Martin Faber*. The expansion of the original "Sketch of the Crescent City" into a full-blown "Tale of the Crescent City" apparently got underway in 1848 or earlier, for, in his November 20, 1848, letter to James Lawson, Simms mentioned that Israel Post, publisher of the then projected *American Metropolitan Magazine*, "wants me to write at $5 per page for a new magazine. . . . I have written to him that I will send an article probably next week, to be paid for when printed" (*Letters*, II, 456). The "article" Simms sent Post was "The Egyptian Masque; a Tale of the Crescent City," one installment of which was published in February, 1849 (*American Metropolitan Magazine*, I, 69-73), with which issue the new journal died. The texts of "The Unknown Masque" and "The Egyptian Masque" are basically similar in content, but Simms has so altered, shifted, and expanded the fragmentary second version that a collation chart is not feasible, despite the fact that in a few instances the phrasing is identical. The unconcluded "The Egyptian Masque" is estimated to be about 4,750 words; the completed "The Unknown Masque," about 4,550 words. (In Simms's estimate, the final form of "Marie de Berniere" is approximately 53,000 words.) Thus, even though it is not certain what "The Egyptian Masque" would have become if the *American Metropolitan Magazine* had not failed (see Simms's letters of February 5, May 6, 1849, to Lawson; *Letters,* II, 474, 513), it is certain that Simms already envisioned a new, much longer piece of fiction; and "Marie de Berniere; A Tale of the Crescent City" was first published in *Arthur's Home Gazette* in seven installments in February and March 1852. It was later included as the title-piece in *Marie de Berniere: A Tale of the Crescent City, etc. etc. etc.* (Philadelphia: Lippincott, Grambo, and Co., 1853), pp. 13-189; and reissued in *The Maroon; A Legend of the Caribbees, and Other Tales* (Philadelphia: Lippincott, Grambo, and Co., 1855), pp. 13-189. In 1866 "Marie de Berniere" was published under a new title, *The Ghost of My Husband. A Tale of the Crescent City* (New York: Chapman & Company [1866]), as No. 2 in "The Sunny Side Series."

The 1845 publication of "The Unknown Masque" in the *Southern and Western Monthly Magazine and Review* is used as copy-text.

Table I: Emendations and Textual Notes

Listed here are all changes made in the copy-text of "The Unknown Masque." The original reading appears to the left of the bracket, the emended Centennial edition reading to the right.

200.12 it] ~.
200.32 twenty-one] ~.
203.33 fortunes] ~.
203.36 him."] ~‸
207.2 him] her

MESMERIDES IN A STAGE-COACH; OR, PASSES EN PASSANT.

This unusual story reflects its author's great interest in mesmerism. Simms was fascinated with the subject: he read books on it, discussed it frequently in his correspondence, attended lectures on it, and wrote about it in his magazines. On October 7, 1842, he wrote to James Lawson, his New York friend who had promised an article on mesmerism for the *Magnolia* (which Simms was then editing): "I shall look for your articles . . . with some anxiety, particularly that on Magnetism. The subject has already excited my attention. Townshend's book I have read. Dr. Ellet, whom I saw a few days ago in Columbia related to me several interesting experiments of his own, particularly upon negroes. I learn that Dr. Dickson, who has just returned from the North has also been making some experiments there. I expect to converse with him, very shortly, upon the subject. Your articles will come seasonably to give us provocation" (*Letters*, I, 323-324). When Simms incorporated parts of Lawson's essay into his own "Editorial Bureau" (*Magnolia*, n.s., I [Nov., 1842], 324-327) rather than publish it separately under Lawson's name, he incurred the New Yorker's temporary wrath. Simms explicitly related to Lawson, in a letter of November 17, 1842, the reason for his editorial action: "You wished by the title to have operated a surprise on the good people of Charleston, without knowing as I did, that we were already largely familiar with the subject . . . . it struck me that it would be more likely to answer your purpose, to take from it such portions as would not have this effect, and to embody the extracts in an Editorial, as if made from a private & unelaborate letter" (*Letters*, I, 330). In addition to Lawson and fellow South Carolinians such as Dr. W. H. Ellet, professor of chemistry, mineralogy, and geology at South Carolina College ("Here in Charleston, every third man is a mesmerist," Simms wrote on April 6, 1843; *Letters*, I, 347), Simms discussed mesmerism with Bryant, Cooper, and Kennedy. It is barely possible that Kennedy may have given Simms the "germ" for "Mesmerides in a Stage-Coach," for after a visit to Philadelphia Simms wrote to Lawson on September 16, 1843: "Kennedy told us of some curious cases of mesmerism in his experience, some of the most remarkable indeed. I may let you hear them at a moment of greater leisure" (*Letters*, I, 367). A review of a book entitled *Gregory's Letters on Animal Magnetism* in the *Southern Quarterly Review* for 1852 is another good barometer of Simms's unflagging interest in the subject (see *SQR*, n.s., V [Jan., 1852], 229-231).

Though such writers as Franklin, Brown, and Poe were interested in mesmerism, Simms's story, published three months before Poe's "Facts of the Case of M. Valdemar," is one of the earliest in American literature to base its main action upon the powers of hypnosis. But the scientific, or pseudo-scientific, is not the point of "Mesmerides in a Stage-Coach"; in it Simms gives a vivid yet humorous portrayal of the blending of courtliness, worldliness, provincialism, and chivalry in early nineteenth-century rural Georgia.

Explanatory Notes

208. Epigraph Tempest, I, 2, 184-186; Epilogue, 9-10.
210.14 the North river: i.e., the Hudson River. In Scrapbook A of the Charles Carroll Simms Collection is a poem entitled, "Written on the North River in 1833," the subject of which is the Hudson River.
212.13 "Habet!": Meaning "he has it," it was used at gladiatorial contests to signify that one of the combatants had been seriously wounded.
223.8 The quotation is from Dante's *Divina Comedia, Inferno,* Canto 5, l. 142.
224.32 Dr. Buchanan: Joseph Rodes Buchanan (1814-1899), American writer and medical-spiritual practitioner. He graduated (1842) from the Medical School of the University of Louisville, where his interest in phrenology and cerebral physiology formed the basis of the two alleged sciences he later outlined: "psychometry" and "sarcognomy."

Textual Introduction

"Mesmerides in a Stage-Coach; or, Passes en/Passant" has never before been reprinted since its original publication in *Godey's Lady's Book,* XXXI (Sept., 1845), 111-119.

Table I: Emendations and Textual Notes

Listed here are all changes made in the copy-text of "Mesmerides in a Stage-Coach." The original reading appears to the left of the bracket, the emended Centennial edition reading to the right. Where no bracket appears the reading is the same in both texts and the refusal to emend is explained in parentheses.

212.26 Few minutes delay (There is some temptation to add an apostrophe after "minutes," but the phrase is sufficiently idiomatic
216.9 mine.] ~"
223.29 "At] ‸~
226.32 hands."] ~‸
227.4 its] it's

227.13 not ?] ~?
227.18 Whose] Who's
228.4 cetainly] certainly

THE MAROON: A ROMANCE OF THE CARIB.

In "Spanish Influences on the Fiction of William Gilmore Simms" Stanley T. Williams commends Simms for "his imaginative use of Spanish history and Spanish subjects in his fiction" and terms him "an unusual pioneer interpreter of Spanish influences in our fiction" (*Hispanic Review*, XXI [July, 1953], 222, 228). Though Williams curiously relegates it to footnote mention only (p. 226n.) in his discussion of Simm's "Spanish" works, "The Maroon" ranks among the more artistically pleasing of the generally undistinguished by-products of the Charleston writer's interest in and knowledge of Spain and its literature. The use which Simms makes of Spanish song, tradition, and character in "The Maroon" is well subordinated to the action of the story, yet remains an integral and important part of it, supporting it and giving it flavor. Though in this case the Hispanic predominates, J. Wesley Thomas finds in "The Maroon" a German flavor as well, pointing to plot parallels in it and Fouqué's *Undine* ("German Sources," p. 137).

Though not a great story, "The Maroon: A Romance of the Carib" is a good one, a picturesque and fast-moving romance with unusually effective, almost realistic, portrayal of strengths and weaknesses in the main character, Lopez de Levya. It is also noteworthy that Simms's treatment of the love play between Lopez and Amaya, and of Lopez's later sexual possession of Maria, is once again surprisingly frank and explicit for the times.

Explanatory Notes

230. Epigraph These lines have not been identified; perhaps they are Simms's own.

261.35 ballad of "Belerma": The legendary Spanish hero Durandarte, who fought with Roland under Charlemagne, had as his dying wish that his heart be cut out and carried to France to his wife Belerma. His friend Montesinos is supposed to have performed the task. In Book II of *Don Quijote* reference is made to this story.

Don Quijote enters the cave of Montesinos, asks Montesinos if the story is true, and hears from the lips of the enchanted Montesinos himself that the whole story is true as it is in the ballads except as to the instrument he used in cutting out the heart.

261.37 Zingali: Zincali, Spanish gypsies. See George Borrow, *The Zincali; or, An Account of the Gypsies of Spain*, 2 vols. (London: John Murray, 1841). The preface to the second edition (1843) says that the book had been reprinted in America.

262.1-4,6-9,22-25 The two stanzas from the ballad of "Belerma" which Simms quotes are included, with English translations, in Thomas Rodd, *History of Charles the Great and Orlando, Ascribed to Archbishop Turpin; Translated from the Latin in Spanheim's Lives of Ecclesiastical Writers: Together with the Most Celebrated Ancient Spanish Ballads Relating to the Twelve Peers of France, Mentioned in Don Quixote; With English Metrical Versions* (London: Printed for T. Rodd, 2, Great Newport Street, Long Acre; and T. Boosey, Old Broad Street, 1812), II, 300-303, as follows:

Quando viò aquel corazon
Estando en èl contemplando,
De neuvas gotas de sangre
Estaba todo bañado.

As she view'd the heart before her,
As she fondly view'd it round,
With fresh drops of blood 'twas cover'd,
Slowly falling on the ground.

Corazon de mi señor
Durandarte muy preciado,
En los amores dichoso,
Y en batallas desdichado.

"Precious heart of Durandarte,
"Heart of him I lov'd so well!
"Blest in love, but cross'd in battle,
"Where the bleeding hero fell:

It is apparent that though Simms may have gotten the original from Rodd (or a similar collection), the translation is his own.

263.25 Baldwin: Baldovinos, another of the legendary heroes of the time of Roland. Like Durandarte, he fought at the battle of Roncesvalles. One of the twelve peers, he was killed by Carloto, son of an emperor. When he was dying, he was found by his uncle, the Marquis de Mantua, who heard him make the prayer quoted in "The Maroon." The prayer is also quoted—and translated into English—in Rodd, *History of Charles the Great . . . .*, II, 64-67. Once again, it is easily possible that Simms may have depended upon

Rodd for the original, but his translation into English idiom differs greatly from the translation in Rodd's book.

A Sir Baldwin also appears in "Sir Otuel" as being one of the knights who heard and answered Roland's call at Roncesvalles. "Sir Otuel" is printed in *Specimens of Early English Metrical Romances* edited by George Ellis. Bulfinch's *Mythology* gives an account of the battle of Roncesvalles in which Baldwin is the first to see the wounded Roland and go for help.

263.26-37 and *264.2-13* The quotation and an English translation (cf. 262.1-4,6-9,22-25) are included in Rodd, *History of Charles the Great* . . . ., II, 64-67, as follows:

O Santa Maria Señora, No me quieras olvidar, A tì encomiendo mi alma, Plegate de la guardar,	"Holy Mary, deign to hear me, "Nor thy suppliant now forsake; "Lo! my soul to thee commending, "Keep it for thy mercy's sake.
En este trance de muerte Esfuerzo me querais dàr, Pues a les tristes consuelas Quieras à mì consolar.	"In the hour of death approaching, "To thy throne for strength I fly; "Cheer my heart with heav'nly comfort, "Hear my piteous piercing cry!
Y à tu precioso Hijo, Por mì te plega rogar, Que perdone mis pecados Mi alma quiera salvar.	"Thy dear Son entreat to pardon "Ev'ry sad offence I gave; "And my soul from hell and Satan "Forth to stretch his hands to save!"

Once again it appears that the translation is Simms's own.

289.26-27 Robertsonian method: a possible reference to Henry Robertson, M.D., *A Concise Grammar of the Modern Greek Language, chiefly composed from the "Nova Methodus," &c. of Father Thomas* . . . . (London, 1818).

293.9-294.12 THE LAY OF THE CARIB DAMSEL: poem by Simms first published in the *Album*, I (Sept. 17, 1825), 96; later included in *Lyrical and Other Poems* (1827), *The Book of My Lady* (1833), and *Poems Descriptive, Dramatic, Legendary and Contemplative* (1853).

Textual Introduction

Simms found the germ for "The Maroon" (variously subtitled, as will be explained later, "A Legend of the Caribees" and "A Romance of the Carib") in his short sketch entitled "A Legend of the Pacific" published anonymously in the *New York Mirror*, X (Oct. 13, 1832), 117-118, and shortly thereafter republished under the same title in *The Book of My Lady* (1833), pp. 244-256. Though clearly the origin for the full-length tale, "A Legend of the Pacific" bears so little resemblance to "The Maroon./A Legend of the Caribbees" as first published in the *New York Illustrated Magazine of Literature and Art*, III (Jan.-June, 1847), 8-12, 54-59, 112-115, 149-154, 219-224, 291-296, that they must be considered separate stories, bearing approximately the same relationship to one another as do, for instance, the "Confessions of a Murderer" and *Martin Faber*.

First mention of "The Maroon" occurs in Simms's despondent letter of October 23, 1846, to Lawson, in which after confessing that "Carolina has been a region of tombs for me, and my worldly prosperity is by no means such as to make me desire to continue here," Simms told his New York friend: "I shall probably send you a Tale in three parts, for each of which you will demand $20 cash, unless you prefer the $3 per page arrangement" (*Letters*, II, 195-196). His letters to Lawson throughout the fall and winter of 1846-1847 reflect the tragic circumstances under which Simms wrote "The Maroon," displaying the author's constant concern with collecting his meager pay and his indecision (probably influenced by economic considerations) about the ultimate length of "The Maroon"—or at least about the number of parts or installments in which it was to be published. On or about November 6, and again on November 19, 1846, Simms wrote Lawson instructions for collecting his due from Lawrence Labree, editor of the *New York Illustrated Magazine*, and added, "I have sent *three* parts of the story to Labree, and when I send the fourth, or concluding part, it will be to you" (letter of Nov. 19; *Letters*, II, 204-205, 211). Simms's statement in his letter of December 12, 1846, to Lawson, though not directly inspired by his difficulties in collecting for "The Maroon," probably best reveals his frustration at the time: "Never was poor devil so harrassed by publishers as myself. I am cheated and bamboozled on all hands" (*Letters*, II, 238). Finally, though Labree had written to Simms on December 31, 1846, that "I like it ['The Maroon'] much. Please send on soon the concluding part—the *fourth*" (quoted in *Letters,* II, 262n.), Simms announced to Lawson that "The Maroon" was to contain six parts, exactly double the number (and double the pay) originally anticipated: "I forwarded to Labree, a few days ago, the *fourth* part of a story, for each part of which I require $20. There are two other parts which I shall send to you. The six parts will be $120—the drafts in your favor are $50. When I send you these parts, I will send you two other drafts for the balance" (letter of Jan. 26, 1847; *Letters,* II, 262). On February 15, 1847, Simms wrote Lawson, "Enclosed I send you the fifth part of the story which I am furnishing Mr. Labree for his Magazine" (*Letters,* II, 268); and on March 2 the Charlestonian wrote his New York friend and agent: "In a day or two I will send you the sixth part of my story for Labree which it may be well to keep *until called for.* He may be rich, but—we are poor and terribly in want of our sixpences" (*Letters,* II, 274). Two days later Simms sent the following:

dear Lawson

I enclose & send you by the hands of Mr. Richards, the Sixth and Last part of "the Maroon" for Mr. Labree's Magazine. Below you have a statement of the account & an order for the balance. You can say to Mr. Labree that I will send him something farther very shortly or bring it myself in Season for his July issue.

Love to all

Yours Ever &c
W. G. S.

Lawrence Labree Esq.
To W. Gilmore Simms

To 6 nos. of the Maroon @ $20 each	$120.00	
By Drft to Mr. J. Lawson	$ 25.	
" " " "	25.	
" " " "	25.	75.00
Bal. Due		$45.00

Lawrence Labree Esq. Ed Illd. Mage.
Dear Sir—Please pay above balance of forty Five dollars to Mr. James Lawson & oblige Yr. obt. Serv.
March 4. 1847. W. Gilmore Simms

[*Letters,* II, 280]

Despite the pressure under which it was written, Simms thought well of "The Maroon" and republished it, with minor revisions, under the title "The Maroon. A Legend of the Carribees" in the *Southern Literary Gazette,* III (May 4, 11, 18, 25, June 1, 8, 1850). It appeared again substantially unchanged from the 1850 text in *Marie de Berniere: A Tale of the Crescent City, etc. etc. etc.* (1853) under the title "The Maroon; A Legend of the Caribbees" (pp. 190-319). *Marie de Berniere* was reprinted in 1855 from the same plates and reissued as *The Maroon; A Legend of the Caribbees, and Other Tales.* During the 1860's, when Simms conceived the idea of publishing the best of his long fictions under separate covers, he included "The Maroon" in his unsuccessful efforts. To this effect he wrote to John R. Thompson on January 10, 1863:

> . . . I write to you to entreat a little favour at your hands. Having concieved the idea that a series of my minor tales or novels, such as Martin Faber, Castle Dismal, Helen Halsey, The Maroon, Marie de Berniere, &c. would be good selling books especially now, & for reading in camp and along the highways—[(]small volumes each of 150 to 200 pages,—& bringing from 50 to 75/100) I wrote to that effect to Mess'rs West & Johnson. To this letter I got no answer. There is a Mobile publisher with whom I had some correspondence before the war, respecting a series of Southern publications; but Mess'rs W & J. seem to have got the start of him, and as I believe that one good publisher is quite as much as we need at present, I am unwilling to open negotiations with any other, till I hear from these Gentlemen. Will you then do me the favour to see them, and ascertain if my letter was recieved. If recieved, their silence, is perhaps sufficient answer. [*Letters,* IV, 420]

The publishing house of West & Johnson (John M. West and Thomas Johnson), founded in Richmond in 1860, apparently was not interested in Simms's project, nor was Sigmund H. Goetzel, the "Mobile publisher" referred to, but Simms did not drop plans to reissue "The Maroon" in book form. In the South Caroliniana Library is printer's copy for a projected new edition of "The Maroon": a copy of the story extracted from the 1853 *Marie de Berniere* collection (or the identical 1855 re-issue) with seventy-four minor revisions pencilled in by Simms in the wide margins, and with a separate title-page prepared in Simms's hand to read as follows: "The Maroon:/a Romance of the Carib/By W. Gilmore Simms, Esq./Author of 'The Yemassee'/'Eutaw' 'The Partisan'

&c/Columbia S. C./Evans & Cogswell/publisher [very faint]/1865." A line struck through the place, publisher, and date undoubtedly signifies the failure of hopes for the publication of the volume as planned.

Although it must remain only speculation, it seems reasonable that the destruction by fire of "the magnificent manufactories of Evans & Cogswell" after Sherman's occupation of Columbia in February, 1865, terminated the arrangement between author and publisher (see Simms's *Sack and Destruction of the City of Columbia, S. C.: To Which Is Added A List of the Properly Destroyed*, Columbia, S. C.: Power Press of Daily Phoenix, 1865, pp. 18, 68). Further support for this theory comes from Simms's statement in a letter of September 9, 1865, to E. A. Duykinck: "A few months ago, I had a volume in press here. The advent of Sherman was fatal to its publication" (*Letters*, IV, 518). Although here Simms's reference is to a proposed new edition of *As Good as a Comedy* which also failed, there is nothing to preclude the possibility that plans for a "new" edition of "The Maroon" ended for the same reason. But whatever the reason, "The Maroon: A Romance of the Carib" escaped publication, and in the greater evils of the time Simms never made mention of it or his aborted hopes for it.

The first periodical publication of "The Maroon" serves as copy-text, but has been emended as follows: (1) substantive revisions, including chapter headings and paragraphing, which seem to have authority in the 1850 text; and (2) all substantive and accidental changes recorded in Simms's handwriting for the proposed Evans & Cogswell edition of 1865.

A Note on Paragraphing in "The Maroon"

The 1850 text of "The Maroon" incorporated fifty-two paragraphs not appearing in the 1847 *New York Illustrated Magazine* version. In revising for the proposed 1865 Evans & Cogswell edition, Simms called for sixty-four additional paragraphs. The beginning points of these 116 paragraphs are identified in the following tabulation keyed to the Centennial edition text. Those paragraphs Simms specified in his revision for the proposed 1865 edition are designated by asterisks *.

231.10*	253.16*	271.3*	284.21	295.32	302.12
231.24*	253.23*	271.35*	286.6	296.11	302.14*
232.3*	254.31*	272.8*	286.21*	296.25	302.34
233.6*	255.1	272.14*	286.28*	297.1	303.16
245.15*	255.10	272.23*	287.8	297.32*	304.38*
245.23	255.23*	273.1*	287.15	298.9*	305.26
246.5*	256.12	273.16*	287.22*	299.15	306.15
246.22	257.5	274.5*	288.5	299.16	306.31*
246.24	258.29	274.20*	288.27	299.17	308.22*
247.33	259.14	275.23*	288.34	299.19	308.35*
247.36	260.15	276.30*	289.16*	299.22	309.27*
249.7*	261.3*	278.22*	289.29	299.23	311.6*
249.20*	262.26	278.38*	290.15	299.24	311.23*
249.36*	263.8	280.10*	290.25*	299.35*	312.1*
250.7*	264.1	280.23*	291.30	300.17*	312.9*
250.21	265.18	281.33*	292.5	300.32	312.25*
250.35	267.23*	282.14*	292.27	301.6*	313.1
251.11	270.14*	283.11	292.36*	301.14*	313.4
252.29*	270.26*	284.1	294.19	301.35*	313.5*
253.1*	270.35*	284.8*	295.14		

Table I: Emendations and Textual Notes

Listed here are all changes in the copy-text of "The Maroon." The 1847 copy-text reading appears to the left of the bracket, the emended Centennial edition reading to the right. Where no bracket appears the reading is the same in both texts and the refusal to emend is explained in parentheses. Where an explanation of the change is necessary it follows in parentheses.

230. <epigraph> (The epigraph is placed before the part heading rather than after, as in copy-text. The epigraph does not appear in 1850, 1853, or 1855 publications.)

230. PART I.] CHAPTER I.

230.19 the] was the

231.15 lovely] graceful

232.14 of a] of

232.18 face of] face

233.16 her lip] lip

233.22 those of the] the

233.24 gaze] look (This type of change is characteristic of Simms's revisions; it avoids repetition of the word "gaze" in the following line.)

233.29 has] had

234.5 now know that] know that

234.5 ar] are

235.4 of] than usual

235.8 that you] you

235.11 Gitano] Gitana

235.17 could] should

235.20 resumed] resumed but

235.24 is] is so

235. <no chapter>] *CHAPTER II.*

235.32 woman] ~.

236.2 as] was

236.28 sea-dandy] a sea-dandy

236.37 the] their

237.25 of refuge to] of

237.26 hat] that

239. <no chapter>] *CHAPTER III.*

239.28 nothing] nothing left

239.29 forth.] ~"

240.1 injuiry] inquiry

240.3 Senor] Señor

240.6 proceeded] preceded

240.13 features. But] ~, but

240.14 and] or

240.17 him, and his] him. His

240.21 consciousness] exultation

240.30 hateful] thankful

240.31 buised] busied

240.32 Juan; for] ~. For

241.10 meant] mean

242.1 ob use] obtuse

242.29 one] me

242.35 they] thy

243.1 lease] least

243.13 trust that] trust
243.19 titles] tithes
243. PART II.] *CHAPTER IV.*
243.27 Sylva] Silva
243.33 the] by the
243.34 than] then
244.2 pride of] pride to keep up
244.16 bitter, sweet] ~-~
244.16 which] of revenge which
244.17 and revengeful nature] nature
244.34 word,] single word,
244.35 Sylva] Silva
245.26 make] make a
245.33 fondness] gratitude
246.19 the] his
246.28-29 store <. . .> were thrown (Refusal to emend for the sake of subject-verb agreement.)
247.8 friend again] friend
247.10-11 help] help me
247.25 color ("Color" is retained, though 1850 reading is "collar." Either is possible, but "color" seems the better word and "collar" could easily be a printer's error.)
248.3 country.] ~, (The tail of the comma appears broken off in copy-text.)
248.5 Sylva] Silva
248. <rule>] *CHAPTER V.*
249.13 glow] grow
249.25 came] dawned (The substitution of "dawned" for "came" in 1853 is significant because by doing so Simms avoids repetition; see "came" at 249.23.)
249.27 fierce ("Fiery" in 1850 is probably the result of an eye skip on the part of the printer; "fiery" appears immediately above "fierce" in the 1847 text.)
249.34 horizon,] horizon, and
250.17 gliding in (In the 1853 book publication "gliding in" became "gilding it," presumably because of a printer's error. In making revisions in 1865, Simms, forgetting the original form but objecting to "gilding it," wrote in "balming it." Though "balming it" is a

good revision, it is not what he had originally written and forgotten. "Gliding in" seems the best reading of the three—the one closest to the author's intent.)

250.22 of] of the
250.27 existence] existences
251.24 fiendish] a fiendish
252. <rule>] *CHAPTER VI.*
252.23 not one] not
252.31 cöoperated] coöperated
253.6 person] person upon her vengeance
253.10 other] other one
253.13 his tastes] to his tastes
253.13 with] as they did with
253.15 and] and lack of
253.17 she yet] she
253.25 the] in the
254.7 battle] baffle
254.11 movement] movements
254.16 love] loved
255.2 *Gitáno*] *Gitana*

255.6 three weeks (This is a refusal to accept a possible correction in the 1850 text, which reads "two weeks." The last paragraph of Chapter VI indicates that "three weeks" is the more accurate reading. If Simms made the 1850 revision, perhaps to emphasize Maria's seductiveness, he had confused the chronology.

255.16 dialogue. is] dialogue. His
255.17 him tain] him to retain
255.21-22 while] even while

255.24 it (The passage has not been emended although "he" would seem more appropriate.)

255.25-26 had] himself had
255.32 answer] ~.

257.1-2 Dian de Burgos (Though the first reference, at 230.19-231.1, is to the "Diana de Burgos," beginning here and in all later references, some in dialogue, Simms reduces "Diana" to "Dian"—a spelling which, in changing the feminine form to the masculine, possibly calls for emendation.)

257.3 his (Though the 1850 text has "her," it is probably a printer's error.)

257.3 slowly (Once again, the 1850 reading—"lowly"—seems more likely to be a compositorial error than an authorial change.)

257.10 my affections] me in subjection (The emended reading was made by Simms in 1865.)

257.22 as] as a

257.22 over] over the

257.34 Yet ("Yes" in 1850 was probably a compositorial error.)

258.3 the] her

258.7 nurtured] murdered

258.11 Sylva] Silva

258.11 thy ("Thy" seems immensely superior to "my," the 1850 reading, a change almost certainly without authority.)

258. PART III.] *CHAPTER VII.*

258.25 Sylva] Silva

258.25 not] not very

258.30 Linores] Linares

258.32 Sylva] Silva

259.5 not a man] a man not

259.6 with;—and his] ~. His

259.17 discontent] ~.

259.18 withdrawn] withdrawn from her

259.27 Sylva] Silva

259.32 Lanares] Linares

260.3 Sylva] Silva

260.8 Sylva] Silva

260.10 but] save

260. <no chapter>] *CHAPTER VIII.*

261.14 Sylva] Silva

262.6 As] When

262.14 ſilence] silence

262.16 not] not so

262.17 My] Thy

262.22 senor] señor

263.4 of] of a

263.5 these] his

263.26 Senora] Señora

264. <no chapter>] *CHAPTER IX.*
264.15 for] equally for
264.33 Dolorosa] Dolores
265.7 murmured] answered
265.19 terrible] dreadful (In 1850 Simms changed "terrible" to "dreadful" to avoid repetition of word "terrible" in same line.)
265.25 shriek was] shriek, were
265.33 Sylva] Silva
265.36 "The] ‸~
266.8 the conviction] in the conviction
266.9 which] whom
266.9 always] once
266.9 fully] wholly
266.10 exalting] exulting
266.24 knowest] knewest (One reluctantly accepts "knewest"—1853—for "knowest"—1847—because it eliminates the play upon "know" at 266.26, the kind of word-play Simms so liked.)
266.24 dost] didst
266.34 charms] subtleties
266.38 I] that I
267.3 dogs. I will live—I wiil] ~ will (The 1850 text has "dogs—I will" This revision is rejected on the theory that the printer experienced eye-skip and overlooked "I will live.")
267.5 unwillin gspirit] unwilling spirit
267.7 which] for which
267.8 this] the
267.12 suddenly been] been suddenly
267.14 the whole weight (Although the 1850 text has omitted "whole", this change is more likely a compositorial error than Simms's revision.)
267.24 pacified] satisfied
267.27 Sylva] Silva
267.28 delared] declared
267.30 "The Maroon—Lopez de Levya!" (In the copy-text there is space both above and below this line. The compositor may have been following extra space in Simms's manuscript, but there seems no justification in following it on the printed page.)
267.32 Lovers] ~.

267. PART IV.] *CHAPTER X.*
268.24 and] and the
270.20 shubbery] shrubbery
271.1 treetops at his head] tree tops
271.9 it] ~.
271.14 quarter,] quarter, he discovered what
271.17-18 like] like a
271.34 capacious] capricious
271.37 slander] slender
273. <no chapter>] *CHAPTER XI.*
274.1 small] narrow
274.13 contributed to afford] afforded
274.38 shreds] shreds of hair
275. <no chapter>] *CHAPTER XII.*
276.2 perceptable] perceptible
276.5 He chose it for his couch that night. The] The
276., <no chapter>] *CHAPTER XIII.*
276.13 awaking] awakening
276.31 but] and
277.3-4 possessions] ~.
277.12 guided] girded
277. <no chapter>] *CHAPTER XIV.*
277.18-19 sky at the same moment] sky, on the return of night,
278.4 atoms] atom,
279. <no chapter>] *CHAPTER XV.*
279.15 the Cayman (The phrase "the Cayman" in copy-text became "a Cayman" in 1850; in the proposed 1865 edition Simms changed it back to "the cayman.")
279.34 breast] heart
280.5 a hidden fire lay] from a hidden fire
280.19 to] of
280.26 brought] bore
280.32 this] the
280.36 victim?] ~?
281. <no chapter>] *CHAPTER XVI.*
282.15 answered] answered her
282.28 his own] his
282. PART V.] *CHAPTER XVII.*

283.30 that] they

283.31 from which] whence (In changing "from which" to "whence" Simms either failed to strike through "from" or the printer failed to follow his instructions.)

284.14 his chamber] the chamber

284.24 and] and to be

285.4 exhiliarated] exhilarated

285.21 *token*] *totem*

285.21 breast,—badge,] breast,—

285.24 token] *totem*

285. <no chapter>] *CHAPTER XVIII.*

285.28 Without, (In the 1853 text the comma is omitted. In the copy corrected in Simms's hand, the comma is restored, as in the original publication.)

286.22 uucovered] uncovered

287.7 of the wood] of wood

287.8 hers, She] ~. She (In the 1853 text the comma was retained, and "She" became "she."

289.11 was] is

289.19 primeval] primal

289.35 their] her

289.36 devote their] devotes the

290. <no chapter>] *CHAPTER XIX.*

290.8 this comparative] the comparative

290.19 had slept] lay

290.35 sign] sigh

291.10 loving] losing

291. <no chapter>] *CHAPTER XX.*

291.15 fears] hopes

291.16 hopes?] fears?—

291.19 Omaya] Amaya

291.21 rights] rites

291.23 lessonings] teachings

291.31 rejoiced] rejoicing

291.32-33 language—as] ~. The

292.30 hurried to] yearned for

293.14 Lo! thousand] Lo! snow white (The emended reading was made by Simms in his 1865 revision.)

294.28 since] indeed, since
295. <no chapter>] *CHAPTER XXI.*
295.2 while] whilst
295.21 the return of the] the
296.5 in turn in a like] in like
296.17 dusky recesses] dusky interior (Emended reading made by Simms in his 1865 revision.)
296.33 rock] hope
297. <no chapter>] *CHAPTER XXII.*
297.33 attachments] an attachment
298. PART VI.] *CHAPTER XXIII.*
299.11 a] near a
299.12 safety] ~.
299.35 chained] provoked
299.35 of] than the alarm of
300.30 compeled] compelled
300.34 proud] too proud
301.10 he] he had
301.12 alarm] occasion
302.5 next] rest
302.10 own] own languor
302.14 his own heart, whieh rose in the mind of the Maroon] his heart
302. <no chapter>] *CHAPTER XXIV.*
302.29 recesses] ~.
302.36 comple] complete
303.18 every] at every
303. <no chapter>] *CHAPTER XXV.*
305.3-4 from the hearing, by] from their propriety, as he heard, more than once,
305. <no chapter>] *CHAPTER XXVI.*
306.13 "Maroon·"] "Maroon."
306. <no chapter>] *CHAPTER XXVII.*
306.31 had] had both
307.1 seamen] seaman
307.26 outpouring] outpourings
307.27 scene] sense
308. <no chapter>] *CHAPTER XXVIII.*

308.12 similar hopes] their mutual hopes (It is noteworthy that Simms here, in 1853, made this change, echoing "their mutual delights" in the same line.)

308.25 stood,] ~‸ (The comma was deleted by Simms in his 1865 revision.)

308.27 beholding] surveying (In contrast to his technique at 308.12, Simms here more characteristically changed "beholding" in the copy-text to "surveying" in 1850, to avoid repetition of "beholding" two lines above.)

309.9 severs] sever

309.14 that she] she

309.23 satisfation] satisfaction

310.14 swam ("Swam" appeared as "swan" in 1853; Simms corrected it in his own hand in the Charles Carroll Simms Collection copy.)

310. <no chapter>] *CHAPTER XXIX.*

311.28 sing him] sing to Lopez (Emendation adopted from Simms's revision of 1865.)

312.3 cabin] ~.

312.9 *Mader*] *Madre*

312.16 Whispered] whispered

312.25 masess] masses

312.28 recal] recall

312.29 impulses] impulsions

312.35 middle.] ~,

313.4 where] Where

Table II: Textual Variants

Below is a list of the variants between "The Maroon" in the 1847 *New York Illustrated Magazine*, the 1850 *Southern Literary Gazette*, and the 1853 *Marie de Berniere* texts.

Reading from left to right the chart of variants has the following text sequence:

LEFT MARGIN: Centennial edition key
FIRST READING: 1847]
SECOND READING: 1850]
THIRD READING: 1853

230. 8. PART I.] 1.d. I.] 190. CHAPTER I.
230. 8. <epigraph>] 1.d. <no epigraph>] 190. <no epigraph>
230.1 8.a.1 Caribbean] 1.d.1 Carribean] 190.1 Caribbean
230.1 8.a.1 sea] 1.d.1 ~] 190.1 Sea
230.15 8.a.18 were,] 1.d.25 ~] 190.19 ~∧
230.17 8.a.21 levels] 1.d.29 revels] 191.2 revels
230.19 8.a.23 well built] 1.d.33 ~] 191.5 ~-~
230.19 8.a.24 the] 1. d.33-34 was the] 191.5 was the
230.19 8.a.24 "Diana de Burgos,"] 1.d.34 ~] 191.5-6 ∧~∧
231.2 8.a.26 day,] 1.d.37 ~] 191.8 ~∧
231.2 8.a.26 modeling] 1.d.37 ~] 191.8 modelling
231.3 8.a.27 succeeded,] 1.d.39 ~∧—] 191.9 ~
231.8 8.a.33 consciousness] 1.d.47-48 con∧| sciousness] 191.15 consciousness
231.12 8.a.38 new world] 1.d.55 ~] 191.20 New World
231.14-15 8.a.41-42 "Diana de Burgos"] 1.d.59 ~] 191.23-24 ∧~∧
231.15 8.a.42 lovely] 1.d.60 graceful] 191.24 graceful
231.17 8.a.45 fight,] 1.d.64 ~;] 191.27 ~
231.18 8.a.46 sceptic] 1.d.66 ~] 191.28-29 skeptic
231.30 8.b.11 prevails] 1.d.87 prevail] 192.13 prevail
231.34 8.b.16 little,] 1.d.94 ~∧—] 192.18 ~
231.37 8.b.20 inquiry,] 1.d.100 ~∧] 192.22 ~,
231.37 8.b.20 suggestion,] 1.d.101 ~∧] 192.22~
232.4 8.b.23 groups] 1.d.105 group] 192.25 group
232.14 8.b.37 of a] 1.e.14 of] 193.8 of
232.17 8.b.41 short,] 1.e.20 ~∧] 193.13 ~
232.18 8.b.42 face of] 1.e.21 face] 193-13 face
232.20 8.b.44 appearance] 1.e.24 appearace] 193.15-16 appearance
232.20 8.b.45 laboring] 1.e.24 labouring] 193.16 laboring
232.24 8.b.49 grisly] 1.e.31 ~] 193.21 grizzly
232.31 9.a.8-9 female] 1.e.44 ~] 193.30 ~,
232.32 9.a.9 features,] 1.e.45 ~] 193.31 ~∧
232.32 9.a.9 wild] 1.e.45 wildly] 193.31 wildly
232.32 9.a.10 makes] 1.e.46 make] 193.31 make
233.8 9.a.27 lips] 1.e.70 ~,] 194.18 ~
233.10 9.a.30 swerve,] 1.e.74 ~;] 194.21 ~

233.14 9.a.35 then,] 1.e.81 ~] 194.26 ~‸
233.14 9.a.35 seen,] 1.e.82 ~] 194.27 ~‸
233.16 9.a.37 her lip] 1.e.85 lip] 194.29 lip
233.21 9.a.43-44 look out] 1.e.93 ~] 195.5 ~-~
233.22 9.a.45-46 those of the] 1.e.96 the] 195.6 the
233.24 9.a.48 gaze] 1.e.99 look] 195.9 look
233.29 9.a.54 has] 1.e.108 had] 195.15 had
233.34 9.a.60 gipsy] 1.e.117 gypsy] 195.22 ~
233.35 9.a.62 God] 1.e.119 ~ 195.23 ~,
233.37 9.a.63 you, ~,] 1.e.121 ~‸] 195.25 ‸
234.3 9.a.68 threatened!——] 1.e.128 ~] 195.30 ~—
234.5 9.b.1 course,] 1.e.131 ~‸] 196.1 ~,
234.5 9.b.1. now know] 1.e.131 know] 196.1 ~,
234.5 9.b.1. ar] 1.e.131 are] 196.2~
234.9 9.b.6 musician.] 1.f.7 ~] 196.6 ~?
234.9 9.b.7 face] 1.f.8 ~] 196.7 ~,
234.19 9.b.19 true!——] 1.f.25 ~] 196.19 ~—
234.25 9.b.27 guitar player] 1.f.34 ~] 196.27 ~-~
234.27 9.b.29-30 impertinence] 1.f.38 ~] 196.29-30 ~,
234.31 9.b.34 Say!] 1.f.45 ~?] 197.4 ~
235.4 9.b.48-49 less of that cat-like] 1.f.64 less than usual of that cat-like] 197.17-18 less than usual of that catlike
235.7 9.b.52 fear,] 1.f.69 ~‸] 197.21 ~,
235.8 9.b.53 that you] 1.f.70-71 you] 197.22-23 you
235.11 9.b.57 Gitano] 1.f.76 gitano] 197.26 ~
235.17 9.b.65 could] 1.f.87 should] 198.3 should
235.20 9.b.69 resumed] 1.f.93 resumed but] 198.7 resumed, but
235.21 9.b.69 disappointment.] 1.f.93-94 ~:] 198.8 ~—
235.24 10.a.3 Dios!] 1.f.98 ~?] 198.11 ~
235.24 10.a.3 is] 1.f.98 is so] 198.11 is so
235.25 10.a.5 Juan!] 1.f.101 Juan !] 198.13 Juan!
235.26 10.a.5-6 guitar player] 1.f.102 ~] 198.14 ~-~
235.28 10.a.8 Lady] 1.f.105 ~] 198.16 lady
235.29 10.a.9 it,] 1.f.108 ~] 198.18 ~‸
235. 10.a. <no chapter>] 1.f. II.] 198. CHAPTER II.
235.32 10.a.13 woman] 1.f.112 ~.] 198.21 ~
235.32 10.a.14 sunk] 1.f.113 ~] 198.22 sank

236.2 10.a.20 as] 1.f.122 was] 199.2 was

236.4 10.a.22 capacity] 1.f.125-126 ca–| pacity] 199.5 capacity

236.5 10.a.23-24 passion] 1.f.127 ~,] 199.6 ~

236.9 10.a.29 if,] 1.g.6 ~] 199.11 ~‸

236.15 10.a.36 oily] 1.g.15 ~] 199.18 ~,

236.20 10.a.42 cat-like] 1.g.24 ~] 199.24 catlike

236.28 10.a.53 sea-dandy] 1.g.39 a sea-dandy] 200.5 a sea-dandy

236.33 10.a.59 him] 1.g.48 ~] 200.11 ~,

236.37 10.a.66 the] 1.g.57 their] 200.18 their

237.2 10.a.68 scorn,] 1.g.61 ~;] 200.20 ~

237.10 10.b.10-11 accents, "Beware] 1.g.77 ~] 201.1-2 ~‸ Beware

237.10 10.b.11 Maria,] 1.g.77 ~] 201.2 ~;

237.16 10.b.18 said—] 1.g.86 said,] 201.9 ~

237.20 10.b.24 that—] 1.g.94 ~?—] 201.15 ~

237.22 10.b.25 What!] 1.g.96 ~] 201.16~‸

237.22 10.b.25 you where] 1.g.96 ~] 201.16 ~, ~

237.23 10.b.26 are,] 1.g.97 ~] 201.17 ~?

237.23 10.b.26 lady] 1.g.98 ~] 201.17 ~,

237.25 10.b.29 of refuge to] 1.g.101-102 of] 201.20 of

237.26 10.b.30 hat] 1.g.103 that] 201.21 that

237.28 10.b.33 Alas!] 1.g.106 ~] 201.24 ~,

237.28 10.b.33 no!—] 1.g.106 ~‸] 201.24 ~

237.35 10.b.41 guitar;—] 1.g.118 ~.‸] 202.2 ~

237.36 10.b.42 you——] 1.g.120 ~—] 202.3 ~

238.1 10.b.46 serpentlike] 1.g.125-126 serpent-like] 202.7 ~

238.5 10.b.51 so!—] 1.h.1. ~‸] 202.12 ~

238.6 10.b.52 fate] 1.h.3 ~] 202.13 ~,

238.14 10.b.62 lofty] 1.h.17 ~,] 202.23 ~

238.23 11.a.4 here,] 1.h.32 ~‸] 203.3 ~

238.35 11.a.19 away!] 1.h.52 ~.] 203.18 ~

239.6 11.a.27 turned] 1.h.63 ~] 203.27 ~,

239. 11.a. <no chapter>] 1.h. III.] 204. CHAPTER III.

239.9 11.a.32 Sir] 1.h.69 sir] 204.1 ~

239.10 11.a.33 uncle] 1.h.70 ~,] 204.2 ~

239.12 11.a.36 prayer,] 1.h.76 ~‸] 204.6 ~

239.13 11.a.37 argument,] 1.h.76 ~‸] 204.6 ~

239.13 11.a.37 balk] 1.h.76 baulk] 204.6 balk
239.15 11.a.39 dark] 1.h.80 ~,] 204.9 ~
239.17 11.a.42 resolution!] 1.h.83 ~?] 204.11 ~
239.18 11.a.43 Sir—] 1.h.84 sir.] 204.12 ~
239.18 11.a.43-44 but—"here] 1.h.85 ~] 204.12-13 ~"—~
239.20 11.a.45 but,] 1.h.87 ~‸] 204.14 ~
239.25 11.a.52 despair] 1.h.97 ~,] 204.22 ~
239.28 11.a.55 nothing but] 1.h.102 nothing left but] 204.25 nothing left but
239.29 11.a.56 forth.] 1.h.103 ~"] 204.26 ~
239.32 11.a.59 upon,] 1.h.108 ~‸] 205.2 ~
240.1 11.a.63 —was] 1.h.112 ‸~] 205.6 ~
240.1 11.a.63 intelligible] 1.h.112-113 intelligigible] 205.6 intelligible
240.1 11.a.63 injuiry] 1.h.113 inquiry] 205.6 ~
240.3 11.a.65 Senor] 1.h.115 Señor] 205.8 ~
240.6 11.a.68 scene;] 1.h.118 ~,] 205.11 ~
240.6 11.a.68 and] 1.h.118 ~,] 205.11 ~
240.6 11.a.68 proceeded] 1.h.119 preceded] 205.11 ~
240.7 11.a.69 two soldiers] 1.h.120 twosoldiers] 205.12 two soldiers
240.7 11.b.1 manacled,] 1.h.121 ~‸] 205.13 ~
240.10 11.b.5 dark] 1.h.127 ~,] 205.17 ~
240.12 11.b.6 beheld,] 1.h.129 ~‸] 205.18 ~
240.13 11.b.8 person,] 2.a.2 ~‸] 205.20 ~
240.13 11.b.9 features. But] 2.a.3 ~, but] 205.21 ~
240.14 11.b.10 and courage] 2.a.4 or courage] 205.22 or courage
240.15 11.b.10-11 paleness,] 2.a.5 ~—] 205.23 ~
240.17 11.b.13 him, and his] 2.a.9 him. His] 205.25 him. His
240.18 11.b.14 countenances] 2.a.11 countenances] 205.27 countenance
240.21 11.b.18 consciousness] 2.a.16 exultation] 205.30 exultation
240.23 11.b.20-21 conspicuous,] 2.a.19 ~‸] 206.2 ~
240.27 11.b.25 Oh,] 2.a.25 ~‸] 206.6 ~,
240.30 11.b.28 hateful] 2.a.30 thankful] 206.9-10 thankful
240.31 11.b.29 buised] 2.a.31 busied] 206.10 ~

240.32 11.b.31 Juan; for] 2.a.33 ~. For] 206.12 ~
240.32 11.b.31 reserved;] 2.a.34 ~?] 206.12 ~
240.32 11.b.32 mean,] 2.a.34 ~∧] 206.13 ~
240.33 11.b.32 mercy?"] 2.a.35 ~∧] 206.13 ~"
240.34 11.b.33 freedom!] 2.a.36 ~,] 206.14 ~
240.35 11.b.35 that——] 2.a.38 ~] 206.16 ~—
240.36 11.b.36 mercy!] 2.a.39 ~,] 206.17 ~
241.3 11.b.42 Levya] 2.a.48 Leyva] 206.23 Levya
241.6 11.b.46 limbs—] 2.a.54 ~.] 206.27 ~
241.7 11.b.48 addressed—] 2.a.56 ~;] 206.29 ~
241.10 11.b.50 meant] 2.a.59 mean] 206.31 mean
241.16 11.b.56 pause!] 2.a.67 ~.] 207.7 ~
241.20 11.b.61 mercy,] 2.a.74 ~∧] 207.12 ~
241.20 11.b.61 forgiveness,] 2.a.75 ~∧] 207.12-13 ~
241.20 11.b.61 generosity,] 2.a.75 ~∧] 207.13 ~
241.21 11.b.63 Velasquez;] 2.a.77 ~,] 207.14 ~
241.22 11.b.64 hear,] 2.a.78 ~∧] 207.15 ~
241.24 11.b.66 resumed:] 2.a.82 ~] 207.18 ~—
241.33 12.a.8-9 intended,] 2.a.98 ~∧] 207.29-30 ~
241.34 12.a.9 into the] 2.a.98 into] 207.30 into the
241.35 12.a.11 culprit] 2.a.102 ~,] 208.1 ~
241.36 12.a.12 himself] 2.a.103 ~,] 208.2 ~
242.1 12.a.14 ob use] 2.a.106 obtuse] 208.4-5 ~
242.3 12.a.17 Lopez;] 2.a.109-110 ~,] 208.7 ~
242.5 12.a.19 distance,] 2.a.113 ~∧] 208.9-10 ~
242.8 12.a.23 hills,] 2.a.118 ~∧] 208.13 ~
242.9 12.a.25 wild fowl] 2.a.120 wild-fowl] 208.15 ~
242.11 12.a.28 discovered,] 2.a.124-125 ~∧] 208.18 ~
242.11 12.a.29 time,] 2.a.125 ~∧] 208.19 ~
242.16 12.a.34 Love] 2.a.133 love] 208.25 ~
242.17 12.a.35 it] 2.a.135 ~,] 208.26 ~
242.17 12.a.36 Lovers,'—] 2.a.136 ~∧] 208.26 ~
242.18 12.a.37 said;—] 2.a.137 ~,∧] 208.27 ~
242.19 12.a.38 crown,'—] 2.a.139 ~∧] 208.29 ~
242.20 12.a.39 merit] 2.a.140 ~,] 208.30 ~
242.21 12.a.41 desire security] 2.a.142 desiresecurity] 209.1 desire security
242.22 12.a.41 love,] 2.b.1 ~∧] 209.1 ~

242.24 12.a.45 him:] 2.b.6 ~,] 209.5 ~
242.25 12.a.46 apprehension,] 2.b.7 ~‸] 209.6 ~
242.26 12.b.1 of a] 2.b.9 of] 209.7 of
242.27 12.b.2 meditation,] 2.b.11 ~‸] 209.8 ~
242.28 12.b.3 proceeded:] 2.b.12 ~] 209.9 ~:—
242.29 12.b.4 one] 2.b.13 me] 209.10 me
242.31 12.b.6 we] 2.b.17 We] 209.12 ~
242.33 12.b.9 honor] 2.b.20 honour] 209.15 honor
242.34 12.b.10 Henceforth,] 2.b.22 ~‸] 209.16 ~
242.35 12.b.11 Levya;] 2.b.24 ~,] 209.18 ~
242.35 12.b.12 they] 2.b.24 thy] 209.18 thy
242.35 12.b.12 empire,] 2.b.24-25 ~‸] 209.18 ~
242.36 12.b.12 Lovers'] 2.b.25 ~,'] 209.19 ~
243.1 12.b.16 lease] 2.b.31 least] 209.23 least
243.2 12.b.18 sight,] 2.b.34 ~‸] 209.25 ~
243.5 12.b.21-22 tenderness,] 2.b.38-39 ~‸] 209.28-29 ~,
243.5 12.b.22 parties,] 2.b.39 ~‸] 209.29 ~
243.8 12.b.25 fixed,] 2.b.44 ~‸] 210.1 ~
243.12 12.b.30 Juan:] 2.b.51 ~] 210.7 ~.
243.13 12.b.31 son,—] 2.b.52 ~‸] 210.8 ~
243.13 12.b.31 trust that] 2.b.52 trust] 210.8 trust
243.13 12.b.32 said,] 2.b.53 ~‸] 210.8 ~
243.14 12.b.33 him,] 2.b.55 ~‸] 210.10 ~
243.18 12.b.37 time, doubtless,] 2.b.61 ~‸ ~‸] 210.14-15 ~
243.19 12.b.38 subjection,] 2.b.62-63 ~‸] 210.16 ~
243.19 12.b.39 titles] 2.b.63 tithes] 210.16 tithes
243.21 12.b.41 fly;—] 2.b.66 ~,‸] 210.18 ~
243.23 12.b.43-44 which he] 2.b.70 he] 210.21 he
243.24 12.b.45 one] 2.b.72 ~,] 210.22 ~
243.24 12.b.45 least] 2.b.72 ~,] 210.23 ~
243. 54. PART II.] 1.a. IV.] 210. CHAPTER IV.
243.26 54.a.1 pronounced—] 1.a.1 ~] 210.25 ~;
243.26 54.a.1-2 executioner,] 1.a.2 ~,—] 210.25-26 ~‸—
243.27 54a.3 Sylva,] 1.a.3-4 ~] 210.27 Silva ‸
243.28 54.a.3 victim,] 1.a.5 ~,—] 210.27 ~;
243.33 54.a.10 around,] 1.a.14 ~] 211.6 ~‸
243.33 54.a.11 the] 1.a.15 by the] 211.7 by the
243.34 54.a.11 crime,] 1.a.16 ~] 211.7-8 ~‸

243.34 54.a.11 than] 1.a.16 then] 211.8 then
243.35 54.a.12 soul,—] 1.a.17 ~] 211.8 ~,^
243.35 54.a.12-13 moments—] 1.a.17-18 ~] 211.9 ~,
244.1 54.a.14-15 pride of] 1.a.20 pride to keep up] 211.11 pride to keep up
244.2 54.a.15 appearances—] 1.a.20-21 ~] 211.11 ~;
244.2 54.a.15 struggle] 1.a.21 strggle] 211.11 struggle
244.3 54.a.16 firmness—] 1.a.22 ~] 211.12 ~;
244.3 54.a.17 sunk] 1.a.23 ~] 211.13 sank
244.4 54.a.17 imbecility] 1.a.24 ~] 211.14 ~,
244.8 54.a.23 Juan,] 1.a.32 ~^] 211.19 ~
244.9 54.a.24 tyrant,] 1.a.34 ~^] 211.21 ~
244.13 54.a.29 to] 1.a.40-41 to the] 211.25 to the
244.13 54.a.29 supplications,] 1.a.41 ~^] 211.26 ~
244.15 54.a.32 glowring] 1.a.45 ~] 211.29 glowing
244.16 54.b.1 bitter, sweet] 1.a.46 bitter-sweet] 211.29 ~
244.16 54.b.1 which] 1.a.46-47 of revenge which] 211.30 of revenge which
244.17 54.b.2 and revengeful nature] 1.a.48 nature] 211.31 nature
244.17 54.b.3 eyes,] 1.a.48 ~^] 211.31 ~
244.19 54.b.5 entreaties] 1.a.51-52 en-|entreaties] 212.2 entreaties
244.21 54.b.8 nothing,] 1.a.56 ~^—] 212.5 ~
244.22 54.b.9 tyrant,] 1.a.57 ~^] 212.6 ~
244.24 54.b.12 woman,] 1.a.61-62 ~^] 212.9 ~
244.25 54.b.13 half suppressed] 1.a.63 ~] 212.10 ~-~
244.26 54.b.14 teeth!—] 1.a.65 ~^] 212.11 ~
244.29 54.b.18 Yet] 1.a.70 ~] 212.15 yet
244.31 54.b.20 blow,] 1.a.73 ~] 212.18 ~^
244.33 54.b.22-23 tyranny!] 1.b.3 ~.] 212.20 ~
244.34 54.b.24 Beware!"—] 1.b.4 ~^] 212.21 ~
244.34 54.b.24 word,] 1.b.4 single word] 212.21 single word
244.35 54.b.25 Sylva] 1.b.6 ~] 212.22 Silva
244.35 54.b.26 worse] 1.b.7 ~] 212.23 worst
244.36 54.b.26 Would'st] 1.b.8 ~] 212.24 Wouldst
245.3 55.a.1 and,] 1.b.18 ~^] 212.31 ~
245.6 55.a.5 emotion,] 1.b.22 ~^] 213.3 ~

245.6 55.a.5-6 conspicuous,] 1.b.23-24 ~] 213.4 ~∧
245.7 55.a.6 instant,] 1.b.24 ~] 213.4 ~∧
245.7 55.a.7 unseen,] 1.b.25 ~∧] 213.5 ~
245.10 55.a.10 commands] 1.b.30 command] 213.9 command
245.20 55.a.22 of] 1.b.47 Of] 213.21 ~
245.22 55.a.24-25 answered—'I] 1.b.50-51 answered: ¶"~] 213.23-24 ~—¶~
245.23 55.a.25 Lopez;—] 1.b.52 ~∧] 213.24 ~
245.25 55.a.28 Know'st] 1.b.55 ~] 213.27 Knowest
245.26 55.a.29 make] 1.b.57 make a] 213.28 make a
245.28 55.a.32 fortune,] 1.b.61 ~∧] 213.31 ~,
245.29 55.a.33 and,] 1.b.62 ~] 214.1 ~∧
245.31 55.a.35 now,] 1.b.65 ~] 214.3 ~∧
245.31 55.a.36 son,—] 1.b.66 ~∧] 214.4 ~
245.32 55.a.36 Prince] 1.b.67 ~] 214.4 prince
245.33 55.a.38 fondness."] 1.b.68-69 gratitude.] 214.5 gratitude."
245.34 55.a.39-40 hesitated,] 1.b.71 ~∧] 214.6-7 ~
245.37 55.a.42 mercy,] 1.b.75 ~] 214.9 ~;
246.1 55.a.45 purposes] 1.b.79 purpose] 214.12 purpose
246.3 55.a.48 and,] 1.b.83 ~] 214.15 ~∧
246.7 55.a.53 strength,] 1.b.89 ~∧] 214.20 ~,
246.8 55.a.54 wonderful] 1.b.91 wonderrul] 214.21 wonderful
246.9 55.a.55 passionate,] 1.b.92-93 ~] 214.22-23 ~∧
246.10 55.a.57 two, alone,] 1.b.95 ~] 214.24-25 ~∧~∧
246.10 55.a.57 whom] 1.b.96 ~] 214.25 which
246.11 55.a.58 immovable] 1.b.97 immoveable] 214.26 immovable
246.12 55.a.59 scurril] 1.b.98 ~] 214.27 scurrile
246.12 55.a.60 suggestion] 1.b.99 ~] 214.27 ~,
246.13 55.a.61 tauridor,] 1.b.101 ~] 214.28 ~∧
246.15 55.a.64 sea despot] 1.b.104-105 ~] 214.31 ~-~
246.18 55.a.67 and] 1.b.109 ~] 215.3 ~,
246.19 55.a.68 the] 1.b.110 his] 215.4 his
246.19 55.a.68 which,] 1.b.111 ~] 215.4 ~∧
246.19 55.a.68 evident,] 1.b.111 ~∧] 215.5 ~
246.31 55.b.13 the Maroon,] 1.b.129 "~"] 215.19 ~
246.35 55.b.18 countrymen,] 1.c.7 ~] 215.24 ~∧

246.35 55.b.18 Pedro—is it] 1.c.8 ~ it is] 215.24 Pedro, it is

246.36 55.b.19 thus—is it] 1.c.8-9 ~] 215.25; ~; it is

246.37 55.b.20 doom.] 1.c.10 ~!] 215.26 ~

247.2 55.b.23 downward,] 1.c.14 ~‸] 215.29 ~

247.4 55.b.25 island;—] 1.c.17 ~] 215.31 ~;‸

247.5 55.b.26 land,] 1.c.18 ~] 216.1 ~‸

247.7 55.b.29 face,] 1.c.22 ~‸] 216.4 ~

247.8 55.b.30 friend again] 1.c.23 friend] 216.5 friend

247.10 55.b.33 worse than] 1.c.27 ~] 216.8 worset han

247.10 55.b.33 death.] 1.c.27 ~] 216.8 ~?

247.10 55.b.33 help] 1.c.28 help me] 216.8-9 ~

247.13 55.b.36-37 moment,] 1.c.32 ~‸] 216.11-12 ~

247.14 55.b.37 suddenly,] 1.c.33 ~‸] 216.12 ~

247.15 55.b.39 him—] 1.c.36 ~,] 216.14 ~

247.17 55.b.41 Surely] 1.c.39 ~] 216.16 surely

247.19 55.b.44 desolation!] 1.c.42 ~] 216.19 ~?

247.20 55.b.45 other; "Jest] 1.c.43 ~] 216.20 ~ "jest

247.23 55.b.49 Prince] 1.c.49 ~] 216.24 prince

247.25 55.b.51 truly,] 1.c.51 ~] 216.26 ~‸

247.25 55.b.51 color] 1.c.52 collar] 216.26 ~

247.27 55.b.54 Lady] 1.c.56 ~] 216.30 lady

247.27 55.b.54 mine!] 1.c.56 ~,] 216.30 ~

247.29 55.b.56 say'st] 1.c.59 ~] 216.31 sayest

247.30 55.b.57 addressed,] 1.c.60 ~‸] 217.1 ~

247.33 55.b.60-61 death,] 1.c.65 ~‸] 217.5 ~

247.38 55.b.66 Prince] 1.c.73 ~] 217.12 prince

248.3 55.b.69 country.] 1.c.77-78 ~,] 217.15 ~

248.3 56.a.1 faces,] 1.c.78 ~] 217.15 ~‸

248.5 56.a.3 Sylva] 1.c.81 ~] 217.18 Silva

248.9 56.a.8 shore;] 1.c.89 ~‸] 217.23 ~

248.16 56.a.17 she!—] 1.c.101 ~‸] 218.1 ~

248.18 56.a.20 always] 1.c.105 alwys] 218.4 always

248.21 56.a.23 Gradually,] 1.c.110 ~] 218.7 ~‸

248.24 56.a.28 Then,] 1.c.116 ~'] 218.11 ~‸

248.25 56.a.29 hope,—] 1.c.118 ~‸] 218.13 ~

248. 56.a. <rule>] 1.c. V.] 218. CHAPTER V.

248.33 56.a.38 favorite] 1.d.3 favourite] 218.22 favorite

248.33 56.a.38-39 indulgence.] 1.d.3 ~.—] 218.23~‸

248.34 56.a.40 offended,] 1.d.6 ~] 218.24 ~∧

249.1 56.a.42 false,] 1.d.8 ~] 218.26 ~∧

249.1 56.a.42 wounded,] 1.d.8 ~∧—] 218.26 ~

249.2 56.a.43 sides;—] 1.d.10 ~] 219.2 ~∧

249.2 56.a.44 passions] 1.d.11 ~] 219.2 ~,

249.3 56.a.45 set;—] 1.d.13 ~] 219.4 ~∧

249.13 56.a.57 glow] 1.d.30 grow] 219.16 grow

249.18 56.a.63 comrades,] 1.d.39 ~] 219.22 ~∧

249.25 56.b.3 ever chiding] 1.d.49 ~] 219.29 ~-~

249.25 56.b.3 ocean;] 1.d.50 ~] 219.30 ~∧

249.25 56.b.4 came] 1.d.50 dawned] 219.30 dawned

249.26 56.b.5 Eastern] 1.d.51-52 ~] 219.31 eastern

249.27 56.b.6 fierce] 1.d.54 fiery] 220.2 ~

249.28 56.b.8 sun,] 1.d.56 ~,—] 220.3 ~∧—

249.30 56.b.9 youth,] 1.d.58 ~] 220.5 ~∧

249.31 56.b.11 when] 1.d.60 ~,] 220.6 ~

249.31 56.b.11 sunset] 1.d.61 ~,] 220.7 ~

249.34 56.b.14 horizon,] 1.d.66 horizon, and] 220.10 horizon, and

249.35 56.b.16 rescue.] 1.d.67 ~.—] 220.11 ~∧

249.37 56.b.18 night] 1.d.70 ~] 220.13 ~,

250.3 56.b.23 wild fowl,] 1.d.77-78 ~] 220.19 ~-~∧

250.5 56.b.25 waters] 1.d.81 ~] 220.21 ~,

250.17 56.b.39 zephyr] 1.d.101 ~,] 221.4 ~

250.17 56.b.39-40 gliding in] 1.d.101-102 ~] 221.5 gilding it

250.21 56.b.45 scene,] 1.d.109 ~] 221.11 ~∧

250.22 56.b.46 possession] 1.d.111 the possessions] 221.12 the possession

250.27 56.b.52 existence] 1.d.119 existences] 221.18 ~

250.27 56.b.52 sky;] 1.d.120 ~] 221.18 ~,

250.31 56.b.57 men] 1.d.127 ~] 221.23 ~,

251.7 57.a.5 object,] 1.e.20-21 ~∧—] 222.10 ~,∧

251.11 57.a.11 people,] 1.e.29 ~] 222.17 ~∧

251.13 57.a.12 lamentations,] 1.e.31 ~] 222.18 ~∧

251.13 57.a.12 entreaties,] 1.e.31-32 ~] 222.18 ~∧

251.14 57.a.13 hand,] 1.e.33 ~] 222.19 ~∧

251.14 57.a.14 consolation,] 1.e.34 ~] 222.20 ~∧

251.16 57.a.16 Savior] 1.e.37 Saviour] 222.22 ~

251.19 57.a.19 passed] 1.e.42 ∼] 222.26 ∼,
251.21 57.a.22 days] 1.e.45 day] 222.28 day
251.22 57.a.23 night] 1.e.47 ∼] 222.29 ∼,
251.23 57.a.25 sea,] 1.e.49 ∼] 222.31 ∼‸
251.23 57.a.25 themselves;] 1.e.49-50 ∼,] 222.31 ∼‸
251.24 57.a.26 fiendish] 1.e.51 a fiendish] 223.1 a fiendish
251.27 57.a.30 lay] 1.e.56 ∼] 223.5 ∼,
251.30 57.a.33 palm leaves] 1.e.61 ∼] 223.9 ∼-∼
251.36 57.a.42 himself,] 1.e.73 ∼] 223.17 ∼‸
252.2 57.a.45 islet,] 1.e.78 ∼] 223.21 ∼‸
252.5 57.a.49 whom] 1.e.84 ∼] 223.25 which
252. 57.a. <rule>] 1.e. VI.] 224. CHAPTER VI.
252.6 57.a.52 woman] 1.e.86 women] 224.2 woman
252.7 57.a.52 was,] 1.e.87 ∼‸] 224.2 ∼
252.7 57.a.52 degree,] 1.e.87 ∼‸] 224.2 ∼
252.9 57.a.55 so.] 1.e.91 ∼.—] 224.5-6 ∼
252.10 57.a.56-57 attachment] 1.e.93 attatchment] 224.6-7 attachment
252.14 57.a.61 woman] 1.e.99 women] 224.11 woman
252.14 57.a.61-62 fearless] 1.e.100 fearles] 224.11 fearless
252.15 57.a.62 shown,] 1.e.101 ∼] 224.12 ∼‸
252.15 57.a.62 had] 1.e.101 ∼] 224.12 ∼,
252.15 57.a.63 probably] 1.e.101 ∼] 224.12-13 ∼,
252.17 57.a.65 one,] 1.e.105 ∼‸] 224.15 ∼
252.18 57.a.67 slave;] 1.e.107 ∼‸—] 224.17 ∼
252.18 57.a.67 add,] 1.e.107-108 ∼‸—] 224.17 ∼
252.23 57.b.5 not one] 1.e.116 not] 224.23 not
252.25 57.b.8 will.] 1.e.120 ∼.—] 224.27 ∼
252.31 57.b.15 cöoperated] 1.f.2 co-operated] 225.7 ∼
253.2 57.b.24 bondage] 1.f.15 ∼] 225.16 ∼,
253.5 57.b.28 fate] 1.f.21 ∼] 225.20 ∼,
253.6 57.b.28 person] 1.f.21-22 person upon her vengeance] 225.20-21 person upon her vengeance
253.10 57.b.33 other] 1.f.29 other one] 225.26 other one
253.13 57.b.37 Levya—] 1.f.34 ∼,—] 225.30 ∼‸—
253.13 57.b.37 his tastes] 1.f.34 to his tastes] 225.30 to his tastes
253.13 57.b.38 with] 1.f.35-36 as they did with] 225.31 as they did with

253.15 57.b.40 and] 1.f.38 and lack of] 226.2 and lack of
253.17 57.b.42 she yet] 1.f.42 she] 226.4 she
253.19 57.b.45 mind,] 1.f.46 ~‸] 226.7 ~
253.21 57.b.47 done] 1.f.48 ~,] 226.9 ~
253.22 57.b.48 thought,] 1.f.50 ~‸] 226.10 ~
253.25 57.b.52 the] 1.f.55 in the] 226.14 in the
253.26 57.b.53 keen] 1.f.56 ~,] 226.15 ~
253.29 57.b.57 this] 1.f.63 ~] 226.20 his
253.30 57.b.58 he,] 1.f.64 ~‸] 226.21 ~,
253.30 57.b.58 whisper—] 1.f.64 ~,] 226.21 ~
253.31 57.b.59 struggle!] 1.f.65 ~!—] 226.22 ~
253.34 57.b.63 conclusion:] 1.f.72 ~] 226.26-27~‸—
253.36 57.b.65 No!] 1.f.74 ~] 226.29 ~,
253.36 57.b.65 he,—] 1.f.74 ~.‸] 226.29 ~
253.36 57.b.65 die—] 1.f.75 ~] 226.29~;
254.7 58.a.9 battle] 1.f.92 baffle] 227.12 baffle
254.7 58.a.9 vigilance;"—] 1.f.92 ~,"‸] 227.12 ~
254.8 58.a.11 how!—] 1.f.95 ~‸] 227.14 ~
254.9 58.a.12 this;] 1.f.96 ~‸] 227.15 ~
254.11 58.a.14 self conceit] 1.f.99 ~-~] 227.17 ~
254.11 58.a.15 movement] 1.f.100 movements] 227.18 ~
254.12 58.a.16 quaintly cut] 1.f.101 ~] 227.19 ~-~
254.16 58.a.22 love as] 1.f.109 loved as] 227.25 loved as
254.17 58.a.23 enough] 1.f.110 ~] 227.26 ~,
254.36 58.a.45 you;] 1.g.11 ~‸] 228.17 ~
255.3 58.a.51 dance] 1.g.19 ~] 228.23 ~,
255.6 58.a.54 three] 1.g.25 two] 228.27 two
255.6 58.a.55 the "marooning"] 1.g.25 "the marooning"] 228.27-28 ~
255.15 58.a.66 before.] 1.g.41 ~.—] 229.10 ~.‸
255.16 58.a.68 is] 1.g.43 His] 229.11 His
255.17 58.a.68-69 him tain] 1.g.44-45 him to retain] 229.12 him to retain
255.21 58.b.6 while] 1.g.53 even while] 229.18 even while
255.25 58.b.10 had] 1.g.59-60 himself had] 229.23 himself had
255.29 58.b.15 silence] 1.g.66 ~,] 229.28 ~
255.32 58.b.19 answer] 1.g.71 ~.] 229.31 ~
255.38 58.b.26 continued:] 1.g.80 ~] 230.7 ~‸—
256.3 58.b.30 pain,] 1.g.86 ~.] 230.11 ~;

256.4 58.b.30 now"——] 1.g.86 ~] 230.11 ~‸—"
256.5 58.b.31-32 right—] 1.g.88 ~] 230.13 ~;
265.5 58.b.32 you;] 1.g.88 ~?] 230.13 ~‸
256.7 58.b.33 spirit!] 1.g.90 ~] 230.14 ~?
256.8 58.b.34 Yes!] 1.g.91 ~] 230.15 ~,
256.8 58.b.35 character?—] 1.g.92 ~?‸] 230.16 ~
256.10 58.b.36 beauty] 1.g.95 ~] 230.17 ~,
256.10 58.b.37 but"——] 1.g.95 ~] 230.18 ~‸—"
256.11 58.b.38 But,] 1.g.96 ~‸] 230.19 ~
256.11 58.b.38 what!] 1.g.96 ~] 230.19 ~?
256.18 58.b.46 know] 1.g.108 ~] 230.28 ~,
256.20 58.b.49 may,] 1.g.110 ~] 230.30 ~;
256.20 58.b.50 treachery,] 1.g.111 ~] 230.31 ~‸
256.21 58.b.50 falsehood,] 1.g.112 ~] 230.31 ~‸
256.21 58.b.50 meanness,] 1.g.112 ~] 230.31 ~‸
256.24 58.b.54 so,—] 1.g.118 ~‸—] 231.4 ~;‸
256.26 58.b.56 be,] 1.g.120 ~] 231.6 ~;
256.28 58.b.58 demand] 1.g.124 ~] 231.8 ~,
256.29 58.b.60 fear,] 1.g.126 ~‸] 231.10 ~
256.32 58.b.63 you,] 1.g.130 you, and] 231.13 you,
256.32 58.b.63-64 command,] 1.h.1 ~‸] 231.13-14 ~
256.33 58.b.65 but no!] 1.h.3 ~] 231.15 ~,
256.34 58.b.67 feel,] 1.h.5 ~‸] 231.17 ~
256.38 59.a.1 isle] 1.h.11 ~] 231.20 ~,
257.3 59.a.6 upon his] 1.h.17 upon her] 231.25 upon her
257.3 59.a.6-7 finger,] 1.h.18 ~‸] 231.26 ~
257.3 59.a.7 slowly] 1.h.18 lowly] 231.26 lowly
257.4 59.a.7 ears—] 1.h.19 ~:] 231.26 ~‸—
257.5 59.a.8 something,] 1.h.20 ~] 231.27 ~;
257.5 59.a.8 Silva,—] 1.h.21 ~,‸] 231.28 ~
257.6 59.a.9 uncle!——] 1.h.22 ~] 231.29 ~!—
257.7 59.a.10 Maria;—] 1.h.24 ~‸—] 231.30 ~;‸
257.8 59.a.12 so;—] 1.h.26 ~‸] 232.1 ~
257.10 59.a.14 affections—] 1.h.28-29 ~] 232.3 ~;
257.10 59.a.14 if,] 1.h.29 ~] 232.3 ~‸
257.12 59.a.16 solely,—] 1.h.31 ~‸—] 232.5 ~,‸
257.16 59.a.22 but—] 1.h.37 ~—.] 232.11 ~‸
257.21 59.a.28 that,] 1.h.44 ~‸] 232.17 ~,

257.21 59.a.28 Juan;—] 1.h.44 ~‸—] 232.17 ~
257.22 59.a.29 as] 1.h.45 as a] 232.18 as a
257.22 59.a.30 over] 1.h.47 over the] 232.19 over the
257.23 59.a.30-31 uncle!] 1.h.48 ~] 232.20 ~?
257.24 59.a.32 him!—] 1.h.49 ~!‸] 232.21 ~
257.24 59.a.32 Enough!] 1.h.49 ~!—] 232.21 ~
257.24 59.a.32 Think'st] 1.h.50 ~] 232.21 Thinkest
257.25 59.a.33 Think'st] 1.h.51 ~] 232.22 Thinkest
257.27 59.b.2 spoils.] 1.h.55 ~] 232.25 ~?
257.28 59.b.3 thou ——"] 1.h.56 ~] 232.26 ~"—
257.30 59.b.5 should'st] 1.h.59 should't] 232.28 shouldst
257.34 59.b.11 still,] 1.h.66 ~‸] 233.3 ~
257.34 59.b.11 Yet] 1.h.67 Yes] 233.3 Yes
257.35 59.b.12 can'st] 1.h.68 ~] 233.4 canst
257.39 59.b.17 Yet] 1.h.74 ~,] 233.9 ~‸
258.2 59.b.20 separated] 1.h.78 seperated] 233.12 separated
258.3 59.b.21 the] 1.h.80 her] 233.13 her
258.4 59.b.23 Ay!] 1.h.82 ~] 233.15 ~,
258.4 59.b.23 methinks,] 1.h.82 ~‸] 233.15 ~
258.6 59.b.26 sister,] 1.h.86 ~] 233.18 ~‸
258.7 59.b.27 nurtured] 1.h.88 murdered] 233.19 murdered
258.11 59.b.32 Sylva] 1.h.95 ~] 233.24 Silva
258.11 59.b.33 thy] 1.h.96 my] 233.25 my
258. 112. PART III.] 1.a. VII.] 234. CHAPTER VII.
258.13 112.a.1 favorite] 1.a.1-2 favourite] 234.1 favorite
258.17 112.a.6 Burgos.] 1.a.8 ~.—] 234.6 ~‸
258.17 112.a.6 young,] 1.a.9 ~‸] 234.7 ~,
258.19 112.a.8 board,] 1.a.12 ~‸] 234.9 ~
258.25 112.a.16 Sylva] 1.a.23 ~] 234.17 Silva
258.25 112.a.16 not] 1.a.23 not very] 234.17 not very
258.30 112.a.21 Biscayan] 1.a.31 ~] 234.22 ~,
258.30 112.a.22 Linores] 1.a.31 ~] 234.23 Linares
258.31 112.a.23 habitually;—] 1.a.33 ~;‸] 234.24 ~
258.32 112.a.25 Sylva] 1.a.35-36 ~] 234.26 Silva
258.33 112.a.25 it] 1.a.36 ~,] 234.26 ~
258.35 112.a.29 interfered,] 1.a.41 ~;] 235.2 ~
259.2 112.a.30 sought,] 1.a.43 ~] 235.4 ~‸
259.2 112.a.31 civilities,] 1.a.44 ~‸] 235.5 ~

259.3 112.a.32 cheap,] 1.a.45 ~‸] 235.5-6 ~
259.5 112.a.34 parties;—] 1.a.49 ~,‸] 235.8 ~
259.5 112.a.35 not a man] 1.a.49 a man not] 235.9 a man not
259.6 112.a.35-36 with;—and his] 1.a.50 with. ‸His] 235.9 with. ‸His
259.7 112.a.37 of the] 1.a.52 of] 235.10 of the
259.8 112.a.38 only.] 1.a.53 ~.—] 235.12 ~.‸
259.8 112.a.38 rankled,] 1.a.54 ~‸] 235.12 ~,
259.8 112.a.39 re-opened] 1.a.55 ~] 235.13 reopened
259.12 112.a.43 resentments,] 1.a.61 ~] 235.17 ~‸
259.16 112.a.47 sometime] 1.a.68 some time] 235.21-22 some time
259.17 112.a.49 discontent] 1.a.69-70 ~.] 235. 23 ~
259.18 112.a.50 withdrawn] 1.b.1-2 withdrawn from her] 235.24 withdrawn from her
259.19 112.a.51 possesses] 1.b.3 possess] 235.25 possess
259.24 112.b.5 listen,] 1.b.13 ~] 236.2 ~‸
259.26 112.b.7 together;] 1.b.16 ~] 236.3 ~,
259.27 112.b.9 Sylva] 1.b.18 ~] 236.5 Silva
259.31 112.b.15 arouse] 1.b.26 a arouse] 236.11 arouse
259.32 112.b.15 Lanares] 1.b.26-27 Linares] 236.11 ~
259.33 112.b.17 subsequently] 1.b.29 ~,] 236.13 ~
259.34 112.b.17-18 Velasquez,] 1.b.30 Velesquez;] 236.14 Velasquez;
259.36 112.b.21 possession] 1.b.34-35 possesion] 236.17 possession
259.36 112.b.21 Besides] 1.b.35-36 ~,] 236.17-18 ~
260.1 112.b.24 No!] 1.b.40 ~] 236.21 ~,
260.1 112.b.24-25 Biscayan,—] 1.b.41 ~‸—] 236.22 ~;‸
260.3 112.b.26 testimony,] 1.b.43 ~] 236.23 ~‸
260.3 112.b.26 mine,] 1.b.43 ~] 236.23 ~‸
260.3 112.b.27 Sylva] 1.b.44 ~] 236.24 Silva
260.3 112.b.27 mightest] 1.b.44 might'st] 236.24 mightest
260.4 112.b.28 would'st] 1.b.45 ~] 236.25 wouldst
260.5 112.b.30 not,] 1.b.47 ~] 236.27 ~‸
260.5 112.b.30 crew!——] 1.b.47 ~] 236.27 ~!—
260.7 112.b.32 should!—] 1.b.49 ~!‸] 236.29 ~
260.8 112.b.34 Sylva] 1.b.52 ~] 236.31 Silva

260.9	112.b.35 Let] 1.b.53 ~] 237.1 ~,
260.9	112.b.35 then] 1.b.53 ~] 237.1 ~,
260.9	112.b.35 can'st] 1.b.54 ~] 237.2 canst
260.10	112.b.36 but] 1.b.55 save] 237.2 save
260.12	112.b.39 But,] 1.b.60 ~] 237.5 ~^
260.14	112.b.41 vessel——] 1.b.62 ~] 237.7 ~—
260.16	112.b.42 friends—] 1.b.64 ~] 237.9 ~;
260.21	112.b.49 thee] 1.b.74 ~] 237.16 ~,
260.22	112.b.50 conspiracy."] 1.b.75 ~] 237.17 ~.^
260.24	112.b.53 behold] 1.b.79 ~,] 237.20 ~
260.	113.a. <no chapter>] 1.b. VIII.] 237. CHAPTER VIII.
260.29	113.a.6 still,] 1.b.88 ~^] 237.26 ~
261.9	113.a.23-24 sadness] 1.b.112 ~,] 238.16-17 ~
261.10	113.a.24 too,] 1.b.113 ~] 238.17 ~^
261.14	113.a.30 Sylva] 1.b.121 ~] 238.23 Silva
261.15	113.a.31 well feigned] 1.b.122 ~] 238.24 ~-~
261.17	113.a.33 Maria.] 1.b.126 ~] 238.26 ~?
261.21	113.a.37 did'st] 1.c.1 ~] 238.30 didst
261.22	113.a.38 that] 1.c.3 ~] 239.1 because
261.22	113.a.38-39 irresolute,] 1.c.3 ~^] 239.2 ~
261.27	113.a.44 now] 1.c. 11 ~,] 239.7 ~^
261.27	113.a.45 thee,] 1.c.12 ~] 239.8 ~^
261.35	113.a.55 "Belerma,"—] 1.c.27 ~^] 239.18 '~'
261.35	113.a.55 favorite] 1.c.28 favourite] 239.18 favorite
262.2	113.a.59 en èl] 1.c.32 èn el] 239.22 ~
262.5	113.a.62 rendered:] 1.c.35 ~] 239.25 ~—
262.6	113.a.63 As] 1.c.36 When] 239.26 When
262.11	113.a.68 powerful,] 1.c.41-42 ~^] 239.31 ~
262.14	113.b.3 silence] 1.c.47 silence] 240.4 ~
262.16	113.b.5 not] 1.c.50 not so] 240.6 not so
262.16	113.b.6 Maria] 1.c.51 ~] 240.7 ~,
262.17	113.b.6 My] 1.c.51 Thy] 240.7 Thy
262.19	113.b.9 beauty] 1.c.55 ~] 240.10 ~,
262.19	113.b.9 would'st] 1.c.56 ~] 240.10 wouldst
262.22	113.b.12 mi,] 1.c.60 ~^] 240.14 ~
262.32	113.b.23 should'st] 1.c.73 ~] 240.26 shouldst
262.32	113.b.23 uncle] 1.c.74 ~] 240.27 ~,

262.32 113.b.24 mine;] 1.c.74 ~,] 240.27 ~

263.3 113.b.29 Juan,] 1.c.81 ~] 241.1 ~;

263.4 113.b.30 of] 1.c.83 of a] 241.2 of a

263.5 113.b.31 these] 1.c.84 his] 241.3 his

263.5 113.b.32 footstep?] 1.c.86 ~] 241.4-5 ~!

263.6 113.b.33 Gomez;] 1.c.87 ~,] 241.6 ~

263.13 113.b.40 conclusion] 1.c.98 ~] 241.14 ~,

263.17 113.b.46 extricate] 1.c.106 ~,] 241.20 ~∧

263.17 113.b.46 condition,] 1.c.107 ~] 241.20 ~∧

263.21 113.b.50 round] 1.c.113 ~,] 241.24 ~

263.23 113.b.53 form,] 1.c.116 ~] 241.27 ~∧

263.25 113.b.56 Baldwin:] 1.c.121 ~] 241.30 ~:—

263.28 113.b.59 ti] 1.c.124 tì] 242.3 ~

263.30 113.b.61 muerte] 1.c.126 ~,] 242.5 ~

263.33 113.b.64 mi] 1.c.129 mì] 242.8 ~

263.35 113.b.66 mi] 1.c.131 mì] 242.10 ~

264.1 113.b.69 thus:] 1.d.2 ~] 242.13 ~—

264.3 114.a.2 cries,] 1.d.4 ~] 242.15 ~;

264.8 114.a.7 terror] 1.d.9 ~] 242.20 ~,

264.8 114.a.7 drinking,] 1.d.9 ~] 242.20 ~∧

264.10 114.a.9 son] 1.d.11 ~] 242.22 Son,

264.10 114.a.9 entreating,] 1.d.11 ~] 242.22 ~∧

264.12 114.a.11 soul,] 1.d.13 ~∧] 242.24 ~,

264. 114.a. <no chapter>] 1.d. IX.] 242. CHAPTER IX.

264.14 114.a.13 Hymn] 1.d.16 hymn] 242.26 ~

264.15 114.a.14 Velasquez,] 1.d.17 ~∧] 242.27 ~

264.15 114.a.14 for] 1.d.17 equally for] 242.27 equally for

264.15 114.a.15 ears,] 1.d.18 ~∧—] 242.28 ~

264.16 114.a.16 human] 1.d.19 ~] 242.29 humane

264.18 114.a.18 Heaven,] 1.d.22 ~] 243.1 ~∧

264.22 114.a.23 Hymn] 1.d.29 ~] 243.6 hymn

264.27 114.a.29 Thy] 1.d.38 The] 243.13 The

264.27 114.a.29 Hymn] 1.d.38 ~] 243.13 hymn

264.30 114.a.33 Hymn] 1.d.45 ~] 243.18 hymn

264.33 114.a.36 blind,] 1.d.49 ~] 243.20 ~∧

264.33 114.a.37 Dolorosa,] 1.d.49 Dolores,] 243.21 ~∧

265.2 114.a.41 Hymn] 1.d.56 ~] 243.26 hymn

265.4 114.a.44 to-night.] 1.d.59 ~] 243.28 ~,

265.7 114.a.48 murmured] 1.d.65 answered] 244.1 answered
265.10 114.a.51 strength.] 1.d.69 ~!] 244.4 ~
265.11 114.a.52 strength?] 1.d.71 ~!] 244.5 ~
265.11 114.a.52 Juan!] 1.d.72 ~] 244.5 ~?
265.12 114.a.54 help.] 1.d.74 ~!] 244.7 ~
265.14 114.a.55 Maria] 1.d.77 Marria] 244.10 Maria
265.18 114.a.59 go'st] 1.d.83 ~] 244.14 goest
265.18 114.a.59 rightly] 1.d.83 ~] 244.14 ~,
265.18 114.a.60 Juan?"] 1.d.84 ~‸] 244.14 ~
265.19 114.a.60 terrible] 1.d.85 dreadful] 244.15 dreadful
265.23 114.a.66 Now! now!] 1.d.92 ~~] 244.21 ~,~,
265.23 114.a.66-67 Quick!—] 1.d.93 ~‸] 244.21 ~
265.25 114.a.68 shriek] 1.d.94 ~,] 244.23 ~
265.25 114.a.68 was] 1.d.95 were] 244.23 were
265.29 114.b.4 agony,] 1.d.102 ~‸] 244.29 ~
265.29 114.b.4 help,] 1.d.102 ~] 244.29 ~‸—
265.31 114.b.6 uncle,] 1.d.105 ~] 245.1 ~‸
265.31 114.b.6 traitor,] 1.d.106 ~—] 245.1 ~‸—
265.33 114.b.8 Sylva,] 1.d.107 ~] 245.3 Silva ‸
265.34 114.b.9 captain.] 1.d.109 ~!] 245.4 ~
265.35 114.b.10 crew.—] 1.d.110 ~‸] 245.5 ~
265.37 114.b.13 confederate] 1.d.114 ~] 245.8 ~,
265.37 114.b.13 Gomez] 1.d.114 ~] 245.8 ~,
265.38 114.b.15 devised,] 1.d.116 ~‸] 245.10 ~
266.1 114.b.16 subtleties,] 1.d.118-119 ~] 245.11 ~;
266.3 114.b.18 doomed] 1.d.121 ~,] 245.13 ~
266.9 114.b.25 which] 1.d.130 whom] 245.20 whom
266.9 114.b.25 always] 1.d.130 once] 245.20 once
266.9 114.b.25 feared,] 1.d.130-1.e.1 ~] 245.20 ~‸
266.9 114.b.26 fully] 1.e.1 wholly] 245.21 wholly
266.9 114.b.26 power,] 1.e.1 ~] 245.21 power; and
266.10 114.b.26 exalting] 1.e.2 exulting] 245.21 exulting
266.11 114.b.28 worn.] 1.e.4 ~—] 245.23 ~‸
266.12 114.b.29 toward] 1.e.5 towards towards] 245.24 towards
266.12 114.b.29 clamorous] 1.e.6 clamourous] 245.24 clamorous
266.13 114.b.30 Maria;] 1.e.7 ~] 245.25 ~!

266.13 114.b.30 captive;] 1.e.8 ~∧] 245.25 ~
266.13 114.b.31 men,] 1.e.8 ~] 245.26 ~∧
266.17 114.b.34 friend,] 1.e.13 ~] 245.29 ~∧
266.18 114.b.36 woman!] 1.e.15 ~] 245.31 ~?
266.20 114.b.38 nigh] 1.e.18 ~] 246.2 ~,
266.23 114.b.41 Maria] 1.e.22 ~,] 246.5 ~
266.23 114.b.41 me!] 1.e.22 ~] 246.6 ~?
266.24 114.b.43 knowest] 1.e.24 knewest] 246.7 knewest
266.24 114.b.43 dost] 1.e.25 didst] 246.7 didst
266.26 114.b.44 fiend—] 1.e.26 ~] 246.9 ~;
266.33 114.b.52 This then] 1.e.37 ~] 246.18 ~, ~,
266.34 114.b.53 charms.] 1.e.39 subtleties!] 246.19 subtleties!
266.37 114.b.57 Oh!] 1.e.44 ~] 246.23 ~,
266.38 114.b.58 Think'st] 1.e.46 ~] 246.24 Thinkest
266.38 114.b.58 I] 1.e.46 that I] 246.25 that I
266.38 114.b.59 such] 1.e.47 ~] 246.25 such a
267.3 114.b.61 off!—] 1.e.51 ~∧] 246.28 ~
267.3 114.b.62 dogs.] 1.e.51 ~∧—] 246.28 ~
267.3 114.b.62 will live—I wiil!—] 1.e.52 will!—] 246.28-29 will!—
267.5 114.b.65 unwilling spirit] 1.e.56 unwilling spirit] 247.1 unwilling spirit
267.7 114.b.66 which] 1.e.58 for which] 247.3 for which
267.7 114.b.67 strength] 1.e.59 ~] 247.3 ~,
267.8 114.b.68 this] 1.e.61 the] 247.5 the
267.8 114.b.69 moment.] 1.e.61 ~—] 247.5 ~∧
267.12 115.a.4 suddenly been] 1.e.68 been suddenly] 247.9 been suddenly
267.14 115.a.6 bulwarks.] 1.e.71 ~—] 247.12 ~
267.14 115.a.7 Suddenly] 1.e.72 ~,] 247.12 ~
267.14 115.a.7 the whole weight] 1.e.72 the weight] 247.12 the weight
267.17 115.a.11 hoarse] 1.e.78 horse] 247.16 hoarse
267.20 115.a.15 Gomez,—] 1.e.83 ~∧] 247.20 ~
267.21 115.b.1 of] 1.e.84 ef] 247.21 of
267.21 115.b.1 death-struggles] 1.e.85-86 ~∧~] 247.22 ~-~
267.24 115.b.4 pacified] 1.e.89 satisfied] 247.24 satisfied
267.27 115.b.8 Sylva] 1.e.94 ~] 247.28 Silva

267.27 115.b.9 Mistress] 1.e.95 ~] 247.28 mistress

267.28 115.b.9 Linares,] 1.e.96 ~‸] 247.30 ~

267.28 115.b.9 delared] 1.e.96-97 declared] 247.30 declared

267.29 115.b.10-11 <one line lead> "The] 1.e.98-99 <normal lead> ¶ "The] 247.30-31 <normal lead> "The

267.31 115.b.12 obeyed—] 1.e.100 ~;] 248.1 ~

267.32 115.b.14 Lovers] 1.e.103 ~.] 248.3 ~

267. 149. Part IV] 1.e. X.] 248. CHAPTER X.

267.33 149.a.1 "Maroon."] 1.e.104 ~] 248.4 ‸~‸

267.34 149.a.2 island,] 1.e.105 ~‸] 248.5 ~

268.1 149.a.5 dangers,] 1.e.110 ~] 248.8 ~‸

268.2 149.a.7 indeed,] 1.e.112-113 ~] 248.10 ~‸

268.4 149.a.9 well] 1.e.115 ~] 248.12 well as

268.4 149.a.9 suffering,] 1.e.116 ~] 248.12-13 ~‸

268.8 149.a.13-14 succumb] 1.e.122 succomb] 248.17 succumb

268.8 149.a.14 usually,] 1.e.123 ~] 248.17-18 ~‸

268.11 149.a.18 and] 1.e.128 ~,] 248.21 ~

268.12 149.a.19 themselves,] 1.e.129 ~] 248.22 ~‸

268.12 149.a.19 sufferer,] 1.f.1. ~] 248.22 ~‸

268.15 149.a.23 resistance] 1.f.7 resistence] 249.1 resistance

268.16 149.a.24 farther,] 1.f.8 ~] 249.1 ~‸

268.17 149.a.25 fails,] 1.f.10 ~] 249.3 ~‸

268.18 149.a.27 developments,] 1.f.11-12 ~] 249.4 ~‸

268.20 149.a.29 which,] 1.f.15 ~] 249.6 ~‸

268.21 149.a.30 necessity,] 1.f.16-17 ~] 249.8 ~‸

268.24 149.a.35 and] 1.f.23 and the] 249.12 and the

268.27 149.a.38 weapons,] 1.f.28 ~‸—] 249.15 ~

268.32 149.a.45 was indeed] 1.f.37 ~] 249.22 was, indeed,

268.33 149.a.46 wild fowl] 1.f.38-39 ~] 249.23 ~-~

268.36 149.a.50 punish] 1.f.44-45 ~] 249.28 ~,

269.1 149.a.53-54 consciousness] 1.f.49 conscionsness] 249.31 consciousness

269.5 149.b.1 Velasquez] 1.f.57 Velasquex] 250.5 Velasquez

269.14 149.b.12 palm trees] 1.f.72 ~] 250.16-17 ~-~

269.16 149.b.14 instrument,] 1.f.76 ~‸] 250.19 ~

269.18 149.b.17 engulphing] 1.f.80 ~] 250.22 engulfing

269.19 149.b.18-19 forebore] 1.f.82 ~] 250.23 forbore

269.22 149.b.22 it,] 1.f.87 ~] 250.27 ~‸

269.32 149.b.35 favorite] 1.f.104-105 favourite] 251.9 favorite
269.32 149.b.35 palm trees] 1.f.105 ~] 251.9 ~-~
269.33 149.b.36 mother,] 1.f.106 ~] 251.10 ~∧
269.33 149.b.37 a while] 1.f.107 ~] 251.11 awhile
269.36 149.b.40 indicated by] 1.f.112-113 indica- | by] 251.14 indicated by
270.7 149.b.52 examination.] 1.f.128 ~—] 251.25 ~∧
270.12 150.a.1 verdure] 1.g.6-7 ~] 252.1 ~,
270.15 150.a.4 sand hills] 1.g.11 ~] 252.4 ~-~
270.15 150.a.4 sea,] 1.g.11 ~‘] 252.5 ~,
270.18 150.a.8 had,] 1.g.17 ~] 252.9 ~∧
270.19 150.a.9 places] 1.g.18 ~,] 252.9 ~∧
270.20 150.a.10 shubbery] 1.g.20 shrubbery] 252.11 ~
270.21 150.a.12 breadfruit] 1.g.22 ~] 252.12 ~,
270.22 150.a.12 pine apple] 1.g.23 ~] 252.13 pineapple
270.34 150.a.28 heaven] 1.g.44-45 ~] 252.29 Heaven
270.36 150.a.30 footsteps] 1.g.48 ~,] 252.31 ~
271.1 150.a.34 tree tops at his head,] 1.g.53 tree tops,] 253.4 tree-tops,
271.3 150.a.35-36 “Maroon”] 1.g.55 ~] 253.5 ∧~∧
271.6 150.a.40 point,] 1.g.62 ~∧] 253.10 ~
271.9 150.a.44 it] 1.g.67 ~.] 253.14 ~
271.11 150.a.47 until] 1.g.71 ~,] 253.17 ~
271.14 150.a.50 quarter,] 1.g.76-77 quarter, he discovered what] 253.20-21 quarter, he discovered what
271.17 150.a.54 like] 1.g.82 like a] 253.25 like a
271.22 150.a.60 forward.] 1.g.90 ~—] 253.30 ~∧
271.24 150.a.62 eminence] 1.g.93 ~] 254.12 ~,
271.24 150.a.63 rose,] 1.g.94 ~] 254.2 ~∧
271.25 150.a.64 beach,] 1.g.96 ~∧] 254.3 ~
271.25 150.a.64 feet] 1.g.96 ~,] 254.3 ~
271.28 150.a.67-68 bigger] 1.g.101 ~,] 254.7 ~
271.28 150.a.68 seem] 1.g.101 ~,] 254.7 ~
271.29 150.a.69 them] 1.g.103 ~] 254.9 ~,
271.32 150.b.4 points] 1.g.108 ~] 254.12 ~,
271.33 150.b.5 currents] 1.g.110 ~] 254.14 ~,
271.34 150.b.6 capacious] 1.g.111 capricious] 254.14 capricious
271.36 150.b.9 beyond,] 1.g.115 ~] 254.17 ~∧

271.37 150.b.10 slander] 1.g.117 slender] 254.18 slender

271.37 150.b.10 speck] 1.g.117 ~] 254.19 ~,

271.38 150.b.11 with] 1.g.119 wich] 254.20 with

272.5 150.b.17 disappear,] 1.g.127 ~] 254.26 ~‸

272.11 150.b.26 lay,] 1.h.8 ~] 255.3 ~‸

272.11 150.b.26 glinting] 1.h.9 ~] 255.3-4 glistening

272.13 150.b.27-28 sun- | light] 1.h.11 sun-light] 255.5 sunlight

272.14 150.b.28 esplanade,] 1.h.11 ~‸] 255.5 ~,

272.14 150.b.29 inviting,] 1.h.12 ~‸] 255.6 ~,

272.15 150.b.29 "Maroon"] 1.h.13 ~] 255.6 ‸~‸

272.16 150.b.31 steps] 1.h.15 ~,] 255.8 ~

272.17 150.b.32 hillside] 1.h.16-17 hill- | side] 255.9 hill-side

272.18 150.b.33 imagine,] 1.h.19 ~] 255.10-11 ~‸

272.19 150.b.35 footsteps,] 1.h.21 ~] 255.12 ~‸

272.23 150.b.39 along] 1.h.27 ~] 255.17 ~,

272.25 150.b.41 and] 1.h.30 ~,] 255.19 ~

272.29 150.b.47 then] 1.h.38 ~,] 255.24 ~

272.31 150.b.49 love,] 1.h.41 ~] 255.26 ~‸

272.34 150.b.53 sunk] 1.h.46 ~] 255.30 sank

272.35 150.b.55 lay,] 1.h.49 ~] 256.1 ~‸

272.36 150.b.55 moaning,] 1.h.49 ~] 256.1 ~‸

272.36 150.b.56 till,] 1.h.50 ~] 256.2 ~‸

272.36 150.b.56 once,] 1.h.50 ~] 256.2 ~‸

272.37 150.b.56 him,] 1.h.51 ~‸] 256.2 ~

273.1 150.b.60 Starting] 1.h.56 Startling] 256.6 Starting

273.5 150.b.66 looked,] 1.h.64 ~] 256.13 ~‸

273.6 150.b.66 threatening,] 1.h.65 ~] 256.13 ~‸

273.9 151.a.2 moss] 1.h.71 ~] 256.17 ~,

273.14 151.a.9 "Maroon,"] 1.h.80-81 ~] 256.24 ‸~‸

273.19 151.a.15 gradual,] 1.h.89 ~] 256.30 ~‸

273.25 151.a.22 he,] 1.h.99 ~] 257.7 ~‸

273.25 151.a.22 length,] 1.h.100 ~] 257.7 ~‸

273. 151.a. <no chapter>] 1.a. XI.] 257. CHAPTER XI.

273.30 151.a.29 echos] 1.a.2 echoes] 257.13 ~

274.1 151.a.37 small] 1.a.14 narrow] 257.21 narrow

274.2 151.a.38 cavern.] 1.a.15 ~.—] 257.22 ~.‸

274.5 151.a.42 "Maroon"] 1.a.21 ~] 257.26 ‸~‸

274.6 151.a.43 rock,] 1.a.23 ~;] 258.2 ~
274.10 151.a.49 vaultside] 1.a.30 ~] 258.7 vault-side
274.11 151.a.49 adventurer,] 1.a.31 ~] 258.8 ~∧
274.11 151.a.50 presence,] 1.a.32 ~] 258.8 ~∧
274.13 151.a.52-53 contributed to afford sufficient] 1.a.34-35 afforded sufficient] 258.10-11 afforded sufficient
274.16 151.a.57 sometime] 1.a.40-41 some- | time] 258.15 some time
274.17 151.a.57 this] 1.a.41 ~] 258.15 ~,
274.17 151.a.58 spear,] 1.a.42 ~] 258.16 ~∧
274.17 151.a.58 length,] 1.a.43 ~] 258.16 ~∧
274.30 151.b.4 gum,] 1.b.16 ~] 258.31 ~∧
274.31 151.b.5 fragments,] 1.b.18 ~] 259.1 ~∧
274.31 151.b.5 wood] 1.b.18 ~] 259.2 ~,
274.32 151.b.7 what,] 1.b.20 ~] 259.3 ~∧
274.32 151.b.7 beside,] 1.b.21 ~] 259.3 ~∧
274.33 151.b.8 "Maroon"] 1.b.22 ~] 259.4 ∧~,∧
274.34 151.b.9 fine] 1.b.23 ~] 259.5 ~,
274.34 151.b.10 hung,] 1.b.25 ~] 259.6 ~∧
274.35 151.b.10 volumes,] 1.b.25 ~] 259.7 ~∧
274.37 151.b.13 large,] 1.b.29 ~∧] 259.9 ~
274.38 151.b.15 shreds] 1.b.31 shreds of hair] 259.11 shreds of hair
275.2 151.b.16 shriveled] 1.b.34 ~] 259.13 shrivelled
275.4 151.b.20 arrows,] 1.b.38 ~] 259.16 ~∧
275. 151.b. <no chapter>] 1.b. XII.] 259. CHAPTER XII.
275.8 151.b.25 Here] 1.b.45 ~] 259.21 ~,
275.8 151.b.25 then] 1.b.45 ~] 259.21 ~,
275.9 151.b.26 days] 1.b.47 ~] 259.22 ~,
275.10 151.b.28 Scarcely:—] 1.b.49 ~] 259.24 ~;∧
275.15 151.b.34 whence?.] 1.b.57 ~—] 260.4 ~∧
275.19 151.b.39 degrees] 1.b.64 degress] 260.9 degrees
275.20 151.b.41 purpose.] 1.b.67 ~—] 260.11 ~∧
275.21 151.b.42-43 gum,] 1.b.69 ~] 260.12 ~∧
275.23 151.b.44 "Maroon,"] 1.b.71-72 ~] 260.14 ∧~∧
275.28 151.b.51 fragments,] 1.b.81 ~] 260.21 ~∧
275.29 151.b.52 glass,] 1.b.82 ~] 260.22 ~∧

275.29 151.b.52 and,] 1.b.83 ~] 260.22 ~‸

276.2 151.b.62 perceptable] 1.b.97 perceptible] 261.1 ~

276.4 151.b.64 himself,] 1.b.100 ~] 261.4 ~‸

276.5 151.b.65-66 He chose it for his couch that night. The] 1.b.102 The] 261.5 The

276.7 151.b.69 cavern,] 1.b.105-106 ~] 261.7 ~‸

276. 152.a. <no chapter>] 1.b. XIII.] 261. CHAPTER XIII.

276.13 152.a.7 But] 1.b.115 ~,] 261.14 ~

276.13 152.a.7 awaking] 1.b.115 awakening] 261.14 awakening

276.17 152.a.12 doubt—] 1.b.123 ~] 261.19 ~;

276.21 152.a.17 Caribbean] 1.c.2 Carribean] 261.24 Caribbean

276.21 152.a.17 man,] 1.c.3 ~] 261.24 ~‸

276.24 152.a.21 "Maroon."] 1.c.8 ~] 262.2 ‸~‸

267.28 152.a.27 influence.] 1.c.16 ~—] 262.8 ~‸

276.31 152.a.29 but] 1.c.19 and] 262.10 and

277.1 152.a.35-36 sunlight.] 1.c.28 ~—] 262.17 ~‸

277.3 152.a.38 possessions] 1.c.32 ~.] 262.20 ~

277.8 152.a.44-45 sacrifice,] 1.c.41 ~;] 262.26 ~

277.11 152.a.48 favorite] 1.c.46 favourite] 262.30 favorite

277.12 152.a.49 plane] 1.c.47 ~] 263.1 plain

277.12 152.a.50 guided] 1.c.48 girded] 263.1 girded

277. 152.a. <no chapter>] 1.c. XIV.] 263. CHAPTER XIV.

277.14 152.a.51 "Maroon."] 1.c.50 ~] 263.3 ‸~‸

277.18 152.a.57 sky] 1.c.58 ~,] 263.9 ~

277.18 152.a.57 at the same moment] 1.c.59 on the return of night,] 263.9-10 on the return of night,

277.20 152.a.59 aspect of] 1.c.62 aspect] 263.12 aspect

277.21 152.a.61 waters,] 1.c.64 ~] 263.13 ~‸

277.22 152.a.61 speck,] 1.c.64 ~] 263.13 ~‸

277.26 152.a.66 be land] 1.c.72 ~] 263.19 ~,

277.26 152.a.67 cloud,] 1.c.73 ~‸] 263.19 ~,

277.31 152.b.4 say] 1.c.81 ~] 263.26 ~,

277.31 152.b.4 Brother!] 1.c.82 '~] 263.26 "~"

277.34 152.b.8 brother] 1.c.87 ~] 264.4 ~,

277.35 152.b.9 "Maroon"] 1.c.89 ~] 264.5-6 ‸~‸

278.4 152.b.15 atoms] 1.c.96 atom,] 264.11 atom,

278.6 152.b.18 sees;] 1.c.101 ~] 264.14 ~^

278.12 152.b.25 Caribbean] 1.c.112 Carribean] 264.22 Caribbean

278.13 152.b.26 spear,] 1.c.113 ~] 264.23 ~^

278.13 152.b.26 cross-bow] 1.c.113 ~] 264.23 crossbow

278.16 152.b.31 favorite] 1.c.119 favourite] 264.28 favorite

278.20 152.b.34 stay,] 1.c.125 ~^] 265.1 ~

278.22 152.b.36 first] 1.c.128 ~,] 265.3 ~

278.22 152.b.37 copse] 1.c.129 ~] 265.4 ~,

278.25 152.b.40 fruit;] 1.d.5 ~,] 265.8 ~

278.26 152.b.41 situation] 1.d.6 ~] 265.8-9 ~,

278.34 152.b.51 hair,] 1.d.21 ~^] 265.19 ~

278.34 152.b.51 shell,] 1.d.21 ~^] 265.19 ~

278.35 152.b.52 arrows,] 1.d.22 ~^] 265.20 ~

279.2 152.b.59 cave] 1.d.32 ~] 265.27 ~,

279.3 152.b.61 days] 1.d.35 ~] 265.29 ~,

279.3 152.b.61 least] 1.d.35 ~,] 265.29 ~

279.4 152.b.62 safe keeping] 1.d.36 ~] 265.30 ~-~

279.5 152.b.63 of] 1.d.38 ~,] 265.31 ~

279.5 152.b.63 convenient] 1.d.38 conveniently] 265.31 conveniently

279.6 152.b.65 And] 1.d.40 ~,] 266.2 ~

279. 152.b. <no chapter>] 1.d. XV.] 266. CHAPTER XV.

279.10 152.b.69 canoe,] 1.d.47 ~^] 266.6 ~

279.11 153.a.2 Caribbean] 1.d.49 Carribean] 266.8 Caribbean

279.14 153.a.6 bore] 1.d.54 ~,] 266.12 ~

279.15 153.a.6 figure head] 1.d.55 ~] 266.12 ~-~

279.15 153.a.7 the Cayman] 1.d.55-56 a Cayman] 266.13 a cayman

279.16 153.a.8 beside] 1.d.58 besides] 266.14 besides

279.18 153.a.10 stern,] 1.d.61 ~] 266.17 ~^

279.18 153.a.11 course] 1.d.62 coarse] 266.17 course

279.19 153.a.12 oarsmen] 1.d.63 oars-men] 266.18 oarsmen

279.21 153.a.14 pearl,] 1.d.67 ~^—] 266.21 ~

279.22 153.a.16 Each] 1.d.69 ~,] 266.22 ~

279.22 153.a.16 hands] 1.d.69 ~,] 266.22 ~

279.24 153.a.18 gums,] 1.d.72 ~] 266.24 ~^

279.24 153.a.18 a wood] 1.d.72 wood] 266.24 wood

279.28 153.a.22 she] 1.d.79 ~] 267.3 ~,

279.28 153.a.23 stern,] 1.d.79 ~‸] 267.3 ~,

279.32 153.a.28 Caribbean] 1.d.87 Carribean] 267.9 Caribbean

279.33 153.a.30 Spaniard,] 1.d.89 ~‸] 267.10 ~

279.34 153.a.30 moments,] 1.d.90 ~] 267.11 ~‸

279.34 153.a.31 breast] 1.d.90 heart] 267.11 heart

279.35 153.a.32 teints] 1.d.92 tints] 267.12 tints

280.5 153.a.40 a hidden fire lay] 1.d.103 from a hidden fire] 267.21 from a hidden fire

280.7 153.a.41 powder] 1.d.105 ~] 267.22 ~,

280.10 153.a.44-45 oars- | men] 1.d.109 oars-men] 267.25-26 oars- | men

280.13 153.a.49 chaunt] 1.d.115 ~] 267.29 chant

280.13 153.a.49 "Maroon"] 1.d.116 ~] 267.30 ‸~‸

280.15 153.a.51 oars,] 1.d.119 ~‸] 268.1 ~

280.19 153.a.56 to] 1.d.125 of] 268.5 of

280.21 153.a.59 ridge] 1.d.129 ~,] 268.8 ~

280.26 153.a.64 brought] 1.e.8 bore] 268.14 bore

280.26 153.a.65 solicitude,] 1.e.9 ~‸] 268.15 ~

280.29 153.a.69 "Maroon"] 1.e.15 ~] 268.19 ‸~‸

280.32 153.b.4 this] 1.e.20 the] 268.23 the

280.34 153.b.6 —to] 1.e.23 ‸To] 268.25 ~

280.35 153.b.6 god—] 1.e.24 ~,] 268.26 ~

280.36 153.b.8 victim?] 1.e.27 ~ ?] 268.27 ~

280.37 153.b.10 chaunt] 1.e.29 ~] 268.29 chant

280.38 153.b.10 stern] 1.e.30 ~,] 268.29 ~

281.1 153.b.12 wo] 1.e.32 ~] 268.31 woe

281.1 153.b.13 boat—] 1.e.33 ~] 269.1 ~;

281.8 153.b.21 awful] 1.e.44 ~] 269.9 ~,

281. 153.b. <no chapter>] 1.e. XVI.] 269. CHAPTER XVI.

281.9 153.b.22 "Maroon"] 1.e.45 ~] 269.10 ‸~‸

281.14 153.b.28 billets] 1.e.53-54 ~,] 269.16 ~

281.16 153.b.31 hands] 1.e.57 hand] 269.19 hand

281.20 153.b.36 incantations,] 1.e.65 ~‸] 269.25 ~,

281.21 153.b.38 chaunt] 1.e.67 ~] 269.26 chant

281.25 153.b.43 Then,] 1.e.74 ~‸] 270.5 ~

281.25 153.b.43 sounds,] 1.e.75 ~] 270.6 ~‸

281.26 153.b.44 paused,] 1.e.75 ~‸] 270.6 ~

281.26 153.b.44 and,] 1.e.76 ~‸] 270.6 ~

281.27 153.b.45 fragments] 1.e.78 f‸agments] 270.8 fragments

281.29 153.b.48 chaunt] 1.e.81 ~] 270.10 chant

281.30 153.b.49 ceased,] 1.e.83 ~;] 270.12 ~

281.30 153.b.49 and,] 1.e.83 ~] 270.12 ~‸

281.33 153.b.52 chaunt] 1.e.88 ~] 270.15 chant

281.35 153.b.55 words] 1.e.92 ~,] 270.18 ~

282.1 153.b.56 women,] 1.e.93 ~] 270.19 ~‸

282.3 153.b.58 neck] 1.e.96 necks] 270.21 necks

282.6 153.b.62 "Maroon,"] 1.e.102 ~] 270.25 ‸~‸

282.11 153.b.69 sea shore] 1.e.111 ~] 271.1 ~-~

282.13 154.a.1 altar place] 1.e.113 ~] 271.3 ~-~

282.13 154.a.2 matron like] 1.e.114 ~-~] 271.3 ~

282.15 154.a.3 answered] 1.e.116 answered her] 271.5 answered her

282.15 154.a.4 cry] 1.e.117 ~] 271.5 ~,

282.25 154.b.5 "Maroon,"] 1.f.6 "~‸"—] 271.18 ‸~‸‸—

282.25 154.b.6 event,] 1.f.7 ~‸—] 271.19 ~

282.28 154.b.9 his own] 1.f.11 his] 271.22 his

282.29 154.b.10 spirit] 1.f.13 ~,] 271.23 ~

282. 219. PART V.] 1.f. XVII.] 272. CHAPTER XVII.

282.30 219.a.2 prostrate] 1.f.16 ~] 272.2 ~,

282.35 219.a.8 nature—] 1.f.25 ~] 272.8 ~,

282.35 219.a.8 training—] 1.f.25 ~] 272.8 ~,

283.3 219.a.11 life,] 1.f.30 ~] 272.11 ~‸

283.6 219.a.15 "Maroon."] 1.f.35 ~] 272.15 ‸~‸

283.8 219.a.18 shame] 1.f.39 ~] 272.18 ~,

283.9 219.a.19-20 rashness—] 1.f.41 ~] 272.19 ~,

283.9 219.a.20 courage,—] 1.f.42 ~] 272.20 ~‸

283.13 219.a.24 life] 1.f.47 ~] 272.24 ~,

283.17 219.a.29 snapt] 1.f.55 ~] 273.3 snapped

283.17 219.a.30 them] 1.f.55 then] 273.3 them

283.17 219.a.30 altar] 1.f.55 ~] 273.3 ~,

283.18 219.a.31 supply,] 1.f.57 ~] 273.4 ~‸

283.19 219.a.32 ceremonies] 1.f.58 cremonies] 273.5 ceremonies

283.23 219.a.37 chaunt] 1.f.66 ~] 273.11 chant

283.25 219.a.40 virgin] 1.f.70 vigin] 273.14 virgin

283.30 219.a.47 that] 1.f.80 they] 273.21 they

283.31 219.a.48 which] 1.f.81 whence] 273.22 whence

283.31 219.a.49 alone] 1.f.82 ~] 273.23 ~,

283.32 219.a.49 left?] 1.f.82 ~] 273.23 ~.

283.36 219.a.54 moans and] 1.f.89 moans the] 273.28 moans, the

283.36 219.a.54-55 murmurs,] 1.f.90 ~] 273.28-29 ~^

283.37 219.a.57 sensibilities] 1.f.93 ~] 273.31 ~,

283.38 219.a.57 chaunt] 1.f.93 ~] 273.31 chant

284.8 219.b.9 destined] 1.f.108 ~,] 274.11 ~

284.8 219.b.9 herself] 1.f.109 ~,] 274.11 ~

284.8 219.b.10 priestess] 1.f.109 ~,] 274.12 ~

284.9 219.b.11 in] 1.f.111 ln] 274.13 in

284.9 219.b.11 same,] 1.f.111 ~] 274.13 ~^

284.10 219.b.13 least] 1.f.113 ~] 274.15 ~,

284.11 219.b.13 which] 1.f.114 ~,] 274.15 ~

284.11 219.13 rapid] 1.f.114 rapld] 274.15 rapid

284.12 219.b.14 "Maroon"] 1.f.115 ~] 274.16 ^~^

284.12 219.b.15 Perhaps,] 1.f.116 ~^] 274.17 ~

284.13 219.b.16 doubtful,] 1.f.117 ~] 274.18 ~^

284.14 219.b.17 his] 1.f.119 the] 274.19 the

284.21 219.b.26 Aborigines] 1.g.2 ~] 274.28 aborigines

284.21 219.b.26 new world] 1.g.2 ~] 274.29 New World

284.24 219.b.29 and] 1.g.7 and to be] 275.1 and to be

284.25 219.b.30 wits] 1.g.8 ~] 275.2 ~,

284.26 219.b.31 chosen,] 1.g.10 ~] 275.3 ~^

284.27 219.b.33 especial] 1.g.12-13 especlal] 275.5 especial

284.28 219.b.34 guardian.] 1.g.13 ~—] 275.5 ~^

284.29 219.b.34 favor] 1.g.14 favour] 275.6 favor

284.30 219.b.36 friendly] 1.g.16 friendiy] 275.7 friendly

284.30 219.b.36 favoring] 1.g.16-17 favouring] 275.8 favoring

284.31 219.b.37 courage] 1.g.18 ~] 275.9 ~,

284.33 219.b.40 labors] 1.g.22 labours] 275.11 labors

284.34 219.b.41 sex] 1.g.24 ~,] 275.13 ~

284.34 219.b.42 their] 1.g.25 thelr] 275.14 their

284.36 219.b.43 from] 1.g.27 froom] 275.15 from

284.36 219.b.44 frequent] 1.g.27-28 f‸equent] 275.16 frequent
285.1 219.b.47 Isolation] 1.g.32 ~] 275.19 ~,
285.2 219.b.49-50 enflame] 1.g.35-36 ~] 275.21 inflame
285.4 219.b.51 exhiliarated] 1.g.37-38 exhilarated] 275.23 ~
285.5 219.b.52 knew,] 1.g.39 ~] 275.24 ~‸
285.5 219.b.53 system] 1.g.40-41 ~,] 275.25 ~
285.6 219.b.55 sustenance;] 1.g.42 ~] 275.26 ~,
285.8 219.b.57 and] 1.g.45 ahd] 275.28 and
285.13 220.a.5 heard,] 1.g.53 ~] 276.3 ~‸
285.17 220.a.10 young,] 1.g.60 ~‸] 276.9 ~,
285.18 220.a.11 favorite,] 1.g.62 favourite,] 276.10 favorite
285.18 220.a.12 visions] 1.g.63 visiions] 276.11 visions
285.20 220.a.13 tribes—] 1.g.65-66 ~] 276.12 ~,
285.20 220.a.14 most—] 1.g.66 ~] 276.13 ~,
285.21 220.a.15 *token*] 1.g.68 *totem*] 276.14 *totem*
285.21 220.a.16 breast,—badge,] 1.g.69 breast,—] 276.15 breast—
285.22 220.a.17 middle ages] 1.g.70 ~] 276.16 Middle Ages
285.22 220.a.17 from] 1.g.71 f‸om] 276.16 from
285.23 220.a.17 favorite] 1.g.71 favourite] 276.16 favorite
285.23 220.a.18 lives—] 1.g.72-73 ~] 276.17 ~;
285.24 220.a.19 Europe,] 1.g.73 ~‸] 276.18 ~,
285.24 220.a.19 token] 1.g.74 *totem*] 276.18 *totem*
285.25 220.a.20 surcoat] 1.g.75 ~] 276.19 ~,
285.25 220.a.20 pennon,] 1.g.75 ~] 276.19 ~‸
285.25 220.a.21 new world] 1.g.76 ~] 276.20 New World
285. 220.a. <no chapter>] 1.a. XVIII.] 276. CHAPTER XVIII.
285.28 220.a.25 "Maroon."] 1.a.3 ~] 276.23 ‸~‸
285.28 220.a.25 Without,] 1.a.4 ~] 276.23 ~‸
285.29 220.a.25 except] 1.a.4 ~,] 276.23 ~
285.30 220.a.27 cocoanut trees] 1.a.6 ~] 276.25 ~-~
285.31 220.a.28 chaunt] 1.a.8 ~] 276.26 chant
285.33 220.a.31 altar.] 1.a.12 ~—] 277.3 ~‸
286.1 220.a.35 "Maroon"] 1.a.17 ~] 277.7 ‸~‸
286.1 220.a.35 fire,—] 1.a.18 ~] 277.7 ~‸
286.3 220.a.37 distinct] 1.a.20 ~] 277.9 ~,
286.3 220.a.37 eyes] 1.a.20 ~] 277.9 ~,

286.4 220.a.38 well marked] 1.a.22 ~] 277.10 ~-~

286.5 220.a.39 office] 1.a.23 ~] 277.11 ~,

286.9 220.a.43 favorable] 1.a.29-30 favourable] 277.16 favorable

286.9 220.a.44 sunk] 1.a.30 ~] 277.17 sank

286.11 220.a.46 employed as] 1.a.34 employed] 277.19 employed as

286.12 220.a.48 nights] 1.a.35 ~,] 277.20 ~

286.15 220.a.51 concealment.] 1.a.40 ~—] 277.24 ~‸

286.17 220.a.54 ante-chamber] 1.a.45 ~] 277.27 antechamber

286.22 220.a.58 uucovered] 1.a.50-51 uncovered] 277.31-278.1 ~

286.27 220.a.65 sky] 1.a.60 ~] 278.7 ~,

286.35 220.b.6 lessen] 1.b.11 lesson] 278.17 lessen

286.37 220.b.8 structure] 1.b.15 ~] 278.20 ~,

287.4 220.b.14 emotions.] 1.b.22 ~—] 278.25 ~‸

287.7 220.b.18 of the wood] 1.b.28 of wood] 278.29 of wood

287.7 220.b.18 Thus she] 1.b.28 Thusshe] 278.30 Thus she

287.8 220.b.19 "Maroon"] 1.b.30 ~] 278.31 ‸~‸

287.8 220.b.20 hers, She] 1.b.31 ~] 279.1 ~ she

287.15 220.b.28 Levya,] 1.b.42 ~] 279.9 ~‸

287.17 220.b.29 pleasing,] 1.b.45 ~;] 279.11 ~

287.22 220.b.36 unfavorable] 1.b.53 unfavourable] 279.17 unfavorable

287.23 220.b.36 damsel.] 1.b.54 ~—] 279.18 ~‸

287.24 220.b.39 ordeal,] 1.b.58 ~] 279.20 ~‸

287.28 220.b.44 measure] 1.b.64-65 ~,] 279.25 ~

287.30 220.b.45 Aborigines] 1.b.67 ~] 279.27 aborigines

287.31 220.b.47 breast,] 1.b.70 ~‸—] 279.29 ~

287.32 220.b.48 "Maroon"] 1.b.71 ~] 279.29 ‸~‸

287.35 220.b.52 them.] 1.b.76 ~—] 280.2 ~‸

287.36 220.b.53 smiled,] 1.b.78 ~] 280.4 ~‸

287.37 220.b.55 spoke,] 1.b.81 ~] 280.6 ~‸

288.6 220.b.64 speak,] 1.b.93 ~‸] 280.14 ~

288.13 221.a.3 sunk] 1.b.105 ~] 280.23 sank

288.13 221.a.4 spoke,] 1.b.106 ~] 280.24 ~‸

288.17 221.a.9 Spirit] 1.b.113 ~] 280.29 spirit

288.20 221.a.12-13 man,] 1.b.118 ~] 281.1 ~‸

288.30 221.a.25 inforce] 1.c.5 enforce] 281.14 ~
288.34 221.a.30 favor] 1.c.13 favour] 281.19 favor
288.35 221.a.31 aspect] 1.c.14 ~] 281.20 ~,
288.36 221.a.32 invocations.] 1.c.15 ~—] 281.21 ~^
288.37 221.a.33 approach,] 1.c.17 ~] 281.22 ~^
288.37 221.a.34 won,] 1.c.18 ~] 281.23 ~^
289.1 221.a.35 long continued] 1.c.19 ~] 281.24 ~-~
289.5 221.a.39 done,] 1.c.25 ~] 281.28 ~^
289.6 221.a.41 reptile,] 1.c.27 ~] 281.30 ~^
289.8 221.a.43 favored] 1.c.31 favoured] 282.2 favored
289.11 221.a.47 was] 1.c.37 is] 282.6 is
289.14 221.a.51 favored] 1.c.42-43 favoured] 282.10 favored
289.16 221.a.53 their] 1.c.45 ther] 282.11 their
289.17 221.a.54 successful] 1.c.47 successsful] 282.13 successful
289.19 221.a.57 primeval] 1.c.51 primal] 282.16 primal
289.20 221.a.58 heaven] 1.c.52 ~] 282.17 Heaven
289.33 221.b.4 both.] 1.c.73 ~—] 283.1 ~^
289.35 221.b.6 favored] 1.c.76 favoured] 283.4 favored
289.35 221.b.7 Deity] 1.c.77 ~] 283.4 deity
289.35 221.b.7 their] 1.c.78 her] 283.4 her
289.36 221.b.7 devote their] 1.c.78 devotes the] 283.5 devotes the
290. 221.b. <no chapter>] 1.c. XIX.] 283. CHAPTER XIX.
290.8 221.b.18 this] 1.c.93 the] 283.15 the
290.13 221.b.25 abode,] 1.c.103 ~] 283.22 ~^
290.19 221.b.32 had slept,] 1.c.113 lay] 284.4 lay,
290.21 221.b.35 countenance] 1.c.117 countenancc] 284.7 countenance
290.24 221.b.38 divine] 1.c.121 ~] 284.10 Divine
290.24 221.b.38 favor] 1.c.121 favour] 284.10 favor
290.26 221.b.40 voice,] 1.c.123 ~] 284.11 ~^
290.27 221.b.41 appreciate] 1.c.126 appreciathe] 284.13 appreciate
290.30 221.b.45 life,] 1.d.2 ~] 284.16 ~^
290.32 221.b.47 as well as] 1.d.5 as well as] 284.19 as
290.32 221.b.47 life,] 1.d.6 ~] 284.19 ~^
290.33 221.b.48 progress,] 1.d.7 ~] 284.20 ~^

290.34 221.b.50 grove,—] 1.d.9 ~‸] 284.21 ~
290.34 221.b.50 bird,] 1.d.9-10 ~] 284.22 ~‸
295.35 221.b.51 fruit,] 1.d.11 ~] 284.23 ~‸
290.35 221.b.52 sign] 1.d.12 sigh] 284.23 sigh
290.36 221.b.52 smile,] 1.d.12 ~] 284.24 ~‸
291.2 221.b.55 sounds,] 1.d.16-17 ~] 284.27 ~‸
291.10 221.b.66 loving] 1.d.31 losing] 285.6 losing
291. 221.b. <no chapter>] 1.d. XX.] 285. CHAPTER XX.
291.12 221.b.69 them.] 1.d.34 ~‸-] 285.9 ~.‸
291.15 222.a.3 fears] 1.d.39 hopes] 285.12 hopes
291.16 222.a.4 hopes?] 1.d.40 fears?—] 285.13 fears?—
291.19 222.a.8 Omaya] 1.d.46 Amaya] 285.17 Amaya
291.21 222.a.11 heaven] 1.d.50 ~] 285.20 Heaven
291.21 222.a.11 rights] 1.d.50 rites] 285.20 rites
291.23 222.a.13 lessonings] 1.d.53 teachings] 285.22 teachings
291.23 222.a.14 "Maroon."] 1.d.53-54 ~] 285.23 ‸~‸
291.26 222.a.18 supplications] 1.d.59-60 ~,] 286.1 ~
291.27 222.a.18-19 evening] 1.d.60 ~] 286.2 ~,
291.28 222.a.20 confessed,] 1.d.62 ~] 286.3 ~‸
291.30 222.a.23 began] 1.d.67 ~] 286.7 begun
291.31 222.a.24 rejoiced] 1.d.69 rejoicing] 286.8 rejoicing
291.32 222.a.25-26 language—as] 1.d.71 language. The] 286.9-10 language. The
292.1 222.a.30 chaunt] 1.d.77 ~] 286.14 chant
292.7 222.a.37 practice] 1.d.87 ~] 286.22 practise
292.11 222.a.41-42 persue] 1.d.94 pursue] 286.26-27 ~
292.13 222.a.44 Here] 1.d.97 ~,] 286.29 ~
292.20 222.a.52-53 "Maroon,"] 1.d.109 ~] 287.7 ‸~‸‸
292.21 222.a.54 He too] 1.d.111 ~] 287.8 ~, ~,
292.30 222.a.66 hurried to] 1.d.128 yearned for] 287.21 yearned for
292.31 222.a.67 famous.] 1.d.129 ~—] 287.22 ~‸
292.34 222.b.1 wild] 1.e.6 ~] 287.26 ~,
292.34 222.b.2 gambolled] 1.e.6-7 gamboled] 287.27 gambolled
292.38 222.b.7 artifices,] 1.e.13 ~] 287.31-288.1 ~‸
293.1 222.b.8 awkward] 1.e.14 awkwark] 288.1 awkward

293.2 222.b.9 Caribbee] 1.e.16 Carribbee] 288.2 Caribbean

293.3 222.b.11 ditty—sometimes] 1.e.19 ~] 288.4-5 ~‸. Sometimes

293.4 222.b.12 melancholy,] 1.e.20-21 ~] 288.6 ~‸

293.6 222.b.14 rocks,] 1.e.23 ~;] 288.7 ~

293.6 222.b.14 hollows] 1.e.23 ~,] 288.8 ~

293.8 222.b.17 following:] 1.e.28 ~] 288.11 ~—

293. 222.b. <no periods after Roman numerals I-IX>] 1.e. <no periods after Roman numerals I-IX>] 288.-289. <periods after Roman numerals I-IX>

293.10 222.b.19 sea,] 1.e.30 ~] 288.13 ~;

293.17 222.b.26 chrystal] 1.e.37 ~] 288.20 crystal

293.22 222.b.31 rest,] 1.e.42 ~] 288.25 ~‸

293.25 222.b.34 climes] 1.e.45 ~] 289.1 ~,

293.25 222.b.34 delight,] 1.e.45 ~] 289.1 ~‸

293.26 222.b.35 night,] 1.e.46 ~] 289.2 ~;

293.28 222.b.37 fruits,] 1.e.48 ~] 289.4 ~‸

293.29 222.b.38 bring,] 1.e.49 ~] 289.5 ~;

293.30 222.b.39 sing,] 1.e.50 ~] 289.6 ~;

293.31 222.b.40 weep,] 1.e.51 ~] 289.7 ~‸

294.1 222.b.42 little,] 1.e.53 ~] 289.9 ~‸

294.2 222.b.43 Thy] 1.e.54 The] 289.10 The

294.2 222.b.43 bestow,] 1.e.54 ~] 289.10 ~‸

294.4 222.b.45 O!] 1.e.56 ~] 289.12 ~,

294.5 222.b.46 thee,] 1.e.57 ~] 289.13 ~‸

294.6 222.b.47 sun,] 1.e.58 ~] 289.14 ~‸

294.7 222.b.48 hopes,] 1.e.59 ~] 289.15 ~‸

294.7 222.b.48 woes,] 1.e.59 ~] 289.15 ~‸—

294.8 222.b.49 flow'rs] 1.e.60 ~] 289.16 flowers

294.13 222.b.55 "Maroon,"] 1.e.66 ~] 289.22 ‸~‸

294.20 223.a.6 interval,] 1.e.78 ~] 290.1 ~‸

294.28 223.a.15 since] 1.e.90 indeed, since] 290.10 indeed, since

294.31 223.a.19 and] 1.e.96 ~,] 290.14 ~

295. 223.a. <no chapter>] 1.e. XXI.] 290. CHAPTER XXI.

295.2 223.a.24 while] 1.e.103 whilst] 290.20 whilst

295.2 223.a.25 "Maroon"] 1.e.104 ~] 290.21 ‸~‸

295.4 223.a.26 cavern,] 1.e.106 ~] 290.22 ~∧
295.6 223.a.30 sight] 1.e.110 ~] 290.26 ~,
295.12 223.a.37 visitor] 1.e.121 ~] 291.8 ~,
295.13 223.a.38 Velasquez] 1.e.122 ~] 291.8 ~,
295.14 223.a.39 "Maroon,"] 1.e.124 ~] 291.11 ∧~∧
295.15 223.a.41 The] 1.f.1 Tue] 291.12 The
295.16 223.a.42 companion,] 1.f.2 ~] 291.13 ~∧—
295.18 223.a.44 name;] 1.f.5 ~] 291.15 ~∧—
295.20 223.a.47 Levya,] 1.f.9 ~∧] 291.18 ~
295.21 223.a.48-49 the return of the] 1.f.12 the] 291.20 the
295.22 223.a.50 return] 1.f.13 ~] 291.21 ~,
295.23 223.a.51 Velasquez] 1.f.14 ~] 291.22 ~,
295.23 223.a.52 motive] 1.f.15-16 ~] 291.23 ~,
295.24 223.a.52 curiosity] 1.f.17 ~] 291.23-24 ~,
295.26 223.a.55 him] 1.f.20 ~] 291.26 ~,
295.28 223.a.57 own,] 1.f.23 ~] 291.28 ~∧
295.32 223.a.63 creature] 1.f.31 ~] 292.4 ~,
295.35 223.a.66 newly gotten] 1.f.36 ~] 292.7 ~-~
296.1 223.a.69 secret] 1.f.39 ~] 292.9 ~,
296.5 223.b.5 ledge,] 1.f.46 ~∧] 292.14 ~,
296.5 223.b.5 in turn in a like] 1.f.47 in like] 292.15 in like
296.8 223.b.9-10 manner, and] 1.f.53 ~; ~,] 292.19 ~
296.13 223.b.14 Spaniards,] 1.f.59 Spaiards—] 292.24 Spaniards—
296.20 223.b.23 trembling still] 1.f.72 ~] 293.2 still trembling
296.20 223.b.24 Velasquez,] 1.f.73 ~] 293.3 ~∧
296.21 223.b.25 "Maroon"] 1.f.74 ~] 293.4 ∧~∧
296.29 223.b.33 surly] 1.f.86 ~] 293.12 ~,
296.30 223.b.36 "Maroon"] 1.f.89-90 ~] 293.15 ∧~∧
296.33 223.b.39 restoration] 1.f.94 ~] 293.18 ~,
296.33 223.b.39 rock] 1.f.95 hope] 293.19 hope
297. 223.b. <no chapter>] 1.f. XXII.] 293. CHAPTER XXII.
297.1 223.b.44 favorable] 1.f.100-101 favourable] 293.23 favorable
297.6 223.b.51 man,] 1.f.110 ~] 294.4 ~∧—
297.9 223.b.54 own.] 1.f.113 ~—] 294.7 ~∧

297.11 223.b.57 point,] 1.f.118 ~] 294.10 ~‸—
297.12 223.b.58 others,] 1.f.119 ~] 294.11 ~‸—
297.13 223.b.59 inflexible.] 1.f.120 ~—] 294.12 ~‸
297.13 223.b.59 But,] 1.f.121 ~] 294.12 ~‸
297.18 223.b.66 "Maroon"] 1.g.1 ~] 294.19 ‸maroon‸
297.20 223.b.68 Impatient,] 1.g.4 ~] 294.21 ~‸
297.21 223.b.69 woman] 1.g.6 ~] 294.22 ~,
297.22 224.a.2 her,] 1.g.8 ~;] 294.24 ~
297.22 224.a.2 and] 1.g.8 ~,] 294.24 ~
297.25 224.a.6 hiding place] 1.g.14 ~] 294.28 ~-~
297.28 224.a.10 case] 1.g.19 ~] 295.1 ~,
297.29 224.a.10 strong,] 1.g.20 ~] 295.1 ~‸
297.32 224.a.14 "Maroon"] 1.g.25 ~] 295.5 ‸~‸
297.33 224.a.15 attachments,] 1.g.27 an attachment ‸] 295.7 an attachment,
298.5 224.b.3 dowry,] 1.g.41 ~] 295.17 ~‸
298.5 224.b.4 herself,] 1.g.42 ~] 295.17 ~‸
298.10 224.b.9 his,] 1.g.49 ~] 295.22 ~‸
298.19 224.b.20 to see] 1.g.65 te see] 296.3 to see
298. 291. PART VI.] 1.a. XXII.] 296. CHAPTER XXIII.
298.21 291.a.1 "Maroon"] 1.a.1 ~] 296.6 ‸~‸
298.23 291.a.3 islet,] 1.a.4 ~] 296.8 ~‸
298.25 291.a.6 periled] 1.a.8 ~] 296.11 perilled
298.26 291.a.7 sacrifices,] 1.a.9 ~] 296.12 ~‸
298.27 291.a.9 love,] 1.a.12 ~] 296.14 ~‸
298.30 291.a.12 Velasquez,] 1.a.17 ~] 296.17 ~‸
298.35 291.a.19 aspects,] 1.a.26-27 ~] 296.24-25 ~‸
299.1 291.a.20 fruits,] 1.a.27 ~] 296.25 ~‸
299.1 291.a.20 abode,] 1.a.28 ~] 296.25-26 ~‸
299.3 291.a.23 youth,] 1.a.31 ~] 297.2 ~‸
299.4 291.b.1 least] 1.a.33 ~] 297.3 ~,
299.5 291.b.2 "Maroon."] 1.a.35 ~] 297.5 ‸~‸
299.6 291.b.3 gipsy] 1.a.36 ~] 297.6 gypsy
299.7 291.b.4 realize,] 1.a.38 ~] 297.7 ~‸
299.8 291.b.6 Heaven] 1.a.41 ~] 297.9 heaven
299.11 291.b.10 a] 1.b.3 near a] 297.12 near a
299.12 291.b.10 safety] 1.b.4 ~.] 297.13 ~
299.24 291.b.20 *We*] 1.b.23 ~] 297.27 ~,

299.24 291.b.21 then] 1.b.23 ~] 297.27 ~,
299.29 292.a.4 sea] 1.b.31 ~] 298.2 ~,
299.30 292.a.5 shore. The] 1.b.33 ~] 298.3 ~;—the
299.31 292.a.6 wing,] 1.b.34 ~] 298.4 ~^
299.32 292.a.8 midnight. The] 1.b.37 ~;—the] 298.6 ~
299.34 292.a.11 isle] 1.b.41 islet] 298.9 islet
299.35 292.a.12 chained] 1.b.42 provoked] 298.10 provoked
299.35 292.a.12 of] 1.b.42-43 than the alarm, of] 298.10-11 than the alarm of
300.1 292.a.17 and] 1.b.49 aud] 298.15 and
300.1 292.a.17 beasts,] 1.b.50 ~] 298.16 ~^
300.5 292.a.22 fruit] 1.b.56 ~] 298.20 ~,
300.8 292.a.26 "Maroon;"] 1.b.62 ~] 298.25 ^~^
300.9 292.a.26 till] 1.b.63 until] 298.25 until
300.10 292.a.27 seashore,] 1.b.64-65 sea- | shore,] 298.26 sea-shore ^
300.11 292.a.28 side,] 1.b.66 ~] 298.27 ~^
300.17 292.a.36 question.] 1.b.76 ~—] 299.4 ~^
300.18 292.a.36 treasure,] 1.b.77 ~] 299.4 ~^
300.19 292.a.38 damsel,] 1.b.79 ~] 299.6 ~^
300.23 292.a.43 devotion,] 1.c.5 ~] 299.11 ~^
300.25 292.a.45 injustice.] 1.c.8 ~—] 299.13 ~^
300.30 292.a.52-53 compeled] 1.c.18-19 compelled] 299.20 ~
300.33 292.a.55 childish,] 1.c.23 ~] 299.23 ~^
300.33 292.a.56 indeed,] 1.c.23-24 ~^—] 299.24 ~
300.34 292.a.57 proud,] 1.c.25 too proud] 299.25 too proud
300.36 292.a.60 love] 1.c.29 ~] 299.28 ~,
301.2 292.a.65 behavior] 1.c.36-37 behaviour] 300.2 behavior
301.7 292.b.2 gained,] 1.c.45 ~] 300.8 ~^
301.10 292.b.5 he] 1.c.49-50 he had] 300.11 he had
301.12 292.b.8 alarm] 1.c.54 occasion] 300.15 occasion
301.17 292.b.13 which,] 1.c.60 ~] 300.19 ~^
301.21 292.b.18 own.] 1.c.68 ~—] 300.25 ~^
301.23 292.b.20 seashore] 1.c.71 ~] 300.27 sea-shore
301.24 292.b.21 them—] 1.c.73 ~] 300.28 ~^,
301.24 292.b.22 footsteps,] 1.c.73-74 ~] 300.28-29 ~^
301.26 292.b.24-25 "Maroon."] 1.c.77 ~] 300.31 ^~^
301.35 292.b.36 Maria] 1.d.11 Marie] 301.11 Maria

301.36 292.b.37 in a] 1.d.13-14 ~] 301.13 in

302.1 292.b.41 "Maroon"] 1.d.18 ~] 301.16 ∧~∧

302.4 292.b.45 it is] 1.d.24 it] 301.20 it is

302.5 292.b.45 next] 1.d.25 rest] 301.21 rest

302.8 292.b.50 sky] 1.d.32 ~] 301.26 ~,

302.8 292.b.51 shore] 1.d.32 ~] 301.27 ~,

302.10 292.b.53 own] 1.d.36 own languor] 301.29 own languor

302.13 292.b.55-56 slept?"—such] 1.d.40 ~∧ Such] 302.1 ~

302.14 292.b.56-57 his own heart, whieh rose in the mind of the Maroon.] 1.d.41 his heart.] 302.2 his heart.

302.22 292.b.68 snug] 1.d.55 ~] 302.12 ~,

302.23 292.b.68 "Maroon."] 1.d.56 ~] 302.13 ∧~∧

302. 292.b. <no chapter>] 1.d. XXIII.] 302. CHAPTER XXIV.

302.25 293.a.2 step,] 1.d.60 ~] 302.16 ~∧

302.29 293.a.6 portal] 1.d.65 ~] 302.20 ~,

302.29 293.a.6 recesses] 1.d.66 ~.—] 302.21 ~∧

302.35 293.a.14 now] 1.d.78 ~] 303.3 ~,

302.36 293.a.15 comple] 1.d.78 complete] 303.3 complete

303.4 293.a.20 reflections,] 1.e.6-7 ~] 303.9 ~∧

303.5 293.a.21 way] 1.e.8 ~] 303.10 ~,

303.6 293.a.22 and] 1.e.10 ~] 303.11 ~,

303.11 293.a.28-29 fire- | place] 1.e.19 fire-place] 303.18 fireplace

303.18 293.a.37 trembled,] 1.e.31 ~∧] 303.27 ~

303.18 293.a.38 every] 1.e.32 at every] 303.28 at every

303.20 293.a.40 scrutiny; his] 1.e.35 ~.His] 303.30 ~

303.28 293.a.51 trembling.] 1.e.50 ~—] 304.10 ~∧

303.33 293.a.57 newborn] 1.e.58-59 new- | born] 304.16 new-born

303.33 293.a.57 woman] 1.e.59 women] 304.16 woman

303. 293.a. <no chapter>] 1.e. XXIV.] 304. CHAPTER XXV.

303.36 293.a.60 night] 1.e.63 Night] 304.19 Night

303.36 293.a.60 rapidly] 1.e.64 ~,] 304.19 ~

304.1 293.a.61 were] 1.e.66 ~,] 304.20 ~

304.7 293.a.69 sea,] 1.e.76 ~] 305.2 ~∧

304.13 293.b.8 enjoyment.] 1.e.86 ~—] 305.10 ~∧

304.13 293.b.9 Linares] 1.e.87 ~] 305.11 ~,
304.14 293.b.10 heir to] 1.e.90 heir to] 305.12 heir of
304.15 293.b.10 Velasquez] 1.e.90 ~] 305.12 ~,
304.17 293.b.13 newly gotten] 1.e.94 ~] 305.15 ~-~
304.22 293.b.19 billows,] 1.e.102 ~] 305.21 ~ʌ
304.23 293.b.20 bright] 1.e.104 ~] 305.22 ~,
304.26 293.b.25 palms] 1.e.110 ~] 305.27 ~,
304.38 293.b.38 "Maroon"] 1.e.129 ~] 306.9 ʌ~ʌ
304.38 293.b.39 feelings] 1.f.1 ~] 306.10 ~,
305.2 293.b.42-43 though fascinated] 1.f.6 though fascinated] 306.14 fascinated
305.3 293.b.44 from the hearing, by] 1.f.8-9 from their propriety, as he heard, more than once,] 306.15-16 from their propriety, as he heard, more than once,
305.5 293.b.45 hiding place] 1.f.10 ~] 306.17 ~-~
305.7 293.b.49 suspicions,] 1.f.16 ~] 306.21 ~;
305.8 293.b.49 and] 1.f.16 ~,] 306.21 ~
305.9 293.b.50 Velasquez] 1.f.17 ~,] 306.21-22 ~
305.9 293.b.51 "Maroon"] 1.f.18 ~] 306.23 ʌ~ʌ
305. 293.b. <no chapter>] 1.f. XXV.] 306. CHAPTER XXVI.
305.10 293.b.53 wane,] 1.f.20 ~—] 306.24 ~
305.12 293.b.55 slept,] 1.f.24 ~] 306.26 ~ʌ
305.13 293.b.56-57 "Maroon·"] 1.f.25 ~] 307.1-2 ʌ~ʌ
305.14 293.b.59 stirred] 1.f.28 ~,] 307.4 ~ʌ
305.19 293.b.65 grasp,] 1.f.37 ~] 307.10 ~ʌ
306.1 294.a.18 As] 1.f.67 ~,] 308.1 ~
306.1 294.a.18 "Maroon"] 1.f.68 ~] 308.2 ʌ~ʌ
306. 294.a. <no chapter>] 1.f. XXVI.] 308. CHAPTER XXVII.
306.6 294.a.24 "Maroon"] 1.f.75-76 "Maaoon"] 308.7 Maroon
306.8 294.a.26 brands] 1.f.79 ~] 308.9 ~,
306.8 294.a.27 forth,] 1.f.80 ~] 308.10 ~ʌ
306.8 294.a.27 course,] 1.f.80 ~] 308.10 ~ʌ
306.11 294.a.31 dark,—] 1.f.85 ~] 308.14 ~ʌ
306.17 294.a.38 gusty!] 1.f.95 ~?] 308.22 ~.
306.23 294.a.44 treasure] 1.f.104 ~] 309.2 ~,

306.26 294.a.47 bosom,] 1.f.108 ~] 309.5 ~‸

306.29 294.a.51 top] 1.f.114 ~] 309.9 ~,

306.30 294.a.52 complete,] 1.f.116 ~‸] 309.10-11 ~

306.31 294.a.53 had] 1.f.117 had both] 309.12 had both

306.32 294.a.54 faintly] 1.f.119 ~] 309.13 ~,

306.33 294.a.56 gusts] 1.f.121 ~] 309.14 ~,

307.1 294.a.58 seamen] 1.f.124 seaman] 309.17 seamen

307.3 294.a.61 horror,] 1.g.1 ~] 309.19 ~‸

307.3 294.a.62 those] 1.g.2 these] 309.20 these

307.8 294.a.67 happy,] 1.g.10 ~‸] 309.26 ~,

307.10 294.b.2 stept] 1.g.14 ~] 309.29 stepped

307.21 294.b.14 refinements] 1.g.32-33 ~,] 310.11 ~

307.22 294.b.16 "Maroon"] 1.g.35 ~] 310.13 ‸~‸

307.23 294.b.17 Pacheco,] 1.g.36-37 ~] 310.14 ~‸

307.26 294.b.21 outpouring] 1.g.42 outpourings] 310.18 outpourings

307.26 294.b.22 exultation] 1.g.43 ~] 310.19 ~,

307.27 294.b.22 scene] 1.g.43 sense] 310.19 sense

307.30 294.b.26 disquiet] 1.g.48 ~] 310.23 ~,

307.30 294.b.26 lessen] 1.g.49 lesson] 310.23 lessen

307.32 294.b.29-30 good anchorage] 1.g.53-54~-~] 310.26-27~‸~

308. 294.b. <no chapter>] 1.g. XXVII.] 311. CHAPTER XXVIII.

308.2 294.b.37 "Maroon"] 1.g.64 ~] 311.2 ‸~‸

308.8 294.b.45 tyrannic] 1.g.74 tyranic] 311.10 tyrannic

308.12 294.b.50 similar hopes] 1.g.82-83 their mutual hopes] 311.16 their mutual hopes

308.13 294.b.51 and] 1.g.83 ~] 311.16 ~,

308.14 294.b.53 "Maroon"] 1.g.86-87 ~] 311.19 ‸~‸

308.15 294.b.54 were] 1.g.88 were] 311.20 was

308.16 294.b.55-56 milk-white,] 1.g.90 ~] 311.21 ~‸

307.17 294.b.56 treasures,] 1.g.90-91 ~] 311.21-22 ~‸

308.17 294.b.56 lap] 1.g.91 hap] 311.22 lap

308.18 294.b.57 neck.] 1.g.92 ~—] 311.23 ~‸

308.27 294.b.67 beholding] 1.g.106 surveying] 312.6 surveying

308.32 295.a.5-6 "Maroon,"] 1.g.116 ~] 312.13 ‸~‸

308.36 295.a.9 every thing] 1.g.121 ~] 312.17 everything

309.3 295.a.14 trampled] 1.g.128 trambled] 312.22 trampled

309.5 295.a.16 "Maroon."] 1.h.2 ~] 312.24 ∧~∧

309.7 295.a.20 stone,] 1.h.7 ~] 312.28 ~∧

309.9 295.a.21 severs] 1.h.9 sever] 312.29 sever

309.14 295.a.28 that she] 1.h.19 she] 313.5 she

309.15 295.a.29 death,] 1.h.20 ~∧] 313.6 ~;

309.23 295.a.40 satisfation] 1.h.35 satisfaction] 313.17 ~

310.3 295.a.63 arise] 1.h.66 ~] 314.9 rise

310.14 295.b.8 swam] 1.h.86 ~] 314.23 swan

310.15 295.b.10 rest.] 1.h.88 ~—] 314.25 ~∧

310.18 295.b.13 high mettled] 1.h.94 ~] 314.28 ~-~

310.25 295.b.23 dreamed] 1.h.107 ~] 315.7 ~,

310.26 295.b.23-24 consolation,] 1.h.108 ~] 315.8 ~∧

310. 295.b. <no chapter>] 1.h. XXVIII.] 315. CHAPTER XXIX.

310.30 295.b.28 sea.] 1.h.113 ~—] 315.12 ~∧

310.32 295.b.31 island,] 1.h.118 ~] 315.15 ~∧

311.3 295.b.40 "Maroon"] 2.a.1 ~] 315.24 ∧~∧

311.13 295.b.51 periled] 2.a.17 ~] 316.10 perilled

311.13 295.b.52 nature—] 2.a.18 ~;∧] 316.10 ~

311.14 295.b.53 periled] 2.a.19 ~] 316.11 perilled

311.14 295.b.53 vain—] 2.a.19 ~,∧] 316.12 ~

311.20 295.b.60 re-assure] 2.a.29 ~] 316.19 reassure

311.21 295.b.61 caresses,] 2.a.31 ~∧—] 316.20 ~,

311.22 295.b.62 justification.] 2.a.32 ~—] 316.21-22 ~.

311.23 295.b.64 heard,] 2.a.34 ~] 316.23 ~∧

311.24 295.b.65 "Maroon"] 2.a.36 ~] 316.24 ∧~∧

311.25 295.b.66 faint] 2.a.37 ~,] 316.25 ~

311.30 296.a.3 chrystalline] 2.a.46 chrystaline] 316.31 crystalline

311.31 296.a.5 sea weed] 2.a.48-49 ~] 317.1 ~-~

311.35 296.a.10 burdened,] 2.a.56 ~∧—] 317.6 ~

311.37 296.a.12 "Maroon"] 2.a.58 ~] 317.8 ∧~∧

311.37 296.a.13 terror.] 2.a.59 ~,] 317.9 ~.

312.2 296.a.15 Pacheco,] 2.a.62 ~] 317.11 ~∧

312.3 296.a.16 cabin] 2.a.64 ~.] 317.12 ~

312.4 296.a.17-18 darkness] 2.a.66 darknes] 317.14 darkness

312.9 296.a.23 *Mader de Dios*!] 2.a.73-74 *Madre de Dios!*"] 317.19 Madre de Dios!
312.16 296.a.31 that] 2.a.85 ~,] 317.28 ~
312.16 296.a.31 Lopez! What] 2.a.85 ~] 317.28 ~?—what
312.16 296.a.31 this?" Whispered] 2.a.86 ~?'~] 317.28 ~?—whispered
312.20 296.a.36 struck,] 2.a.92 ~] 318.3 ~∧
312.20 296.a.37 "Maroon,"] 2.a.93 ~] 318.4 ∧~∧
312.25 296.b.4 masess] 2.a.102 masses] 318.10 ~
312.26 296.b.5 shudder] 2.a.103 ~,] 318.11 ~
312.28 296.b.7 recal] 2.a.106 ~] 318.13 recall
312.29 296.b.9 impulses] 2.a.109 impulsions] 318.15 impulsions
312.33 296.b.14 pinnacle.] 2.a.115 ~—] 318.20 ~∧
312.34 296.b.15 half awakened] 2.a.117 ~] 318.21 ~-~
312.35 296.b.16 middle.] 2.a.118-119 ~,] 318.22 ~∧
313.1 296.b.20 Pacheco,] 2.a.124-125 ~] 318.27 ~∧
313.2 296.b.22 "Maroon."] 2.a.126 ~] 318.29 ∧~∧
313.3 296.b.23 roar,—"where] 2.a.128-129 ~.∧¶"Where] 318.30-31 ~
313.4 296.b.23 Lopez—] 2.a.129 ~] 318.31 ~?—
313.8 296.b.28 forward,] 2.a.136 ~] 319.5 ~∧
313.10 296.b.31 pieces,] 2.a.140 ~∧—] 319.8 ~
313.11 296.b.32 him,] 2.a.141-142 ~] 319.9 ~∧
313.14 296.b.36 chaunt] 2.b.5 ~] 319.13 chant
313.16 296.b.38 "Maroon"] 2.b.8 ~] 319.15 ∧~∧
313.16 296.b.38 conscious] 2.b.8-9 ~,] 319.16 ~
313.17 296.b.39 sea nymph,] 2.b.9-10 ~] 319.16 ~-~—

MAIZE IN MILK.
A CHRISTMAS STORY OF THE SOUTH.

Though he wrote longer and more successful stories of Southern plantation life in *Castle Dismal, or the Bachelor's Christmas: A Domestic Legend* (1845) and in *The Golden Christmas: A Chronicle of St. John's, Berkeley* (1852), Simms likewise gives an interesting and knowledgeable account of the customs and traditions of Christmas in the Old South in "Maize in Milk. A Christmas Story of the South." The strength of the story lies not in its contrived plot and stereotyped characters, but in the spirit and atmosphere of its setting. The reader interested in understanding the social order and philosophy of the Old South will find much of it captured here, including the paternalistic concept of the Negro slave so inimical to Simms's reputation. That "Maize in Milk" is best read as a reflector of nineteenth century Southern thought and manners is suggested by Simms's own terse evaluation: "It is simply descriptive" (Letter to Duyckinck, Feb. 25, 1847; *Letters*, II, 273).

Explanatory Notes

314. Epigraph The quotation is from "The Ceremonies for Candlemasse Day," included in *The Works of Robert Herrick* (Edinburgh, 1823), II, 124. Perhaps Simms's source is William Hone, *The Every-Day Book*, I (London, n.d. [1826]), column 204. See *Letters*, III, 10.

327. Epigraph The "slightly altered" quotation is from the first verse of "A Christmas Carroll" in the added material at the end of *Faire-Virtue, the Mistresse of Phil' arrete Written by Him-selfe* (London, 1622). A possible source for Simms is Hone, *Every-Day Book*, I, column 1631, which (except for accidentals) differs from Simms's version only in the last line: "And let us all be merry" instead of "And down with melancholy."

328.11-15 The quotation is from *Hamlet*, I, i, 160-164. Hone, *Every-Day Book*, I, columns 1641-1642, is very likely Simms's source, though slight differences, primarily in punctuation, exist in the two versions.

328.30-31 This quotation has not been identified.

329.5-8 These lines from an ancient English carol are included in Hone, *Every-Day Book*, I, column 1603.

330.4-19 The source for these lines is unknown.

332.1-17 The source for this carol is unknown.

343.5-24 Simms's source for "Carol for Christmas Eve" is unknown.

344.3 M. Chateaubriand: François René Chateaubriand (1768-1848), French romantic author whose writings were widely read in America.

354.10-23 With changes in spelling, punctuation, and wording, this carol is included in Hone, *Every-Day Book*, I, column 1620.

355.18 "seriously incline": *Othello*, I, iii, 146.

Textual Introduction

Simms probably began writing "Maize in Milk" in March, 1846, for on March 17 of that year he said in a letter to E. A. Duyckinck: "I wrote recently to W. & P [Wiley and Putnam, who in 1845 had published *The Wigwam and the Cabin*] suggesting to them an American Tale of Christmas, for which I have the scheme of a very pretty story" (*Letters*, II, 152). Wiley and Putnam apparently did not take to the suggestion, for some five months later, having just returned to Charleston after a visit to New York, Simms wrote to James Lawson: "I succeeded in transacting my business, in some degree, with Godey, having arranged to write him a nouvellette descriptive of Southern Life—a sort of tale for Christmas, to occupy two or three numbers of his Book, and thus to complete the year" (*Letters*, II, 177). "Maize in Milk. A Christmas Story of the South" was first published in *Godey's Lady's Book,* XXXIV (Feb., March, April, and May, 1847) 62-67, 146-152, 199-204, 249-258. It was subsequently republished as "Maize in Milk; A Christmas Story of the South" in *Marie de Berniere: A Tale of the Crescent City, etc. etc. etc.* (1853), pp. 320-422, and in *The Maroon; A Legend of the Caribbees, and Other Tales* (1855), pp. 320-422. There is at least some evidence that Simms toyed with the idea of reissuing "Maize in Milk" about 1865. The copy of *Marie de Berniere* that Simms used in preparing printer's copy for a contemplated 1865 edition of "The Maroon" (see Textual Introduction to "The Maroon," above, pp. 709-710) has in it, written in Simms's hand on page 320 above the title of "Maize in Milk," the phrase: "Contains 31000 words." Since Simms had written "Contains 36000 words" above the title of "The Maroon" some time during the process of pencilling in revisions and preparing the title-page for the proposed new edition, there is reason to speculate that he had similar, uncompleted plans in mind for "Maize in Milk." The fact that "Marie de Berniere" has been extracted from the copy (now in the South Caroliniana Library) perhaps lends support: is it possible that Simms used the torn away pages as printer's copy for the separate edition of "Marie de Berniere" published in 1866 under the title *The Ghost of My Husband*?

Since the changes in accidentals introduced to "Maize in Milk" in the 1853 edition (and 1855 reissue) do not appear to be authorial (there are no substantive changes), the 1847 publication in *Godey's* serves as copy-text.

Table I: Emendations and Textual Notes

Listed here are all changes made in the copy-text of "Maize in Milk." The original 1847 reading appears to the left of the bracket, the emended Centennial edition reading to the right. Where no bracket appears the reading is the same in both texts and the refusal to emend is explained in parentheses. Where an explanation of the change is necessary it follows in parentheses.

319.7 Bessy,] ~‸

323.36 havn't (Though Simms customarily wrote "haven't" [see 324.12], no attempt has been made to regularize spelling.)

325.17 asl awyer] as lawyer

327. <Epigraph/Chapter heading>] <Chapter heading/Epigraph> (In copy-text the epigraph is placed above the chapter number; the epigraph is placed below the chapter heading in the Centennial edition text.)

328.11 "*The* (Though the italics may be a printer's error, the decision is not to depart from copy-text.)

337.36 black puddings (Refusal to regularize is maintained, despite "black-puddings" at 337.32 and "black-pudding" at 337.38.)

343.5-24 Where . . . (Another refusal to emend: other quoted songs in "Maize in Milk" are in double quotes.)

343.24 Christ is born] Christ is born! (End punctuation is added, but the comma to regularize is not.)

343.25 <no chapter heading>] *CHAPTER III.*

343.27 St. Mathews] St. Matthews (Misspellings of city or town names are corrected.)

346.10 Dick] Harry (The sense of the passage calls for "Harry.")

349.18 (*here*)."] *(here).*" (Parentheses and quote marks immediately preceding or following italicized words are also italicized.)

349.25 voice.] ~,

354.11 *landes*] *laudes*

358.34 expensive (There is a possibility that the reading here should be "expansive.")

362.16 $718,44] $718.44
371.8 errror] error
371.34 gentleman] gentlemen
373.32 Charlestou] Charleston
374.7 (*Signed*)] *(Signed)*
375.9 deco ration] decoration
379.35 event,'"] ~,"

Table II: Textual Variants

Below is a chart of the variants between the *Godey's* text of "Maize in Milk" (1847) and the text of "Maize in Milk" in the *Marie de Berniere* volume (1853). (The texts of "Maize in Milk" in *Marie de Berniere* and in *The Maroon* [1855] are identical.)

From left to right the chart of variants has the following text sequence:

LEFT MARGIN: Centennial edition key
FIRST READING: 1847
SECOND READING: 1853

314. 62. MILK.] 320. ~;
314. 62. <poem precedes CHAPTER I.>] 320. <CHAPTER I. precedes poem>
314.3 62.a.4 army worm] 320.3 ~-~
314.3 62.a.4 catterpillar] 320.4 caterpillar
314.8 62.a.12 loving,] 320.10-11 ~‸
314.11 62.a.15 shall] 321.1 should
315.10 62.a.37-38 Christmas] 321.22 ~,
315.26 62.b.20 that] 322.13 ~,
315.26 62.b.20 log] 322.14 ~,
315.31 62.b.26 gathered] 322.19 gathered in
315.38 62.b.36 thee] 322.28 ~,
315.38 62.b.37 home] 322.29 ~,
316.11 63.a.8 corn] 323.12 ~,
316.15 63.a.13 neighbor] 323.17 ~,
316.22 63.a.24 you] 323.26 ~,
316.23 63.a.25 opposition] 323.28 ~,
317.1 63.a.44 tea-cup] 324.16 teacup
317.11 63.a.58 conducted] 324.29 conducting

317.17 63.b.7 terror] 325.6 ~,

317.26 63.b.19 nature] 325.17 ~,

317.29 63.b.23 logic] 325.21 ~,

317.31 63.b.26-27 venture therefore] 325.24 ~, ~,

318.1 63.b.38 good humor] 326.4 ~-~

318.15 63.b.57 Harry] 326.21 ~,

318.19 63.b.62 Years] 326.26 Year's

318.28 64.a.13 table,] 327.7 ~;

318.29 64.a.14 Madeira] 327.8 ~,

318.34 64.a.21 dogs] 327.15 ~,

318.35 64.a.23 you] 327.16 ~,

319.2 64.a.29 scarlet berries] 327.22 ~-~

319.4 64.a.33 no——] 327.26 ~—

319.16 64.a.48 know——] 328.10 ~—

319.18 64.a.50 that] 328.12 ~,

319.27 64.a.63 answer] 328.24 answer that

319.31 64.b.6 knows——] 328.30 ~—

319.35 64.b.11 the——] 329.4 ~—

319.37 64.b.14 spiggot] 329.7 spigot

320.2 64.b.18 Bond] 329.11 ~,

320.3 64.b.20 continent] 329.12 ~,

320.5 64.b.22 Homer——] 329.14 ~—

320.7 64.b.24-25 anybody——] 329.16 ~—

320.9 64.b.28 usual,] 329.19 ~ʌ

320.30 64.b.56 Europe] 330.13 ~,

320.31 64.b.57 now-a-days] 330.15 nowadays

320.31 64.b.58 horns] 330.15~,

320.37 65.a.1 owe] 330.21 ~,

321.11 65.a.18-19 years——] 331.6 ~ —

321.17 65.a.27 continued—] 331.13 ~:

321.19 65.a.29 years] 331.15 ~,

321.20 65.a.30 mince-pies——] 331.16 ~—

321.22 65.a.33 citron] 331.19 ~,

321.23 65.a.34 killed——] 331.20 ~—

321.24 65.a.35 anxiety then] 331.21 ~, ~,

321.34 65.a.51 do indeed] 332.3 ~, ~,

322.1 65.a.57 alone:] 332.9 ~;

322.4 65.a.62 world——] 332.13 ~—

322.16 65.b.15 some] 332.28 ~,
322.20 65.b.21 fashion—] 333.1 ~;
322.21 65.b.22 me] 333.2 ~,
322.27 65.b.31 that!] 333.11 ~.
322.29 65.b.34 far.—But] 333.14 ~∧— But
322.30 65.b.36 dog—] 333.16 ~;
322.31 65.b.37 Tom] 333.17 ~,
322.31 65.b.38 you.] 333.17 ~!
323.4 65.b.52 chair] 333.30 ~,
323.12 65.b.62 exultation] 334.8 ~,
323.23 66.a.15 wild cat] 334.24 ~-~
323.30 66.a.24 it,] 335.2 ~∧
323.35 66.a.30 said—] 335.7 ~:
323.36 66.a.31 havn't] 335.8 haven't
323.37 66.a.32 then——] 335.9 ~—
324.4 66.a.37 farther——] 335.14 ~—
324.9 66.a.43 Ay] 335.19 ~,
324.28 66.b.5 No.] 336.13 ~!
324.28 66.b.5 ask] 336.13 ~,
325.7 66.b.27 negroes] 337.3 ~,
325.10 66.b.30 these] 337.6 ~,
325.10 66.b.31 child] 337.7 ~,
325.17 66.b.40 asl awyer] 337.15 as lawyer
325.25 66.b.52 earnest] 337.26 ~,
326.1 67.a.6 And then] 338.12 ~, ~,
326.7 67.a.15 game] 338.20 ~,
326.17 67.b.1 things,] 338.31 ~;
327. 146. <poem precedes CHAPTER II.>
] 340. <CHAPTER II. precedes poem>
327.1 146.poem.1. joyful'st] 340.poem.1 joyfulest
327.13 146.a.3 south] 340.3 South
327.19 146.a.12 oak] 340.11 ~,
327.22 146.a.31 son] 341.7 ~,
327.22 146.a.31 traveling] 341.8 travelling
328.15 146.b.15 hallow'd] 341.31 hallowed
328.21 146.b.23 mansion house] 342.7 ~-~
329.12 147.a.15 midnight?"] 343.9 ~.∧
329.15 147.a.19 you have] 343.13 you may have

329.36 147.a.49 a] 344.9 the

330.4 147.a.54 Bethl'em,] 344.14 ~∧

330.23 147.b.14 below] 345.2 ~,

331.3 147.b.32 wife!] 345.18 ~?

331.13 147.b.46 prankt] 346.1 pranked

331.30 148.a.9 berries:] 346.23 ~;

331.34 148.a.13 stairs,] 346.28 ~.

332.13 148.a.31 this blessing] 347.15 his blessings

332.16 148.a.34 o'er:] 347.18 ~;

332.17 148.a.35 "Welcome <double quotes overhang one space beyond left margin>
] 347.19 "Welcome <double quotes flush with left margin>

332.33 148.a.58 bamboo,] 348.8 ~∧

332.36 148.a.62 wreaths] 348.11 ~,

333.5 148.b.8 re-arranged] 348.18 rearranged

333.12 148.b.16 own pony,] 348.25 pony

333.16 148.b.21 marshaled] 348.30-31 marshalled

333.19 148.b.25 Sure] 349.3 ~,

333.21 148.b.29 high sheriff] 349.6-7 ~-~

333.23 148.b.31 nightly—] 349.8 ~;

333.23 148.b.31 shrewd,] 349.8 ~∧

333.36 148.b.50 ash] 349.26 ~,

334.9 149.a.2 tree tops] 350.8 ~-~

334.10 149.a.3 beside,] 350.9 ~∧

334.10 149.a.4 squirrels,] 350.10 ~—

334.11 149.a.5 black] 350.11 ~,

334.11 149.a.5 gray,] 350.11 ~—

334.15 149.a.11 rise] 350.16 ~,

334.16 149.a.12 fields] 350.17 field

334.17 149.a.13 grasses] 350.18 ~,

334.20 149.a.18 or hundred] 350.23 or a hundred

334.23 149.a.21 towering] 350.26 ~,

334.24 149.a.24 frost as to] 350.28-29 frost to

334.32 149.a.35 fruit—] 351.8 ~;

334.33 149.a.36 fields,] 351.9 ~—

334.35 149.a.39 period,] 351.11 ~—

335.2 149.a.48 agoing] 351.19 going

335.8 149.a.56-57 proceeded—] 351.27 ~:

335.19 149.b.9 gum] 352.11 ~,
335.21 149.b.11 deep,] 352.13 ~^
335.22 149.b.13 river,] 352.14 ~;
335.23 149.b.14 front] 352.15 ~,
335.33 149.b.28 banner] 352.28 ~,
335.34 149.b.31 staff] 352.30 ~,
335.37 149.b.34 Dick] 353.3 ~,
336.15 149.b.58 Milk] 353.24 milk
336.29 150.a.13 arrived—] 354.10 ~;
337.2 150.a.29 semi-transparent] 354.24-25 semitransparent
337.5 150.a.33-34 consistency,] 354.29 ~;
337.5 150.a.34 soft] 354.29 ~,
337.6 150.a.35 hard] 354.30 ~,
337.12 150.a.44 fast] 355.7 ~,
337.20 150.a.54 corn] 355.16 ~,
337.21 150.a.55 plantation—] 355.16 ~;
337.24 150.a.60 market] 355.21 ~,
337.26 150.a.62 staple—] 355.23 ~;
337.28 150.b.3 breadstuffs—] 355.26 ~;
337.31 150.b.6 corn beef] 355.29 ~-~
337.32 150.b.8 black-puddings] 355.31 ~^~
337.38 150.b.15-16 black-pudding] 356.7 ~^~
338.2 150.b.19 eye] 356.10 ~,
338.3 150.b.21 and perhaps] 356.12 ~, ~,
338.6 150.b.24 Log] 356.15 log
338.21 150.b.46 ploughs] 357.4 ~,
339.9 151.a.20 Milk] 358.7 milk
339.10 151.a.20 gentlemen] 358.8 gentleman
339.14 151.a.25 Spanish] 358.12 ~,
339.14 151.a.25-26 brimstone] 358.13 ~,
339.22 151.a.37 Milk] 358.23 milk
339.25 151.a.42 sympathize,] 358.27 ~;
339.38 151.a.59 Butler,] 359.12 ~^
340.4 151.b.2 Col.] 359.18 Colonel
340.4 151.b.2-3 practicing] 359.18-19 practising
340.5 151.b.4 hurriedly,] 359.20 ~^
340.7 151.b.7 frame,] 359.22 ~^
340.33 151.b.42 sturdy,] 360.23 ~^

340.33 151.b.42 clear,] 360.24 ~^
340.36 151.b.46 objects] 360.27 ~,
340.37 151.b.48 Col.] 360.29 Colonel
341.9 151.b.63 Col.] 361.11 Colonel
341.17 152.a.10 Col.] 361.21 Colonel
341.26 152.a.23-24 traveled;] 362.2-3 travelled,
341.31 153.a.30 man,] 362.8 ~^
341.37 152.a.39 Milk] 362.17 milk
342.8 152.a.50 passes,] 362.27 ~^
342.13 152.a.57 Log] 363.3 log
342.18 152.b.4 could,] 363.9 ~^
342.19 152.b.6 wood-pile] 363.11 woodpile
342.23 152.b.11 tend,] 363.15 ~^
342.23 152.b.11 degree,] 363.16 ~^
342.27 152.b.17 tamborine] 363.21 tambourine
342.32 152.b.24 eggs —] 363.27 ~;
342.38 152.b.32 Milk] 364.4 milk
342.38 152.b.33 never,] 364.4 ~^
343.1 152.b.33 before,] 364.5 ~^
343.11 152.b.45 grace,] 364.16 ~;
343.18 152.b.52 Token'd] 364.23 Tokened
343.20 152.b.54 fill'd] 364.25 filled
343.21 152.b.55 Cheer'd] 364.26 Cheered
343.22 152.b.56 "Tidings <double quotes flush with left margin>] 364.27 "Tidings <double quotes overhang one space beyond left margin>
343.24 152.b.58 Christ is born] 364.29 ~, ~ ~.
343. 199. <no chapter>] 365. CHAPTER III.
343.26 199.a.3 Milk] 365.3 milk
343.27 199.a.3 Mathews] 365.3 Matthews
343.30 199.a.8 song birds] 365.8 ~-~
343.30 199.a.9 forest^ birds] 365.8 ~-~
343.33 199.a.12 feel] 365.12 ~,
344.1 199.a.14 So,] 365.13 ~^
344.5 199.a.18 because,] 365.17 ~^
344.6 199.a.21 fox] 365.19 ~,
344.7 199.a.22 Milk] 365.21 milk
344.12 199.a.28 noon-tide] 365.26 noontide

344.12 199.a.29 apprehension,] 365.27 ~;
344.15 199.a.33 morning,] 366.3 ~‸
344.28 199.b.1 song birds] 366.20 ~-~
344.33 199.b.8 short,] 366.26 ~‸
344.35 199.b.10 But,] 366.29 ~‸
345.2 199.b.17 twigs,] 367.4 ~‸
345.3 199.b.19 finally,] 367.5 ~‸
345.4 199.b.21 Milk] 367.7 milk
345.5 199.b.21 household,] 367.8 ~‸
345.16 199.b.37 Milk] 367.23 milk
345.21 199.b.44 revolution] 367.29 Revolution
345.21 199.b.44 tory] 367.29 Tory
345.24 199.b.48 Dick] 368.1 ~,
345.25 199.b.50 south] 368.2 South
345.28 200.a.3 customs] 368.6 ~,
345.37 200.a.16 protegé] 368.17 *protégé*
346.3 200.a.20 Milk] 368.21 milk
346.6 200.a.24 pendant] 368.25 pendent
346.6 200.a.25 Dick] 368.25 ~,
346.7 200.a.26 fire-place] 368.27 fireplace
346.10 200.a.30 Dick] 368.30 Harry
346.11 200.a.31 shoes] 368.31 ~,
346.14 200.a.35 Bond] 369.4 ~,
346.16 200.a.38 fire-place] 369.7 fireplace
346.20 200.a.44 him,] 369.12 ~;
346.21 200.a.44 over-all] 369.13 overall,
346.23 200.a.47 him,] 369.16 ~;
346.25 200.a.50 girls] 369.19 ~,
346.25 200.a.51 that] 369.19 ~,
346.29 200.a.56 gifts!—] 369.23 ~‸
346.32 200.a.60 knife] 369.27 ~,
346.32 200.a.60 and] 369.27 and a
346.32 200.a.61 flagelet;] 369.27 flageolet,
347.6 200.b.14-15 common-prayer] 370.12 ~,
347.14 200.b.26 parties] 370.23 ~,
347.18 200.b.32 again] 370.28 ~,
347.20 200.b.35 you,] 370.31 ~‸
347.22 200.b.38 mother] 371.3 ~,

347.23 200.b.39 sister] 371.3 ~,

347.26 200.b.44 morning] 371.8 ~,

347.29 200.b.47 Butler] 371.11 ~,

347.36 200.b.58 hue,] 371.20 ~∧

348.6 201.a.7 egg-nogg] 371.31 eggnog

348.10 201.a.12 ramble] 372.5 ~,

348.13 201.a.16 Milk] 372.9 milk

348.16 201.a.20 wild cat] 372.12 ~-~

348.19 201.a.24-25 Maize-in-Milk,] 372.17-18 "Maize-in-milk,"

348.28 201.a.36 chaunt] 372.28 chant

348.29 201.a.38 halt] 372.29 ~,

348.31 201.a.42 great, great grand-children] 373.2 great-great-grandchildren

348.35 201.a.47 mute,] 373.7 ~;

348.36 201.a.47 one-armed,] 373.7 ~;

348.36 201.a.48 Polly] 373.7 ~,

348.36 201.a.48 half-witted,] 373.8 ~;

349.2 201.a.53 this,] 373.12 ~∧

349.4 201.a.56 good,] 373.15 ~;

349.4 201.a.57 heir-looms] 373.16 heirlooms

349.9 201.a.63 Col.] 373.22 Colonel

349.13 201.b.6 Christmas?] 373.28 ~,

349.14 201.b.8 chillans." These] 373.29~;" these

349.16 201.b.10 school-boys:] 373.31 ~:—

349.25 201.b.19 voice.] 374.9 ~,

349.26 201.b.20,21 <lines indented deeper than others>] 374.10,11 <normal indentation>

349.30 201.b.26 pedlar's] 374.15 peddler's

349.33 201.b.29 scissors;] 374.18 ~,

349.33 201.b.29 shawls] 374.18 ~,

350.2 201.b.31 cards,] 374.21 ~∧

350.5 201.b.36 masques] 374.24 masks

350.14 201.b.49 fullness] 375.6 fulness

350.14 201.b.49 hogmeat] 375.6 ~-~

350.21 201.b.59 discussion,] 375.15 ~;

350.28 202.a.8 *rôle*] 375.24 ~,

350.32 202.a.13 Whipple] 375.28 ~,

350.34 202.a.15 Butler] 375.30 ~,

351.1 202.a.21 Bond] 376.5 ~,

351.17 202.a.44 leaves] 376.26 ~,

351.17 202.a.45 cottage] 376.27 ~,

351.24 202.a.53 Milk] 377.4 milk

351.26 202.a.56 Colonel] 377.7 colonel

351.31 202.b.1 college,] 377.13-14 ~;

351.34 202.b.5 and] 377.18 ~,

352.7 202.b.19 Milk] 377.31 milk

352.13 202.b.27 go so soon] 378.8 go soon

352.20 202.b.37 silent] 378.17 ~,

352.22 202.b.40 suffice, that] 378.20 ~^ ~,

352.24 202.b.43 new comer] 378.22-23 ~-~

352.25 202.b.44 company,] 378.23 ~^

352.34 202.b.57 Milk] 379.4 milk

352.37 202.b.61 emerge,] 379.8 ~^

353.3 203.a.4 himself] 379.13 ~,

353.3 203.a.4 what,] 379.13 ~^

353.4 203.a.5 sense,] 379.14 ~^

353.8 203.a.11 man,] 379.19 ~^

353.9 203.a.12 selfish,] 379.20 ~^

353.12 203.a.16-17 title sneeringly] 379.24 ~, ~,

353.23 203.a.32 good humour] 380.7 good-humor

353.26 203.a.37 instance] 380.12 ~,

354.4 203.a.60 appearance] 381.2 ~,

354.6 203.a.62-63 rosemary] 381.4 ~,

354.11 203.b.5 *landes*] 381.9 *laudes*

354.27 203.b.22 south] 381.25 South

354.32 203.b.29 pastry,] 382.1 ~^

354.34 203.b.33 denomination,] 382.5 ~^

355.2 203.b.38 ale,] 382.9 ~^

355.4 203.b.40 north] 382.11 North

355.4 203.b.41 peanuts] 382.12 ~,

355.6 203.b.44 mincepies] 382.15 ~-~

355.12 203.b.52 feast,] 382.22 ~^

355.16 203.b.58 it, and] 382.27 ~; ~,

355.17 203.b.59 south side] 382.28-29 ~-~

355.24 204.a.8 Dick] 383.6 ~,

355.27 204.a.12 tamborin] 383.9-10 tambourine

355.28 204.a.14 Butler] 383.11 butler
355.33 204.a.20 tamborin] 383.17 tambourine
355.38 204.a.28 Still] 383.25 ~,
356.7 204.b.3 awkwardness,] 384.2-3 ~^
356.8 204.b.5 remember accordingly] 384.4 ~, ~,
356.10 204.b.7 Milk] 384.6 milk
356.12 204.b.10 Bond] 384.9 ~,
356.13 204.b.12 nay] 384.10 ~,
356.14 204.b.13 Milk] 384.12 milk
356.23 204.b.26 possums] 384.23 ~,
356.24 204.b.27 bread] 384.24 ~,
356.26 204.b.29-30 manufacture—] 384.27 ~,
356.27 204.b.30 cider,] 384.28 ~^
356.29 204.b.33 Milk] 384.30 milk
356.29 204.b.34 wrapt] 384.31 wrapped
356.31 249.a.2 Milk] 385.2 milk
357.1 249.a.9 aspect] 385.9 ~,
357.6 249.a.16 unfriendly] 385.15 ~,
357.7 249.a.19 inundated] 385.17 ~,
357.10 249.a.23 army worm] 385.21 ~-~
357.16 249.a.30 Milk] 386.1 milk
357.19 249.a.35 pest] 386.5 pests
357.21 249.a.37 low] 386.7 ~,
357.24 249.a.43 toward] 386.12 towards
357.26 249.a.45 mind] 386.14 ~,
357.36 249.b.10 approach] 386.27 ~,
357.38 249.b.13 dinner parties] 386.30 ~-~
357.38 249.b.14 pleasure parties] 386.30 ~-~
358.15 249.b.35 change—] 387.18 ~;
358.24 249.b.47 College] 387.30 college
358.27 249.b.51 Clinton] 388.2-3 ~,
358.32 250.a.6 them] 388.9 ~,
358.34 250.a.10 scrupulous] 388.12 ~,
359.4 250.a.21 importance which] 388.23 ~,~,
359.4 250.a.22 man] 388.23 ~,
359.8 250.a.27-28 exclaimed—] 388.28 ~:
359.10 250.a.29 How] 388.30 ~,
359.16 250.a.38 way—] 389.7 ~;

359.17 250.a.41 dem] 389.9 ~,
359.18 250.a.41 say] 389.10 ~,
359.18 250.a.41 *I*] 389.10 I
359.19 250.a.43 say] 389.12 ~,
359.31 250.a.59 daily] 389.28 ~,
359.31 250.a.60 months] 389.28 ~,
359.33 250.a.63 wild cat] 390.1 ~-~
360.4 250.b.9 destined] 390.9-10 ~,
360.6 250.b.11 was] 390.12 was a
360.9 250.b.16 time—] 390.16 ~;
360.14 250.b.22 left] 390.22 ~,
360.18 250.b.28 poplar] 390.27 ~,
360.25 250.b.38 disquiet] 391.6 ~,
360.26 250.b.39 forebodings] 391.67 ~,
361.26 251.a.28 days] 392.22 ~,
361.27 251.a.30-31 silence—] 392.24 ~;
362.2 251.a.46 north] 393.8 North
362.3 251.a.47 apples] 393.10 ~,
362.3 251.a.48 and——] 393.10 ~—
362.8 251.a.55 interest] 393.16 ~,
362.16 251.b.3 down] 393.26 ~,
362.16 251.b.3 mistake—] 393.26-27 ~,
362.16 251.b.3 $718,44] 393.27 $718 44
362.18 251.b.5 payment] 393.29 ~,
362.19 251.b.7 wish that there] 393.30 wish there
362.19 251.b.7 were] 393.30 was
362.38 251.b.33 and——] 394.23 ~—
363.16 251.b.55 everything—] 395.12 ~;
363.23 252.a.3 children] 395.23 ~,
363.24 252.a.3 usual, and] 395.23 ~; ~,
363.31 252.a.13 high——] 396.2 ~—
363.32 252.a.14 grocers] 396.3 ~'
364.12 252.a.40 cordiality,] 396.27 ~;
365.7 252.b.23 you,] 398.9 ~∧
365.12 252.b.28 sufferer] 398.14 ~,
365.16 252.b.32 executioner] 398.18 executor
365.27 252.b.46 states] 399.1 States
365.36 252.b.59 sir—] 399.12 ~;

366.9 253.a.15 Hem] 399.28 hem
366.13 253.a.20 manner] 400.2 ~,
366.14 253.a.22 all] 400.3 ~,
366.22 253.a.34 crops] 400.13 ~,
366.27 253.a.41 Openheart] 400.20 ~,
366.37 253.a.54 securities] 401.1 ~,
367.3 253.a.62 but to put] 401.8 but put
367.5 253.b.2 so—] 401.11 ~:
367.10 253.b.8 property,] 401.16 ~;
367.16 253.b.16 would in] 401.24 would
367.24 253.b.29 conduct.] 402.4 ~?
367.29 253.b.37 one—] 402.11 ~;
367.30 253.b.38 me] 402.13 ~,
367.31 253.b.39 affairs] 402.13 ~,
367.36 253.b.46 frankness—] 402.20 ~:
368.2 253.b.51-52 and——] 402.25 ~—
368.4 253.b.55 sir—] 402.28 ~;
368.5 253.b.56 me—] 402.29 ~;
368.5 253.b.56 yet—] 402.29 ~;
368.8 253.b.61 aristocrat,] 403.3 ~;
368.9 253.b.62 frank] 403.3 ~,
368.15 254.a.7 and] 403.11 ~,
368.16 254.a.8 congress] 403.12 Congress
368.24 254.a.20 fields] 403.23 ~,
368.30 254.a.29 meeting!] 403.31 ~?
368.31 254.a.30 slowly] 404.1 ~,
368.35 254.a.36 rein] 404.7 ~,
368.37 254.a.39 "with] 404.10 ‸~
368.38 254.a.39 But] 404.10 "~
368.38 254.a.40 exertion—] 404.11 ~;
369.13 254.a.57 country] 404.27 ~,
369.22 254.b.6 Still] 405.6 ~,
369.25 254.b.10 said that they] 405.10 said they
369.26 254.b.11-12 establishment and have to] 405.11 establishment, and
369.30 254.b.18 and——] 405.17 ~—
369.34 254.b.23 sir—] 405.22 ~;
370.6 254.b.36 *father*] 406.3 ~,

370.11 254.b.42 counsel] 406.8 ~,
370.14 254.b.47 delicacy,] 406.13 ~;
370.16 254.b.49 you—] 406.14 ~;
370.17 254.b.51 Openheart] 406.17 ~,
370.26 254.b.63 Why,] 406.28 ~‸
370.26 255.a.1 particular—] 406.29 ~;
370.27 255.a.2 category] 406.30 ~,
370.38 255.a.15 dialogue] 407.13 ~,
371.8 255.a.28 errror] 407.26 error
371.18 255.a.42 landholder—] 408.7 ~;
371.19 255.a.42 noble,] 408.7 ~‸
371.22 255.a.48 watchfulness] 408.12 ~,
371.31 255.a.60 Bloomdale] 408.23 Bloomsdale
371.34 255.b.1 gentleman] 408.27 gentlemen
372.10 255.b.23 astonishment,] 409.16 ~;
372.12 255.b.25 lawyer] 409.18 ~,
372.13 255.b.26 daughter] 409.19 ~,
372.28 255.b.47 declaration] 410.7 ~,
373.1 255.b.63 sweetness] 410.22 ~,
373.4 256.a.5 gentleness.] 410.26 ~:
373.12 256.a.16 jury] 411.5 ~,
373.15 256.a.19 Openheart] 411.8 ~,
373.16 256.a.22 ill-concealed] 411.10 ~‸~
373.21 256.a.28 forebore] 411.16 forbore
373.21 256.a.29 apologetic] 411.17 ~,
373.23 256.a.31 warmly] 411.19 ~,
373.29 256.a.39 sorrows] 411.26 ~,
373.29 256.a.40 might] 411.27 ~,
373.32 256.a.42 Charlestou] 411.30 Charleston
373.32 256.a.43 Bloomdale] 411.31 Bloomsdale
373.33 256.a.45 money] 412.1 ~,
373.35 256.a.47 truant] 412.4 ~,
373.36 256.a.49 Bloomdale] 412.5 Bloomsdale
373.38 256.a.52 handsome] 412.8 ~,
374.5 256.a.59 Cripps. "Sense] 412.15-16 ~ ¶ ~
374.7 256.a.61 &c. With] 412.17-18 ~ ¶ "~
374.7 256.a.62-63 &c. (*Signed*)/"Richard
] 412.18-19 &c. ¶ (*Signed*,) <long space> "Richard
374.9 256.b.2 palm] 412.21 ~,

374.27 256.b.26 Col.] 413.12 Colonel
374.35 256.b.38 foreborne] 413.23 forborne
375.9 256.b.55 mantel] 414.7 ~,
375.9 256.b.55 deco ration] 414.7 decoration
375.26 257.a.15 cold,] 414.27 ~^
375.29 257.a.19 enclosure] 414.31 inclosure
375.34 257.a.27 guests] 415.8 ~,
376.1 257.a.32 remarked—] 415.13 ~:
376.3 257.a.35 counseled] 415.15 counselled
376.9 257.a.45 assembled] 415.25 ~,
376.12 257.a.49 articulate—] 415.29 ~;
376.18 257.a.58 sickness] 416.6 ~,
376.21 257.a.61 sheriff—] 416.9 ~:
376.25 257.b.5 answer—] 416.14 ~;
376.26 257.b.5 you;] 416.14 ~,
376.28 257.b.9 once."] 416.17 ~^
376.33 257.b.15 said—] 416.23 ~,
377.3 257.b.26-27 Good morning] 417.3 ~-~
377.3 257.b.27 good morning] 417.3-4 ~-~
377.13 257.b.40 negroes] 417.16 ~,
377.16 257.b.44 SIR:—] 417.20 SIR:
377.21 257.b.52 leisure—] 417.27 ~;
377.29 257.b.62 handsome] 418.8 ~,
377.32 258.a.3 negroes] 418.11 ~,
378.35 258.a.56 pocket inkstand and] 420.1 ~-~-~
378.36 258.a.57 obligation] 420.2 ~,
379.2 258.a.63 him,] 420.8 ~;
379.2 258a.63 bowed] 420.8 ~,
379.3 258.a.64 good morning] 420.8-9 ~-~
379.11 258.b.11 you] 420.18 ~,
379.14 258.b.13 away] 420.21 ~,
379.32 258.b.36 disquiet] 421.12 ~,
379.32 258.b.37 mortifications] 421.12-13 ~,
379.35 258.b.41 event,'"] 421.16 ~,"
380.8 258.b.57 mockbird] 421.31 ~-~
380.9 258.b.58 warm] 422.1 ~,
380.11 258.b.60 dance—] 422.3 ~;
380.12 258.b.62 unconsciously—] 422.5 ~,
380. 258. <omitted>] 422. THE END.

FLIRTATION AT THE MOULTRIE HOUSE.

Flirtation at the Moultrie House is a light farcical comedy of manners which gently satirizes fashionable Charleston society.

The Grand Costume Ball it describes is not fictitious; it actually took place at the Moultrie House on Sullivan's Island on August 29, 1850, under the sponsorship of the Junior Managers and Senior Managers (one being "W. G. Simms Esq.") listed in the Appendix (see also "Grand Costume Ball," *Charleston Courier*, Sept. 5, 1850, p. 4). But Simms added to the facts of the well-known social affair the fictitious main characters and their presumably fictitious love entanglements: the 1850 census of Georgia does not show any citizens named either Appleby or Kirkland living in Habersham County (Clarkesville); nor does it list a Richard Meriwether in Coweta County, although the census of Coweta County does show two farm families, the P. L. Merriwethers and the James Merriwethers, neither with a son named Richard. Although Colleton is a well established family name in South Carolina, Augustus Colleton is also the creation of the author's imagination. For his characters Simms selected names that have the ring of authenticity, yet are unidentifiable.

To add to the air of reality of *Flirtation at the Moultrie House*, Simms, it must be assumed, planted in the *Courier* of September 5, 1850, the newspaper account which he later incorporated into *Flirtation* as its Appendix (see Table II, pp. 785-792). It is also assumed that no one was deceived by Simms's ingenious device of establishing the identity of his fictitious characters by including them among the host of actual persons named (or partially named) in the *Courier* story and in the Appendix, and that the small circle of knowing Charlestonians who received copies of *Flirtation* would have enjoyed this "deception" as a private joke.

Flirtation at the Moultrie House is apparently Simms's only attempt at fiction in epistolary form. It is also his only effort to present his story primarily through the eyes of a female character, who is even more gently satirized than the Charleston society she views. Although *Flirtation* is of interest to Simms scholars primarily because it represents a type of fiction almost wholly different from that characteristically associated with the prolific South Carolinian, he did make other thrusts toward light satire; e.g., *Father Abbot*, *or; the Home Tourist, a Medley* (Charleston: Miller & Browne, 1849); the fragmentary "Major Martinet; or, the Lost Half Hour," *Cosmopolitan Monthly*, I (Jan., 1870), 1-6; and the unpublished manuscript, "Will O' Wisp; or the Irish Baronet," now in the South Caroliniana Library. Simms himself probably considered *Flirtation* too light an effort to take seriously, an attitude which perhaps accounts for the fact that he apparently never acknowledged his authorship.

Explanatory Notes

386.28-29 The quoted lines have not been identified.

393.23 Robert le Diable: The reference is probably to the hero of a medieval legend which perhaps owed certain details to the cruelty and daring of Robert, third Duke of Normandy (1028-1035), father of William the Conqueror. According to Norman tradition, the wandering ghost of Robert the Devil will not be allowed to rest till the Day of Judgment. The legend is the basis for Meyerbeer's opera *Robert le Diable* (1831), a great success in its day. In the opera the duke is depicted as a libertine, and Meyerbeer shows the struggle in Robert between the virtue inherited from his mother and the vice imparted by his father. Simms's allusion is probably to a famous scene (in the third act of the opera) in the ruined convent of St. Rosalie in which unfaithful nuns rise from their graves and dance around Robert, enticing him to do evil. (See *Kobbé's Complete Opera Book*, New York, 1954, pp. 688-690.) Simms apparently saw *Robert le Diable* when it was performed in New York in the summer of 1845. In Notebook G in the Charles Carroll Simms Collection is an unsigned clipping, dated "New-York, Sept. 23, 1845," which reads in part: "I have seen, at this house, (Niblo's) the two operas (in French,) of '*Les Huguenots, ou le Massacre de la Saint-Barthelemy*,' and '*Robert-le-diable*,' both written by M. Scribe, with the music of Meyerbeer. The latter piece I had seen before in French and English, and it is one of those pieces in which I always took great delight;—though it strikes me that their subject is susceptible of much more admirable use than Scribe has made of it."

398.17-21 JUNIOR MANAGERS: (1) E. M. Beach is listed as a merchant, 23 Meeting Street, in the Charleston Directory *(CD)* of 1849; (2) Wilmot Gibbes DeSaussure (1822-1886), was a Charleston attorney; (3) F. J. [P?] Porcher was probably Francis

Peyre Porcher (1825-1895), physician and friend of Simms; (4) R. D. Spann was possibly Russell Spann, identified as a widower in 1833 (see *South Carolina Historical and Genealogical Magazine*, XXXIV, 186)—otherwise unidentified; (5) Henry C. King, husband of minor writer Susan Petigru King (1824-1875), is listed as an attorney, 68 Tradd Street, in the 1849 *CD* ;(6) a John J. Edwards is listed as wharfinger, Central Wharf, 2 State, in the 1849 *CD*; (7) A. Herbemont, Jr. was possibly the son of Nicholas Herbemart, professor of French at South Carolina College, 1807-1817, and a producer of South Carolina wine (*Letters*, IV, 143); (8) Lt. J. B. J. Weld, U.S.A., has not been identified; (9) Theo. Stoney was probably of the family of C. F. Stoney, druggist of the firm Stoney and Wiltberger at 245 King Street, Charleston: 26 Hasell is given as the residence of a T. Stoney (*CD*, 1849; see *Letters*, IV, 83n.); (10) C. K. Prioleau cannot be identified, unless possibly he is the son (or relative) of Dr. Philip Gendron Prioleau, in whose office Simms's friend Samuel Henry Dickson read medicine; (11) Edward C. Jones, architect, planned the Charleston Custom House and Magnolia Cemetery (see *Charleston Courier*, March 7, July 20, 1850; *Letters*, III, 25); (12) Motte A. Pringle is listed as clerk, 9 King, in the 1849 *CD*.

398.29-35 SENIOR MANAGERS: (1) Jacob Bond I'On (1782-1859), Yale graduate, served as president of the state senate for many years, once ran unsuccessfully for governor (1825), and owned the famous plantation Fairlawn, near the head of Wando River (see *Courier*, July 18, 1859, for obituary); (2) James Louis Petigru (1789-1863), prominent attorney—one-time attorney general of South Carolina—to whom Simms dedicated *The Vision of Cortes, Cain, and Other Poems* (1829); (3) the author himself; (4) William A. Carson, purchaser of 3,100-acre Dean Hall plantation in 1821 (see *S.C.H. & G. Mag.*, XXIV, 27); (5) Charles T. Lowndes, nephew of Jacob Bond I'On, was a well-known planter identified in 1853 as a "friend" of the *Southern Quarterly Review*, then edited by Simms (see *Letters*, III, 209 and 209n.); (6) William John Grayson (1788-1863), attorney-statesman-author, is best remembered today for the widely read poem, *The Hireling and the Slave* (1856); (7) James Gadsden (1788-1885), who served as a director of the Bank of the State of South Carolina and president of the South

Carolina Rail Road Company, negotiated the Gadsden Purchase while acting as minister to Mexico (see *Letters*, II, 419n., 422; V, 342n.); (8) A. Herbemont, Sr., was possibly [Alex?] Nicholas Herbemont, mentioned in the notes to 398.17-22; (9) Henry Workman Conner (1797-1861) was president of the Bank of Charleston (1839-1840, 1843-1850) and president of the South Carolina Road Company from 1850 to 1853; Conner supported Simms as a delegate to the Southern Convention in Nashville in June, 1850 (see *Letters*, III, 9n.); (10) Otis Mills is listed as a corn merchant, 36 Meeting Street, in the *CD* of 1849; (11) Robert Hume is listed as a planter, 6 Lynch Street, in the 1849 *CD*; (12) Philip Johnston Porcher (d. 1871), Charleston broker, married the sister of James Louis Petigru (see *S.C.H. & Mag.*, XXXVIII, 11); (13) William Bull Pringle, prominent planter, 9 King Street, was a member of the "friends" of the *Southern Quarterly Review* and a correspondent of Simms (see *Letters*, III, 209, 209n., 300-301n); (14) Edward Gamage is listed as a planter, 65 Broad Street, in the 1849 *CD*.

401.13 The quotation has not been identified.

404.36-37 old song, which says, "I won't be a nun!": Perhaps the allusion is to "I will sing willingly an old song" from Meyerbeer's *Finita è pei frati.* See Minnie Earl Sears, ed., *Song Index* (New York, 1926), p. 259.

406.4-5 The quotation is from Byron's "She Walks in Beauty," Stanza I, included in *Hebrew Melodies* (1815).

406.11 "sylph of the season,": Washington Allston, *The Sylphs of the Seasons* (1813).

Textual Introduction

Though Simms does not mention *Flirtation at the Moultrie House* in his voluminous correspondence and no unequivocal evidence of his authorship has been discovered, there seems little doubt that he was the author; Trent's unhesitating ascription of it to Simms (perhaps on the basis of evidence available in 1892 but since lost) is in itself convincing argument for Simms's authorship, for Trent exercised such admirable caution in compiling his "A Partial Bibliography of Simms's Writings" (*Simms*, p. 336) that no errors of ascription have been found.

Circumstantial evidence also supports Trent's testimony. The year before the publication of this farcical contrast of the manners of piedmont Georgia and coastal Carolina, Simms had visited upper Georgia—including Clarkesville—and recorded his impressions in a series of newspaper articles signed "The Wanderer." Though the newspaper in which they appeared has not been identified, clippings of the articles have been preserved in Scrapbook E in the Charles Carroll Simms Collection. It is particularly interesting to note that "The Wanderer" wrote at least three of his accounts—apparently in the form of editorial correspondence—from Clarkesville, carrying the dates of August 20, August 24, and September 14, 1849. In these commentaries Simms describes the travel conditions (particularly from Athens to Clarkesville), the weather, the mountain scenery, and the customs of upper Georgia, with his most telling remarks coming in an undated clipping signed "WANDERER":

> The days when Judge Longstreet wrote his cock fighting, horse swapping, gander pulling, and sham fighting Georgia scenes, . . . have passed by and become obsolete . . . . We have been in Georgia upwards of five weeks, witnessed a Commencement at Athens, been among the miners at Nacoochee Valley, visited the Tallulah and Toccoah Falls, and Yonah Mountain [all near Clarkesville], and travelled upwards of 140 miles in stage coaches about the country, and have never seen a drunken man, witnessed a fight, or heard even of a cock fight or gander pulling.

Because his personal correspondence reveals that Simms visited Sullivan's Island—"one of our watering places" (*Letters*, II, 550)—as well as "the mountains of Geo." (*Letters*, II, 544) during the 1849 summer months, the Charleston author had cause to contrast the two widely divergent cultures during the year before the publication of *Flirtation*. Other clues include the use of the pseudonym "Colleton" to sign an undated article describing a fancy dress ball—and giving a list of participants—at "Madison Springs, Georgia"; and a demonstrated interest in the beauties of Clarkesville women—"they are American women, and breathe the pure air of Alleghany mountains" (clipping signed "The Wanderer," dated Aug. 20, 1849.)

The full title of this story of manners in epistolary form reads as follows: *Flirtation/at/the Moultrie House:/In a/Series of Letters,/from/Miss Georgiana Appleby,/to Her/Friends in Georgia, showing the Doings at the/Moultrie House, and the Events Which/Took Place at the/Grand Costume Ball,/on the 29th August, 1850;/with*

Other Letters (Charleston: Printed by Edward C. Councell, 1850). Its publication was announced (under the heading "Will Be This Day Published") in the Charleston *Mercury* of September 10, 1850, with the additional comment: "This *Brochure* will also contain a revised and full account of the various characters and costumes with the names of parties, &c. To be had at the office of the publisher where subscribers will please call for their copies. A few copies for sale at store of Messrs. Courtney & Weinges, and by the subscriber. Price 25 cents. ED. C. COUNCELL, No. 119 East Bay. Sept. 10."

Flirtation at Moultrie House has never before been reprinted.

Table I: Emendations and Textual Notes

Listed here are all changes made in the copy-text, the original 1850 publication. The original reading appears to the left of the bracket, the emended Centennial edition reading to the right. Where no bracket appears the reading is the same in both texts and the refusal to emend is explained in parentheses. Where an explanation of the change is necessary it follows in parentheses.

385. <no rule>] <rule added between 385.27 and 385.28> (In copy-text there is no rule between Letter Third and Letter Fourth, for Letter Third ends at the bottom of the page. The line has been added to conform with the copy-text practice of using rules as dividers between letters.)

388. <no rule>] <rule added after 388.37> (See 385.)

390. <no rule>] <rule added between 390.8 and 390.9> (See 385.)

391. <no rule>] <rule added between 391.17 and 391.18> (See 385.)

392.2 Merriwether's] Meriwether's

393.6 "precious of hearts jewels," (The addition of the apostrophe is not necessary to clarify the meaning.)

393. <no rule>] <rule added between 393.15 and 393.16> (See 385.)

394. <no rule>] <rule added between 394.26 and 394.27> (See 385.)

395.13-14 before. Ever your] before./Ever your (Copy-text has "Ever your" on the same line as the last line in the letter to prevent the signature's running over to the next page.)

395. <no rule>] <rule added between 395.15 and 395.16> (See 385.)

396.21 let's] lets

397.6-11 (This note signed "Publisher" appears on a separate page in copy-text.)

399.32 appartments (Spelling has not been regularized.)

402.9 C——h——m (Long 2 em dashes have not been emended to customary 1 em dashes because the added dash length may have meaning.)

402.10 B-d-g ("B-d-g" has not been regularized to "B—d—g," as in paragraph above. There is a slight possibility of a different meaning.)

404.1 F. ower] Flower

404.30 Mrs S-th] Mrs. ~

405.4 "Soubriettes," (Spelling has not been corrected.)

406.5 skies," (A period to end the sentence has not been inserted.)

Table II: Textual Variants

Below is a list of the variants between the appendix to *Flirtation at the Moultrie House* (1850), pp. 31-46, and "Grand Costume Ball at the Moultrie House," *Charleston Courier*, September 5, 1850, p. 4.

Reading from left to right the chart of variants has the following text sequence:

LEFT MARGIN: Centennial edition key
FIRST READING: 1850 book
SECOND READING: 1850 newspaper

397.21 31.14 found,] 2.98 ~^

397.23 31.17 Island,] 2.101 ~^

397.24 31.17 summer] 2.102 Summer

397.24 31.18 erection,] 2.102 ~^

397.28 31.23 epidemic] 2.107 ~,

398. 32. <list of Junior Managers written in small capitals, after initial large capital, except for the "R" of "Jr.", col. 2.1>] 2.129 <list of Junior Managers uses lower case, except for initial letter>

398.17 32.18 Jr.] 2.130 Jr.,

398.24 32.25 Young] 2.137 YOUNG
398.25 32.26 Pine] 2.138 PINE
398.25-26 32.27 Eugene Bell] 2.139 EUGENE BELL
398.31a 33.4a W. G.] 2.145a W. Gilmore
398.29b 33.2b A.] 2.143b Alex.
398.29b 33.2b Sr.] 2.143b ~,
398. 33. <list of Senior Managers set up as for Junior Managers>] 2.142 <list of Senior Managers set up as for Junior Managers>
398.29 33.2 Sr.] 2.136 Sr.,
399.3 33.12 in at] 2.153 into
399.5 33.14 committee] 2.155 Committee
399.6 33.16 faery] 2.157 fairly
399.8 33.18 Bell] 2.158 BELL
399.14 33.26 drapery] 2.166 ~,
399.15 33.28 bearing,] 2.168 ~‸
399.16 33.28 letters,] 2.168 ~‸
399.16 33.28 Moultrie] 2.169 MOULTRIE
399.18 33.31 of] 2.171 of the
399.19 33.32 The] 2.172 THE
399.21 34.3 disposed] 2.175 ~,
399.25-26 34.8-9 one hundred by thirty-eight feet] 2.180 100 by 38 feet
399.31 34.16 committee] 2.187 Committee
399.32 34.17 appartments] 2.188 apartments
399.32 34.18 ball] 2.188 ~,
399.33 34.18 house] 2.189 House
399.35 34.21-31 dances. ¶ These were numerous, we may say in this place, and were continued, with little intermission, from 9 o'clock, P. M., to 2, A. M.; allowing only the proper intervals for the supper. They alternated agreeably from the cotillion to the waltz, and from the waltz to the polka. Many of the dancers were not simply prepared to *walk* through the figures, but to enter with great enthusiasm into the full spirit of the movement, with equal grace, taste, and propriety. But let us not anticipate. We have described the scene; it is time
] 2.191-192 dances. ¶ Thus much for the scene. It is time

400.9 35.2 non-descripts] 2.196 nondescripts
400.15 35.11 ranks,] 2.204 ~∧
400.17 35.13 G—m—ge] 2.206 G——E
400.20 35.17 McPh–s–n] 2.210 McP——
400.20 35.17 confessor,] 2.210 ~∧
400.29 35.28 of the most] 3.6 of
400.30 35.29 blazed;] 3.7 ~,
400.32 35.32 H—r—t] 3.9 H——T
400.34 36.2-14 set. We remarked, however, nothing sinister in his countenance; certainly, nothing of that murderous occult purpose which Kean, in Richard, does not entirely conceal from the audience, even when playing the lover to the princess whom he had widowed. We were disposed to find fault with Mr. H—r—t, for the exceedingly small development of *hump* between the shoulders. No doubt the Richard of history was a much more *personable* man than Shakspeare has made him; but Mr. H—r—t, should have dressed according to the dramatist. ¶ Other] 3.12-13 set ¶ Other
401.6 36.15 Gr–y–on] 3.14 G——ON
401.7 36.17 of a] 3.16 of
401.8 36.18 bodice] 3.17 boddice
401.8 36.18 over-skirt] 3.17 over skirt
401.13 36.24 poet,] 3.22 ~∧
401.15 36.27 Fl—m—g] 3.25 F——G
401.15 36.28 Hermit] 3.26 ~,
401.20 36.33 F—rd] 3.31 F——D
401.21 37.2 bodice] 3.33 boddice
401.22 37.3 sleeves;] 3.34 ~,
401.23 37.4 hung] 3.35 being
401.28 37.12 Fanny P–k–r] 3.42 FANNY P——R
401.29 37.13 Rebecca,] 3.42-43 ~∧
401.32 37.17 velvet] 3.46 ~,
401.37 37.23 faith,] 3.52 ~∧
401.38 37.25 Wilfrid] 3.54 Wilfred
402.1 37.26-32 appearance. In his absence, however, we perceived that the close devotions of Mr. B—d—g, representing "The Southern Traitor," were by no means stinted; and

we did not see that the fair Jewess was at all scrupulous in bestowing her smiles upon the ultra-Carolinian. ¶ Here] 3.55-56 appearance. ¶ Here

402.6 37.32 followed, in odd contrast] 3.56 followed in odd, comparison

402.7 37.33 Ben. T–p–r,] 3.57 B. T——R

402.9 38.3 C——h——m] 3.60 C——H——M

402.10 38.4 B–d–g] 3.61 B——G

402.11 38.6 State;] 3.63 ~‸

402.12 38.7-8 cotton, rice,] 3.64 Cotton, Rice

402.13 38.8 palmetto] 3.64 Palmetto

402.13 38.9 Dan'l L–n–e] 3.65 DAN'L. L——E

402.14 38.9 boatman,] 3.65-66 ~;

402.15 38.11 DeS–s–re] 3.67 DES——E

402.16 38.12 T–v–u] 3.68 T——U

402.17 38.13 his *prey*] 3.69 *his* prey

402.17 38.14 picturesque,] 3.70 ~‸

402.18 38.15 inexpressibles] 3.71 small clothes

402.19 38.16 M–ni–d] 3.71 M——D

402.20 38.17 O'H——a's] 3.73 O. H——A's

402.21 38.19 a fit] 3.74 a

402.22 38.21 Thos. Fr—st] 3.76 THOS. F——T

402.25 38.24-25 Julius Bl—ke's] 3.79-80 JULIUS B——E's

402.29 38.30 Be—ch] 3.85 B——H

402.37 39.7 Sm–th] 3.94 S——H

402.38 39.8 Scott's] 3.95 SCOTT's

403.1 39.9 one] 3.96 ~,

403.1 39.11-16 arm. The costume was probably derived from that scene, in the rocky hermitage of the Priest or Santon,—the mad Saint,—where the Prince of Scotland first beholds the beautiful Princess of England,—the sister of the fierce Richard Cœur de Leon. ¶ Miss Julia Ma–g–lt] 3.97-98 arm. ¶ Miss JULIA M——T

403.6 39.16 *poblana*] 3.98 Poblana

403.12 39.24 St–n–y] 3.106 S——Y

403.14 39.26 C–t–r] 3.108 C——R

403.17 39.30 evoked] 3.112 worked

403.18 39.31 nereid] 3.112 nereiad

403.21 40.2 Y–t–s] 3.117 Y——S

403.22 40.2 postilion,] 3.117 ~‸

403.23 40.4 black] 3.119 ~,

403.25 40.6 A–h–by] 3.121 A——BY

403.26 40.7 Wil–ie] 3.122 W——IE

403.26 40.8 marshal] 3.123 Marshal

403.27 40.8 M–ot] 3.123 M——T

403.27 40.9 El–ott] 3.124 E——OTT

403.28 40.9 C–n–y] 3.124 C——Y

403.28 40.11 C–n–r] 3.125 C——R

403.29 40.11-12 Mr. D. P–i–u] 3.126 Mr. P——U

403.33 40.17 come] 3.131 came

403.34 40.18 C–rt–r] 3.132 C——R

404.1 40.24 M–l–s] 3.138 M——S

404.1 40.25 F.ower] 3.139 Flower

404.3 40.26 in] 3.140 In

404.5 40.29 A–l–by] 3.142 A——Y

404.5 40.30 Scott's] 3.143 SCOTT's

404.7 40.32 heroine] 3.144 ~,

404.8 40.33 Texian] 3.146 Texan

404.9 41.1 Richard M–iw–r] 3.147 RICHARD M——R

404.10 41.3 C–nn–r] 3.148 C——R

404.10 41.3 Charleston] 3.148 ~,

404.15 41.10-14 <list of last names set in regular type>] 3.155-158 <list of last names set in small capitals except for the initial letter, a large capital>

404.17 41.12 Connor] 3.157 CONNER

404.17 41.12-13 Screven, Jones, Whitaker] 3.157 SCREVEN, WHITAKER

404.18 41.13 Cheesborough] 3.158 CHEESEBOROUGH

404.19 41.15 when] 3.159 were

404.21 41.17 costumes] 3.161 costume

404.23 41.20-31 <list of names> Hu—e / M–l–r / M–ls / H—be—t / T–y–r / E–m–e / P–ch–r / B–y–n / P–k–y / F–m–n / C–lc–h / E–ns / H–ry / V–dy–e / W–l–ms / S–th / B–ks / G–l–son / L–a–s / McN–ty / D–ve / W–lt–r / W–ng–n / S–th / C–t–r / T–m–r / N–th /] 3.164-175 <list of names: first letter in large capital

followed by long dash and final letter in small capital. Exceptions noted below>

404.23 41.20 M–ls] 3.164 M——

404.27 41.25 E–ns] 3.168 E——s,

404.30 41.29 Mrs S–th] 3.173 Mrs. S——<?>

404.33 41.32 M–nk] 3.176 M——K

404.34 42.1 dignity] 3.178 ~,

405.1 42.6 G—d—n] 3.182 G——N

405.1 42.6 of —] 3.182-183 ~ ——

405.2 42.7 Nun,] 3.184 ~‸

405.4 42.9 B——ke] 3.186 B——E

405.6 42.11 Ga–l–d] 3.188 G——D

405.7 42.13 K–kl–d] 3.189 K——D

405.10 42.16 C—ll—n] 3.193 C——N

405.13 42.20 Ellen Fl—n] 3.196 ELLEN F——N

405.15 42.23 H—a—d] 3.199 H——D

405.18 42.26 G–lm–n] 3.202 G——N

405.20 42.29 Hu—d] 3.204 H——

405.22 42.32 flowers.] 3.207 flower<?>

405.22 42.33 Hu—d] 3.207 H——D

405.25 43.2 moustaches] 3.210 moustache

405.25 43.3 eyes] 3.210 eye

405.26 43.5 M–l–r] 3.212 M——R

405.28 43.7 P–kn–y] 4.1 P——Y

405.32 43.12 P–ti–u] 4.5 P——U

405.32 43.13 ball] 4.5 b<e?>ll

405.34 43.14 R–g–r] 4.7 R——R

406.1 43.19-24 head. The costume was a very striking one, as if intended to realize the poetic atmosphere with which Byron seeks to clothe his oriental damsel:—

> "She walks in beauty, like *the night*,
> Of cloudless climes and starry skies,"

¶ Miss R–g–r
] 4.11-12 head. ¶ Miss R——R

406.9 43.27 S–h–k–r] 4.15 S——R

406.9 43.28 in an] 4.15 in

406.10 43.29 W—ner] 4.17 W——R

406.12 44.1 Sw—in] 4.19 S——N

406.15 44.3 attendants;] 4.22 ~,

406.17 44.6 P-kn-y] 4.24 P——Y

406.18 44.7 M—ig—t] 4.26 M——T

406.18 44.8 Provisional] 4.26 Provincial

406.19 44.8 R. M—w—r] 4.27 M. W——R

406.19 44.9 Texian] 4.27 Texan

406.21 44.11 Geo. Re—d] 4.29 GEO. R——D

406.22 44.12 S-on-y] 4.30 S——G

406.22 44.13 Sm—th] 4.31 S——TH

406.24 44.15 W—k—r] 4.33 W——R

406.24 44.15 fancy dress] 4.33 Fancy Dress

406.25 44.16 M—ns, B—e, O'H—a and Sch—ffer] 4.34 M——S, B——E, OH——A and Sc——ER

406.25 44.17 members] 4.35 Members

406.26 44.17 Provisional] 4.35 Provincial

406.27 44.18 W—ld] 4.36 W——D

406.28 44.19 Sm—th] 4.37 S——TH

406.29 44.21 Sc—n] 4.39 Sc——N

406.29 44.21 W-ld-n] 4.39 W——B<N?>

406.31 44.23 B—e] 4.41 B——E

406.32 44.24 H-w-t] 4.42 H——T

406.34 44.26 E—w—ds] 4.44 E——DS,

406.35 44.28 W-k-r] 4.46 W——R

406.36 44.29 S-m-ns] 4.47 S——NS

406.36 44.29 last] 4.47 ~,

406.36 44.30 least,] 4.48 ~‸

406.37 44.31 record,—] 4.49 ~,‸

407.1 44.32 R—g—r] 4.50 R——R

407.2 44.33 which] 4.51 of which

407.2 45.1 equally] 4.51 equailly

407.3 45.3-4 <about a 4-line break in text, with a rule in middle>] 4.53-54 <end of ¶. New ¶> <no break>

407.8 45.9 many] 4.59 ~,

407.11 45.14 aptly] 4.63 amply

407.12 45.14 excellently,] 4.64 ~‸

407.13 45.16 Pine] 4.65 PINE

407.15 45.19 fruits,] 4.68 ~‸
407.19 45.24 Pine] 4.72 PINE
407.19 45.24 Young] 4.73 YOUNG
407.23 45.29 until] 4.78 till
407.26 46.4 ball] 4.81 Ball

EPHRAIM BARTLETT, THE EDISTO RAFTSMAN.

"Ephraim Bartlett, the Edisto Raftsman" is a slight, but interesting backwoods sketch in which Simms combines his interest in folklore, his love of the supernatural, and his knowledge of local customs and traditions. The opening paragraphs effectively establish the setting along the banks of the Edisto River and set the mood for the tale that follows, but since they contribute little to the action of the story, they seem disproportionately long. Once he gets to the story told in Ephraim Bartlett's own words, however, Simms has found his true medium—the tall tale told in the dialect of the backwoods. Almost immediately the language comes alive, not only because of Simms's remarkably sensitive ear for dialect, but also because of his skillful handling of the conversational interplay between the two companions on a raft, Ephraim and Bram, white man and black, whose human understanding of one another transcends a master-servant relationship.

Textual Introduction

"Ephraim Bartlett, the Edisto Raftsman" is the title which the editor has given to the fourth installment of "Home Sketches, or Life along the Highways and Byways of the South" published in the *Literary World*, X (Feb. 7, 1852), 107-110. The full sub-title of this installment of "Home Sketches," by "the author of 'The Yemassee,' 'Guy Rivers,' 'Richard Hurdis,' 'Katharine Walton,' &c.," is as follows:

IV.

Ancient Settlements along the Ashley.—/The Cooper.—Izard's Camp.—Game.—Su/perstitions.—Ephraim Bartlett, the Edisto/Raftsman.—Bram.—The Haunted House./—The Spectre Hunt.

Other installments of "Home Sketches" appeared in the *Literary World*, X (Jan. 3, Jan. 10, Jan. 24, 1852), 1-3, 31-32, 63-65; XI

(July 31, Sept. 11, Nov. 20, Dec. 11, 1852), 73-76, 163-166, 323-324, 378-379.

First mention of the plan to do "a series of sketches of Carolina life" occurs in Simms's letter of c. December 19, 1848, to E. A. and George Long Duyckinck, editors of the *Literary World.* In the letter Simms enclosed "a specimen" for the brothers' perusal; he also indicated that Evert Duyckinck had mentioned to him "the rate of $5 per page" (*Letters,* II, 467). Simms's correspondence reveals that the "Home Sketches" were submitted to E. A. Duyckinck, usually through James Lawson, periodically for several years before Duyckinck began publishing them (*Letters,* II, 469, 474-475, 513-514, 533, 551, 559); finally in a letter of November 10, 1852, after two months had passed since the publication of one of the installments, Simms unburdened himself to E. A. Duyckinck: "You do not publish my sketches? I confess I should like them disposed of; yet do not care, if you do not relish them, to have them burden your pages. Deal frankly with me, and say they do not suit. You shall not annoy or offend me by so doing. I know that it may be objectionable to put forth the fragmentary residue, and the only recommendation for it, is the glimpse which it affords at the condition and superstitions of a particular region & peculiar class of people. The lack of completeness may well cause a doubt of the propriety of publication; and I tell you candidly that I can promise you no sequel" (*Letters,* III, 206). Shortly after receiving this letter, Duyckinck published the last two "Home Sketches" to appear in the *Literary World,* in the November 20 and December 11 issues. Though the other seven sketches are best classified as essays, articles, or letters, "Ephraim Bartlett, the Edisto Raftsman" is an interesting example of Simms's use of folklore and dialect in fiction dealing with his native region.

The 1852 publication in the *Literary World* is copy-text.

Table I: Emendations and Textual Notes

Listed below are all changes made in the 1852 copy-text of "Ephraim Bartlett." The original reading appears to the left of the bracket, the emended Centennial edition reading to the right. Where an explanation of the change is necessary it follows in parentheses.

413.29 put on] put ("On" and "upon" are redundant; Simms apparently forgot to strike through "on" in manuscript when he added "upon" three words later.)
414.36 drunk] ~"
414.37 'Nebber] "~
414.37 time,'] ~"
415.1 ''Bram] "'~
415.2 up.'] ~"
415.3 'Ha] "~
415.6 you.'] ~"
415.7 'You] "~
416.13 "I'speck] "I 'speck
418.6 someth'ng] something ("Someth'ng" could easily be a printer's misreading of Simms's manuscript "something," though there is a possibility of eye dialect.)
418.23 was] ~.
420.14 neat] near

HOW SHARP SNAFFLES GOT HIS CAPITAL AND WIFE.

If it is true that in "The Maroon" William Gilmore Simms successfully used a German source in fostering a Spanish tale, it has also been claimed that he followed a German lead even in the composition of his distinguished backwoods tale, "How Sharp Snaffles Got His Capital and Wife." J. Wesley Thomas states that Simms's "tall tale parallels very closely the well-known experience of Baron Munchausen with the flock of ducks" ("German Sources," p. 139). A more specialized study, Alexander E. Jones, "A Source for William Gilmore Simms's 'Sharp Snaffles,'" *Journal of American Folklore*, LXX (Jan.-March, 1957), 66-69, develops the same idea more fully.

Two recent studies, as yet unpublished, refute the emphasis on German sources for "How Sharp Snaffles Got His Capital and Wife." Before his death Donald Davidson kindly sent to the editor a copy ("A Crude Summary of Projected Article," Davidson called it) of his partially completed "Origins and Background of Simms's 'Sharp Snaffles,'" and Mrs. Davidson has generously given permission for its use here. Though granting that "It is of course entirely possible, perhaps not unlikely, that Simms sometime, somewhere had encountered the Munchausen 'influence,' directly or indirectly," Davidson asserts: "Much more credible, if not near to certainty, is the conjecture that Simms got the tale, in its essentials, from oral recitation by a mountain hunter, during his camping trip in the autumn of 1847 to the vicinity of Mt. Tryon in North Carolina . . . ." Davidson points out the "remarkable degree of correspondence" between Simms's 1847 Notebook (in the Charles Carroll Simms Collection, South Caroliniana Library) "and characters and scenes in the Sharp Snaffles story" (eight examples are cited in Explanatory Notes to individual lines). Calling attention to the fact that most of Simms's story "cannot possibly be attributed to Munchausen as a source," Davidson gives other traditional sources for elements of "Sharp Snaffles," including the possibility that Simms borrowed the dominant "capital" theme from William Crafts' "The Sea Serpent, or the Gloucester Hoax," which he saw performed in Charleston in May, 1821, and wrote about in "Our Early Authors" in the *Nineteenth Century* for September, 1869 (pp. 281, 282). James E. Kibler, Jr., in a paper entitled "Folk Motifs in William Gilmore Simms's 'Sharp Snaffles,'" written for the Simms seminar at the University of South Carolina in 1967-68 (now accepted for publication in the *Southern Literary Journal* for Spring, 1972) fully supports Davidson's thesis that "How Sharp Snaffles Got His Capital and Wife" is in the most meaningful sense an authentic American folk tale, though his and Davidson's conclusions were arrived at independently. Kibler identifies the "three important strands of folklore" in "Sharp Snaffles"—(1) "the wonderful hunt"; (2) "the man being carried into the air by wild geese"; and (3) "the hunter being pulled from a hollow tree by holding onto a bear's tail"—and cites numerous examples of variants of these motifs published in American periodicals and books during Simms's lifetime, including at least one found in Simms's own scrapbook (Scrapbook E, Charles Carroll Simms Collection, South Caroliniana Library). This clipping, entitled "Old Long John—The Bear Hunter" and published in the Charleston *Evening News* of February 7, 1850, reads in part:

I thot I hearn something nestling inside the stump; so I tuck off my shoes and up it I went; when I come to the top, I looked in, *I did;* and what do you think I seed? Why two *cub bar,* be God sirs, rolling and playing down thar jist like two little niggers. Well, says I, you're jist the critters I have been wantin for a long time, for pets for the children. So I jist lumbered righ down among them, *I did* . . . . Then, for the first time, I seed my sitivation. Now the holler of the stump was heep bigger at botom nor it was at top, and I could get no foothold to climb out by . . . . All at once I was a studyin about it, I heard the all-firedist rippet, outside, you ever heard; the Old She had come sure enough; Oh! I was mad then, I was; all at once a thought struck me; I knowed that an Old She, (nor a bar of any kind, indeed, could not bear to be *fingered behind* much, so I intended to act accordin. When she entered the top of the stump, she made all look dark below, I tell you. she did! I got on my feet and waited twell I could jest cleverly reach her, I did; you know they allways come down tail formost. As soon as I could reach her, I grabbed her behind with both hands, and I give her the whoop, I did; if ever you saw a *skeered* bar—and I was mad, be God, sir. She took me faster than any railroad car, twell she landed me about ten foot from the root of the stump, flat on my belly, she did; Oh man! I was mad! but *sort a stuntified-like* by the fall. Before I could get old death, she was clean outen sight, and a running.

Though "Sharp Snaffles" has attracted more scholarly attention recently than any other story by Simms, recognition of its merit has been slow coming. Trent, for instance, ignores it, though he knew of its existence; Ridgely dismisses it in a sentence (p. 30) in his book, as do Current-Garcia (p. 65) and Morris (p. 33) in their articles on Simms's stories. The first scholarly awareness of its artistic achievement appears to have been Donald Davidson's 1952 pronouncement that it "stands almost without a peer, surely, among the 'tall tales' recorded or written in the United States" (Introduction, *Letters,* I, lii). Edd W. Parks, "Simms: A Candid Self-Portrait," *Georgia Review,* XII (Spring, 1958), 94-103, more recently called it "one of the finest tall tales ever written by a Southern humorist" (p. 101).

It seems logical to assume that neglect of "How Sharp Snaffles Got His Capital and Wife" will soon end.

Explanatory Notes

The notes furnished by the late Donald Davidson are designated by an asterisk *.

421.2-4 A similar passage in Simms's 1847 Notebook (p. 6) reads: "The close of the third day brought us to our camping ground at the foot of the balsam range."*

421.6-7 *Names of hunters:* In the 1847 Notebook (pp. 6-7), Simms wrote: "Meanwhile, we had been joined by Jim Fisher a famous hunter. . . . Nathan Langford—Bill Langford—the strange hunter, Green."*

421.17-18 Closely paralleling this statement is Simms's commentary in the 1847 Notebook (p. 6): "Our point of destination was about 60 or 70 miles, through a country comparative destitute—a country of wilderness, in which save at two or three isolated points, we could hope to find no settlements."*

421.26-28-422.1-7 In the 1847 Notebook Simms wrote as follows (p. 6): "Our cortege was a tolerably large one consisting of six persons, each well mounted and one baggage wagon carrying all the utensils for cookery, camping, clothing, to say nothing of food, of which we made ample provision."*

422.29-34-423.1-11 There is a long, almost identical passage in the 1847 Notebook (pp. 14-15) describing the cooking of deer.*

422.32 Delmonico: Lorenzo Delmonico (1813-1881), American restauranteur, introduced European gastronomy into the United States.

423.24-26 In the 1847 Notebook Columbus Mills, a relative of Simms's wife, is referred to as host of the hunting party, which stops at his house. He is frequently mentioned throughout.*

423.29-36 The 1847 Notebook is filled with jottings on hunters as tale tellers. Examples: "Hunter's bragging, about horse, dog rifle—what they have done, what they will do & what nobody else has done or can do" (p. 8); "The bragging of hunter's is not merely empty boasting. . . . they are not lessened in the proprieties of a convention which makes modesty a virtue" (pp. 12-13); Jim Fisher "has seen the entrails of his favorite no less than nine times"—which entrails Fisher sewed up after each bear-fight his dog engaged in (p. 23).*

424.19-20 A very similar passage in the 1847 Notebook (p. 6) reads: "Meanwhile, we had been joined by Jim Fisher a famous hunter.—Jim was about 70."*

425.24 "Leave off your damnable faces and begin.": *Hamlet,* III, ii.

451.10-11 Nicholas Biddle (1786-1844) was president of the Bank of the United States, 1823-1836. President Andrew Jackson fought against the bank and in 1836, when its charter lapsed, he did not recharter it. Instead of the bank's paper money, the hard currency which Senator Thomas Hart Benton (1782-1858) advocated was used; hence, "Benton's Mint Drops."

Textual Introduction

Though "How Sharp Snaffles Got His Capital and Wife" was not published until after Simms's death (June 11, 1870) in *Harper's New Monthly Magazine* for October, 1870 (XLI, 667-687), there is evidence that Simms may have begun gathering notes for it as early as 1847 when, during August, September, and October, he visited the mountain region of North and South Carolina. Simms's 1847 Notebooks in the Charles Carroll Simms Collection give an elaborate account of this camping trip to the Mt. Tryon area with a group of hunting companions including Columbus Mills, friend and kinsman who served as unofficial host (see Explanatory Notes for illustrations of Simms's use of these notes). Even in writing to James H. Hammond from Charleston on July 15, 1847, of his plans to "take my folk to the mountain region" on "the 10th or 12th Aug.," Simms stated his purpose of "gleaning scraps & glimpses for revolutionary & other illustration" for "a book descriptive of Carolina—its history, manners of its people, scenery &c." (*Letters,* II, 330; see also *Letters,* II, 333, 345, 346, 349). On September 23 Simms wrote to James Lawson from Spartanburg: "Tomorrow, I expect to set off on a visit to the mountains of North Carolina . . . . My purpose is to visit as much fine scenery, and to see and hear as much as I can. I shall make a book of it. 'A chiel's among *'em* taking notes, & i' faith, he'll prent 'em!" (*Letters,* II, 350). On October 19, 1847, after his return to Charleston, Simms said in a letter to Robert Taylor Conrad: "I am here again, on the seaboard, after a two months ramble among our mountains. I have been for some weeks the occupant of a camp among the hunters, beyond our remotest bounds of civilization. I have slept with the howling of the wolf & the sudden shriek of the panther in my ears, and have eaten my steaks of venison, fresh from the haunches of the buck, eight hundred feet above the Atlantic levels. I could make you a series of descriptive sketches that might tell much better than most of our foreign travel,—and may do so" (*Letters*, II, 351; see also *Letters*, II, 355). But, as usual, it was to James Lawson that Simms sent his most revealing letters; on October 20, 1847, he wrote Lawson from Charleston: "I have been among the mountaineers, in the very realm of wolf & panther, bear, deer, and other small vermin, with a budget sufficiently stored for a volume" (*Letters*, II, 356); again, approximately five months later, in a letter of March 23, 1848, Simms referred to "one month . . . spent in a mountain camp, in the midst of hunters where I gathered notes for a volume" (Letters, II, 404). Knowledge of his working habits leads to the conclusion that the 1847 mountain visit provided Simms with the basic material for both "How Sharp Snaffles Got His Capital and Wife" and "Bald-Head Bill Bauldy," though he was not to bring his experiences to artistic fruition until some twenty years later.

It is not possible to determine when Simms completed the writing of "Sharp Snaffles" since the manuscript does not exist and he never refers to the story (by title, at least) in his correspondence. One possibility is that he had completed writing it by mid-1865, submitted it to the Harper brothers for consideration, and that they held it, perhaps half forgotten, until his death jogged them into a decision to publish it. At least it is known that Simms planned to submit several "articles" to *Harper's* in 1865 and that nothing attributable to him was published in that magazine after that date until the appearance of "Sharp Snaffles" in 1870; on June 13, 1865, Simms stated in a letter to James Lawson: "I have two or three articles on hand, suitable for their [Harper brothers] monthly and which I deem very good. These, I will revise in a few days, & forward by the next opportunity" (*Letters*, IV, 500). There is, however, no certainty that Simms got the manuscript to *Harper's* at this time. Two days after his letter to Lawson, he wrote to Duyckinck, also, that he had "a few articles in hand now, suitable for Harper's Magazine" which he would "revise & forward . . . by the next opportunity" (*Letters*, IV, 503). In another letter to Lawson, on June 27, 1865, Simms requested the New Yorker to "see what

Harper & Bro. will advance me on the strength of articles to be furnished them hereafter" (*Letters*, IV, 508). Still later, on August 12, Simms wrote once more to Duyckinck: "It would be much to me, if Harper & Brothers could be persuaded to remit me a few hundred dollars on the strength of papers, tales &c. for their magazine, which I would proceed to prepare as soon as I can get things decently settled at the plantation" (*Letters*, IV, 515).

Another possibility, then, is that Simms actually did not complete the writing of "How Sharp Snaffles Got His Capital and Wife" until some time much closer to its date of publication. Simms visited New York during the summers of 1866, 1867, 1868, and 1869 largely for the purpose of placing his works with publishers, and could have deposited the manuscript of "Sharp Snaffles" with his old friends, the Harpers, on any of these occasions. (The editor's search through the publisher's archives of Harper & Row failed to uncover any trace of "How Sharp Snaffles Got His Capital and Wife.") But, however and whenever "Sharp Snaffles" came into *Harper's* possession, the correspondence of Simms's hectic final years contains frequent references to unidentified literary work in progress, from which neither "Sharp Snaffles" nor "Bald-Head Bill Bauldy," that other excellent backwoods story never mentioned by title by its author, can always automatically be excluded. For instance, though the reference of September 9, 1865, to the "new romance" which Simms proposes to "make equal to any thing I have yet done" (*Letters*, IV, 519) is almost certainly not to "Sharp Snaffles" (see also *Letters*, IV, 524), one cannot be positive about his statement to Duyckinck on December 19, 1865; "I hope shortly to begin my 'Sensation' Story, of the progress of which you shall have periodical report" (*Letters*, IV, 528). Other ambiguous references to work contemplated or underway occur in Simms's correspondence as follows (through 1868; for a listing of similar references in Simms's letters of 1869-1870, see Textual Introduction to "Bald-Head Bill Bauldy," below, pp. 809-810):

Date of Letter	*Addressee*	*Volume and Page of* Letters
c. October 2, 1865	E. A. Duychinck	IV, 523-524
March 5, 1866	E. A. Duyckinck	IV, 541
March 5, 1866	James Lawson	IV, 544-545
March 24 [1866]	W. H. Ferris	IV, 547-548

Date of Letter	*Addressee*	*Volume and Page of* Letters
May 25, 1866	James Lawson	IV, 560
May 25, 1866	W. H. Ferris	IV, 562-563
July 1, 1866	E. A. Duyckinck	IV, 574
July 7, 1866	E. A. Duyckinck	IV, 577
July 11, 1866	E. A. Duyckinck	IV, 580
December 13, 1866	E. A. Duyckinck	IV, 625
December 20 [1866]	W. H. Ferris	IV, 626
June 20, 1867	James Lawson	V, 63
July 2, 1867	E. A. Duyckinck	V, 65
August 22 [1867]	Eugene L. Didier	V, 77
September 2, 1867	J. E. Cooke	V, 83-84
January 14, 1868	T. A. Cheney	V, 103
March 13, 1868	Charles E. A. Gayarré	V, 115
May 9, 1868	J. E. Cooke	V, 130
[June, 1868]	W. G. Simms, Jr.	V, 140
June 29, 1868	W. J. Widdleton	V, 141,142, 142-143
July 25, 1868	E. A. Duyckinck	V, 153
October 29, 1868	E. A. Duyckinck	V, 170
November 1, 1868	Anna Augusta Roach	V, 173
November 15, 1868	James Lawson	V, 176
December 1, 1868	M. C. M. Hammond	V, 177
December 5, 1868	Joseph Henry	V, 180
December 11, 1868	Anna Augusta Roach	V, 184
December 25, 1868	M. C. M. Hammond	V, 188, 189

A few passages not included in the letters listed above seem important enough to quote directly. For example, though Simms commented rather frequently on the increasing demand for short stories by the American reading public, one of his most telling observations, revealing recognition of his own strength as well as of the publisher's market, occurs in a letter of August 3, 1866, to E. A. Duyckinck, of whom he asked: "What the proper pay, for a tale running through eight or ten pages of the same [octavo] size? As a tale writer especially I have achieved a great many successes; and I do not believe that my right hand hath lost any of her cunning" (*Letters,* IV, 589-590). Four months later, on December 13, 1866, Simms confided to Duyckinck that "it will be my hope, policy &

expectation, to provide an original work of prose fiction at least once a year" (*Letters,* IV, 625). If, with this new resolution in mind, Simms repaid a visit to the mountains of North Carolina in September, 1867, as he reportedly did (". . . he is found at that time among his favorite North Carolina mountains, shooting deer, listening to hunters' yarns, making notes on the proper construction of bear-traps,—in a word, gathering materials for other stories with his customary care" [Trent, p. 306]), it is not difficult to guess the direction in which he now focused his creativity. But perhaps the most significant clues to the composition of "Sharp Snaffles" are contained in the letter to Duyckinck dated June 30, 1868. In it, Simms first stated that, though he was "dull & depressed," necessity probably "will force me to the preparation of prose contributions, each complete, for some one or other of the Magazines" (*Letters,* V, 144). He then added: "My contributions to the newspapers here, which are frequent yield me little more than my tobacco and *eau de vie,* or rather *uisque*baugh. You are aware that whiskey is the contraction of the Irish word, and means eau de vie literally." Not only does this paraphrase of the author's first footnote to "How Sharp Snaffles Got His Capital and Wife" (see above, p. 422) suggest that Simms recently had "Sharp Snaffles" on his mind, but his comments later in the same paragraph strongly support the idea:

> If I could get contracts enough, and could rely upon the Publishers for my compensation, I could easily provide fresh matter, salient & picturesque, the very stuff for magazines. I have an abundance of the very sort of material . . . . I have sundry things, on hand, some as I think, which would cause sensation enough, & of the right kind, but these are the very things which startle common men out of their propriety. As a general rule, I have found Editors, & readers for publications, the least capable of deciding correctly, whenever article or book is out of the beaten track. [*Letters,* V, 145]

Whether this "fresh . . . salient & picturesque" material "out of the beaten track" is "Sharp Snaffles," "Bald-Head Bill Bauldy," or neither, it is nevertheless demonstrable that in the early summer of 1868 Simms was thinking thoughts consistent with the creation of the backwoods tale. (Further evidence that Simms was "backwoods" conscious in 1868 is his use of the phrase "what the backwoodsmen call 'a dead Horse'" in his letter of December 26, 1868, to John Esten Cooke, *Letters,* V, 190). Perhaps the most plausible theory is that Simms went to New York in the late summer of 1868 with "Sharp Snaffles" in mind or in hand, talked with *Harper's* representatives about it ("I have some negotiations going on," he wrote his son from New York on August 26, 1868, "which may result in giving us bread & meat for another year . . . ." [*Letters*, V, 155]), and promised them the completed manuscript, however delivered. (For still another alternative, see Textual Introduction to "Bald-Head Bill Bauldy," below, pp. 807-809).

"How Sharp Snaffles Got His Capital and Wife" has been reprinted, under the title "The Big Lie; A Hunter's Story," in A. R. Spofford and Charles Gibbon, eds., *The Library of Choice Literature* (1883), III, 324-338; and in Addison Hibbard, ed., *Stories of the South: Old and New* (1931), pp. 32-90. Copy-text is of course the first periodical publication, the only text with authority.

Table I: Emendations and Textual Notes

Listed below are all changes made in the copy-text of "How Sharp Snaffles Got His Capital and Wife." The original reading appears to the left of the bracket, the emended Centennial edition reading to the right. Where no bracket appears the reading is the same in both texts and the refusal to emend is explained in parentheses. When an explanation of change is necessary it follows in parentheses.

422.4 usquebaugh] uisquebaugh (Simms's usual spelling, as in his note on page 422 and in "Bald-Head Bill Bauldy," is "uisquebaugh.")
422.16 Bumpo] Bumpo
422.31 dear] deer
423.10 *haut gout* (Emendation to *haut goût* has been rejected since clarity of meaning is not involved.)
436.5 three-old-year (Although "three-old-year" may be the result of printer's eye skip—or author's hand slip—it may also be part of Sharp Snaffles' distinctive dialect.)

BALD-HEAD BILL BAULDY.

"Bald-Head Bill Bauldy" (as the story Simms entitled in full " 'Bald-Head Bill Bauldy,' and How he went through the Flurriday Campaign!—A Legend of the Hunter's Camp—" shall be known) is another example of Simms's excellence in the genre of Southern and Southwestern humor. It serves as a sequel to "How Sharp Snaffles Got His Capital and Wife": it is the "Big Lie" narrated the "Second Saturday Night" of the hunting camp which one week earlier had produced the legend of Sam Snaffles. Like "Sharp Snaffles," "Bald-Head Bill Bauldy" makes use of traditional devices found in stories of this genre: framework narrative; backwood setting; "tenderfeet" or "greenhorns" in contrast to the backwoodsman (the professional hunter who tells tall tales to fool and entertain the amateurs); and comic realism. In "Bald-Head Bill Bauldy" as well as in "Sharp Snaffles" Simms achieves this comic realism through a multiplicity of means: (1) dialect, which in addition to lending authenticity to the speech of characters, emphasizes the contrast between the amateur and the backwoods storyteller (in "Bald-Head Bill Bauldy" Simms has an amateur tell a slightly humorous story not at all comparable in merit to the tale of Bill Bauldy; (2) concrete details at crucial points, thereby giving a note of veracity to an otherwise impossible situation; and (3) sensuous or suggestive scenes employing imagery and language unacceptable in the polite literature of the time. In addition, again like "Sharp Snaffles," after a concrete beginning "Bill Bauldy" takes breathtaking flights into fancy (the big lie), with the amount of exaggeration fluctuated so skillfully that the reader is uncertain what to believe and what to disbelieve.

The merit of "Bald-Head Bill Bauldy" is probably best revealed, however, in its differences from other fiction in the same tradition. Its length alone (it is even longer than "Sharp Snaffles") separates it from most writing in this genre; few other writers of tall tales had the skill and talent to sustain a comic atmosphere through 25,000 words, as Simms here does. In a very real sense "Bald-Head Bill Bauldy" is an American mock epic forged out of truly indigenous material. It turns the traditional epic upside-down: it has a journey to a battle, fighting, capture, escape, journey, capture, descent into the underworld, and so forth; but it lacks (and thereby satirizes) the epic hero and heroine, the lofty purpose, and the elegant language. And, in addition to mocking the established European epic, "Bald-Head Bill Bauldy" also pokes fun at one of the oldest American traditions in literature, the captivity narrative, as Stephen E.

Meats has convincingly demonstrated in an as yet unpublished article entitled "The Captivity Narrative, William Gilmore Simms, and Captain John Smith."

"Bald-Head Bill Bauldy" ranks with "How Sharp Snaffles Got His Capital and Wife" at the top of Simms's literary achievement.

Explanatory Notes

468.4 Famous cruse of the widow: The allusion is to I Kings 17:10-16, Elijah's encounter with the widow woman. She had meal in a barrel and oil in a cruse, which Elijah made to replenish themselves.

468.33 McCord's Ferry: According to a 1836 map of South Carolina, McCord's Ferry was on the loop of the Congaree River approximately five miles above its junction with the Wateree.

472.7 Goodwyn's Regiment: Colonel Robert H. Goodwyn commanded a regiment of mounted South Carolina volunteers during the Second Seminole War. See John K. Mahon, *History of the Second Seminole War, 1835-1842* (1967), pp. 156, 158.

472.25 Dade's Regiment: Major Francis L. Dade commanded the 4th Infantry Regiment which was massacred by Indians on December 28, 1835, six or seven miles north of the Withlacoochee River (Mahon, pp. 104-106).

473.7 Osceola (c. 1803-1838) was leader of the Indians in the Second Seminole War. Major General Edmund Pendleton Gaines (1777-1849) led an expedition in the Second Seminole War and was wounded at Withlacoochee.

473.9 General Duncan Lamont Clinch (1787-1849) commanded at the battle of the Withlacoochee, December 31, 1835. He later served as congressman from Georgia, 1844-1845.

473.11 General Winfield Scott (1786-1866) was commissioned in 1835 by President Jackson to prosecute the war against the Seminoles and Creeks.

473.36-474.1 Bedell in Columbia: The reference is probably to C. A. Bedell, whose house and stores in Columbia were burned during Sherman's occupation of the city in February, 1865. (See Simms, *Sack and Destruction*, pp. 63, 71, 74.) Bedell apparently made a quick business recovery, however, for in the Charleston *Courier* of

June 25, 1867, Simms (using the pseudonym "SAGITTARIUS") described Bedell's new store as "not only the most spacious and beautiful one in all Columbia, but I doubt if there be a dry goods store in Charleston which approaches it in size."

474.31 Amy Dardan: According to the *American State Papers 1789-1838* (serial 036), p. 377, a petition of the widow Amey Dardin was brought before the 11th Congress, 2nd Session. On February 26, 1781, a Lieutenant Rudder took a stud horse from David Dardin in Mecklinburg County, Virginia, to be used in the Continental Army. General Greene had the horse returned when he learned of its value; but the horse was taken again by another officer on July 17, 1781. Dardin brought the case before the Mecklinburg County Court, which referred him to the Virginia Assembly in 1782. The legislature referred Dardin to the High Court of Chancery of Virginia, which dismissed the suit in June, 1793.

But Dardin was not easily discouraged. Petition was first brought before Congress in February, 1794. After being brought before one branch or the other of the U. S. legislature perhaps twenty times, the petition was passed by the House. The Senate, however, refused to read the petition on February 17, 1815 (*Debates and Proceedings in the Congress of the United States*, Vol. 27, pp. 1123-1124—13th Congress, 3rd Session, Feb. 6, 1815).

The petition was read again in the House in January, 1832, and passed on January 27, 1832 (*Debates and Proceedings . . . .*, Vol. 8, pt. 2 [1831-1832], pp. 1669-1673). By this time the Dardin widow had died and the claim passed to her children.

Records of the First Auditor of the Treasury Department show that the account was finally settled on December 3, 1832, when $1,500 was paid to Robert Y. Overbey, administrator of the estate of David Dardin, deceased.

477.17 'long nine': Slang for a siege gun.

485.24 'Hampton's Race Course': The reference is evidently to the track of the Columbia Jockey Club, of which Colonel Wade Hampton was the first president. The club was established in the spring of 1828 and the first meet took place the following December. See *American Turf Register and Sporting Magazine*, I (July, 1830), 560.

492.4 Fortygraph: Although photography was not available in 1835 at the time of the Second Seminole War, it was at the time of the story-telling—hence, probably another example of the story-teller's intentional exaggeration.
494.24 Old Johnson: Colonel William R. Johnson, famous horse-breeder and racing enthusiast of Oakland, Virginia, apparently raced his horses in South Carolina frequently. See *American Turf Register and Sporting Magazine,* I (Aug., 1830), 584, 617-620; IV (Sept., 1832), 9-12; IV (April, 1833), 421; V (July, 1834), 579.
499.23 'Columbian orator': In the 1847 Notebook (p. 11) Simms wrote that the "Columbian orator" was the name given to Jim Fisher's rifle. In "The Cub of the Panther," Simms again used the "Columbian orator" as the name of a famous rifle, but in this instance Jim Fisher was not the owner: "Every rifle of these mountain hunters, you must know, has a name if it has a reputation. The rude weapon of Sam [Fuller] he called, 'The Columbian Orator,' . . ." (*Old Guard,* VII [Jan., 1869], 13).
520.33 The sixty nine particles: Could this be a pun on Martin Luther's thirty-nine articles? The Lutheran Church was particularly strong in the Dutch Fork area, Lexington District, South Carolina, in the nineteenth century.

Textual Introduction

" 'Bald-Head Bill Bauldy,'/and How he went through the/Flurriday Campaign!—A Legend of the Hunter's Camp—" (herein referred to in short-title as "Bald-Head Bill Bauldy") is published for the first time in the Centennial edition. The manuscript—evidently Simms's rough draft—is included in the Charles Carroll Simms Collection in the South Caroliniana Library.

Since Simms makes no mention of the story in his correspondence or notebooks, it is impossible to say precisely when it was written, other than probably between 1865 and 1870—that is, later than "Sharp Snaffles," for which Simms apparently had time to prepare fair copy, and probably also later than "The Humours of the Manager," which he had completed in "rough original" in 1868 and for which he had begun preparation of greatly revised fair copy before his death. Another indication that "Bald-Head Bill Bauldy" is the work of fiction Simms last completed is the handwriting, pre-

Manuscript page of "Bald-Head Bill Bauldy," in Charles Carroll Simms Collection, South Caroliniana Library.

sumably that of the author's terminal years when rapidly declining health made even desk work painfully difficult. Nevertheless, because of its close relationship to "How Sharp Snaffles Got His Capital and Wife," to which it is a companion-piece, "Bald-Head Bill Bauldy" is placed in the Centennial edition before "The Humours of the Manager." Another editorial justification might be the fact that "Bald-Head Bill Bauldy," like "Sharp Snaffles," appears to have germinated from Simms's 1847 visit to hunters' camps in the North Carolina mountains (see above, pp. 798-799), though a return trip Simms reportedly made to the region in September, 1867 (Trent, p. 306), may have acted as catalyst.

It is of course possible that some of Simms's ambiguous references to work in progress during 1865-1868, cited in the Textual Introduction to "Sharp Snaffles" (pp. 800-801), point to "Bald-Head Bill Bauldy," but it seems more likely that allusions to its composition, if any, would occur in the correspondence of 1869-1870. In a letter of January 18, 1869, to Edward Roach, Simms stated: "I have been working very hard, & have written & sent north, some 1300 pages MS. on two works—one of them finished, since I reached here Oct. 21. This apart from 2 or 300 other pages MSS. not to speak of my correspondence" (*Letters*, V, 196). The "two works" are presumably *Voltmeier* and "The Cub of the Panther," but since the "2 or 300 other pages MSS." cannot be identified, "Bald-Head Bill Bauldy" among others is a possibility. An indication of Simms's intellectual involvement with "legends of the hunter's camp" comes in a letter of January 26, 1869, addressed to J. N. Robson, in which Simms mentioned the "superiority" of gunpowder "of Duponts manufacture" and lightly added: "This powder with the use of the drop shot, is all potent & persuasive with duck & deer, squirrel & partridge, and, when it is once known that the sportsman uses it the fowl, beast or bird, is apt to cry out to him, in the language of the Coon to Capt. Scott—'Don't shoot, Captain—I'll come down!" (*Letters*, V, 200). This pointed reference to a "typical tall tale of the frontier . . . told of Capt. Martin Scott, David Crockett, and Daniel Boone" (in the words of the footnote in the *Letters*) seems a good clue to the workings of Simms's imagination in early 1869. Later letters in 1869 and early in 1870 contain comments about literary labors not positively identified (see *Letters*, V, 203, 209, 214, 217, 221, 225, 238, 241, 245, 247, 250, 263, 270, 279, 296-297), and it is conceivable that some of them refer to "Bald-Head Bill Bauldy"—as, for instance, the unelaborated reference in a letter to Duyckinck of May 13, 1869, to "two or three smaller [than *Voltmeier* and 'The Cub of the Panther'] tales" Simms had recently "completed" (*Letters,* V, 221). Perhaps particularly relevant, however, in the light of Simms's known late concentration upon backwoods tales of the common man, is the observation he made to John Esten Cooke in a letter of August 5, 1869: "I find the general objection to me, that I cannot write down to the level of the popular comprehension & desires, who find sufficient grandeur in the vulgar" (*Letters,* V, 242). Even if Simms had completed the manuscript of "Bald-Head Bill Bauldy" as early as March, 1870, it is no wonder that he failed to prepare fair copy: ". . . I can no longer sit up to write," he confessed to Paul Hamilton Hayne on March 26. "My back begins to ache, and my body to writhe" (*Letters,* V, 304). Though Simms made the tremendous exertion to write *The Sense of the Beautiful* for his last public performance, on May 3, his final months were too marked with suffering to permit reasonable belief that the proud, enfeebled author expended creative energy other than that motivated by a personal appearance—in reality honoring him—before the citizens of his home city. Even earlier, on April 14, 1870, he had confessed to Duyckinck—"the exhausting effects of my malady, leave me too wretchedly feeble for the assertion of will or the exercise of faculty" (*Letters,* V, 310).

Table I: Emendations and Textual Notes

Listed here are all changes made in the copy-text of "Bald-Head Bill Bauldy," the manuscript in the Charles Carroll Simms Collection. The original reading appears to the left of the bracket, the Centennial edition reading to the right. Where no bracket appears the reading is the same in both texts and the refusal to emend is explained in parentheses. Where an explanation of the change is necessary it follows in parentheses.

466. I. Second Saturday Night.] *I.*/Second Saturday Night. (Chapter titles have been regularized throughout the story and the volume.)

466.13 &] and

466.22 bucks &] ~ and

467.1 &] and
467.4 furs &] ~ and
467.10 & <. . .> &] and ~ and
467.19 hunter's] hunters
467.22 &] and
467.36 &] and
468.3 honey, &] ~ and
468. II] *II.*
468.chapter title river] River
468.14 &] *and*
468.19 &] and
469.5 more &] ~ and
469.9 &] and
469.17 &] and
469.18 polling (Spelling has not been regularized, though in the language of Major Henry "poling" is perhaps more likely than "polling.")
469.22 &] and
469.23 remained, &] ~ and
469.25 "Scrub."] '~'
469.28 Cudjo] "~
469.30 &] and
469.33 Cudjo <. . .> &] "~ and
469.35 "Misser] " '~
469.36 sense!"] ~'
469.37 "What <. . .> Cudjo?"] " '~'
470.1 "Wha'] " '~
470.4 &] and
470.5 &] and
470.7 water &] ~ and
470.14 sweat!"] ~'
470.15 "How <. . .> country?"] " '~'
470.16 "Misser] " '~
470.18 see?"] ~'
470.19 "I <. . .> alligator."] " '~'
470.20 "Das] " '~
470.23 Congaree!"] ~'
470.24 "Well <. . .> enough!"] " '~'

470.25 “I] “ ‘~
470.27 &] and
470.31 & <. . .> &] and ~ and
470.38 sense!.”] ~∧’
471.1 “But <. . .> boat?”] “ ‘~’
471.3 The] “~
471.5 “Misser] “ ‘~
471.6 dat?.”] ~∧’
471.7 Holding] “~
471.8 “That’s <. . .> thumb!”] “ ‘~’
471.9 “Ah!] “ ‘~
471.10 ribber.”] ~’
471.11 “But <. . .> river?”] “ ‘~’
471.12 “Well] “ ‘~
471.13 down.”] ~’
471.14 “But,” <. . .> “suppose] “ ‘~’ ~ ‘~
471.15 Cudjo?”] ~’
471.16 “My] “ ‘~
471.19 ribber!”] ~’
471.20 “But] “ ‘~
471.22 him?”] ~’
471.23 “My] “ ‘~
471.24 ebbry ’ting?”] ~∧
471.26 ribber!”] ~’
471.27 “But] “ ‘~
471.29 bottom?”] ~’
471.30 Here] “~
471.31 &] and
471.34 “Ah!] “ ‘~
471.36 kin!”] ~’
472. iii] *III.*
472.3 & fidgetting] and ~ (The manuscript could possibly be read “fiidgettey” instead of “fidgetting.”)
472.19 &] and
472. iv.] *IV.*
472.chapter title volunteers <. . .> fight] Volunteers ~ Fight
472.24 & skrimaraging] and ~

472.28 &] and

472.29 &] and

472.31 &] and

473.3 & children] and ~

473.4 down &] ~ and

473.9 &] and

473.13 &] and

473.14 low &] ~ and

473.15 bush &] ~ and

473.18 beat, &] ~ and

473.19 &] and

473. <missing leaf> (In the manuscript of "Bald-Head Bill Bauldy" leaf 23 is missing; an additional problem is the fact that manuscript leaf 22 [beginning "give fair notis . . ."—see 473.13] does not appear to be in Simms's handwriting. One possible theory is that Simms made extensive revisions of leaves 22 and 23, and asked someone—perhaps his daughter Anna Augusta Simms Roach, with whom he lived when he visited Charleston in his last years—to copy them. In the process one leaf may have been misplaced. Fortunately, the missing leaf does not seem to be crucial to the meaning of the story, but one cannot be certain.)

473.27 tooth &] ~ and

474.2 &] and

474.11 &] and

474.13 &] and

474.22 &] and

474.23 &] and

474.27 &] and

475.5 "misery,"] '~'

475.6 ossifer's] ossifers

475.9 "This <. . .> &] "'~ and

475.10 him?"] ~'

475.13 "He] "'~

475.14 Bauldy?"] ~'

475.17 "I'm] "'~

475.20 cook!"] ~'

475.21 "We'll] "'~

475.22 do!"] ~'

475.28 &] and
475.29 &] and
475.36 hams, & <. . .> plenty, &] ~ and ~ and
476.4 dinner &] ~ and
476.5 & wait] and ~
476.6 &] and
476.7 "*scullion*"] '~'
476.8 Twas] "~
476.9 "parquizites,"] '~'
476.23 They] "~
476.24 "*Plantation*"] '~'
476.32 side, &] ~ and
477.4 & <. . .> & <. . .> &] and ~ and ~ and
477.5 "thick,"] '~'
477.6-7 "plantation"] '~'
477.10 Meantime <. . .> "Scullion"] "~ '~'
477.12 plates & <. . .> pots &] ~ and ~ and
477.13 'gin (Use of apostrophe is not regularized except to prevent possible misreading, usually with reference to possessives.)
477.15 a'ternoon's] a'ternoons
477.16 "thick"] '~'
477.17 down & <. . .> "long nine"] ~ and ~ '~'
477.23 blue &] ~ and
477.30 & <. . .> &] and ~ and
478.1 &] and
478.12 "long nine"] '~'
478.20 "long nine"] '~'
478.23 up, &] ~ and
478.30 &] and
478.32 "thick"] '~'
478.36-37 "Big Lie,"] '~'
479. <rule>] <no rule>
479. V.] *V.*
479. <rule>] <no rule>
479.chapter title lost his] Lost His
479. <rule>] <no rule>
479. <rule>] <no rule> (At this point Simms began a new leaf of manuscript and repeated designations for the new chapter.)

479. V.] <no V.>
479. <rule>] <no rule>
479.12 skill &] ~ and
479.14 & which] and ~
479.18 &] and
479.32 & <. . .> &] and ~ and
479.33 One] "~
480.4 "thick"] '~'
480.9 &] and
480.12 "long nines"] '~'
480.16 up &] ~ and
480.17 & <. . .> &] and ~ and
480.18 tops & <. . .> &] ~ and ~ and
480.27 "long nines,"] '~'
480.30 & carrying] and ~
480.34 There <. . .> shots &] "~ and
480.36 beating &] ~ and
480.39 cook; &] ~ and
481.5 &] and
481.7 & Kept <. . .> "thick"] and kept ~ '~'
481.9 shooting &] ~ and
481.11 closer &] ~ and
481.14 &] and
481.17 finger's] fingers
481.20 "parquizites" <. . .> &] '~' ~ and
481.22 &] and
481.24 &] and
481.27 &] and
481.32 rifle, &] ~ and
481.33 When] "~
481.34 head, &] ~ and
481.37 I] "~
482.9 &] and
482.15 "misery"] '~'
482.21 "Hegh <. . .> chee!"] "'~'
482.23 &] and
482.24 &] and
482.27 &] and
482.30 &] and

483.4 "Hegh <. . .> Etchee-ma-la-la!"] " '~'
483.13 &] and
483.21 up &] ~ and
483.23 &] and
483.24 head &] ~ and
483.29 Siminoles &] ~ and
483.31 rigiment, &] ~ and
484. vi] *VI.*
484.chapter title rescued <. . .> torture] Rescued ~ Torture
484. <rule>] <no rule>
484.2 &] and
484.9 &] and
484.15 &] and
484.17 in & <. . .> rifle &] ~ and ~ and
484.18 &] and
484.19 side &] ~ and
484.21 &] and
484.32 marching &] ~ and
484.33 & more] and ~
485.12 me &] ~ and
485.15 &] and
484.18 But <. . .> &] "~ and
485.20 &] and
485.24 Columbya (Manuscript shows that Simms had first written "Columbia," then changed to vernacular "Columbya.")
485.26 men &] ~ and
485.28 'gin (See 477.13.)
485.29 Then] "~
485.30 &] and
485.31 &] and
485.35 minnit, &] ~ and
485.39 &] and
486.3 &] and
486.3 its (See 477.13.)
486.7 long &] ~ and
486.8 face &] ~ and
486.10 hands &] ~ and

486.11-12 "It's <. . .> now!] '~'

486.24 & arrows, &] and ~ and

486.28 laugh &] ~ and

486.37 &] and

487.3 "Hegh!"] "'~'

487.6 face, &] ~ and

487.7 woman &] ~ and

487.13 &] and

487.16 September!] ~"

487. vii.] *VII.*

487.chapter title relieves] Relieves (At this point Simms began a new leaf of manuscript.)

487. <rule>] <no rule>

487. vii] <no vii>

487.23 coatee &] ~ and

487.29 "double quick," <. . .> &] '~' ~ and

487.33 Jamaica &] ~ and

488.21 kicked &] kicked and

488.23 wood &] ~ and

489.17 &] and

489.38 *now!"*] ~‸

490. viii.] *VIII.*

490.8-9 <rule>] <no rule>

490.chapter title runs] Runs (At this point Simms began a new leaf of manuscript.)

490. <rule>] <no rule>

490. viii] <no viii>

490. <rule>] <no rule>

490.16 Kicked, & knifed, & sculped, &] kicked, and ~ and ~ and

490.19 this, &] ~ and

490.24 "double quick,"] '~'

490.26 &] and

490.32 &] and

491.6 &] and

491.11 &] and

491.16 &] and

491.17 &] and

491.18 &] and
491. IX] *IX.*
491.chapter title fight] Fight
491.22 "That <. . .> fix!] '~'
491.25 &] and
492.3 box & pipe, &] ~ and ~ and
492.9 &] and
492.21 "Who is you?"] '~'
492.25 &] and
492.27 &] and
492.28 &] and
492.33 eyes & <. . .> &] ~ and ~ and
492.34 &] and
493.1 &] and
494.3 "by <. . .> Gentleman!"] '~'
494.8 less!] ~"
494. X.] *X.*
494.chapter title down <. . .> bottomless depths] Down ~ Bottomless Depths (At this point Simms began a new leaf of manuscript.)
494.8-9 X. <no X.>
494.8-9 <rule>] <no rule>
494.11 &] and
494.12 &] and
494.13 spurring &] ~ and
494.16 My] "~
494.19 whip &] ~ and
494.27 nothing &] ~ and
495.1 & on, &] and ~ and
495.18 &] and
495.24 down, &] ~ and
495.30 drowning, & <. . .> massacr*ee*.] ~ and ~"
495.30-31 <rule>] <no rule>
495. XI] *XI.*
495.chapter title depths] Depths
495. <rule>] <no rule>
496.1 &] and
496.2 &] and

496.4 &] and
496.5 I] "~
496.7 "I'm] '~
496.8 last!] ~' (This quote could be closed almost anywhere in the remainder of the paragraph.)
496.16 &] and
496.20 &] and
496.38 I?"] ~∧
497. XII] *XII.*
497.chapter title after <. . .> experience, is made <. . .> type] After ~ Experiences, Is Made ~ Type
497.14 I] "~
497.17 A'ter] "~
497.19 I] "~
497.21 &] and
497.26 &] and
496.28 Thar] "~
497.30 &] and
497.31 &] and
498.1 &] and
498.2 &] and
498.23 shells &] ~ and
498.25 &] and
498.27 big, &] ~ and
498.28 me, &] ~ and
498.34 By <. . .> &] "~ and
498.35 &] and
499.8 &] and
499.10 &] and
499.11-12 "I <. . .> that!"] '~'
499.18 "Bauldy <. . .> lie!"] "'~'
499.20 &] and
499.23 "Columbian orator"] '~'
499.29 skear'd, &] ~ and
499.32 I] "~
499.33-34 chrystals &] ~ and
500.5 &] and

500.7 She] "~
500.13 fellows] fellow's
500.15 And] "~
500.19 &] and
500.30 "What's <. . . .> &] "'~ and
500.31 another.] ~'
500.32 But] "~
500.33 &] and
500.37 &] and
501.10 Gineral's] Gineral ("Gineral's" in the manuscript is probably the result of Simms's thinking ahead to "Scott's.")
501.12 &] and
501.16 &] and
501.20 "I'm <. . .> agin!"] "'~'
501.23 &] and
501.32 &] and
501.36 front &] ~ and
501.37 &] and
501.38 &] and
502.4 &] and
502.6 "March!"] "'~'
502.8 &] and
502.9 They] "~
502.9 & and] and
502.12 &] and
502.14 &] and
502.17 But] "~
502.20 &] and
502.26 &] and
502.28 "What's <. . .> next?"] "'~'
502.30 &] and
502.33 &] and
503.11 upon.] ~"
503. <rule>] <no rule>
503. xiii] *XIII.*
503.chapter title discovers <. . .> places <. . .> & <. . .> excitement <. . .> escapes] Discovers ~ Places ~ and ~ Excitement ~ Escapes

503. <rule>] <no rule>
503.18 &] and
503.22 She] "~
503.30 cheeks &] ~ and
503.32 But] "~
503.33 &] and
504.3 &] ~ and
504.5 I] "~
504.17 &] and
504.19 shrimps & clams &] ~ and ~ and
504.24 She <. . .> me, &] "~ and
504.25 &] and
504.26 I] "~
504.27 But] "~
504.29 &] and
504.31 When] "~
504.32 some, &] ~ and
504.34 But] "~
504.35 &] and
504.37 &] and
505.4 &] and
505.5 I <. . .> &] "~ and
505.7 &] and
505.10 When] "~
505.12 & seed <. . .> hyar &] and ~ and ~ and
505.21 &] and
505.25 There] "~
505.35 Them] "~
505.37 & <. . .> &] and ~ and
505.38 shirks (The fact that Simms put an apostrophe in parenthetical "shark's" implies that the omission of an apostrophe in "shirks" is eye dialect.)
506.4 &] and
506.7 & <. . .> &] and ~ and
506.16 It] "~
506.17 &] and
506.25 &] and
506.26 neck &] ~ and

506.29 &] and
506.30 I] "~
506.37 But] "~
507.1 natured &] ~ and
507.2 &] and
507.4 &] and
507.6 off, &] ~ and
507.8 boats, & <. . .> river, &] ~ and ~ and
507.10 &] and
507.14 I] "~
507.17 Twas <. . .> &] "~ and
507.18 &] and
507.19 &] and
507.20 I] "~
507.21 &] and
507.22 "Whoo <. . .> Whoo!"] '~'
507.23 And] "~
507.26 & never] and ~
507.30 &] and
507.34 &] and
508.1 "You <. . .> woman!"] "'~'
508.7 down &] ~ and
508.8 sarched &] ~ and
508.11 broad &] ~ and
508.14 & <. . .> &] and ~ and
508.15 & <. . .> Ingin &] and ~ and
508.24 &] and
508.25 And] "~
508.28 And] "~
508. <between 32 and 33> <rule>] <no rule>
508.34 & thar] and ~
508.35 &] and
509.5 &] and
509.8 &] and
509. <between 14 and 15> <rule>] <no rule>
509.16 & swim, &] and ~ and
509.19 &] and
509.24 I] "~

509.27 Then] "~
509.32 on on] on
509.34 Twas <. . .> &] "~ and
509.36 And] "~
510.3 And] "~
510.4 &] and
510.7 &] and
510.8 &] and
510.12 What] "~
510.18 & <. . .> &] and ~ and
510.19 &] and
510.23 Oh] "~
510.25 I] "~
510.26 & waded] and ~
510.32 "good bye"] '~'
510.33 &] and
511.1 And] "~
511.4 And] "~
511.7 &] and
511.12 &] and
511.15 Twaur] "~
511.16 &] and
511.18 When <. . .> &] "When ~ and
511.26 & honey] and ~
511.27 now?] ~"
511. <rule>] <no rule>
511. xiv.] *XIV.*
511.chapter title & his escape from] and His Escape From
511. <rule>] <no rule>
511.31 &] and
512.2 &] and
512.4 &] and
512.5 Then] "~
512.6 & <. . .> &] and ~ and
512.12 &] and
512.18 pulled &] ~ and
512.19 eyes &] ~ and
512.24 "Oh <. . .> last!"] "'~'

512.27 “Hello] “ ‘~
512.28 haird!”] ~’
512.29 &] and
512.30 “It’s <. . .> desarter!”] “ ‘~’
512.31 “Desarter!”] “ ‘~’
512.32 “Yes,” <. . .> “a] “ ‘~’ ~ ‘~
512.35 shot!”] ~’
513.4 “Keep] “ ‘~
513.5 martial.”] ~’
513.8 calkilated, &] ~ and
513.10 nine’s] nines
513.15 & <. . .> &] and ~ and
513.23 &] and
513.24 &] and
513.27 &] and
513.30 &] and
513.33 “What <. . .> scoundrel?”] “ ‘~’
513.35 & I] and ~
513.37 “He] “ ‘~
513.38 Adwokit!] ~’
514.2 &] and
514.3 &] and
514.8 &] and
514.11 &] and
514.14 cigars &] ~ and
514.16 ’em &] ~ and
514.17 & <. . .> &] and ~ and
514.25 &] and
514.27 “thick”] ‘~’
514.31 “thick”] ‘~’
514.37 & <. . .> & <. . .> &] and ~ and ~ and
515.1 Did] “~
515.8 “thick”] ‘~’
515.9 “long nine”] ‘~’
515.18 “And <. . .> scoundrel!”] “ ‘~’
515.18-19 “What <. . .> yourself?”] ‘~’
515.22 thoughts &] ~ and
515.24 &] and

515.27 “We’ve <. . .> days.] “ ‘~’

515.28 “Oh!” <. . .> “but <. . .> ago!”] “ ‘~’ ~ ‘~’

515.29 Then <. . .> “What] “~ ‘~

515.30 on, <. . .> go on!”] ~,’ ~ ‘~’

515.31 And] “~

515.34 me, &] ~ and

515.35 “Why <. . .> about,”] “ ‘~’

515.35-36 “The <. . .> now!”] ‘~’

515.37 & <. . .> wig.”] and ~‸

515.38 “But,” <. . .> “whar’s <. . .> one?”] “ ‘~’ ~ ‘~’

516.1 “Why <. . .> pocket!” <. . .> “I] “ ‘~’ ~ ‘~

516.3 it!”] ~’

516.10 &] and

516.11 easier, &] ~ and

516.14 &] and

516.15 &] and

516.17 “But,” <. . .> “let] “ ‘~’ ~ ‘~

516.18 amusing!”] ~’

516.21 & <. . .> &] and ~ and

516.22 back, & rode him, &] ~ and ~ and

516.23 &] and

516.25 & <. . .> &] and ~ and

516.27 & <. . .> & <. . .> &] and ~ and ~ and

516.29 “thick,” <. . .> less!”] ‘~’ ~‸

516.29 less!”] ~

516.30 laughed!”] ~‸

516.31 “And to think!” <. . .> that] “ ‘~’ ~ ‘~

516.32 Bauldy,”] ~’

516.33 “How <. . .> camp?”] ‘~’

516.34 “Well,” says I, “Gineral] “ ‘~’ ~ ‘~

516.36 abouts!”] ~’

516.37 “Now,”] “ ‘~’

516.38 “Now] “ ‘~

516.39 dinner?”] ~’

517.2 “Yisterday, Gineral!”] “ ‘~’

517.5 “We] “ ‘~

517.8 breakfast.] ~’

517.11 Then <. . .> & <. . .> “Blox] “~ and ~ ‘~

517.13 went!”] ~’
517.14 “So] “‘~
517.16 &] and
517.21 marcy!”] ~’
517.30 I’ve] ‘~
517.31 “I <. . .> &] “‘~ and
517.33 “I] “‘~
517.34 “I] “‘~
517.35 hugged & kissed &] ~ and ~ and
517.36 yit—”] ~’
518.2 baby, &] ~ and
518.5 &] and
518.7 “Now] “‘~
518.9 &] and
518.13 guilty!] ~’
518.14 “Guilty!”] “‘~’
518.15 “What <. . .> punishment?”] “‘~’
518.16 “Death!”] “‘~’
518.17 “How <. . .> die!”] “‘~’
518.18 “Shot <. . .> death!”] “‘~’
518.19 “Hung!” <. . .> “Shooting’s <. . .> man.”] “‘~ ~ ‘~’
518.20 And] “~
518.22 A’ter] “~
518.23 “Gentlemen] “‘~
518.28 &] and
518.29 &] and
518.31 &] and
519.2 &] and
519.7 &] and
519.10 down &] ‘~ and
519.12 “It’s <. . .> vartue!” <. . .> to] “‘~’ ~ ‘~
519.13 &] and
519.14 &] and
519.15 &] and
519.16 &] and
519.17 &] and
519.21 &] and

519.29 onst!"] ~'
519.33 table, &] ~ and
519.34 ate; &] ~ and
519.35 &] and
519.36 &] and
519.37 "Gentlemen] "'~
519.38 one!"] ~'
520.3 & <. . .> &] and ~ and
520.4 &] and
520.4-5 red-/skin (This is the one time in the manuscript that Simms clearly wrote "red-/skin" as a single word or a hyphenated word. All other times he wrote "red skin[s].")
520.6 &] and
520.7 Bauldy's] "'~
520.9 musket!"] ~'
520.10 At <. . .> &] "~ and
520.17 &] and
520.19 Gineral &] ~ and
520.21 "Bauldy] "'~
520.25 bottom!"] ~'
520.26 "Ah, Gineral!" <. . .> "getting <. . .> "that] "'~' ~ ‸~ '~
520.27 &] and
520.29 Mar'maids."] ~'
520.30 "Well," <. . .> "I] "'~' ~ '~
520.33 particles!"] ~'
520.34 What] "~
520.35 &] and
520.36 pepper & <. . .> allspice, &] ~ and ~ and
520.37 inyon's] inyons
521.8 &] and
521.9 "I've] "'~
521.11 me!"] ~'
521.12 The] "~
521.16 &] and
521.20 &] and
521.23 Amen!] ~"
521. <under 23> <rule>] <no rule>

THE HUMOURS OF THE MANAGER.

"The Humours of the Manager," left in manuscript at its author's death, is perhaps the best example of Simms's humor in a story of manners. In it Simms combines several of his recognized talents: his ability to draw upon actual experiences and persons in creating fiction; his skill in sustaining humorous narration and dialogue; his ear for language (in this instance, German-American dialect); and his knowledge of the manners and mores of the theatre in New York and Charleston. At times in "The Humours of the Manager" Simms displays, with considerable skill, the Chaucerian knack of writing with tongue in cheek; the humor is light and two-edged, leaving the reader uncertain whether the author's intent is entertainment or satire or both.

A good example is Simms's use of "The Female Assassin" as the title of the "lost" drama in "The Humours of the Manager." The humor—as well as the possibility of satire—is increased with the knowledge that as a youth Simms himself had written a play identically titled—and that later, with good humor, he spoke condescendingly of it. In a letter of October 16, 1841, to James Lawson, Simms confided to his friend: "At 14 I wrote a Tragedy called 'The Female Assassin'—you may readily conjecture the sort of stuff which followed such a title" (*Letters*, I, 285). The tone here is one of amusement—the same amused tone which in "The Humours of the Manager" mocks the indignation of the pretentious, inept young author whom the cavalier Gilfert so unscrupulously and patronizingly handles. Thus, in a sense Simms may be privately poking fun at himself—"privately" in that almost no one else would know that "The Female Assassin" was one of his own early titles. But that Simms also had deep feelings on the impropriety of theatre managers controlling and exploiting authors is revealed by his long statement in the preface to *Count Julian; or, The Last Days of the Goth. A Historical Romance* (Baltimore and New York, 1845), which, incidentally, lends additional support to the idea that "The Female Assassin" episode in "The Humours" is at least partly autobiographical:

> The conquest of Spain, by the Moors, was an event which, at a very early period, seized upon and influenced my imagination; and, at the immature age of seventeen, I had planned the rude draught of a tragedy upon the subject . . . .

The drama, thus written, was submitted to the manager of a theatre—was accepted, announced and put in rehersal [*sic*]. But theatrical management in modern times is something of an absurdity. The secondary position which the author holds to the actor—reversing the order of things, as they were when the drama was successful—of which my first association behind the scenes soon gave me sufficient evidence, was quite too offensive to my self-esteem to be endured patiently. My tragedy was withdrawn and quietly consigned to the closet. With a passionate fondness for the drama—with a pressing conviction, not yet surrendered, that, as a literary man, in this department of fiction lay my *forte*—I was yet thoroughly satisfied that the day had gone by, or had not yet come, when it would be becoming in a man of pride and character—of sensibility at least—to present himself at the door of a manager, soliciting to be heard through this medium. I felt that nothing but necessity—the defeat of theatricals on every hand—the utter desuetude of the drama—would ever open the eyes of the actors to the suicide course which substitutes their art for that of the poet in whose labors only do they find exercise and employment. I took for granted then—and subsequent experience confirms all my conjectures—that the day must come, when, in the utter neglect of the stage by the great body of the public, the manager would discern the secret of its renovation to lie in the novelty of the fiction itself, and not in the variety of styles in which different actors would present to the multitude, the same old story with which they had become a thousand times familiar. For that day, however reluctantly, I was prepared to wait, sooner than forfeit any of my self-respect by unmanly concessions to a system falsely recognized as a legitimate medium of communication with the public. [pp. v, vi]

Though there is little evidence that he made direct use of them, Simms must have been familiar with John B. Irving's reminiscences of the Charleston theatre published in the *Charleston Courier* between 1857 and 1859 (under the title "The Theatre as It is and as It was") and, later, in March and April of 1870 (under the title "Early Days of the Drama in Charleston"). In fact, Irving dedicated his "second series" to Simms in "sincere token of my admiration of your genius" (*Courier*, March 18, 1870) at the very time that Simms must have been at work on his fair copy manuscript—a timing which leaves open to question which writer influenced whom. It is worth noting that Simms portrays Gilfert as an adroit gambler and confidence man much as does Irving, and that the striking details of Gilfert's death in "The Humours of the Manager" closely resemble those in Irving's account (see Emmett Robinson, ed., "Dr. Irving's Reminiscences of the Charleston Stage," *South Carolina Historical and Genealogical Magazine*, LI [1950], 125-131, 195-215; LII [1951], 26-33, 93-106, 166-179, 225-232; LIII [1953], 37-47).

Explanatory Notes

522.2 John Wakefield Francis (1789-1861), New York physician and author, a close friend of J. F. Cooper and E. A. Duyckinck, taught medicine at Columbia and Rutgers. He wrote *Old New York, or Reminiscences of the Past Sixty Years* (1858; reprinted 1866 with a memoir by H. T. Tuckerman).

522.13 Frederick Swartwout Cozzens (1818-1869), wine merchant of New York City, wrote humorous articles for the *Knickerbocker* and other periodicals under the pseudonym Richard Hayward. He was editor of *Cozzens' Wine Press: A Vinuos, Vivacious Monthly*, 1854-1861. His writings were collected in *The Sparrowgrass Papers* (1855) and *The Sayings of Dr. Bushwhacker and Other Learned Men* (1867).

523.3 "damnable faces": *Hamlet*, III, ii, 263.

523.27 the eminent Dr. Swedenborg: Simms must have created this character, perhaps named in honor of Emanuel Swedenborg (1688-1772), the Swedish scientist, philosopher, and mystic.

524.5 Dr. Mucklewhabber: Although Scott uses "Muckle-" in several of his characters' names (e.g., Mucklebackit in *The Antiquary* and Mucklewrath in *Old Mortality*), Dr. Mucklewhabber has not been identified.

524.7 Hugh Miller (1802-1856), Scottish man of letters and geologist, was the author of the well known *The Old Red Sandstone; or New Walks in an Old Field* (1841).

524.21 Mr. Tuckerman or Mr. Duyckinck: Henry Theodore Tuckerman (1813-1871), critic, essayist, and poet; and Evert A. Duyckinck (1816-1878), the close friend and correspondent of Simms.

524.23 a late publication: Joseph N. Ireland, *Records of the New York Stage from 1750 to 1860*, 2 vols. (1866-67). Simms made extensive use of Ireland's work in the preparation of "Humours of the Manager," citing it at length, for example, in his footnote at pp. 544-545.

526.9 Charles (or "Charley") Young was a colorful actor prominent on the Charleston stage for some eighteen years after joining Gilfert's company in 1817. According to John B. Irving's "Early Days of the Drama in Charleston" (which originally appeared in the *Charleston Courier* for April 12, 1870), it was Young who challenged Gilfert to the duel, because of the manager's "too marked" attentions to Mrs. Young, a beautiful actress; see Robinson, ed., "Dr. Irving's Reminiscences of the Charleston Stage," *SCHGM*, LII (1951), 225.

526.13-17 Louis Trezevant Wigfall (1816-1874) fought a duel with Preston S. Brooks in 1841 before moving in 1848 to Texas, where he served as U. S. Senator. See C. W. Lord, "Young Louis Wigfall: South Carolina Politician and Duelist," *South Carolina Historical Magazine*, LIX (1958), 96. One possible allusion to "Cogdale of Charleston" and his duel with Louis Kigfall's "kinsman" occurs in a footnote to Lord's article (p. 96n.): "Louis Wigfall's brother, Hamden, was killed in a duel with a fellow-student of South Carolina College. Written statement of D. W. Youngblood, M.D. (grandson of Eliza Wigfall Youngblood), Apr. 22, 1938." According to William L. King, *The Newspaper Press of Charleston, South Carolina* (1882) p. 166, a Toby Cogdell and a T. T. Wigfall fought a duel in or near Charleston about 1826.

526.19 Miss Holman: Agnes Holman Gilfert (1793-1833), English-born actress, first played Lady Townly (in Vanbrugh and Cibber's *The Provoked Husband*) on October 3, in New York. See Ireland, *Records of the New York Stage*, I, 289.

526.30-31 the great Siddons: Sarah Kemble Siddons (1755-1831) played Lady Macbeth at Drury Lane in February, 1785.

527.38-528.1 The quoted line is from Thomas Campbell, "The Pleasures of Hope," Part I, line 7.

528.2 The proverb "Familiarity breeds contempt" comes from Aesop, "The Fox and the Lion"; cf. *Merry Wives of Windsor*, I, i, 258, 259: "I hope, upon familiarity will grow more contempt."

531.23 blue pill: References to "blue pill" in Simms's letters of 1867-1869 reveal that it is a cure-all—probably a patent medicine—taken to relieve symptoms ranging from chills and fever to nausea and dyspepsia. See *Letters*, V, 29, 56, 58, 76, 245. Since the unpublished "Diary of William Porcher Miles from January 1st, 1870 to the end of the year, Oak Ridge, Nelson Co., Va." (Southern Historical Collection, University of North Carolina Library) also contains many similar references to "blue pill," it must have been a popular and well-known remedy of the times.

531.24 Congress water: A mineral water from Congress Spring, Saratoga, New York.

534.14-17 Mrs. Gray, Mrs. Hughes, and Miss Tilden are all mentioned in John B. Irving's accounts of the early Charleston stage (see Robinson, ed., "Dr. Irving's Reminiscences of the Charleston Stage," *SCHGM*, LI, 131; LII, 97, 100, 232).

535.25 Benefit of the Greek Cause: In early February, 1824, Gilfert gave three benefit performances for the Greek Fund (Greek cause for independence). See Charleston *Courier*, Feb. 4, 6, 10, 1824.

535.31 Dan G—— and *536.19* Colonel Bondy: Daniel Gaillard and Colonel Thomas D. Condy. One of John B. Irving's anecdotes tells of a summer visit to Saratoga Springs by two prominent patrons of the Charleston theatre, Gaillard and Condy, who enroute stop at Albany to see Gilfert and actor Charley Young. See Robinson, ed., "Dr. Irving's Reminiscences of the Charleston Stage," *SCHGM*, LII, 95.

537.17 North river: The Hudson River. See Explanatory Notes to "Mesmerides in a Stage-Coach" (210.14), p. 739.

540.18-19 "Throw physics to the dogs!": *Macbeth*, V, iii, 47.

540.36 Nova Zembla, or Novaya Zemlya, is a group of islands in the Arctic Ocean, between the Barents Sea in the west and the Kara Sea in the east.

541.18 Benton 'Mint Drops': See Explanatory Notes to "How Sharp Snaffles Got His Capital and Wife" (451.10-11), p. 000.

546.6 Tom Hilson: Thomas Hilson (1784-1834), English-born actor, was engaged by Gilfert to play in Charleston in 1817. He is listed as a member of Gilfert's stock company for the seasons of 1817-1818, 1819-1820, 1820-1821, 1821-1822, and 1822-1823. See W. Stanley Hoole, *The Ante-Bellum Charleston Theatre* (1946), pp. 15, 82, 84, 86, 87, 88.

Textual Introduction

During his visit to New York during the summer and early fall of 1866 Simms must have conceived the idea of doing a fictionalized account of some humorous episodes in the life of Charles Gilfert (1787-1829), flamboyant theatrical manager of Charleston and the Bowery. First reference to the idea occurs in the letter that Simms wrote to James Lawson on October 25, 1866, shortly after returning to Charleston: "I wish you would prepare & send on by Jimmy [Lawson's son, who was to visit Simms's son Gilmore], your anecdote of Gilfert. It is too good to be lost, & I wish to employ it with other matters. Be particular in giving all the details" (*Letters*, IV, 617). Several months later, on February 8, 1867, Simms again wrote to Lawson urging the New Yorker to supply what information he could about Gilfert: "Let me beg you also, while ice bound at Yonkers to send me the details of that vivid sketch of Gilfert in his latter days, not omitting names of place, or any item of interest, & especially give me a description of his personal appearance at that time & when you knew him, & of his mode of speech & general manner" (*Letters*, V, 14). Simms once more jogged Lawson's memory in a letter of March 7, 1867: "Thanks for your *promise* about Gilfert. I trust you will prove yourself something more than a *merely promising* youth" (*Letters*, V, 21). Ten days later, on March 17, the persistent Charlestonian again wrote his forgetful or reluctant friend, "I wish you to make an effort, some rainy day when you do not go down to the city, to make the notes about Gilfert" (*Letters*, V, 27). Not to be denied, Simms chided Lawson good humoredly when on May 14, 1867, he still had not received the requested notes: "Of course you have done nothing with the Gilfert anecdote. You are an ancient humbug. You talk to me of having no regular employments & speak of your drudgeries, at the very time when Jimmy is describing you as seldom visiting your office, taking your luxurious ease . . ." (*Letters*, V, 52). Such persistence must finally have paid dividends, for by June 30, 1868, Simms had completed "The Humours of the Manager"; his letter of that date to E. A. Duyckinck reads in part:

> I have been writing a magazine paper, about which I would have you say nothing, but it will report the substance of one of our *soirees* at the house of your old friend, Francis, when I think that you were present with several others, and when Charles Gilfert was the topic. I had some anecdotes of Gilfert in Charleston to deliver, & there were others. Dr. F. himself gave us a vivid picture of the last hours of Gilfert whom he attended—a sublime enthusiasm. I have worked this matter up into an article which I call, "The Humors of the Manager," & think to send it to Lippincott who paid me promptly & well for the only article I sent him. The material I think remarkably good, & I trust the dressing will not fail it. [*Letters*, V, 145]

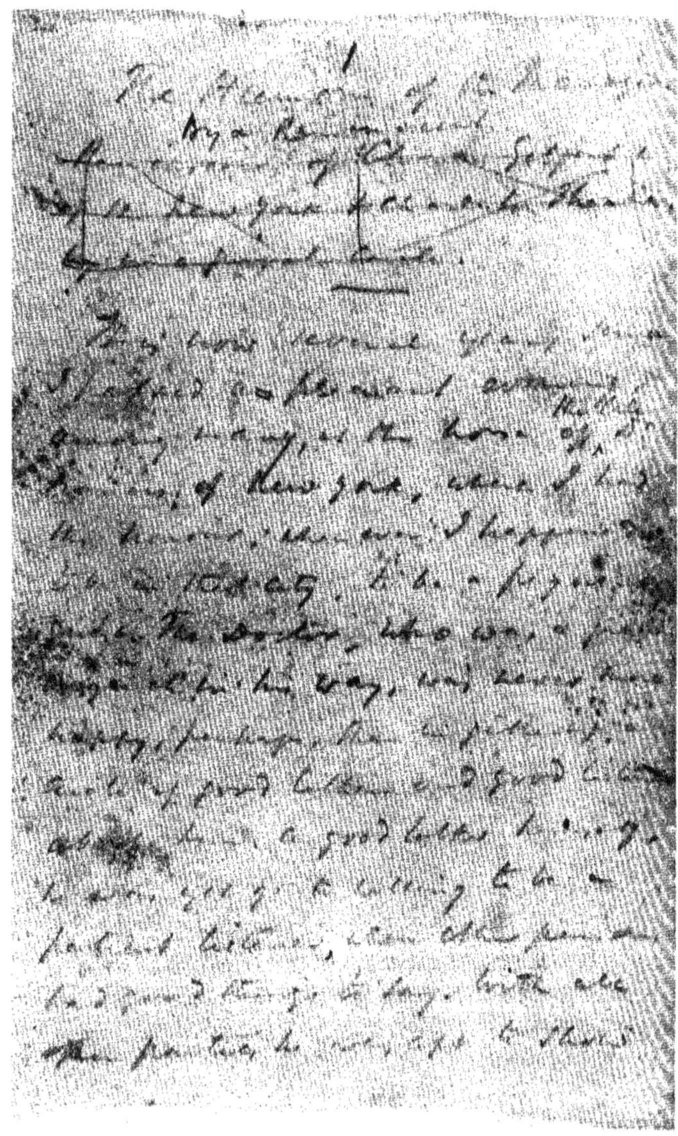

First page of Simms's rough draft of "The Humours of the Manager," in Charles Carroll Simms Collection, South Caroliniana Library.

First page of Simms's incomplete fair copy of "The Humours of the Manager," in Charles Carroll Simms Collection, South Caroliniana Library.

The editor of *Lippincott's Magazine*, John Foster Kirk, apparently did not accept "The Humours of the Manager," however, and Simms made one more effort to get his manuscript published. In another letter to Duyckinck, dated July 25, 1868, Simms informed his friend:

> I will, as soon as I can get the rough original (in pencil) copied, send you the article on Gilfert. It is called "The Humours of the Manager," and is, in fact, a series of sketches of Gilfert in various attitudes,—some of them stories which you will possibly recal, for I think you were present at Dr. Francis's with me, when they were narrated. I brought up the subject to Dr. F. Lawson, also, furnished me with some items. It is a gossippy, anecdotical thing, which will, I think, prove lively and attractive. Lippincott's Editor is of the opinion that Manager Gilfert's career would not constitute an interesting subject,—as if, however biographical, the Manager is any thing but a lay figure. But such are the blockheads we have to deal with in too many of our periodicals. [*Letters*, V, 152]

For whatever reason, Simms did not succeed in getting "The Humours of the Manager" published. One complete manuscript of the story (presumably the "rough original" referred to in the letter of July 25, 1868) and one partial manuscript (presumably the fair copy Simms never completed) are in the Charles Carroll Simms Collection of the South Caroliniana Library. Both bear identical titles written on a single line. The fair copy manuscript (18 leaves) is used as copy-text for as long as it goes; at the point where the fair copy stops, Simms's pencilled "rough original" manuscript is resorted to for copy-text (at leaf 58 of the 107-leaf MS.).

Table I: Emendations and Textual Notes

Listed here are all changes made in the copy-text—i.e., the combination of the existing eighteen leaves of fair copy manuscript and leaves 58-107 of the rough draft, as explained above. The copy-text reading appears to the left of the bracket, the emended Centennial edition text to the right. Where no bracket appears the reading is the same in both texts and the refusal to emend is explained in parentheses. Where an explanation of the change is necessary it follows in parentheses.

522. <no chapter>] *I.*
522.2 Dr] Dr.

522.3 D^{r}] Doctor
522.5 he] he had
522.10 buoyant &] ~ and
522.11 agreable ("Agreable" was acceptable nineteenth-century spelling.)
522.11 &] and
522.21 &] and
522.22 &] and
522.23 &] and
522.27 &] and
523.1 & <. . .> D^{r}] and ~ Dr.
523.4 &] and
523.7 &] and
523.10 &] and
523.11 &] and
523.12 & <. . .> D^{r}] and ~ Dr.
523.22 D^{r}] Doctor
523.23 &] and
523.27 D^{r}] Dr.
523.29 &] and
523.31 D^{r}] Dr.
524.5 D^{r} <. . .> D^{r}] Dr. ~ Dr.
524.7 &] and
524.16 &] and
524.18 D^{r}] Dr.
525.12 &] and
525.16 &] and
525.25 &] and
526.1 M^{rs} <. . .> &] "Mrs. ~ and
526.4 &] and
526.5 &] and
526.6 Nor] "~
526.12-13 "the <. . .> Honour"] '~'
526.16 &] and
526.18 M^{rs}] "Mrs.
526.22 &] and
526.26 &] and

526.38 held it] held (Simms must have intended to strike from this line either "which" or "it." "Which" is retained because it parallels the "which" at 526.37.)

527.5 &] and
527.11 &] and
527.17 "Ah] "'~
527.23 thing.] ~" (The unclosed quote seems to end most appropriately here.)
527.31 & <. . .> recieve &] and ~ received and
527.32 recieve] receive
528.4 & <. . .> &] and ~ and
528.14 eyes."] ~'
528.15 And] "~
528.16 &] and
528.20 last.] ~" (Double quotes are added at the seemingly most logical place.)
528.21 <no ¶> One (The paragraphing is not regularized because of the uncertainty of the author's intent.)
528.22 &] and
528.27 "The <. . .> Assassin"] '~'
528.28 "Abollin <. . .> Bandit,"] '~'
528.29 "Schinderhannes"] '~'
528.37 &] and
528.38 "the <. . .> Assassin"] 'The ~'
528.39 recieved] received
529.3 *sang azul* (Simms apparently confused his French and Spanish in writing this phrase.)
529.10 Gilfert's &] Gilfert and (Simms must have first intended to write "Gilfert's coterie"; when he change the phrasing, presumably to "Gilfert and his coterie," he neglected to strike out the possessive "s".)
529.14 &] and
529.16 &] and
529.25 earnest &] ~ and
529.29 recieved] received
529.31 recieved] received
529.34 "Ah] "'~
529.36 &] and

529.38 Mrs <. . .> concieve] Mrs. ~ conceive

529.39 sensation."] ~'

530.3 &] and

530.4 &] and

530.12 "Your <. . .> sensation!"] '~'

530.13 "The <. . .> is," <. . .> "I] "'~' ~ '~

530.14 &] and

530.18 &] and

530.20 &] and

530.21 sensation.] ~'

530.24 &] and

530.26 &] and

531.13 "Ah!] "'~

531.15 & <. . .> Theatre."] and ~'

531.17 &] and

531.19 "My] "'~

531.24 morning."] ~'

531.25 "Thank] "'~

531.25 Mr] Mr.

531.27 Mr] Mr.

531.28 to—"] ~'

531.29 "Don't] "'~

531.33 then—"] ~'

531.34 "I] "'~

531.34 Mr] Mr.

531.36 Drama."] ~'

531.37 "W-h-a-t] "'~

532.3 &] and

532.5 &] and

532.8 grandest——"] ~' (In this instance it is doubtful whether Simms intended the long dash to indicate an interruption or an omitted word.)

532.9 "Thank] "'~

532.9 Mr] Mr.

532.10 Mr] Mr.

532.11 longer."] ~'

532.12 "Delude <. . .> friend."] "'~'

532.13-14 "Ay <. . .> Mr <. . .> piece."] "'~ Mr. ~'

532.15-16 “Not <. . .> that.”] “ ‘~’
532.17-18 “The <. . . .> benefits.”] “ ‘~’
532.19 “And] “ ‘~
532.25 played.”] ~’
532.26-27 “Thank <. . . .> Mr <. . .> M.S.”] “ ‘~ Mr. ~’
532.28 There] “~
532.32 “d——est <. . .> sensations.”] ‘~’
532.37 “It] “ ‘~
533.7 chambermaid——”] ~’
533.8 “There <. . . > Gilfert.”] “ ‘~’
533.8-9 indignantly] ~.
533.10 ‘To] “ ‘~
533.12 earnest?”] ~’
533.13-14 ‘I <. . .> MS.”] “ ‘~’
533.15 “Mein <. . .> bien!”] “ ‘~’
533.16 And] “~
533.19-20 “Ah! <. . .> yours?”] “ ‘~’
533.20-21 “What <. . .> sensation?”] “ ‘~’
533.23 “And] “ ‘~
533.25 faculty.”] ~’
533.26 “My <. . .> Assassin!”] “ ‘~”!’
533.29 “Female Assassin!” “Female Assassin’] ‘ “~”!’
533.31 “Tis <. . .> there!” <. . .> &] “ ‘~’ ~ and
533.34-35 “Tis <. . . .> Assassin.”] “ ‘~” ’
533.38 “You <. . .> lost!”] “ ‘~’
534.1 “Lost] “ ‘~
534.3 them.”] ~’
534.4 Female Assassin] ‘~’
534.5 “Where <. . .> Female Assassin!”] “ ‘~ “~”!’
534.6 “You <. . .> Sir!”] “ ‘~’
534.9 “It <. . . .> here.”] “ ‘~’
534.11 &] and
534.12 “Female Assassin”] ‘~’
534.13 “Some] “ ‘~
534.14 Mrs] Mrs.
534.17 Mrs] Mrs.
534.23 & I’ll] and ~
534.27 treasury.”] ~’

534.28 "My <. . .> doubt!"] " '~'
534.29 "My <. . .> copy!"] '~'
534.30 Savage] "~
534.32-33 "Lost <. . . .> money!"] " '~'
534.34 "My <. . . .> M^{r} <. . .> play!"] " '~ Mr. ~'
534.35-36 "Mein <. . . .> women."] " '~'
534.37 "D——n <. . .> women!"] " '~'
534.37-38 "I <. . .>tragedy!"] '~'
535.1 "Oh!] " '~
535.3 Assassin!] ~'
535.6 "I] " '~
535.8 pieces,"] ~'
535.8 "Take] '~
535.10 d——n!"] ~'
535.11 This] "~
535.17 performance!] ~"
535. ii] *II.*
535. title How Gilfert made a trip to Saratoga. How he bled the Cashier, and Completed his professional education.] How Gilfert Made a Trip to Saratoga. How He Bled the Cashier, and Completed His Professional Education.
535.21 "Female] '~
535.22 Assassin,"] ~'
535.24 &] and
535.29 &] and
535.32 &] and
536.1 fun &] ~ and
536.10 Danl] Daniel
536.14 &] and
536.16 The] "~
536.17 &] and
536.18 &] and
536.22 pleasantries &] ~ and
536.27 &] and
536.29 But] "~
536.31 &] and
536.32 exclaimed: (At this point the fair copy manuscript ends, and Simms's rough draft becomes copy-text.)

536.33 “Mein] “ ‘~

536.35 do?”] ~’

536.36 “Oh! <. . .> Gilfert,” <. . .> “You] “ ‘~’ ~ ‘~

536.38 us.”] ~’

537.1 Gilfert] “~

537.2 “Bondy] “ ‘~

537.3 & <. . .> Dan[l]] and ~ Daniel

537.8 begin.”] ~’

537.9 What] “~

537.14 From <. . .> &] “~ and

537.15 & <. . .> &] and ~ and

537.18 &] and

537.20 But] “~

537.23 &] and

537.25-26 “Pay <. . .> steamer.”] “ ‘~’

537.27 Bondy] “~

537.28-29 “What <. . .> yesterday?”] “ ‘~’

537.30 Dan.] “~‸

537.31 “Patience <. . .> & <. . .> cards.”] “ ‘~ and ~’

537.32-33 “Yes! <. . .> expense!”] “ ‘~’

537.34 Without] “~

537.37-38 “Bondy <. . .> please.”] “ ‘~’

538.1 The] “~

538.2 “The <. . .> good,”] “ ‘~’

538.3 “Nothing <. . .> *way;*”] “ ‘~’

538.4 As] “~

538.8-9 “My <. . .> morning.”] “ ‘~’

538.10 By] “~

538.12 “Where] “ ‘~

538.17 longer!”] ~’

538.18 Dan] “~

538.20-21 “Patience <. . .> faith!”] “ ‘~’

538.22 “Faith,] “ ‘~

538.24 purse?”] ~’

538.25 “He] “ ‘~

538.29 &] and

538.31 days.”] ~’

538.32 “And] “ ‘~

538.35 Tom."] ~"'
538.36 There] "~
538.37 "To] "'~
539.2 Grandy] ~"
539.3 end."] ~'
539.4 As] "~
539.7 "I] "'~
539.14 death!"] ~'
539.15 It] "~
539.16 "just <. . .> end!"] '~'
539.17 "Gilfert," <. . .> "is] "'~' ~ '~
539.19 night!"] ~'
539.20 "Oh] "'~
539.22 Bills."] ~'
539.23 He] "~
539.25-26 "I <. . . .> good."] "'~'
539.27-28 "You <. . . .> now."] "'~'
539.29 The] "~
539.32 love &] ~ and
539.34 The <. . . .> &] "~ and
540.5 He] "~
540.7 "Another <. . .> $200."] "'~'
540.8 Gilfert] "~
540.9 "Bondy] "'~
540.23 jerk."] ~'
540.24 The] "~
540.25 "John," <. . .> "Do <. . .> that?"] "'~' ~ '~'
540.26 Holding] "~
540.27 "Now <. . .> gentlemen."] "'~'
540.28 John] "~
540.29 "You] "'~
540.33 relief."] ~'
540.34 John] "~
540.35 "Now] "'~
540.36 Vesuvious] Vesuvius
540.38 allways ("Allways" is retained despite the possibility that Simms intended either "always" or "all ways.")
541.3 reappear!"] ~'

541.4-5 "Great <. . .> drinks?"] "'~'

541.6 Bondy] "~

541.7 "To] "'~

541.9 Bondy."] ~'

541.10 Bondy] "~

541.11 Gilfert <. . .> &] "~ and

541.13 "Dan," <. . .> "you] "'~' ~ '~

541.16 Look!"] ~'

541.17 Here] "~

541.18 "Mint Drops"] '~'

541.20 The] "~

541.24 "Drink] "'~

541.30 &] and

541.35 Bondy—"] ~'

941.36 Here] "~

541.38 "A <. . .> repay!"] "'~'

542.1 Bondy's] "~

542.2 &] and

542.3 "A <. . .> Bondy."] "'~'

542.4-5 Bondy <. . .> "Eight <. . . .> d——d!"] "~ '~'

542.6-7 "Bondy <. . .> education."] "'~'

542.8 "Education!" <. . . .> "Education!"] "'~' ~ '~'

542.9 "Yes] "'~

542.18 proffession] profession

542.20 you!"] ~'

542.21 Bondy] "~

542.22 "But] "'~

542.24 so!"] ~'

542.25 Bondy] "~

542.26 concieving] conceiving

542.26-27 "only <. . .> man"] '~'

542.28 "Yes] "'~

543.2 '*good hope*'] "~"

543.8 yourself!"] ~'

543.9 With <. . .> &] "~ and

543.11 gold &] ~ and

543.14 "Help] "'~

543.17 &] and

543.22 figures."] ~'
543.23 Whether] "~
543.24 &] and
543.25 &] and
543.27 "cool hundreds,"] '~'
543.29 morals.] ~"
543. <no chapter number>] *III.*
543.31 *literateur*] *litterateur*
544.9 "How <. . .> Gilfert,"] "'~'
544.9-10 "I <. . . .> garment?"] '~'
544.11-12 "Ah! <. . . .> breeches!"] "'~'
544.13 The] "~
544.14 &] and
544.16-17 "Heavens <. . . .> awkwardly!"] "'~'
544.18 "Ah] "'~
544.21 &] and
544.26 tights!"] ~'"
544.27 D[r]] Dr.
544.29 &] and
544.33 "Much <. . .> Nothing,"] '~'
544.34 "La <. . .> Coquette,"] '~'
545. <no chapter number>] *IV.*
545.5 &] and
545.7 final &] ~ and
545.10 infinity] infirmity (Although the manuscript reading appears to be "infinity," Simms must have intended "infirmity.")
545.22 &] and
545.23 &] and
545.31 *March*] "~
545.32 &] and
546.3 Melpomenene (Simms may have intended to write "Melpomene," but "Melpomenene" may just as easily be taken as Gilfert's pronunciation.)
546.6 milk &] ~ and
546.10 &] and
546.13 &] and
546.19 "Do <. . .> me?," <. . .> I?] "'~?‸' ~.

546.20 “Know you,” <. . .> “haven’t <. . .> honour.”] “ ‘~’ ~ ‘~’

546.21-22 He <. . .> “Well” <. . .> “you <. . .> Bowery.”] “~ ‘~’ ~ ‘~’

546.23 “Bowery” <. . .> “what’s that?”] “ ‘~’ ~ ‘~’

546.24-25 “What <. . .> gentleman” <. . .> “you <. . .> Theatre?”] “ ‘~’ ~ ‘~’

546.26 “I <. . .> not,”] “ ‘~’

546.27 “Not] “ ‘~

546.29 possible.”] ~’

546.30 “No <. . . .> Park?”] “ ‘~’

546.31-32 I <. . .> “Of <. . .> Hilson?”] “~ ‘~’

546.33 “Have <. . .> honour,”] “ ‘~’

546.34-35 “What <. . . .> him.”] “ ‘~’

546.36 “Have <. . .> honour.”] “ ‘~’

546.37 “Honour] “ ‘~

547.1 lying &] ~ and

547.3 & <. . .> pretences.”] and ~’

547.6 &] and

547.7 “I <. . .> business.”] “ ‘~’

547.8 “Well,”] “ ‘~’

547.9-10 “Well” <. . .> “if <. . .> generally?”] ‘~’ ‘~’

547.11 “New York:” <. . .> “what’s that?”] “ ‘~’ ~ ‘~’

547.12 “What <. . .> York?”] “ ‘~’

547.13 “No!”] “ ‘~’

547.14 & the] and ~

547.16 “Well,” <. . .> “my] “ ‘~’ ~ ‘~

547.18 know!”] ~’

547.19 To] “~

547.20 “Then,”] “ ‘~’

547.21-22 “of <. . .> Earth.”] ‘~’

547.23 “Yes] “ ‘~

547.25 here.”] ~’

547.26 “Indeed!”] “ ‘~’

547.27-28 “Well,” <. . .> “Saint <. . .> seat & <. . .> leisure.”] “ ‘~’ ~ ‘~ and ~’

547.29 “No <. . .> won’t,”] “ ‘~’

547.30 “What!” <. . .> “you <. . .> in?”] “ ‘~’ ~ ‘~’

547.33 gentleman &] ~ and

548.1 "Can't!" <. . . .> "Impossible!"] "'~' ~ '~'

548.2-3 "Look <. . .> fellow," <. . .> "you <. . . .> where!"] "'~' ~ '~'"

548. <no chapter number>] *V.*

548.6 &] and

548.11 &] and

548.20 &] and

548.26 murdered?" Mr Gilfert?] ~,∧ Mr. ~"

548.29 Mr] Mr.

549. <no chapter number>] *VI.*

549.4 Dr] Dr.

549.11 &] and

549.13 conspicious] conspicuous

549.14 &] and

549.15 & playfuly] and playfully

549.24 &] and

549.26 &] and

549.29 &] and

549.32 &] and

549.33 form &] ~ and

550.6-7 "The Frankenstein"] '~'

550.7 Mrs] Mrs.

550.11 &] and

550.18 &] and

550.30 "Ah] "'~

551.7 forever."] ~'

551.8 And] "~

551.9 &] and

551.11 soul!] ~"

Table II: Textual Variants

Below is a list of the variants between the rough draft of "The Humours of the Manager" and the fair copy manuscript.

From left to right the chart of variants has the following text sequence:

LEFT MARGIN: Centennial edition key
FIRST READING: rough draft
SECOND READING: fair copy

522.title The Humours of the Manager. By a Reminiscent.] The Humours of the Manager.

522.1 1.2-3 evening, among many,] 1.2 evening

522.2 1.3 house] 1.2 residence

522.2 1.4-7 Francis, of New York, where I had the honour; whenever I happened to be in that city, to be a frequent guest. The Doctor, who was a great
] 1.2-3 Francis of New York. Nobody needs be told that the D^{r} was a famous

522.3 1.8 way, was] 1.4-5 way, was one of the most remarkable of the reminiscents of the city, and was

522.5 1.9-2.3 happy, perhaps, than in gathering a circle of good talkers and good listeners about him. A good talker himself, he was yet quite willing to be a patient listener, when other persons had good things to say. With all other parties he was apt to show himself somewhat impatient. I need not say—to the New Yorker, at least—
] 1.5-9 happy than when he about him a circle of good listeners. Not that he was at all unwilling, himself to listen, when other parties had any thing to say. ¶ I need hardly mention, to those who knew him

522.11 2.7-8 grateful reminiscent.] 1.12-14 agreable talker, while his anecdotes of persons & events perpetually opened new avenues for conversation.

522.13 2.8 Our] 1.15 ¶ Our

522.13 2.9 friend] 1.15 humourist

522.13 2.9 litterateur] 1.15 Litterateur

522.14 2.11-12 old Gentleman, in a recent volume, in the character of Dr Bushwhacker
] 1.16-17 reminiscent in the character of Dr Bushwhacker, in a recent volume

522.15 2.13 natured,] 1.18 ~‸

522.16 2.14 give] 1.18 occasion

522.17 2.16 manner—] 1.19 ~,

522.18 3.1 him] 1.20 ~,

522.18 3.1 burly, and] 1.21 free, burly, in brief,

522.19 3.3 a Boreas] 1.22 Boreas

522.19 3.4 fresh and full of geniality.] 1.22-23 fresh, and as full of stimulating geniality, as a stiff breeze in November.

522.21 3.5 in it,] 1.24 ~∧
522.21 3.6 and] 1.24 always enjoyed it, &
522.22 3.8 observation,] 1.25-26 observation &
522.24 3.10-11 vitality & interest] 1.27 vitality
522.24 3.11 experiences of] 1.27-28 long professional as well as private association with
522.25 3.13-14 specially his intimacy, for] 1.29 his intimacy, especially, for more than
522.27 3.16 cities] 1.30 American cities
522.27 3.16-17 all his] 1.31 lively
522.28 4.1-2 life-like freshness] 1.32 lifelike freshness,
523.2 4.6 had none of those long] 1.34 was none of those demure
523.4 4.9-11 dashed into his subject, *in medias res*, as the poet counsels,
] 2.1-2 had something to tell & told it,—dashing into his subject, as the Poet counsels, *in medias res*,
523.6 4.12 Cavalry,] 2.3 ~∧
523.7 4.13-16 & free, was that of a good-humoured & well bred gentleman at his dinner table;—and so
] 2.4-6 & full of bonhommie, was that of a liberal and portly Virginia Host at his dinner table: and so, with a spirit and humour all his own,
523.10 5.2-3 recollections of the parties in the past whom
] 2.7-8 memories of the past, in men & things, which
523.11 5.4-5 curious present] 2.8 curious,
523.11 5.5 and] 2.9 &
523.12 5.6 tastes,] 2.10 ~∧
523.13 5.9 order,] 2.11-12 class or profession
523.15 5.11 young.] 2.13 young in art and letters.
523.16 5.12-17 with the young was of equal mental and physical benefit to the old. There you met the savant, or the eminent author—poet or painter—from other states & countries.
] 2.14-15 of age with youth was equally beneficial to both parties.
523.17 6.1 untill these] 2.15 for this untill the
523.19 6.6-10 the amateur or incipient genius, whether in art or letters. He could encourage these with hope, and quietly guide them with counsel.

] 2.18-20 or incipient genius, in any province. He could quietly guide them with counsel, and pleasantly encourage them with hope.

523.22 6.12 Doctor,] 2.21 D^{r}

523.23 6.14 pleasant, and] 2.22 grateful &

523.24 6.16 pleasant] 2.23 grateful

523.25 7.1 in,] 2.24 ~—

523.25 7.1 happened,] 2.25 ~—

523.26 7.2 ——in] 2.25 —to use

523.26 7.3 D^{r}—] 2.26 host:—

523.29 7.8-9 adventures] 2.29 adventures & experiences

523.30 7.10 had] 2.30 enjoyed some

523.31 7.12 D^{r}] 2.31-32 Sir Isaac Newton, Lord Bacon, D^{r}

523.32 7.14-8.7 Third; all of which he is preparing for the press of our friends, Harper & Brothers, who welcome his revelations with a degree of appreciation which stints at no amount of money in making itself evident. By the way, the D^{r} gives them no encouragement for the circulation, in the shades, of Webster's dictionary.

] 2.33-36 Third, the last of whom he describes as having quite recovered his wits, though the measure of development is still appropriately small for a crowned head. Of these conversations we shall no doubt have a full report as soon as the publishers are ready.

523.36 8.7-8 all these things we have to wait.] 2.36-37 these we shall need to wait awhile.

523.37 8.9 journies] 2.37 adventures

523.37 8.9-10 him, as you see;] 2.37-3.1 him as you may see,

523.38 8.11 progress] 3.2 material progress

524.1 8.12-13 have done] 3.3 now boast

524.1 8.14 steamboats,] 3.3-4 ~‸

524.2 8.15 rail ways] 3.4 railways

524.2 8.16 electric telegraphing] 3.4 telegraphing

524.3 9.1-2 somewhat to the use of the latter,] 3.6 in this direction,

524.4 9.3 establishing better relations] 3.6-7 a direct intercourse

524.4 9.4-7 world. On this subject, I must refer you to my dear friend & brother in the art, Professor Hare of Philadelphia,—D^{r}

] 3.7-8 world. . . . ¶ "Dr
524.5 9.8 Mucklewabber;] 3.8 Mucklewhabber,
524.6 9.9-10 Scotch Peripatetic philosopher] 3.9 German peripatetic Philosopher
524.6 9.11 hour] 3.10 hour, on foot,
524.7 9.11-12 Miller, yet] 3.10 Miller, &
524.7 9.12 mineralogized,] 3.10-11 ~^
524.8 9.13 moralized,] 3.11 ~^
524.8 9.14 progress.] 3.11-13 progress. He too has his book in preparation, five volumes quarto, with thirty thousand illustrations.
524.11 9.16 together."] 3.15 ~—
524.12 10.1-2 *degagie* yet hearty] 3.16 hearty jovial
524.12 10.2 loud sonorous] 3.17 sonorous
524.13 10.3 a lively] 3.17 lively
524.13 10.3 a great] 3.17 great
524.14 10.6-7 something of our old friend, and remarkable] 3.19 the portrait of our venerable
524.15 10.8-9 reminiscences, confined mostly to New York,] 3.20 recollections
524.16 10.10 portly] 3.21 pleasant & portly
524.16 10.10 but the volume is] 3.21 which is yet very
524.17 10.12-14 local in character, and illustrative of the manners & morals of men deserving of record,] 3.22-23 illustrative of his experiences among men; full of interest,
524.18 10.14 Francis] 3.23 F.
524.18 10.15 knowingly in society,] 3.23 knowingly,
524.19 10.15 supply] 3.24 furnish
524.19 10.16 of such] 3.24 of
524.19 10.16-12.9 volume; but this will task the memories of other reminiscents. Mr H. T. Tuckerman has made his tribute memorial, in a graceful & highly appreciative biography. In any future publication, of local memoirs, Dr F. will not only merit a conspicuous place, but, were his conversations recalled, the work could be made one of very singular interest. ¶ But, it was not my purpose to say much of the Doctor himself, and my notice of him must be recieved as the tribute of one who remembers gratefully the cordiality

of his receptions, and the pleasant graces of his circle. He has been recalled to me especially by a recent publication, two volumes of a history, or chronicle rather, of the New York stage, prepared by an amateur, and industrious compiler of that city. Happening upon certain passages in these volumes, devoted to Charles Gilfert, manager at different periods of the Bowery and Charleston Theatres, I was reminded of one of the many pleasant evenings, at the house of D[r] F., where Gilfert was brought upon the carpet. There happened to be present several gentlemen of letters, most of whom had known Gilfert personally, as well in Charleston as New York, and all of whom had something to say about him.

] 3.24-4.5 volume, which might be made one of singular interest. Such a volume might be commended safely to M[r] Tuckerman or M[r] Duyckinck. ¶ One of the evenings passed at the house of D[r] Francis, has been recalled to me by happening, in a late publication, a chronicle of the New York stage, upon certain passages relating to the once well known Charles Gilfert, famous for his music, and manager, at different periods, of the Bowery and Charleston Theatres. Francis was intimate with Gilfert, was his physician, as he was frequently employed by the leading actors, and the subject of Gilfert's humours being adverted to by one of the company, they became the subject of the evening's conversation, mixed up with incidental references to famous performers. Several gentlemen were present who had also known Gilfert as well in Charleston as in New York, as well in the full flush of his fame as a musician, and late in life, when, hopelessly insane, the strings of the fine instrument were all jangled, and out of tune. Each of these persons had something to contribute to the topic.

524.36 12.11-12 generation now entering upon the stage of life—] 4.6 present generation,

524.37 21.13 it] 4.7 it forever

524.37 12.13 original;] 4.7 ~,

524.38 12.14 humour—] 4.8 jest, of gay capricious humours,

525.2 12.17-18 great tact, great shrewdness & cleverness in many] 4.10-12 equal tact and improvidence, shrewdness and recklessness,—cleverness in sundry

525.4 13.2 reckless] 4.13 capricious

525.4 13.1 life;—] 4.12 ~;

525.4 13.2 mood,] 4.13 ~;

525.4 13.3 *vivant,*—] 4.13 ~‸

525.5 13.4 *bon hommie;*—] 4.14 noble charities;

525.5 13.5-6 brief, a singular & contradictory compound of the *Genus Homo.*
] 4.14-17 brief one of those anomalies in endowment and character, the very caprices of whom have been too often supposed the certain indicatives of genius.

525.9 13.9 though] 4.19 ~,

525.10 13.10 periods,] 4.20 ~‸

525.10 13.11 Christendom,—] 4.20 ~,

525.11 13.14 fredom] 4.22 freedom

525.11 13.14 many various circles—] 4.22 various circles

525.12 13.15 was] 4.22 became

525.12 13.16 of mind] 4.23 in mind

525.12 13.16 & character.—] 4.23 & manner.

525.13 13.17 every situation—] 4.23-24 all situations—

525.13 13.17 cool,] 4.24 cool self possessed and

525.14 13.18-19 conversation;] 4.25 ~,

525.15 13.19-14/15.1 conceptive capacity, which enabled him readily
] 4.25-26 power of conception, the fruit of a lively fancy,—he had the art

525.16 14/15.3 company, and] 4.27 company &

525.17 14/15.4 guise] 4.28 character

525.18 14/15.6 droll] 4.29-30 humourist and Droll

525.19 14/15.6-7 reminiscents,] 4.31 ~‸

525.19 14/15.7 *re-union*] 4.31 reunion

525.19 14/15.8-9 I now speak, in the house of Dr Francis, each had] 4.31-32 we write, had each

525.20 14/15.10-13 to make to the conversation, illustrative of some one or other of the moral phases, or pecularities, of Charles Gilfert.

] 4.32-33 of anecdote illustrative of these characteristics.

525.21 14/15.14 said—] 4.33 told the following:

525.22 14/15.15-17 "I remember Gilfert when I was quite a boy, and after I had grown up to be a man. He] 4.34 "Gilfert

525.22 14/15.17-16.6 loose of build, and wore green spectacles. Over these spectacles, & sometimes under them, he had a trick of looking at you, when his mood was quizzical, when] 4.34-15.1 of heavy build, somewhat loose of limb, careless in his gait, and remarkable by his green spectacles, under or over which he was accustomed to look, when he was disposed to indulge in a sly mood & when his humours were quizzical, or

525.26 16.6-9 or when he desired to provoke the smile of his companions for the time. He was careless in business matters,] 5.1-4 without in any way discovering himself. His green spectacles, could upon occasion, as we shall see, be exchanged for blue. Careless in business,

525.29 16.10 his debts. He] 5.4-5 debt, to which he

525.29 16.11-16 reluctant, at acts of this nature, as Sheridan, and had as many clever subterfuges by which to escape his creditors, baffle them for the time, and even procure fresh loans. His credit, finally became

] 5.5-9 reluctant as Sheridan, he also possessed that happy art of Sheridan by which he could not only baffle his creditor for the time, but even procure additional loans. With all his cleverness, however, his credit grew finally

525.32 16.17 Charleston, in this respect,] 5.9 Charleston

525.33 16.18 him; and,] 5.10 him, and

525.34 17.1 Manager] 5.10 manager

525.34 17.1-3 old Charleston Theatre, at the west end of Broad Street,] 5.11 Theatre in that city,

525.35 17.4 credit] 5.12 ~,

525.35 17.5 *her*] 5.12 her

525.36 17.6-11 in part, having assistants. He was too careless, too fond of pleasure & society, to be very methodical or capable of business, no matter how large the interest.

] 5.13-14 and just as careless in the management of the Theatre, as he was in his private affairs.

526.1 17.11-12 His wife, on the contrary,] 5.15 Mrs Gilfert

526.1 17.13 Charleston.] 5.15-17 Charleston, not only as a noble actress, but as a woman of elevated tone and character.

526.3 17.14 purity & character free] 5.17 purity

526.3 17.15-16 freedoms & familiarities] 5.18 familiarities, the freedom & levity

526.4 17.16-19 stage, with a degree of dignity and self esteem that compelled the respect of all.
] 5.18-20 stage; while her bearing was as dignified & lofty, as her character was above question.

526.7 18.2 man] 5.22 person

526.7 18.3 honour,] 5.22 fair name

526.8 18.4 person,] 5.23 ~‸

526.8 18.6-8 actors,—Young or Caldwell, I forget which—in a duel, for attempting some liberties
] 5.24-25 actors—Young, I think, in a duel because of some liberties taken with her person,

526.10 18.9 situation,] 5.26 ~‸

526.11 18.11 was, I believe,] 5.26 was

526.12 18.12 and] 5.28-29 and was tenacious of what, in that day, was called "the Point of Honour.

526.13 18.14 Cogdale,] 5.29 ~‸

526.14 18.14 to] 5.30 for

526.14 18.15 Wigwall] 5.31 Wigfall

526.14 18.16-17 District—an elder brother, I believe,] 5.31 District, a kinsman

526.16 18.19 and] 5.32-33 & more recently

526.16 19.1 Army of the Southern Confederacy] 5.33 Confederate armies

526.18 19.2-3 a noble actress as well as a fine woman.
] 5.34-35 unquestionably one of the most finished of actresses in her day in America.

526.20 19.5-15 in the dramatic art.* She belonged to the Siddons School. Her ròle was chiefly High Comedy & tragedy; and certainly her Lady Townly, Lady Macbeth, her Queen Catharine & other similar grand parts in the higher drama, were rarely surpassed or equalled on the American Stage,

within my memory. She lingered too long upon the stage for her reputation, as an actress,—
] 5.36-6.13 especially in Dramatic Art. She had been highly educated, and few women have ever shown themselves more capable of appreciating & nicely discriminating the characters which they sought to personate. She was equally eminent in Tragedy, and in High Comedy. Her Lady Townly was a conquest over art and nature; and, by all contemporaries was admitted to be superior in finish & general excellence to any previous or contemporary performance of the part. Her Lady Macbeth was one of those grand representations which fasten upon the imagination forever. It was never surpassed in this country, and was held by good judges at the time to be second only to the personation of that character, by the great Siddons, to whose school she belonged. She survived her reputation, lingered too long upon the stage,

526.33 19.17 became] 6.14 grew

526.33 19.18-20.1 neglect, & the decline of favour which
] 6.14-15 the decline of public favour, which, as is usual in such cases,

526.35 20.2-4 power. She resented the public neglect, and, I remember, perfectly,
] 6.16-17 power in herself. I remember perfectly

526.36 20.6 hostile,] 6.18 hostile towards her,

526.37 20.7 carriage] 6.19 ~,

526.37 20.8 held to be] 6.19 considered

526.38 20.8-10 dignified while the public fancied it to be arrogant &
] 6.20-21 dignified, but which her audiences held it to be arrogant and

527.2 20.12 finally failed, after several experiments.] 6.22 failed.

527.2 20.13 musician, however,] 6.22 musician,

527.2 20.14-15 cherished in Charleston; and,] 6.23 greatly esteemed, and

527.3 20.16 a] 6.24 also a

527.5 21.1 violinist & pianist—the latter chiefly—] 6.25 pianist & violinist,

527.5 21.1-5 taxed, for performance on the stage, as an attraction still to be relied upon to secure an increase of audience. He was however chary of these exhibitions.
] 6.26-29 taxed on the stage as an added attraction to the dramatic performance. He was chary of these appearances, and the announcement of them was always welcomed by a good audience.

527.9 21.6 But] 6.30" ~

527.9 21.7-8 for him, as a practical musician,] 6.30-31 of his music, as a performer,

527.10 21.9-13 he suffered the public to know that he was also a *Composer*, and that they were commonly in the enjoyment of his pieces, published from
] 6.31-33 the Charleston public knew him also as a fine composer. He kept his secret, though composing much, & published his compositions

527.12 21.13-22.5 *nom de plume*. The music of these pieces was mostly engraved in Germany; though some perhaps, were published, as from Germany, by Seigling a worthy German music dealer & publisher in Charleston. Gilfert assumed a title with his *nom de plume*. The pieces were usually published as by
] 6.34-35 nom de plume—that of a German nobleman—

527.13 22.6 *von*] 6.35 von

527.14 22.7-9 —When this practice became known to some of his friends, one of them asked him
] 6.36 When asked

527.15 22.11-13 in the local reputation which he enjoyed, as a musician. He
] 6.37 by reason of his local reputation, he

527.16 22.15 English:] 7.1 ~—

527.18 23.1 the] 7.3 as

527.18 23.2 violinist &] 7.4 violinist and

527.19 23.3 are] 7.4 are apt to be

527.19 23.3-4 author's when they] 7.5 author's who

527.21 23.5 people that] 7.6 persons who

527.22 23.7 yes,] 7.8 ~!

527.22 23.8 well,—*but to compose*] 7.8 well—but composition!

527.23 23.9 thing!] 7.9 thing.

527.23 23.10-12 But there are other reasons. Music & poetry, and all the fine arts,
] 7.9-15 They will be willing to admit that you are something, and somebody, but you must not be too much thing or body. That makes them jealous. Besides, there is another good reason. The people of this country have too little selfesteem, to venture to judge for themselves, in matters of the fine arts, without the sanction of foreign opinion. The arts

527.29 23.13-15 water before this people will acknowledge them to be good. You see, your
] 7.15-16 water, like old maderia, to be recognized as legitimate. Your

527.30 23.16 provincial. They *recieve*] 7.17-19 provincial now. They will outgrow it; but now, & for a good many years they recieve & will continue to recieve their

527.32 23.17 *make*] 7.19 make

527.33 23.18 opinion.] 7.20 opinion in matters of art.

527.33 24.1 afraid always] 7.20 afraid

527.33 24.2 at; and they feel] 7.21 at, and find

527.34 24.3-4 sneer, and turn up their noses] 7.21 sneer

527.34 24.4 *home* productions] 7.21 home production

527.34 24.5 to risk their credit,] 7.22 risk their reputations

527.35 24.5 critics,] 7.22 ~∧

527.36 24.8 where] 7.23-24 my friends that where

527.36 24.9 make their own] 7.24 *make*

527.37 24.10 can not] 7.24-25 cannot

527.37 24.10-12 reputation.—No! they wait for the verdict, and the wine, from across
] 7.25 reputation. The wit as the wine must cross

527.38 24.14 Poet.—"Tis *distance*] 7.26 Poet. "Tis Distance

528.1 24.15-16 view." It is true in this thing.] 7.27 view."

528.1 24.17 away the] 7.27 all the

528.1 24.18-25.2 object. What says the proverb—I believe it is from the Scriptures—
] 7.28 object.

528.3 25.5-6 streets, or in the market-place] 7.29 market place

528.3 25.6-7 beef and] 7.30 my little basket of beef &
528.4 25.7-8 and pork & onions,—] 7.30-31 mutton & onions and other things—
528.5 25.9 specks, &] 7.32 ~ and
528.5 25.10 along, just] 7.32 the streets
528.5 25.11-12 of the Mill among themselves—] 7.32-33 the Miller,—nay, perhaps,—who knows—
528.7 25.14-15 some of you] 7.34 you
528.7 25.15-26.1 quite unable to keep myself from grazing the wall, or embracing, the lamp-posts—how should how] 7.35-37 not always able to keep a right line as I go,—perhaps, embracing the wall, or a lamppost, to preserve my equilibrium—how
528.10 26.2-3 a Grand Master of Musical] 7.37-8.1 one of the Grand Masters of Musical
528.11 26.4 composers that shall] 8.1-2 great geniuses that expects to
528.11 26.5 posterity,] 8.2 ~‸
528.12 26.7-8 masters—in the character of the Baron Von &c."] 8.3-6 composers. They will believe it of the Baron Von, &c. whom they have never seen, but not of Charles Gilfert, who is but five feet seven inches in their eyes."
528.15 26.9 close] 8.7 close his rambling harangue
528.16 26.10 side] 8.8 sides
528.16 26.11-27.4 inquiring companion. ¶ Gilfert was very proud of his music, very confident of its future, as well as present triumphs, and, whatever its acknowledged merits at the time, he was never quite satisfied that the acknowledgement made any approach to the real claims of his genius. Genius, it was, in the opinion of many, as in his own conviction; and one] 8.8-14 companion, & staring at him, through his green glasses, with the most comical expression. He had seriously spoken, however, when he affirmed his own convictions of his rank as a musical genius. Here, his self esteem was indomitable, and he continued firm in this conviction of his future fame to the last. One
528.21 27.4-5 anecdotes given of him, during] 8.14 anecdotes of

528.21 27.5 evening,] 8.14 ~‸
528.22 27.7 hope, and] 8.15 ~‸ &
528.22 27.7 aspirations,] 8.15-16 ~‸
528.22 27.7 imagination,] 8.16 ~‸
528.23 27.8-10 this hereafter.* ¶ Our] 8.16-17 of this hereafter. Our
528.24 27.11-28.7 reminiscences. These, by the way, I have summed together, for the sake of order, though they were given in a desultory manner, in the way of conversation, rather than narrative; the company, most of whom knew Gilfert, interposing with suggestions of doubt & inquiry occasionally, which led to frequent discussion. The main facts, however, were generally assented to. The Charlestonian proceeded.
] 8.17 reminiscences.
528.25 28.9 manager] 8.18 Proprietor
528.26 28.10 a tragic drama] 8.19 an original tragic Drama
528.28 28.15-18 Bandit," "Schinderhannes the Robber of the Rhine," and "The Robbers" of Schiller, were] 8.22-23 Bandit" Schinderhannes" &c. were the
528.30 29.1 hear] 8.23-24 hear, in our times,
528.30 29.2-3 talk now-a-days of the sensational in novel writing; but
] 8.24-25 critical talk, in regard to the sensational in literature. But
528.31 29.4 sensational] 8.25-26 sensational *not* an element
528.32 29.5-30.12 drama—nay, even in music, painting & statuary—not a recognized element in all the arts which appeal to the sensuous, to human passions, and—briefly—to an impure, uneducated vulgar taste? Society, itself, is every where the creature of the sensational. Athens, with all her grand masters, &, in all her glory, was a people highly sensational, perpetually curious, demanding novelty, and as sneered at by Demosthenes running about & asking "What Philip is doing?" We must be content to accept even the vulgar sensational, if only as evidence that there is an anxious stirring of the popular mind, craving curiously after mental excitements, which, in their untrained conditions

must necessarily be morbid & sensuous to a large degree. "*The Female Assassin*" was of this very character. Gilfert recieved the MS very courteously &
] 8.26-35 Drama, and briefly in every province of the fine arts. Athens, in the days of her greatest glory, under Pericles, was quite as sensational as New York, but without the myriad agencies of the latter city, in diversifying and accumulation of those sensational objects which appeal to the sensuous nature—to human passion, curiosity & the love of change.— ¶ "Enough, that "the Female Assassin"—the new drama, anticipated some of the monstrosities of the modern stage. Gilfert recieved the manuscript very

529.1 30.14 him,] 8.36 ~‸

529.2 30.15-31.1 F.F.S.C.'s—a gentleman of the genuine *blue* "*sang azul*", pure in 30 quarterings running through as many generations. This gentleman
] 8.36-9.2 fashionable gentlemen of the city—one of the genuine *sang azul*—who could number thirty quarterings on his escutcheon. Such a man

529.4 31.1 He] 9.2 Besides, he

529.5 31.3 drama; a regular patron &] 9.3 Drama, a constant

529.5 31.4-6 theatre; a person who kept his stud, was
] 9.3-4 theatre—a man of fancy, who kept a famous stud,

529.6 31.7-9 Jockey Club of S.C.; ran a blooded nag, and—*bled freely!* He
] 9.5-8 jockey club, who entered his blooded horses annually for the turf. He was also fond of cards, and—bled freely. These qualifications commended him especially to Gilfert's favour, and he

529.10 31.10 theatre] 9.9 Theatre

529.10 31.11 Gilfert] 9.9 Gilfert's

529.10 31.11 coterie,] 9.9 ~‸

529.11 31.12 all] 9.9 most of

529.11 31.12 circles,] 9.10 ~‸

529.11 31.13 where] 9.10 in which

529.11 31.14 &] 9.10 and

529.12 31.14-15 gentleman] 9.11 amateur Dramatist

529.12 31.16 & was] 9.12 was

529.13 31.17 & at] 9.12-13 and at
529.13 31.17-18 rehearsals,—where he] 9.13 rehearsals, and
529.14 32.1 actresses] 9.14 & sprightly actresses
529.14 32.2-3 Though somewhat *passée* himself,] 9.14 Though
529.15 32.4-8 he was yet to be conciliated. He gave fine supper & dinner parties. His cellar was stocked with old madeira. He was liberal. He gave handsome presents; and the] 9.15-19 the heroines of the stage gave him such welcome as would better comport with one more youthful of age & aspect. They too had reasons for conciliating his favour. He was rich, liberal, gave fine dinners, delicious suppers, and occasionally very handsome presents. The
529.20 32.9-16 actress, secured her, the next day, some costly ornament, or jewel, ruby, pearl or diamond, which, it sufficiently gratified the donor's heart, if displayed upon her head or bosom, at the next nights performance] 9.20-24 actress were apt to be rewarded with some rich jewel, ruby or diamond, which it sufficiently delighted the Donor's heart, to see displayed the next night, upon the damsel's head or bosom
529.23 32.16 But] 9.25 "~,
529.23 32.17 sportsman] 9.25 sporting
529.23 32.17 proclivities,] 9.25 ~‸
529.24 33.1 of our] 9.26 of the
529.24 33.2-3 authorship, was quite as fervent & as] 9.27-28 dramatic authorship was paramount, and quite as earnest &
529.26 33.5 triumph.] 9.29 triumph. It was to glorify him.
529.27 33.7-9 theatre should crown him with a sudden glory. The deference, &] 9.30-31 theatre, were to lift him to the seventh heaven of self satisfaction. The
529.29 33.9 delight,] 9.32 ~‸
529.29 33.11 his drama,] 9.32 the MS.
529.31 33.14-15 week he called at the Theatre. He] 9.34 week, he
529.31 33.15 manager's room. ¶] 9.34 manager.
529.32 33.17 There was] 9.35 He was surrounded by
529.32 33.17-34.13 fellows around him—the regular *habitues*—such as are to be found in all theatres; actors, amateurs,

editors, *et id omne genus*, in which we include the Lounger, the gamester, the *bon vivant*, the small critic, the *roué* & occasional bore! Wine stood in portly decanters upon the table, and cigars were in abundance. ¶ "Happy to see you, my friend"; cried Gilfert embracing the incipient dramatist. "You are just in time. Come, gentlemen, a seat & a glass for Col ———. Ah! my friend, you are welcome.

9.36-10.1 fellows. He broke through the circle, embraced the amateur, and cried out— ¶ "Ah! my dear friend, I am so happy to see you.

529.35 34.14 drama] 10.2 play

529.35 34.14 yours!] 10.2 ~.

529.35 34.15 h———] 10.2 ———

529.35 34.15 sensation!] 10.3 ~.

529.36 34.16-17 and most magnificent situations!] 10.3-4 & magnificent sensations.

529.36 34.17 Fred.] 10.4 ~∧

529.37 34.18-19 hero! He is the very man for it!
] 10.4-6 hero—Mrs Hughes the heroine. I have concieve all the cast already. It is a grand thing.

529.38 34.20 grand d———d] 10.6 ——— grand

529.39 34.20 sensation!] 10.6 ~.

530.1 35.1 dramatist] 10.7 delighted Dramatist

530.1 35.1-3 seat delighted. His glass was filled with Madeira; emptied & refilled.
] 10.7-8 seat, amid the circle. The Madeira was put in circulation.

530.3 35.4 and] 10.9 &

530.3 35.5 author. The author] 10.9 author, who

530.3 35.6 speech] 10.10 speech in reply

530.4 35.7-13 it; and, slapping the aristocrat on the shoulder, congratulated him with the showers of glory that were to envelope him so soon as the "*Female Assassin*" should be given to an admiring world. And all
] 10.10-12 it, & slapping the amateur upon his shoulders dubbed him with all of his anticipated fame. All

530.5 35.13-14 merry as the] 10.12 merrily as

530.6 35.14-19 Glass after glass of Madeira wound up the scene & the parties, & the dramatist, so soon to be glorified, went off with his head in the skies, and his feet treading on air!] 10.13-16 The Madeira continued to circulate. The circle squared into a whist party; and the dramatist, somewhat lighter of pocket, went off, with head in the skies, and feet treading the etherial plains.

530.9 36.1 So,] 10.17 "~∧

530.9 36.1-8 week, the Dramatist, sought the Manager, to be hailed with the same sort of welcome; to be assured of the same successes; always dismissed with the declaration, that "*The Female Assassin*" was destined to make a grand d———d sensation!
] 10.17-21 week elapsed, and at every visit of the author to the manager, he met with the same enthusiastic reception; was assured of his successes, and dismissed with the passionate phrase, "Your play will make a most ——— grand sensation!"

530.13 36.9 said] 10.22 quoth

530.13 36.9 manager—] 10.22 ~,

530.13 36.10 build upon your tragedy] 10.22-23 build, my dear Colonel, upon that grand drama

530.14 36.11-12 public, & with] 10.24 public &

530.15 36.14 time] 10.25 season

530.16 36.14 d———d] 10.26 ———

530.16 36.15-18 taste. You see for yourself. The house is rarely full. We are playing half the time to empty boxes.
] 10.26 taste for theatricals.

530.17 36.19 up;] 10.27 ~—

530.17 36.19 theatre;] 10.27 ~—

530.18 36.21 d———d] 10.28 ———

530.18 36.21 and] 10.28 &

530.18 36.21 de new] 10.29 the new

530.18 37.1 era when there shall be a general] 10.29 era of

530.19 37.3-4 —Yes, my dear friend, your piece] 10.30 Your play

530.20 37.4 us] 10.30 us, my friend

530.20 37.5-6 grand d———d great sensation!"] 10.31 ——— grand & glorious sensation.

530.22 37.7 Fancy] 10.32 "~

530.22 37.7 assuances, given] 10.32 assurances repeated

530.22 37.8 week] 10.32-33 week, throughout a tedious term of three months

530.23 37.9 dramatist] 10.34 Dramatist

530.24 37.9-10 always received with] 10.34 hailed with equal

530.25 37.12 one, he] 10.35-36 one class and

530.26 37.13 and gave] 10.36 gave

530.26 37.13-14 presents. Gamed] 10.37 presents; gamed

530.26 37.14 Manager, and] 10.37 manager's circle &

530.27 37.15-38.5 gentleman!—"Talked Horse" with the Jockey Club, and occasionally joined in a sweepstakes; but regularly, every Saturday, he sought Gilfert in his office, only to listen to the same flatulent eulogies upon the tragic bantling, which was kept in such judicious reserve, in order to renovate the falling fortunes of the theater, at the perilous moment. ¶ But
] 11.1-4 gentleman. Gilfert still enthusiastic in his assurances, in behalf of the new tragedy, had yet shown no signs of putting it upon the boards. ¶ "But

530.30 38.5 told,] 11.4 ~‸

530.30 38.5-6 deferred hope,] 11.4 hope deferred

530.31 38.7-8 Weeks, rolled on,—months slipt away; the
] 11.5-7 Our dramatist was no longer satisfied with the fine speeches of the manager. The theatrical season was passing rapidly away;

530.33 38.10 at hand, and,] 11.8 approaching, and

530.34 38.10 warm] 11.9 hot

530.34 38.12 likely] 11.9 apt

530.34 38.12 find] 11.9-10 find much

530.35 38.13 May;—] 11.10 ~,‸

530.35 38.14 dramatist] 11.11 Dramatist

530.36 38.15-39.7 things; but the grand assurances of Gilfert kept him in heart, though doubting oftentimes. But, one morning, he was startled to find the announcement in the Newspapers that one of the actors was to take a benefit. The next day it was a stock actress; the third day another benefit, and so on through the week. ¶ On this Saturday he could stand it no longer. He began to suspect
] 11.11-17 things, and began to doubt the good faith of

the manager. He was in this mood when he was suddenly startled one morning at seeing the announcement of a Benefit for one of the actors. The next day, a stock actress took her benefit. And so through the week. The endurance of our amateur was at an end. He felt

531.3 39.10 managers;] 11.18 ~—

531.3 39.11 dramatic authors;] 11.19 Dramatic authors

531.4 39.12-13 selfishness, & stupidity,] 11.20 ~‸ and ~‸

531.4 39.13 pieces; &] 11.20-21 ~—and

531.5 39.15 F.F.S.C.,] 11.21-22 fashionable gentleman

531.7 39.16 He] 11.23 "~

531.7 39.16-17 theatre. He] 11.23 theatre where he

531.8 39.18 well-known] 11.24 ~‸~

531.8 39.19 table] 11.25 round table

531.9 39.19-40.1 old Madeira; glasses & goblets convenient, &—] 11.25-27 corpulent decanter of old Madeira; with convenient goblets; and there too, ready for use, were

531.10 40.2 cards!—] 11.27 ~.

531.11 40.4 welcome. An] 11.28 welcome—an

531.11 40.5 time,] 11.29 ~‸

531.12 40.6 German] 11.29 fervent German

531.13 40.7 friend,] 11.30 ~;

531.13 40.8 there,] 11.31 Gentlemen—

531.14 40.9 ———] 11.31 ———.

531.14 40.9 let us drink,] 11.32 we will drink

531.15 40.10-11 your play, and] 11.32 that grand tragedy &

531.16 40.12 But] 11.34 "~

531.16 40.13-16 dignity. Once persuaded that he had been trifled with—perhaps laughed at—he was not to be soothed by any of the usual *placebos* of speech.
] 11.34 dignity.

531.16 40.16 sit—] 11.35 be seated &

531.17 40.17-19 drink—declined all civilities—was, in brief, upon his dignity! ¶ "Why, my
] 11.35-12.1 drink. Gilfert, with the tenderest consideration, taking his hands fervently within his own, exclaimed: ¶ "My

531.19 41.1-2 sit—you] 12.2 sit. You

531.20 41.2-3 drink—And, now. I look at you,] 12.2-3 drink! Ah! I see. I look into your eyes and see that
531.22 41.5-6 liver, my friend. That d———d] 12.5 liver! That ———d
531.22 41.7 liable to these irregularities.] 12.5-6 getting out of order.
531.23 41.8 physic. Take the] 12.6 some blue
531.23 41.9 to night,] 12.6 tonight
531.24 41.10 to morrow. That shall make you all right.] 12.7 in the morning.
531.25 41.11-14 I believe I am all right. I am conscious of no such irregularities as you suggest. My skin is free.] 12.8-9 but I have no complaint to make of my liver.
531.26 41.14 good;] 12.9 is good, and
531.27 41.16 I have come—Sir] 12.10-11 My object here, Mr Gilfert, is to
531.30 41.19 inactive,] 12.13 ~;
531.30 41.20 unmistable] 12.14 unmistakable
531.31 42.2 half-circle] 12.15 ~‸~
531.32 42.4 your liver] 12.16 the liver
531.33 42.5 and] 12.17 and then
531.34 42.6 you] 12.18 ~,
531.34 42.6 Gilfert; but] 12.18 Gilfert. But
531.34 42.7-8 for any prescription. I do not need any.] 12.19 in search of medical advice.
531.36 42.10-11 the MS. of my drama] 12.20 my Drama
531.37 42.12 —Return] 12.21 return
531.37 42.12-13 the MS. of your drama] 12.21 your Drama
531.37 42.13 friend!] 12.21 dear friend.
531.38 42.14 mine] 12.22 my
531.38 42.15-16 the play] 12.23 that play
531.39 42.16 fortunes] 12.23 fortune
531.39 42.17 theatre.] 12.23 ~!
532.1 42.18 man] 12.24 sinner
532.1 42.19 d——dest] 12.25 ——dest
532.1 42.19-43.3 that was ever made in Charleston, or any where, I may venture to say,] 12.25 ever yet made

532.2 43.3-4 —My friend, it] 12.26 It

532.2 43.4-5 impossible! How can you ask it?] 12.26 impossible!

532.2 43.6 suicide! To blow] 12.27 suicide. Blow

532.3 43.7-8 pistol! To swallow arsenic] 12.27-28 pistol. Swallow laudanum & arsenic

532.4 43.8-9 go drown myself,] 12.28 go

532.4 43.10 off,] 12.29 off and drown myself

532.5 43.11 river;—] 12.29-30 river, well

532.5 43.12 and crabs, & eels,] 12.30 crabs & eels

532.6 43.13 Charles Gilfert's carcass] 12.31 the poor carcass of Charles Gilfert

532.6 43.14 after!] 12.32 ~.

532.7 43.15 play] 12.32 tragedy

532.8 43.16-18 very long; and, when it does, there shall be the grand d——d sensation.
] 12.33-34 long, and you shall witness the grandest——

532.9 44.1 "Thank] 12.35 ¶ ~

532.9 44.1 but,] 12.35 ~‸

532.9 44.2-4 it shall *not!* I have heard this story long enough, and often enough, and, you will permit me to say, it
] 12.35-37 my play shall not be presented on these boards. These fine words, Mr Gilfert

532.11 44.5 longer!] 12.37 ~.

532.12 44.6 friend?] 13.1 ~.

532.13 44.7 Ay,] 13.2 ~‸

532.13 44.7 me!] 13.2 ~.

532.13 44.8-9 satisfied that all these professions & protestations amount to nothing. You
] 13.2-3 satisfied, Mr Gilfert that you

532.14 44.10 mean, Mr Gilfert,] 13.3 mean

532.14 44.11 piece!] 13.3 ~.

532.15 44.12 Do not] 13.4 Not

532.15 44.13 sensational drama] 13.4 Drama

532.15 44.13 How] 13.5 and how

532.16 44.14 know that?] 13.5 knows that.

532.17 44.15 season] 13.6 theatrical season

532.17 44.15-17 over, Sir. The hot weather is coming on, and, for all this week, I see that your
] 13.6 over. Your

532.19 44.19-45.8 Nothing." ¶ "I know what it means very well, Sir! I know that it is a sure sign that the theatrical season is over, & that you are about to close the Theatre." ¶ "It means nothing of the kind! It is a *ruse de guerre*, my dear friend. It is just as if we told the people, "Come one, come all, before it be too late." Now, Sir, though we call these the benefits of particular actors & actresses, we shares with them!] 13.8-10 Nothing! That, my friend, is a mere *ruse de theatre*. We shares with the actors all these benefits.

532.21 45.9-10 popularity, whatever it is,] 13.10 popularities,

532.21 45.10-11 house. We divides the profits with them.] 13.11 house.

532.21 45.12-19 There is no good reason why the theatrical season in Charleston, should end in April;—why it should not last through May; for the Theatre is coolly, is most beautifuly situate on the water; open to the South & West & East, & the five other points of the compass;—and we are always cool, my friend! Come, dont
] 13.11 Come! Come, my friend; don't

532.22 45.19-20 unreasonable; sit down &] 13.12 unreasonable. Sit down, and

532.23 45.20 little stoup] 13.12 bumper

532.23 45.20-46.1 this this] 13.12 this

532.23 46.1 Madeira] 13.13-15 Madeira, with all these gentlemen, your friends and mine. They will turn out strong as thunder when your piece is played

532.26 46.2-3 Gilfert, but I must decline!] 13.16 Gilfert; but no more of this.

532.27 46.4-5 restore me my MS.] 13.17 return my M.S.

532.28 46.7 this; Gilfert going] 13.18-19 this, in spite of the dogged resolution displayed by the amateur. Gilfert went

532.30 46.9 promising, and] 13.21 and

532.30 46.10 up, always,] 13.21 up

532.30 46.10-11 frequent assurance,] 13.21 frequently repeated assurance

532.31 46.12 played,] 13.22 ~;

532.32 46.13 be a "grand d——d sensation] 13.23-24 prove the "d——est, grandest of all Dramatic sensations

532.33 46.14 It was all] 13.25 All

532.33 46.14 vain!] 13.25 ~.
532.33 46.15 F.F.S.C., was up, and] 13.25 amateur was
532.34 46.16 any sedatives;] 13.26 the old sedatives,
532.34 46.17-47.1 Gilfert rose and went to his escritoir, exclaiming—¶ "It is very
] 13.27-30 Gilfert proceeded to look up the precious M.S. Throwing open his escritoir, he soliloquized in the following fashion for the benefit of the author. ¶ "It is terrible
532.37 47.2 great] 13.30 such great
532.38 47.2 that drama!] 13.31 this drama.
532.38 47.3 grand d——d] 13.31-32 most grand monstrous
533.1 47.4-5 not been profitable] 13.32-33 had such losses
533.2 47.6 up—would] 13.33-34 up! Would
533.2 47.7 treasury!] 13.34-35 Treasury. Mein Gott! Mein Gott!—
533.3 47.8 earnest] 13.35 in earnest
533.3 47.8 friend] 13.35 ~,
533.3 47.8 resolute,] 13.35 ~‸
533.4 47.9 play played] 13.36 piece played,
533.4 47.10 present it, with Frederick] 13.37 put it on the boards—with entire new scenery—with Fred
533.5 47.11 and M^rs] 14.1 —M^rs
533.6 47.12 and] 14.1-2 —~
533.7 47.13-15 —Ah! well!—Eh! Mein Gott!—" ¶ "I *am*
] 14.2-9 and Mrs Gray as the chambermaid——" ¶ "There is no chambermaid in my tragedy, Mr Gilfert."—indignantly ¶ 'To be sure there is no chambermaid. How I should make that blunder.—But, what say you now, my friend. You are really not in earnest?" ¶ "I am
533.13 47.15-17 Gilfert. I give up all hope of seeing my play produced this‸ season. I
] 14.9 Gilfert; and
533.14 47.18-19 M.S." ¶ "Eh! bien!—"] 14.10-12 MS." ¶ "Mein Gott!—Demand! Eh bien!" ¶ And
533.16 47.19-48.2 from a shelf in the escritoir, a huge bundle of MSS. and turning them over. ¶ "Ah! my friend,
] 14.12-16 a huge pile of MSS. from a shelf, he proceeded to turn over, and canvas their titles. Here, a new dilemma

beset him, and turning to the author, some what awkwardly, he said— ¶ "Ah! one thing, my dear friend—

533.19 48.3 grand d——d play] 14.17 famous grand drama

533.21 48.5 What!] 14.18 ~,

533.21 48.5 don't know even] 14.18 do not even remember

533.21 48.6 play that] 14.19 drama which

533.23 48.8 And] 14.20 ~—

533.23 48.8 name?] 14.20 ~!

533.24 48.11 remembers] 14.22 remember

533.26 48.13 play is the "Female Assassin."] 14.23-24 play, Sir, is called "The Female Assassin!"—

533.27 48.14 &] 14.24 and

533.28 48.15 Gilfert] 14.25 "~

533.28 48.15 piles] 14.25 pile

533.28 48.16-19 MS. one by one, and muttering over each, "Female Assassin," "Female Assassin," as he lifted MS. after M.S." ¶ "It is
] 14.25-28 MS.S. play by play, kept muttering, "Female Assassin!" "Female Assassin!' till he had gone through the whole collection. ¶ "Tis

533.31 48.19 there.] 14.28 ~!

533.31 48.19-20 that bundle. He drew another,] 14.28-29 the one collection & taking down another

533.32 49.1 bulk, from another shelf, and] 14.29-30 dimensions, with which he

533.33 49.2-4 process. ¶ "Female Assassin! Female Assassin!" 'Tis] 14.30-32 process, with a like result. ¶ "Tis

533.34 49.5-11 is dat d——d female assassin. Ah!" ¶ Here he found another bundle, which he examined with the same result. He was bewildered. ¶ "Where the H——l is that female assassin?"
] 14.32-35 the d——l is that d——d "Female Assassin." ¶ "A third pile resulted in no discovery. The manager was evidently gravelled. The author grew frightened.

533.38 49.13-14 lost!" cried the author, now in visible alarm.] 14.36 lost!"

534.2 49.17 lost,] 15.1 ~‸

534.2 49.17 always able] 15.1 sure

534.2 49.18 Ah!] 15.2 Ah! Stop!

534.3 49.19-50.3 —Taking a nother pile from a drawer, and going over it with as little profit as all the rest. ¶ "Where] 15.2-6 And, from a fourth receptacle, he drew another pile of MSS. But the Female Assassin still eluded his search. ¶ "Where,

534.5 50.3 H——l] 15.6 d——

534.5 50.3-4 "female assassin?"] 15.6 Female Assassin!"

534.6 50.5 Sir?] 15.7 ~!

534.6 50.6-7 now turning over the huge piles] 15.8-9 who now proceeded, with trembling fingers, to turn over the several piles of MS.S.

534.9 50.8 here!"—] 15.10 ~."‸

534.9 50.8 Gilfert, now] 15.10 Gilfert utterly

534.9 50.9 wits] 15.10 wit's

534.10 50.10-11 to other shelves, to other drawers, but all in vain.] 15.11-14 from shelf to shelf, from drawer to drawer, untill he had explored every possible hole & corner which could possibly hide the "Female Assassin," but without result.

534.13 50.12 d——d] 15.15 d——

534.13 50.12 women] 15.15 woman

534.14 50.15 where] 15.17 ~,

534.15 50.16 copies, and she's as curious as H——] 15.17-18 play books and she's curious as ——

534.15 50.17 pieces!] 15.18 ~.

534.16 50.18-19 she takes it off. And] 15.19-20 —a grand thing, like your play, she carries it off; and

534.17 50.20 Tilden;] 15.20 ~,

534.18 51.1 when] 15.21 whenever

534.19 51.3-4 "female assassin", they carries it off] 15.22-23 Female Assassin—they seizes upon it,

534.19 51.4 study] 15.23 study it

534.20 51.5 fit] 15.23 suit

534.21 51.7 the heroine!] 15.25 that heroine.

534.21 51.7-9 it. They'll all be scuffling for the heroine!—] 15.25-26 it, just as sure as if I see them at it now.

534.22 51.9 some where] 15.26 somewhere

534.22 51.10 them.] 15.26-27 them, my dear friend, &

534.23 51.10-11 it, my dear friend, & then,] 15.27 it; and then, my dear friend,

534.24 51.14 it,] 15.29 it,—why,

534.25 51.14 Gott,] 15.29 ~!

534.25 51.15 piece,] 15.30 play;

534.26 51.17-18 d——d—t Sensation which would fill the poor treasury!] 15.31 d——t sensational that ever filled a treasury.

534.28 52.1 "My] 16.1 ¶ ~

534.28 52.1 —gone—lost—missing] 16.1 gone—missing—lost no doubt

534.28 52.2 despair] 16.2-3 a fit of despair for which Gilfert had no consolation

534.30 52.4-5 Savage eyes were upon Gilfert. ¶ "I tell you," says he, "nothing
] 16.4-6 Savage were the eyes which he fastened upon the manager, who could only repeat, helplessly, ¶ "Lost! Nothing, I tell you, my dear friend,

534.33 52.6 but] 16.7 but the

534.34 52.8 piece, Mr Gilfert] 16.8 play, Mr Gilfert! My play

534.35 52.9-11 you see! It is not here! I will look. I will ask these women. They've got it."
] 16.9-11 What shall I do! What shall I say. It is not here, you see. But I will look with all my specks. I will go to these women."

534.37 52.12-13 women! My piece, Sir,] 16.12-13 women!" was the ungallant response. I say, Sir; my piece,

535.1 52.14 be angry now!] 16.14 you be angry, my friend.

535.2 52.16 piece.] 16.15-16 piece. That is all I can say.

535.3 53.1 Assassins!" Then,] 16.16 Female Assassin! *(sotto voce.)* Then

535.3 53.1 author] 16.7 wretched author

535.3 53.2 foamed & fumed about] 16.17 bestrode

535.4 53.2 apartment,] 16.17-18 apartment, almost speechless with rage,

535.4 53.3-4 despair, cried out—impatiently—] 16.18-19 desperation:—becoming impatient himself, exclaimed—

535.6 53.6 Col.] 16.20 Colonel

535.7 53.7 thing!] 16.21 ~.

535.7 53.7-8 find your piece; but] 16.21-22 recover your play. But

535.8 53.9 any one] 16.22 any

535.8 53.10 pieces. Take] 16.22-23 pieces," —pointing to the enormous piles of MS.S. "Take

535.9 53.11 dem! They is] 16.24 them, if you please! There's

535.9 53.11 them] 16.24-25 them that's

535.10 53.12-13 d——n!"— ¶ Here] 16.25.27 d——n!" ¶ This was the *coup de grace*, designedly administered. Here

535.12 53.13-15 author, in a rage that rendered him speechless, rushed out of
] 16.27-30 author's rage, now at white heat, rendered him utterly speechless, and glaring at the manager, with eyes of a hyena, he darted headlong from

535.14 53.15 Gilfert,] 16.30 ~∧

535.15 53.17-54.1 circle that had witnessed] 16.31 circle, which had beheld

535.16 54.1 rare,] 16.32 ~∧

535.16 54.2 merriment,] 16.32 ~∧

535.16 54.2 affair.—] 16.32-34 affair—a scene quite as dramatic, perhaps, as any in the lost performance!

535. 54. <No chapter division>]17. ii / How Gilfert made a trip to Saratoga. How he bled the cashier, and completed his professional education.

535. 54.2-3 <no rule>] 17.3-4 <rule>

535.18 54.3 ¶ "It] 17.1-4 ¶ The Carolina Reminiscent continued his narrative, illustrating the "Humours of the Manager" in a new province. ¶ "It

535.20 54.4 season,] 17.5-6 season, which did *not* bring forth the grand sensational Drama of the "Female Assassin,"

535.22 54.6 most frequent] 17.7 Charleston

535.23 54.7 make a visit to] 17.8 visit

535.25 54.11-12 occasions, in public, as an amateur,
] 17.10-12 public occasions, for the Benefit of the Greek Cause, and other objects of popular concern,

535.27 54.15 wonder,] 17.14 surprise

535.29 54.18 and] 17.16 &

535.29 55.1 art] 17.17 ~,

535.30 55.3 would seem] 17.18 seemed

535.30 55.3-4 a crime] 17.18 criminal

535.31 55.5-6 Certainly, our friend Daniel ——— though] 17.19-21 It is very certain that Dan G——. could do nothing half so well as tread the stage & face the footlights.

536.1 55.7 & capable of a good] 17.21-22 prompt at retort, and good at an

536.2 55.9 was] 17.22 he was

536.3 55.10-11 graceful of person &] 17.24 fine of figure, graceful of

536.3 55.11-12 quick & keen perception, &] 17.25-26 keen quick perception of what the part required, and

536.5 55.13 the susceptibilities of character, we] 17.26 its susceptibilities, I

536.5 55.15 a] 17.27 any

536.6 55.15-16 completely and entirely] 17.27 completely

536.7 55.18 animated, humourous,] 17.29 humourous, droll, animated,

536.8 56.2 lively &] 18.1 ~ and

536.9 56.4 illuminated,] 18.3 ~‸

536.10 56.5-6 discourse, Danl — —] 18.4 ~; Danl G——

536.10 56.6 men,] 18.5 ~‸

536.12 56.10 content simply] 18.7 ~, ~,

536.14 56.15 foils & no] 18.10 foils, & rarely an

536.16 56.17 trip] 18.12 excursion

536.16 56.17 Gilfert] 18.12 ~,

536.17 56.18 lawyer,] 18.13-14 lawyer, of some literary proclivities,—

536.18 56.19-57.3 popularity. We will hide his true name under the *nom de guerre* of Col. Bondy.
] 18.15-17 popular in society. I will slightly cover the true name under that of Colonel Bondy,—for he was a Colonel—in the militia—as well as a lawyer.—

536.20 57.3 young—] 18.18 ~,

536.21 57.5-7 excitements—delighted with its freedoms & pleasantries, and admitted

] 18.19-20 excitements—happy in its pleasantries & freedoms, and admitted, because of his fellowship with Gilfert,

536.23 57.8-9 He was one of Gilfert's favorites, and he] 18.21 He

536.24 57.10 & of] 18.22 and

536.24 57.10 temper] 18.22 temperament

536.24 57.11 his] 18.22 these

536.25 57.12 valuable] 18.23 grateful

536.25 57.13 Gilfert,] 18.23 ~^

536.26 57.14 his two] 18.24 the two

536.26 57.15-16 Saratoga. ¶ But, hardly] 18.25-27 Saratoga, looking forward to the beyond, of Montreal & Quebec. It was to be an excursion for the summer. ¶ But, scarcely

536.29 57.17 at their hotel in] 18.27 in

536.29 57.18 York] 18.27-28 York, safely housed at the most fashionable hotel of that day

536.30 57.18 Gilfert, with] 18.29 Gilfert made a most startling discovery. With

536.31 58.1-2 his face and manner, exclaimed—] 18.30 face & manner, he exclaimed:

APPENDIX

WORD DIVISION

Note: The word "copy-text" as used in this appendix includes emended substantive additions to the original copy-text (as, for example, the 1837 additions to the 1833 *Martin Faber*).

Table A

The following possible compounds, hyphenated at the end of a line in the Centennial edition of *Stories and Tales*, appear as one word in copy-text. All other compounds that are hyphenated at the end of a line in the Centennial edition text (except those listed in Table C) are hyphenated within the line in copy-text and are omitted from this table.

19.36-37 fire-|side
185.12-13 moon-|light
227.9-10 blood-|shed
241.27-28 whirl-|pools
247.8-9 country-|men
270.36-37 foot-|steps
286.28-29 foot-|steps
289.33-34 lone-|some
315.3-4 sun-|shine
320.4-5 gray-|beards
334.26-27 over-|spreads
335.39-336.1 blunder-|buss
337.21-22 wise-|acres
355.32-33 grand-|son
370.35-36 false-|hood
373.38-374.1 well-|bred
402.23-24 boat-|man
461.3-4 fore-|finger
473.27-28 toe-|nail
487.10-11 tom-|hogged
487.33-488.1 hand-|ful
490.16-17 tom-|hogged
490.28-29 boat-|man
493.17-18 tick-|tacks
513.22-23 thunder-|storm
518.4-5 thunder-|storm

Table B

Listed here are compound words that fall within the line in the Centennial edition of *Stories and Tales* but whose intended form is ambiguous because they are hyphenated at the end of a line in copy-text. Where other examples of the same compound have been found within the line in the copy-text of the applicable story, the form (hyphenated or one word) most frequently used has been adopted. Where no other examples of the same compound could be found within the line in the copy-text of the applicable story, the Centennial edition has attempted to adopt the form of the compound which is most consistent with the copy-text's handling of similar compounds and with Simms's handling of the same compound in other writings of approximately the same date.

4.37-5.1 To-morrow
12.22 arch-enemy
14.28 childhood
29.3 dwelling-house
34.16 starlight
38.20 nightshade
60.1 everyday
65.2 high-souled
67.35 new-born
72.20 alongside
80.13 gunpowder
90.18 wonder-loving
91.11 granddame's
97.14 midnight
97.28 daredevil
113.14 childhood
121.1 outstretched
147.16 pathway
162.21 footsteps
166.29 overhung
211.10 tobacco-chewing
225.1 overcome
244.14 manhood
280.10 oarsmen
286.23 afternoon
299.8 childhood
303.11 fireplace
306.4 headlong
318.27 plum-puddings
326.16 headstrong
326.29 to-morrow
328.21 mock-birds
331.37 grandsire
339.14 brimstone
345.31 graybeard (Cf. "graybeard," *Voltmeier*, 90.27; but see Table A, 320.4-5)
347.6 common-prayer
351.18 gentle-hearted
360.19 evergreens
361.13 simple-hearted
365.4 corn-stalks
370.25 fireside
374.34 horseback
383.35 headland
390.11 blow-out
393.13 to-morrow
396.5 unwomanlike

399.25 well-lighted
409.22 re-awakened
409.37-38 hunting-ground
418.30 mealy-mouthed
420.21 *bald-face*
423.5 gridiron
433.11 turnip-bed
436.25 bedside
443.24 chestnut
445.11 hindquarters
448.18 bee-tree
449.23 bee-tree
451.16 shot-bags
457.20 wedding-breeches
458.20 to-night
458.21 to-day
461.25 handsome-looking
463.22 to-night
464.20 forefinger
467.25 moonlight
477.36 Lawd-a-marcy
("Lawd-a-|marcy" in copy-text)
481.21 a'ternoon
492.38 a-thinking
510.6 pine-knot
524.1 steamboats
535.32 footlights

Table C

Listed here are compounds, or possible compounds, which are hyphenated at the end of a line in both the copy-text and the Centennial edition text.

199.4-5 here-|after
(i.e., hereafter)
332.24-25 chubby-|cheeked
(i.e., chubby-cheeked)
442.28-29 day-|peep
(i.e., daypeep)
520.4-5 red-|skin
(see textual note)
546.37-38 church-|going
(i.e., church-going)

www.ingramcontent.com/pod-product-compliance
Lightning Source LLC
Chambersburg PA
CBHW022036120726
47899CB00004BA/1047

* 9 7 8 1 6 1 1 1 7 4 8 1 6 *